JANELLE TAYLOR

JANELLE TAYLOR

Three Complete Western Love Stories

First Love, Wild Love
Sweet Savage Heart
Midnight Secrets

WINGS BOOKS
New York • Avenel, New Jersey

This omnibus was originally published in separate volumes under the titles:

First Love, Wild Love, copyright © 1984 by Janelle Taylor
Sweet Savage Heart, copyright © 1986 by Janelle Taylor
Midnight Secrets, copyright © 1992 by Janelle Taylor

This edition contains the complete and unabridged texts of the original editions. They have been completely reset for this volume.

This 1995 edition is published by Wings Books,
distributed by Random House Value Publishing, Inc.,
40 Engelhard Avenue, Avenel, New Jersey 07001,
by arrangement with Zebra Books, an imprint of Kensington Publishing Corp.

Random House
New York ● Toronto ● London ● Sydney ●Auckland

Printed in the United States of America

Library of Congress Cataloging-in-Publication Data
Taylor, Janelle.
[Novels. Selections]
Three complete western love stories / Janelle Taylor.
p.   cm.
Contents: First love, wild love — Sweet savage heart — Midnight secrets.
ISBN 0-517-14924-9 (hardcover)
1. Man-woman relationships—West (U.S.)—Fiction. 2. Frontier and pioneer life—West
(U.S.)—Fiction. 3. Love stories, American. 4. Western stories. I. Title.
PS3570.A934A6 1996
813'.54—dc20
95-23566
CIP

8 7 6 5 4 3 2 1

Contents

First Love, Wild Love

For:

Tony W. and Stanley W.,
my terrific brothers and best friends
who shared my "tomboy" days.

and for:

Peggy C. and Sylvia T.,
two very special friends for many years.

I wish to express my gratitude to the staff of the Texas Ranger Museum in Waco and to the staffs of many Texas Tourist Bureaus acrosss the Lone Star State for graciously and unselfishly sharing their time, knowledge, and research materials with me. I also wish to thank Debby Pitzer for sharing interesting facts about Texas and the famed Rangers, of whom her uncle was a past member. I'm indebted to Trace Taylor for supplying the Spanish diaogue. For their assistance on the history of Texas railroads and factual train robberies, I am beholden to Oliver Brown and Anne Jones.

". . . *The character of the Texas Ranger is now well-known by both friend and foe. As a mounted soldier he has had no counterpart in any age or country. Neither Cavalier nor Cossack, Mameluke nor Mosstrooper are like him; and yet, in some respects, he resembles them all. Chivalrous, bold, and impetuous in action, he is yet wary and calculating, always impatient of restraint, and sometimes unscrupulous and unmerciful. He is uniformed, and undrilled, and performs his active duties thoroughly, but with little regard to order or system. He is an excellent rider and a dead shot. His arms are a rifle, Colt's revolving pistol, and a knife.*"

—Giddings, "Sketches"

"*A Texas Ranger can ride like a Mexican, trail like an Indian, shoot like a Tennessean, and fight like a devil.*"

—observation of a noted Texas Ranger

SILVER SPURS AND RED SATIN

Adorned in Red Satin, part woman, part child;
Meeting by chance in a land raw and wild.
Without her red satin, she captured his heart;
Tall, golden stranger branding love's mark.
Stolen moments together, Duty tearing them apart;
Passion burning brightly, Flame of his heart.

The gunslinger, a loner, skilled in diversity;
A hero in an age of a half-savage country.
Symbol of Justice, so strong and so vital;
Averting violence with iron will and metal.
His ivory-handled Colts flashing a deadly glint of steel;
A shiny star, his trademark on a silver heel.

Becoming a woman, both cautious and just;
With grit, trading chantilly for denim and dust.
Unaware of her bonds to a prosperous empire;
Breaking her spirit, tho' challenge her deisre.
Drifting in and out of her life, this golden stranger;
By Fate of his purpose, there to rescue her from danger.

Dark secrets of the past gradually unfold;
No more haunting memories ravish his soul.
Black magic Ranger, deft in his art;
Lady in Red Satin, Flame of his heart.
Fast rides the Ranger through an unsettled town;
To trade in Silver Spurs for her Red Satin gown . . .

—Penny M. Thomas and Janelle Taylor

Chapter 1

UNUSUALLY WARM AND HUMID WEATHER assailed the four people confined inside the jolting stagecoach for Fort Worth. The steady pounding of hooves mingled with the creaking of wood and the grinding of metal to noisily assault the passengers' ears. Deep ruts in the well-travelled road prevented all comfort, even if the hard wooden benches would allow any. The narrow, oblong windows refused to allow any refreshing breezes that might have soothed irritable minds and cooled damp bodies. Although the distance between Dallas and Fort Worth was only twenty miles, the bumpy journey seemed lengthy and monotonous. By now, muscles were stiff, bodies were bruised, and restless minds sought any source of distraction.

Hoping to improve her comfort, Calinda Braxton shifted against the torturous seat as she courteously pretended to listen to the droning voice of Cyrus Peabody as the boastful man spun his enlarged yarns of the West, Texas in particular. Seemingly endowed with endless vitality, the gregarious newspaperman embellished his accounts of many violent episodes in the area's past and present. Although Cyrus sounded as if he had personally staged and reported those deadly events, Calinda thought he was full of hot air. Without a doubt, at the first sign of trouble or peril, a bold yellow stripe would shine brightly down the back of the talkative owner of the *Austin Examiner*.

As Cyrus droned on and on, Calinda assumed a pleasant and attentive look as her mind wandered hundreds of miles from the bleak reality and loneliness before her. As much as she wished she could prevent their intrusion, the haunting memories came calling once more. Resigned to their relentless invasion, Calinda allowed her mind to retrace her puzzling and painful past.

Calinda vainly attempted to recall life with her father, Elliott Braxton, whom she hadn't seen since 1863 when he had demanded his wife and four-year-old child sail to relatives in England to avoid the war that was spreading viciously and rapidly toward their Georgia home. The following fifteen years had passed slowly, as she grew from a skinny and awkward child with carrot-colored braids to a graceful and bright young lady with golden red curls.

She wondered if her vague recollections of her father were a result of a poor memory or a defensive effort to protect herself from anguish. Without her locket, could she even envision his image? She touched the golden object beneath her dress. How cruel for a father to be only a face in a locket.

After the Civil War, her father had written to say he was heading for Texas to buy land and build a new home; he would send for them when all was ready and safe. As the years passed, his letters grew more and more infrequent, until finally none came at all. Calinda's uncle had written to her father to reveal her mother's sudden death in 1870. Elliott's last response had been, "Since Calinda is only eleven and this area is too rough for a child, please keep her in school there until I am firmly established here and can come for her."

Calinda had borne her loneliness, disappointments, and grief and completed her schooling. But Elliott had not kept his promise; he had never come for her or sent for her. Now, Calinda was almost nineteen and school had been over since last summer. It was time to discover the reason for her father's five years of silence. Rankin Cardone was the only clue to her father. She had nothing to lose in England. To begin a new life, she must settle her old one. The first step along her daring journey was to seek out Rankin.

Whether or not Elliott Braxton admitted it or desired it, she was his responsibility, one ignored too long. How did she feel about this stranger who was her father? What if he didn't love her or want her? No, that was unthinkable, unacceptable.

When her uncle, verging on financial destitution, had sailed for America in April to settle some pressing business, he sought to relieve himself of one financial burden which he said he had covered long enough and brought Calinda along so she could join her father. Calinda had been only too happy to begin a search for her errant father and to be free of her relatives' guardianship. She was grateful to be away from the Simpsons' control and selfish demands. Her aunt and uncle would have been only too glad to keep her around if she had agreed to wed one of the wealthy suitors who came courting, one who might be persuaded to divest the Simpsons of their careless money problems in exchange for Calinda's coveted hand in marriage.

The Simpson family had never approved of Elliott Braxton. To make matters worse, Miranda Braxton and her four-year-old child had been "dumped" on them during a terrible period of history, then practically "ignored and abandoned by that selfish, worthless rake." As long as Miranda was able to protect Calinda and Elliott sent money for their support, their existence in England had been tolerable. But after Miranda died and Elliott halted his support and letters, matters had slowly deteriorated.

After arranging Calinda's train passage to Dallas, Thomas Simpson had placed Calinda in charge of her own safety and fate. In Dallas, she purchased a stagecoach ticket to Fort Worth; from there she would send word to the Cardone Ranch. In her father's last letter, he had written that Rankin Cardone was his "closest friend and eventual partner in a cattle spread west of Fort Worth." In that letter he had promised Calinda that she would come to live on the Cardone Ranch in Texas just as soon as the partnership was finalized and she had completed her schooling in England. Why had her father ignored her since then? Soon she would have answers.

Despite her eagerness and suspense, the trip west had been uncomfortable and intimidating. Along the way, Calinda had purchased books and newspapers to acquaint herself with her imminent new surroundings. The gentle and impressionable girl had been alarmed and dismayed to read of a rugged, lawless land. The paper novels had recounted tales of infamous outlaws, vengeful Indian raids, greedy cattle-rustling, lynchings and riots, brazen gunfights on town streets, and bloody battles with Mexicans. But there were also stories of heroic men who fought against immense odds and under terrible conditions for "law and order."

Calinda halted her mental roamings to listen to Cyrus' versions of recent train-robberies conducted by a gang of unknown desperadoes. There had been four daring attacks around Dallas since February. Cyrus almost sounded disappointed that their train hadn't been attacked. Calinda smiled to herself. She had a feeling Cyrus would have fainted from fear if one of those bandits had stuck a gun to his hawkish nose and demanded his money or his life.

Calinda was delighted her stay in Dallas, the self-appointed headquarters for large groups of heavily-armed detectives and bounty hunters, had been brief. The town was bursting with Pinkerton detectives, railroad detectives, bounty hunters, a U.S. marshal with countless deputies, special agents from the express companies, and secret agents from the U.S. government. Strangely, she hadn't seen even one Texas Ranger.

To distract Cyrus from his monotonous narration, Calinda asked him about the Texas Rangers. Cyrus was only too willing to expose his opinions and knowledge, especially to a beautiful woman. He recognized fine breeding and intelligence when he met them. But never had he faced them in such a charming and beautiful package. He had furtively admired the arresting contrasts of Calinda's stunning appeal many times along this route. Her eyes were large and expressive, colored like velvety green leaves. The softness and shading of her unmarred complexion enchanted him. She possessed a body destined to be envied by women and desired by men. Her tumbling curls were light auburn with highlights of brassy gold; when the sun danced over them, they glowed as if containing an inner fire. Surely it was a punishable crime to look like Calinda Braxton, a sinful temptation! He leaned forward as he spoke, anxious to impress her.

"The Rangers started back in '35; they were dissolved during the War. But when the military pulled out and things got real bad, the Rangers were reactivated in '74. They're a special unit of men, around four or five hundred for the entire state." He grinned.

"How large is Texas?" Calinda asked.

"Bigger than the country of France," Cyrus boasted.

"If you have marshals and sheriffs, why do you need special Rangers? Are things that awful here?" she inquired worriedly.

"This territory's big and wild. Sheriffs have to remain near their own towns. Marshals usually work the big towns or deal with the problems that affect the American government, like the theft of U.S. mail and money. Rangers can go anywhere. Rangers don't bow to anybody or anything. They're feared and hated by outlaws throughout the state. Whenever there's trouble, a Ranger isn't far behind," he said proudly.

"I haven't seen one yet," Calinda remarked.

"Probably wouldn't know if you did. They don't wear uniforms, just lots of weapons. Some say they make their own law, but they do their duty. Braver, more cunning men were never born."

"They sound like powerful and proud men," she commented, pleased to have gotten Cyrus talking about something so interesting.

"The ones I've met are surprisingly modest and reserved. They are very intelligent, and most are well-educated men from the best families. A Ranger can stare death in the face and never bat an eye."

"You make them sound infallible," she pressed curiously.

"They're cool-headed and wary. Most of them work alone or in small groups. One Ranger can bluff or capture five to ten desperadoes just on his reputation as a Ranger. Sometimes they don't even have to fight or shoot; a Texas Ranger turns even a smug and desperate outlaw into a coward. They never give up on any mission, even into hell. I've printed true stories about one or more Rangers riding into a riotous mob or large band of marauding Indians or Mexican bandits and winning the fight. I've heard they would die before yielding to any threat. We westerners are known for our courage and daring," he bragged.

Calinda was about to ask Cyrus about Rankin Cardone when shots rang out behind the stagecoach. The driver whipped the team of horses into a swift run, his shouts encouraging the animals to move faster. The two male passengers were nearly tossed into the laps of the two females as the stage thundered precariously down the road. The guard and outlaws exchanged ominous gunfire as the bandits closed in on their target. The combined din of metal, wood, gunfire, and hooves nearly drowned out the driver's commands to the six-horse team. The landscape flashed by so rapidly that it became a blur of abundant ecru and scanty green.

As Calinda turned to glance out the window, Cyrus grabbed her shoulder and shouted to keep her hands off the windows or she might lose a finger or two. Calinda's dark emerald eyes widened. "They're shooting at us?" she asked incredulously.

"Keep your head down; don't give them an easy target!" Bill Farns, a Fort Worth merchant, yelled at her as he slumped in the wooden seat, silently praying the baggage bound to the rear would prevent a lethal bullet from entering his back.

As if this were a common occurrence, the two men began looking for hiding places for their money and valuables. Neither man drew his weapon. Apparently, they had no desire to fight. Everything seemed predestined: the exchange of gunfire, the futile and mandatory flight of the stagecoach, and the inevitable surrender.

The other female passenger didn't panic—she had nothing worth stealing. Calinda had even given her money for food at their last stop. Twenty-year-old Callie O'Hara was heading for her new job at the Red Satin Saloon in Fort Worth. Calinda had tried to converse with the remote and haughty Irish lass several times during their trip, but Callie was decidedly cold. Now she just stared straight ahead, seemingly unfazed by the danger they all faced.

Several bullets smashed into the fleeing stagecoach. The mingled noises of horses' hooves and gunfire drew closer. Above the clamor, the guard shouted, "I'm hit!," then his Winchester was silent.

But the stubborn driver continued his hasty fight toward town. As the perilous drama raged on, Calinda stared at the two men inside the coach. "Why aren't you shooting at them?" she demanded.

"Won't do any good," Bill vowed fearfully. He had stuffed his money into his boot and covered it with his pants leg. Pale and shaky, he was clinging to the seat for dear life.

Calinda tried once more. "They're shooting at us; we could get killed! Why won't you defend us? You heard the guard—he's wounded. This stage can't out-run their horses. We'll be robbed!"

"Robbed is better than murdered," Cyrus informed the naive Calinda. "If we fire at them, they'll make us pay when we're stopped. It's best to give in and let them take what they want."

"Give me your gun. I'm not afraid to defend myself. I'm not a coward. They won't rob me without a fight," she bravely shouted.

"You gonna kill 'em?" Bill Farns sneered. "That's the only way to stop 'em. All you have to do is wound one of them and they'll fight like crazed cocks. You ain't gonna get us killed playing heroine."

Before Calinda could voice her outrage, the stage slowed to a halt. The ex-hausted team was lathered and wheezing; it was time to surrender. The stage was instantly surrounded by a masked gang of eight men. Each bandit had two pistols pointing at the driver and his anxious charges. When one outlaw demanded that their guns be tossed to the ground, all four men complied.

Next, the stage occupants were ordered to step outside. The driver and wounded guard remained on their lofty perch. The two male passengers de-scended to the dusty ground, then helped the two women out. One outlaw, probably their leader, prodded his horse forward to within a few feet of the small group. Above his black bandanna, his eyes showed cold amusement as they viewed the terror of the two men, mild indifference as they drifted over Callie, and visible pleasure as they slowly raked over the auburn-haired treasure.

Calinda trembled, but her face appeared impassive and her poise unruffled. She didn't like the way the bandit leader was staring at her. For an instant, she was relieved she hadn't shot at them and drawn their anger. Then she decided that armed resistance might have driven them away.

Two outlaws remained on their horses as guards while the others dismounted to carry out their plans. The driver was ordered to hand down the U.S. mail and a strongbox with money. The male passengers were searched and relieved of their money and watches. Callie convinced the bandit before her that she was penniless and jewel-free. The self-assured leader then approached Calinda, holding out his hand for her drawstring purse and jewelry.

There was still a glow in his eyes which Calinda noticed and dreaded. Still, she moved her purse behind her slender back and obstinately shook her head, tawny red curls shimmering over her shoulders with her defiant movement. The leader's eyes registered surprise, then humor.

"The money, Ma'am," he demanded as he holstered his weapon, placed his hands on his hips and assumed a confident stance.

"No," Calinda refused. "It's mine."

"You'll have your life if you obey before my patience wears out," he retorted mirthfully.

He was playing with her. She was sure he was grinning beneath that triangular mask and her chin jutted out in continued rebellion. "I've never heard of outlaws murdering innocent women over a small amount of money," she boldly bluffed.

"Give it to him, Miss Braxton," Cyrus anxiously encouraged.

"No," Calinda recklessly stood her shaky ground. Violence was an unknown force to her, one she failed to recognize or wisely respect.

"Need some help with that little filly?" another bandit offered, laughing. A chorus of chuckles filled the stuffy air, altering the mood of the leader.

"I'm in a hurry, Miss B. I don't normally go around roughing up beautiful women, but I can if you force me. The jewelry and money," he demanded imperiously, his voice and gaze now chilly.

Calinda took a few steps backward and shook her head. If she were going to be robbed, it wouldn't be with her cooperation! Besides, she needed what little money there was in the purse. She would be in a terrible state if her father had left this area. She tried to reason with him. "Please, it's all I have until I can locate my father. I don't have any friends or relatives here. If you take the money, how will I survive? Surely my meager cash cannot be that vital to you?"

A curious look filled the insolent stranger's eyes. He almost appeared tempted not to rob her. "Sorry, Miss B," he finally said, then reached for the purse she clutched tightly behind her.

Calinda struggled for possession of the purse. Within moments, she found herself breathless, her dress torn, and her purse in the hands of the leader. One man held her securely while the leader removed a sapphire ring and an inexpensive cameo brooch.

Finally realizing she was helpless, Calinda ceased her resistance. But her torn dress had revealed a hidden treasure, more precious to Calinda than the money or other jewelry—a locket with her parents' picture. The bandit snatched it, leaving a gradually reddening streak on her ivory neck. Calinda fought with renewed determination and strength.

"Take the money and jewels, but not the locket. Please . . ."

The outlaw eyed the gold locket in his sweaty palm, then the beseeching look on the girl's face. He flipped it open, and saw the reason for her battle. "Your folks dead?" he unexpectedly asked.

Hoping her answer would convince him to return the prized locket, she nodded, her entrancing eyes misty. "Please don't steal it," she pleaded softly.

"If you hadn't cost me so much time and trouble, I wouldn't." After checking her purse, he glanced at her and asked, "This all the money you have? Any hidden? Maybe I should search you."

His words sent shivers of alarm over Calinda. She went rigid and silent, wondering if he would carry out his petrifying threat. "No," he said then. "You wouldn't have fought for this measly bit of money if you had more." He chuckled when she exhaled loudly in relief. "Let 'er go."

As she was released, Calinda surged forward to snatch the locket. When the outlaw instinctively reacted to her unexpected attack, she was shoved backwards and landed with a loud thud against the stage. This harsh treatment instantly spurred the injured guard into action; he reached for a concealed rifle. One of the outlaws shot him before he could take aim.

Calinda screamed and ran to kneel over the fallen man. The locket hadn't been worth a man's life. She looked up at the masked leader in disbelief, her face white and her expression frozen. For a moment, no one spoke or moved as Calinda Braxton stared at the notorious Sam Bass. What shocked her most was the outlaw's total lack of remorse or concern, which he flaunted with a cocky stance and laughing eyes. Clearly and belatedly, she knew this man was lethal and ruthless.

Driven beyond all caution and wisdom, Calinda stood up and squared her shoulders proudly. Glaring coldly at the bandit, she held out her hand. "Give me the locket; he paid for it with his life."

"You're a stupid girl, Miss B. I've killed more men than you have fingers and toes. Don't tempt me to add a female notch to my gun," he warned.

"You murder men, then boast about it? You're an animal," she sneered.

Sam's eyes appraised this girl who was as stubborn and brave as any of his men. He respected courage, except when it was a hindrance. To end this crazy stand-off, he shoved Calinda aside. She fell backward and struck her head against the stage wheel, then slid unconscious to the ground. Sam resisted the urge to check her injury and ordered his gang to search the baggage.

More money and valuables were added to the gang's pile as they looted the men's luggage. When they opened Calinda's, the thieves were delighted with the expensive gowns and frilly lingerie and took Calinda's baggage as gifts for their women.

When Calinda awoke, all she had was the dirty, torn dress she wore. Unable to stem her anger, she berated the two men for their cowardice, but was told she had only herself to blame for her injuries and losses. Callie O'Hara remained silent and watchful. She was glad to see the gently-reared beauty defeated, but didn't dare show her viciousness before the men who might be her customers. The driver carried the guard's body on the stage, shaking his head at the rash loss of life; still he felt a begrudging respect for Calinda's courage. Bill, however felt no such admiration.

"If you hadn't fought them, they probably wouldn't have searched our baggage. Or stolen yours for spite. If that guard hadn't tried to help you, he wouldn't be dead," Bill angrily heaped his charges on Calinda to ease his own humiliation. It galled any man to play a coward, even if he was one.

"If you two had helped the guard shoot at them, we might have scared them off!" she shouted back at him. "Those outlaws wouldn't be so bold if they weren't allowed to rob people like us so easily!"

"You fought 'em, and what did it get you?" Bill scoffed.

"One person couldn't battle eight, but four could have. Besides, at least I have some pride."

"That's all you have left, girly," the driver added sullenly.

"Stop this bickering. We've got to get to town and tell the sheriff," Cyrus interrupted their quarrel. "Maybe the posse can help us."

Calinda sat in the corner as they made their pensive trip into Fort Worth. At least she could get that much closer to her father and the Cardone Ranch. She would contact the sheriff and have him send word to Rankin Cordone of her arrival, if her letters hadn't already reached him. But what would she do until help reached her? She felt vulnerable, doubtful, and afraid. She certainly couldn't ask Bill or Cyrus for assistance, not after her brazen tirades and insults. Perhaps they had been wiser after all. Perhaps it was best to swallow pride and allow the bandits their way until the law could pursue them. It was clear her resistance had been futile and costly.

After their late arrival in Fort Worth, Calinda's problems mounted by the hour. The town was rough and the men rowdy, just like the descriptions in the paper novels. She didn't know anyone, except the passengers, who had all disappeared. Even the stage office was closed by the time she discovered that the sheriff and his deputies had been out pursuing bank robbers since that morning. Most of the stores were closed.

Dusk was gradually enveloping the town, and the streets were slowly filling with noisy men and horses. She could hear music, but it was coming from run-down saloons. Calinda had approached two boarding houses and one hotel, to learn none of them would accept her presence with only the promise of repayment when her father arrived. To her further alarm, Calinda discovered that her father's name was unknown in town. And when she mentioned Rankin Cordone, she was met with skepticism. It was apparent her father was not that powerful man's partner. Her claims only inspired mistrust and her apprehensions and doubts increased with the shadows.

Calinda stood on the wooden walkway pondering her next move. Angry and frightened, she had no place to go. Several men paused to offer crude solutions to her predicament. What kind of place was this? Would no one help a young woman in terrible straits, a woman robbed near their town, a woman without family or money? Did they feel no concern or responsibility toward her? Soon, any hope for assistance vanished as family people went home for their evening meal. Only saloon girls and cowpokes were on the street. Calinda honestly didn't know what to do or where to turn. She berated herself for her dwindling courage, independence, and resourcefulness.

"You be Miss Braxton?" a gruff voice inquired from behind.

Calinda turned and nodded, tears misting her eyes. A hefty woman with faded blonde hair and a painted face stepped forward. Her scarlet dress was snug-fitting over her round body. Yet there was a gentleness in her expression as she smiled at Calinda.

"I be Nelle O'Hara, Callie's cousin. Callie told me 'bout yore troubles on the stage and the money you give her. Women like us don't git such kindness from ladies like you. I owns the Red Satin Saloon down the street. You be welcomed ta stay there till you kin locate yore kinfolk. The place's noisy, but she's clean and safe. Won't nobody harm you whilst you're under my roof." Nelle kept it to herself that the ungrateful and cold-hearted Callie had laughed at Calinda's predicament.

"I . . ." Calinda started to refuse her generous invitation, but fell silent. How could she stay in such a place. How could she not? It was the only help she had been offered. She couldn't stand here all night in this dangerous cowtown. "I don't have any money to pay you." Calinda was beginning to understand the full extent of the danger she was in today. Still, she had to stay until she could locate Rankin.

"Don't you be worryin' yore pretty head none. You kin stay with us till the sheriff gits back, then he kin help you. I knows it ain't the kind of place you're used to, but you'll be safe. I seed you standin' here alone and scared; folks 'round these parts don't take ta strangers, not without some price I doubts you'd be wantin' ta pay. Decent folks, me big toe. Can't even help a lady in trouble," Nelle muttered. As she awaited the girl's answer, Nelle shifted uneasily. Maybe this girl reminded her too much of her own daughter who was back East in school, away from the crude life in a saloon.

"But how can I repay your kindness?" Calinda fretted anxiously.

"No need. Jus' come along. We'll git you a hot bath and some warm victuals. I'll have Maggie stitch yore dress fur you. By mornin' you'll be feelin' sunny," she said confidently, taking Calinda in tow.

Nelle and Calinda made their way to the Red Satin Saloon and went inside. They walked through the noisy crowd of working girls, appropriately attired in red satin dresses trimmed in black lace, and rough-looking men. Calinda's face flamed as men approached them to check on Darlin' Nelle's newest girl. Nelle quickly and cheerfully corrected the bewitched cowboys and fancy gamblers. Embarrassed and vexed, Calinda cautiously held her tongue and temper, not daring to offend her only source of help.

Calinda tightly gripped her torn dress as the two women wove through tables and chairs in the cluttered room, then climbed the stairs and walked down a long hallway. Nelle halted before a door and unlocked it. She went inside and motioned for Calinda to follow her. Nelle lit two lanterns and turned to smile genially at the exhausted girl. Calinda was glancing around, pleased and surprised to find the room was nicely furnished and exceptionally clean.

"See, tain't so bad," the older woman encouraged.

Calinda smiled at her and nodded.

"You makes yoreself at home, Miss Braxton," Nelle said. "I'll fetch you some hot food and a bath. Jus' rest and calm yourself. You've had a rough day."

As Nelle was leaving, Calinda said, "Thank you, Nelle, and please thank Callie for me."

Nelle chuckled and smiled again. After she'd gone, Calinda dropped into a plush chair and stared into space, trying to relax her tense mind and body. She hadn't moved when Nelle and a black man appeared with her food and a wooden tub. Nelle chatted freely while Calinda ate and the man hauled in hot water for the tub. Nelle actually blushed when she handed Calinda a red satin dancehall dress like ones they'd seen below and a fiery-colored flimsy nightgown edged with what looked like wicked ebony lace.

"I'm sorry, Miss Braxton, but that's all the clothes I has ta offer here at the saloon. I'll have yours repaired and washed and I'll return 'em in the mornin'." They talked a while longer and Calinda told her about the robbery and her motives for coming West alone, touching the tender-hearted Nelle with her plight and courage.

Calinda thanked her again before Nelle left her. After the bath, Calinda slipped into the seductive dress that exposed the upper portion of her creamy bosom, unable to put on the revealing nightgown. Soon, a knock sounded at her door. Apprehensive, she asked who was there. It was a drunken customer at the wrong room. For a time, he was determined to come inside and he rattled the doorknob and bumped the door with his shoulder. As he spouted curses at the delay, the besieged girl cringed against the wall, trying to shut out his vulgar words. For a horrifying moment, she feared he was going to break down the door and assault her, but Nelle came along and pointed him in the right direction, then entered to calm Calinda's distraught nerves.

After the tub and water were removed by the lanky black man, Nelle stayed with Calinda, who was suddenly overcome by all that had happened. She began to shake and cry softly, and her distress tugged at Nelle's heart. Although she could be a tough businesswoman, and was stern with her working girls, Nelle was also a gentle and caring person. She just couldn't afford to show it most of the time.

"You poor child," Nelle softly encouraged. "That noise'll go on far into the nite. I brung some medicine to calm yore nerves and help you sleep. I knows you must be bone-tired and scared stiff."

At Nelle's order, Calinda managed to force down a teaspoon of laudanum. "Now, you git ready fur bed. This here's a private room; my friend won't mind you using it while he's away. Don't you fret none; you'll be fine when the sun shows its face. I'll take you ta see the sheriff. Afore you kin think, you'll be home safe agin."

Nelle left Calinda alone. As she lumbered down the hallway, she worried over the fact that she had placed Calinda in the privately rented room of a special customer, an irresistibly handsome loner who wasn't supposed to show up for weeks. But it was the only room fit for such a charming lady. And the mysterious cowboy would never know.

Nelle sighed as she thought about him. That golden stallion was a complex and private man, one who thrived on his freedom and daring adventures. Although she had known him for years, she really didn't know him at all. He was a natural-born charmer when the mood struck him, but was very selective with his female companions. Nelle doubted there was a woman alive who wouldn't give her soul to corral that untamed creature. If she were younger and prettier . . . She chided her foolishness; that Texan would never wed a tainted woman, if he ever wed. Not that he was arrogant or cynical, he just appeared unsusceptible to love, a man content to feed his passions when they demanded appeasement. He was a perfect specimen of a man. His appeal to women was a vivid fact, a fact he nonchalantly accepted. He was quick to reveal he made no promises to any female, nor did he take kindly to those who tried to force their attentions on him.

It was known the cunning and clear-headed rebel feared nothing and no one. He was an expert horseman and crack shot. Few men challenged him or his ivory-handed Colts. But he was wary and mysterious, and kept to himself a great deal. Alert and agile, he had never lost a fist or gun fight. He was feared, respected, or envied by most men and desired by all women whose eyes feasted on him. He was a self-assured and easy-going devil, but the cowboy could be tough and cold when a situation demanded it. He had the money and power to come and go as he pleased. He could be a coveted friend or a deadly enemy.

Nelle fretted over facts she wished she didn't know, but a woman in her position often learned closely guarded secrets. Miss Braxton was here to seek her father through Rankin Cardone. What would Calinda do and say when she discovered the last man who would aid her was Rankin Cardone? Rankin was a wealthy and powerful man, a man who dealt fairly with friends and ruthlessly with enemies.

It was obvious from Calinda's earlier confession that there were many things the girl didn't know. She was so naive about the perils before her. Nelle wondered if she should enlighten Calinda. She quickly decided no, since Rankin wasn't a man she'd like to have as an enemy. If that girl knew what was hovering over her lovely head, she would run like the wind!

Nelle also had Callie O'Hara to worry her. Callie was refusing to work! That hateful cousin of hers had a temper to match her fiery hair. But tonight, Nelle had an even more pressing matter on her mind. Her beloved trail-boss had arrived and was waiting in her room. Giggling with joy, Nelle dismissed both girls from her mind.

The loud music and raucous laughter from downstairs drifted into Calinda's borrowed room. Her head was spinning from the potent drug and she was tormented by thoughts of her harrowing episode. She reluctantly changed into the flimsy nightgown, tossing the red satin gown over a chair. She stumbled to the bed and slipped between the clean sheets. Crying softly, Calinda soon fell asleep.

Downstairs, a man attired in jet black entered the saloon and casually tossed down two whiskies. He had removed his dark hat to run lean, deft fingers through a tousled mane of amber hair which blazed like ripened wheat beneath the sun. He exuded an undeniable contempt for danger and a matchless confidence. He was over six feet tall and his body rippled with well-toned, flexible muscles. His flesh had been lovingly and deeply kissed by the sun. A tangible air of brute strength and keen alertness clung to him. His violent and demanding lifestyle had honed his stalwart body and sharp mind to an impressive degree—his sole goals were success and survival. His physical prowess and intelligence made him a formidable opponent. Not even a minuscule glimmer of self-doubt could be sighted in that tawny gaze; his eyes were as perceptive and intimidating as a crafty lion's. And to the women present, it seemed that beneath that black outfit was the form of a bronzed god.

Several saloon girls rushed over, eagerly vying for his attention; but the distracted man wasn't in such a mood tonight. Flashing them a beguiling and falsely rueful grin, he pleasantly refused their company. After a few words with the bartender, he took a bottle and headed to his room. As he agilely mounted the steps, he admitted he was growing weary of this secret work with the Texas Rangers with its countless sacrifices and demands. He had had enough of battling renegade Indians, Mexican bandits, and an abundance of outlaws and cutthroats. He was bored with foiling fence-cutters and rustlers, tracking train and stage robbers, dogging wanted men, living among disgusting outlaws to learn their plans and identities. If he couldn't openly and proudly be a Ranger, why keep endangering his life? He didn't like the reputation he was attaining as a superior gunslinger and arrogant rebel. Since he couldn't deny his deeds or give the reasons behind them, he was rapidly becoming an unsavory legend. And glory-hungry, gun-toting fools loved nothing more than unseating legends.

After roaming around for two years, he had gone into secret service for the railroad and U.S. government at the age of twenty. When his job began to send him across the West in '76, he had joined up with the Rangers. He usually liked being on the move, but here in Texas certain personal matters controlled his thoughts and needs, even after so many years. He had craved the excitement and distractions which his work had offered; he had needed them, still needed them. But something was going crazy inside his head these days. He was becoming dissatisfied, moody, and tense. What was this loneliness or emptiness that plagued him? What was this wild and urgent desire to find the missing element in his life? He possessed so much, had the means and talents to obtain anything he desired; what was left to win or to gain? Yet, how could even a clever and fearless man vanquish an intangible desire?

Maybe it was time to end this work and settle down at home to face other responsibilities. Just as soon as he solved the Sam Bass question, perhaps he would. But so far every attempt to hook up with the Bass gang had failed, and he couldn't accept that. It was clear Bass was working these parts, but the outlaw was sly and deadly. With Major John Jones arriving nearby, perhaps together they could end Bass's career quickly and efficiently. For now, he would rest himself and his horse, then head for Dallas at first light.

He grinned as he climbed the last few steps. Only two men were aware of his identity, but many criminals knew of a daring and unknown Ranger who left his mark of victory on their saddles or holsters: a tiny star that symbolized law and revealed a deadly warning. But this man wanted what other Rangers possessed, respect. The mere mention of a Ranger's name could inspire fear and reluctance in foes. Since he kept his identity concealed, he always had to battle to prove himself or to survive.

The lithe cowboy unlocked his door and walked inside. Noting the softened glow of a burning lantern, he was instantly on alert, his left hand lightly grazing the butt of his pistol. Soundlessly laying his saddlebag and hat in a chair, he headed for the bed and stared down at the enchanting bundle asleep there. His gaze flickered from the discarded red satin dress to the beautiful creature clad in a revealing nightgown; the sheet had been shoved aside in the stuffy room and all of the vixen's treasures were revealed to his surprised eyes.

With fluid movements, he headed to the window and opened it to invite fresh air inside. He unfastened his hand-tooled double-holstered leather belt and hung it over the chair. He bent down to remove his spurs, and added them to his pile of discarded possessions. The girl hadn't moved yet. Going over to the bed, he sat down, the mattress sinking under his weight. Still, no response to his arrival.

He stared at the unfamiliar girl for a time. His loins instinctively and vexingly tightened, but he restrained his physical urge. He was too fatigued to play games with an audacious saloon girl—one as beautiful as this must have had numberless men in her life. All he wanted was her absence and a good night's sleep. He reached over and shook her, but she didn't respond. She was stupid and brazen to invade his privacy, but her lesson could be taught later when he was revived.

"Up, pretty lady, I'm too tired tonight," he said in a mellow voice, thinking it easier to use fatigue as an excuse for his lack of interest.

Deeply entrapped by drugged slumber, Calinda didn't react to his presence or his voice. His gaze eased over her fiery chestnut curls and breath-taking form. Her flesh was smooth and creamy. She was slim, but shapely. Her transparent gown left nothing to his imagination. She was the most beautiful woman he had ever seen. As he pondered how many men had caused her exhaustion tonight, he was irrationally provoked by how she was affecting him. She was a whore, probably a very busy one! He shook her, roughly and firmly. "Get your eyes open and your feet moving, Ma'am." He desired her, but would never stand in a lengthy line for the attentions that paid for her crude survival.

Calinda stirred and fluttered her green eyes, hazily taking in this image of irresistible manhood.

"What's your name?" he asked.

"Ca . . ." she dreamily attempted to answer, but couldn't force her name past her dry tongue. She tried to focus on the arresting illusion clad in devilish ebony hovering over her.

"Callie?" he assisted here, recalling the bartender's words about a lovely newcomer with that name. Fuzzily hearing the name her mother had called her as a child, she nodded. "What are you doing in here, Callie? This is a private room."

"No other place to go," she murmured hazily.

"Why did you come to my room?" he persisted, intrigued.

"Only safe place . . . Had to get away . . ."

"Did Nelle send you here?" he continued in a lazy drawl.

"Yes. Said stay here until I work out these . . ."

"Where did you live?" he asked. "Safe . . . Get away . . ." his keen mind echoed. Probably from customers and their abundant demands!

"No home . . . Mama dead . . . Papa . . . Lost everything . . . Must stay . . ." The unfinished, hazy words tumbled out to form mistaken conclusions in his befuddled mind and inflamed body.

"Ever work in a saloon before?" he demanded casually, sensing something different and haunting about this delicate girl.

"Never," she mumbled in answer to the strange question.

"I see," he thoughtfully murmured. His investigative mind went to spinning with questions and doubts. Had she completed her first day in this kind of job? Or would she begin tomorrow? Was she here of her own free will? Had that mischievous Nelle sent her for his enjoyment? For certain, this would be his only chance to enjoy this unselfish gift, before she was tarnished from months of visits to countless beds of any male who could afford her price. Common whores didn't appeal to him, but there was nothing common about this girl. From her looks, she would be in popular demand. How could any female condemn herself to such an existence? Surely one such as Callie could have her choice of husbands. Was she a penniless widow? A runaway from a terrible home? Why would she choose such a degrading life over a respectable one? Despite the temptation this proud Ranger was reluctant to take advantage of this enticing set-up.

"I'm thirsty," Calinda managed to say, feeling the room spin around her.

All he had was a bottle of superior whiskey. He poured her a glass and helped her sit up to drink it, supporting her lax body against his strong one. The biting liquid was strong, but wet. Calinda automatically thanked him, before her senses went rushing around again.

He placed the empty glass on the table, then eased Calinda down on the bed. He grinned in amusement; she clearly wasn't used to potent drinks and she possessed good manners. When she smiled up at him, he lazily stretched out beside her, hesitating to end this pleasing contact. He reclined on his left side, his jaw cupped in his hand. He absently shoved a straying vibrant curl from her ivory face. His finger made a compelling trek over her forehead, down her cheek, across her pert nose, past her dainty chin, and to her inviting lips. At the tickling sensations, she smiled and shifted, those verdant green eyes pulling his gaze to hers.

"Do you want to be here with me, Callie?" he inquired tensely, despite the thunderous warning inside his head that screamed of the danger she presented, a warning he helplessly denied.

"Yes," the spoken word escaped her lips softly, as she tried to clear her somnolent wits, too late . . .

Chapter 2

THIS SPECIAL RANGER was adept at handling emergencies or hazards; he usually knew how to prepare for them and master them with unerring accuracy, speed, and courage. But this situation was uncommon. Even his many skills couldn't tell him what to do with this particular crisis. He suspected this new saloon girl had heard of his daring exploits and good looks, and perhaps found him desirable on reputation alone. Was she lurking here to guilefully cast her spell over him? As he eyed her compelling beauty, he grew inexplicably angry. Maybe it was because she looked so innocent and vulnerable. Unlike the other saloon girls she was unpainted and presented a soft seductiveness which was overwhelming. She looked as if she belonged in elegant silk gowns rather than in the garish red satin one, and he was struck by the dangerous appeal of the sheer nightgown in bright crimson which made a startling contrast to her creamy flesh. Callie was as bewitching and devious as his mother. No, he wouldn't permit that selfish bitch to torment him tonight.

Still, that tiny comparison sparked more anger within him, adding dashes of fierce spite. Damn any *puta* who could retain such a look of purity and charm while she coldly trampled on lonely and unsuspecting male hearts, especially his! How dare this creature set a provocative trap for him! How dare she steal inside his head!

Even as she slept, her lips curled up in an inviting smile that played havoc on a man's senses. Evidently she wanted to begin her new career in Fort Worth with him as her first prize. She had probably brazenly entered his hide-away to seduce him, perhaps to prove she possessed the power to captivate even the cynical and elusive Unknown Ranger.

A beguiling and devilish grin tugged at the corners of his wide and full lips. His tawny eyes glowed with mischievous lights. He ran his strong fingers through his curling mane of dark blond hair. Strangely, he was no longer tired and bored; his senses were alive and alert. It had been a long time since he had taken a woman in bed, and he found Calinda utterly arresting. A soft chuckle escaped his lips as he decided to accept her implied invitation.

The intrigued Ranger stood up and stripped off his clothes and boots. Filling the wash-basin, he removed the trail-dust from his face and hands, leisurely taking the time to shave. He removed the covers and drank in the invigorating sight, then joined her. Drugged with Nelle's laudanum, the Ranger's whiskey, and her own exhaustion, Calinda didn't react as the impulsive stranger undressed her to admire her beauty. He bent over and captured the lips which seemed to beg for his. With expertise, he skillfully stormed her body with deft hands and bedeviling lips, exploring curvy regions and flat planes.

Calinda lacked the strength, awareness, or logic to resist him as she surrendered to the intoxicating kisses and stirring caresses of the golden man of her dreams.

As Calinda's arms unknowingly encircled the man's iron-muscled body and her lips answered the call from his, his resentment melted away. All he wanted was to make tender and passionate love to this mysterious siren. If Calinda's mind had any intention of freeing her from its torpid state, the thought was quickly dismissed as she revelled in the warmth, protection, and heated desire of this enchanting stranger. Nature took over her blurry senses and demanded she respond to his urgent messages and unleash her unbridled passion to match his.

The now enraptured Ranger eased between her thighs and tenderly, yet persistently, probed at her maidenhead, ignoring its meaningful presence. Ensnared by potent desire and her eager encouragement, he was hurled beyond control or reason. She smelled as fresh as a field of wildflowers and her loving was as sultry as the hottest summer day. As the barrier against his possession gave way, her small cry of discomfort reached his fuzzy brain. Virgin! The word ricocheted through his confused mind like a perilous gunshot, then gradually receded in a fading echo.

Governed by the insistent throbbing within his manhood, he entered and withdrew gently until her brief struggle halted. Her skin was as soft and white as the petals on a loquat flower. The peaks on her taut breasts were firm and sweet. As Calinda's arms eased around his tantalizing body and her lips yielded to his kisses, logic escaped him for a time as his hungry body urged him to feast on the fruits of his labor and to submit to her bewitching pervasion of his senses.

Blissfully appeased, the sated rogue eased to her side, retaining his possessive hold on her. He shifted his head to gaze down at her; she was snuggled peacefully into his embrace. A curiously warm and happy feeling flowed over him. Bemused by the odd sensations and thoughts which assailed his mind and body, he couldn't seem to pull his eyes from her serene face. Watching and touching her gave him intense pleasure. Normally one sexual union was sufficient to satisfy his needs. But he fiercely desired this girl again this moment! He bent over to nibble at her lips, then passed his tongue over them. His body was simmering with desire, preparing to boil with molten passion. There was no way he could go to sleep yet. With renewed vigor, he enticed her once more, whispering, "Love me again, my fiery vixen."

Calinda stirred, her green eyes dreamily focused on his tawny gaze. She caressed his tanned cheek and nestled against his coppery frame, sighing contentedly. In Calinda's whiskey- and laudanum-dulled mind, all she heard was the mingled pounding of passion's fiery blood and the muffled instructions of her bronzed lover. As his lips and hands worked magic upon her quivering body, his voice and face vanquished all but this undeniable craving to forge their bodies and hearts. What knowledge instinct didn't supply, he did.

Calinda relaxed into the softness of the bed, allowing him full control of the situation and abandoning her will to his. When the wildly wonderful invasion became too bittersweet to simply enjoy, Calinda feverishly matched his movements. Their bodies and spirits blended into one driving force, one commitment to shared pleasure.

Calinda's senses reeled with the exquisite enticements. In the pit of her womanhood, an aching need fused with ecstatic delight. She was striving urgently for a goal she didn't comprehend until she was forcefully rocked by the stunning climax to her sensual drama. Her body stiffened momentarily, then tingled and warmed. Her hold on her dream lover tightened; her lips meshed with his as entreating moans slipped from her throat. Her body writhed and pressed upward to glue her moist flesh to his until each rapturous spasm ceased. After willingly sharing this intoxicating and enlightening experience, she settled down to savor the tranquil aftermath.

Calinda's cheek lay against his chest, her eyes closed dreamily. His strong fingers wandered through her silky hair and over her naked shoulders as his lips dropped tiny kisses over her temple. Her head moved slightly as she relished the feel of his damp and firm shoulder against her satiny cheek; she inhaled the manly fragrance which filled her nostrils. She felt so warm, safe, and happy in his arms, so empty of cares and doubts. Like a newly bloomed flower in a field of ripened wheat, she was totally content to be a part of his golden domain.

As her fingers played with dampened curls on his muscled chest, a mellow voice rent the romantic silence when it murmured, "I've never met a woman so beautiful and innocent, yet so skillful she steals your mind. I'm afraid you're going to be unforgettable. I surely wish I didn't have to ride out at dawn."

The Ranger inhaled deeply, then allowed the air to escape his lungs quietly. He hugged her tightly, then chuckled as he questioned his good fortune, "Why me, love? You could have any male around." He knew now that he had never experienced real passion until tonight, until this female. Never had he been so aware of each instant of lovemaking. It was so different with her, so stimulating, so consuming, so utterly satisfying. Yep, there was plenty to learn from this unique treasure.

Even as he spoke these words, the laudanum and whiskey were gradually losing their potent and wit-dulling effects. The reality of the naked body cuddled next to hers registered in her whirling brain, as did the implication of their intimate position. She swallowed with difficulty, gaping at the brawny chest within inches of her wide eyes, fearing to lift her head to view the face of her mysterious lover.

Her movements caught his attention. He opened amber eyes to discover startled green ones locked on him. He smiled, causing her stupefied gaze to rivet to his sensual lips, then back to his beguiling gaze. Instantly, he knew something was amiss.

Calinda blinked her eyes and shook her head to test this shocking reality. She knew this man—didn't she? From where? When? How had she come to be in bed with this handsome devil, naked in his strong arms? Why was she boldly fondling his chest! How could she recognize his face and voice, and yet not know his name or when they met? Remember . . . Her fantasy . . . The mental pictures which flashed across her warring brain stunned her. It hadn't been a dream?

When she tried to free herself, the golden stranger refused to release her. "Let go of me, you beast," she ordered hoarsely, shoving at the immovable chest. "If I had a gun, I'd kill you," she warned as her voice strengthened. What black magic had lured her into this compelling demon's bed? He was behaving as if he owned her body and soul! "Take your filthy hands off me!" she panted when he retained his painlessly firm embrace as his piercing eyes observed her.

When the girl began to thrash angrily like a frenzied badger in a steel trap, he captured her wrists and pinned her nude body beneath his. "What the hell!" he stormed at her unexpected behavior. "What's wrong with you, woman? You make love to me, then attack me like a wildcat! Calm down and explain yourself!"

"You break into my room and ravish me, then act the victim? Release me this instant, you vile brute! I'll have you arrested for this wicked crime against me. I'll scream," she warned as his tawny eyes frosted visibly at her threat. Calinda had been about to fight him tooth and nail for her freedom, but his glacial stare inspired trepidation and warned her to use caution and defensive guile. She must get free.

"Your room? Ravish you?" he repeated the unexpected charges, then chuckled at their absurdity. "I don't know what trick you're trying to pull on me, but it won't work. Sorry if I hurt you, green eyes, but you should have warned me you'd never made love before. Still it doesn't justify you accusing me of rape. As for breaking into *your room*, that's another mistake in this scheme of yours," he mockingly scolded. "Didn't Nelle warn you to stay out of my private quarters? I know you're new here, but it's dangerous to sneak into a fellow's room and bed." He didn't smile as he watched the curious array of emotions which came and went on her ashen face.

"Your room and bed?" she echoed in sarcastic fury, instantly recalling Nelle's allusion to this being a privately owned room. *His?*

"Yep. You were lying in wait for me tonight, weren't you? How'd you know I'd be arriving so soon after you hired on? Besides what made you believe I wouldn't toss you out on your pretty tail? I must confess, you were a nice surprise." Having been the first man in her life, he felt great relief, excitement, and heady power. Could she be persuaded to become his private property? She was too lovely and unique to endure a whorish life.

His mocking words were frightfully enlightening. "I wasn't waiting here for you or anyone! If this is your private room, then Nelle made a terrible mistake.

I'm not a saloon girl; I'd never work in a horrible place like this. Even if what you claim is true, you still assaulted me!" she hotly accused. "Get off me!"

"Not until you explain what you're doing naked in my bed," he flatly refused. "Either speak up, or we'll be here like this all night."

Calinda was panicked by his determination. She tried to forget her innocent part in his wild charade. Was he the owner of this room? Had he mistaken her identity and reason for being here? What harm could the truth do? "Nelle let me stay here tonight because I didn't have anywhere else to go. I was robbed today outside town on the stagecoach."

"Then why didn't you say something or stop me?" he asked, an uneasy feeling washing over him, one oddly mingled with elation.

"I was too dazed. It must have been the sleeping drug Nelle gave me." As she eyed his bare chest, she swallowed loudly. Tears welled in her limpid eyes as she fought to move away from his warm touch, his flesh like a soft coppery blanket stretched tightly over a sturdy and exquisitely molded frame of iron.

The Ranger was just as disquieted and confounded as she was. To his acute dismay, he discovered himself in the novel position of feeling ashamed and thoroughly unsettled. He needed to get to the bottom of this dark well of mystery.

If she was telling the truth about being in his room and being drugged, that meant . . . Those arresting green eyes bright with unshed tears plagued him. "When I found you sprawled in my bed with little but your skin on, what was I supposed to think? You told me Nelle sent you, and you said you wanted to be here with me! Darnit, woman, you kept smiling at me and encouraging me! You did respond to me, green eyes, like no other female I've known," he defensively asserted. "The bartender told me about a new girl with fiery locks."

Those shocking remarks caused her to miss his last statement which would have clarified the misunderstanding. "What kind of beast ravishes a woman while she's senseless!" she charged angrily. "Even if Nelle made a mistake letting me sleep here, you didn't have to take advantage of me! Would you rape any woman found in your bed?" she berated him, as hazy memories of their lovemaking, alarming memories which she pushed aside, unclouded in her steadily clearing mind. "You're no better than those outlaws who attacked and robbed me, or those selfish people in this town who wouldn't even help me! How dare you mistake me for a wh . . . saloon girl."

"You can't put all the blame for this mistake on me. What kind of father would turn loose an innocent beauty like you to go roaming around in a dangerous territory? Nelle was crazy to put you in my bed dressed like that. Nobody uses this room but me. Any man would have lost his head in a set-up like this!"

"Evidently Nelle wasn't expecting you, but she could have warned me. And I wasn't 'roaming around'! I was riding a stage under guard. How do you people live under such violent conditions? Who are you?" she abruptly asked the rigid stranger with eyes entreating and piercing.

"Tex," he offered, not wanting her to learn his identity and risk complications. With luck, she would be gone tomorrow. At least, he would be. Instantly that knowledge piqued him. How could he leave her in trouble and danger, without money or protection? He knew nothing about virgins—had he hurt her on this first sexual encounter?

"Considering I'm partly to blame for this . . . mix-up, I'll give you some money to get home," he offered sullenly, failing to comprehend why he was speaking and acting in this insensitive way. He was having a terrible time holding his tough exterior in place.

Humiliated and angered, Calinda inhaled sharply. "You vile scoundrel! Your money can't pay for this outrage! Get out of here!" she ordered coldly, pounding on the sturdy chest. She needed solitude to decide how to deal with this staggering episode.

"Aren't you forgetting this is my room? If you don't like my company, dress and leave," he playfully suggested, waiting for her next move in this stimulating contest of wills. "I want to help you."

"What?" she blurted, staring at him. He had casually stolen her purity and was now tossing her out of this questionable room? She had no clothes or money! He wouldn't dare! He was the villain here!

"Get a room at the hotel," he added, grinning roguishly. "I apologized for my error, but I could lose control of myself again," he hinted, rolling to his side and propping on his left elbow to observe her.

"Error? You call what you did a simple error?" she demanded sarcastically, emerald eyes narrowed in outrage and distress.

"My first one," he informed her, as if shocked himself, then chuckled at her expression. "I guess I'm not perfect after all," he added.

Incensed, Calinda snapped. "You're despicable!"

"I've been called worse," he casually parried her insult.

"You are," she added, gritting her teeth at her helpless position. She had believed it could be no worse, but it was. She had no possessions or a weapon. Even her sharp wits were betraying her! She hated her scant choices. Either she could summon the sheriff and let everyone know she had been ravished by this carefree devil, or she could dress and leave as he so insensitively suggested. If she didn't accept his money, the hotel wouldn't accept her. If she did, she would be no better than the girls here who sold their bodies! Damn him!

"You're right, Callie," he agreed contritely as he witnessed her dilemma. She was so beautiful and vulnerable. "Callie what?"

"None of your business," she said frostily. When she found her father, she would have him discover this man's name and punish him! But punish him without permanently staining her reputation!

"Go to sleep, Callie. I'm exhausted. I promise you'll be safe tonight," he suddenly coaxed her, sounding serious and looking sincere. To steady his own nerves, the cowboy sat up and turned his back for a drink. Calinda couldn't help but see that the twisted sheet didn't conceal his firm buttocks. After the whiskey was poured and downed, he sat quietly for a time.

Calinda was about to spew forth another stinging tirade. When she turned in that direction, she couldn't speak. Caught unaware by the sight which greeted her gaze, she helplessly allowed her entranced eyes to wander over his coppery body of rippling muscles. He was lean and tall, his skin was smooth and unscarred. His tawny hair curled under at his nape and was full and wavy. Calinda found herself wondering who and what he was, this cunning seducer. When his hand went up to ruffle his hair, she stared at it, recalling how sensuously it had tormented and stimulated her body. The white statues of Apollo and Adonis couldn't match the perfection of his golden body. Growing warm and tense, she hurriedly pulled her eyes away from him.

"Well?" he split the silence, bemused by her lack of vengeful threats from her family and the law. He abruptly recalled her mumblings about no home and family. Maybe she had been dreaming. He was instinctively aware of her previous scrutiny. "Staying or leaving?" he clarified unnecessarily. "You know how it'll look if you traipse over to the hotel at this hour in that outfit? You can go to the law if you wish, but I wouldn't advise it. I didn't rape you, love. You know I'll have to tell my side of this mix-up. We're trapped together, Callie. Admit it and turn in. I know this has been a frightening day for you, a crazy experience for both of us. But I swear I won't hurt you or touch you again." His voice was as soft and warm as a summer day.

"Stay here with you?" she furiously scoffed, vexed by the way his words and voice affected her. "You're mad!" To gain thinking distance, she snatched the discarded coverlet and wound it about her trembling body. Being naked made her feel even more defenseless and hazy-headed! She wanted to pounce on him and beat him soundly; but she knew she hadn't the strength to hurt him. She couldn't allow him to go free, unpunished. But it was foolish to provoke him tonight; her revenge must be postponed until she had favorable odds.

"Why not? You have my word I won't . . ." he began.

"Don't you dare turn around!" she shrieked, adjusting the protective covering as humorous chuckles escaped him.

To appease her distraught senses, he relented to her panicky request. "It's easy to see you're a lady who's found herself in a perilous and embarrassing position. In spite of what happened earlier, I'm not a heartless animal. I don't force myself on any woman, especially not on a defenseless creature as beautiful and delicate as you. I can't erase tonight, but I can offer you my protection and hospitality."

"How chivalrous," she sneered, eyeing him suspiciously. Somehow she sensed she could trust him. Why, she couldn't explain or comprehend, unless it was the look in his mesmeric eyes or the tone to his stirring voice. Small rays of gentleness filtered through the tiny holes she had pierced in his hard facade, illuminating traits she found strange and pleasing. "I'll find Nelle and see if she has another place I can sleep."

"I wouldn't disturb her, she's busy with her sweetheart. Besides, this is the safest room here, even with me in it. I doubt the customers and working girls will take kindly to you tapping on their doors this time of night. Where were you heading?" he inquired.

Calinda cautiously lied, "To a town called Austin. My father's there and I was heading to join him. I've been in school back East." It was absurd to be carrying on a conversation with this rake.

Perceptive, the man knew she had spoken only half-truths, but he didn't want to reveal excessive interest by pressing her or contradicting her. She should have known those lucid green eyes read as easily as a marked trail. Too bad he didn't have time to study this exquisite girl more closely. He could sense her uncertainty and fear. She reminded him of a trapped rabbit, and twinges of remorse and tenderness pulled at his heart and mind. He was about to tell her she could stay in his room as long as necessary, but ruefully changed his mind. Once she contacted her father and revealed tonight's events, he didn't need an irate father tampering with his tight schedule or endangering his secret identity. They would meet again —Callie couldn't be difficult to trace . . .

"Evidently you have no intention of leaving, so I will. Would you please wait outside while I dress?" she said in an acid tone. "After what you did, you would leave me alone if you were any kind of gentleman." When the trailing coverlet tangled her bare feet, the top portion nearly escaped her tight grip as she reached for the bedpost to steady her balance. He wouldn't be grinning if she could reach one of his guns! But if she made a try for it, he would be on her in a moment. Besides, she didn't know how to use it!

He laughed as her cheeks burned a vivid red, aware of her longing gaze on his Colts. Her dismissal of that idea revealed her intelligence, not cowardice. When she glared at him, he playfully crossed his heart and huskily vowed, "I promise I'll be a perfect gentleman, Callie. If I hadn't been sleeping on the hard ground for weeks, I'd sleep on the floor. Been looking forward to my soft bed and there isn't enough cover to make a comfortable pallet. I'm afraid that sofa's too short for a man six-four," he added before she could suggest it. "This bed's big enough to share. If I was truly a dangerous brute, Callie, I could hold you here by force or just as easily toss you out. Come to bed. We're both tired and confused."

"I can't sleep like this," she argued his ridiculous solution. He was a smug and beguiling devil! Was he crazy as well as daring!

The flustered man assumed she meant sleep naked as he watched her clutch the cover to her bare body, as if fearing it would dislodge during the night or their bodies would make perilous contact. He reached for the nightgown, then changed his mind. "You might as well wear nothing as that see-through garb," he stated, looking about anxiously. If he was going to keep his vow, he couldn't be overly tempted! Then again, just looking at her accomplished that feat. Never had his control been so sorely strained!

He flung her his shirt and laughingly said, "This should protect you from my lecherous eyes, my wild vixen." Their gazes locked on the black shirt, both knowing how easily it could yield to his strength.

"You make this sound like some kind of mischievous game," she sneered at him, taking it and slipping it on. "If you lack the decency to let me stay here tonight, I insist you give me privacy to change," she ordered, chafed by his playful manner.

"I know it isn't a game, Callie. I've asked you to stay." He softened his words and gaze. How could he leave her so soon?

"To stay here with you! I'm not some whore, Tex! One of us has to leave," she persisted, a note of pleading edging her voice.

The Ranger suspected she might visit the sheriff's office if he forced her out tonight. He couldn't afford trouble. Besides, he was riding out early in the morning. He might as well sleep in the stable loft. Who knew what his generosity could earn him on a future day . . .

"All right, Callie, have it your way," he yielded. "Do you want to turn your back or wait outside while I dress?" he teased.

"You'll leave?" She couldn't believe she'd won.

"I can't have you traipsing around looking for a place to sleep. I will need my shirt," he hinted, laughing at her skeptical expression. "If you want that modesty to remain intact, best turn around, love."

Calinda slipped off his shirt and tossed it on the rumpled bed, then turned away. She waited anxiously as she heard the bed squeak. She closed her eyes tightly and leaned against the bedpost, praying he was being honest.

As he dressed to depart, the puzzled man was trapped in pensive reflections. Clearly he had misjudged her and this situation, but it wasn't entirely his fault. He was almost annoyed Callie hadn't laid a trap for him. At least he wouldn't feel so strange and remorseful if it had been a pre-planned deed. Her fiery passion couldn't be forgotten. Question was, had it been spontaneous or involuntary, a result of drugged senses? Would he ever see her again? These emotions were new and potent and he didn't know how to resist or accept them. Why did this slip of a girl offer such an alarming threat? What made her so different from other women? He didn't even know her! Yet he was actually giving up his comfortable room and bed for a stranger, one who viewed him the blackguard of all time! *Caramba!* He must be bored and fatigued to be thinking and feeling such contradictory emotions!

He pulled on his snug ebony pants and boots, then reached for the shirt she had been wearing. He strapped on his holsters and dropped the two Colts into place, ignoring the tightening in his pants as he viewed her slender back and inhaled her fragrance on his shirt. He berated his crazy indecision, this impulse to refuse to leave, this impulse to storm her with passionate kisses and stirring caresses. He flexed his strong hands as they itched to wander over her stimulating territory, upon which he had mentally staked a claim.

"Sure you want me to leave you alone in this dangerous place?" he inquired so close to her face she could feel the warmth of his breath.

She jumped, her eyes opening. "I'll be fine after you're gone," she sassily informed him before their gazes met to fluster her.

His eyes roved her face, the simple action pleasing to him. "Perhaps we'll meet again, Callie, under better circumstances."

"I pray I never set eyes on you again," she panted, her anger curiously returning as he made ready to leave.

The Ranger studied her flushed face and guilt-riddled look for a time. He was tempted to sweep her into his arms and prove her words a desperate lie. "If a certain gunslinger has his way, you might get your prayer answered before this week's out," he stated, watching for a reaction.

Calinda briefly fell for his ruse, but quickly controlled herself. She watched him place the dark hat on his tawny head before swaggering to the door. Tossing his saddlebags over his shoulder, he grinned and winked. "Nite, Callie, see you around," he murmured, then left. Calinda rushed forward to lock the door, forgetting he had a key.

She paced the floor for a lengthy time. It was hard to believe such things had taken place in one short day. She had another demanding day tomorrow; her head was throbbing and she needed sleep. She noticed the bottle left behind; she poured a drink and forced it down. This time, she removed the cover from her body and slipped nude between the mussed sheets. She sighed loudly and relaxed into the softness of the bed, inhaling his lingering fragrance on the pillow. Incredibly, she was soon sleeping peacefully. Maybe it was the dangers and violence she had witnessed and endured this day that made her feel safe in this particular room. Or perhaps it was the incredible nature of this day's events and emotions that made what happened this night seem unreal. Suddenly, it all seemed only a dream again . . .

The Ranger made his way toward the stable just as a heavy rain began. Before he could reach the entrance, he was soaked. As he stepped inside the enclosure, he cursed this strange day. The air was crisp at this late hour. He shivered and chided his sacrifice. He was tired, chilly, and miserable: all for a stubborn female! What did it matter if he had endured worse conditions? Tonight, his discomfort was self-imposed. He paced the dirt floor, berating himself and the girl sleeping warm and secure in his bed.

His whiskey should warm him. But he had left it behind. She would be panicked by his return, but what the hell! He could suffer only so much for an innocent mistake. He headed for the saloon, not bothering to run since he was already thoroughly saturated.

He quietly unlocked the door and peeked inside. She appeared to be sleeping. As if for a frightened child, the lantern had been left burning. As Calinda rolled to her side, the sheet slipped away to reveal most of her slender back. His white teeth gleamed as he grimaced, his arms aching to ease around her. Calinda sighed tranquilly and curled into a tight ball, fiery curls spreading over the white pillow.

The Ranger couldn't find the willpower to move, remembering how it had felt with the girl nestled against him. He irrationally cursed himself for giving his word not to touch her again; his loins ached for her. He yearned to feel those soft hands wandering over his body again, to bury his nose in that fragrant hair, to ride over the stirring hills and peaceful plains with a first love, a wild love. He had never broken his word, and he wouldn't start with this tempting treat. But watching her was as painful as falling into a thistle of bull nettles. He fretted over the novel emotions he was experiencing. The instinctive hair on the back of his neck seemed to bristle in warning. It was past time to get the hell out of this room!

Feeling slightly ridiculous, but trained to be wary and careful, the lawman soundlessly searched the room and under the edge of the mattress for a weapon or concealed clue to this delightful creature. Finding none, he sighed gratefully for that good luck. After all, some women were known to be vengeful and selfish . . .

Calinda stirred again, as if restless. Before she turned to her stomach and snuggled into his deserted place, he studied her intently, as if he could ever forget a line or curve on her ravishing face and body. He went to the corner table. He took a piece of paper and scribbled a note, then placed it and some money on her pillow. If Nelle was up before he rode off, he would question her about this mysterious girl. If not, then he would do so the next time he came to Fort Worth. He glanced at her a final time, wondering why he was having such a difficult time breathing, and departing. It wasn't like him to allow any distractions to his duty. Having never before avoided a threat or a challenge, he scurried from both in her.

He returned to the stable and stripped off the wet clothes, pulling on a pair of lightweight longjohns to ward off a chill. He took several large gulps of whiskey and snuggled into the wiry hay and scratchy blanket. As the Ranger continued to lie there awake and restless, defensive doubts badgered his keen mind. Was it possible two redheads would show up at the same saloon, the same day, with the same first name? Would Nelle loan his private room to a total stranger? If Nelle had been swayed by this girl's troubles, why didn't she loan her two dollars for a hotel room? If Callie was playing some game, she had selected the wrong man to dupe. It didn't seem logical for a "lady" to be travelling alone in the wild West. Surely this girl wasn't a female detective, out to use him for information? Several cattle barons, one in particular, were under investigation; but would they hire a beautiful vixen to waylay him? Perhaps his undercover job made him too leery, but there was one powerful *haciendado* he couldn't ignore . . .

The wily Texan had slain many men, some in the line of duty and some from challenges that couldn't be handled any other way. Could she be a vengeful sweetheart, daughter, or sister? Improbable, he concluded, but not impossible. Her prior innocence ruled out vindictive widow. He was relieved that Nelle had been warned never to reveal his name or location to any curious person. It was a difficult search, but the persistent drifter finally located dreamland and entered its enticing gates. It was only a few hours before he was up and dressed, riding off to Dallas to meet with Major Jones, not daring to check on Callie again.

Hours later, Calinda stirred. Slowly her hazy mind and heavy eyes cleared. She bolted up in the bed and looked around; something was different. The window was closed; the lantern was out; the bottle was gone. Staring at her naked body, she fumed at his unforgivable action. He had returned while she was sleeping! She hurried to make certain the door was locked, sighing when it was though she knew he had a key. Her gaze touched on the money on the pillow, bringing a flush to her face and anger to her mind. Was he paying her like some harlot? She stalked to the bed and seized the unsigned note. Stunned, she read it a second time:

Callie,

Sorry about our delightful mistake last night. Buy some clothes and a gun. Get to the hotel and stay put until you can get on your way home. Next time we meet, my flame-haired beauty, my chivalrous promise will be worthless. Rest assured, we will meet again. Keep a sharp eye over your lovely shoulder. One day I'll ride up behind you when you least expect it.

Calinda was addled, but annoyingly warmed. How dare that arrogant rebel order her around! "Our mistake," she scoffed. But he had kept his word, and he had left her some money. "No doubt you'll expect payment for it if we do ever meet again," she whispered apprehensively, then scolded herself for the surge of eager suspense that followed. Even if it had been a misunderstanding, she had a right to this money in view of what he had taken from her. As soon as her dress was repaired, she would take his suggestions. She would shop for clothes and buy a gun, then register at the hotel and wait for the sheriff to assist her. If Tex came around again before her departure, he would find himself on the barrel end of the gun he had generously purchased!

Yet as Calinda waited for Nelle to appear, she found herself thinking about the trespasser who had abruptly invaded her world and selfishly changed it, then just as mysteriously departed. Was his note a promise, a threat, or a joke? As she reflected on his touch and kisses, she trembled. How could a beguiling stranger cause her body to sing such forbidden and romantic songs and entice her traitorous heart to dream of meeting him again. She must be going daft!

When Nelle came to bring her garments and breakfast, Calinda didn't mention Tex's nocturnal visit. Nelle appeared flustered and rushed this morning, quickly leaving with the promise to return later. Recalling the stranger's words about Nelle's sweetheart, Calinda decided Nelle was either spending every available minute with him or was bidding him a sad farewell. Calinda ate slowly, then dressed, after which, she impatiently sat waiting for Nelle's return.

Just before noon, the hefty and genial woman returned. When Calinda casually inquired about the owner of her room, Nelle told her not to worry, that he wouldn't mind her staying here one night. When Calinda pressed for more information about him, Nelle reluctantly told Calinda he was Cody Richards, a wealthy rancher's son from down Laredo way. When Calinda asked how often he came to town, Nelle said he only showed up about every six weeks to relax and have some fun.

It would be dusk, when Jake Tarply the bartender came to work, before Nelle would learn of the cowboy's unexpected visit. A new mystery would be added to Nelle's immense collection. She would wonder why Calinda had kept silent. And again today, Nelle had her guileful cousin to fret over, for the audacious Callie had stolen money and vanished at dawn, after having been seen in the company of a notorious gunslinger!

Calinda was shown to the sheriff's office, then Nelle went about her flurry of business. Calinda related her story to the sympathetic man, who promptly informed her there was little chance of getting back her possessions. Calinda was distraught. She told the sheriff he could keep everything as a reward if he only recovered the locket. After promising to do all he could, Calinda went to the hotel to register. The owner was surprised to see her again this morning. If she had any other choice, she wouldn't stay in his hotel.

Later, she went to the telegraph office to hire a messenger to deliver two letters to the Cardone Ranch, one to her father and one to Rankin Cardone in case her father was absent. When that task was finished, she headed for the mercantile store to purchase the needed garments. There was little to choose from in her size, so Calinda purchased two simple dresses, cotton underwear, toiletries, and a plain nightgown. Having nothing to occupy her time until her father or Mister Cardone appeared, she purchased another book to while away the hours and to distract her from thoughts of Cody.

Knowing Nelle deserved a brief explanation, Calinda went to see her later that afternoon. Nelle sensed her embarrassment, tension, and reluctance as Calinda told her false story. Calinda said the banker had loaned her money until her father or Mister Cardone arrived. She tried to pay Nelle for her kindness, but Nelle refused. When Calinda asked about Callie, Nelle dropped several enlightening clues to the event of last night. Nelle was surprised when the young woman hugged her fondly and thanked her before leaving.

As Calinda returned to the hotel, she realized how the beguiling stranger had made such a tormenting error; he had been told about the arrival of Callie and had mistaken Calinda for the new girl. In light of the crazy set of coincidences, the outcome was logical. Yet, he had made love to the wrong woman, if only she hadn't been dazed! Had Cody learned of his error? Was that why he had returned to leave the money and note? Or did he still think she was Callie O'Hara . . .

Calinda slept fitfully that night, but dreamed about the bronzed stranger with tawny eyes. For two days, she paced the wooden floor of her room, waiting and praying. The tall stranger didn't return to town; or if he did, Calinda never saw him from her window which faced the main street. The sheriff called once, to tell Calinda there was no news on the robbery. In the raw cowtown, Calinda dared not go out alone, especially not after her initial experiences here in Texas. After each meal, she would return to her room to wait.

By the third day, she was growing anxious. If she didn't hear something today, she would send another message and speak bluntly with the sheriff. Surely it couldn't take much longer for her message to arrive and to get a response. Calinda dreaded to think about her future if her father was gone. Her only friend was a tender-hearted saloon madam. If only Cody . . . he had probably dismissed her from his mind the instant the door closed behind his towering and virile frame. She cursed Cody for his hold over her mind and body.

To her dismay, she suddenly wondered how to deal with another problem— what if Rankin Cardone didn't live around here anymore? He was the only clue to her father! She hastily dismissed that fear, for the messenger had taken her money and agreed to deliver her letters.

Mid-morning, a loud knock sounded on her door. When she asked who was there, a masculine voice replied, "Rankin Cardone, *Senorita*. May I come in and speak with you?"

Relieved and excited, Calinda unlocked the door and opened it. Her smile froze in place when she saw he was alone. She dreaded to hear the meaning behind her father's absence.

"You wanted to see me?" Rankin asked crisply, eyeing her intently. He obviously held an inner strength which matched his supple frame.

"Yes. Please come in," she offered politely, then stepped aside.

—— *Chapter 3* ——

❧

THE FORMIDABLE *HACIENDADO* entered her room and sat down in a chair, his movements fluid and controlled. It was impossible to miss his aura of wealth, power, and self-assurance. As if a man at ease anywhere, he crossed his right ankle over his left thigh. Rankin Cardone presented a most distinguished figure, tall and muscular. Though he must have been nearly fifty, he certainly did not look his age. Impeccably dressed, he wore garments that suggested a Spanish flair. Except for a white shirt, he was clad in black. A narrow length of black silk was tied around his collar, its tails dangling down the front of his ruffled shirt. He casually removed his hat and placed it on his lap, his fingers caressing the braided band as a child would stroke a furry kitten. His boots were highly polished; for a moment Calinda wondered if she could see her face reflected there.

His sable hair was peppered lightly with silver at the temples. He wore a thin mustache which curled slightly on both ends and a neatly trimmed Vandyke beard. His features bore an aristocratic mien. Suddenly his last name struck a note, Spanish or Mexican? His forceful gaze seemed to penetrate Calinda's flesh, making her uneasy. The expression on Rankin's face was resolute, his thoughts and feelings unreadable. He gazed at her as if assessing a new breed of stock. Although Calinda was accustomed to meeting people of wealth and prestige, this man tampered with her poise and confidence.

Calinda walked forward and sat down on the edge of the bed. "I'm sorry if I'm inconveniencing you, Mister Cardone. Why didn't my father come? Why did he send you? Is he busy or away?" she asked, hardly knowing where to begin.

One brow lifted inquisitively and his dark eyes intentionally clouded with confusion. "Your arrival and frantic summons came as a complete surprise to me. Since your message sounded so urgent, I felt I should respond personally. I am greatly puzzled, *Senorita*. Why are you seeking Elliott Braxton at the Cardone Ranch?"

"You're saying my father doesn't work or live at your ranch?" she questioned apprehensively, her eyes pleading for a negative reply.

"Where would you get such ideas, *Senorita?*"

"His last letter told me about you and the ranch. I was supposed to join him when I finished school in England," she replied hoarsely.

To test her depth of knowledge or questionable intentions, Rankin probingly disputed, "Impossible. Brax has been gone for years. Who are you, *Senorita?* Why did you really come?" he asked unflinchingly.

Bemused, Calinda arose quickly and gaped at him, her face paling. "He's gone?" she asked in a strained voice.

"Probably dead," Rankin declared to test her reaction.

The room spun dizzily, then went black as Calinda slipped to the floor in a faint. Rankin was spurred into motion, coming to her side. He lifted her limp body and placed her on the bed. Taking a wet cloth, he mopped her ashen face until she stirred. In spite of his calm facade, Rankin's mind was whirling with wild speculations. What did this girl expect from him? Was she really Calinda Braxton? She didn't favor Brax at all. Bitterness and hatred smoldered within Rankin. Aware of the stakes, he quickly warned himself to be cautious and alert.

When Calinda began to sob, Rankin quietly said, "I'm sorry, *Senorita* Braxton: I should not have been so blunt. We only assume your father is dead; he vanished years ago. All of your letters to him were returned. Why did you come here?"

Her voice trembling with emotion, but edged with new hope, she told Rankin what had brought her to this moment. "I'm just as confused as you, sir. If you returned my letters, they never reached me. Why would he leave without telling me? I never imagined you wouldn't be able to help me." She tried to master her tears and grief.

Rankin didn't know what to think. Perhaps this girl was ignorant of the turbulent past. But did he owe anything to the daughter of his treacherous enemy? Still, her fear and sadness, if they were real, touched and disarmed him.

"Why would you come this far without hearing from Brax for years? I cannot understand why Brax didn't inform you of his departure."

Calinda explained her reasons and predicament, adding details of the recent robbery. Rankin concluded either she was an excellent deceiver or she didn't know the truth. This girl and curious situation could be dangerous. She could accidentally or rashly uncover the buried past . . . He needed time to observe her, to glean more facts.

A genial smile flickered on Rankin's lips as a plan formulated in his keen mind. "There is but one action to take. You'll come to the Cardone Ranch until we can decide what to do with you."

"I couldn't impose on you, Mister Cardone," she weakly argued.

"Don't be foolish, *Senorita* Braxton. Of course you'll come. You can hardly remain here accepting charity. Besides, this is no place for a young lady alone. You'll be my guest for as long as you wish." No matter what her motive, she must go with him.

A sunny and trusting smile brightened Calinda's face, softening her eyes. "You're very kind, Mister Cardone. Do you think there's any possibility my father's alive? Did anyone search for him?"

"Yes, *Senorita* Braxton. I personally conducted a lengthy search, then hired a Pinkerton detective. Nothing. When so much time passed without word or a clue, we gave up all hope. Brax was always craving new adventures and chasing dreams. Perhaps he'll return one day."

In her distracted state, Calinda missed the coldness in Rankin's voice and eyes and the intensity of his observation. Within the hour, she was packed and on her way to the Cardone Ranch, under the eagle eye of Rankin and several of his men.

To prevent her from asking too many questions, Rankin conversed on Texas, cattle, local events, and the landscape. Calinda was amazed by the scenery. She had never seen such openness, such seemingly endless grasslands and pale blue skies. Mountains could be viewed in the distance. In some areas, no trees or bushes existed. In others, they sparsely dotted the land in scattered clusters or stood singularly like a lonely person. Wild cactus and white yuccas were abundant, as were a variety of colorful wildflowers. Some fields appeared sown in thousands of goldenrods, Indian paintbrush, or blue bonnets. To take her mind off her dilemma, Calinda turned this way and that to take in the panorama, a ruggedly beautiful setting.

As they passed fenced areas, she watched healthy cattle and sleek horses as they grazed or moved about aimlessly. Sometimes mounted cowboys could be seen herding them or kneeling beside fires with branding irons. When Calinda asked if branding hurt the animals, Rankin eagerly launched into an explanation of the necessary task.

"A brand is like your name. Any man can capture and sell mavericks, unbranded cattle that roam free. It's important to use a mark that can't be changed by rustlers or be read in another way by some dishonest rancher. Branding might sting for a minute, but it's quickly forgotten. We try to do horses and cattle while they're young. There's a certain way to read a brand. It starts from top to bottom, then from left to right. If a letter is in a slanted position, it's called tumbling. If it's lying on its side, it's called lazy. Naturally a rocker on its base means rocking something, or wings on its sides means flying something. I'll show you all about them on the ranch."

"That sounds most intriguing," she said, eyes aglow.

"Do you know how to ride and shoot?" he asked curiously, glancing at the exquisite lady in the cheap, cotton dress.

"I'm a good rider, and I can handle a rifle. From what I've observed so far, both traits appear vital out here."

"Most assuredly, *Senorita* Braxton. I'll have one of my men teach you how to fire a pistol. One never knows when one's life might be in jeopardy." He chuckled at her hasty agreement.

"Do you have any family, Mister Cardone?" she inquired.

"One son. My wife . . . is no more."

Calinda graciously dismissed the grim mention of his deceased wife. "I look forward to meeting your son. I hope he won't mind my intrusion." Calinda was charmed by his easy manner and stimulating personality, taking an instant liking to this man. Despite their unlikely meeting, they had discovered an easy rapport.

"Lynx is rarely home. He prefers to roam. This area often inspires wildness in young bucks. I'm hoping he'll be ready to settle down soon." Calinda's arrival had been a shock to Rankin, and he was feeling more talkative than usual in his troubled state. It was uncanny, but she possessed a rare talent for liberating him of doubts and restraints.

Calinda noted the trace of sadness in Rankin's expression as he unknowingly allowed it to surface. Her heart went out to him; he must be terribly lonely with his wife dead and his son off sowing wild oats. If Lynx favored his father, he must be a handsome man. "How did he get such an unusual name?" she asked politely.

Rankin gazed off as he told her the fascinating story of his son's birth. "That was before the ranch was settled and our house was ready. Laura and I were living in a cabin at the edge of the mountains, waiting for winter to let up. I was trapping and hunting. One day I returned to find my only son arriving early. When he made his howling entrance, the first thing I grabbed to wrap him in was a lynx hide. Might add, he seems to have grown up as wild and cunning as one."

Traveling a road from his past and exploring Calinda's reactions, Rankin talked on. "Lynx was terribly upset when Laura was taken from us. He couldn't seem to sit still a minute. He became moody and reckless. Every time he rides off, I wonder if he'll get home alive. He's been in more gunfights and fistfights than I care to recall. I think that reputation of his has him bewitched; sometimes he acts like he can challenge and defeat Satan himself. In fact, I wouldn't be at all surprised if he did. I've scolded and reasoned for years. Hasn't done any good. God help any fool who crosses him." From the corner of his dark eyes, Rankin watched the girl sitting next to him. If any of those facts were familiar to her, it didn't show; nor did she seem to doubt or fear him. Rankin couldn't allow Calinda to discover what had happened with Brax, nor to become mistrustful of the Cardones.

Calinda felt Rankin had been speaking about himself as much as his carefree son. This Lynx should be ashamed of his selfishness; it was clear his father needed and loved him. She wanted to ask more questions, but didn't want to be impolite. When she tried to probe into her father's departure and past life on the ranch, Rankin asked her to wait until later when they could speak in private.

By dusk, the Cardone Ranch was in sight. They travelled for miles after Rankin told her they were on his land, then for many more miles after passing under the gatepost with the "C" over the "R". Evidently the Cardone Ranch was massive. The landscape was peaceful and lovely. Large herds of cattle and groups of horses could be seen at intervals. She was filled with awe and excitement.

When they approached the house, Calinda's eyes widened in astonishment. It was a two-story, oblong structure which hinted at a *hacienda* facade. The exterior was adobe, sheathed in sandy-colored stucco. The roofs on the house and the verandas were covered with mission tile, dull red terra cotta. The front portico spanned the full length of the house, displaying five large arches through which the downstairs doors and windows were visible. The curved arches were edged with muddy red adobe blocks, as were all windows on the first and second floors. Two private balconies were set on either end of the top floor, each with a front and side arch for views. The house and private yards were enclosed by an irregular stone wall. With cactus gardens scattered around, the scene was enchanting and heart-warming.

A short distance away, there were other structures, well-kept and solid. She noticed three stone bunkhouses with a separate cookhouse, two lofty barns, several supply sheds, a windmill and watertower, sturdy corrals, and miles of fencing. She couldn't help but wonder why her father would desert such a lovely locale and good man.

When the carriage halted, Rankin helped Calinda down. A dark-haired, dark-eyed young woman left the house to join them, halting near Rankin to glower at Calinda with visible displeasure. She was introduced as Salina Mendoza, housekeeper and cook. Salina's colorful skirt swayed as her shapely body moved. She was wearing a white peasant blouse that hinted at a large bosom. Her mouth was painted red; her skin was olive and smooth. Midnight hair tumbled over her dark shoulders; her nearly black eyes were chilly and mocking. She merely nodded when Calinda spoke to her. Tossing a *"Disculpa,"* excuse me, over her shoulder, Salina turned and strutted inside with Calinda's small bundle clutched beneath one arm.

As they stepped into the entry hall, Rankin was telling Calinda she would need clothes made very soon. He suggested a party in the near future to introduce her to his neighbors, implying a lengthy stay. He could hardly keep his past friendship with her father a secret, so he used it as the motive for helping her. For now, he simply needed to discover how much she knew and why she had appeared suddenly.

Rankin doubted that Brax had confided in a distant family which he had abandoned and betrayed. The question remained, was Calinda Braxton as genuine and naive as she claimed and appeared? The best solution was to wait until Lynx came home. With Lynx's intuition, intelligence, and charming prowess, he would extract the truth and deal with it. If she was guilty, *Que lastima . . .*

Just inside the doorway, Calinda visually explored her new surroundings. To the left, a bowed arch revealed a striking dining room. An open door beyond it exposed the kitchen. Straight ahead, there were steps leading upstairs. Beside the stairs, she could partially view the bedroom used by Rankin. To her right, double wooden doors opened into an immense living area. To the rear of that room was Rankin's office, with doors opening into it and his bedroom.

Salina returned to show Calinda to a guest room on the second floor, a spacious and feminine room with a small front balcony and a large veranda to the rear. Salina spoke little and seemed to enjoy revealing her dislike of the beautiful stranger. Salina left her alone.

The moment the nasty girl left, Calinda examined her room. The furnishings were Spanish; the color scheme was in shades of blue, gold, and ivory. There was a sitting area to the front which opened onto the private balcony. She peered out the double glassed doors to the rear. A roofed veranda went from one end of the house to the other, again with three large arches before three sets of double doors. After freshening herself, Calinda donned a plain dress and went downstairs for dinner.

Rankin was relaxed in this controlled setting. Tonight, he chatted easily and smiled freely. The roast and fresh vegetables were delicious, a rare treat after her recent meals. Salina cleared the table as Rankin and Calinda went into a very masculine living room for a glass of sherry.

Calinda wandered around the spacious area as she sipped her sherry. As they sat, they conversed on the heavy and skillfully carved furniture, the chair made of horns from steers, the swords and guns displayed on one wall, the large buffalo head mounted over an enormous fireplace, various objects of Spanish art exhibited, and tapestries which added color and enchantment to the rectangular room, as did several multi-colored rugs placed on the highly polished wooden floor. Rankin pointed out the *"vegas,"* ceiling beams in cottonwood, and *"rajas,"* split cottonwood molding vertically attached to the walls every three feet. As with the exterior, the interior adobe walls were sheathed in beige stucco. There were two sets of double glass-doors, one leading to a side portico and one leading to the front veranda. Even though it lacked a feminine touch, Calinda found it appealing. To one end, there was a billiard table. Rankin said he would teach her that game.

The hour grew late as Rankin told Calinda carefully selected tales of how he and her father had spent earlier days. There were only a few hired hands still around from those years; they had been warned not to mention Brax or those past times. Calinda heard how her father had fought Indians and nature side-by-side with Rankin while he was carving out this empire which rivaled the King Ranch to the south near Laredo and the XIT to the northeast. Rankin disclosed many colorful past adventures, all of which Calinda found stimulating. She warmed at the slight mention of Laredo . . .

Rankin told Cal that Brax "just up and left one day," never to return or send a message of his whereabouts. "Brax made a terrible mistake, Calinda. We would have been great partners. If things had been different, both you and Lynx would be living here." Once again, Rankin gingerly questioned Brax's letters to her in England.

Calinda felt embarrassed about her father's actions toward her and her mother and to this generous man. Evidently her father had become greedy, selfish, and ungrateful. Rankin was surprised when Calinda apologized for her father's conduct. "I don't know what I would have done if you hadn't shown up, Mister Cardone. Considering how my father repaid your kindness, I'm amazed you did. Why would he leave here? Why didn't he confide in you or contact me?"

"In those early days, Brax and I were best friends, Calinda. I could hardly allow his daughter to fend for herself. Brax was like a man driven by some inexplicable force; maybe he found life here dull after the danger was past and the challenges were fewer. But I am sorry for what he put you through. You can stay here as long as you wish. I've missed laughter and beauty in this house. Come and go as you wish. Ask for anything you want or need. I owe Brax plenty. You have no place to go. I doubt you wish to return to England, and you have no other kin." He felt those reasons should hold her here until this precarious mystery could be solved. Besides, he desired her to remain.

His hospitality and friendship were godsends, and Calinda was drawn to them. "I insist on helping out, Mister Cardone. I can cook and clean. This is a large house for Salina to manage alone."

"A special guest doesn't work, *Senorita*," he teased mirthfully before they went their separate ways.

When Calinda awoke the next morning and went downstairs, she found Rankin gone and Salina busy with chores. When she offered to help, she quickly discovered Salina wasn't receptive to that idea. In fact, Salina waited on her as an honored guest in this house, as Rankin had ordered with the hope of disarming Calinda.

Calinda walked around the house and yards, trying to avoid Salina's glacial path and sharp tongue. She couldn't decide why the Mexican girl was so hostile. It seemed best to ignore Salina and evade her. If she stayed very long, she would find a way to halt this silly conflict with that tempestuous girl. Calinda wasn't one to accept charity or to laze around. But she had suffered several defeats and needed time to regroup her thoughts and to make future plans. Although she had never thought of getting a job, it seemed the only course for survival. The idea of teaching or sewing for the rest of her life sounded repulsive and boring. But what else could a woman do?

Calinda ate lunch in the quiet dining room, feeling very small at the lengthy table. Afterwards, she boldly explored the upstairs while Salina was occupied with laundry. At the top of the stairs, a hallway ran in either direction. She went to her left, to locate a room on the end which matched hers in size and shape. Obviously, from the manly decor, it was Lynx's room. On both sides of the stairway, she found two smaller rooms; one hinted at a previous nursery and the other was a storage room for linens and so forth. Between her room and Lynx's was another, but smaller, guestroom.

She walked to the veranda, promptly aware all three bedrooms opened onto it. As with the front two balconies, it had a waist-high adobe railing for safety. She strolled to each of the three back arches and two side ones to scan the picturesque setting. From her lofty position, she could see a distance in many directions. She leaned over the edge, mildly surprised to see the bottom floor revealed only windows. She did notice two other entrances, one for the kitchen and one she would learn was Salina's room. She sat in one of the chairs and allowed her placid senses to be engulfed by the splendor of nature before her gaze.

When Rankin hadn't returned by evening, Calinda questioned the sullen Salina about him and his return. The girl's eyes flung daggers at Calinda as Salina informed her Rankin wouldn't be home until tomorrow night, that he had gone to purchase her some clothes in several nearby towns. The Mexican girl bade Calinda goodnight and went to her room in the rear of the house, with only an outside entrance.

Calinda went to the sitting room and selected a book from the shelves. She read for a while, then went to bed. Why hadn't Rankin told her his plans? A surprise? But why take such pains and expense with her? Evidently he was very lonely and wanted to keep her around.

Lying in bed, Calinda's mind rebelliously chased a sunny-haired man with mocking tawny eyes. How she wished she could forget Cody and his bedeviling touch. Why did little twinges pain her when she realized she would never see him again? His smiling face with its twinkling eyes loomed before her dreamy vision. She snuggled into the bed, recalling how his embrace had felt, how he had smelled, how his shirt had felt clinging to her nude body. Her fingers trailed over her lips as they craved to taste his again.

She felt warm and edgy, but didn't know why. She shifted this way and that, trying to find a comfortable position. He was like a pesty insect, buzzing around inside her head, refusing to leave her in peace. *Cody Richards,* her mind murmured softly, *damn you for haunting me.* Did she dare ask Rankin about this mysterious Cody?

Suspense filled Calinda's heart as dreams of what she would say and do if Cody discovered her identity and pursued her flashed through her mind. Would he check on her when he returned to Fort Worth and the Red Satin Saloon? Had he only been looking for a good time that night? Nelle had said that was the reason for his room and trips there. What if he was married? She hadn't even asked Nelle about that possibility. What was Cody really like? How far away was this Laredo? Would he bother to look her up one day? Probably not. A man with Cody's looks and wealth could have any woman, many women. Even though he had cunningly seduced her, he no doubt felt he didn't owe her anything since he had left her money and a crafty apology! But he did owe her something. He had forced himself into her life and heart and made an unforgettable impression there. By now, Cody had probably forgotten all about her and their night together . . .

To the east of Dallas, Major John Jones was having a meeting with his undercover Ranger, the mysterious and irresistible man who filled Calinda's dreams. Major Jones possessed all the traits demanded for a successful leader: he was a man with superior intelligence, a man feared and respected for his courage and daring, a man with a cool head and unerring judgment, a man who would give quarter and never ask for it. Jones was short and slender for such a powerful force, standing under five-nine and weighing less than one hundred and forty. Yet, he exuded strength and confidence.

Lynx Cardone listened as his superior told him General Steele had ordered Jones to Denton County to study the violence and crimes there. When Lynx remarked he was growing weary of his secret service, Major Jones reminded him of the importance of his undercover work. He listed several examples, two of which included getting into tight places and giving advanced warning of planned Ranger assassinations like he did in June of '77. A man in Lynx's stealthy position could ride into a troubled area, study it, then report to the arriving Rangers. Lynx's clues often aided their work and safety. But the perceptive Jones sensed a novel tension in his friend and fellow Ranger. As Jones watched Lynx, his penetrating eyes saw a noticeable glow of vitality and gentleness, a sensitivity and alertness which were rare.

A quiet and deliberate man, Major Jones laughed softly and said, "Maybe we'll have help on this problem. The Pinkerton men are holed up at LeGrand, and Marshal Russell and his deputies are over at the Windsor Hotel. We've got more bounty hunters, special agents, and detectives in town than Texas has cattle." He lightly stroked a thick mustache which almost concealed his upper lip. He was the perfect image of the aristocratic Southern gentleman.

"Is Armstrong coming in on this mission?" Lynx asked, watching Jones's dark eyes twinkle.

"He's working the southern area, down Kerrville and San Antonio way. Here's your crime book, Lynx. Don't lose it," he jested.

Lynx scanned the vital book which listed the names and descriptions of wanted men. Lynx sipped his coffee as Major Jones tossed his gear on the bed. Lynx's gaze eased over the supplies which all Rangers carried: Winchester rifle, Colt pistols with their eagles carved on ivory handles, Bowie knife, blanket, gum coat, riata, ammo, salt, and sweetened and dried corn for relieving thirst.

"It won't be much longer before you can wear your badge, Lynx. Be patient, son, you're doing us a valuable service. You've figured out it's the Bass gang that's operating around here?"

Lynx nodded his head. Jones continued, "I'm setting Peak on his trail. See if you can latch on to any of Sam's men. Here's a list of their names; memorize it and burn it."

Lynx read the seven names listed under Sam Bass's. There was an eighth name with a question mark beside it. Jones explained, "We're not sure about Murphy. Just be aware of him. Bass seems to be favoring the Texas Central and the Texas & Pacific Railroads. I'm checking their schedules now. I'll fill you in later. I sent for Lieutenant Reynolds, but don't know when he'll arrive. Quick as I get this matter studied, I'll decide how many Rangers we'll be needing."

"Where's McNelly?" Lynx asked, leaning back in the chair.

"Down Palo Alto way. He's needed there right now."

"I'll hang around the Split Horn Saloon a few days."

Jones halted his work to glance at his friend. "That's a rough place, Lynx. Be careful. Been home lately?"

Lynx sighed heavily and stroked his bristly chin. "Not in months. For the time being, that seems best." He chuckled wryly.

"Rankin still flaying your hide?" Jones teased knowingly.

"He will until he learns the truth."

"Won't be much longer," John Jones encouraged once more.

"I hope not, sir." Lynx didn't tell Jones about the flame-haired girl who continued to haunt him, even though he struggled to erase her from his mind. Maybe he should ride over to Fort Worth tomorrow and see if Callie was still around and if she was all right. He wasn't sure if he dared see her this soon, but this ignorance was sheer torture.

When Lynx rode to the Red Satin Saloon that following night, only Jake Tarply knew of his coming or going. When he discovered Jake out back taking a break for fresh air, Lynx questioned him about the redhead who had arrived by stage a few days past. After learning what he had come for, Lynx mounted and raced the wind to Dallas, cursing Callie O'Hara all the way and berating himself for even caring about her.

The little vixen had fooled him completely, an uncommon mistake on his part, one which rankled for several reasons. When Callie's outlaw sweetheart discovered Lynx Cardone had bedded his stunning *zorra* first, perhaps a future showdown would result from his reckless night of passion. Lynx chuckled coldly. He might enjoy this one!

Anger and revenge gnawed at Lynx. He shouldn't have given Callie another thought. Why had he allowed that conniving bitch to burn through his tough hide? Apparently the only truth to leave her soft lips concerned the stage hold-up and her losses, which she deviously recovered at his and Nelle's expenses. But the traitorous Callie would pay dearly if and when their paths crossed again! Cousin or not, how dare Callie betray darlin' Nelle! Tonight, the flame in his heart smoldered brightly with fury, not passion . . .

Like a child at birthday or Christmas time, Calinda squealed with excitement and pleasure as she opened the boxes Rankin had placed on her bed. His taste was excellent and his generosity extravagant. Everything Calinda could need or want was there. Rankin had taken one of her dresses and an outline of her shoe for appropriate sizes. He had even purchased jeans and boots for riding, as western women could dress and ride like men. There were dresses, nightgowns, underwear, shirts, pants, skirts, blouses, shoes, boots, and a gun with a leather holster.

Calinda argued against the expense but Rankin said, "While I was in town on business, I remembered the robbery and your losses. Your father left before I paid him for the last cattle drive. I only spent the money due him; he shouldn't mind."

That last lie eased Calinda's conscience. But she knew from Salina that Rankin had gone specifically to shop for her. Evidently he was proud and didn't want her to guess his kind motives. Rankin was slightly flustered when the young girl hugged him and thanked him over and over. "A lovely young lady should be dressed in silks and satins, but that's the best they had to offer nearby. Next time I go to Wichita Falls or San Antonio, you can tag along and choose some more clothes. When I show you off to my friends and neighbors I want you to be the prettiest girl in Texas."

As Calinda admired the clothes, Rankin watched her closely. She possessed many fine qualities. Even if she had originally come here to cause trouble, Rankin would soon have her too indebted and charmed to do so. If she was anything like she seemed, she wouldn't have the stomach or desire to deceive or betray the Cardones.

Impressionable and susceptible, Calinda was overwhelmed by Rankin's plans and actions. The next few weeks saw her adjusting easily and quickly to life on the Cardone Ranch. As she eased into the ranch routine, she showed a freshness and warmth which appealed to Rankin. During these past years, Rankin hadn't realized how lonely and barren his life had become. Rankin found himself enjoying Calinda's wit, charm, and intelligence. She sparkled with life and made him feel vital and young again. A budding fondness and delight in her companionship came to pass during those following weeks after her arrival, deepening in spite of his lingering doubts and resistance.

Frequently they were seen riding together, laughing freely and getting to know each other as Rankin introduced Calinda to his cattle spread and way of life. During meals, they would engage in stimulating conversation. Calinda's eyes would shine with enthusiasm as Rankin told her the history of the west and his ranch. She came to respect and admire him and to love the ranch and her new existence. Helpless to alter her situation, she eagerly accepted it. Each task learned or observed was done with carefree adventure and gay spirit.

True to his word, Rankin taught Calinda how to play billiards, then cards. Many nights their laughter and wagers could be heard above the stillness of the night. Calinda learned to ride a horse western style. She watched calves and colts being branded. She perched on the corral fence in her jeans, boots, and colorful shirt as cowboys broke wild horses. She rode beside Rankin as he checked on herds or fences. Each passing day drew them closer, a respect and admiration for each blooming steadily. Neither mentioned Calinda's departure, as if it were unthinkable.

At times, Calinda thought she noted strange looks in Rankin's eyes, but dismissed them as tricks of light or attributed them to fatigue. It almost seemed Rankin wanted to fully accept her permanent residence and affections, but was afraid to do so. Sometimes, Calinda sensed he was withholding facts from her, that he was telling her only what he wanted her to know. She scolded herself for harboring such unkind suspicions. When Rankin was distant or moody, she concluded it was from loneliness for his son or perhaps painful memories which her feminine presence inspired. Calinda decided that Rankin was a wary man, a man afraid to share too much of himself, a man afraid of being hurt or deserted. To Calinda, Rankin was a special and uncommon man, a private man who defended his home and feelings. It didn't take long for the ranch to seem like home and Rankin like family.

Rankin dreaded the facts this girl might uncover, facts he wanted to remain buried. He knew he was becoming extremely fond of Calinda; he was beginning to trust her. He was torn between two warring emotions. It was difficult to see Calinda as Brax's child, but she was. Was it dangerous or insane to keep her around? Should he give her money and send her away? How could a sweet, artless child survive alone? Calinda hadn't said or done anything unusual. Rankin fretted over this affection which was destroying his clear head and lessening his desire for revenge. But Rankin selfishly ignored his qualms, deciding to deal with Calinda's reality and future some distant day.

One night, Calinda was asking Rankin if there was anything they could do to try to locate her father. Rankin stiffened and grew silent, taken off guard by her unexpected question. His voice was bitter and sullen as he advised her to accept her loss. When she rejected that harsh suggestion, she was stunned when Rankin reminded her of her father's abandonment, and told her Brax had been selfish and insensitive.

"How can you speak of him this way?" she asked sadly.

"You forget, Cal," he stated, calling her by his chosen nickname, "I knew him for years, but you haven't seen him since you were a baby. A man can change greatly in that length of time. Looking back, I doubt I knew him at all. I'm sorry if you find the truth painful and upsetting, but you persist in learning it. Do not press for facts which will hurt you. Brax helped me carve this ranch out of a dangerous wilderness, then deserted it before we could enjoy our success. He was like my brother; Lynx loved him and looked up to him. I think that's part of Lynx's problem. My son has never gotten over what happened that day." Angered, he had made a careless slip.

"I don't understand," she murmured, observing him closely, hearing an odd inflection in his words.

To gain Calinda's sympathy and to prevent more discussion, Rankin said, "I've told you all I can; the past is a painful subject, Cal. You see, we . . . lost Laura that same day. It was hard for a teenager to lose two people in one blow. Sometimes I think Lynx loved and respected Brax more than me."

A twinge nipped at Calinda. What had destroyed the closeness between Rankin and her father? Why would Brax abruptly disappear? There was a mystery here which Calinda felt she shouldn't question now, but would study later. Rankin had shown some strong feelings which alarmed Calinda: resentment, anger, and coldness. She recalled their first meeting with rising curiosity. Rankin had surely mistrusted and disliked her. Why? Very strange . . .

As if ignorant of his slips, Rankin stood up and stretched. He suggested they turn in for the night. Calinda went to her room with mounting intrigue to keep her company. Clearly, Rankin Cardone didn't want to discuss her father or the muddy past. Did Rankin blame her father for adding to their misery and grief, for Lynx's departure and continued absence? Did he also blame her? Apparently her father and Lynx had left at a painful moment in time, left Rankin to suffer and to recover on his own. If such talks made him edgy and unhappy, Calinda, as his guest, shouldn't broach them, for now.

Another storm was brewing in the Cardone house. Witnessing the growing bond between Rankin and Calinda, Salina did everything she could to prove Calinda didn't belong in Texas and that she was taking advantage of Rankin's charity. Salina tried to inspire resentment toward Calinda, to make Calinda appear a haughty and soft lady who should be asked to leave. The fiery tempered and envious Salina wanted Calinda gone before Lynx's return. She was determined to do anything to become the mistress of this ranch, the wife of Lynx Cardone. Her snide remarks and jealousy soon grew visible to the men and to Rankin, all of whom dismissed it as harmless feminine rivalry.

When Salina continued her hatefulness toward Calinda, Rankin warned the feisty girl to behave, but that only increased Salina's envy and malice. It didn't help matters when Calinda insisted on doing her own chores: washing and ironing her clothes, helping to set and clear the table, and cleaning her own room. Such tasks only proved Calinda wasn't soft and vain, much to Salina's chagrin.

Calinda was well-liked and received by the ranchhands. She was a breath of fresh air on a stifling day. She was taught to shoot and ride as well as the men. Each day her knowledge and skills increased.

On Saturday, Rankin took Calinda along to a neighbor's barbecue and dance. Her winning charm and freshness helped her make friends quickly and easily. As Rankin watched her talking and learning to square-dance, a new idea came to mind . . .

Rankin reassessed his situation. Calinda was resilient and well-bred. She was beautiful and friendly. If his plans could be carried out, Calinda would be the ideal choice for a Cardone, a perfect wife for his wayward son. An heir would solve all of his problems. Was it possible to entice Lynx to marry her? A striking wife and child might persuade Lynx to remain home. With so much at stake, could Lynx be compelled to respond to his duties just once? Surely one look at Cal and Lynx would accept his vital role as husband and father . . . Too, Lynx was a man to turn a woman's head. If Lynx agreed to his scheme, Calinda shouldn't be able to resist his charms and prowess. After all, if Cal made trouble, Lynx would be the eventual loser. After a marriage between them, it wouldn't matter what Calinda discovered . . . Besides, Rankin trusted and adored her.

When Salina noticed Rankin elaborating on Lynx's good looks and strong character and hinting at how he needed to settle down, she sensed what the older man was plotting. She fumed and ranted in her room at night. Calinda Braxton would never get Lynx Cardone!

That next day, Salina initiated her own scheme. When Calinda entered the kitchen for the dishes, Salina glanced at her. "*Mi amor* will be home soon," she stated casually. "*Tengo muchos ansioso. He is so caronil, so intrepido. Tanto guapo, un ardiente pasion,*" she stated dramatically, sighing as if caught in the throes of fiery passion.

Calinda turned to look at her. "I beg your pardon?" she said, doubting her ears. Had the girl actually spoken to her? The Spanish words were unknown to Calinda, but she'd recognized that sensual tone.

"*Cobre piel . . . Dorado ojo . . . Rubio cabello,*" she sighed passionately as she described Lynx's golden appearance.

"I don't understand Spanish, Salina," she told the dreamy girl.

"I said, my love is coming soon. He is so virile, so handsome, so intrepid, and so passionate. I quiver with eagerness. When you see him, *Senorita* Braxton, remember, he is taken," she seductively warned, continuing calmly with her chore.

"Taken? By whom?" Calinda asked. Rankin hadn't mentioned a sweetheart. What was Salina up to now?

"By me," the girl smugly claimed, tapping her chest. "Lynx has eyes for me alone. We are *mucho* close," she alleged, crossing her fingers as an example. "When he is home, I have no time for chores. You wish to help? Work while I am with him. He is *mucho* tempting, so remember you are a *dama*, a lady," she stressed sarcastically. "Do not charm him or sneak into his room. I do not carry this knife without reason," she brazenly threatened, pulling up her skirt to expose the shiny blade strapped to her inner thigh. "Lynx Cardone is mine. You have the *hidalgo encantado . . . Senor* Cardone bewitched, but do not toss your charms on Lynx. A real lady would not be living off a *caballero*. Return to where you belong."

"I belong here as long as Rankin wants me to stay," Calinda calmly stated. "As to Lynx, you have no worries about me. If he was a real man, he would be home where he belongs."

"I would not speak so to Lynx. He has a short fuse and quick gun. No one, including his papa, tells him what to do. He is like a blue norther: powerful, cold, destructive. You should hide in fear while he is home. *Senoritas* like you he chews up and spits out like old tobacco. Be on guard, *Senorita* Braxton, Lynx is a *hombre* as you have never met before. But do not be fooled by his charms and good looks; he uses them as weapons, always with a purpose. I will slit the throat of any girl who forgets he is mine."

Calinda realized the Mexican girl was doing her best to intimidate her, to speak understandable English in that thick accent of hers. She smiled sweetly and inquired, "What does *Llama de mi corazon* mean?"

Salina gaped at her for the silly question, then sneered, "Flame of my heart; why? Did you not hear my warnings?" she demanded.

"No warning is necessary; I don't chase men, any man." She left the kitchen without explaining herself, mentally savoring the endearment Cody had murmured that fateful night, wondering why it had flashed across her mind.

Naturally Calinda didn't relate that ridiculous conversation to Rankin. In fact, she and Rankin spoke little that night at supper. His mind seemed on a matter far removed from her. Shortly after their meal, Rankin entered his office to do bookwork.

Calinda went to her room to read before bedtime. Salina's words and warnings chewed at her. Were Lynx and Salina in love? Did the Mexican girl fear

Calinda could replace her? Would this wealthy and handsome son marry a servant? Evidently from the recent conversations, this mysterious Lynx was due for a visit soon. Calinda's ears had been flooded with stirring tales and descriptions of Lynx. As Salina's resentment had increased and she was now voicing a claim on Lynx, Calinda was sorely tempted to vex Salina by boldly flirting with Lynx when he came home. She couldn't behave like that.

Calinda wondered about Lynx. He was said to be a handsome and dauntless rogue. The wranglers and Salina made him sound larger than life, a compelling legend, a man of matchless prowess. Calinda laughed softly. What if this Lynx was actually clumsy and plain? What if he was only a boastful and insipid bumpkin? On the other hand, what if he was invincible, arrogant, cold, and deadly . . .

After the magnetic stranger in the Red Satin Saloon, could she ever desire another man? Could any man match Cody's prowess and looks? Calinda was plagued by memories of him and doubts of her future. She couldn't and wouldn't return to England. How could she search for Brax in this vast and wild territory? Should she leave and begin a new life? Where? How? Doing what?

Life was peaceful on the Cardone Ranch. She felt safe and happy. She couldn't bear the thought of leaving this security to face unknown dangers and fierce challenges. What to do? At times, Rankin was so odd. Yet, he seemed to care for her and about her. He claimed he wanted her to remain, but for how long? As long as she complied to his terms, he enjoyed her company. But what was the truth about her father? Without money and protection, she was literally trapped here. Besides, she wanted to meet this Lynx just once . . .

The next afternoon, Calinda received another startling surprise. Several trunks were brought to her room, trunks filled with clothes and jewels which had belonged to Laura Cardone. Rankin insisted she take and use whatever fit and was still in good repair. Pressed, Calinda accepted this added act of kindness and generosity. She was astonished by the elegant gowns and costly jewels in the trunks. And each garment she tried on fit perfectly. She wished Rankin would show her a picture of Laura, but he didn't.

When Calinda questioned Rankin about her future, he smiled and told her not to worry, that she was welcome to live here forever. "But, Rankin," she reasoned, "I'm not even family. What will people think if I continue to live here? At least put me to work," she coaxed.

"Who cares about idle gossip? Who would dare to speak against Rankin Cardone? From this day on, you are as family. You don't want to leave, and I wish you to stay. Why must we be miserable to please others? No more silly talk about leaving," he ordered sternly, affectionately cuffing her chin.

The next afternoon, Calinda went to her private balcony to catch a breath of air. She looked out over the grassy terrain before her line of vision. She saw Rankin on horseback in the distance, talking with another man whose back was to her. She observed them for a time, then leaned against the solid corner portion between the two arches, concealed from view. Without spoiling the closeness between them, she needed to persuade Rankin to clarify the past, to learn more about her father, to decide if and how to locate Elliott Braxton. She needed to make a decision: to live here or to go look for Brax. It dismayed her to realize she was calling and viewing him more and more as Brax, a stranger, not as her father . . .

"So, you've finally come to visit," Rankin commented merrily.

"You don't look pleased to see me, father," Lynx teased, a broad grin making tiny creases near his amber eyes and full mouth. "Should I have requested a visit before surprising you?" he joshed.

"I'm always happy when you come home. But I'd be happier if you'd stay. I also have a surprise for you; we have a guest, a beautiful one," Rankin hinted, dreading his son's reaction.

Lynx wailed humorously, "Not another rancher's daughter to toss in my lap? I thought you'd grown tired of matching me up to fillies."

Lynx's smile was rapidly replaced by a frigid scowl as he listened to his father's startling news. "You're not serious, father? Do you realize the trouble she can make?"

Rankin explained what he had discovered about Calinda Braxton and his impressions of her. Lynx straightened in his saddle as he unwillingly absorbed the incredible story. He was astonished and vexed when Rankin alleged Calinda's innocence and ignorance, then expounded on her good virtues and beauty. "I can't believe you would allow a slithering viper to nest in our home," he scolded angrily. "What if she's playing you for a fool, father? If not, what if she discovers the truth?"

"Cal isn't like Brax, son. I doubt Brax told Miranda or Cal anything. I'm positive she is honest and vulnerable."

"You don't mind if I decide for myself? Let's go have a look at your Cal," Lynx said coldly, sitting rigid in his saddle.

As they were riding in, one of the men shouted to the others, "Lynx is home, boys. He's coming in with the boss."

That news caught Calinda's attention. She remained concealed behind the wide span on the balcony, peering out to see this legend for herself. As Rankin and Lynx halted and dismounted, Calinda's eyes blinked rapidly in disbelief, then stared at the tall figure of the man greeting his friends below. Cody Richards! Tex! Lynx Cardone . . .

As Lynx joked and talked with the cowpunchers who gathered around, Calinda listened to the mellow and stirring voice she would never forget. It was undeniably and terrifyingly clear the mysterious stranger and Lynx Cardone were the same man. Why had dear Nelle lied to her? It was impossible for Nelle not to know who this wealthy and irresistibly handsome man was. Had Lynx discovered who she was after leaving her that night? Was that why he had left the money? Was this the meaning of the last words of that note . . .

Cal wouldn't humiliate herself and her gracious host by confronting his son with his wicked conduct in Fort Worth. Yet, how could she calmly stroll downstairs and act as if they had never met? How would Lynx react to seeing her again, in his home? Maybe Salina was right, she should hide in her room! No, she couldn't do that.

Resentment and spite filled Calinda as she watched him laugh happily as if he were without a care in the world. Surely the note had been a jest! Doubtlessly he had assumed their paths would never cross again. Calinda suddenly realized she possessed the delightful element of surprise; Lynx would be shocked and distressed by their unexpected meeting, especially under these circumstances. He wouldn't dare do or say anything wrong before his father. Dreams of revenge challenged her to repay him, to teach the arrogant rogue a lesson. She would see him squirm in dread of her devastating revelation of his vile behavior, squirm and worry. It vexed Calinda to admit perhaps Salina's description of him hadn't been exaggerated at all. No doubt they made a fine pair!

Calinda remained out of sight until the two men entered the house, then she hurried into her room. She rushed to her closet and searched it for a particular dress which had belonged to Laura, one in elegant red satin and trimmed in expensive black lace. This outfit should certainly jog his memory. When she was ready for the evening meal, she brushed her fiery chestnut locks until they bounced and shone with golden lights. Even if the dress clashed with her hair, no matter.

She answered the knock at her door; it was Salina coming to tell her of Lynx's arrival and the dinner hour. The girl's dark eyes narrowed in rage as they slipped over the exquisite Calinda.

"Have you forgotten my warning, *bruja?*" she purred venomously.

"Perhaps if we go downstairs and you repeat it before both men, then I shall always recall it," Calinda warned in return, rankled by the girl's antagonistic manner and taut with apprehension. "I could care less about you or Lynx Cardone. Threaten me once more, and I will make certain Rankin learns of it instantly. Is that clear, Salina?"

Salina was shocked by Calinda's sudden display of mettle and daring. She nodded, then disappeared. Calinda gracefully walked down the stairs, her legs shaky. As she was about to knock on the closed door, Rankin opened it and came out into the entry hall.

Since it had become their habit to dress for dinner, Rankin never suspected Calinda's mischievous and dangerous ploy. He looked her over and smiled in pleasure, imagining his son's reaction to this lovely creature. He glanced inside and said, "Lynx, this is Calinda Braxton. Cal, my son Lynx." As Rankin made the introductions, he failed to witness Calinda's feigned look of surprise and following glare of fury which she cunningly dismissed before he turned to her again. But Rankin alertly caught the astonishment and another unknown emotion which flashed over his son's face. He hastily decided his son was pleasantly surprised to find Calinda Braxton so entrancing. "You two get acquainted while I go tell Salina we're ready for dinner to be served." With that, Rankin left them alone, pulling the door shut.

Neither Calinda nor Lynx moved or spoke for a short time, each deliberating how to handle this precarious situation. His gaze mocking, Lynx scoffed sarcastically, "You're Calinda Braxton?"

"Yes, but you aren't Tex, or Cody Richards," she sneered.

"Cody Richards?" he repeated in confusion.

"When I asked Nelle about the room's owner that next morning, she told me your name was Cody Richards," Cal said.

Lynx stared at her skeptically. "How could you ask anything about me when you skipped out at dawn with Cousin Nelle's earnings? Didn't I leave enough money? I must have been dazed with fatigue; I never pegged you as a thief and a liar. What did your lover say about your night with me? Or didn't anyone tell you he's a deadly killer? Just what are you two trying to pull on the Cardones, Miss Callie O'Hara?" Lynx sarcastically responded. Was this girl more cunning and daring than he could imagine? Whatever she was trying to pull, he would enjoy defeating her!

It was Calinda's turn to look puzzled, then all at once she understood. She laughed coldly, relishing his dismay as she corrected his mistaken impressions. "My mother was the only one to call me Callie; she's dead now. In my stupor that night, I answered to it. To my misfortune, you persist in confusing me with Callie O'Hara, Nelle's cousin. Unfortunately, we arrived on the same stage, and we're both redheads. I have never been a thief or a harlot. As to being a liar, surely you know why I misled you about my destination, to prevent any future contact with a lecherous beast. As you can see, Mister Cardone, you have the wrong Callie again, as you did that night. If you doubt me or my word, go ask Nelle," she frostily suggested.

Lynx's keen mind seized these facts, quickly sorting and storing them. Had he been set up by Elliott Braxton's treacherous and beautiful daughter? What were the odds against Calinda Braxton accidentally landing in his bed and arms? *Two Callies?* He strolled forward and halted before her. His hand came up to stroke her fiery cheek as he huskily remarked, "From where I'm standing, I'd say I have the right one, for a change, Miss Callie Braxton. Red satin suits you after all. But you certainly go to rash lengths to meet and charm a cowpoke."

Calinda drew back her hand to slap the smug look off his mocking face. Lynx painlessly captured it before it could complete its task. He chuckled. "At least you're wide awake tonight. I'd like some straight answers later. I didn't realize you'd use my money to settle yourself in my home," he teased, oddly delighted to see her tonight.

"Considering how we met, Mister Cardone, I'd say I earned your monetary assistance. But if I had known who you were, I wouldn't be here right now. It appears lying about your name was another error."

His tawny eyes travelled over her furious expression. "What else do you think you've earned, Callie?" he asked, his voice deceptively soft.

"I don't understand," she replied, trying to pull free. "If you think I'm here because of you or what happened, you're vastly mistaken."

"We'll see, won't we?" he hinted mysteriously, then released his hold and stepped away from her. He turned his back to retrieve his brandy, his senses whirling madly at her nearness.

Calinda's hand impulsively reached out as if to snatch his gun. "I wouldn't if I were you, Callie," he warned coldly without moving or turning. "I have a reputation for dealing harshly with people who pull guns on me."

"You have eyes in the back of your head?" she snapped nervously.

"A man in my position must to survive." As he turned and faced her, he said, "Don't ever draw a gun on anyone unless you intend to use it. They might not be as even-tempered or forgiving as I am."

"What if I intended to use it?" she challenged.

Lynx didn't flinch when he stated seriously, "If you dare to challenge me, be prepared to pay the price for defeat." Calinda couldn't tell what challenge he was referring to at that moment.

"If you dare to ravish a female in her sleep, you should be prepared to pay the price for your crime." she warned in return.

Abruptly Lynx filled the room with lusty laughter. "I must admit, you're one brave and reckless gal, Calinda Braxton. It seems we've gotten off on the wrong foot again. Would another apology settle those ruffled feathers?" He leaned against the billiard table and crossed one booted foot over the other, observing her with a roguish smile. Maybe his father was accurate in his assessments. Even so, she would be a stimulating riddle to solve.

"An apology is insignificant for what you did, Mister Cardone."

"Tonight, or back in Fort Worth?" he playfully jested, as they both recalled the implication in his note. "I did plan to seek you out one day soon, but I never expected to find you waiting here for my return. This looks to be a most interesting reunion. Just imagine, you and me living under the same roof. Think we should let Father in on our little secret?" He chuckled when she blushed and stiffened.

"You wouldn't dare confess what you did to me! But if you come near me again, I'll tell him! If you think your money absolves you of guilt, you're wrong. I'm not afraid of you, but I wouldn't want to hurt your father by telling him what a villain you are. From what I hear, your visits are short and rare; thankfully," she scoffed to nettle him. His smoldering eyes seemed to scorch her.

He laughed heartily. "Maybe I should make some exceptions and changes this trip. What do you think, Callie, *mi bello flor?*"

Before Calinda could reply, Rankin returned to tell them dinner was ready, cognizant of the fiery sparks between them. Setting down his glass and straightening, Lynx smiled sensuously at her and waved her forward. "After you, Callie. It sure is nice to be home, Father."

Calinda shot him a look of warning before she turned to follow Rankin into the dining room with Lynx closely behind her.

Chapter 4

As THE MEAL WAS SERVED and eaten, Calinda was hard pressed to remain poised enough to prevent curiosity or suspicion in Rankin or Salina. She wondered how a lady was supposed to act under such trying circumstances. Here she sat having dinner and sharing the company of the man with whom she had slept, the man who had claimed her purity, the man who inflamed her senses with his very presence, the man who seemed to comprehend his provocative effect upon her and was playfully taking advantage of her discomfiture and necessary silence. She wanted to hate him and to punish him, but could do neither.

Rankin sat at the end of the long table, with Calinda on the right side and Lynx on the left, facing each other. Calinda politely dined and listened while the two men did most of the talking. Never had she seen Rankin's eyes glow with such warmth and pleasure, proclaiming his love and need for his son. Calinda was fascinated with the easy rapport and genial manner between the two men. Not a single cross word or surly expression had passed between them. They appeared overjoyed with this visit, delighting in every moment and word.

The conversation waxed between the ranch and Texas happenings. Calinda watched the variety of emotional reactions come and go on the beguiling face of a man who was no longer a stranger. Except in character, he was perfect, a fact which disturbed her. His features were strong and well-blended to promote a facade of strength, looks, and self-assurance. She could mentally envision the tall, steely-muscled body in smooth bronze beneath his snug black pants, baby blue shirt, and black leather vest. She shifted in her chair and tore her probing eyes from the magnetic Lynx. She found herself wanting to run her fingers through that enticing head of brandy-colored hair and to gaze longingly into those amber eyes. What had gotten into her? She was as nervous as a yearling around a hot branding iron.

A man keenly versed in making many observations simultaneously without appearing to have but one object of interest, Lynx was all too aware of the fetching girl before him and her furtive study of him as he attempted to focus his full attention on his father and their talk. Lynx was utterly intrigued by this stimulating turn of events. Later, he would make some inquiries in town, just to be certain there were two Callies indeed.

There was something about Callie and her abrupt arrival which troubled him. Since Lynx had never found any woman irresistible or unforgettable, he didn't realize it was the powerful attraction between them which plagued him. He attributed his uneasiness to suspicions. There were several unacceptable answers to this stunning mystery: she could be a clever spy or a money-grubbing imposter; she could be a malicious and sly conspirator; or she could be real . . .

The perceptive Rankin witnessed the undercurrents passing between Lynx and Calinda, swift currents which both were trying to dam and control. His heart soared with satisfaction. By mutual attraction or wily coercion, he would come out the winner if those two got together. Lynx and Calinda were both intelligent and stubborn. To avoid suspicions and rebellion, Rankin decided to allow Mother Nature to take her course first, and she seemed mighty busy already.

To draw Calinda into the conversation, Rankin spoke of her harrowing experience on the way to Fort Worth and dilemma after her arrival. Amusement sparkled in Lynx's eyes and he grinned raffishly. Calinda demurely lowered her lashes as if embarrassed about something, her cheeks glowing strangely. Rankin studied these reactions and wondered about them. It appeared those two shared a compelling secret. How was that possible since they had just met? Why was Calinda being so quiet and nervous? Why was Lynx so devilishly playful and attentive?

"I hope you learned a valuable lesson, Cal; don't fight odds greater than you. Some men are very dangerous and impulsive," Lynx beguilingly remarked. "You were lucky to come out unscathed. You're fortunate to have lost nothing more than clothes and jewels."

Calinda stared at him, then stated, "They had no right to steal my possessions or to threaten my life. In the same circumstances, I'll react the same way. I doubt you would give in willingly, even with overpowering odds against you," she added calmly, fuming inside, her words carrying dual meanings which he astutely understood. How dare he so boldly and rashly hint at their intimate misadventure! Did the unflappable rogue lack all manners, caution, and wits?

"But I'm a man; I carry a set of Colts which itch to speak for me. Perhaps I should teach you how to protect yourself while I'm home," he audaciously suggested. "I'm good at self-defense, and a *bello mariposa* is a tempting treasure." Yes, with her vivid beauty and delicate air, she presented the illusion of an exquisite butterfly.

"Rankin gave me a gun, and he taught me how to fire it. Next time, if there is a next time, the odds won't be so one-sided."

"I'll give you a piece of advice, Cal; men like those are deadly. They'd kill even a woman if she caused trouble, shoot her and never glance back or think twice about it."

"Those are nearly the same words that bandit leader used to frighten me. I hope your knowledge and advice don't come from excessive experience," she remarked accusingly, wanting to ask for a translation of the softly spoken Spanish words. "You do have quite a reputation."

"Where females are concerned, from observations only. I've had my share of gunfights with men who simply want to see if they can out-draw me. Since I'm sitting here tonight, that should tell you who was the fastest and smartest," he said, without arrogance and with a subtle hint of dissatisfaction with his uncontrollable reputation.

"The hazard of being a famous gunslinger?" she probed.

Through clenched teeth, Lynx informed her, "I've never shot any man who didn't demand it, one way or another."

"What about your famed Texas Rangers? Why can't they clean up this lawlessness and keep the peace here?"

"They're trying their damnedest. Texas is a huge territory, too many warring factions, too many people looking out for themselves."

"What warring factions?" she inquired, listening intently.

"The Comanche and Apache Indians, Mexican bandits, and a wide assortment of American criminals. We're flooded with escaping convicts, rustlers, outlaws, gunmen, and such. Down South, Mexican bandits cross the border to rob and raid, then return to safety. The Rangers have pursued them many times, but the government doesn't like them encroaching on Mexican soil." Lynx couldn't bring himself to tell about the Alamo, where too many Rangers had died in defeat.

"To make matters worse for the Rangers, even supposedly law-abiding men cause trouble. We've had range feuds, fence-cuttings, riots, lynchings, and bouts of revenge. The Rangers spend as much time on battling ranchers and farmers as they do fighting crime."

"It sounds like an awful place to live. Why don't the ranchers and town people help the Rangers keep peace?"

"Texas was practically lawless after the War ended in '65. The soldiers who returned here or remained here afterwards were too used to the killing and violence. When anyone challenged them or harmed them, it was natural to fight back with bloodshed and strength. The South was bound together during the War. After it, everyone was out for himself. When the railroads pushed into Texas to haul cattle and sheep, train-robbers followed their progress to get rich. The biggest conflicts came with fencing. Grasslands and water-holes were claimed and protected by cattlemen. The farmers and squatters didn't care for barriers against them; neither did the sheep-herders. Many a killing and feud's been over those barbed strips."

Calinda and Rankin were most impressed by Lynx's span of knowledge. Calinda found herself mesmerized by his mellow drawl. The tone of Lynx's voice thrilled Rankin, for it told him there was much he didn't know about his grown son. Rankin found the emotions exposed there pleasing and enlightening. He smiled at Lynx, who didn't notice it as he and Calinda gazed enraptured at each other across the table. For a time, Rankin felt they didn't even acknowledge his presence.

"Lynx, why don't you take Cal for a stroll," Rankin suggested to give them time to be alone. "I promised to ride over to Rafe's to discuss his water problems," he added to remove himself graciously.

Lynx stood up, his agile frame drawing Calinda's eyes to it. Salina entered the room, heading for Lynx, smiling provocatively. As if she hadn't heard Rankin's words, Salina asked coyly, "When I finish my chores, can we take a walk, Lynx?"

Lynx tugged a dark curl and chuckled, his eyes glowing with a response which piqued Calinda, as he had intended it to do. "*Mañana*, Salina. I'm taking Cal for a stroll. Been good since I left?" he teased lazily.

Claro esta, mi famoso vaquero," Salina promptly replied, eyes sending messages which even a dull-visioned man could read.

"You get your chores done, and I'll see you later," Lynx advised, as if planning some romantic rendezvous.

Calinda masked her warring emotions, hands clenched tightly on the edge of the table, as she arose. She must avoid this cunning devil. "I'm very tired, Mister Cardone. Perhaps Salina would accept the stroll in my place. I'll go to my room, then you can visit privately."

Neither man missed her inflection on the last two words. Rankin was relieved when he didn't have to insist their guest come first, since Lynx quickly took her unintentional bait. "It appears we're becoming sister and brother, Cal. We should get acquainted before I ride off again. No telling when I'll be home again."

Not wishing to cause more resentment in the Mexican girl, Calinda tried once more to dissuade him, inwardly afraid of being alone with him. "I'm sure there will be plenty of time tomorrow for us to talk, Mister Cardone. Salina has been looking forward to your homecoming. You don't want to disappoint her. Goodnight."

As Calinda turned to make a floating exit, Lynx was at her side, gripping her elbow. She was shocked when he teased, "Afraid to stroll in the dark with your new brother? I'm perfectly harmless; ask my father. Cardones are famous for their hospitality and manners."

Calinda reluctantly accepted the enforced invitation. "I'm well acquainted with the Cardone traits. If you insist," she casually yielded.

"I insist, Callie; and the name is Lynx."

After they left the room, Rankin turned to the furious Salina and stated coldly, "Need I remind you, Salina, you are my servant? Cal is a guest, and I will not tolerate such rude and brassy behavior. I should also remind you, Lynx is a Cardone. Don't interfere in his life. I will not speak further on these issues," he tersely warned.

Salina acknowledged his warnings, but dismissed them. Besides, the night was young and Lynx was within her reach once more. This time, he would discover she had become very much a woman. This time, she wouldn't accept another rejection from him.

Calinda and Lynx silently walked toward the corral, to halt there and to watch the moonlight dance off the shiny hides of the sleek horses. An Appaloosa stallion came trotting over for Lynx to nuzzle him affectionately. She witnessed the strong attachment between the mottled steed and his bronzed master. As Lynx fluffed Star's mane, Cal noted the stirring gentleness in his mood and expression. This man was capable of feeling and displaying a wide range of complex emotions.

"He's very beautiful," Calinda said softly.

"Out here, a man needs a tough and smart horse. If his mount isn't quick and alert, he can find himself in great danger. Go, Star, visit with your friends," he told the animal, who seemed to understand his words and returned to a small group on the far side of the corral.

As Rankin rode off, they both smiled and waved. After a few moments, Lynx asked, "You want to stroll or sit over there and talk?" pointing to a swing beneath an arched trellis which was covered with fragrant yellow roses, a highly romantic setting in the moonlight.

"Neither," she replied, tense and alert. "We have nothing to discuss. I only agreed to a walk to avoid a scene. Just stay clear of me."

When he took her hand to lead her to the swing, she yanked it away and glared at him. He laughed and taunted, "I don't bite, Cal."

"I think you do," she too quickly snapped, then flushed.

"*Por Dios,* you are afraid of me," he teased as if surprised.

Calinda ignored his taunt to sit down on the stone enclosure, instead of the swing which would allow him to be too close for comfort or attention. She might as well settle this trying matter. The uneven, adobe wall encirled the house, except for gates at intervals. Although it wouldn't deny entrance to wild animals, it offered a striking appearance and allowed privacy from the other structures. Without thinking about the stones snagging the red satin gown, Calinda defensively sat on a two-foot-high ledge, nestled safely between the four-foot-high posts.

Lynx pretended not to notice her action, one which exposed her anxiety. He negligently leaned against the pier to her right. "Tell me about yourself, Cal," he encouraged, gazing ahead.

"What?" she asked, as if her attention had strayed.

"I'm at a disadvantage. If I know Rankin, you're well-informed about me; but I know little about you."

"Well-informed? I only know you're a nasty villain. Dare I ask, are the rumors true? Is your reputation justified or exaggerated?"

Lynx turned to rest his left shoulder on the post and looked into her upturned face. "I'd be lying if I said no. Westerners demand legends and love creating them. I just happen to be their target right now. Like I said, I've never killed an innocent man."

"Innocent in your eyes or the law's? How can you calmly take another man's life? Those bandits who attacked my stage murdered the guard. It didn't seem to bother any of them."

"If I didn't keep a cool head, I wouldn't be able to hesitate until the last minute before firing. If a man has a gun pointed at you and won't listen to reason, it's you or him. Frankly I don't care to have the thirsty ground drinking my blood."

"But what about the law? Can't they arrest such men?" she continued the grim talk, but wanted to ask much different questions.

"The law is rarely in the same place at the same time. Somehow it's impossible to stall a determined man until a Ranger or marshal can appear. This isn't England or the East, Cal; don't ever forget it."

"If you refused a challenge, would he kill you anyway?"

"Most would. To turn tail and run brands a man a coward. Cowards have a tough time out here. Men keep pushing them until they either leave or they fight. Since I live here, I'm forced to fight."

"Does killing become easier, as natural as a reflex?" she pressed.

"Not to me. I've set out to intentionally take only one man's life." He flattened his back against the cool stones, bending his knee and placing the bottom of his boot on the post near his other knee. He remained impassive as he chewed on a blade of sweetgrass.

"Who? Why?" she asked when he didn't expound.

"Perhaps I'll tell you one day, if you hang around." He glanced at her, a half-grin curling up one side of his inviting mouth.

"Did you kill him?" she persisted, having a need to know.

"Nope." He inhaled deeply, then slowly released it, as if mentally soothing a raw nerve which she was exposing.

"You changed your mind?" she continued softly.

"Never found him. Finally stopped wasting my time and energy," he murmured in a tone which mutely implored her to cease this topic.

She didn't. "If you located him today, would you kill him?"

There was a long and somber silence before Lynx said, "I honestly don't know. I'd have to see him again to learn if his crimes still matter to me. Isn't this a gloomy subject?" he hinted clearly.

"I'm sorry," she murmured to placate him.

He turned and gazed down at her. "Why?" he almost demanded.

Calinda's eyes were soft and her lips compelling as she replied, "Because he must have done something terrible to you to earn such hatred. Is he the reason you've stayed away from home so long, why you've grown so hard and cynical?"

"Am I cold and ruthless, Cal?" he asked unflinchingly.

To elude the snare which she had unwittingly set, she continued, "I don't know what you are, Lynx. I've never met anyone like you before. Sometimes I see the same pain and loneliness in your eyes and in Rankin's. You're both very good at covering your feelings. Why don't you come home, Lynx? Rankin misses you and needs you here."

"What about you, Cal? Do you miss me and want me around?"

Calinda blushed and looked away. "Why should I? We're strangers. Besides, I won't be living here much longer," she added for some absurd reason. Thoroughly unsettled, she couldn't think clearly.

Lynx grasped her chin and lifted her head. "Why not?"

"I can't go on accepting your father's charity indefinitely; it isn't right. He's been wonderful to me, and I'm very fond of him."

"Where will you go? How will you live?" he asked curtly.

"I don't know." For a moment, she looked very young and vulnerable and afraid. "Do you mind if I stay here until I decide?"

"Why should I?" he inquired, drilling his gaze into hers.

"It is your home, and we . . ." She hastily fell silent.

"We, what, Cal?" he probed, searching her rosy face.

"Nothing," she verbally denied him an answer which her expression boldly supplied. She had rashly stepped into her own trap!

Lynx captured her face between his hands and lowered his head. His intention clear, she whispered fearfully, "Don't, Lynx."

Trapped between him and the confining posts, Calinda couldn't halt his action. His lips came down on hers in a tantalizing kiss. When she tried to turn her head, he held it securely, his lips parting hers and forging their mouths together. His strength superior and his desire great, he pulled her to her feet and imprisoned her in his embrace.

As his mouth seared over hers, Calinda struggled to retain her wits and control. She quivered as a dangerous wildfire licked at her body, wanting to burn away her resistance. As his lips moved from hers, she hoarsely demanded, "Stop it, Lynx."

The tall Texan leaned back and gazed into her panicky face. This wasn't the time or place to force the reality of their shared passion on her. "Sorry, Callie," he mumbled huskily, loosening his grip. "You are too damn beautiful and bewitching for your own good. We'd better go inside before I forget myself again."

Shaken, Calinda didn't respond. Lynx slipped his arm around her waist to escort her back to the house, aware of the tremors in her body. They said goodnight inside the door and Cal ascended the stairs on trembly legs. After watching which room she entered, Lynx grinned. He doubted his father would have given them such provocative solitude if he had known about their prior meeting and its results. Whatever happened from this point on with Cal, Lynx would never expose that night. Did he dare take advantage of their adjoining balcony . . .

An hour later, Calinda sat up in bed and strained to detect an unusual noise. Unable to fall asleep, she was lying there with her eyes shut and her mind open.

Again a sharp "ping" was heard, then another. Knowing Rankin hadn't returned, she wondered if that devilish son of his was up to daring mischief. Cal eased out of her bed and cautiously went to peer out the rear door. Moonlight invaded the open spans between the arches, softly illuminating the shadowy veranda.

As Lynx walked to the railing to answer Salina's persistent summons, he was cognizant of the slit which appeared in Cal's door. No doubt Salina's less-than-quiet messages had alerted Cal. He was tempted to inspire jealousy in Calinda, but realized she wasn't the kind of woman who would accept a midnight rendezvous with a sultry Mexican servant. If Callie presumed there was something between him and Salina, she wouldn't look at him twice after tonight. If he was going to get any answers from himself and his father, he needed to polish his tarnished image. Anyway, he was annoyed with Salina's hot pursuit every time he came home. It was clear Salina desired him, but she craved a position as his wife even more. Lynx rebelled at such greedy deceit. It was time to make himself clear to the wanton Salina. This was the perfect set-up to get Salina off his back and to enchant Calinda into trusting him. "What gives?" Lynx asked crisply.

At his brusque tone, she petulantly said, "I missed you, Lynx. Why not come to my room? We can have a drink and . . . talk."

"I'm exhausted, Salina; it was a long and dusty ride."

"I could fix you a hot bath and scrub your back," she tempted.

"I just had one, but *gracias*," he stated, running fingers through blond hair which was nearly dry, then over his clean-shaven face.

"A drink and massage might loosen those stiff muscles . . ."

"I've had my limit. A good night's sleep will do more for me tonight," he responded. Although they were passing words back and forth in muffled voices, Lynx knew they could be heard. He plotted what he wanted Cal to learn, without alerting Salina. Lynx realized Salina was purposely using English. Was this more than a seduction attempt? A sly game to irk Cal? If not, why hadn't the Mexican tart stolen into his bedroom?

"I doubt your bed or sleep could relax you as quickly and enjoyably as my hands," she wickedly pressed, easing the neckline of her white blouse down to expose olive shoulders and the cleft of her bosom.

"You're a brazen hussy, Salina. *Vaya a la cama*," he tested her.

"I go to bed, if you join me," she entreated seriously, wetting her lips and swaying erotically. "What do you say?" she coaxed.

"Don't you ever get tired of flirting with me? You should know by now the boss's son is off-limits," he made himself clearer, now that he was on to her sport. He didn't like to be duped for any reason.

"Whose rule is that? *El patron's?*" she challenged, undaunted.

"Mine," he stated casually, watching her twitch as if she had hot embers or chiggers in her drawers.

"Afraid I might be too demanding?" she teased.

"I just like to choose my own woman, Salina."

"Perhaps I am too much woman for you to handle," she mocked his male ego. "Perhaps you have lost your magic touch?"

"Perhaps not enough woman," he insultingly came back.

"*Inquieto? Pollo?*" She mockingly called him a frightened chicken. She cursed this foolish trick as she hoped Cal was asleep.

"I'm not afraid of anything; and you know it."

"You *encantado* with the little *senorita* your papa brought home? *Es barato puta* is trouble, Lynx," she angrily suggested, trying to inspire a spewing forth of stinging insults about Cal, if she were awake.

"I'll have to admit, she's a most enchanting lady. A mighty tempting treat for any man. But you could hardly call her a tart," he confessed slyly, then chuckled softly.

"A gunslinger and a *dama?* You don't stand a chance with her."

"Didn't say I wanted one. Don't have time for a woman right now, any kind. I'll be heading out again in a few days."

"Remember, *guapo diablo,* I am here if you change your mind."

Lynx watched her swaying movements until she disappeared from sight, no doubt heading to find someone else to douse her fiery passions, which was frequent from what he'd heard. One day those flames would engulf her. Lynx stretched and yawned, then returned to his room.

Calinda carefully closed the door, afraid to turn the lock for fear of his hearing it. It was impossible for anyone to climb to the balcony, so she decided to bolt it later. She didn't want Lynx to discover her furtive action. She smiled to herself, knowing Salina had lied about them. But why was she so ecstatic about that news? Funny, she was finding herself drawn to Lynx Cardone, even to his roguish manner. Maybe she should despise him for his seduction and spurn his nonchalant manner, but she didn't. He possessed such potent magic.

She stared at the wall, imagining that virile body stretched out on a bed next door. She knew too well what his lips and hands did to her body and mind. Was it possible to change a man like Lynx?

She paced the floor for a time, then halted with her back to the veranda doors. She whirled suddenly to head for her bed, nearly bumping into Lynx. Before she could shriek in alarm, his hand closed over her mouth and he shushed her. "Rankin's home, love."

When she regained her poise, he removed his hand. "What are you doing here? How did you sneak in?" she whispered.

"The door was unlocked. You were so deep in thought, you didn't hear me. Can we talk for a while?"

"Get out of my room. It's late, and I'm not dressed for company." She knew she should put on her robe, but she didn't move.

"I'm not company, and you're wearing more tonight than the last time I saw you. We need to talk, Callie."

"You arrogant, sneaky rogue. If we have anything else to say, it can be done tomorrow, downstairs," she told him.

"I doubt we'd want anyone to hear this discussion. I want to know what happened in Fort Worth after I left," he softly demanded.

"You dare to come here to question me about anything?"

"I want to know everything you said and did," he stressed, gripping her elbows and pulling her closer to him.

"You don't have any right to interrogate me," she panted.

"I'm not leaving until I have the truth, all of it."

"I'll scream," she threatened, noticing his look of determination.

"Be my guest," he invited, not the least concerned.

She gaped at him as he hastily slipped out of his shirt and boots. "What are you doing? Are you daft?" she asked in panic.

"If you're going to scream, I might as well help you look the injured party. Wonder what Father will say when he knocks on the door to find his only son half-naked in your room . . ."

"You wouldn't dare humiliate and hurt him like that." She snatched up the discarded shirt and slammed it against his hard chest.

"I'm too intrigued to consider anybody's feelings but mine."

"I don't understand you, Lynx. Aren't you afraid I'll tell Rankin what happened in town? Why wait until now to come here? Why are you interested in what I said and did after you left?"

"I have my reasons," he stated flippantly, trailing a finger over her bare shoulder, then lifting her chin when she lowered her head. He had noticed the sullen inflection on her last few words.

"Such as?" she scoffed, shoving at the disturbing hand.

"I'm not here to answer questions, Callie, just to ask them."

Calinda fretted briefly. Her silence wasn't important. She just hated to yield to his insufferable demands. She related the account of her time in Fort Worth, then answered any remaining questions. He then insisted on practically hearing her life's story. Calinda was rankled, but complied, "Is that all, Mister Cardone? Do I pass inspection?"

"Father is becoming quite attached to you, Cal. I just wanted to make certain you deserve his help and affections. You pass all of my inspections," he ventured in a mysterious tone.

"If you're so concerned about Rankin, why don't you hang around and make sure I don't take advantage of him," she sneered.

"I just might do that, in a few months. Right now, I've got some vital matters to settle elsewhere."

"If you don't get killed first," she stated.

"If I don't get killed first," he infuriatingly mocked her. "Don't forget to lock your door this time," he taunted, grinning at her. "But you needn't worry; I won't be back, unless invited."

"That day will never dawn," she informed him.

"Don't be so positive. I seem to recall a fiery nature concealed beneath that lady-like exterior. One day, you'll realize you desire me as much as I desire you, even if you keep it a secret." Before Calinda could vent her anger on him, he seized her and kissed her soundly. When Calinda tried to break free of his powerful embrace, he tightened it. His lips seared over hers as he pressed her trembling body to his. As his lips teased over her eyes and ears, she pleaded for him to halt.

What was the matter with her? Even as she threatened to scream, all she wanted was to respond to him! In spite of their first meeting, she was weakening. If only he wasn't so magically overwhelming. His body was sending hers sweet and forbidden messages, which she must refuse. Drawing on what little strength and will she possessed, she struggled to halt this enticing madness.

Lynx yielded to her panic. He leaned back and smiled. "You say no, Callie, but you want to say yes," he murmured as his thumb passed over her throbbing lips. "I know you have reason to fear me and doubt me, maybe even despise me; but I hope you'll change your mind. You're the most desirable and refreshing vixen I've ever met." He left quickly while she was still stunned. "Goodnight, *Llama de mi corazon*," he lazily tossed over his shoulder at the last moment.

Calinda rushed to the door and bolted it, quivering. She fumed as she heard him chuckle merrily. She leaned against the door and sighed. This arrangement would never work. How could she remain here if Lynx decided to come home permanently? How would she ever resist him if he pressed her? She would die of embarrassment and shame if Rankin learned about them. She prayed he would leave quickly, then scolded herself for wishing he wouldn't. His parting words flowed over her as a gentle wave, "Flame of my heart." Why did he call her that in such a seductive tone? Why did he have such power over her?

Chapter 5

❧

CALINDA AWOKE SLUGGISH AND EDGY, for she hadn't slept well after her confrontation with Lynx. Calinda didn't trust this mercurial man whose appeal was much too powerful and tempting. She was as much afraid of his contradictory behavior as she was of her own crazy emotions. As implausible as it was, she wanted to yield to him as much as she needed to resist. She frowned as she realized she was being just as contradictory as he was.

She found it hard to deal with the fact that Cody Richards was Lynx Cardone, a man whom she presumed she would never see again. What did Lynx want from her? Other than physical desire, did she have any effect upon him? Did he merely view her as an entertaining diversion, a convenient object upon which to sate his carnal urges? She couldn't get involved with that carefree rogue.

How would she feel and act if they had actually met for the first time last night? But they hadn't; there was a stolen night of passion between them. Too, Lynx's smug attitude dismayed her. Last night, he had boldly insinuated her eventual and uncontrollable surrender. Surely her gaze and tremors had exposed her feelings to a man of Lynx's experience. To deny his effect would be absurd.

She dressed in pants, boots, and a cotton shirt before going downstairs. She had brushed her hair and caught it back with a yellow ribbon. It was mid-morning, and the men were riding the range. Salina was outside, hanging up freshly scrubbed laundry. Calinda made her breakfast and sat down at the kitchen table to eat it.

When Salina returned, she was just taking the last bite. "What is this? I allow no one to mess up my kitchen."

"Don't start on me this morning, Salina. I'll clean up any mess I make. Find someone else to aggravate. Just leave me alone today."

"Too hot to sleep after your stroll?" she hinted suggestively.

Calinda was fed up with Salina. This morning in particular she didn't feel like matching words and wits with this malicious female. "I take it you were. Next time you make a late call on Mister Lynx Cardone, would you be a little quieter?"

"You were spying on us?" she hotly accused.

"I didn't have to. You made no attempt to conceal your plans. I'm sure you staged that little charade for my benefit. Too bad Lynx wasn't forewarned to comply with the proper role. If he's yours as you claimed, he seems ignorant of your close relationship."

"*Bruja!*" Salina sneered. "Stay away from Lynx; he is mine."

"You don't say?" Calinda purred like a feisty cat. "He gave me the impression he was free for the taking," she boldly hinted.

"Don't you two think it a bit early in the day to be arguing over me?" Lynx's lazy drawl chided them from the doorway. Both women turned to watch him swagger into the room, chuckling. "Salina, I think it would be wise for you to watch your naughty tongue to our guest. As for you, Callie, please don't go harassing the hired help; it's hard to find good servants this far out."

Embarrassed, Calinda rebelled at his scolding, "She started it."

"You did," Salina quickly injected. "Stay out of my kitchen, and stop treating me like the dirt you walk on. I was here first."

"Calm down, Salina. Callie is free to come and go anywhere in this house, at any time," he stated, casting Calinda a mocking look.

"But, Lynx, she has been under foot for weeks. Is time for her visit to end, *si?*" Salina pouted, coming over to him to caress his muscled arm. "*Que me cuenta?*" she anxiously entreated.

"I say, you're acting like a spoiled child, Salina. I know you've had free run for a long time, but Callie isn't leaving any time soon, if at all," Lynx said clearly and firmly as Salina stared at him.

Calinda surged with anger; they were discussing her as if she were not present. "I'll leave when I please, Lynx," she stated tersely.

Lynx walked over and took her arm. "Let's go for a ride, Callie."

"I don't want to go riding with you," Calinda refused flatly.

"I didn't ask. I'm telling you. Let's go," he ordered, nearly dragging her out of the house. "Stop being so childish and hateful."

"Let go of me, you brute," Cal panted, trying to pull free.

Out of Salina's hearing, he released her and scolded her again. "Don't ever lower yourself to cat-fight with a hired servant. She works here and takes orders, if you're strong enough to give them. Salina's a good worker, just bull-headed. If you let her, she'll walk all over you. Put her in her place, and she won't give you any more trouble or backtalk. Otherwise, we're going to have a war on our hands. Once it's out of control, either you'll leave or she'll quit. Where's some of that pluck and spirit you rain on me? You trying to run her off and take her place? You bucking for an excuse to remain here without charity?" he slyly taunted and unsettled her.

"Of course not! She's been like that ever since I arrived. I've tried to be nice, but it isn't my place or right to correct her. This morning I was tense. I'm sorry if I caused trouble."

"I'm glad to see you didn't get any more sleep than I did. What was Salina's thorn today?" he inquired in a lazy tone.

"The same as the other day, you. She's afraid . . ."

When Calinda stalled, he asked, "Afraid of what? You have this annoying habit of halting in mid-sentence. Say what you mean."

"Nothing," she snipped defiantly, turning her back to him.

He walked around her stiff body and bent forward, cocking his head to look up into her lowered face. "Afraid you'll steal me from her?" he jested as their gazes locked.

"Yes," she replied icily. "But I told her she needn't worry."

"You're a bright girl, Callie. Surely you realize there's nothing between me and Salina, never has been. She can stake a claim, but it doesn't make it legal or true. Jealous?" he teased.

"Of course not. She thinks she has a claim on you. She even threatened me with a knife to stay clear of you." Calinda flushed in irritation. She hadn't meant to tell Lynx that.

Lynx filled with fury. He straightened, capturing her jawline between his fingers and thumb. "She what?" he stormed.

"She didn't exactly pull it on me. She just showed it to me and gave me several warnings about you. It's strapped to her thigh."

"If she ever draws a weapon on you, I'll break her hand," he threatened, totally serious.

"She wouldn't really, Lynx; she was just trying to scare me. I promise to behave from now on," she stated sarcastically.

"Salina has a temper, but she isn't stupid. I'll have a talk with her." His hold on her softened, as did his expression.

"Please don't. I'll take your advice and make my own stand."

"If you don't, I will. I won't allow her to terrorize you." His forefinger left her jawline to caress her cheek. For a brief and wild moment, it seemed as if he was about to kiss her right there in the open.

"You do enough of that," she vowed, glaring at him as she came to her senses. Why did he have his hypnotic effect over her?

"I don't mean to, Cal. You just have a way of provoking me to mischief. It isn't smart for us to quarrel in front of her. I know we met in a crazy way; but if you'll give yourself a chance to get to know me, I'm not as terrible as you think. How about a pardon?"

"What about our ride?" she reminded him, dropping the subject.

"Let's go," he took her defensive hint.

Lynx was amused when she insisted on saddling her own horse. They mounted up and rode off, heading toward some nearby foothills. Lynx waited near a bluff for Calinda to catch up with him. "It's lovely, Lynx; how can you bear to leave it so often?" For a girl who had been drilled in the social graces, she felt so unsure with him. She didn't know how to behave or how to converse with this unpredictable man.

She observed his warm gaze as it seemed to proudly caress the landscape. "The Cardone Ranch stretches as far as you can see in all directions, Cal. It's one of the largest and most successful spreads in the state. One day, it will all be mine," he added absently.

"You love this place, don't you?" she inquired.

"I helped steal it from the wilderness. I've got sweat, blood, and tears on nearly every acre. Look over there," he pointed to a dark splotch on the grassland. "That's some of the best cattle anywhere."

For the next few hours, they trotted or raced over the countryside. Lynx showed her lovely meadows, peaceful streams, cool clusters of trees, line-shacks, rolling hills, deep gullies, arroyos, and large spans of grasses and wildflowers which she had all seen before. But she viewed it differently under his guiding hand and descriptions. As they watered their horses in a sparkling pond, Lynx directed her attention to a lofty hill. "If I had been the first owner of this spread, I would have built the ranch-house there. You can see the sunrise and sunset, and you could look down on what you built and lived for."

He sat down and reclined, propping on his elbows and crossing his ankles. He removed his hat and fluffed his damp hair. He inhaled the freshness and sweet odors wafting on the breeze. He lay down and closed his eyes, relaxing. Lynx had never been more aware of how much he loved this ranch, of how ready and eager he was to come home.

Calinda assumed he was permitting the horses to cool and rest. She sat down near Lynx on the plush grass. It was very warm, so she removed her boots, planting her bare feet near her buttocks. She crossed her arms, rested them on her knees, then placed her chin on them. She watched the horses drink, then munch on grass near their hooves. She also inhaled the sweet aromas of blended nature. She was pleasantly fatigued and calmed. In this serene setting, she didn't feel threatened by anything or anyone, including her fiery passion for Lynx.

"Why don't you lie back and relax, Cal?" he suggested.

Without even thinking twice, she did. Closing her eyes, Calinda felt like a cloud drifting peacefully. When she opened her eyes later, Lynx was propped on his side, watching her. Their gazes fused. It seemed an eternity before Lynx bent over and kissed her.

After the heady kiss, Lynx caught her shoulders as he asked, "Why did you really come here, Cal? What do you want from us?"

Calinda assumed he was referring to their first meeting. "I told you everything, Lynx. What happened between us at the saloon wasn't entirely your fault. I'm not here seeking vengeance or chasing after you. I swear I didn't know about you. Why don't you trust me?"

"You and your story are too good to be true," he confessed.

"But they are true, Lynx," she argued, missing his real point.

Lynx's grip tightened unknowingly as he pressed, "Swear you're telling the truth, Callie. Swear our meeting was only a coincidence."

"You're hurting me," she cried out, wincing in discomfort.

"Swear it," he insisted, loosening his hold. "You know the odds against Calinda Braxton winding up senseless in Lynx Cardone's bed."

"I swear it," she vowed, although she felt he wouldn't harm her if she refused. Was it his male pride, that survival instinct? He was afraid it was all a trick? "What happened with my father, Lynx?"

Lynx moved to get up. "Let's go; it's getting late."

Calinda grabbed his shoulder, causing him to topple against her. "Tell me the truth. Why did he leave the Cardone Ranch?"

"I can't say. You'll have to ask him, if you ever find him."

"Do you know where he went? Where he is?"

"No," he replied, a strange coldness filling his eyes.

"Swear it," she used his previous demand.

"I swear it," he replied honestly. "Brax and I were close friends. He didn't tell me he was leaving and I don't know where he went. He never wrote and told you anything about his plans?"

"For the last five years, I didn't receive any word from him. His letters were always few and sketchy until mother died. He told my relatives it was too wild and dangerous for a child out here. He persuaded them to keep me in school there. He promised he would send for me after it was over. He never came. I know very little about him. What was he like?"

"Then why did you come this far searching for him?"

Calinda explained about the Simpsons again. "I just don't understand him or what happened, Lynx. Isn't there anything you can tell me?" she pleaded. "Is my father the reason you don't trust me?"

"Do you trust the Simpsons? Do you think they might have kept some letters from you?" he speculated, dodging her questions.

"It's possible. But if they knew he wasn't here, why would they send me to join him? If they knew where he had moved to, wouldn't they tell me? Unless . . ." She became pensive.

"There you go halting again. Unless, what?" he probed.

"Unless he was sending money all along. If they were keeping the money, they couldn't tell me about his letters. If he mentioned he was leaving here without telling anyone, they might assume I'd never locate him to discover their deceptions."

"Were they capable of such plots?" he asked, needing to know if there was a letter telling about the past, or just as importantly Brax's new location. Perhaps the Simpsons allowed her to come here because they knew the truth. Perhaps they intended to let her settle in and then make demands on her new wealth as repayment for their care and support. He would warn his father to watch for any mail to Calinda from the Simpsons, or a visit by any English strangers.

"I hate to admit it, but I wouldn't doubt it. They were awful people. I'm glad to be free. But I never expected to walk into a den of cutthroats and thieves. I honestly thought my father was here."

"Were they cruel to you?" he demanded, annoyed at that idea.

"Not physically. They were pressuring me to marry some rich man so they could entice money from him to pay their debts. They lost all feeling and concern for me when I refused. I might have been raised like the English, but I deplore arranged marriages. Why should I ruin my life to help them out of a dilemma which they created?"

That told Lynx they probably didn't know anything. Her explanation also told him why she was so eager and desperate to flee them. "I'm sorry you came all this way for nothing, Cal. I wish I knew where Brax is; I honestly don't."

She smiled unexpectedly and confessed, "I'm not sorry. I've been freer and happier here these last few weeks than I was there for years. I have Rankin to thank."

"You're very fond of him, aren't you?"

"Yes, he's a very special man. You're lucky to have such a father, Lynx. I hope you realize it and appreciate him."

"You've missed having your parents and a home, haven't you?"

"Yes, especially on holidays. After Mama died, the Simpsons always made me feel so left out. They constantly harped on my father's foul deeds. I wanted to prove them wrong, but I guess I can't. You're fortunate to belong in a special place; I'm envious."

Lynx turned his head to listen to a muffled noise in the distance. "What is it?" Calinda asked, noting the echoing sound of a bell.

"Dinner time. Father is calling us home. We rarely use that bell anymore. My mother used to . . ."

He jumped up and bent over to take her hand to pull her to her feet. "Supper's getting cold, Miss Braxton."

He guided her to her horse and was about to give her a hand up. Warmed by his charming and sensitive face, she flashed him a smile and said, "I can manage. Thanks."

"I'm sure you can," he jested, then agilely mounted.

He leaned over and gripped her saddle-horn, grinning into her face. "Want to race me home? Winner chooses a prize?"

"No way, Lynx Cardone. I doubt any horse can beat yours. In fact, I doubt you would make any wager you weren't certain of winning. Now if I can race Star, you're on," she counter-challenged.

"Sorry, love, but Star doesn't allow anyone but me on his back."

His hand went behind her head and pulled it to his, sealing their lips for a breath-stealing kiss. When he straightened in his saddle, he laughed and said, "I reckon I deserve a reward for being good."

He flicked his reins and his horse galloped for home. Calinda laughed softly before speeding off after him. Lynx Cardone was proving to be a complex man, a man of many pleasing facets and emotions.

After dinner, Lynx took Calinda for another walk. They headed toward the bunkhouse where some of the men were sitting on the porch playing music. Calinda listened to the joyful sounds while Lynx joked and chatted with several men, allowing her another insight to him.

"Want to dance?" he asked, grinning and taking her hand.

"Here?" she debated, fearing contact with that hard frame.

"Why not?" he playfully reasoned, eyes glowing appreciatively.

"I'd feel silly," she argued, but he swept her into his arms and whirled her around, his merry laughter stirring her blood. He was an excellent dancer, but she should have known Lynx could do anything.

After the lengthy song ended, the cowhands clapped and howled. Lynx thanked them and led Calinda back toward the house, winded and unsettled. As they neared the stone fence, he plucked a wild yellow rose and handed it to her. He left her at the door, saying he was going for a late ride, sounding as if he needed solitude.

Calinda went inside, miffed he hadn't asked her to go along. Surely he wasn't going to call on some rancher's daughter? Instead of heading for her room, Calinda changed her mind and went to the water shed to take a cool bath. The shed was a wooden structure about eight by eight square, located near the back fence. There were tubs for washing and rinsing clothes, and a very large one for bathing dusty bodies. Soap and linens were always there, and it was simpler to bathe here than to carry endless buckets of water to one's room. The water tower was nearby, supplying all the fresh water one needed, warmed by the day's sun. If it was winter, there was a wood stove for heating it.

Calinda latched the door. She walked to the oversized tub which reminded her of an immense keg without a cover. She took the huge cork and plugged the hole which allowed the tub to empty itself through a small trough behind it. She enjoyed this cask-like tub which was roomy enough for two people and even had a seat on one side. She pulled the cord and allowed it to fill with tepid water. She stripped and immersed herself, relaxing carefree for a time. She took scented soap and lathered up from head to waist. She dipped over and over to rinse. She stood up and scrubbed her tingly flesh from the waist down. Afterwards she sat on the wooden seat and pulled the cord to thoroughly rinse her hair. Her head was leaning backwards and her eyes were closed as she allowed the water to splash over her long tresses.

"Need me to hold that rope for you?" Lynx asked.

Startled, her eyes and mouth flew open. Calinda hadn't released the cord, causing water to gush into them. She jerked aside, coughing and gagging, letting the cord free, wiping her eyes. "How dare you come in here!" she ranted at the chuckling man, folding her arms over her bare and wet chest, sinking to her neck in the water.

"I thought the latch was hung up, Cal. I didn't realize anyone would be in here this late. Did you need a cold bath?" he helplessly teased, his gaze taking in her face and upper body before she protectively sank behind the edge of the deep tub, leaving only her neck and head in view. Her cheeks were colorful and her eyes were stormy.

"Then why didn't you show some manners and leave when you found it occupied?" she panted in distress.

Lynx grinned, then negligently leaned against the wall. "Need any help? I'm good at scrubbing backs."

"I'm positive you've had plenty of practice, but no thanks. I thought you were going riding," she reminded him nervously.

"Changed my mind. Thought I'd enjoy a relaxing bath more. Seems you had the same idea. Care if I join you?" he murmured huskily.

"Don't you dare, Lynx Cardone," she shrieked in panic. Lynx was a man who did as he pleased, and Calinda feared he might just take advantage of this heady situation. It was so difficult to think clearly when he was this close. At times, he was so magnetic, playful, attentive, and romantic. Other times, he was cool, insolent, and cynical. Calinda never knew what mood or behavior to expect from him.

Laughter came forth. "Be quiet," she warned, "Someone might hear you. What about that pardon you wanted?"

Lynx strolled forward. A few steps and a low platform had been constructed beside the tub to assist entrances and exits. Lynx sat down, the rim of the tub striking him at heart level. "Then I suggest we whisper. We certainly don't want anyone to learn our little secrets," he boldly teased, as if he had no intention of leaving soon. He propped his elbow on the edge of the tub, then rested his chin on his balled fist. He realized just how tempting, pleasing, and stirring she was.

To conceal her body, Calinda was given no choice but to snuggle against the edge of the tub, her chin resting on the rim to deny his softened gaze a clear view of anything, placing her in dangerously close proximity with him. "You're a devil, Lynx Cardone."

He chuckled softly and winked at her. His fingers grazed her scarlet cheek as he moved wet curls from her upturned face. As he shifted the heavy tresses to her back, his fingers made disturbing contact with her moist shoulder, then slipped down her back as he asked, "Sure you don't need any help? You can return the favor."

He was leaning forward, his face much too close to hers. "Please leave so I can dress," she entreated, her gaze locked on his face.

The cuff of his shirt was soaked as his fingers traced her spine. "You really know how to spoil a lonesome cowboy's fun. I'm enjoying the view. Never had a chance to share a lady's bath."

"Well, you're not sharing this lady's," she informed him. His touch and nearness were intimidating, but she dared not move.

"You're much too modest, Cal. After all, we have slept together. You don't have anything to hide from me."

"I didn't sleep with you; you slept with me," she disputed.

"Is there a difference?" he taunted, tracing her collarbone.

"Yes, a big one," she declared, nettled by his smug poise. He was thoroughly enjoying himself.

"How so, Callie?" he pressed mirthfully, covering her cold hands with his warm ones, leaning so close his breath touched her face.

"The end result was just as delightful."

"Please go away," she rashly cried. "I was distraught that night. I didn't know what I was saying or doing."

"You look rather distressed right now. Why?"

"You know why. You're embarrassing me," she accused.

"Surely you're not afraid I'm going to try to kiss you or seduce you? Why, Calinda Braxton, how could you think such insults?"

"Because you deserve them, Lynx Cardone. I don't trust you for a minute. You're always trying to disarm me. Stop teasing me, you rake. Didn't your father teach you any manners?"

"Guess I wasn't around long enough. You interested in giving me some lessons?" he mischievously inquired.

"You don't need lessons in anything. It must be nice to be perfect. But it certainly gives one a swollen head and vexing personality. Evidently I'm your only mistake."

"I didn't realize you possessed such a high opinion of me. I guess that means I'll have to live up to it, much as I'll hate myself for doing it. Chivalry is damned expensive." He stood up and shrugged. "Shall I wait outside, or do you intend to play a while longer?"

"I won't be much longer," she said, watching his departure.

She eyed the closed door, then hesitated before leaving the water. She hurriedly dried off and struggled into her clothes, wrapping a thick cloth around her wet hair. When she couldn't dislodge the cork, she called Lynx to help her. "It's stuck."

"I'll take care of it. You go inside and work on that hair if you don't want to turn in with a wet head," he politely offered.

"Thanks, Lynx," she murmured softly.

"Callie?" he called out as she started to leave.

She turned and responded, "Yes, Lynx?"

"Don't I get a goodnight kiss for being so helpful and courteous?"

Feeling protected by her clothing, Calinda smiled and placed a brief kiss on his cheek. "Thanks, and goodnight."

"That wasn't a kiss," he mocked, pulling her into his arms.

"It wasn't?" she daringly taunted.

"This is a kiss," he said, closing his mouth over hers.

Calinda's arms were trapped between them. If not, they would have eased around his narrow waist. Yet, her lips eagerly surrendered to his exploratory ones. His embrace tightened; his mouth refused to leave hers. The kiss became demanding and urgent, as did his passion. He removed the covering on her hair as his lips covered her face and roamed to her ears and throat.

He groaned in mounting desire. "You're a dangerous temptation, Calinda Braxton," he murmured hoarsely.

"So are you, Lynx Cardone," she replied in a strained voice as she pushed away from him, fighting to regain control of herself.

He caught her face between his hands, drilling his smoldering gaze into her matching one. "I want you, Cal," he stated simply.

"We can't, Lynx; it isn't right," she argued weakly against something she fiercely wanted.

"We already have," he reminded her, dropping kisses on her nose and eyes. "I need you. You're driving me crazy."

"Please don't, Lynx. We can't. I can't. I know what happened between us before, but it was a mistake. I can't sleep with you again."

"Damnit, Callie, you want me as much as I want you."

"I know," she confessed. "But that still doesn't make it right."

"Then don't tease me," he rebuked her responses.

"I didn't. You kissed me first," she protested, hurt.

"Don't you feel this need between us?" he irritably asked.

"But we aren't married, Lynx. I can't sleep with you like some harlot. Please don't spoil our truce. I want us to be friends."

"I can't marry anyone, Callie. I'm not ready to settle down. I've got some important things to do first. I need you. I can't even think straight with you around."

"Would you rather I leave the ranch?" she asked, wondering if he was hinting in that direction.

"Hell, no. I want you right here where . . . where I know you'll be safe and happy. But I want you, Callie, all of you."

"You can have me, Lynx, except in bed. If we slept together every time you came home, I'd be nothing more than your mistress. I'm not like that, Lynx. I don't think you know me at all."

"I want to know everything about you, Callie." Lynx was dismayed by her mention of marriage, a nice resolution to her problems.

"Then give it time, Lynx. It's hard enough to relax around you after what happened at the saloon. We need to discover each other first."

"I don't have time, Callie; I'll be leaving in a few days."

"Then make time, Lynx. No one's forcing you to go. If you really care for me and want me, then stay here and show me."

"I can't. I've given my word to help out a friend with a problem. You should recall, I always keep my word, even when it's hard."

"Does this friend need your help, or the aid of your guns?"

"Both, if it comes to that. I'm hoping I can settle his problems without shedding blood. It could be weeks or months before I get home."

"Please don't go, Lynx," she suddenly begged him. Fear and desire battled to be the dominant emotion in her expression.

Lynx realized Calinda felt more than passion for him, but what? He was baffled by that discovery, intimidated by it. First, a bold hint at marriage; then, hints at love and possessiveness; and then, hints at blackmail to keep him home . . . Inflaming her body and feeding her affections were dangerous actions. Callie was a woman, and he couldn't allow any holds over him at present. Callie was bright; she could start to put her nose where it didn't belong if she became determined to have him. He backed off.

"Go to your room, Callie, before I say or do something I'll regret. Since our timing is wrong, perhaps we should steer clear of each other while I'm home. If you're still around next time, maybe we can study this attraction between us. If not . . ." He shrugged.

Calinda stared at him. He was calmly dismissing her! Was this a cunning trick to entice her into his bed? He was making her refusal appear a stinging rejection. He wasn't being fair to demand all or nothing. He was just too accustomed to having his way. If he wanted to pretend there was nothing between them, let him. "That's fine with me, Mister Cardone," she scoffed, turning to leave.

"Callie?" he murmured again.

"What?" she snapped as she whirled to face him.

He grinned and tossed her the discarded cloth. "You forgot something," he teased as the cloth struck her in the chest.

She instinctively reacted and caught it. "So did you, Lynx," she stated myste-riously, then left in a huff.

Knowing Lynx would probably take a long time in the water shed, Calinda stood on the balcony to allow the warm breeze to help dry her hair. She muttered to herself as she worked the tangles free and fiercely brushed it. When her task was completed, she walked into her room and went to bed, to toss and turn for hours before slumber released her from her doubts and tension.

The next day was tormenting for both Lynx and Calinda. He rode out with the men at dawn to distract himself from that puzzling piece of fluff in his house. He worked the fence-line until he was weary and sweaty. He didn't return until nearly dinner time. He headed for the water shed to remove the traces of dirt, sweat, and leather from his firm body. Afterwards, he went to his room to dress in Spanish trousers and a blood red silk shirt, which was left open to his heart. He tossed his dirty clothes in a corner, then pulled on his boots. He picked up his silver spurs and tossed them on a chair. He left his room to join his father.

Calinda had spent much of her day alone. Nearing the dinner hour, she had changed into a lovely dress in muted shades of green, enhancing the color of her eyes. Lynx hadn't been home all day, and she dreaded to see him tonight. Would he still be angry and sullen? She collected her nerves and headed to join the men.

Lynx nodded at her when she entered the room, but didn't make conversa-tion or even smile. He was lazily sprawled in a comfortable chair, sipping a whis-key. Calinda glanced at him and spoke guardedly. She walked over to Rankin and smiled warmly. They chatted for a few moments before Salina came to announce dinner.

Salina flashed Lynx a seductive smile, which he returned in like manner to annoy Calinda. Calinda pretended not to notice. Dinner was long and painful for her, as Lynx totally ignored her. He talked genially with his father, but left her out of the conversation. When Rankin would draw her into it by choosing a mutual topic, Lynx would promptly change the subject back to ranching and cattle, or some business or event of which she was uninformed.

Calinda sat quietly and politely, knowing Lynx was intentionally excluding her, making her feel unwelcomed and saddened. Clearly he was attempting to make a point, to unsettle her. To verbally spar with him at the table would only enlighten Rankin to a problem between them. Being well-trained and well-bred, Calinda suffered in silence. Her poise and pleasant expression didn't reveal the battle within her.

But Rankin witnessed clues which tugged at his imagination. It wasn't like Calinda to be so reserved, to keep her lashes lowered so frequently, to absently toy with the food on her plate. Neither was it like his son to be so talkative, nor was it like Lynx to be subtly rude or to dominate the conversation. Lynx appeared overly carefree and energetic tonight. Rankin knew his son was playing some game with Calinda. But why? What was going on between those two? After dinner, Rankin suggested the two young people take a walk.

Calinda stiffened noticeably, then forced herself to relax. She didn't have time to formulate an excuse before Lynx was saying, "Not tonight. Sorry, Callie. I think I'll stroll down to the bunkhouse and visit with the boys a while. I might head into the high country tomorrow to look around before I leave. See you two later." He was up and gone before either Calinda or Rankin could speak.

Rankin persuaded Calinda to play a few games of billiards. She was distracted, and allowed him to win easily. He teased, "You aren't yourself tonight, Cal. Something bothering you?"

"I guess I just feel out of place here. I'm not used to so much free time and luxury. I know I should have made a decision by now, but I haven't. What do you suggest, Rankin?" If Lynx wanted her gone, would Rankin comply? Would Lynx make unreasonable demands on her if she remained?

"Maybe I should put you to work as one of my ranch-hands and burn off some of that excess energy and boredom. There's no decision to be made, Cal; you'll live here as long as you please."

"But what about my father, Rankin?" she implored.

"There's nothing you can do about Brax, Cal. If he ever returns, you'll be here waiting for him. If he writes you in England, the Simpsons will let you or him know where to find you. Accept it, Cal, you're better off here than anywhere else."

"I suppose you're right," she concurred. "But I would feel better if I did something around here to earn my keep."

"Then I'll look around for an appropriate chore for you. Does that ease your worries?" he teased her.

She smiled and nodded. They played one last game before they turned in for the night. It was nearly eleven, and Lynx hadn't returned. Her nerves were as tight as a miser with his money.

Calinda entered her room and slipped into one of the sensual nightgowns which had belonged to Laura Cardone. She stroked the silky garment, admiring its cool softness and lovely shade of deep green. She decided that either Laura or Rankin had extravagant and excellent taste in clothing; the gown was exquisite and provocative, one to stir a man's blood and daze his senses. How she wished Laura was still alive. It would make things so much easier for her.

Too keyed up to sleep, Calinda paced the floor again tonight. She went to the fireplace and rested her forehead against the mantel, gazing into the dark hole which lightly smelled of past fires. Right now, her future was as obscure as the blackness behind the hearth.

Why were life and love so complicated, so demanding, so frightening? Why was it all right for a man to yield to his passions, while a woman was compelled to subdue and deny hers? Just thinking about Lynx rekindled those forbidden flames of desire. She wanted him and needed him. Did she dare play such a perilous and costly game? Was she falling in love with him? Did he feel anything other than carnal desire for her? Was he with another woman? How long could she resist this hunger for him, conquer these yearnings? At least it would be harder, rather impossible, to be tempted once he left. Left? That word tortured her. She sniffled as if weeping, inhaling raggedly.

Strong hands gently grasped her shoulders from behind. She jumped and turned to face Lynx. Had she left the door unlocked again? Intentionally? She couldn't make out his face in the darkness, but she could sense his gaze roaming over her body, seeming to brand it.

"You're up mighty late, Callie. Missing me already? Worried about my safety?" he teased, his face hidden from her probing gaze.

She wanted nothing more than to fling herself into his embrace. Instead, she responded in a quavering voice, "Don't be absurd."

He craftily provoked her, "You're just as attracted to me as I am to you. You just won't admit it. Frankly, it's a most inconvenient time to be troubled by such cravings. I'd be obliged if you'd hang around until I come home again; I'd like to find out why I find you haunting me all the time. When Jake gave me all that phony information, I was ready to strangle you. What is it about you, Callie, that makes my guts twist and the hair on my neck stand up in warning?"

"If these are compliments, Lynx, they're the most unusual ones I've ever received. I haven't made any attempts to catch your eye."

"I know. Why not? Am I too repulsive for a well-bred lady?" he speculated, his hands leisurely moving up and down her bare arms.

"I find you insufferable and exasperating, but not repulsive," she admitted cautiously. "I doubt you and I have anything in common."

"More than you imagine, Callie," he whispered hoarsely.

"You're mistaken, Lynx; we're nothing alike."

"Won't be my first mistake where you're concerned, will it?"

"Do you mind if we forget about that night?" She felt shaky, innocently resting her palms against his chest to steady herself. Warmth, firmness, and a heavily thudding heart tantalized her sensitive hands.

"I can't. Have you? Was it a fatal error, Callie?" he asked, his hands halting their journey. He watched her in the scant light.

"Fatal error?" she repeated, losing his meaning, wishing she could see his expression. She didn't know her face was vaguely visible.

"Did it kill any hope of our becoming friends?"

"Us, friends?" she echoed, sadness flooding her eyes.

"Why not? Looks like we'll be living in the same home."

"Only until I can leave. And you don't live here."

"You have no family or money, Callie. Just where can you go and do what? Jobs for women are few, with lousy pay and harsh conditions. You're safer and happier here. Why leave?"

"It just doesn't seem right to live with two strange men, especially when one resents me and harries me all the time."

"You can hardly call me or Father a stranger. Besides, you . . ."

When he halted and dropped his hands to his sides, she asked, "I'm, what?" Her gaze filled with intrigue and attention. Her hands had detected the sudden increase in his heart-rate and his rigidity.

"You're welcomed by both of us," he said.

Calinda knew that wasn't what he had started to say. She wondered what new sport he was attempting now. "Thanks, but I still don't feel comfortable accepting extended charity."

"Would it help if I begged you to stay?" he tested a suspicion.

"Would you?" she challenged, straining to see him.

"Nope, but I would ask seriously. I never beg for anything."

"At least you're honest," she said too quickly. "It's late. You'd best leave now before we quarrel again. After the way we acted tonight, I'm sure Rankin wonders what's going on between us."

"Do I get a goodnight kiss from my new sister?"

"I doubt you view me as such, or ever would."

"You're right, Callie. I hope you don't mind if I call you that." Lynx cursed this visit home which seemed to be exposing the missing facets to his life, facets which he couldn't explore or claim at present.

"Do as you please," she stated unthinkingly.

"Right now, I please to kiss you," he murmured, then swept her into his arms. "I guess I was a little asinine last night and today. I don't meet many ladies. You give a man strange ideas, Callie."

Calinda's hands braced against his hard chest. "No."

"But you said I could do as I pleased," he mocked her resistance.

"Leave before Rankin learns you were in my room. We must be careful. There's no telling what he would do if he learned about us. Are you trying to get me thrown out? You've already seduced me. Now you're sneaking in here trying to . . ."

Without warning, Lynx released her. At the torturously familiar words, he rubbed his forehead as if it ached unmercifully. His expression changed drastically, his eyes chilling and narrowing as the past threatened to devour him. He glared at her for a moment, then asked, "Have you been wearing my mother's clothes? That's her gown, isn't it?"

"Yes, why?" She was startled by his harshness.

"How dare you presume to do something like that?" His voice was harsh with anger. My God, why hadn't he warned his father? Why hadn't he seen Brax for the snake he was? Now Callie was in Laura's clothes and home, trying to take her place.

"Your father gave them to me and insisted I use them. If it upsets you, I won't wear any of them again." Calinda assumed his lingering grief had inspired his outburst, and the anguish in his eyes kept her from throwing angry words back at him. When he continued to glare at her, she touched his arm and promised, "It won't happen again, Lynx. I'm sorry."

He stared at the sensual gown, then her. "It doesn't matter. They should have been burned. It just shocked me. See you tomorrow." With that, he left quickly.

Both their doors had been left open during his hasty flight. Calinda could hear Lynx pacing his floor and mumbling to himself. Her tender and warring heart reached out to him. It had been years since Laura's death, and he was still resisting the healing process. Or so Calinda assumed. Evidently he had been too surprised by her presence to realize whose clothes she had been wearing. When it struck home, it had been devastating. There must be something she could say or do . . .

Calinda walked to Lynx's room and went inside, closing the door behind her out of habit. He was in bed now. He turned his head on the pillow and looked at her. Slowly Calinda went forward to stop and glance down at him. He looked so troubled. "Lynx, I'm truly sorry. If I had known how it would hurt you, I would never have worn them. Rankin told me about your mother's death. I know it hurts deeply, but you must let go, let the wounds heal. When my mother died, I was numb for a long time. You must accept it. Don't you see what it's doing to you?"

"It isn't that easy, Callie. You don't understand."

"Would you like to talk about her? Sometimes that helps. She wouldn't want you to suffer like this."

Lynx laughed coldly. If Laura had truly loved him, she would never have deserted him. Lynx could almost understand her falling out of love with her husband and falling in love with Brax, but sacrificing her only child and home for another man . . . The least she could have done was leave a note, or send some word over the years. "I don't ever want to hear her name again. She never loved me or wanted me."

Calinda sat down on the edge of the bed. "You can't possibly think such a terrible thing, Lynx. How could a mother not love her child? You're letting grief and resentment destroy you. She didn't betray you or desert you by dying," she tried to console him.

Lynx captured Calinda's hand and held it between two strong ones. "I know the truth, Callie, because she told me so, many times over the years. Laura Cardone was devious, cruel, and selfish. She proved she didn't love me or father. Her only desires were . . . money and power." Just in time, he caught himself before saying passion and Brax. "It's over, Callie; let it alone."

Calinda stared at him, reading the honesty in his anguish-lined face. "I'm so sorry, Lynx. I didn't know." A tear eased down her cheek, feeling she understood Lynx's rebellion and cynicism, feeling she now grasped Rankin's reluctance to discuss his wife and the past.

Lynx pulled her face down to his chest, stroking her hair. He tenderly whispered, "Don't worry about me, Callie; I'll survive."

Calinda lifted her head and gazed into his eyes. "But you deserve more than surviving, Lynx, especially how you're doing it."

"Do I deserve an angel like you, Callie?" he asked, kissing her, needing her warmth and touch to repel the agony she had revived.

When the kiss ended, Calinda smiled and said, "Yes."

"Because you feel sorry for me, pity me?" he asked.

"No," she murmured honestly. "I feel sorry for the suffering you've endured, Lynx, but I don't pity you. You're a very strong and brave man. Why is it so difficult for you to accept your feelings and deal with them? You have defeated everything but your worst enemy, yourself. Come home, Lynx; Rankin needs you, and you need him."

"What about you, Callie? Do you want and need me here?"

His mouth closed over hers. Calinda didn't resist his silent plea for her response. He pulled her over his body and down beside him. Eventually he was lying half on her eager body. Her arms went around his neck and she held him tightly to her. Their mouths meshed in unison; their bodies touched and pleaded. Their desires couldn't be ignored.

This time, Calinda was not dazed by drugs or sleep, but by forceful passion. This time, Calinda was aware of each caress and kiss, but mindless with smoldering desire. This time, Calinda wanted to learn why Lynx filled so much of her mind and heart. She needed to comprehend this fierce urgency, this bittersweet torment.

Lynx's hand drifted down to unlace Calinda's gown and expose her creamy flesh to his lips and quivering hands. She hadn't realized Lynx was nude beneath the sheet. She didn't resist when he eased her gown off and their fiery bodies made staggering contact. She only knew she wanted Lynx to halt this raging fire and end this tormentingly sweet agony. She surrendered to his blissful touch and possession.

Lynx had just enough presence of mind not to hurriedly make passionate and savage love to her. He had dreamed of her for weeks. His daring caresses tempted her until she was aquiver with urgent need. She moaned softly and writhed as his tongue lavished moisture on her firm breasts and his hands stimulated her womanhood. He murmured into her ear, "Do you want me, Callie?"

"Yes, Lynx, yes," she feverishly responded.

He entered her and rode wildly and freely until she stiffened briefly and then clung desperately to him. As if starving for him, she greedily encouraged him to feed her fiercely and quickly. When both were rapturously sated, Lynx was drenched in perspiration. He rolled to his side, mentally willing his drumming heart and swift respiration to slow to normal. Never had he felt as whole as he did at this moment.

Callie didn't mind the moisture on his chest as her fingers drifted over it and she laid her face against his damp shoulder. They lay quietly for a time, then Lynx propped on his elbow to study her. "Are you all right, Callie?" he asked, as if this was her first time to make love.

She smiled serenely and nodded. "You have a way of hypnotizing a woman, Lynx Cardone. Perhaps I should watch you closely and be on guard every minute."

Lynx tenderly caressed her cheek and smiled. "I hope that won't be necessary or desirable, Callie. You're the most intoxicating woman I've known. Promise you won't leave here while I'm gone. I'll get back as soon as possible, then we can work out something about us."

"Must you leave?" she entreated, missing him already.

"Yes. I promised a man I'd do some work for him, but I can't tell who or where." His thumb moved back and forth over her lips.

"Is it dangerous?" she worried aloud.

"Living is dangerous, Callie," he side-stepped her question.

"You will be careful?" she insisted, knowing he wouldn't tell her more than he had stated.

"I promise. Give me your word you'll be here next time."

"I promise. I'd better go," she said reluctantly.

"Don't," he urged, hugging her tightly.

"Your father would be most upset and disappointed with me if he discovered the truth about us." She suddenly laughed.

"What's so amusing?" he inquired, eyeing her curiously.

"I don't believe this. I'm lying in bed with a near stranger, calmly chatting after making love. You are a wicked and potent temptation. You should be ashamed of yourself for demoralizing me. This is the most illogical and incredible thing I've ever done."

He chuckled. "Count me in. I'm just as astonished and confused. I'm glad I met you first. You'd best be on your guard, woman; I'll probably shoot the first cowpoke who looks at you sideways."

"How could I possibly notice him when my eyes are for you alone?" she quipped, caressing his smooth jawline.

"Just make sure you remember that while I'm gone. I wouldn't want to challenge some new sweetheart the moment I returned."

"Aren't you mighty possessive for a man who has no claim on me?" she teased, snuggling up to him, savoring his words and new mood.

Lynx shifted to remove a cross of pounded Spanish silver from his neck. He slipped it over her head and vowed, "That says you're mine." Lynx tried to ignore a stunning reality: he hadn't felt this happy, carefree, or excited in years. His only regrets were bad timing, mandatory silence, and a defensive reluctance to trust this woman so quickly and completely or his own unpredictable feelings. Until he was certain of what he wanted and needed, he must bind her to him without making rash promises or perilous confessions. A man would be a fool to douse such flames without a good reason . . .

"How shall I mark my claim?" she hinted playfully.

As he chuckled, she bit his shoulder gently. "There, that's my brand. However you read it, it says Calinda Braxton. Perhaps I could alter the bottom of the C/R branding iron and make one to use on you," she gleefully ventured.

"You wouldn't want to inflict such searing pain on me."

"Rankin told me it only smarted for a minute."

"On a horse or cow, but I'm a man," he amusingly wailed.

"That you are, Mister Cardone," she agreed dreamily.

Lynx's gaze fused with hers, then his mouth came down to begin a leisurely session of lovemaking . . .

Lynx's tongue drew moist circles around her breasts as she watched with smoldering eyes. Oddly, she felt no shame at this intimate and erotic behavior. The look in his gaze told her everything she needed to know at this special moment; this was love, their first love, love wild and free. Her heart surged with joy at that realization.

A radiant smile flickered over her face. Her fingers drifted through his curling mane, the ecstasy of their contact flooding her heart and soul. For a time, he seemed content to engulf her beauty and to lovingly stroke her satiny flesh. This moment had been long in arriving and demanded to be savored to the fullest.

When their play grew serious and hungers mounted, he entered her and held her possessively. Each blissful stroke urged another, then another. Soon they were caught up in the swirling vortex of fierce passion. As if submerged in water, he seemed to surround her completely. She wondered why she had ever resisted him. His love offered all she wanted or needed. Regardless of the past or future, Lynx Cardone was a vital part of her existence now. She loved him.

With skill and persistence, he timed their release perfectly. They clung together as rapture enslaved and rewarded them. Afterwards, he held her with such

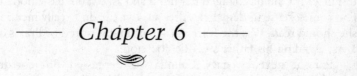

gentleness she wanted to cry with joy. She nestled into his arms, knowing she never wanted to leave them.

"You're mine, Callie," he whispered against her forehead.

"Yes Lynx," she instantly agreed, hugging him tightly.

Wrapped in each other's arms, they slept until passions demanded another feeding . . .

Chapter 6

WHEN CALINDA YAWNED AND STRETCHED CONTENTEDLY the next morning, she discovered herself in her own bed! As her mind cleared of dreamy cobwebs, she recalled Lynx gathering her drowsy body in his arms and returning her to her room. She smiled as lovely memories of last night returned. It was definite; she was in love with Lynx Cardone. After his actions last night, surely he felt the same. She hopped out of bed and dressed, eager to see him. She prayed he hadn't left for the range yet, but he had promised to take her riding with him.

When she went downstairs, the house seemed empty. Finally she located Rankin in his office, poring over the ranch books. He glanced up and smiled fondly at her, quickly closing the books. She returned his smile, then asked if she was disturbing him.

"Not at all, Cal, come in. You look mighty chipper this morning." He opened a drawer and slipped the two books inside, then closed and locked it.

"I suppose I was out of sorts yesterday," she excused her mood. "I didn't see Salina or Lynx around," she remarked to withdraw information. She was trembling with excitement at seeing her love.

"Salina's gone into town with one of the men for supplies. I'm sorry to say, that son of mine took off for parts unknown at daybreak."

Calinda's smile faded. "He's gone?" she asked without caution.

"Is something wrong, Cal? You look pale," he said.

"He said he was taking me riding this morning. I guess he forgot he was leaving." Calinda didn't conceal her disappointment.

"He was in a strange mood last night," Rankin said. "How did you two get along?" he probed.

"Fine," she murmured, not really paying attention.

"He left me a note. Want to hear it?" he asked.

"No thanks," she almost whispered, her eyes sad.

"He mentioned you," Rankin tempted.

Her face brightened. "He did?"

"Told me to take real good care of you. I think you made quite an impression on my son. I was hoping you might encourage him to stay home. Seems he still has wander-dust in his boots."

Calinda blushed. "You two are lucky to have each other. Did he say when he'd be home again?" she asked, trying to sound casual.

"Afraid not. Maybe knowing you're here, he'll hurry back."

That news put a curious sparkle in her eyes and smile. Rankin suppressed his grin and pleasure. Clearly these two had something going. But why had Lynx taken off like that? Had Rankin's hints at marriage panicked Lynx into defensive distance? If Calinda changed her mind and asked to see the note, he would have to find some excuse to deny her. After all, Lynx hadn't really mentioned her in terms she should read. Was the fearless Lynx running scared of Brax's daughter? Or was Lynx avoiding his father's gentle coercion?

For the next few days, Calinda was depressed. She couldn't believe Lynx would make such passionate love to her, then leave without a word. He had shown trust in her by exposing such bitter and private feelings. Had he felt threatened by the revelation of his emotions? Had her sympathy and fiery responses merely been soothing for him?

As promised, Rankin found Calinda a chore to eat up time and energy. She was responsible for feeding and watering the new colts and their mothers. Later, she asked to help with the extra saddles to keep them in condition. Wherever possible, she took on little chores and performed them skillfully and eagerly. She cleaned and blued Rankin's guns, and she rode fence with him while he taught her more each day. As with Rankin, she came to love the openness and beauty of the landscape. But she missed Lynx terribly. After learning about the other event which occurred the day of her father's disappearance, she comprehended the two men's reluctance to discuss that agonizing time. How could she probe her father's actions without refreshing the haunting memory of Laura? She let the matter slide for now.

When Salina became busy with canning fruits and vegetables for winter, Calinda found household tasks to drive her body to fatigue and her mind to distraction. She helped one of the men in the floral gardens; she assisted with cleaning the balconies and outside furniture; she scrubbed the stone floors on the porches; and she made herself useful in many other ways. Still Lynx haunted her day and night.

Carly Jones, a dependable and amiable ranch-hand, worked with Calinda many times. He taught her to handle a lasso and small calves. Some days they practiced roping and shooting. Other days, she accompanied him on his fence rounds. It was imperative to locate any holes cut in the fences and to repair them quickly to prevent expensive cattle from being stolen or wandering off. Calinda came to realize that rustling and fence-cutting were common occurrences. After she learned to manage a wagon and team of horses, she frequently delivered barbed wire and supplies to the cowboys on the range.

Some days, when Salina wasn't present to prevent it or to harass her, she would prepare special treats or cool drinks and take them to the men who worked within riding distance of the house. The men became fond of her and her company.

During the first week of June, Calinda sought out Rankin to beg a favor. She handed him a letter and asked him to mail it for her the next time he went into town. "I wrote to the Simpsons," she told him. "I asked them to let me know if they heard from my father. I doubt it will do any good, but I felt it was the only action I could take."

Rankin smiled indulgently. "Why don't you go into Waco with Steve tomorrow? You can mail the letter and shop. You've worked hard these last weeks, Cal. Steve will look after you. You deserve a rest and diversion." Rankin wasn't worried about the Simpsons. He knew he would intercept any response.

Two days later, Calinda was in Waco, "Six-shooter Junction." This large town was bustling with activity, prosperity, and people. Though Waco was quite modern, it wasn't uncommon to have a gunfight on the main street every day. A center for education and culture, Waco was often labeled the "Athens of Texas." It boasted of churches, opera houses, and flourishing businesses. There were many schools, including Baylor University. She was surprised by the immense size and architecture of the buildings, many flaunting lofty spires or turrets. There were stockyards on one end of town, for cattle being sent by train to the market. There were a variety of stores, and Calinda had a fat purse which Rankin had given to her.

Steve Garrison, a trusted ranch-hand and close friend to Lynx, took Calinda to see the sights after their arrival. Steve related tales of early longhorn cattle drives through this area before the railroads came. He told her how fencing and windmills had altered Waco's landscape and way of life. Besides cattle, this was a heavy agricultural region, with vegetables and cotton the main products. Calinda was surprised to discover a large Texas Ranger post at Fort Fisher. Perhaps they could offer help with her dilemma.

Steve hired a buggy and showed her the cotton mills, expounding on the days when "Cotton was King." He gave her a brief history lesson on Waco during the Civil War, adding that Confederate uniforms were made from local cotton and on machinery smuggled through the enemy blockade. He drove her to see the suspension toll bridge over the Brazos River which had been completed in 1870. Steve pointed out how many buildings and homes were constructed of Waco-made pink brick. She saw the McLennan County Court House, the Cotton Belt Depot, and the famous Waco Square. Then, having business to handle, Steve left her to herself later that afternoon.

As Calinda was leaving a dress shop to return to the hotel, a pair of startled golden eyes trailed her movements. When she was safely inside, Lynx headed for his meeting. He kept wondering what Calinda was doing alone in a wild town like Waco. Surely she hadn't left the ranch? Later, he would check out this mystery.

Lynx pulled up a chair and sat down across from Major Jones. "Things going smoothly up Dallas way?" he queried absently.

"Peak is dogging the Bass gang. I'm going to need your help, Lynx. Murphy is ready to turn traitor to Sam. He'll need a contact."

"Where do I find him?" Lynx asked, propping elbows on the table.

"Sam's planning another big robbery. Murphy's going to inform me as soon as it's set. I'll need you to stick close until word comes in."

"You sure it isn't the James gang?" Lynx inquired.

"Yes. The Jameses are working out of Arkansas and Kansas right now. But we do have two other problems: Rube Burrow and Cole Stevens. Burrow has been hitting the Southern Express heavily. He's got Pinkerton detectives roaming the woods after him." Jones shoved some papers into his saddle-bag and focused his piercing eyes on Lynx.

"Burrow's description wasn't in the crime book."

"He's a mean one, Lynx; don't take any chances if you happen on him. Blue eyes as cold as winter; nerves like iron. He's tall and gangly, but strong as an ox. He thinks nothing of using his 44's on anyone. He also likes to use disguises, so he's hard to trace."

"What about Stevens?" Lynx questioned, leaning back in his chair, his hands dropping across his lap.

"He's a sly one, Lynx. He hits banks, trains, and stages at their peaks. I don't see how it's possible, but it appears he knows when and where to strike. Mighty strange . . ." Jones murmured.

"Who's riding with him?" Lynx asked, coming to full alert.

"Six men and a skinny lad."

They talked on for a time, then Lynx left by the side door. He headed for the hotel. It was nearly nine o'clock by then. Lynx encountered Steve coming out of a saloon. He questioned his friend about Callie's presence, relieved to learn why she was in Waco.

Lynx decided it would be best not to see Callie and went to his own room in the same hotel. The longer he lay there thinking about her so close, the tenser he became. Why was he afraid to love her and trust her? Finally, he got up, dressed, and headed to her room.

Concluding it might attract the attention of others, Lynx didn't knock. He used his acquired skills to unlock her door and sneak inside. He walked to her bed and stared down at the lovely sleeping face. Could she betray him too? Could he handle her and the resulting situation if he allowed her to get too serious and too close? He clenched his teeth and turned to leave, as soundlessly as he had entered.

"Lynx?" Calinda spoke softly. "Is that you?" she asked, fearing she was asleep, dreading she wasn't.

He faced the shadowy bed, hands on gun-butts, boots planted apart. "It's me, Callie. I didn't want to disturb you. I saw you in town earlier, but I've been in a meeting. I talked with Steve; he explained what you're doing here. Must say, I was surprised to see you."

Fully awake by now, she recalled their last parting. "Why bother to say hello? You were too busy last time to say goodbye. You do have a cunning way of sneaking in and out when it suits your purposes. Just leave; I don't want to see you again. Ever," she added tersely.

"I didn't sneak out; I left you a note," he argued, expecting her anger, but not her coldness and rejection.

"You left your father a note; that isn't me," she told him. She removed the silver cross and threw it at him. "Take your little ruse and try it on someone else. I don't have time for users and liars."

"User and liar? What's gotten into you, woman? I told you in the note I'd be home within two months." Lynx was vexed at being insulted, challenged, and forced to explain anything. Just as he had feared, she was becoming possessive and demanding with closeness!

"The note you forgot to write?" she sneered.

"I left it on your pillow when I put you to bed, Callie," he snarled. "If you're playing games with me, I don't like it, woman."

She sat up. "There wasn't any note on my pillow."

Lynx's hungry gaze roamed over her partially concealed features. His tone softened. "Then look under the bed; it must have fallen off."

"I've cleaned that room many times; there wasn't any note."

Lynx came over to sit down beside her. "Is that why you're so angry with me? I swear, Callie; I left a note on your pillow."

"I never found one," she disputed his claim. "You could have said something before taking off. I didn't even know where you'd gone or for how long. You're greedy, Lynx Cardone; you think only of yourself. I was a fool to trust you or let you come near me again."

"Didn't Salina tell you a man came for me early that morning?"

"No," she snapped at him like a testy diamondback rattler. "Don't go creating phony notes and messengers to pacify me."

The truth settled in. "That little *serpiente!* Just wait until I get home. Don't you see, Callie? She must have taken the note while you were still asleep. She wanted it to look like I took off without a word. Probably hopes it will send you running. Damn her!"

"Are you saying Salina took your note?" she asked skeptically.

"She must have. When Tom came by, I had to pull out in a hurry. It was dawn, too early to disturb you without exposing us. I didn't have time to hang around until you were up. Besides, I didn't want any trouble. I was afraid you would cry and beg me not to leave. Salina must have seen me write the note and put it in your room," he sullenly defended himself.

"You are wrong, Mister Cardone. I would never cry like a baby or beg for affection or attention from anyone. If I'm such a dark secret, then I'm not worth your time and energy. Afraid I might impair that carefree, cold-hearted image of yours? Are you ashamed to be seen with me, for anyone to learn we care about each other? I don't understand you at all, Lynx. I'm fine to sleep with, but nothing else?"

"That isn't true, Cal," he argued, witnessing her rising fury.

"Then what is the truth, Lynx?" she demanded.

"I'm enchanted by you, Cal. But right now, I just don't have time to deal with you," he murmured tenderly, but sternly.

"You certainly find time to sleep with me," she sneered.

"Damn it, Cal. I didn't force you into my arms. Both times, you were in *my* room and in *my* bed," he informed her, stressing his claims. "You're being unreasonable. You wanted me as much as I wanted you. I haven't misled you. What do you expect from me?"

"You think I'm chasing after you?" she asked incredulously.

"Are you?" he unwisely teased.

"You conceited ass, no. To think I actually felt sorry for you that night and wanted to comfort you. Was it only an act to disarm me?"

Calinda's forceful words struck Lynx the wrong way. In the heat of her anger, she hadn't meant them as they sounded to him. "You slept with me out of pity? What are you trying to do to me, Cal? At least my feelings were open and honest. I don't need your pity or self-sacrifice." He glared at her before standing up to leave. "I was a fool to get tangled up with another Braxton. If that's the way you want it, Cal, I'll leave you alone. Just remember, it was your decision."

As he stalked toward the door, Calinda shrieked in panic, "Lynx, don't go. I'm sorry; I didn't mean it like that. You're so darn sensitive! Oh, forget it! I'm tired of battling a situation and a person I don't understand."

Lynx came back to the bed and seized her by the shoulders. "Then what did you mean?" he insisted, staring down at her.

"I don't know. But I didn't yield out of pity. How could you even think such an awful thing about me? It's just that one time you behave like I'm special to you; then the next, you act as if you don't give a fig. I don't know where I stand with you," she vowed, frustrated.

The implications of her words stunned him. "What do you mean by, where you stand with me?" he anxiously inquired, stalling for time to think out the consequences of his explanation either way.

"You heard me," she murmured, compelled to press the issue now that she had foolishly opened it with this jittery creature.

"Are you falling in love with me, Cal?" he blurted out, then scolded himself for his bluntness.

"Does it matter to you?" she asked another explosive question, rather than dousing the fuse to the one already lit.

He sat down on the edge of the bed, his back to her as he pensively stroked his taut jawline. "Do you think we've known each other long enough to have such serious talks and feelings?" he asked, trying to handle the volatile subject without it blowing up in his face.

They had known each other long enough to spend two nights in bed together. Was intimacy easier to accept than deep emotions? Was he resisting a commitment to her? Did he feel a vow of love would entrap him, would entice her to expect marriage? He was being awfully hesitant and evasive. How should she interpret his moods and actions?

Calinda recalled how Lynx had looked and sounded when he had spoken of his mother. Had Laura Cardone actually denied this troubled man love? Had she scarred him so deeply that he resented loving a woman, resisted sharing himself? What had Laura done to Lynx to make him so cynical and defensive? How could she repair the damage?

Calinda had never confronted anything like this. Perhaps Lynx was just as emotionally assailed, confused, and panicked. If such was true, she shouldn't pressure or corner him. It was possible that Brax's desertion and selfishness inspired mistrust toward her.

"Lynx, I think it's best if we drop this subject permanently. I've been under a great deal of stress these last few months, and I suppose I'm still not thinking clearly. The situation between us happened too quickly and unexpectedly. You needn't worry about my pursuing you, because I won't. The smartest thing for me to do is find a way to search for my father. Under the circumstances, I don't think it's wise for me to live in your home. I'll speak with Rankin when I return and see what can be worked out about my leaving the ranch. I wouldn't want you to be reluctant to come home because I'm there."

Lynx turned to observe her for a lengthy time. She was serious. "Afraid I won't come home, Cal? Or afraid I will?" he speculated.

"Either way, the situation isn't right, Lynx. It's time I stopped being a coward and started making my own decisions. Rankin has been very kind and generous to me, and I'm grateful to him. Perhaps he'll loan me the money to make a new start on my own somewhere. Goodbye, Lynx; I should be gone before you come home again."

"You can't mean it, Cal. This isn't England. Haven't you seen and learned enough to know you can't up and leave the ranch? If we couldn't find Brax with a hot trail, how do you expect to locate him on one that's been cold for years?" he anxiously tried to reason with her.

"I don't know. But I plan to try. I'll start tomorrow at the Ranger post. Perhaps they can tell me how and where to begin." Cal tried to master the telltale quivering in her voice and body.

"You'll be wasting your time, Cal. Rankin hired the best detectives around to look for Brax and . . . If they couldn't find him, you surely can't. You'll only hurt yourself and endanger your life." Lynx berated himself for pushing her into such a precarious action.

"Since you love to roam around, why don't you help me search for him? Why were you and Rankin so anxious to find my father?" she asked, abruptly aware of the determination revealed in his voice. They had paid detectives to search for a deserter of friendship?

"We wanted to solve the problem which made him leave. I'm not heading out on another futile chase, so drop this crazy idea."

"Is there something you and Rankin aren't telling me? I get the feeling there's more to Brax's departure than either of you have said. I sense bitterness and resentment when you two talk about him and the past. Why, Lynx? What really happened?" she implored.

"I've told you all I can. He's gone, and he'll never set foot on the Cardone Ranch again. If he dared to show his traitorous . . . Just drop it, Cal. You can have a good life on the ranch, if you'll just let the past stay buried. Please," he urgently coaxed.

Calinda shifted to sit beside him. "You hate my father, don't you? Why, Lynx? What did he do before he ran off? Please tell me the truth; I must hear it. Why did you say 'traitorous'?"

"Leave it be," he stated firmly, regretting his careless slips. "I don't want to hurt you, Callie," he added mysteriously. What was wrong with him? Where were his wits and self-control?

"If you don't tell me, I'll ask Rankin," she rashly threatened.

Pinning her face between his hands, he warned through clenched teeth, "Do so, and you'll answer to me, Cal. Rankin has suffered enough. He took you in and cared for you. You want to repay him by tormenting him? If you can't accept us and trust us, get off the Cardone Ranch. If you stay, forget about Elliott Braxton."

"But he's my father, Lynx," she reminded him.

"Was he ever a real father to you, Cal? If so, he would have contacted you and you wouldn't be wondering where he is now. He hurt and disappointed us, just like he did you." He forced devastating facts into her bruised heart, with a coldness and insensitivity which he hadn't intended.

Her chin and lips quivered as tears ran down her cheeks. "You despise me as much as him, don't you? Is that it, Lynx? Revenge? You can't get to Brax, so you're punishing me in his place? Befriend and charm, then reject, like Brax did to you? That's cruel, Lynx."

Her assumptions shocked him. The anguish and accusations in her eyes plagued him. He had said too much. Now, he must say more to correct matters. "You're wrong, Cal. It isn't like that. I'm not going into the whole story, but I will tell you certain facts. First, I want your promise you won't mention this or the past to Rankin again."

"What are you talking about, Lynx?" she asked, puzzled.

"Give me your word, Cal, or I won't tell you anything."

"You have it," she complied, her heart beating wildly.

"Brax doesn't deserve your loyalty and love, Cal; he never deserved ours. He did some terrible things years ago. That fall before your father vanished, Brax and my father completed a very lucrative cattle drive, 1500 cattle at $30 a head. That next afternoon, Brax stole the $45,000.00 and our ranch deed from Rankin's desk. My father caught him packing to leave hurriedly, and they fought. Brax cheated him, beat him, and disappeared without a trace. Afterwards Rankin became cynical and remote. If a man couldn't trust his best friend, who could he trust? If a man who was like his brother could rob him and beat him, anybody could. Brax turned love and faith into cruel jokes. Those things are hard for a man to accept, Cal; they color his whole outlook on life and people. Brax escaped that same day, and he hasn't been seen since. After my mother . . . I searched for Brax. I never found him." Lynx had spoken the truth, but only selected parts of it. He had to persuade her to forget her search.

"Were you going to kill him?" she asked reluctantly.

"I don't know what would have happened if I had located him. I was angry and bitter. I loved your father almost as much as my own; I even spent more time with him than with Rankin. I had trusted him and respected him. I'd followed him around like an innocent, blind pup. He made fools of us. Men have been hung for a lesser offense. Rankin went through hell; first Brax, then mother. We thought it was over, until your arrival. We felt guilty every time you begged for answers, but we didn't want to tell you such terrible things about your father. Leave it be, Callie. We've all suffered too much."

"You're certain Rankin's hired men never located him and . . ."

She didn't finish, but her insinuation was clear. "No, Cal, he didn't have your father killed. When you first arrived, we both suspected Brax might have sent you to nose around. We wondered if he'd run through all that money and was scheming for more. Since you don't favor Brax, father wasn't convinced you were Calinda Braxton."

"If he didn't believe me and resented I might be a Braxton, why did he invite me to the ranch? Why does he want me to stay on there?"

"At first, to be honest, he wanted to watch you; I agreed. If Brax was up to something, you could clue us in or lead us to him."

"Why would he come back? If he wanted to reach me, he would have contacted me in England, long ago. Do you still want revenge after all these years? Is the stolen money that important?"

"I was like you are now; I was confused and I needed to know the whole truth from Brax. Betrayal is hard to swallow, Cal. After it happened, I went searching for him. I couldn't believe Brax would do such things without some reason. When I realized I'd never find him, I couldn't make myself go home that soon. There were too many painful memories at the ranch. In a way, I had chosen Brax over my father for years; I couldn't face Rankin with all that guilt inside. As time passed, I liked going from place to place and doing exciting things. It made me too tired and busy to be tormented. But every time I went home, I was reminded of mother and Brax. I needed to make a man of myself, Cal. I had to test myself, learn who and what I was. I needed to conquer my inner demons. I also needed to prove myself for Rankin. Like you said, Cal, grief and hate are vicious diseases."

"But what about me, Lynx? Where do I fit in at the ranch?"

He chuckled, slowly relaxing. "You're one bewitching and stubborn bundle. It didn't take long for us to realize you're nothing like Brax. You brought a change of pace, new life and sunshine to the ranch. It appears Rankin observed you too closely. He became fond of you, Cal. Course you're mighty hard to resist. When he decided he could trust you, he felt you should stay at the ranch. I think he's being selfish; he likes you and likes having you around. Besides, you can't be punished for being Brax's daughter."

"What about you, Lynx? Do you honestly want me to stay?"

"Frankly, I was furious and shocked when I came home to find Brax's child living in my home. I was fully prepared to hate you and determined to kick you out that same day. Trouble was, I didn't expect Calinda Braxton to be Callie. Luckily we had met, and most provocatively I might add. I found myself in a most uncomfortable position. There you were again, and I didn't know what to do about you."

"Do you think my father might return one day?" she asked, switching to a safer topic.

"I don't know, Cal. He nearly killed Rankin in that fight."

"Why would my father steal the ranch deed?"

"We suspected he might try to take the ranch by altering it. He loved the ranch and did a lot of work on her. Or he could use it to make a false sale to some rich fool. If the records office ever burned, we'd have a hard time proving Cardone ownership without it. It's impossible to say where it is or what he'll do with it. It's clear he didn't mail it to you for safe-keeping."

"Lynx, does it bother you that Brax is my father?"

He looked away. "Sometimes," he admitted. "I guess we don't want to see you in that light, but you seem determined to keep reminding us."

"You're still observing me and testing me, aren't you?"

He looked her straight in the eye and nodded. "Can you blame us? You invaded our lives and turned them upside down. You're forcing us to face emotions and decisions we're not ready to deal with, Cal. As for me, I care about you and want you; beyond that, I'm just not sure yet. It takes courage and daring for a man to accept a connection to an enemy." He was finally saying "I," instead of "we."

"I don't see you as man short on courage or daring. I seem to recall a very bold man in the Red Satin Saloon and the water shed."

"That wasn't daring, Cal. You just drove me past the point of control or wisdom. Both times you cunningly set up irresistible traps for me, and I rashly got caught," he jested.

"You poor thing, you must be exhausted from your struggles for escape," she taunted him playfully, forcing his confessions from her mind until later when she could absorb them.

He fell back to the bed and sighed heavily. "You're right." It was easier to corral and tame a wild mustang than Callie Braxton.

"Up and out, Mister Cardone, it's late," she hinted softly, knowing where things might lead if she didn't stop them. Lynx must learn that he couldn't stroll in and out of her life at will. If he wanted her and she was important to him, then he needed to make it clear to both of them. If he was allowed all privileges without a commitment, he would stall making one. She would not force him into making a hasty decision, but she would avoid giving him reasons to evade one.

He turned his head to gaze at her, his expression revealing his imminent plans. "It's been weeks, Callie; I want you. I need you."

"Not tonight, Lynx. Too much has been said. I need time alone. Will you be around tomorrow before I leave?" she asked.

"No. If I go now, we won't see each other for a long time. Do you want me, Callie?" he asked huskily, waiting tensely for a reply.

"That has nothing to do with it. You've given me a lot to consider. We'll talk when you come home again, whenever that is."

Lynx felt she would relent if he ardently tempted her, but that wasn't fair. "Don't forget your promise, not one word to Rankin."

"I'll remember everything you told me. You have my word. Lynx, what about your mother? When did she . . ." she cautiously probed, knowing that harmful malady couldn't heal until excised.

"If you don't mind, Callie, I don't want to discuss Laura Cardone, now or ever. Let the past die, all of it," he said inflexibly.

Calinda read the anguish in Lynx's tawny eyes. She knew he had been describing his emotions and reactions as much as Rankin's. The two people Rankin and Lynx had loved most had hurt them deeply. Since she was Brax's child, she felt responsible for gleaning the truth or an explanation to ease their torment. Brax owed each of them that much. She knew she could not discuss this painful subject with Rankin, and she realized she could never borrow money from the Cardones to seek the man who had done such evil in their lives and home.

Lynx couldn't beg for her touch, so he left. Afterwards, Callie allowed his words to flood her mind, as tears flooded her eyes. It was hard to accept the truth and she resisted it. If what Lynx said was the truth, how could he and his father stand to look at her? There must be more to it. Brax's crimes might explain his lack of contact with her; perhaps he thought that if he wrote to her, they could trace him through his letters. But why had they pursued her father, unless to punish him? Why had they taken her into their home? Why would they think Brax might return to the scene of his crime? Curious inflections, questions, and looks from the two men returned to make an impression in her mind. Somewhere there were other pieces to this unfinished puzzle . . .

But there were realities Calinda couldn't ignore. Her father had abandoned her and ceased to support her, as if she meant nothing to him, with not one letter of apology or explanation. He had taken a path of crime, at the expense of good friends and his family. How could he do such wicked things? Surely there had to be more to the man her mother had loved and married, more to the man the Cardones had trusted and loved? What had changed her father? He had sacrificed everything and everyone; why? It was senseless.

The next day, Calinda went to the Ranger post. She asked to speak with the man in charge. Without giving facts she had promised Lynx to keep concealed, she explained her dilemma to Major Jones. He was kind, attentive, and patient. But he told her there was nothing the Rangers could do to help. He suggested she locate a picture of her father, then hire a detective to hunt for him. Lastly, he told her there was little, if any, hope of locating a man who had vanished long ago, adding that Rangers couldn't be involved in personal matters.

Calinda thanked him and returned to the hotel. She didn't have either a picture of Brax or any money to hire a detective. She was still trapped at the Cardone Ranch and dependent on them. Knowing this, she felt uneasy about returning there. To discover how tight her web was, she spent all morning seeking a job. By the time Steve was ready to leave Waco, Calinda knew she had no choice but to return with him.

Calinda didn't know that Lynx was having her watched, for her safety. When the man reported to Lynx after her departure, he was baffled and annoyed by her visit to Major Jones and her attempts to find work in Waco. Evidently she hadn't fully accepted his words and was still determined to locate her father. Too, she seemed resolved to leave the Cardone Ranch. Was it to elude him, or was she suspicious of them now? What if she sought work in Fort Worth, Dallas, or Wichita Falls? What if she pressed Rankin for more clues? Where was that critical ranch deed? What was Brax planning to do with it?

Lynx couldn't help but wonder if his mother was still alive somewhere. Had she ever regretted her traitorous actions? Had she ever been tempted to return home? After what his own mother had done to him, could he blindly trust another woman, rashly offer his heart and soul? Even to his beautiful and gentle Callie? Why was he reluctant to reach out and take something he wanted so desperately? Because he feared his dream would dissipate as wind-assailed smoke.

Lynx couldn't allow his love to desert the ranch or place herself in danger. But if she pressed his father for answers, Rankin would make her leave rather than tell her the whole truth. He headed to see Major Jones about a two-day leave, needing to settle this matter with Calinda before it was too late for all concerned. He cursed his careless revelations to her; he berated this weakness, this overwhelming and aching desire for her. How could he stop her departure and also distract her from the past? The problem was, he was on a tough assignment; it could be weeks before Jones gave him permission to go home. Time might be a new enemy . . .

Chapter 7 ❧

CALINDA HAD BEEN HOME for less than two days when a harrowing episode began on Thursday morning. She had kept her word to Lynx; she had not mentioned their unexpected meeting in Waco and she hadn't asked Rankin any questions or dropped any clues. Calinda had returned late Tuesday evening; Rankin had departed early the next morning for Graham to meet with the Southwestern Cattle Raisers Association. He would be gone for over a week. Calinda was relieved by his absence—she needed time to adjust to the stunning information Lynx had supplied. Caught up in the excitement of her return and preparations for his departure yesterday, Rankin hadn't noticed a change in Calinda. But she was more observant and subdued, with a slight gleam of remorse and sadness in her eyes.

Shortly after Rankin left, Calinda had confronted Salina with her daring theft of Lynx's note. Naturally Salina denied the charge, a charge which told Salina the infuriating Calinda had been with Lynx in Waco. The jealous Salina threatened to reveal their "wanton affair" to Rankin, shrieking that Rankin would never allow such goings on in his home with his son. Their volatile quarrel had nearly erupted into a fight, but Calinda had wisely prevented it by suggesting they halt their private war before Lynx and Rankin got involved and were forced to choose between them.

Salina had smiled deceptively. If her revenge was to succeed, she couldn't openly expose herself as a bitter enemy of Calinda's. Once Calinda was removed from their home, she must look innocent. Something strange had taken place between Calinda and Lynx in Waco, for the hated girl alluded to being afraid of the Cardones' rejecting her.

Calinda unknowingly stepped into Salina's long-planned scheme to be rid of her when she had stated unflinchingly, "I'm not leaving, Salina. I like living here on the ranch with Lynx and Rankin. Besides, I don't have a home or family anywhere. So you're stuck with me."

"What about your papa? You do not care if you find him or not. It was a trick to steal into this home," she hotly accused.

"That isn't true! While I was in Waco, I went to see Major Jones of the Rangers to gain their help and advice," Calinda shouted back at her, continuing angrily with the whole meeting. "And I'm not accepting charity from the Cardones! I've been working hard for my keep. I checked around in Waco; there weren't any decent jobs. I have no choice but to stay here, so stop trying to run me away."

"If you say so," Salina skeptically responded, her mind racing wildly with excitement. This was the event and time she had anticipated. She finally had an opportunity to send Calinda a misleading note about her father, a note to lure her into danger and to inspire trouble between her and the Cardones. It was perfect.

That next morning, Salina supposedly left early to go into town for supplies. After Calinda straightened her room, she went to the water-shed to do her laundry. When it was hanging on the line, she went to the kitchen to prepare a lunch of scrambled eggs and coffee, as she had skipped breakfast. Afterwards, she went to her room to rest.

There was an unpost-marked letter on her pillow. Calinda glanced around; her room was empty. Who had placed the envelope there? She hadn't seen anyone come near the house all morning. She lifted it and read it.

> Miss Calinda Braxton,
>
>   You must forgive this manner of delivery, but there are reasons which I will explain when we meet. I have uncovered distressing news of your father. You must come to the Keystone Hotel in Lampasas with all speed. The Butterfield Stageline runs between Fort Worth and here. The trip will take two days. You must tell no one of this letter or your plans, even the Cardones. I cannot sign this note, but you asked my help and should know who has written it. Come quickly, before it's too late.

Calinda's mind was in a flurry of thoughts. Major Jones? Was her father in danger or trouble, or both? Why didn't the Ranger want the Cardones to know about his help? Of course, they would follow her and arrest her father. Did she dare go and meet him? If so, would she finally uncover the missing link in this chain of events? But how could she disappear for days, five at least? She couldn't claim to be visiting friends or shopping for that length of time. She had enough money to carry out this journey, thanks to Rankin. But how would he and Lynx react to her seemingly traitorous actions? There was no simple answer to this crisis. Yet, this might be her last and only opportunity to confront her father and hear his side.

Calinda paced her room, trapped by indecision and worry. Suddenly she raced out and searched the house and surrounding yards, finding no one. She hurried to the stables to speak with the two men working there; they hadn't seen or heard anyone come or go. When they questioned her behavior, she smiled and told them she thought she had heard someone arrive while she was bathing, but found no one when she was dressed. They grinned when she cunningly hinted she thought Lynx might have come home. They shook their heads and said no. Calinda went to the house, halting by Salina's door to knock. There was no answer. Clearly Salina hadn't returned from town . . .

Calinda went back to her room to give this grave matter more thought. Two hours later, Salina slipped out of her room and stole into the supply shed. She carried several bags to the kitchen, loudly slamming the door on her last trip.

Calinda went downstairs to find Salina putting away supplies. She asked the sullen girl if she had seen anyone around the ranch or on the road earlier this morning.

Salina turned to glance to her. "Were you expecting company? Lynx does not return home so quickly after leaving," she sneered, making it sound as if Calinda was hoping he had changed his ways now that she was here. "It would be fun with old papa away so long."

"I wasn't thinking about Lynx, Salina. Several times I thought someone was in the house, but I couldn't find anyone when I searched. Do you ever have bandits come around?" she tried to prevent any suspicion in the Mexican girl who was watching her strangely.

"We have rustlers on the range, but no *bandido* has dared to enter this *casa* to rob a Cardone. It must have been your imagination, or perhaps wishful dreaming," she hinted playfully.

"Perhaps," Calinda flippantly agreed to end the matter. She must make a decision this afternoon. If she could come up with an acceptable excuse, she could make the two-day trip to Lampasas, speak with Jones or her father, then make the two-day trip home. A five-day journey could be carried off before Rankin's return in six or seven days. If she could sneak off, the men wouldn't think anything about her absence on the range since Rankin wasn't home to escort her. The problem was Salina. That malicious witch would enlighten Rankin the moment he returned. Since Calinda couldn't lie to Rankin, it might spoil everything. What to do?

Calinda remembered her laundry and went to fetch it. When she returned to her room, Salina was standing near her bed with the letter clutched tightly in her hand, cunningly plotting how to help Calinda solve the problem of Salina.

Calinda entered the room and halted instantly. She raced forward, throwing her clothes on the bed and snatching the letter from Salina. "How dare you read my mail!" she shrieked at Salina. "What are you doing in my room? I told you never to set foot in here again."

"I came to make a truce. You are right about our battles causing trouble. I sat down to wait for you to come back. I saw the letter on the bed. I could not help but see what it said. What does it mean?" she asked, pointing to the letter.

"Since you so boldly read it, you know as much as I do," Calinda snapped in irritation, viewing the girl as a kink in her plans.

"Are you going to meet him?" Salina inquired, eyes wide.

"How can I? Rankin and Lynx would be furious with me. I don't even know who sent it or how it got in my room."

"Who do you think sent it?" Salina questioned innocently.

"I suppose that Major Jones, the Ranger from Waco."

"Why does he want you to come in secret like a thief? Why would your papa not come here to see you?" Salina pressed.

"I don't know, unless my father is in some danger or trouble."

"But you said the Cardones would be angry with you; why?"

Calinda wondered how much, if anything, Salina knew about the past. "How long have you lived here?" she asked. "Did you work for Laura Cardone?"

"No. My sister worked here until she married. I took her place. You did not say, why will they be mad if you seek your papa? If you came to look for him, why do you not rush to answer this message?"

Calinda chose her words carefully as she said, "My father used to work here. He was Rankin's best friend. For some strange reason, he vanished five or six years ago. Rankin and Lynx were upset because he left suddenly without a word to any of us. He treated us badly, so they would be angry with me if I rushed to him now that's he's decided to come forward after all this time." Calinda observed Salina closely. If Salina had learned anything since coming here or her sister had revealed any facts to her, it didn't show on her face or in her voice.

"Men are silly creatures, so proud. How can you refuse over a quarrel so long ago? If your papa is in trouble, why would a Ranger send for you? He would arrest him. Perhaps your papa is a secret agent. That could explain why he moved so quickly, why he could not get in touch with you, and why they are helping both of you. *Si?*"

"Your sister never mentioned Elliott Braxton? He was called Brax. I would think sisters shared all secrets and gossip."

"She was my step-sister. We never liked each other. She always thought she was better than me. She hated her mother for marrying my father. She left home as soon as possible. She did not even tell me about the Cardone job; my father did."

"Do you think she would tell you anything she remembered if you wrote to her? I would like to know what happened to him."

"Then why do you not go to see him? Perhaps he will only confide in you. If he leaves on a mission again, you might never see him."

"My father couldn't be an agent, Salina. He was a rancher. Something happened to either drive him away or to scare him off."

"Then why do you not find the reasons which keep him from you?"

"I told you why," Calinda panted in exasperation.

"Which is more important, *senorita?* Your own papa or the Cardones and your life here on the ranch?" Salina artfully challenged.

"I see what you're trying to do. You want me to leave. You hope they'll be furious and will refuse to let me come back."

"I care nothing for your truth or papa. *Si,* I wish you to leave and never return. If you find your papa, perhaps it will be so. My tongue does not run wild. If there is a slim chance your papa will take you away from here, I will keep silent for you to chase it. Even if I told them about your trip, they would probably forgive you and I would look bad in their eyes. They take your side against me. There is time for you to seek your answers before *Senor* Rankin comes home. If you are here to stay, I also wish to know."

"Why would you cover for me? You despise me."

"I told you. If you cannot find your papa, you will remain. If that is to be, I wish to know now. Then I must decide if I am to go or stay. If your trip and success can bring home answers for both of us, then I beg you to go. If you resist because you do not want the Cardones to know of your search, then I will keep silent. But I swear to you, Calinda, I will deny I knew of your departure and its reasons. You must promise to never tell anyone I knew of your plans. If they discover your actions and question me, I will tell them it was none of my business.

They said you were free to come and go. Who am I to stop you?" Salina shrugged her shoulders and sighed.

"What if I don't find him and return? You would seek trouble and spite by telling them or by threatening to tell them. I don't trust you." Calinda and Salina stared at each other. Calinda was so confused and intrigued that she couldn't observe this situation wisely. She was so desperate to hear the truth and to see her father just once that she unconsciously allowed herself to be charmed and convinced.

"If you return, then I must leave or we must make peace. If there is trouble, they will send me away before casting you out. You can clean the house and cook, and they like you more. You are the one not to be trusted, Calinda. You have come here and tried to take my place and my family," Salina accused grimly.

"That isn't true, Salina. The only reason they've been upset with you is because of the mean way you've treated me. I don't want to take your place. There's no reason we can't be friends. Why must you hate me so much?"

"Friends? You do not wish me to leave so you can take over the house? You do not wish to turn them against me?"

"Of course not. I've never seen a more qualified housekeeper and cook. I could never handle everything with the skills you do. You've been here a long time, Salina; they're very fond of you. They know how special you are and how hard you work. They also know you love them and love working here. If you're angry about Lynx, I'm sorry. Lynx has had a difficult time growing up. I've been trying to convince him to come home, that Rankin needs him on the ranch. But he wouldn't listen. If you think I'm chasing him, you're wrong." If Lynx was the major problem between them, Calinda wanted to clear the air today.

"You are very beautiful. I saw how he watched you. It was as I feared; he desire you. You are a lady, and *hombres* hunger for them. He will not come to me with you here," she voiced her jealousy.

"Desiring and loving are two separate things, Salina. Lynx doesn't love me. I'm not sure he's capable of loving any woman, at least not yet. I think his mother hurt him deeply; now, he doesn't trust any woman. He's afraid to feel anything or share himself. Even when he's ready, I doubt he would select me."

"But you also desire him, do you not?" Salina asked with a deceptively calm and sad voice. "If you wish, you could win him easily."

"I like him very much, Salina. But Lynx is a mistrustful man. We're very different. He is charming and handsome, but that doesn't justify love. I only want him to be happy."

"What if he chooses me? Would you stay here if he did?"

Calinda's face betrayed her answer, but she didn't voice one. "I don't think we should discuss him like this, Salina. But I will promise you one thing; I won't ever chase after him."

Salina had her answers. She sighed dramatically and nodded. "You are right, Calinda. A woman cannot force a man to desire or love her. But I will promise you something; I will go after him until the day he marries another woman. Until then, he is free to be taken."

Calinda couldn't suppress a smile. "You and Lynx are much alike, Salina. You're both proud and strong. You both know what you want and you go after it with all your might. I envy such daring." Calinda had caught herself before including mercurial and stubborn on her list of similar traits. Could she trust Salina? The girl's arguments were logical, even selfish; and Salina freely admitted to her feelings. Right now, they were both trapped in the middle. Calinda's quest could solve many of their problems.

"Are you going to Lampasas?" Salina queried.

"I'm afraid to go, and I'm afraid not to go," she replied honestly. "I don't even know where it is or how to get there. It could be dangerous. If you recall, the first stage I rode here was robbed."

"You said you envied my daring and courage. If you challenge nothing, you win nothing. Find the truth, Calinda. Then we can settle this confusion between us. I swear to hold my tongue silent."

"But what if someone sees me or tells them? What if Rankin comes home early?" Calinda fretted aloud.

"I can not tell you what to do, Calinda. But I will help you. In doing so, I help myself. I can not risk earning their wrath, so I must deny everything if you get caught," Salina reminded her.

"If I don't get caught, you promise to say nothing? Even if I come back to the ranch?" Calinda pressed anxiously.

Salina withdrew a silver cross from beneath her blouse and held it tightly between her fingers as she said, "Upon this cross, I swear never to tell anyone where you went or why. If anyone should come home early, I will swear I know nothing of your departure. I swear only you will explain when you return, if you do."

Calinda sighed with relief and gratitude. Salina demanded, "Now, you hold the cross and swear you will say nothing of my knowing such things."

Calinda held the silver cross between her fingers and murmured softly, "I swear to tell no one of your knowledge or help." She released the cross and sat down on the bed. "Now, all I have to do is figure out how to get to this Lampasas."

"*Manana,* I must go to town to get more supplies. You can ride with me to the stage office. It will take you to Lampasas. But you must stay there or return in five days. I do not wish to lie to *Senor* Rankin unless it cannot be helped. Agreed?"

"Agreed. Thank you, Salina. I promise things will be better when I come home," Calinda naively and wistfully implied.

Home, Salina mentally sneered. *You will never return. Lampasas has many outlaws and dangers. One will surely claim you. He will see to it for me. Even if you escape this trap, you will return too late to keep their love and trust . . .*

"You must pack tonight. We will leave as soon as the hands have left for the day. It is best no one sees you leave with me." Salina eagerly planned the one-sided conspiracy.

"Will you have dinner with me tonight?" Calinda offered.

"That is not permitted, but *muchas gracias.* I have promised to see an *amigo.* If Lynx finds another woman, then I must be prepared with another man. I will soon be past my age of beauty when husbands are harder to find and trap," she teased happily, knowing her revenge and dreams would soon be met, denying Calinda's offer of friendship.

Calinda smiled and remarked, "You're very smart, Salina."

Salina left thinking, *more than you know, senorita. . .*

In Waco, Lynx was trying to reason with Major Jones, and having no success. For the past three days since Calinda's departure, he had been working feverishly to complete this present mission. Finally today, he had gained the information and names which Jones needed. He had asked for a short leave on Monday, but had been refused. Now, he was asking again Thursday, but was receiving new orders instead.

"I'm sorry, Lynx, but you just had a leave home. I can't spare you or another Ranger to take your place right now. I've got explosive problems all over the state threatening to go off at any time. I need you in Kimble County within the next few days. You're the only Ranger those men won't recognize. As soon as that fire's put out in Junction, you must come back here. From Murphy's reports, Bass is heading this way for the biggest job he's ever pulled. If we don't nail him this time, it could be ages before we sniff the right trail again."

"What's so vital in Kimble?" Lynx asked, annoyed but resigned. He had never been one to shirk his duty or to put personal feelings above them. Calinda would just have to wait another few weeks.

"You see all these letters?" he asked, directing Lynx's attention to the sliding stack on his desk. When Lynx nodded, Jones continued. "They're from terrified citizens, nervous local officials, and eagle-eyed Rangers. There's been a heavy rain of fear and crimes in that county. You name it, and Kimble has it: rustling, robbery, murder and beatings. There're so many outlaws operating in that area that the two Rangers I have assigned there can't handle all of them. It's like a viper's nest; little snakes crawling all over and hiding everywhere. You've got desperados working alone and in gangs. The citizens are banding together and carrying weapons. Could be another vigilante or regulator group forming. You know what that means: violence and lynchings. Innocent people get caught in the middle, Lynx. Those people are so touchy, a sudden thunderstorm could set them off. What few lawbreakers the sheriff captures are stolen from jail and hung. Some of those men could be innocent. Things are getting out of hand, Lynx. I need you to scout around and report to Ranger Clark with any news. No one else, Lynx, just Clark," he stressed.

"Yes sir. I'll pack and leave at dawn," he accepted his duty.

"Lynx, if it becomes necessary, use your badge. I don't want you killed down there. But I hope to keep you a secret a while longer."

"I understand, sir," he said, then left.

That night, all Lynx could think about was Calinda. He tossed and turned until he was tense and exhausted. He worried over his distraction, as survival demanded a clear head. He wasn't much good to anyone in this state, especially himself. Calinda was proud and stubborn. He recalled a gleam in her eyes which troubled him. If he pulled out at dawn and rode hard, he could swing by the ranch before heading to Kimble. If he could just see her and talk with her a few minutes, he could settle her fears and his nerves. If things were that bad down Kimble way, he might not come out of this one alive or soon. He must see her again before riding into the face of death. He had to make certain she would wait at the ranch for him. If need be, he would give her a good reason to hang around, a promise of marriage. If he really pushed himself, his arrival in Kimble would be delayed only a few days. What could possibly happen in three days to change things?

After all he'd done for the Rangers, they owed him this one lapse. He loved Texas, the Rangers, and the law. But he also loved something else now. He chuckled to himself at that realization and admission; he actually loved Calinda Braxton. He had wasted a lot of years and emotions, but not any more. He would complete these last three assignments, then go home for good. Rankin was a sly devil; this time he was right. Calinda was the perfect woman for him.

It was like a heavy weight had been lifted from his chest. He felt deliriously happy and excited. He would hurry home and confess his love for her, then secure her promise to wait for him. Rankin should be delighted with his decisions to marry and come home soon. In fact, it was time to confide in his father about everything . . .

Nearing town that next morning, Salina reined in the team of horses and told Calinda to get out. "If Rankin questions anyone, I do not want us seen together. Just get home by Tuesday."

"Thanks, Salina. If things do work out with my father, I'll send word to you. I'll sign the letter Maria. If they don't, I'll be at the stage office Tuesday afternoon. I'll hire someone to bring me out to the ranch. If Rankin's home, I'll handle everything."

"Do not forget your promise," she cunningly reminded Calinda.

"I won't. Thanks again. Goodbye."

"*Adios*, Calinda," the girl stated, thrilled by that word.

As Calinda made her way to the Butterfield Stageline, Salina headed for the telegraph office. Simultaneously, her deadly telegram was flying across the wires faster than the stage was carrying Calinda to her fate. By Saturday, Calinda would be at the Keystone Hotel and battling the dangerous surprise Salina had in store for her . . .

It was late Friday night when Lynx tied Star's reins to the hitching post before his home. He quietly entered the house, trying not to alert Rankin until he had spoken with Calinda. He found her room empty and her bed rumple-free. It was late. Where was she? His heart began to drum madly. Surely she hadn't . . .

He walked to Rankin's room, whose bed and room were also empty. Could they be at a neighbor's this late? Rankin's mutual absence calmed his tension. He would wait for them. He poured himself a drink and stretched out in a chair. But his peaceful mood was transient; he fumed as he imagined Calinda with another man. She was beautiful and available, perhaps hurt by him or desperate to flee this ranch. Jealousy chewed at him. The hour passed to midnight without their arrival. Could they be on a trip somewhere? That was unlikely.

Lynx hated to disturb Salina this late, but he needed some answers. His time was limited and precious. Was there a problem? Since Rankin was also missing from home, it would cover his questions at this hour. Besides, it didn't matter what Salina thought.

Salina opened her door without even asking who was there. She rubbed her sleepy eyes and stared at Lynx. "Lynx!" she squealed happily. "*Entrar*. When did you get home?" With Rankin and Cal gone, his timing was perfect. What a night they could share . . .

"Where is Rankin? I've been waiting to see him. I have to leave at first light."

"He went to Graham Wednesday for the cattlemen's meeting. He said to expect him home late next Wednesday or early Thursday. Shall I give him a message?" she offered.

"Did he take Calinda with him?" he tried to ask casually, his gut turning in dread. But he was too upset to care, even too distracted to notice the nearly naked Salina who was posing seductively before him.

"No. Are you sure you can not stay this time?" she coaxed. "You look tired, *amante*," she noted, stepping closer to him.

"Then where is she?" he demanded, ignoring her sultry appeal.

"You have checked her room," she concluded petulantly.

"I did. Where is she?" he demanded again, wondering if she had left the ranch or was out with another man. Both thoughts rankled.

Salina rested her back against the jamb, causing her ample bosom to flaunt itself as she revealed Cal's departure. "*Senorita Braxton irse hoy*. She did not tell you?" she asked, feigning innocence.

"Where?" he shouted in disbelief.

"*Que se yo*, and I did not ask. I was ordered to leave her alone. You said she could come and go as she pleased. It pleased her to pack and leave today. Why are you screaming at me? I did not run her off. *Ciertamente*," she stated defensively.

"She didn't tell anyone where she was going or why?"

"I can not speak for *Senor* Rankin. Why would she tell me; we despised each other. *Me allegre tanto*," she expressed her pleasure.

"How? When?" he probed, his fury and panic rising by the minute.

"She was packing when I went to town for supplies. I came home, she was gone. *Es lastima*," she murmured sarcastically.

"Damn right, it's a pity," he mocked to irk her. "Come on, Salina, surely she said something to you?"

"*Nada*. When I saw her last, she was holding a letter in her hand. She told me she was leaving. It was not my place to pry or stop her. Maybe the letter was from *Senor* Rankin asking her to join him."

"She would have told you. She didn't say anything about someone coming for her?" he speculated. Was Salina devious or only delighted?

"No. But she must return. I was curious, so I checked her room. She did not take all of her clothes," she hinted as if annoyed and disappointed. "*Que te pasa?*" she questioned his anxiety and interest.

"Who brought the letter?" he asked, recalling that curious fact.

She shrugged. "In case you forget, I have chores to occupy my time and attention. Maybe it was an old letter."

That couldn't be true, for he had thoroughly searched her room the last time he was home. Rankin was to check her mail, but he was gone. Where? Why leave secretly? "Tell me the truth, Salina," he demanded fiercely, grabbing her shoulders and squeezing tightly, suspecting she knew something she wasn't sharing.

"You hurt me, *diablo*. I know not where she is or why she left. I asked Charlie who took her away; he saw nothing. When I told him she had left, he asked the other men. None of the hands took her away or saw her leave. At least they said they did not."

"Did Charlie say if there was a horse or carriage missing?"

"He checked; no. Someone must have come for her."

"*Que mas?* She didn't leave a note?" he suggested an overlooked clue as Salina shook her head.

"I saw *nada* when I cleaned. There is nothing more to say."

"You didn't by some chance get rid of it like you did mine?" he asked, his teeth clenched tightly as his rage increased. He captured her wrist and put pressure on it until she cried out in discomfort.

"No!" she panted. "I swear she left no note. If you do not believe me, look for yourself. Or ask her when she comes back."

"If she doesn't return, that would suit you just fine, wouldn't it?"

"*Si!* She causes trouble. I hope she never shows her face again. Why are you so eager to see her tonight? If you made her mad the last time you were home, she took her time leaving. She knows *Senor* Rankin will be home next week. Maybe she just took a little trip while he was gone. Maybe she has another *amante* somewhere."

Lynx threw her backwards against the door before he could stop himself. "Don't you dare talk about Cal that way! She'll be back."

Salina's eyes widened in astonishment. "You love her!" she shouted in spiteful jealousy. "You came home to see her, not Rankin." Salina burst into chilling laughter. "So, the wary Lynx has gotten himself trapped by a sneaky *zorra*. *Digame,* Lynx, what will you do if she has run off with another *hombre* and made a fool of you?"

"Calinda isn't like you, Salina," he stated insultingly.

"How do you know what she does when you are not home? She did sneak off. I wonder how she will explain it when she returns, if she does. *Que le vaya bien, bestia,*" she mockingly wished him good luck.

"If I discover you had anything to do with this, you'll be sorry," he warned, then stalked off.

He went to the bunk-house and aroused Charlie. He fumed when he got the same answers from Charlie as he had gotten from Salina. But Charlie added another alarming clue; Calinda's odd actions the day before leaving. Had she been expecting someone? Had she merely checked to see if the hands had noticed anything suspicious? He told Charlie to search for Calinda and bring her home if he found her, by force if necessary. Charlie was confused by those orders, but promised to carry them out, scratching his head as Lynx swaggered to the house.

Lynx couldn't sleep, so he mounted up and rode off. If Calinda had packed clothes, she wouldn't be returning tonight or tomorrow. The letter Salina had mentioned worried him. Could it be from Brax? Or the Simpsons? Did Calinda know where to locate her father? Had she gone to meet him? Rankin wouldn't send for her in secret or without an escort. Why would she rush off without leaving word? Maybe she just used Rankin's absence to flee the ranch. Maybe they had quarreled. No, Calinda would keep her vow of silence; she would wait for Lynx to return before leaving the ranch. Something was going on, but what? It was doubtful she would take off alone.

There was only one rational explanation: Brax. After what Calinda had gone through, she wouldn't hurry into danger without good reason. If Brax had returned and told her the truth, it would ruin everything. He wanted to search for her, but he didn't have the time. Without clues, it could take days or weeks to track her down. There was nothing he could do but wait and pray, pray she loved him and trusted him enough to return to the ranch. At least she should grant him the chance to explain and to prove his love. Since she had left things behind, it must mean she planned to return. There was another possibility; she might be looking for a job to halt her dependence on them. If so, she would send word or come back. All he could do was head for Kimble and Junction, then telegraph Charlie for news. He wished he hadn't come home; he was more distracted now than before!

Chapter 8

THE STAGE HALTED in front of the Keystone Hotel in Lampasas. Ensnared by conflicting emotions, Calinda had hardly noticed the changing scenery along her journey or the passage of time. Fortunately she had been the only passenger since the last stop along the Butterfield route. Yet, she hadn't given any study as to her planned response to her father. As if numb with shock, she had stared out the window for hours at land which was becoming harsher and drier by the mile.

She accepted her bag from the driver and glanced around. This instantly depressing town was small and crowded. She noticed the common western structures: the hardware store, the gunsmith shop, the smithy and stables, a bank, an adobe sheriff's office and jail, a saddle-shop, stage depot, barber shop and a bath house, two saloons and one cantina, a combination church and schoolhouse, and other mercantile and specialty shops, all of which were ramshackle or soon would be. Decrepit houses could be seen on either end of the dusty and pitiful town. The vegetation present was sparse and thirsty.

The hard-packed street was noisy with rickety buckboards, wagons, and mangy horses. Decaying hitching posts and murky water troughs were conveniently placed before each building. Calinda was distressed and alarmed by what her wide gaze discovered. What an awful place; why would anyone wish to live under such conditions? She had to admit the Keystone Hotel looked the cleanest, most durable structure in Lampasas.

What concerned and panicked her most was the abundance of squalid men. She saw men dressed in grimy and wrinkled clothes, men unshaven and unkempt in all manner, men loud and crude, men armed with one or two guns and sometimes knives and rifles. If there were any decent women around, she didn't see them. Several saloon girls were basking in the sun on porches overlooking the main street, resting or enticing passing males. Calinda couldn't believe their vulgar chatter or their indecent clothing. Three men halted to speak to her, eyeing her up and down and grinning lecherously. Others gaped at a distance or called their friends' attention to her. She promptly concluded she didn't like this place or feel safe here.

She ignored the offensive cowboys and walked inside the hotel to register. She questioned the bug-eyed, scrawny clerk about Major Jones. When he found his tongue and used it, he told her he didn't have any Jones staying there. She hastily inquired about Elliott Braxton and received the same reply. After telling the clerk she was expecting either or both men, she registered. She would freshen up and then find the sheriff of this disgusting and intimidating town. Evidently Jones had been delayed. Perhaps the sheriff had news for her. She didn't like the appearance or the mood of this town and its inhabitants; she would make her powerful contacts known quickly.

Calinda selected her most modest gown when she bathed and changed. She donned a bonnet to conceal as much of her face and hair as possible. She didn't want to draw any more attention than necessary to herself. She asked the clerk for directions to the sheriff's office, even though she knew where it was located. She was hoping he would suggest he escort her along that crowded street. He didn't.

Summoning her courage, Calinda left the hotel and walked down the wooden-planked walkway. Since there were saloons on both sides, she had no choice but to pass one or the other. Rowdy men were standing in the batwing doorways or perched on hitching posts, as if they had nothing better to occupy their time and energies in the middle of a workday. She recalled her mother saying that idle hands and bored minds were the devil's playland. Squaring her shoulders, she lifted her chin proudly to reveal false courage, then steadily continued her walk. Cowboys on horses slowed to observe her progress and beauty. The men she passed halted their talks to stare openly at her, some turning to watch the gentle swaying of her skirt as she moved away.

She received admiring glances and brazen greetings, all of which she haughtily ignored. As she approached the dreaded saloon, her heart began to run ahead of her. She increased her pace to get by it quickly.

"Howdy, Ma'am," one cowpoke said, flashing a broad grin.

Calinda didn't slow or speak. "Yer new 'round these parts, ain't you?" his friend attempted to catch her attention.

"What's yer big hurry? How's 'bout sharin' yer name and a little talk?" the first man tried again, reaching for her arm.

Calinda jerked it away and glared at him. "You will kindly keep your hands and words to yourself, sir," she admonished him.

"I'll swan', Pete, uh fancy lady," he remarked, not the least discouraged. "She don't cotton to us'ens. Uh plumb shame."

"Yeh, pretty 'un too," his shabby friend agreed.

"Caint blame 'er. Yer smells wors'n kee-arn," he joked merrily.

"You boys ain't pestering this lady, are you?" a steely voice spoke from behind her. "You need some help and protection, Ma'am?"

Calinda kept moving. The tall gunslinger moved forward to block her path, nearly causing her to tumble against him. "How dare you accost me, sir! Move out of my way this instant," she demanded.

A lop-sided grin captured and twisted his lips; his blue eyes sparkled with amusement and pleasure. His playful expression revealed two things: mischief and determination. "It's a hot and dusty day, Ma'am. Why don't we go to the cantina to wet our throats? Looks like you need a strong hand and fast gun to defend you against all these hungry wolves. Why I'd be obliged to take care of you."

"I don't need or want your assistance, sir. I'm on my way to the sheriff's office, and I can find it alone," Calinda informed him, fighting to control her tone of voice and trembling.

"You got a long wait, Ma'am; he's out at the Hardy Ranch. You'd best come along with me till he returns. This here ain't no safe town for a lady." His gaze leisurely scrutinized her.

Calinda watched the devilish lights play in his blue eyes. He wasn't dissuaded. "Then I shall return to the hotel and wait for him."

She turned to leave, but Clint Deavers wouldn't allow it. "Unhand me this instant or I'll scream," she warned.

Clint laughed. "Ain't no need to do that, Ma'am. Wouldn't matter anyway. See these guns? No man here would challenge them, including that lily-livered sheriff. Now you don't want to go making Clint angry. Let's have us a nice drink and get acquainted."

"I don't care to drink or converse with you. Release me!" she shouted at him, trying to pull free.

Clint patiently waited for her to realize she couldn't get away and no one would come to her aid. She looked around. No one had moved. Anyone watching them seemed afraid of going against those guns Clint had boasted of earlier. It was apparent she was defenseless. She wished she had the gun Rankin had purchased for her. If so, this ruffian wouldn't be treating her in this vile manner.

"If the sheriff is out, then perhaps my uncle has arrived. I can assure you he will not be bullied as these other so-called men. Do you know if Major Jones of the Texas Rangers has arrived to meet me?" She desperately attempted to trick this persistent man.

"Your uncle's a Ranger? He's coming here?" he asked, trying to conceal the panic which glimmered in his eyes before he could hide it.

So, she hastily decided, it was true; all men feared the Rangers, even a solitary one. Her lagging courage returned. "Yes. Why else would I come to a horrible town like this! If you do not show me the respect due to a lady, my uncle will deal severely with you."

"He ain't here now, and he might not come," Clint called her bluff, grinning as if undaunted by her claims or the Rangers' power.

"When he does arrive, he will be furious at your treatment. Have you ever known a Ranger to be denied the man he seeks? And I can assure you, he won't rest until he finds you and punishes you."

"I think Major Jones will be happy I took such good care of you."

"I doubt Major Jones will view your conduct in that same light," she sarcastically sneered, sensing this man wasn't going to back down.

"Well, I tell you what, Miss Jones; when your uncle arrives, I'll be the first to see if he minds you having a drink with Clint Deavers."

"You'll be wasting your time, Mister Deavers. My uncle doesn't permit me to associate with gunslingers or strangers, nor to partake of strong spirits." With that refusal, she pulled her arm free and headed for the hotel, forcing her steps to be light and confident.

Once inside her room, she cried softly to release her tension and terror. She decided she would leave this horrible place tomorrow if Jones or her father failed to appear today. Why had Jones asked her to come to such a dangerous place and then be late? She was distressed by the terrifying confrontation with Clint Deavers. He appeared a man who didn't take no for an answer, one who would rebel against deceit and resistance. If he suspected her trickery and vulnerability, he might press her again. It was petrifyingly clear that the daring gunslinger feared only the Rangers, and there were none around.

When Cal finished her evening meal and stood to leave, she froze in trepidation as she sighted Clint Deavers leaning negligently against the doorpost, watching her every move. He tipped his felt hat and smiled seductively at her. He pushed himself away from the doorframe, winked and smugly swaggered outside.

Calinda wished she had known of his intense observation. If so, she could have prevented the telltale alarm from crossing her pale face. Her unmasked panic would inspire more aggressiveness in him. She wanted to know the truth, but not this badly. It was crazy to stay here. She shouldn't have come. She would leave in the morning.

Calinda sounded the bell on the desk many times before the clerk came to answer her summons. "Has there been any word from Major Jones or Elliott Braxton?" she inquired first.

"Nope," he said, vexed at being disturbed.

"I see," she murmured thoughtfully. "I don't wish to wait any longer in this awful place. I'll leave a message for them, if that's all right with you, sir. What time does the stage leave for Fort Worth?"

"Ten o'clock . . . next Saturday," he sluggishly replied.

"Next Saturday!" she exclaimed incredulously.

"Yep. She runs once a week, to and from Fort Worth, each Saturday," he said, unconcerned by her dismay.

"But surely there's another stage sooner?" she helplessly debated.

"Nope. Didn't you check the schedule back there?"

"I just assumed it ran every day or at least every other day. I was planning to buy my return ticket here, after I saw my uncle. He must have been delayed. Please don't take offense, sir, but I dislike your town. You have so many ruffians. It is not the place for a lady."

"Yep," he readily agreed. "This here area has the reputation as an outlaws' stronghold. I kin see why your uncle would come here, being a Ranger. But I don't gain a reason for him 'viting you to meet him." The weaselly fellow was looking at her oddly, doubtfully.

"I'm certain he felt I would be perfectly safe under his protection, even under his name alone. I'll send a telegram to Waco tomorrow and check on his delay," she announced shakily.

"Can't. Telegraph office ain't open on Sunday."

"Can I pay you to deliver a message to the sheriff? I don't care to walk those streets again with so many rude cowboys lining them."

"Can't tonight, but I'll take your money come sunup. Sheriff's out to the Hardy Ranch collecting a horse thief afore those Hardys stretch his neck. Anything else tonight?" he asked impatiently.

"Nothing, thank you. I'll speak with you in the morning."

Calinda went to her room and locked the door. Just to be on the safe side, she propped a chair beneath the knob and checked her window. Her room was on the second floor and had no porch, so she felt safe leaving the window open for fresh air. She fumed over the clerk's behavior; he almost appeared delighted over her troubles. She scolded herself for her carelessness. She hadn't even considered the stage schedule. What if neither man arrived? She was trapped here for another week! She was afraid to leave this hotel. But she needed to send a telegram and see the sheriff. With luck and a little money, she might get the sheriff to come here. If fate was agreeable, things might work out.

As the hour grew later and darkness engulfed the town, Calinda dared not undress for bed. She reclined on the lumpy mattress, but didn't close her eyes. Her heart refused to keep a normal pace, and she couldn't halt her tremors. How she wished she were sleeping peacefully in her room at the ranch, instead of lying awake here in this perilous town and quaking in terror.

As the clamor from the street below increased in volume, Calinda wondered what was taking place. Surely such rowdiness didn't occur every night? She rolled off the bed and went to the window. The wooden sidewalks and dusty street were filled with boisterous men. As her curious gaze travelled down the way, she noticed a group of about fifteen men who were the center of attention and the cause of the commotion. Her green eyes widened as she watched them.

The band of men was heavily armed, their heads and identities concealed by dark hoods. It didn't require a keen mind to realize something criminal and dangerous was taking place near the jail. Many of the men were carrying fiery torches. A gunshot rang out over the din of ominous noise. Then a man's screams and pleas could be faintly heard. Calinda didn't want to see what was going on, but she couldn't pull herself away from the open window.

From her lofty position, she saw a struggling man dragged from the jail into the street, then thrown into the dust. Masked men crowded around him, kicking and cursing at him. She could make out only a few words: "Horse-thief . . . Get yore due . . . Example . . . Skittish sheriff . . . Law of the West . . ."

As if hypnotized by violence, she helplessly waited and watched. A rope was tossed over the beam which held the sign reading, "Sheriff's Office." A noose was skillfully made, then placed around the man's neck. He was squirming and shouting his innocence. Chilling laughter and shouts of "caught in the act" and "guilty as sin" rang out in answer. The lanky man began to cry in fear and plead for mercy. He was ignored and shoved to a waiting barrel. He was placed on the deadly perch, and the rope around his neck was tightened. The leader of the crazed mob shouted, "Die like a man, you filthy rustler! The sheriff ain't gonna stop us; he's anxious to live a day longer!"

The leader kicked the barrel from beneath the man's feet. The beam groaned in protest of the weight placed on it with this wicked deed. The alleged rustler's body jerked spasmodically and gagging sounds left his lips, then he was still silent. The group quieted down as they watched the limp body sway to and fro. Shortly, they dispersed, slowly parting as if leaving a friendly barbecue. The crowd which had witnessed and encouraged this foul action gradually scattered. Soon, only a few men were left on the darkened street along with the body which continued to swing aimlessly in the still night.

Calinda's attention was drawn to a sudden flash of light directly across the street from her window. She went rigid as the dancing flame of a match revealed the man's face as he lit a cigar. His face was held upward and his hat was pushed back from his forehead. He seemed to purposely hold the lighted match close to his face so she could identify him. He stepped into the street, his taunting gaze never leaving her window. He swept off his hat and grinned. "Goodnight, Miss. I'll see you tomorrow," he smugly vowed, then headed for the Mexican cantina, patting the late telegram in his pocket.

Calinda couldn't move or scream. As Clint Deavers passed the suspended body, he laughed coldly and started the dead man to swinging again. The rope and beam sent forth their combined sounds of eerie warning. She inhaled raggedly, knowing that repulsive rogue would definitely be around tomorrow. Before she left the window, a man approached the body and cut it down. He carried it inside the jail, then appeared once more to return the barrel to its proper place under the water spout on the corner of the jail. Tears began to ease down her flushed cheeks as she fearfully watched the pale moonlight glittering on the silver star which announced him as the town sheriff. *My God,* she sobbed silently. *If a man of the law can't halt a lynching, how can he possibly help or protect me?*

That night was the longest one Calinda had ever known. When she dozed, she was plagued by nightmares. Once, she slipped into restless slumber for half an hour, to awaken in a drenching sweat, sobbing and thrashing on the bed. She splashed her face with tepid water, then sipped some to moisten her aching throat and dry mouth. She could almost hear Lynx's past warnings echoing across her weary mind. Why hadn't she listened? Why was she so obstinate and impulsive. When she got back to the ranch, she would never leave it again! She began to cry once more. What if they wouldn't let her stay this time? If she couldn't get out of Lampasas until next week, she'd never be able to keep this futile quest a secret.

Finally about four in the morning, Calinda fell asleep from sheer exhaustion. The rapid sound of gunfire around ten o'clock jerked her to full awareness. She jumped up and ran to the window. She instantly berated herself for looking. In the street below, Clint Deavers was lazily replacing his pistols in their holsters. Down the street, two men lay dead or wounded, while Deavers hadn't received even a minor scratch. "Take 'em away, my good man; they won't be troubling me again," he told the black-garbed undertaker.

The door to the jail opened and the sheriff came forward. "Dang you, Clint Deavers! I done told you to do your shooting out of town," he declared, as if mildly correcting a mischievous child.

"Now, Sheriff, I didn't start anything," Deavers innocently remarked, a tone of indulgence and a total lack of respect lacing his strong voice. "What was I supposed to do? Let them two gun me down? It was a fair fight, two against one. Ask anybody; they drew first. I was only defending myself."

"Yeh, like you claim every time you hand over a dead body. I'm trying to gain some peace and order in this town, Clint. I can't have you battling on the street all the time. What am I gonna do with you?" The sheriff could have been talking to himself.

"Ain't nothing you can do. I drew last. I can't help it if I'm faster and better. If I wasn't, ole Greeley there would be stuffing me into a pine box instead of those two." Clint discussed the two killings as if they were a joke.

"One day, it is gonna be you if you don't stop challenging any man who looks at you sideways. You're itching to get killed, Deavers, and some man's gonna oblige you," the sheriff warned.

"There ain't a man alive who can beat my guns from their holsters. You gonna arrest me?" he teased lightly.

"For what?" the sheriff scoffed, then ambled away muttering.

When Clint focused his attention on Calinda's window, she quickly ducked behind the curtains. Clint laughed merrily as he watched their enlightening movement. "Sorry about the noise, Miss Braxton. I hope I didn't disturb your sleep. Care to join me for supper?"

Before thinking, Calinda slammed the window shut. She could hear the satanic laughter from Clint Deavers at her foolish action. "Is that fearless uncle of yours here yet?" he shouted at her.

Calinda shuddered. He was making fun of her, trying to frighten her. He knew her name—evidently he had questioned the clerk. What had that stupid man told him? Even if Deavers knew her name, he couldn't be sure Major Jones wasn't her uncle as alleged. There was no way for him to know the truth . . .

She was hungry and she needed to send a message to the sheriff, even if it was ridiculous. That old man would never antagonize a ruthless gunslinger. Cal was afraid to leave her room, but she couldn't remain locked in here for a week. It would be wiser to show a brave front and try to continue her bluff.

Calinda went to see the obnoxious clerk to hire his service. She was disconcerted when the stolid man informed her he was too busy to run an errand for her, even with pay. She argued and reasoned with him, but she couldn't change his mind. When she turned to enter the area where food was served, Clint Deavers was poised in the open doorway. He strolled forward and smiled confidently.

In a lazy drawl, Deavers asked, "Having problems, Miss Braxton? Looks as if that uncle of yours has forgotten all about you. Now he shouldn't go letting a pretty thing like you go roaming around in such a dangerous area. Ready to settle for my help and company?" he murmured suggestively, tugging on one of her shiny chestnut curls.

Calinda slapped his hand away and commanded, "Stay away from me, Mister Deavers, or you'll regret it. My uncle was probably delayed on Ranger business, but he'll arrive very soon. You might use your guns and colorful reputation to frighten the local people, but I'm not afraid of you. And I don't like you. So keep your hands off me, or you'll discover what an excellent shot I am."

Deavers captured her hand, finding it cold and shaky. He was a man who depended on his keen observations and instincts to stay alive. He could read Calinda's panic at twenty paces. He noted the enlarged pupils of her deep green eyes. He watched her moisten her dry lips several times. He caught the rapid rise and fall of her chest. He could see the throbbing of the pulse in her neck. Too, the letter which the clerk had refused on his orders was quivering in her tight grasp.

Calinda yanked on her imprisoned hand, but Clint didn't release it. He chuckled, then said, "That's the first time I've ever been challenged by a woman, a beautiful one at that. Where you want this showdown to take place, Miss Braxton, in the street or in your room?"

"You vile creature," she gasped. "Leave me alone."

"I can't rightly do that, Calinda. You have me all heated up over you. You don't mind if I call you Calinda, do you?"

Calinda stared at him. He was playing with her, mocking her. "Yes, I do mind. You appear a proud man, Mister Deavers; won't it damage your ego and reputation to harass a lady because she rebuffs you and your rude manner?" she icily struck at his immense pride.

"Just think how it will improve my 'reputation' and 'manner' when I win you over. Haven't been turned down by a female yet."

"There's always a first time, Mister Deavers, and this is it. I'm sure you try to terrify any woman who catches your gaze. But I gravely doubt any one of them would . . ."

When she flushed and stammered, he laughed. "Well, Calinda, people usually do try to keep on my good side."

"You don't possess one," she scoffed, her disdain visible.

As it was noon by then, several men entered the hotel to eat, including the incompetent sheriff. He walked like a rolling wave, his slumped shoulders reminding her of the curl on its crest. She called him over to them. "Sheriff, would you please tell Mister Deavers I do not wish his company or conversation, today or any other day. He seems intent on forcing both on me."

The sheriff's eyes rolled backwards in irritation. "Come on, Clint, ain't you had enough fun and excitement for one day? Move along," he ordered, his voice lacking any serious conviction or force.

"I was only offering my protection and assistance to Calinda," Clint insouciantly replied, retaining his grip on her hand.

Calinda knew it was time to press her advantage and get away from this man. "Release my hand! Sheriff, my uncle, Major Jones of the Rangers, will hold you responsible for this mistreatment."

"Your uncle's a Texas Ranger?" the sheriff asked nervously.

"That's correct, sir. I came here to meet him, but he's obviously been detained. Mister Deavers has been harassing me since yesterday. I would appreciate it if you would handle this matter promptly," Calinda demanded boldly.

"Head on out, Clint. We don't want no trouble bringing Rangers to

Lampasas. You can see the lady ain't interested in you," the older man cautioned, sounding serious this time.

Clint shrugged as if the sheriff's words had been convincing. "I guess you're right. I hear you're gonna be mighty busy between now and Saturday. Guess you won't be in town too often this week," he spoke casually, but Calinda seized his implication and paled.

"That's right. I got to head into the brush and see if I can flush out those other rustlers. But I don't want no trouble from you while I'm gone. I'm leaving Deputy Barnes in town," the sheriff told him, unaware of the part he was playing in Clint's impending scheme.

"Old Barnes?" Clint jovially hinted, then chuckled wickedly. "Why old Barnes is fifty if he's a day."

"What's wrong with that? So am I," the sheriff muttered.

"Why, I think he's the best man you could leave behind. I'll be seeing you later, Sheriff. Calinda," he added, then nodded. A guileful leer spread over his face after revealing how helpless she was.

"You want to sup with me, Miss Jones?" the sheriff offered.

"Yes, thank you. I was planning to see you today and discuss my problem. I headed for your office yesterday, but you were out. That's when I ran into Mister Deavers; he's been pestering me since. Your townspeople aren't very friendly or helpful," she stated grimly.

After they were seated and served, Calinda told him her carefully constructed story. The sheriff sympathized with her, but said there was nothing he could do to solve her troubles. She concluded this man was a discredit to his badge and to law and order. She felt no respect or confidence in him; he was useless to this town and to her. She knew her only safety lay in sticking to her false claims. She dared not trust this man with the truth. It was also futile to plead for his protection, so she didn't. She was tempted to flaunt Lynx's name for added protection, but changed her mind. An egotistical man like Deavers might try to use her peril as a challenge to Lynx.

As they finished their meal in stony silence, the sheriff stood up to leave. He lingered to offer, "If you'll write out a telegram to your uncle, I'll send it out for you." He smiled affably.

Calinda was pleased and relieved. Since she had been told the telegraph office was closed today, she assumed her message would go out in the morning. The sheriff sat down again for another cup of black coffee while she borrowed pen and paper from the sulky clerk to write out her message. Cornered, she fretted over how to word the message to indicate her dangerous position without making Jones think she was touched in the head and without giving away her deceitful claims.

Finally it was ready. Cal handed it to the sheriff and withdrew the money to pay for it. He accepted it, bid her farewell, then left, promising to bring any response which came in later. She quickly made her way upstairs before Deavers could return to torment her. As before, she propped the chair under the doorknob.

Deavers watched the sheriff head for the telegraph office and enter. He decided to check out this action before seeing the beautiful redhead again. He waited until the sheriff had left and disappeared into his office. He ambled over to the telegraph office.

"What's doing, Slim?" Clint asked the chubby man behind the desk.

Slim glanced up and tensed. He didn't like this man who wore his guns low on his hips and tied securely to his muscled thighs. Slim pulled his beady eyes from the roguishly handsome face and chilly blue eyes. "Nothing, Clint. Kind of quiet today."

"I saw the sheriff leaving a while back. Did he hand you a telegram to send out?" he asked, his expression relentless.

"Yes," Slim hesitantly replied. "It wasn't about you," he quickly added.

"The sheriff made a mistake, Slim; he doesn't want that telegram to go out after all. Just hand it to me and I'll take it over to him." Clint didn't even try to make his lie sound plausible.

"You know I can't do that, Clint; it ain't legal," Slim weakly argued. "Anyway, it's too late; I just tapped it out."

Clint's eyes narrowed and frosted. His rigid stance exposed his anger. "What did it say? Where did it go?" he demanded coldly.

"Clint, please. You know that ain't allowed. I could get in big trouble. Telegrams are the same as U.S. Mail; they're protected by law. It was personal business for some lady stranded here."

"Smart people say the law is made by the strongest man and fastest gun," Clint hinted lucidly, pulling out one of his weapons and lazily fondling it as he spoke. "I got my eye on that little gal, Slim. If she's planning to leave town, I need to know. Who's to know if I take a look-see at her telegram?" His voice was smooth and firm.

Slim knew from observation that Clint always spoke and acted in this deceptively calm and sportive manner when he was seething with lethal fury. What did it matter? "Just don't you tell anyone," he acquiesced, fetching the handwriting sheet.

Slim could tell that Clint didn't like what he was reading by the way he moved his jaw from side to side and frowned. Slim shook his head, delighted he wasn't in Miss Calinda Braxton's shoes.

Clint's sharp mind took in the facts on the page:

Major J.B. Jones, Fort Fisher Ranger Post, Waco,
Came to Lampasas as your letter requested. No Elliott Braxton. No Major Jones. Why? Town unsafe. Stranded. No help in sight. Please explain delay. Must return home. No stage for six days. Send message promptly. Hurry. Calinda Braxton, Keystone Hotel, Lampasas.

Clint's gaze lifted to pierce the distance between him and the stocky man who was trembling in dread. "You're positive this has already gone out to Jones in Waco?"

"I'm sorry, Clint, but the sheriff said it was important."

So, Clint reasoned, that old buzzard wasn't as dumb as he seemed. He was trying to help Calinda, even if that meant bringing a Ranger here. Clint glanced over the missive again, then chuckled. He had the girl worried and frightened. It would take days for anyone to arrive, if Jones didn't think her crazy. Still, the weird telegram might stir Jones's curiosity. If his time was limited now, he should halt this silly game with that ravishing flower. Clint glared at the station agent. "When the answer comes in, Slim, you best bring it to me first. Understand?"

"You'll give it to her after you read it, won't you? If they find out she didn't get it, them Rangers could get nosy and nasty."

"I'll see she gets the message, loud and clear, Slim." Clint's chest rumbling with laughter, he strolled out into the afternoon sun. This was turning out to be a most rewarding favor . . .

Dusk began to lightly drop into dark shadows. Calinda had been sealed in her room since mid-day. If a response didn't come tomorrow, she would be on slippery ground. Perhaps Jones had run into trouble; perhaps he wasn't coming; perhaps he wasn't in Waco to receive her urgent plea for help. If he was absent, would anyone read his messages, or hold them until his return?

Calinda had spent the last two hours huddled by the window, remaining out of sight, watching for any sign of Clint Deavers. What kind of town and people were these? A lynching on Saturday night and a gunfight on the main street on Sunday morning . . . A town where a villain held more respect and authority than the law . . . A town where a decent lady wasn't safe . . . This peril and fear reminded her of her danger and situation in Fort Worth. Since coming west, she had found no safety or serenity except at the ranch. When a knock sounded on her door, she jumped and nearly screamed.

When she didn't answer it, the sheriff called out, "You in there, Miss Braxton?"

Calinda rushed to open it, sighing in relief. She never thought she'd be delighted to see this particular man. It was strange how a person could get extremely hungry when sitting around with nothing to occupy her mind or hands, and her stomach was growling softly.

"I wanted to drop by to say there's been no word yet. I been busy, so I came over to eat before heading home."

Calinda quickly asked, "May I join you? I haven't eaten yet."

"Surely, Miss Braxton," he replied, suspecting why she hadn't left her room. He had heard the scraping of the chair on the floor when she had removed it. Poor child . . . But he was retiring next month, and he was finishing his duty without endangering himself. A man would be a dead fool to challenge Clint Deavers, and he didn't want to be one. More accurately, he didn't want to be another notch on a gun. He had done all he could for her; he had sent her telegram.

They talked little as the meal was consumed. While they were having coffee and pie, Calinda asked about the violence she had witnessed last night. Recalling the fragility of men's egos from the stage incident, she didn't ask why he had done nothing to stop it. She listened as he talked of rustlers and armed citizens resisting the outlaws. He even excused his cowardice last night by saying they would have killed him if he had interfered; one man was no match for a riled mob with loaded guns and functioning on hatred.

"If you think this town is wild and lawless, Miss Braxton, you should visit Junction in Kimble County. It's south of here, two days' ride. This town is peaceful compared to Junction. I'm too old for this job. I'm retiring next month when the election is held. Gonna do myself some fishing and hunting. Gonna read some books and rest plenty. This job needs a man with iron in his back and courage in his blood. I used to have plenty of both." He sighed heavily. It was difficult for a man to accept growing old and useless.

Calinda watched his sad expression. Her heart went out to him. She couldn't blame him for her crisis or for wanting to survive. She smiled warmly and thanked him for his help. As he was leaving, he whispered, "I wouldn't worry about Deavers tonight. He's over to the cantina. Once into a card game, he usually stays the night."

She smiled gratefully and thanked him again. Before going up to bed, she approached the clerk about some water for her room. She wanted to freshen up before turning in. The clerk groaned as if in pain. She was shocked when he told her there were buckets by the door and guests were responsible for fetching their own water.

"Surely the hotel charge covers such services?" she argued.

"Just the first day, Miss. We ain't got time to do more 'an cook meals and clean rooms after that," he lied.

"You can't be that busy; you have only three guests. Shall I pay extra?" Cal sarcastically asked, feeling he was cheating her.

"Don't have time, Miss. I was turning in. The well's by the door and there's a light. See you tomorrow."

Calinda gaped at him as he hurried to his room. What a rude and selfish man! Surely he could take a moment to fetch water for her, at least go along with her. She hesitated to go for the water. But it was humid and hot today, and she knew she would rest better if she washed off before bed. The sheriff had said Clint was busy for the night. And no one else had bothered her since Clint had made it clear he was pursuing her.

Calinda went to the door and unbolted it. She picked up a bucket and walked outside, finding the well nearby as informed. She lowered the pail, allowed it to fill, then drew it up again. She dumped the water into her own bucket. Before she could lift it, she noticed a man's legs behind her as she leaned over for it.

Cal shrieked in alarm, straightened, and whirled around. "How dare you sneak up on me!" she declared in a strained voice.

A sinister chuckle escaped his mouth before he teased, "I do believe your temper is as fiery as your hair, Missy."

Calinda was filled with panic. She deserted the water bucket in a vain attempt to hurry inside and bolt the door. Just as she reached it, it was slammed and locked from the inside. Taken by surprise she crashed into it, wincing in pain as she forcefully struck the immovable object. She hammered the door with her balled fist. No one responded. Terror seized her wits and dazed them.

Cal realized a trap had been set for her, and she had naively fallen into it. The clerk was definitely involved, but was the sheriff? She slowly turned to face her tormentor. She tried to imagine any way to battle him and escape, but her petrified mind refused any assistance.

Clint walked forward purposefully. He halted before her, placing an outstretched hand on either side of her shoulders, resting his palms against the sealed door, confining her between two well-muscled arms. His boots were planted apart, his body lax. Calinda's hands were clenched into fists, positioned near her chest for impending defense. Her respiration had increased, her efforts to conceal her panic futile.

Clint leaned forward as he spoke, his face ominously close to hers. She could feel his warm breath and smell the whiskey on it. "I thought it was time you and I had a private talk," he hinted. "You've been avoiding me, Calinda, and that don't sit well."

Calinda rammed her shoulder against one arm, trying to break his confinement. When that failed, she pounded his chest and shouted, "Leave me alone! Let go of me! My uncle will kill you for this outrage!"

Clint laughed wickedly. "Plenty of men have tried. I been real patient with you, Missy. Why don't we stop this horsing around? I bet your blood is just as fiery as that temper and hair."

"Not for you! Get out of my way!" Cal screamed at him, rashly grabbing for one of his pistols. When Clint imprisoned her wrists, she shrieked, "You're hurting me! When I get free, I'll kill you!"

"You're wasting your time and breath," Clint warned huskily.

"You'll be wasting more than that, Deavers, if you lay one finger on Cal," another voice spoke through the shadows.

Deavers spun around with lightning speed, his fingers touching his guns. Calinda bolted toward the stirring voice as she cried out, "Lynx! Where are you?" she asked, straining to find him.

"Here, Cal," Lynx verbally directed her toward him.

She ran into his arms and embraced him. "How did you find me?"

Lynx kept his arms hanging loose at his sides, his fingers limber and ready. "What's going on here, Cal?" he asked, alerting Clint to their acquaintance. "I've been tracking you for days, woman. Why the hell did you leave home? What are you doing outside this late? I should thrash you soundly for falling for such a dangerous trick."

Calinda assumed Lynx was referring to Clint's trap, but Lynx was setting one of his own to avoid a bloody conflict. He was fully aware of Deavers' short temper and lethal reputation. Lynx's mind was working fast as he tried to analyze this crazy situation.

"I'm sorry, Lynx," Calinda murmured apologetically, then briefly explained about Jones' letter and her perilous journey.

Clint remained stiff and alert, straining to catch their muffled words. There could be only one man with that unusual name. But what was his connection to this girl? Why hadn't he been warned about Lynx?

Calinda realized Lynx was up to something when he declared angrily, "I saw the letter on your dresser at home. You're a foolish woman, Cal. Don't you realize it was a trap to lure you here? I had a drink with Jones in Waco three days ago; he was heading for Dallas. If he wrote you, he would have said something when I talked about you. He didn't send that letter. Why didn't you wait and talk to me?"

Clint moved forward a few steps. Lynx slowly turned Calinda to face Clint, holding her left hand behind her. She felt him slip a ring on her finger as he asked

Clint, "Are you in this kidnapping plot, Deavers? If so, you'll answer to me," he threatened coldly.

"What kidnapping? She came here on the stage to meet her uncle. We were making friends until you showed up. Get lost, Cardone."

"We were not!" Cal shrieked, blurting out how Clint had been terrorizing her since her arrival.

"I ain't never known you to fight over a woman, Cardone," Clint remarked.

"This one I will; she's my wife. Somebody lured her here with a phony letter, and I plan to discover who and why," Lynx alleged.

"She ain't your wife; she's Calinda Braxton. Who you trying to fool? If she was married to Lynx Cardone, she would 'a tried to use your name to scare me off," Clint debated smugly. Cardone had to be lying; nobody was fool enough to dupe Clint Deavers . . .

"I didn't owe you any facts about me!" Calinda stormed at him. "I thought I was here to meet my uncle. If I had mentioned who my husband was to a man like you, you would have caused more trouble just as a challenge to him. I'm surprised you didn't notice this while you were harassing me," she sneered, holding up her hand for the gold ring to twinkle in the moonlight.

Calinda had immediately comprehended Lynx's scheme to avoid violence. She recalled his past words about trying to settle disputes without bloodshed: "I've never killed an innocent man. If I didn't keep a cool head, I wouldn't be able to hesitate until the last minute before firing."

To prevent distracting that cool and cunning head, Cal waited tensely to see if Clint would buy their story and relent. Calinda shivered in fear, recalling how Clint had easily gunned down two men at the same time. Clint was dangerously arrogant. Was Clint too vain or dull-witted to realize a peaceful compromise was not a defeat? Was Lynx faster? Could her love talk Clint out of a fatal confrontation? Lynx would never reveal cowardice, but why risk his life for her?

—— *Chapter 9* ——

TIME SEEMED IRRELEVANT as the two men stood there deliberating their next moves, as if nonchalantly deciding if life or ego was more important. Calinda turned and eased her arms around Lynx's waist and snuggled her face against his brawny shoulder. Perhaps this show of affection would influence Clint's decision. "I'm sorry, Lynx. I promise I won't ever leave home again without your permission. But your business was taking so long, and the letter sounded urgent."

Lynx allowed her to speak freely, hoping her words and actions would entice

Clint to walk away. Clint was vain and quick, but he wasn't stupid. To date, Clint had been sly enough to carry out his crimes without being apprehended. Lynx fretted, *if only my reputation wasn't greater than his* . . . . That alone could encourage Clint to fight him. But Calinda was in danger; she could get in their crossfire. If anything happened to Lynx, she would be at Deavers' mercy. Lynx was self-assured and talented, but there was always that one chance that another man would be faster or craftier. If it became necessary, should Lynx use his badge to prevent deadly trouble? How would Lynx explain revealing himself over a woman and a gunfight? He prayed Calinda wouldn't be a witness to his lethal self-defense. As for himself, Lynx wasn't afraid or insecure. In fact, it required immense self-control to prevent him from beating Deavers to a pulp.

Clint had seen Lynx Cardone in two gunfights and was aware of his speed, accuracy, and fearless courage. As much as it rankled, he knew Lynx could probably beat him to the draw. Clearly Lynx knew and wanted this girl; Lynx wouldn't back down. It was a rule of survival: know your enemy and his skills. "Seems there's been a misunderstanding, Cardone; I didn't know she was married. I don't fight men over their wives, even one this beautiful and tempting. I ain't got no quarrel with you," Clint skeptically informed Lynx. But Clint wasn't convinced of Lynx's legal possession of this treasure. Someone owed him a satisfactory explanation for this deception . . .

Lynx knew better than to insult a man's pride and courage over a sensible move. But Lynx didn't trust Deavers or that gleam in his eyes, a curious glimmer which implied Clint had a wicked secret. "Know anything about that phony letter?" Lynx asked.

"Don't know anything about a letter or kidnapping. Nobody's made a move against her. You got me to thank for keeping her out of danger. If I was you, I'd give her a good spanking and scolding. Could be your little woman was just running off," Clint gibed boldly.

"That's a lie!" Calinda shouted at the gunslinger.

"He's only teasing, Cal; settle down," Lynx advised astutely, the situation still tense. "Let's go inside and figure out this puzzle," he suggested, affectionately cuffing her chin. "You've got plenty of explaining to do, woman. See you around, Deavers. If you hear anything about this mix-up, I'll pay well for the information."

Deavers turned and stalked off without replying. "You all right, Cal?" Lynx suddenly asked, noticing how pale and shaky she was. She nodded faintly. "Let's get inside before Deavers changes his mind."

As Lynx reached the door, Cal said, "It's locked. Someone slammed it and bolted it after I came out for water."

Lynx's hand was already on the knob, which opened easily. He half-turned to gaze at her. "Maybe it was stuck," he hinted oddly.

"It was bolted! Slammed in my face and locked!" she shrieked in confusion, stressing her points angrily. "That mean clerk wouldn't fetch any water for me, and the sheriff told me at dinner that Clint was busy for the night. It was a trick to get me alone!"

"Could be," Lynx too calmly agreed. "Deavers could have threatened them into helping him. I'll check into it tomorrow. Naturally they'll deny it, but I can tell if they're lying. Even so, Cal, what do you want me to do about it? Shoot all of them as punishment?" He had spoken lightly, but his expression was grave.

"You mean you can't do anything? But I could have been hurt or killed. Or worse! I know that sneaky clerk was in on this plot," Cal heatedly accused, then told Lynx of his previous mischief.

"Sounds logical, but we couldn't prove his guilt. How do we ride out of town after making such charges against so many men? I know you're angry and upset, Cal, but sometimes justice isn't worth the cost. I'm here now, and you're fine. If you want me to press it, I will. I just want you to understand the consequences. I have a tall reputation, Cal, and men fear it. They might tell me what they think I want to know. In that case, some innocent person could be accused and injured. It's over; do you need to press it?"

"You don't understand, Lynx. He was going to attack me. I don't understand your code of justice. Why are men like that allowed to go around terrorizing people, forcing them to do evil things, then get away with it? If they aren't arrested and punished, they'll keep on doing as they please. What about another unsuspecting woman who comes here? She might not be as lucky as I was."

"I keep trying to tell you things are different out here. If you're going to stay in Texas, you'd best learn that quickly to avoid danger and trouble. Next time, help might not arrive in time. Let's get inside and you can fill me in," Lynx said firmly, taking her arm.

When they were safely in her room, he demanded, "Let me see that letter; maybe the handwriting will give us a clue."

"I don't have it; I burned it," Cal told him anxiously.

"*Cielos,* Cal! How can I solve this mystery without a clue?"

"I was afraid someone would find it," she excused her action.

Lynx angrily snarled, "You mean Father or me! Why the hell would you take off like that alone? Tell me what it said, word-for-word."

Calinda slowly complied, watching the anger increase in his tawny eyes. "Who delivered the letter?" Lynx inquired.

"I don't know." Cal told him how she'd found the letter, then related her search of the house and grounds, then her questioning of the men. "Why would Major Jones do this to me?"

"I can promise you it wasn't from Jones. He would never send you to a dangerous place like this. If he discovered any news of Brax, he would have contacted the Cardones, not you. Aren't you forgetting Brax is on the run from the law? He stole a great deal of money and assaulted my father," he reminded her icily.

"Then who sent it?" Cal fumed in exasperation.

"Whose help did you ask for besides Jones?" Lynx pressed her.

She reflected for a time, then responded, "Only the sheriff in Forth Worth. I've been at the ranch since then. But it's no secret who I am and why I came here. Are you positive Brax couldn't have sent it?"

"If he's here, he would have shown himself by now."

"What if he was waiting to see if I was followed or if I told someone? It said to come in secret," Cal reminded the furious man.

"No way, Cal. Seeing the danger you were in with that Deavers, Brax would have come to your aid," he stated, oddly defending her father. "Why in blazes did you pack up and leave?" the query stormed out of his taut lips.

To lessen his fury and irritation, Cal explained her motives. When Lynx debated them, she added, "Don't you see, Lynx? I haven't seen Brax since I was four. You've told me the horrible things he did, but they're only words. I didn't witness those events; they don't seem real to me. I must learn what changed him. A man doesn't suddenly rob and beat his best friend without some desperate reason. Something panicked him and drove him away. You knew him for years; could you have been so wrong about him? Don't you care about the truth? I owed him this one chance to explain. He's my father! I also wanted to uncover the past for you and Rankin. It can't end until it's resolved. If I had waited around for your return, he might have panicked again and left. If I had brought you with me, he might not have revealed himself. I know it was impulsive, but there wasn't time to think clearly or to lollygag. Surely he knows you hate him and would kill him on sight." she finished breathlessly.

Lynx didn't deny her last statement, hurting her. "You've got to give it up, Cal; it's too dangerous. Someone is after you. It's lucky I stopped here tonight; I almost by-passed Lampasas."

"What are you doing here?" Cal promptly asked, intrigued.

"I was heading for Junction to see a man. I should have been there by now. I would have if I hadn't swung by the ranch to check on you," he sullenly declared.

"Why did you go to the ranch?" she inquired curiously.

"I was worried about you. I wanted to make sure you were all right. I was stunned when Salina told me you'd packed up and left without telling her anything. I suspected she was lying. I forced the truth out of her. I had to make sure you hadn't left me or Father a note. She told me about a letter which enticed you away," Lynx told her.

Calinda stiffened. "What did she say? How did she know?" she gingerly pressed to see how much Salina had revealed.

Lynx repeated their conversation. Calinda decided Salina had kept most of her promise, but why had she mentioned the letter? Surely she wasn't afraid of Lynx. But if he had been furious, it might have slipped out in panic. It really didn't matter; at least he knew there was a letter. For a time, he hadn't looked convinced.

"Did you leave a message for either of us?" he questioned.

"No. I thought I could get here and back before either of you realized I had left," she admitted contritely. "There's been so much conflict between Salina and me that I doubted she would say anything about my short absence. How was she to know Rankin hadn't given his permission? Besides, it would make it appear she was only trying to cause more trouble. It really doesn't matter now, you know everything."

"Are you certain Salina didn't leave that note on your bed?" Lynx questioned suspiciously, a revealing scowl on his face.

Calinda wondered if Lynx was intentionally casting doubts on Salina. Was there a reason he didn't want them to become friends? "She couldn't have. She left early that morning for supplies. Salina didn't get back home for several hours. While I was washing clothes, it appeared as if by magic. I searched the house and grounds, but couldn't find anyone. I even questioned your men, nothing."

"I know; I questioned them too," he calmly disclosed. "You can be very sly and impulsive, Cal. I underestimated your cunning and daring."

Calinda feared he was about to question her as to how she slipped off the ranch, and she couldn't improvise a believable tale under this pressure. To distract him, she asked, "If the letter is gone and Jones didn't send it, how can we learn who did?"

"We can't. From now on, don't you ever set foot off that ranch without telling me or Father. You might have an enemy trying to get rid of you," Lynx stated to frighten her into compliance and caution. This situation was perplexing. He sensed she was withholding other facts, but didn't press her. It struck him she was trying to explain without lying, and he didn't want to compel her to begin. Later he could pull more information from her. As he did frequently, she was attempting to tell only the facts she wanted him to know and in such a manner as to inspire the desirable conclusions. Still, Brax could be behind this weird incident . . .

"What if Rankin doesn't want me to stay there when he learns what I've done?" Cal speculated worriedly. "I can't get back before he returns, and I can't deceive him. He'll be hurt and angry. I didn't know the stage wouldn't run again until Saturday. I'm stranded here. When must you leave for Junction?" Fear brought moisture to her eyes.

"If you think I'll leave you here with Deavers or some other enemy around, you're loco. Damnation, woman! You've ruined my tight schedule. First that rash trip home, now this new delay. There's no choice; I'll have to take you back to the ranch tomorrow. I'll send a telegram to Junction explaining things. Some excuse, a mule-headed female!" Lynx growled in consternation.

"Why did you stop in Lampasas?" Cal probed again, thinking this stroke of good fortune very strange. Who had lured her here? How had Lynx timed his arrival and rescue so perfectly?

"I told you. I've been riding for two days and a night trying to make up the time I lost worrying over you. I was so exhausted, I had to stop here. Lampasas is on the trail to Junction. When I hitched up out front, I heard the commotion out back. Needless to say, Cal, I recognized that voice of yours. I didn't have the vaguest idea what was going on or why you were here." His gaze was penetrating.

"Then why did you rescue me?" she asked foolishly.

"*Que demonios!* I might not know you well, Cal, but I do know enough to realize you wouldn't be tangled up with Deavers," he said, shaking his tawny head in exasperation.

"Why did you slip this ring on my finger?" she pressed to see if her conclusions had been accurate, gazing at the golden circle.

"That's the only reason he relented. I've had it a long time; a man who owed me money used it as payment for a job. It's been like a good-luck charm. I knew Clint would think twice before fighting over another man's wife, especially mine. You see, Cal, sometimes a colorful image is valuable," he teased light-heartedly.

"What if he finds out you tricked him?" Cal fretted aloud.

"I don't want to alarm you, Callie, but this didn't end it with Deavers. He'll seek another time and place to get to me, and you. A man like Deavers doesn't give up something he wants that easily, and he wants you and my notch on his reputation. As soon as I send that telegram in the morning, we'll head for home," he announced.

"Will we get there before Rankin?" she ventured quizzically.

"I doubt it. He'll probably think you took off to look for a job."

"That isn't true; I couldn't lie to him," she protested.

"Don't worry about it tonight, Cal; I'll take care of everything. If he isn't home, I'll leave him a message. I've got to get to Junction before I lose this job and my boss's respect. Let's turn in; I'm exhausted." Lynx walked to the chair and began to undress.

Cal gaped at him. "You can't sleep in here. What will people say?" she argued his bold intentions, suspense washing over her body.

"Are you forgetting about Deavers? Wouldn't it look suspicious if a husband didn't sleep with his wife? I'd like to get out of Lampasas without more trouble. Nobody knows the truth about us."

"What about when they discover we aren't married?"

"Doesn't matter what they think or say," he stated casually.

"It does to me!" Cal snapped. Having a secret affair was one thing, but flaunting it was another. "Are you sure you didn't lure me here so you could play around again?" she hinted saucily to ease her tension.

"Sounds like a crafty idea, but I'll have to disappoint you. I never expected to find you in my path. You had me worried, Cal. If I'd had the time, I would have hunted you down and strangled you."

"It does seem odd that we keep running in to each other."

"You're right about that. You sure you aren't pursuing me? Was there a letter, Cal? How do you keep track of me and set up these meetings?"

She laughed, relaxing as time passed and his nearness assailed her senses. She played along with his joke. "It isn't easy, but I'm doing fairly well so far. But this time I outsmarted myself; I didn't plan on exposing us to Rankin. If he beats me home, the game is up."

"I hope not. I'm enjoying the chase," Lynx replied, pulling her into his arms. She laid her face against his thudding heart. "Ready to turn in?" he murmured, his lips against her hair.

Her gaze turned serious. The moment she had dreaded, yet fiercely craved, had arrived. She yearned to taste and share his beguiling tenderness and torrid passion; yet, she feared another flight of mindless ecstasy. When he caressed her body and stole her breath and reason with intoxicating kisses, she was as eager and pliant as clay in a gentle sculptor's hands. He controlled and designed her responses as deftly as a treasured piece of earthenware in a master potter's grasp.

When Calinda didn't verbally respond, Lynx gazed down at her, reading the unspoken submission in her eyes. His tawny gaze studied her indecision. His hands slipped into sunny red hair on either side of her head and tilted her face upwards. Her lips were parted as if to speak, but no words came forth. She didn't want to say no, but neither could she boldly say yes. Her dreamy green eyes locked with his, as two emeralds sinking leisurely into a tranquil pool of amber liquid. Mentally poised on the edge of a shadowy region, she feared to wave aside the obscuring veil to seek what her body and heart desired.

Mesmerized by his powerful gaze, Cal did not move or resist when Lynx undressed her, nor when his admiring gaze wandered over the creamy flesh before it. His hands went to her shoulders, then lazily slipped down her arms and over to her waist. He leaned forward to tantalize her warring senses with moist kisses on her breasts. She stiffened and inhaled as the blissful sensation attacked her spinning mind. His lips came up to fasten hungrily to hers.

Like an artist's tools, his lips and hands moved lightly over her body, preparing and honing and creating a prize worth possessing. When he leaned backward to look into her passion-gazed face, Calinda's arms around his waist shifted to withdraw his shirt from his pants. Longing to make contact with his virile frame, she shamelessly unbuttoned it with quivering fingers, then eased it over his broad shoulders and allowed it to float to the wooden floor. Her palms flattened against his coppery flesh and drifted from his throat down a hard chest covered with curling hair down to a flat stomach, only to begin her stirring journey upward again, this time to ease over darkly tanned arms with their smooth and powerful muscles.

Lynx shuddered as he tightly controlled his rising passion which strained at the crotch of his pants. He caught her hands and brought them to his lips, placing kisses on each finger tip and in each palm. "I want you, Cal," he murmured in a tight voice, recalling her last rejection, dreading another one.

"I want you, too," she promptly concurred, quivering.

Lynx swept her into his arms and deposited her on the bed. He hastily removed the rest of his clothes and his boots, then reclined beside her. His mouth seared over hers, branding it his. Her head dug into the pillow as his lips continued down her neck to place his mark of ownership on every inch they encountered. Ever so lightly his fingers moved over one breast point as his lips drew magical nectar from the other one, to later shift from one to the other driving her wild with pleasure. Even if this was wrong, Calinda didn't care.

Soft moans of urgency escaped her lips as his exploratory mouth sensuously travelled down her chest to tease at her navel as his seeking hands mapped out the silky territory along her thighs and most private region. As his hands climbed a small peak located there to travel back and forth with stimulating resolve, she sighed in tormenting ecstasy and clung to him, pleading for this hunger to be sated. When Lynx had her straining against him with a fiery intensity which matched his own, he dared to enter her.

Each time Lynx partially withdrew and briefly hesitated to cool his rampant flesh, Cal groaned as if fearing the feverish object would never again plunge into her receptive and entreating body. Her body was a savage blending of ecstasy and torment. As she fervidly matched her pace to his, he huskily cautioned her to master her ardor.

His warnings were futile. Cal writhed beneath him, tightening her grip around his body, twisting her mouth into his. "Don't, love," he pleaded hoarsely. "I'm barely restraining myself. You're driving me wild, Callie. I can't hold out much longer. Be still a minute."

"It doesn't matter, my love. Take me now. Now, Lynx," she sobbed passionately into his mouth.

As love's music played over their minds and bodies, its tempo increased in pace and volume. Blood pounded in their ears as urgency consumed them. Faster and louder the strains filled the room, until a powerful crescendo thundered in her ears. Their fused bodies worked in perfect unison as love's strings yielded the sweet chords of a pleasure beyond words. Never had love's tender passion sent forth such romantic and stirring notes, such a harmonious blending of spirits.

Contented and sated, they nestled together in spite of the heat and their damp bodies. The mood demanded a silent touching and sharing. Safe and happy, they gradually surrendered to slumber's arms.

After dressing and eating the next morning, Lynx began preparations to leave. "You stay here with the door locked until I return," he ordered softly. "Don't open it to anyone but me. I'll be ready to pull out after I get you a horse and send that telegram. Keep this in case you need it," he commanded, giving her one of his pistols.

Lynx headed for the stable to make a deal. Once the purchase of a sleek sorrel was completed, he told the man to have both horses ready to leave in fifteen minutes. He handed him the saddle purchased on the way to the stable, then left.

At the telegraph office, Lynx wrote out his message to Major Jones in Dallas and told the agent to send it out while he waited. Knowing the code, he always made certain his messages went out exactly as worded. He listened to the clicking noises of the metal key as the words formed in his mind:

Advise Clark of three-day delay. Trouble in Lampasas. Calinda lured by foe. In danger. Rescued. Returning her to ranch. Will head out from there. Hold her message for me. Excuse delay. Will explain later. L.X.

"Miss Braxton didn't receive any answer to her telegram to Jones?" Lynx questioned, furtively watching the apprehensive agent.

"No sir. I guess he didn't get it yet. I was supposed to give it to the sheriff and he was to take it to her." The man fidgeted.

"What did Clint Deavers say about her telegram when he read it?" Lynx queried astutely, reading the man's alarm.

The pudgy man went pale and quivered. "I can't allow anybody to read other people's telegrams. It ain't legal."

"I'm in a big hurry, so I'll only ask this once more," Lynx sought to intimidate the man into a confession. It was doubtful Clint hadn't either demanded the telegram or its contents, not after the way he had been chasing and frightening her. "Did he stop you from sending it? Or just read it later?" Lynx had pulled out his Bowie knife and was carefully passing his finger over the sharp blade.

"Her telegram went out; I swear it, Mister . . ."

"Lynx Cardone," he nonchalantly ended the man's ignorance, but birthed his mounting panic.

The man sank into his chair, growing paler if possible. He stammered, "I . . . sent it . . . out while the sher . . . sheriff was still here. You can . . . ask him."

"But Deavers did force you to let him read it? I know he's a dangerous man; I don't blame you for giving in to his demands," Lynx cunningly reasoned with the terrified agent. "I can assure you, I'm more dangerous than he is if I'm crossed.

This baby can peel a man's hide as skillfully as an Apache. Calinda's my wife, and I want to know if Deavers saw her message."

"He'll kill me," the man blurted out in unleashed fear.

"I won't tell him you confessed. I'll be leaving town as soon as you speak. I like to know when to guard my backside. You know this Deavers has been after her. I want to get her out of town before he presses me. I'll deal with him the next time we meet, when my wife's safely at home. Speak up, my good man."

The agent jerked open a drawer and pulled out the copy of her telegram. "Here, this is what he read. He threatened to kill me if I didn't give him the response when it came in. But it hasn't; I swear it."

"I'm sure of that; Jones is in Dallas, not Waco." Lynx skimmed the contents of her urgent message. Evidently she had told the truth, most of it. He tossed it back to the agent. It fluttered before Slim could seize it, then it noisily crackled in his sweaty grip.

Lynx took a pen and paper from the counter, then scribbled another message on it. He held it out for the agent and ordered, "Burn the first one. If Deavers comes in to check on mine, give him this one."

"Burn it?" the man echoed. "But that's against the rules."

"Burn it right now," Lynx demanded, then watched the man hastily comply. "Do as you're told, and Deavers won't suspect a thing. If he's planning on calling my hand after we ride out, that should send him in the wrong direction. He'll figure I tricked him, not you."

The nervous agent read the message:

Found Calinda. Lured to Lampasas. Both safe. Returning her to ranch. Swinging by Waco. Seeking Jones' help. Will discuss trouble. Must solve plot. Arrive ranch four days. Lynx.

The phony telegram was addressed to Rankin Cardone near Fort Worth. The man glanced up at the towering and cunning Lynx. He grinned and nodded. "I'll handle it, Mister Cardone." Slim wondered if he should tell Cardone about another telegram, but quickly decided he didn't want to get involved in a conflict between two famed gunslingers.

"I'm sure you will. I'd hate to swing by here again soon." His implication was clear. Lynx smiled to calm the man, turned and left.

Before returning to Calinda's room, Lynx made a call on the sheriff and the hotel clerk. He let them know how furious he was with their actions. He informed both men the Rangers would receive a full report on the happenings here in Lampasas and their parts in them.

Clint Deavers watched Calinda and Lynx ride out of town on the trail heading toward Waco. As Lynx suspected, Clint went to the telegraph office and demanded to see his message. The clerk handed the phony words to Clint, who read them and grinned wickedly.

Clint headed for his rented room behind the Mexican cantina. He packed a saddle bag and headed out of town to skirt the Waco trail and find a perfect spot to ambush them. Clint rode swiftly and purposefully, allowing Lynx time to feel confident in their escape and to lower his guard. What man, even a husband, could retain a clear head with a beauty like that beside him? Clint knew Cal and Lynx had spent an envious night together in the same room. If he could lay a trap for Lynx and get the drop on him, he just might allow Lynx to witness his lusty pleasure before killing him. That should punish the smug gunslinger for thwarting his plans and for forcing him to settle their dispute with words only. Too, with Lynx's life in danger, that fiery redhead should be willing to do anything to save her lover's hide.

Five miles out of Lampasas, Lynx motioned for Cal to follow him as he left the deserted road to head off across rugged country, a loamy terrain which discouraged all life. He quickened his pace, compelling her to pursue his galloping steed, denying any chance for conversation. Her bag, tied securely to his saddle, bounced precariously as he nudged Star into a steady run. Her sorrel needed little encouragement to tag along. Her tender buttocks were bruised as the saddle pounded against them along the rough and hasty route. Her dress kept pulling free of its confines under her thighs to flutter wantonly in the breeze which their rush created.

The pace continued for thirty minutes until he spotted a cluster of trees with their branches which hung like an umbrella. Lynx headed that way, halting and dismounting beneath their concealing shade. When Calinda reined in, she was breathing hard; perspiration was trickling down her face and neck and was gluing wet curls to her face.

Lynx helped her dismount, grinning as she mopped the moisture from her upper lip and forehead, then inhaled and exhaled slowly to steady her respiration. Her cheeks were flushed and her clothes were damp. He pulled the canteen off his saddle-horn and offered her water. Calinda accepted it and drank greedily.

As Lynx took his turn at the canteen, she asked, "Why the rush? And why did we leave the road? This route is awful."

Lynx sat down and motioned for her to do the same. He told her about the incident at the telegraph office and his precautions. She stared at him, then asked, "Do you think he's trailing us?"

"Nope. If I know Deavers, he'll get ahead of us and set a trap along the Waco road. By the time he figures out I've tricked him, we'll be long gone. Plus, I have to get you home as fast as I can. I'm late for a meeting in Junction. You sure are a lot of trouble, Cal."

"You're the smartest and bravest man I've ever known, Lynx. I appreciate your help. I'm just sorry I'm detaining you. Are you still angry with me for coming here?" she coyly wheedled.

"Damn right, I am! Do it again, woman, and I won't be so lenient or understanding," he thundered at her.

"You don't have to get upset again. I explained and apologized." Cal realized she was twisting the ring round and round. She pulled it off and held it out to Lynx. "Thanks for loaning me your magic charm."

"Keep it; with that impulsive and defiant streak, you might need it another time." His voice became mellow and mocking as he ventured, "Tell me, love, what can I say or do to make certain you don't pack up and run off again? Even if another letter arrives and claims to be from Brax?"

"I've learned my lesson, you mean brute. If Rankin doesn't toss me out, I'll stay put this time." She turned her back to him.

"I need to make sure I can trust you," he murmured thoughtfully. "How can I hold you there without locking you in your room?"

Cal whirled and watched him in astonishment. Lynx sounded serious. "I know," he finally spoke again. "You need a home and a family. Why don't we change your name to Calinda Cardone?"

"You want me to become your sister?" she cried.

"Cal, Father's been on my back for two years about settling down. He says it's past time for me to find a wife and have my own son. Why not? That would settle both our problems," he reasoned flippantly. "When we get to the ranch, I'll marry you before I head out again. It's perfect," he smugly congratulated himself.

"Marry you?" she echoed in disbelief.

Observing her reaction, Lynx playfully chided, "You don't have to make my proposal sound like an insult, Cal."

"Then don't issue it like one!" she panted in distress, anticipating a spiteful game. "You make marriage sound like a joke or a business deal: my safety and life on the ranch in exchange for appeasing your father and producing a Cardone heir. Marriage is very serious, Lynx."

Lynx threw back his golden head and laughed heartily. "I suppose I did word it a bit strangely. I conceitedly assumed you were in love with me. Aren't you?" he challenged, grinning devilishly.

"Are you in love with me?" Cal parried his question.

"Why would I ask you to marry me?" he avoided responding. "Have you got something against marrying me and staying at the ranch?"

"Of course not. I just didn't expect a proposal from you," she anxiously confessed.

"Neither did I. That little trick gave me the idea. Sounds like a perfect solution for both of us. Well?" he pressed for her answer.

"I thought you recently said we didn't know each other well enough to have such serious feelings and conversations. I thought we agreed to drop this subject. We hardly know each other, Lynx."

"I didn't agree to any such thing, Cal. Besides, once we're married, we'll have plenty of time to get acquainted." His tawny eyes gleamed with passion and suspense. "Father won't make you leave the ranch if you marry me. He'll think you ran off to seek a job; I pursued you and convinced you to marry me so I could hold you captive. He'll be thrilled by the idea. As soon as I finish these two . . . jobs I agreed to do, I'll be coming home for good. It'll be easier for us to live in the same house if we're married," he hinted suggestively.

"If you get killed, what then?" she speculated in dread.

"You win either way. Father would never cast out my loving widow," he replied, then chuckled at her look of astonishment.

"It's crazy, Lynx," she muttered anxiously. He hadn't declared any love for her, but maybe after they were married . . .

"I know, but it sure sounds enticing. I love challenges, Callie, and you're one stimulating vixen to tame. Does it take that long to give a simple yes?" he teased roguishly when she eased into silence.

"It isn't a simple question," Cal blurted out.

"How about we analyze this matter carefully? One question at a time. Do you want to stay at the ranch?" Lynx began. Cal nodded. "Do you . . . Shall we say, find me desirable?" She flushed and nodded. "Are you at least deeply fond of me?" Her flush deepened in color, but she nodded. "Then why not marry me?"

She hesitated, then murmured hoarsely, "All right."

"You sound like a person heading for the hangman's noose. Is it so difficult to say, I want to marry you, Lynx," he teased.

"I want to marry you, Lynx," she complied, then grinned. "I also have a penchant for challenges, but I doubt anyone could tame you."

"Then it's settled. We'll tie the knot as soon as we make home."

"Are you positive you want to do this, Lynx?" she asked quietly.

"Yep," he stated laughingly. "That should keep you bound to me and the ranch. Let's get moving. I don't want Deavers to catch up and alter our plans. My time's fleeing fast. If we don't hurry, I'll lose any time with my bride." A lazy grin crossed his features.

"You're a rake, Lynx Cardone," she chided him, warming to his insinuation. She watched the beguiling grin deepen on his bronzed face, then settle in his smoldering eyes.

"I know, but you love me anyway," he remarked blithely.

"You're right," she concurred saucily, sticking out her tongue.

Lynx gazed at her, then pulled her into his arms. "I wonder what our first child will look like when your red hair mixes with my blond," he speculated happily.

His gaze was tender and seductive. He kissed the tip of her nose. "If he looks anything like you, he'll be irresistible," she said.

"And if she favors her mother, she'll be utterly enchanting."

His mouth closed over hers, sealing their bargain most provocatively. When senses began to enflame to a danger point, he pulled away and huskily warned, "If we don't get moving, Deavers could find us in a most perilous position. You're clouding my senses."

"Are you sure you'll have to leave the ranch so quickly?" she asked, recalling last night in vivid and stirring detail.

He chuckled, restraining his passion by sheer force. "I promise to get home without delay, Cal. Just trust me and wait for me."

There was an odd inflection to his voice, but she dismissed it. "Be careful, Lynx. I would die if anything happened to you," she raggedly confessed, caressing his cheek.

"As long as I know you're waiting for me in safety, then I can keep a clear head. I'll be all right. I have lots of sons to make."

Their gazes fused and locked. They laughed and embraced. "Since we can't start them here, we'd better ride," she boldly hinted, confidence born from his proposal and disarming mood.

With merry laughter ringing, they mounted up and headed off again. With luck, they could make the ranch by tomorrow evening. He would stop by the next town and send Rankin a telegram. This news should entice his father home by Tuesday night. He wanted Rankin there for the hasty wedding, and he needed to explain a few things . . . .

——— *Chapter 10* ———

LYNX AND CALINDA RODE HARD ALL DAY with few stops. When they did halt, it was mostly for the horses to rest or drink. Nearing six o'clock, they entered the town of Comanche, shortly before the telegraph office was to close. Lynx tied their reins to the hitching post, then guided Calinda inside the small building. She collapsed wearily into a chair while Lynx wrote two telegrams, one to Rankin in Graham and one to Ranger Clark. He waited patiently as the agent sent the messages over the wire. He paid the man, thanked him, and turned to collect his woman.

Calinda's head was resting against the wall, her eyes closed. Her respiration was so steady that he thought she had fallen asleep. He nudged her and called her name, "Cal?"

She stirred, her eyes fluttering open. "Yes?"

"Let's get some hot food before we head out again," he suggested, helping her to rise.

"Head out?" she wailed. "Aren't we going to spend the night here?" When he reluctantly shook his head, she grimaced. "But we've been riding hard all day; I'm exhausted. I need a bath and some sleep."

"Sorry, *pelirrojo*, but we're overdue now," he reasoned, smiling.

"Can't your schedule be changed?" she pleaded.

"You've already delayed it by six days. We'll eat and rest, then move on. You'll have plenty of time to laze around when we get home. You want to wait in the hotel restaurant or go with me to see about our horses?" he asked, leading her outside to talk privately.

"I'm sticking with you, Cardone," she quickly stated. "But I don't see why we can't get a bath and sleep for at least a few hours," she added peevishly, frowning at him. "You didn't allow much rest last night," she pointedly refreshed his obviously lagging memory.

"You know why, Cal; you're not thinking clearly," he chided.

"I'm too tired and dirty to think at all," she came back at him.

"I promised to be in Junction last Friday night. Here it is Monday, and I'm on my way to the ranch with you. By the time we get home, marry, and I head out, it will be Wednesday. If I break my neck, I'll be lucky to reach Junction by this coming Friday."

"What difference does it make, Lynx?" she questioned irritably.

"I promised to do a job there, four days ago," he replied.

"You have the ranch; why do you need to work for other people?"

"That isn't the point. I gave my word to help a friend."

"A man doesn't marry every day. Under the circumstances, can't you break it or change it?" she wheedled.

He sighed heavily, then stated unrelentingly, "No, Cal; I can't. A man's word is his bond and respect; without them, he's worthless. I'm doing all I can to solve two problems at the same time. Don't be selfish and stubborn; please," he added to soften his demands.

"You're not being fair," she gently scolded, inhaling wearily.

"You're the one who isn't being fair, Cal. First you pack up and run off into danger; then, you treat me like this after I toss everything aside to rescue you, escort you home, and marry you. I made promises before all your problems cropped up to delay them. I'm doing my damndest to help and protect you first."

"We've been through this before. I promise to be a good girl from now on. Will a few hours' rest be that terrible?"

"Then be good and stop pressuring me," he coaxed fretfully.

"All right. Even if you drive us into the ground, I won't say another word," she declared sassily. "Let's eat; I'm starved. You did say we have time to fill our tummies?" she sarcastically stated.

He groaned in exasperation. "Fine," he agreed crisply.

Lynx walked away from her, seizing the horses' reins to lead them to the stable for rest and care. He began strolling down the street, the horses following him. Cal watched him, then rushed forward.

"You beast! You're mean and cruel, Lynx," she accused.

He glanced over at her and grinned roguishly. "Then perhaps you should give my proposal further consideration. If you prefer, stay here and rest, then take the stage home. I could head for Junction tonight, then you can give me your answer when I make it home."

Cal halted in her tracks, but he kept walking. Leave her alone in this strange town? Risk Deavers catching up with her? Delay their marriage? Perhaps change his mind altogether? Was he that annoyed with her or merely that rushed? Falling for his crafty ploy to put some energy into her fatigued body, she ran to catch up to him. She grabbed his arm and forced him to stop. "Are you serious?" she demanded, eyes glittering in doubt. "Your proposal was a trick all along!"

"If you want to marry me any time soon, Cal, it has to be Wednesday. No matter how I feel about you, I'm keeping my word. If you can't accept that, you don't know me or love me at all. You'll be safe here until the stage arrives. If we can't make the ranch late tomorrow and marry Wednesday, then I'm wasting my time by going home. I'm putting you first as long as I can. Well, which do you want: me or sleep?" he challenged.

"I don't know why, but you," she confessed, frowning.

"Good," he responded, smiling at her and tenderly caressing her cheek.

"Come along, woman. One day we'll look back on today and laugh. You're a demanding vixen, *pelirrojo*."

"What does *pelirrojo* mean?" she bravely inquired.

He chuckled. "Redhead. In case you ever need to use it, *'yo te quiero'* means 'I love you,' " he slyly added, winking at her.

They left the animals to be fed, watered, and rubbed down. They headed for the hotel to eat a hot meal. Lynx didn't permit her to linger over it, even though she tried to stall. As they remounted, Cal groaned. "My fanny and back are killing me. It's obvious you're used to driving mindless cattle, not people."

"I'll rub 'em good when we get home. You can stretch out on my bed and relax while I ease those pains and aches. Or I could give you a rub-down in the tub," he hinted seductively.

"With a promise like that to urge me on, let's get going." She knew she couldn't change his mind, so she wisely relented.

They laughed and rode out of Comanche. They moved steadily through the night, then halted at dawn to catch a short nap. Lynx knew he couldn't push her any harder or faster. But an hour later, he had her up and going again, amidst grumbles and pleas.

When Calinda realized they were heading straight to the ranch, she argued his plans once more. She wanted to stop at the hotel in Fort Worth, to bathe and change clothes. Cal told him she couldn't arrive at the ranch filthy and exhausted. When Lynx adamantly refused, she scolded him and pleaded for some consideration. When he wouldn't budge, she sank into peevish silence for the rest of the journey.

It was nine o'clock when they reached the Cardone house. A flurry of talk and actions commenced instantly. Charlie hurried over to take care of their horses and to greet them on their safe return. Rankin came outside, staring at them with a mixture of confusion and pleasure, his probing gaze going from one to the other.

Salina was about to rush out to greet Lynx, but faltered when she saw Calinda at his side. Her eyes widened in disbelief. How had Lynx found her? How had she gotten away from Clint? Rage filled Salina at the sight of her thwarted plans. She whirled and returned to the kitchen to complete her chores before they entered the house. She would flee to her room and stroke her fury into cautious calm while she made new plans for this vexing girl.

Numerous questions rolled past Rankin's lips before Lynx could answer the first one. When Rankin halted breathlessly, Lynx said, "Calinda's exhausted, Father. I've been pushing her hard. We'll let her bathe and turn in. I'll explain everything."

"You all right, Cal?" Rankin asked worriedly.

"I'm fine, sir, just numb and sleepy. I'm sorry for the trouble," she apologized, smiling faintly.

"What trouble?" Rankin asked, intrigued.

"I'll explain later. You want me to get you some food, Cal?"

"Just some sherry after I bathe. I'm too tired to eat."

"You go to the water-shed; I'll fetch you some night clothes," Lynx offered unthinkingly.

She blushed. "We aren't married yet, Lynx. I'll fetch them."

"You two are getting married? No joking?" Rankin pressed, hoping his surprise plans hadn't been made unwisely.

"*Si. Mañana.*" Lynx and Rankin exchanged a curious look which Calinda noticed but didn't analyze.

Cal went to get a clean gown and wrapper. She left for the water-shed as the two men entered the house to talk. She didn't linger in the water, but bathed quickly. After dressing, she sneaked into the house and up the stairs. She was asleep the moment her drowsy head and sore body touched the comfortable bed.

When Lynx tapped lightly on her door, she didn't answer it or call out. He peeked inside. He smiled to himself, then downed her sherry in one swallow. He joined his father, a serious talk long overdue.

Rankin opened the conversation. "I must admit I'm delighted with your plans, son. But I'm a little confused and surprised. Why the rush? Where did you and Cal go?" Since the telegram had stated Lynx would explain everything, Rankin hadn't questioned him since his unexpected return at mid-day.

Lynx stroked the two days of stubble on his face, then ran his fingers through his mussed hair of ripened wheat. "Fix us a brandy while I get comfortable," he entreated. He removed his spurs, hat, and guns, hanging them on the hooks by the door. He dropped into a chair and accepted the glass from his father.

Rankin sat down near him and waited impatiently for the news. "I don't quite know where to begin, Father; there's so much to tell," Lynx stated mysteriously. As he stalled to choose his words, Rankin suggested he begin with their sudden marriage plans.

"Calinda . . . Now there's a fetching and exasperating problem. You've been trying to get something going between us ever since her curious arrival. You've been after me for years to marry, settle down here, and give you a grandson for the Cardone line. As you hinted the last time I was home, Calinda Braxton is the perfect choice, for many reasons," Lynx told his father.

Their gazes touched and spoke mutely, knowing Lynx's meaning and agreeing with it. "Is that why you're marrying her?" Rankin asked.

"Hell, I don't know myself. I hadn't imagined Lynx Cardone settling down with a wife anytime soon. But she's here now, and a marriage can solve many problems for all of us." Lynx drew in a long breath, then released it, aware of the weighty burden on his shoulders.

Rankin observed his son; for a man known for his self-assurance and control, Lynx looked edgy and indecisive. "Are you doing this for us, or do you love her?" Rankin boldly inquired.

Lynx stiffened noticeably. Just in case he was misjudging Calinda and her motives, he couldn't confess such powerful emotions this early. He had been wrong about Brax and hurt his father deeply. Now, he was accepting Brax's child into his life. "She's a beautiful and spunky lady. I find her desirable and intriguing. She's bright and charming, easy and fun to be around. She's proven she has the mettle and stamina for living out here. From what I've witnessed, she'll make a good mother and a pleasing wife. She has a lot to offer. It seems logical. As for loving her, I'm not sure I would recognize that emotion in me."

"Does she love you?" Rankin dauntlessly continued.

"I think so," his son muttered in response, sounding wishful.

"Why else would Cal go off with you?" Rankin reasoned. "Cal's a lady, and ladies don't usually act so boldly or impulsively."

"She didn't," Lynx informed him. "She packed and left; I tracked her down." Lynx carefully allowed the incident to unfold for his startled father, explaining how he had convinced her to marry him and to stay put on the ranch. He even told him the phony story he and Calina had created for Rankin, then swore his father to secrecy. "With a home and family here, she won't take off again. With us, the house, and children to occupy her time and hands, she'll forget about Brax and the past. Besides, I honestly don't want her hurt anymore."

"Then you're sure she's genuine?" Rankin said happily.

"Unless she's the best actress around, I think she is. But I sure would like to know who sent that letter and why," he said, a look of puzzlement filling his eyes.

"You're positive there was a letter? And that she burned it?"

"Yes," Lynx readily answered. He explained about her telegram to Jones, then added he would investigate it further.

"If Brax has wheedled Jones' help and friendship, he won't tell you anything, son. Running off like that is mighty queer."

"If there's a man alive I can trust, it's Major Jones." Lynx stared his father in the eye as he finally disclosed his secret identity as a Texas Ranger. While Rankin was speechless, Lynx continued with tales of his past, present, and imminent assignments. He let his father know he had two remaining missions to carry out before he would be coming home to settle down permanently.

"Why didn't you tell me? Does Cal know?" Rankin asked, stunned and thrilled. His son, the famous Ranger who used the coded star? Pride and respect flooded Rankin's heart.

"Cal doesn't know anything about me. She thinks I'm a famous gunslinger and carefree rogue. She won't learn anything until my work is over, if then. It might be best to keep my identity a secret, in case the Rangers need me again in the future. You can't tell anyone, Father, not even hint at it. I'm sorry I couldn't tell you sooner, but my role was safer and stronger with my father treating me as the rebellious son. If you'd gone around with that proud smile, it could have been dangerous for me and my missions."

"Why are you telling me now?" Rankin probed.

"These next two missions are tricky and deadly. If I don't . . . get home again, I wanted you to know the truth about your son. Few Rangers know my cover, and no one else. I report to Major Jones; that's how I know I can trust him. If anything had happened to me, he would have contacted you with the truth." Lynx continued with his present orders. "Now you see how late I am? I'll have to pull out as soon as the wedding's over. I know it's moving too fast, but I've got to keep her on the ranch. I want both her and the ranch, Father," he stated simply.

"If you're not in love with her, son, you're wavering on the edge of it," Rankin said. "I'm proud of you, Lynx."

"Maybe I'm just too wary to trust anyone, especially a mysterious female, and certainly a Braxton. I can't risk feeling too much for her until I'm positive it's worth it," Lynx candidly admitted.

"I know what you mean," Rankin concurred. "She does have a way of stealing your affection. I pray she deserves it."

"The only step she might take now would be a letter to or from the Simpsons. Make sure you intercept all mail except from me," Lynx cautioned once more. "I'll try to keep you informed as to my location. If she says or does anything unusual, send word to me. I'll sign myself as Wade. Now, all I have to do is round up the preacher for the wedding."

"That won't be necessary, son. He's coming here for the wedding at two o'clock. I also invited a few of our closest neighbors. Can't have a Cardone married without a little show." Rankin smiled.

"But I've got to pull out right after the wedding," Lynx argued.

"To marry in secret could inspire gossip. If anyone tries to hang around past four, I'll send them on their way. It'd look strange if you ride off in front of them. Anyway, son, you need some rest. Why not leave early Thursday?" Rankin suggested.

"*Valgame Dios!* She surely has complicated my life."

"If you leave after the wedding, that means no time alone with your new bride. I doubt Calinda will accept such treatment. Besides, it might be wise to work on a son before heading into danger," Rankin hinted slyly.

Lynx caught himself before confessing to past work on a son. He suddenly realized this hasty marriage was best for another reason: what if Calinda was already pregnant? He was shocked at having overlooked that possibility. He recalled his fears in the Red Satin Saloon about a shotgun wedding, then chuckled at the private joke.

"What's so funny, son?" Rankin asked.

"Who would have ever thought Lynx Cardone would marry Elliott Braxton's daughter?" he parried the loaded question.

"It's one of the smartest moves you've made, son. Looks as if we'll finally outsmart Brax, ironic justice. You do realize the legal implications in marrying Cal? A wife can't harm her husband?" When Lynx ruefully nodded, Rankin added, "We'll make a nice family." They exchanged smiles, then shared hearty laughter.

"Well, this future groom is bone-weary. We'll talk in the morning. Goodnight, Father. Pretty soon, you'll be sick of having me around daily. You and I do have a way of challenging each other. Maybe we're too much alike," Lynx devilishly speculated.

Like Calinda, Lynx scrubbed quickly and went to bed. Shortly, the entire house was asleep.

Rankin and Lynx were up and drinking coffee when Salina entered the kitchen. She glanced at both men, pondering their smug grins and cheerful moods. If Rankin was furious with Calinda, he didn't show it. Salina puzzled over what had taken place in Lampasas and after their return last night. She dreaded what Calinda may have said to the men. Yet, if they were annoyed with her, they didn't offer any clues.

"Ready for breakfast?" she asked.

They both nodded. "Is the *senorita* up yet?" she inquired, trying to sound casual, turning her back to conceal her expression.

"Not yet. We're letting her sleep a while longer. She's got a busy day ahead," Rankin hinted, laughing merrily.

"Busy day ahead?" Salina echoed suggestively.

"Cal and Lynx are getting married at two," he stated.

"*Ca . . . casada?*" she stammered the devastating word, whirling around to gape at the insouciant Lynx.

Rankin declared, "That's the size of it, Salina. I want you and Charlie to help get the house and food ready. We'll be having neighbors over for the wedding. See if you can round up some flowers to brighten things up a bit. It isn't everyday a Cardone gets lassoed."

"*Hoy? Por que?* How can we prepare for a *boda* on such short notice? When did this happen?" Salina questioned, stunned and distressed. *Se quieren mucho?* No, they could not be in love!

"We'll have to make do; Lynx is leaving in the morning," Rankin nonchalantly stated, grinning mischievously at his son.

"*Que te pasa?*" she queried, fearing Calinda was pregnant, or claiming to be to force a marriage with Lynx.

"*Nada.* Why wait? I asked and she accepted. I'll be coming home to stay within the next two months. A wedding ring will hold her put till then," Lynx humorously alluded.

Although Lynx was laughing roguishly, Salina knew something was going on between them. She pressed boldly, doubting him, "*Que se ha hecho de el astuto solo lobo?* You asked her?"

"*Si,*" he replied, furtively watching her for revealing clues.

"*No importa.* I did not realize you and Calinda were *enamorado, tomar casamiento en consideracion,*" Salina deviously explained her surprise at their wedding plans, having failed to score with her mocking taunt about the careless snaring of the Lone Wolf.

"Surprised me, too," Lynx declared playfully. "Calinda didn't feel right staying on here. When she packed up and left to find a job, I went after her and forced her to come home. A wedding ring's the only way to keep her where she belongs. I was getting used to that vixen."

Salina realized Lynx hadn't mentioned love. He made it sound as if he was going to any measure just to keep her on the ranch. Why? Did it have something to do with this Brax and the past? Did he want to prevent her from locating her father? It was awfully suspicious . . .

Feeling she must respond, Salina murmured, "*Que le vaya bien.*" He would need good luck, but she would never congratulate him.

"*Gracias,* Salina, I'll probably need it to tame that wild filly."

Salina set to cooking their breakfast, her mind working steadily and maliciously. There was nothing she could do or say to halt this event. Evidently Calinda had lied about her reason for going to Lampasas. That flame-haired witch had somehow compelled Lynx to marry her. Even if Lynx was bewitched by Calinda, he wouldn't rush into a confining marriage, unless there was a vital reason. If Salina confessed her lies to Lynx about the letter and trip, Lynx would think she was trying to cause trouble. She dared not do anything which might entice them to fire her. She must stay here to sever this marriage!

Salina decided on her future path. She would disarm Calinda with feigned resignation to this marriage and gradual friendship. She would keep her eyes and ears open to solve this riddle, then use the information gleaned to destroy Calinda and win Lynx. Time, cunning, and patience were all she needed. No, she hastily concluded; she didn't have time. A *bebe* could complicate matters further! How dare that haughty bitch enjoy what Lynx had denied her for years! *Jamas!*

While the men were discussing ranch matters after breakfast, Salina eased upstairs to awaken Calinda. She needed to learn what Calinda had said to Lynx. She aroused the sleeping girl, putting on a controlled expression. "You must get up, Calinda; they have planned the wedding for two," Salina revealed to the sluggish girl. "The neighbors have been invited, and there will be a *fiesta*."

"What?" Calinda shrieked, coming to full awareness. They had altered the plans without even consulting her? "But I thought Lynx and I were riding into town to see the preacher there. A wedding here? Guests? But I don't have an appropriate dress," she fretted nervously.

"Use one of Laura's," Salina suggested, wanting to slap her foe. "I must start the cleaning and cooking. First, I wanted to know about your talk with Lynx. What did you say about me?"

Calinda explained the terrifying incident to Salina, omitting personal parts. Salina in turn related Lynx's arrival and fury. "I mentioned the letter before thinking. I have never seen him *hecho una furia*. I told him it might be an old one. He was *cierto* it was not. Could he figure out who sent it?"

Calinda asked for a translation, then told her no and why. She apologized for getting Salina involved. "Well, it did prove valuable; Lynx proposed," Salina remarked.

"I suppose so, but he was furious with me. I can't blame him. It was a stupid idea. Thanks for the help, Salina," Cal said, throwing the covers aside and getting out of bed. She would need to hurry.

"Why do you marry Lynx, Calinda?" the girl inquired gravely.

Calinda blushed, then replied, "I'm sorry if you're upset with me, Salina. I didn't mean for this to happen. But Lynx is so . . . irresistible and forceful. I do love him. I know this is awfully sudden, but I don't have any choice. If I stall him or refuse, he might never ask me again. He's so proud and obstinate. I just wish there was more time and he was staying home."

Salina didn't press her luck by asking if Calinda was pregnant. She shrugged and sighed. "I should not be shocked. I saw the way you two stared at each other. Knowing Lynx always gets what he desires, I should have realized he wouldn't release you; he wants you badly."

Becoming uneasy with this intimate conversation, Calinda smiled and said, "I'd better get busy. Thanks again, Salina."

Salina glared at her back as Calinda stood before the closet trying to select a dress for her wedding. *You might marry him today, my cunning foe, but you will not keep him long,* Salina mentally plotted.

When Calinda went downstairs, Lynx and Rankin were out riding. She ate breakfast, sensing she would be too nervous and busy to eat before the wedding. She washed her hair and bathed, then sat on the balcony in the sun to dry the vibrant curls. She had selected a teal blue gown in satin, one of Laura's prettiest.

She spent most of the morning in her room preparing for this major change in her life.

Lynx didn't come to Calinda's room, but that didn't surprise her. After most of the guests had arrived, Rankin came to fetch her. He stood back and admired her beauty and softness. The rich blue gown complimented her creamy coloring, golden-red hair, and dark emerald eyes. The billowy skirt swayed gently when she moved, sending forth a muted rustle. Her slender waist looked as if he could reach around it with two hands. He complimented her on her choice, knowing whose gown Calinda was wearing, bitterly recalling the last time he had seen it.

"I hope it's all right, Rankin. It was the only one which seemed appropriate. You don't think Lynx will mind, do you?" she fretted.

"Certainly not. Why would you worry?" Rankin inquired, pondering if Calinda knew something she shouldn't.

Calinda lowered her lashes as she told him how displeased and upset Lynx had been the last time she had worn one of Laura's gowns. She modestly didn't tell what kind of gown. "I don't favor her, do I?" she asked, that horror suddenly entering her anxious mind.

"Not at all, my dear. Lynx favors his mother a great deal: the same eyes and hair, the same expressions. Sometimes when he smiles or laughs, it's like a small echo or mirror of Laura's. Maybe that was why he and I had such conflicts after she . . . was gone. Maybe I saw too much of Laura in our son," he murmured remorsefully.

Calinda was warmed by the confession. There was such anguish in his eyes and voice, emotions Rankin rarely exposed. It gave her another insight into the troubled past, especially into the relationship between these two men. Had Lynx mistaken his father's unconscious resentment as a lack of love and need? Had Rankin unknowingly punished his son for Lynx's love for Brax? Perhaps Lynx had also blamed Rankin for driving Brax away, perhaps suspecting jealousy as the motive. Had Lynx somehow blamed his father for Laura's early death? Surely it was tormenting to gaze into a matching face of a lost loved one. How sad they had taken their grief and bitterness out on each other. How tragic to waste so many years and so many emotions. Perhaps she could draw them closer. Evidently time had eased some of those pains and differences, for they appeared to get along fine now. If only Lynx would halt his roaming and come home. If only Rankin would gentle his grip to prevent Lynx from needing solitude and excitement elsewhere. If only they would talk to each other and work out their differences, or wisely accept their similarities.

Cal grasped his arm and smiled into his face. "But things are better now, Rankin. I've seen the love and rapport between you two. Lynx has changed since those wild days; he's a very special and strong man. When he comes back to stay, I know everything will be wonderful."

"You love him very much, don't you?" Rankin asked.

Cal flushed, but felt she should admit such an emotion. After all, it was their wedding day. She wondered how Lynx had responded to this same question, for surely his father had broached it. "I've never met any man like your son, Rankin. He's handsome, charming, smart, and brave. He swept me off my feet. I hope our sudden plans didn't upset you," she hinted.

"Not in the least. Surprised me, yes; but I'm delighted, Cal. Lynx and I had a long talk last night and this morning. Before we know it, he'll be home to stay. Until then, you and I can have fun running this ranch. He did tell you he must leave first thing tomorrow?"

"Yes," she replied sadly. "I tried to change his mind, but he wouldn't listen. Seems your son is a proud and stubborn man."

"If there's one thing I know about my son, he's a man of his word. Lynx has always been reliable and relentless. If he gives his promise to do something, he'll fight the demons of hell to keep it. That speaks highly of a man out here, Cal. Lynx made some promises before you came along, now he must keep them. If he didn't, he wouldn't be the man you love. Be patient and understanding while he's gone. He'll come home as soon as he can; he'll have a pretty wife to lure him back quickly. You ready to come downstairs?"

"I'll be there in a moment. Is everything ready?"

"I think you'll be amazed and pleased," he said, sparking her curiosity.

After Rankin left her alone, Calinda sat down on the edge of the bed. What was going on between them? Why was Rankin expounding on Lynx's good traits and defending his departure? Rankin's sudden change of heart about his son's behavior inspired speculations. Getting married wasn't the answer, for Lynx was taking off almost immediately. If they didn't have guests, he probably would. In Rankin's eyes and mind, how had Lynx gone from carefree rebel to "reliable" and unquestionably honest and honorable? Until now, Rankin had been arguing and threatening Lynx to come home; now, he was coaxing her to be "patient and understanding." Evidently Rankin knew where Lynx was heading and why, and he clearly agreed with Lynx's motives. If Lynx could confide in his father, why not in his wife? She was miffed and disappointed. It was almost as if they were conspiring to keep secrets from her, conspiring to hold her on the ranch. That was ridiculous, she hastily decided. Maybe her jittery nerves were playing tricks on her mind. She must join them before they wondered what was keeping her. As Cal removed the silver cross Lynx had given her, she abruptly realized it matched the one which Salina wore. She stiffened. Instantly, she scolded her jealousy and suspicions, dismissing them.

When Calinda gracefully walked down the steps, she was amazed and pleased, as Rankin had stated. The house was filled with beautiful and colorful wildflowers. Delicious odors from the kitchen assailed her nose. She could hear laughter and muted conversation coming from outside and the next room. She summoned her courage and entered the room. It was crowded with people. Had they invited everyone nearby?

Lynx glanced up and grinned. He came forward with agile steps. He caught her cold hands and smiled into her tense face. He leaned over to kiss her cheek, whispering, "Relax, *querida;* they aren't here to devour you. Let's give 'em a good show of love and happiness."

Cal met his gaze and smiled faintly, his last words echoing across her mind. "I'm scared stiff," she murmured to hide her doubts.

"Me, too. But we've gone too far to back down now," he teased.

Several neighbors came over to congratulate them. Calinda smiled and spoke genially, her anxiety seeming natural for a bride. Soon, Rankin announced it was time for the ceremony. The crowd gathered on the veranda as Calinda and Lynx were directed to stand before the preacher. Within a blurred twenty minutes, Lynx was slipping the gold band on her finger again, this time for good.

As she stared at it, he lifted her chin and kissed her soundly. Cheers went up as they parted. A bright flush greeted Lynx, who chuckled in amusement. "Well, Mrs. Cardone, how about a toast?"

The party began. There were platters of barbecued beef and pork, fried chicken and baked ham, bowls of fresh beans and peas, stacks of "rowsinears" as they called corn-on-the-cob, fragrant bread, and mounds of creamed potatoes. Besides steaming coffee and tea, stronger spirits were offered in abundance. Afterwards, there were many tempting desserts to choose from, or a slice of wedding cake. Calinda stared at the lovely cake which was Salina's prized creation.

The new bride nibbled on the food Lynx placed in her hands or lap. She chatted with neighbors, accepting their compliments or teasing jokes. She carefully sipped very little wine, knowing how long this day might be. With the assistance of her new husband, she looked every inch a happy bride very much in love.

But Rankin's plans for a short celebration were thwarted by merry neighbors. Several men had brought along musical instruments. They joined together to encourage dancing. Without rudely ordering everyone to leave, Cal and Lynx had no choice but to go along with their friends' good intentions.

As the bride was enticed to dance with many friends, the hour grew late. She had danced several times with Lynx, but it was always a lively tune. With all the excitement, they were granted little time alone. As Calinda was dancing with Rankin, she longingly gazed at Lynx who was genially chatting with friends.

Rankin whispered in her ear, "I'm sorry, Cal. I know this is stealing most of your time with Lynx. But our friends don't know he's leaving at dawn. They should start heading home soon."

Cal looked up at him and smiled. He, too, had good intentions, but costly ones today. "Everyone loves a party, especially a wedding. They'll hang around as long as possible. Don't worry about it."

Rankin caught his son's eye and sent him a message to join his wife. When Lynx claimed her hand for a dance, Rankin asked the musicians for a slow tune. A devilish grin flashed over Lynx's handsome face as he gathered her tightly against him.

Cal mildly protested, but he didn't loosen his embrace. She sighed and accepted what she felt was an immodest closeness even for newlyweds. As they seemingly floated around the grassy area, Lynx boldly kissed her forehead, then nuzzled her ear.

"Lynx, stop that," she softly warned. "We're in public."

"Maybe they'll take a hint and leave," he said.

"It wouldn't matter, if you stay home another day."

He looked down at her and taunted mischievously, "Missing me already? Afraid you won't have enough of me tonight?"

Calinda stared at him. "What's gotten into you?" she asked. "Have you been drinking too much?"

"I'm trying my damndest to stay loose, but thoughts of getting you alone are tying my nerves into knots. You look beautiful today, Cal. I could almost make love to you right here," he informed her.

"Behave yourself; you're embarrassing me," she scolded, but a telltale tremor passed over her.

"I could behave, if I didn't recall our last night together. You realize tonight will have to last us for weeks?" he hinted wryly.

Calinda was about to make a naughty comment, but realized they were the only ones dancing. As she gazed around, Lynx did the same. He threw back his head and chuckled, then hugged her tightly. Before she realized what he was doing, he boldly swept her into his strong arms and announced to the laughing crowd, "If you folks don't mind, my bride and I will take our leave. Please continue." With that, he carried her into the house and up the steps to his room.

Shocked by his conduct, she didn't speak until he dropped her on his bed. "How dare you do something like that to me," she ranted.

"If I hadn't, they would stay around half the night. Damnit, Cal, you're driving me wild. If you think that embarrassed you, this would have more," he declared, pointing to the bulge against his tight britches. "See what you were doing to me out there? When the music ended, we were in trouble. Don't worry; they'll find it amusing."

Calinda's face was as fiery as a sunset. Lynx murmured, "You're the first woman who's ever stolen my self-control. I started thinking about tonight, and nature took over. What are you doing to me, woman? I must not have the same effect on you, but I'm as heated up as a piece of dry wood in a roaring fire."

Calinda's anger was replaced with passion. She grinned and replied, "You don't affect me like that because we don't have the same parts, my darling husband, in case you haven't noticed."

"I have noticed. That's why my pants got so tight and uncomfortable. Let's just see if I can inspire a similar effect."

Lynx pulled her to her feet, turned her around, then started unbuttoning her dress. "What are you doing?" she asked in alarm.

"Getting us ready for bed," he cheerfully replied, continuing his task at hand.

"Bed," she shrieked. "But we have guests outside. Surely you don't plan to stay in here while they're still out there?"

"Why not?" Lynx fenced, spreading kisses over her neck.

"They'll know what we're doing," Cal wailed anxiously.

"Maybe it'll heat the men up so they'll race home to do the same thing," he mirthfully teased her.

"You're awful, Lynx Cardone," she declared.

"But you're ravishing, Mrs. Cardone," he retorted.

"This is embarrassing, Lynx. What will they think about us?"

"We're married, Cal. This is a natural act to follow a wedding."

"But during our own party?" she debated, turning to face him.

"In less than six hours I'll have to ride out for weeks. Do you want to spend most of it entertaining guests who should have enough intelligence and consideration to go home?" Lynx reasoned.

"But they don't know my beloved husband is deserting me right after our wedding," she countered angrily.

"Let's don't quarrel tonight, Cal; time is short," he coaxed, easing her dress and chemise down to torment her senses.

He gently kissed each soft tip, then travelled up to eagerly devour her parted lips. The palm of his hand moved over her breasts, enticing them to crave their lingering pleasure. When his lips roamed to her ear and asked, "Do we stay here or return to our party?", she was lost.

"You win, Mister Cardone, but most unfairly," she helplessly relented. She freed herself to finish undressing, then returned to his waiting bed. He was quickly out of his clothes and lying beside her.

"I'm going to miss you terribly," she murmured against his shoulder. "When people find out you left so quickly, they'll think something's wrong between us. It isn't natural for a bridegroom to leave home the day after his wedding, a hasty one at that. They'll probably think I'm pregnant," she apprehensively speculated.

"You could be, Cal," he said softly, lifting his head to gaze down at her. At her shocked expression, he teased, "That does happen when two people make love, and this isn't our first time."

"But . . ." She actually paled and shuddered. "Is that why you married me before heading off again?" she fearfully questioned.

"No, love. I didn't even consider it until last night. But it isn't impossible. Would that upset you, Cal?" he asked seriously.

"No, I just haven't thought about a baby."

"Our baby," he corrected her, then smiled warmly. "Promise me you won't go running off again, not even to chase after me."

"I promise. But do you have to leave?" she entreated a last time.

"We'll talk about it later. Right now . . ." he hinted, then seared her quivering flesh with fiery kisses and burning caresses.

He shifted to lie half atop her. His mouth came down on hers, exploring and tasting the sweet desire within her. He embraced her so tightly and fiercely that she feared she couldn't breathe, but didn't care at that moment. Eagerly seeking her unbridled response, Lynx hungrily took her mouth with skill and resolve.

Cal's arms had encircled his waist and her hands slipped up his back. How intoxicating he was, as some potent drug which dazed her. Surely there wasn't a spot on her body that he hadn't set to tingling with his tantalizing actions. She was alive with molten flames, as was he. Lynx seemed to control and stimulate the very essence of her being. His warm breath caused her to tremble as he murmured words of passion into her ears. His insistent hands roved her sensitive body, as if stirring each inch to life and awareness.

As his hands became bolder, they soared over her slender and shapely figure. Soon her entire body urged him to conquer and claim her willing territory, to invade it, to explore it, to map it, and to declare it his sole possession. Wild and wonderful sensations attacked her senses, enslaving her. Cal wanted to savor this special union, but her need was too great to linger.

Her hand went into his hair and drew his mouth closer to hers. As his hand provocatively slipped down her flat stomach to seek out the secret place that summoned his skills and heightened his desires, Cal moaned and writhed in unleashed passion. Her fingers roamed down his sleek sides to brazenly claim a prize she had not dared to touch before tonight, a prize which possessed the power and talent to drive her mindless with pleasure and blissful torment. She stroked it gently, relishing its warmth and smoothness. His body shuddered as a groan came from deep within his muscled chest.

Moments later, Lynx shifted between her parted thighs. His body so taut and enflamed, he swiftly and urgently entered her. The contact was staggering to his senses. He moved leisurely and deliberately, fearing his self-control would vanish too soon.

Her hands wandered up and down his strong back, feeling the muscles rippling at his movements. As Lynx probed her body again and again, she arched to meet each entry, moaning at each exit. Her responses told Lynx when she was ready to conquer her rapturous challenge. He increased his pace and invaded her with a savage gentleness.

A muffled cry of victory was torn from Cal's lips as the powerful release claimed her. As if a signal to charge his own defenses, he quickly and eagerly pursued her successful journey. His body shook with the force of an equally potent release. His mouth engulfed hers, blending them as one until every spasm had ceased and his body was as sated as hers.

They snuggled together in his bed, caressing and kissing until their passions were reborn. They made love once more, slowly and relentlessly. Lynx murmured instructions into her ear, which she quickly and readily followed, increasing their pleasures. When they lay exhausted and moistened in each other's arms, he whispered fiercely, "You're mine, love; I'll never let you leave me. If you did, I would hunt you down and . . ." When he realized what he was saying, he made a light joke of it. "I'll hunt you down and punish you by tormenting your body and senses. I'll make you beg with hunger, then refuse to feed you. I'll make you burn with desire, then let the flames go undoused."

Cal twisted her head to gaze over at his roguish expression. "That kind of torment runs in two directions, my love. Whyever would I leave you; you're mine now. But if you don't come home soon, I'll punish you in said manner when you do show that handsome face and virile body," she laughingly threatened.

"I promise you, when I come home, we'll be too busy for games." He kissed her lightly, then they fell asleep without moving.

It was mid-morning when Calinda stirred, smiling contentedly. As dreamy memories flooded her mind, her body responded with rising passion. Her lips hungered for his; her body flamed to join with his. As Cal turned over, her hand reached out to touch her love. She sat up, the covers falling to her lap, exposing flesh which quivered with desire. She looked around, but Lynx wasn't in the room. She snuggled into the softness of his bed, waiting to see if he would return soon. She held out her arm to gaze at the gold band which thrilled her soul.

When time passed, Cal decided she must dress and look for him. Lynx was more than likely eating breakfast or talking with his father or making preparations to leave. That last thought spurred her into hasty action. It never crossed her mind her husband would ride off for such a lengthy separation without awakening her to say goodbye in a proper manner for deliriously happy newlyweds. Cal hummed merrily as she pulled on a paisley dress. She hurriedly brushed her hair, then rushed downstairs, to discover Lynx had ridden off before dawn.

— *Chapter 11* —

❧

To MAKE MATTERS WORSE for Calinda, it was Salina who informed her of Lynx's departure. Salina gave the facts in succinct words, her tone crisp and mocking. The Mexican girl offered Calinda nothing more. Calinda would not dismiss her pride to press the girl, who was inexplicably hostile again.

As she was about to prepare her own breakfast, Calinda did ask where Rankin was this morning. If there was more to learn about her husband, she would do so from her new father-in-law.

Salina told her that Rankin had gone into town on business. Calinda was forced to ask when he would return. Salina stated indifferently, "*Buenas tardas,* late afternoon," she clarified.

When Calinda reached for an iron skillet, Salina asked frostily, "What are you doing?" When Calinda said she was going to cook her breakfast, Salina snapped, "Not in *my* kitchen. No one works in here but me. What would you like this morning, Mrs. Cardone?"

At Salina's caustic tone and bold order, Calinda looked at her. "What's wrong with you, Salina? I always do this. If you think you'll have to wait on me now, that isn't true."

"I do not plan to wait on you, Mrs. Cardone. But I allow no one to take over my kitchen or prove I'm not needed anymore."

"This isn't your private domain, Salina. Lynx and I are married now. I can enter and work here anytime I choose," she stated defiantly.

"*Senor* Rankin and Lynx do not agree. Before Lynx left, they talked of me. They said I was needed and wanted. They said, just because you live here now, it changed nothing, *nada,*" Salina joyfully emphasized her allegation. "That means, you are still a guest and I am in control of this *casa*. If you do not believe me, ask *Senor* Rankin. In fact, I dare you to ask him. Your husband is gone, poor thing."

Calinda's mouth fell open at her hostility and daring. "I thought you and I had a truce, Salina. Why are you being so hateful?"

"A truce and peace are *mucho diferente,*" Salina replied.

"So, it's back to the secret war again?" Calinda surmised angrily. "I doubt Rankin and Lynx will accept your demands and spite."

"They know me longer than you. If you tattle or treat me badly, they will think you try to run me off. I will see they do not believe you. This was my *casa* and family *primero*. You are foolish, blind."

"How dare you! Lynx and I are married now," Cal shrieked.

"I know not how you forced him into marriage, but it was not love. If Lynx married you, he had *bueno* reasons. Did you claim to be *encinta,* with child?" she coldly challenged, glaring at Calinda.

"No! But even if it were true, it's none of your business! Lynx proposed on the way home from Lampasas, and I accepted."

"*Pero por que,* that is what I wish to know," she sneered.

"When Rankin comes home, we'll have a long talk about this," Calinda warned the surly girl, mutely praying she wouldn't get pregnant too soon and give Salina cause to gloat.

"Do so, *senora;* I care not. I will tell you what else *Senor* Rankin said this morning. He said be nice to you; he does not want you to run off again. He does not want you to know Lynx told him all about your *poco aventura,* little adventure, in Lampasas. *Senor* Rankin thinks you will be upset and *nervioso* around him," she murmured balefully, placing her hands on her rounded hips.

"I don't know what you're trying to prove or pull, Salina, but I won't allow it. Lynx is my husband, and you'll have to accept it. I won't allow you to be rude or cause trouble."

"Your *esposo?*" Salina scoffed. "Tell me, *Senora* Cardone, do you have any idea where he is right this minute, or when he will be home, or what he is doing? No. I wonder how much a husband loves his wife when he keeps his life a secret from her. Must be nice to have a hot-blooded wife at home, then be able to roam around the state doing anything you please, with anyone you please," she hinted audaciously and crudely. "I wonder who he is with today . . ."

Fury and resentment surged through Calinda. She nearly slapped the girl, but realized she couldn't dispute the statements. "When Lynx comes home, we'll settle this matter once and for all, Salina. I'm going to confess everything."

A cynical smile claimed the girl's lips. "He already knows everything, Cal. Did you really think I would lie to my love? Tell him the truth. He knows you deceived him before. To confess now will only inspire suspicions for your change of heart. He will think you are the one trying to pull a trick. You will look the trouble-maker."

"You have the arrogance and gall to threaten me! To blackmail me! You're a fool, Salina. Lynx would never take a servant's word over his wife's." Calinda and Salina glared challengingly at each other.

"I proved I can be trusted, but you have not. I do not plan to blackmail you, *Senora* Cardone. I just want you to stay out of my path until Lynx grows weary of you and tosses you out. Lynx is used to freedom, privacy, and lots of women. Once he comes home to stay, you will strangle him with your constant presence and demands. I doubt you are woman enough to hold his interest very long. I will do my work and bide my time until that day comes, which it will."

"You're wrong, Salina; I'm here to stay. I love him," she boldly confessed to vex Salina. "He married me, didn't he?"

"We will see, will we not, Cal? I bet you will be gone before the fall round-up. Lynx will never change. Even if he permits you to hang around for a respectable image, you will tire of his ways."

"I don't want him to change; I want him just as he is. I'll never tire of him, and I'll make sure he doesn't get bored with me."

"Would you care to know where your loving *esposo* has gone?"

"I know," Calinda declared smugly. "To Junction."

Mirthful laughter filled the quiet kitchen. "The business in Junction was lost because of you. He goes to Waco to meet with Major Jones, something to do with your telegram to him. You see, *Senora* Cardone, your trusting *esposo* is checking out your wild story."

"No, Salina, he's trying to discover who sent the phony letter."

"No, Cal, he does not believe you," Salina refuted.

"Lynx knows there was a letter which lured me there!"

"He knows there was a letter, but he is not convinced it was a trap as you pretended. Two reasons: he knew it was not an old letter because he searched your room on his first trip home; and you suspiciously burned the letter to prevent him from seeing the message and the handwriting. He is what I call a devoted *esposo*," she scoffed.

"I don't believe you! I'll ask Lynx when he comes home."

Salina laughed maliciously. "I would not corner a fierce wolf. Lynx is sly, ruthless, and deadly. Do you honestly think he will confess such things to you? You play the fool! He will lie to you or attack. Will you risk either reaction?"

"If such things are true, how did you learn them?" Calinda questioned, her sarcastic tone voicing her doubts of Salina's honesty.

"I saw Lynx searching your room, and I heard him tell his father many things. That is how I know you will not last long. If I am right, Lynx married you to trap you here while he investigates you. It is strange they do not want you seeking your own father . . . I wonder what they hide from you . . ." she mumbled thoughtfully.

"At least you're being open with your resentment and hatred. If I ever catch you spying on any of us, I'll force a choice between us. No matter who wins or loses," she told Salina, then went to Lynx's room to do some heavy thinking.

Calinda paced the floor as distressing questions stormed her mind. Lynx hadn't left a note this morning. Did he feel he owned her now, that it wasn't necessary? Perhaps he had given Rankin a message to pass along to her. But why had he confessed the truth to Rankin, then sworn him to secrecy? If such was true, it was painful.

Why was she allowing that vicious girl's statements to haunt her, to inspire mistrust? Why had the men drawn Salina into their schemes and confidence? If Salina had repeated Rankin's words accurately, they didn't want or plan for Calinda to take over anything. But she was Lynx's wife, the new mistress of this house! How could they allow a mere servant to have more authority and power?

Had Salina lied to her? Had Salina deviously misled the two men? Had that tempestuous Mexican girl told Lynx everything? If so, no wonder Lynx didn't trust his wife. Cal didn't like him searching her room, but she couldn't blame him for his mistrust back then. But now? Investigate his own wife? Was there a vital reason for marrying her quickly and holding her here on the ranch? Yet, she begrudgingly agreed with Salina; they were withholding facts.

Calinda knew she had trusted that sly vixen too easily. Perhaps Salina knew more than she was telling; she was behaving awfully smugly and brazenly. If there was future trouble between them, Salina would try her best to make certain

Calinda was blamed for it. Calinda scolded herself for being so trusting, naive, and gullible. She should have known that little witch wouldn't take their marriage calmly. As surely as the sun was up, Salina was plotting and practicing more mischief. It would be wise to keep a close eye on that devilish girl.

Calinda was distressed and alarmed by their deceptions and her husband's sneaky departure. So much for his statement of discussing it this morning. He had avoided a scene by slipping out early. She vowed to clear the air with everyone the moment Lynx came home.

Rankin returned shortly after five. He was in a cheerful mood, smiling and chatting with the subdued Calinda. He grinned and teased her about missing Lynx already. He told her he had gone into town to send telegrams to their distant friends, to reveal Lynx's marriage. He didn't tell Calinda he had sent the announcement to newspapers over the state, nor that he had done so to take a last stab at luring Brax out of hiding. If anything would draw Brax out of conceal- ment, his daughter's marital entanglement with a Cardone should do it . . .

Calinda asked Rankin where Lynx had gone and when he was expected to be home again. Rankin sighed and told her, "He was heading back to Junction, if it isn't too late to carry out his . . . business there. What do you say to some cards and sherry?" he tried to distract her, but they both caught his slip.

Calinda pretended not to notice it. She smiled and nodded. As they played cards and sipped sherry, she asked Rankin what kind of work Lynx did. Her head was lowered to prevent Rankin from noticing her close observation. "He used to take odd jobs for excitement and a good reason for staying away from home. Now, he's trying to locate two bulls for breeding. In cattle country, it's important to keep good blood in the breeding line. He'll be traveling around to several ranches to check out their stock. Plus, he's setting up the plans for the next cattle drive to market."

"How long will he be away?" she continued, knowing Rankin was deceiving her.

"I would venture a guess at three or four weeks. Are you mad at him, Cal?" Rankin asked anxiously.

"I'm just disappointed that breeding bulls are more important than a new bride," she said, letting him know she was indeed rankled. Evidently her new father-in-law had forgotten that both men had vowed the honorable and reliable Lynx was heading south to keep a promise which his pride demanded he fulfill. Now, Rankin was telling her Lynx was merely checking out bulls and round-ups! Didn't he realize such lies didn't excuse Lynx's hasty flight and absence at this special time?

"Is something bothering you, Cal?" he asked in panic.

She glanced up, her expression innocent. "No, I was just studying my hand. Someday I'll have this cunning game under control. I'm never sure when to bluff or fold. It's difficult to tell which hand is better." Rankin didn't realize that Calinda wasn't referring to their card game, but he did note the odd inflection in her voice.

"Maybe your concentration is bad tonight," he teased.

"I think you're right. Yesterday was a busy day and late night. I think I'll turn in, Rankin. See you tomorrow." As she stood up, she halted to ask, "What about my new duties around the house?"

"New duties?" he queried confusedly.

She laughed brightly. "I am Lynx's wife now, the new mistress of the Cardone Ranch. Surely I will assume part of running the house?"

"That isn't necessary, Cal; Salina can handle everything. You don't need to slave here when we have an excellent housekeeper and cook. Why don't you spend your time re-doing the bedrooms? You could also use some new clothes. It's the custom to visit the neighbors and get better acquainted, to invite them over occasionally for dinner."

"You make it sound as if I'm to be a hostess and decoration around here," she jested cunningly. "I should learn how to run the house, Rankin. What if Salina got sick or left? I would be lost; I hardly know where to find anything," she reasoned logically for his reaction. She waited for Rankin to think up a good excuse.

"We could make do for a few days if she took ill. But why would Salina leave? She loves it here."

"She's a young and pretty woman, Rankin. She might find someone to marry. If so, she would want her own home and family."

"Salina marry?" he mocked playfully. "That girl's too wild; she likes too many men to settle for one. She doesn't strike me as the wifey, motherly type. Is there some problem between you two? Do you want her to leave?" A look of concern washed over his face.

"That isn't what I meant, Rankin. I don't want to take her place; I doubt I could run this house alone. I haven't had any experience. I just wanted to help out and learn everything. That is the custom for a wife, isn't it?" She laughed softly to disarm him.

"Only if she isn't lucky and wealthy enough to have a servant. Salina's a feisty girl, Cal. She doesn't like anyone in her way. Could you wait a while before making your new role known to her? Let her get used to having you here. If she starts to feel unwanted or in your way, she might take offense and leave. As you said, you can't run this big house alone. Just give it some time," he coaxed.

"But she won't even let me help with little things, Rankin," she softly argued, her fears and doubts concealed from him. Besides Salina had been given plenty of time to get adjusted to her presence.

"She's just insecure right now, Cal. Your arrival and marriage have been shocks for her, big changes. She'll settle down. Just relax and be patient. Besides, you'll need your energy and rest if a baby comes along," he hinted, grinning wistfully.

A baby, Calinda mentally sneered. *How can I get with child when my husband isn't around enough to make love to me!* "If it will cause dissension, I'll do as you say. But I'll need something to occupy my time and hands."

"There'll be plenty of work when Lynx comes home."

Calinda wanted to scoff, but what about until then? She didn't. "I suppose so. Goodnight, Rankin," she said in a muffled voice.

Leaning against the wall outside the open double-doors, Salina smiled to herself. She stealthily made her way to her room, concluding Rankin had played right into her devious scheme and put Calinda in a wary and uncomfortable position. That should teach Cal a thing or two!

When Calinda got to her room, she sat in the middle of her bed, ensnared by depression and worry. Evidently Salina had spoken accurately; that deduction infuriated and troubled her. Something was terribly wrong in this house and with the two men. Perhaps she shouldn't have married Lynx so hurriedly, so impulsively. It almost appeared they had more confidence in Salina, more affection for her, more fear of offending her than Calinda. She needed to unravel this mystery confronting her, but first she needed more evidence or clues. She fretted over this new situation. Just as she was solving one puzzle, a new one appeared; or was it merely unexpected pieces to the old one? It saddened and alarmed her to suspect she couldn't trust her new family.

To prove her new position, Calinda dressed for bed and went into Lynx's room. She would show that little witch! Let her do all the plotting and grinning she wished, but it wouldn't change things. After all, it was a natural arrangement, one which might irritate Salina. Hopefully that vixen would squirm in her bed downstairs, knowing Calinda was occupying Lynx's room and bed right above her. That should teach her a much needed lesson! Calinda wasn't normally a spiteful person; but something was troubling her deeply, something which she didn't quite recognize or comprehend.

Calinda spent a restless night in her love's room. His manly odor still lingered on the wrinkled sheets. The masculine decor loudly announced its intoxicating owner. She was haunted by his past presence and his tormenting absence. She fretted over the facts which she had discovered today. Her body hungered for his touch; her heart cried at his actions; her mind spun with the plaguing riddle.

Cal awoke early, the bed rumpled from her tossings. Having slept little, she was jittery and fatigued. After pulling on her clothes and brushing her hair, she closed the door and reluctantly went downstairs for coffee, relieved Salina wasn't around. When she returned to Lynx's room with the cup in hand, the door was standing open. She went inside to find the room empty. She stared at the sheets which showed the signs of their heated night of lovemaking and the vivid evidence of her restive night alone. Besieged with anger, she yanked off the sheets to change them.

"What are you doing now?" Salina shrieked at her from the doorway, startling Calinda. "Get out of here; I have work to do."

"If you aren't blind or simple-minded, Salina, it's obvious I'm changing the sheets," she quipped bitterly.

"That is my job. This is Lynx's room; I am responsible for cleaning it. Go back to your room where you belong," Salina commanded.

"This is my room, too! I'll take care of it from now on. As Lynx's wife, here is where I belong and plan to stay. Don't set foot in here again without my permission!" she shouted at the venomous girl.

"Did Lynx say you could move in here?" Salina brazenly pressed.

"He didn't have to! I'm his wife!" she stressed to vex Salina.

"He will be angry. He loves privacy."

"If he didn't want me around, he wouldn't have married me, idiot! I'm moving my things in here today," she sassily informed Salina, outraged and angered by the girl's audacious behavior.

"I wouldn't until he agrees," Salina told her.

"You don't honestly think we'll have separate rooms or that he'll kick me out of *our* bedroom?" Calinda sneered smugly.

"Do not forget I warned you. Even so, I am the housekeeper. You do not fool me, *puta*. If you are trying to hide the truth, you are *tarde*. Either you did not sleep with him, or it was not the first time. There is no virgin's blood staining them," she vulgarly announced.

Calinda was shocked by Salina's unforgivable language and actions. "How dare you, you bitch!" Calinda screamed at her.

Suddenly Rankin was standing in the doorway. "What's going on in here? Cal, I could hear you screaming all the way downstairs."

"Tell him," Salina wickedly suggested. "About the sheets," she maliciously added, her insinuation clear to Calinda.

Calinda mastered her poise and temper, knowing she had rashly stepped into Salina's trap. "I'm sorry for my outburst, Rankin. I'm just tired and edgy this morning; I didn't sleep well last night. Something I ate didn't sit well in my stomach. I suppose I'm still adjusting to Salina's spicy cooking. I was trying to *explain* to Salina that I prefer to take care of mine and Lynx's room, that I would like some privacy in here. I was annoyed when she barged in without knocking, then *ordered* me to leave and let her do my chores. I'm not accustomed to being waited on like a baby or invalid; I will perform my own personal chores. Salina feels I'm usurping her authority and position by changing the sheets on my own bed. I hardly feel it's important to quarrel over such a small task. When Salina disagreed, I asked her to stay out of my room, to never enter again without knocking or asking permission."

"Then why the shouting and screaming at her?" he asked, sure Cal wasn't telling him everything.

"She informed me it was Lynx's room and I would need his permission to move in here. Is that true, Rankin?" she challenged, her gaze piercing and frosty. Salina had forced this confrontation, so she could face the consequences. If they preferred to side with Salina, it was best to know immediately. Calinda's nerves were frayed and sensitive. At that moment, she didn't care what truth spilled forth; she didn't care what Salina exposed or alleged. Salina was trying to intimidate and torment her, and Calinda was pressed against the wall.

"I don't know what's gotten into you two women, but this argument is silly. Settle down, Cal. It was a simple mistake. Salina is used to coming and going at will; she probably forgot you would be in here. It sounds awfully unfriendly to order her to never enter this room. You're just tired. Why don't you let Salina clean up in here while you rest? If you demand your privacy, she won't come in here again. Salina knows Lynx's quirks; she assumed he would like to be asked about the move before it takes place," he stated diplomatically.

Calinda's gaze slipped over Rankin's shoulder to witness the taunting sneer on Salina's smug face. "I will take care of this room myself; I prefer total privacy in here. Surely with the entire house under her control, she has more than enough to keep her busy?" she stated distinctly, stressing most of her words, refusing to back down or soften her chosen stance. She would discover just how much power that little witch possessed!

Rankin sensed a deeper problem here than either of them revealed. He wondered how he should handle it. Was it simple female rivalry? "Of course you can have full control of your own room, Cal, if that's what you demand," he stated finally, using words which nettled Calinda. "But I do wish you would try harder to get along with Salina. She did a marvelous job with the wedding party and decorations yesterday. And she does work hard for us."

"I offered Salina a truce, Rankin; she doesn't want one. She seems intent on making me feel a stranger here, an undesirable one at that. She takes offense at everything I say or do; she constantly corrects or scolds me like a bratty child. I don't plan to spend my days walking on eggshells around her. If she dislikes me and my presence so much, perhaps she would be happier working elsewhere."

"*Senora* Cardone, surely you do not ask him to fire me?" Salina carefully wailed, phony tears coming to her cold eyes. "I was only trying to help you. Why do you despise me? The Cardones are like my family, the ranch like my home. Where would I go?"

"I have never despised you, Salina, but I do resent your hateful attitude and surly manner when no one else is around. I also dislike your phony politeness and friendliness when they're present. Your two faces are wearing thin. Either accept me here and be friends, or one of us should leave. If we can't be friends, at least stop being my enemy. I'm not taking any more of your insults and threats. If Rankin and Lynx hold more affection and respect for you than me, then perhaps you were right moments ago when you said I didn't belong here." Calinda glowered at Salina; *let her get out of those charges,* she decided.

Salina realized she had pushed too hard this soon; she slyly relented. "*Perdon* if I treated you badly. Perhaps I am overly tired and tensed from the extra work from the wedding. It will not happen again. I am a bossy and out-spoken person by nature; I did not mean to anger you. I will try not to be so sensitive to your help. Would you like for me to wash those sheets for you?" she sweetly inquired.

Calinda saw through her ploy to make her the villainess. She smiled and nodded. "If you mean it, Salina, that's fine with me. I'm even willing to meet you more than half way. I have tried to convince you I have no intentions of taking your place or encouraging you to leave. When Lynx comes home and we start a family, we'll all need your loyalty and help. Then, after the baby comes, I'll need to spend most of my time with our son, or daughter."

"*Bueno,* that's a start," Rankin complimented both women, sighing in relief, ignoring the seriousness of their conflict. "I'll see you two later; I have some work to finish."

After he left, Calinda reached over and gathered the sheets. Tossing them to Salina, she smiled confidently and stated, "Thanks for the help, Salina. Where are the clean linens kept?"

"I will bring them," the girl replied, observing the dauntless Calinda with new vision. It was clear this *cerdo* would get in the mud to battle if pressed. Salina knew she had underestimated Calinda's determination. She must be more careful in the future . . .

Calinda spent the afternoon moving into Lynx's room. She took possession of drawers unused or nearly empty. She placed Lynx's clothes in the drawers down the left side of his dresser, then placed hers in the drawers down the right side. Since there was little space available in his closet, she left most of her dresses and gowns in the other room. She hung her daily garments of shirts, vests, riding skirts, and pants in his room. If Salina dared to inspect the two rooms, she would find Calinda settled in with Lynx.

Cal was pleased with her accomplishments. But one small drawer near the top of the dresser kept attracting her attention. Since it was locked and she hadn't found a key, she assumed he kept private possessions inside. Her curiosity chewed on her all afternoon. What did it contain? Why was it locked? Secrets about Lynx? She couldn't break it open, so its secrets remained hidden.

For the next few days, Calinda and Salina were on their best behavior. They were polite around Rankin, but avoided each other when he wasn't present. Calinda found things outside to occupy herself, trying to keep out of the path of Salina and her baleful tongue. Rankin foolishly believed things were going fine between them.

But Calinda was determined to reveal poise and confidence. If Salina got to her, she didn't let it show. The same was true with Salina. If Calinda wanted to perform some household chore, she would cunningly wheedle in front of Rankin, compelling Salina to comply. Too, Calinda furtively observed everything, learning more and more about the house, watching Rankin and Salina.

Calinda would take advantage of Salina's occasional absences. She would practice her cooking skills, but wisely give the food or treats to the working hands. Sometimes she would entertain the men with tales of England or the East, or read stories to them, or play games with them. The men came to appreciate and accept her company. She quickly realized she was winning them over with her kindness and charms. As she worked around the ranch, the hands noticed how her skills increased. She was always willing to take on or share in any chore, no matter how difficult or dirty, gaining her their respect and friendship.

A week had passed without even a note or telegram from Lynx. Calinda pretended not to notice, but it pained her deeply to be ignored or taken for granted this quickly. She had gradually learned to sleep peacefully alone in the new room.

When Lynx was mentioned, Calinda exposed her loneliness and disappointment to Rankin, but concealed her vexation. She didn't challenge Rankin's explanations or excuses, but Lynx wouldn't have the same leniency when he came home! As the days passed, she came to realize that Rankin was caught in the middle of her dispute with Salina and her baffling husband. She couldn't hold him responsible for either, so she gradually relented and pressed for a closer relationship. He had suffered greatly in the past and she didn't want to cause him more pain.

Rankin instantly warmed to her overtures of friendship. As their bond tightened, Salina became more secretive with her hatred and picking at Calinda. The early days of July were dry and hot. Many times an afternoon swim became part of Calinda and Rankin's schedule. When weather-confined to the house, they played billiards, talked, read, and played cards.

As Rankin relaxed and opened up his emotions to Calinda, a mellowing took place. As Calinda spent more time with him and observed him, she was disarmed by his warmth and admiration. She chided herself for past suspicions, not allowing any new ones to take hold in her mind. She was content, except for her husband's absence. Clearly his father felt a loyalty to Lynx which he couldn't break or betray. She finally accepted that facet of Rankin. It was apparent Rankin was extremely fond of her and enjoyed her companionship.

But each time Calinda dusted her room, the locked drawer fascinated her. To date, Lynx had been gone for nine days, nine days without contacting her, nine days of Salina pointing out that fact. Did the drawer contain some secret to Lynx's work or character? He would be furious if she opened it. And she knew how.

During a stifling night when a violent thunderstorm prevented sleep, Calinda's curiosity was overwhelming. She took a curved knitting needle and jimmied the lock. She slowly opened the drawer and peeked inside. She was surprised to find it contained boyhood treasures: a watch, a rabbit's foot, two sets of snake rattles, a raccoon tail, the ear of a mountain lion, an Apache necklace, a rusty knife, a child's toy, and other such objects. Why would he keep a drawer with such innocent souvenirs locked? Her gaze touched on two objects of interest, the watch and two jealousy-inspiring lacy handkerchiefs.

Cal lifted the gold watch and studied it. It was rather large for a boy and clearly expensive. She pressed the button to flip open the cover. Her gaze widened as she read the incredible inscription:

"To Lynx, a son I never had. Brax. 8/17/72"

Her hand trembled as she stared at the portentous wording and the date. It didn't make sense. If her father had loved Lynx that much, how could he leave soon after that date? When and how had such affection turned to bitterness and hate? Why did Lynx despise and resent Brax so much, when Brax had clearly adored him? An irrepressible and unbidden pang of envy assailed her. A parting memento?

Cal returned the tormenting watch to the drawer, then reached for the lacy kerchiefs, monogrammed with lovely "LC." As she lifted them in her quavering grip, another object caught her eye. "No, it can't be," she murmured. She threw the kerchiefs aside to pick up the mesmerizing item. She examined it closely, then opened it. Tears slipped down her cheeks; her heart drummed wildly. How could this be possible? Why would he keep it from her? How had he gotten it?

Her mind was spinning with confusion and anguish. Cal stared at the tiny golden circle: her precious locket, the one stolen during the stage hold-up, the one which had cost the guard his life . . .

—— *Chapter 12* ——

❧

CALINDA MINDLESSLY WALKED to the bed and sat down, her brain too stunned to think about anything or anyone, too dazed to ponder this monumental discovery and its meaning. She didn't want to think about this devastating mystery; it was too painful.

She blankly stared at the locket for a lengthy span. Her finger traced the delicate artwork; her misty eyes roamed the smiling couple—her parents—who stared unseeingly back at her. When she could no longer shut out her accusatory questions, she asked herself why Lynx would do this cruel thing to her. She had told him about the stolen locket; she had related its precious meaning, her anguish at its theft. Even if he had come upon it accidentally, he must have known it was hers; he must have recognized her father's picture inside. Why had he hidden it from her? Why hadn't he returned it?

Why? Why? Why? the words echoed across her warring mind, as loudly and ominously as the rolling thunder outside. How could he possibly explain this foul deed? Did she mean so little to him? Why had he married her, if he was going to treat her so vilely? Where was he? What was he doing? With whom? The mystery surrounding Lynx grew larger and darker. Calinda realized how very little she knew about her husband. Who and what was the man who held her soul in his grasp? His secrecy and reputation stormed her tortured mind. Surely he was not an outlaw?

Cal wept until exhaustion claimed her, to free her from her agony and doubts. By the time the sun rose, Calinda was plagued by relentless suspicions. Lynx had been gone two weeks. This demanding enigma was rapidly becoming a cruel maze. Each time she pursued a liberating path, she found herself facing an obscuring hedge, more lost and confused than before. When would she escape and what solution would greet her senses?

Calinda felt she must get away from the ranch for a while, away from Rankin and away from Salina and away from her torment. She dressed in a tawny pantsskirt, a dark blue shirt with colorful designs in sunny yellow, and western boots. She snatched her felt hat off the rack and headed downstairs. Salina had better watch her step and tongue today; Calinda was ready to explode from tension and fatigue.

Fortunately, Salina was busy in the water-shed with the laundry. Calinda walked to Rankin's office and knocked. Rankin opened the door and smiled. Calinda only faintly returned it, her thoughts vividly somewhere else. She told

Rankin she was riding into town to shop for the day. She requested that Charlie go along as her driver and escort. Naturally Rankin agreed.

Calinda left immediately, without breakfast or coffee. She would eat in town while she settled her nerves. Charlie hitched up the carriage and helped her up into it. They headed off toward town. An unseen rider quickly mounted up and rode off swiftly behind them.

Charlie tried to make conversation with Calinda, but she was quiet and distracted. As they rounded a bend in the road, Charlie hastily reined in the horse. He grumbled at the fallen tree which was blocking the road. It would be impossible to go around it. He told Calinda he would move it aside, then jumped down to do so.

From the nearby rocks and trees, masked riders surged forth and surrounded them, their guns pointing at Charlie and Calinda. Charlie wisely didn't go for his weapon, seeing they were out-numbered. "Take our money and ride off," he suggested to the outlaws. "If Mrs. Cardone is injured, you'll be chased to hell and back," he warned.

"We know who she is," one desperado announced. "Take her," he gave the order to a mounted outlaw near her side of the carriage. "The Cardones will pay plenty to get her back safely."

A kidnapping? Her, for ransom? Leave with these vicious men? As the man reached for Calinda, she carelessly pulled her gun from its holster to defend herself. Taken off-guard, the outlaw responded with a blow from his pistol to her forehead. She screamed and lost consciousness, falling sideways on the padded seat.

Charlie moved to aid her, but the leader warned, "Move one muscle and you'll die. Take Cardone a message. Tell him I want $50,000 for her return. I'll give him three days to come up with the money. Monday, I'll send him a message where to deliver the money. If he comes after us, we'll put a neat little bullet hole through her head."

"But Lynx isn't home. We don't expect him back for another few weeks," Charlie fearfully told him.

"Then old man Cardone can handle it for him," the leader snarled.

"But that's a lot of money to gather in three days," Charlie argued, dreading the coldness in these men.

"Then I suggest he get his ass to town before the bank closes today," the leader responded casually. "Take her," he shouted again.

Charlie watched the gang ride off with Calinda. He jumped into the carriage and raced wildly for the ranch to inform Rankin. He jumped off the carriage and ran into the house, yelling for his boss.

Rankin hurried out of his office to see what the commotion was. Charlie babbled almost incoherently. Rankin hushed him, then told him to slow down and speak clearly. His eyes widened and his face paled as the daring tale came forth. "Get the sheriff! They won't get away with this outrage! The posse will hunt them down and shoot 'em!"

"That won't do no good, boss. They could be anywhere by now. You'd best try to get the money before they contact you. They mean business, boss. They'll kill her for sure," Charlie wailed anxiously.

Before Salina could come inside and learn the truth, Charlie and Rankin were heading for town at breakneck speed. Rankin went to the bank first, to arrange for the money. He told the banker he would return shortly, after he sent Lynx a telegram in care of Jones.

Three hours later, Rankin was sitting in his office, worrying and praying. He had the money, and the telegram was on its way to Lynx, if Jones could locate him. All he could do now was wait and hope.

Calinda gradually struggled to seek freedom from the tormenting black void which had imprisoned her for an hour as the outlaws galloped toward their hideout. Nearing it, on rugged terrain, the men had slowed their pace to a leisurely ride. Her head was throbbing, her body was being shaken to pieces. She had just enough wit about her to remain still and silent until she could clear her dazed head. She comprehended her dangerous situation and uncomfortable position: she was lying on her stomach across a man's thighs, the man who had kidnapped her. The rocking motion came from the steady walking of his horse. Her injured head and bruised ribs aggravated this humiliating and painful position. She dared not attempt any struggle until she could think of a promising escape plan. Cal was not amused by the thought which flashed across her mind; during the last robbery and knock on the head, the bandits had stolen her possessions, not her. She endured this agony and listened as they talked freely, assuming her still out to the world and their words.

"You know Cardone's gonna come after us. Taking his woman and demanding $50,000 won't sit well. You think it was smart to strike on him? He ain't one to tangle with," one man remarked.

"Don't matter. He'll never find us in here. Farley's been covering our trail. After we get the money, we'll lay low for a while," the leader replied. "After we split the money equally, we'll have ten thousand dollars apiece," he added, telling Calinda there were five of them to defeat. Impossible.

"What about that payroll stage to Abilene? We still gonna take it Friday? Oggie said it leaves Fort Worth about ten."

"Yep. We'll strike right after she slows to cross Big Sandy Creek. That ought to give us plenty of money for a long rest."

"Sandy Creek?" the man shrieked. "Ain't that too close to Rangers? They'll be madder'n a dogie caught in a barbed fence!"

"That's why it'll work; who would suspect a robbery in that area?" the leader boasted, chuckling with pride in himself.

"Did Little Red scout it out good?" a third man asked.

"Yep. Won't be no problem," he smugly stated.

"Little Red know about that bundle in your lap?" he teased.

Cole Stevens glanced down at Calinda, eyes slipping over her shapely figure and striking hair. "Little Red suggested it. But Red didn't want her harmed, unless we can't avoid it." He winked at his men.

"Harmed, or touched?" the second outlaw teased, then burst into lecherous laughter, the others quickly joining in with amusement.

"Neither," Cole sneered, as if Little Red had anything to say about his gang or plans. But Little Red did offer certain advantages.

"The way Little Red handles that six-shooter and fiery temper, I wouldn't challenge either. I wonder if all redheads are hot-blooded."

Little Red's britches are getting a mite too big. It's time for the boss to cut 'em down to size, he mused to himself, growing weary of Red's bossy air and his men's tauntings. Red could never be a leader!

Calinda almost sighed in relief. Whoever this Little Red was, she prayed he held the power to control these crude men. For certain, it wouldn't do for her to antagonize them, especially Little Red.

As the outlaws began joking about their daring attack and the hopeful results of the kidnapping, the whole story unfolded for Calinda. Could Rankin get his hands on that much money? Would they truly release her afterwards? Where was her husband? If he had been home, this danger wouldn't have befallen her!

Calinda couldn't ride in this position any longer. She felt it best to alert them to her arousal. She began to moan softly and move gingerly. The leader halted his animal to lift her into a sitting position before him. Her hand went to her temple and she winced with pain. She opened her eyes and looked around. "Where am I? What happened?"

Cal pretended to be too weak and fuzzy headed to struggle for escape. She glanced around, observing four men with masks. "Who are you? Why did you kidnap me? And hurt me?" she asked sluggishly.

Cole Stevens related the facts she needed to know, prompting her to act stunned and alarmed. She gave the same arguments Charlie had given to them; Cole laughingly debated each one. "Just be a good girl, and you won't get hurt. Before you know it, you'll be at home."

"Surely you wouldn't kill an innocent woman for money?"

"Nope. But we will if we don't get it," Cole said to frighten her.

They rode on for another thirty minutes, weaving around tall boulders and scattered trees until a wooden shack came into view. Cole reined in and dismounted, then lifted her down. To carry off her part, Calinda swayed precariously and grabbed his right arm to steady herself.

To her amazement, the leader said, "Sorry about that, you shouldn't have gone for a gun. You've got a nasty cut and bruise."

"What did you expect me to do when you attacked us? How was I to know you didn't plan to rob and murder us? My head aches. May I have some water?" she asked politely, drawing on her manners to disarm him and force him to realize she was a lady. He was a confusing, complex man. He was cruel and cold; yet, his eyes and voice could wax warm and gentle at times. Could this man murder her? Was he second in command to this absent Little Red?

"Let's get you inside. I'll see if I can round up a bandage. I'll warn you now, Calinda Cardone; don't try anything foolish. If you do—" He halted dramatically to imply a deadly warning, then left the ominous threat hanging in mid-air.

Calinda was taken inside, through a large room, and into a smaller one. After she was given water, she thanked the carefree leader. He smeared something on her wound, saying it was an Indian remedy, then bound her head with a bandanna. He tied her wrists securely, then told her to lie down and rest.

When she asked his name, he laughed merrily and stated, "You don't want to know that, little lady. If you learn who we are, then we can't free you later. Don't get up or leave this room. Savvy?"

Cal nodded and thanked him for his assistance, inwardly wanting to spew forth threats and curses on his sable head. She knew it was best to play the delicate and gentle-minded beauty to inspire any hope of escape. She couldn't say how Rankin would respond to this danger. Had he contacted Lynx? Even so, Lynx could never find her. She could only pray for the Cardones' cooperation, or a daring escape.

The door was pulled to an angle which allowed the men to remove their masks without Calinda seeing their faces. She dared not risk learning their identities, just in case the leader kept his word.

Later, she was given food and water by the masked leader. After she ate, she was bound again. Her headache was lessening by the hour. She closed her eyes and fell asleep.

When Cole came to check on her, her steady respiration told him she was resting peacefully. He stood beside the bunk for a time, staring down at her. She was very beautiful. Her skin was fair and unblemished. Her hair sparkled like a roaring blaze. Her eyes were as green as spring grass. Her lips were the kind which drew a man's eyes to them. The tip of her dainty nose turned up slightly. Her voice reminded him of sweet music. How had Cardone captured this fragile creature? Why had this lady married a man like Lynx Cardone? Maybe Little Red was right: no family, no money, no home. But Little Red was a thorn in the side to be removed very soon.

Cole dashed aside tuggings of fierce desire for her. For some crazy reason, he liked her. She was spunky and bright. But if he laid one hand or lip on her, Little Red would punish her for tempting him. The minute his back was turned, Little Red would be maliciously handing her over to his men for their pleasure.

Cole wondered if it was time to send Little Red down another path, a separate one from him and his men. Little Red had proved valuable to his gang, but was getting cocky and demanding. Cole didn't like anybody infringing on his leadership and manhood. If Little Red could be dumped before this job was over, perhaps . . .

He shrugged his shoulders and left the room, closing the door. He and his men played poker and drank until late, then turned in.

In Dallas Saturday morning, Major Jones sent one of his Rangers to fetch Lynx at the hotel. He was pacing the floor when Lynx arrived, an uncommon action for the steely-nerved and calculating man. Lynx noted this curious behavior, then asked, "Trouble, sir? I was packing to leave for Waco. I shouldn't be far behind Bass and his men."

Jones halted his wanderings to meet Lynx's steady and probing gaze. "You recall that suspicious incident with your wife recently?"

"You mean that phony letter and Lampasas?" Lynx asked. Why was Jones bringing up that matter again? They hadn't been able to come up with any logical explanation or additional clues. Since Lynx had left home, he hadn't even been allowed to write or telegram Cal, to avoid giving away his location. Jones had hinted she couldn't come chasing after him if she didn't know where to look.

"Evidently someone did lure her there, but not to find Braxton."

"You know something I don't," Lynx hinted warily.

"A telegram came for me last night, but wasn't delivered until this morning. Your father wanted me to locate you and send you home. Does that mean he knows all about you?" Jones questioned calmly.

Lynx sighed heavily and nodded, giving his reasons for confiding in Rankin. "Is it that important, sir? He'll keep it to himself."

"I'm not worried about Rankin, Lynx. It's your wife."

"My wife? What has she got to do with this? Father wouldn't tell Cal anything about me and my work," he said confidently.

"Calinda's been abducted by outlaws. They want $50,000 by Monday. Do we let your father handle the ransom? Or do we send you home?" Jones waited patiently for that fact to settle in.

That news was like a perfectly landed blow to a tender gut. Fear, alarm, and fury attacked Lynx. "Was she injured? Do they know who's involved?" he inquired tensely.

"No. You think you should take care of it?" Jones asked.

Lynx almost shouted, Are you loco! Nothing could stop him! "Even if Father pays the ransom, they might not release her. I've got to head home, sir. Maybe I can ferret out the snakes. If she's harmed, I'll track them down and kill 'em," he vowed coldly. "I'll head for Waco the moment she's home safe."

By noon, Lynx was riding hard for the ranch, fear his companion. He halted only once: to eat, flex his muscles, and rest Star. He fretted over who had taken Calinda and worried if she was all right. No doubt she was as furious with him right now as she was terrified. As he drank from his canteen, his keen senses heard a branch snap behind him. In one flash of action, the canteen was tossed aside, he had whirled around, and his gun was in his hand. A challenging bullet whizzed past his shoulder; his gun quickly answered.

The man howled and struck the ground, then writhed in pain. Lynx waited but a moment before going over to the fallen back-shooter. When Lynx shot or killed a man, he wanted to know who and why. He searched the man's pockets, finding a handwritten note. He read it, then stuffed it into his pocket. He would deal with the contents of the note later; right now, time was short and imperative.

Blood was flowing from a chest wound on the cut-throat. The man was groaning in pain, pleading for help from the very man he had tried to murder. "You'll get help after you tell me who you are and why you tried to kill me," Lynx snarled. "If not, I'll stand here and watch you bleed to death."

Lynx's nerves were taut as he heard the man relate his tale. At one point, the man decided to keep silent. Lynx booted him in the ribs, demanding his answers. The man grimaced in agony, but stubbornly refused, appearing afraid to reply. Lynx pulled his large knife and declared he was going to give the man a few more wounds to increase his bleeding and suffering.

The man related the facts, sensing Lynx meant what he said. By then, the man had lost a great deal of blood and was very weak. Lynx was all too aware of his fleeting time. Should he leave this filth here to die, or should he carry him back to

Fort Worth to the doctor? If he patched him up and left him, the man might miraculously survive. If he took the time to find the doctor or sheriff, it could be too late for Calinda. The man probably wouldn't survive the ride.

Lynx withdrew his father's urgent message and read it again. This was late Saturday; Calinda had been taken yesterday morning. The ransom was due Monday—that gave him one day to ease his father's worries, to get the whole story from him, and to save Cal. Lynx wasn't usually a man without mercy or sympathy, but too much was at stake. This man had tried to kill him, just to rob him. His decision was unavoidable. He gritted his teeth and mounted up, leaving the outlaw to die there.

As he rapidly covered the dusty trail, he kept thinking about the first time he had met Calinda Braxton Cardone. Clad in a red gown, she had appeared part woman and part child. Even when he sought every chance to steal even a blissful moment with her, his duty was always coming between them, tearing them apart without even an acceptable excuse. From that first meeting, he had instinctively known he must change drastically to win her. A gunslinger and a lady, the words flashed across his mind. He grimaced in wry humor; it was as if he were being compelled to surrender his silver spurs to gain a lady who had innocently worn red satin on a fateful night. Was the trade-off worth it? Yes . . .

As Lynx raced to rescue his love, he was consumed by worry, fear, and anger. He kept thinking, *what will I do if anything happens to her?* His tormented mind refused to even guess.

Chapter 13

CALINDA WAS SLIPPING in and out of light slumber when she sensed someone near her. She forced her mind to clear and her eyes to open. The bandit leader was propped lazily against the wall near the bunk, one ankle crossed over the other, his arms folded over his chest, his mask securely in place over the bridge of his nose. His sparkling sapphire eyes told her he was grinning beneath that red bandanna.

Cole shoved himself up and walked toward her. Calinda shrank away from his approach. He saw her fearful response and halted. "No need to be afraid, Calinda," he coaxed playfully.

"You kidnap me, terrify me, threaten to kill me—then say I shouldn't be afraid?" Cal disputed skeptically, her gaze detecting a lean and hard physique beneath those dusty and snug garments.

"I didn't know if I should let you sleep or wake you up for breakfast. Hungry?" he asked, hunkering down beside the bunk.

Calinda's eyes flew to the window. The sun was shining brightly. It was morning! "What time is it?" she asked, sitting up.

"About ten, Why, are you going some place?" Cole teased.

"That's very amusing," she scoffed angrily, glaring at him.

He chuckled. "Don't worry. You'll be leaving me soon."

Calinda wondered if that was disappointment in his voice. "Have the Cardones agreed to pay the ransom?" she asked, sounding doubtful.

"I gave them until Monday noon to get the money together."

"If they refuse?" Cal speculated, eyes misty.

"Why would they refuse?" Cole reasoned confidently.

"They might. That's a great deal of money, and they haven't known me very long," she answered.

"From where I stand, you're worth it," he said too warmly.

"Maybe not to them," Cal disagreed. "If they refuse, will you really kill me?" she questioned seriously.

Cole's eyes narrowed in deep thought. "I suspect you married Cardone for protection and security. But why did he marry you?" he boldly questioned, watching her startled reaction which implied, how did you know that? Cole was intrigued when she actually blushed.

"I married him because he asked me. Why else?" she sneered.

"But why did he ask you?" Cole pressed the proud beauty.

"You abducted me for money, not my life story," Cal parried his too nosy question. "When will you know if they accept your terms?"

"One of my men will bring their answer tomorrow night. If all's set, they'll be told where to leave it Monday. I've got two . . . men watching the trail and town to prevent a double-cross," Cole responded. "You're afraid they won't pay, aren't you?" he challenged.

Her flush deepened. "If they can get the money, they will," Cal stated, but her tone and look belied her words and confidence.

"Where's Lynx? When's he expected home?" Cole demanded, his tone insinuating close knowledge of her mysterious husband.

Calinda looked out the window. "I don't know. His father said he was away on business. Could you open the window? It's stuffy."

"What kind of business?" Cole continued, pushing up the sash.

"Something about buying new bulls," she answered. "Do you know Lynx?" she abruptly inquired.

"How long has he been away?" Cole asked another question, to her dismay and rising tension. "When is he returning?"

"He left the day after we . . ." She caught her foolish slip and changed it, "after he settled some business at the ranch."

"You mean, the day after you married him, don't you?" he astutely challenged, his curiosity piqued. "Some marriage," he sneered.

Calinda wanted to hide when her face went crimson. "I need to be excused. May I go to the little house?" she asked.

Cole gazed at her turned head. Why would a man leave his bride of one day, if he loved her? Could Lynx Cardone love any woman? It wasn't a secret he normally avoided them. Maybe his father had selected this girl for a respectable wife. Maybe old man Cardone had used some hold over Lynx to force their marriage. If so, Cardone might pay for her return, but Lynx might not . . . Perhaps it was best Lynx wasn't home. Just maybe those two had trapped this girl. That could explain her fear of them not paying. If Lynx refused to meet his terms . . . No, Lynx wouldn't let anyone take his property, whether he valued it or not. This sweet little game would serve two purposes: victory over Lynx and plenty of money. He smiled . . .

Cole went to the door and told his men to cover their faces. He came back and untied Calinda. She swung her legs off the bunk and rubbed her chafed wrists, remarking on the rope's excessive tightness. Cal followed him to the wooden out-house. After warning her against recklessness, Cole stopped a short distance away. As she relieved herself, Calinda peeked out cracks in all directions to assess her surroundings. Her predicament didn't look good.

She returned to Cole's side, wincing as she tested the injury on her forehead. "Still hurt?" he inquired as if honestly concerned.

"It throbs when I move. Why am I so dizzy and weak?" Cal asked, setting her plans into motion. If they felt she was disabled, they wouldn't expect her imminent actions.

"He cracked you pretty hard. Let me look at it," he said, removing the bandage. Cole studied the swollen area which presented a small cut, reddish blue coloring, and dried blood. As his gaze lowered to hers, his hands propped on his hips. "Should heal nicely."

Her right hand lifted slightly, then went back to lock with the other one. "Why didn't you jerk off my mask, Calinda?"

She blushed and lowered her head. Cole grasped her chin and lifted her head, drilling his blue eyes into her green ones. "Well?"

"I remembered what you said about surviving if I couldn't identify you and your men. I was just wondering how an outlaw looks." To disarm him and win his sympathy, she related the stage hold-up incident.

"And you believed me?" Cole queried strangely, eyes alert.

"I don't have any choice. I pray you'll keep your word."

"I will, Calinda, unless you force my hand."

"What if . . ." Again she halted. "I'm hungry. Do prisoners get to eat around here?"

Cole guided her back to her confining room, then brought the food prepared by one of his men. Cole didn't like the way she was getting to him, so he left the room. As Calinda ate her meal, she pondered this perplexing and dangerous episode. She had better keep quiet and remote from now on; that bandit leader was getting too friendly. He was mistaking her desperate attempts to save her life as flirtation. She had unwisely thought a man would have more trouble slaying a friend or someone he had gotten to know. But her scheme might go awry. He was developing a gleam in his eyes which troubled and frightened her. He wasn't feeling sorry for her; he was feeling desire for her. When would this Little Red arrive and prevent problems?

Supper came and went, with dusk on its tail. As the hours slowly crawled by,

Calinda became panicky. Her fate would be settled in less than two days. She had already decided she wouldn't plead for her life, nor offer this outlaw any bribe to spare it. If he attempted anything before killing her, she would fight him to the death.

What troubled Cal most were the two men in the next room. They were becoming restless and rowdy. They had been playing cards and drinking for most of the afternoon. Several times their leader had entered her prison to chat with her, annoyed when she rebuffed his company and conversation. The last time, two hours ago, he had snarled, "Don't talk, little lady, some things don't require it," then stalked out and slammed the door.

Suddenly the door opened slightly and the bandit returned. Alarm filled Calinda when he strolled over to the bed and sat down. He stared down at her, the expression in his eyes concealed by the darkness in the room. Her face was illuminated by the light from the other room, her fear plain to Cole. "What happened to all that trust, Calinda?" he asked, his voice blurred by whiskey. "Why this sudden freeze?"

Tears glimmered on her lashes. "Please go away," she whispered.

"What if I say no?" Cole fenced, watching her terror mount. He shifted to light the lantern on the table by the bed.

"You promised . . . to return me safely," Cal reminded him.

"Did I say that, Callie?" he taunted mischievously, trailing the back of his rough hand over her smooth cheek.

"Yes, you did," she replied, her voice strengthening.

As he casually let his finger drift over her quivering lips, Cole murmured, "Well, I tell you what, Calinda Cardone; if I get that money, I'll set you free just the way I found you. If not . . ."

Cole placed his finger against the throbbing pulse on her neck. When Cal tried to move away from his touch, he chuckled, placing his hands on the bed on either side of her, causing him to bend forward. "You know, you're a very beautiful woman, the best I've seen. If I don't get paid with money, I might think of some other way for you to buy your freedom. We've still got another whole day to become good friends." His meaning needed no further clarification.

"Don't waste your time or energy," she vowed softly, her voice quavering, her respiration erratic. "I'm not a saloon harlot."

"Your life's worth lots of Cardone money, but nothing else? I'm sure my men will demand some kind of reward if the Cardones refuse payment. Course, my men don't bother good friends of mine. Think we can become good friends, Callie?" he asked, stressing "good."

"I'll let you know at noon Monday," she bluffed him to stall for time, to keep him away from her as long as possible. She recalled the two missing men, knowing she would have five to deal with on Monday.

He chuckled smugly. "Then we'll talk at noon, Callie," he surprisingly agreed. He stood up, stretched, and headed for the door. At it, he hesitated to say, "I'll leave this open, just in case you get a wild notion to test my patience and temper. But I hope you won't."

Cal snuggled her face into the pillow, tears rolling down her cheeks to be absorbed there. She would never come out of this alive. Lynx probably thought she had been raped and abused by now. He wouldn't want a ravished wife back in his arms. Even if they did pay for her release, it would never be the same between them. They had begun their relationship with a stormy breach between them, one which had widened with time.

Calinda kept remembering that odd letter; it couldn't have been from this gang, for she hadn't been a Cardone then. She reflected bitterly on the locket and Lynx's mysterious life. How could they ever find love, happiness, and trust when he kept so much of his existence and self from her? Maybe she was just a pleasing convenience.

Her gaze aimlessly shifted to the window, then froze abruptly, her lips parting as she inhaled in astonishment. Lynx! He lifted a finger to his lips and shook his tawny head to signal her to silence. Was she dreaming? Hallucinating? How had he found her in this den of outlaws? What if they caught him? Her warring emotions ceased to battle within her; her painful reflections halted their keen study. Resentment and anger fled as she stared at the man so near to her.

Cal lifted her head to glance at the door into the other room. It was standing ajar, but she couldn't see into the next room. Her gaze went back to Lynx outside the window. His features were taut with determination and fury. He smiled encouragingly, white teeth gleaming at her. He examined the window, deciding it would be noisy to open. His gaze went to the lantern and analyzed its revealing danger. Calinda watched him closely, comprehending his two obstacles. Lynx suddenly moved aside, removing himself from her view. Why did he go away, she fearfully wondered.

Cal had her answer when the leader strolled into the room. "Want any coffee?" Cole asked moodily.

"No, thank you," Cal responded faintly. "I'm tired, and my head is pounding again. Could you lift the window for some fresh air; it's smothering in here."

"And let you get hurt sneaking out during the night?" he teased.

"If you tie my hands to the bedpost, I couldn't possibly escape," she suggested sassily. "Besides, I'm not stupid. You would kill me."

Cole came over and tore a long strip from the dirty sheet. He took her hands and secured them to the post. "That should hold you."

Cole lifted the window sash and propped it open. When he leaned forward and gazed outside, she nearly fainted. He inhaled the muggy air, then came back to her side. "Anything else, Callie?"

"Will you put out the lantern? I want to go to sleep."

"You're just full of demands tonight," he murmured. "One good deed without a nice reward is enough. Now, if I was to get a little kiss, I'd be glad to help you."

Calinda tensed in dread. If she didn't kiss him, he wouldn't douse the lantern to safeguard Lynx's rescue attempt. If she did, he might get aroused and demand more than a mere kiss. How could he be so nice, then turn so mean? One minute he was gentle, the next savage. What to do? If he tried to attack her, surely Lynx would try to stop him. If Lynx tried to stop him, there were other armed men to confront. They could both be killed. She hesitated in doubt.

"What's wrong, Callie? Don't trust me to have self-control?"

"You'll give me your word of honor, just one kiss?"

"My word of honor, just one kiss, until Monday," he added.

"But if you remove your mask to kiss me, I'll see your face."

"Not with the lantern out. Well?" he eagerly pressed.

"All right," she reluctantly acquiesced, wondering how Lynx felt about this necessary action.

Cole doused the light, then lifted his mask when he was near her lips. His mouth seared over hers in a demanding and greedy kiss, to which she didn't resist or respond. Cole forced her lips apart, fusing his mouth to hers as if to devour her. He made the kiss last as long as possible. When his mouth left hers, he taunted, "That wasn't a fair deal; a kiss can't be one-sided."

She replied angrily, "You gave your word. You didn't say I had to respond."

"I said, if I was to get a little kiss, not take one," he argued.

"That wasn't a little kiss," she snapped, feeling duped. "You're trying to trick me; I shouldn't have trusted you."

"Maybe you're right. But Monday at noon, make sure you understand my meaning," Cole warned. If he wanted her to be willing, he couldn't press her tonight. Anyway, he had all day Sunday to work on her resistance and hopes. He walked out, whistling.

Calinda's gaze went from the nearly closed door to the darkened lantern, to the open window. She had done all she could; the rest was up to Lynx. Her heart was racing happily; he had tracked them down and was going to rescue her, just as in Lampasas. Funny, every time she was in trouble or danger, Lynx inexplicably showed up to help. She waited; he didn't appear at the window. Had they seen him and captured him? She trembled with growing suspense. She fretted over the perilous full moon which might expose his presence.

A towering shadow moved before the window. She held her breath as Lynx stealthily crawled through it. He stood up and paused, cocking his head to listen for a minute. Her eyes grew large with astonishment; he wasn't wearing his guns or boots. If that outlaw entered the room again, Lynx would be helpless! Was he so self-assured that he felt he could lick three men with his bare hands?

Lynx gingerly moved forward, careful of creaking boards. He bent over her, placing his lips to her left ear. He whispered, "Don't talk or move, Callie. I'm getting you out of here."

Lynx withdrew a large blade from his waist, then severed the ropes binding her wrists. Cal wanted to throw herself in his strong arms, but didn't dare move as ordered. He leaned over again, saying, "Be still while I take off your boots."

Lynx removed one, then the other, bobbling the second one before he had control of it. She tensed in alarm, then relaxed. The intoxicating rogue grinned playfully, as if this was a game. He scooped her up in his arms and set her down near the window. Her clever love reached for some blankets and fashioned them into a body-like roll on the bed. He placed her boots in a position which indicated she was lying on her side. He covered the handmade dummy with the dirty sheet, except for the boots which were peeking out near the foot. He took her hat and placed it where her head should be. He stepped back to eye his creation. In the darkness, it should pass for Calinda's frame.

Lynx grinned in satisfaction. That should give them time to escape, if Cole Stevens didn't try to enchant her again tonight! Naturally Lynx had recognized the man's voice. When Calinda was out of danger, he would take care of Stevens and his reckless gang.

Lynx warned her again in silence, then slid her out the window. Cal waited anxiously as he agilely eased over the sill and joined her. He caught her head between his hands and pulled it forward. She was piqued when he didn't kiss her, but only whispered, "See those rocks over there?" He pointed to them and waited for her to nod. "Get behind them pronto, but don't make any noise. I'll stand guard. If I don't come right behind you, get the hell out of here fast."

Calinda flung her arms around his waist, briefly craving his comforting contact. Lynx hastily seized her arms and loosened her grip. He warned, "We don't have time for that, Cal. Get going."

After what she'd been through, Cal yearned for a moment of solace. It had been weeks since she had seen him and touched him. Cal was too distraught to consider their danger. At that time, all she could think about was the safety of his arms.

At her hesitation, he murmured into her ear, "If you don't get moving, we'll be caught and shot. I didn't risk my life for nothing."

Calinda jerked her hands from his brawny chest, then glared at him. She whirled and headed for the assigned hiding place, gritting her teeth as the sharp rock snipped at her socked feet. Lynx stepped behind the corner of the shack and waited there until she vanished from his sight. He stepped back to the window, then fished a small object from his pocket. He placed the tiny silver star he had removed from a broken pair of spurs on the windowsill where Cole would be sure to notice it. He reached behind a bush and lifted Farley's gunbelt, digging an impression of a small star into the scuffed leather, symbol of justice and the unknown Ranger. He hung it over the sill, then snatched up his own gunbelt and boots.

As quietly as possible, Lynx hurried to join the waiting Calinda. Once concealed by the large boulder, he dropped his boots to fasten on his gunbelt, tying a holster down to each muscled thigh. He pulled on his boots. He glanced at her and smiled broadly. "So far, so good, Callie. Let's move out before Cole realizes that isn't you in that bed."

"Cole? How could you know him with a mask?" She despised the suspicions which chewed viciously at her, inspiring rash anger.

"I recognized his voice when he was trying to seduce my wife. Don't worry; I'll repay him after you're home safe," he vowed coldly. "How's the head? Did they . . . hurt you, Cal?"

"Some scrapes and bruises, nothing serious," she replied. When his hand reached out to move aside her hair to check the injury, she twisted away from his touch and panted, "We don't have time for that! It's fine; just a little crack on the head. How did you find me?" she demanded, her voice exposing a strange note of accusation. "I'm surprised you took the time from your busy schedule. But I suppose a man like Lynx Cardone prefers to pay such debts with vengeful pride rather than money. No promising bulls for sale?" She had remembered all at once how he had deceived her. Was he an outlaw? What if he were killed or captured? How could she live without him? Fears and doubts clouded her reason and compelled her to strike out in fury and spite.

"What are you babbling about, woman? I think that lick on the skull is playing havoc with your senses. I've finished my work in Junction; we trapped some fence cutters and rustlers. I was heading home when a man tried to back-shoot me, one of Cole Stevens' men. That's how I learned about the kidnapping and your location."

"I see," she murmured skeptically. "What happened to that code of honor amongst thieves, to die in brave silence?"

"I told him I'd kill him if he didn't speak up and fast," he casually informed her, wondering at her frigid manner.

"How did you know he had anything to tell you?" she pressed.

"I'll explain everything later. We can't stand here jawing. Follow me," he commanded, then headed off into the scattered rocks.

Calinda decided his story sounded a little too incredible and convenient. Why had Stevens called her Callie? As in Lampasas, Lynx had appeared just in the nick of time to rescue her from peril. By generous fate or Lynx's unknown purpose? It was past time for some truthful answers. When they reached home, she would demand them. Her stockinged feet began to gingerly pick a path between sharp rocks and cacti in pursuit of her exasperating husband, dressed in satanic black as usual.

When Lynx turned to realize how far behind she was and why, he hurried back to her. He scooped her up in his arms and walked off with her, despite her muted protests. "There isn't time to argue, Cal. Just shut that lovely mouth and follow my instructions."

She fell into stony silence. When he set her down, she murmured sarcastically, "You don't seem very glad to see me safe and sound, dear husband." She knew she was being asinine, but couldn't halt it.

"In this predicament, I'm not," he growled. "You're one bag of trouble, Calinda Braxton."

"It's Calinda Cardone, in case you've conveniently forgotten."

"I haven't forgotten. If I had, I wouldn't be here tonight. I've been waiting around for hours until dark. It's been driving me wild."

"How did you locate me so quickly?" she inquired.

"I'll tell you later. For someone just rescued from killers, you sure have a funny way of showing your appreciation," he scolded. "What's gotten into you, Cal? You sound like I'm responsible for this dangerous situation." His gaze searched her expression, trying to unravel this curious puzzle.

"You are. If you'd been home where you belong, instead of gallivanting all over the countryside in search of adventure, they wouldn't have dared kidnap me. Obviously this golden band isn't a magical charm. I believe you said for me to stay home where I'd be safe and happy. Well, dear husband, I haven't been either. I hate Texas. It's a land of violence, deceit, and peril. I shouldn't have agreed to marry you or remain on the ranch," she bluntly informed the startled man. She kept herself from adding, if you can't be honest with me. She was tired of secrecy and separation which she didn't understand. If he loved her . . .

"You did, so you'll have to make the best of both. Come on; I'm sure Father's half out of his mind by now." He mounted up. He held out his hand and told her to mount before him.

Calinda didn't want to be in his line of vision or within his stimulating embrace. She much preferred his less demanding broad back. "I'll be more comfortable riding behind you."

"You'll also be in the line of fire if they discover you're missing and come after us. Stop behaving like a spoiled child, woman. We've wasted precious escape time as it is."

The tension too much to contain, she angrily vented some of it, "How do you expect me to act after what I've endured? I could have been ravished or murdered, for all you care."

"If I didn't care, my rebellious wife, I wouldn't be here." His amber eyes narrowed. How could she blame him for this crime? Why was she so cold, sarcastic, and ungrateful? For the first time in his life, he had experienced real fear and a lack of confidence in his own abilities. He was trying to save both their lives, but she was determined to pick a silly fight! Maybe it was a reaction to her shocking ordeal. But they had to get out of here; if they were caught, that star left behind would expose his identity.

"If you're shot in the back, I don't want to be left alive to face those crude men. Let me sit behind you—they might be reluctant to shoot a woman. They think I'm a valuable prize," she reasoned fearfully.

"You're worth far more than fifty thousand dollars. But they'd kill both of us before allowing us to escape. I'm larger and stronger. I could survive a bullet in the back easier than you could. Now, hush and get up here," he ordered firmly, his gaze daring her to refuse.

"All right," she agreed, placing her hand in his.

Lynx gave Star his lead. The animal sensed danger from previous training and experience, and walked for a lengthy distance from the hideout before picking up his pace. At a steady gallop, they made the ranch in less than three hours, time for her silly anger to vanish.

The moment they arrived, Calinda and Lynx were surrounded by gleefully shouting people. In a flurry of excitement and greetings, the daring tale of their escape spilled forth.

"I shore am glad to see you, Mrs. Cardone," Charlie stated.

"Not as happy as I am to see your face again," she replied.

"How did you find her son?" Rankin shrieked. "I had the money all ready to go at their signal. I guess you got my telegram?"

Calinda glanced at Lynx. Rankin had sent for him? He had known Lynx's location? Lynx smiled at his father, then nodded. Calinda's anger and hurt returned two-fold at that news. Lynx related the incident on the trail with Farley, whose pocket contained the instructions for the delivery of the money, the message to be delivered to the Cardone Ranch Monday at noon. "I'm sorry I couldn't stop by and tell you my plan to rescue her; there wasn't time. When I discovered it was Cole Stevens behind it, I headed for his hide-out. I doubt Cal would have been safe for another day and a half."

Calinda captured the dual meaning to his statement. How did Lynx know Cole Stevens so well? Why not, both were noted gunslingers! Had uncanny luck aided Lynx's rescue, or was there more to it? Perhaps her roguish love had connections to many outlaws. After all, there was the stolen locket in his possession.

She wanted to challenge him about it, but was afraid to let him know she'd searched his room.

"You're a courageous and cunning man, son," Rankin affectionately complimented Lynx. "You're a lucky girl, Cal."

Dazed by their deception, she murmured, "I want to thank you for offering to pay them so much money, Rankin. I'm just relieved you didn't lose it. I promise to be more careful in the future. Right now, if you'll excuse me, I want to get out of these filthy clothes and take a soothing bath. This has been quite a harrowing experience, and I'm exhausted." Suddenly, she felt utterly drained.

"I'm sorry we didn't protect you better, Cal," Rankin apologized.

"It wasn't your fault. Lynx, I did hear something you should pass on to the sheriff, if this Cole doesn't change his plans now," she began, then related the overheard details for the robbery Friday.

"I doubt Cole and his gang will be smart enough to alter those plans. The sheriff or Rangers can set up a trap and take 'em Friday. Wouldn't do any good to return to their hideout; they've cleared out of there by now." He looked at his father and said, "You'd best post guards around the ranch, just in case Cole doesn't give up easily. Cal, make sure you stay within sight of the house until Cole's gang is captured."

"You needn't worry; I will. Goodnight." She entered the house, passing Salina without a word or nod. Gathering her needed items, she went to bathe. Afterwards, she would sleep in her old room. The strain of her many ordeals demanded solitude. She feared the reasons for Lynx's dishonesty and the effect it was having on their relationship.

Both Lynx and Rankin noticed Calinda failed to hug or kiss her heroic husband. They went into the study and closed the door. "Is something bothering Cal? She was acting strangely."

"Then it wasn't just my imagination. I don't have the vaguest idea, father, unless the tension of this ordeal. Maybe she'll settle down after a bath and a sherry. She's been a little peeved since the moment she saw me. I don't know what's going on, but I'm glad she's safe. She had me scared out of my wits."

"Tell me everything," his father coaxed, wanting to hear of his son's intelligence and daring.

Lynx went through the whole episode in minute detail.

"You left one of your marks behind? What happens when they learn Lynx Cardone snatched his wife from their evil clutches? They'll know you're the unknown Ranger. That wasn't smart, son," Rankin scolded him.

"I was too furious at the time to think clearly. Anyway, by Friday, Cole and his men will be under the Rangers' control. I'll head out at first light for the Rangers; we'll be ready and waiting for them to strike. I have a personal score to settle with Stevens."

"Tonight, you have something else to settle, with your wife."

"You haven't given Cal any hints about me or the ranch? I'm worried about the way she's acting and looking at me."

Rankin filled in Lynx on the happenings since he left weeks ago. Lynx was troubled by the conflicts between his wife and Salina. "I don't think Salina should be allowed to treat my wife like that, father. I know Salina's a valuable servant, but not irreplaceable. I don't like her harassing Cal. You think Cal's merely upset by Salina's attitude? Cal might be disturbed by what she views as ill treatment from us if we allow Salina to pester her. Cal's a proud, stubborn woman. It's only natural for her to want to run her own home, at least be in control of it. It's unfair to allow Salina to have more authority. I think we'd better settle this tomorrow before I pull out."

"I guess you're right, son," Rankin concurred.

Salina had just made her way near the open doors, to boldly eavesdrop on the men's conversation. She tensed and fumed at their last words. If she didn't soften her covert attack, that little bitch would force a showdown! Too bad Lynx had bravely rescued her!

"You don't think there's any way she's learned anything, do you?" Lynx worried aloud. "Salina doesn't know anything to maliciously pass along, does she? For certain, something has my wife inflamed."

"You're forgetting, Marie was away for several days during the trouble with Brax. She couldn't reveal anything to Salina."

As the two discussed what had taken place years ago, the staggering truth was devoured by the greedy Salina. When Lynx said he was going to talk with Calinda, Salina waited until he left the room before slipping away from her hiding place. She danced around her room, hugging herself, congratulating herself for her good fortune. So, that explained why Lynx and Rankin were so desperate to keep Calinda here, to hold her captive with a wedding band, to prevent a search for Brax? If something happened to Calinda . . . Surely their shows of affection were phony, just devices to ensnare her, to disarm her? Surely they hated the daughter of the man who had done such evil to them? No doubt they were waiting for the proper time to get rid of her . . .

Lynx went to his room; Calinda wasn't there. He went to the next room, both the hall and balcony doors were bolted. He tapped lightly and called out, "Cal, are you all right? I want to talk to you."

Why had she returned to her old room? he fretted anxiously. When she didn't respond, he warned, "If you don't open the door, I'll do it myself. You've got some explaining to do, wife."

Calinda walked to the balcony door and unbolted it. "I'm tired, Lynx. What can't wait until morning? Or will you even be around then?"

"I'd like to know why you're being as chilly and aggressive as a blue norther?" he stated, moving her aside to enter the room.

The weary girl turned and gazed at him. Dare she demand the truth? She closed the door and came forward to stand before him. "You're most selfish and inconsiderate, Lynx. You know what I've been through since this terrifying incident began. Why do you insist on talking tonight? I just want to relax and unwind." Her cloudy gaze prevented his piercing eyes from ascertaining her crazy mood.

"We're both drained. I've been crazy with worry, Cal. I've had little sleep or rest in days. If I was unresponsive back there, I'm sorry. I just wanted to get you away safely. I've missed you, woman."

"You had enough time to give me plenty of insults, terse orders, and scoldings. That wasn't what I needed or wanted. But I am grateful for your second timely assistance. It appears you know a great deal about outlaws, Mister Cardone."

"What's that supposed to mean?" he demanded, piqued by her tone and manner. "I told you how I found you."

"Ah, yes, the miraculous clue to my misfortune and location," she murmured skeptically. "You do have an uncanny way of showing up in the nick of time, don't you? First the saloon, then Lampasas, and incredibly at the scene of my captivity. You must possess immense insight, luck, and intelligence. I'm learning quite a number of lessons, my talented husband." Please remove my doubts, she prayed.

"I don't like the insinuations in your frosty tone, Cal."

"And I don't like being kept in the dark about my own husband," she instantly retorted. "Mainly, I don't like being deceived."

"What are you talking about, Cal?" he asked seriously. His baffled gaze eased over her tumbling chestnut hair, her stormy green eyes, and her silky skin. Her complexion looked as if she hadn't been out of the house since her arrival in sultry Texas.

"The next time you leave home, which is probably at dawn, you should get your excuses to match your father's. Even Salina knows more about you and your movements than I do. I suppose you've never heard of letters or telegrams home?" Cal hinted in rising vexation.

"You knew I was heading for Junction to do a job delayed by a willful and crafty young lady. I don't know what my father said, but he was probably trying to ease your concern and loneliness. But you're right about my leaving at dawn; I'm going to set a trap for Stevens. Besides what he did to you, he's wanted for numerous crimes. I'm heading over to the Ranger camp to see that he's put out of action for good. I know I should have contacted you sooner, but I kept thinking I would be finished and heading home any day. It won't happen again, Cal; I promise. Now, what's this about Salina?" he asked, returning to a clue which had caused her eyes to glimmer with fury.

Wanting to clear the air and make her position a known fact to all of them, Calinda revealed what Salina had said to her. Lynx tensed, realizing Salina must have discovered information to use to her advantage. He must caution his father to avoid any future conversation which might be enlightening and hazardous. He would deal with Salina's brazen conduct!

"Listen to me carefully, Cal, I swear to you I went to Junction to help a friend. Afterwards, I rode to Dallas to meet another friend, to complete one last promise so I could come home. As soon as I warn the Rangers about Stevens, I'll head for Waco and be done with this separation. I know you said you would handle matters with Salina, but clearly you haven't. If you let that tempestuous girl order you around or insult you again, I'll turn you over my knees and spank you. If she's going to treat my wife like that, then she'd best get the hell out of my home. The first time she ordered you out of your own kitchen, you should have flung a skillet at her, preferably a hot one. And don't ask her which chores you can have; do whatever you please. Rankin's just become dependent on her, but I don't think he realizes how bad it is between you two. I'm deadly serious, woman. You'd best recall, you're the wife and she's the servant. As for moving into my room, you didn't need to ask. In fact, I'd have been awfully hurt and curious if you hadn't. Trust me a while longer, Cal. I just need a few more weeks, then I'll be home for good."

"You have so many secrets, Lynx; you're like a total stranger to me. How can I trust you when you don't trust me?" she asked sadly.

"I'll explain everything when the time is right, Cal. I'll be frank with you; there are certain things I can't tell you at present, some things I don't want to tell you, and some things I'll never tell you. But I will say enough to explain matters, to justify what I'm doing right now. I just need a little time and privacy for a while longer."

"You've been shutting me out of your life ever since we met. You expect blind faith and unquestionable loyalty. Don't you understand how difficult and demanding that is over such a long period of time and distance? I'm weary of all the excuses, deceits, and mistrust. I'm so confused and exhausted, I don't even know if it's worth it anymore." She sighed heavily in frustration.

"There's more to it, Cal," he speculated astutely, reaching to pull her into his yearning embrace.

She moved aside, denying him his quest. "Don't, Lynx. I'm not in the mood to be touched. Tonight, I need some time and privacy," she informed softly. She turned away from him, locking her arms over her abdomen, closing her eyes, and inhaling raggedly.

His hands gently grasped her shoulders. "I'll be leaving soon, Cal. We've been through hell. I need you," he stated huskily. Even if she didn't want to make love tonight, he wanted to hold her tightly and kiss her time after time. He wanted to vanquish her coldness and painful rejection. He wanted her to feel the love within him.

"What about my needs?" she challenged in a hoarse voice.

"If I've hurt you and disappointed you, Cal, I'm truly sorry. If you don't feel like making love, at least come to bed with me. I need you near me tonight. Do you realize how close I came to losing you?" he asked, his voice and gaze tender and compelling.

"Would it really matter if you did?" she asked shockingly, alarming him with the gravity of her dejected tone.

"How can you even ask such a question?"

"If you care so much, why have I seen my husband for less than a day since our blissful marriage? If you care so much, why haven't I received even the tiniest note? If you care so much, why do you keep your life a secret from me? If you care so much, why are you leaving within hours after I escape from the jaws of death?"

"If I don't head for the Rangers tomorrow, this might be our last chance to snag Cole Stevens and his gang. Don't you see, Cal, the timing is perfect to capture him? Do you want me to allow him to go on killing, robbing, and terrorizing the countryside? Perhaps kidnap another woman?" he questioned in exasperation.

"Do your duty, Lynx; I won't try to stop you. I won't cry or plead or scream. Just don't expect me to calmly accept your running in and out of my life whenever it suits your fancy. I hate this place; I wish I had never come here," she falsely vowed.

"You don't mean that, Cal. You're just upset and tired."

"Yes, I do mean it. It's been awful since the first day of my arrival. How do you think I should feel about Texas? I was robbed before I even got to the ranch," she placed the bait on her hook.

"I know you're angry about the hold-up. I wish I could find your possessions. I can't. The sheriff never caught who was responsible."

"I don't care about the money or clothes or other things, just my locket. I told the sheriff he could keep everything as a reward if he could only locate and return my locket. It means so much to me," she said, dangling the baited hook before him.

"I'm sorry about the locket, Cal."

"No, you aren't. And stop saying you're sorry. If you were, you would help me find it," she continued to fish for the response she wanted so desperately.

"How am I supposed to do that?" he asked strangely.

"You're very successful at solving mysteries about me. You seem to be acquainted with plenty of outlaws and gunslingers. Find out who has my locket and get it back for me. Maybe my locket will turn up in as timely and unexpected a manner as you do," she tried another area.

"I wish I could hand you the locket right now, Cal."

Calinda turned and faced him. Her heart began to thud heavily, "Why can't you, Lynx?"

"Because I don't . . ." He halted and stared at her. He had a gut feeling she was trying to imply something. But what?

"Perhaps I should teach you how to complete sentences, my devoted and heroic husband. Shall I assist you? Because I don't have it?"

Lynx's heart skipped a beat. He stiffened slightly. He grabbed her chin and forced their gazes to fuse. "You know, don't you?" he asked simply, fearing the worst.

"Yes, my loving husband, I know you have it," she replied, her gaze never leaving his as it narrowed and hardened. "But what I would like to hear is why you kept it from me, knowing how I felt?"

"Why did you open that locked drawer, Cal? Why?" he demanded.

"I wanted to know who and what my husband was, since he refuses to tell me."

"I don't believe what I'm hearing," he stated softly.

Calinda observed the unexpected reaction on his bronzed face; he actually looked betrayed and disillusioned. She had thought he would be furious, but he was hurt. "I wanted and needed to understand you. Why do you keep me at arm's length? Why do you and Rankin feed me false tales and words which even a starving fool would choke on? I'm not stupid. Is it me, Lynx; is there something terrible about me?" she inquired in a near whisper.

"All right, Cal, I'll tell you about your locket. I took it off a man I fought in Dallas. He was a member of Sam Bass' gang, the ones who held up the stage. When I went to see the Rangers to give them the information, Major Jones asked me not to give away their identity yet; they're tracking him down to capture him. That's how I knew Jones didn't have anything to do with that letter. I had the locket with me when I found you in Lampasas risking your lovely neck to find Brax. I didn't give it to you for several reasons. First, I didn't want you to have a picture of Brax; I was afraid you would use it to hire a detective to search for him. A search would cost you lots of money, futile time, and more anguish. I wanted you cut off from the past so you would stay here with us. Second, I didn't want you wearing it here. I saw Brax's picture inside. I didn't want my father and me having that constant reminder flaunted in our faces. Last, I didn't want to explain how I came to be in possession of it. Your image of me was already dark; I didn't want anything to make it worse. Believe it or not, I was planning to return it some day. I knew how much its loss pained you; I couldn't throw it away."

Oddly, Calinda felt he was telling the truth. "What about the watch? I'm so confused about the past, Lynx."

"Some day, I promise to tell you everything I know, Cal. Please, not tonight. We've been through hell for three days. If it bothers you that much, I'll give you the locket right now. Just don't wear it for a while longer," he urged.

"Keep it for me. As long as I know it's here, that's all that matters. You're a very complex and puzzling man, Lynx Cardone."

"I suppose you're right, Cal. I've never had to answer to anyone before now. Maybe I am too damn proud and stubborn. Sharing and loving come hard for me, I've had no experience," he teased.

"I think certain kinds come too easily, Lynx. You share yourself and your skills with your friends. And you positively know a great deal about loving," she murmured, her implication clear.

"If I promise to try harder at everything, am I forgiven?" he coaxed, trailing his fingers over her silky cheek. "You're a challenge to me, Cal; and I'm having a devil of a time accepting it. Taking you into my life and heart requires heavy changes; it's difficult, love."

"You drive a hard bargain, Lynx. Stop grinning at me like that, or I might forget my anger. You're a heartless devil and you know it. When it comes to you, I must be a naive and gullible fool. You're dangerously irresistible." She returned his smile, mellowing as time passed. She should have waited for his explanations before jumping the gun. He had a beguiling way of justifying anything. When he was near and enticing, all other thoughts fled her mind.

She yawned and stretched, her lids droopy and her body going lax. "Let's go to bed, husband; I can hardly hold my eyes open."

"No wonder, it's nearly morning," he said, tugging on a stray curl, leading her into his room. "To bed with you, wife."

She looked up into his arresting face. "But you'll be leaving soon."

He chuckled. "Not before you wake up, love; I promise."

She smiled as he pulled the covers over her, then kissed her lightly on her injured forehead. He undressed and joined her, pulling her into his possessive embrace. He kissed her tenderly, then murmured, "Go to sleep, *Llama de mi corazon;* you're safe now."

"I love you, Lynx," she murmured drowsily at his endearment, leisurely sailing off on a peaceful journey to dreamland.

"*Yo te quiero,* Callie, *mi vida, mi aliento, mi corazon,*" he responded, but she didn't hear him. He was relieved she had accepted his truthful explanation about the locket. With loving determination, he was gradually constructing a bridge across the river of mistrust and bitterness which kept them apart. In the near future, he would complete his compelling task when he removed the final obstacles between them. But he must be very careful to allow nothing to destroy his steady progress; for she was indeed his love, his life, his breath, and his heart. Soon, Lynx was fast asleep.

——— *Chapter 14* ———

❦

It was approaching noon when Calinda awoke. Subdued rays of sunlight gently pierced the translucent curtains on the balcony doors. She sat up, staring down at the empty place where Lynx had slept. Had he broken his promise and left without telling her? Had the abduction and rescue been stygian dreams? No. Cal flung the covers aside and jumped up to search for an inexcusable note.

The door opened quietly as Lynx tried to steal inside without disturbing Cal. When he saw her standing by the dresser, he smiled and closed the door. "*Buenos dias*, Mrs. Cardone," he said warmly.

A bright smile flickered over her face. "I was looking for a note, Mister Cardone; I feared you had left already," she confessed.

"I promised I wouldn't leave before you could give me a good scolding for my terrible behavior lately," he teased, strolling toward her. "But I was beginning to think you were going to sleep away all our time together. I was trying to be patient," Lynx ventured merrily.

"It must be awfully late. Why didn't you awaken me?"

"You needed your sleep, *mi amor*. I gave my word to remain. You've got to learn to trust me, Cal," he advised, stopping within inches of her, assailing her senses with his arresting aura.

"I know," Cal contritely replied. "I suppose all newlyweds go through this demanding period of adjustment and confusion."

"Hungry?" Lynx hinted, his amber eyes sparkling as sunbeams dancing upon a glass of golden sherry.

Hungry? Cal mentally challenged. *Certainly not for food!* How could she think of anything when he was standing before her wearing nothing but a wrapper around his hips! It was obvious that he often went shirtless, as his appealing body was darkly tanned from the waist up. His taut flesh was as smooth and firm as hardened taffy. His muscles were flexible and strong. Not an ounce of excess fat marred a frame Apollo would envy. Despite having been in so many fights, his splendid body was scarless.

Lynx reminded her of a magnificent male animal, lithe and sleek. He was as quick and nimble as a prized stallion. His arms and legs rippled with each movement. His shoulders were broad, his chest covered with a dark gold mat of curly hair. His stomach was flat and taut, his waist narrow. Cal smiled as a crazy thought touched her mind; he even had pretty feet.

As her brazen study travelled up from the floor, it hesitated briefly on the noticable bulge beneath the wrapper which covered him. Her respiration quickened; she warmed and tingled. When her gaze reached his handsome face, his parted lips exposed even ivory teeth that added charming allure to his sensual smile. His tawny eyes smoldered like a pool of amber liquid. As if his gaze was magnetized, it drew and held her tightly.

His hands cupped her face, a thumb moving over her lips in a provocative manner. "You're beautiful, Callie. Do you have any idea how you affect me?" he asked huskily, his voice thick with passion.

Her hands came up to rest on his chest. She murmured, "I hope the same way you affect me, Lynx."

His hands wandered up into her fiery hair, relishing its satiny feel. He pushed aside the curls falling over her temples, his gaze locking on the contusion and angry red line. His eyes chilled and squinted. "I should kill him for hurting you," he stated glacially, a deadly gleam telling of his inner rage.

Cal snuggled her face against his furry chest, her arms slipping around his taut body. Lynx was so tall compared to her medium frame that he could lay his face on the top of her head, which he did after kissing it. "Don't think about it now, Lynx. Our time is so short." She lifted her head to look up into his features. "Can't you wait until the holiday is over? Thursday is July fourth. There's going to be a celebration in town; Rankin's taking me. Couldn't you join us, at least a few hours? Surely everyone wonders why a new bride is always alone."

Lynx sighed heavily. "If I stay, Cal, there's no way I can get to the Rangers to trap Stevens. If he steals that money, he'll lay low for a long time. Don't you see I have to do this, for all of his victims?"

As much as Cal wanted to debate his logic, she couldn't. She knew from experience how dangerous that outlaw was. "I'm sorry, Lynx. I won't ask again. Of course you're right. But I don't have to like it," she added laughingly, punching him in the back very softly.

"How do you like this, Mrs. Cardone?" he asked playfully, nibbling at her ear. "Or this?" he added, searing his burning lips over hers. His deft fingers removed her gown, then pulled her naked body to his bare chest. He groaned at the staggering contact of her warm flesh against his cool body. As he shifted from side to side to tease her sensitive breasts with his hairy torso, he hinted knowingly, "Or this?"

"I can think of something better," Cal hinted bravely. "If you have time to return to bed," she speculated seductively.

He leaned backwards to study her inviting expression. "Then show me what you have in mind," Lynx coaxed eagerly.

Cal took his hand and led him to the rumpled bed. She released it to straighten the covers. She glanced at him and smiled, "Would you care to lie down first?"

"At your pleasure, *Llama de mi corazon, mi cuerpo,*" he retorted, stretching out on the inviting bed.

"What does that mean?" she probed in undisguised curiosity.

"Flame of my heart, my body," he sensuously responded.

Calinda sat down beside him, grinning mischievously. Salina's words about his growing bored with his wife kept racing through her mind. If he ever did, it positively wouldn't be today. She would show her adventure seeking husband what excitement and fulfillment he was missing at home! If she dared to use the stimulating actions which she had overheard at school and from careless English servants . . .

"Then relax, my love, and let me discover what pleasures you," she hinted suggestively, emerald eyes dancing with intrigue.

Lynx stared at her suspiciously. "If I didn't know any better, I'd think you were up to something, Mrs. Cardone."

Calinda felt very confident and daring today. Her senses were alive with suspense and desire. Her hand casually roamed over the hard mound which was concealed from view as she innocently replied, "It appears, my love, that you are the one . . . up to something. I wonder what it could be," she murmured, coyly pursing her lips.

When Lynx reached over to draw her down to him, she pushed his entreating arms aside, saying, "Relax, love. I'm in full command."

His eyes glittered with amusement and interest. His arms fell back against his pillow on either side of his head. "If you're brave enough to become the leader, I'll gladly surrender that rank."

Calinda lay half over his body, her breasts threatening to burn holes in his chest. She dropped feathery kisses over his nose and eyes. She confined his head between her hands, seeming to attack his mouth with feverish intensity. As she drifted from his lips to one ear, then back to his mouth to eagerly trace each inch in the other direction, he moaned in rising need of her. As his arms instinctively reached for her, she chided, "No, my tempting mate. I must teach you how to relax, how to enjoy new experiences."

"Relax?" Lynx taunted skeptically. "How can I possibly relax when you're heating me up to a boiling point?"

"Then you'll just have to control yourself and simmer a while longer, Lynx. This is fun." She covered her giggling mouth.

"You're a sadist, love; you're just trying to torture me," he playfully accused, chuckling in pleasure.

"Torture you?" she murmured. "You call this punishment?"

"Nope. I call it sheer heaven," he admitted raggedly.

"Then you best savor your brief visit; perhaps this will entice you to return sooner," Cal easily scored a point in her favor.

Her lips created tremors as they worked their way down his neck, nibbling at the hollows there, then at his shoulders. He stiffened briefly as her tongue drew moist circles around his breasts, discovering the unknown fact that his could be as susceptible and sensitive as hers. She took his left hand and kissed each finger, then his palm. Each spot she touched and teased tingled and flamed. For a man who was well versed in sex, Lynx was learning something new and exciting.

When one of Calinda's hands trailed lightly over his taut stomach and released the wrapper to encircle his manhood, he shuddered and groaned with tormenting bliss. His hips squirmed as her light journey tickled over his groin area and upper thighs. Ever so gently she caressed the two round objects beneath his vividly aroused manhood. As her hand slipped up and down the pulsing shaft, he wanted to grab her and make savagely sweet love to her. Thrilling to this unexpected facet of his modest wife, he dared not halt her dauntless adventure.

Lynx's blood surged with fiery life when she moved to drop brazen kisses on the throbbing, rearing stallion. He was quivering all over, his body a sheet of tingling sensations and roaring flames. "Blazes alive, Callie, you're driving me wild," he stated breathlessly.

After a few more stirring kisses and caresses, she moved up to his face. "Then douse our flames, my love," she wantonly entreated.

He rolled her to her back, assailing her breasts with intoxicating skill. He wanted to see her passion glazed eyes and flushed cheeks as he gave her mutual satisfaction. He lifted her legs and shifted to his knees near her buttocks, sinking his aching shaft into her receptive sheath, burying it to the hilt within her quivering body.

As Lynx tantalizingly invaded her body over and over, he inspired fiercer yearnings within them. His control was sorely strained from her daring trek. Cal moaned in urgency, her head rolling from side to side as he masterfully explored that molten region. As a sleek and powerful mustang, he rode up and down her dark canyon which presented no obstacle against his wildly rapturous invasion.

Back and forth he galloped the distance of her womanhood, mutely enticing her to follow his lead. He hungrily claimed and branded his private territory which willingly yielded to his control and ownership. He charged forward with daring and skill, then retreated slightly for another successful assault.

Calinda was fascinated and bewitched by the erotic sight of their bodies blending to seek fulfillment, fusing as if they would never part. Mesmerized, she watched the wickedly wonderful motions. Her darkened gaze went up to his, their eyes joining to speak silently of shared needs and emotions, of seemingly predestined love.

When their passions reached the point of no retreat or denial, he urged his tightly reined manhood to race for the summit of victory which loomed before them. With confidence and talent, he galloped toward it, setting his pace to allow her to arrive at their destination only seconds before him.

A muffled cry of triumph left her throat as she topped ecstasy's peak, quivering and savoring her victory before sliding down the other side into the peaceful valley which compelled her forward. He freed her legs to lower himself on her damp body, his mouth taking hers as he thundered after her approaching contentment. He extracted the sweet nectar of love from her lips until his body was sated.

At last, he lifted his head and met her glowing eyes. His expression became serious and thoughtful. "What is it about you, Calinda Cardone, that makes you so unique and enchanting? You can't imagine how many nights I've lain awake thinking about you and a moment like this. Sometimes your face appears before my eyes even during the day. Sometimes I want you so badly it scares me. Other times I wonder what I would do if I lost you. You're like a part of me; I feel denied when I'm away from you. Pretty soon, you'll get sick of me and my constant demands on you. Because when I come home, I won't let you out of my sight for more than an hour."

"I can hardly wait," Cal happily announced. "As to getting sick of you, that day will never dawn. As implausible as it sounds, I love you and want you with all my heart and soul." The confession had accidentally slipped out, but she didn't correct or withdraw it.

"I'm probably the luckiest man alive to have you. Have I ever told you how glad I am you came? You're the most important thing that's ever happened to me, Cal. I never knew such feelings existed in me. No woman had even lingered in my mind, but you. Do you comprehend what a terrible distraction you are?" he teased.

"I would prefer to be a wonderful attraction," she quipped.

"I'm gonna have to keep a sharp eye on you, woman. If I don't, you'll be leading me around like a horny bull in mating season."

"Then we should both be overjoyed that you possess such stamina and talents, my love." Her verdant eyes twinkled. "Now, all we need is time to take advantage of them. Just remember I'm waiting at home."

"That's one of my problems, I can't seem to forget it when I'm away. You take up so much of my time and attention, I work slowly and carelessly. You're a dangerous obsession, Callie."

Her features softened with a contented smile. "Good."

"Now that one appetite has been fed, how about some breakfast?"

"Only if I can prepare it," she hinted. "But first, I need to visit the watershed. I might find it difficult to concentrate on cooking with your manly fragrance clinging to me."

Lynx chuckled. "You're a wanton hussy, my fetching wife. What's happened to you? You were never this carefree before."

"You happened to me, Lynx Cardone. Besides, we're married now. Am I behaving improperly for a wife? God, how I've missed you," she wailed, throwing her arms around his neck, drawing his mouth down to join with hers. "I can't bear the fact you're leaving."

"We're matched perfectly. We'll have a wonderful life together. Your appetite is as insatiable and ravenous as mine."

"It's your fault; you created it. If you're sorry, you've only yourself to blame. Since you're home so rarely and briefly, there isn't time for modesty or manners. I'd best stuff myself before my tasty food leaves again. Alas, how shall I face another period of starvation?"

Lynx threw back his head and chortled. "What's so amusing?" she asked, staring at him as the peals of joyful laughter subsided.

"I never knew a woman could be so much fun, especially not a wife. A man's supposed to feel trapped and bored, but you don't permit it. You never cease to amaze me, Callie," Lynx avowed.

"I hope I never do, my love."

As his mouth leisurely feasted at her breasts, she teased in rapidly rising passion, "I thought you were hungry."

"Starving, but not for breakfast just yet."

Her fingers tousled his dark gold hair. A tranquil sigh slipped out of her chest.

He set a deliberately titillating pace to arouse her to another quest for rapture. Locked in each other's arms, they invaded the heady realm of passion's ecstasy and easily conquered it.

Her boldness most rewarding, Cal didn't protest when Lynx joined her in the overly large bathtub. They splashed and played as two children, laughing and teasing, soaping and rinsing each other. When Lynx's laughter would increase in volume, she would giggle and caution him to lower his voice. He would wink at her and declare he didn't care who heard him, after all they were married.

Lynx sat on the submerged wooden seat and pulled her down across his lap, her spread legs dangling over his thighs. Cal hugged him tightly as he trailed his lips over her shoulders and neck. When he fastened his mouth to a taut breast, she glanced down at his face. His eyes were closed dreamily as his lips and tongue played on the tiny summit. How was it possible to want him again so soon? How did his mere touch tempt her beyond reason? As if they hadn't made love for weeks or months, her body fiercely craved his.

When a hand sneaked below to investigate a small peak there, she lay her cheek on the top of his head and snuggled against him. Even if the water had been ice cold, it couldn't have cooled her body and passions. "Lynx, I want you so much. Why are you tormenting me here?"

"What's wrong with here, Callie?" he inquired thickly.

"We can't make love in a bathtub," she replied sultrily.

"Why not?" he debated, looking up into her glazed eyes.

A look of astonishment claimed her features. "You can?" she asked seriously, naively.

Lynx chuckled softly as he shifted his body and entered her, seizing her hips and gently forcing them tightly against his groin. Her eyes widened, then she burst into muffled laughter. "If you were home for longer periods, my love, you could teach me such lessons."

"You'd be shocked by how much I can teach you, Callie."

"I doubt it. But I'm a bright and willing student," she whispered, causing him to shudder with anticipation as her tongue traced the contours of his ear before working on his sensitive earlobe.

Lynx artfully stirred her passions for a time, then withdrew. "Why did you stop?" she asked in lucid disappointment.

He stepped out of the tub and placed a padding of thick linens on the platform. He reached for her, lifting her out of the tub and placing her on her back on the make-shift bed. He entered her again as his mouth took possession of hers. Soon, they were riding the stormy waves of passion which eventually crested and ebbed into a serene pool.

Afterwards, he returned her to the tub and washed her from head to foot. After completing his own bath, he dried her off with a provocative slowness which threatened to re-whet her greedy appetite. "Now, Mrs. Cardone, does that earn me a sturdy farewell meal?"

"That, my love, earns you anything you desire from me."

"I think I've tied myself to a lecherous and demanding vixen. Are you trying to kill me, woman?" Lynx gleefully accused.

"I don't want a single hair on that devilish head harmed. I was just trying to give you a sample of Calinda Cardone, so you'll hurry home again. At least, maybe you'll be as lonely and miserable as I will."

"I knew it," he declared. "You're trying to disease me and drive me wild with discomfort. You know my only cure and appeasement is you. You're a sly vixen, Callie. Whatever shall I do with you?"

"Love me and keep me forever," she responded instantly.

"If I ever wanted to do anything more in my life, I can't imagine what," he informed her, grinning.

They returned to Lynx's room to dress, then Calinda cooked Lynx a big breakfast. As they were eating and chatting in the kitchen, the back door opened and Salina strolled in, her hips swaying and her lips sending out sultry messages to Lynx. She came to the table and spoke to Lynx, totally ignoring Calinda.

"I am late returning, Lynx. I see your *esposa* is feeding you properly. Will you be here for dinner?"

Lynx's left hand captured Calinda's right one beneath the table and squeezed it. "If you don't mind, Salina, Cal and I would like to be alone while we eat. We have some talking to catch up on before I leave soon." His smoldering gaze engulfed his wife's joyful expression.

"I have supplies to put away, Lynx. Surely I will not be in your way?" Salina reasoned petulantly, trying to spoil their contentment.

"I'm afraid you will, Salina. Run along until we're finished."

At his playful dismissal, Salina actually blushed for the first time in her life, a scarlet covering of mingled anger and embarrassment. She glanced at the serene Calinda who was forcing her loving gaze to remain locked on her love's face. "If that is what you want," she hinted.

Calinda was determined not to look at Salina and gloat smugly. Her heart was singing with happiness. Lynx placed their interlocked hands on the corner of the table, causing Salina's eyes to widen.

"That is what I want, Salina. Your chores can wait for me to say goodbye to my wife. Run along, and close the door behind you."

Salina unknowingly gritted her teeth. "Would you like anything before I am tossed out? Coffee? More food?" she asked sassily.

Lynx glared at Salina. "You're getting a wee bit large for your fancy britches, Salina. I think you're forgetting who lives here and who just works here. One of those positions can change quickly," he warned subtly. "I was asking nicely. But now I'm telling you; get out of here before I lose my temper. If I need or want anything else, I have a most capable wife sitting beside me. I think it's past time you realize Calinda Cardone is the mistress of this house and ranch; don't force me to remind you again. I'm fully aware of your *hinchado*."

"But," Salina opened her mouth to dispute his statements.

"No buts!" he snarled. "You think I don't know how you've been treating her. I'm surprised she hasn't fired you or punished you."

Salina bit her tongue to keep from blurting out, she wouldn't dare! "What has she been telling you?" Salina asked, emphasizing the "she." "I do not understand why you act and talk this *salvaje* way."

"I spoke with Rankin about the conflict between you two. Callie didn't want to cause trouble, so she's kept silent. From now on, I'm demanding she tell me everything. She's been taking your crap for months to avoid problems. No longer, Salina. If you work for the Cardones, that includes my wife. If you can't endure her, then I suggest you start looking elsewhere for another job," he stated coldly.

Salina paled. "Where would I go? I have lived and worked here for five years! Where? How?"

"Things have changed, Salina, but you're refusing to accept those changes. It's time you decide if you want to remain with us."

"Lynx, let me give you my side," Salina entreated fearfully.

"*Alto! Ya se acabo!* That's what I'm talking about!" he thundered, switching to English for his wife's benefit. Exasperated, his fist struck the table, sloshing coffee from their cups, causing both women to jump in surprise. "There are no sides to be taken! I've never met anyone easier to get along with than Cal. If you give it some help, you two could get along fine. Is that clear?" When Salina nodded, he said, "Good, now leave us alone."

Salina left quickly. Lynx looked over at his wife, frowning. "Think I was too harsh?" he speculated.

"I should say yes, but I can't. I don't know if that scolding will help or hurt. But I promise to do my best with her, Lynx. She just resents me so much. Thanks," she murmured sweetly.

"It will help if you constantly remember you're a Cardone."

She lifted her left hand and gazed at her ring. "I will."

Calinda stood in the yard watching Lynx ride away from home, failing to move until even his dust vanished. She sighed, this time happily rather than angrily. For the first time, she was convinced they had a bright future together. She resolved that nothing and no one would dampen her gaiety or destroy her trust and happiness.

Today was Monday, July 1, 1878. With good luck and smiling fate, Lynx should be home before the end of this month . . .

Chapter 15

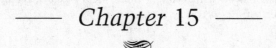

As THE DAYS PASSED, Rankin noticed a pleasing change in Calinda. There was a serene glow to her cheeks and a happy sparkle in her eyes; she hummed merrily as if the entire world was in love and at peace. She didn't appear the least worried about her close call with peril. It was obvious; Calinda was deeply in love with Lynx.

As they talked, dined, and played cards, her laughter was bubbly and frequent. When Lynx was mentioned, a twinkle filled her eyes and spread warmth over her face. They didn't discuss his location or purpose. They merely enjoyed each other's company and wit.

To Salina's surprise, Calinda didn't become bossy and smug. It was as if Calinda was content to let Salina continue with her chores in her own way. When Calinda wanted to perform a particular task or help with one, she didn't ask; she simply did it. Salina couldn't believe the lack of gloating in the victorious Calinda. The new Mrs. Cardone seemed too preoccupied to notice what went on around her or be troubled by any menial problems.

Salina wisely accepted this curious behavior, observing it closely with intrigue. Until things settled down, she would make herself as unnoticeable as possible. She would be as quiet as a field mouse and as sweet as wild honey! Her time would come . . .

When Thursday arrived, Calinda told Rankin she didn't want to go to the July fourth celebration in town. She explained her motives for wanting to stay home, which included her absent husband. She told Rankin she didn't want to risk running into any of Stevens' men or Stevens himself, just in case they had hung around this area. When Rankin debated her points, Cal reminded him she couldn't identify any of the bandits. That notorious outlaw could stroll right up to her face, and she wouldn't know when to scream or run.

"They lost $50,000 on me, Rankin, surely more than any stage carries. They might try to snatch me again. I'd feel safer and happier here. I would be asked buckets of questions about Lynx's constant absences; I hate making phony excuses. I'm not a good liar or actress. I don't want people playing guessing games or starting rumors. Besides, it's hot and noisy in town. I heard you assign half the hands as guards this morning and half of them for this afternoon. I'll be perfectly safe."

"I suppose you're right, Cal. But I'll miss you with me today. It'll be hard to explain your absence since we don't want to let anyone know about the kidnapping. I warned Salina and my men not to say anything to anyone." But Calinda didn't know the real motive behind keeping it quiet, to protect Lynx's identity. Still, he didn't want any gossip about his family. From what Lynx had said, he had rescued Calinda just in the nick of time to spare her any degradation.

So, the holiday passed with Calinda under heavy guard, reading a book while Rankin had a merry time in town.

Under Ranger McNelly's leadership on Friday, Lynx and Tom Peters set a trap for Cole Stevens and his gang. Five miles before reaching Big Sandy Creek, they halted the stage. The three passengers were taken aside to be picked up after the foiled robbery; they were to wait in the wagon until the lawmen returned with their prisoners. The three Rangers hid themselves inside the coach and headed to defeat the outlaws. McNelly told them to wait until the stage was stopped and the bandits were nearby, to shoot anyone who tried to escape.

All went as planned. As the driver slowed to ford the wide creek, the stage was approached by four heavily armed outlaws. As instructed, the driver and guard didn't make any precarious moves.

"Throw down that strong-box, and we'll be on our way without any shooting," Cole ordered the driver, lazily propping his crossed wrists on his saddle horn, his gun pointing negligently into the air.

The guard struggled to lift the heavy metal box and tossed it to the ground. Instantly he and the driver sank into the protective area in the shotgun box at their feet. The coach door sprang open, McNelly bravely exposing himself as Tom and Lynx simultaneously appeared in the windows. The three Rangers sent forth warning shots.

McNelly shouted, "Rangers! Throw down your guns or be killed!"

Two of the outlaws quickly obeyed, tossing away their guns and lifting their hands. Oggie and Will didn't want to challenge such deadly odds. As if prearranged, Little Red and Cole Stevens fled in opposite directions. The three Rangers bounded from the stage. Tom trained his two pistols on Oggie and Will. Glancing in both directions, McNelly shouted to Lynx. "You take Stevens! That way."

McNelly knew how much Lynx wanted to defeat his foe, so he fired at the fleeing carrot-haired Little Red, winging him with skill.

Lynx fumed at Cole's flight. Lynx wanted to yank Cole off his saddle and beat him senseless. Without Star to pursue him, Lynx had no choice but to shoot or let Cole make his escape. He aimed his Colt and squeezed the trigger twice, striking Cole in the left thigh and right arm, the one gripping his reins. The bandit wavered and fell off his horse, the frightened animal continuing his terrified pace.

Lynx rushed to where Cole had fallen. Cole was holding his wounded arm across his stomach and gripping the profusely bleeding wound on his leg with his left hand. When Lynx swaggered to where Cole sat in agonizing pain, Lynx towered over him, grinning in pleasure.

Cole stared at him. "What the hell are you doing here?"

"Helping the Rangers clear this land of rattlesnakes," Lynx sneered, kicking his injured leg, recalling Cole's treatment of Calinda.

Cole grimaced in anguish. Lynx snarled at him, "You'd best be glad you didn't hurt my wife any worse than you did, Cole, or you'd be choking on your own blood right this moment. The Rangers will put you away a long time, if they don't hang you, you bloody bastard!"

Cole scoffed, "You're just riled that Unknown Ranger saved her instead of you. Did the little wife fall for that courageous man?"

"How could she? She's in love with me," Lynx stated smugly.

"Didn't look that way to me. She was even willing to do anything I said to earn her freedom. She's a damn good kisser with fiery blood."

"Forget it, Cole. The Ranger was outside the window when you forced her to kiss you to gain some fresh air. It might interest you to know that's why she asked for the window up and the light out. If her hands hadn't been tied, she would have scratched out your eyeballs. She said she nearly puked when she followed the Ranger's orders."

Cole stiffened in fury. "That good for nothing bitch! If I ever get my hands on her again, I'll . . ."

Lynx grabbed Cole by the front of his shirt and yanked him to his feet. He delivered several blows into Cole's face and gut with lightning speed and forceful strength. "I'll kill you if you even think about her in passing," Lynx warned ominously at Cole's threat.

Cole doubled over with pain. Blood seeped from cuts at the corner of his mouth and left eye. A shirt sleeve and pants leg were saturated with crimson liquid. "If I ever get loose, Cardone, I'll kill you for this," he mumbled, spitting blood on the dry ground.

Torn between a desire for revenge and a duty to justice, Lynx scathingly declared, "If those Rangers weren't standing over there, Cole, you'd be a dead man. I'm a fool all right; I should have come alone and dealt with you. I'll see that you either hang or rot in prison. Mark my words," he vowed confidently.

When Lynx dragged Cole over to the waiting stage, Cole began protesting his beating, claiming a man wasn't guilty until tried.

McNelly glanced at the bloody Cole and stated calmly, "I didn't see Cardone lift a finger against you, other than to prevent you from escaping after an attempted holdup which I personally witnessed and will testify to in court. Seems I was busy with your surprise."

Lynx gaped at the belligerent and lovely female with fiery red curls. Little Red was a woman! He promptly realized how the successful scouting was carried out. Who would suspect an attractive woman of spying! His astonishment mounted when he learned her name, Callie O'Hara. "So you're Darlin' Nelle's cousin," he murmured reflectively, absorbing the image of past misconceptions. Two fiery-headed Callies.

"So you're Calinda Braxton's husband," she sneered hatefully. "Too bad Cole didn't let his men work her over good. I doubt a Cardone would have taken back used goods."

McNelly glanced at Lynx, but Lynx merely smiled satanically at Cole and Callie. Lynx hoped McNelly didn't suspect the truth. With each mission, more Rangers were discovering his identity and more people were suspecting it. He wished he could confide in McNelly, but he needed to keep silent a while longer. The more who knew, the less effect he had. Since Tom was Lynx's contact with Jones, Tom was one of the few who knew who left that warning mark behind. How he wished he could tell Cal.

McNelly promised to take care of Cole and his men before Lynx headed out for Waco to catch up on the news of the Bass gang. From Murphy's traitorous reports, the gang was heading south from Dallas, their target either Waco or Round Rock. Murphy was to let Jones know something definite this week. Lynx had been ordered to remain at Waco until word arrived. Before leaving the Rangers, Lynx sent a telegram home, telling Rankin and Calinda about the defeat of the Stevens gang. He said he would send word again when possible.

Lynx paced his room in Waco for three days before word came from Murphy, saying the target was the bank at Round Rock on Friday, either July 12 or 19, according to how things looked in town when they arrived. Most of the time Lynx could cover his involvement with his gunslinger reputation as a paid assistant or as a favor to a Ranger friend. But this mission would unavoidably reveal his identity to several noted lawmen. On July 8, Lynx rode out of Waco, heading for Round Rock to meet with Major Jones and other famed Rangers.

It was Lynx's assignment to mingle in the saloons, watching for any sign of Bass or his men. When Friday the twelfth came and went, it was concluded Bass would strike the next Friday. An urgent message came from Murphy: Round Rock Bank on the nineteenth.

Lynx had a week to while away in that rowdy cowtown. He missed Calinda and wanted to get home. None of the Rangers were allowed to send telegrams or letters out of Round Rock—it was vital that they maintain a low profile. The days were arid and boring; the nights, long and stuffy. For the first time in his Ranger career, Lynx became edgy and restless. It had been over two weeks since he'd been with Calinda, with over another week to go before he could even think of heading toward her arms.

At the ranch, things were going much the same for Calinda and Rankin. With the capture of the Cole Stevens gang, Rankin didn't lower his guard. He was concerned over another outlaw trying where Cole had failed. Calinda often went riding with Rankin or helped with the stable chores. When the day was too hot or was rainy, she found tasks inside to occupy her mind.

Lynx had sent a telegram on the sixth, but nothing since then. She fretted over his safety and the lack of word from him. Neighbors came to call several times, giving Calinda a chance to get better acquainted and to entertain. Twice she and Rankin went to visit friends of his, staying for dinner both times.

It had been seventeen days since Lynx cheerfully rode away from the ranch. As if in a lull before a powerful storm, Calinda and Salina had practiced good conduct. They had been careful to avoid arguing or fencing; even their thinly veiled insults had ceased. They were civil to each other even when Rankin wasn't around. It seemed as if each was finally resigned to the other's role in the Cardone house.

As the days slowly drifted by, Calinda experienced mild discontent and loneliness; she was too inactive. She missed Lynx terribly, but she also missed female companionship and the engrossing facets of society and civilization. She longed for exciting evenings at amusing plays, elaborate dinners, and gay parties. She missed the enthralling shops which larger towns offered. She loved Rankin and the ranch, but there was little to do but dreary chores or the same masculine games each day. Cal was educated and vivacious; she missed fascinating people and enlivening events. She liked the hired hands, but there was little in common with them. Amusement here might include a swim in the pond or a raucous game of horseshoes. If she were really lucky, there might be a taxing dinner or barbecue where the conversations centered on cattle, horses, the weather, or violence. The people here were kind and nice, but their sole interest appeared to be daily existence. Surely she would get accustomed to the monotonous routine and lack of diversions. If only she had at least one female friend, but the women here were too busy for such relationships.

Calinda wondered if the hardships, sacrifices, boredom, and loneliness were the factors behind Laura's misery and malicious behavior. Had Laura taken her unhappiness out on her husband and son? Calinda recalled Lynx's allusions to Laura's love of money and power; out here, those were critical defenses, means for survival. She couldn't be right, for Laura had been blessed with her husband's and son's presence.

When word failed to arrive from Lynx, Salina's old suspicions surfaced and blossomed. She told herself that nasty scene in the kitchen had been for Calinda's benefit, to further disarm and enchant her. Evidently Calinda didn't feel secure in her role, or she would be taking over by now. Was Calinda afraid to test her importance? Perhaps Lynx had given her a scolding in private, warned her to behave or be sent on her way. Still, Calinda was settling in too firmly. Something had to be done to shake her confidence and trust. Salina's resentments had festered with time and suppression; they were ready to burst open and spew forth their viciousness. Salina couldn't forget that revealing conversation between Rankin and Lynx, those dark secrets in her favor . . .

It had been pouring rain for two days, and Calinda was confined to the house. Lightning slashed across the dark sky. Violent claps of thunder rattled the windows; twice, windy gusts blew them open, allowing rain to soak the floor. The house was immaculate; laundry had to be postponed. There was little to do; Rankin was in Fort Worth on business.

Calinda had read constantly for the past two days. She was bored and tense. An idea came to her restive mind; she could clean the attic. Attics were always fun. Hidden treasures were discovered; adventures could be imagined. Perhaps there was something of value stored there, perhaps old furniture which could be refinished and used. Perhaps it contained boyhood prizes of her husband, items to warm her heart and lighten her mood on a dreary day. She almost invited Salina to go along, for she had been pleasant lately. Since they were the only two women around, it was foolish to be enemies. Calinda decided against it, dreading her invitation would send Salina off on one of her unpredictable tirades. At least, they were speaking and not quarreling. Perhaps in time . . .

Calinda took a lantern and mounted the steps. Once inside, she glanced around. She grinned in pleasure. The attic was filled with boxes and trunks, old furniture, and such. She inched her way around, peeking here and there. She abruptly laughed. Never had she thought the day would come when a musty, cluttered attic was the highlight of her existence! But it would be different when Lynx came home.

To her disappointment, most of the trunks were empty. She realized those were the ones which had contained Laura's clothes. Two other trunks were sealed by rusty locks. There was an interesting crate of old books which she could check later. She found a beautifully carved wash-stand which would be lovely if refinished. She found boy's clothing, snuggling them to her heart. She wondered what it would be like to have her own child, Lynx's baby. There were two crates of old toys, some in excellent or fair condition and others irreparable. She trailed her fingers over a cradle, trying to envision her love tiny and crying inside of it. There were odds and ends which should be discarded.

On the far wall was a painting covered with a moldy sheet. Cal removed the filthy covering, sneezing as dust scattered around her. She stared at the exquisite woman in the portrait. The woman was small, but very shapely. Her skin looked as if the radiant sun itself had kissed it gently with a golden tan. Her silvery gold hair hung to her waist, curling ever so slightly. Her eyes appeared as tawny as precious topaz. There was no doubt; the woman was Lynx's mother.

Calinda moved closer, holding the lantern up for more light. If the oils didn't lie or exaggerate, there was a vivid sparkle of life in Laura's exquisite face, especially her compelling eyes. Her features were delicate, she had a face which could stun a man speechless. Lynx definitely favored his breathtaking mother. Cal understood what Rankin had meant by seeing Laura in Lynx's smile and twinkling eyes.

As Calinda turned her head to one side, she observed a curious aspect which she hadn't noticed at first glance. On closer study, there seemed to be a softly provocative countenance about Laura Cardone. Perhaps it was the artist's interpretation or a trick of the lighting. But Laura's expression and pose created an impression of untameable wildness, a radiant and carefree spirit, a playful seductiveness. It was as if Laura knew she was a beautiful creature who could take or give if it suited her purpose, a woman accustomed to having her way. How Calinda wished she had known this unique woman.

Standing there, Calinda couldn't imagine this ravishing beauty as a deprived pioneer in a raw and dangerous land, or screaming in pain in a lonely mountain shack while giving birth to Lynx, or tranquilly enduring the kind of existence which Calinda was living now. Laura Cardone was a woman who seemed to belong in expensive gowns and jewels, in a large town where civilization was at its peak, or on an English estate with countless servants and a husband with the king's ear. Laura Cardone definitely didn't appear the cowgirl type.

Laura must have loved Rankin deeply to share his earlier days in this rugged territory. Rankin must have loved her, for he still carried scars from her death. And Lynx, how could this vital creature deny all love for her only son? Could it be she hadn't wanted children? Could it have been the harsh circumstances around his birth which caused her to resent him, to avoid having other children? Surely some tragic misunderstanding was at the bottom of their problem? Oddly, Laura's image didn't imply arrogance, but immense pride and self-assurance. Calinda couldn't find any traces of coldness and cruelty. Obviously, Laura had changed drastically after the flattering portrait.

The painting was splendid, but the heat and moisture were taking their toll. Had they placed it here to keep from facing it each day, a painful reminder of her loss? Would seeing it again re-open those unhealed wounds? It was too costly and beautiful to be ruined in the attic. If they didn't want it hung downstairs, she should at least clean it and store it properly. One day, the anguish would be gone; one day her children would like to view their grandmother.

Calinda carried the painting downstairs to the kitchen. She carefully placed it on the table to scrub gently. She would return it to the attic and cover it tightly to prevent damage. As she worked, Calinda wondered about this ravishing creature.

Also bored, Salina was straightening the pantry. She heard Calinda come into the kitchen. Strange noises reached her ears, enticing her to investigate. When Salina moved to glance into the kitchen, she couldn't believe the sight before her wide eyes. Surely Calinda wasn't planning what she thought! Rankin and Lynx would be furious when they came home, to find that treacherous harlot's picture hanging again! Salina smiled maliciously. *Let Cal do as she pleased* . . .

Another thought flashed through Salina's wicked mind. They would simply claim grief and take it down. They would never tell Calinda the truth. Somehow she needed to inspire mistrust in Calinda. This was the perfect moment to expose one damaging secret . . .

Salina sauntered into the kitchen, sighing wearily. "If you will not tattle, I will sneak a brandy," she murmured. "What are you . . ." She dramatically halted and gaped at the object of Calinda's attention. "Where . . . did you get that?" she stammered as if shocked.

Calinda glanced over at Salina, puzzled by her behavior. "What's wrong? I'm not harming it. It shouldn't have been hung in the attic; it's nearly ruined. Perhaps a good cleaning will have it lovely again."

"You cannot hang that down here," Salina fearfully mumbled, staring at the painting as if mesmerized by a horrifying demon.

"You look as if you're seeing a ghost, Salina. It's only an old painting of Laura Cardone, a very good one. It would be terrible to allow it to deteriorate," she explained.

"What are you planning to do with it?" Salina continued her game to spark Calinda's intrigue. Matters had gone so well between them recently that Calinda shouldn't suspect a thing. Salina was aware of Calinda's friendly overtures and genial manner lately. Salina had been pretending to gradually mellow toward Calinda. For the past two days alone, she had compelled herself to converse politely with Calinda.

"I don't know. Why?" Calinda asked in rising intrigue. Salina was behaving so strangely—she looked panicky; why?

"If I were you, I would put it back this *momento*," Salina advised, her voice strained and her gaze wary.

Calinda halted her work to look at Salina. "Why?" she asked.

"*No importe*," Salina stated, her gaze staying locked on Laura.

There was a knock on the front door. Calinda said she would see who was there. It was one of the hands checking on them for Rankin. Salina peeked around the corner, watching Calinda speak with Charlie, then close the door and head her way. She hurried over to the painting and stared down at it, muttering, "If she knew the truth about you and her papa, you traitorous *puta*, she would burn it."

Salina turned to fetch her brandy from the front room. She jumped as if startled by Calinda's presence and a quizzical stare. "Who was it?" she asked, trying to sway Cal. "Want a brandy?" she offered.

"What truth, Salina?" she demanded tacitly.

"Truth?" she repeated, her black eyes darting around as if trying to think of a hasty explanation.

"I heard you. What about my father and Laura?"

"I do not know what you are talking about," Salina declared, exhibiting phony panic and noticeable dishonesty.

Calinda walked over to the table and gazed down at the image. "Why did you call her a traitorous *puta*? What is a *puta*? Why did you say I would burn it if I knew the truth?" Calinda pressed stubbornly.

"You must have misunderstood me. I was just . . . just muttering about a saloon girl in town who is making eyes at my *hombre*," the Mexican girl alleged saucily.

"You're lying," Calinda charged.

Salina forced herself to look even more edgy and secretive. "Do not be silly. Do you want a brandy?" she asked again, acting as if she were trying to pacify Calinda.

When she tried to leave the kitchen, Calinda seized her arm and prevented her flight. "I heard you plainly, Salina. Now tell me what you were talking about," Calinda persisted. "What do you know about my father? Don't lie to me," she commanded sternly.

"I never met your papa; he was gone before I came to work here. My chores are finished. I will rest for a while. Do you want me to cook your dinner tonight?" the malicious girl offered sweetly.

"What I want is an explanation, now," Calinda demanded.

"About what?" Salina stalled intentionally.

"Damnit, Salina! If you don't speak up, I'll question Rankin."

Salina inhaled sharply and rapidly shook her head. "No, you cannot!" The words seemed to burst forth uncontrollably. "I am in *mucho* trouble here because of you. Have you not noticed how good I have been lately? You will spill your guts the minute *Senor* Rankin or Lynx returned, just like you did about Lampasas," she accused.

"I didn't tell Lynx anything except what we agreed on. You're the one who betrayed our bargain!" Calinda retorted angrily.

"No, I did not! I only said I did to aggravate you."

"But why?" Calinda inquired.

"I wanted to make you miserable, to leave. I never expected them to ask you to live here. I was shocked when Lynx married you. I love him for years; then you stroll in and take him without even lifting a finger to snare him. Things were fine until you came. I was happy; they were like my family. But you have changed everything; all they care about is you and keeping you happy. I know part of the trouble was mine. I wanted to prove you did not belong here with us. Maybe I am wrong, but I do not trust you."

"If I've made you unhappy, Salina, I'm sorry. It wasn't intentional. You've known Lynx for a long time. Can you blame me for falling in love with him? But I don't want to push you out. Why can't we make a fresh start and become friends? We're the only women for miles. It would be fun to work together and talk. Is that impossible?"

"It is too late, *senora*. We have been too mean to each other. We could never trust each other," Salina cunningly hedged.

Challenged, Calinda argued, "That isn't true, Salina."

"You would suspect everything I say or do. If I confided in you, you would run to the Cardones, and they would get rid of me. I feel I live on borrowed time here. I have tried to be nice to you since Lynx left, *si*? But I do not see how we can become *amigas*."

"I've proven I can be trusted, Salina. Haven't I tried to ease your concerns and stay out of your way? I can see how these changes have been difficult for you, but you must accept them. Please."

As Salina pensively mused on Calinda's words, Calinda asked, "What are you trying to conceal from me about my father?"

Salina shifted nervously. "If I dared open my mouth, you would tell them. You could not help it. You would insist on more facts or try to solve the problem. You cannot. What is done is done, *senora*. Forget about your papa and the past. It is trouble for all of us."

"If you weren't here, how could you know anything vital? Do you spy on the Cardones?" Cal asked, trying to trick Salina into a defensive disclosure.

"No!" Salina shrieked. "But I could not help but learn certain things over the years. Sometimes they forget I am around and talk too freely. But I do not listen at door cracks, so do not accuse me of such."

"What did you overhear, Salina?" she insisted firmly.

"I cannot repeat it," Salina defied her demand.

"I'll ask Rankin to explain your statements, if you don't."

"If you speak to him about this, you will be *mucho* sorry, *senora*. If he does not lie to you, you will regret forcing the truth from him. Do not remind *Senor* Rankin or Lynx you are a Braxton. Hide the picture and forget Laura Cardone and your papa."

Something about the provocative inflection on those two names linked together inspired suspicion in Calinda. Both left the same day. Lynx had called her father traitorous; Salina had called Laura traitorous. Everyone refused to discuss either. "I might be sorry later, Salina, but I'm going to unmask the truth."

"You do not hear me, *senora;* everyone will suffer. They will demand to know how you discovered such clues. I will be fired, perhaps beaten!" she blurted out anxiously.

"I swear to you I'll keep silent," Calinda vowed desperately.

"Not after you learn why he ran!" Salina shouted at her.

"I promise you, I'll never mention either of them or the past if you'll tell me what you know," Calinda tried once more to convince her.

"*Demonio!* I am trapped between devils and demons!" Salina ranted. "If I keep silent, you will talk with *Senor* Rankin. If I speak, you still might. Either way, I am doomed. Why did you have to come here causing trouble and digging up the past? Why would you even take my word? You will think I lie just to hurt you! There is no guessing what they will do to me. You are too damn tender-hearted! You will try to ease their pains; I know you will," she panted, as if that trait were an insult. Both girls jumped as thunder crashed nearby.

"If you lie to me out of malice, Salina, I'll make you sorry."

"That is the problem! You will think so," she charged heatedly.

"This has gone far enough. If you don't explain yourself, I'll speak to Rankin the minute he returns. If you tell me, I give you my word I won't repeat it to them, no matter what it is."

Salina guilefully paced the floor, fretting and thinking. "All right, *senora*, but I warned you. *Primero*, I need a brandy." She fled into the other room and quickly downed two glasses, pouring another to sip. She handed Calinda a sherry. "You might need that, and you must sit down," she advised gravely.

Salina roamed the spacious area for a time. Calinda said, "Stop stalling, Salina." Salina turned and met her probing gaze.

"I was trying to decide where to begin," she murmured.

"Why not at the beginning?" Calinda suggested, annoyed.

"I do not know the beginning, only the end. I know why your papa vanished, and I know why the Cardones hate him."

Salina sank into a chair, acting as if this confession was weighty. "Your papa was *Senora* Cardone's lover. When *Senor* Rankin discovered their affair, he confronted them together *en cama,* in bed. There was a terrible fight, and *Senor* Rankin was injured. While he was unconscious, your papa stole money, *mucho* money, and escaped. Lynx was the one who found his bloody papa. Lynx loved your papa. You can imagine how the truth hurt him. Your papa betrayed them, used them, and destroyed their family. Can you see how *Senor* Rankin felt when he learned his wife was whoring with his *amigo? Peor,* in his *cama,* his *casa?* That is why Lynx hates women and does not trust them," she vowed.

Calinda was gaping at her in stunned disbelief. Salina went on, "How could they allow you to step foot in this *casa* after what your papa did to them. I suspected *venganza,* revenge; they could punish or trap your papa with you. As a *presa,* they could lure your father out of hiding. But when Lynx married you, I was confused. He would not go that far to punish *el enemigo.* He must love you to lose his freedom."

When Salina halted to catch a breath, Calinda still remained silent and stiff. "Do you see why they will not speak of the past and your papa? Do you see why you cannot hang that picture? I will never understand why they did not burn it and her things. Why would *Senor* Rankin give her clothes to you, to see such reminders of that *bruja?*"

"What is a *puta?* A *bruja?* What happened to Laura? Did Rankin kill her in a fit of rage? Did she take her own life? She was too young to die naturally. If my father loved her enough to do such things, why leave her behind?" Calinda questioned in a strained voice.

"If you repeat this, I will deny every word. That grave on the hillside is for protection, to save face. *Bruja* is witch; *puta* is whore. *Senora* Laura is not dead; she ran away with your papa. She sacrificed her *casa, esposo, nombre,* and *hijo* for your papa. She has sent no word to Lynx since she left. That is why he went to roaming the countryside, searching for them. *Acaso* he still looks for his *madre.* When *Senor* Rankin healed, he told everyone your papa had run off to new pastures; he said *Senora* Laura died of a sudden illness. Very few people know the truth. See why I feared to speak such words?"

"How could they do such a cruel thing? If they loved each other, why didn't Laura divorce Rankin and marry my father? How could she desert her own child? Never see him again? Never communicate with him?" Cal reasoned in anguish.

"Your papa did the same to you and your *madre, Senora* Cal," Salina added softly, to send her incisive point home.

"It can't be true, Salina," she argued against the searing truth.

"You must tell no one of our talk. *Tener cuidado,* be careful. Do not keep reminding them you are Braxton's *hija.* Your papa will never return here and risk his life. He dares not contact you and give away his location. Forget him; you have sided with the Cardones."

"I can't! I must learn why it happened," Calinda stated dejectedly.

"Why does anyone fall in love? Why is anyone selfish and cruel? There are no *bueno* answers to such questions. If you go seeking more answers or your *mal* papa, you will lose Lynx and *Senor* Rankin," she warned anxiously. "You are lucky to live here, more so to have Lynx."

"How could they stand to even look at me?"

"You know the truth. Can you stand to look at them? Does it change your *amor* for Lynx?" she craftily pointed out such emotions to gain Calinda's trust and imperative silence. Let Cal be plagued with doubts and insecurities, but suffer in agonizing silence.

"Where could they be?" Calinda mused aloud.

"Anywhere, *Senora* Cal. They would be *loco* not to put a great distance between them and the Cardones."

"But what about that letter for me to come to Lampasas?"

"*Acaso* that is why Lynx was so alarmed. He knew it could not be from your papa. Do you think Cole Stevens sent it?"

"No. Maybe it wasn't from my father, but it might have been from a contact of his. If I was being lured into a trap by an unknown enemy, nobody showed up to seal it. Still, I'm glad Lynx came along," she murmured gratefully.

"That was lucky for you. It did teach you how dangerous this area can be and how much you need the Cardones. It also inspired Lynx to marry you. So, it was not all bad," Salina dropped little seeds to take root in Calinda's mind and to grow entangling vines there.

"Are you positive that's what happened, Salina?"

"I can only repeat what I heard; I cannot swear it is true."

"You're right about one thing; I can't discuss this with them." Calinda missed Salina's satanic smile.

It was working beautifully. Salina asked, "Would you like me to put that picture where it belongs, in that dark attic? You did not say; do you want me to cook dinner before I leave?"

"Leave?" Calinda inquired.

"I go to town. A *buen mozo vaquero*," Salina lied skillfully.

After Salina interpreted her words about meeting a very handsome cowboy, Calinda said, "You go along and dress. I can take care of dinner and the portrait. There's little else to do tonight."

Salina headed for the door. She stopped and glanced at Calinda, relieved Calinda was too distraught to remind her of the storm outside. Within the hour, Salina would be forcing Lynx from her mind in the arms of some man yet to be selected for that urgent purpose. Besides, her body was aching for a man's passionate touch. "You have no reason to trust me, *Senora* Cal, but I swear your papa and *Senora* Cardone ran away together. You will not tell?" she pressed, as if anxious.

"No. Thank you, Salina. Would you like to borrow a dress to wear tonight?" Calinda generously offered.

"I do not wish to wear anything of that *puta's*," she refused.

"Neither do I," Calinda concurred absently.

Salina tensed in panic. "If you stop wearing them and start acting strange, they will know something is wrong," she speculated.

"Not if I buy new clothes." Calinda solved that dilemma.

"It must be nice," Salina sighed dreamily, envious.

"I'll buy you a new dress, too," Calinda decided aloud.

"You must not; that will look just as odd," Salina remarked.

"Not if we keep it a secret," she refuted, smiling faintly.

"I do not think we wear the same kinds of clothes," Salina discouraged any show of kindness from her rival.

"Then I'll give you the money to select your own."

"*Por que,* why?" Salina asked seriously, amused.

"An offer of friendship," Calinda declared honestly.

"Perhaps I have been wrong about you," Salina hinted.

"Maybe we've both been in error," Calinda added, smiling.

"See you in the morning. Do not forget to lock up," Salina reminded her, sauntering out of the room. She wanted Calinda to be alone in the quiet house, to have privacy and time to think . . .

Calinda sat in the shadowy room for a long time, then went into the kitchen. She lifted the portrait and stared at it, trying to envision this woman in past reality. She mentally placed Laura beside her father, or how he had looked long ago. Truthfully, she might not even recognize him today if she passed within a foot of him! Surely he had changed with time and age.

Was selfish, wanton love the answer she had been seeking to his disappearance? Real love was precious and rare; could the desire for it entice such cruelty and betrayal? Had they been so desperate to be together? Or had they simply fled out of discovery and fear? Hadn't she and Lynx deserved just one letter from them? Were they still alive somewhere? Had they regretted their decision, if only once? Were they happy? How could they be happy when they had obtained it with the sufferings of others?

Calinda never doubted Salina's words; for that shocking revelation logically explained her father's actions and the Cardones' behavior and innuendoes. Although she felt Salina had told the truth, Cal helplessly suspected malicious motives. She returned the portrait to where she had found it, wishing she had never laid eyes on it or Salina had tricked her into pressing for the truth. She wandered around the house, locking and checking doors and windows. She went to the room shared with her husband when he was home. She pried open the drawer and withdrew her locket. She opened it and studied the stranger.

"Why, Father? How could you do such evil things?" she asked.

She sat down on the edge of the bed, sobbing. How she wished Lynx were here to comfort her. Yet she couldn't even hint at this devastating discovery. How could she pretend she didn't know? How could she keep it from him? Still, she must.

Now that she knew the truth, their silence was understandable. A mingling of male pride and affection for her had imprisoned their tongues. In fact, they had never said Laura was dead. They always said "gone" or "left." It was painfully clear why they didn't want to talk about Laura or Brax or the past: they were all interconnected. Laura's betrayal had crushed Lynx; he had justifiable reasons for doubting her love. The truth explained so much about Lynx. He had cause to be bitter and cynical.

Calinda was glad they had met before he learned her identity. If they hadn't, Lynx would never have given them a chance. "Oh, Lynx, I'm so sorry for what Brax did to you. I wish I could erase the past and your pain, but I can't. Let the past die. Please don't punish us for our parents' deed. Please don't seek revenge against them."

Punish, the word rang across her mind. Her weeping abruptly subsided. "Stop it!" she ordered herself. "Don't even vaguely consider such vile thoughts."

But the speculations grew larger and wilder in her warring mind as the storm outside increased its fury. Revenge . . .

Cal couldn't deny they had wanted to keep her at the ranch. She couldn't rationally explain her hasty marriage. She knew they had kept the truth from her, had tried to stop her search.

It couldn't be true! Lynx wouldn't marry her just to lure her father back. A more ominous thought forced itself into her dazed mind; would he entrap her with love and marriage, then seek revenge or appeasement by copying her treacherous father's actions? Could Lynx hate her father that deeply, that obsessively? Could Lynx seek to repay Brax by destroying his child? Were Lynx and Rankin in on some treacherous plot? But who was their intended victim, she or her father? Was she only a pawn in a vindictive game?

Calinda's mind raced backward to her arrival, then slowly walked forward to this moment. She didn't like what she was thinking. What had Lynx said that day when she ventured, "Love me and keep me forever"? He had replied, "If I ever wanted to do anything more in my life . . ." Wanted to do? Had he ever said, I love you? He usually said, "need" or "want." Was physical desire enough to compel marriage? No. She analyzed the damaging clues.

The locket . . . Had Lynx been one of the bandits that day? Had he known who she was that night in the saloon? Positively, he wasn't that roguish and lecherous leader. But were they friends? Was he a merry bandit, seeking daring challenges while keeping his identity a secret? Was that why he had kept the precious necklace from her, preventing discovery?

The letter . . . Had Lynx planted that mysterious letter to lure her into danger, danger from which he would rescue her, danger which would bring her under his control? A rescue to indebt and beguile her? Was Clint Deavers another friend and assistant?

Waco . . . How had they accidentally run into each other? Had Rankin informed Lynx of her visit, to allow Lynx to work his charms on her? Had Lynx been watching her to see if her father would contact her? Lynx had discouraged her about seeking the Rangers' help. Why?

Cole Stevens . . . Had Lynx planned that terrifying scheme? What new lesson was it supposed to teach her? Cole had called her Callie. Had Stevens truly been captured? Perhaps Lynx had warned his outlaw friends!

Lynx had too many secrets, too many connections to dangerous men, too many timely rescues! The newspaper announcements . . . Were they crafty enticements for Brax?

"No!" she cried out in torment. Why was she doing this to herself? It was all a series of coincidences and strokes of good fortune!

Calinda remembered something Lynx had said about mistrusting her in the beginning. Surely they didn't think she and her father were plotting some mischief? For what? They knew Brax wouldn't return here; he had taken Laura with him. They couldn't possibly believe she would help Brax and Laura alter that missing deed to steal the ranch!

If Lynx didn't trust her, why would he marry her? If anything happened to him and Rankin, the ranch would be . . . hers. *My God,* she fretted, *surely they wouldn't set themselves up as targets for Brax and Laura?* If the Cardones were removed, those two could return home and take everything. That logic was insane! Or desperately evil and vengeful . . .

Calinda forced such terrible speculations from her mind. She knew and loved both Lynx and Rankin. They could never plan and carry out such evil. Her mind was playing tricks on her. It must be the gloomy solitude and the violent storm, one which was raging as wildly outside the house as the emotional one inside of her.

They might have mistrusted and disliked her in the beginning, but not now. It just wasn't possible. Surely they were only protecting her from anguish and themselves from shame. Missing puzzle pieces were causing her imagination to run crazy. She returned the locket and went to bed, ordering herself to forget this entire day.

—— *Chapter* 16 ——

⮞

BY FRIDAY, JULY 19, there were six Rangers hiding out in Round Rock: Major Jones, Dick Ware, Tom Peters, George Harrell, Chris Connor, and Lynx Cardone. In addition to the Ranger force, the sheriff and several deputies were available. It was decided that the Rangers would remain concealed, but the local lawmen would move around as normal to prevent suspicion. The waiting had begun when the bank opened; it was presently mid-afternoon.

Connor was visually scouting the street from the grimy windows, the other men relaxing after their turns. They had consumed cold ham and biscuits, washed down with strong coffee. As time continued to crawl by like a sluggish snail, someone said that Bass had probably changed his mind. Murphy had reported that Bass and his men were watching him like a hawk, so something must have gone awry.

The deputies were milling around aimlessly, or so it appeared to the innocent eye. The day was hot and clear. Each man sensed this could be his last one and mentally prepared for a deadly confrontation.

"Anything, Chris?" Jones inquired from his chair.

"Three cowpokes just rode in. Stopping at the saloon. No sign of trouble or Murphy." Connor's eyes scanned the entire street.

"From the last message, there should be four of them. You all have Murphy's description; he'll be impossible to miss."

In the saloon, Sam Bass and two of his men swaggered over to the wooden bar and ordered whiskies. They headed for a table and sat down to relax. Trying to get a message to the Rangers about the change in plans, Murphy had claimed his horse had a sand crack in his front hoof, halting by the stable to get help. The nervous traitor stalled for a lengthy spell, just in case he was being watched. He had to locate a lawman and tell him the robbery would take place tomorrow; he wanted out of this perilous bargain as quickly as possible.

Two deputies walked over to the saloon to check out the three strangers, one waiting outside and one entering. The deputy nodded to the bartender and wandered about the nearly deserted saloon. When he came to the strangers, he remarked genially, "I see you cowpokes are still toting yer sidearms. Ain't allowed in town. Check 'em with the barkeeper or ride on through. Ain't seen you fel . . ."

The deputy didn't complete his sentence before one of the outlaws drew his gun and fatally shot him. The deputy waiting outside looked over the batwing doors. He, too, was killed instantly by the panicky gang, the frail wood splintering as two bullets blasted through it and into the unsuspecting lawman's body. His torso struck forcefully by the gunfire, the second deputy was hurled backward into the dusty street. The outlaws raced out the door and fled toward their horses.

Ware shouted, "Bet it's them!"

The Rangers surged out of the building, opening fire and shouting instructions to halt. Seaborn Barnes was struck by a lethal bullet before he could cross the dirt street. Bass took a direct hit and staggered. Frank Jackson reached the horses and mounted frantically. Seeing Bass was wounded, Jackson fetched both horses and helped the injured Bass to mount. Both men galloped out of town, bullets and dust flying all around them. Out of range, the shooting ceased.

When the dust and suspense settled, Murphy revealed himself, reminding Jones he was their helper and was supposed to go free. A small posse was formed under the leadership of the Rangers. They quickly pursued Sam and Frank. The lengthy chase was on . . .

The search continued far into the night, until it was too dark to see anything. The posse camped to rest and eat. At first light, the search was on again. Around noon, Tom sighted a fallen man beyond them. When they reached him, the man proudly informed them he was the notorious Samuel Bass.

When they reached town with the wounded outlaw, Sam was questioned about Jackson. A man of curious honor, Bass refused to betray one of his men. He endured his agony without complaints. By Sunday morning, the infamous Sam Bass was dead. As if fate had stepped in, Sam died on his twenty-seventh birthday on July 21, 1878.

When Sam was buried on Monday, the whole town turned out for the short ceremony, behaving as if it were a mournful occasion. His colorful and daring exploits were related time and again. Flowers were placed near his tombstone. Several witnesses were teary-eyed. Strangely, it seemed they were laying to rest a beloved legend.

Lynx noticed a photographer as he made picture after picture of the historical episode; as usual, he tried to conceal his presence. Normally he avoided exposure with ease and skill, but today he knew he had been captured on film several times. Only two Rangers present knew why Lynx was there, so he could slip away without joining the victory celebration. In Waco, he would send a telegram home as soon as the reports were signed and filed. First, he needed to locate that photographer and see if he could confiscate that perilous film—that would force him to hang around another day. This secrecy was a pain in the neck! At the earliest, he could make the ranch by Friday.

While Lynx was completing the business of Sam Bass in Round Rock, Calinda was experiencing her second and third shocks in less than a week. Since her stunning discovery about Brax and Laura, neither she nor Salina had mentioned it again. Salina had been calm and cheerful, pressing her advantage by revealing a genial acceptance of Calinda, delighting Rankin and fooling him completely. The guileful Salina had even begun to use her nickname to display fondness.

The day after that stunning incident, Calinda had been pensively reserved. Rankin concluded she was missing Lynx and working too hard. For Calinda did push herself for the next five days with chores, any task which would drive her body to exhaustion so her mind could rest at night. She adamantly refused to recall that devastating episode, blocking such thoughts from mind when they tried to assail her. She kept telling herself all would be fine when Lynx came home. She told herself there were logical explanations for each coincidence or deceit.

On Tuesday, she had labored hard polishing saddles in the barn. She had gone riding with her father-in-law later. When she entered the house to gather her things to bathe, Salina hastily approached her. The Mexican girl glanced behind her to make certain she was alone. "I did not think *Senor* Rankin should see this. The man delivered it while you were riding; it is a letter from England. You must see this, too, before *Senor* Rankin comes home," she added, handing Calinda the newspaper. "I feared he would hide it to avoid a problem."

Calinda's brow lifted inquisitively. "See what?" she asked, gripping the Simpsons' fat letter tightly in her shaky hand.

Salina pointed to the story about the slaying and burying of Sam Bass. Calinda met her curious gaze and said, "I don't want to read about violence and outlaws."

"Just look at the pictures," Salina encouraged slyly.

"No," Calinda refused, recalling her perilous episodes with Cole Stevens, the stage bandits, and Clint Deavers.

"Lynx is in several of them," Salina came to the point.

Calinda almost snatched the paper from her. There were three printed photographs and a lengthy account of the deadly drama. The first picture was taken immediately after the shooting. People were crowding around a dead man lying in the dusty street; in the background was Lynx Cardone. The next picture was taken when the wounded Sam Bass was brought into town after his capture; Lynx was standing beside Star in the left corner. The last picture was at Sam's burial; standing again in the background was her missing husband. She hurriedly scanned the story which told of a daring shoot-out with five Texas Rangers: Peters, Connor, J.B. Jones, Harrell, and Ware. Two bandits had been killed and one had escaped. Cal remembered Lynx telling her Sam Bass had robbed her stage and stolen her locket, now in Lynx's possession. Why was Lynx at the scene of another Bass crime? Attending the funeral of a friend? Had Lynx been involved in this foiled crime? She scanned the story once more; there were no mentions of Lynx.

"Why would Lynx be in Round Rock?" Calinda wondered aloud.

"He is always where there is danger or excitement. Too bad he did not help them and become famous. Sam Bass is a legend."

"He was an outlaw, Salina; he robbed and killed," Calinda softly chided her. "So much for all the enlarged tales about Rangers. I was led to believe it merely required one Ranger to handle such a tiny battle with only three men. How far is this Round Rock?"

"I think a little less than two hundred miles south of Fort Worth."

"But he was only sixty miles west when he sent that telegram! Why would he go that far away? It'll take him days to get home."

"Is he heading straight home from there?" Salina guilefully asked.

"How should I know? He doesn't tell me anything!" she panted, before thinking. "He just said he would be back in a few weeks," she tried to correct her rash outburst. "I guess I'm just tired and hot."

"It is all right, Cal. It must be irritating to learn your *esposo's* whereabouts from a *periodico*. It is time you learn, *hombres* can be thoughtless creatures at times, especially in those circumstances."

"I suppose you're right. I'll get my bath now."

"What about the letter?" Salina hinted curiously.

"I'll read it later. If I know the Simpsons, they probably want money or a favor. Frankly, I'm not in the mood for them."

Salina returned to the kitchen while Calinda went upstairs. She locked her door and sat on the bed. Cal tore open the envelope and withdrew a nearly illegible note and another unsealed letter, noting the vaguely familiar handwriting on the envelope which bore no return address. She expected the note to be from the Simpsons; it wasn't.

> Missy Calinda,
> I promised ye any news of ye papa. I be leavin me work here and caint gits in no more trouble. I be cleanin the lady's room and found this here letter hiding there. They be wrong to keep it from ye. I prays it be good news. I won't be here to send no more letters to ye.
> Martha

Wrong to keep it from me? she mentally questioned. Calinda wondered what the baffling message meant from Martha Drummond, a dear servant in the Simpson household who had befriended her for years. When she had left England, sweet Martha had promised to forward any news from or about her father. Perhaps she should at least send news about her marriage. She glanced at the enclosed letter. Who would write to her from America in 1872? America, 1872 . . .

Suddenly Calinda went pale; her hands began to tremble so violently that the paper rattled noisily. Could it be . . . She ripped open the envelope, flipping the page to check the signature. Her vision blurred with tears as her father reached across time to haunt her.

Her hands sank to her lap. She leaned her head backward and closed her eyes, inhaling and exhaling several times to slow her racing heart. They had dared to read her letter, then steal it! Why not burn it? They had lied about not receiving any word! But why hide it and keep it for years? Did they plan to return it some day? What didn't they want her to read? Yet, what news needed saving? Dare she read it after all these years? 1872, the year he had left her existence . . .

My dearest daughter Calinda,

I write you this letter with great sadness and guilt. I will be leaving the Cardone Ranch soon. How I wish you could see it, my child. My heart is heavy at such losses, too many sacrifices. I have worked hard to earn something special and beautiful; now I must walk away forever from a dream too costly to claim.

I know I have been remiss as your father. I beg your understanding. I know you will find this difficult to believe, but I love you with all my heart. Forgive the pain and loneliness which you have endured because of me, my selfishness, my cowardice. For they still rule my world, and I must say farewell for a long time. One day, I promise to locate you and explain my coming actions. At present, I can offer you nothing but my love and prayers as I go to seek a new life. Where, I do not know.

I beg you not to hate me or forget me. I also ask that you do not seek to find me, for it won't be possible. I have given the Simpsons ten thousand dollars to care for you until you wed. Find true love, my precious child, for it is the richest of all dreams.

When the time is right, I will contact you through the Simpsons. Only in a life/death crisis, contact Kyle Yancey, a lawyer in Austin (Texas). Remember my love.

Your devoted father

Calinda stared at the date: August, 1872. So, the Simpsons had lied to her; his letters had ceased, but money had been sent: ten thousand dollars less than six years ago! How guilty they had made her feel over every shilling spent on her education, entertainment, and clothing. How dare they steal from her! They were no better than these western bandits. Then, to send her away with less than fifty dollars was criminal. She would rather those bandits had taken it than her so-called family. Evidently, Thomas had wasted her money along with his. It would serve him right to become destitute. If he dared to beg one sixpence from her, she would sneer in his face. All those years of feeling abandoned by her father, when he had sent money and word . . .

From the date and wording of her father's letter, he must have been planning to leave the ranch before Rankin's discovery of his foul deception. The "sacrifices" he must "walk away" from must have been Laura and Lynx and his life here. But he dallied with Laura too long and got caught. He was right; he was selfish, a bloody coward. True love? she scoffed. He didn't know the meaning of real love. Real love wasn't selfish, or cruel, or destructive.

How dare Brax try to condone his actions. How dare he ask for her love, understanding, patience, and forgiveness; he didn't deserve any of them! "How cunning you are, Father. You never mentioned your wanton affair. Your blood money couldn't replace what you took from me! I hate you," she vowed sadly, weeping softly.

Distraught, Cal tore the letters to shreds. "That's what I think of you and your promises. I don't need you or your love."

As Salina had speculated, Rankin didn't show her the paper or even mention it. Cal toyed with her food at dinner, staring at her plate. Resentment flooded her. She didn't know who or what to believe anymore. She felt deceived and dejected. She no longer knew what was truth or reality. She was trapped in illusion, help- lessly waiting for others to make their dreams or desires known.

"Cal, is something bothering you?" Rankin inquired in concern.

"When will Lynx be home, Rankin?" she asked a question instead of respond- ing to his. "This waiting and silence are stifling."

"I would imagine very soon, probably the end of the week. You miss him, don't you?" he teased happily.

"If he doesn't return soon, I might forget him," Cal scoffed, dropping her fork to her plate and sighing heavily.

Taking her statement as a joke, Rankin chuckled. "It's just the heat and humidity. You aren't used to them yet."

"Does anyone ever get accustomed to such conditions?" she debated his words. "I'm so bored. I think I'll ride into town tomorrow and go shopping. I might stay a few days and have some new clothes made, if that's all right with you."

"But Lynx should be arriving in a couple of days," he remarked.

"So? I've waited around for him for weeks. The least he can do is wait a day or two for me. He shouldn't worry; at least he'll know where I am," she sneered irritably.

"Are you feeling all right, Cal?" he asked, watching her.

"Stop staring at me; I'm fine," she responded.

"Spite is a two-edged sword, Cal," he warned softly, worried about her state of mind.

"I wouldn't know; I've never drawn or used that weapon," she commented flippantly. "I'll go crazy if I don't get some relief."

"Is there trouble between you and Salina?" he ventured.

"No; we're getting along fine now."

"I know you, Calinda Cardone; something isn't right," he insisted.

"Do you, Rankin?" she asked strangely, gazing at him.

"I think I do," he said.

"Sometimes I don't think I even know myself." Why was she calmly accepting this offensive treatment? Why was she too fearful to challenge Rankin and Lynx for the truth? Why forget about Brax?

"What do you mean?" he inquired, leaning forward to listen intently. Was it merely the demands of Lynx's absence on a new marriage and bride? She looked so melancholy, so insecure.

"Nothing. I'm just moody tonight. I'm sorry."

Calinda didn't go into town that week. She worked in and around the house until Friday afternoon, then took off to go swimming in the pond over the hill. As she swam in the oblong body of water, she reflected on her letter to the Simpsons which she had given to Salina this morning to mail when she went into town for supplies. Thankfully Martha couldn't be punished for her aid. By now, Salina should be home and the strongly worded letter should be on its way to the Simpsons.

Cal tried to imagine their reactions to her demand for an accounting of the

$10,000. She stated if she didn't receive an accounting and the balance due, she would turn the matter over to a lawyer. She told them her father was away on business; and by the way, she was married now to a wealthy and powerful man who would see that justice was done. She really didn't expect to hear from them, but maybe the threat would prevent future contact. Where had Brax gotten that money?

Calinda left the soothing water and stretched out on the grassy bank. She closed her eyes and gave herself over to dreamy relaxation. Her life was such a puzzle, with a mysterious golden stranger at the center of it. She loved him and wanted him, but could she trust him?

Cal's body felt light and drowsy. His lips were sweet and stirring as they softly captured hers. She sighed as her arms automatically encircled Lynx's body, greedily sealing her mouth to his and embracing him fiercely. As his lips drifted down her cheek to nibble playfully at her ear, she slowly aroused to learn she was not dreaming.

Her startled shriek of his name sent his ear ringing. Lynx raised his tawny head and shook it, grinning down at her. Her gaze slipped over his tousled hair which reminded her of wind tangled stalks of ripened wheat. His coppery features were lined with mischief and warmth.

"When did you get home?" Cal asked, without even a slight trace of a pleased smile. Her hands fell to the ground near her head, palms upward. Her expression was guarded and her eyes fathomless.

A pang of disappointment surged through Lynx as he witnessed her lack of a happy greeting. If he didn't know any better, he might be tempted to think Cal wasn't glad to see him. He flashed her a wide grin, deciding she was just peeved with his long absence. She shouldn't act so surprised; he had sent a telegram to expect him Friday. To make certain he reached home today, he had ridden as if the demons of hell were chasing him. Lynx was nettled by her chilly reception.

"Just in time to grab a fresh horse and ride over here," he informed her. "I tossed my things in our room, turned Star over to Homer, and high-tailed it to see my wife."

When he leaned forward to drop a kiss on the tip of her nose, he teased, "You shouldn't lie around like this, Cal; it's dangerous." He motioned to her dark blue shirt with missing sleeves and her cut-off jeans with their ragged bottoms which exposed most of her shapely calves. He chuckled when she looked annoyed.

"I'm fully clothed, Lynx, and perfectly safe," she told him, pointing to the gun lying in the grass near her.

Lynx refuted, "You were asleep, love; I did sneak up on you. But I was referring to the scorching sun and this cloud-white flesh."

Calinda placed her hand in the middle of his sturdy chest and pushed him aside to sit up. "Afraid I'll freckle instead of tan?" she said, her mind elsewhere.

He placed his elbows on the grassy earth to recline slightly with his torso propped up, one knee bent with a boot resting near his buttocks. "I've never seen a redhead with even a threat of golden skin."

"In your numerous travels, I'm certain you've met plenty of them. Have you seen your father?" she inquired casually.

"Nope. Don't tell him, but you're the one I wanted to see."

He sat up beside her as she challenged his husky claim, "If that were true, Cardone, you'd stay home more."

Lynx made the mistake of grinning ruefully and teasing, "Been missing me and it's got your dander up? Well, I'm here now." He leaned forward to rub his lips over a bare shoulder.

Calinda jerked away and stood up to leave. "I need to bathe and dress. It's getting late."

He bounded to his feet and caught her wrist to stop her. "Let's stay here and talk, Cal; we can skip dinner," he coaxed, his voice thick with rising passion, his eyes dark with it.

"I skipped lunch, so I'm starving," Cal responded tersely.

"I'm starving too," the playful rogue replied, reaching for her.

Calinda stunned him when she shoved his arms away and glared at him. "Is that all you care about? Sometimes I think that's the only reason you come home for brief visits! You run in, stuff yourself, then ride off again until hunger pangs nibble at you. In case you don't know it, Mister Cardone, a marriage requires more than sex!"

"What's gotten into you, Cal? You feel the same way about me. We need each other. If you're riled because I've been away so long, I'm sorry. I got home as soon as possible."

"How do you expect me to welcome you, my devoted husband? We've been married forty-two days, of which I've spent one and a half with you. Since we met seventy-five days past, I've been generously given a total of six days in your company, mostly in your bed. Is that all I'm good for, Cardone? We don't have time to discover each other."

"All I've wanted for weeks was to be home with you, Cal. I made promises, and I have friends who needed me," he reasoned.

"You also made promises to me! I needed you! Obviously your stimulating life and friends are more important to you. So go hug and kiss your carefree life and snuggle up to your numerous escapades of daring and danger. Obviously they give you more satisfaction than I do. Why even bother to come home?" she shrieked at him. "I'm sure you were having more fun and excitement in Round Rock."

"Round Rock?" he echoed anxiously. Damn! That photographer must have printed his picture. How else would she know about Round Rock? How could he explain to her without lying? Lynx had managed to keep a low profile at countless Ranger victories, until Round Rock. He didn't know Jones was gaping at the papers this very moment, praying no one would start adding up such damaging and enlightening figures.

Lynx captured her chin and lifted her head, probing her gaze which was a baffling mixture of sparkling fury and misty anguish. "My God, Callie, have I hurt and disappointed you this much?" he asked.

"How could you? You aren't around long enough to do anything to me or for me. I didn't even know when you'd be home."

"What about my telegram?" he debated.

"That was weeks ago. Or does time pass too swiftly and happily to notice? I see you didn't receive any scars from your run-in with Cole."

"I'm talking about the telegram from Waco two days ago," he clarified, his own temper steaming.

"What telegram? If one arrived, your father hasn't mentioned it. He also didn't mention your visit to Round Rock. You take a very good picture, my love. Your handsome face was emblazoned all over the paper he thought I didn't see before he concealed it. Three of them, all in Round Rock where the action was. Is there some reason your whereabouts should be kept secret from your wife?"

He murmured thoughtfully, "What did the paper say?"

"I'm sure your father saved it for you. For some reason, he didn't feel I should see it or your telegram. I wonder why."

"There's an explanation, Cal," he stated softly.

"Isn't there always some tidy excuse to explain away your mysterious life? When you're ready to come home to me, really come home, Lynx, let me know. Until then, don't trouble yourself."

"What's been happening here, Callie?" he probed in dread.

"Such as?" she questioned innocently.

"You're angry with me about more than my absence. Would you please explain?" he asked quietly, a worried frown lining his forehead.

The weeks of suspicions, demands, boredom, and loneliness attacked her very soul. So much had been kept tightly constrained. Tears began to ease down her cheeks. "It isn't working, Lynx."

"What isn't working, Cal?" he asked, pulling her into his arms.

She rested her flushed face against his chest as she sobbed in anguish, her shoulders trembling. How could she get answers without questions, questions which she dared not ask? When she brought her tears under a small measure of control, she lifted her face and stated simply, "Us."

"What about us, Callie?" he sought to comprehend her meaning.

"Don't you understand, Lynx? There is no us, because you won't allow it. I don't know you at all, and you don't know me," she stated hoarsely. "How can we work on a real marriage like this?"

"I'll be home for a week this time, Callie. Then, I only have one last promise to fulfill before I'm here to stay. Bear with me a while longer. Please," he urged her.

"Why? Will it change anything?" she challenged dejectedly.

"I hope our love and desire don't change. I thought you felt the same way. Are you trying to say you don't love me? You want out of our marriage?" he asked fearfully, dreading her response.

"My feelings aren't in question; yours are," she told him.

"But you know how I feel about you," he argued, confused.

"No, Lynx, I don't," she replied honestly.

"*Por Dias,* woman! I love you. I need you. I want you. Whenever I'm away from you, I think I'll go mad before I can get home. I dream of holding you, kissing you, making love to you. What more do you want from me? You're the most important thing in my life."

"That isn't how it looks to me," she contested painfully.

"How can I prove it to you, Callie?" he asked seriously.

"Show me with actions, not words," she replied bluntly.

"But you just spurned my touch," he pressed in bewilderment.

"I know you find me desirable, Lynx. I wasn't referring to sex. You don't let me share your life. You tell me nothing. You stay gone for weeks. Did you hear what I said? Less than two days out of forty-two since our marriage. Just six out of seventy-five since we met. And you ask why I doubt your affections and loyalty?"

"I swear by all I hold dear and sacred, Callie, I love you with all my heart. I don't think I could survive if I ever lost you. I didn't even realize I was capable of feeling such powerful emotions, of knowing such fears, until I met you. You're the most wonderful and exciting thing to enter my life. If I've given you reasons to doubt me and my love, I'm sorry. I never intended to hurt you or shut you out. When this last job is over, I promise to tell you everything."

Calinda gazed into his entreating eyes, eyes which declared his honesty and love. What a fool she had been. How wildly and crazily her imagination had tormented her. There was no vengeful plot against her. Lynx was trying to change, with difficulty. He loved her . . .

Cal smiled at him, tears glistening on her lashes. "Do you know that's the first time you've ever said such things?"

Lynx chuckled. "I suppose I've always been a man of few words. I thought you knew how I felt about you. I guess a man should speak his mind once in a while, even if it's hard to learn how. Well, Calinda Cardone, I love you, pure and simple love you. It scares the hell out of me, even shocks me, but it's true," he declared roguishly.

"I know what you mean, my love." she concurred. "But it's more frightening when you feel it's one-sided."

"When we get to the house, we'll see why Rankin hid the telegram and paper. If I know my father, probably to surprise you. I believe you said you were starving, Mrs. Cardone. Let's go home."

"Would you believe my appetite has changed drastically?"

A beguiling grin flickered over his arresting features. "In what way, Mrs. Cardone?" he queried huskily.

Calinda unbuttoned his shirt to the waist, then snuggled against his firm chest. "I bet with a little cunning and investigating, you might gain a clue," she hinted seductively.

Lynx grasped her chin to lift her head, fusing their gazes. "Is sex all you think about, Mrs. Cardone?" he teased.

"Only for the next week," she saucily replied, her lips meeting his as his arms surrounded her.

They sank to the grassy earth, their love shared at last . . .

Chapter 17

❧

As Lynx spread enticing kisses over Calinda's face and mouth, her body was consumed by a great need for him. He was so absorbing, filling her mind with thoughts which prevented any distractions, consuming her body with urgent passion, blinding her warring heart to all emotions except her love and his nearness.

During their mild argument and blooming of desires, dusk gradually wrapped them in an ever-darkening blanket. Without taking his lips from hers, Lynx gathered her in his arms and carried her to a copse of small oaks and placed her there for privacy, his lithe body partially covering hers. It was possible someone might come riding by or might come to search for them when they failed to respond to the dinner bell; yet ravenous emotions demanded to be fed and sated.

Within a few minutes, Lynx had removed her scanty garments and his own clothing. Semi-surrounded by bushy trees and cloaked by shadows, Calinda felt no modesty or resistance. She had doubted his love and suspected his motives; she needed to destroy those feelings. She clung to his sinewy frame, thrilled by its wondrous contact with her tingling flesh. She yielded to his lips, intoxicated by their ability to stir her senses to a wild frenzy. She vanquished all worries and mistrust, allowing her love to lead her where he willed.

The sun could have blazed down upon them and revealed their feverish actions to the entire world, and she couldn't have prevented their imminent union. If anyone had confronted them, she would have been too engrossed with him to notice their arrival. Lynx filled her senses as no other force had ever done, not even air or life itself.

He was so strong, yet his touch was as gentle and light as rays of sunshine dancing over her quivering flesh, its heat warming her very soul. Her body seemed as helpless as a blade of grass being swayed to and fro by a powerful breeze. Her will was as pliable as dough in a baker's hands.

Like a daring and skillful explorer, he let his hands search her enticing regions. They travelled, mapped, invaded, trespassed, conquered, and claimed nearly every inch of her willing body, as his lips did simultaneously with hers. A welcomed interloper, his tongue forded her lips and tasted the eagerness of her mouth. Accepting him as a seasoned and talented guide, she followed his lead.

Yet, Lynx didn't enter her unguarded paradise too quickly. He tantalized and stimulated her appetite until she pleaded for his expedition into that conquerable territory. At last, he boldly eased inside the dark passage which was moist and trembling with anticipation. His manhood journeyed from end to end many times, often swiftly, then with tormentingly sweet leisure. He calculated how long he needed to bring her to the point of victory at his side, then lovingly labored at that pace.

Their bodies and spirits united to strive for that rewarding goal, they sought it with stirring suspense. Soon, the moment of ecstasy seized them and carried them away on waves of blissful rapture. They lay entwined until respirations returned to normal and a quiet contentment filled them.

A light breeze played over their nude bodies, cooling and refreshing them. "Thank God I don't have to leave soon because I couldn't," he murmured softly into her fragrant hair, nuzzling her ear.

"A week is very soon, my love," she debated tranquilly.

"In another month, we'll forget all these separations. We'll never be apart again, Callie. Wherever I go, you'll come with me. I'm eager to work on some little Cardones," he teased mirthfully.

"Ah, ha," she playfully mused, "so that's why you married me."

"Why not?" he genially accepted her jest. "I can't think of a better choice for the mother of my children."

The moment the word "mother" left his lips, she noticed a slight tensing in his body. Knowing the truth, her heart ached for the anguish he had endured because of Brax and Laura. Never would she treat her children in such an evil manner. "You'll make a wonderful father, Lynx. I can envision you now, trying to teach our son to ride and herd cattle. I only pray you don't share any of your wandering spirit with him; I'd like him to hang around longer than you. One expert gunslinger and carefree roamer is enough for me," she teased.

"He'll never have a reason to leave, Callie; I'll make certain."

Although Lynx didn't know she caught the dual meaning in his statment, she responded to it as she gazed into his impenetrable eyes, "So will I, my love; I swear it."

There was a haunting gleam in his eyes when he tenderly coaxed, "Please don't ever get weary of life on the ranch, Callie. I know trading silks and towns for jeans and dust is a big change for you. But don't lose faith in me, in us. If you're unhappy or angry, tell me quickly. Don't let bitterness fester until it sickens you and drives you from me. I don't know how I would survive if you ever walked away from me, if you stopped loving me. It's damn scary to love and need another person so much," he whispered in a deeply emotional tone.

Cal snuggled into his protective arms and hugged him tightly. "How can you even think of such an impossible thing?" she softly scolded him, but she knew why. "You would have to take a whip to me to drive me away from your side. I love the ranch and jeans. Who needs silks and civilization when I have you? I love you, Lynx, and nothing will ever come between us again."

Lynx's sharp mind picked up her last word and mentally questioned it. "You mean nothing I say or do will change things for us?" he tested for more information.

Cal twisted her head to meet his probing gaze. "What could you possibly do or say to shatter our love and promises?" she parried his oddly voiced question. "I'm holding you to your vows, Lynx. If you break them, I'll make you sorry," she warned merrily.

Her innocent threat brought a curious reaction to his face. "You trying to intimidate me, wife?" he asked, failing to mask an odd concern. "If I don't ride straight, what would you do to punish me?"

"I don't need to use energy planning for something which will never take place. If you love me and want me, why would you try to damage our relationship? One day, I want to know anything and everything about you. All right?"

"Nosy little critter, aren't you?" he insouciantly claimed.

"Only because you make it necessary. One day I want to hear all of your secrets," she whispered conspiratorially, then laughed.

"I doubt it, Callie. If you knew them, I would lose you for certain. I'm really a devil in disguise, after your beautiful and trusting soul," he murmured huskily.

"Then your wicked task is over, Sir Demon; you own me body, heart, mind, and soul. What more can I offer to win you for eternity?"

"That's quite a valuable collection, woman. You sure you trust me to take care of them?" he ventured, chuckling with renewed life.

"If I can't trust you, Lynx, then I can trust no one," she stated gravely, her voice muffled and strained.

Lynx captured her quivering chin, alarmed by the moisture on her lashes and the panic in her voice. "Do you trust me implicitly, Cal?"

She glanced away as she light-heartedly declared, "Why shouldn't I? You're my husband, perhaps soon to be father of my children."

"Is there something I should know, woman? You've been acting awfully strange and tense," Lynx speculated an impending announcement.

"About what?" Cal asked, her fretful gaze and voice guarded.

"A baby?" he hinted cleverly. "Is that why you're so edgy?"

"Not that I know of, Lynx," she replied honestly, delighted his keen mind was running in that false direction. She cautioned herself to relax and to avoid bringing up any stressful points. She had been attacked by too many pains and problems lately. Soon, he would be home permanently; then, they could discover each other and share their lives. During this visit, she wanted to prevent quarrels.

Clever and perceptive, Lynx knew she was keeping something from him, something which was plaguing her deeply. Maybe they just needed time together to teach her to accept him and his words. He hadn't been much of a husband, lover, or friend since their marriage. Her hesitation and mistrust were natural. He would give her the time and love she needed to win her loyalty and contentment. He would grant her the time to come to him and talk openly about what was troubling her. His many secrets and separations couldn't help but distress her. In time, she would understand them. She had said to "prove" himself to her; he would make every effort to do so. Yet, her unhappiness and boredom tormented him, panicked him. He could never release her. He allowed the matter to pass for now.

"Let's freshen up in the pond, then get something to eat. I'm starved. If you want me to hang around home, you best take real good care of me, Mrs. Cardone," he teased her.

"Do you know how much I love you and need you?" she asked.

He cupped her face between his hands and studied her serious expression. "More than anyone else in my life, Callie," he answered.

For a brief moment, her eyes misted and her lips quivered. He thought she was about to cry, but she controlled that reaction. "Are you so miserable here at the ranch, Callie? Is it me?"

"I just miss you so much, Lynx," she confessed raggedly.

"I'm sorry, love. It won't be much longer," he promised.

She flung herself into his arms and whispered fearfully, "I hope not. I'm so afraid something will happen to you."

His embrace tightened as he said, "Nothing will happen to me, love. Please don't upset yourself like this."

"Every time you leave, I fear it will be the last time you hold me, or kiss me, or I see you. Am I so terrible or life here so dreary that you can't stay home very long?" she challenged.

Her insecurities and loneliness flooded her words, startling him with their depth. "Look at me, Callie," he softly commanded.

When she did, he stated distinctly, "I love you, woman. If you don't believe anything else I say, at least know for certain that's the God's truth. I promise to take you with me if I ever leave again. If you'll recall, I do keep my word," he hinted slyly, grinning at her.

"I hope so, my darling. But if you start this secretive roaming again, Lynx, I might not hang around to be convinced of your love and needs. I can't live like this much longer, me always waiting alone and in fear while you gallivant around the countryside for reasons you can't even share with me. That isn't a good marriage or a real commitment; it's only a convenience for you. I'm going to trust you to keep your word, unless you prove otherwise. One final separation," she compromised softly.

The haunting words sounded as if they had been carved from her soul with an incisive honesty and sent forth with much agony. "I won't let you down, Callie. One last trip," he concurred joyfully.

"I pray you mean it, Lynx. If I ever discovered you didn't, I would leave that very day. I want so much to know you, to understand you, to share everything with you, to help you, to love you blindly."

"Is there any reason you can't?" he questioned.

"You," she stated simply. "You don't allow it to happen."

"Then prepare yourself to be stormed with answers and love," he playfully warned Cal. "Bargain?"

"I've been ready and eager since that night we met in the saloon. Did you honestly think I was Callie O'Hara?" she asked merrily.

"Yep, but that wasn't such a terrible mistake after all. It did get us acquainted before . . . Did you know Callie turned into an outlaw?" He hurriedly tried to cover a slip which she had caught. He went on to reveal the Irish lass' unmasking during the hold-up and her planning of Calinda's kidnapping. He was surprised when Calinda's intrigue was small. Watching her intense observation of him, he lazily rolled into the telling of the Round Rock incident, alleging himself as a witness and spectator without outright lying.

"That's what I meant earlier, Lynx; you're constantly in danger."

"I'm perfectly safe. Haven't you seen me with these Colts?"

"What's the saying about there's always someone else faster?" she craftily rebutted his confidence. "A reputation as large and colorful as yours is mighty tempting to a rising legend. Perhaps I should come along to guard your back."

"No way will I endanger your life again, woman. I'll kill the first man who threatens you," he warned ominously.

"How soon do you propose to defend me at such a distance? As we both recall, you weren't around when Cole Stevens grabbed me," she reminded him, her fishing expedition in full swing. With the right bait, she might catch some enlightening answers or clarifying clues.

"I did rescue you, my ungrateful and demanding wife," he retorted, his intuition alive and working overtime.

"You do have that stimulating ability to sense when I'm in peril. We must have a mental link, or fate is guarding us. And I am most appreciative of all you do for me, Lynx. But alas, I admit to being demanding and selfish; I want more," she stated comically.

"Do you deserve more from me, you sly vixen?" he taunted.

"All you have to offer," she replied smugly.

"Demanding and selfish don't cover the half of it, woman."

"We'll see, won't we?" she cheerfully hinted.

"I think I'm in deep trouble," Lynx playfully sighed.

"You are, Lynx. You haven't seen anything yet. Let's get moving before we miss dinner," Cal reminded him.

They quickly bathed and dressed. She was mounted before he could assist her. "See you at home, love," she threw over her shoulder as she raced off across the meadow, heading for the rolling hill beyond.

Lynx jumped into his saddle and raced off in pursuit, easily catching up with her. She slowed her pace to ride beside him. "You're a damn good rider, Callie," he complimented her.

"Good shot, too," she informed him. "Maybe good enough to challenge you," she laughingly added.

"I'd be a dead man; I'd never be able to draw a weapon on you."

"Any kind?" she speculated with a giggle.

"If I can help it, Callie, I'll never hurt you."

"Bribery and flattery are sly tricks to win my favor."

"I have it, don't I?" he smugly declared.

"Yes, my love, you do," she readily agreed.

When they arrived at the stable, Charlie took possession of their horses. They locked hands and strolled to the house. They were greeted by a grinning Rankin. "I see you found her, son. She's been fretting over your arrival for weeks. I saw you in the papers from Round Rock. I didn't dare show them to Cal; I didn't want her tearing off in search of her adventurous husband and getting into danger again. I even kept your telegram a secret; I wanted her to be surprised tonight," he cunningly enlightened Lynx.

"You underestimate my wife's intelligence, Father; she knew about both. She's been annoyed with us for keeping her in the dark. She's been raking me through the fires," Lynx replied in that same sly communicative way, failing to deceive an alert Calinda.

"I'm sorry, Cal," Rankin said. "Now I see why you've been so irritable and distant with me. We won't trick you again."

"Any food left from dinner?" she asked, dropping the nettling game. "We're both famished."

"In the oven. Salina's gone for the night."

Calinda stopped her pleased response from leaving her lips. "You relax, dear husband, while I get it ready. Talk with Rankin."

"We can talk later or tomorrow. I'm not letting you out of my sight in that crazy mood," Lynx informed her, a gleam of mischief in his tawny eyes. "I'd best learn my way around this house again."

Together, they set the table, retrieved the food, and sat down to eat. Hungry and weary, Lynx and Cal ate in relative silence. Afterwards, Lynx helped her with the dishes. "Watch it, Lynx, this could become a habit with me. I like having you around."

"Excellent. Would you like to take a walk?" he offered.

"Not tonight. That work and swim drained me. I think I'll turn in. You coming along, or staying to talk with your father?"

"I'll be along shortly, love. I think I should speak with my father for a little while tonight," he said, stroking her silky hair.

"I'll be waiting," she murmured, smiling seductively at him.

"I'm counting on it," he responded, his smile tugging at her.

Calinda went to their room and dressed for bed. While she waited for Lynx and Rankin to visit, she read and dozed. If only she'd known he was coming home today, she wouldn't have worked so hard. Now that she was bathed and fed, her fatigued and sated body was lax. After thirty minutes of straining to focus on the book, it fell into her lap and closed; Calinda was fast asleep.

Downstairs, Lynx and Rankin were sipping brandies and chatting about the ranch and impending round-up. They discussed his recent adventures and accomplishments. Lynx told his father that his last mission was to trace Rube Burrow and apprehend the vicious bandit. After which, his career as a secret Ranger would be complete. They spoke about children and Calinda. Time passed as the two mellowed men really talked for the first time in years, enjoying each other's company and intelligence.

Rankin leisurely filled in Lynx on the happenings at the ranch, each man delighting in the women's truce. But Lynx fretted over the moods of Calinda's which his father revealed. Evidently she wasn't as happy here as he assumed or hoped. But things would change soon . . .

When Lynx noticed the late hour of midnight, he hurriedly downed his brandy and bid his father good-night. He mounted the steps with eagerness, his loins throbbing at the thought of what awaited him. When he slipped into his room, he was dismayed slightly to find her sleeping peacefully. Her position and the book indicated she had tried to wait for his appearance. He could hardly blame her, for his father had enlightened him as to how hard she labored each day.

He eased out of his clothes and doused the lantern. He gingerly slid into bed and drew her into his arms. She sighed softly and murmured his name, her eyes never opening. As soon as Lynx forcefully cooled his smoldering passion, he joined her in slumberland.

* * *

An early riser, Lynx was up and eating with Rankin shortly after dawn vanquished the shadows of night. When Rankin suggested he ride to the north pastures with him, Lynx accepted, thinking Calinda would sleep late.

But, as if her body-clock was attuned to his presence, Calinda was awake and up by eight o'clock. She dressed and went down to join her husband. She was peeved to find he had left at seven-thirty. When he hadn't returned by lunch, she grew annoyed. So much for spending time with her while home! She fumed, *no doubt I'll only get him at night!*

Lynx and Rankin found traces of attempted fence-cuttings in three locations. It would be wise to plant guards at those areas tonight. Rankin told his son that he suspected at least one hundred steers had been rustled during the last three weeks. Whoever was behind it seemed to know their routine, their weaknesses, and strengths. Rankin asked his son to help solve this crisis while he was home, if he didn't mind.

When Lynx returned to the house near four in the afternoon, he discovered his wife had gone riding alone. Considering her past jeopardy and the allusion of rustlers nearby, he was furious with her. "What the hell could she be thinking to go out alone!" he snarled.

"Probably hoped to link up with her beloved," Salina hinted.

Lynx turned and scowled at the Mexican beauty. "I'll make sure she doesn't do it again," he stated confidently, his jaw set in angry lines.

"She does it all the time. She has not found trouble yet," Salina remarked, hoping to halt his future demand which could foil any distant plans to place Cal in danger. "She is a grown woman, Lynx; she carries a gun. She will resent your harsh orders, treating her like a *nena*. She gets bored around here with nothing to occupy her days and thoughts. Riding on the ranch is far better than going to town for a diversion."

"How do you know she's bored?" Lynx inquired sternly.

"Anyone who does ranch chores or cleans attics must be at their wit's end for amusement. Any other female would be sewing or such. Sometimes I think Cal wishes she were a man. If she were, she would roam around like you do," Salina stated with phony giggles.

"She cleaned the attic?" he queried tensely.

"*Si*. And she polishes saddles, drives the wagon, feeds animals, and you would not believe what else. Sometimes, she evens helps in the house, when the wifey mood strikes her. She is actually a good cook; did you know that?" she hinted slyly, knowing he was distracted by her guileful hint. How she wished she dared tell Cal everything . . .

"No, I didn't," he replied absently, then excused himself.

As Salina assumed, he headed for the attic to check out a nagging dread. It was clear his wife had found his mother's portrait. He worried for a time, then dismissed his anxiety when he realized she couldn't know anything about Laura. It would appear natural for them to remove such a haunting picture. He stared at his ravishing mother for a long time, wondering if she had ever regretted her decision. He tormented himself with questions. Did she ever think about him? Did she ever want to contact him or come home again? Was she even alive and well? Why had she given up so much for Elliott Braxton? Had it been worth her present life? Would he ever learn her fate or see her again? God help him if Cal was anything like Laura.

Lynx threw the sheet over the painting and went to the study to toss down two brandies. He must not think about his mother; she wasn't worth the mental energy or his concern. Yet, new apprehension chewed at him. What if his lovely Cal became that restless and unhappy? What if life here was too demanding, empty, and despicable for his love? Would Cal run away from him and the ranch? No, Cal loved him.

"Lynx," Salina called out from the doorway.

He turned slowly and caustically responded, "Yes?"

"There is something you should know about Cal. After the past trouble between us, I was not sure if I should tell you. I was afraid you might not believe me or think I am only trying to start more trouble. I am not, honestly. She and I are becoming friends, but I worry about you. If you repeat what I say, she will never trust me again and we will return to battling every day. Maybe she has already told you about it," Salina slyly speculated as if nervous.

"Stop dodging cowflops, Salina; spit it out. What about my wife?" he demanded, stressing Calinda's position to him.

"Did she tell you she got a letter from England?" she opened the vindictive conversation. If she were going to halt this marriage farce, she needed to inspire conflicts on both sides, but cautiously.

"When?" he asked, his question admitting his ingorance.

"Tuesday, the same day the papers arrived with your pictures in them." Salina went on to repeat Calinda's words and actions that day, and Calinda's curious moods afterwards. "If you question her about the letter, she will think I spy on her for you. She will make certain I learn nothing more to tell you. Besides, she might be waiting for the right moment to tell you. Whatever it said, it surely had her upset. She sent the Simpsons a letter yesterday. She asked me to mail it. You might be furious with me, but I saved it for you."

"Where is it?" he growled coldly, piqued by their conspiracy.

"In my room. Did I do the right thing?" she fretted aloud.

"No, Salina, you didn't. If you ever tattle on her again or betray her confidence like this, you're fired. Calinda is a Cardone now. Don't ever presume to spy on her or trick her," he stated icily, even though he was relieved to see at least one letter. He sat impatiently while she fetched it. He would search their room for the other one, but Cal had doubtlessly destroyed it. Why hadn't she mentioned it yesterday? No matter, he couldn't give Salina any weapons to use against his wife or any power to deceive her. If Cal needed watching, his father would handle that dreadful matter. Anyway, Cal would probably tell him the truth before the week was out.

Lynx snatched the letter from Salina's hand and glowered at her. "Don't you ever do anything like this again. Just to prevent any conflicts, we'll forget about today. Understand?" he warned.

. As he left the room, Salina smiled maliciously. She knew he was going upstairs to tear open the letter and devour its contents. He didn't have her fooled one bit.

He simply didn't want her to know how much he mistrusted his little wife. He wouldn't tell Cal anything; he would watch and wait for the instant to pounce on her. As she worked, she hummed, envisioning her seeds sprouting in his mind.

Lynx paled and shuddered when he read the sarcastic and intimidating message about her father's 1872 letter which had been kept secret from her for years. His eyes widened as he scanned the contents which included her vow to expose their deception to her father, her threat to make trouble for their theft of the $10,000 balance which her father had sent for her support, the announcement of her marriage to him, her allegation of their possible theft of other letters from her father, and a warning to never contact her again.

Lynx couldn't believe what he was reading. Surely there was a logical explanation? Who had sent her a letter from Brax, even an old one? He was puzzled and worried. What had it said? Where was it?

He studied the letter and its implications. What had Brax revealed to Calinda? What had her so secretive? Why had she gone to the attic and examined his mother's portrait? *My God,* he worried, *did Brax tell her the truth?* He paced the room like a caged beast. Suddenly, he laughed at his foolishness. No, Brax hadn't confessed; her behavior proved she still loved and trusted her husband . . .

Between his secretive absences and the unexpected letter from the past, no wonder Cal was distracted and moody. She would tell him later, he concluded. Lynx went to the water-shed to bathe and dress for dinner. He waited for his wife's return.

Knowing she would bathe when she returned, Calinda had left her things on the shelf in the water-shed. When she came to the house afterwards, she was carrying her damp and dusty riding clothes. As she passed through the kitchen, she spoke to Salina, but didn't ask about her husband. She headed upstairs to hang the garments on the balcony railing to dry before placing them in the laundry.

"I see you made it home safely," a mellow voice teased from behind her as he propped negligently against the doorframe.

Cal halted and turned, her expression impassive. "Did you think I had run off?" she retorted, lacking any smile or merriment.

"It's dangerous to ride alone, Cal," he mildly scolded her.

"I've grown accustomed to being alone, my wayward husband. I'm surprised you had time to notice I wasn't around."

"I've been home for several hours. What took you so long?"

"Nosy critter, aren't we?" she copied his quip of yesterday.

"Just concerned, love," he replied, staring at her oddly. "Anything wrong, Cal?"

"What could possibly be wrong now that my husband is home and generously granting me his precious time and attention?"

"Can we take that stroll now and talk?" he suggested, needing to comprehend her new mood and to stroke her ruffled feathers.

"I should help Salina with dinner," she responded warily. Why was he looking at her in that curious manner? Why the interrogation?

"Salina's done it alone for years. Surely she can manage tonight. I'd like to spend time with you, Cal," he seemingly wheedled.

She appeared to ponder his invitation for a short time, then shrugged in resignation. "Why not? Let me hang these out to dry first. I'll be down shortly." She hurriedly vanished from his piercing gaze.

When Cal returned, Lynx hadn't moved from that spot. He waited for her to descend the steps, watching her with a smile. "You could let me explain my tardiness before getting so angry," he teased.

"You don't owe me any excuses, Lynx," she told him, then walked outside without waiting for him to tag along.

Cal sat down in the yard swing and gazed off across the hills, recalling the night she hadn't dared sit in this swing with him. He came to join her, frowning at her petulance. She didn't appear to be listening as he related his reasons for being gone nearly all day. When he halted, she didn't debate or comment on them.

Calinda wasn't being attentive. She knew he was telling the truth, and she had no real cause to me mad or unreasonable. The letters were plaguing her. If she and Lynx were going to have a new beginning, it must be with honesty and openness. She couldn't fool him; he sensed something was troubling her. It would be a lie to say everything was fine; yet, she couldn't confide too much this soon.

"Cal?" he said for the second time before breaking her stiff concentration. "What's wrong, love?"

She inhaled deeply, then released it slowly. "Lynx . . ." She hesitated, then turned to meet his worried gaze. "Something happened while you were gone. I . . ." she faltered again, then related the letter episode in a quavering voice. "I was so confused and distressed I ripped it to shreds. I should have saved it for you to read; I'm sorry. I don't trust the Simpsons; I'm furious with them. I wrote and told them so. I couldn't tell them the truth, that I don't know where my own father is. Maybe if they think I have you and him they'll leave me alone. I know I'll never see that money, and I don't care about it. How could they be so cruel and evil? They made me feel like a lowly beggar all those years. At least I understand why they took the care to have me well-educated and clothed; they feared my father might turn up someday. How do I know that was the only letter from him? What if he wrote and told me the truth or where he is now? I hate them!" she shrieked in renewed anguish at their deceits.

"Don't worry, love. I'm glad their tricks sent you to me. Tell me what the two letters said," he coaxed gently, trying not to distress her further, needing to hear her repeat her letter accurately.

She regained control of her poise and speech, relating her letter nearly verbatim and then exposing the contents of her father's. For some reason, she didn't tell him about Kyle Yancey in Austin, although that was undoubtedly the reason the letter was kept. She told herself it was to prevent him from chasing that fleeting clue. She focused a tormented gaze on his unreadable one. "What could he have meant by guilt and sacrifices? He sounded as if he loved it here; why would he leave? What dream would be too costly to claim? He said he was a selfish coward, but I don't understand. Was he trying to buy my forgiveness and love, Lynx? Surely after so many years, he could have contacted me?" the questions tumbled out with hopes he would match her trust and confide in her. She had opened the door; would he walk inside and join her or would he close the door instead?

"You think he was referring to being guilty about stealing the money and sacrificing his life here? He had dreamed of a ranch in Texas; could that be what he meant by walking away from one?" When she didn't respond either way, he continued, "He proved he was selfish by his treatment of you, and he was a coward to leave after the theft. He made himself a criminal, Cal; to contact you might involve you in that life of running from the law. If he's still alive, love, he may never try to reach you. I know that's painful, Cal, but you must face it."

Calinda lowered her gaze, tears clouding her vision. Not at his gentle and torturous words as he assumed, but at his cunning way of deceiving her with questions which were intended to sound like speculative answers. When Lynx lifted her chin, she burst into tears and nestled her face against his chest. She sobbed quietly, praying he could one day confess his own anguish to her. If she could bare her inner soul to him, why couldn't he do the same? Perhaps it was more humiliating and painful to him, for he had lived it and not read it. Perhaps he feared it would alter her feelings for him.

Lynx embraced her tightly. "Don't cry, love. You have me now. I'll never desert you or hurt you, Callie," he promised tenderly.

She looked up at him, her face streaked with tears. "Will we ever know the truth, Lynx?" she asked sadly.

"I hope so, Callie; God, I hope so," he agreed honestly. "I wish I had been here when you needed me. I'm sorry you went through it alone."

"You're here now," she said, smiling up at him.

"Try to forget about it, Callie; it only brings pain and unhappiness. We have our life to think about," he reminded her.

"Yes, we do. I feel better now that you know. I was afraid to tell you; I know how the past disturbs you. I thought I could ignore it, but it kept haunting me, I felt I was being dishonest with you. There are too many secrets between us, Lynx. One day, I hope it won't be this way. I hope we can tell each other everything, anything."

He chuckled. "If that's a hint for my confession, it'll have to wait a while longer. Please, love," he entreated. "A few more weeks?"

To his relief and surprise, she smiled and nodded. "Do you think that $10,000 was part of the money stolen from your father? I would feel terrible if it was used on me." Surely the mention of the stolen money explained why the letter had not been given to her.

"I don't know, but it doesn't matter. What better investment than in my wife? Forget the money and the Simpsons."

"Will you promise me two things, Lynx?" she asked mysteriously.

Intrigued, he nodded. "Promise me the past is dead and you won't go looking for my father again. But if you do accidentally run into him, walk away without trouble. Please do this for me, for us. Don't allow him or the past to come between us."

"I will, if you'll promise the same things," he offered.

"I promise," she stated quickly.

"I promise," he vowed, smiling at her. He couldn't change the past. Nor could he kill Brax if he confronted him; to do so would place a wedge between him and his wife. Brax had taken something special from him; but in a way, Brax had replaced it with something more valuable. Besides, the letter revealed something Lynx hadn't considered before; Brax had intended to walk away alone. Something had changed Brax's mind: either Laura had done so, or Rankin had caught them saying farewell. Whatever the reasons, it was over now . . .

──── *Chapter 18* ────

❦

THAT NIGHT CALINDA AND LYNX had made passionate love for hours, to awaken the next morning to another fiery and leisurely bout of sensual pleasure. Calinda felt it was best to accept her husband as he was until he could effect drastic changes in his life and thoughts. With her love and loyalty proven, that day couldn't be far off.

When they came down for breakfast, they appeared utterly happy and bewitched with each other. The amorous looks and cheerful banter between them vexed Salina. Evidently the sly Calinda had confessed everything and disarmed Lynx. Did Calinda have a new and powerful hold over him? She wondered why Lynx kept Calinda around, now that he had everything he wanted from her. Was there another vengeful challenge to be met? Salina was more determined than ever to devastate their marriage, to make certain Cal learned why this golden treasure had pursued and married her . . .

Calinda and Lynx went riding after breakfast, to return later for a picnic lunch to carry to the pond. Calinda raced upstairs to retrieve her outfit for swimming; Lynx took care of another task. While they were gathering needed items for their outing, Salina set one of her plans into motion before packing the envious basket . . .

Lynx tied the basket and other bundle to his saddle and mounted. He grinned at Cal and challenged, "Beat me to the pond and you can share my lunch." With that playful statement, he clicked his tongue and raced off toward the end of the corral to wait at their starting point.

Calinda jumped into the saddle. Before she could knee her chestnut roan, he frantically pawed the ground and reared, flaying his hooves in the air and neighing in outrage. The saddle shifted to the right and Calinda was thrown to the hard ground. Manuel ran forward and grabbed the horse's reins before he could trample her legs. Before anyone could notice, he furtively removed the burr which he had planted beneath her saddle. He quickly removed the loosened saddle and tossed it aside, then guided the animal over to the fence and tied his reins.

Salina's first cousin went to Calinda to assist her. "Are you all right, *Senora* Cardone? Anything broken?"

Seeing the incident, Lynx came racing back to her, hopping off Star's back and rushing to his fallen wife. "What happened? Are you hurt, love?" he inquired apprehensively, kneeling beside her.

Calinda was still struggling to breathe, the wind knocked from her lungs by the heavy thud. Finally she nodded. Lynx helped her to stand. She rubbed her right hip and winced. "Just banged up a bit. The horse went crazy when I mounted, then the saddle slipped."

"Didn't you check it after our ride? You know it loosens after a swift run and good sweat," he chided her perilous oversight.

"I did check it after we returned. It was snug. Why would he act like that?" she inquired, nettled by his scolding, suspiciously eyeing the contented beast at the fence.

"I'll check him out," Lynx said, then went to see if there was a problem. He examined the saddle and found nothing. He studied the horse for any injury. Manuel had wiped the spot of blood from the sharp burr, leaving no evidence of its previous presence to alert Lynx.

"Everything looks fine," he told his sore wife.

"Except me," she retorted. "My fanny feels terrible."

"Think I should fetch the doctor to check you over?"

"Don't be silly. It wasn't my first fall, and won't be my last. What I need is a soothing swim. How about I ride with you?" she asked.

He grinned. "That's the craziest trick to finagle a ride, woman."

"Got to get your undivided attention some way," she teased, attempting to restrain her wild imagination. Who had intentionally loosened her girth?

He chuckled as he helped her mount behind him. "Slowly, love, no slapping this sore rear with a bouncing pace," she hinted merrily.

At the pond, Lynx eyed her closely and questioned, "Are you sure you aren't hurt, Cal?"

"Just my pride and seat. Somebody loosened that saddle, Lynx," she informed him unexpectedly, thinking it wise to air her suspicion.

He stared at her. "Come on, Cal. Who would do that?"

"I don't know, but someone did. I checked that girth and tightened it. You were standing there watching me, remember?"

"I saw you lift the stirrup and work with it. Are you sure you tightened it, not loosened it?" he asked, fretting over her charge.

"I get thrown and you don't care. I tightened the damn girth! Forget it!" Cal snapped, heading for the water with a limp.

He surged forward and halted her progress. "If you're certain, Cal, I'll check into it. I'll ask Manuel if he saw anything."

Her face brightened, then glared coldly. "He's Salina's cousin, isn't he?" she asked suddenly, her mind spinning with that idea.

"Yes, why?" he inquired curiously.

"Nothing. Let's go swimming. I'm hot and achy."

"Just a minute, woman. What were you hinting at?"

"If I didn't know any better, I'd accuse that little witch of pulling this trick," she heatedly announced, lightly rubbing the sensitive area. "She has been nice lately, but . . ." she halted pensively.

"You're wrong, Cal. Manuel's been with us for years. Why would he let Salina get him fired? Or worse, beaten by me!"

"Salina's been here for years, too," she responded irritably. "Maybe her truce isn't so peaceful and sincere. She did flip sides very easily."

"I'll question Manuel tonight," Lynx told her, dismayed.

"No, let it ride. But I'll be watching both of them from now on," she decided aloud. If Manuel and Salina weren't behind this accident, that left only Lynx. For certain, it wasn't her oversight! Why was she always in trouble when he came around?

As Cal removed her boots and socks, Lynx observed her. If he didn't know any better, he might think she suspected him. She could have been injured badly. She wouldn't risk death or broken bones to gain his attention, not when she already had it. Surely it was a freak accident. Then again, maybe he should check out this curious event. Hopefully she hadn't deceived him yesterday with her revelations of the letters. Hopefully she hadn't learned of Salina's mischief and sought revenge by implicating her.

As he removed his own boots, he scolded himself. What was wrong with him? Too many years of loneliness, cynicism, and wariness. If he couldn't trust his wife, he couldn't trust anyone. Clearly, someone was trying to harm her, and he would discover who and why.

Her right side throbbing, Calinda merely played in the water for a time. She left the refreshing liquid to lie on a blanket in the sun, turning to her stomach to allow the sun's warmth to dry her clothes and to relax the stiffening in her right buttock. She wanted to dismiss her suspicions, but she couldn't. Too many past perils added to this one to alarm her. Who was behind them? Why? It was possible for Salina to be involved in this one, but not the others. Perhaps she was jumping the gun by accusing Salina and Manuel . . .

Lynx came over to join her, lying down beside her prone body. He moved her lengthy hair aside and nuzzled her neck. She squirmed and giggled. "I hope your passions aren't as fiery as the sun's heat, my love. I refuse to place this hip against the hard ground," she teased.

"Maybe I can think of something," he playfully hinted.

Without lifting her head, Calinda peeked through curls fallen over her face. She smiled in amusement. "Always hungry, aren't we?"

He pushed aside the flaming locks which blocked a clear view of her lovely face and compelling eyes. His left arm went across her shoulders as he laid his face near hers. "Yep," he cheerfully agreed.

She shifted to her left side and curled against him, kissing the tip of his nose, then gingerly bit the strong chin. "You know, you're delicious," she said provocatively.

He turned to his right side and drew her closer to his stalwart frame. As she snuggled into his possessive embrace, the furry mat on his chest pillowed her damp head. Her fingers wandered through it as if passing through golden dried grass upon firm soil. Her hand roamed over his broad shoulder and slipped under his arm to fall over his side. She listened and thrilled as his heart-rate increased. She was intoxicated by her effect on him. How could her contact and simple actions stir his passions so fiercely? The same way his affected her! When she was in his arms, she felt so loved and protected, so barren of any thought but him. In his close proximity, no haunting enigmas existed, no riddles haunted her mind, no uncertainties harassed her heart. Was it safe and wise to love so strongly, gullibly, and deeply?

When she moved and groaned, he asked tenderly, "Hurt much?"

"Yep," she insouciantly answered. "It's only a bad bruise; it should be better by tomorrow or Monday."

"I was afraid you'd say that," he wailed humorously.

"If I can wait around for weeks to be with you, my love, surely you can manage a day or two for me," she taunted his disappointment.

"Right now, I'm having a helluva time, but tonight will be easy."

"How so?" she mocked his alleged control later.

"I promised Rankin I'd set a trap for those fence cutters. We're losing too many cattle to them. If I get home tonight, it'll be late."

"Lynx!" she shrieked in annoyance. "You were gone all day yesterday, and you just got home."

"In your condition, it might be wise to sleep out," he jested.

"What happened to friend, as well as lover?" she taunted.

"You think I could hang around you for that long without touching you?" he murmured skeptically. "Besides, it'll be our ranch one day, Cal. We have to protect our property. Who knows, perhaps one of those rustlers sneaked up and tampered with your saddle, hoping to send my thoughts in your direction instead of theirs. I don't like having bandits this close to my woman and home; I want them gone before I am."

She smiled and caressed his cheek. "Then you'd best hang around and protect both," she sweetly suggested.

"I plan to," he said. "Ready to eat?"

"I don't think I can sit up yet."

"Then I'll feed you lying down," he solved her problem.

They rested on their stomachs with elbows propped, eating the sumptuous fare and drinking wine. "Who's the thoughtful one?" she inquired, nodding at the wine and glasses.

"Me, naturally," he stated proudly. "While you were upstairs."

They enjoyed the romantic setting another two hours before heading home. After a lengthy span in a tub of hot water, Lynx asked, "Think I should rub some liniment on that lovely backside?"

"Don't you dare touch it," she declared fearfully.

"Let me have a look," he insisted, removing the bath sheet from her slender body. He walked behind her and gazed at the large area of blackish blue. "Lie down on the bed, Cal. This needs to be checked. You sure nothing's broken?"

She followed his gentle order, stretching out on the soft mattress. "This might be touchy, love; bear with me," he coaxed.

She clenched her teeth as he probed her hip-bone. He shifted down to her upper thigh and examined it, then up to check her ribs. "Move to your left side, then wiggle it back and forth," he instructed.

She did so, but muttered how foolish she felt. "Any sharp pains when you move it around?" he inquired.

"Just soreness," she replied through gritted teeth.

"It doesn't seem broken, but there could be a crack. I think it's best if you stay in bed for a while," he concluded cautiously.

"That's the craziest trick to wrangle me into bed," she teased.

He frowned at her, then chuckled. "Since you're new at this set-up, I should tell you that a wife always obeys her husband."

"Is that a fact? Where is that marital law written?"

They both laughed. "You just want me out of everyone's hair. Think I'll be irritable and obnoxious?" she murmured coyly.

"I hope you'll be frustrated as hell," he sassily stated.

"Then, you're wasting your time, love; I already know that uncomfortable feeling. And you're to blame."

"Me?" he hinted beguilingly.

"You probably loosened that girth to keep me confined while you work all night," she speculated, her hand covering her giggling mouth. "If you want to trap me in bed, you shouldn't do it with a hindering injury."

"Not a bad idea, but too rash. I want you in bed, but not disabled. Think a hot, wet cloth will help ease the aching?"

"I can picture me lying here naked with a bandage on my rear."

They burst into shared laughter again. "Sounds appealing to me."

"You, Lynx Cardone, are a brute," she charged as she gingerly rolled to her back, the bed cushioning the injury.

He leaned over and kissed her, stealing her breath. "But a nice one," he debated, trailing his fingertips over her breasts.

She captured his enticing hand and playfully bit the area between his thumb and forefinger. "Ouch," he shrieked as if hurt.

"With an injury like that, you should be put straight to bed."

"You dangerous and wily vixen. I'd spank you if that lovely rump could take the earned punishment." His eyes glowed with deviltry.

"Do I get served dinner in bed?" she inquired, smiling at him.

"Food only," he mocked her double entendre.

"Yes, master dear," she pouted.

Lynx set a small table near the bed and placed her dinner on it. When she asked why he couldn't eat with her, she learned he was leaving to set his rustler trap. He kissed her and asked if she needed anything else. She sighed and shook her head. He kissed her again, this time a lengthy and sensual span. When Calinda wildly responded, he drew back and inhaled with a shudder. "You're a tormenting hussy."

"I know," she flippantly responded. "But you love me anyway."

"Damn right, I do. I best git while I can." He flashed her a woeful grin and left.

Calinda picked over her meal, then read. When Salina came for the table and dishes, the Mexican girl inquired about the fall. Guarded, Calinda astutely claimed it was a silly accident. From now on, she would keep her eyes and ears open.

Most of the night, Cal varied between quick naps and restless tossings. Once she awoke in a cold sweat, a nightmare torturing her: she could see those flaying hooves descending toward her helpless body, crushing her time and time again.

Twice she got up and walked around to loosen taut muscles. When she returned to bed the second time, the door opened and Lynx slipped inside. It was five in the morning.

"Can't sleep, love?" he inquired worriedly.

"Now I can," she decided aloud, cuddling up to him on her left side, her arm lying over his iron-muscled chest. "Any success?"

"Nope. It's like they were warned off tonight. We'll try it again tomorrow night after we check around for a scout."

"Must you?" she asked.

"I've already explained, Cal. Don't make me go through it again. It's late and I'm exhausted. Can you slide over? It's too hot to snuggle," he growled, feeling frustrated and tense.

"It wouldn't be too hot if I weren't injured," she snapped, hurt.

"Why the hell do you think I'm so hot and miserable? I've been at boiling level all day. It's got me edgy. Woman, I need you," he confessed in a hoarse voice. "Do you know how you get to me?"

She smiled to herself. Her hand played over his flesh as it drifted downward to comprehend his aroused state. "Please, Callie, don't," he pleaded huskily, tremors passing over his body.

"You said you would think of something," she reminded him.

"You're hurt, love," he argued at his raging passion.

"Some pains are worse than others," she rebutted.

"I don't want to hurt you, Cal," he reasoned, his body aflame.

Abruptly Calinda recalled their sensuous adventure in the watershed. She threw the sheet aside and walked to the armless rocking chair. "Come over here, Lynx," she requested warmly, feeling wonderfully wanton and brazen.

"Please, Callie," he entreated.

"Shut up, my love, and come here," she commanded sternly.

When he reluctantly indulged her, she told him to sit down. "What are you doing, woman?" he asked, taking his seat.

"Remember that day in the tub?" she hinted, then sat in his lap, each of her legs crossing one of his. She boldly and bravely grasped his manhood and slipped it within her eager womanhood. She eased forward to lock their bodies together, her feet pressing against the backs of the rockers. "Now, Lynx, the rest is up to you."

He groaned in blissful torment. "You sure this won't hurt you?" he asked, praying for a negative reply.

"Not enough to make me want to stop," she said, leaning forward to seal her lips to his.

His arms encircled her waist as he carefully worked his pulsing shaft deeper into that inviting recess. As her lips tantalized his and her breasts threatened to burn his chest, he feared his manhood would explode instantly at the sheer ecstasy of her contact. As he began to move gently, the rocker swayed back and forth to match his steady rhythm. When her lips strewed kisses over his face and nibbled at his ears, his head fell back against the chair. He thought he would go wild with rapture when she seductively writhed her hips against his flaming torch. When her mouth returned to his, she seemingly devoured it with feverish savagery, her tongue outlining his lips several times.

"Merciful heavens, Callie, you're killing me," he moaned.

"Can you think of a better way to die, my love?" she reasoned, her breath warm in his ear as she nipped gently at his lobe.

"Never," he agreed, laboring to sate this desire before her position became unbearable to her. Soon, love's fiery heat was washing over him as the potent spasms staggered his control.

Exhausted and appeased, his hands rested on her thighs, his head leaning back against the chair as he sought to master his rapid breathing and pounding heart. She drew a chuckle from him when she nonchalantly said, "You owe me one, love. I won't let you forget it."

"Nothing could repay such generosity, love," he debated.

"Your love can and does, Lynx," she freely admitted.

"Then you have no debt against me, for I love you, Calinda Cardone." He pulled her tightly against him, holding her for a long time. Such love and tenderness filled him, warmed him.

"Now, can I snuggle?" she teased, laughing softly.

"Now, you can do anything you please."

He lifted her and carried her to bed. For the next seven hours, they were lost to reality and fate's demands.

After rising and dressing quietly, Lynx stood by the bed gazing down at his serene wife. He had never experienced such love and contentment. Calinda Braxton Cardone belonged to him of her own will.

Monday passed tranquilly for both. Lynx went riding with his father to make plans for tonight's snare. Calinda rested for most of the day. When Rankin and Lynx returned by mid-afternoon, they chatted and snacked together. Later, Rankin pored over the ranchbooks in his office while Calinda nestled in Lynx's arms as he read aloud the local paper. When he tossed it aside and pulled her closer to him, he related the events of a large round-up and cattle drive to market.

Salina entered the enormous room and asked if they needed anything before she prepared dinner. Lynx and Calinda gazed longingly into each other's eyes and told her "nothing." Salina raged inwardly as Lynx stroked Calinda's cheek and murmured unknowingly, "I have everything I need right here."

Calinda's eyes softened and glowed. "Me, too," she replied.

Neither noticed Salina's hasty retreat from the infuriating sight, nor her glare of hatred and jealousy. She went into the kitchen, warning herself not to slam pots around in her irate condition. "When he sates his lust for you, *bruja,* your day is coming," she whispered balefully.

At dinner, Lynx brought a soft-bottomed chair to the table so Calinda could join them for the evening meal. The two men exposed their new plans to Calinda as they dined. Afterward, Lynx assisted Calinda to their room and into bed. "Think you can sleep better tonight?"

She grinned and nodded. "I have some dreams to create."

He bent to kiss her before leaving, to spend another useless night lying in wait for rustlers who had been warned of their concealed presence in three logical locations. It would be lunchtime on Tuesday before Rankin and Lynx learned where they'd struck.

In spite of Calinda's annoying torment, she slept fitfully all night. She hardly stirred when Lynx came to bed near dawn.

When she went downstairs past lunch the following day, Lynx and Rankin had left to check on Steve's report of a cut fence on the northern border of the ranch. Beside the number of steers taken, many had escaped through the opening and compelled the hired hands to search for them. The two owners realized it was time to do serious thinking about who was tipping off the rustlers. They rode to a private spot to discuss this unsettling mystery, wondering who couldn't be trusted.

Before they could dismount, someone opened gunfire on them. Lynx was off Star's back with one agile leap, concealing himself behind a slender live-oak. Rankin's startled horse reared and threw him. For three minutes, they were pinned down by the ominous gunshots. When Lynx heard the assailant's horse galloping off, he couldn't pursue him; Rankin was injured and bleeding.

He went to his father's side. Rankin sat up, cradling his left arm. "Broken?" Lynx hinted.

"Don't know," his father answered, grimacing.

"Let's get you to the house. I'll send Charlie for Doc."

"What about that bushwacker?" Rankin inquired angrily.

"He's long gone. Here, let me help you to mount."

When they reached the stable, Lynx told Charlie to fetch the doctor. Charlie took control of their animals before saddling another horse. Lynx assisted Rankin to the house. He asked the fretting Salina to tell Calinda they were home and his father was hurt. To his amazement, Salina told him Calinda had gone riding.

Rankin sank into a chair, then hastily told Lynx to go find Calinda. He could see how distressed his son was over Calinda's absence. What if she confronted that dangerous villain? Rankin had never seen his son so panicky.

Lynx remarked tensely, "I'll be right back, Father. Don't move. I've got to locate her before . . ."

When he didn't complete his anxious thought, Rankin encouraged, "I'll be fine. Go get her."

Lynx went to question Charlie as he was just leaving. Charlie told him he had saddled a horse for her an hour ago. She had headed up the lengthy road toward the gate, walking unsteadily beside the animal. Lynx thanked him and accepted a double-back ride in that direction, if that was the one she had truly taken . . .

When they met her returning to the ranch, she was strolling cautiously, the horse trailing behind. Lynx slid off Charlie's horse, then waved him on to town. Charlie took off at a swift pace, kicking up dust behind him. Calinda turned and watched the rider, then focused her curious attention on Lynx as he inexplicably and verbally assailed her.

"Where in tarnation have you been!" he thundered at her. "I told you not to go riding alone. I thought you were injured!"

"What's chewing at you, Lynx?" she asked in bewilderment. "I went walking to loosen up my stiff backside. I'm tired of lazing around. Why are you shouting at me?"

"You shouldn't ride in your condition," he snarled in tension.

"I didn't!" she snapped back. "And stop ordering me around like a child or dim-wit! I've got to do something to ease my nerves."

"Then why did you take a horse?" he demanded.

"In case I couldn't get back on my own two feet. If a problem came up, I thought I could throw myself over the saddle and let him bring me home. I don't require your permission to leave the house. Shut up and leave me alone!" she warned frostily, her fanny aching.

"Damnit, Cal! We were attacked by a gunman on the range. Rankin is hurt. Charlie's gone for the doctor. If you ever ride out alone again, I'll spank you, sore tail or not!" he shouted.

When his stormy gaze shifted to the gunbelt and weapon at her waist, she trembled at the horrifying gleam in his tawny eyes. "If you're wondering if it's been fired, Lynx, the answer is yes. If you care to wander up the road a piece, you'll find a very dead rattler with several bullets in him."

"Don't be ridiculous, Callie!" he stated sarcastically. "Why would you shoot at us?" he asked, revealing his line of thought.

"To gain ownership of this illustrious ranch?" she sneered, angered by his unnerving mood and harsh words.

"It's partly yours now!" he yelled, perturbed. "Why be greedy?"

Forgetting about Rankin during their implausible quarrel, she scoffed, "If I got rid of you two, I could be a wealthy and powerful widow. I could own everything in sight," she stressed, waving her hand.

He grabbed her by the shoulders and roughly shook her. "But you wouldn't have me around to give you pleasure and excitement!"

The argument silly, she still continued it. "Which times have been rare since we met! When you're like this, I'd just as soon be alone! Sometimes I wonder why I stay here to take such abuse!"

"Why do you?" he snarled coldly as she rashly provoked him.

"Because I love you, you bastard!" she shrieked in frustration. "Why, I don't know myself!" she added, jerking free of his grip.

"Let's get you home. Doc can check you over, too," he stated, berating his stupid words and actions which fear had borne.

"No, thank you. I don't care to have some strange man eyeing my naked derriere. Once was sufficient," she purred cattily.

"I'm being an ass, Callie. I'm sorry. I was worried about you, and I'm upset over Rankin," he suddenly apologized, leashing his temper and tongue. "I'm used to being shot at, but he isn't. This whole rustler affair has me edgy and fatigued. I shouldn't take my fury out on you. You just have a way of provoking me at the wrong time."

He looped the bridle reins over the saddle horn, then slapped the horse's rump to send him racing for the stable. He scooped her up into his arms and headed for the house.

"Put me down this instant, Lynx!" she demanded, wildly thrashing her legs to show her vexation.

"Stop that, or I'll drop you on your sore bottom. You've had enough exercise for today. Enjoy the free ride."

"Nothing's free around you, Lynx. Afraid I'll antagonize my injury and inconvenience you?" she taunted helplessly, still piqued.

He infuriatingly ignored her barb and kept walking. When they entered the house, he carried her into the den and set her down beside his father. She ruefully asked, "How are you, Rankin?"

"I haven't decided," he replied with a strained laugh.

She looked at his gradually swelling wrist. "Lynx, get a wide strip of cloth. We need to bandage this tightly to halt the swelling. Rip up an old sheet," she suggested, taking charge of the situation.

"We best wait for the doctor, Cal," he argued softly.

"We can't. He'll be too long arriving. I've seen injuries like this. I know what to do," she informed him. "And get Salina to bring me some salty water to clean this cut on his forehead."

When Lynx left to follow her instructions, she muttered, "He should have taken care of you rather than stalking me down."

"He went wild when you weren't here, Cal. I've never seen my son so panicky. He was afraid you had run into that cutthroat. He set me down and dashed out to rescue you again. I suspect my son has a bad case of love fever," he explained Lynx's behavior to a stunned wife.

Calinda was plagued by guilt over her conduct. Why did Lynx refuse to expose his great concern? Why was he so defensive and secretive about his emotions? He was so unacquainted with love, sharing, and fear that he didn't know how to deal with them!

When her sullen mate returned with the torn sheet, she smiled at him and thanked him. "Hold this, love," she told him, pointing to the cloth ends on Rankin's lower arm. Lynx placed his fingertips where she indicated. She carefully and snugly rolled the strip around the injured area. She informed Rankin it would be tight and uncomfortable, but it would prevent more swelling. When the bandage was secured in place, she cleansed the small cut on his temple where his head had struck a jagged rock. "That should do it until the doctor arrives, unless you want a brandy to ease the pain and settle your nerves," she hinted.

When she appeared to have trouble arising from her kneeling position, Lynx took her hands and helped her to her feet. She smiled into his wary expression. "You could use a stiff drink, too, my love."

"Did you see any strangers while you were out?" Lynx asked.

"No, I wish I had. But I wouldn't have known enough to shoot at him."

"Please don't go out alone, Callie," he gravely entreated.

"I know I'm a bad girl at times, too willful and impulsive," she confessed. "I'll do my best to correct those terrible traits."

"That sounds like excellent advice for both of us, including curbing these sharp tongues," he whispered softly, tapping her lips and his. "You scared the pants off me, woman," he admitted shamefully.

She didn't care if Rankin was in the room, she hugged him tightly. "What's this?" Lynx asked mockingly.

Her eyes said, "I love you; thanks," as did her radiant smile.

They sat together on the couch waiting for the doctor. She heard about the alarming episode on the range and their mutual suspicions about the thefts. The doctor was on another emergency, and it was several hours before he arrived.

After examining Rankin, the elderly doctor glanced at Calinda and smiled warmly. "You didn't need me, Rankin; she did everything possible in such a case. I would have treated you the same way. Rest easy, you're in good hands." He gave Calinda an approving nod and instructions for Rankin's care. "If you ever decide to become a nurse, let me know. I could use a smart and alert helper."

"Thank you, Doctor Weaver, but I can't stand the sight of blood. I get nauseous and faint," she told the amused man.

"Too bad," he murmured.

After the doctor was gone and Rankin was resting comfortably in the den, Lynx and Calinda went to their room to freshen up for dinner and talk privately. Lynx noticed a letter on the bed the moment he entered the room. He swaggered over and retrieved it; it was addressed to his wife. He turned and asked, "What's this, Cal?"

She glanced over at the item in his grasp, her eyes widening in puzzlement. "I don't know. Why?"

"It's a letter for you," Lynx casually announced.

"From where?" she inquired, coming toward him. "I hope not another one from the Simpsons," she fretted.

"It didn't come by mail," he stated, holding up the envelope with her name scrawled across the front.

Her face went pale and she trembled. "That's the same handwriting as the first one. How did it get here?" Cal asked fearfully.

"I'll ask Salina; you wait here." He left the room as she sank down on the edge of the bed, oblivious to her aching hip.

When he returned, he told her Salina hadn't seen anyone around, that she and Charlie had been cleaning the supply shed and checking the stock there. "You didn't see anyone come around?" he pressed. "How long were you out earlier?"

"I don't know; I didn't notice the time. I guess about an hour. But I didn't see anyone," she told him. "What does it say?"

"There's very little to block the view, Cal. How could someone ride up and away without you seeing him?" he probed.

"The same way no one else noticed a stranger! The same way one attacked you two and got away without revealing his identity! There are plenty of things to block the view: the house, stables, and sheds! Are you accusing me of lying?" she demanded breathlessly.

"I just don't understand how these mysterious messages keep appearing from nowhere. I don't like the idea that someone can sneak in and out of my home at will. I think we had better keep the doors and windows locked, and maybe post a guard for a while."

"What if I hadn't taken that walk? I could have been in worse danger than you two. Clearly this mystery man doesn't want to be recognized. But how does he get close enough to watch the house for an opportunity to make a stealthy visit and then carry it out?" she reasoned in alarm.

"Let's see what our villain has to say this time. I wonder why he would leave it while I was home," he deliberated aloud.

"Burn it," Cal pleaded, a foreboding sensation washing over her.

"After he went to such trouble and peril to deliver it?" he teased.

"Who's doing this to me, Lynx? Who's trying to be rid of me? I bet it's just another lure. It won't work this time. I don't care what it says; I'll never leave this ranch again."

Lynx opened the envelope and silently read the message:

> My dearest daughter,
>
> Forgive this manner of contacting you, but do not be afraid. The others will be distracted to give you time to find and read this message in secret. You have grown into a very beautiful young lady and I am proud of you. I saw you in Lampasas, but could not risk coming to your side. I watched you for two days. My enemy was lurking in the shadows waiting to spring on me and slay me. We must meet and talk. There is much you should know about the Cardones. You have trusted them too soon, my child, and I fear for your life and happiness. They have used you and tricked you. It is urgent you come to Dallas. Let no one see you leave. I will contact you there and explain. Please trust me, daughter. Leave the ranch today. I will take steps to protect you from them.

A tic formed along his clenched jawline and he went rigid. His eyes narrowed and hardened. "I'm riding over to Dallas to check out this invitation," he coldly announced from his pensive study.

Cal jumped up and seized his arm. "No! You can't! Don't you see, Lynx? That note isn't for me; it's to lure you away. Please don't leave," she urged him frantically, eyes wide with terror.

"How do you know? You haven't read it," he remarked oddly.

"If it was for me, idiot, he wouldn't have left it where you were certain to see it. Besides, why wouldn't I give it to you? I have this awful feeling that letter means trouble."

"You burned the first one, then took off in secret," he said.

"That was before we had an understanding. I told you I wouldn't leave again. I've related the contents of all my messages."

"Read it, Calinda," he said firmly, holding out the paper, curiously calling her by her first name.

"No, I don't want to," she refused, turning her back. "If he can't be open with me, I don't trust him. It must be a trick."

"Him, who?" Lynx inquired casually, as if trying to entrap her.

"How should I know? I just assumed it was a he."

Lynx insisted, "I'll read it to you. My dearest daughter," Lynx began icily. He looked over at her and sneered, "From Brax."

She slowly turned and stared at him, her body trembling and her face draining of natural color. Her lips parted as if to silence him, her tormented gaze wide and beseeching. Tears glistened in her sad eyes. She looked at him as if he had plunged a hot knife into her heart. As her chin and lips began to quiver, she looked on the verge of racking sobs. She sat on the edge of the bed and stared at him.

Lynx observed this strange reaction, holding silent until she composed her-self. Her head remained lowered for a time as she was lost in deep thought. Finally she lifted it and met his searching gaze. "Shall I read the contents?" he asked when she didn't speak.

Her eyes and voice were dulled as she murmured faintly, "I don't care who it claims to be from, Lynx; I don't want to hear it. Why are you being so persistent and cruel? You recently told me to forget him and the past," she painfully rea-soned. "Why must you torment me this way? My father has been lost to me for years. Don't bring him back to life."

"The past can't be over, Cal, not as long as he's trying to reach you. He was waiting for you in Lampasas. He didn't show his miserable face because of me. He's trying to set up another meeting."

"I was there long enough for him to come forward before you suddenly appeared. You're not saying you were there all along while that gunslinger Deavers was terrifying me?" she inquired in dread.

"No, Cal, I arrived that night. But your father thought I was lurking around," he concluded. "This note isn't a trick, Cal. From what it says, only Brax could have written it."

"He's never been a father to me, so stop shoving him down my throat! I don't want to see him! I don't want to speak with him! There's nothing he can say to justify his actions! I hate him! Is that clear enough, Lynx?" she panted in anguish.

"If you hear him out, Calinda, we could both learn the truth and be free of the past," he suggested to her astonishment.

The letter intrigued her, but pained her deeply. Reading the hatred and cold-ness in his eyes and tone, she accused angrily, "You mean, set a trap for him so you can gun him down!"

"Do you care?" he asked indifferently.

"He's a person, Lynx; I don't want you killing anyone. No matter how wicked he's been in the past, he's my father. If you slay him, we could never be happy together. Please, I'm begging you; don't chase this vengeful dream. Rankin and I need you here. Have you forgotten about the rustlers and that man who tried to gun down you two? Are you forgetting someone can slip in and out of this house?"

"Your messenger takes the blame for that incident, to stall us out there until you found this note," he frigidly informed her.

"You mean he's that dangerous, and you want me to walk into his den? I don't believe what I'm hearing. My God, you westerners are all crazy and violent! I won't go!" she stated defiantly. "And if you do, don't expect to find me here when you return!" she added. Suddenly she was furious with him. He was acting as if she were conspiring with her father. "If my father is so evil and yellow that he can't come to me here, then he doesn't deserve to see me again. He made his decisions long ago; he'll have to abide by them. It's over."

Lynx began to chuckle. "Excellent, my love," he murmured happily, winking at her. Shocked by his genial mood, she gaped at him. "I just wanted to be certain you wouldn't feel drawn to him again. I was afraid his letter would compel you to

Dallas. Now, I know I'm more important to you than he is. You're right, love; it's finally over."

Calinda glared at him, breathing heavily. She balled her fists and pounded on his chest until he seized them and stared at her in confusion. "Damn you, Lynx Cardone! How dare you pull a trick like that! It's unforgiveable! Your little note scared the wits out of me! Do you know how you frightened me, to think someone could sneak into our bedroom unnoticed! If you don't trust me by now, I don't belong here. How could you be so cruel and spiteful! Get your lousy hands off me!" she shrieked.

"Hold on a minute, love," he demanded, tightening his grip to keep her from pulling free. "I didn't have anything to do with the note! I was just trying to make sure it wouldn't entice you to follow its urgent summons. That's why I was picking at you. I had to know what you were feeling. I didn't write it, Cal; I swear."

Their gaze fused. Each was speechless as the other's words and actions settled in. "You didn't write it?" she inquired shakily.

"No, love, I didn't. I was just as shocked as you were."

She ceased her struggles. "Then who did?" she agonized.

"I hate to say it, Cal, but Brax. Read it and you'll see why," he coaxed, his gaze unreadable, as was his tone of voice.

Calinda glanced at the letter still clutched in her love's tight grip. She longed for the truth. But could she seek it at any price? Could she allow her father to keep torturing them in this cruel manner? Even if she followed the letter's instructions, it might be another wild-goose-chase. To go to her father might appear a betrayal of the Cardones. Besides, she had plenty of clues about her father's actions. There was nothing he could say to justify his evil deeds.

It was a difficult decision, but she made it. She shook her head, tears welling on her lower lids and threatening to spill over their narrow banks. "You know what that other letter did to me; I can't punish myself like that again. He killed himself to me, and I must let him remain buried in the past. I want him out of our lives, to stop causing a breach between us. Don't you see, Lynx? No matter what he says, he can't ever be a part of my life again, not after what he did to you and Rankin. Swear you won't go to Dallas. I could never forgive either of you for hurting the other. If I must choose between you two, I want my husband, the man I love more than life itself. If you truly love me, swear it."

Lynx pulled her into his arms and hugged her fiercely. How could he ever love her more than he did at this very moment. Yet, if he didn't do something about Brax, her father might continue to interfere in their lives. Brax held certain weapons which he could use against the Cardones, weapons to possibly destroy his life with Cal. Still, he had to handle this matter in such a way as to remain honest with her. "I won't go to Dallas, love," he vowed, mentally adding, *but I will go to town tomorrow and send a telegram for a friend to check out this riddle . . .*

—— *Chapter 19* ——

W̲EDNESDAY AND T̲HURSDAY WERE RELATIVELY CALM DAYS on the ranch. For some unknown reason, the rustling and fence-cutting abruptly halted. Lynx insisted on running the ranch while Rankin nursed his injured arm for a few days. Between Calinda's healing bruise and Rankin's disabled arm, they spent more time together. They played cards and took short walks. They even planned a large barbecue for early September when Lynx should be home to stay.

Lynx was out most of both days, giving orders or checking on various chores. This time of year hinted at the approaching fall when all ranches were active with round-ups, solitary ones if the ranch size allowed it or a joint one when several smaller ranches banded together for protection along the trail to the stockyards near the train depot.

At night, Rankin and Calinda would join Lynx and other cowboys as they played or listened to music, tossed horseshoes, or re-lived olden days when life was perilous and challenging. Some of the men would sit around the table in the bunk houses drinking coffee and playing poker. It was the rule that hard drinking could be done only on Saturday night or Sunday, when the men were off, except for the few selected for that weekend's chores.

Friday was an exciting day. To practice for the fall round-up and to provide tension-breaking entertainment, the ranch-hands were involved in a mock-rodeo. Volunteers took turns breaking-in captured broncos, wild stallions and obstinate mustangs. There was a stirring bout of calf-roping, then a delightful session of trick roping. Rankin told Cal the men weren't permitted to ride bulls to prevent injuries. They rode horses, instead.

After observing the dangerous bronco-busting for a while, Calinda was relieved her husband didn't attempt such sport. But she could see the gleam of desire in his eyes; she could sense the eagerness to be on the back of one of those bucking stallions. When the hands encouraged Lynx to try it, he laughed and told them, "Next time," saying he couldn't risk an injury today. Knowing Lynx Cardone was exceptionally brave and daring, they accepted his explanation.

When Steve suggested they have target practice and a shooting contest, Calinda was given a first-hand observation of how fast and accurate Lynx was with his Colts. He could draw and fire in the flicker of an eye. She shook her head several times during the contest, wondering how the target could explode before she saw Lynx react to the "fire" shout. His movements were so fluid and swift, one moment he was poised ready and in a flash he was limber and the action was over! It almost seemed as if Lynx hadn't moved a muscle, as if he had wished the target shattered. It looked a greased reflex, so easy and natural, as if man and weapon were briefly one. Lynx never missed a target or failed to be first. In each instant, the gun was back in his holster before the others had drawn and fired. Cal was amazed.

At dinner, Cal kept staring at Lynx in astonishment. When he grinned and asked why she was watching him so strangely, she said, "You're so fast; if I blinked, I missed your shot. You hit every one, Lynx. No wonder you've never been beaten; I doubt any man could."

Laughter spilled forth into the room. Lynx winked at her and teased, "I thought you said there was always a better challenger."

"That was before I saw how perfect you are. I suppose I should relax now, but it frightens me even more," Cal confessed.

"Why?" Lynx asked, bemused and flattered.

"Too many gunslingers will demand to take your place. Don't you get tired of the killing and fighting? It's like one endless nightmare of death and violence. What if eager men pursue the colorful legend here?" Cal sadly expressed her fears.

"I don't kill or fight unless there's no other way out, Cal. Once I retire from the scene, they'll forget about me, be glad I'm gone."

"I recall reading about Wesley Hardin. Did the Rangers forget him when he fled Texas? No, they relentlessly pursued and captured him. Legends don't retire so easily, my love," she asserted warily.

Calinda wondered why both Rankin and Lynx had tensed at her mention of the Rangers, but she didn't question their reactions. If Lynx was in trouble, she would have heard about it. "Wes killed for the fun of it, love; I don't. Besides, he was an outlaw; I'm not."

"If you weren't rich, would you use your expert talents in that line?" Calinda stunned Lynx with a curious and serious question.

He threw back his head and laughed heartily. "No way, love."

To alter the topic, Lynx dropped his dismaying news on her. "I'll be leaving tomorrow for the last time, so you best get prepared to lose your privacy. I got a telegram today, and I'm needed."

Calinda's head jerked up as she protested, "Leaving? Tomorrow? But you can't. What about the problems and dangers at home? We need you, don't we, Rankin?" she sought Rankin's assistance.

Rankin sighed heavily, knowing the details of his son's trip. "I'm fine, Cal. The sooner Lynx leaves and gets this matter settled, the sooner he'll be home for good. I can't complain; this was his longest visit in years. I think you're responsible for the change in him."

"You can't be serious," she refuted Rankin's words.

"This wrist is nearly healed. I can manage things now. Those rustlers have moved on to other pastures. We'll be all right until he gets home," the man reasoned, smiling at his son. "I've been on my own a lot longer than Lynx. I can defend my land and family."

Calinda's stupefied gaze shifted from one man to the other. How could Lynx leave his home and family at a time like this? Why would his father encourage it?

Witnessing their determination, she knew further debate was useless. "Where are you heading?" she asked.

"To Waco, then San Antonio," Lynx reluctantly deceived her. The telegram from Jones had said Dallas, then Austin. If he told her where he was heading, Cal would think he was breaking his promise. He would explain later when he returned from the state capital.

"For how long?" she asked distantly.

"Anywhere from one to six weeks," he confessed uneasily, watching her reaction to that displeasing information.

"Six weeks would put it at mid-September. What about the round-up and barbecue?" she pressed dejectedly.

"I'll try to make it home before then," Lynx subtly promised.

"The barbecue can be cancelled, but not the round-up. We won't do social planning until we hear when you'll be home," Cal wisely yielded to this vexing situation. At least he had added eight more days to their time together. But if this didn't turn out to be his last time-consuming adventure, they would need to have a very serious discussion about their marriage and his feelings . . .

After dinner, Lynx and Calinda went to their room to spend time together before his imminent departure. Most of the soreness was gone from her hip, but it still boasted loudly of a purplish-blue reminder. On the surface Lynx was in a mellow and romantic mood, but inwardly he was dreading and resenting this new separation. He knew how it must appear to her at this trying time. He had no choice but to stall an explanation until his return. On this journey he would send frequent messages home to keep himself alive in her mind.

Calinda was exceedingly quiet and almost unresponsive tonight. Each time Lynx sought to draw her out of her remote shell, she would sigh heavily and make some nonsensical comment. She determined she wouldn't quarrel with him tonight, or plead for him to remain with her. But she was dismayed by how easily and readily he could pick up and leave after what they had shared recently and the new dangers around them. Her confidence in their closeness was slowly vanishing.

"You planning to pout and rub that icy shoulder against me all night?" he playfully ventured to bring an end to her distance.

"Surely you don't expect me to be cheerfully resigned to your leaving? You haven't even left and I miss you terribly," she said.

He laughed softly as he pulled her into his entreating arms. "If you were glad to see me leave, I'd be worried sick, woman."

Cal was so tempted to break her promise to herself, to cry and beg him not to go. What hurt most was knowing she couldn't do anything to alter his plans. She wanted to scream and argue with him; she couldn't. But neither could she behave as if all was wonderful.

Following two hours of blissful lovemaking, Lynx lay awake for a long time. He fretted over the way Calinda had struggled to control her responses to him, how she had tried to accept their lovemaking dutifully and not give passionately. He could almost read a resentful glitter in her eyes at his power to sway her masked resistance to mindless surrender. Lynx sensed she rebelled inwardly against her greedy body's power over her warring senses. Finally Cal had dismissed her futile guard and given herself over to his prowess and will, submitting wildly to tantalizing ecstasy. He worried over the way she had turned her back to him and wept softly after she thought he'd fallen asleep. Was it merely his departure which was affecting her this way? Was she doubting his love and commitment? What more could he say or do?

At seven on Saturday morning, Lynx nudged his wife and called her name to awaken her. He dared not slip off again. Besides, leaving her was the last thing he wanted to do. He craved a warm send-off.

Calinda yawned and stretched, opening her eyes. Lynx smiled down at her, fluffing her hair. "You want to sleep longer or eat breakfast with me before I ride out?" he inquired.

"What time is it?" she asked, trying to clear her hazy mind.

"Seven. I need to eat and pack a few things. I'd like to get going before that sun's too high and hot. I know you're tired, Cal, but I needed to spend time with you this morning," he revealed.

"Give me a few minutes to dress, then I'll prepare our breakfast."

"Salina should be up; she can do it," her husband suggested, wanting her with him every minute.

"If you don't mind, I would prefer to cook my husband's last meal home. In case you aren't aware of the fact, I'm a good cook."

He smiled roguishly. "You're good at many things, love. If Salina enters the kitchen, tell her we want to be alone this morning."

"She'll love that," Calinda scoffed under her breath.

"Who cares what she thinks, love?" he asked breezily.

"I did, but no longer. I'm tired of going beyond half way for peace with her. It's time you and Rankin accept the fact, she will never like me or my presence. I've never been a quitter, but I give up on her. I have other matters to consume my concentration."

"Cal, are you feeling all right this morning? You look a bit pale. I think you're working too hard," he noted.

"The harder I work, the better I sleep when you're gone."

"How can I debate that stirring excuse?" he murmured.

"I shouldn't have told you; now, you'll never get your hat on the enlarged head," she jested, deciding to play it lightly this morning.

"Zat a fact, Mrs. Cardone? You adding conceit to my long list of bad traits?" he teased.

"I think you're so self-assured that it comes across as enormous ego and arrogance. I think you're too accustomed to getting your way and wishes. No doubt I'm the first problem you can't settle with those blazing Colts and your great prowess," she remarked saucily.

His chest rumbled with laughter. "You're right, Cal. You're the most exasperating, challenging, and refreshing task I've confronted. Sometimes I can't decide if I'm coming or going with you."

"I can tell; it's usually going, too much and too long," she quipped as she brushed her tangled hair, her gaze flickering over him.

"I'll remind you of your demands when you grow weary of having me underfoot," he said, trying to sound stern.

"Save your breath, love, because I won't," she retorted coyly.

"We'll see," he mused aloud, passing his tongue over his lips.

"Yes, we will," she concurred. "See you downstairs."

"I'm coming with you. I'd like to see my wife in action."

"Afraid I'll poison you? Make you sick so you can't leave?"

"I wouldn't put any trick past you, woman," he told Cal.

"Why, Lynx Cardone, how wicked of you."

Lynx sat at the table sipping coffee and watching Cal as she prepared their breakfast. Salina had left in a huff when Lynx dismissed her from her duties. When all was ready, Cal served him with a bright smile. "See, I'm not utterly helpless."

They ate in near silence, the weight of his remaining time sinking down on them. Afterward, Lynx told Cal to leave the dishes for Salina and to keep him company while he packed his saddle-bags. She didn't argue or refuse, but followed his lead upstairs.

Cal stood at the end of the bed, clutching the tall post as if she required its support. Suddenly, she couldn't think of anything to say. She simply watched Lynx, her eyes easing over his arresting face and virile body. How was it possible to love and need another person so much that it hurt to be separated from him. With his departures, he seemed to take the air and sunshine from her life. Unlike a morning glory with the blazing sun, she folded her petals when his heat vanished.

Lynx walked past her several times as he retrieved and stuffed several shirts, pants, underwear, and pairs of socks into his bulging saddlebags. He added a sharp razor and shaving soap. His camping gear and supplies were packed and waiting in the stable with Star, along with a rain-slicker, his rifle, and extra ammo. He grabbed an extra vest and crammed it into the leather bag. Occasionally he would glance over at her and smile. Her gaze never left him.

Lynx read such loneliness in her eyes that he could hardly bear to look at her; Cal was so subdued now. He mentally begged her not to cry or debate this necessary last trip, which she didn't. He lifted his gunbelt and checked his pistols, then laid them beside his bags. He drew the large Bowie knife from its sheath and tested its sharpness with his finger, then replaced it. His keen gaze drifted along his holster belt, checking to make sure each hole contained an extra bullet.

Lynx went to his closet one last time, seeking some papers he wished he had packed earlier. He withdrew them from a hidden pocket in a winter jacket. Calinda turned to speak to him as he approached the bed, bumping into him and sending the loosely held papers in his hand fluttering to the floor. She was about to help him gather them when he grinned and distracted her with, "I've got 'em, love. Grab me a few bandannas; I sweat heavily on the trail."

As Cal responded to his request, Lynx retrieved the papers. He folded them and stuffed them into the bag, to read later. He walked to the coat-rack near his door to get his silver spurs and black hat, adding them to the items on his bed. He glanced around the room in deep thought. "That's about it, love. I wish I had your picture in a locket to carry with me," he surprisingly told her.

"I wish I had yours here," she agreed with his touching words. "Perhaps we can have a painting done when you come home."

Cal's gaze trailed Lynx as he prepared to leave. His stance and movements always suggested immense self-assurance and pride. She wondered what it was like to fear nothing and no one. Lynx was so valiant and intelligent in most areas, so why couldn't he understand how she felt about his absences and halt them? Why weren't she and the ranch enough for him? If he loved and needed her as vowed, how could he endure so many separations? Even now, Lynx remained a golden stranger who was as impenetrable as his black attire.

Lynx dropped his saddlebags by the locked door and placed his hat on them. He returned to the bed to fasten on his spurs and gunbelt. Calinda went to him and murmured, "How about my farewell kiss and hug before you get all loaded down?"

Lynx tossed the gunbelt back to the bed and reached for her. His mouth came down on hers as his arms went around her as a steely band. Her hands slipped up his back and held him tightly, dreading to release him. At first his kisses were gentle and exploratory, but soon they became forceful and demanding. Placing his palms near her shoulder blades, he crushed her to his hard frame. Silky curls danced over his hands as her head twisted to hungrily grind her mouth against his.

He kissed the corners of her mouth, then tugged on each lip in turn. He dropped kisses on her nose, chin, and each brow before travelling to her ear. His voice was thick with emotion when he muttered, "Your lips are softer than moonlight. God, Callie, I need you . . . I'm hotter than a hunk of beef spit over a roasting fire."

"Love me before you go, Lynx," she entreated passionately.

He was dressed and packed, but it didn't matter at that moment. Last night she had been restrained; presently, her need for him was urgent. He knew it wasn't a stalling tactic; he could feel the tension and desire within her, feelings which matched his own. He pulled away and picked up his gunbelt and spurs.

"Please, Lynx, just for a short time, let me be first in your life and thoughts," she pleaded, thinking he was about to leave her in this highly agitated state. What if she demanded he remain home?

"You are, Callie," he confessed, pulling the covers aside and gingerly dropping his possessions on the floor beside the bed. He held out his inviting hand to her, tawny eyes glistening with unleashed desire.

Tears of joy glimmered in her eyes as she placed her hand in his. He drew her forward and slowly undressed her. His smoldering gaze wandered over her body from head to foot. His hands pinned her jawline between them as he fused his eyes with hers. "Your skin is as silky and soft as a gentle rain. I can't even glance at you without wanting you. Do you know how beautiful and bewitching you are?" he asked proudly, his embrace and gaze possessive.

As her trembling fingers unbuttoned his ebony shirt, she replied, "Do you know how staggering you are to my senses?"

He yanked his shirt off, dropping it to the floor, his boots and dark pants quickly following it. He lifted her and lay her down, then joined her. His tongue flicked over her breasts and she quivered. His mouth captured one peak and tantalized it, then stimulated the other one. His hands caressed her body, fondling each curve and mound it encountered. It wasn't necessary to arouse her, but he savored his stirring effect on her. He played and tempted her until she was breathless and pleading. Her body was as thirsty as a desert; her skin as smooth as a serene pond. Her mood was as fiery as her hair when the blazing sun caressed it.

His manhood entered into her gently. He charged and retreated leisurely until their passions demanded he hasten his feverish task. Tingles and warmth covered her body as the delightful series of sensations attacked her senses.

Cal arched to meet his entries, wanting nothing more than his total love and commitment to her. For a time, he was her entire world and being as their joined bodies strove for mutual completion. When tormented desires were appeased, they lay locked in each other's arms. Neither spoke for a time, relishing this special sharing.

When she shifted her head to look into his face, he smiled and said, "I love you, Callie; don't ever doubt it or forget it."

She wondered if he had been about to add, no matter what happens. She smiled tenderly and caressed his cheek. "I love you, too."

Lynx rolled to his back and placed one hand beneath his head. "Whew, now I need a bath and a nap. I'm drenched and exhausted."

"I could wash your back; I'm very good in the tub," she hinted seductively, her gaze exposing mischief and contentment.

"Oh, no, you won't," he wailed humorously. "If I let you join me, I'd never get going today."

"Perhaps next time?" Cal speculated mockingly.

"I'll hold you to that promise. Right now, I'd best get busy."

When she started to rise, Lynx pushed her into the mattress and pinned her beneath his body. "You stay here and rest, woman; I don't trust that gleam in those green eyes." He kissed the tip of her nose.

When he moved to get out of bed, she caught his arm and chided, "What's this, Lynx? No farewell kiss?"

He eyed her suspiciously. "That's why I'm in bed rather than on the trail. I don't dare risk taking one."

"How about accepting one?" she teased, undaunted.

"The next kiss you get from me, woman, will be a greeting. You rest; you're pale and you've got dark smudges beneath your eyes. And this time, don't drive yourself into the ground," he cautioned.

"Yes sir," she stated gaily at his pleasing perceptions.

Lynx stood up and pulled on his clothes. When he glanced down at her, Cal was grinning at him. "Don't you dare cast those bewitching eyes on me," he playfully warned. "I'm getting a bath and leaving while I can. Keep the bed warm; I'll be home soon. And I'll send you a telegram every few days," he added, winking at her.

She snuggled into her pillow. "Good. That might help me remember I have a carefree husband somewhere."

"Forget it one minute, and I'll thrash you soundly," he jested, trying to glare sternly at her, but laughing instead.

As he reached the door to gather his things, she called out, "Lynx, please be careful. I love you."

Lynx threw the saddlebag over his shoulder and put his hat on his tawny head. With the gunbelt swinging over one arm, he came over to the bed. He bent over and kissed her lightly. "I love you, Callie."

When the brief kiss ended, Lynx studied her face once more, then left. After a

quick rinse in the watershed, he headed for the stable to complete his preparations. Rankin joined him. Lynx asked his father to watch after Calinda, telling him
she seemed overly tired and pale. Rankin credited her appearance to her recent fall
and emotional upheavals.

"Keep a guard posted around the house. I don't want her getting any more of
those strange notes; they frighten her. If she gets any mail, hold it until I come
home. I don't want her upset while I'm away. And make certain she never goes
riding alone," Lynx requested.

"Not to worry, son; she'll be fine," Rankin assured him.

Calinda decided she would dress and wave goodbye to her husband. She
stood up and swayed precariously, grabbing the post to steady herself. Her head
was swimming. She sat down, then reclined. Maybe it was just the heat or excitement. Or maybe she was pushing herself too hard with unfamiliar strenuous
chores. She had been feeling slightly weak and very sleepy lately. As she heard the
pounding hooves of a departing horse, she realized it was too late to see him. She
sighed wearily and curled into bed, falling asleep within minutes.

Lynx and Star boarded the Texas & Pacific Railroad to get to Dallas late that
night. While Star rode comfortably in a cattle car, the undercover Ranger relaxed
in the passenger section. When the train halted in Dallas, Lynx hurried to his
stealthy rendezvous with Major Jones at the Windsor Hotel. With perseverance
and courage, he might have that ruthless and wily Burrow in custody before the
week was out.

After placing Star in the livery-stable, Lynx strolled down the street, his perceptive gaze and keen senses engulfing sights and sounds. He had confronted
many perils and criminals, but none which sent sparks of apprehension through
him as this gaunt villain with an iron nerve, a lack of feelings, and a hair-trigger.
That truculent character had been known to terrorize whole areas. The one thing
about Rube Burrow that worried Lynx was that the killer had no fear of dying.
Normally, even the worst criminals feared capture and death, but not Rube. That
made him deadly and unpredictable.

Lynx slipped in the back door to the hotel and made his way to Jones' room.
Once inside, Lynx was given a pleasant surprise. He sat down to listen to his
commanding officer's words.

"You don't need to hang around Dallas, Lynx. After hitting the T & P five
times, Rube made off for Mississippi and Alabama. Guess he's getting nervous
about having Rangers chasing his tail."

"Who's going after him?" Lynx asked, perceiving that Jones wasn't going to
hand him that assignment.

"He's got the Pinkerton men and several railroad detectives in hot pursuit.
We'll let them harry Rube awhile. If he shows his guns here again, we'll be ready
and waiting."

"Has Tom learned anything about the telegram I sent earlier?" Lynx inquired
reluctantly.

"He's done plenty of checking around, but nothing so far. He's got the
descriptions of the man and woman you mentioned, but they aren't here. He's

been keeping an eye on the train depot to see if anyone seems to be waiting around for your wife."

"Is Deavers in town?" Lynx questioned, his eyes and voice cold.

"I did some checking on him; he's in San Antonio. Whatever the plot and whoever the instigator, I can't figure them yet. It sounds to me as if someone just wants her off the ranch, or in trouble with you. Anyone come to mind with that speculation?"

Lynx frowned. "Salina," he concluded. When Jones questioned his assumption, Lynx explained the Mexican girl's rivalry for him.

Jones chuckled. "You know the old saying about a spurned woman, Lynx. That could explain the mysterious notes. Living there, she's probably overheard enough to make them sound convincing. I think you'd best be careful with jealous ears around," he warned astutely.

"When I get home, I'll settle this matter once and for all. I should have reasoned this out before," he reprimanded himself.

"Something tells me you have other things on your mind when you're home," Jones teased his good friend.

"If Burrows is gone, does that mean I'm finished?" Lynx stated hopefully, grinning entreatingly at Jones.

Jones thoughtfully twirled his thick mustache. "Since you've already set aside the time, how about handling another matter for us? You can have your choice: Jim Miller or Kid Curry. Miller's operating around Abilene, and the Kid's trying to take on every gunslinger near Kerrville. Since you need to finish your work in Austin, Kerrville is the nearest. We've decided to reveal your identity as you retire. Knowing you're a past Ranger should make most outlaws leery of following you home to challenge that gun of yours. We want you to keep your badge just in case you need it to prevent trouble; we owe you some peace and protection after what you've done for us."

Lynx anxiously inquired, "What if Curry's left by the time I get to Kerrville? You want me to dog him and arrest him?"

"That won't be necessary. I know you're eager to get home and settle down. Just send any word you can get on him. I'll put another Ranger on his backside. Don't get too eager and head home before you visit the capital; you've got to testify for us," Jones reminded him.

"I'll take care of the Kid, my court session, and retiring before I head home," he agreed. "If you can spare him, I would appreciate it if Tom can make sure Braxton isn't around these parts. I don't want him interfering in Cal's and my lives anymore. When I leave Austin, I want my next stop to be home, permanently."

"Consider it done. After all, Braxton is wanted for assault and robbery."

"If you locate him, send the message to me, not home," Lynx cautioned. Jones nodded, then they discussed Kid Curry.

Calinda lazed around most of Saturday and Sunday. She couldn't seem to shake this sluggishness which was plaguing her. Between nightly slumber and naps, she was getting plenty of sleep; so why was she so tired and drowsy all the time?

On Monday, she decided to deny her annoying weakness by cleaning her room. As she was sweeping, she heard a rustle under the bed. She sat on the floor and peered beneath it. Sighting a paper, she used the broom to retrieve it. Evidently Lynx had dropped it while packing. She lifted it and glanced at the telegram. Dismay filled her. He wouldn't break his word to her; besides, he had sent her a telegram this morning from Waco. He couldn't be in Dallas!

> Lynx,
> Urgent. Waiting in Dallas. Windsor Hotel. Come Saturday. B running. Must pursue. News in Austin after Dallas. J.B.J.

That last mysterious message had summoned Cal to Dallas. Kyle Yancey was in Austin. Was Lynx chasing the unexpected clue to her father? Had he sent someone a telegram to investigate matters in Dallas for him? Was that why he hadn't taken off last Monday? Was he waiting for a reply and allowing time to mislead her? Who was this "B"? Brax? This "J.B.J."? How could she discover if Lynx was in Dallas? How could she reveal mistrust in him? Yet, her suspicions were overwhelming.

There was only one way to end her doubts and assuage her fears; send a telegram to the sheriff in Dallas. She could say it was urgent to locate her husband. She could wait at the telegraph office for a reply. Yes, she would do just that tomorrow . . .

Tuesday morning in the telegraph office, Calinda paced the floor while she awaited an answer from Dallas. Each time the keys clicked noisily, she became excited and frightened. One hour later, the agent smiled ruefully and handed her the sheriff's reply: he was sorry he couldn't help her, but Lynx Cardone had left Dallas on Monday, and his location was unknown.

Calinda was crushed by this staggering news. Lynx had lied to her. She wanted to send another telegram to ask if there had been trouble or a shooting there, but she couldn't. Lynx couldn't kill her father in revenge; Laura was just as guilty! Cal had to face an indisputable reality; if Lynx had deceived her about Dallas, what else had he lied about or secretly done? She reflected on their days together.

Austin! The word rifled through her mind. Was Lynx heading for Austin? Had Lynx learned about Kyle Yancey? Was her disloyal husband stalking her father at this very minute?

Cal unsteadily approached the agent once more, to send another telegram. She wrote out the message and handed it to him.

> Mr. Kyle Yancey, Lawyer, Austin.
> Told to contact you by Elliott Braxton. Please send his address.
> Urgent I locate father. Waiting your reply in Fort Worth station.
> Calinda Braxton.

This time, Calinda was given a curious response within forty-five minutes:

Calinda Braxton. Have important papers for you. Will deliver. Explain. Meet here, Thursday. Awaiting response. Kyle Yancey.

Without hesitation or remorse, Calinda instantly fired a telegram back to the lawyer, requesting they meet in Fort Worth at the Canton Hotel. There was only one way to solve this weighty enigma and to halt its power over them; she must meet with this Kyle Yancey. If her love couldn't or wouldn't be honest with her, she would find someone else to do so! Perhaps then she might understand Lynx's deceptions and reluctance. God, how she despised and dreaded this furtive path of action, but Lynx was making it necessary.

As Charlie drove Cal home in the buggy, a flood of emotions and thoughts saturated her body and mind. *What papers? What explanation? Why a lawyer? Why in person? Why was she being so secretive?* There was an answer only to the last question . . .

—— *Chapter 20* ——

WHEN CALINDA RECEIVED A TELEGRAM on Wednesday from Lynx, she realized how beguiling he was; clearly someone was helping him send messages from where he was supposed to be, not where he actually was. The first one had said Waco, when Lynx was in Dallas. This one alleged San Antonio, when she suspected he was in Austin. Cal agonized over her mistrust and her furtive actions. She fumed at Lynx and Rankin for compelling her to investigate like this. But this destructive mystery must be conquered and dismissed promptly. She and Lynx could never be happy as long as the dark past continued to assail them, and Lynx willfully created new mysteries. She prayed Kyle Yancey had left Austin before Lynx's arrival. When her husband came home, she wouldn't be so gullible and lenient. This time, she would demand frank answers.

Calinda had planned her strategy well. Tuesday she had hired a local seamstress to make her a new gown for Lynx's homecoming; she used this excuse to return to town on Thursday. She sat in the eating area of the hotel, nervously sipping coffee and squirming in her seat. The train from Austin was late; she prayed nothing had gone wrong, yet she dreaded to hear Yancey's words.

Cal was ensnared by pensive study when a man tapped her on the shoulder and asked if she was Calinda Braxton. Since she was the only lady present, it was a natural assumption. She turned and looked up into his face, a pleasant one with sharply defined features. His eyes were like warm chocolate. His hair was nearly gray, hinting at his advancing age. His manner and expression implied he was of a gentle nature. She gradually relaxed and nodded.

"You cannot imagine how glad I was to hear from you, Miss Braxton. I have been deliberating what to do with this packet. It has been in my safe for years," Kyle hastily began as he took a seat near her.

"I don't understand, Mr. Yancey. Where is my father?" Cal asked softly, her voice laced with a noticeable quiver as she stared at the ominous packet.

Kyle eagerly explained, "When Elliott Braxton gave me these papers for safe-keeping, he said he was leaving Texas. He instructed me to turn them over to you if he didn't reclaim them within six years, which is next month. He paid me handsomely to safeguard them, to deliver them to you if necessary."

"You mean you haven't seen my father or heard from him since then?" Cal murmured in dread.

"I'm afraid not. I was wondering how I was supposed to locate you, since you didn't respond to my letter two months past. I see you decided to come to America rather than write to me."

"What letter, Mr. Yancey? I've never received any messages from you. I've been living at the Cardone Ranch since May. I'm married to Lynx Cardone. I came to America to locate my father, but it's been impossible. He's been missing for years. A lost letter was recently delivered to me which told me to contact you. Why, I do not know. I was hoping you had news of him. I find this matter confusing. Is my father still alive?" she asked uncontrollably.

"I have no way of knowing, Mrs. Cardone. I was retained to hold this packet. If he didn't recover it within six years, it was to go to you. As you can see from the date, the deadline is near. Perhaps I am pre-shooting the assigned schedule, but I hardly feel he will return at the last moment. Since I have fortunately located you, surely your father will forgive my eagerness in settling this matter. Its contents are unknown to me, other than letters and a legal document. I was paid well to make certain this packet fell into no hands other than his or yours; that's why I personally delivered it," Kyle expounded.

"May I see the packet?" she asked apprehensively.

Calinda couldn't halt her hands from trembling as she accepted the time-yellowed packet. She inhaled deeply and slowly released it before breaking the wax-seal. She withdrew four papers. The largest one captured her attention first, the missing deed to the ranch. Why would her father place a stolen deed in her possession, making her an unbidden accomplice to his crime? She placed the other papers beneath it, to focus her concentration on the legal document. She paled as she read over it; the deed was for the Cardone . . . Braxton Ranch! She read it several times, then asked the lawyer to explain it to her.

Kyle glanced over the document, then informed her, "In essence, the ranch is jointly owned by Rankin Cardone and Elliott Braxton. In the event of the death of either or both men, their halves will be inherited by Lynx Cardone and Calinda Braxton. In case of mutual deaths in either family, the other family inherits every-thing."

"Are you telling me my father owned half of the Cardone Ranch?" Cal in-quired dubiously, gaping at him. Surely Yancey was mistaken.

"Not owned, owns, unless he's deceased. In such case, you own half of the ranch and all entailed," he casually clarified, unaware of the shock of his devastating news, intrigued by her astonishment.

"That isn't possible, Mr. Yancey," Cal debated. "My father never owned any part of that ranch; he only worked there. He and Mister Cardone were close friends, never partners," she refuted.

Kyle Yancey peered over his spectacles to study the befuddled lady. To prevent any error, he closely examined the document again. "This deed is legal and binding, Mrs. Cardone," he evidenced, confused by her ignorance of this matter in light of her marriage.

"Then my father must have sold his half to the Cardones," Cal reasoned earnestly, dreading the implications of this new riddle. Had the proclaimed stolen money actually been for a sale? Had they lied about the theft because of her father's adulterous betrayal?

"See if there's a record of the sale in the packet," he suggested.

Calinda sought the next paper; it was a will. She handed the paper to the lawyer, who studied it. "According to this deed and will, Braxton transferred his half-ownership to you at his demise. I suppose it's safe to assume he's no longer alive, since he never returned. What did the Cardones tell you? You are married to this . . . Lynx Cardone?" he questioned, glancing at the deed for her husband's name. He mused, was her husband the famed gunslinger and insolent rebel?

Calinda flushed, then confessed they had told her nothing of this matter. "These papers are of little consequence at this date; your husband owns half of the ranch with his father. In the event of Rankin Cardone's death, Lynx Cardone will be the sole owner. Are you aware, a wife's property falls under her husband's control after marriage?"

"You're saying, they actually own the entire ranch now because of my marriage?" the dismayed girl asked for total clarity.

"That's the size of it," Kyle reluctantly concurred.

"And that's legal? No recourse?" she asked cautiously.

"None. Why would you ask?" he quizzed curiously.

Calinda didn't want to ask her next question, but forced herself. "If Lynx and I weren't married, where would I stand now?"

"You would own half and the Cardones would own half. By marrying one of them, it legally passed into their hands and control."

"Are you positive my father didn't sell it to them?" Cal probed desperately, consternation biting viciously at her heart and mind.

"Impossible, Mrs. Cardone. He left these documents with me before leaving Texas. To sell his portion, he would need to reclaim the deed as proof of half-ownership. He hasn't," Kyle stated simply.

"Then this deed is vital to prove his claim?" she pressed.

"Yes, or your claim," he gave the answer she feared, the answer which told why they were so intent on locating it and her father.

"If my father took $45,000 of the ranch's money with him when he left, would that constitute a verbal sale of his portion? Would it be viewed as theft, a criminal offense?" she probed anxiously.

"Both partners should agree to such financial matters, but it could hardly be called criminal to take money from your own ranch. No matter, unless sale papers were signed, witnessed, and filed, it doesn't change anything. As you see, the deed has not been altered or stamped," he further expounded, holding out the unmarked deed.

"I see," Cal murmured pensively. She owned half of the ranch? Why hadn't they told her? Why had they treated her as if she were penniless and dependent? She could have claimed and taken half of that cattle empire, a spread worth a fortune? Owned, that was the key word. Through her hasty marriage, the Cardones possessed everything . . . In exchange for Laura, they had stolen her inheritance.

Calinda didn't like what she was thinking and feeling. Yet, she couldn't explain why they had withheld many critical facts. Didn't they know her by now? Didn't they realize she would have signed her half over to them because of her father's theft and betrayal? Her father had lost all rights to the ranch; she would never have demanded anything.

It was apparent why they had been suspicious of her in the beginning. It was evident why they suspected Brax might return one day. It was obvious they wanted revenge, and it was noxiously clear how they had obtained it. That final missing piece to the pernicious puzzle fell rapidly and agonizingly into place, forming a picture which she didn't want to view. She had been ignorant and trusting; why had they used her for such a wicked plot? After knowing her, why did they continue their malicious tricks? They had gained possession of the ranch; what more could they want? To lure her father and Laura back . . .

Calinda lifted her tormented gaze to ask a question. "Mr. Yancey, where would I stand if I left Lynx and the ranch?"

Surprise and bewilderment registered on the elderly lawyer's face. "Even if you abandoned both, the ranch will remain in your husband's control. That's the law, Mrs. Cardone."

"You mean, I wouldn't get anything? I've lost all rights by marrying Lynx? I couldn't even demand payment for my share?" she persisted painfully. "If they wished, could they force me to leave?"

"I take it you're asking me these questions in confidence as a lawyer?" he astutely hinted before responding.

"Yes, Mr. Yancey. Whatever your fee, I want this conversation to remain private between us. I must clarify this matter in my mind."

"Do you feel you've been duped, Mrs. Cardone?" he probed.

"I don't know. They never told me anything." Calinda slowly related relevant facts and how she had been treated since her arrival. She revealed the story of her father's disappearance and her attempt to locate him. "I'm confused by this secrecy and deception. If Lynx married me just to gain control of my half, it doesn't appear that way. Surely their affections and acceptance can't be false?"

Kyle realized the young woman was on the verge of tears. He saw how vulnerable and distressed she was. "I'm well-acquainted with your husband's reputation, Mrs. Cardone. I'm sorry to say, but I feel some miscarriage of justice has taken place. The fact they withheld this information from you suggests dishonesty. However, legally our hands are tied. We're dealing with two powerful, cunning, and wealthy men. Even if you vowed deception, we couldn't prove it. Unless the Cardones forced you to marry Lynx and are holding you prisoner, there's nothing we can do. I'm afraid you've given up any claim to the ranch. Evidently your father suspected something might happen to him, so he entrusted the papers to me for your protection. I doubt he envisioned a complication like this. But I do find it strange and hopeful that they are keeping you at the ranch. Perhaps they care more for you than you realize. Perhaps their desire for revenge has been sated. You're a beautiful and charming woman; any man would be pleased to have you as his wife. Why don't you ask your husband about this situation?"

"I can't decide how they would react to my knowledge of this matter. I know this might sound unfair, but I pray they aren't using this trick on me to lure my father out of hiding. Perhaps I'm safe only as long as I'm in the dark," Cal stated uncontrollably.

The moment that statement left her lips, memories of past dangers and mysteries attacked her mind. If anything happened to her . . .

"Aren't there other papers?" Kyle inquired gently, hoping there was an explanation to this injurious scheme.

"A letter and a note. I'm not sure I want to read them," she confessed, her whole world seeming to come apart.

"Would you like me to read them to you?" Kyle offered.

"I'd better do it myself," she refused softly, since the affair with Laura might be mentioned, the one point she hadn't revealed.

Calinda struggled to restrain her tears as her bleary gaze took in the note, then the heart-racking and revealing letter. Her shaky hand covered her dry lips; she feared she would be ill right there on the floor. Her face was extremely pale; her once lively gaze was now empty and moist. She rested her arms on the table, crushing the two letters in her tight grasp, staring unseeingly at them. Her shoulders were slumped in despair, as if the burdens of the world had been placed on them. Her head was lowered; she appeared to hardly breathe. Sensing a traumatic shock in those letters, the sensitive lawyer remained silent while she mastered her emotions.

At last, Cal understood the motive behind Laura and Brax's actions. Each time she was positive every incisive axe had fallen, another obscure blade hovered over her head before slashing down to sever a vital part of her. God, how this gradual evisceration racked her body and soul. She didn't know if she should be bitter, understanding, or furious. Right now, she was too distraught to think about anything. Later at home . . . Home? She could never call the Cardone Ranch home again. Yet, she had to return there, at least for a while.

She thanked Kyle Yancey for his kindness and assistance. When she tried to pay him, he smiled and refused. "I'm sorry if I've been the bearer of dire news. If you need my services again, please don't fail to contact me," he urged, touched by this suffering child.

"Promise me you won't breathe a word of this to anyone?"

"I promise, Mrs. Cardone. I truly hope things work out for you."

She smiled faintly and said, "They will; I'll make certain."

Calinda left him to spend the night in the hotel room and return to Austin tomorrow. As Charlie drove her home, she was remote and sad. In response to Charlie's concern, she told him she was merely exhausted. At the ranch, Rankin was out riding and Salina was busy with chores. Calinda reluctantly mounted the stairs to the room shared with Lynx when he was home. She went inside, locked the door, and flung herself on the bed to sob in anguish.

Cal didn't want to ponder the insinuations in her discovery of the ranch deed and the joint betrayal of their parents. Was she a naive pawn in a monstrous game of revenge? She and Lynx had known each other for three months and had been married for nearly two. Yet, she knew so little about him and his existence, and too much about their interlocked pasts. She could justify his secrecy about Laura and Brax, but not about the ranch. His continued silence painted him guilty.

One suspicion bred with another to produce a litter of rapidly growing doubts. So beguiling and irresistible, Lynx had used his prowess to disarm and enchant her, to fool her completely. How could he do such terrible things to her, if he truly loved her? Was it possible he had set a trap for her, then carelessly ensnared himself by falling in love with his prey? Had she unknowingly managed to alter Rankin's resentment and hatred into trust and affection? Did they feel it was harmful to reveal their deceptions and initial motives? Was Lynx afraid of losing her if the truth was exposed at this late date?

So many previously unnoticed clues entered her mind. Cal remembered that night in bed when they had joked about brands. She knew his feelings toward his traitorous mother were more than lingering grief. So many of his past words and expressions assailed her groping mind, especially their discussion of that lost letter when he had refused to be candid. What had Lynx blurted out after Rankin was shot: "It's half yours now!" Other slips from the two men filtered into her crowded mind, to swim around in her mental ocean of turbulence.

Cal recalled the many times Lynx had alluded to a fear of losing her. Had Lynx left home to destroy all clues to the past, to protect their love? What would he say if she confronted him with these newly discovered facts? How would this letter and note affect him? Would they ease his lingering anguish and sever any remaining ties to the past? Or would it serve to breed more trouble and bitterness? She read the heart-stabbing letter again:

My dearest daughter Calinda,

Since this packet has been given to you as prearranged, it means I am permanently out of your life. Please do not grieve for me, but accept me as dead. I do not deserve your respect. I pray you will try to understand and forgive me. If you will read further, I will attempt to explain events which changed many lives, including your own.

I know grave mistakes which I have made. One was in not sending for you and your mother. If you two had been with me, such dire events might never have happened. You were too young to realize the lack of love between me and your mother. We both married for selfish reasons. I, for her social rank and family wealth; she, because I was the best of her suitors and an escape from her father's family.

As I lived and worked in this exciting and challenging territory, I met a beautiful and unique woman whom I came to love beyond all reason or caution. She consumed my thoughts and feelings. I forgot all responsibilities and morals. I tried to fight my hunger for her, but I failed. I knew it was wrong to desire her, but I was helpless to resist. Once I even planned to leave Texas to halt this powerful temptation.

You see, my daughter, the woman is Laura Cardone, the wife of my closest friend and mother to a boy I love as a son. I could go for pages telling you about her and our fated love, but it would justify nothing in your eyes. When I forced myself to see what our love would do to Rankin and Lynx, I tried to desert her and the ranch. I could not.

There was a complication, my daughter. Laura discovered she was carrying a child. There was no doubt that the child was mine, and not her husband's. We were forced to make a costly decision. I had to take money and betray my friends to get my true love and our unborn child away. Once this decision was made, we could never look back or return. When Rankin discovered our affair and plans, we fought bitterly. I dared not leave Laura behind, so the money was vital for our safety and survival. How I wish you could have met the flame of my heart and known her.

If you ever meet the Cardones, please give them patience and respect. I know they must hate me and desire revenge. To prevent them from locating us, we must flee far from Texas. Laura and I are grieved over the loss of our two children, but we must protect ourselves and our new child. I know your resentment must be great, but please forward this letter to Lynx, as he also deserves an explanation. You and Lynx must forget us. We have brought much pain into your lives. A total break is best for all of us.

In time, I pray you will find understanding in your heart for us. If you wonder if we regret our costly love and harsh decision, we cannot say this early. Believe me, Calinda, when I swear our love was uncontrollable. We will do our best to find happiness and peace together with our new child. If you ever meet Rankin and Lynx, I'm certain you will realize what special men they are, if they allow you the chance to get to know them.

By now, you are a young woman. I hope you are strong enough to accept these stunning facts and deal justly with them. Please don't hold the Cardones responsible for my actions and weaknesses; please don't make them suffer more for what I have done in the past.

If I am rambling in this letter, it is because I hardly know what to say in our final communication. Be happy and find true love, my child.

Your father, Elliott

Calinda lifted the note which had been attached to the deed and forced its reality into her warring thoughts.

For your many sacrifices, I give you all I have left to offer, my undying love and half of a prosperous ranch which I helped carve from a wilderness with my own sweat and blood, at the side of my closest friend Rankin Cardone and his beloved son Lynx, who were like my brother and son.

If you are living in England, please do not come to America with hopes of finding me. If you are in Texas as you read this letter, I regret any vengeful battle you might face to claim your inheritance. Kyle Yancey is an honest and talented lawyer; use him to gain what is rightfully yours. I do request you find the means to repay a debt of $45,000 to Rankin, ranch money which I took to begin my new life elsewhere. Possibly you can sell him a portion or all of your claim, or repay him from monies earned from the ranch and cattle if you decide to retain possession.

I used the money from the sale of our Georgia home to buy land and cattle in Texas with Rankin, except for the $10,000 which I sent to Thomas for your support. With time and work, the Cardone/Braxton Ranch became one of the most successful spreads in the West. God, how I love this land and agonize over leaving it forever. I know this is not a fair exchange for a father, but I want you to have my share. I pondered selling my half to Rankin for ruining his life, but I owed you something more. I beg you to give Rankin first choice at any sale. If you want no part of the ranch, please sign the deed over to Rankin. I owe him this and far more. Forgive me.

Calinda put the papers inside the packet and went into her old room. She opened the closet door and pinned the packet beneath one of the billowing gowns which had belonged to Laura Cardone. Some other less painful time, she would decide what to do with it. She returned to her room and locked the door.

All she could do was wait and observe. She couldn't make any plans, for there was too much she didn't know, too much to consider. Her reactions depended upon the feelings of Rankin and Lynx, feelings she must discover soon. Until Lynx returned, she must wait. Maybe there was a logical and reasonable explanation . . .

For now, Cal was mentally, physically, and emotionally drained. An idea came to mind; from this day forward, she would lock her room to prevent any more mysterious letters from appearing on her bed. She would observe and listen to everything which surrounded her. She was positive those furtive messages were not from her father. Someone was trying to lead her away from the ranch or to cause dissension with the Cardones. Maybe she should study Salina more closely. If her life was in jeopardy from some evil force, she must be more careful and alert. She must avoid anything which hinted of a perilous trap. The most difficult and expensive task would be to uncover the motives of the Cardones . . .

One piece of this obscure puzzle kept returning to unnerve her; Lynx was always around when one of these dangers or mysteries occurred. But if he wanted her harmed, why did he always rescue her? Since the Lampasas episode had resulted in their marriage and her loss of the ranch—why the kidnapping, her dangerous fall, his declarations of love, and the inexplicable letters? If a marriage hadn't lured her father back, why would a series of accidents? Surely they realized Brax and Laura wouldn't remain anywhere near Texas? Even so, how could Brax learn Cal was in danger? Could the return of the ranch deed satisfy the Cardones? Cal shuddered as if chilled. What if her father or Laura had lied? What if the child was Rankin's? The money, his child, the ranch, and his wife would certainly supply Rankin with plenty of hatred, an obsession for vengeance. It was so complicated.

All Cal wanted was Lynx and the truth. They could have the ranch; she didn't care. But if Lynx didn't confess when he returned, she must consider leaving. She couldn't live under this shadow of delusion and mistrust. It was settled; everything hinged on Lynx and his love. Cal would do as her father had asked, consider him dead.

Cal wished it wasn't so, but she understood mindless and irresistible love. She had met a handsome and unique man whom she had come "to love beyond all reason and caution," as with Brax to Laura. Her father's words pained her deeply —"consumed my thoughts and feelings . . . forgot all morals . . . helpless to resist . . ."—it was as if Brax were describing her relationship with Lynx . . .

By Friday, much of Calinda's anguish and disappointments had altered to smoldering anger and fierce determination. She wasn't a child or a simpleton to be protected; she wasn't a stranger to this affair, one who didn't deserve any facts. This situation had become wearisome and intolerable, it was time to end it.

A telegram had been delivered late yesterday, one from Brownwood which informed them Lynx was on his way home. Rankin had told her that town was only a day's travel from the ranch. Any time now, her husband should come riding up to his home. Was she ready to face him? How should she behave? What was there to say?

Cal was moody and cool today. Rankin asked, "Is something wrong, Cal? You don't seem yourself today. Eager to see Lynx?"

"Would you please stop fretting over me? I'm fine," she declared peevishly. "I'll be convinced he's home to stay when I see it. How's everything going on your ranch?" she inquired innocently.

"Never better, Cal," he replied, smiling proudly.

"You really love this place, don't you? I imagine it was awfully expensive to buy; it's so large. Did your family have money to loan you?"

Assuming Cal was opening a simple talk, Rankin calmly replied, "No. I earned the money and staked out the land. Some of it I fought Indians and Mexicans to hold. It was dangerous back in those early days. A man held his possessions by his gun, courage, and determination. I've worked hard to make this ranch what it is today."

Cal wouldn't dispute that Rankin had made this empire what it was at present. Infuriatingly, she could understand why the Cardones must feel that her father didn't deserve any portion of it or the increased profits. She could comprehend their desire to protect their home and labors, their fear of her walking in and demanding an enormous share of everything. But she was a Cardone now, and none of that mattered anymore. "How long did my father work here?" Cal boldly and unexpectedly asked. "If you don't mind answering," she slyly added.

Rankin stiffened and frowned. "Would you understand if I said I preferred not to discuss your father or those days? You know we parted on bad terms." He waited tensely for her reaction, having been told of the arrival of Brax's misplaced letter.

"I won't press you, Rankin. I just wanted to know something about him. If I didn't have his picture, I doubt I could recall him. It just troubles me sometimes to know so little about my own father. This place is so beautiful and so special; I can't understand why he would leave."

"I know it must be confusing and painful, Cal. Maybe one day we can discuss him in detail," he relented slightly.

If Cal was mistaken about Rankin, she could hurt him deeply by probing into Laura's memory. She decided against any questions or mention of her. "Could I ask one last question, Rankin?"

He nodded, but his face was lined with worry.

"Do you ever resent me because Brax is my father? Does it make you uncomfortable for me to live here?" She kept her gaze locked on his face.

"That's two questions," he teased to calm his frayed nerves. "To be honest, at first I was leery of you. But you got under my tough skin and won my heart. If there's one thing I've learned in life, each man stands on his own. Another can't take his punishment or rewards. To answer your last question, not in the least. In fact, I love having you around. You're about the most delightful creature I've met. I'm proud and pleased you're a part of the Cardone family."

If Cal was any judge of character, he was being honest. But then again, she was too naive and trusting; she wanted and needed to believe him. She had misjudged the Simpsons. Too, the Cardone men hadn't been frank with her. "Thank you," she said, smiling faintly.

"Think we should plan a special dinner for Lynx? You can wear that lovely new gown," he hinted, fretting over her strange mood.

She sighed heavily, then blithely answered, "I'll wear the gown, but Salina can handle dinner. Our truce is too nice to spoil at this special time. I think I'll take a short ride before I bathe and dress."

Rankin reminded her, "Lynx doesn't want you riding alone. Take Manuel with you. Charlie's probably working on the hands' chow."

"That won't be necessary. I'll stay within sight of the house."

"I would go with you, but I need to work on the books. I've got to do some figuring on expenses until we make our fall sale."

His statement opened the door for her to probe, "I wish there was some way to replace what my father stole from you and Lynx."

Rankin's smile faded instantly. "What did you say?" he asked warily, alerting Calinda to her reckless slip.

She quickly covered it by explaining, "I wish I could replace the joy and trust my father stole from you and Lynx. Why?" she queried.

"Forget about it, Cal," he said sternly. "You've more than repaid us. Be happy here; that's all we need. Besides, you're part of this family now."

"You know something? You've been more of a father to me than Brax. I truly appreciate what you've done for me, Rankin," she tested his reaction to those statements.

To her astonishment, he hugged her fondly. "One day, my grandson will own all of this. I look forward to you and Lynx having a child. You've brought sunshine back to the ranch, Cal."

Cal smiled through misty eyes. If they had a son and he inherited the ranch, she will have lost nothing. Horror filled her as a wicked thought flashed through her warring mind; what if they took her child to replace the one stolen by her father? Both men frequently mentioned a baby. Their revenge would be complete: the ranch and a child, compliments of the enemy who had stolen both long ago.

Cal shook her head to vanquish her wild imagination. What was the matter with her? She was going crazy! No one could be that evil! She must get away from this haunting house for a time and clear her wits. Cal felt she was going around in a vicious and tormenting circle. If only she weren't so fretful and jittery these days. If she could just shake this sluggishness and this urge to burst into tears at every turn. She needed privacy and a good self-scolding to get rid of this pressure and despair. She was a grown woman, a resilient and smart one. Why couldn't she think and act like one? She had to put a bridle on her wild imagination! She had to pull herself together before Lynx arrived and questioned her irrational behavior.

How long could she wait for Lynx to reveal the truth? It was imperative that Lynx confess everything to her willingly, not from compulsion. She silently and desperately prayed that love, not vengeance, was the true flame in his heart. After reading her father's letter, that endearment was no longer special or beautiful . . .

—— *Chapter 21* ——

➣

ONCE MOUNTED, Calinda rode straight for the hillside where Laura Cardone was alleged to be buried. She halted the snowy animal and dismounted, tying his reins to a bush. She scanned the tranquil setting where several trees and many wildflowers seemed to offer beauty in the face of dark treachery. She walked to the headstone and read. So timely and so false: September 15, the day her marriage would be three months old and Laura was claimed dead six years past.

Cal was an adult, a Cardone. Why couldn't she know the truth? She tried to envision Brax and Laura together, then Rankin and Laura. Were Brax and Laura happy now? How could they be after the trail of pain left behind? How ironic that she should love Lynx as wildly and uncontrollably as Brax had loved Laura, as if cruel fate were determined to mingle the two family lines. In similar circumstances, could she sacrifice all to have Lynx? What if Lynx had been married when she arrived here? Would she have fallen in love with him? If so, could she have destroyed lives to have him for her own? Could true love be so malicious and costly?

Suddenly a rifle-shot thundered across the landscape, startling the forlorn girl. A searing pain racked Cal's body as a bullet hurled through her left shoulder. At the stunning invasion of hot metal, Cal was jolted forward and thrown to the ground, across Laura's make-believe grave. Despite dazed senses, she had enough wits to play dead.

As Cal lay there, she heard pounding hooves as an unseen rider fled this evil deed. She fearfully realized she would be dead now if she hadn't flinched at the lethal sound. As her head had jerked upwards and shifted her body, the death-intended bullet had missed its mark.

Cal moaned as she attempted to move; pain and nausea washed over her as she glanced down at her torn shirt above her left breast where blood was flowing rapidly to soak it. She drew her gun and placed it on the ground beside her for defense if her assailant returned. She accepted the knifing pains as she tested her shoulder and arm for a break; they moved, but produced immense agony and each movement increased the flow of fiery liquid.

Her fingers touched the wound, her blurring vision staring at their crimson tips. Shot, someone had actually shot her! Why? Who? Cal pressed her shaky hand against the wound to staunch the heavy flow of blood, her action tormenting the injury. She struggled to rise; she knew she must reach her horse and get home. She swayed precariously, her senses whirling in ominous warning.

If she passed out and no one found her soon, she would die. She crawled to the nervous animal and used her quickly vanishing strength to yank the reins free of the bush. If she could manage his back before losing consciousness . . . She commanded her head to clear and her body to function. Cal gripped his foreleg and attempted to pull herself up to the saddle, smearing scarlet fluid over his white hide. She grabbed the horn, but blackness challenged her. Slowly she sank to the ground, leaving a bloody trail down the saddle and animal.

Cal was too weak and fuzzy-headed to mount. In desperation, she lifted a fallen branch and thrashed the animal's legs, startling him and sending him racing off. She prayed he would run for home and not halt to graze. His solo return should entreat someone to come looking for her. She rolled to her back, her right arm falling over the earthly mound beside her. Cal tried to resist the threatening blackness, but it was too powerful. The last thought she remembered was watching the leaves gently over her head and thinking, if I die . . .

"Don't tell me you let her go riding alone," Lynx chided his father on his return to discover their nettling disobedience.

"She'll be fine, son. She said she'd stay close by. You're just annoyed she isn't here to greet you," Rankin teased his son.

"I didn't see her when I rode up," he argued, an uneasy feeling coming over his lithe frame. For some inexplicable reason, he recalled her jest about a mental link with him, especially in times of peril. He implausibly shuddered. "You know how stubborn and impulsive she is. She could be anywhere. I'll go find her."

Rankin chuckled at his son's displeasure. "Think you'll return in time for dinner?" he jested, recalling their tardiness on his last visit.

"Maybe. Maybe not," Lynx quipped, grinning mischievously.

"You just missed her; she left about thirty minutes ago," Rankin informed him. "I'll walk you to the stable. I need to ask Steve a question. You and I can talk later."

As they approached the corral, a noise drew their attention to the east; it was a riderless horse coming in. Rankin hastily shouted, "That's the horse Cal was riding when she left!"

Lynx ran toward it, then seized his reins. The bright red blood stood out alarmingly against the horse's ivory hide. "It's blood!" Rankin shrieked as he joined his son, who was gaping at the stains and tensing in panic. For a moment, Lynx thought his heart had stopped.

"He came from the east slope. I'll go after her," Lynx stated in a deceptively calm voice, his insides turning as he re-saddled Star. He tested the blood smears. "They're fresh. She must have been thrown and injured," he concluded as he swung into his saddle. "Damn her!" he snarled angrily in mounting apprehension. "Get some of the men to help search for her. Fire three shots when she's located."

"I'll come with you," Rankin called out.

"No time to wait," Lynx shouted over his shoulder.

Lynx headed in the direction from which the horse had arrived, his eagle eyes scanning the terrain as he galloped along. On the crest of the first hill, he halted and looked around, seeing nothing. He raced wildly to the pond, finding nothing there. Dread filled him. She could be bleeding to death in some hidden location! The one thing which gave him hope was the realization she had attempted to mount.

As Lynx guided Star one way, then another, he noticed hired men had joined his frantic search. Lynx kept recalling the appearance of mysterious letters, Cal's previous kidnapping, her peril in Lampasas, the day he and his father were bushwacked, that tampering with her saddle girth . . . Why had he ignored so many warnings?

Suddenly, three gunshots pierced the silence. Lynx's head jerked in that direction, then he encouraged Star to a swift pace. Before he reached the location, a coldness attacked his senses as he became aware of where he was heading.

Jed and Seth were bending over a prone body near his mother's grave. He jumped off Star's back before the animal halted. Taut with suspense, he ran to Calinda's limp body and dropped to his knees. The front of her shirt was saturated with blood; even her sleeve was soaked as the ominous red stream flowed to the ground. She was very pale and motionless. Never had Lynx experienced such anguish and terror.

"Is she . . ." Lynx didn't finish the unacceptable thought.

"Still breathing, but bad off, Lynx," Seth replied first.

"Get the doctor, Jed! I'll carry her home," Lynx ordered.

"Best patch her first, boss; she's bleeding fierce. She was back-shot. Looks like the bullet passed clear through," Seth told him.

Lynx yanked off his shirt and wrapped it tightly around her shoulder. He carefully lifted her into his arms. Seth held the precious burden as Lynx mounted and reached for her. Jed raced off for town. Lynx gently kneed Star and headed for home, praying all the way.

Rankin caught up with him and rode along, fearing to ask any questions. Without accepting any help with her, Lynx slipped off his horse and carried her to their room. Rankin rushed into the kitchen for water and bandages, telling Salina what the commotion was about.

As he left Salina, a merry twinkle danced in her eyes. *Too bad, Calinda, but I said you'd never survive here.* She wondered who she should thank for this thrilling assistance . . .

Lynx ripped off Calinda's shirt and studied the wound. He rolled her to her side; thankfully the bullet had indeed passed clear through. He placed a thick bandage beneath her shoulder and laid her down. He pressed another one to the jagged tear on her chest. She was spilling too much blood, he fretted. He couldn't lose her; he couldn't . . .

Lynx had seen plenty of gun-wounds, but he was too overwrought to assess the severity of this one. Likewise, he was too worried to analyze this shooting astutely. Fury chewed at him. He exploded, "By God, I'll kill whoever did this!"

"You want me to wash the blood off her arm and hands?" Rankin offered, needing to do something to ease his own anxiety.

"Not yet. I want to keep her as still as possible. Cal?" he called to her, but she was beyond hearing him. "Who would do this?"

"Maybe those rustlers are back, or whoever's been sending those notes," Rankin suggested with a shaky voice.

"But she's never hurt anyone," Lynx debated.

"I'll go tell Steve and the boys to scout around. Maybe they can find a clue," Rankin suggested, then left.

Lynx sat down beside Calinda. Tears moistened his eyes, and his voice exposed his pain as he whispered, "Don't you go and die on me, woman. It took me too long to find you. I love you, Callie; I need you. Please don't leave me. I promise you, I'll find whoever did this and make them pay," he swore furiously.

Lynx was near a frenzy by the time the doctor arrived. Rankin had to force him to move aside to allow the doctor to examine her. Lynx hovered on the other side of the bed, his gaze never leaving her ashen face and limp body. Normally cool-headed and durable, he absently twisted his hands over and over as he watched the dire scene and realized what it could cost him.

The doctor dabbed at the rebellious wound and frowned. "What is it?" Lynx fiercely demanded, his self-control strained.

The doctor glanced up at the towering man with his darkly tanned bare chest and agitated expression. The older man's forehead wrinkled in concern and concentration. "There's a lot of bleeding, and I can't tell what the bullet struck. It's a crazy angle."

"But it passed clear through," Lynx argued, tensing in consternation, awaiting news he didn't want to learn.

"I wish it hadn't. Now we have two places for infection to attack. But it isn't as bad as it looks, son. I'm going to doctor and patch the hole in her back first, then stitch that front wound. That exit injury is the worst of our worries. When I sew it shut, I'll put some medicine on it. You best settle yourself, son; I'll need you to help me, just in case she comes to," he explained, doubting she would this soon. How horrible that such a charming creature had to face such violence and pain.

A moanful noise left her dry lips. "Can't you give her something?" Lynx insisted, caressing her creamy cheek.

"Don't want to rush things, son. The sooner she wakes up, the better her chances for licking this battle."

"What do you want me to do?" Lynx inquired hoarsely.

"We'll do the back first. I'll need you to hold her still."

Calinda was shifted to lie crossways, her head near the edge. Lynx was instructed to hold her still. "When we start on that front, even if she wakes up or screams, don't let her move an inch. Understand?" the doctor expounded.

Lynx took his assigned position. He had witnessed lots of bleeding and pain, but none had affected him as hers was doing. She moved slightly as the doctor cleaned it and placed a medicinal salve there. He washed away the surrounding blood and dried the area to bandage it.

"Now, let's do the front," the doctor stated. "Turn her over gently, Lynx. This is the tricky one. Appears a rifle shot."

Lynx carefully rolled her to her back and straddled her waist, confining her body between his legs, positioning himself to prevent any movements from her. He locked his fingers around her wrists and imprisoned her hands near his bent knees. "I'm ready, Doc."

"This is gonna hurt, Lynx. Even if she stays out cold, she's gonna struggle instinctively. I'm gonna try it without drugging her. I need to ask her some questions. Don't let go of her hands," he cautioned.

The doctor worked several minutes trying to see through the flow of blood from the torn flesh. Finally, he pinched the two sides together and took his first stitch. Calinda jerked and groaned. When he took the second stitch, she tried to twist away from the excruciating pain. Lynx tightened his grip on her wrists and increased the pressure on her body with his knees.

On the next stitch, she cried out in agony and thrashed her head from side to side. Cal attempted to fight the forces which were inflicting more pain on her and preventing her escape, but Lynx refused to allow her body any damaging movement. The doctor waited a few minutes to let her settle down. When he began anew, she screamed into the imprisoning blackness, "No . . . Stop . . ."

"It's all right, love," Lynx tried to comfort her. "We'll be finished soon. I'm here with you, Callie."

The doctor took another stitch as her eyes flew open wide. Calinda shuddered and screamed. Perspiration glistened on her face, as well as on Lynx's. He couldn't bear to see her suffering like this, but he couldn't prevent it. Damn, he felt so helpless, a new and distressing emotion. "How much more? She's coming around."

"Just one, Lynx. Ready?"

Lynx nodded. Calinda tried to uncloud her vision, her feet pounding the bed as she screamed, "Stop! No . . ."

"Please, doc, give her something. Anything," he urged.

"Not yet, Lynx. I can't stop now. In a moment. I know best," the struggling man explained hurriedly, resolved to hasty completion.

Calinda didn't arouse fully, but she didn't settle down. Amidst her frantic exertions, her cheeks stood out like red patches on a snowbank. Her body quivered spasmodically as if she were freezing. Her respiration was erratic. Drops of blood seeped between the tight stitches. The wounded area was fiery red and puffy, but for the whitened spots around the stitches. Tears were rolling into her tousled hair.

"You want me to release her, doc?" Lynx asked, watching his wife in shared anguish.

"Not yet. She might claw at the stitches. Let me bandage her first. She should settle down soon. Don't worry, son; she's dazed."

As the doctor cleansed the wound, she cried out, "Lynx!"

"I'm here, love," he responded, carelessly loosening his grip.

Cal's hand flew upwards to rub the throbbing area. Lynx grabbed it before it made contact. She yanked to free herself, crying.

"I'm sorry, love," he murmured sadly, cursing his inability to help her.

When the wound was bandaged and the blood washed away from her upper body, the doctor suggested Lynx put her in a gown. "You'll need to sit with her. Don't let her tamper with that wound. She appears to be breathing fine; I hope that means the bullet missed her lungs. I can't feel any breaks. I'll give her something for pain and rest. When she comes to, try to get some soup into her. If she starts to run a fever or get delirious, send for me immediately."

"I'll take care of her, doc," Lynx vowed. "She'll be all right?" he was compelled to ask, eyes tenderly roaming her grimacing features.

"I think so. She might sleep all night. Her body's had quite a shock. But if she comes to in pain, give her one teaspoon of this," he instructed, handing Lynx a small bottle from his scuffed bag. "No matter how much pain she has, no more than one spoonful every six hours. Make sure you keep it out of her reach; people in agony get desperate," he cautioned, forcing the drug between her lips.

"Right, doc. What if the bleeding doesn't stop?"

"I don't expect it to halt for hours. It'll take time for those cuts to settle down. Those stitches are gonna be sore; she'll want to pick at them when she's asleep. If you get tired, tie her hands to her sides before you fall asleep. If she tears open that wound again, won't be nothing I can do. And don't let her get out of bed," he added.

Rankin saw the doctor out and came upstairs. Lynx related the action and the doctor's advice. "I can watch over her while you sleep, son. We'll take care of our girl."

"Thanks, Father, but I'll take care of her myself. If anything happens to Cal, I'll never forgive myself. I shouldn't have left her alone. She's been in danger since she arrived. Who's doing this to her?"

"I think we best find out soon," Rankin suggested.

It was an hour later when Rankin returned to the somber room. He told Lynx he would watch over Calinda while his son bathed and ate. For the first time since this drama began, Lynx realized he wasn't wearing a shirt and had dried blood on his hands and chest. He nodded and left reluctantly, too weary and anxious to talk.

As Lynx ate quickly in the kitchen, Salina asked, "Is she all right, Lynx? Nobody will tell me anything," she stated as if worried.

Lynx's haunted gaze lifted to stare at Salina. "I doubt you give a damn,

Salina, but we don't know yet. When I discover who's behind those mysterious letters and this shooting, I'll kill the bastard, or bitch," he added, sending his intimidating and crafty point home.

"You mean she might . . . die?" Salina probed incredulously.

"Not if I can stop it. And by God, I'm doing all I can. If she does, this land isn't big enough for her killer to escape me," he snarled.

"Who would shoot her?" Salina murmured.

"Just as soon as she's out of danger, I'll find out," he vowed.

"Is there anything I can do?" Salina offered guilefully.

"Stay clear of her," Lynx demanded harshly in surprise.

"What is into you, Lynx?" she asked petulantly.

"The devil, Salina, and he's battling to break free."

She watched him closely. "Are you accusing me of having something to do with this accident?" Salina questioned his surly mood.

"Accident?" Lynx growled skeptically. "You could hardly label cold-blooded murder an accident. I've been doing some thinking, and I've decided someone is trying to use any method to get her away from the ranch and me. You wouldn't have any idea who might try something reckless and deadly like that, would you?" Although he continued to eat with his head lowered, Lynx was furtively observing Salina.

"*Como!* Are you *demente* with grief?" she panted in alarm.

"The fires of hatred and revenge burn brightly and fatally, Salina. You were eager to spy and tattle on her before. Is there anything new you think I should know?" he quizzed the nervous girl.

"She has been acting very strange since you left, if that is your meaning. I saw her restless and sad. She went into town Tuesday and Thursday. Both times she returned in crazy moods. She spends much time alone in your room. Does that help any?"

"What else?" Lynx pressed, glaring coldly at her.

Salina thought for a time, then added, "Maybe she is not well. She has been pale and tired lately. She cries a lot in her room."

"How would you know that?" Lynx demanded tersely, engulfing her with that burning gaze which seared off even a brave man's courage.

"The signs, Lynx. Puffy and red eyes?" she hinted, unable to battle that forceful gaze which was glacially intimidating.

"Why would she cry so much?"

"Maybe she was missing you or upset with you," she replied flippantly. "How should I know? You ordered me to steer clear of your wife." Salina realized it was time to cease her dangerous game; it was getting out of control.

"Who went into town with her?" Lynx persisted with resolve.

"I think Charlie," she replied, ready to end this conversation.

Since it was too late to speak with Charlie tonight, Lynx returned to his room. "Anything, Father?" he asked instantly.

"Not a peep or move, son. She'll make it, won't she?"

"She must," Lynx replied wistfully, plagued by Salina's words.

Lynx stretched out beside Cal and waited for her resilience to take command of her weakened body and to strengthen it. Several times, she stirred and moaned, but didn't arouse. When she attempted to reach for the injury, he would capture her hands and hold them until she settled down once more. When she became so restive that he dreaded further injury, he forced more medicine between her lips. Gradually she quieted. Off and on, he tested her forehead for a fever, finding none and saying a grateful prayer. But by dawn, the front bandage exposed signs of fresh crimson stains.

Lynx had slept little that night, each muffled utterance or movement catching his attention. His father entered the room around seven to check on both of them. He stayed with Calinda while Lynx flexed his stiff muscles and went for coffee. Lynx was back in the room within minutes. Lynx felt like a splotch on a cowhide, providing nothing but its decorative presence.

Around eight o'clock, Calinda began to squirm in distress and send forth muffled whimpers. As her hand went upward to rub her groggy eyes, Lynx surged forward and seized it, cautioning, "Don't aggravate it, love. Lie still."

There was a terrible aching on her chest and back; she shifted in discomfort, sending sharp pains through her body. She cried out, fighting to reach the level of awareness. "Callie, can you hear me?" Lynx's voice probed the encasing shadows.

Cal struggled to open her eyes. She moistened her dry lips, breathing raggedly. She couldn't understand why she was in such agony and why she couldn't awaken. She could hear Lynx talking to her, but she couldn't respond. Her head rolled from side to side as she resisted the encompassing blackness. "Help me, Lynx," she murmured, before slipping beyond communication.

"I'm here, love," he told her, but he knew it was too late for her to catch his words. She was having a terrible time seeking, and yet resisting, consciousness. Lynx couldn't endure her anguish. After checking the time, he forced more medicine between her lips.

Hours passed and the doctor arrived. He questioned Lynx about her condition. They talked for a few minutes, then he removed her bandages to examine the wounds and change the dressings. He glanced at Lynx and smiled. "So far so good, son."

As Calinda yanked to free her hands, she screamed, "Let go!" Her lids fluttered and her slumberous eyes touched on Lynx who was confining her. Pain racked her body as she hazily recalled the shooting. Why was he being so cruel to her? Why couldn't she think clearly? "Why . . . do you want me . . . dead?" she asked unknowingly, stunningly. "I've . . . given you . . . every . . . thing," she sobbed. "Don't . . . kill me," she pleaded groggily, senses deluded by medicine and pain.

Lynx was shocked into speechless disbelief. He stared at his ailing wife. The doctor noted his incredulous expression. She thrashed on the bed, crying and begging. "Callie?" Lynx finally brought an entreating word from his tormented body. "What are you saying, love?"

In a brief flash of awareness, she shrieked, "Don't touch me! You won't deceive me again," she whispered, slipping beneath that cloak of protective darkness once more where breathing didn't hurt.

Lynx's palm flew to her face to test for fiery warmth. "Is she delirious? Did you hear what she said?" he yelled in dismay.

"She's just confused and in pain, Lynx. She doesn't know what she's saying. There's no fever or infection yet. She's out of her head."

"But she called my name," he debated anxiously.

"That's natural, son," the doctor tried to calm him.

"Natural to think I did this?" Lynx stormed in bewilderment, for that was how it had sounded to him.

"It's the pain and drug talking, Lynx, nothing more," he tried again to quiet the distraught man.

"You sure, doc?" Lynx challenged skeptically, worriedly.

"Yep. Is there any truth to her wild rantings?" he teased.

"Hell, no!" Lynx thundered from rising tension and fatigue.

"Then forget it. We can't have her upset over saying something she won't even remember. She recognized you standing over her when she's tortured with pain; that's why her dazed mind held you to blame."

Lynx nodded, but wasn't totally convinced. For a brief instant, there had been full awareness in her expression, one of inexplicable fear and accusation! Unable to question her actions and words, he was compelled to let them pass. He observed her lovely, unblemished face. Some natural color had returned and her cheeks weren't bright red anymore. She was weak, but alluded to inner strength. All of which the doctor pointed out to him as encouraging signs.

"Unless you need me, son, I'll check on her tomorrow afternoon. She's doing just fine. Keep her quiet and still," he reminded.

Off and on for hours, she briefly came to wakefulness, then quickly sank back into her plaguing darkness without speaking. As she battled unseen foes, she mumbled incoherently. It was nearing the dinner hour when Calinda regained full consciousness. Lynx jumped up from his chair near the bed the moment she sighed in misery and wiggled slightly. She forced her drowsy senses to clear and her heavy lids to open. As Lynx sat down beside her and smiled, her baffled gaze shifted to him. "What . . . happened, Lynx? Merciful Heavens, I hurt."

"You tell me, love," he coaxed gently, moving damp curls from her face. "I've been crazy with worry and fear since yesterday."

"Yesterday?" Cal echoed as she fought to recall the memory.

Lynx explained how he had arrived home and found her missing, how her horse had returned with blood on him and the saddle, how they had searched for her, and how he had found her wounded near his mother's grave. Lynx observed her closely for all reactions.

"Laura's grave?" Cal repeated, simultaneously trying to recall and to forget the pernicious episode.

"What were you doing out there alone, Cal? Who shot you?"

"Shot me?" she continued her repetitious confusion. "I . . . You . . . found me? I . . . remember a shot. I saw blood . . . on my fingers. I couldn't . . . mount. There was a horse . . . galloping off. I passed out. It hurts," she said, grimacing and reaching to soothe the pain.

"Don't touch it, Cal. The doctor said you were to stay quiet and still. We don't want that wound opening or those stitches breaking. You didn't see anyone? Think hard, Callie."

"The doctor was here?" she asked, blinking her eyes to stay alert and awake. "It's throbbing, Lynx." Tears rolled down her cheeks.

"I know, love, but you can't touch it. You didn't see who fired the shot?" he pressed cautiously, tenderly dabbing the moisture.

"No. It happened too quickly. I didn't die?" she murmured suddenly, as if astonished she was alive. Was she suppose to survive?

Lynx smiled. "No way would I lose you, woman. You sorely tried to desert me, but I wouldn't allow it. I stayed with you all night and today. I even helped Doc stitch you up. You were determined to fight us; I had to sit on you and hold you down," he stated merrily, joy and relief coursing through his body and mind.

"How long was I out?" she asked, her lids drooping.

"Since yesterday when it happened. It's nearly dinner time. Think you can drink or eat something if I help you?" he coaxed.

She yawned, groaning as the reflex enticed needling torment. "I'm so sleepy and weak," she whispered faintly. She closed her eyes, surrendering to sleep before answering. But she didn't rest long before she began tossing and crying.

Lynx came to her side, entreating, "Relax, love."

Cal looked up at him. Slowly her mind cleared. "How about a stiff brandy to dull this agony, Lynx?" She gritted her teeth.

Lynx chuckled at her attempt at humor. "Afraid not, love. But you can have soup and some medicine," he counter-offered.

"I'm not hungry. I'll take some water and the medicine."

"You need some food in that tummy, Cal. It's been over twenty-four hours since you were . . . injured. You lost a lot of blood, and you're very weak. Please take just a little soup," he beseeched her.

"I'm not hungry, Lynx, just in pain," she argued sullenly.

"I'm sorry I wasn't here to protect you, Cal. I promise it won't happen again. Please, let me take care of you and get you well. Do you know how I felt when I found you lying on the ground, bleeding to death? If my heart didn't stop, it skipped many beats. It tore out my guts to watch you suffer yesterday while we were working to save you. For a time, Cal, we didn't think we could, I've been sitting here all night, afraid to leave you, praying for your survival. For the first time in my life, Cal, I was petrified. I felt useless. You cried and screamed and begged me to help you, but I couldn't do anything. When I find out who did this, I'll kill him!" he declared forcefully, a glimmer of fierce rage and ominous resolve in his stormy expression.

Calinda gazed at him, witnessing the tenderness and anguish in his expression. But were they real? How could she doubt him? How could she think clearly and calmly. Her thoughts were controlled by pain, drugs, and weakness. "When you search for him, be careful; he's a crack-shot, as you call it. If I hadn't been startled by the gunfire, the bullet would have been accurate, right in the heart."

"Thank Heavens he didn't check on his accuracy. Why did you go riding alone, Cal; you promised you wouldn't," he softly scolded her. "If your horse hadn't raced home with blood on him, you might have died out there."

"Is that how you knew I was hurt?" she asked, shifting gingerly.

Lynx related the few untold events of yesterday, unaware of how they settled in her warring mind. Another timely arrival and rescue? The bloody horse had alerted others, besides him, to her peril? If the animal hadn't returned to the stable, how long would Lynx have waited before seeking her, long enough for her to die? "You didn't see anyone?" Cal inquired; he shook his head ruefully. "I guess I was lucky," she murmured, looking down at her bandaged body.

"Damn lucky, woman," Lynx corrected her, wondering at her piercing and unreadable gaze. What was she thinking? "Can I play doctor, Mrs. Cardone?" he asked, trying to lift some curious burden.

She focused on him, then remarked, "You look terrible. You need a shave and some sleep. I'll be fine." She forced all thoughts from her mind, except getting well and easing the pain.

"I've had something, rather someone, more important on my mind." He bent forward and kissed the tip of her nose. "Soup?"

She stifled a yawn and winced, tears coming to her eyes as she trembled. "I'll try, after the medicine," she reasoned desperately.

"Fine," Lynx promptly agreed. "Don't move until I return."

After he left the room, she clenched her teeth as she tried to check the extent of her injuries. Cal fought to keep from crying and screaming as she shifted on the bed. There was a bandage on her back and front, and she could detect the stitches beneath the front binding. She noticed the crimson traces on the front bandage; it was still bleeding a little. Her nerves were tight and tense; the stitches nerve-racking. Her weakness was most noticeable, and hindering.

Cal glanced at her surroundings; the room was messy. Clearly her husband had been at her side since the shooting, but why? To see if she survived? Or died? Playing the concerned husband? For whom? Salina and Rankin couldn't care less about her! Who had tried to murder her? Why? They had possession of the ranch; they didn't need her dead. If they wished her gone, all they had to do was force her off the ranch. It was senseless!

Cal told herself she was foolishly mistaken. Lynx would never do such a vile thing. He might be capable of vengefully taking the ranch or wanting to hurt her emotionally, but never murder her. She had to figure out who was fatally pursuing her . . .

How she wished she could change her recent past. She wouldn't look at Laura's portrait or hear Salina's words. She wouldn't go to Lampasas. She wouldn't send word to Kyle Yancey or converse with him. There was so much she wished she didn't know; but she did, so many haunting coincidences and complexities.

When Lynx returned, she was sobbing. "Please don't cry, love," he entreated, coming over to her. "You might injure yourself." How he wanted to pull her into his arms, but he dared not risk her movements.

"It hurts so much, Lynx," she wailed, meaning the combination of physical and emotional pains. Yet, she needed his solace.

He took the bottle of medicine and poured out one spoonful. He said, "Take this, love. It'll ease the pain."

Without thinking or hesitating, she swallowed the nasty-tasting liquid. As she choked and coughed, she shrieked in pain and twitched. "Be still, Cal," he advised sternly. "You'll rip open that wound."

"That's easy for you to say! You're not the one in agony!" she shouted, ordering herself to lie motionless after paying for her outburst.

Lynx captured her face between his hands and shouted, "Like hell, I'm not! Damn you, Cal, if you break those stitches, I'll hold you down and replace them myself," he threatened harshly to calm her.

"I'm sure you love torturing me, you beast! Do something!" she hoarsely pleaded, shuddering with torment, clenching her teeth.

"What?" he asked in frustration, wringing his hands.

"Kiss me!" she replied angrily, knowing the power of his lips to blind her to reality. "Just hold me and kiss me."

"But you're hurt!" he debated. "You've got a fever!" he fretted.

"Use that potent magic on me; give me something else to think about until that medicine works," she frantically reasoned.

His lips covered hers as he concentrated on keeping his hands off her body. For what seemed hours, but was only minutes, the feverish kissing and throbbing pain continued. Gradually, both softened. Lynx felt her still body begin to relax. He leaned back and looked down at her. "Well? Did I help any?" he murmured huskily.

The drug alleviating her distress, she smiled. "You're the best treatment I know, Cardone. Thanks."

"For what, love?" he asked, watching her mood mellow.

"For saving my life again, and for easing the pain."

"That's the medication," he refuted happily.

"Perhaps," she stated skeptically. "If you want any of that soup in me, you best hurry. I'm getting awfully sleepy."

He sat on the edge of the bed and carefully spooned the soup into her mouth. "If it wouldn't hurt so much, I would laugh at this ridiculous scene," she murmured, forgetting all but him.

"I think it's fun," he remarked mischievously.

"Then perhaps I'll shoot you and become your amused nurse."

Minutes later, Cal's lids were very heavy. Each time he went for her mouth with the spoon, he had to tap her lower lip and say, "Open up, lovely mouth."

Finally her eyes closed and she didn't respond. She was sleeping peacefully for a change. He set the bowl and spoon on the dresser and headed for bed, relatively calm for the first time in two days. Suddenly he realized he might roll over on her and inflict more damage or pain. He fetched his sleeping roll and reclined on the floor, his senses alive and alert to her every sound even in slumber.

Chapter 22

❧

WHEN CALINDA AWOKE around six the next morning, she lay very still as she summoned the courage to assess her strength. Her entire shoulder area ached and complained, but she felt stronger and more alert this morning. The tight stitches nagged at the sensitive wound, especially with movement. She felt her cheeks for any warmth, relieved to find no exceptional heat residing there. She stalled her impending action as her mind swept away all lingering cobwebs.

Using her right arm, Cal tried to shove herself to a sitting position. The strain on her disabled left side harassed her immediately. She panted, "Ouch!", then gently eased back to the mattress. She attempted to hold her breath until the throbbing lessened.

Lynx bounded up from the floor and approached her. "What's wrong?" he asked in alarm.

Her startled gaze flew to his worried frown, unshaven face, and mussed hair. He stood there barefoot and bare-chested, attired in snug-fitting jeans. He reeked of masculinity. "Where did you come from?" Cal asked in amazement. Her gaze was a loving brush and his virile frame a receptive canvas, as her eyes moved over him.

"I was sleeping on the floor," Lynx answered quickly, inflamed by her appreciative study of him.

"On the floor? Why?" she quizzed, meeting his warm gaze.

"I was afraid I might hurt you during the night. I do have a habit of snuggling up to you," he merrily ventured.

"Why didn't you sleep in the other room?" she reasoned curiously.

"And leave a willful and impulsive vixen alone all night?" he jested. "Doc says you can't leave that bed, so I stayed here to make certain you followed his orders. I do have a stake in you, love."

"Surely you didn't think I would hop up and dance around?" she played along with his insouciant mood.

"From what I've seen, Mrs. Cardone, you have a defiant streak which I don't trust. Am I wrong, or were you trying to get up?" he challenged, making his point. "Looking for me, afraid I'd deserted you in your hour of need?" he roguishly hinted.

"If there's one thing I've learned, husband dear, it's knowing you'll always show up in the nick of time. How do you manage such cunning?" she asked saucily, veiling her seriousness with a smile.

"Fate," he nonchalantly replied. "Somebody's keeping an eye on us, giving us guidance and protection."

Cal motioned to her condition and speculated, "You call this protection? Our guardian angel was snoozing this time," she charged.

"Not for long. You were found quickly, and you're better this morning. Right?" Lynx gingerly sat down on the bed near her waist.

"I'll decide later. Any clues on my would-be assassin?"

"None yet, but don't worry," he advised, smiling broadly.

"Why should I? I have my fearless and powerful husband here with me," she murmured, her gaze fathomless. "To answer your earlier question, I wasn't trying to get up, just determine my damage."

Lynx seized a trace of a curious resentment in her tone. "Do you blame me for this, Cal?"

She tensed, then forcefully relaxed. A flush sped over her face; her gaze lowered briefly. "Why should I blame you, except for being absent when I obviously needed your protection?" she asked in a tone which was perplexing and alarming. "You didn't shoot me, did you?" she tried to jest lightly, but failed to deceive him.

"If you have even the slightest reservation about me, Cal, then we're in deep trouble, love. I wouldn't do anything to harm you."

"Wouldn't you?" she debated gravely. "You keep secrets from me; that hurts me. You stay away from home for ages; that hurts me. You can't protect me from danger because you're too busy defending your unknown friends; that hurts me. I can't make you happy or content; and that hurts most. You can halt one stab of pain by ceasing this distressing conversation. May I have my medicine now?"

"You need to eat first, Cal. That drug makes you pass out," Lynx entreated, following her request for a truce for the time being.

"I'd rather be out, Cardone; that way no pains attack me."

"You've got me worried, Callie. Do you honestly think I had something to do with the shooting?" he pressed earnestly.

"No, Lynx, I don't believe you shot me," she replied.

"From the look on that lovely face, you think I'm capable of doing it, don't you?" he demanded, piqued.

"Please don't do this, Lynx. I'm just tired, and confused, and miserable. It was a joke. If I recall, you made the same jest when you and Rankin were attacked. Don't pay any attention to my irritable mood and stupid rantings. I just want everyone to leave me alone."

"Including me?" he speculated in dread.

"Right now, my nerves are tight, I'm in terrible pain, and I need to rest and think. My heavens, Lynx, someone tried to murder me! It's hard to accept the fact someone hates me that much. After that last mysterious note appeared, I told you I sensed danger or evil lurking nearby, but you assumed I was trying to trick you into staying home. You listen to your own instincts, but deny feminine intuition."

"Since we don't know who did it, we also don't know the motive. Some outlaws think nothing of gunning down anybody in their path. It could have been one of those rustler scouts who thought you saw him or the same person who ambushed father and me. Or it could have been our mystery man trying to deliver another letter. Maybe whoever did it didn't realize you were a woman," Lynx speculated.

"I don't pass for a man, Lynx. If it was that sneaky villain, why kill the person he's trying to contact?" she rebutted.

"If those letters were meant to lure you away into danger, he didn't need to deliver it after he caught you alone and helpless! I told you to stay home or ride with someone, not alone!" he snarled.

"Stop being so bossy! In spite of that marriage certificate, you don't own me! I'm weary of your terse orders and defensive attitude!" she snapped at him. "I'm also damn tired of your secretive conduct!"

"I'm just trying to protect you, wife," he growled sullenly.

"From another town?" she scoffed sarcastically.

"That's really what's chewing your tail, isn't it? My private trips and long absences?" he challenged to unmask her resentful anger.

"Where did you go, if that's not too nosey?" she asked frostily.

Perceptive, Lynx noticed the alerting hint in her voice. "Why? I told you before I left where I was heading; I sent messages home."

"I didn't ask where those messages came from or where you were suppose to go. I asked where you went after you left the ranch."

"If you already know, why the question?" Lynx fenced warily.

"Would you hand me that box of writing paper?" Cal asked, more than ready to begin a journey toward the truth.

"You can't work like that. You've got to take care of yourself."

"Hand it to me, or I'll fetch it myself," she said stubbornly.

Cal opened the box which he placed in her lap. "This might explain my irrational and unreasonable annoyance, my devoted husband."

Lynx unfolded the paper, recognizing it immediately. A tremor washed over him. "Where did you get this? You searched my things?"

"When you were packing that morning, you dropped some papers; remember? Evidently this one went under the bed; I found it Monday when I was sweeping. What logical excuse do I receive this time for deceiving me? I suppose you're going to deny you went to Dallas?"

"No. I went to meet Major Jones, at his request, as you know from reading my mail. I didn't tell you because I was afraid you'd think I was breaking my word. I didn't look for your father, Cal; I swear it."

"Being dishonest is easier than explaining? Am I so dense or untrustworthy that you must constantly deceive me?" she sneered icily.

"Before you ask, woman, the 'B' stands for Burrow, a man Jones wanted me to locate for him. I had my reasons for keeping quiet."

"You always do, Lynx, about many things," she stated coldly.

"What's that supposed to mean?" he inquired, eyeing her warily.

"Nothing, Lynx, it doesn't matter anymore. I'll follow that old adage, ask me no questions and I'll tell you no lies . . ."

"Why did you go to town twice this week?" he asked unexpectedly to catch her off guard. He had a bad feeling about her trips.

She paled, then stammered, "To . . . get a new dress for your homecoming.

I selected the material and hired a seamstress Tuesday, then picked up the dress Thursday. Looks as if I'll wear it later.''

"Why the rush job for a husband who has you infuriated?"

"You were expected home Friday, remember? As you know, I'm impulsive; I decided at the last minute to wear something special.''

"But you found the telegram Monday, *Llama de mi corazon*. You had me painted black by Tuesday," he debated her half-lies.

Briefly Calinda went rigid as she stared at him. "All the more need to look ravishing when I'm trying to bewitch my own husband into sharing his life with me, to explain why he can't be content and honest with me," she sought to mislead him. "And please don't call me that.''

"I told you I'd clear up any problems between us when I got home. Couldn't you wait to hear me out before judging me guilty?"

"That was my exact intention, but a nasty bullet got in my way. Tell me, Lynx, does someone want me dead or just off this ranch? Even a fool can decipher this many hazardous clues. I want to know who's declared himself my enemy and why," she stated bluntly.

"It isn't me, love; but I aim to discover who it is. Nothing suspicious happened while I was gone?" he probed.

"Can you interrogate me later? I'm hungry and hurting," she avoided the subject with truthful excuses. "Didn't you return too quickly?" she questioned, realizing this contradiction in his plans.

"You sound disappointed I rushed to finish and hurry back. I'll get you some breakfast and medicine, if you promise to stay put until you're well." He refused to move until she gave her word.

"Yes, boss," she replied, smiling tightly.

When Lynx attempted to kiss her, she turned her head and pleaded, "Not now, Lynx. I feel terrible.''

"*Llama de mi corazon* isn't an insult, Callie," he told her, wondering at her glacial reaction to the endearment. "It means . . .''

"I know what it means; I asked Salina to translate," she injected.

"What did she say?" he questioned, assuming the worst.

"Flame of my heart. I simply dislike words I can't understand.''

That morning birthed three days of fencing and probing on both sides. Calinda wasn't allowed out of bed. She depended on the medicine to keep her out of his verbal reach during those first few days after the shooting. She ate, slept, and rested. When Lynx would enter the room, Cal would often pretend to be asleep, unaware that she didn't have him fooled at all. When he tried to entertain her, she would politely ask him not to be so amusing, that laughter aggravated her wounds. When he tried to help her with meals, she would tell him that was her only means of diversion and feed herself. She refused to allow Salina to visit her, and Lynx agreed with that decision. Rankin would come by for a few moments, but she would feign fatigue to keep his trips to her room brief.

Lynx slept in the other room, but checked on her frequently. He realized she was very guarded and remote, but couldn't decide why. Cal remained pensive and moody, quick to deny his assistance and company. Lynx fretted over her lack of warmth and her resistance to him. She watched him strangely when he was in the room. She permitted his kisses, but hers lacked honesty. After that first morning, she hadn't questioned him again; it almost seemed she didn't want to converse with him on any topic.

When the doctor came around, they would chat genially and she would exchange smiles with the elderly man. He told her the stitches could be removed in a week. Both were delighted that no infection set in on either injury. He jovially commented on Lynx's excellent care of her while Calinda stared at her lap. The doctor said he wouldn't need to drop by for several days unless there was a problem. He showed Lynx how to change her dressings, then said she could begin sitting up for short periods each day. "A while in the morning and afternoon. Nothing strenuous, my girl. Lots of rest and good food. No lifting anything," he issued his orders cheerfully.

"I'll make sure she obeys, doc," Lynx said firmly.

"Just be patient, Calinda, don't rush this," he added.

She smiled and nodded. "I'll be up and around before long."

"Not before I give the word, girl," he reminded her.

Four more days passed. Lynx would prop her up on pillows each morning and afternoon so she could read. When she tried to lengthen her schedule, Lynx refused to allow it. He would bring his meals to the room to eat with her, finding it difficult to draw her out. When he insisted, Cal would play a game of cards with him. He continued to sleep in the other room, becoming restless and moody himself. To relax her, he persisted in sponging her off each night before bedtime, to her arguments and rebellion. When she demanded a real bath, he denied it until the doctor said she could exert that much energy.

Being close to her and unable to touch her was sheer torment. At least she could grant him some affectionate kisses and bright smiles! At least she could talk to him, tell him what was troubling her! This chilling silence was gnawing at him, reeking pain and injury. Why couldn't he reach her, soften her? It was frustrating.

By the tenth day, a storm was brewing in Lynx. He had been working hard to drive himself into exhausted slumber, recalling her past confession of a similar desperation. He had reached his limit of patience and understanding. It was time to clear the tainted air between them. Cal had punished and tormented him enough! It was time for her self-pity and reserve to end. He left the range early to confront her.

When Lynx arrived home, she was in no condition to settle anything with him. The doctor had been there to remove the stitches, and she was nervous and uncomfortable. She constantly wiggled her foot to get rid of some of her anxiety. Her cheeks were flushed a bright red, and she was pale around her mouth. He strolled over to the bed and sat down. Her gaze darted around the room like a busy insect.

"I saw Doc leaving. How does it feel?" he asked solicitously.

"Like hell, Cardone," she unnaturally snapped at him.

"Need something for the pain?" he tried to help her again.

"Doc says I can't have anymore of his magic fluid. Sometimes he's as mean as you are. I want some sherry," Cal declared.

"Did Doc say you could have any?" he inquired, trying to keep his composure. She was as squirmy as a captive on an Apache antbed.

Cal glared at him. "I didn't ask. But if I don't get some relief, I'm going to scream my head off. It's easy for you and Doc to give orders; you two aren't injured or upset," she panted breathlessly.

When Lynx continued to observe her, she added, "Please."

"Let me see your chest and back," he said unflinchingly.

"After the sherry," she informed him crisply.

"Before the sherry," he called her bluff, their gazes meeting and silently battling. "I'm serious, Calinda Cardone."

Lynx comprehended her distress when she readily agreed when he knew she wanted to scream a refusal at him. "Doc just put on new dressings," she tried to prevent his touch and nearness.

"I'll re-do them," he dismissed her excuse, grinning. "You shouldn't be embarrassed, love; I'm well-acquainted with what's beneath that gown," he hinted provocatively.

"It's ugly and sickening," she taunted him.

"Is that why you're shutting me out of your life, afraid a tiny scar will repulse me? Isn't that cold-shoulder getting heavy by now?" he probed.

"If you've come here to start another quarrel, Lynx, I'm not in the mood. What's unbearably heavy is this bed and room. I want some fresh air, sunshine, and exercise before I go mad. How would you be feeling if you'd been laid up for over a week with no end in sight?"

"Ornery as a trapped badger," he roguishly replied, then chuckled. "I know it's hard to laze around in pain and boredom. One sherry coming up," he stated, bowing at the waist before leaving.

When Lynx returned and Cal reached for the glass, he held it away from her and reminded, "My inspection first, Callie."

She spread her arms on the bed and invited, "Proceed, tyrant."

He carefully lifted the front patch and studied the fiery area with its sealed white line. The surrounding flesh exposed yellowish purple bruising. He gingerly replaced the bandage, then checked the back injury where a fairly healed hole greeted his vision. When he was satisfied, he handed her the glass. "Looks marvelous to me."

She smiled indulgently and sipped the golden liquid. Lynx remained silent, his body rigid. A haunted expression filled his tawny eyes. Mentally he seemed to be far away from her, so sad, so miserable. "Lynx, why are you staring at me like that?" she asked.

He straightened and shrugged. "I was just thinking how close I came to losing you. Now that I have you, Callie, I can't imagine my life without you. For the first time, I realize what my father went through years ago when Mother . . . I don't know which is worse, the agony or the fear of facing life alone. I'll see you later," he murmured hoarsely, then turned to leave, berating his show of vulnerability.

"Lynx," she called to him, drawn to that sensitive facet.

Expecting an apology for her treatment of him lately, he slowly turned and waited. "Tell me about your mother," she entreated instead.

"I can't, Callie," he said, shaking his head.

262 ⚜ JANELLE TAYLOR

"It's been nearly six years according to the date on her tombstone. How long will you suffer like this?" she asked quietly.

"I wish I knew. Sometimes it seems like yesterday. Sometimes, as if she never existed. If only I knew . . . Why were you at her grave?" he asked, twisting the conversation around to her.

Cal was prepared for a reply. "I saw her portrait in the attic. She's very beautiful. I was wondering what she was like; you two favor so much."

"That's why it was so hard on Rankin back then. Every time he looked at me, he saw glimmers of her. It was tearing him apart. I thought if I left for a while, those painful memories would end. I discovered something terrible; you can't leave problems behind when they're inside your head."

"You can't grieve forever, Lynx. Why can't you let her go? You expect me to do that with my father," she reminded him softly.

"There's a big difference between us, Callie. I had my mother until I was seventeen; you were a small child, too young to recall Brax. If it was as simple as speaking words, I could," he murmured softly.

"Words aren't simple, Lynx, not from you."

"When you're better, we'll talk, love, not tonight." He smiled at her, then headed for the door again.

Before she realized what words were forming in her mouth they had spilled forth to halt and stun him. "She isn't dead, is she?"

Lynx whirled and faced her, then stalked forward to the bed. "What did you say?" he demanded fiercely, all tenderness gone.

Bright and quick, she cunningly deceived him, "In your heart, she isn't dead yet. She's like a ghost haunting you."

"You're wrong, Callie; as far as I'm concerned, she's dead."

Calinda's heart screamed, *why can't you confide in me?* Not that it mattered, but he hadn't lied to her, just misled her, again. "So we're just supposed to forget our parents?" she inquired sadly.

"We have no choice, Callie; they're gone forever. Do you want me to join you for dinner tonight?" he asked for the first time since her perilous battle with death.

"Need you ask?" Cal parried as if honestly surprised.

For a brief moment he looked like a vulnerable boy as he said, "Something tells me I do. I won't ask why; you'll tell me when you're ready to discuss it. Until then, know this, woman; I need you."

Tears glistened in her eyes. "I need you, too. But we have some problems to work out before things can be right between us."

"Yes, I know. But this isn't the time. See you later," he told her, then left. As he walked down the steps, Lynx was curiously exhausted. Not once since his return had she said, I love you . . .

He headed for the stable. It was past time to speak with Charlie and to investigate her depressing trips into town. Maybe some vital clues or an answer could be located . . .

When dinner came and went without her husband's appearance, Calinda wondered why Rankin had brought her meal and why Lynx had ridden into town and stayed so late. While she ate, she deliberated this situation. Had she carelessly tipped her hand? She admitted she had been acting suspicious. Just in case that cunning rogue discovered something, she must prepare her defense. Mastering her weakness and pain, Cal retrieved Brax's will and letter and placed them where Lynx could find them, if he made a search. It was too soon to let him see the note and deed, for they revealed things which Lynx should confess willingly, mainly the ranch ownership. After conning another sherry from Rankin later that evening, she was entrapped by slumber when Lynx arrived near midnight.

Lynx walked into the room and stood beside the bed, staring down at his wife. Why would Cal meet with a lawyer from Austin? Why keep it a secret? Why send that phony telegram about him to the sheriff in Dallas? What papers had the man brought to her?

Lynx possessed a calculating and crafty mind. He was well-versed on intense investigation. These clues tumbled over in his keen mind like a colorful kaleidoscope until a devastating picture formed before his mind's eye. She had learned things he wished she hadn't, but what was the extent of her knowledge?

Tomorrow he would unravel this entwined mystery. He cautioned himself as he gingerly searched the room, fearing to awaken her. When he located two papers hidden beneath her underwear, he seized them to read in the other room, immediately recognizing the handwriting on those pages, alarmingly noting the dates. Lynx dreaded confronting her, knowing he couldn't avoid it. This discovery explained her interest in the portrait and Laura's grave. It explained her distance and mistrust. If she knew everything, it was frightfully clear why her imagination was running wild about the shooting . . .

In the other room, Lynx unfolded a paper which turned out to be a will. He quickly scanned it, finding no mention of the ranch. He was shocked and confused to learn he was Brax's heir if anything happened to Calinda. He tossed the will aside to devour the contents of the lengthy letter. Lynx couldn't believe his eyes; Brax had confessed to the affair with his mother. Calinda knew Brax was guilty of theft and adultery! Did she understand why he and his father had kept silent about that painful betrayal? That knowledge explained why she had given up her search. But the reason for the hasty departure of Laura and Brax staggered him; somewhere he had a half-brother or half-sister . . . But so did his suffering wife! No wonder she was so confused, frightened, and saddened!

Chapter 23

IN SPITE OF HIS LATE AND RESTLESS NIGHT, Lynx was up early the next morning. He wanted his chores done by mid-afternoon so he could have plenty of privacy and time with Calinda. With Brax's will and plaguing letter, his wife had just enough misleading evidence against him to damage their relationship, but hopefully not enough to destroy it. Lynx tried to force the words in Brax's letter from his mind, but he couldn't. At last, he had some answers, but not the ones expected or imagined. Oddly, he felt unshackled from the past; yet, he was still fettered by unbroken links in that fateful chain.

Lynx planned his strategy all morning. He would discuss Brax and Laura with Cal, fill in the gaps about what happened long ago. He would beg her forgiveness for keeping that affair and betrayal a secret. When Cal was well enough to be left alone a few days, he would place her under Steve's guard, then head for Austin to question this Kyle Yancey. Before Lynx revealed the truth about his connection with the Rangers and her ranch partnership, he must know everything she and Yancey had discussed. When he returned to her side, there would be no more secrets between them. Somehow he would make her understand his deceptions and accept his love. He had been a fool to keep such facts from her this long! If she accidentally discovered the truth about the ranch, there was no telling how she would interpret it. Telling his love everything wasn't as risky as keeping silent. Whatever it took, Lynx must force her to understand.

When he arrived home, he carefully prepared himself with a bath and fresh shave. He pulled on snug jeans and a baby blue shirt, hoping to cast a boyishly innocent facade. He left his tawny hair fluffy and his shirt opened beneath his heart level. He left off his spurs and gunbelt. Lynx was aware of how he affected her, he must use that to sway her.

When he swaggered into their room, he halted and gaped at her. Cal was sitting on the floor beside a tub, her naked body glistening with beads of water, her freshly washed hair dripping into the tub over which her chin was resting on her folded arms. Her daring offense was blatantly evident, as was its exhausting effect on her. Lynx hurried over to Cal and lifted her limp body, heading for the bed. "What the hell are you doing, woman?" he thundered angrily. "You're supposed to be taking it easy. Doc said no lifting or exerting."

"Taking a bath, idiot," the disobedient girl weakly panted. "Take me to the balcony to dry my hair; I'll soak the bed."

"Don't you know you're too weak to bathe alone, much less wash your hair?" he scolded as he wrapped a sheet around her nude body.

"I couldn't stand this greasy hair and filthy body a day longer. I thought I could make it if I hurried," Cal said softly, battling to control her nausea and woozy head.

"You thought wrong!" he declared in annoyance.

"Please don't fuss at me, Lynx. I feel awful; I think I'm going to faint," she told him, hoping he would cease his tirade.

He carried her outside into the warm sunlight and sat down with her in his lap. "I'm soaking your shirt," she whispered.

"It doesn't matter, love. Just relax," he coaxed her tenderly, his fury vanishing as he realized how helpless she was.

"I need my brush. If my hair dries like this, it'll be in a thousand tangles. Please," she entreated.

"Serves you right, woman. As punishment, I'll enjoy removing each one.

Whatever possessed you to push yourself like that? Couldn't you wait until I was home to help?" he scolded in frustration.

"I was miserable, Lynx. I didn't know I was that weak. Besides, I've been enough trouble for you." Cal began to weep softly from tension and fatigue. As she sniffed, she murmured, "I'm sorry."

Trying not to hurt her, he snuggled her against him. "I know you've had it rough lately. Things will be better soon; be patient."

When part of her trembling and weakness passed, he sat her in the chair to fetch a towel and her brush. He lifted her and placed her in his lap again. Lynx gently dried her hair, then worked to unmat the curls with her brush. When Cal told him she could do it, he chuckled and vowed he would handle the stimulating problem. Lying in his arms with nothing but a sheet around her, Calinda was intensely aware of his sensual body and manly appeal.

"Lean your head over my arm," Lynx instructed.

She did as told, her cascading tresses falling over it. With sweeping strokes, he soon had her wavy curls silky and shiny. Sunlight danced over her hair and slowly dried it, bringing its fiery glow to life. She closed her leafy green eyes and relaxed completely. The sun was warm; the breeze was refreshing; his embrace was intoxicating; and she was fatigued from her exertions.

As her respiration became slow and even, Lynx smiled. His admiring gaze shifted over her delicate and striking features. She had the cutest nose and most inviting lips. Her neck was long and slender, her shoulders creamy, but for the darkened area which exposed her recent brush with death. He quietly dropped the brush to the floor to allow his fingers to trail over her satiny flesh; they travelled as if mapping her slender arms, her softly rounded shoulders, and exquisite features. Not even the smallest blemish marred her compelling face. How could a woman be so beautiful and enchanting without recognizing the power and extent of her magic? His artless wife accepted her ravishing looks as easily and unnoticeably as her breathing. The fact that Cal never used her beauty and power over him as weapons touched Lynx deeply.

It had been so long since their last passionate union that his body ached for hers, his heart yearned for her loving responses. He had hurt her deeply by deceiving her, regardless of his motives. Did she doubt his love, too? He had destroyed what faith she had in him. He had disappointed her and confused her. As he watched her sleep peacefully, he silently prayed for her forgiveness and understanding. She appeared so fragile, yet she was strong in many ways. Her traits reminded him of the yucca, also white and lovely, so stubborn and resilient, so vulnerable to destructive forces. He sighed heavily.

His confessions must be postponed until tomorrow. Cal wasn't strong enough in mind or body to delve into such a weighty matter. Since her father's letter hadn't mentioned his partnership with Rankin, Lynx assumed Cal didn't know that injurious fact. Lynx was relieved Brax's will had stated nothing more than Calinda was his sole heir. But Lynx was bewildered and disturbed by the last line in the bequest which granted all of Brax's possessions to Lynx Cardone, in the event of the death of Calinda Braxton . . . For love or retribution?

Lynx was intimidated by the evidence against him, but what difference could one more day make? Her face nestled closer to his shoulder as Cal snuggled up to him. Careful of her left shoulder, his arms embraced her possessively. With her in his arms, Lynx didn't care how long she slept. His heart was bursting with pride and love; he could never lose her, no matter what.

Salina observed the tender and infuriating scene on the balcony as she came to discard the bathwater and remove the tub. She soundlessly made her way to the door and peered outside. Sensing her presence, Lynx glanced over at Salina, placing his finger to his lips. Salina eased onto the porch and looked down at the sleeping Calinda. Her gaze lingered on the remains of Calinda's misfortune, one Salina wished had been fatal. As her eyes slipped up to Lynx's partially concealed face as he also stared at his wife, the truth was never clearer to her: Lynx was actually in love with Calinda.

Lynx motioned and mouthed for Salina to complete her task, to leave them alone. Salina nodded and left, masking her new defeat. There was no one to thank, not the powers of heaven or hell. How she hoped Calinda would be terrified into fleeing the ranch and Lynx.

Lynx watched the blazing sunset to the west, calmly allowing her to sleep until she was fully recovered. When she sighed heavily and moaned in discomfort, he concluded her position was bothering her. He carried her to bed, gently tucking her beneath a light cover. He would change clothes before dinner. Perhaps that black outfit which always glued her eyes to him . . . Or that red silk shirt . . .

When Cal awoke in the bed and saw she was alone, she quickly checked the drawer to test her unsettling theory; the papers were there, but not as she purposely left them. A stand-off was certain as each would wait for the other to approach the dismaying subject. She had piqued him into seeking an answer, but how had the clues affected him? Would Lynx ignore them or confess? She would follow his lead.

"Feeling better now?" he asked tenderly when he returned to find her supposedly stirring for the first time. He took a seat at her side.

Cal lifted her head and looked around, aware of the passage of time and their enticing solitude. If Lynx was a black-hearted villain, how could he be so tender and gentle? As his right palm moved up and down her arm, she smiled and thanked him for his concern and care.

"Any pain, love?" he inquired, his tone lacking any anger.

"Just a dull ache with little twinges every so often. It seems to be healing nicely. Now, all I have to do is regain my strength. You make a comfortable bed, Cardone," she teased, recalling his embrace, needing this brief sharing of tenderness.

"Speaking of bed, that's where you're staying, woman. No more defiance until you're well. Agreed?" he whispered against her forehead, then kissed it, thrilled when she didn't retreat from him.

"That's the best rest I've had in weeks. I think I'll keep you around as my doctor," she teased playfully, feeling better than she had since his last visit home. She looked up into his arresting face and asked, "Still mad at me?"

"A little. I was planning to take you outside to the swing, but you've had too much activity for one day." He smiled raffishly.

"Tomorrow?" Cal wheedled. "If I'm good?"

He grinned and nodded. "Otherwise, I'll tie you to the bed," he jested. "Ready for dinner?"

"Starved, for a change," she hastily accepted.

As they dined in the room, Lynx waited for her invitation to return to their bed, but Cal didn't extend one. He wouldn't press her tonight; she needed another few days to fully recover. To avoid upsetting her, he let their talk slide until another day. She was still insecure and leery tonight, but he knew why. He turned on the charm to beguile her. Instead of creating a serene mood, his romantic overtures made her uneasy. His assumption was accurate; she doubted his love and sincerity. It shouldn't surprise him, but it did trouble him. Winning her over would be a stirring and difficult task.

They made light conversation for an hour, then he cleared the small table. Following a heady kiss, he tucked her in and said goodnight.

During the next few days, Lynx watched her get stronger each hour. Cal was permitted to sit up and to be assisted outside for short periods. Between generous nature and his constant attentions, her improvements increased and the wounds gradually healed. With the continued schedule of nourishing food, lots of rest and sleep, light exercise, fresh air and warm sunshine, and his assistance, she was managing nicely by the fifteenth day after the shooting. Her spirits enlivened and her tensions lessened. She was irresistibly drawn to his agreeable mood.

By the twentieth day, Calinda could get around by herself. She would take her meals with the two men in the dining room. She would sit downstairs for a couple of hours each afternoon and evening, listening to the men's conversations, joining in when they persisted. When they tried to discuss the barbecue, she persuaded them to wait until she was as good as new.

Salina stayed out of Calinda's sight as much as possible. She performed her chores as usual, but spent most evenings away from the ranch. She had become evasive and remote lately. Calinda wondered if Salina was thinking about a new life away from them. Salina made no attempts to converse with Calinda, but politely responded when addressed. Perhaps Salina now realized nothing and no one would drive Cal from the ranch and Lynx. Although the Mexican girl wasn't hateful, neither was she cheerful. Something had changed Salina's resentful and sarcastic manner, but Calinda didn't know what. In fact, the girl almost seemed frightened of something, displaying a subtle wariness and reluctant resignation. But Calinda had problems of her own to solve. Tomorrow would be three weeks since her attack. Yet, Lynx had said nothing about the letters he had secretly read. He was being so damn carefree and jovial! There was a smugness and confidence in him which vexed her. Why wouldn't he talk about the papers? He was behaving as if nothing uncommon had transpired, as if he intended to ignore and forget the entire matter. Why was he being so loving and charming? Yet, he put no pressure on her to share his bed again. He appeared content with their present arrangements, too patient and genial to suit her. She was cognizant of his piercing gaze and proximity. He guarded her so closely that she almost felt a prisoner.

Cal prayed her enemy would soon be captured, and that he would be exposed as a callous stranger. What foe was smart as to leave no clues, so skilled as to be an excellent marksman? The assailant had to be an expert shot, so Cal did not suspect Salina. Salina was malicious and conniving, but surely no killer. Brax's will presented another suspicion—if Lynx had known about the bequest, which would have come first: marriage or . . .

Calinda received a startling jolt that next afternoon. As she gingerly strolled outside with his strong arm supporting her, Lynx nonchalantly told her he would be away at the state capital for two or three days. Although she had enough strength to walk alone, he still insisted on aiding her. He was in a blithe mood today, joking and smiling.

When Lynx made his unexpected announcement, Cal halted abruptly and turned to stare at him. He swiftly expounded, "I was planning to take you with me, Cal, but it's too soon for you to make a tiring trip. I've put it off too long as it is. I couldn't leave until you were better. I've asked Steve to guard the house until I get back. Will you promise not to over-do and stay inside the fence?"

"Why do you have to go to the capital?" she inquired, acting as if she didn't know Austin was his impending destination . . .

"You recall that story in the newspaper from Round Rock about the Bass gang?" When she nodded, he went on, "Major Jones, you recall him, asked me to help him locate two members. You see, I can get in places and speak with men the Rangers can't. J.B. Jones and I have been friends for years, so I agreed to keep an eye out for Sam Pipes and Frank Jackson, two of Sam's men. They passed through Waco when I was there, so I followed them. I have to testify at their trials because I witnessed a bank robbery. Jones had the cases put off while you were so ill. The trial is set for Monday; I'll take the train from Fort Worth tomorrow. As soon as I tell the court my side, I'll come straight home. No more than four days, I promise," he informed her, truthfully preparing her for his impending confession.

Cal wondered why he hadn't mentioned his close friendship with Jones when she met the imposing Ranger. How convenient that the trial would be in Austin where Kyle Yancey resided. How convenient that the Ranger who had discouraged her search was his close friend, a friend linked to the peril in Lampasas. Even if Lynx hadn't learned about her meeting with Yancey in town, the letter had revealed his name to Lynx. Was he planning to question the lawyer before confronting her, to see just how much she knew before telling her too much? That explained why he hadn't said anything to her yet.

"I want to go with you," Cal told him. "Lynx, you promised no more solitary trips. I can relax on the train, then wait in our hotel room while you're in court. If I take it easy, I'll be fine. Besides, I'll have my doctor with me," she reasoned evocatively.

Lynx shook his head. "I swear you can go next time. It's too soon for such a strenuous journey. This isn't a new promise, love. It's an unfinished part of our last separation; I came home early because they weren't ready for the trial. I had planned to take you with me. If I can testify early, I'll catch the train home that same day. You get well, woman; you and I have some serious talking to do."

"All right, boss," she relented, knowing they could both use some privacy to think and plan. He couldn't be lying about the trial for it would be too easy to check out his reason. She prayed Yancey would hold her confidence about the ranch deed until she decided how to handle that distressing matter. But Lynx was an intimidating, powerful, wealthy, and relentless man; he might be able to persuade Yancey to talk.

"You understand? You don't mind?" he probed at her silence.

Cal responded light-heartedly, "I know you have to go and do your duty for law and order. I don't have to like it, but I won't interfere. Too bad you never joined the awesome Rangers; they could use a man with your skills and courage."

He chuckled roguishly. "What man could make a proper Ranger with a wife like you waiting at home?" he murmured playfully.

"Texas's loss is my gain?" she ventured coquettishly.

"I hope so," he mirthfully replied. "Is it?"

"A lack of self-assurance has never been one of your weak points, Lynx. I would say you're a man who's never heard the word no or accepted defeat. Have a nice time and a safe trip."

"You don't have to sound so eager for my departure," he mischievously chided her when she smiled saucily.

"I thought I was being very lenient and bright this time by not pestering you with childish tears and quarrels. Are husbands so hard to please? Which do you prefer, futile hysterics or mature resignation? A word of caution, don't let Jones fill your head with new adventures and challenges. I'll expect you home by Tuesday. You don't want me coaxed out of bed to come seeking my errant husband, or to be enticed to seek a more devoted and appreciative *esposo*."¿¿

"You leave that bed or this house, woman, and you'll answer to me. Savvy?" he demanded seriously.

"Don't return by Tuesday, and you'll answer to me. Savvy?" she captured his taunt and flung it back at him, then laughed.

"You're a mighty demanding vixen," he stated with a chuckle.

"On the contrary, I'm not demanding at all," she corrected him. "In fact, I'm the best thing that's ever happened to you."

"I can't argue that point," he promptly concurred.

"I'd better go inside now; I'm a little shaky. What time is your train?" she inquired as they made their way into the house.

"Eight, so I'll say farewell tonight. I'll need to ride out at dawn."

They ate a quiet dinner downstairs, then chatted with Rankin for a short time. Since Lynx had to get up early, they headed upstairs. He kissed her goodnight after packing, then headed for the borrowed room, resolved this would be his last night to sleep alone.

Calinda tossed on the bed for hours. Perhaps she should go and see if Lynx was still awake. Wouldn't it be better to settle one topic before he left, rather than battle over several when he returned? For surely he would pull the devastating information from Yancey. She needed to know just how much he would confess before he learned she knew everything. If she could take him unprepared, she might learn more. If she gave him time to come up with some plausible explanation . . .

That was the best solution, to get Laura and Brax out of the way before the ranch issue must be dealt with later. If he didn't contact Yancey, she would reveal everything on his return. The stress of remaining silent and uncertain was intolerable.

Cal threw the covers aside and headed for the door. Even though Salina's room was downstairs, it was beneath this one. Cal didn't want that nosey witch to hear her trip to the guestroom at the other end of the hallway. Cal tiptoed to the door and stealthily eased it open a small amount. She listened to make certain there was no noise from downstairs. Before Cal fully opened the door to step into the hallway, she froze and witnessed a stunning sight: Salina was slipping into Cal's old room, dressed in a transparent nightgown!

Mesmerized, Calinda stayed there for a few minutes. If Salina was merely delivering a message, why was it taking so long? If she needed to speak with Lynx about something, why wait so late? Why be so sneaky? Why dressed in that sexy nightgown? A luscious Mexican beauty had no business in her husband's room this time of night and hardly attired! It had been four weeks since they had made love, but was Lynx this desperate for a woman? Like mother, like son?

Cal paced the room as her fury mounted. How dare those two commit such an unforgiveable betrayal! Were they having an affair right under her nose? A new one? An old one? Was Lynx punishing her for the letters? For the past? My God, was he using Brax's type of treachery to destroy her? Make her fall in love with him, then betray her with another woman, in their own home? How could he be so cruel and vindictive?

Salina had stolen into the room where she knew Lynx was sleeping alone, had been sleeping alone for weeks. A man of his virility must need a woman by now. Her decision to leave the ranch had been made; she would join Clint Deavers in a few days. Before she left, she would have Lynx Cardone one time. He owed her for all the years she had waited for him, craved him, endured his teasings and rejections. Once Lynx departed, she would make certain Cal learned about tonight and the ranch! She would devastate them with one blissful night.

Salina walked to the bed, gazing down at the sleeping figure. He was magnificent, lying naked on the covers. His natural instincts were dulled at home where he must feel safe and content. She removed her gown, running her hands over her sultry body, envisioning a passionate night with this bronze god. Before he could clear his head, she would have him writhing in need! Maybe he would mistake her for Calinda if she kept silent. Before Lynx became aware of who she was and what was taking place, they would be making savage love. If there was one thing Salina knew, it was how to use her hands and lips to drive a man wild with desire, to entice him beyond reality or wisdom.

Salina gingerly lay down beside Lynx. His body was so perfect and appealing, she didn't know where to start or which temptation to use. She had waited for this night too long. As her deft hand reached for his manhood, the door flew open and lantern light flooded the room.

When Salina shrieked in alarm at untimely discovery, Lynx stirred and jerked upwards. Simultaneously his keen senses took in many facets of this baffling situation: he and Salina were in bed together naked; and Calinda was standing in the doorway with a lantern, glaring at them. "What the hell's going on here?" he snarled.

"It's obvious, my adulterous mate," Calinda sneered coldly. "You animals deserve each other! I hate you!" She whirled and slammed the door. She rushed to her room and bolted the lock.

"You lousy *puta!*" Lynx shouted at the shrinking Salina. "How dare you sneak in here and cause trouble! Get the hell out of my room! Better still, you malicious whore, get out of my home!"

Salina cowered beneath Lynx's full-blown rage. She begged to explain, but Lynx wouldn't listen. He cursed and berated her, threatened to beat her if she didn't leave instantly. When she groveled and cried, he grabbed her and shoved her toward the door. Still she resisted and pleaded. Lynx forcefully yanked her fingers from the door and pushed her into the hallway. "Get out of my sight before I forget you're a female! If you ever step foot on this ranch again, I'll strangle you!" he thundered at her, flinging her gown into her furious face.

Rankin came rushing to the bottom of the steps. "What's happening, son?" he asked, then his eyes widened as they observed the naked Salina, clutching a gown and swearing at his son.

"Throw her out, father, or I won't be responsible for controlling my temper! She sneaked into my room and tried to seduce me, right in front of Cal! Take care of her; I've got to speak with my wife."

Lynx pounded on the sturdy oak bedroom door, but Calinda refused to open it. He tried to reason with her, explain his innocence. When she kept silent with the door locked, his anger increased. He beat on the door, demanding she let him inside to talk. "Damnit, Cal! I was asleep, dreaming. I didn't know she was there. Honestly, I didn't. I swear I haven't touched another woman since we met. Please let me in."

As Calinda sat on the bed listening to his quarrel with Salina and hearing his shouts of innocence, she knew what must be done. Guilty or not, she must leave the ranch before he returned from Austin. If he loved her, they would work something out after both had been given time alone. She needed to get away from him, the ranch, and these demands for a while. If she couldn't trust him, she shouldn't be married to him. Lynx had been given ample chances to be honest with her; he had rejected each of them. After he departed tomorrow, she would leave for Georgia and get her head and nerves together. She hadn't been herself in weeks, too jittery, too weepy, and too listless. With all this added trouble of the past and the recent shooting, she needed time and solitude, away from Lynx and these continual dangers.

When Lynx circled to the balcony doors, he thundered, "Open up, Callie, or I'll kick them down! We're gonna talk right now!"

Calinda walked to the doors and unlocked them. Tonight, she would say goodbye to him, for a short time or forever. Either way, Lynx Cardone would know what he was missing, or losing. When he stormed inside, she closed the door and bolted it.

He seized her shoulders and shouted. "I'm not guilty, Cal!"

"You're hurting me, Lynx," she murmured softly. "You don't have to explain. It's over."

He loosened his grip. "Please believe me, Callie," he urged, fearing the addition of this spiteful ruse to her stack of misconceptions.

"Make love to me," Cal astonishingly commanded.

"What?" he quizzed in bewilderment. They were quarreling over another woman and Cal wanted to make love?

"Make love to me right now," she repeated distinctly.

"But you're still mending. If you think I need a woman that badly, love, you're wrong, Callie. I don't want Salina or any other woman. I need you. When I return, I'll prove it," he mysteriously vowed.

"I need you now, tonight," she stubbornly insisted.

"You're hurt, Callie," he reasoned, noticing how pale she was in the moonlight. "I didn't mean to squeeze your shoulder. I was just frightened by what you must be thinking. Is it all right?" he fretted.

"There are different kinds of pain, Lynx. Right now, I want you so much it hurts deeply. How can I think about anything else when you're around? You've become the only reality for me. You block out everything and everyone. I need that. Please."

"Do you believe me about Salina?" he pressed.

"Even if it were true, it doesn't matter tonight," she parried.

"You love me that much?" he questioned incredulously.

For one last attempt to elicit a truthful explanation before she carried out her desperate plan, she said evocatively, "I could forgive you anything, just once."

"I swear there's nothing to forgive tonight, Callie," he responded. "I didn't invite her to my room and I didn't touch her."

"Then love me before you leave," she enticed sadly.

Lynx was enchanted by her urgency. He lifted the gown over her head. Before he could lift her and carry her to the bed, she turned and went to it, reclining there, holding out her hand in sweet invitation, her liquid green eyes beckoning, her seductive aura overwhelming. He came forward and joined her.

Her desire was as tangible as a physical caress. He sat on the edge of the bed, filling his greedy senses with her stirring nuance. Her hand reached out and caressed his golden chest, playing over the lean muscles of his stomach and rippling bulges on his shoulders. A bittersweet aching surged through him, plaguing him until she became his one thought. His gaze drifted over her full, taut breasts with their darkened peaks. His tawny eyes glowed with fiery passion as they travelled down her sensual curves and graceful limbs.

Weeks of starved senses ignited his body to smoldering flames, fires which licked dangerously at his resolve to take her leisurely. His molten passion engulfed her, sharing his seething warmth. He was almost afraid to touch her, lest his control be quickly vanquished and he took her swiftly and urgently. She was an overpowering force.

When Calinda's hand moved over his ribs and passed his narrow waist to draw little circles around his groin, he shuddered and moaned. "Your hesitation reeks of distraction and disinterest, my love, but he does not agree," she boldly taunted, trailing the backs of her fingers over the stiffened shaft. "He shouts of an appetite to match mine."

Lynx leaned over and tantalized her breasts with his lips, his hand moved downward to stimulate her as was he. He labored lovingly and deliberately, tearing away her reason. When his mouth sealed upon her parted lips, the kiss fused into a savage and feverish blend. Their need so compelling, he slid within her body, halting instantly to master his wavering control. Never had he known a female who enticed his manhood to seek bliss the moment he invaded her womanhood.

Calinda arched to meet his hips each time he withdrew and entered again. Her body took his instinctively, as her heart absorbed his tenderness. The sensations were so pleasurable and intense that she feared she would faint from their rapturous torment. Like a morning glory, her release burst forth into full bloom, bearing its beauty to the blazing sun above her, enticing him to feed her with his power. When her love's day was past, she gradually folded her exquisite petals.

Lynx pressed fleeting kisses upon her brow, her nose, and her lips. As his own sated passions brought a covering of contentment, his kisses softened on her lips. "Surely you know you are the only woman for me?" he murmured huskily against the silky flesh of her shoulder.

"And you, the only man for me, my love," she replied, her tears hidden in the darkness of the room.

"Sleep, my love, when I return, all will be right between us."

"How can I sleep when I crave you again and you stay so near?" she whispered raggedly. "There is so much I need from you."

Lynx wondered at the anguish and desperation in her voice. How he longed to speak his heart to her, but not when he was leaving for days. What must be said between them would take more time than he had left. He had done everything to prove his love and need with actions during these last weeks. How could she deny what she witnessed and perceived? It seemed as if she compelled his touch as proof of his feelings, a way of entreating reassurance from him.

"As I said, a demanding and greedy vixen," he teased, his tongue flickering over her breasts.

"Oh, Lynx," she cried out as if in torment. "Why must love be so complicated and painful?"

"Only when you resist it or question it, *mi amor,*" he told her.

Her arms tightened around him as she sought appeasement for a yearning deeper than her sexual desire. They loved until exhaustion claimed them, to take them far away to a land where only peace and love reigned . . .

Far into the night, Calinda awoke. She watched her love sleeping so peacefully at her side while she agonized over the dark span between them. If after tonight he still couldn't come to her fully, there was no way for her to reach him. Some evil monster was standing between them, and her husband was refusing to slay the destructive beast. Was her love for him so blind that she refused to see the truth? If he truly loved her and needed her beyond all else, he would prove it. He would not; therefore she must leave this traitorous haven. He knew how deeply she was troubled, how frightened and confused. Yet, some dark secret was more powerful than her love. Until that secret came to light, she could not live here with him.

He was heading out at first light to learn just how much she knew. She could not be here when he returned to confront her, too late to matter. If it must end between them, then let it be so before more damaging evidence was brought to light. If somehow there was hope for them, he would locate her and convince her. If not . . .

Silent tears washed down her cheeks until merciful slumber ended her anguish for the present.

Chapter 24

✒

As Lynx tiptoed out of their bedroom at dawn, Calinda awoke. She hesitated but a few minutes before slipping into her robe and heading downstairs, her barefeet treading inaudibly on the floor. At first, she told herself she was going to have breakfast with Lynx, to send him off properly; then, she warned herself to honesty, as there was so little of it in this house. Cal was intensely aware that Lynx realized that she knew many things about the past. She was worried and frightened by his silence. Why wouldn't he confess the truth? Was there more she didn't know? This ceaseless mystery was tearing her apart. Unanswered questions loomed darkly and suspiciously in her mind.

She made her way near the kitchen to learn if Salina was present, to see if there was something she should know about them before he left. She pressed herself tightly against the wall, ears alert, breath held in suspense as she prayed for a clue to change her plans.

Rankin was sipping coffee at the table while Lynx prepared their breakfast. For a time, the two men were silent. Rankin broke it when he asked, "Did you tell her anything, son?"

"No. I'm waiting to see what this Kyle Yancey revealed first. I'll go to his office after I finish in court," Lynx responded thoughtfully.

"You think he told her about the ranch?" Rankin worried aloud, dreading explaining their deception to Cal.

"If he did, she hasn't let on. From that letter, all she knows about is Brax and mother. Can I ask you a personal question, Father?" he inquired seriously, daring to state his curiosity for the first time since reading that provoking letter.

"About the child?" Rankin guessed astutely. When Lynx nodded ruefully, Rankin sighed heavily. "If there is a child, it could be mine. Either Brax lied in the letter to Cal, or your mother lied to Brax. As if they didn't hurt me enough with their betrayals, now they add more anguish and doubts; I might have another son or a daughter out there somewhere. I thought it was over, son, but it isn't. *Demonio!* I was willing to let the past die until Cal showed up in May. We've got to locate them, Lynx. I can't allow them to steal anything more from me. No son of mine will grow up without his rightful name and heritage."

"How could we be certain whose child Mother carried away with her?" Lynx questioned, musing on this unknown relative.

"Since she was sleeping with both of us, I suppose we can't. This new child might favor her as you do. Only if the child resembles Brax or Cal would we know the truth. But I'm confused, son. If Cal has the deed, why is she keeping it a secret from us? She is your wife."

"For the same reason she kept all those mysterious letters and her visit with Yancey a secret," Lynx reasoned. Having discussed this matter before, they didn't relate their assumptions again, leaving Calinda's curiosity unsated. But Cal was alerted to the fact the Cardone men hadn't known about the child.

"What will you do if Yancey told her everything?" Rankin asked.

"There's only one thing I can do, use my charm and cunning to convince her it was a terrible mistake," he said, winking at his father and grinning broadly, feeling renewed confidence in their future after their night of love. "I doubt she knows where Brax is."

"I doubt you'll need to woo her; you have her dazzled as it is."

"Cal's a bright girl, Father," Lynx stated playfully.

"I always heard that love was blinding," Rankin retorted.

"Maybe before the shooting, but she's too wary and skittish now. We'll have to be very careful what we say and do for a while. She's faced lots of dangers and gathered plenty of evidence; we don't want her spooked into running away. Cal's seen me in action. You know she's got to think it's awfully strange I haven't captured her attacker. Make sure you or Steve guard her until I return. Once she realizes I'll never let her leave the ranch, she'll settle down and accept it. Besides, she doesn't have any money or a place to go." He proclaimed smugly, "Calinda Braxton is mine."

"Does she know the truth about you and Jones? Does she have any idea where you go and what you do?" Rankin inquired to make sure he didn't expose anything Lynx hadn't told Cal.

"None. She'll be shocked when I enlighten her," Lynx jested.

As Lynx spooned up the scrambled eggs, Calinda stealthily returned to her room, false impressions storming her senses. When Lynx returned, they would hold her captive to prevent trouble and embarrassment. She must escape while he was gone!

All day, Cal prepared to seek her freedom. When she discovered Salina's absence, she asked herself if Salina had taken off alone or with Lynx. Perhaps his little tirade had been for his wife's benefit. Damn him for using her, for hurting her! She had fallen into his clutches so readily and willingly. She was a fool! Now, she had lost everything. If only she'd learned about the ranch and treachery sooner; she might have prevented this tragedy.

All morning she had battled nausea to pack lightly and to conserve her energy. That afternoon, she took a long nap, having decided to slip out during the night. Even if she wanted to flee the moment Lynx rode off, she couldn't because of a sturdy guard named Steve. When she awoke later, she felt much better; the curious sluggishness and queasy feeling had passed. She decided it must have been her nerves or a lingering result of her wounds. Thankfully they had healed to the point of mild discomfort. But there was no time to spare.

To prevent any suspicion, Cal cooked dinner for Rankin and herself. But he chided her for her exertions, saying Charlie would cook for them. Calinda brushed aside his soft scolding and forced a disarming smile to her lips. After the meal,

Rankin helped her clear the table and do the dishes. When he invited her to play cards or to read together, she told him she needed to lie down and rest.

"See, I told you not to work so hard," he taunted her gently.

"I'm fine, Rankin, just taking it easy like my husband ordered. Perhaps we should have invited Steve to eat with us; I'm sure he's tired of sentry duty by now. Is this caution really necessary?"

"Yep. He's only around during the day; at night, I'm here if you need anything. I'll make sure the doors and windows are bolted before I turn in. Give a shout if there's a problem. Goodnight, Cal."

"Goodnight, Rankin," she replied, knowing this was the last time she would see this traitorous man she had come to love more than her own father. But how critically she had misjudged him.

"Is something wrong, Cal?" he inquired at her somber gaze.

"I was just thinking, you've been more of a father to me than Brax. I hope you realize how much I appreciate all you've done for me."

He shifted nervously, remorseful over his past actions. Soon, everything would be settled, there would be no more guarding secrets or stepping lightly. He smiled. "I couldn't be more fond of you, Cal, if you were my own child. You're a very special young woman."

She thanked him, grimacing inwardly at his deceit. She went to her room to lie down, to wait for the proper moment to slip out. Since tomorrow began a new week, the hired hands should be asleep soon. She dozed for a while, checking the clock each time she looked that way. At one o'clock, she stood up, summoning the courage to head for safety and peace of mind. She would carry out some plans here first, then take a horse and ride northward to the train depot in Wichita Falls. When they started a frantic search for her, surely it would be eastward toward Fort Worth.

Barefoot for silence, Cal made her way to Rankin's work-room, gratified to find the door between his office and bedroom shut. Inside, she closed the other door and cautiously placed a Spanish shawl on the floor to prevent any light from sneaking under it to alarm him. Cal lit the desk lantern, but wisely kept the wick low. She jimmied a drawer and withdrew the cash-box. She shivered in suspense, fearing discovery before she could make her escape. There was no time left to deliberate whether she was right or wrong; she only knew she had to get away for a while. When she had regained her stamina and confidence, she would contemplate a message to Lynx. She counted out three hundred dollars and stuffed it into her shirt pocket. She retrieved two sheets of paper and sat down to write on them.

> To whom it may concern:
>
> I, Calinda Braxton Cardone, do willingly surrender all legal and moral claims to my half of the Cardone Ranch to Lynx Cardone on this date September 1, 1878, in exchange for my marital freedom and the sum of $45,300 in said debts to Rankin and Lynx Cardone. Neither I, nor any of my heirs or relatives, will have future claims against this land from this date forward. Nor will Elliott Braxton, proclaimed deceased last month, nullify this agreement should he ever return and lay claim against it.

Cal signed the statement and placed it with the official deed which her father had stolen years ago. On the other paper, she wrote a letter to Lynx. She sighed painfully before ending their stormy affair. What did one say in light of such treacherous betrayal? How did one say goodbye forever to the love of her life? What words could halt this vicious circle of despicable vengeance?

Lynx,

As you have doubtlessly learned by now from Kyle Yancey and the letters which you found in our room, I know the dark secrets which you and your father withheld from me about our parents and the ranch. The letters were placed there intentionally for your discovery. Many times I have opened the door for your admissions, but you refused to enter and banish your deceptions to the past where they rightfully belong. Your secrecy speaks loudly and painfully. I can understand your mistrust and silence in the beginning, but not after our marriage and your vows of love. I have no knowledge of the whereabouts of Laura and Brax, nor will I make any attempt to locate them. To avoid more suffering on everyone's part, I'm leaving the ranch and yielding its deed and ownership to you. I know this is unnecessary as the unjust law states our marriage relinquished my claim to you. Even with the truth and the deed, I would never have placed any claim on your ranch. I also give you everything which I leave behind to dispose of as you wish.

With the deed in your possession, you have what you desired from me. Surely your hatred and revenge can be sated with this substitute victory over Brax? Please don't come after me, but allow this tragic matter to end; bury the past and find peace and happiness.

I must apologize for taking money as my treacherous father did, but surely half of this ranch is worth $45,300? I will consider all debts and obligations fulfilled from both parties. I shall never understand your cruel deceits. How I wish we could have discovered the trust and happiness which my father prevented. Don't concern yourself over my safety and health. Perhaps one day you will regret all you have sacrificed for an earthly mistress without warmth or feelings, as your dirt vixen is far more demanding than I.

I don't know how many of my troubles and dangers were at your hands, and I hope I never learn that final secret. I give you back your freedom, as I retrieve mine. Knowing everything, how I loved you and needed you . . .

Calinda

She folded the letter and placed it inside an envelope, dropping her wedding band inside, then sealing it and writing his name on the front. In a neat row, Cal placed the deed with her relinquishing statement, her father's will and letter for proof of her past ownership, and the heart-rending letter to Lynx. She stared at the line of multiple betrayals, then went upstairs.

Cal gathered the small bag with the few things she would need for her journey. She didn't know what she would do when she reached Georgia, but she would find a way to survive. If she had learned anything since coming here, it was how resilient and bright she was. She slipped out of the house and to the stable. She saddled a horse and walked him far from the yard before mounting, denying the twitches in her shoulder. She sat on the animal's back and gazed at the hacienda style home she had shared with two unknown foes for many months. It was over, this cycle of tragedy which her own father had initiated.

She clicked the reins and rode off without glancing back. Cal knew which road headed off from this one toward the north. She shifted her gunbelt to be ready for any trouble ahead. She was wearing a light jacket to conceal her feminine figure, her flaming curls tucked beneath her hat. She had separated the money, hiding some inside her hatband, some inside her right boot, and some inside her jeans pocket. If she were robbed, chances were they wouldn't find all of it.

She chose a steady pace and rode for hours, halting to rest the animal as the sun peeked over the distant horizon. She travelled within sight of the dirt road, but a safe distance away from anyone who might come along. She would eat and rest later, once she was assured of her success. Besides, she was too queasy to eat so early. Usually that lingering annoyance faded by lunchtime.

As the sun rose higher in the pale blue sky on this humid September Monday, Cal became warm and damp. She headed for a cluster of trees to rest and cool herself and the horse. She slowly consumed the cold ham and biscuits which she had prepared yesterday. She watched the horse as he grazed peacefully at the thirsty covering at his hooves. She was so weary and sleepy, but she dared not doze this soon. She needed to travel most of today and tonight, then sleep around daybreak. After her initial caution, she would ride at night and sleep in some hidden place during the day to prevent being seen or accosted. As she looked over the rugged landscape, pangs of loneliness and trepidation assailed her. Was she mistaken, impulsive, rash?

When she came to an area which was fenced off on both sides, she had no choice but to ride along the dusty road. When Cal noticed a single rider approaching her, she tensed, checking her pistol for readiness. The man passed her and nodded in greeting. Calinda noticed how well-armed he was, but his expression was genial and his gaze friendly. Calinda rode on, unaware of the way he twisted in his saddle to stare at the retreating back of a beautiful woman with blazing hair sneaking from beneath her tan hat. Intrigued, he shrugged and rode on toward Fort Worth, assuming she lived nearby.

Mid-afternoon, Calinda reached a large stream. She reined in her horse and slid off his back, allowing both of them to drink. She refilled her canteen and splashed her face with tepid water. When she heard the mournful sounds of cattle nearby, she panicked; for cattle meant cowboys, witnesses to her passing. She mounted up and headed off again, her attention northward. Cal refused to think about what she was leaving behind or what she was facing. She tried to defensively block-out all realities, but for her arduous trek.

Calinda had planned on Rankin's normal schedule to aid her flight. But the concerned man returned home early since Salina was gone. Near three in the afternoon, Rankin headed toward the house from the stable. He greeted Steve and went inside, dismissing him from his watch since early that morning. He glanced around curiously as he entered the quiet house. He called Calinda's name, but there wasn't any response. He went into the empty kitchen, then the den.

Rankin decided Cal must be napping, so he headed for his office to do book-work. As his eyes touched on the neat line of papers, an ominous chill walked over his body. He snatched up the ranch deed to scan it and her attached paper, freezing in consternation. He noticed the letter and will which he had read another night. He lifted the envelope with his son's name on the outside. He cast aside any reservations and ripped it open, shocked and alarmed by the words which greeted his eyes. He tossed the papers aside and rushed upstairs. She wasn't in her room. He looked in every room, checking beside and behind furniture to see if she had passed out somewhere. He looked on balconies and finally realized the astonishing truth.

A hopeful thought tugged at his mind. How could she leave with Steve on guard? Surely Cal was outside somewhere, perhaps hiding and waiting to sneak off tonight. He rushed to the stone fence and called Steve back to the house. Rankin questioned the guard about her absence. Steve told him he hadn't left the porch all day, even to eat. He said Charlie had brought his food and had tried to offer some to Mrs. Cardone, but she didn't answer their knock. They assumed she was resting upstairs. Steve hadn't seen Cal all day.

"That's strange; I can't find her," Rankin worried aloud.

Steve said he would search around the house and ask at the stable. If she left, it was by the kitchen door. Steve checked the water-shed, the supply sheds, the stable, and the surrounding yard. He questioned Charlie and several other men, to no avail.

When Steve returned with his unsettling news, Rankin was panicked by her incredible departure. How could she run away? What should he do? How long ago had she left? To go where?

Rankin chose his words carefully when he spoke with Steve. "She hasn't been herself since that shooting, Steve. She's scared and sick. Get some of the men to search the ranch. Bring her back whatever she says. I'm heading into town to warn Lynx. I'm putting you in charge of getting her home."

Steve nodded and went to issue those orders to the men who had returned from the range. The desperate search for Calinda was on within minutes. Rankin and Seth headed for town at a swift pace. It was five o'clock when he sent his telegram to the Texas Timbers Hotel in Austin. He paid the agent to remain open until he received an answer from his son, offering the agent on the other end the same amount from his son to pass their urgent messages along.

At six-thirty, Lynx returned to the hotel from his tormenting meeting with Kyle Yancey. It had taken heavy persuasion to pull the facts from that elderly man. As Lynx had feared, Calinda had the ranch deed and her version of the truth. He cursed his distance from her and the train which didn't leave until morning. As certain as the changing seasons, his love had been subtly probing for his confessions. He understood how his refusals must have appeared to his confused wife. He raged at what she must be enduring at this very moment.

The clerk called Lynx over, handing him an urgent telegram. He told the puzzled Lynx that the sender was awaiting a response at any hour. Lynx unfolded the paper and shuddered in terror:

Lynx, Have ranch deed. Cal knows truth. Said nothing. Ran off. Can't
locate. Send advice. Hurry home.
Rankin.

Lynx rushed to the telegraph office and pounded on the door. The man let
him inside after he gave his name. He composed his response:

Rankin. Search everywhere. Ask sheriff for help. Horse too slow. No
train until morning. Home at two. Meet me. Must find. Saw Yancey.
Looks bad. Wire Dallas sheriff. Check trains. Stages. Lynx.

Lynx paid the man for his delay and assistance. He rushed to Major Jones'
room at the hotel and poured his troubles and fears out to his friend. Jones said he
would send messages to all his men to be on the lookout for her. Jones felt great
sympathy for his friend, but gently scolded Lynx's actions. "There's no fair swap
for truth, son, not even with good intentions," he finished sadly as they parted.

The violence and dangers of this wild frontier having been forced upon her,
Calinda stubbornly drove herself onward until her head and shoulder throbbed
and tears threatened to choke her as she tried to govern her pain and emotions.
She had been riding since two this morning, and the moon's angle indicated it was
nearly midnight. But for rest and water stops, she had been on this deserted trail
for over eighteen hours. Surely it was safe to slow her flight.

Cal had made a wide detour around one small town and concealed herself
when a stagecoach thundered past her. Fortunately, there had been cedar brakes
and live oak stands or arroyos to offer her protection from wary eyes. She had
continually observed all directions to prevent anyone from approaching her unseen, a time-consuming measure, but a vital one. She had controlled the reins with
her right hand, but the jolting motion of her pace was plaguing her sensitive
injuries. Each time the horse's hooves touched the ground, pains shot through her
chest and back. The muscles around the wound had grown stiff and angry; her
head was pounding. Her body ached all over; Cal was exhausted. She was forced
to give in to her body's demands.

Lynx couldn't sleep all night; he paced his room until it was time to catch the
train to Fort Worth. Along the journey the clicky-clack of the rails seemed to
chant, "She won't come back. She won't come back. She won't come back . . ."
Lynx heard that ominous message until he was tensed and haunted. For someone
alleged to be cunning and fearless, he had been a cowardly fool.

Whatever it took, he would locate her and force her to listen. He didn't care
about the ranch if he lost her. Even from an unknown distance, Brax was hurting
him; the traitor was stealing another love from his life, one more precious than his
devious mother.

When the train slowed, Lynx bolted off and ran toward his father before it
halted. Rankin's forlorn expression said everything; no news. Lynx accepted her
letter and read it, quivers passing over his towering frame. Could he blame her?

But she was wrong. She was still mending. There was no telling what kind of perils she was confronting along the trail. But what trail?

He listened to Rankin's revelations of yesterday, tormented by her desertion and desperation. Lynx tried to think as she would. Where would she go? She had nearly two days on him. But she was a woman, and she wasn't fully healed. He had to make certain he chose the same direction to overtake her. He grimaced at the thought of his beautiful and vulnerable wife out there alone somewhere, a temptation to any man who saw her, too weak or untrained to defend herself.

"You checked the stagelines and trains?" Lynx asked.

"Everything I could imagine, son. She took a horse," he hinted.

"She could catch either anywhere along the line," Lynx fretted.

"They've been told to watch for her and alert us if she's spotted," Rankin tried to encourage his distraught son and himself.

A tall, lanky man ambled toward them. He smiled genially and spoke to Lynx. "You look like a puma with a thorn in his paw, Lynx."

"I've got a terrible problem, N.O.," Lynx began, then explained it to Lieutenant N.O. Reynolds of the Texas Rangers, one who had been at Round Rock and knew of Lynx's secret identity.

"What does she look like?" Reynolds inquired sympathetically.

When Lynx described Calinda, Reynolds beamed in pleasure. "Sounds to me like the lady I saw on the road to Wichita Falls yesterday," he casually informed Lynx, then gave his impression of her and the horse.

"She was alone?" Lynx fearfully inquired.

"Yep. Thought it strange, but didn't question it. Figured she lived around there. Too pretty to be out riding alone."

"When? Where?" Lynx asked, his hopes building by the minute.

"About forty miles south of Jacksboro, that's where I was coming from, around threeish." Reynolds flexed his aching muscles.

Lynx quickly tallied how far ahead she must be by today. Even riding all day and night, she couldn't make Jacksboro by now. He had to reach her before she entered that rowdy and hazardous town. "Why don't you hop that train to Taylorsville, then head southwest to intercept her?" Reynolds offered the same solution Lynx was planning.

"You hold the train while I rent a horse and get some supplies," Lynx entreated Reynold's help.

"I brought Star and supplies, son. I figured you would head out quickly as you arrived," Rankin informed the optimistic man.

While Rankin went for Star at the livery-stable, Reynolds and Lynx made arrangements with the conductor to take Lynx to Taylorsville. By six Tuesday evening, Lynx was heading northwest on the AT&SF Railroad. Within two hours, he would be riding Star to reach the Jacksboro road about ten miles south of town. He would follow the road southward with the hopes she hadn't reached that far yet. In her weakened state, Cal must be travelling slowly and cautiously.

Lynx guided Star off the train at the water-stop and leaped on his strong back. As if sensing his beloved master's urgency, the mettlesome and nimble beast galloped off in the assigned direction. Possessing great stamina and intelligence, the animal raced swiftly, his keen ears pricked for any hint of danger.

Steadfast and unrelenting, the two travelled as one to rescue the love of Lynx Cardone. Besieged with panic, Lynx wondered where his wife was beneath this same full moon which hopefully lit his path toward her. What if she had altered her course? What if she were battling some villain this very moment? What if she had fallen ill beneath her reckless pressures? Somewhere in this vast and precarious territory, his woman was defenseless and suffering.

He urged Star to an even faster pace. With at least a twenty-hour headstart, she could be anywhere and in any danger . . . Lynx recognized he had several advantages over Calinda: he and Star were fresh and anxious after their train ride; and they could make better time than she could since she would be compelled to ride cautiously to appease her disabled body. He was around thirty miles from the Jacksboro road; considering where Reynolds had seen her, she had to be around forty miles to the south. If Cal made fifteen to twenty miles tomorrow, he should intercept her at least that many miles below that turbulent settlement, if she held true to course and didn't collapse. If Fort Richardson hadn't been abandoned in May, he could have telegraphed there for assistance. He glanced at the moon, assessing the time as ten o'clock. If he travelled all night, he could make up for her lead.

Lynx tried to focus his attention on another subject to distract his troubled mind. He recalled his last talk with Jones when he had refused to continue with the Rangers. Someone else could battle the aggressive Apaches who were stirring up again in the Pecos area, and someone else could struggle against the forces of Mexican *banditos* and American desperadoes.

Calinda had slept restlessly for several hours last night, then urged herself to halt this murderous pace and yield to short naps. Her fatigue was increasing, as were her morning bouts with nausea. Preoccupied, her symptoms failed to register accurately in her muddled thoughts. She continued to believe the squeamish feeling was connected to her injured condition and physical distress. The mixture of blazing sun, hard riding, and painful agony took its toll as the day passed from ice blue skies, to a brilliant sunset, to deepening shadows of impending night. Planned as the moment to switch from day riding to night riding, she was coerced by inflexible and merciless nature to suspend her trek until morning or until sufficiently rested.

Just before eleven, Cal walked the animal into a dry gulch and gingerly dismounted. She tied his reins to a small mesquite bush, then denied her fatigue and anguish to remove his saddle. She drank from the canteen and sighed listlessly. Too lacking in spirit and strength to consume the unappealing nourishment, Cal spread a blanket on the sandy ground and was quickly devoured by sleep.

Lynx journeyed all night, halting as streaks of pinkish gray dawn filtered across the landscape. While Star caught his wind, grazed, and watered, Lynx quickly prepared a small fire for enlivening coffee. He tossed down three cups of the black liquid and some dried beef with biscuits. He rinsed the dishes and pot in the river, then stripped and dove in. He splashed himself and ducked many times to refresh his lagging spirits and depleted energy. If he came upon trouble, he must be revived and alert. He packed up his gear and headed off again.

When Calinda awoke around eight she felt terrible, she wanted to cry like a baby. She was sore and miserable. After sleeping so long, she was still drained. She choked and heaved several times, but her stomach was too empty to eject anything. She felt dizzy and wobbly. She wondered how she could saddle the horse or ride in this weak state. But she realized Lynx must be aware of her escape by now. Was he tracing her flight this very moment? Did she even care?

She reclined on her back to settle her whirling head and agitated stomach. She sipped water, dabbing at the fluid which dribbled down her chin from her shaky hands on the canteen. She poured some into her cupped hand and rubbed it over her ashen face. She lay down again. Nothing seemed to help. How she longed for a bath and a soft bed.

Cal had to lie there in misery until mid-morning before nature showed her any sympathy and assuaged the unfamiliar harassment. She forced one biscuit down with water, but feared it wouldn't remain inside very long. Placing most of the weight of the saddle on her right arm, she tossed it over the horse and fastened the girth beneath his belly. She tied the blanket behind the saddle and pulled herself up on his back. She wanted to sob hysterically when she realized she hadn't untied the reins from the bush and they were refusing to be yanked free. Was everything and everyone against her?

Cal dismounted and untangled the leather strip, gritting her teeth in vexation. She leaned forward as the horse climbed out of the coulee and follow her command. Ignorant of what menacing threats lay ahead, the quest for unwanted freedom was underway again . . .

Chapter 25

THE FIRST TWO HOURS WERE HELLISH for Calinda. Her stomach was still churning feebly. Her head was aching; her shoulder was screaming for relief. How she craved some of Doc's magical elixir. Two fiery patches flamed on her cheeks against her milky complexion. She was colorless around her pale lips, which were dry from her erratic respiration. Dark smudges lingered beneath her somber green eyes.

Calinda swayed precariously in the saddle, leaning forward countless times and gripping the horn to keep from tumbling to the hard ground. Her appetite had vanished; all she desired was soothing water, liquid which her tummy battled to accept. At that moment, she would have given all of her money for a sip of medication and a soft bed. By now, she didn't care if Lynx overtook her; in fact, she found herself praying he would, reflecting on his tender and loving care after her injury. Never had she felt worse in her life, not even during or after the shooting. Oddly, his supposed betrayal didn't pain her as much as her own body did at this time.

Calinda feared she was going to faint soon. She weaved to and fro on the horse, struggling to retain her senses and balance. Her jumbled thoughts told her Lynx had had a logical explanation for his actions. She shouldn't have fled so recklessly. No matter what she assumed Lynx had done, he had always rescued her from peril and taken care of her. Why had she run away before giving him the chance to explain?

Cal felt so alone and wretched. She was afraid, afraid of life without Lynx, afraid of her worsening illness, afraid of the path ahead. She even feared she might die out here alone. She was swiftly becoming too hazy and weak to fend for herself. A hysterical sob came forth as she realized the seriousness of her predicament.

What was her love thinking and feeling? Was Lynx glad to be rid of her? Would he honor her request not to pursue her? Or was he alarmed and worried about her? Had her desertion cut him deeply? Was he furious with her? What if he did come after her? How would he know where to look? She cursed herself and the burdensome past, hoping she hadn't been too cunning for his tracking skills.

Her dazed vision noticed a thick cluster of trees ahead. Knowing she couldn't stay alert or in the saddle much longer, Cal headed the horse in that direction. To conceal them from dangerous eyes, she guided him into the center of the leafy copse.

Suddenly a man bolted forward and seized her reins. She wavered dizzily. She vaguely took in a tousled blond head and steely eyes. Between rapid blinks, her blurry vision momentarily settled on the pistol in his grip. Her stupefied mind couldn't analyze her danger. She could hear his voice, but couldn't make out his words as her ears buzzed precariously. Her eyes closed and she fell over into the arms of the astonished outlaw.

He stared at the beautiful bundle in his grasp, then smiled. He deposited her on the spot which he had hastily deserted. He holstered his sixgun and secured the reins of her horse to a tree beside his stallion. He swaggered over to kneel beside her, taking in her unique beauty and sorry condition. He removed her hat, allowing the fiery curls to spread around her head, dabbing her face with his handkerchief.

He shoved one eye open, enchanted by the rich greenness of it. He ran his rough fingers over flesh which was creamy and smooth. Clearly she was real sick. He removed her light jacket to allow her body to cool. Unfastening the top three buttons on her shirt to assist her breathing, he tingled as his fingers made contact with silky skin. She certainly was a looker. Probably around his age.

Why was she out here alone? He removed her gunbelt and put it out of reach, should she awake soon. He slipped off her boots, knowing how refreshing that was to a warm body. When the money fell to the ground, he chuckled and stuffed it into his pocket. He searched her, finding the other two hidden sums. He grinned; she was a bright gal.

Where was she heading? What was wrong with her? She was ravishing, but in sore shape. Running away from some vicious father or a horrible husband? How vulnerable and childish she looked. Yet, her face and body declared her very much a woman. His loins flamed, tugging against the restraint of his jeans. He threw back his yellowy blond hair and laughed coldly; what Billy Bounet wanted, Billy took. Billy lazed against his saddle, observing her as she slept. The famed outlaw glanced at the sun and smiled salaciously; it was early, around two. This fragile filly was no match for him . . .

Even at eighteen, Billy was fearless and deadly, with a string of murders and robberies to his credit. He was a dreaded legend who terrorized the areas of Santa Fe, Brazos Forks, the Panhandle, and Plains. Some knew him as William Bonnet, Henry McCarthy, or Kid Antrim. Most knew him as Billy the Kid. With his Winchester rifle, Smith & Wesson pistol, Mexican blade, and his steely eyes Billy could frighten most men into backing down. This girl would be no trouble at all.

Lynx had connected with the southern road from Jacksboro, but he still had at least twenty miles to ride before catching up to his wife. He halted everyone he passed to question them. When he could find no one who had seen Calinda along the trail, Lynx prayed it was her bright mind which allowed her to elude discovery and not some other force which had taken her off the trail: illness or peril.

As Lynx rounded a bend in the road, he came face to face with no other than Salina Mendoza and Clint Deavers! His heart lurched to find these two on the same trail as his missing wife. Clint reined up instantly, glaring at the golden image clad in black. Salina whitened and had difficulty controlling her horse.

"Well, well, who do we have here, Salina?" Clint muttered, his gaze lethal and frosty. Clint hadn't forgotten how this man had tricked him and called his bluff, acts which still riled the gunslinger.

"Lynx, why do you ride this way?" Salina asked weakly.

"I might ask the same of you, Salina," Lynx snarled. "That's bad company you're keeping. I wondered where you'd flown to."

"Were you looking for me?" she asked wishfully, her eyes and face brightening, much to Clint's annoyance.

Lynx laughed sarcastically and shook his head slowly. Lynx appeared utterly relaxed and unruffled, but he was tense and alert. "Did you notice Callie along the trail?" he casually inquired, observing their reactions for clues he dreaded. "Seems your malicious trick worked after you left. Any idea where she went?"

"You mean Cal ran off again?" Salina asked in amusement.

"You've been scheming to run her off ever since her arrival. What did you expect after she caught you naked in my bed?" Lynx ventured, pleased with the effect of his enlightening words on Clint. "If I hadn't been so busy trying to calm her down the other night, I would have beaten the daylights out of you for that malicious prank," he sneered scornfully.

Salina flustered. She glanced over at the nettled man beside her. "He lies, Clint. I have never slept with you," she charged hotly.

"Only because I kicked you out on your lustful ass. I've been telling you for over two years that I'm not interested in a slut like you. And don't go looking insulted! Only a cheap *puta* would sneak into a married man's room while he's sleeping! It takes a daring, heartless bitch to crawl naked into his bed with his injured wife in the next room. Ask Deavers, who would look at you even once with Cal around?" Lynx added harshly, noticing the gleam of agreement in Clint's eyes.

"If Cal had not been wounded and an invalid for weeks, you would not have needed a woman so badly," she shot back at him.

"Wounded?" Clint echoed in surprise. "That pretty little thing got shot? Who did it?" he demanded as if he deserved to know the identity of anyone who would dare such an outrage. He hadn't been able to forget her since their meeting in Lampasas.

"I'd bet my boots Salina knows. I learned how cruel and devious she is when she tried to pin an adultery charge on me," Lynx announced.

Stressed, Salina exposed a look of guilt before she could control her expression. She stammered, "Don't be . . . absurd! Why would . . . I shoot Calinda? She is a pain in the rump, but that's *loco*."

Clint stared at Salina. Lynx drilled his intimidating glare into her frightened face. "You little bitch!" Clint thundered at her. So much for their plans of kidnapping that spicy redhead for her revenge and his pleasure! Salina had promised him money and Calinda if he aided her plot. All along, she had wanted to kill the sweet lady!

"He just tries to anger you, *mi amanta*. Do not listen to him," she pleaded, her nerves jittery between two powerful males.

"Where is she, Salina?" Lynx demanded suspiciously, capturing a curious interaction between them. "What have you done to her now?"

"*Que se yo, diablo!*" she screamed at Lynx in rising panic.

"The hell you don't know!" he stormed back, eyes blazing in fury.

"We haven't seen her, Cardone, but I'll gladly help you search. This ain't no safe area for a lady like that," Clint merrily offered.

"*Caramba!*" Salina cursed at the grinning outlaw.

"Shut up, Salina," Clint warned in mounting repulsion.

"You two were behind those mysterious notes, weren't you?" Lynx questioned, but didn't expect any answer. He was astonished when Clint responded almost immediately.

"This *chica* planned the whole thing. I should have known she was up to no good. If you'll recall, she wasn't your wife at the time. I knew you were lying, but I had a soft spot for her. Can't blame me for falling under her spell. Must be powerful to snare you. If she's run off from home, I take it she's available again?" he baited Lynx.

"*Vete al infierno!*" Salina heatedly damned them to Hades.

Lynx was too aware of the passage of time. But before he rode off, he had to make certain these two weren't involved in Calinda's disappearance. What if they forced her to write those notes and leave? What if Cal assumed he would pull clues from the letter? What had it said? Lynx tried to envision it, but he was distracted by Clint's cold blue gaze and palm resting on the butt of his pistol. It was rash to think of other things in the face of death . . .

Stalling for time, Lynx exposed Salina's plot the other night. He icily added, "No Deavers, she ain't available and never will be."

"Well?" Clint hinted guilefully. "Need my help? If Calinda's finished with you, I'm ready and willing to marry her."

"Damn you, bastard!" Salina screamed at Lynx, watching him thwart her final plan. Once Clint had taken his fill of Calinda and she had driven her small dagger into that witch's heart, Salina had planned to return to the ranch and offer herself to the grieving Lynx. "I wish Manuel's aim had been accurate; she would be dead! Too bad that horse did not trample her! I should have told Clint to rape her that first night in Lampasas! You are a fool, *diablo!* Manuel should have killed you that day on the range! She is a *puta!* A *feo gata!* A *sucio bruja!*" she shouted rashly, going for the gun at her waist. If she couldn't have this irresistible devil who haunted her, no woman would!

Lynx was about to lurch forward to slap her vulgar mouth, pushed beyond reason and control as that bitch spouted crude insults about his beloved. But Clint viciously slapped Salina's face three times as he growled satanically, "No, you don't, you slut! He's mine! Trick me, will you!"

Salina couldn't recoil swiftly enough to avoid those bruising blows. Tears rolled down her face. Her dark eyes were wide with terror and disbelief. She begged for Lynx's protection. Deavers clearly wasn't done with her yet.

Clint laughed wickedly. "Let me see you use that ugly face to fool any more men! Get out of here before I break your arms!"

Again the Mexican girl appealed for Lynx's help. "Sorry, Salina, but I have to be going." Right now, Cal could be in more trouble than Salina was. Lynx despised such brutality, but he didn't have the time to help this girl who had maliciously played havoc with his life and his wife's. He chilled his heart and conscience to her sufferings. Salina had chosen this path and must ride it to the end. Besides, Deavers was too edgy to suit him.

"Not so fast, Cardone. It's time you and I settle our differences, here and now."

The puissant Texan leveled his potent gaze on Clint. "We have no quarrel, Deavers. Don't force me to kill you," he stated clearly, unshaken by the outlaw's threat. But it was his way to avoid death if possible. He would reason first, bluff second, and shoot last.

"You're wrong, Cardone. You made a fool of me in Lampasas; I don't take that insult lying down. Let's dismount and see who's the fastest," Clint suggested stubbornly, wishing he hadn't shot off his mouth so quickly. Now, he couldn't back down.

"I don't have time to argue with you, Deavers. Cal's out there lost somewhere, maybe in danger. Let it pass for today," he entreated.

"How long does it take to die, Cardone?" Clint scoffed. "If you survive, you go after her. If I survive, then I'll take your place. It's very quick and simple, the winner gets her."

"I'd kill you before I let you near her again," Lynx snarled.

"You'll have to," Deavers replied, grinning at his rigid foe.

"No, I won't," Lynx said lightly. "I'm a Texas Ranger; you're under arrest." He gingerly withdrew the badge from his pocket and flashed it before Clint's infuriated eyes.

Abruptly Clint burst into taunting laughter. "You're a Ranger about as much as you were Calinda's husband in Lampasas. No more sneaky tricks, Cardone. Get off your horse," he demanded.

"I'm a Ranger, Deavers, and you're a bloody fool."

Clint and Lynx challenged each other with their combative gazes. Clint wavered in doubt, then scoffed, "You're married. You wouldn't join the Rangers with a wife like that at home. You're lying."

"Will you relax a minute while I prove it?" Lynx asked.

"How?" Clint skeptically queried.

"Like this," Lynx replied negligently, lifting his boot and swiftly digging his spur into the leather of Clint's saddle. "Recognize that?"

Clint gaped at the tiny depression in the shape of a star, then lifted his apprehensive gaze to the impassive face of Lynx Cardone. "You?" Clint hinted incredulously.

"Me," Lynx answered nonchalantly, not a tiny trace of dishonesty or fear on his face. "What's it to be, Deavers?"

Clint glanced from the imprint of the star to the confident look on Lynx's face. He hesitated in doubt. Lynx was fast and accurate, and the Unknown Ranger was untouchable in courage and daring.

"You've got ten seconds to dismount or ride off," Lynx stated.

Clint wiped the moisture from the corners of his mouth as he assessed the situation. Salina was bending over her saddle, weeping. Her gun was on the ground; no help to him. Could he take this man who was two daring men in one? His irrational pride mocked him.

"I don't want no trouble with Rangers. Another day?"

"Another day," Lynx calmly accepted, wary of this man.

Clint reached over and took Salina's reins. He glared at Lynx, then headed past him. "Count on it, Cardone," he sneered.

Lynx didn't move a muscle, but watched the man closely. Clint spurred his horse and rode off, pulling Salina's along with him. Lynx nudged Star in the ribs to move out, his keen instincts alive.

The moment Clint halted and yanked his Winchester from his saddle to backshoot Lynx, the intrepid Ranger went into lightning action. In one graceful movement, Lynx had whirled and drawn his Colt and fired at Clint's left shoulder. The rifle flew to the ground as Clint yelped in pain, the bullet lodging beneath his shoulder blade. Even at that distance, Lynx was accurate.

"Another day, Deavers!" he shouted, then prodded Star into a fast run. Wounded, Deavers would be forced to head for Jacksboro. When Lynx had time, he would wire the Ranger there to arrest him and Salina for their crimes. In their condition, they wouldn't get far. When he returned home, Lynx would deal with Manuel. Besides being Calinda's attacker, he was doubtlessly the rustlers' informant.

Lynx's eyes flickered to the sun's angle. He ranted at the loss of time; it was nearing five o'clock and he had a lengthy distance to cover before darkness. Soon, he would be forced to slow his pace to search the sides of the trail. Lynx didn't want to ride past her!

Ten miles southward, Calinda was stirring for the first time since early afternoon. Her hand went to her forehead as she mechanically mopped the beads of perspiration from it. She inhaled and exhaled deeply as she tried to clear her senses. When her eyes opened, there was a roughly dressed man hunkered down beside her. She caught her breath in panic and surprise. Her eyes darted around, assessing her location and situation. Her hand eased down to her waist, finding her gunbelt missing. She tensed in panic.

Billy noted each of her actions and expressions. She was a feisty little beauty. "Good morning. Or is it good afternoon?" he playfully murmured, caressing his knobby chin with his left hand.

"Who are you? What happened?" Cal asked shakily.

"Don't know what happened, little lady, but I'm called Billy," he smugly announced, sitting down beside her.

Calinda struggled to sit up, but her head swam. "Best lie down a while, Ma'am. You don't look so good," Billy advised.

"May I have some water?" she asked politely, amusing him.

He handed her the canteen and helped her rise to drink. As she relaxed with her head against his saddle, she asked, "Where am I?"

"Just south of Jacksboro. Where you heading alone and in this sorry shape?" he asked, intrigued and stimulated.

"I was meeting my husband there, but I became ill. I guess I'm lost," she responded cautiously, slyly.

"No ring on your finger," Billy informed her.

"I lost it. He's buying me another one. May I have some more water? I must have a fever. I'm so thirsty," she told him to stall for time to think and plan.

"A good shot of Irish whiskey will do more for you," he offered.

"No thank you. I don't partake of strong spirits," she alleged.

"What do you partake of, Ma'am?" he asked alarmingly.

"I beg your pardon?" Cal replied, trying to disarm him with manners and innocence.

"Got me a real lady on my hands," he congratulated himself aloud. "What about that? Billy the Kid with a lady, imagine that."

Billy was slightly miffed when she failed to recognize his notorious name and the reputation that went along with it. He had expected to strike terror into her heart with it. "What should I do with you?" he asked absently, running his fingers through his shaggy hair.

"Do you live around here? Will your family help me get home?"

Chilling laughter came forth from this belligerent man. "Nope!"

"You don't live around here, or they won't help me?" she asked softly, as if for clarity, but actually for time.

"I don't live anywhere, and I ain't got no family," he declared.

"Then I must head for Jacksboro before night comes," she stated, glancing at the enclosing shadows. "If my husband isn't there or searching for me, I'll stay in the hotel."

"That ain't a good idea, Ma'am," Billy murmured.

"Why not?" Cal asked, focusing trusting eyes on him.

"Lots of reasons," Billy replied, eyeing her strangely.

"Such as?" she continued this desperate talk which prevented any actions for the present. *What to do?* she fretted mentally. She had to get away from this leering man, but how? She wisely realized she musn't offend him. She must portray the distressed lady perfectly, and hopefully play on any chords of decency at the same time. Cal noticed her missing boots and jacket; worse, she was aware her shirt was opened to the cleft between her breasts. Obviously, Billy had discovered the money in her boot and shirt pocket, but what more did he want from her?

"Such as, that's a dangerous town for a lady alone. Such as, you ain't strong enough to ride that far. Such as, I don't want you to leave," he added the reason which struck terror into her heart.

"You needn't worry, Mister Billy, I'll be fine," Cal tried to sound light and brave. "My husband taught me how to shoot. I appreciate what you did for me. If you'll give me your address, I'll see you're paid for your trouble and kindness. Where's my gun?"

"Over there," he told her, pointing to where it lay near her saddle. "But you won't be needing it. I'll take care of you."

"That's nice of you, sir, but I'm feeling some better now. I should be heading out," she remarked, attempting to rise.

Billy warned, "Stay put," then placed his hand against her injured shoulder to push her down. Cal screamed in pain and went white. Billy came to full alert as she cradled her left arm and tears spilled forth. He confined her wrists in one hand and pulled the shirt aside to check her baffling action. She was inhaling raggedly; her eyes squeezed tightly as she endured the agony which knifed her body.

He stared at the astonishing area, then gaped at her tormented expression. "That's a gunshot," he stated in wonder.

"Get your hands off me," she commanded faintly, grimacing.

"People don't order Billy Bonnet around," he snapped at her. "What's your name?" he demanded forcefully.

"You arrogant brute! Leave me alone. Can't you see I'm hurt and sick?" she panted breathlessly.

"Don't pain me none," Billy retorted as if utterly insensitive.

"Please, Mister Bonnet," Cal entreated softly.

"Please, what?" Billy taunted, his mood becoming larkish.

"Please take your filthy hands off my wife before I put a slug in your miserable hide," Lynx warned icily from behind him. Billy the Kid! His blood ran cold. He'd need all his skill to get Cal safe this time.

Billy flung himself to his back, ready to snatch his gun from its holster. He halted that reflex as he eyed the barrels of two ivory-handled Colts pointing down at him. On the shirt pocket of this audacious man was a shiny Ranger star. On the towering man's face was an expression of coldness and determination.

"Lynx," the name slipped from Cal's dry lips as her astonished gaze glued to his stern face. Lynx didn't look at her, keeping his gaze glued on the pugnacious outlaw. She sensed the gravity of this moment and fell silent to avoid distracting him. Her heart surged with relief and love. Again, Lynx was at her side when danger struck; and this time, Cal knew positively he wasn't behind this new peril.

But how did he get that Ranger star? Had his friend Jones let him borrow it to help him out in just this kind of situation? No, she thought, he probably stole it and if it'll scare Billy I'm glad he did!

Billy insouciantly reclined on his back, propping up his lean torso with his flexed elbows. He grinned conceitedly. "Surely there's only one man with a crazy name like that," Billy murmured. "Didn't know you were a Ranger, Cardone. I ain't committed no crimes in Texas. What's your beef with me?"

"None today, Billy, if you release my wife," Lynx played along with Billy's deceptively genial mood.

Both men appeared to be complaisant and even-tempered, but were cunningly ready to spring into action. It was a ploy of the best gunmen; throw your opponent off with a slack body and placid manner. Each man was aware of the latent force behind the other.

Billy didn't fear any man, not even one behind a badge. Neither was afraid to die; but it was a part of life somewhere down the trail. He was acquainted with the reputation and might behind the man called Lynx Cardone. Billy never doubted he was faster than Lynx, but he pondered if this situation was worth the trouble. Having incompetent sheriffs after you was one thing, but enticing the Rangers to hotly and rashly pursue you was another. But who would know what happened out here? Unless he boasted of having Cardone's notch on his gun. But why kill a famous man if you couldn't take credit for it?

"How's the shoulder, love?" Lynx inquired, cunningly lacing his words with tenderness, revealing an emotion which was lethal to challenge. Yet, his pleasant gaze remained on the smiling Billy.

"Terrible. What took you so long to find me?" Cal asked, taking his unspoken clue and using it. "I fainted on the trail and Billy found me. Up to now he's been a perfect gentleman." She wondered if Lynx would use the same ploy on Billy which had worked on Clint, or was he planning to use that stolen Ranger badge to win this battle?

"You do have an infuriating way of getting into mischief, woman. When I get you home, I plan to tan the seat of your britches. Father's out of his mind with worry. We've got Rangers everywhere looking for you," Lynx gently scolded her. "You sure you're alright?"

Calinda played along with his deceit, amazed by the realization that they often communicated without words or with sly ones. Acting the contrite wife, she lowered her head and murmured, "I'm sorry, Lynx. If you'd stay home, I wouldn't get crazy and come looking for you."

"Is that a promise or a threat?" Lynx teased her, using their playful banter to mellow the wary outlaw.

"Both," she stated petulantly. Now that he was here with her, she wasn't afraid of anything, even confronting the past with him. She wondered if Lynx would get into legal trouble for posing as a Ranger.

"Well, Billy, do we call a truce and go our separate ways; or do we battle over my wife? You and I have no quarrel. I just want Cal."

Well aware of Lynx's reputation for fairness and extreme prowess, Billy mused on his decision. His gaze flickered over to the injured beauty. She was too pretty and spunky to die. And she would die if he killed her husband, for she would fight him to the death. Perhaps another day he would challenge this man to a duel. This wasn't the time or place, for his mind wasn't into killing either of them. The spark of love between them tugged strangely at his heart.

Calinda cringed in fear as she awaited the outlaw's choice of behavior. "Please, Billy, don't fight him. I don't want him to kill you any more than I want you to slay him. I love him and need him."

Lynx was moved by her words. "Can you ride, Cal?" he asked.

"I'm feeling better; I think so," she answered him.

"Take Star and ride out," Lynx commanded tenderly.

"What about you?" she worried anxiously.

"If Billy insists, we'll handle our business after you go. Leave now," he ordered again. "I'll bring your horse."

Calinda didn't move. She merely stared at her husband. He wanted her away safely, even at the cost of his own life. How could he make such a sacrifice if he didn't truly love her? She wanted to run into his arms and beg for his forgiveness. The dire circumstances prevented it. What if Lynx was killed or wounded?

"Move, Cal," he warned sternly. "I've had enough of your defiance. We wouldn't be here if you had stayed home where you belong."

"That won't be necessary, Cardone. You have my word you two can ride out together," Billy suddenly announced, grinning.

Lynx eyed him intently. His guns remained where they were and his gaze continued to study this imposing rival. Years of training and experience took command of his senses. Lynx had played similar scenes many times. Rarely had he misread a man's intentions or honesty. He smiled and nodded, slipping his Colts into their holsters, to her shock.

Calinda was frozen in mid-step. She couldn't believe what Lynx was doing. He was actually putting away his weapons and turning his back on this truculent man. He calmly saddled her horse and called her over. She couldn't budge, her lips parted and her eyes wide.

"Callie, let's go home," Lynx coaxed indulgently.

Calinda shook her head, then gaped at both men. "Billy gave his word; that's good enough for me. Let's ride, woman. I'm hot and tired and mean-spirited right now. I've been dogging you for days. If you ever pull another stunt like this, I'll thrash you soundly."

Lynx trusted this outlaw? What kind of western code of honor was this?

"Cal!" Lynx stormed, breaking her trancy state and propelling her forward with his potent tone.

Lynx helped her to her mount, then told her to head out before him. Confused and alarmed, Cal did as told and waited near the edge of the worn trail. Though it seemed hours, it was only minutes before he joined her. Unaware of holding her breath in tension, she slowly released it when he was beside her. She wondered what the two men had said to each other after her departure. She looked over at the thicket. Billy was leaning against a slender tree watching them, a wide grin on his nicely featured face. Billy waved to her, then chuckled before disappearing into the thicket.

"Lynx," she began softly, but was cut off instantly.

"Shut up and ride, woman, before Billy changes his mind. We'll talk later. Right now, I'm not in the mood to hear anything but hooves."

Stunned, she stared at him. Lynx slapped her horse's rump to send him running forward. Cal lurched in the saddle and caught her balance. She promptly reined up and snapped at him, "Don't you dare order me about! I don't care to talk to you now or later! You go your way and I'll go mine. But thanks for another of your timely rescues."

Lynx's attempt to give her strength through anger and fear backfired on him. "Woman, if you don't get moving, I'll spank you right here. I want some distance between us and Billy. Do you know who that man was?" he asked. He hastily enlightened her on the lethal and infamous Billy the Kid. "I trust him to keep his word for the moment. But I don't plan to give him time to change his mind. You damn fool, don't you realize how weak you are? We'll be doing good to make five miles without stopping. Not that it matters to you, but he's probably faster and better with a gun than I am. If you don't want to be returned to him, stop stalling with this foolishness or you just might find Billy again," he warned.

"You think he'll come after us?" she asked fearfully.

"Wouldn't surprise me none. Now, get moving before I lose my temper. Anything else you want to know can wait until later."

"Have you been home yet?" she asked in dread.

Lynx drilled his volatile gaze into her nervous one, suddenly and irrationally furious and impatient with her, harsh emotions born of tension and relief. "No, I didn't have time. Rankin met me at the train Tuesday. I've been after you since then."

"I see," she murmured, pondering his radical change in mood.

"No, Callie, you don't see anything yet. But you will," he vowed sullenly. Lynx seized her bridle and headed off at a gallop.

Calinda had no choice but to hang on tightly and to weather the storm before her.

Chapter 26

EXCEPT FOR THE INCESSANT POUNDING of the horses' hooves, Lynx and Cal rode in strained silence for a lengthy time, each trying to master their warring emotions. Following their initial brisk run to put distance between them and the notorious outlaw, Lynx set their rate of movement at a steadfast pace: inflexible, resolute, and indisputable. He rode slightly ahead of her, never glancing backwards.

Peeved by his harshness, Cal followed in rigid disquiet. A flurry of conflicting thoughts and emotions filled her. She knew he was serious about that criminal behind them. Yet, her fears had dissipated, allowing resentment and puzzlement to flood her mind. Lynx was behaving as if she were at terrible fault! He knew the truth, both sides, but was holding his tongue for now. *What will he say later when we stop? He's returning me to the ranch, but why? What don't I see?* She eagerly anticipated, yet dreaded, their imminent discussion.

Cal observed the assertive and moody man before her. In Billy's camp, Lynx had evinced a courage and cunning which amazed her. Did the man lack all traces of fear and hesitation? He was so dashing, intelligent, and daring. When he had joined her afterwards, she had absently noticed a quivering tic in his darkly stubbled jawline, the unnatural anxiety in his gaze, and the glacial edge to his stirring voice. Mingling with that novel tension, fury had danced wildly and brightly in his tawny eyes. Even now, his tightly leashed anger could be detected in his taut body as it swayed rhythmically with the motion of his mottled steed. His vexation was like a tangible object.

Lynx was dressed in that pitch-black again: snug shirt, pants, shiny boots, and felt hat. He wore a fiery red bandanna around his throat, a startling contrast to the inky attire. The color of it seemed to match his now leashed rage; it fluttered capriciously in the breeze which he was creating. His corded muscles were strained against the tight material of his shirt and pants. His skin was so bronzed by the sun that only his wheatish hair and red bandanna denied a satanic facade. Was that the intention of his ebony outfit, to intimidate, to charm?

Her gaze drifted down to the gunbelt around his firm waist, displaying a row of coppery colored bullets in small loops and flashing two weapons with creamy butts. From her angle, Cal noted the way the tooled leather holsters were securely strapped to his sinewy thighs to prevent interference when he needed to extract his guns quickly. What a mesmerizing vision of imposing looks and immense prowess.

Lynx rode as if a temporary appendage of his stallion, their traits seeming to blend and match. The splendid beast was eye-catching with its ebony mane, tail, and legs. Star's belly was a dull white, with small sooty splotches here and there; his rump was like midnight. His majestic head was charcoal, but for a large white patch beneath his dark mane. She assumed that marking had labeled him Star. He was sleek and fast, intelligent and loyal to his master. Uncannily, Star almost seemed human.

Cal wondered when they would cease this tiring journey and delve into his suspicious chicanery. If Billy wasn't trailing them, they must be two hours ahead of him. Dusk was gradually closing in on them with the disappearance of the sun. It must be around eight or nine o'clock by now. She had rested late this morning and napped this afternoon, but her energy and stamina were vanishing as the light.

Lynx had remarked on her weakness this afternoon, so he was aware of it. Why did he keep pushing her in this unfeeling and relentless matter? Was he trying to punish her, to lower her guard, to lessen his anger, to drain her fighting spirit? What pretext would he claim for his trickery? He was responsible for her problems and misconceptions, if they were misconceptions. He was responsible for alienating her and driving her away. The first move should be his, but she was reaching the point where she couldn't wait for it. She was exhausted; her injury pained her; she was hungry and thirsty; she needed some privacy.

When Cal observed a grove of trees to their right, she headed for it, shouting over her shoulder, "I'm stopping whether you do or not."

She nudged her horse to go in that direction. Astonishingly, he didn't argue, but trailed her. When she reached the stand of trees, she alighted and tied her reins to one. She headed for a deep ravine not far away and disappeared over the side. After she excused herself, she reluctantly and sluggishly rejoined him, sitting down beside a tree and leaning against it with her eyes closed.

Lynx noted the way she cradled her left arm and breathed deeply. She was pale, but rosy-cheeked. He heard her tummy growl softly. How did one open the type of conversation they needed to share? There was so much explanatory ground to cover, and she was in a sorry state to begin such a vital and taxing journey toward honesty and love.

Lynx retrieved his canteen and walked over to hunker down beside her. "Water?" he offered, holding the container out to her.

Cal opened her eyes and accepted it, drinking slowly, then moistening her lips. Returning it, she thanked him and relaxed against the tree trunk again. She had kept her gaze on the canteen, then lifted it to stare at the hovering tree above her. As if wary with him, she didn't speak. Her tummy signaled its craving once more. Her right hand caressed it lightly, as if trying to comfort it.

"I'll start a fire and get us something to eat. You rest," he stated matter-of-factly, standing to carry out his task.

Her leafy eyes shifted to his chest, settling on the silver star pinned to his pocket, a vivid contrast to the ebony shirt. "What are you doing with that Ranger badge?" she asked in a muffled tone. "Did you steal it or did Jones persuade you to join up with them? You won't be staying home?"

Lynx sank to one knee and propped his elbow on it, cupping his chin and fusing his fathomless gaze to her uneasy one. This was the perfect moment to correct one misconception. "I've been an undercover Ranger since I was twenty-two. Jones has been my commanding officer for two years; he's one of the few men who knows my secret identity. Before the Rangers, I was a detective for the railroad and a covert agent for the government. My little trips that riled you so much were missions for Jones and the Rangers. To protect lives and carry out critical assignments, I couldn't expose myself to anyone, not even the Rangers I worked with. Most thought I was a paid gunslinger, or I was helping out Ranger friends as favors. That's why I couldn't explain myself before now. I told Father the last time I was home, but I wanted to wait and tell you everything when my stay was permanent. I didn't want you worrying over my safety or accidentally dropping any clues which might endanger your life and mine or hinder my missions. I asked you to trust me, Cal, until I could explain things. After I testified against those two men I arrested, I resigned in Austin on Monday. They let me keep this badge for protection. With each mission, more people were learning or suspecting my position. It was hard to keep silent, love. I had to or lose any chance of success. That's why I was so upset about my pictures in the paper. I'm not an effective secret anymore."

"You've been a Ranger all this time?" she probed incredulously.

He brought her saddle over and dropped it on the ground. "Ever hear of the Unknown Ranger who leaves a star as his mark after each secret mission?" he inquired, watching her carefully.

Cal nodded. As with Clint, he demonstrated his enlightening point by forcefully striking his spur against the smooth leather of her saddle, leaving a star indention there. "Does that tell you anything, my mistrustful wife?" he ventured playfully. He withdrew a small and shiny star from his pants pocket and placed it in her palm. "That night I rescued you from Cole Stevens and his gang, I left one of those on the window sill. It was a rash move; that's why I was so antsy to get out of there. Getting the picture, Cal?"

She leaned forward, her trembling fingertip touching the tiny depression. She looked at the matching size in her damp palm, then stared at the silver spurs attached to his ebony boots. She let these clues and his words filter into her mind and settle there. As he hunkered down beside her and met her astonished gaze, she murmured, "You?"

"That's right, love, me. In case you've been wondering, I'm not a gunslinger or an outlaw. I've been on a mission every time I left home, not pursuing your father or crazy adventures, and certainly not luring my wife into danger just to play hero. That's also why I was always around or not far behind where there was trouble. To carry out my assignments, I had to get to know outlaws and suspicious characters and mingle with them to gain clues about past and future crimes. As long as no one knew who or what I was, I could come and go as I pleased; that made me valuable to the Rangers and the law. With my colorful reputation and secret identity, it was exciting and simple. At least it was until you walked on the scene. Since that night at the Red Satin Saloon, my life and guts have been turned inside-out by one infuriating and rebellious young lady."

"Your life?" she scoffed. "What about mine?"

"What about yours, Cal?" he probed in a mellow voice.

"Since the day I arrived out here, I've endured one violent episode after another. If anyone had told me what Texas was like, I would never have come. I would have wed one of those fops the Simsons shoved on me. I hate this place and these evil people!"

"Including me and the ranch?" he inquired lazily.

Her face grew scarlet and warm. She lowered her fiery gaze and squirmed nervously. "No," she bravely replied, her tummy pleading audibly as she made the stirring admission.

"Good," he casually remarked. "After we've eaten and rested, we'll settle our differences. It's past time you and I reach an understanding," he informed her mysteriously. "Relax, Callie. Believe it or not, but you're perfectly safe with me. Before I start the coffee and supper, I want you to know one thing which might expel some of that mistrust and fear. I know who's responsible for those strange letters and the shooting: it was Salina. She'll be arrested tomorrow."

"Salina?" she murmured pensively.

"I'll explain it all later, but I swear it was her. Neither Rankin nor I had anything to do with it. Why don't you lie down a while? How's the shoulder feeling?" he altered the subject for now.

"I ache all over, but it's not the worst aggravation at present. If I lie down, I'll probably fall asleep, and I'm starved."

"I can tell," he muttered in amusement. "When did you last eat?"

"Just a biscuit and water this morning," she confessed ruefully.

Lynx shook his tawny head and chided her, "If you're planning any future travel, you best learn how to prepare for it. I hope you've learned a valuable lesson with this dangerous mischief."

"I've learned quite a few valuable lessons lately," she purred cattily, frowning at him.

"School isn't over yet, Cal; it hasn't even begun," he hinted.

"It's about time to be educated on certain matters, don't you agree my devious husband?" she sullenly inquired.

His expression waxed serious. "All the time I've been dogging you, I've been praying it wasn't too late for that education. Is it?" he challenged, tensed in dread of her reply.

Following a pensive moment, she replied guardedly, "That depends on you, Lynx, and how you explain those matters."

She was bemused when he admitted freely, "I won't say it wasn't intentional, Cal. But I did have reasons."

"I'm sure you did. When I hear them, then I'll decide my course."

"Agreed," Lynx acquiesced. "Now, rest until supper's ready."

He spread out his sleeping roll and motioned for her to lie down. His tenderness and concern chewed at her irritation and bitterness, devouring them bite by bite. Cal stretched out and sighed in relief as her body thanked her for being kind to it. She yawned, then curled to her right side to watch him as he worked.

Every so often, Lynx would glance over at her and smile, as if making certain she was still there. When the coffee was ready, he poured a cup and brought it to her. Cal sat up, accepted it, thanked him, and began to sip it gingerly. Soon, fragrant odors wafted on the breezy currents of warm air.

Lynx had set a tin plate of fried bacon and steaming beans on the grass before her, cautioning, "Careful, they're hot." He took her cup and refilled it, adding sugar. He brought the cups over and set them on the ground, dropping a hunk of bread on her plate. Retrieving his own plate, he asked, "Mind if I sit this close?"

"After this service, of course not," she murmured merrily.

He took a seat beside her and worked on his supper. The beans and bread were easy to get down. But her sensitive stomach rebelled against the greasy bacon; even its smell repulsed her. As her tummy churned unexpectedly, Cal swallowed hard several times to combat her sudden nausea. She took a few sips of the coffee and inhaled in suspense, relieved when the sensation passed.

"You all right, Cal?" he asked, noticing her curious behavior.

"Just a little queasy. I guess because my stomach's so empty." She set down the plate and cup, resting her face between her hands.

"You don't look too good, woman. What's the problem?"

Her voice and hands were trembly. Her face had lost most of its color, leaving it chalky. "I'm just exhausted. My head's spinning and my ears are ringing."

He gently seized her shoulders and pressed her to the bedroll. He grabbed the canteen and yanked off his bandanna, wetting it and wiping the beads of moisture from her face. He examined the wound above her left breast, relieved it wasn't inflamed or infected. It appeared to be healing properly. He fretted over this curious state.

"Does it still hurt, Callie?" he asked apprehensively.

"A dull ache most of the time, but it rarely throbs anymore. I feel so awful, Lynx. So weak and shaky. How long will this last?"

Unless there was some internal problem, her condition had nothing to do with the gunshot. She had no fever. Was she merely worn out from lingering misery or assailed by intense stress?

"Why did you run off in this shape, woman?" he muttered.

"Because I was frightened and confused and miserable. I don't want your damned old ranch! After all this time, Lynx, didn't you two know me better than that?" she asked sadly, tears of tension escaping. Cal snuffed and wiped at the embarrassing droplets. "I hate cry babies! And I seem to be crying so much lately," she berated herself.

"I know, Salina told me," he unthinkingly remarked.

"I bet she told you lots of things which were none of her damn business!"

"I'm sorry she hurt you so many times, love. I didn't realize things were that bad between you two," he apologized.

"How could you know? You were never home! When I found your mother's portrait, she was delighted to tell me all about the treacherous Laura Cardone and my despicable father. I hate them both!" she cried, some of her spirit and strength returning as she reclined. "I hope I never lay eyes on either of them as long as I live."

"Which won't be long, Callie, if you don't take better care of yourself. When did Salina tell you about them? I wasn't aware she knew anything about the past."

"She was always spying on all of us. I tried to warn you two about her. But I was viewed as the outsider, the troublemaker. She told me a week or so after you rescued me from Stevens. Then she relished pointing out your pictures at Round Rock. No doubt she knew everything and was savoring the slow release of her facts."

"Why didn't you tell us what she was doing to you?"

"Ha!" she sneered sarcastically. "Do you recall how you acted when I accused her of being behind that fall I took? I know that girth was secure. Either she did it or Manuel did at her request."

"But why would she do such things?" he entreated craftily as the truth of her torments came to light, wanting her to solve the riddle.

"She told me when I arrived that you were hers. I told you she threatened me with a knife if I got near you. If she isn't in love with you, she wants you desperately. She's dangerous and wicked."

"Not anymore," he informed her, relating the confrontation with Clint and Salina.

"My God, Lynx," she said softly. "I wouldn't wish a man like Deavers on anyone, even her."

Lynx went on to explain his knowledge and theories about Lampasas and the letters. He told her how he had discovered where Cole was imprisoning her. He revealed who the "B" was in that telegram which she found beneath the bed. He repeated how he had come into possession of her stolen locket and why he had concealed it from her. He expounded on his Ranger career and last few missions.

"I never lied to you, Callie. But I'll confess I allowed you to misread certain events and people. I worded sentences to keep you in the dark. I didn't clarify misconceptions you had. I disarmed you with love. But I did it so you wouldn't be hurt anymore. I loved and respected your father deeply. You can't imagine how he hurt me. As for my mother, I'll never accept or understand what she did to me and father," he vowed bitterly.

He was seated beside her, his left hip touching hers as he gazed down at her, his palms flat on the ground on either side of her body. "Don't you see why I couldn't reveal their treachery and betrayal? God, Callie, it knifed me up every time I heard or spoke their names. We didn't even know about the baby until we saw that letter you concealed. I don't know who lied, but Rankin assures me it's my half sister or brother."

"It's been so many torturous years, Lynx. They're gone for good, no matter whose child it is. Why can't their malicious hold over all of us be broken?" she sobbed.

"For us, Callie, it can, if we're willing to allow it. But for my father, it isn't that simple. He loved Mother and trusted her. He would have given his life for your father. If it were your child, could you forget about it? If it was the person you loved more than life itself, could you accept the betrayal and loss?" he reasoned sadly.

"I wish Brax had never written that letter," she murmured.

"At least we know why they ran," he debated her words.

"How could something like that happen? To betray and sacrifice your husband and child for a man like my father?" she scoffed.

"You never knew him, Callie. One day soon, I'll tell you about Brax and those early days when we were all a happy family."

"Why did you marry me, Lynx?" she asked helplessly.

"We've talked enough tonight, Callie. You need to sleep and recover. I promise we'll discuss the rest tomorrow. I can't let you walk out of my life. If you force me to hold you a prisoner at the ranch, I will," he told her gravely.

"But you have full control of the ranch now. What more do you want from me?" she panted in exasperation and anguish.

"Damn the ranch and that blasted deed! I love you and need you, woman. If you don't believe that, we don't stand a chance."

"You don't have to shout at me," she reprimanded him.

"Don't I? You take off and nearly get yourself raped and killed, and I shouldn't be furious with you? When I met up with Deavers and Salina on the Jacksboro Road, I nearly went crazy with fear. I swear to you, Callie Cardone; if you ever step foot off that ranch again without my permission or knowledge, I'll hunt you down and lock you in your room! As to the ranch, I'll sign half of it over to you the first chance I get. That should prove I didn't marry you to take control."

"But why didn't you say anything about it?" she pressed.

"At first, we didn't trust you. Now that you know the truth, can you blame us? I was pressed for time when I found you in Lampasas. I married you because I love you and wanted to keep you home safe. I told you I would reveal everything soon. I guess I was waiting for us to get to know each other better. When I realized you were truly in love with me, I panicked. I couldn't risk exposing my deceit until I was home to deal with your reaction. Then when you were shot and suspecting me, I tried to prove how much I loved you and wanted you. When that matter came up in Dallas, I knew how you would take that news. Then word came about the trial in Austin. I figured you needed time to fully recover. And I needed to learn everything Yancey had told you, in case some of it was lies. I swear I was going to spill everything the moment I got home. I saw those letters from Brax, and they had me plenty worried. I caught your little clues and enticements to confess, but I didn't know you had the deed. I felt you weren't in any condition to be jolted with the past. I'm sorry, love; I honestly didn't mean to hurt you or deceive you. I can't lose you, Callie; I love you with all my heart and soul." He waited anxiously for those words to sink into her mind.

In her gut and heart, Calinda knew he was being totally honest. In a way, her own deceptions had blocked the truth. As these revelations settled in, she remained quiet and thoughtful.

"Callie? Do you believe me?" he asked hoarsely.

She looked him in the eye and murmured, "Yes."

A whoop of joy and relief rent the air. A broad smile claimed his lips. "You'll come home with me? You won't leave again?"

"Yes. No," she cheerfully replied, smiling up at him.

He fell to his back on the grass, sighing loudly. She rolled to her side and asked, "May I go to sleep now? I'm beat."

"Sleep as long as you wish, love. I'll be right here," he stated, patting the ground as his gaze caressed her.

"How about if you be right here?" she retorted, patting the bedroll, eyes heaped with smoldering embers of desire.

"In your condition, just for protection and sleep," he teased, warming to the fires in her green eyes.

She laughed and pouted, "For tonight."

"Think I can move back into our room when we get home?"

"If you don't, I'll hunt you down and hold you prisoner," she jested, laughing happily and honestly for the first time lately.

"I'm already your prisoner, Callie," he told her huskily.

"And I, yours, my love," she seductively responded.

"No more secrets, Callie; I swear it," he promised sincerely.

Cal leaned over and kissed him, provocatively and sweetly. Lynx gingerly pulled her into his embrace. They snuggled together on the bedroll as she relented to the strong callings of slumber. He watched her for a time, then closed his eyes.

They rode for two days, halting frequently to relent to her need for rest and to master her dizziness and nausea during the mornings. When they camped that second night near a river, she bathed and splashed joyfully as she refreshed her body and spirits. When she grew queasy at dinner, Lynx studied her closely. He hadn't noticed any change in her figure when they made love, but he suddenly recalled how sensitive her breasts had been.

Striking as swiftly and unexpectedly as a lightning bolt, a suspicion jolted him.

Lynx eyed her intensely. She was relaxing on the bedroll in a lively mood. He sat down beside her and asked, "Cal, is there something you haven't told me?"

Baffled, she met his piercing gaze. "Such as?" she hinted.

"This illness of yours, tell me about it," he coaxed.

Naive, Cal related all of the symptoms which had been plaguing her of late, excluding one which she had failed to notice. "When's the last time you . . . you . . ." he faltered as he tried to select the appropriate word to use in her presence.

"When I what, Lynx?" she pressed in bewilderment.

"When you did what all women do every month?" he stated, actually blushing in modesty. "Are you pregnant?" he asked abruptly.

"Pre . . . pregnant?" Cal stammered in astonishment. Her mind went to whirling with that added clue. "Am I?" she asked him.

Lynx chuckled. "You do have all the signs. Right?" he teased as she reasoned on his assessment. "When was the last time, Cal?"

"Before I was kidnapped," she told him shyly.

"That doesn't pin down any date, love. Since we were married?" Lynx aided her deliberation.

"I didn't marry you because I was carrying your child," she informed him, if that was his implication.

"It doesn't matter. If you were, it was my doing," he jested.

"The last time was three days after our wedding. Since then, I haven't . . . I suppose it happened after you rescued me from Stevens."

"From your symptoms and our timing, that should make it about two months into blooming," he concluded, patting her flat abdomen.

"Are you angry?" she fretted anxiously.

"To be expecting a son or a daughter from my beautiful wife? Never, love. Our first baby, imagine that?" he stated at the pleasing wonder of it. Chills suddenly washed over him. "Are you sure you're all right?" he queried.

"I suppose I'm normal, if your judgment is accurate."

"I mean about the shooting and all the pressures you've been through lately? You were pregnant during that fall. I could kick myself for endangering you and our baby like that," he criticized himself.

With this discovery, she felt better immediately. She wasn't sick or dying; she was carrying her love's child, their child. She lovingly caressed the area which would soon expand and tell everyone. "Our baby," she murmured in ecstasy.

He looked at her, fierce love and pride storming his body. He captured her face between his hands to engulf the radiance there. "I love you, Callie. I promise everything will be fine now."

"I know, my love," she quickly and joyously agreed. "Our baby," she stated again, giggling softly. "There's so much I'll need to learn. Heavens, Lynx, I don't know anything about babies or having them," she vowed, suddenly apprehensive and insecure.

"That makes two of us, but we'll learn together."

A bright and serene smile greeted him as she said, "Yes, we'll learn together. I love you, you arrogant and mysterious rogue. You with your sneaky silver spurs," she jested, playfully striking one with her finger and watching the tiny stars fly round and round, glittering in the moonlight. "A golden stranger in magical black," she teased.

"Never would I have believed I would marry a girl I met in the Red Satin Saloon, lying seductively in my bed in that sleazy red and black gown. You can't imagine the contrast in my first thoughts and feelings compared to them right this minute."

"Knowing you, Lynx Cardone, I can well imagine," she stated.

"Good thing I didn't toss you out of my room that night. Then some other man would be experiencing this special moment."

"Fate, my love, that guardian angel you mentioned. After I met you, mean and lecherous though you were, I could think of no man but Cody Richards," she murmured dreamily.

"What?" he shrieked.

"As you recall, that's the name I was given for my late caller, that mysterious drifter in devilish black with hair and eyes of gold."

"I owe fate a large debt for withholding my identity until we could meet again. Hearing it at the ranch, you would have surely fled."

"Maybe not," she whispered softly, revealing her ruse that night.

They both laughed as they reflected on their first meeting at the ranch. "You think you can stay home and take care of your greedy husband and child? Or should I use this spur to place my mark of warning and ownership on a lady who carelessly wears red satin?"

They exchanged playful looks and laughed. Calinda softly parried, "I'll make you a bargain, my love; you hang up those silver spurs and I'll promise to never wear red satin or visit another saloon. Besides, my fierce and cunning Lynx, your ownership is much too vivid as it is, or soon will be," she insinuated, tapping her abdomen.

Impassioned, he murmured seductively into her ear, "I love you, *Llama de me corazon, mi alma, mi mente, mi vida* . . ." Catching his slip and knowing why she had once rebelled at that endearment from her father's letter, he leaned back and apologized, "I'm sorry, love; I forgot. But I never knew Brax called Mother that."

She smiled provocatively and replied, "Honestly, it doesn't matter anymore. But I would like to know what you're saying. Perhaps I should have lessons in Spanish? When my other education is completed, if ever," she speculated mirthfully.

Lynx tenderly grasped her face between his strong and gentle hands, whispering huskily, "I love you, flame of my heart, my soul, my mind, my life . . ."

Her rapturous gaze devoured his compelling features. "*Yo te quiero, mi amante;* that's all the Spanish you taught me."

"That's more than enough, Callie Cardone." His lips covered hers as they sank entwined on his bedroll, the musical sounds of a lovely September night offering serenity to their passionate lovemaking beneath the Texas moonlight.

—— *Epilogue* ——

ON THE PROSPEROUS CARDONE RANCH, it was late spring of 1881. In March of '79, Calinda Braxton Cardone had given birth to a son. The child had been named Travis Cardone, in memory of Colonel William Barrett Travis who had commanded the ill-fated and heroic stand by the Texas Rangers at the Alamo. Except for Lynx's silver spurs and badge in a drawer, the name Travis was his only link to past days with that dauntless force. Also keeping her promise, Calinda had never worn Laura's red satin gown again.

Following Lynx's last rescue of his wife and their return home, the ensuing months had been peaceful for the Cardones. Manuel, Salina, and Clint Deavers had been arrested for their crimes. Their names were never mentioned again on the ranch.

To Calinda's relief and joy, not once since his retirement from the Rangers had Lynx appeared restive or discontent. He seemed too busy with the ranch, his adoring wife, and growing son to have time or energy to desire anything other than what he proudly possessed. Neither had thought it possible, but their love and passion had increased with time. Even Rankin had been snared by love; he had been seeing Eliza Adams, a lovely widow from a nearby ranch, for over eleven months.

At two, Travis was a happy and active child. He was bright, daring, and confident. Mischievous and determined, Calinda was constantly chasing after her small son to keep him out of danger. Travis was frequently seen riding with his parents or keenly witnessing the exciting facets of ranch-life. Even though he was so young and small, Travis Cardone thought nothing of climbing the ladder into the stable loft, or sneaking under the corral fence to get closer to the horses, or unwisely testing the heat of a branding iron out of curiosity, or showing his strength by "helping" with chores.

Often when Travis attempted something too difficult or perilous, Calinda would sigh and shake her head, playfully warning her husband, "Merciful Heavens, Lynx, he's as daring and stubborn as you. But he's also as handsome and smart. His skin's as bronze as yours and his hair is just as tawny. I hate to imagine how many hearts he'll break."

Lynx would chuckle and retort, "But he had your mysterious and expressive green eyes, *mi corazon*. I must confess, he is a handsome and roguish devil already."

"I do wish you'd stop filling his head with all those tales of Rangers and their colorful exploits. If not, he'll join up the moment he's of age. Do you regret leaving the force? Do you miss it?"

Lynx would gaze into her lovely and entreating face to declare honestly, "Never, *llama de mi corazon.*"

Only once, three months ago, had Lynx left home without Calinda. As the dark secrets of the past had unfolded, they had been conquered by their love and serenity. Unexpectedly, a letter had arrived from California, a stunning letter which demanded attention and action. Both Rankin and Lynx had journeyed to San Francisco to sever the last remaining tie to their turbulent past.

In California, a startling tale had awaited the two Cardone men on a windy and chilly March day in '81. Upon arrival, the two men learned that Laura Cardone had died in childbirth in February, alone and probably terrified. As merciful fate would have it, the ailing child had not survived. According to local authorities, Elliott Braxton had vanished six months earlier, proclaimed dead at the hands of hostile Indians in Colorado where he was supposedly checking out a silver claim he'd purchased.

Letters found in Laura's and Elliott's possessions had exposed their ties to the Cardone family in Texas; thus, Rankin and Lynx had been notified of the three deaths and a lingering problem: Carlotta Braxton, eight years old . . .

Laura's body was returned to the Cardone Ranch, to finally and perhaps fatefully occupy that grave on the hillside. While Rankin was discovering and claiming his lost daughter and Lynx was meeting and seeing his sister for the first time, Travis Cardone was celebrating his second birthday, without his father or grandfather . . .

There was no doubt Carlotta "Lottie" Braxton was the daughter of Laura and Rankin. Lottie's hair was as black and shiny as coal; her large eyes were as dark as midnight. An undeniable resemblance to Rankin was stamped on the girl's face. Almost immediately upon returning, Lottie had been officially declared Carlotta Cardone, another heir to this vast and opulent empire.

It hadn't taken long for Calinda to notice several dismaying and saddening facets to this curious child. For the tender age of eight, Lottie was exceptionally mature and disturbingly withdrawn. Calinda realized the girl was slightly spoiled and willful. Lottie had given both Calinda and Travis a difficult time after her arrival. To make matters worse, Rankin overly indulged and excused the audacious child, seeking to make up for her suffering.

Calinda decided she would become just as beguiling as Lottie, to win her affections and trust. Only then could she effect any changes in Lottie. Surely a grown woman could outwit a defiant child? Perhaps Lottie's behavior was defensive. Perhaps Lottie needed correction and instructions. Perhaps Lottie wasn't to blame for her offensive traits and actions.

With time, effort, affection, and patience, Calinda made tremendous progress with the little minx. As time passed, Lottie began viewing Calinda as her big sister. Before summer ended, peace and love ruled on the Cardone Ranch, and the past was dead forever.

When Eliza Adams finally won Lottie's affection and trust, the romance between her and Rankin flourished, The timing was perfect for Calinda to encourage

Lynx to build that dream-house on the bluff not far away, the one they had discussed and planned for so long.

With Eliza and Lottie in Rankin's heart and future, perhaps that was a perfect solution for all. They would be close, but not too close.

When Calinda seriously broached the subject of the new house, Lynx was very receptive to the idea. Rankin had been hinting strongly at a new family of his own. Plus, Lynx was noticing some changes in his beloved's body which boldly hinted at another child, and Lynx was eager to point them out to her. Another child with his only love, his first love, his wild and wonderful love . . .

Sweet Savage Heart

For:

Kay Garteiser, a dear friend who has such a special and supportive
"romantic spirit;"

Virginia Brown, my very good friend and a superb writer;

Virginia Driving Hawk Sneeve, from whom I've learned so much about the
Sioux chiefs and the inspiring Dakota Nation.

Raised on the Plains with a spirit just as wild,
Lives an Indian princess half woman, half child.
On her wits and courage she was taught to depend,
Now, to the whiteman's way, she is forced to bend.
Will it be justice or only a selfish game?
Who will step forth her wild heart to tame?
Indian is her heart, but white is her skin;
Is there a way for her two facets to blend?
Once free as the air, is this deed right or wrong?
Blithe child of nature, now where does she belong?
When fate opens a new path, where will it end?
For who has the power to tame a wild wind?

Chapter 1

IT WAS A BUSY TIME of year with the spring buffalo hunt and the constant flood of whites onto the ancestral lands of the Sioux. It was a time of great peril and many changes—for the Oglala tribes in the Lakota branch of the Dakota Nation and for a white girl who had lived for ten years as the daughter of Chief Soaring Hawk of the Red Arrow Band. Sadly, tragically, Soaring Hawk had been slain; the band was now ruled by his son, Lone Wolf. Indeed, times were rapidly and painfully altering for the flaming-haired, blue-eyed girl who was trapped between two warring cultures and who seemingly belonged to neither world. But she desperately wanted to find inner peace and the answers to the mysteries and influences that controlled her life and continuously plagued her mind and daily existence during these troubled times. The North/South war had ended and the whites had turned eyes of conquest toward the west; now an ominous conflict was brewing in these lands and another one was brewing within the heart and life of Wild Wind.

The warrior Buffalo Slayer urged his horse toward the mottled stallion that carried their new chief, Lone Wolf. The younger brave informed the stalwart warrior of the inquisitive "wild wind" who was rapidly blowing down their backs. The seasoned warrior glanced over his bare shoulder, frowned in vexation, and told his braves to continue toward their meeting point with other Oglala and Hunkpapa hunting parties while he halted to order his adopted sister back to camp. The warriors and braves were amused by the willful but beautiful Indian princess who would have gladly performed the Sun Dance to become a warrior. Many in this group had been rejected by her, but in such a way as to inspire more hunger rather than resentment or discouragement.

Lone Wolf dismounted and tied his reins to a bush. He fretted over *Watogla Tate's* ceaseless streak of defiance, her impulsive ways, her annoying independence, her refusal to obey his commands. She wanted to race the wind on her white stallion, which only she could mount and master. She wanted to perform the duties and practices of warriors—to hunt, track, raid with his band, and sit in the ceremonial lodge and be a part of the talks and votes. She still wanted to shadow him as she had since becoming his sister ten winters ago. It was time she realized they were no longer children, he mused in annoyance. It was too late to change past years, when he and his recently deceased father, Soaring Hawk, had allowed her to do as she pleased and had actually enjoyed and boasted of her immense skills. How foolish that had been.

He asked himself if it mattered that she could ride and fight better than many braves. Did it matter that her lance or arrow never missed its mark? Did it matter that she could swim as skillfully as the otter? Did it matter that she could track a disguised or aged trail? She was a female! He had been chief one full moon. His band and others were observing his leadership and prowess. If he could not properly control his own tepee, they would look upon him unfavorably.

He knew he must convince her that a woman cannot change her sex, or her role in life; such things are controlled and decided by the Great Spirit.

Lone Wolf reluctantly admitted that he and his father had been too lenient with *Watogla Tate*. During the past year, his father had been too weak from a soldier's bullet—it was this viciously consuming wound that had finally claimed Soaring Hawk's life—to battle this headstrong creature who had been thrust into their lives long ago and had been accepted by them at the direct command of the Great Spirit, *Wakantanka;* and he, Lone Wolf, had been too ensnared by his responsibilities, his love for her, and his many adventures to realize what was happening to his cherished white sister. But now, with Soaring Hawk gone, it was up to him to discipline and train her.

Yet the constant verbal fights they waged were wearing thin on the warrior, for he had more vital matters to consider and handle. Feeding and protecting his people and guarding his sacred lands against white conquest weighed heavily in his mind and heart. These days she provoked his anger faster and caused it to run deeper. Others were teasing both him and her. During these perilous times, he needed the full respect and support of his band and their Lakota brothers. He could allow no mark of weakness or ridicule to stain his face or threaten his leadership and the Lakotas' survival. His sister had left him no choice; she would have to be forced to obey his orders!

Lone Wolf wondered how he could reach her, how he could stop these foolish dreams of hers. He hated to force her into a marriage to settle their war of words and wills, but he must, or all that he knew and was could be in peril. The hostilities with the white man were increasing; he needed the total confidence and loyalty of his people. Her misbehavior was casting bad shadows over both of them. She was closing off all paths to escape, except one. Countless braves and warriors from their tribe and other tribes desired her. She had spurned each one. Soon she would have to marry and begin her own family. Perhaps a mate and children would tame her wild spirit.

Lone Wolf stood tall and alert as he awaited his audacious sister. She had become aware that her presence had been discovered and she had ceased her stealthy approach. He was glad he had told Buffalo Slayer to guard their backs, for now he could force her home before their Lakota brothers discovered her embarrassing defiance.

Her hair was unbraided, and the wavy mane swirled and tangled in the breeze she created with her fast pace. As the locks whipped wildly in the wind, they seized the sun's rays and reflected its fiery glow. If she had not been his sister, he might have been stimulated by the shapely legs, revealed by her raised skirt, as they deftly gripped the horse's sleek body. His sister was slender, but firm and nimble. She could move as rapidly and agilely as a bee but appear as lovely and delicate as the flower upon which it landed. Although her flesh was nearly as tanned as most Indians, it was a different shade, a color that favored newborn colts in early spring. He envisioned her compelling winter-sky eyes, no doubt filled with determination and eagerness. Truly she was a beautiful and body-stirring creature, though one who had refused to use such magic to lure a mate.

The girl's shapley body grew larger against the horizon as she closed the remaining distance between them. Lone Wolf worried over her conduct and his necessary response to it. He wondered if it was her white blood that was causing the unrest and rebellion within her. After all, *Watogla Tate* was his adopted sister; she was all white. She had once been a captive of the fierce Kiowas, until his brave father had attacked their camp after they had encroached on Oglala lands. He had won many *coups* by stealing weapons and horses and by taking many captives. This white girl had been nearly eight winters old then, and a sacred vision had commanded Soaring Hawk to adopt her.

Lone Wolf could close his dark eyes and recall the pathetic creature whom his father had brought into their tepee after that raid. She had been so dirty and afraid, too scared to talk or move or cry. There had been bruises and scratches on her skinny body and tangled knots in her filthy hair. Her grimy dress had been torn in several places, but thankfully she had not shown any feminine traits at that early age. Those gray-blue eyes had appeared so large and so full of terror and sadness. She had been a slave to the Kiowa chief's second wife, and she had been intimidated and abused by the hateful woman in this demeaning position. To reflect upon such cruel treatment of an innocent and helpless child evoked new anger in him against his enemies, the Kiowas. Silently he raged. A small child should never be treated as an enemy!

The day Soaring Hawk had returned from that raid, the Great Spirit had spoken to him through a vision, telling him to take that captive child into his tepee as his daughter and to name her *Watogla Tate,* Wild Wind, for Soaring Hawk had won his victory and her capture during a violent wind storm: it was a name well suited to the girl, who could behave just as unpredictably as a wild wind. From that moon to this one, the white girl with flaming hair had lived with them. How she had changed during the past years! he reflected now.

Wild Wind had learned to protect herself, physically and emotionally. She had worked on defensive skills and had sharpened her senses as if her very life had depended on them. She had once confessed to him that she would never allow anyone or anything to hurt her again. Perhaps that persistence and determination and the motives behind them were the reasons why he had assisted her in her training, training that had done as much damage as good for her as well as him. Many times he had dreamed that her destiny did not lie with his people. Many times he had dreamed of her leaving their camp to travel a long and dangerous path, a path that led to the destiny she had been born to live. For years he had been preparing her to face and conquer that perilous challenge. But with her practiced skills and honed instincts had come the belief that she was as effective and as proficient as any male warrior. And, he vexingly confessed to himself, perhaps she was. Yet she had become an Indian maiden and would have to exist as one.

For many years they had not spoken of the deaths of her white family or her abuse at the Kiowas' hands. Perhaps with a wounded mind, the injuries to body and spirit were suppressed, as her white childhood had been. Perhaps secret resentment against her Kiowa captors was inspiring her to refuse marriage to any Indian. Maybe deep inside she did not feel as if she belonged here. Perhaps she was training and waiting for the Great Spirit to return her feet to her destined path. If outsiders had not continued to mention her white skin and blood, it would have been forgotten by her, his people, and their Lakota brothers. But the more they endured this vicious war with the whites, the more her white skin, blue-gray eyes, fiery hair, defiant ways, and high rank were noticed and scorned by his and other bands. Too many saw a white enemy in a place of honor in the Oglala camp, not Soaring Hawk's daughter or Lone Wolf's sister. It was a tormenting situation, which needed a swift and acceptable resolution.

No matter what his sister did or said, he knew she had a tender and caring spirit. She was as lively as a muskrat. She was as gentle as a doe. Her smile could be as warming as the sun and her laughter as musical as a watery cascade. Sadly, Wild Wind rarely let such special traits show, as if exposing them would endanger her hard covering and bring about more anguish.

The Indian princess now pulled on the reins to halt her stallion. She tossed her leg over his back and gracefully dismounted. It did not require keen eyes or a sharp mind to detect the change in her brother's attitude today. Quivers of uneasiness teased over her body and a knife of cold reality stabbed into her racing heart. The fact that Lone Wolf had reached his limits in patience and tolerance was exposed boldly in his ominous gaze and rigid stance. He did not smile or relax as she joined him. She was alarmed by the resolve and barely leashed anger that she read in his expression, though fear was something she detested in herself and in others. It was as if she were trapped upon a landslide, and she sensed there was no way she could halt her movements or prevent her injuries.

She wondered why she felt an outsider with the people who had rescued her, adopted her, and raised her as one of their own. She could not comprehend why she seemed so restless. Even if she did not think and behave like the other women, this was the only life she knew; yet she could not accept her designated role in it. There was an unknown hunger that ate at her heart and mind daily and denied her peace and forced her to disobey. It was as if an uncontrollable force was pushing her toward a vital challenge that continued to elude her. *Help me, Great Spirit,* she prayed. *Help me understand who I am a seeking. Help me find my rightful place. Help my brother and our people understand and accept why I cannot be as they desire me to be.*

Exasperated, Lone Wolf decided to take a rash but stern path with his sister. "*Tokiya la hwo? Takca yacin hwo?*" he queried, tersely asking her where she was going and what she wanted. Before Wild Wind could respond, Lone Wolf scolded to embarrass her, "Why does my sister race after warriors as a fool without honor and wits? Anger fills my heart and head, *Watogla Tate.* Have you no pride, no shame, no sense of duty and loyalty? Do you not see how you are destroying my love and respect for you? Do you not see you are stealing the peace in our tepee? Does it mean nothing that you are staining my honor and rank? Do you think only of Wild Wind and her desires? You—"

"I want to observe your first talk with the Hunkpapas as our chief. Pride fills my heart and excitement clouds my head. I will stay hidden, my brother. It is a great day for us. Please, let me—"

"*Inila!*" Lone Wolf harshly ordered her to silence, rebuking, "Do not cut into the words of a warrior, your chief! Have you learned nothing of our customs and laws since living with us for so many winters? You defy our ways and bring dishonor to your family. I can allow no more disobedience," he warned coldly. "You bring shame to the tepee of Chief Lone Wolf and to our band of Oglalas. You shame Wild Wind. We made you the daughter of our chief and the sister of Lone Wolf. We loved you and protected you. Why have you dishonored and pained us? You cause my warriors and others to laugh at me. How can warriors ride behind a fool? How can they follow the commands of one who cannot control his own tepee? Your disobedience and dark pride prove that there is no Indian heart within a body without Indian blood. Each moon you become more white than Oglala. It brings sadness and anger to my heart to view such evil within my chosen sister."

Wild Wind was stunned momentarily by his vehemence and incisive words. He had become annoyed with her of late, but never had he spoken in such a manner or behaved so coldly toward her. Something was terribly wrong today. Though she was one who normally could control her expressions and reactions, she helplessly paled beneath the golden glow of her silky flesh. Eyeing him intently, she asked, "Why do you speak such cruel words to your sister, Lone Wolf? I have lived by your side for many winters, and I wish to be like you. Can you deny that I am as trained and skilled as your best warrior? Why must I waste such skills and prowess when my people are in danger of being no more? When I see wrongs, where is there honor and bravery in remaining silent? What excitement and courage is involved in gathering herbs and wild vegetables, or putting up a tepee and taking it down, or rubbing foul brains into a hide to cure it, or cooking meals and serving men like a slave? Such acts require no skill or wits. They can be done by old women or young girls, or by our captives. They can be done asleep!" she shouted at him in an unusual display of anger. "I do not want to be enslaved by a tepee, by a woman's boring life. I want to feel the sun and wind upon my body. I want to feast on danger and freedom as you do. I want to put my skills against fate's powers. I wish to be a warrior, not a helpless woman! Let me help our people."

Lone Wolf shook his head in mounting frustration. "You are a female, Wild Wind. You are the most beautiful creature alive. Why do you make yourself ugly with shame and defiance? If you love me and honor me, find a worthy warrior and join him. Be as you are, my sister, a woman of great value and pride and courage," he urged.

"You wish me to marry and leave our tepee? You wish me to be miserable? You wish me to let our people suffer and die because the pride of warriors will not allow women to join them in battle? I must not! I cannot!" she blatantly refused, her eyes sparkling with fury.

"You are eighteen winters old, a woman. It is time to accept your place as Grandfather willed it. Do not force me to—" At her wounded expression, he halted briefly. He was softening, and he could not permit that to happen if he wanted to win this battle.

"Force you to do what, my brother?" she quickly demanded, her heart pounding in trepidation.

Lone Wolf breathed deeply, wearily. "I am your brother and chief, and I must be obeyed. If you do not cease your childish and rash behavior, I will be forced to punish you before the entire tribe. Then you will feel the shame that you bring to me and my camp. If you do not find a mate before the Sun Dance, I will choose one for you and have you joined after the ceremony. I have spoken."

Wild Wind could not believe what she was hearing. "You would not do such brutal things to your sister!" she debated fearfully, for she perceived the danger and seriousness in this threat from him.

"You are my sister only as long as you behave as my sister. For many moons you have behaved as white. If you are my sister and you are Indian at heart, you will obey the laws and ways of our people," he shockingly informed her, his voice clear and crisp and intimidating.

"Father would not wish you to hurt me and punish me this way. It is wrong, my brother," she argued frantically, though she knew Lone Wolf saw the situation from a completely different viewpoint. She had been raised by the Oglalas and she knew their customs and ways; yet something strange and powerful was pushing her away from them and was preventing her from sealing her life with them. If only she could understand and explain what was influencing her thoughts and actions, she reflected miserably.

"Father is with the Great Spirit, Wild Wind. He was too weak to battle you. If love and respect lived in your heart and head, you would not shame and hurt your brother and people. Do you wish to make us regret you are Soaring Hawk's daughter? Is there hatred and bitterness hiding within you toward all Indians? Do you seek to punish all with red skin for the cruelty of our enemies? In the past three winters, you have become more white than Indian. I fear such changes will bring much trouble to our camp and to those of our Lakota brothers. There is a powerful force that is driving you from us."

"You words are not true, Lone Wolf!" she shrieked in dismay. She licked her suddenly dry lips and tried to slow her racing heart. "I love you and loved our father. I would do nothing to hurt you or our people."

"Your words do not match your actions, my sister," he replied, refuting her frantic claims. "There is no deeper wound than dishonor. You know the way of my people: it is better to die in honor than to live in shame. If you are truly Oglala, become one with us in all ways."

"Do you say that the only way to prove my love and loyalty is to marry a man I do not love or want? Must I deny all I am and feel just to prove I am your sister and the daughter of Soaring Hawk? If you loved me as I love you, brother, you would not wish such an empty and cruel life upon me. Perhaps I have acted too boldly and recklessly, but it was to seize your attention and to earn the right to defend our lands and people. If I cannot live in peace and love in our tepee, then I will leave our camp and your life," she warned him.

She expected him to relent slightly. Instead, he responded, "Perhaps that would be best for all, Wild Wind. Your will was too strong for Father to master, and it pained him to watch your arrogance and rebellion grow as swiftly as the spring grasses. I cannot reach you. Soon, I will be forced to put my people first. I cannot allow you to darken my honor and rank. I cannot waste time and strength correcting or punishing you each sun. Think on Rides-Like-Thunder of the Cheyenne as a mate. He is a great warrior with many *coups*. By all females he is called handsome, and he has many skills upon the sleeping mat."

Her cheeks grew as fiery as her hair at his last remark and her gray-blue eyes widened with astonishment. He continued slowly and confidently, "It is time for my Cheyenne brother to have his own tepee. He has many horses and skins to trade for a wife. He is strong and brave; he can protect his family from all evil. In his camp, you will forget your foolish ways and words. He has spoken with me about you. He wishes to join soon. I say we accept his offer. Do you agree?"

Anguish and panic ruled her senses. "You despise my white blood so much that you would send me to another camp, to a stranger, to become his slave by the joining law?" she inquired anxiously. Tremors assailed her body as she observed his resolve. Normally she would have battled him with obstinate words and actions, but she knew he was gravely serious. She dared not push him today.

"Many warriors have asked for you as their mate; each day the offers for you grow larger. Black Hawk and Prairie Dog have asked to approach you. No maiden has received such great offers of trading. The other women grow jealous and angry. You must not reject so many noble warriors. The warriors challenge each other and joke over who will tame the wild wind. For peace, you must choose one, or I will do so. Is there a warrior who stands taller and braver than than Rides-Like-Thunder?"

"You would sell your own sister for the biggest price? I do not wish to marry your Cheyenne brother or any other warrior. I am young, Lone Wolf. I am not ready to become a wife and mother. There is much to learn and see. I do not love or desire any of them," she protested. She had allowed several handsome braves to steal kisses, but they had had no effect on her. What was so special about the joining of bodies on sleeping mats? she wondered. Once she was wed, her freedom and joy would be lost forever, and her restless spirit would be corralled. If only Soaring Hawk were still alive . . . Her Indian father had understood her hunger for life, her many differences from the others of the tribe. Sometimes they had talked for hours of the mysteries of life and the variations in people. He had never pressed her to be anything more than she was. Why had he been taken from her during this confusing period in her life? Why could she not consent to her brother's commands? She knew why: somewhere there was a special existence and a man awaiting her. She would have to resist Lone Wolf's orders until her destiny was revealed to them. If only the Great Spirit would open her brother's eyes to the truth, he would understand why she was refusing to comply with his wishes, and perhaps he would find a way to help her locate her path to happiness.

"I will invite Rides-Like-Thunder to visit our tepee. You will see that he is the best choice for the daughter of Soaring Hawk and sister of Lone Wolf. Do not rashly close your heart and mind to him. He is a good man and my friend. You are my sister and I love you. That is why I choose the best man for you. Accept him and my words," he coaxed. He did love her, and this matter was difficult for him. He was distressed by her rebellion and selfishness. How could he reach her?

"Would Rides-Like-Thunder be the best choice if he were of our tribe? Or is he the best because he will take me away from your camp and tepee? Am I so repulsive that my own brother wishes to be rid of me?" she challenged him, her emotions in turmoil. "Why are you blind to the truth, Lone Wolf? Grandfather must guide my steps."

Lone Wolf reasoned, "Good changes will be made in Wild Wind in another camp. If you remain here, you will not try to become a good wife. Your defiance will vanish in the Cheyenne camp, for you will learn that such ways and words are wrong. You will learn to be Indian again. You will find love and desire. If you wish to choose another warrior, do so before the buffalo hunt ends. If you do not, I will accept my friend's offer after our tribes hunt together. I will allow him to take you as his mate after the joint Sun Dance. If Rides-Like-Thunder were of this camp, my choice would be the same," he added honestly. "If you desire Black Hawk or Prairie Dog and promise to become a good Oglala wife, I will accept your choice of either warrior. I do not wish to hurt you, my sister. Do not make it so."

Unaccustomed tears glimmered in her eyes, for she could not alter or resist the Indian ways. She had lived with the Oglala Sioux long enough to know she must obey Lone Wolf's words or be banned from her tribe. Where could she go? How would she survive? Did she want freedom that badly? Even if Rides-Like-Thunder was the best choice for a mate from any tribe, she did not love him or want to marry him. She wanted happiness and freedom; she wanted to comprehend this fierce and intangible hunger that chewed at her mind and body. She wanted and needed . . . what the Great Spirit had not yet revealed.

How could she yield to defeat when such a powerful urge to seek her real destiny pulled at her? As surely as the sun rose, it was wrong to marry Rides-Like-Thunder, or any man, just now. But how could she prevent it until she understood who and what she was? Why must she sacrifice her joy, her freedom, and her body to another person? What about her desires and her honor? Was she of such little importance?

"*Niksapa hantans ecanu kte,*" Lone Wolf encouraged her tenderly.

Wild Wind bravely fused her blue gaze to Lone Wolf's ebony one and mentally questioned his last words: "If you are wise, you will do it." Suddenly she lost the will to resist him. This battle between them was too vicious and demanding and destructive. If the Great Spirit had other plans for her, He would see them exposed and fulfilled before it was too late. For now, peace with her brother and people was the important thing. She replied, "As you command, I will choose a mate by the Sun Dance, or I will leave our camp forever. If you open your senses to the words and desires of the Great Spirit, you will know your order is wrong. I beg you, Lone Wolf, seek His will for our lives before you stubbornly go against it. Your words and anger have pierced my heart as fiery arrows. I was a child when I came to the tepee of Soaring Hawk and Lone Wolf; you have made me as I am. Now you punish me for the skills I have learned and the hungers I feel. I know I am a female, for I experience the sting of that sex each day. Why must being a woman destroy my chances for happiness? A captive could perform the same duties you ask of me. Why can there not be more to my life, Lone Wolf? Why is it wrong to ride with the sun and wind? Why is it wrong to learn and practice warrior skills? Is it not best for a woman to be able to protect her tepee and family when her warrior is gone? Have you forgotten how many camps have been raided and destroyed while warriors were hunting or fighting?"

Her voice became strained with heavy emotion as she continued, "Why are women not taught to defend their camps and lives? Why must they flee into the forests or be abused by their captors? Without homes and families, the warriors will have nothing and will cease to exist, as the white man cunningly plans. You know their clever strategy: leave nothing and no one behind and the Dakota Nation will perish. Why is it wrong to know how to track and hunt when the warriors are away and food is needed? Must women, old ones, and children suffer and die because of male pride? Why can we not listen to the words of the council, which also affect our lives? Did not Grandfather also create females? Did He not also give us cunning and courage? Why must we hide these traits? Women have feelings and wishes; why can we not speak them? We are allowed to do no more for our families and people than animals do for their own kind or slaves are commanded to do for their owners; yet we are above animals and slaves in all ways. Women are Oglalas too, Lone Wolf, the children of the Great Spirit. Where and when has Grandfather said we are beneath males? The taste of cowardice is bitter, my brother. Explain these things that trouble me, and I will obey all orders," she vowed.

Lone Wolf declared impatiently, "We have spoken of such matters many times, my sister. It is our way. Grandfather chose the paths for males and females long ago, and He has not changed them. Oglalas must be Oglala. I will waste no more words and strength on such useless talk," he told her, for he could not think of words to refute her arguments, and this dismayed him. "You refuse to see right and to do it. I wish it were not so. Think on your honor and deeds, my sister, and we will speak when I return." He secretly hoped his wits would not fail him at such a trying time. If only her words did not sound so logical, or go against all he had been taught . . .

"It is useless to speak further, my brother and chief. You see only your feelings and thoughts; you care nothing for mine. All people are not the same, Lone Wolf. One day you must face this truth and you must learn the value of women. If you could become a female for only one sun and moon, you would learn much. I agree that many of my deeds are rash and my words are often too quick and sharp, but my honor exists only as long as I remain true to myself and all that I believe. We will not speak on this matter again. I will obey your wishes or I will leave before the buffalo hunt," she announced, a new confidence filling her at that irrevocable decision. If her brother felt she would leave before complying with his commands, he might back down . . .

Lone Wolf watched his adopted sister mount and ride for camp. Wild Wind was smart and brave. She would think on his words and her behavior, then yield to his orders. After the passing of one full moon, she would become the mate of his Cheyenne friend or another of her own choosing, and all would be as it should be . . .

Wild Wind returned to camp and closed the flap to her tepee to signal privacy. She had much thinking to do but did not know where to begin. For as long as she could remember, or would permit herself to remember, she had lived as an Oglala.

Yet she was not Indian, and the trader's looking glass impressed this reality upon her more and more each day. She had tried to be like all of the other Indian maidens but had failed. She was making Lone Wolf and others angry and sad, yet she could not help herself. She wanted and needed something more than this confining life offered her. She was not Soaring Hawk's daughter, but she could not recall her dark past. Who was she? Where did she belong? How could she become all she wanted to be? "Help me, Great Spirit, for I am lost in mist and cannot find my rightful path. I do not wish to dishonor or sadden my brother, Lone Wolf, but I cannot yield to his commands. Please show him I am not like the females of his kind. Please reveal my purpose in life to him. My time is short, Grandfather, and I need your help and answer. Do not fail me because my skin is white, for my heart is Indian."

Suddenly she began to weep, for the truth pounded inside her head: No, Wild Wind, you are not Indian and your place is not here . . .

A similar confusion was taking place far away in Texas, near Fort Worth. Rancher Nathan Crandall was wondering if he was experiencing a cruel joke or a miracle as he digested the news he had just received. He swallowed to remove the lump in his throat that temporarily prevented him from questioning the astounding mystery that had been presented to him. The hands that gripped two breathtaking canvases by renowned artist Thomas Mallory were wrinkled by advancing age and scarred by countless hours of hard manual labor often done in harsh weather. His grayish blue eyes glanced from the two small portraits of an Indian princess to a large portrait of his deceased daughter, Marissa Crandall Michaels, which was hanging over his fireplace. The deteriorating portrait, which Thomas Mallory was now studying intently, had been painted in 1847, when Marissa had been eighteen. Nathan found himself wondering in confusion how the two portraits he held could look like Marissa when they had been painted so recently and his daughter had been dead since '56?

This talented and adventurous artist had arrived in Fort Worth three days ago. Nathan's foreman, Travis Kincade, had met Thomas in the Silver Shadow Saloon and had become intrigued by his work and tales. Travis had learned that Thomas had been traveling the West for the past three years, painting portraits of trappers, soldiers, Indians, and settlers. When he was not doing portraits, he was painting landscapes, portrayals of customs and adventures, and wildlife. Nearing the end of his often perilous trek and before returning east, Thomas had traveled to Texas to capture rugged lawmen and infamous outlaws in evocative oils.

Returning home, Travis had informed Nathan of the master craftman's arrival. As Marissa's portrait was in dire need of expert attention, Nathan had sent Travis back to town to bring Thomas to the ranch to examine his daughter's portrait and to discuss its restoration.

At first glance, the eagle-eyed artist had gaped at the portrait that he was being asked to revitalize. To explain his curious reaction, Thomas had pulled two canvases from an oversized leather satchel, unwrapped them, and handed them to Nathan. "I brought along some of my favorite paintings to let you judge my work for yourself. Now you can understand my astonishment, Mister Crandall. They could almost be the same person. Such resemblance . . . It's incredible."

The owner of the Rocking *C* Ranch tried to master his shock in order to think clearly and calmly. "Who is this girl? When did you paint these? Where?" Nathan demanded hoarsely, the questions suddenly tumbling over each other from his dry mouth.

Thomas Mallory pulled his probing gaze from Marissa's portrait and focused it on the anguished expression of his eminent host. "Her name is *Watogla Tate*. She's the daughter of Chief Soaring Hawk of the Sioux. I spent most of the winter and spring traveling through the Dakota Territory, painting chiefs and warriors. When I saw that girl, I had to paint her. So much beauty and vitality for a maiden of eighteen years. No artist or healthy male could ignore a face like hers. Nor that one," he added hoarsely, motioning to Marissa's fading portrait.

"*Wato* . . . what?" Nathan asked anxiously.

"*Wa-to-gla Ta-te*," Thomas repeated. "It means Wild Wind. Clearly she isn't Indian, not with that red hair and those gray-blue eyes. I wonder how those Sioux got hold of her and why they made her a chief's daughter." He turned to continue his study of the painting, which was desperately in need of repairing and retouching.

Nathan placed the smaller paintings on either side of Marissa's portrait and stared at the images side by side. The sixty-three-year-old man ran shaky fingers through mussed hair, the color of which shifted more from blond to silver with each passing year. As time seemingly halted, Nathan visually compared the Sioux Indian princess, *Watogla Tate*, to his deceased daughter, Marissa. His heart began to pound forcefully.

With an eye for detail, Thomas Mallory pointed out each matching or similar feature. Both women had large eyes, but Marissa's were a cornflower blue, whereas Wild Wind's were the color of a Texas winter sky just before dusk, an entrancing gray-blue. Each set of eyes exposed an air of mystery and sensuality. Thick red hair in masses of waves and curls tumbled over slender shoulders to small waists, hair that came alive with fiery color, that seemingly flowed wild and free like the rain-swollen river whose banks could not confine its abundance and energy. Marissa's portrait had been painted inside while *Watogla Tate's* had been painted outside, and therefore Wild Wind's tresses revealed golden highlights that Marissa's lacked. Both women seemed to exhibit a love for the outdoors, displaying sun-kissed golden flesh with a barely noticeable smattering of pale freckles. The shapes of their noses, faces, and chins matched perfectly. It was eerie. "This resemblance is fascinating. I would like to meet your daughter. Perhaps she could pose for a new portrait after I complete my repair work on this one. I would guess it's around . . . twenty years old?" he hinted as he critically eyed the aging portrait.

Nathan nodded. Despite his reluctance, he had to think, to remember those painful times. "I'm afraid that isn't possible, Mister Mallory. Eleven years ago, Marissa was murdered by Kiowa Indians. The red bastards attacked her stagecoach and slaughtered everyone on it but my seven-year-old granddaughter. They kidnapped her. For years I searched for Rana and offered large rewards for her return. Nothing. I couldn't bear the thought of her being enslaved and abused by those murdering savages, so it seemed easier to accept her as dead, like her mother. She was eighteen this March, if she's still alive." Nathan's eyes were glued to the canvases. "After years of torment and doubt, have I found my little Rana? Look at her. She's the spittin' image of my Marissa. It has to be my granddaughter. But how did the Sioux get her away from those Kiowas? Their territories are far apart and they're fierce enemies. How could a white captive become a Sioux chief's daughter? How can she look so dadburn happy?"

Mallory turned and glanced at the distressed man. "It seems I've brought the image of a ghost to your home, sir. I'm truly sorry." After looking at the portraits and at Nathan again, he shook his head and refuted his words. "Not a ghost, but wonderful news of your missing granddaughter. She has your eyes, sir. How marvelous to create such a happy event. You must be ecstatic to discover she is safe and happy."

"Hell, no!" Nathan shouted. "The only thing that will please me is to get her back home where she belongs. And, by God, I will."

"But what can you do to recover her, Mister Crandall? Even if you can prove she's your granddaughter, Chief Soaring Hawk wouldn't turn his daughter over to a white man. Most of those Sioux despise white men. You can't blame them, with whites and soldiers taking their lands, killing off hundreds of them, and herding the survivors onto reservations like cattle. Those treaties are worthless to both sides. I had a terrible time getting into their camps and getting permission to paint some of them. Conflicts are brewing all over that territory; that's why I had to get out so fast. Settlers are pouring in, and the Indians don't like it. If this girl is your granddaughter, perhaps she doesn't even recall her childhood. Eleven years is a long time away from family and civilization. Chief Soaring Hawk and his son, Lone Wolf, seemed crazy about her. Besides, those Indians are nomads. How would you locate her and steal her? I was told the Sioux are the largest and mightiest Indian nation in the West. It could cause a war."

"I'll get her back the same way those Indians snatched Rana from her home and family—by force! She's my granddaughter; she belongs here with me. Travis will help me get Rana back," Nathan declared confidently, nodding toward the young man who had been his ranch foreman and like a son to him for seven years.

Travis Kincade had gone unnoticed during the conversation between Nathan Crandall and Thomas Mallory. He had been sitting in a large chair in the rear of the room and had listened intently as his friend and boss had questioned the artist about the intoxicating girl in his paintings, a woman whose expression and pose blended perfectly with the wildness and striking beauty of the landscape behind her.

"What do you think, Travis? Is this my Rana?" Nathan asked, even though he knew without a doubt that she was Marissa's child. He was charged with a variety of uncontrollable emotions as he looked into the face that mirrored his lost child's features.

Travis joined the men before the fireplace. Seeing the girl's clothing had brought to life a flood of haunting memories and suppressed feelings. Long ago he had lived as a Lakota warrior, and an Indian maiden had gotten him into peril; she had not only ruined his existence but had also nearly cost him his life. Repressing his past, he compared the two women. Both were of medium height and possessed shapely figures of the variety that could entice moisture above a man's upper lip and a tightening in his pants, though such reactions only supported his belief that most women were nothing but trouble. He unknowingly focused his full attention on the fascinating creature in a heavily beaded white buckskin dress. Her unmarred complexion glowed as if the sun had turned to lather and had bathed her in its golden foam, permanently staining her silky flesh.

In one portrait, the girl's hair was in braids and she was wearing a beaded headband and matching braid ties. In the other, his favorite, her thick hair fell wild and free to her waist. If the sun's rays had not caused it to seemingly burst into fire, her wavy tresses would have appeared a medium auburn shade. A small medicine wheel, made of quills in the sacred colors with a breast feather dangling from its center, was secured just above her right ear. Travis knew a Sioux medicine wheel had to be earned before one could wear it, as a warrior must earn a *coup* feather. He wondered what brave deed had prompted her tribe to gift her with it. As more turbulent memories stormed his vulnerable mind, he tried to deter them, as he had for years. He could not quite succeed.

Travis's green eyes settled on the girl's winter blue ones. Unlike Marissa's knowing look, which revealed she had tasted some of life's wanton offerings, Wild Wind's alluring gaze had a glow of innocence, a glow that hinted at eagerness to explore life. Oddly, he warmed at the undeniable spark of magic and vitality that flowed out to him from *Watogla Tate's* expression. She was a rare beauty who could strike a man speechless or halt him in his tracks. She was trouble of the highest degree and had probably crushed many men. For years he had noticed Marissa Michaels's portrait and beauty, but it was the Indian girl's image that affected his respiration and pulse; it was Chief Soaring Hawk's adopted daughter who caused his curiously susceptible mind and body to do more than stare. And this was most unusual considering his sardonic attitude toward women, an attitude that had been forced on him.

Travis became aware of the silence and the fact that the two men were staring at him. He scolded himself for his foolish reaction to a mere painting of a beautiful woman, one who doubtlessly used her looks as a potent weapon. "It could be her, Nate, or just a wild coincidence. But you'll surely pay hell if you try to steal her from Soaring Hawk and his Oglala band. Didn't you hear Mallory? She's considered the chief's daughter."

Nathan and Travis stared at each other as if speaking without words. Nathan realized his mixed-blooded, twenty-seven-year-old foreman knew what he was talking about, for Travis Kincade had been born and reared as Hunkpapa, one of the most powerful tribes in the Lakota branch of the Sioux Nation, as was the Oglala tribe, which had his granddaughter. Before settling on the Rocking C Ranch seven years ago, Travis had been a defensive and wary loner, a drifter, and a devilish rogue who had been a master of many skills and charms and had used them without mercy or hesitation whenever necessary. Born and trapped between two warring cultures, Travis had grown up too fast and too hard. Although he and Travis were now very close, Nathan knew there were things Travis had never told him or anyone, things that haunted the young man and had made him cynical and rebellious.

After leaving the Indians at the age of eighteen, the troubled youth had wandered from place to place, observing and learning about life and people, and constantly honing his skills and body. The fearless and cunning man had worked many jobs inside and outside of the law. Even when he had ridden as an Army scout and U.S. Marshal, he had owed loyalty to no man or force but himself. Travis had become a man of immense physical prowess. Confident and self-contained, he had always sought the danger, excitement, challenge, and intrigue of any new and stimulating adventure. Then Nathan had crossed Travis's path.

Travis was also recalling his first meeting with Nathan Crandall. It had been the second time the young man had almost lost his life. The first had been at the hands of Indians and, when Nathan found him, Travis had just experienced the treachery of a spiteful white vixen. Nathan had come across the critically injured youth near St. Louis, during a Rocking *C* cattle drive. The older man had personally doctored him back to health. Some of the most difficult challenges Travis had had to face had been controlling his restive spirit, learning to trust and love, and yielding to his new fate during his physical and emotional healing process. Nathan had brought him to this ranch to recuperate, but he had been persuaded to stay on as foreman. Over the years the two had formed a deep, strong bond of friendship, dependence and loyalty. Nathan had become like a father to him and had made vast changes in his character and his way of life. This ranch had become his home and part of his responsibility. He had found acceptance and respect here; he had found happiness and a sense of belonging; he had found himself, his place in life—things that had been stolen from him nine years ago . . .

He had been born the mixed-blood son of a Hunkpapa woman and a white man, and had been raised in the Lakota way. When he was eighteen and a seasoned warrior, a lethal and unjust travesty had destroyed all he had been and had known and loved. His mother's people had accused him of being a traitor and had tried to slay him. Their treachery and betrayal had cut him deeply and painfully; it had sapped his belief in good and evil, and had shaken his faith in the Great Spirit. It was as if all he had done and had become had been in vain. If they could believe he was guilty of such wicked deeds and could order his torture and death, their past love and acceptance had been lies; his entire life had been a cruel lie. Because of one man's and one woman's greed and treachery, he had been forced to become a renegade.

Even after all these years, reflecting on that betrayal sliced through his heart and soul like an enemy's white-hot knife. By turning against him so bitterly, the Hunkpapas had robbed him of many precious things: his very existence, his honor, his trust, his hopes and dreams, his confidence. And, for awhile, they had stolen his heart and soul. They had made him become leery, resentful, hostile, hard. They had taken part of his self-esteem and, for the first time in his life, had made him feel worthless, scared, weak, helpless. For a man's desperate lie and woman's selfishness, he had been sentenced to death by his own people and, fleeing that injustice, he had become an outcast, forever estranged from his Indian lands and ways.

Two years after that tragic episode and just as he was beginning to feel and to care once more, an evil white woman had attempted to ensnare him, and, failing that, destroy him. His bitterness, mistrust, and cynicism had increased. To avoid being hurt or betrayed again, he had tried to resist any feelings or contacts that could lead to more anguish and rejection. Then Nathan Crandall had entered his life . . .

Nathan had accepted him for himself and had proved there were people who were not selfish or traitorous. Despite what the Kiowa Indians had done to his daughter and granddaughter, Nathan had not resented him or held him accountable, though most whites hated all Indians and they persecuted all of them for the evils of a few. As for "half-breeds," they were despised and scorned by both sides. It was only because his mother had been a war chief's daughter that the Indians had accepted him, until a grasping foe had maligned him and turned his mother's people against him.

Not so with this white friend. Nathan was a rare man, a good and kind man. Nathan would never turn against him unless he was convinced Travis was guilty of some crime; then Nathan would doubt it until he was given absolutely unquestionable evidence. And, despite such evidence, Nathan would probably try to rationalize the deed and pardon him. After all this man had done for him and was to him, Travis hated to think of Nathan being hurt by this fantasy of regaining his missing granddaughter. By now, that girl was no longer white, no longer his family . . .

Nathan saw Travis's look of deep concern and affection. "That's my daughter's child, my own flesh and blood. Surely you don't expect me to sit here and do nothing?" he asked softly.

"Of course not. We'll just have to do some clever planning before we take off to Soaring Hawk's camp. If that's Rana, there's no telling what she's been through since her capture. We'll need to walk this path slowly and carefully, Nate. First, we have to make certain she is Rana Michaels; then we'll have to figure out a safe way for you to stake your claim on her to get her free of the Oglalas and back home. She's probably been there a long time and might not want to leave. This won't be quick or easy, Nate."

"Nothing good or right ever comes fast and easy. I'm used to hard work and patience, Travis; but this time, it's damned difficult to practice them." What if Travis was right? Nathan reflected silently. What if Rana had forgotten her family? What if the Indians refused to release her or she refused to come home with him? After all, during her childhood Rana had seen him only a few times. He looked at Thomas Mallory and asked, "Can I buy those two portraits of Rana? Name your price."

Thomas replied, "Normally I would say no; but this time I'll agree. We can discuss a reasonable price later." He glanced at the clock. "I must be hurrying along. I have a dinner engagement tonight. The restoration of your daughter's portrait should require five to seven days. If we have a deal, Mister Crandall, I'll complete my work in Fort Worth tomorrow and return here Sunday afternoon."

Nathan shook hands with the artist. "I'll have one of my hands pick you up at the hotel around three Sunday afternoon. Thank you for bringing me the news of my granddaughter's survival and her location."

"I wish you luck in accomplishing her return. As your man said, it won't be an easy task to recover her. We can discuss her and your impending journey Sunday evening when we have more time."

Travis remained before the immense fireplace while Nathan escorted the artist to the waiting buggy. When Nathan returned, he poured himself and Travis a whiskey. The younger man turned and watched his older friend as the man collapsed wearily into a chair. "I know this must be hard on you after all this time of considering her lost forever. Are you sure it isn't best to leave her where she is, Nate? Stealing her back could be as traumatic for her now as her abduction was years ago. Look at her, Nate. That isn't the expression of a miserable, lowly captive. Clearly she's done well for herself. Those Oglalas are her family now. I would think long and hard before I interfered. I know what it's like to be caught between two warring peoples, and I know how hard change is. She can't replace Marissa." Travis almost hated the idea of a "Marissa" coming to live with them. She could turn their lives inside out and wreak havoc on their emotions. He instantly realized that his was a selfish attitude and scolded himself. If she was Rana, she deserved to be rescued and given another chance.

Nathan drained the last sip of whiskey from his glass, then placed it on a side table. "Even after all these years, Travis, it's impossible to understand Marissa's behavior. If she hadn't taken off with that conniving gambler, she would still be alive. I can close my eyes and picture her sashaying into this very room to announce she was eloping with Raymond Michaels. I tried everything to change her mind. We argued for hours. I threatened to whip her and lock her in her room. Hell, I even threatened to have Michaels beaten and jailed. I refused to give them my blessing or permission. I told Marissa she would be disinherited if she ran off with that piece of cow dung; I thought that would change Michaels's mind about latching onto a wealthy girl. I knew Marissa was spoiled and headstrong, but I didn't think she would give up all she had for a man whose reputation was as black as his hair or that fancy suit he wore. It was like Michaels had cast some evil spell over her. I was a fool to call a gambler's hand. I always thought he would drop her before the wedding, but that greedy bastard held out with dreams of getting his filthy hands on my money. Perdition, I would spend it all to get Marissa and Rana back!"

"You can't blame yourself for Marissa's mistakes."

Nathan sighed heavily. "I'm to blame for some of them, Travis. I let her have her way too long. If my Ruthie hadn't died with that fever when Marissa was ten, she would have known how to handle our feisty child. When I realized Marissa was dead serious about running off, it was too late to stop her. Hell, I would have married her off to one of the neighboring ranchers or one of my cowpunchers! How could a girl raised so easy choose a hard and dangerous life like Michaels offered? Traveling from one dirty town and loud saloon to another; always being around drunks and whores and gunslingers; going up and down that treacherous river on one of them big boats so Michaels could lie and cheat while he plied his dirty trade. You know what kinds of things go on in those saloons and riverboats. It wasn't any place for a lady like Marissa or a small child. Surprised me Michaels kept them around for seven years. I kept hoping Marissa would come to her senses and return home. She never could see the evil in that man, or wouldn't admit she could to me or herself."

"You sure you want to dig this up tonight?" Travis asked. He knew how painful this subject was for Nathan. Besides, he had heard most of this tale before and it always made him angry. Travis loved and respected the older man; he would risk any peril to defend him. During the seven years since Nathan Crandall had saved his life, Travis had learned much about Nathan, and his defiant, selfish daughter.

Travis had met plenty of vixens like Marissa and had forgotten all except two vicious bitches. Conniving, greedy females rubbed him the wrong way. He despised vain, spoiled creatures who only cared about themselves. Marissa's eyes told wicked tales and seemed to shout them louder than a cannon roared, though Nathan was too much the loving father to hear them. It had taken years after that horrible incident for Nathan to find happiness and peace of mind, and he had still been suffering when they had been thrown together. Maybe that mutual need for love and peace had sparked the rapport and bond between them. Together they had healed each other's wounds. Now some evil force was thrusting this imposing girl into Nathan's life and emotions. She possessed the power to hurt Nathan as deeply as Marissa had, and he could not allow it. If she was like her mother, she could destroy Nathan Crandall.

"Maybe I am partly to blame, Travis. Maybe I should have let Marissa have her way. Maybe I should have tried to buy off Michaels. Hell, I made sure Marissa learned about his other women and deceits. She wanted to stay deaf and blind to his weaknesses; she refused to believe my reports. Michaels turned her into a spineless, empty-headed fool who would follow him anywhere! Maybe I was too busy with the ranch to see what was happening to my little girl. Maybe if I had remarried and had given Marissa a mother who could supply love and guidance, then she wouldn't have gone bad. Women can be such fools when it comes to a handsome face and charming front. Michaels thought all he had to do was outwait me, then move in here and take over. I've wished a hundred times I had shot the bastard. Hell, he tried to have me killed twice! If those Kiowas hadn't murdered him, me and him would have tangled eventually. If Michaels had truly loved her, I would have done anything to help them. Why didn't my little girl listen to me?"

Nathan picked up his glass and poured himself another drink. Travis remained silent and observant, a lingering trait from his Indian upbringing. "If it had been anyone but my child, I would have said she was getting what she deserved. I loved that girl, Travis. If only she could have admitted she was wrong and let me help her get away from that snake. If we'd only been given a little more time . . ."

Travis empathized with Nathan as the older man was forced to retrace a torturous path. "Just before she was murdered, she and Michaels seemed to be at their last stand. I told her over and over that she could return home with Rana any day or night. Maybe I shouldn't have sent money for food and clothes. Maybe poverty and shame would have opened Marissa's eyes and driven her home. But I couldn't let them go hungry and naked and sleep in barns or over saloons. I wonder if he even let her keep the money. Knowing that beast, he probably took it and gambled it away. Those two girls saw plenty of hard times. No, I should have given in to her pleas; maybe they would still be alive."

"No, Nate," Travis argued. "Marissa would have had to have been the one to break it off with Michaels. He would have destroyed you and this ranch. Let this matter rest," he urged. Travis had never seen Nathan so insecure, so determined to place the blame on the wrong head. He knew that Nathan was being plagued by doubts and self-recrimination, but the man did not deserve them, for Nathan had done what he had thought was right for his child and for himself. That was not true of his own father. Jeremy Kincade had duped and betrayed his child for selfish reasons.

"I can't, Travis. I have to think about Rana. You and her are all I have left. If you had been here years ago, Marissa wouldn't have looked at another man. I could have left the ranch to you two. You know I think of you as the son I never had. If I can't get Rana back, it's yours. If I do, you two will share it."

Travis smiled. "You've done plenty for me, Nate. I wouldn't be alive now if you hadn't found me and taken me in. I know I gave you lots of hard times and smart mouth, but you turned me around. If Michaels hadn't been pulling at Marissa with pretty words and smiles, you could have turned her around too," he encouraged his friend, even if he did not believe these last words. He wondered how Marissa had turned out so badly with a good father like Nathan Crandall.

"The last time I saw Rana, she was a beautiful, vivacious child. Marissa had brought her to visit me for a month, probably trying to change my mind about taking them in before winter started. I could tell she was getting tired of always moving around and ignoring Michaels's lies. She was tense and moody. She was weakening, Travis. I should have pressed her harder. She looked so weary and sad. I think Michaels was starting to give her a hard time, maybe threatening to get rid of her and the child if she couldn't get any money out of me. You should have seen those two girls together, Travis. Little Rana had arrived a quiet, shy, frightened child. She loved it here on the ranch. I watched her open up and come to life. After a few days, she was full of laughter and chatter, always following me and the boys around and asking countless questions. I think that was the first time since her birth she was getting enough food and rest and play. She thrived on the sunshine and attention, and she wasn't timid or afraid anymore."

Nathan's voice and expression went cold and harsh. "They only stayed two weeks. That no-good Michaels showed up and took them away. The minute he walked in the door, I saw a change come over Marissa and Rana. He sapped the life and joy right out of their bodies. He was a cold and clever bastard, but I saw through his little game. He had been giving me a taste of what I was missing. He figured I would relent. I was hoping my daughter had regained some of her pride and spunk and she would stand up to the vermin. God forgive me for saying that only Marissa and Rana would be welcome here. Michaels called my bluff and I lost Marissa. If she hadn't died, I think she would have returned home within a month. She's gone forever, Travis, but I can get Rana back with your help. Will you take me to Soaring Hawk?"

Even if he disagreed with Nathan's explanation and plans, Travis realized he had to yield to his friend's plea. The truth was that he did not know how he felt about this matter. "I'll do what I can to get her back for you. Just make sure you understand the consequences if she and the Oglalas don't agree with our actions. You know the government sent every Union soldier they could find into that area to subdue the Dakota Nation. Maybe they have rounded up and fenced in some of the tribes, but those Oglalas and Hunkpapas will never make peace with whites who are stealing their lands. Those ex-Yankees don't realize who they're challenging in Red Cloud, Gall, Sitting Bull, Crazy Horse, and Soaring Hawk. Blind lambs to the slaughter, Nate. Even if we can get in and out alive, bringing Rana back with us will be nearly impossible. We could stir up more trouble and danger for the whites and Indians by stealing part of Soaring Hawk's family. Do you want to risk causing a new bloodbath?" Travis observed the effect of his words on Nathan. Travis was not afraid to risk his life, but he did not want to risk Nathan's.

"I want her, Travis. I need her. Help do this the right way. Once Soaring Hawk hears the truth, surely he'll let Rana return to her real family. If necessary, I'll get on my knees and beg him."

"When, and if, we reach the Dakota Territory, promise you'll let me handle everything. Promise you won't interfere with whatever I say or do. Maybe we can come to some peaceful compromise."

"How soon can we leave?" Nathan questioned eagerly.

Travis reminded Nathan, "We're already running weeks behind on our spring roundup and cattle drive. I don't see how we can take off for the Oglala camp until we return from Sedalia. Say six to eight weeks. Then we should be able to reach the Dakota Territory within three or four weeks. If all goes well, we might have her home by mid-August."

"That's two or three months! If things are as bad as you said, Rana could be injured or killed before we reach her," Nathan protested.

"Soldiers wouldn't kill a beautiful white girl."

"Even if she behaves like a Sioux enemy?"

Travis dodged that question by focusing attention on another problem. "Have you forgotten that Harrison Caldwell is breathing fire on your neck? Last summer and winter were bad for us, Nate; we borrowed plenty of money to get through. If we don't get those cattle to market soon, he'll force Mason's bank to call in your loans so he can buy them up. If we lose that sale or get there too late for good prices, we're in deep trouble. He's already found ways to take over nearly every neighboring spread and close us in on three sides. That only leaves us protected by the river and McFarland's spread. I don't like the idea of being surrounded by that snake. Do you want to lose the Rocking C Ranch to that rattler while we're off chasing a ghost? Patience, Nate, or you won't have a home to bring Rana back to. Not unless you don't mind my having to marry Clarissa Caldwell to get it back for us," he teased cunningly to relax Nathan's tension and concern.

"I'll thrash you with a leather strap if you ever seriously glance in that vixen's direction. You just keep leading her down a flowery trail to keep an eye on her old man. Harry will hang back as long as he thinks he can get hold of this ranch through you and his daughter." Nathan cautioned, "We'd best make sure he doesn't learn about Rana, or he might see her as a kink in his dirty plans. Just keep letting that pretty vulture believe she's got her talons wrapped tightly around you and we'll be fine." He chuckled. "Little Clarissa and her father won't be none too happy when they get a look at my beautiful granddaughter."

Both men's gazes went to the mantel to eye the girl mentioned. Travis grinned and devilishly agreed, "Nope, Miss Clarissa Caldwell won't take kindly to Rana Michaels's arrival at all. I wonder just how accurately Soaring Hawk named his adopted daughter. *Watogla Tate*, Wild Wind . . . Lordy, Nate, we might have us a tough taming job ahead."

Later, at supper, Travis's keen instincts were alert. He asked, "You've thought it over carefully and you're sure you want to do this?"

Nathan's blue eyes locked with the lively green ones of the man who was like the son he had never had. He sighed deeply and nodded. Travis had given him back his spirit, his vitality, his pride; Travis had brought him happiness and a new reason for living. He knew something of the hardships, loneliness, anguish, and humiliation the younger man had endured. But those emotions and experiences had toughened Travis; they had made him nearly invincible; they had honed his talents, instincts, and body into a powerful force that few men rashly challenged. Over the years since coming here, Travis had lost much of his brittleness and wariness. Nathan knew that his love, acceptance, and help had changed that coldness and filled that emptiness. He knew he had done as much for Travis as Travis had done for him, and understood that Travis might be leery of returning to the people he had rejected for the whites.

Nathan asked soulfully, "What would you do if she were your flesh and blood, Travis? If she were your daughter or sister or wife? I owe her, son. I'm the reason she was born, and maybe the reason she was captured. If not for my self-righteousness and obstinancy, Marissa would be alive and Rana would be at home tonight. I should have found the courage to kill that bastard she married!" Nathan declared, some of his old guilt and rage returning to plague him.

"You've got to face reality, Nate. What if she isn't Rana? This trip will be long and dangerous. It could take weeks to locate Soaring Hawk's camp. We can't just ride in and demand her return. If we ask too many questions along the way, word will spread and they'll get suspicious. We could get killed before we reach her."

Nathan fused his worried gaze on the man who was half-Indian and a highly trained warrior—a fact known only in these parts by Nathan Crandall. Travis's knowledge of the Indians and their language could be vital to his success. Yet the search for Rana did not have Nathan as concerned as asking Travis to return to the Dakota Territory with him, for Nathan suspected the emotional and physical agonies that this fearless man had experienced there. While doctoring Travis's muscular body years ago, Nathan had viewed the scars of the Sun Dance and those of a brutal torturing. To force Travis to enter that territory again might refresh those painful years, those horrible events, those traits that had taken Nathan a long time and a lot of love to alter. He asked himself if he dared risk losing Travis to death or to the "old ways," in order to rescue a girl who might not wish to be returned home. Yet, there was no one who could better understand and deal with this present Rana or the hazardous conditions in the Sioux territory than Travis "White Eagle" Kincade.

"There's only one way to find out if she is my granddaughter. Rana had an accident during her last visit here; that injury would have left a permanent scar on her left ankle. If she wasn't wearing those beaded leggings, I'd point it out to you. She also has a birthmark on the underside of her left arm." Nathan paused briefly before saying, "I have no right to ask you to go with me, Travis, but I wish you would. I can put Cody Slade in charge of the ranch and Mace Hunter in charge of the cattle drive to Sedalia. We won't tell anyone where we're going."

Travis loved and admired this older man and told him, "I don't want to see you hurt again, Nate. You know what you always tell me: don't climb on a wild mustang who's sure to buck you off and cripple you."

Nathan shook his graying blond head and smiled stubbornly. "We both have a gut feeling it's her, Travis. You know better than most what kind of existence that is for a captive female, especially with all this fighting between the whites and Indians. Can we allow Rana to be slaughtered during a cavalry raid on their camp? What do you think either a white or Indian captor would do with such a beautiful girl? Make her his whore," Nathan declared with a sneer. "It's too dangerous for her to remain in the Dakota Territory, no matter what she says or thinks. I'll risk any danger or pay any price to get her back."

Travis knew why Nathan hesitated over asking him to go. His love and concern were obvious. Travis wondered how he would feel returning to his mother's lands and people after all these years, and if it would be safe for him to enter Hunkpapa territory. He wondered if he was emotionally strong enough to deal with the feelings and situations that could arise during this journey. He could feel a lingering bitterness rising within him. He had tried to come to terms with his past and thought he had, until this matter had come up today. He could now admit that the "evidence" against him had looked bad then, but the Hunkpapas should have trusted him, at least given him the chance to defend himself. He did not know if he could ever totally forgive them for that denial. Travis could not help but wonder, if he were to tell Nathan about his past, which life he would choose to protect—his or Rana's. No, Travis decided unselfishly, the truth would compel Nathan to make a distressing choice.

Besides, he hated to think of Nathan's granddaughter being captured, raped, or killed. There was something about this girl that pulled at him, something that no woman had been able to do before. If she was part of Nathan, she belonged here with them. And he wanted to meet her, even if she were not Rana Michaels. Nathan needed him, and perhaps the girl did too. Maybe she was not as happy or as free as she appeared. Maybe she was not like the other women he had known, the ones who had made him so cynical and wary. Like him, this girl was trapped between two warring peoples. She was part of Nathan's family, and the Lakotas should not be allowed to take anything else of real value from him. He owed Nathan, and he owed himself.

As he envisioned Wild Wind, Travis's green eyes brightened and he grinned. He stroked his stubbled jawline. "I haven't had a decent challenge in a long time, Nate. Rana or not, that ravishing creature will make for a stimulating quest. We'll get supplies ready tomorrow and leave at dawn Sunday." Travis mentally added, *May the Great Spirit help us if she's anything like Marissa or Raymond Michaels,* but Travis did not share with Nathan his overwhelming sense of foreboding . . .

—— *Chapter 2* ——
❧

Dakota Territory
May 24, 1867

WILD WIND CEASED HER SWIMMING, for it had failed to relax her taut body or distract her troubled mind. Time had escaped without giving her answer to her dilemma. She left the still-chilly water to stretch out on the spring grass in a secluded area along the riverbank. She closed her eyes and allowed the afternoon sun to dry and warm her shapely body and fiery hair. Neither she nor Lone Wolf had mentioned their last quarrel of weeks ago. Yet each knew it weighed heavily on the other's mind, just as each wondered what the other would do. The Sun Dance ritual and buffalo feast were approaching rapidly. If she did not make her own decision soon, the problem would be settled for her.

Wild Wind sat up and crossed her feet. She absently scratched a white scar on her left ankle, which sometimes itched when she was angry or tense. Her arms encircled her legs and she rested her chin on one knee. She had not changed her mind about marriage, especially to Rides-Like-Thunder, who was always trying to steal kisses or put his hands where they should not touch. She was tired of being the butt of jokes and teased. How could she marry a man who did not take her seriously, a man who thought mastering her was an amusing game?

Wild Wind was not afraid of animals or wilderness dangers; she could protect herself with weapons and cunning. She would not starve, for she knew how to hunt and cook. But secretly she had witnessed evil deeds of the man-beast enemy, and this caused her to hesitate over leaving her camp and people. She could not live in the forest or mountains alone; and once she rejected her people's laws and departed, she could never return. Was there no answer other than a forced marriage?

She leapt to her feet and paced back and forth along the riverbank until her bare feet made a path through the supple blades of grass. Needing solitude to make a decision, she had been here since dawn, but she had not achieved success. How she wished these lovely surroundings would share part of their tranquillity with her. How she wished *Tunkansila* would hear her prayers and respond, for Grandfather was supposed to know all things and to have love and mercy for His people. She was so confused, so torn by what should be a simple and happy decision for an Indian maiden: the choosing of a mate and the settling down to married life. Why was she troubled by a terrible sense of foreboding? Why was she resisting and lingering here when she had only two choices: marry or leave?

Wild Wind inhaled deeply and loudly. Perhaps she was overly tired today, for she had slept little the night before. She sat on her drying blanket and stretched out once more. If any peril approached, *Mahpiya* would warn her. She glanced at the cherished white stallion whom she had named Cloud. The highly intelligent animal loved and obeyed only her. He was sleek and swift, and he responded instantly to the slightest hint of danger to her. She smiled, then closed her eyes.

Travis Kincade and Nathan Crandall had been waiting over an hour beside the coulee for the young brave to return with Chief Soaring Hawk or with a message from him. Nathan glanced at Travis and asked, "Do you think he'll come to parley, or send a war party to kill us?"

Travis did not pull his scanning gaze from the harsh landscape before him as he replied, "From what I can recall about Soaring Hawk, he's a man of great honor and courage. I doubt he would kill us before letting us speak our piece. 'Course, things and people have changed a great deal since I left. You heard what those soldiers at Fort Wallace had to say. The Army's got several bands of Oglalas and Hunkpapas givin' 'em hell. Captain Clardy at our last stop told me they've been sending replacements up this way for months to squash Red Cloud and his followers. He said Red Cloud has been able to keep that Boseman Trail through the Powder River country and most of their forts closed for over a year. You know that doesn't sit well with the Army. If those Yankees think they can whip the Lakotas like they did the Rebs, they're in for a rough awakening. One Lakota tribe is hard enough to conquer, but several tribes banded together . . . No way, Nate."

Nathan leaned against the same large rock as Travis. "From the way those soldiers were talking and preparing, these Sioux Indians have 'em plenty nervous. Afore this matter is settled, I'll wager the Army's gonna regret teaching the Indians about massacres and broken promises. Hell, it's only been five months since Crazy Horse wiped out Colonel Fetterman and his entire troop. If you ask me, Travis, that's one warrior the Cavalry had better watch very closely."

"You're right, Nate. Crazy Horse is smart and fearless, and he's tired of watching the whites try to annihilate the Dakota Nation. He's a born warrior, the same age as me. Put him with Soaring Hawk, Red Cloud, Gall, and Sitting Bull, and those soldiers are as helpless as newborn pups in a blizzard. The Army's filling a powder keg on Indian lands, Nate, and we're smack in the middle of its explosion area."

Nathan looked tired and worried. "Maybe we shoulda just sneaked into their camp and snatched Rana. I bet these Indians don't trust any white man. Once he learns why we came here, you think he'll . . . ?"

Nathan fell silent as Travis straightened to full alert and reflexively checked the Remington Army .44 pistols that were strapped to his muscled thighs. Travis had selected these particular weapons because they were more accurate and sturdier than the Colt .44. His green eyes narrowed briefly as he forcibly relaxed his taut body, which had stiffened in a careless show of fear or uncertainty. "They're here, Nate. Stay calm and quiet. Try not to look nervous. Remember, no shouting or arguing."

Nathan's hands shook and he wiped his suddenly moist palms on his trouser legs. Nathan glanced around. "I'll let you handle everything like I promised. Where are they? I don't see or hear anything."

"I make out eight of them, two on each side of us. Soaring Hawk should arrive soon. Relax, Nate. If he wanted us killed or captured, we wouldn't be standing here right now." Travis's keen senses had detected the stealthy approach of the Oglala warriors. Alone, he could have taken on eight warriors and probably defeated them, but he had Nathan's life to protect. He had to handle himself and this matter gingerly and wisely. He knew Indians liked to eye a situation before encountering it. His sharp senses did not perceive any immediate threat of danger; but if he was mistaken, he was prepared to deal with it. His Winchester .44 rifle, which fired seventeen rounds, was lying on the hard dirt before him in case he had to drop to the ground and seize it quickly. His pistols were ready for firing, and he carried two concealed knives, which he could use with lethal skill.

Travis cautioned the older man, "Keep your hands away from your weapons, Nate, unless I give the attack signal. Then hit the dirt and fire right and front. I'll take left and rear. Stand here while I make contact. I need to let 'em know what we want." Travis stepped away from the gulch where their horses and supplies were waiting. He lifted his hands and gave the sign for "peace," his hands before his chest, the left palm turned upward and the right hand grasping the left one snugly.

Travis knew he had to depend on his skill in sign language to get his points across to the concealed warriors. He lifted his right hand to shoulder level. With the index and middle fingers extended upward and held together and with the other fingers and thumb closed toward the palm, he gave the sign for *kola*, "friend." He continued his mute one-sided conversation by giving the signs that he had come to make a trade for one of their white captives, the granddaughter of the man who was waiting with him. Travis silently entreated Chief Soaring Hawk to come and bargain with him for the girl's release. To show the warriors he knew of their arrival and their locations, he faced the other three directions and repeated his message. The sable-haired man waited a few minutes, but no one responded to his claims or his summons.

Travis knew his patience and courage were being tested, so he made certain his expression remained calm and his stance remained poised. Travis decided to reveal his Indian identity to Soaring Hawk and his band, for tribes rarely related the humiliating and painful news of a warrior's betrayal and punishment to outsiders. Unless the traitor posed a threat to allied tribes, the personal and embarrassing matter was usually kept private. And since all those involved in that treachery had been slain or driven far away, there would have been no remaining danger to the Hunkpapas or their Lakota brothers. Travis hoped that some of these warriors who were closing in on him might recall the famed and fearless half-blooded warrior, White Eagle. What he had to do was recover Rana, then get them out of this area before the Hunkpapas heard of his return and labeled him a threat to their Lakota brothers, as well as unfinished business for them.

Travis gave the sign for "color" by rubbing the fingertips of his right hand in a circular pattern on the back of his left hand. Then his hands formed the signs for *wanmbli* and *ska*, indicating his name of White Eagle. Lastly, Travis revealed he was part Lakota by giving the signs for "half-Indian" and "Sioux" with the "throat-cutter" movement, then signaled his bond to the Hunkpapa tribe. Again he motioned that he had come in peace to bargain with Soaring Hawk.

It was only moments before a lone Indian approached him on a brown and white Appaloosa whose painted markings exposed the numerous and daring exploits of his bronze skinned master. The man proudly carried a *coup* lance with feathers attached from one end to the other, a counting stick for his many deeds. A bow and quiver of arrows were hanging over his broad back, and a war shield was clutched securely in his left hand. A leather sheath that held a buffalo jaw hunting knife was secured at the right side of his waist. The markings on the arrow quiver, buffalo shield, knife sheath, and horse's rump worried Travis. They were symbols of the Black War Bonnet Society and boldly announced his membership in that fierce and determined "war medicine" brotherhood. Clearly this was a man of great prowess and high rank.

The Indian, who appeared to be in his mid-twenties, did not dismount or speak. A long mane of shiny black hair settled around the warrior's brawny shoulders, and a beaded headband with geometric designs kept it from falling into his ruggedly handsome face and piercing eyes. The Indian's pleasant features were strongly defined. He was dressed in a breechclout and low-cut moccasins, leaving most of his well-developed body in view. His dark skin revealed white scars here and there, signs of past battle wounds and the Sun Dance. Around his neck there was a *wanapin*, an amulet in the shape of a wolf's head, with bared teeth, keen eyes, and ears erect and alert. Around his large biceps were secured arm bands with special *coups* colorfully etched on them and from which beaded thongs and feathers dangled.

"*Hau,*" Travis greeted the warrior genially, fearlessly. The amulet implied that the warrior was Lone Wolf, and Travis assumed he had been sent to investigate this matter for his father. As Travis eyed the striking man who possessed Wild Wind, incredible jealousy sparked within him until he reminded himself that she was living as the Indian's sister.

Eyes the color of greased coal roamed the full length of Travis's body and settled on his face. The Oglala warrior asked, "*Nituwe hwo? Taku ca yacin hwo?*" It meant "Who are you? What do you want?"

Travis easily responded in the Lakota tongue of his mother's people, saying, "We have come to bargain with Chief Soaring Hawk for the release of a white captive. By the whites I am called Travis Kincade and by my Hunkpapa people I am known as White Eagle. Soaring Hawk, Chief of the Oglalas, is called a man of great courage and cunning. Why does he send another warrior to speak and stand in his place?"

Lone Wolf stared at the man with intensely green eyes, deep golden skin, and nearly black hair. The white man's expression and stance told Lone Wolf that he was a man of great physical and mental prowess. Black eyes lingered for a moment on the red cloth band that was secured around Travis's forehead in the Apache style. He noticed that the man was clad in fringed buckskin shirt and pants and was wearing knee moccasins. Something was suspended on a leather thong around his neck, but it was hidden beneath his sienna-colored shirt. "*Iyeciciye sni yelo,*" the warrior remarked, telling Travis that he had not recognized him. He contin-

ued in his tongue, "Many times Mother Earth has renewed her face since I heard
Hunkpapa tales of the half-white warrior with fire in his heart and head. My own
eyes witnessed his skills and courage when our tribes camped together for the
buffalo feast and trading season. You have been gone many winters, White Eagle.
Why do you return this sun to seek words with my father?"

Travis said, "*Nawin Upizata he kci wowaglaka,*" telling the intrepid warrior
that he wished to speak with Soaring Hawk. "*Tokiyaya hwo?*" the ranch foreman
continued, asking where he was.

The warrior replied in Oglala in a tone of confidence, "My father lives with
the Great Spirit. His life was stolen by the burning ball of a bluecoat's firestick. I
am Lone Wolf, son of Soaring Hawk, chief of the Oglalas. Many changes have
come to our lands, White Eagle, since you vanished. I believed you dead these
many seasons. Oglalas joined the Black War Bonnet Society. Oglalas carry the
signs of death and danger. Oglalas speak and wear war medicine. Many of our
Dakota brothers have made treaty with the white dogs and have given away their
lands and freedoms to end the white man's war, to save their people. Surrender
did not stop the white man's war. The white-eyes seek defeat of all Dakota tribes
and conquest of all Indian lands."

Lone Wolf watched Travis intently. "Oglalas say, 'What is life without freedom, sacred lands, and honor?' But the white-eyes come swiftly and heavily as the
winter snows. Many Lakotas are too old and weary to fight. Many have no warriors or weapons to battle our foes. Many have no place to run or horses to carry
them. Soldiers attacked and burned many camps in the winter past; many starved
and many died from the cold. The soldiers give little time to gather medicine
herbs and to make weapons and to hunt game. They are sly and vicious as the
badger. Many Lakotas live inside the fences that the whites called reservations!"
he stated with repulsion, his eyes flickering with black fires of hatred and anger.
Quickly he mastered his display of emotion.

"It is not so with the Oglalas and Hunkpapas. We fight our white and Indian
enemies. Those who refuse to sign the white man's treaties are called renegades,
hostiles, savages! The white man seeks to defeat them and slay them. To stand
against the bluecoats becomes a challenge to destroy us. They declare war on
those who will not yield their freedoms and lands to greedy whites. Many soldiers
and weapons have been sent to this land to conquer the Lakotas. We have painted
death on our shields and robes, and we paint the mark of the Black War Bonnet
Society on our faces when we ride to battle our white foes. The Hunkpapas join
with the Oglalas to fight this white enemy, to drive him from our lands. White
Eagle has not been in our lands and battles for many seasons. You dress and speak
as white, the path you have chosen to walk. Gall is war chief of the Hunkpapas; he
is the adopted brother of the medicine chief, Sitting Bull. Sitting Bull draws all
Lakotas together with his words. Grandfather gave him the power to see beyond
this sun to those to come. When he speaks, all Lakotas listen and obey, as you
once did, White Eagle."

Knowing it was a show of bad manners to interrupt a warrior when he was
talking, Travis remained silent and attentive as Lone Wolf spoke. "Red Cloud,
Crazy Horse, and Lone Wolf of the Oglalas defeat more of the whites than all
other tribes together. The soldiers fear us and wish us dead. We cannot drive them

from the lands they have taken from our brothers, for they are many and they carry magic weapons. But we will fight to hold our lands until no Oglala or Hunkpapa warrior is alive. Our Cheyenne brothers fight beside us. No white-eyes is safe in our lands. Your white blood has chosen the white man's world. Go, and do not return while you side with our enemies."

Realizing that Lone Wolf was unaware of the dark secret that had driven him from these lands years ago, Travis relaxed slightly. "I do not side or fight with the white soldiers, Lone Wolf. I left our lands to find peace and acceptance in another place many suns' ride from our sacred Black Hills, a place where I am not forced to take my father's or my mother's side in a cruel war. I did not choose to be born with warring bloods. I rode from these lands to seek a place where the fires within my heart and head could cool. Seven winters past I found my place of honor and happiness with the white man who travels with me. I live on his ranch on the lands that once belonged to the Kiowas and Comanches. We come to claim his grand-daughter and take her home with us. She was taken captive by your tribe many winters past. She is white, so she is not safe in your lands. Your tongue has spoken the many reasons why she must be sent home to her family. Hear my words of truth, Lone Wolf, and release her to us, for she is loved by you and your people and you wish no harm to come to her."

The warrior's stoic expression did not change. Travis continued, "Your people need supplies for survival and defense, Lone Wolf; the man called Nathan Crandall will give you much money for her return to buy those supplies: food, blankets, knives, guns," he offered temptingly. "We come in peace. Let us sit and make trade." When Lone Wolf did not react, Travis reasoned, "What is the value of one white captive in exchange for needed supplies and weapons? You are chief. How will you help your people survive without food and weapons?"

"How much of the white-eyes money do you offer for one white captive? What is the girl's value to White Eagle and his friend?"

"Her value is as large as the heaven, Lone Wolf, but we do not have enough money to fill it. His reward to the Oglalas for rescuing his granddaughter and caring for her will buy many supplies."

The warrior did not glance at Nathan during this talk. "How can Lone Wolf buy supplies from white-eyes? Trading posts are guarded. Do you speak false, White Eagle? Do you set a trap for the Lakotas?"

Anger flared briefly in Travis's leafy green eyes, but he quickly suppressed it. "I am half Lakota, Lone Wolf. I do not wish to see my mother's people massacred. The whites are wrong to take Indian lands and lives. Many whites and bluecoats are bad; they seek to kill any Indian, even women and children and the old ones. The whites are countless, Lone Wolf, and I see great suffering and death for many Lakotas. The bluecoat war chiefs and soldiers battled another white enemy with numbers and weapons greater than those the Lakotas possess, and they won a painful victory. They are powerful warriors, Lone Wolf. They carry hatred for the Indian and hunger for his lands in their hearts and minds. As a stormy river, they cannot be halted or controlled. If you cannot make honorable peace, you must have weapons for your battles and hunts so your people can live. The old ones must not suffer in their last days or die on land far from the sacred hills. The women must not mourn the deaths of sons and husbands who are defenseless against the soldiers' fire sticks and longknives or be left to the charity of others who have little themselves. And what of the children? Must they suffer or grow under the shadow of white fear or be denied their lands and heritage? Must they be raised as slaves of the white-eyes?"

Travis fused his gaze to Lone Wolf's so the warrior could read his honesty and sincerity, praying that Lone Wolf did not know of his dishonor long ago. "I will help you get the supplies to make this war even. This very sun, many supply wagons are unloading at the Chambers Trading Post, two days' ride from your camp. We saw this with our metal eyes but did not ride close, for we wished no whites to learn of our journey to the Oglala camp. Nate and I will ride there with the money. The white traders are greedy. If they ask why we buy the supplies, we will tell them for friends to defend their lives and lands. Since we are white, they will not suspect that we buy them for your people. You must use them to fight soldiers, Lone Wolf, not innocent whites who have been tricked into coming here. Defeat the soldiers and make it impossible for settlers to exist on your lands, and they will return to theirs or push further west. Prove you are a man of honor and mercy by driving whites from your lands alive."

"I am to trust you with such a deed and plan?" Lone Wolf asked.

"As I trusted you with my life this sun. Send a band of your best warriors to guard us with the money and to guard the supplies after we purchase them. When we bring them to your camp, you will give the white captive to her grandfather. Do we make trade?" the green-eyed man asked. Travis knew about the 1830 Indian Removal Act, the 1851 Indian Appropriation Act, the numerous worthless treaties, and the many brutal massacres of Indian camps, so he knew why Lone Wolf was reluctant to trust him or any white man, even if he did have a past reputation and identity as a renowned warrior.

The Sioux chief was intrigued. "Tell me of the white captive you risked your life and honor to seek. How do you know we have her?"

Without his awareness, Lone Wolf's expression responded to the shocking words of Travis Kincade as he related the tale of the Kiowa capture of Rana Michaels eleven years ago and revealed the details of the enlightening visit and the paintings of artist Thomas Mallory. "She lives with the Oglala people as the adopted daughter of Soaring Hawk. She is called Wild Wind," he explained. Motioning to Nathan, Travis said, "Her grandfather has come to bargain for her release. She is of his blood and belongs with him."

Lone Wolf said with a sneer, "You wish Lone Wolf to sell his own sister? What trick is this? The fires in White Eagle's head and heart now burn with the black fires of evil and betrayal. My sister belongs with her people. She is to join with Rides-Like-Thunder of the Cheyenne. Why do you seek to help the bluecoats buy her? What do they want with Wild Wind? I should slay you where you stand."

Travis was relieved when Lone Wolf did not mention his traitorous father, for he felt only shame and disgust for Jeremy Kincade's betrayal of his mother, Pretty Bird Woman, and her people. Travis had been ensnared and dishonored by his father's treachery, for he had ridden innocently with him that black day that had ended so tragically for his mother and many Hunkpapas. For a long time he had carried the bitterness, cynicism, and stigma of his father's actions. If a man could not trust, respect, and love his own father, how could he inspire such feelings in other men? he had wondered. But Náthan had taught him how to deal with those destructive emotions. Returning to these lands placed his life in peril, for the Hunkpapas would influence the Oglalas not to trust the son of Jeremy Kincade and would probably seek to slay him. Years ago he had tried in vain to clear his name and had barely escaped with his life. That burden still rode with him; yet there was no way to wash the black stain from his face, for all of the guilty ones no longer existed.

Travis replied in a measured tone that concealed his anger, "No, Lone Wolf, she is not your sister. Nathan wishes to have returned to him what is his, what Soaring Hawk took from the Kiowas and the Kiowas took from my friend, Nathan Crandall, who saved my life and has been as a father to me for seven winters. There is no deceit in our hearts and words. His heart filled with joy when he looked upon her painted face. I have seen the face of his daughter, Marissa; it is as Wild Wind's reflection on the surface of the water. I speak true; she is his grand-daughter. He begged me to come to speak with my Lakota brothers for him. We come in peace, Lone Wolf. We have no quarrel with my Oglala brothers. We do not seek to trick or endanger Wild Wind or your people. She is the child of Nathan's daughter who was slain by the Kiowas. His heart burns only with love and hunger for her."

When the warrior remained quiet, Travis continued, "The bluecoats do not know of our visit to the Oglalas. He has come prepared to reward the Oglalas for their kind treatment and acceptance of his granddaughter and for her rescue from the Kiowas. If you love Wild Wind as we have been told, you will desire only her happiness and safety. We have seen and heard of the increased hostilities between the white man and all Indians, and you have spoken of them. Wild Wind is white. She is not safe here." Travis then recounted the many perils that could befall Rana from the whites and the Indians. "You are chief and your people are at war. Who will protect your sister if you are slain? Would she be safe here or in the Cheyenne camp? No. Let her return to her home and family, Lone Wolf. We will protect her and love her."

"How can you know my sister is the female you seek?"

Travis explained about the scar on Rana's ankle and the birthmark on her left arm. He pointed out the girls' matching histories, ages, and looks. "You know she is Rana Michaels," Travis stated firmly. "Just as you knew she must leave your people and lands one day," he added to test a suspicion of his. "That day has come."

Lone Wolf eyed the mixed-blooded male with renewed interest. The man's eyes and statements were startlingly direct and confident. There was an air about Travis that could cause other men to be consumed with fear or to feel challenged. Yet Lone Wolf was not a man of fear or rashness. Seemingly without trying, the white man had used a tone of voice that suggested he was capable of challenging and defeating almost any foe or peril. Lone Wolf's mind filled with respect for the other man. Yes, he recalled this half-white warrior and his legendary prowess. He knew Travis was speaking the truth and was offering him a tempting path to help his people. Was this the path of destiny that had been calling to his sister for many years? Should he force her feet upon it? He glanced at Nathan Crandall and requested, "*Lel usi yo.*"

Travis told Nathan, "He wants you to come over here. Don't worry, Nate; he can be trusted. Nothing's settled yet, but he's willing to discuss a trade." Travis quickly revealed the warrior's identity, his rank, and the fact that Soaring Hawk was dead. Nathan stepped forward to join them. The two white men stood side by side eyeing the powerful chief.

Lone Wolf slipped from his horse's back. To convince his warriors that there was no danger and to express his lack of fear to the white men, he rested his lance and shield on a nearby rock, then removed his bow and quiver to place them with his discarded weapons. He faced them and, as he did so, instantly decided that his sister favored the older man, especially in the coloring of the eyes. In fluent English, Lone Wolf inquired casually, "What will you do if I refuse to bargain with my sister's freedom? Our peoples are at war."

"If you do not accept our offer in exchange for Rana, I will try to steal her from your tepee. If I fail, her grandfather will bargain with the Army to fight for her release. Do not force me to battle my brothers for what we know is right for all concerned."

"What if I order my warriors to slay you and your father friend? Why do you not challenge for Wild Wind in the Lakota way?"

Travis gently seized Nathan's arm and shook his head in warning when the older man started to interrupt. He smiled affectionately and encouragingly at him, then answered the warrior in Oglala for privacy. "My friend's protection and happiness come first in my heart, for he has given me love and acceptance as no other has. I am as his son. It would pain him deeply to cause my death while seeking the return of his loved one. He is getting old and needs me at his side. If I challenge for her, then she is mine, not her grandfather's. I seek to marry no woman until love is a strong bond between us. We came under truce. If you slay us, your face would be stained with dishonor. If I challenge for Wild Wind, her bargain price and all it buys will be lost to you and your people. Accept our offer, Lone Wolf, for we will not leave the Dakota Territory without her. You must trust me. If I were a man of lost honor and hate, I would have entrapped and slain you and your warriors."

Lone Wolf grinned, for he knew Travis could have and would have done exactly as he had said, and probably would have succeeded. The warrior was cunning and astute. He knew Travis's words were not a threat; they were a sincere warning, a statement of fact. He could tell that the two white men were determined to regain the white girl who had lived as his sister for ten winters. Lone Wolf knew he could refuse Nathan's and Travis's demands and offers, that he could slay both men. But these were men of courage and honor, despite their white skin, and they were offering something his people needed desperately.

Lone Wolf sat and crossed his legs. He had many responsibilities on his shoulders. He needed a clear head for planning their defense against the awesome white attack that was sure to come soon. Worries over his sister constantly clouded his reason and provoked his anger and impatience. He needed the weapons, supplies, and money that Nathan was offering for her recovery. He needed Wild Wind's future settled. Undeniably, Wild Wind was Rana Michaels, and Rana was white. Perhaps she belonged with her true family, away from these conflicts between the Indian and white man. Perhaps the Great Spirit had sent this solution to him, for

White Eagle had lived in both worlds and could help his sister adjust to her old life. Lone Wolf could not help but wonder what Wild Wind would say and do. Perhaps, he mused, it would be best for all if White Eagle and Wild Wind were joined . . .

Travis sat down before Lone Wolf. Black eyes locked with green ones. Travis could tell that the warrior was considering his offer seriously. Yet an air of mystery and a hint of amusement exuded from the warrior, which he tried to comprehend. Travis pressed his advantage by reiterating why Rana should be sent home and why Lone Wolf needed to accept their bargain. Recalling a fact mentioned earlier, he inquired, "Has the joining ceremony been announced for Rana and Rides-Like-Thunder? Is that why you hesitate or refuse to bargain?"

The chief answered candidly, "Many have asked for Wild Wind, but she has rejected all warriors. She threatens to leave our camp if I force her to join on the full moon. She bluffs Lone Wolf; she has no place to go that offers safety and happiness, and she is too proud to disobey before the eyes of our people. She is to choose her mate or leave by the Sun Dance, or I will bind her to my Cheyenne friend. What if my sister refuses to go with her grandfather? What if she chooses Rides-Like-Thunder or another warrior over him?"

Travis smiled at the amusing and strangely pleasing revelations. "She has been raised Oglala, Lone Wolf; she will obey the commands of her chief and brother. Do not give her a choice. Order her to return home with Nathan. Explain the bargain to her; ask her to sacrifice herself for the survival of her Oglala brother and people." Lone Wolf winced and frowned noticeably. "Such a brave and unselfish deed should make her proud and happy, perhaps earn her a tribal feast and *coup*, perhaps a special medicine wheel for her fiery hair," Travis suggested cleverly.

Lone Wolf laughed. He recalled how she had earned her last one by defiantly trailing a hunting party, then warning them of a white ambush in time to crush their foes. "White Eagle has not forgotten the ways of the fox," the warrior remarked, complimenting his cunning. He liked this half-white male, who he was beginning to think might make a good match for his sister. "Wild Wind was raised Oglala, but she carries white blood that makes her stubborn and defiant, as White Eagle was long ago. You have changed, my Hunkpapa friend. You have found peace and honor and acceptance in your new life. Would it be the same for my sister? Can you make her white again? Can I force her to obey me in this? Many times her Indian heart wars with her white skin. If she does not remember her grandfather, she will not wish to return to him. She might fear leaving with strangers to go far from the people she knows and loves. In truth, she desires to be a warrior, not a woman. If I agree to your trade, White Eagle, do you have the strength, cunning, and patience to tame a wild wind for her grandfather?"

Travis scowled in annoyance, dreading to learn if Rana had inherited any of her mother's bad traits or if she were anything like the twenty-eight-year-old Clarissa Caldwell, who could pass for twenty-three. Considering their personalities, it was no wonder those two Texas vixens had become close friends during Marissa's last few visits home, even though Marissa had been ten years older than Clarissa. Lordy, even their names rhymed! he reflected sardonically. It still surprised Travis that Harrison Caldwell's daughter had not persuaded Marissa to stay home and get rid of Raymond Michaels. From what Nathan had told him, the two women had stuck together during that last visit like a tick to a calf's ear. No doubt Rana and Clarissa would take to each other just as rapidly and tightly. His mind ceased its foolish ramblings. "I was afraid she was named accurately. It sounds to me like I'll be taking a problem off your hands. If you release her to us, I'll do whatever is necessary to get her home and get rid of that rebellious streak. Perhaps a good spanking will work magic on her. That's one white man's custom I heartily approve of."

Lone Wolf shook his dark head. "If she leaves with you, you must be kind and patient with her, White Eagle. Have you forgotten how hard it was for you to leave and to change?" he reminded Travis knowingly. "She is my sister and she is Oglala. I must speak with my council before I give you my answer. Come, you will wait and sleep in my tepee. Do not speak of this matter to my sister or to others. She will feel betrayed by our exchange. She does not agree with trading for another person as is done with wives and captives. If we vote to keep her, you must leave in peace as you came. Do not force us to slay good white men, for they are few and we count them friends."

"I cannot agree to leave without her, Lone Wolf, for I have given my promise to return her to her home and grandfather. Do not force me to battle for her. All Oglala warriors and their brave chief are needed to fight a real enemy, not their friend White Eagle."

Lone Wolf pictured himself addressing his council on this matter. He would explain his warring emotions and predicament to the wise and heroic men who sometimes made him feel too young and ignorant to be sitting around the same council fire with them. But he could not make such a crucial and troubling decision by himself. He would ask for the opinions and reactions of each member. He would listen carefully to each reply, then allow each member to cast a vote on whether or not to accept White Eagle's offer. With wry amusement he reflected that the council discussion and vote would be different if the young, unmated warriors of the tribe were deliberating and deciding Wild Wind's fate. He was glad he had not mentioned his imminent decision about enforced marriage to his Cheyenne friend and relieved that Soaring Hawk was not alive to confront his heartrending dilemma. If the vote went as he expected, he would have to convince his sister of his love for her and his desire to do what was best for all concerned, including her.

No one spoke as Lone Wolf continued his silent study of the situation. The Oglala chief concluded that perhaps it was an ironic form of justice that a white man's money and help would clear the tangled path to survival for his people. But there were dangers and obstacles to consider. The council might believe this was a bluecoat trick and order White Eagle and his friend put to death. The council could vote to keep Wild Wind or to allow her to make her own choice. The council could vote to torture the white men until they turned over the much-needed money for supplies and weapons. Or the council could vote to trick White Eagle into getting the supplies and weapons before slaying them. Even as chief, once he went before the council, he could not go against their vote.

To prevent Nathan from hearing his words, Lone Wolf responded in his native tongue. "If the council votes against you, then we will speak of such matters. Come to my camp, I will call the council together. My head and heart belong to this problem and it confuses them. Others must help make this decision. Tell White Eagle's friend to camp here with my warriors until the new sun glows in the sky. He does not know our ways and might interfere or offend. He is eager and afraid; he may speak words I do not wish others to hear. He is white. His words and presence could endanger two lives and our bargain."

After Travis nodded understanding and agreement, Lone Wolf advised, "There is danger for you and your friend, White Eagle, if the council thinks you speak or act falsely. Do not enter my camp if you are afraid to face death or cannot keep your word. You know our ways; the council's word is law even for their chief."

"I fear no one and nothing except dishonor, Lone Wolf."

"Speak to your friend; then we ride for my camp."

Travis sat in Lone Wolf's tepee awaiting the outcome of the council meeting, which had been going on for over an hour. It was near the eating time and Wild Wind had not appeared to prepare her brother's meal. Travis wondered if Lone Wolf had ordered her to stay out of the tepee until his return. He was edgy, for there had been an undercurrent in Lone Wolf's voice and manner that he had been unable to grasp. Yet he did not feel as if the warrior would deceive or betray him. He only wished he felt the same way about his council and tribe.

Time dragged on and Travis's tension mounted. Lone Wolf had not confined him to this tepee, but he wanted to be here when the girl arrived. He wanted to study her privately, to see what he and Nathan would be in for if they secured her release. He was annoyed by his anxiety and lack of patience. Had he forgotten that part of his Indian upbringing? Evidently Wild Wind had, for it was her duty to care for her brother's tepee and needs, and those of his guests.

The village noises became muffled by the buffalo hides forming the Oglala dwellings, for most had gone inside their tepees for the evening meal. Eating at this early hour would allow time for final chores before darkness claimed the settlement.

For the countless time, Travis glanced at the closed flap of the tepee, unaware that his impatience actually had to do with wanting to meet Rana Michaels before Lone Wolf's return. He had not been able to get her image out of his mind since his eyes had touched on it. If she did not come home soon, the fading light would deny him a good look at her, for it was too warm to build a fire inside the tepee this early.

Travis decided to take a short walk to the nearby river to freshen up and to revive himself. Just as he reached the tepee entrance, the flap was thrown aside and Wild Wind ducked to rush inside, slamming her head into Travis's hard chest. Both were caught off balance and tumbled to the ground with exclamations of surprise. Wild Wind landed atop the man in buckskins who was struggling to keep her from being injured from the ramming and fall. An abundance of fiery hair spilled over Travis's face and chest like soft hay falling from a loft and covering him. His senses went spinning at her nearness and her fragrance.

Wild Wind instantly realized it was not her brother she had bumped into and landed upon. She lifted her head and stared at the grinning man beneath her. The smoothly tan face that filled her vision was breathtakingly handsome. In a flurry of observations she noticed the red band secured across his forehead and the wisps of deep brown hair playing over it, which danced in the breeze of her rapid respiration. Her eyes took in his full lips, the tiny cleft in the center of his chin, the strength of his stubbled jawline, those incredibly green eyes that sparkled as they watched her, and teeth that flashed shockingly white against his darkly tanned features. She noted that a *wanapin* with Lakota markings had slipped from beneath his clean, chamois-colored shirt and now rested near the hollow of his throat.

While Wild Wind was studying Travis, he was doing the same to her. From viewing her portraits, he had expected her to have great beauty and allure, but nothing as potent as what he was now observing. All suspicious twinges about women vanished from his entranced mind. She radiated an awesome attraction that set his heart pounding and her scent reminded him of a meadow of flowers on a dew-fresh morning. There was an untamed wildness and earthy sensuality about her, which seemed to convey a powerful yet hazardous magic. Her eyes were large and magnetic, and he felt as if he were being drawn into a blue-gray whirlpool. Lashes and brows of dark auburn set off those arresting eyes perfectly. Her unmarred complexion was smooth and golden, which was unusual for a redhead, though not so the light sprinkling of pale freckles across a dainty nose and cotton-soft cheeks. Her lips were pink and full—the kind that pouted prettily and would kiss delightfully, he mused. From her length against his body, he guessed her height at five feet three or four. Her weight could not be much more than two sacks of grain, he estimated; perhaps a shave over one hundred pounds. With it resting on him, he could tell it was enticingly placed to tempt a man to boldness. His large hands wrapped completely around her slender arms. Compared to his six-feet-four frame, hers seemed tiny and fragile.

Travis sensed that this girl knew what she wanted from life and would risk anything to obtain her desires. Yet there was a compelling aura of softness with her strength, a warmth and vulnerability that her mother had lacked. This girl had a naturalness that other women would envy. He was certain that Lone Wolf had spoken truthfully when he had told him that many men desired her and had made large offers for her. And he was just as certain that this girl could pick from the best warriors and wrap her choice around her finger like a supple blade of spring grass. Thomas Mallory had not exaggerated her beauty. There had been no artistic misinterpretation or tricks of lighting. If anything, she was even more beautiful than her portraits. Mallory had been right; who could forget or ignore this ravishing and radiant creature?

In Oglala, Travis hinted mirthfully, "You must be Wild Wind. Perhaps Lone Wolf should rename you Whirlwind. Do you always make your guests prepare their own meals while you spin around?" he teased.

Wild Wind's cheeks pinkened, first from embarrassment and then from anger. How dare this white man touch her and insult her, compare her to a flighty *wamniomni!* *"Nanpi yuze sni yo!"* she demanded unflinchingly, ordering him to take his hands off her. He was so tall and strong, and so infuriatingly appealing. She was apprehensive about his curious effect on her, though she attempted to conceal her feelings. "*Nituwe he?*" She asked him who he was, questioning his presence and the freedom he was enjoying in her tepee.

Travis could not suppress his unintentionally provoking chuckles as he sat up, easily taking her along with him and setting her beside him on the ground. He had never met a woman who ignited such fierce passions within him. He suddenly felt relaxed; he felt alive and daring. "*Kopegla sni yo, Watogla Tate. Wanmbli Ska kola.*" He shifted to an Indian sitting position and grinned at her.

She glared at him, for he seemed to be making fun of her or perhaps was challenging her to battle him or cry out for help. Though he seemed fearless and powerful, she met his challenge with a proud and willful jut to her chin and a pretty pout on her lips. She held herself straight and still, expressing confidence and self-control as she responded tartly, "I am afraid of nothing and no one. What do you want? A despicable white man can be no friend to my brother and the Oglalas! It matters not if you speak our tongue and give yourself an Indian name. The white soldiers killed my father and attack all Lakotas. My people make war against them. We will drive all whites from our lands, or they will die."

She looked him over for weapons and was surprised to see none. She wondered why he was calmly sitting here unarmed. He did not appear to be a fool or a reckless man, for his eyes and demeanor suggested intelligence and prowess. To test his reaction, she warned, "You steal into the wrong tepee, white dog. When my brother returns, he will capture you and slay you. He is chief of the Red Arrow Band. When he has taken his revenge, there will be nothing left of your body for the wolf or vulture." As she stared into his sparkling eyes and genial expression, she found that such an idea oddly pained her. His gaze was as soft as a feather but as strong as wet rawhide. His eyes made no secret of the fact that he found her beautiful and desirable. She could only hope that her eyes did not mirror those matching feelings, for they surged madly through her mind and body. It felt good to touch him, to look upon him. She suddenly and absurdly wished he would escape unharmed. This was a man who would never need the help of the Elk Dreamer's love medicine to obtain or to hold onto his chosen woman. He could steal any careless maiden's heart and honor easily. Quickly she suppressed such strange thoughts and reactions.

Travis understood her anger and waxed serious. "I am half Lakota, Wild Wind. I offer no danger to Wild Wind or your people. I wait for Lone Wolf to return from the council. We are friends. I came in peace to offer help to your people against the bluecoats. I was born and lived in the camp of the Hunkpapas until seven winters past. I carry two bloods. My father was white and my mother Hunkpapa. Both are dead. I was named White Eagle by our medicine chief, Sitting Bull."

Travis lifted his fringed shirt to expose the scars on his chest muscles. "I was a warrior. Twice I offered my life to Grandfather in the Sun Dance; twice He spared it and honored me with many victories. I am sorry your father, Soaring Hawk, was slain; he was a man of great courage and honor. Lone Wolf fills his moccasins and tepee with the same measure of honor and courage. I live twenty moons of fast riding from your camp, in the land between the waking and sleeping of the sun. Lone Wolf brought me to his camp and tepee. When he returns, he will tell you I am his friend and guest. Are you injured?" he asked when she rubbed the top of her head.

She retorted, "When my brother returns, I will learn if you speak with a split tongue. If your heart is as hard as your body, you will die, White Eagle. You are part white, and I trust no white-eyes."

"Wild Wind is all white. Should a man of Lakota blood not trust her? It is wrong to hate all whites for the evil of some. Tell me how you came to be Oglala, the daughter of Soaring Hawk," he asked politely.

"Only my skin is white; my life and heart are Lakota. We will speak no more until my brother returns and calls you friend or foe. What help did you come to offer my people? You are only one man, a half-white man. How can you help? Why did you leave the Hunkpapas?"

Travis smiled and shook his head of nape-grazing sable hair. "We will speak no more until your brother returns and calls me friend," he playfully retorted to intrigue her. "I did not mean to tease you earlier. My body was restless and my stomach is empty; they clouded my reason. Does Wild Wind know how to gather firewood and cook?" he mischievously teased, though he had just finished apologizing for doing so earlier.

In spite of her resolve to remain poised, Wild Wind narrowed her eyes and clenched her teeth. "Why do you insult Lone Wolf's sister?"

"Why does Lone Wolf's sister treat his guest so badly? It is past the eating time and White Eagle hears thunder in his belly. Do you wish me to hunt and roast my own rabbit?"

"You dare to shame and correct Wild Wind?" she demanded.

"You shame yourself with defiance, unless there is a reason why you come home late and do not prepare food for Lone Wolf's tepee. Perhaps Wild Wind has more than white skin to master."

"I will explain nothing to you, half-breed!" she exclaimed, panting.

"You will explain your lack of manners and disobedience to your brother and chief when he returns to a dark tepee and hungry guest. I was told of Wild Wind's bad ways, but I did not believe one so beautiful and smart could behave so shamefully and defiantly. I see the words and jokes of others hold much truth. It is wrong for a sister to bring such dishonor and unhappiness to her brother and chief. I will seek food and warmth in another tepee until Lone Wolf returns."

Wild Wind frowned in dismay. This arrogant, insufferable man was going to get her into more trouble with her brother and people! As much as it hurt, she held her tongue and forced her manners to surface. "A smart man does not accept the foolish words of loose tongues, White Eagle. I have good reason to be late. My brother will understand and forgive me. I did not expect to find a white man in our tepee, one who tries to cut Wild Wind with his sharp, cruel words. I will return soon with hot food to quiet your rumbling belly and loud manner. I will build a fire to lighten the darkness in our tepee and in your head. You are Lone Wolf's guest and I will treat you as such. But do not speak to me again. Anger and hatred for you fill my heart."

Wild Wind arose gracefully. She brushed off her garments, then checked her hair with quivering fingers. Her stormy blue eyes flashing insults at him, she turned and left quickly. She would go to Myeerah's tepee to obtain food for her brother's insolent guest and information about him. Before the council meeting ended, Lone Wolf's tepee would have a cheery fire and hot food. Then she would see if the half-white man exposed her misbehavior to her brother. If he did, he would be sorry! So would Lone Wolf if he dared to reprimand her before that nettling creature with the devilish grin and mocking eyes!

Yet, as she walked toward Myeerah's tepee, she glanced over her shoulder several times to see if the stranger was watching her retreat; she found herself annoyed that he was not. Much as she tried not to be, she was impressed by him and she quivered strangely. He had a smile that brightened his handsome face and eyes like a fiery sunset. His body and grip told her he was powerful; his movements and responses told her he was agile and alert. He was a superior male and doubtlessly had been a superior warrior. His wit was quick and amusing, even if it had been directed at her. Surely he was a man of many sides and traits, and all seemed most appealing. If only he was not half white, she mused dreamily as she called his image and voice to mind. Suddenly a voice inside her head replied, But you are white too . . .

Chapter 3

As Travis Kincade built a small fire in the center of the tepee, he questioned his behavior toward Nathan's misplaced granddaughter. It was not right to view or to judge Rana in the same light as he did other women, or to treat her so rudely. His initial motives had been to test her character and to see if he could control her with cunning. He had thought that if he made her angry and defensive now, she would comply with his demands later, just to prove that his insulting accusations about her had been false, or at least exaggerated. If he were lucky, she would meet his challenge and would expose her mettle and suppress her disruptive ways. Hopefully she would think twice before "shaming" her brother and herself by being unwilling to accept her new fate or by refusing to behave like a proper Indian maiden of high standing.

Maybe she would use extra effort to impress him, for her initial study of him had been one of appreciation, and he knew women went after things that caught their eyes. She was accustomed to men pursuing her, just as he was used to women desiring and chasing him.

But this girl had been raised differently, raised as he had been, and hopefully without learning dirty, greedy feminine tricks. If he showed little or no interest in such an untamed minx, she might be intrigued into mellowing in order to entice him. One thing he knew for sure was that the girl had spunk. She was proud, and pride might aid his cause if she were led to believe that her departure would be a heroic and unselfish act. No matter what she might say or do to soften him, he would have to stand firm and blind to it, for he felt certain she would yield better and more quickly to a show of strength and persistence, or a display of scorn if she were to conduct herself badly. Perhaps her brother's leniency was the root of Lone Wolf's trouble with her, he mused. Travis felt he had to let this girl know immediately who was boss. He had to weaken her rebellious streak, make her defensive and compliant. Though they might be dirty tricks to play on her, it looked as if she would demand such deception and harshness to master her.

The kindling caught and Travis gradually added small pieces of wood. He sat near the blaze, feeding it when necessary and reflecting on Wild Wind. What an independent and ornery little cuss she was, as Nathan would say. She was going to be one bag of trouble, that mule-headed and irritating vixen . . . that ravishing and arrogant creature who would no doubt use her wits and charms to battle or disarm him. Lordy, this trip home was going to be long and rough! he told himself. Especially if Nathan became enchanted by her and interfered with his lessons and discipline. Without a doubt she would try to escape them at least once, just to annoy him with a display of her unusual skills. So Wild Wind wanted to be a fighter, did she? He would watch her every minute and mile during their trek home.

Travis envisioned her challenging expression and smug air; they reminded him of his own attitude long ago, before Nathan had taken him under his wing. Sakes alive, how he had changed over the past few years! People who had met or had known him before Nathan Crandall would not recognize him now. The thought brought a roguish smile to the ranch foreman's lips and eyes. He recalled certain lessons Nathan had used with him. Nothing made a person do something or do it well quicker than to have another person tell him he couldn't do it or do it right. He couldn't count the times he had behaved himself or had learned something new and had made sure he had done it better than anyone else, only because Nathan had challenged him with clever words or cunning expressions. Sometimes it had been to prove Nathan and others wrong, and other times it had been to show Nathan that he had been right about a hot-tempered, sullen youth who had touched the old man's heart.

Travis wished Lone Wolf would settle this matter tonight, so he and Nathan could carry out their part of the bargain and be gone before any Hunkpapa warriors came to visit. Maybe he had been a fool to let Nathan come here with him, for Nathan could become entrapped along with him if things went badly. If Lone Wolf and the Oglalas discovered why he had left this territory years ago and what his—

"*Loyacin sni he, Wanbli Ska?*" Wild Wind breathily asked, inquiring if he were still hungry and startling the dreamy Travis into reflexive action.

In a blurred instant, Travis was on his feet, crouching and holding a knife that had appeared in his left hand seemingly from nowhere. Poised for an enemy's attack, he saw Wild Wind inhale sharply and back away, her alert eyes never leaving his and her stance preparing to defend herself. Travis instantly relaxed and smiled. He replaced the knife in its sheath beneath his left pant leg. "I did not hear you enter, Wild Wind. You move as silently as the stalking cat . . . or as nimbly as a skilled warrior. Your eyes and instincts are sharp. You have watched and trained well. No foe would be safe around you."

Wild Wind had observed how rapidly and agilely the man had moved. She had intentionally sneaked up on him and she now realized that if his instincts had not been dulled by deep worry over some matter, he would have detected her stealthy approach. She had been wrong earlier, for he was indeed armed. By not blindly lunging at her, which she had desired, he had revealed self-control and the ability to rapidly assess a situation. She had hoped he would react foolishly and cause her to drop the food he had demanded she get for him. Yet when their eyes had fused, she had unconsciously clutched the containers to avoid dropping them and looking clumsy. Reluctantly, she was impressed by his show of superior training and pleased by his flattering remarks. She knelt beside his fire without commenting, retrieved a small wooden platter, and served his food, then handed him a bag with fresh water.

"*Pilamaya,*" he thanked her as he accepted the meal and drink.

"A warrior should not lower his guard so completely, White Eagle. If a lowly female can sneak up on you, how are you safe in the forests? Have you forgotten your warrior's training in the white man's world?"

Travis was amused by the heavy sweetness in her voice and expression. "I saw no need to be on guard in Lone Wolf's tepee and camp. Surely no enemy would dare invade them. As for you, Wild Wind," he ventured slowly and evocatively as his mocking gaze swept over her, "there is nothing lowly about the daughter of Soaring Hawk and the sister of Lone Wolf. You value yourself too little. You should work hard to prove that others are wrong about you," he mirthfully suggested, smugly assuming that his distracting thoughts had allowed her to sneak up on him.

"I can be nothing less than Wild Wind. If others think false thoughts of me, it is a flaw in their minds and hearts, and Wild Wind will not waste time correcting foolish people. Perhaps White Eagle should work hard to prove that Wild Wind is wrong about him," she retorted slyly.

Disconcerting green eyes leveled on the girl who was sitting across the fire from him and waiting for him to complete his meal before she ate, as was the Indian custom. He continued to eat slowly, without taking his eyes from her face. He noticed her cheeks pinken, but she refused to lower her gaze demurely. Her eyes were bright and startlingly direct, as her words had been. In a lazy voice that carried undertones of mischief, he inquired, "What if Wild Wind is not wrong about me? And what if she receives only the actions she provokes?"

Still she refused to pull her stormy gaze from his taunting one. "*Ota wayata he? Inipi he?*" she asked as he halted to stare at her.

"Yes, I had enough to eat; and I am full," he roguishly replied. "It was very good. Please thank your friend for me. You did not answer before. Can Wild Wind cook and tend a tepee?"

Wild Wind glared at him. She was not hungry, but she ate to prevent him from thinking he had stolen her appetite. When she was finished, she cleared their platters and washed them. She wondered why this disconcerting man vacillated back and forth between insults and apologies. What crafty game was he playing with her? She set the earthenware bowl containing Lone Wolf's meal on the flat rocks that encased the fire. She hung the water bag on a side pole. To dispel the unnerving silence in the tepee, she remarked as she worked, "The council meeting runs long. What news did you bring to my people? Why did you not attend?"

"You know it is not permitted for a guest to sit in Oglala council. I promised your brother I would not speak of such matters to anyone. We must wait to hear their vote, and obey it with honor."

Wild Wind observed Travis Kincade. If he had lived in this area, she would have heard of him or seen him before. If he were a friend, why had he never visited them? she wondered. He knew the Lakota customs and laws, and he spoke of them with respect and loyalty. Yet he looked and sounded concerned by the length of the meeting. "Is it good or bad that the council talks long?" she probed curiously.

Travis glanced over at her and shrugged. "*Slolwaye sni,*" he admitted, telling her he did not know. "*Unkomani kte,*" he added, asking her to take a walk.

"Tell me why you come and worry, White Eagle, and I will go."

Travis chuckled and shook his head before remarking, "You are too clever and perceptive for such a young woman, Wild Wind. I worry because the council's decision is important to many people. Ask me nothing more. Soon you will know all."

She did not heed his request. "Important to White Eagle?"

"Yes, because it is important to someone I love and respect, and to the survival of my Lakota people," he responded mysteriously. "Do you know anything about the white man's guns?" he questioned as he pointed to his pistols and rifle on a buffalo mat. When she shook her head, he commanded sternly, "Then do not touch them. They are dangerous. They can injure or slay a careless or nosy whirlwind."

"Do they carry great magic like the warrior's weapons?" she asked, knowing it was wrong for a woman to touch a man's weapons and ceremonial items, especially during her monthly flow.

"Their magic lies in their owner's skill and use of them, nothing more. I will return later. I need fresh air and movement."

As Travis headed for the entrance, she called out, "Do you wish me to go?" She wanted more information and decided that a woman's soft hand could pick him better than a wildcat's claws.

Travis glanced over his shoulder and replied, "If you like." He saw her expression change and knew that was not the right answer for this vixen. "It's nearly dark. As I look more white than Indian and many in your camp do not know of me, perhaps it is wiser and safer for Lone Wolf's guest if you walk beside him." He ducked and left, eager to see if she would swallow his bait and join him. Recognizing that there indeed was truth in his conniving words, he walked slowly and cautiously.

"The meeting lodge holds secrets and dangers this moon. The council speaks in whispers. It is not good," she concluded worriedly as she caught up with his lengthy strides.

Travis furtively eyed her. He could tell from her increased respiration and the tightness around her eyes that she felt intimidated by him and that meeting. She shuddered, suddenly looking very vulnerable and afraid. That unexpected insight warmed him. To distract her, he rashly questioned her past and memory. "Lone Wolf told me you have been his sister for ten winters. He did not explain how a captive white child became the honored daughter of Soaring Hawk."

Wild Wind halted and looked at him strangely. "Why would my brother speak of such matters to White Eagle? I do not know from where you ride or why I have not heard of you. Why do you question me?"

"Is there some evil secret to your capture and adoption?" His crafty response worked, for it kept the conversation on her. "Most prisoners hate their captors, but you do not hate the Oglalas. Why?"

"Oglalas did not murder my family and capture me," she swiftly defended them. Her gaze lifted to the moon, which would reach its fullness within a week, and that sight seemed to panic her. She began to talk dreamily, as if to force the alarm from her mind. "Kiowas killed my family and stole me. They were a cruel and fierce band and I hated them. I do not remember how long I was with them. Then, ten winters ago, Soaring Hawk raided the new Kiowa camp and rescued me. Soaring Hawk explained that the white man had driven the Kiowas from their lands and that the Kiowas were trying to invade Lakota lands. There was a violent storm and many whirlwinds filled the air with dirt. The Kiowas and their horses were blinded by the winds and sands and did not see the Oglalas attack until it was too late. The Oglalas knew of such storms and wore thin cloths over their faces. They could look out, but the sand could not come into their eyes and noses," she related proudly.

She looked and talked as if she had drifted into a trance. "I was frightened. I tried to hide, but the sand burned my eyes and I could not see to run. Soaring Hawk found me lost in the whirling storm and took care of me. That is why he named me Wild Wind. He said the Great Spirit had come to him in a vision and had told him to take me as his daughter. His wife lived with the Great Spirit and his heart was full of sadness and pain. He ordered two Indian captives to care for Wild Wind, Lone Wolf and himself. When my father died, Lone Wolf sold the captives and Wild Wind now cares for his tepee. He is chief now and must take a wife. Soaring Hawk is gone and things are chang—Enough words of Wild Wind. Speak of White Eagle and his mission."

Travis knew the meaning of her incomplete sentence. He pressed, "Do you remember your white family, Ra . . . Wild Wind? Do you know where your real mother and father lived before your capture?"

Wild Wind became nervous and angry. To stop this distressing talk, she lied, "No, I was a small child. Speak of other things. I do not wish to remember those dark suns and moons." She lapsed into pensive silence. Many times in her sleeping and waking dreams she had seen a strange and wicked white man who terrified and injured her. She could hear him shouting awful words at her and see him striking her, his pale face distorted by evil and cruelty, his black hair flying wildly as he jerked his head and body about in fits of pure rage. She had heard herself sobbing and pleading to go home, but he had beaten her and called her filthy names. She had heard his icy laughter fill her ears and she had covered them to close out the wicked sounds. They had to be bad dreams, not memories, for she always saw herself as a grown woman, not as a child. Those terrible dreams were so strange, for she was always wearing white man's garments and her fiery hair was not long and thick as it was in real life and was worn differently. Many times the dreams were petrifying, for her lovely face would be swollen and bruised and bleeding. The older she became, the less the dreams filled her mind. Yet whenever she thought or spoke of the Kiowas, the bad dreams would return for many moons to torment her.

"What frightens you, Wild Wind?" Travis asked in concern.

She glared at him for his painful intrusion. "Go away. White Eagle is mean and bad." She whirled and raced back to her tepee.

Travis waited a short time before returning to the tepee to find her sitting on her sleeping mat, pretending to be beading a pair of moccasins. When he heard a quiet sniffle and saw her inhale raggedly, he walked to her and dropped to his knees. Lifting her chin, he stared into misty blue eyes filled with anguish. As a tear escaped to roll down one cheek, she tried to free herself from his firm but gentle grasp. He could tell she did not like exposing such deep feelings or a loss of control. He wanted to hold her in his arms and comfort her, then cover her face with kisses. He wanted to make love to this half-wild vixen, this part-woman, part-child creature, yet he dared not respond to such tempting hunger. "Do not cry, Wild Wind. I will speak no more of such days of pain and fear. You are very brave and special. Your people must love and respect you greatly. Do not be sad," he entreated, for her pain had had an overwhelming effect on him.

She watched him master the urge to lean forward to kiss her, and oddly she was sorry he had found the strength to do so. He was a man of many emotions and sides, a man of great prowess. Only a man of enormous strength would have the power and courage to reveal tenderness, as tenderness was a strength of its own that few men possessed. She could tell that it was difficult for him to expose such feelings, for the look in his grass green eyes told her that he had once known much suffering. As an Indian, he had been raised to master his emotions and to depend on himself for survival. Obviously he had left the Lakota world, and she wondered when and why. He was a new man, but the old one had not died easily or fully. She wondered which part of him he wished to slay, the Indian or the white, for surely those bloods warred fiercely within him, as they did with her sometimes. It was terrible to be torn between two lands and two peoples, to be neither accepted nor rejected by either. Her gaze seemed to mesmerize him. He appeared capable of experiencing powerful emotions and seemed vulnerable to certain forces, though it was obvious he fought to conceal and control such traits. She liked these impressions, and she liked him when he was this man.

"*Tanyan amaye, Wanbli Ska. Pilamaya.*" She softly explained that she felt better and surprisingly thanked him as if it were because of him.

He smiled. "*Ohan.*" He went to the buffalo mat she had spread out for him, for it was very late, and mused silently, Yes, it was "good" . . .

Wild Wind watched him lie down in his garments and moccasins, his back to her because of the angle at which she had placed his mat. Putting aside her beading, she checked the fire. She added small hunks of wood, mostly knots, for they would burn slowly and give off enough light to chase the darkness and ghosts from the tepee. Then she removed her moccasins and, leaving on her garments, reclined on her sleeping mat. She closed her eyes to envision White Eagle's face, in order to study and admire it. Gradually she allowed herself to drift into light slumber.

Within the hour, Wild Wind was tossing restlessly and mumbling words that Travis could not grasp. She began to whimper and moan, and her head and body thrashed upon the sleeping mat. Travis eased over to awaken her from her nightmare. From the few words that came out clearly, he assumed she was dreaming about the Kiowas, whom he had recalled to her mind. He gently shook her and called her name.

In the horrifying dream, she saw her flaming-haired image fleeing the nighthaired white man as she screamed for rescue. The evil man captured her by long curls of fire and jerked her to her knees. Large blue eyes and a muffled voice pleaded with him to let her go free, to stop hurting her. He sent forth chilling laughter and started pounding her with his fists. She could hear him shouting, "You little bitch! If you try to leave me again, I'll beat you and your sniveling brat senseless. I got you out of a nasty mess, so you owe me plenty, slut. You don't want me to tell your pa the truth about his whoring daughter before I put a bullet in his head, do you? I'm warning you, harlot, the next time you go against me in any way, they're both dead, and you too."

"Please, let us go home. I can't do this anymore."

"We got us a deal—silence for money. If you can't get it from your loving pa, earn it on your back, just like you earned your trouble. I'm broke, so shuck those clothes and git your pretty ass to work. You ain't gonna cost me my next stake by refusing to let Fargo poke you good. He's your best customer. You don't want me telling nobody the truth about you and that brat, so git in there and—" Suddenly the door crashed aside and White Eagle's towering body filled the opening. He called her name, but the brown-eyed enemy held her shoulder tightly and warned, "I'll never let you go; you're my gold mine."

Travis was shocked when she called his Indian name and begged for help. He seized her in his arms and shook her roughly as he told her to awaken: "*Kikta yo, Watogla Tate!*" She fought him and confused him with her Oglala words: "He will slay us if we disobey. He torments us and hurts us. Help us, White Eagle. Make the pain and blood go away. Kill him! Kill him . . ." She began sobbing against his chest.

His arms held her tightly and his voice spoke comforting words. "Do not cry or be afraid, Wild Wind. I will protect you from all evil. Come with me and trust me. No one will hurt you again," he promised in her tongue as he stroked her hair and placed kisses over her face. At last he had met a rare creature, a woman with real feelings, a woman like him, a woman who needed and wanted the same things he did.

Wild Wind reached out to his touch and comforting voice. She clung to his shirt and nestled her face against his. Her lips instinctively and hungrily sought and found his. As they sank to her mat, her arms encircled his body and she greedily feasted at his mouth. Her senses went spinning when his lips tried to kiss each spot on her face and neck. A curious warmth and trembling attacked her passion-inflamed senses. Suddenly he pulled away from her, and she felt lost and scared. Her whirling wits cleared as she watched him sit up and try to slow his rapid breathing. He wiped moisture from his face and turned his back to her.

After a minute, Travis said, "I was not fully awake when I tried to free you from your bad dreams, Wild Wind. I must not touch the dau . . . sister of my friend, Lone Wolf, in this way. Go back to sleep. I will be here to guard you from all evil."

Before he could return to his mat, she caught his arm to stay him and asked, "*Taku eniciyapi wasicun he? Waniyetu nitona he? Nicinca tonapi he? Tohan kin yagli kta watohanl he?*"

Travis half turned and gazed at her, wary of the power of those bewitching eyes and sultry lips. He answered her first three questions in order. "The whites call me Travis Kincade. I'm twenty-seven winters old. I have no children, for I have taken no mate." Not because Nathan had not tried to get him to marry and have children, but because he had not found any woman worthy of those roles. He replied to her last question with a question, "Do you wish me to return here one day?"

"*Slolwaye sni,*" she replied honestly, pulling her gaze from his.

"Why do you not know your thoughts and feelings?" He lifted her flushed face, locking his probing gaze to her wary one. They stared into each other's eyes for a lengthy time and desire flamed between them. He tenderly caressed her cheek and stroked her mussed hair. "Do not fear me, Wild Wind; I bring you no harm. Why do you quiver?"

"Because there is something about you that troubles me. You are a man of many secrets and dangers, a stranger. I do not know why you came to our camp, but I do not think my people will trust you. There is too much hostility between the Indians and whites."

"If they do not trust me, the Oglalas might not survive this war with the white man. The whites are many and powerful, Wild Wind. I fear they are one enemy the Lakotas cannot defeat, and that pains me. If my blood were all Lakota, I would ride into battle with my people. But a warrior cannot fight the white man while he fights the half-breed disease. I am accepted in the white lands, for they do not know I am half Indian, but I am scorned in the Indian lands, for they can see I am half white and it stirs their blood to hatred and cruelty. I wish it were not so. I wish I could share both lands and peoples, for I have missed my Lakota people since I rode far away. Neither side will allow it. Once long ago I was forced to travel a path from my mother's lands. I had to learn many new things and make many changes. It was hard, but a man of honor endures his suffering silently and bravely."

As he continued, his left forefinger absently pushed silky strands of golden-red hair from her face, and his eyes gazed more and more deeply into hers. Her magnetism was a tangible force and caused his voice to become husky. "When Grandfather changes our paths in life, we must not refuse to travel them or many will suffer for our selfishness and blindness. When I return to my wooden tepee in the white man's territory, I will never return to the land of the Dakotas, but I will pray to Grandfather to save His children and sacred lands from total destruction, and I will do the only thing I can to help them."

"White Eagle, tell me why you came to our camp," she urged and found herself wishing he would reply, "For you." She wanted to snuggle into his arms, to feel his touch and to touch him, to share kisses.

"Lone Wolf has my word of honor to hold silent. Go to sleep, Wild Wind. The new sun could bring many dangers for all in this camp. I will allow no harm to come to you and I will awaken you if the bad dreams return. I must leave when the sun rises in the heaven." Travis knew his last statement was not a lie. He would depart to buy the weapons or he would leave with her; and if not with her, then to return later to abduct her. He had promised Nathan he could get her back, and, after meeting her, he was more determined than ever.

Lone Wolf moved away from his tepee as silently as a shadow. He had been listening to and watching Travis and his sister since their walk. Lone Wolf turned and walked toward his tepee, intentionally making enough sound to be heard by the sharp ears of the half-white warrior lying inside his dwelling. He quietly lifted the flap and tossed a small rock on Travis's chest to obtain his attention. When Travis glanced in Lone Wolf's direction, the chief used sign language to command him to silence and to follow him outside for a private talk.

Travis obeyed without alerting Wild Wind to his departure and absence. The two men walked to the nearby river and sat on blankets. Travis tried to conceal his impatience, but he knew he must let the chief speak first.

"The council voted to give White Eagle a chance to prove his words and honor, if we agree to make trade. White Eagle and his friend Nathan will ride to the white man's trading post to buy weapons and supplies. My warriors will ride behind you to protect you and the trade goods. When the weapons and supplies rest in Oglala hands, Lone Wolf will tell his sister that White Eagle has made trade for her. Lone Wolf will command his sister to go with White Eagle. You must leave quickly after I speak words of farewell to her. If she battles my words, White Eagle must tie her hands and take her by force. She is a wild creature, and Lone Wolf has not tamed her with words or punishments."

When Travis grinned in amusement, Lone Wolf warned, "Do not smile quickly, White Eagle. Soon you will feel the sting of her words and endure the troubles of her defiance. She is clever and daring; do not take your eyes or ears from her. If you earn her hatred and anger, do not turn your back to her; she is as skilled as my warriors. I pray Wild Wind will allow White Eagle to be gentle with her. When you return from the trading post, her grandfather must camp where he sleeps this moon. The council refuses to let him enter our camp and interfere with Wild Wind's farewell ceremony. He is old, and blind to our ways. He will not understand how White Eagle will be forced to treat his granddaughter. If he weakens and interferes, the matter will be hard for all concerned."

"It is agreed, Lone Wolf," Travis declared, accepting the exchange terms.

"There is more to hear before you answer, White Eagle."

His smile faded as he eyed Lone Wolf's expression. "Speak it."

"The council says that when you return to our camp White Eagle must join to Wild Wind before you leave with her. She will not be told of her grandfather and our exchange until you are many suns' ride from our camp and lands. She will follow her mate, but she might refuse to return to the land of the whites with strangers. Her mind and heart are troubled and she will think we trick her with claims of family. She thinks I wish to be rid of her and she will doubt our words."

When Travis started to argue this astounding term, Lone Wolf held up his hand and cautioned, "Do not speak until I finish. You will join Wild Wind under Oglala law. Oglala laws do not matter to the white man. Rana Michaels and Travis Kincade are white; they will live in white lands, under white laws. Once you leave our lands, the marriage will not be binding. It is a trick for my sister's obedience and to prevent trouble with the other warriors who have asked to make trade for her. No warrior can offer more than White Eagle's supplies and weapons. The exchange will not be questioned or criticized. The council demands that she leave joined to you. If you refuse to make trade and to join to her, she will be guarded until she is bound to Rides-Like-Thunder and sleeps on his Cheyenne marriage mat. Once her body is mated to his, she will never leave him. Join her and leave in honor, or she is lost to you."

A false marriage . . . Travis raged silently, cursing his bad luck. He knew as well as Lone Wolf that he was trapped, and traps and deceptions riled him. "What if she refuses when I ask her to join to me?"

Lone Wolf chuckled. "Do not play word games with me, White Eagle," he teased mirthfully. "There is no asking in Indian lands, only trading and telling. If she is defiant, she will be bound during the joining ceremony. When you are far away, you can say you pretended to join to her to get her away peacefully to return her to her grandfather. You must tell her the Oglala joining ceremony is not binding in the white man's world. Such words should make her happy, for she has refused to join to any man. But I warn you now, if you sleep upon the marriage mat with my sister, you must promise to join to her under the white man's laws. You must not dishonor Wild Wind or bring pain to her heart. How can she be sad or angry? She will have freedom and her people will be saved by her trade goods. Is it agreed?"

"What if Nathan doesn't agree to these terms? It seems cruel and dishonorable to trick her this way."

"I know Wild Wind, my Hunkpapa brother. If you buy her with trade goods and try to take her away with the truth, my sister will battle you fiercely. She has been raised as Oglala, to hate and mistrust whites. She will fear your claims and she will try to flee them. It is dangerous and foolish to chase an escaped rabbit when the white wolves are running free and hungry. Take her away quickly and safely. Let her ride with White Eagle and her grandfather for many suns so that she might learn to trust and share friendship. When you speak words of truth many moons away, they will touch her ears softly and gently. Do not challenge her to accept strangers and hard words at the same time. Such words will come more easily from trusted friends. Do you know a better way to win my sister's freedom? Does my Hunkpapa brother lack the skills to entice my sister into leaving peacefully with him?"

Travis frowned at the grinning warrior. Lordy, he had never suspected he would be forced to marry the rebellious vixen to buy her freedom! He remembered what had happened when a white woman and her father had tried to force him to marry her. And he recalled the time when an Indian maiden's dreams of having him had provoked the Hunkpapas' rejection and had nearly gotten him killed . . . He forced thoughts of those treacherous days from his mind, for this situation was different; this marriage would not be real or a matter of his survival.

Lone Wolf was right about his needing to get out of this territory as quickly and as safely as possible, but not for the reasons he had mentioned.

Travis considered the matter carefully and gave Lone Wolf the only decision he could make. The men talked for awhile, then headed for Lone Wolf's tepee. Travis realized that when dawn appeared and he rode out of camp, it would be too late to change his mind about this matter. He would explain the council's terms to Nathan, and his friend would have to understand the situation.

Lone Wolf strode along the path in front of Travis Kincade and, as the Oglala chief reflected on what had passed between his sister and the half-white warrior earlier, a mischievous smile slowly crossed his lips.

In his office on the Circle C Ranch near Fort Worth, lawyer and landowner Harrison Caldwell was speaking with his burly foreman, Silas Stern. "I don't know how you found those new men, Silas, but I like them," he remarked, then laughed wickedly, for Harrison recognized men with cold, evil hearts like his own. "You said they're real handy with those guns and rifles and aren't afraid to follow orders? Any orders?"

Silas's brown eyes sparkled with pleasure and arrogance as he grinned at his employer, a man whom Silas was careful never to cross. He knew how greedy and cruel Harrison Caldwell could be, for he had witnessed the man's evil and had obeyed orders that had sometimes curdled his blood. He had seen how Harrison had shrewdly used his power and reach to punish men who opposed or challenged him and how he had widely opened his cash box to or had bestowed favors on those who obeyed him or aided his cause. "I found 'em drinking in the saloon and I knew they weren't lying or spinning tales of past days. I watched and listened close for hours afore I hired 'em. I thought we could use two quick guns and stone nerves since McFarland ain't moving out fast enough; then we got Crandall to deal with soon. They rode with Quantrill during the war; they were in on them bloody raids in Missouri and Kansas. Wes said Jesse James helped 'em half the time. It bother you that Wes and Jack were in on that Lawrence massacre or that fight over in Baxter Springs?"

The ranch owner and lawyer recalled the bloodbath in Kansas that had claimed the lives of one hundred and fifty men, women, and children in August of 1863 as well as the slaying of over one hundred Union soldiers near Baxter Springs. He had been a Southerner to the bone, so what did he care if Union soldiers and sympathizers had been slain during that recent war. Served them right, he decided coldly. "Nope, Silas. Fact is, Wes Monroe and Jackson Hayes did us all a big favor years ago. Those Yankees shouldn't have been so far from their beloved Union. I need men who obey orders for a price and without questions, men who aren't afraid to shed blood or go against the law, or die for their boss if it comes to that. Quantrill trained his men well, and I can use them. Still it wouldn't hurt to keep a sharp eye on them. I'm too close to success to have anyone muddy my waters. Crandall and McFarland are the only holdouts against my controlling this entire area. Once McFarland is sent on his way, I'll own every inch of land surrounding Crandall's ranch, and I plan to squeeze him until it hurts too bad to stay around for winter. Did you learn anything about where he and Kincade went?

It's been weeks, and Cody Slade is still running things over there. He refuses to tell Clarissa anything. Strange they would sneak off during the spring cattle drive . . ."

"All I could get out of his hands is what we already know. Cody's in charge and Mace Hunter took the cattle to market. If'n they knows, ain't nobody saying where they rode off to. You want me to sic Wes and Jack on some of 'em and see what they can learn?"

"No. Right now I have other plans for Monroe and Hayes. Just make sure our boys keep stealing and rebranding as many of the Rocking C calves and horses as possible before Nate returns. That was real obliging of him to get a brand that I can alter so easily. Tell them to make certain they aren't caught, or they're dead men. What I want Monroe and Hayes to do for me is to make sure McFarland gets on his way as soon as possible, any way necessary. In a few weeks, I'll let them make sure the money from Nate's cattle sale comes to me, not him. When he can't repay the bank, I'll force good ole Wilber Mason to take over his ranch, real legal like. When she goes up for public auction, Monroe and Hayes can make sure nobody bids against me. If anything goes wrong, I have other plans in motion. Of course, they'll have to take care of Kincade before we can run off Nate."

Silas scratched his head of unruly black hair. "Miss Clarissa ain't gonna like that, sir. She's had her eye set on Travis for years."

Harrison chuckled. "Then she had best have his ring on her finger and have him working for me real soon, hadn't she?" he jested calmly, even though he knew he could never trust a man like Travis Kincade, who had been under the influence of Nathan Crandall too long. "She's only got herself to blame. It's her fault she didn't get any information out of that traveling painter when he did her portrait. She said he didn't know anything about Nate's sudden trip. If you ask me, I think the timing of Mallory's visit and Nate's rush is a little tight to be coincidental. I should have set the boys on him before he left."

As Harrison poured himself a whiskey, Silas frowned. He did not like the idea of tangling with Travis Kincade, or of killing him. Still, he would never interfere with his employer's desires. As for that dark-eyed, dark-haired daughter of his, Clarissa had been trying to snare the handsome foreman since his arrival, and she had not taken kindly to his resistance. That woman could be a real bitch, in actions and in character, he mused wryly. Every time Travis spurned or denied her, she came home and took it out on everyone present, including the lucky cowhand she chose to release her fiery frustrations on. Of course, none of the boys who rolled in the hay with her would boast on it. If one did, he was dead. Strange, her papa didn't care what she did, as long as she obeyed him and kept her doings secret from the town and their neighbors. Silas admitted he might feel differently about her if she would rub that soft body against him a few times, or just once, in fact. He had seen how she had eyed Wes and Jackson up and down yesterday, and he had refused to warn her to steer clear of those dangerous men, men who were used to taking a woman, whether she said yes or no. Yep, those men were dangerous, but they seemed to have a curious sense of loyalty to whoever hired them. Even bold gunslingers like Wes and Jackson were not fool enough to go against a powerful man like Harrison Caldwell.

"That's all for tonight, Silas," Harrison said and watched the man leave. He wished his daughter could find a man like himself to marry, for he was weary of dealing with the crude Silas Stern. Yet he knew he could trust Silas completely, and he needed him a while longer. But as soon as he had the Rocking C Ranch under his control, Silas would not trouble him further. In fact, he was planning a lethal surprise for all of the men who knew his secret dealings . . .

Harrison sat at his desk and gazed into his whiskey. He was on the verge of possessing a vast and powerful Texas empire, and he would allow no one to stand in his way, including his daughter! When he had everything he wanted, he would govern his only child more rigidly. She would marry and settle down respectably with the man of his choosing or, as with Marissa Crandall, she would be sent into the world on her own. And he never doubted that the she-cat would land on her clawed feet. He was angry with her for failing him with Thomas Mallory. He did not like situations and people whom he could not control. Actually he did not like Clarissa and despised the thought of her inheriting his massive and lucrative spread, but she was the only seed of his loins. A devilish smile curled one corner of his broad lips. Maybe it was not too late to find himself another wife who could bear him a son. After all, he was only fifty-six and still virile. If he worked hard and fast, he could have him a son in a year or so and could rid himself of his spoiled, loose-thighed daughter! Too bad Nathan only had one daughter and she was dead. Marriage to Nathan's heir could have solved all of his problems quickly and simply, after Nathan's death.

"Little Marissa Crandall, what a fiery body and greedy appetite you had," he murmured dreamily, then rubbed the rapidly stiffening effect her memory created. "I wonder what your pa would say if he knew how many times you had climbed into bed with me."

Laughter filled the room as he recalled the things he had taught Marissa before she had suddenly run off with that fancy gambler. It did not matter to Harrison that he had gotten her drunk one afternoon and had taken advantage of her. For six months he had enchanted the vixen into sneaking into his bed at every available instance. He smiled wickedly as he trailed his fingertips up and down his hard member and slowly sipped on his whiskey, reflecting on those stimulating days.

He remembered how Marissa had been enamored of him, secretly eyeing him and flirting with him. He had done the same with her, for the seventeen-and-a-half-year-old innocent had been thrilled by the attentions of a handsome, rich, thirty-five-year-old lawyer and rancher. Their first encounter had taken place unexpectedly, when Marissa had ridden to his ranch to deliver a message while her father was away. He had enticed her to linger and to sample forbidden champagne. The daring, impulsive girl had agreed eagerly. Once her wits had been dulled, he had worked skillfully at seducing her, making sure she enjoyed their afternoon together. At first he had pretended to blackmail her with exposure to entice more visits, until the hot-blooded vixen had admitted how much she enjoyed their wanton bouts; he had always been careful to please her in order to keep her coming back for more, and gradually she had lost all inhibitions.

Marissa had sneaked over while his daughter was at school. He had sent his housekeeper away on errands or had given her time off for her own family. Sometimes, before he and Nathan had become enemies, Marissa had come over under the pretense of tutoring Clarissa or staying with her when his housekeeper supposedly could not. During those times, Clarissa had been locked in her room to keep her ignorant of their liaison. Some nights, Marissa would work him into a heavy sweat and would not let him sleep until the cock crowed. She had wanted to learn everything about men and sexual pleasures. Naturally he had been delighted to be her teacher and her pupil. He had waited for her eighteenth birthday to marry her, but Marissa had refused his proposal, claiming she wanted to enjoy her freedom a while longer. She began seeing other men, younger men, but swore she never slept with any of them. She loved to flirt and tease and bewitch them all. Finally, when she was nineteen, he had demanded they marry and halt this secret affair of one-and-a-half years. She had humiliated and pained him deeply by telling him that his size and stamina and appetite were too small for her, and she had ceased her visits, vowing to claim rape if he came near her again or tried to expose their lengthy, wanton affair. When he had traveled back East on business for several months, she had eloped.

Fury filled him at the memory of her casual dismissal, then sadistic pleasure washed over him as he recalled her brutal demise. He wondered if the Indians had enjoyed her before killing her, and he vengefully hoped they had. At least he had obtained his revenge on her last trip home. Secretly he had sent Clarissa to visit a friend one night, then had cleverly summoned Marissa to the Circle *C* Ranch with a forged note from his daughter, for the two had become friends, despite their different personalities. He trembled with ecstasy as he remembered that last night with Marissa tied to his bedposts and him feeding his savage hungers with her tasty body. He had learned the truth from his man Fargo about how she was being forced by Raymond to whore for her family's support, and he had given her no choice but to endure whatever he chose to do to her. He had threatened to expose their past affair and her current demeaning situation to her beloved father. After all, if she could sell it to strangers to stake her fancy gambler, he had reasoned, then, after what they had shared and she had done to him, she could certainly give him all he wanted or needed. Poor little Marissa; she had really changed, for the girl he had known would not have allowed anyone to use her, and it had seemed she no longer enjoyed sex. He had not cared, as long as she could sate his needs as only she had been able to do. Damn her, he mentally cursed. She had haunted him for years, and still did so on occasion. He shuddered now as he mentally relived that night of bliss and domination.

Perhaps he was the only one who had known why Marissa had run off a few days later with that no-good husband of hers. Besides being tied by the mysterious and powerful hold that Raymond Michaels had over her, she had had the knowledge of what her fate would have been at Harrison's hands—or at least what she had thought it would be. Actually he had intended to slay Raymond Michaels and marry his widow, for even then he had still yearned to possess her. Too bad he had forgotten to reveal his plans to Marissa while he was having the best night of his life. The truth was, Marissa Crandall Michaels had been terrified of her husband, and with just cause, from his reports.

Harrison still remembered the look on Marissa's face when he had boasted of supplying the money every time his man Fargo had copulated with her while seeking information for him. He had laughed at her for not having the guts to leave or to kill Raymond Michaels. Clearly she despised her husband and his cruelties, but the man had had some petrifying hold over her that she had been afraid to break or challenge. How he wished he had guessed their secret. Harrison knew that if he had offered her marriage and protection, she would be lying in his bed this very night, waiting to ease the aching in his loins, and the Rocking C would now be a part of his kingdom.

If only he had known Raymond Michaels would show up early . . . He had wanted to punish Marissa and play with her a few days before changing her life completely. When he discovered that Michaels had taken her away, he had planned to go after her, get rid of Michaels, and marry Marissa. The Kiowas had ended that dream. Too bad, he decided, for Marissa could have given him a handsome son and her father's ranch.

Soon he should begin looking for a wife, an innocent, beautiful young thing like Marissa had been, a girl he could train to his liking and needs. This time, he would not make the mistake of letting her know how pleasurable and rewarding sex could be!

Chapter 4

❧

AT DAWN, NATHAN CRANDALL STARED at his ranch foreman as Travis revealed the unexpected terms for his granddaughter's exchange and his agreement with Lone Wolf. "That's a low-down trick, son, and I don't like it," Nathan declared angrily after learning of the deceitful marriage stipulation and the demand for Rana's ignorance of the truth until they were far away. As he listened, the older man jerked his head around to glare at the band of warriors who were waiting patiently for the two white men to ride out before them, and, as he did so, a silvery blond lock of hair fell over his forehead. His faded blue eyes narrowed and sparked with warring emotions as he absently brushed it aside and put on his hat.

Travis shrugged and frowned. "I know, but we have no choice. The joining won't be legal, so Rana can select her own husband when the time comes. You know I wouldn't take advantage of your granddaughter, even if she is the most beautiful female I've ever seen," he added with a roguish grin. "She's one headstrong filly, Nate. Looked and sounded to me as if she's carrying plenty of Crandall blood and spirit."

As the two men packed their camping gear and Nathan saddled his horse, Travis related his talks with and impressions of Rana and Lone Wolf. "She was one lucky girl to be taken in by Soaring Hawk and his people. But if I've pegged her right, she'll give us trouble just to show her mettle. Lone Wolf has enough problems without adding Rana's defiance or creating dissension amongst the other warriors who have their hearts set on marrying her. I must admit, she's a woman who could blind a man to duty and caution if she had a mind to. If she learned about our deal, she would choose an Oglala warrior to marry just to stir up things. The way me and Lone Wolf plan to handle matters, she won't have time to think or react badly. We have to be strong, Nate, or we'll never get her back to Texas. You have to remember she's been raised to hate and suspect whites since she was a child. If we don't follow White Eagle's suggestions, we're in for a long, rough ride home."

"Sounds crafty, but I still don't like it," he admitted, then asked worriedly, "What happens if we can't get the guns and supplies?"

"First we have to recover the money from where we hid it. Just follow my lead," Travis cautioned, then explained his plan. Next he walked to the Oglala band and gave them their final instructions. Then he mounted, took the reins of the four borrowed packhorses, and rode away with Nathan beside him and the Indians trailing at a safe distance.

Wild Wind awoke with a start and glanced toward the sleeping mat where the bedeviling stranger had slept the night before. She was disappointed to find it empty and felt he had intentionally left before seeing her, a fact she found vexing. She waited for Lone Wolf to awaken so she could question him about the enticing and infuriating stranger.

The young chief smiled and said guardedly, "Do not trouble your spirit, little sister; he will return before the full moon. He rides with Oglalas to buy weapons and supplies for our people's survival."

"I do not understand, my brother. Why does White Eagle side with us against his own people? Can he be trusted?" she inquired.

The astute warrior recognized this opportunity for pushing his sister toward the man she would be ordered to marry. He responded cunningly, "Do you not know that White Eagle is half Lakota? He was born and lived under Grandfather's eyes for twenty winters in the camp of our Hunkpapa brothers. He trained as a warrior and many times I have heard of and witnessed his great prowess. He chooses to side with his mother's people because he feels the whites are wrong to invade our lands and to kill Lakotas. He is a man of great honor and courage. I call him friend and helper. He returned to our lands to obey the words of Grandfather. He has ridden many moons on a mission, and I must help him fulfill it. You must say and do nothing to dishonor him. In his hands is the power to save our people. His heart is good, Wild Wind. Do not hurt him or shame him."

She was surprised by his mysterious words and appealing tone. "What is the meaning of your strange words, my brother?"

"White Eagle has known much pain and sadness from his mixed bloods. Many times he has been rejected and scorned. He covers his heart to prevent more pain and rejection, and he hides his gentleness, for many foolishly think that such behavior reveals weakness. When he fulfills Grandfather's command, he will return to his home. I wish him to leave our camp with happy thoughts and feelings. Do not treat him as you do other warriors, for you have touched his heart and warmed it. Soon he will leave our lands forever. Do not send him away in coldness."

Astonishment widened her blue-gray eyes. Her heart began to pound heavily with excitement and her gaze mellowed dreamily. She had been touched and warmed by White Eagle. She hated to think of his departure, to think she would never be allowed to explore these feelings he inspired within her. "He spoke of me?" she asked eagerly.

Lone Wolf grinned and nodded, then cleverly changed the subject. "The full moon nears, little sister. Black Hawk and Prairie Dog have asked to make trade for you. Do you wish me to say you are promised to Rides-Like-Thunder? Or do you desire another warrior as mate?"

Wild Wind bristled and her cheeks flushed with annoyance. "I desire no man as mate, my selfish brother. Do not rush me. Who will care for Lone Wolf if he sends his sister away?"

"I will make trade for Myeerah," he calmly announced. He added pointedly, "After my tepee has privacy for a first night of mating."

Wild Wind's cheeks grew redder and she briefly lowered her gaze. She thought about her best friend, with her large brown eyes and silky black hair. Myeerah had been in love with Lone Wolf for years. She was smart and genial, the perfect choice for her Indian brother. "Myeerah will make you a good wife, my brother and chief. We have been friends for many winters and she speaks of you each sun."

"That is why my sister should have her own mate before I bring Myeerah to my tepee. It would be hard for her to become a wife and mother while her friend sleeps nearby. Childhood must be put behind her. If Wild Wind remains in our tepee, she would remain a girl. I do not wish her to see and hear how Wild Wind disobeys her brother and chief. It will be good for Wild Wind and Lone Wolf to take mates together on the full moon. We will join, feast, and enter separate tepees."

Her heart lurched in panic, for it seemed that freedom was swiftly deserting her. It would serve him right if she married a white man and moved far away where he could never see her again! That thought jolted her, for she knew who had inspired it. But how could the daughter of Soaring Hawk join to a half-blooded male, one who provoked her to anger and rashness? He was a stranger, and her time was short. No doubt he could have any woman he desired—if he even wanted to take a wife.

Wild Wind placed her back to Lone Wolf to ponder her troubling thoughts and her situation. She did not want to marry any warrior she knew, or one she did not know. Travis's image continued to appear before her mind's eye, warming her more each time. She remembered his stirring touch, his sensual smile, his tenderness, his entreating eyes, and his stimulating kisses. How could she despise his half-white blood and skin when she was all white? Time was her enemy. There was no time or chance to observe him. According to Lone Wolf's words, White Eagle would return the day before or the day of the full moon, when she was to give her promise and her body to her new mate. She inhaled loudly. She had been taught that whites were evil. This half-white male had inspired more bad dreams and rankling fears. Their lives were far apart. It was foolish to dream of him!

Wild Wind faced Lone Wolf. "I will obey, my brother and chief. I grow weary of our quarrels. I ask one thing; let me speak the name of my chosen mate on the sun of our joining day in six moons. I wish to be certain Black Hawk is the best choice for Wild Wind. Do not tell him or others I think on him," she insisted in order to stall for additional time.

Lone Wolf could hardly believe she was yielding, and so easily. He prayed he was not wrong about the reason behind her hesitation to announce Black Hawk as her choice, just as he prayed Travis Kincade would return on or before the full moon, the time of her decision . . .

"You Claude Chambers?" Travis asked the man behind the counter in the sturdily constructed trading post that was two days' ride from the Oglala camp, and three days' return ride with supplies.

The man looked Travis over, then did the same with Nathan. "Yep, that's me, owner of Chambers Trading Post, biggest and best post in these parts. What you fellers be needing today?"

"I'm Bill Saunders and this here is my friend, Thomas Clardy," Travis replied smoothly. "I just took over a wagon train whose scout got itchy feet after a few Injun attacks and run out on 'em. Got me about a hundred wagons of green easterners who don't know the difference between a man's gun and boy's peashooter. I left 'em camped about forty miles south of here while I try to round up some proper weapons and ammunition. I'm surprised the fools got this far alive. How are you set for rifles—Henry .44's and Winchester .44's?"

A broad smile crossed Chamber's face. The idea of a big sale caused his eyes to gleam. In eagerness he rubbed his hands together as he boasted, "I got all the guns you need, mister, and plenty of ammunition and supplies. Folks sure need protection with these renegades running loose, terrorizing and burning ever'thing in sight. How many you looking to buy? Where are your wagons heading?"

"Right into the hands of the Modocs and Shoshones. I tried to get 'em to settle around here, but they're determined it's Oregon. Best I can do for 'em is get 'em proper weapons and teach 'em how to use 'em. As for me and Tom here, we're heading on down to California soon as we get them settlers to the end of their trail. I got me about eighty men and boys who need good rifles and enough ammunition to see us there—about forty boxes should do it. I'll also be needing . . . say fifty knives. Wouldn't hurt 'em none to learn how to fight hand to hand. Let's see," he murmured as if recalling his list of needs. "Them women are complaining about cold nights. You got around forty or fifty blankets? And I need four sacks of cornmeal; some got busted a ways back. What kinds of prices you asking?"

Chambers took a slate and a piece of chalk and began to figure his profit. Travis eyed him and the amount skeptically and shook his head. "I came here 'cause we heard you was an honest man, Chambers. Where's the next trading post? Maybe we can deal better there."

"Hold yer pants. I'll see if I can refigure. You don't know how hard and dangerous it is to get these supplies out this far. A man has to earn something for his troubles. Seventy-five dollars is a good price for a rifle like that." He suggested a slightly lower price for the items.

Travis looked over the list and the addition, then shook his head. "Still too high. I know what I need and how much money I got. I'll have to find me a place where my needs and money match. See ya," he said cordially and turned to leave.

"Then make me a decent offer," the owner challenged hungrily.

Travis returned to the counter and picked up the slate and chalk. After rubbing it clean, he spoke aloud as he wrote and figured. "Forty boxes of ammunition at five dollars each, fifty knives at three dollars each, fifty blankets at ten dollars each, four sacks of cornmeal at fifteen each, eighty rifles or carbines at fifty dollars each, and ninety dollars in sewing supplies, jerky, and coffee for five thousand dollars in U.S. money and gold. Plus I'll need to borrow one of your wagons to get it back to camp. Tom will return it in a few days. Is it a bargain, Chambers?" Travis had added the last three items to prevent suspicion and hoped that his ploy would work.

"You're robbing me blind," Chambers accused deceitfully, knowing Travis's offer was a fair one. He himself was never fair unless he was forced to be. He grinned. "You're a smart feller, Bill Saunders. Them folks are lucky you signed on as scout. I'll let you have everything today except the knives. When your friend returns with my wagon, he can pick up the knives. Might say I have to protect myself in case my wagon don't come home again."

Travis had prepared for this demand. "Ninety dollars is more than enough proof against your wagon not returning. Tom and the others will retrieve the jerky, coffee, and sewing supplies when your wagon comes home. Those items will fit better on packhorses than a crate of knives. And don't go suggesting I leave the cornmeal, 'cause I don't want more sacks busted by bouncing them around on horseback for days. You write out a paper saying them supplies are paid for, just in case you ain't around when your wagon comes home."

"Let's go in the back room so you can look over the rifles," Chambers slyly suggested before Travis could. He led the way into the adjoining room and pried open five oblong crates containing fifteen rifles each, stacked in five rows of three weapons. He placed five carbines across the top of the first one and began stacking boxes of ammunition nearby.

Travis lifted and examined each of the five Winchester .44 carbines, which would fire thirteen rounds before reloading. In the first three crates of Winchester .44's, which would fire seventeen rounds before reloading, he examined a different row of rifles in each wooden box. In the fourth crate, he examined every rifle, as he did with the fifth crate of Henry .44 rifles. He was satisfied with his purchase, knowing his random search would have exposed any deception on Chamber's part.

"Harvey, nail them crates while Mister Saunders checks over this ammunition," Chambers ordered pleasantly.

Travis quickly and sporadically examined boxes of ammunition, then asked to see the knives and blankets. He followed Chambers into another room and waited for the man to count out fifty of each to be checked. Twice Chambers lost his count and had to restart it. As with the other items, Travis randomly selected knives and blankets to study for quality. "I'm going to trust you on the cornmeal. But if I find it bad when it's dumped into barrels at camp, I'm sending it back with the wagon. You set our other supplies aside to be picked up in a few days."

When Travis and Chambers had gone into the other room, Harvey sent Nathan to harness the team and wagon and bring it around to the back door. When Travis returned to the first room, Nathan was watching Harvey and another man load gun crates. Afterward the ammunition, knives, blankets, and cornmeal were loaded by the two men while Travis paid Chambers and waited for a receipt for the goods that supposedly would be picked up later when the wagon was returned.

"You sure it's safe to go riding out with such a valuable shipment and only two guards?" Chambers inquired as he watched the two men climb aboard the wagon and take their seats.

Travis smiled. "I got me ten men waiting nearby in case of trouble. Only a fool would travel alone with that much money or this many supplies. They were to ride in if we didn't show ourselves soon."

Chambers laughed. "Like I said, Saunders, you're a smart man. Been a pleasure doing business with you and Tom."

As the wagon vanished behind a hill, Harvey joined Claude Chambers, who was grinning broadly. "You get them crates swapped?"

"Yep. Good thing we'll be long gone before that Saunders finds out won't more than twenty of them rifles work and most of that ammunition ain't worth as much as this dirt," he said, kicking the sand beneath his filthy boots. "You sure pulled a sly one on him. Like he said, his friend shoulda stayed with us all the time as ordered. Made it real easy."

Between wicked chuckles, Chambers concurred, "Yessirree, the new owner will take over in two days and we can be on our merry way. I sure am glad I didn't have time to return that bad lot of guns and ammunition. Gave me a chance to sell 'em twice and avoid any problems."

"Saunders ain't gonna be none too happy when he gets past the top row in each of them crates. You sure he won't stop and check 'em?"

"He examined them real careful inside and he don't know you and Slim were given time to swap the crates. If they use any of them blankets or knives or cornmeal tonight or pull out any of them top rifles, they'll be fooled by good stuff. He won't discover his mistake for days, and then it'll be too late. We'll be heading for St. Louis."

"Them folks who wants them guns and ammunition ain't gonna be happy with them two scouts. They might even think them scouts are trickin' 'em. Hell, they might even kill 'em. Ain't that a shame?"

"Yep," Chambers agreed. "A cryin' shame. That Saunders thinks he's real clever, but ain't no man been born who can outwit me."

It was the morning of the full moon and Wild Wind was very much aware of the significance of this day in her life. She apprehensively carried out her last chores in Lone Wolf's tepee. Before this sun passed, her life would change drastically. She could not stop her cold hands from shaking or her mind from drifting constantly to the half-blooded man who had failed to return before this awesome moment of decision had arrived. She had been haunted by her strange enchantment by him. She had thought about him and dreamed about him for days. At last a real man had entered her life and she worried that perhaps it was too late to study him and the potent attraction between them, though she believed he had felt it too. She knew he had been told of her "bad ways," and she realized that he might have been merely showing kindness to Lone Wolf's sister. After all, he could be so arrogant and infuriating! How could she reveal this pull she felt toward a white man? How could she reject her Oglala role? She had promised Lone Wolf and herself that she would relent to her destiny, and she dreaded it.

For the past few days, she had encountered curious stares and tension-building silence that had bewildered her, actions she could not understand because she had been on her best behavior. As soon as her Indian brother returned from his latest council meeting, she would have to relate her choice to him. Her heart pounded in panic and dismay. Then suddenly unusual noises captured her attention and set her pulse racing in suspense. He had returned! She put aside her task and went to investigate.

Travis Kincade halted the loaded wagon before the ceremonial lodge and jumped to the ground. The warriors who had traveled with him dismounted and awaited the approach of the chief and the council. Travis and Lone Wolf exchanged smiles and grasped forearms in greeting. A few words passed between them. Sighting her, Lone Wolf called Wild Wind to join them and to share this joyous moment.

Suddenly her feet seemed as heavy as large rocks and her legs as stiff as posts. Anxiety rushed through her. She chided herself for her cowardice. Swallowing with difficulty, she ordered her body to obey the summons. She walked forward and halted at Lone Wolf's side, affectionately gazing at him and ignoring Travis's intimidating presence. She dared not look at him, fearing her expression would reveal her turmoil. She was glad she had scrubbed her hair and taken care with her appearance.

In Oglala, the chief announced to everyone, "Our Hunkpapa brother, White Eagle, has returned with many weapons and supplies for the defense and survival of our people. He has shown much courage, cunning, and generosity. As chief of the Oglalas and friend to White Eagle, I say he has earned a *coup* feather for his deed. What say the Oglalas?" he cleverly asked, initiating his ploy to release Wild Wind.

Sounds of agreement and praise filled the air. Lone Wolf placed the *coup* feather in Travis's headband as he stated, "White Eagle will be our honored guest this moon when your chief takes his first wife."

Wild Wind observed the proceedings, appearing proud and calm before the green gaze that watched her intently and obviously. She was glad she did not tremble and her cheeks did not glow like the fire. She sensed that something was about to happen, but she did not realize what. She was too ensnared by thoughts of how to stall her joining tonight. If only White Eagle had visited her camp sooner!

As he had planned, Lone Wolf queried, "What can Lone Wolf and the Oglalas do to reward my friend and brother for saving our people?"

In an unwavering tone, Travis casually replied, "I desire to join with Wild Wind this sun. I offer all you see in trade for her," he stated, motioning toward the wagon filled with weapons and supplies.

Wild Wind's mouth fell open and her eyes widened in astonishment as she whirled to stare into Travis's unreadable face. When Travis's gaze shifted to hers, he smiled confidently and enticingly. Before she could gather her wits and force her tongue to respond, Lone Wolf had accepted the bargain and everyone around them began cheering. Wild Wind's gaze raced to her brother's grinning face, then moved to the beaming ones of those around them. She did not know what to think or feel at this unexpected turn of events.

Black Hawk instantly stepped forward and declared, "I have spoken for Wild Wind. The daughter of Soaring Hawk must not join to a half-breed."

Silence fell over the assembled group at the insulting claim. Lone Wolf focused angry eyes on the belligerent warrior. "I am chief. White Eagle is called friend and brother. Your words shame you. Lone Wolf did not accept Black Hawk's offer; it was not enough for Wild Wind. Do you offer more than White Eagle for her trade?"

Black Hawk's gaze slipped over the heavily loaded wagon, then he eyed Travis with contempt and hatred. "It is wrong to send the daughter of Soaring Hawk and sister of Lone Wolf away with a half-white man. He lives in the white lands, in the white ways," he argued.

"His heart is Lakota; his deed is Lakota. His honor and courage are high. He is good mate for the sister of your chief. Why do you dishonor Black Hawk and his people with dark words and feelings?"

"Wild Wind belongs with her people," the warrior continued offensively, trying to prevent his loss of the flaming-haired beauty.

Lone Wolf glanced at each council member and asked, "Is there one among you who agrees with Black Hawk?" Because they were all part of this ploy, each man shook his head. Lone Wolf looked at Black Hawk and stated, "Wild Wind will join to the man who brings deliverance from our enemies."

"It is wrong, Lone Wolf. She does not wish to join him and travel away from our lands," the jealous warrior reasoned frantically.

"The sister of Lone Wolf will obey her brother and chief and the Oglala council. She has much courage and honor. She would not refuse to join the man who saves her people and lands. I will speak with my sister and hear her words. Come, Wild Wind," he commanded, taking her arm and leading her inside the ceremonial lodge to talk.

Lone Wolf walked to the center of the large tepee and sat on a buffalo hide. Wild Wind followed his lead. She looked into his entreating gaze and questioned, "Do you truly wish me to marry him and leave our people and lands? I have been raised Indian; I know nothing of the white world. White Eagle is a stranger to me." Even as she argued, she was filled with stirring anticipation. She had wanted time to get to know him, but she had never suspected he would ask for her in joining. He had seemed the kind of man who enjoyed his freedom. He wanted her, and today! But his smile had been mischievous and his look smug. Did she dare relent to her wild desires and his control?

"This is the sun of our joining, my sister. Is there a man with more honor and courage to choose, a man who offers more for Wild Wind and her people? Do you seek to insult White Eagle and dishonor your brother and chief by refusing to join to him?"

She was dismayed and hurt by the seeming ease with which he was bargaining and sacrificing her. "Do you seek to punish me for behaving badly many times? For not choosing Rides-Like-Thunder?"

"No, my sister. I do what is best for you and our people. War covers our lands as the spring grasses. Far away with White Eagle, the sister of Lone Wolf will find safety and happiness. Do you forget that your skin and blood are white? There is no dishonor in joining to White Eagle. Think of your people, my sister, not of Wild Wind."

If only she knew White Eagle and grasped his motives for this unexpected demand, she reflected frantically. He had such a potent effect on her, and she feared losing herself in him. If only he did not insist they join and leave today! Thoughts of being alone with him both alarmed and excited her. "Lone Wolf said that Wild Wind could choose her mate this sun."

"The sun is high and no choice has been spoken. Before the eyes of White Eagle and our tribe I have accepted trade for you. Will you shame me and hurt me with defiance on our last sun together? Do you fear White Eagle?" he shrewdly inquired. "Do you wish him to ask for another in joining? Who can match the beauty and skills of my sister? Who is more worthy to walk at the side of White Eagle?"

"He is white, my brother, and lives far from our lands. He seizes me too quickly. You cannot force me to join to him and leave. Will he refuse to give our people the weapons if I refuse to join to him? Can you not take the weapons from him? Do you fear his power?" she inquired, wondering why this demand for her had not come as a surprise to her brother and why he was so eager to comply. Had this intriguing man asked for her before leaving camp? she mused. After all, they had been powerfully drawn to each other from the beginning.

"Lone Wolf will not answer such wicked questions. Many times you have shamed and angered Lone Wolf and his people. Many times his heart has known great pain and sadness over Wild Wind's deeds. If your heart is Oglala and honor lives within you, you will obey my words. It is the vote and will of our council. Do you refuse him?"

It was not Travis she was refusing; it was his intimidating rush. She felt trapped, helpless; others were ruling and controlling her life. "He will carry me far from my brother and people," she fretted, recalling her fears over her dark dreams and dreading this white challenge. There seemed to be too many changes to accept at the same time.

"Hear my words, sister, for Lone Wolf does not speak falsely of Grandfather's visions." He slowly related his past dreams about her departure and why he had taught her to defend herself. He spoke of his fears for her survival during this war with the whites and for the survival of his people. "The moon Grandfather revealed to me in dreams has come. It is time for my sister to tame the wild winds that blow through her head and heart. Grandfather has chosen your path and you must walk it with pride and courage. Far away with White Eagle, Wild Wind will become the woman warrior she hungers to be."

"I do not wish to become white again," she protested in dread, apprehensive about the shadows that surrounded her past and uncertain about Travis. She wanted more time with him, more time to explore her feelings.

"You are white, little sister," he gently reminded. "Go in peace to seek your new destiny and tame it bravely as I have taught you."

Outside, Travis tried not to appear worried or tense, but he was both. He sensed what was taking place inside the lodge and wondered how he and Lone Wolf would be forced to deal with it. He had to entice her to accept him so they could depart quickly before trouble struck. He wished his offer could have been more than a trick, for he truly wanted her. His gaze shifted to Black Hawk's, whose expression was cold and taunting.

Suddenly the tepee flap was thrown aside. Lone Wolf approached the group awaiting him, pulling the obviously reluctant girl along with him. He placed Wild Wind's hand on Travis's arm. "Lone Wolf accepts the offer of White Eagle and will give his sister in joining."

Immediately Wild Wind pushed past Travis and the others to head for her tepee without speaking or looking at her intended mate or their audience. Although well acquainted with their customs, she felt betrayed by this "exchange," which made her the possession of another. She angrily suspected that the two men had plotted secretly. Her life was changing, and she felt helpless. She was confused by her warring emotions and embarrassed by the degrading situation.

Watching her flight, Travis said, "The joining must take place soon, Lone Wolf. The ride is long and hard and we have been away from our lands many suns. White Eagle and his friend must return home to protect them."

Lone Wolf thought he understood why the man was in such a hurry to claim his adopted sister and be on his way: he did not want to give Wild Wind time to change her mind or to flee and cause trouble. He smiled. "We will prepare for the joining," he announced happily.

Within ten minutes, Travis and Wild Wind were standing before the ceremonial chief and listening to his Oglala words of joining. At the proper time, Travis turned to the silent girl and lifted the edges of the joining robe, which Lone Wolf had lent him. He tensed again as Wild Wind hesitated briefly before stepping to him so he could wrap the feathered cloak around her body to seal their joining. He could feel her slight trembling and she refused to look up at him. Clearly she did not want to marry him or leave these people. He was baffled by her compliance. No doubt her sharp mind was plotting his defeat and her escape this very minute, neither of which he could allow. A few more words were spoken, then the ceremony ended.

The quicker they left, the sooner she could learn the truth and be free of this farce, he mused dourly. Him, too, for his crazy feelings for her scared the hell out of him. Evidently he had misjudged her attraction to him, and that conclusion did not sit well. "Get your belongings and say your farewells, Wild Wind. We must leave," he told her, unaware that his voice and gaze appeared chilly to her.

She looked up at him, her stare challenging and her chin held high. She did not like being forced to comply with a demand that would alter her entire life. She feared his magic and her impending return to the white world. He owned her, and he was being the man she did not like again! The least he could have done was ask her first, or warn her! She whispered angrily, "Do not give Wild Wind orders. You have not taken me from my lands and people yet. I only obey the council's command to save my people and to punish my brother for selling me to a half-breed. I wished to join to Black Hawk or Rides-Like-Thunder; you have ruined all. Perhaps you will be sorry for forcing me to become your mate. Perhaps I will not fit in your white world."

Travis concealed his anger as he grinned and nodded. Perhaps, thinking he would be gone soon, she had been having fun with him. Perhaps she had used him to make Black Hawk jealous. Either she did not like being forced to marry and leave or she had been using her wits and charms to get her way; in either case, she had lost.

"White Eagle has many bad traits. Perhaps trading is the only way White Eagle could obtain a mate," she scoffed insultingly. Why wasn't a man like him joined? she wondered silently. Because he was viewed as a "despicable half-breed"? Did he need a mate and feel she was a good choice because she was white and would not expose his Indian heritage?

"Wild Wind has many bad traits. Perhaps slyly trading her to a stranger was the only way Lone Wolf could be free of her cutting tongue and wild ways," he taunted devilishly. "Perhaps I can tame them before we reach home. Do not forget, your words and honor bind you to me. If you do forget, I will bind you with thongs or punish you."

Without replying, she turned and, with great dignity, walked to her tepee. She was distracted as she collected her possessions and stuffed them into several *parfleches*.

Myeerah entered the tepee and found her immersed in packing. "I wish you did not have to leave," her lovely friend told her.

Wild Wind did not want to dampen her friend's happy joining day or leave in such gloomy spirits. She would not give the other girls reason to pity or ridicule her. Her self-sacrifice must be carried out bravely and unselfishly, or at least appear so. She could not help but recall Lone Wolf's words in the ceremonial lodge. Having been raised by Indians who were firm believers in and followers of visions and dreams, she felt this was the Great Spirit's will, or His test of her courage and obedience. Perhaps some exciting challenge lay before her, even at the side of that mysterious and vexing male. Perhaps her separation from the Oglalas would not be forever. She smiled and artfully replied, "Do not worry, Myeerah. He is very handsome and brave. I must not show eagerness and joy at his trade, for his pride would grow too great. Wild Wind must force him to seek her heart gently and patiently. As the doe, I will dart and run and hide, and he must chase me. He will not tame the wild wind; she will tame a mighty eagle," she teased. "White Eagle does me great honor to choose the sister of Lone Wolf and to offer so many trade goods. But you must tell no one of my secret."

The girl was fooled, and delighted. "My heart is happy that he pleases my friend. His face is handsome and his body virile. He is strong and cunning. If Lone

Wolf did not cause fires in Myeerah, her eyes would settle on White Eagle," she confessed with laughter.

"Be happy with my brother. One sun, Wild Wind will return to visit. I wish to find many children and great joy in this tepee."

Myeerah left to retrieve a parting gift for her best friend and Wild Wind knelt on a buffalo mat as she continued her packing. Her back to the entrance, she allowed herself to become lost in deep thought. Her mind envisioned the evil white man of her nightmares and she murmured, "No white dog will ever harm me or own me."

Her thoughts drifted to Travis. She was nervous about leaving with him. He had not revealed her bad behavior of that first night. He had made her relax and talk freely. But still she wondered, Had he asked for her because she had rashly inflamed his body? Did he need a strong woman of courage, daring, and wits? A white woman to conceal his dark past? "I must not be afraid or bad," she declared aloud as she completed her packing and shifted to sit on the buffalo mat to await her friend's return.

Suddenly her line of vision was filled by the towering physique of her new husband, whose gaze seemed to encompass her. She failed to notice that he had closed the tepee flap to assure their privacy.

Travis came forward and hunkered down before her. His intention in visiting her had been to offer encouragement and to lessen her tension during this difficult period, but this was forgotten as he looked at her and drank in her stimulating presence. Unable to master his feelings and thoughts, he allowed his smoldering gaze to engulf her exquisite features, which set his body aflame with desire for her. It was obvious that he had trouble swallowing as he tried to clear his throat to speak to her. He was quivering with tightly leashed passion and straining to keep himself under control. His respiration became shallow and rapid. All he could think for a time was, She's my wife and I want her. He was sorry he had been rude and harsh, and he was determined to win her approval and help.

Wild Wind's body and emotions reacted to his presence instantly. Her gaze fused with his and she was unable to think clearly. He seemed to dominate her entire world and all sights and sounds of other things were lost to her. Her tongue refused to speak and her body had the urge to fling itself into his arms. Her lips craved a melting against his and her mind begged to let her senses soar like his Indian name. She felt charged with anticipation and energy, yet held fast by weakness and apprehension. She felt bold and brave, yet hesitation and cowardice sneaked into her mind to prevent her from rising, walking to him, and surrendering eagerly to his allure. The drums had never beat more swiftly than her heart at this moment. She did not know what to say or do, or even if she could compel her body to obey her. She was flustered and enraptured, and her reaction annoyed her.

Slowly Travis's body drifted forward until his knees touched the ground and brushed lightly against hers. His shaky hands slipped into her hair on either side of her head, and he looked deeply and longingly into her expressive gaze, which sent forth messages of a matching hunger. Nothing and no one, including himself, could have halted him from touching her and savoring her lips. He lowered his head and brought his mouth down to hers, evoking a shudder from each at the blissful contact. The kiss was tender and exploratory, but gradually it deepened to reveal mutual desire. Travis's strong arms closed around her body and drew her up to lock her possessively within his embrace. His lips skillfully claimed hers and sent their senses spinning.

Wild Wind's hands moved up his hard chest to ease around his neck. Without hesitation or inhibition, she pressed her body against his in a manner that exposed her desire and announced her surrender. An August day could not have warmed her body more than his nearness and passion. She was trembling with feverishly awakened needs. At that moment, she wanted him urgently and was willing to yield without reservation, to follow him wherever he led. He was the only man to claim her heart, her love, her desire, her life, her all.

Abruptly Travis's lips left hers and he pushed their bodies apart. Both were flushed and breathing heavily. She eyed him inquisitively and tried to reclaim her stirring place in his arms. Then she understood the reason for his withdrawal as Lone Wolf's voice called out to him more sternly, "Come, White Eagle, we must complete our trade. This is not the time to begin your life with my sister."

Travis glanced at her as if guilty of some misdeed. His embarrassment and dismay were obvious, and they cooled her ardor. He mastered his respiration, then replied, "I will join you soon, Lone Wolf."

The chief did not enter the tepee or leave his position outside the closed flap. Lone Wolf's sharp instincts and keen senses had absorbed enough to know he should separate them quickly; yet he was tempted to allow Travis and Wild Wind to make this joining a real marriage by sealing their vows with their passion and commitment. He decided it was too soon. "The sun passes swiftly, White Eagle. We must hurry."

"I am coming," Travis answered, then gently caressed her cheek and smiled apologetically. In a few more minutes she would have been his completely. He was shocked by the power of his attraction to her, but he knew she was also taken by him. "I must go. I came to tell you not to fear me or leaving your people. Prepare to ride, and I will come for you soon. Do not allow anger and false pride to spoil your departure. We will speak later." He paused. "Surely what has just passed between us proves that it is I, not Black Hawk, you crave."

Wild Wind watched him rise and leave, closing the flap behind him. She wished her brother had not interrupted them, and she wondered if he and others had guessed what was happening inside this tepee. She blushed and tried to calm herself but found it difficult. His kisses and touches had created a fierce aching within her, an aching she knew only he could appease. There was a magic between them, and she was delighted by it. Now she was ready to leave with him. But then his last words echoed through her mind. Had he been trying to enchant and control her? Trying to ensnare her with her own feelings?

The wagon had been unloaded and Travis was opening the crates to show the warriors how to use the different weapons. "I'm glad this matter has been settled peacefully and quickly, Lone Wolf," Travis remarked. Yet he was uncomfortable. He did not like the way his neck kept itching, a sure sign of trouble. He had not trusted Claude Chambers; it had been the reason he had ordered Nathan not to take his eyes from the crates for an instant. Travis knew that if Chambers had a hundred barrels of water, he could not trust the greedy man to share even a dipper of it with a dying man. A cold shiver ran over the Texan's body as he realized his keen instincts and suspicions were about to be proven accurate.

Lone Wolf noticed the man's reaction to the trade goods just before Travis declared in vivid rage, "That sorry bastard! He switched crates on us! These guns and ammunition are useless. I'll kill the sneaky bastard."

"What troubles you, White Eagle?" the young chief asked.

Travis explained the problem, knowing how the deception would appear to the Oglalas. "We'll have to go back to the trading post. This time, Chambers will reward us with more than our fair share."

Black Hawk stepped forward and accused, "The white-dog lies. He seeks to trick us. He sets a trap for the Oglalas. He betrays us. I say kill him and the white-dog who waits nearby. The trade is no good. Seize him! I challenge for Wild Wind and his life."

Lone Wolf stared at the furious Travis, who was glaring at his hostile warrior. "What trick is this, White Eagle?" he demanded.

Travis met the dark gaze and replied, "I swear on my life and honor that the white trader will pay for this black deed. I will go after the guns and prove White Eagle did not betray the Oglalas."

"The white-dog has no honor or true words. He must die."

"Black Hawk speaks in anger with a swift tongue," he retorted. "The knives, blankets, and cornmeal are good. Many of the guns and bullets are good. I will return to the trading post to replace those that are bad. I will punish the white-eyes who tricked me. I must be allowed to prove my honor and words. Wild Wind is mine."

"No!" Black Hawk declared thunderously. "You must die." The warrior drew his knife and lunged at Travis. Buffalo Slayer and Two Ponies seized the warrior and restrained him until their chief spoke.

Prairie Dog rushed to Lone Wolf's tepee and explained the dangerous situation to Wild Wind and Myeerah. The women hurried to where the argument was taking place. Wild Wind keenly and fearfully observed the confrontation. This man was her husband, she reflected, perhaps her destiny . . .

"Hear me, Lone Wolf," Travis beseeched, "I did not lie or trick you. I demand the right to prove my innocence. I will ride to the trading post for more guns and ammunition. I will punish the trader."

Lone Wolf eyed the man critically, praying that Travis was speaking honestly and wanting to believe him, for he knew how much was at stake. "Buffalo Slayer, ride with Prairie Dog and Two Ponies and bring the other white man to our camp. We will hold White Eagle's father friend and wife until he returns with more guns. If he does not return, I will slay the white man and Wild Wind will join to Black Hawk."

A gasp of astonishment from the girl alerted the debating men to her presence. "Tell me what happens here, my brother," she coaxed.

Lone Wolf explained Travis's dilemma. Her gaze went to the man who was now her husband. Her probing eyes searched his face and observed his stance. No, she decided to herself, this man would not shame himself or risk the life of his friend by tricking her people. He was too clever to be unmasked this easily. It had to be a terrible mistake.

"If he has betrayed us, he must die," her brother told her.

Black Hawk said with a sneer, "I will slay the half-breed for fooling you and shaming you, Wild Wind. He cares not for Wild Wind. He only desires a wild spirit to master. He seeks our shame and deaths. In five moons, he will be dead and you will join to me."

Wild Wind was antagonized by the warrior's words. She was not a fool or a prize! She walked to Travis and studied him, all too aware of what had occurred between them a short time before. She knew that if a man tricked you in one way, he would trick you in others. Surely he could not cause her heart to soar and her senses to cloud if he was evil and deceitful. "Do you lie, White Eagle?" she asked softly.

Travis met her steady gaze and responded, "No. I was tricked. I must slay the man who betrayed and dishonored me." Travis felt as if his personal history was almost repeating itself. Once more the Indians were accusing him of treachery, and again he was innocent. But this time there was more at stake than his life and honor. He inwardly raged against the false charges and his vulnerability, but he was touched by the lack of doubt in her eyes and voice.

When Travis repeated how he had checked the items, then explained that the trader had cheated him by switching them, she knew he was telling the truth. "I will ride with him, my brother. If he lies, I will slay him for my people." She watched the effect of her words on Travis.

Black Hawk shouted, "No! I will ride with the white dog and guard him. You are a woman. Do not seek to protect your new mate."

Wild Wind whirled and shouted back at the nettling warrior, "I am only a woman, but my arrow and knife find their targets more times than yours, Black Hawk! If he has shamed and tricked me and my people, it is my right to slay him. We are joined only in words, and false words can be broken. If you ride with him, I am sure he will not return alive. As does White Eagle, Wild Wind looks white. Only she can enter the white dog's trading post and watch him for tricks. My people need guns and supplies to battle the white-eyes. I joined to him to obtain them for my people. Now I must help him replace those stolen by the evil white dog. Until his words are proven good or bad, his mate lives under this shadow of suspicion with him."

"You cannot ride with me, Ra . . . Wild Wind. It is too dangerous. The trader will expect my return for justice. He will be waiting to trap me. I will need twenty warriors, Lone Wolf. Guard my father friend and wife carefully. I will return for them in five moons."

"Who is this father friend, and where does he camp?" she asked.

Instead of replying, Lone Wolf ordered his braves to capture Nathan Crandall and to bring him to camp. He was not surprised when Travis warned them not to injure the old man. "He will be safe for five moons, White Eagle. On the sun of the sixth moon, he will die and my sister will join to Black Hawk, if you betray us again.

"No, my brother. If I am freed, I will join to Rides-Like-Thunder as you promised," Wild Wind announced, declaring her rejection of Black Hawk, whom she had rashly believed she could easily enchant and master. She was astonished at the clever way in which the warrior had concealed his dark side from them. If anything happened to her new husband, she would not remain here!

"So be it," Lone Wolf concurred, to Black Hawk's fury.

Wanting to give her courage and hope and having a desire to annoy Black Hawk, Travis ignored the eyes watching them as he took Wild Wind's hand and smiled at her. He entreated confidently, "Do not worry. I will prove my honor and words and return for you soon. You are my wife and you must trust me." She nodded and lowered her gaze, and he knew it was to shield her emotions from him and the others. Travis was not given time to await Nathan's arrival and speak with him. Instead he was soon riding off with the band of warriors to seek Chambers.

It had required enormous self-control for Wild Wind not to hug him and kiss him farewell. She had nodded understanding and her agreement with his words, then had squeezed his hand tightly to let him know she believed him and would be waiting eagerly for his return.

After watching Travis and the warriors ride away, everyone went back to their tasks but Wild Wind and Black Hawk, who remained where they were until the band was out of sight. The jealous warrior scoffed, "Be careful of the evil fires of love and passion, Wild Wind. If they burn too swiftly and wildly, they will leave nothing of you but blackened coals. You are a fool to trust him. He is bad, and he has gained control of your will and wits. If you are rash, the eagle's claws will tear your heart and life to pieces. He did not wish to join to you. Lone Wolf demanded that you leave as his mate, not his whore. What is an Indian wife to a white man? Only a lowly squaw to warm his mats until he grows weary of her."

She glared at him and retorted, "The only evil here is within you, Black Hawk. Think of your people, not your wicked desires. You make a fool of yourself before our people and you blacken your face with shame. I will wait for his return, then go where he commands. It is as I wish, and so it shall be. You will see," she declared smugly.

Near the trading post over two days later, Travis pointed to a lone cottonwood in the distance and told the leader of the band, "If I do not show my face by the time the sun reaches the top of that tree, you must attack the post and take the guns. If I am slain in the battle, tell Lone Wolf what happened. My friend will teach the Oglalas how to use the white man's firesticks. When the training is over, he is to release my friend and my wife to return home." He impulsively removed his *wanapin* and handed it to the silent warrior as he said, "Give this to Wild Wind . . . if I die."

Buffalo Slayer took the necklace and gazed at it. It was a circular medallion made of sacred red stone. Upon its surface was scratched a war eagle in flight, one talon clutching a thunderbolt and the other one tightly grasping two broken shafts of an arrow. Around the eagle's neck was suspended a smaller medallion with symbols of the War Bonnet Society. Buffalo Slayer lifted curious eyes as Travis snapped the reins of the harness and headed the wagon toward the trading post.

Once inside, Travis was angered to discover the extent of Claude Chamber's guile. He explained his problem to the new man in charge, who accepted no blame or responsibility for the treachery. And no amount of reasoning could sway the man's unfavorable decision. He would not even honor the receipt for the items already purchased. Travis did learn that Chambers and his two cohorts had not left the post until yesterday morning and were heading for St. Louis.

"Yore quarrel is with Chambers, son. I can't take my time and money to exchange damaged goods you bought from him."

Travis returned to where the Indians were waiting for him. "At dark, we go in and take what's ours. Post some guards, Buffalo Slayer," he gravely advised, hoping to avoid more trouble and another delay.

Travis began pacing with unnatural impatience, musing that darkness could not arrive quickly enough to suit him. He knew he had no choice but to steal the guns and ammunition, or Nathan would be dead and Rana would be lost to them.

Finally, when all seemed quiet in the small settlement near the trading post, Travis cautiously returned to the large, sturdy wooden structure.

"We're closed," a voice called out without opening the door. "Come back in the morning."

"It's Bill Saunders. I've got a deal for you, a thousand dollars."

The bolt was moved aside and the door opened slightly. "What's your deal, Saunders?" the man inquired eagerly.

Travis held out a leather pouch and shook it, making the emptied bullets sound like clinking coins. "A thousand and those useless guns until I can track down Chambers and retrieve my money for the exchange. You'll have the money, plus those guns to exchange for another sale. I'll need twenty rifles to arm my men to go after him. Deal?"

The man pondered his offer and his blank expression. "And what's to keep you from not coming back after you catch Chambers, if you can?"

"The fact that I need eighty rifles more than I need the money Chambers swindled out of me. I've got a wagon train of green settlers sitting practically helpless three days' ride from here. The quicker I can track Chambers and get my money back, the sooner I can arm my people and be on our way to Oregon. You won't be sorry for helping us," he coaxed. "I'll pay you a hundred dollars for your help and trust."

The man seriously considered the lucrative deal. Finally he shook his head and replied, "Sorry, son, but it ain't wise to trust a desperate stranger with so much of my stock."

Travis sighed loudly and grimaced. "I was afraid you wouldn't be obliging." He drew his pistol before the man could slam and lock the door. Pushing the man inside, he bound and gagged him, then rendered him unconscious to prevent a witness to his actions. When a voice called out from the other room, Travis rapidly reacted. Without making a sound, he hurriedly concealed himself near the door to the adjoining storeroom. When the man entered the dim area to see why his boss had not answered him, Travis carefully struck him over the head and he too fell unconscious. Then he went to the door and gave his signal.

As quietly and swiftly as possible, the gun and ammunition crates were exchanged. When the warriors attempted to take more than Travis had purchased, he halted them, saying, "The man who cheated us left. Our battle is with him. We steal nothing from the innocent. You must take the goods to Lone Wolf while I track and punish the man who betrayed me. I will return in a few moons."

"We are at war, White Eagle. We need many guns and bullets."

"If we take more than I paid for, Buffalo Slayer, the new trader will send the white soldiers after thieves. The wagon is heavy and must travel slowly. We do not have time or enough warriors to battle many soldiers. Even in war, men must have honor. If they come after thieves, we could lose everything."

The warrior gave Travis's words deep thought. He smiled and nodded. "We will do as White Eagle says. He is cunning."

Travis wrote a message on the slate, telling the owner he would return soon with the money to pay for the guns and ammunition. He placed the two men where they could not free themselves or send out an alarm for at least a day, then set the slate within the men's line of vision. All he could do was pray the owner would accept his claim.

As silently and stealthily as they had approached the secluded area, Travis and the warriors departed. At a safe distance, Travis advised the band's leader to cover their trail and be careful. He knew that the supplies in that wagon meant Nathan's life and Rana's freedom. Taking his *wanapin* from Buffalo Slayer, he smiled. "I will return to Lone Wolf's camp for my friend and wife after the white man is punished."

"What if the white man or soldiers capture or slay White Eagle?"

Travis inhaled deeply. He knew he was lingering in this perilous Hunkpapa area too long, but he could not allow Chambers to get away with his treachery. "If the Great Spirit does not protect me on this journey, do not let Wild Wind join to Black Hawk. Make sure Lone Wolf remembers his promise to release my friend and his . . . my wife."

"Buffalo Slayer will give White Eagle's words to our chief." The warrior smiled, for he comprehended this man's feelings for Wild Wind.

Travis watched the wagon and the warriors ride away into the darkness and prayed they would reach the Oglala camp within the time limit. As he galloped off in the other direction, visions of Rana filled his mind. He was sorry she was not his wife under the white law that ruled Nathan Crandall's life, for he knew that Nathan would not see their joining as a binding reality. Yet, if there was one truth he knew, it was that he wanted Wild Wind with all his heart and might, and he prayed she felt or would soon feel the same.

Chapter 5

❧

FOUR DAYS HAD PASSED and Wild Wind was becoming more edgy with each new sun. She was disappointed and annoyed that Lone Wolf had postponed his joining day until her predicament could be settled. Joining to a half-blooded stranger and traveling so far away from all she knew and loved was intimidating. She wondered, What if White Eagle were not pleased with his Indian-raised wife? What if she could not adapt to this new existence and people? What if something happened to him once they were far away? She hated doubting herself or him, but such feelings could not be suppressed. If only her suspicions would vanish. One more day, she thought anxiously, then quivered in anticipation.

She had not been allowed to visit the tepee where the man with silvery yellow hair and eyes the color of a stormy blue sky was being held prisoner. He was kept under guard but was treated gently. The way the white man watched her from a distance, she wondered if he blamed her for his friend's perils. She wished she could speak with him, to see if she could learn more about White Eagle and his lands. Sometimes his intense blue stare unnerved her; sometimes its tenderness reached out to her. Sometimes his face frightened her . . .

Wild Wind continued her chores, entrapped by deep thought, just as she was trapped by the unexpected events of the past few days. She knew Lone Wolf was hoping White Eagle could avenge himself and prove his words. She wished he would discuss the alarming matter with her, but he refused. At times he was stern and cool, and at other times he was very kind and warm. She sensed that his feelings were as confused and as tormented as hers. He had been offered a way to help his people, only to have the glorious near-victory threatened by betrayal. She could tell that Lone Wolf realized his leadership would be questioned because he had trusted the white man, that he would be humiliated for being fooled by him and for trading his sister for useless goods. She had grasped the heavy responsibility he carried, and it had mellowed her feelings toward her brother. She had tried her best not to upset him with words and actions. But this waiting and not knowing was eating at her poise and increasing her tension.

On the last moon, she had tried to convince Lone Wolf to carry out his joining to Myeerah, hoping her friend could distract her Indian brother and bring joy into his eyes once more. She had offered to stay with friends to give them privacy. Lone Wolf had told her he could not think of personal and selfish matters at such a critical time.

Whenever she observed Lone Wolf visiting with the friend of the man who had made trade for her, she would discover herself praying that White Eagle would return and save his friend's life and her brother's honor. She had come to accept the reality of what the trade goods could do for her people. Yet she worried over the dreams her Indian brother had revealed to her, wondering where her new path would lead her if White Eagle returned alive. She recalled her own fearful dreams of the evil white man with dark hair and eyes, and she begged the Great Spirit to make them only bad dreams and not visions of moons yet to be.

"Why did you marry me, White Eagle?" she murmured in confusion. "Will you take me far away, use me, and desert me? Will you allow the evil spirit who haunts my dreams to harm me? Why do I fear you and these powerful new feelings?"

Ever since White Eagle's departure, Black Hawk had stalked her everywhere she went. His igneous eyes had visually stripped her garments from her body, then brutally punished her with their fiery heat. He looked at her as if he despised her, yet craved her as well. "I will never let you have me. I will flee or die first," she vowed aloud as she recalled the persistent warrior.

The thought of mating with Black Hawk or Rides-Like-Thunder or any other man dismayed her now, after such close contact with Travis. She had happened upon lovers or animals mating in the forest, so she knew it was a natural part of life or loving. Vividly she remembered being in White Eagle's arms and tasting his kisses. She recalled his tenderness during her dark dreams and their walk. She could almost feel the fires that had inflamed her body at his touch, and the pleasure she had received from his gaze and nearness. Oddly she did not fear his sleeping mat.

Perhaps, she admitted, she had provoked his mischievous and taunting actions. Perhaps he had heard wicked tales of her misbehavior, as he had alleged. Yet he had chosen her and had made the largest trade offer any maiden had ever received. She helplessly questioned his feelings and motives. She did not want to be a tame-the-wild-wind game to him, a game about which she had so often been teased. And, if he had tried to fool her people, had he hoped to leave with her before they learned of his deceit—leave with the sister of Chief Lone Wolf as his hostage? If only she did not sense some great mystery and reluctance surrounding him.

She reflected on her taunts to him after their joining. He could have chosen any maiden, and won her. Why her, an Indian girl? Why had he returned to the land of his birth? Why help the Oglalas? "Who are you? What are you? Why do you ensnare me and trouble my spirit?" she asked aloud.

Surely he would return for his friend, but how would he feel about her and her people for doubting him, for threatening him and his friend? So many questions and mysteries, she concluded nervously, completing her chores and attempting to push her distressing thoughts aside, to no avail.

The morning of the fifth day arrived. Lone Wolf entered the tepee and announced that Wild Wind was to serve food to the white man. She looked at him quizzically, silently questioning his unusual order and his reasons.

In a rare moment of kindness, or weakness, Lone Wolf had yielded to Nathan

Crandall's plea to meet his granddaughter once before he died, if it were to come to that today. Lone Wolf had secured the older man's promise to reveal nothing to her about her past or his reason for coming to the Oglala camp. He told Wild Wind now, "I wish him to see the reason why his friend will return to our camp. He is old and weak and afraid. He knows White Eagle has taken you as his mate. When his senses are filled with Wild Wind, he will trust his friend to return for one whose beauty is greater than Grandfather's flowers. If he must die, he will believe some evil kept his friend from returning. He is a good and gentle white man. He must not suffer for another's dark deed." He paused. "Do you wish me to send another with food and smiles?"

For the second time, Wild Wind felt that her brother was lying to her. Yet she did not expose her doubts and anguish. Another mystery, she concluded sadly. "I will go, my brother and chief."

She was not surprised when Lone Wolf accompanied her and remained at her side. She offered Nathan food and waited for him to consume it. He did so slowly, his eyes seeming to drink in her face and essence. He did not appear afraid, only sad, and seemed overly happy with her visit, as if she were warming sunshine on a cold winter day. Neither did he appear weak, in spirit or in body. This was a man who knew hard work, she realized, who knew courage, who loved and trusted his friend . . .

When Nathan could no longer stall his meal and her visit, he smiled and thanked her, and moisture filled his eyes. He removed a turquoise and silver pendant and handed it to her. It was a curious shape, as if it had once been a circle and someone had cut a small section from its top and sealed it in a point on its bottom. It looked old and precious. As she eyed the lovely treasure, a pain flashed inside her head and she rubbed her right temple to ease it. With quivering fingers, she held it out to him in polite refusal, for it frightened her.

Nathan closed his hand around hers and the pendant, indicating that he was insistent she keep it. Lone Wolf translated Nathan's emotion-hoarse words. "It belonged to his daughter. He wishes you to have it for your kindness. Do not offend a dying man by refusing his generosity." Lone Wolf had noticed her reaction, and he knew it had been the suppression of a memory.

Wild Wind met Nathan's gaze and probed it, learning nothing. She allowed the man to place the pendant around her neck. Again, she was baffled by the curious moisture that brightened his eyes. She could not explain why, but she felt drawn to this man. She smiled and said, "*Pilamaya.*"

"My sister thanks you and accepts your gift. If it pleases her, I will bring her with food before . . . the sun sleeps."

His hesitation was not lost on any of those present. If Travis and the guns did not return in the next few hours, Nathan would not live to eat another meal or to see the sun go to sleep. Lone Wolf had spoken, and he could not change his mind. He dared not tell Wild Wind who this endangered man was, nor did Nathan want her to know under these circumstances.

Anticipating her husband's return, Wild Wind left Nathan and her brother to wash her hair and body and dry herself in the afternoon sun in the company of some of her friends. Her garments and possessions were packed, and she felt a certain satisfaction that the other girls were envious of her and charmed by Travis.

Her pride demanded that she appear trusting and confident around them as well as around her spurned suitors.

A few at a time, the other women left the river, their baths and washing completed. "Are you coming, Wild Wind?" Myeerah asked.

Wild Wind glanced at the sun. It was past the treetops, time to prepare her brother's evening meal. So little time left for White Eagle to return and the man called Nathan to live . . . Would time forever be her foe? she wondered. It always seemed to be battling her.

"Go along, Myeerah. I will return shortly." She needed to be alone, for it seemed the worst was about to happen. Clad in a drying blanket, she stood and began to walk along the riverbank to expend part of her tension. She tried not to think about her fate, yet her mind allowed her to think of nothing else. Time and distance passed unnoticed.

"He will not return, Wild Wind," a cold voice taunted nearby.

She glanced toward her right and her gaze fell on Black Hawk. Although her body was covered, she felt naked, and she was alarmed by his gaze. "Why," she asked angrily, "do you torment me, Black Hawk? Have you no pride and honor? White Eagle will return before dark."

The warrior laughed, and the sound of it was wintry and mocking. "Buffalo Slayer and his band have returned. They took many guns and bullets from the trader's wooden tepee. The white dog did not return with them. His friend will die, and you have no mate."

Wild Wind paled. "Was he slain in battle for the guns?"

The warrior laughed coldly once more. "Buffalo Slayer watched him ride away in the dark. Our warriors did not chase him; they rode swiftly to bring the guns to our camp before soldiers could pursue them. White Eagle is gone. I will demand to track him and slay him, and I will demand Wild Wind as my *coup*. I will not be denied."

"You lie," she accused boldly, her blue-gray eyes chilling.

"My words are true. I spoke against the white dog many times. I said he could not be trusted. I tried to save Wild Wind from his tricks. I must be rewarded for my words of warning. Wild Wind will be mine."

The aggressive warrior yanked her to his hard body and covered her mouth with his. Even when she struggled fiercely, he did not release her. Tightly banding her arms to her body, he clamped his hand over her mouth and dragged her into the concealing bushes, his abrupt movement deterring her from kicking. He fell to the ground with her and pinned her hands to her sides with his strong thighs. Withdrawing a wide rawhide strip from his waist, he secured it over her mouth to cut off her screams for help, then loosely bound her hands with another strip. She could hardly breathe from his heavy weight across her torso and could not wiggle free. His forearm across hers prevented her from striking out or battling him. He shifted to yank off her blanket, exposing her naked body to his crazed senses. His roughened hands moved over her breasts as his eyes grew wilder with lust and determination. When she continued her futile battle, he told her, "Once you are mine, Lone Wolf will be forced to give you to me in joining." His mouth fastened to one breast and he sucked greedily on it.

She freed her tied hands and, for a brief instant, pounded on his head and shoulders. Laughing, he seized them and pinned them to the ground above her head. His legs wrapped around hers to halt her kicks and thrashing. He gave his attention to the other breast, nursing hungrily like a baby starving for his mother's milk.

Suddenly Black Hawk was ripped from her helpless body. Wild Wind watched as her new husband beat her attacker as if he were as crazed by fury and jealousy as the warrior had been with lust. White Eagle showed the man no mercy; clearly he wanted and was trying to kill Black Hawk with his bare hands. Stunned by the warrior's attack and White Eagle's sudden rescue, she merely watched the action as if she were detached from her body. Her wits and control returned finally as the warrior drew his knife and lunged at White Eagle. Shaking violently, she came to her knees and sent forth a gag-muffled scream.

As suddenly as the battle had begun, it was over. The men fell to the ground and, during the scuffle, the knife was shoved forcefully into Black Hawk's chest.

With revulsion, Travis tossed the dead warrior aside and did not even glance at him. He went to Wild Wind and, drawing his own knife, cut her bonds. Before she could throw herself into his arms and thank him, he reached for the blanket and flung it at her, saying, "Cover yourself and return to camp. You should not place yourself in such peril. He was blinded by you. No man takes what is mine and lives to enjoy it." He whirled then and left, heading in the direction of the settlement.

Wild Wind stared at his rapidly retreating back. He was in a great hurry. His face, which was dirty and sweaty, had not been shaven for many suns. His clothes were dusty and his hair tousled. She saw that he walked like a man consumed by fiery rage, one seeking some challenging prey to conquer and burn beyond life or recognition. Surely he did not blame her for Black Hawk's actions! She had done nothing wrong. On unsteady legs, she stood and tried to wrap the cover around her trembling body. It slipped from her grasp, and she cursed it and her weakness. Her reaction filled her with anger, and the anger instilled control.

She rushed past Black Hawk's body without looking at him. Seizing her garments, she yanked them on. Then, grabbing her other possessions, she hurried toward camp. She had to discover the truth, or the peril awaiting him.

Travis entered the camp, and with unsuppressed relief, noticed the wagon standing near the ceremonial lodge. He strode in that direction, scolding himself for cutting it too close for Nathan's and Wild Wind's safety. Lordy, he was too fatigued and worried to think straight! Wild Wind should not have been at the river alone; she was too trusting and tempting! She had this way of causing a man to lose his wits and his control. If he hadn't rushed off, he would have pulled that naked body into his arms and taken her in pure animal heat, right beside his dead enemy! She did crazy things to him, and he was in no shape to resist her.

The shouting of his name called Lone Wolf's attention to Travis's arrival. The chief smiled at him, then wondered at his stormy mood. Nathan, who was examining the guns, turned and saw Travis approaching them. Nathan winced, for he knew Travis's look and walk meant trouble.

Travis greeted his friend with a bear hug and a forced smile. "Have they been treating you right, Nate?" he inquired needlessly as his keen gaze examined the older man's face and body.

"We did not expect White Eagle this moon. Buffalo Slayer told us you rode after the treacherous white dog," Lone Wolf remarked.

"I found the bastard and killed him," Travis informed the warrior as he withdrew a scalp lock from his pocket and handed it to him. "Put that on your *coup* stick for all to see what happens to those who trick or betray the Oglalas." He did not say how easy it had been to locate and battle Claude Chambers and his two hirelings, all of whom had been camped and getting drunk on whiskey purchased with his stolen money. He had ridden like a devil-pursued man to pay the new trading post owner, who had not concealed his astonishment at Travis's honesty. Then he had ridden like mad to make sure he arrived before this sun set, just in case the wagon was late. In five days, he had covered many miles, and most without food or sleep. "I rode like the storm clouds to make sure Lone Wolf did not make another mistake. You see I am a man of honor and truth," he stated coldly, pointing to the wagon and then flicking the small section of hair into the chief's grasp. "Not so, a warrior named Black Hawk. He lies dead near the river for trying to rape my wife." To avoid causing Nathan any further distress, Travis spoke in Lakota. After finishing his account, he ordered himself to calm down, for the dangers to Nathan and Wild Wind were past. He only wanted to get out of this territory before any Hunkpapa warriors passed this way and remembered him. Damn, he swore silently, feeling utterly fatigued, his nerves taut.

Nathan caught his arm and asked worriedly, "Son, you all right?"

"I will be as soon as we're heading home. I was in a little bit of a rush, so I haven't eaten or slept for days. I had forgotten why I left this bloodthirsty land. Seems I've regained some bad traits, which you'll just have to correct again," he stated jokingly to relax the man.

Travis turned to Lone Wolf. "Any more objections to our leaving as soon as we show you how to use those weapons?" he inquired sullenly.

Lone Wolf shook his head. "Where is my sister?"

"Here," Wild Wind answered, pushing her way to his side. She was miffed by White Eagle's coldness and refusal to comfort her at the river.

The young chief eyed her intently. Her hair was mussed, her cheeks were glowing, and signs of minor injuries were visible. "White Eagle says Black Hawk attacked you near the river," he probed.

"White Eagle speaks the truth. Black Hawk is dead and Wild Wind is safe," she responded, but her look at Travis was filled with tiny blades. "White Eagle had to battle Black Hawk to the death to rescue me."

"Is there more?" he questioned sternly.

"No," she replied and pulled her stormy gaze from Travis.

"Your husband needs food and sleep. Do you wish me to have another see to his needs while you recover from your struggle?"

"Yes," she stated, angry with Travis and wanting to avoid him. She left the group and went to Lone Wolf's tepee to lie down, assuming it was surely too late to begin their journey today.

Myeerah and her mother fed a hungry Travis before he went to the river to bathe and change clothes. While Nathan instructed the warriors on the use of the rifles and carbines, Travis collapsed on the sleeping mat rolled out beside Nathan's in the guest lodge. There being no need for him to remain alert and on guard in the safety of the camp, Travis drifted into deep and much-needed slumber.

When Lone Wolf finally entered his tepee long after dark, Wild Wind gazed evocatively at him. He told her he had eaten with Myeerah and her family and would join to the lovely girl after his sister's departure in the morning. Lone Wolf did not offer any information about her missing husband, and Wild Wind was compelled to question his absence.

"He sleeps in the guest lodge with his friend. He will come for you when the new sun appears. He has kept his word and his bargain. You belong to White Eagle," he reminded her, noting her rebellious glare.

"Perhaps, like my brother, he wishes privacy on the first night with his mate," she speculated, then blushed at her bold words.

"I offered to sleep in the guest lodge with his friend. He was weary from his journey and said there will be other nights to claim his mate. He says White Eagle and Wild Wind are strangers, and strangers do not share a sleeping mat. Be happy he is a good and patient man."

Lone Wolf hoped his words would silence her probing questions and would end her curiosity. He claimed his sleeping mat and closed his eyes, aware that she was still gaping at him in astonishment. Soon she would learn that, as he had promised, White Eagle would not take her to his sleeping mat and would free her from her Indian joining vows, which held no power in the white world. Soon she would discover that it had been her grandfather who had desired her freedom. Eventually Lone Wolf's mind drifted to other matters: his joining with Myeerah on the next moon and the defense of his people with Travis's guns.

Wild Wind lay down in a huff. She was sleeping alone on the first night she might have shared with her new husband. She would be humiliated and teased for her lack of appeal to him. How dare he ignore her! It was no excuse that he was exhausted! At least he could have slept in her tepee to prevent gossip. She had been desired by many warriors. They were joined, and joined couples slept together. He would pay for this insult, she vowed irritably.

Early the next morning, Wild Wind sought out Myeerah to help her prepare for her joining to Lone Wolf. The two girls went to a secluded spot near the river. As they bathed and dressed, Myeerah said, "The sun climbs high, Wild Wind. It is time for you to leave." The girl sensed that her friend was intentionally avoiding her new mate, was actually hiding from him. "Do you seek to make White Eagle angry?"

Wild Wind stiffened and her eyes glowed with intense emotion. "For many moons I waited for his return. He can wait one sun for Wild Wind. She must show no eagerness to leave with a stranger. He joined to me, then insulted me by sleeping in another tepee. If he is tired, he must rest before our long journey," she scoffed. "He makes fun of Wild Wind and pretends she is not desirable. If that is so, he should not have chosen her. Let him wait and worry. Let him see Wild Wind does not find him desirable as a mate."

"Do you fear him?"

"I fear nothing and I will not be shamed before my people. Perhaps he will grow weary of waiting and leave without Wild Wind."

Myeerah wisely suggested, "Let us return to camp."

"No. Sit, and Wild Wind will braid your hair. Your fingers are not working well on this happy day. I must see my friend and brother joined. The white man can do nothing to harm me in our camp."

Travis was pacing as he awaited Wild Wind's return to her tepee. He had assumed she was off somewhere preparing to leave or saying farewell to her friends and people. He glanced at Lone Wolf and remarked pointedly, "Wild Wind moves slowly this sun."

Lone Wolf motioned to her belongings, which were ready for the journey. "She will return soon, my friend. She was angry and confused when her mate slept in another lodge. She fears others will laugh and tease her for her husband's action. Let her head and spirit cool. She does not understand why you cannot take her to your mat."

"I gave Lone Wolf and her grandfather my word not to touch her. It's getting late. Where can I seek her hiding place," he questioned, wishing he could have spent the night with her.

"Be strong and patient, my friend. If you show anger, she will be happy for causing it. I must prepare my band. We ride with our Hunkpapa brothers this sun. Two Ponies tell me they come to hunt and feast with Lone Wolf. It is a good day for a joining."

His words struck Travis like a physical blow to an unprotected gut. Without showing any fear or tension, he would have to find Wild Wind and Nathan and ride out as fast as he could. He would claim he had to hurry home to defend his lands, an excuse Lone Wolf would understand. "I will be strong, Lone Wolf. I will find her and take her, by force if necessary. I must show Wild Wind she has to obey, to prevent trouble on the trail."

Lone Wolf shrugged and agreed. "Do as you must, White Eagle. I will not interfere. Her defiance must be tamed for your safety."

Travis went to speak with Nathan. "Listen to me closely, Nate, because we don't have much time. I never told you why I left this area, because it was too painful and humiliating and I wanted to forget it. But it's past the time you heard the truth. My father, Jeremy Kincade, was a trapper and trader in these parts back in the days when Indians would accept and befriend a good and honest white man, or one who appeared to be one. One day he tangled with a pack of wolves and was rescued by a Hunkpapa hunting party. After they tended him, he took up with them and later married my mother, Pretty Bird Woman, daughter of their war chief."

The mention of his deceased mother brought anguish to Travis's eyes and voice. He cleared his throat and continued. "He stayed for years, then went off supposedly to check out the advancing white man. When he returned, I was thirteen, and he said it was high time I learned about my white blood and civilization. He was my father and I was curious, so I obeyed him. We traveled around for two years, but I didn't like what I was seeing and hearing. I was almost sixteen and I was taller and stronger than he was. After some arguing and a shooting in Kansas, we went back to my mother's camp. He trapped and sold furs until the Hunkpapas stopped him for killing too many animals just for their skins. One day he accidentally encroached on sacred burial ground and found gold. He started sneaking off to collect it and hide it. He planned to leave as soon as he had enough—if a greedy man ever has enough gold. Two of his trapper friends showed up and joined him, so he needed more gold for his partners.

"You know what happens when men get too greedy. Four braves caught them panning in the river on sacred land. They shot three of the braves and stabbed one. Jeremy figured it was time to get out quickly. He knew most of the warriors were out of camp, hunting and raiding. He sent his two friends to the nearest fort to tell the soldiers the Hunkpapas had twenty white captives they were torturing and killing; he thought that would keep the warriors busy while they made their escape with the gold. He returned to camp and calmly packed up his belongings and told us he was heading off for a few months. By then I was eighteen and loved being a hard-to-match warrior. He asked me to ride with him to the edge of the Hunkpapa territory to say good-bye. Maybe he was trying to save me from the attack, but it didn't matter to me then and it doesn't now. He was evil and worthless."

Travis inhaled before continuing as he forced the new anguish from his voice. "Like a trusting son, I mounted up and rode off with him to rendezvous with his cohorts. One of the wounded braves reached camp and exposed Jeremy Kincade's treachery. That warning gave the Hunkpapas time to send for their warriors and to summon help from our Blackfeet brothers. The soldiers were defeated, but many Hunkpapas were slain, including my mother." He breathed deeply and for a time cast a fixed stare on the distance.

"A war party was sent after us and pinned us down before they could recover the gold, or mention it to me. I had some rivals and enemies in camp, and I didn't know why we were being attacked; so, like a fool, I defended myself and my father. After his friends were slain, I tried talking to the warriors. They captured us under a false truce and we were dragged back to camp. Trouble was, the brave who had escaped death to warn them claimed I had been with my father, desecrating sacred land and taking part in the killings. Charge-A-Buffalo hated me because the girl he loved had had her evil heart set on me. I guess he figured he'd keep us apart by getting me killed. He died without clearing me. Jeremy tried to convince them I was innocent, but what was the word of a white enemy and half-breed traitor against a renowned warrior who had endured agony to warn his people? They tortured Jeremy all day, then killed him. Before he died, he told me where they had hidden the gold, which was nothing more than yellow rock to the Indians. They didn't care about the gold or its recovery, only our alleged crimes."

He stated bitterly, "They wouldn't even allow me to fight a truth challenge. They tried to torture a confession from me and planned to kill me at dawn. After dark, Pretty Rabbit freed me. Hell, she owed it to me for causing Charge-A-Buffalo to hate me and lie about me. She had fueled his desire, jealousy, and desperation by always comparing him to me unfavorably. Plenty of times she told him if it hadn't been for me she would have loved and married him. She drove him wild with hunger and mad with frustration. Charge-A-Buffalo was clever and proud; he made sure nobody witnessed or learned about his shameful rivalry, so he wouldn't look foolish or bad. Pretty Rabbit wanted us to escape and marry, but she was killed before we got away. Lordy, Nate, wicked vixens have always gotten me into trouble! I'm telling you the truth. If Jeremy hadn't been slain, I would have battled him myself to prove his evil blood did not flow within me. He's responsible for my mother's death and my people's rejection; he didn't deserve to live."

When he paused, Nathan said, "I'm sorry, son. I know it must have been hard losing everything and everyone like that. Sometimes greed takes over and a man don't know what he's doing. I see why you had trouble talking about this or trusting anyone. A betrayal like that would make any man bitter and hostile, especially a boy. The Hunkpapas should have known you by then. It wasn't right to cast you out."

"With so many dead and Charge-A-Buffalo's words against mine, all they saw was my white skin and my father's treachery. Even those who believed me dared not speak or act against the council's vote. There wasn't any way to prove my innocence, so I had to ride and keep on riding. For months I was dogged and attacked. The Hunkpapas won't ever forget what happened or forgive me. That's the problem, Nate."

"What do you mean, son?" he inquired in confusion.

"The Hunkpapas are part of the Lakota Council Fires. Their camp is only a few days' ride from here. If they learn I'm nearby . . . I don't have to tell you what danger me and you would face. I'm sure they're still watching and waiting for me to return for that gold. We've got to get the hell out of here pronto. Lone Wolf says a Hunkpapa hunting party will arrive today. If the Oglalas hear the Hunkpapas' charges against me, they'll think I did try to fool them the other day and that I only replaced the damaged guns to save your hide and mine. It'll start all over again and we won't stand a chance of survival and escape, not with Rana. Besides, we've been gone for over a month. There's no telling what Caldwell is up to now. McFarland is getting on in years; he could get nervous over our lengthy absence."

Nathan's expression revealed his grave concern. "Let's go."

"That's the other problem. Your defiant granddaughter is off hiding somewhere. She's peeved because I spent the night with my friend instead of my wife. Something about feminine ego and pride. I'll explain what I have to do, Nate, and you can't interfere. We've got to ride, hard and fast. You get our horses saddled and ready to leave. I'm going to find Miss Rana Michaels, tie her up, and get us out of here before those Hunkpapas arrive."

Nathan gasped in shock. "You can't treat her like that, son," he protested. "She'll be scared, and them Indians will be plenty mad."

"Better her scared for awhile than us dead. Lone Wolf gave his permission to use force to claim her. Don't forget, she's supposedly my wife now. Defiance can be dealt with harshly, and she does have a reputation for rebellion and stubbornness. Let me handle it my way. We can lose her and our lives if she balks and stalls our departure."

Nathan did not like the idea, but he realized from Travis's words and expression that he was genuinely worried, and when Travis Kincade was worried, he'd better worry too. "All right, son, but be gentle."

"That's up to your granddaughter, Nate."

As Travis and Nathan were leaving the tepee, Lone Wolf joined them. "Wild Wind is at the river with Myeerah. Come, we will get her. It is best for all if others do not see her battle you."

The horses were saddled and Wild Wind's possessions were collected. Then the three men headed for the river and quickly located the two women downstream by their voices. Lone Wolf wisely suggested, "Tell your father friend to wait here with the horses." Nathan obeyed.

Lone Wolf called out to alert the women before he and Travis approached. The warrior chief smiled at his beloved and frowned at his adopted sister.

"Have you lost all pride and courage, Wild Wind?" Travis asked. "You have stalled our departure long enough. We must go," he commanded firmly.

Wild Wind glared at White Eagle, then at Lone Wolf, who did not defend her against such treatment. "Wild Wind will leave when she is ready to leave. I will see my brother and friend joined first," she asserted. Startled that White Eagle had sought her out so boldly, she stared defiantly at the man before her line of vision, for his size and stature seemed to block out everything and everyone else. As her challenging gaze met his narrowed one, a strange warmth passed over her body and she found she was having difficulty thinking and breathing. She realized that if ever a male was masterful in exerting his prowess and in controlling any situation, he stood before her now, and, indeed, he owned her. Yet she was still wary of this man who had so easily enchanted her and alarmed by the emotions he had brought to life. She would not let him think her a coward or a weakling—or his lowly squaw! she stubbornly decided.

When she tried to push past Travis, he captured her arm in a firm yet pain-free grip. "We ride, woman," he commanded sternly. "I have work to do and land to protect. You hide like a frightened rabbit."

"I will ride after Lone Wolf and Myeerah's joining," she replied. She yanked on her arm, but White Eagle would not release it. She scolded him in Sioux, and still he held her securely. A curious panic flooded her body, and her blue-gray eyes blazed with fury. Her other hand attempted to claw free the imprisoned one. White Eagle simply captured it and stared calmly at her, his green gaze mocking her helplessness.

Nettled, she called him names and fought him. Travis looked and behaved as if nothing unusual were taking place. He pulled a rawhide thong from over his pistol and bound her wrists. She was astonished when Lone Wolf did and said nothing to the brazen man with laughing eyes. "Release me, white dog!" she shrieked at him. She struggled fiercely, to no avail. At last she was rendered breathless from her exertions and protests and could do no more than shake with rage at his actions. To make matters worse, Travis lifted her and tossed her over his shoulder. Then he strolled to his waiting horse and stood her beside it.

Bewildered, Nathan asked, "What's going on, son? This can't be necessary."

Travis glanced at his friend and reminded, "Don't forget what I told you, Nate. We need to head for home and she's fighting me. She's demanding to hang around until tonight to watch her brother's joining. This little wildcat will settle down after we get away from here. Please let me handle her and get us on the trail pronto," he urged.

Wild Wind glared at Travis, then spewed forth insults and threats in the Indian tongue. When she added, "*Sunka ska, nanpi yuze sni yo! Mni kte sni yelo!*" Travis removed his bandanna and gagged her so that she would not draw the attention of others. He was glad Nathan could not understand his Oglala words as he refuted, "Yes, you will go with me. And if you call me a white dog one more time, I'll spank you. And I'll put my hands on you anywhere and any time I please, if I please."

Wild Wind soon realized that her Indian brother would make no attempt to come to her aid. But it also seemed obvious that the older white man was annoyed and distressed over her vile treatment. Yet, when her gaze sent an appeal to him for help, he winced and lowered his head as if hurt and embarrassed. Suddenly she twisted, ducked, and forcefully threw her shoulder into Travis's midsection.

He grunted and staggered slightly at the unexpected attack. Then he seized her by her forearms and shook her, warning, "Behave, woman, or I will punish you for acting like a fever-mad raccoon. You are a chief's daughter and sister, and my wife, not a wild she-bear who is wounded. You are making a fool of yourself and shaming all of us."

Nathan helplessly questioned, "Are the gag and bonds necessary? She's only a scared child, Travis. Don't be so rough and mean to her."

Travis Kincade drilled his leaf green eyes into her stormy blue ones. Then he grinned roguishly and quipped, "Damn right, they're necessary, Nate. This little viper would strike without warning if she had the chance. I'll release her when she learns and uses some manners, or when she remembers she's a woman and not a little savage. And she had best learn quickly, 'cause my temper and patience are short. I plan to take real good care of . . . my defiant wife, if she lets me," he murmured, his smoldering gaze slipping over her face and body.

When Nathan started to debate Travis's words and actions, Travis cautioned, "Taking up for her only encourages her to act worse, Nate. We can't stay any longer, and she won't leave peacefully unless I use force. She's only trying to prove to herself and her friends that she can control me. We ain't got time for silly female games. Please, stay quiet."

Wild Wind was overjoyed when her flushed cheeks and flashing eyes did not expose her understanding of Travis's words. Rather, both men interpreted these signs as indications of her anger. As far as these white men would know, she had forgotten English, which could not be considered unusual for a girl captured as a small child who had heard and spoken only Sioux for years. She decided to encourage the older man's friendship and help, for she felt this would annoy her new husband. She would be clever and patient, she mentally plotted, until she could defeat him and escape. She would teach him about manners and kindness, and about Wild Wind.

Travis mounted agilely, then reached down to scoop her up in his powerful arms. When a resentful Wild Wind found herself on the same horse with her white tormentor, she sat rigidly before him, her chin held high and her gaze focused on the distance. Never had she been so humiliated or infuriated or mistreated. Knowing Lone Wolf and Myeerah were witnessing this degrading display, she ceased her struggles, vowing this white devil would pay dearly for shaming and abusing her.

After Travis and Lone Wolf had exchanged parting words, Lone Wolf touched her arm and advised her to be obedient to her new husband and happy in her new life. Wild Wind's gaze settled on the warrior. Her eyes told him she would never forgive him for this deed, even when he asked for her understanding and forgiveness. She shook her head and tore her misty gaze from his entreating face. She would not be forgiving or understanding while she was a humiliated captive who could neither speak nor move. Lone Wolf had the authority to order Travis to remove the bonds and gag so she could hug him and speak words of farewell. Since he made no attempt to do so, he did not deserve her forgiveness. Let him suffer, as she was suffering.

Travis was annoyed by her obstinancy and spitefulness. "Do not worry about her, Lone Wolf. I will make certain she is safe and happy. When her temper cools, she will be sorry she behaved so badly. You did right by trading her to me. I will take good care of her."

"You are a good and wise man, my friend. My sister is strong and proud. Give her time and patience. She will come to accept you and her new life. In time, understanding will fill her mind and heart."

"I wish happiness and long life for my Oglala brothers and Lone Wolf. May you find great success on the hunting grounds and in battle. May the Great Spirit ride with you and protect you from your enemies. Soaring Hawk is proud of his son, a wise, strong chief and a powerful, cunning warrior, as he was. May you find peace and joy with your new mate on this happy joining day. I am proud to call you friend."

Travis smiled when Lone Wolf responded with the heartfelt words, "*Pilamaya, Wanbli Ska. Wakan Tanka ni'ci un. Tanyan yaun nunwe, Watogla Tate. Icantewaste, mitanksi,*" which translated: "Thank you, White Eagle. May the Great Spirit go with you and guide you. Good-bye, Wild Wind. Be happy, my sister."

Travis knew their time was fleeing. He kneed his horse and rode away. When they were almost out of sight of the settlement, the girl began to battle him like a snared badger. She wiggled and thrashed, threatening to send both of them to the hard ground. His horse was well trained, and he released the reins while he struggled to control her and their precarious position. His arms banded her body and he shouted at her, "Stop it, Wild Wind! You do not have to be afraid of me and Nate." When she did not relent, he commanded, "Be still, or you will make me hurt you. We must leave here—*now,*" he stressed impatiently.

The realization of a permanent parting with her Indian brother and her friend Myeerah had struck her hard. Soon all she knew and loved would be lost to her forever. She did not wish to leave in this cold manner, with cruel words between them. She wanted to go back to say she was sorry, but she could not explain this to White Eagle through the gag. She hoped her actions would enlighten him and he would remove it, but all he did was threaten her and shake her. Her anger and desperation grew.

When she attempted to shift herself to peer around his broad chest, Travis saw her pleading gaze and understood her actions. He removed the gag and inquired, "Do you want to say something?"

"I must go back and speak with my brother and Myeerah," she coaxed. "It is wrong to leave this way," she informed him sullenly.

Travis knew he could not comply with her wishes. "There is no time, Wild Wind. The sun is high, and we should have been on the trail long ago. You should not have behaved so badly or wasted precious time trying to provoke me. Lone Wolf knows you are angry and hurt; it is natural. He will forgive you and forget your defiance and cruelty. The trail is filled with enemies. We must become friends or our lives will be in danger. For once, be a good girl," he commanded.

She glared at him, her look scorning his order and his refusal. "*Hiya kola! Wanbli Ska toka!*" she declared heatedly declining his offer of friendship and calling him her enemy. She asked to be untied, but he shook his head and unwisely grinned at her. "You are mean and evil; that is why I resisted leaving with you. I hate you. I will never yield to you. If you try to force me to sleep on your mat, I will claw out your eyes. I will escape and return to my people," she warned coldly.

Vexed at having to behave this way and knowing time was short before the Hunkpapas' arrival, Travis retorted, "If you try to escape or disobey, you will be sorry. When I take a woman to my sleeping mat, it will not be a hateful, defiant child. You are selfish and coldhearted, and you were mean and evil to your brother. Stay my enemy if it makes you feel better. I do not need your friendship or your body, only your obedience. I cannot see why any warrior would chase after a bag of trouble like you. Obviously the jokes about you are true. One of us will tame a wild wind; the choice of who does it is yours."

Incensed, she scoffed, "If you do not wish me as your mate, why did you make trade for me? Did you need a slave for your chores?"

"You are not my slave or prisoner," he replied too quickly. He sighed in annoyance at his slip and added, "Unless you behave like one."

"If I am of no value to you, release me," she responded.

"No. I made trade for you to help Lone Wolf and his people. I offered them many guns and supplies. In exchange, I had to ask for something they viewed as having great value. I could not ask for horses, because your people need them for fighting and hunting. I could not ask for furs, because it is wrong to slay so many animals. There was nothing else of value to ask for in trade. I believed taking Wild Wind as my wife would make the trade one of honor and fair exchange. You are a white woman, and you caused trouble many times for your brother and his people. He was about to trade you just to get rid of your sharp tongue and rebellious ways. You should be glad I rescued you from an enforced joining. Just do as you are told, and we will not have any problems."

He could tell she was getting more angry by the minute. He decided to try reasoning with her. "White women can do the things you desire, things that need to be done in our lands—hunting, riding, fighting, and protecting your family. We thought you would be happy with other whites, and safer during this war between our peoples. I did not choose an Oglala woman, because an Oglala would feel lost and frightened in my white world. Since you are white, you will fit in easily. If you escaped or I sent you home, you would live in shame and ridicule. You would no longer have trade value or pride. You would be dishonoring your chief and the trade that could save his people. I gave you the chance to do something good and unselfish for the people who raised you and loved you. I believed you had pride and courage. I thought you were smart and could relearn the white ways and accept them. You will go with me willingly or by force, but you will not cause trouble and dishonor. I have never raped any woman and I will not start with you, wife or no wife. You have more thorns than a wahoo tree, and I do not like getting pricked on my sleeping mat. Do the chores. I will ask nothing more."

Wild Wind recognized the truth in most of his words. Nothing was as important to an Indian as honor and the survival of his tribe and lands. If she rejected her appointed role in this intimidating episode, she would face shame and ridicule. He knew the Indian ways and the paths of cunning too well. His reasoning had been flawless, except for one point: his motive for claiming her in trade. She was neither blind nor a fool. She recalled that night in her tepee; he was a virile man and he had found her desirable. She was his wife now, and he would not ignore her for very long. Too, she questioned why he had made trade with the Oglalas instead of the Hunkpapas. Or perhaps, she decided, he had made trade with both. She was too angry and confused to be flattered by his compliments, which had been laced around insults or chiding, but she had caught them and now stored them away in her keen mind. She wondered if he would come after her if she were to escape, and she concluded that he would. The only honorable way she could return to the Oglala camp was through his death, and he was not a man who would die easily. She was trapped. "Then I am your captive and you are my enemy," she announced. "I will ride my own horse. I am not a child." For now, all she wanted was to put some distance between them.

Nathan turned back when he saw that Travis was making little progress in his argument with his granddaughter. He fretted over their conflict, asking, "What's wrong, Travis?"

"Just a battle of wits and wills, Nate. I'll explain later. Ride a little ahead and keep an eye out for visitors while I settle her down." He watched as Nathan reluctantly gave in to his order, which Travis knew would keep his older friend from making a slip. To Wild Wind, he said in Oglala, "We do not have time to exchange harsh words. You ride with me until I know you can be trusted."

"No," she protested, and tried to slip from his saddle and arms.

Travis hurriedly caught her, then placed her bound hands over his head and settled them around his waist. "Behave, or I will twist you over my knee and whip your fanny. Maybe that is what you need."

Wild Wind decided to test him and to get free of his unsettling embrace and nearness. It was difficult to locate any extra flesh around his middle and to imprison it between her fingernails, but she worked until she was pinching him painfully. "I will ride Cloud or walk."

Travis grabbed her mischievous hands and held them away from his body, scowling at her. With her teeth, she caught the tender flesh at the function of his arm and chest. She bit him, then gradually increased her pressure as he struggled to break her tenacious hold with his other hand. Nothing seemed to encourage her to stop biting and resisting him. She wanted him to toss her to the ground or place her on Cloud's back, for she realized she did not enjoy his pain. Though she would not unclench her teeth, she added no more pressure.

Travis grimaced in discomfort, but he had endured more pain than she was giving him. He did not cry out or strike her. Instead he stared down into those turbulent blue-gray eyes. "How can someone so beautiful be so damned mean and savage? You're gonna force me to hurt you and cause more trouble between us," he mumbled to himself in English. In Lakota he stated, "Wild Wind, I will have to gag you again when I get that lovely mouth free. If you stop biting and behave, I will let you ride Cloud soon and I will untie you so you can signal your brother."

As he was speaking, he had grasped her head between his hands and indicated his resolve to obtain freedom at any risk or threat of pain. Given an opening, she ceased her reckless action. "Your word of honor?" she probed, implying that his offers were the reasons for her rapid release of his flesh.

Travis nodded, then whispered softly and gratefully, "*Pilamaya*." He tied the bandanna around his neck, showing her that he would not gag her again. "A truce, woman? Your word of honor to behave?" After she nodded, he pulled on the reins to turn around his horse. As he sat her up straight before him and cut her bonds, he muttered in English, "So very beautiful and dangerous, and as cold and wild as a Texas blizzard. You're gonna be one tough and delightful vixen to tame, if any man has the cunning and strength to do it . . ."

Travis watched her use sign language to relate her love and farewell, and her hopes for Lone Wolf's happiness and survival. He watched her ask for forgiveness for her previous action and saw that Lone Wolf returned her signals in kind. Thoughtfully, he noticed that tears brightened her lovely eyes as he saw her send Lone Wolf one final smile and wave.

The flaming-haired beauty with steel blue eyes looked up at Travis and whispered softly, almost seductively, "*Pilamaya, mihigna*."

Travis smiled mysteriously as he responded in Oglala, "You are welcome, my wife. Remember your promise: no more fighting with words or hands. We go home . . . We should take care of that name right now," he suggested, as if an idea had just struck him. "You will need a white name to prevent any hostility toward you and any nosy questions. My name is Travis, Travis Kincade. Can you say it?"

"Travis, Travis Kincade," she repeated obediently.

"Very good," he remarked cheerfully. "I will call you Rana, a soft, beautiful name for a beautiful and hopefully gentle woman."

Rana shuddered as the vaguely familiar name rifled across her mind. She stiffened and paled. "I do not like that name. I am Wild Wind."

"You are my wife, and I am naming you Rana, Rana Michaels," he insisted, perceiving the effect on the name of her and observing her ensuing actions. He hoped that Nathan would not return now and interfere.

Rana unconsciously grasped the heart-shaped pendant that Nathan had given to her and toyed nervously with it. She remembered where she had heard the strange name Rana and had viewed the *wanapin*—in her bad dreams. Or, she fearfully wondered, were they visions of horrible days to come? Suddenly she yanked the pendant from her neck, leaving a red scratch on her satiny flesh. As she started to fling the necklace away, Travis grabbed her hand and prevented her panicky behavior. "I do not like the white name Rana and I do not like the *wanapin;* both are evil. Grandfather sent me warnings about them in bad dreams. Now you, my husband, bring them to life. As I feared, I must not trust you. You have lied to Wild Wind and tricked her; this I know is true from my dark visions. Is this not so, Travis Kincade?"

Travis kept his expression closed to her probing gaze. He knew he could not reveal the truth, not when she was so suspicious of him. As Lone Wolf had said, she needed time to become friends with them before he related the story of her past to her. Evidently she was haunted by bad memories, which she considered dreams or visions. It would be unwise to admit he had lied and duped her. Instead he tried a different path. "I will keep the necklace for you until you realize that it comes from a good heart and not a bad vision. Grandfather was preparing you to face your new destiny, one where you must live as Rana Michaels. Do not resist His revelations and will, Rana. Do not fear the bad dreams or your new life far away. You are my wife, and I will protect you from all harm."

The nightmare she had experienced on the day of Travis's arrival filled her mind. She was confused and alarmed by the unknown, which seemed to be surrounding her. But the man who had rescued her in her dark dreams was now at her side, her husband. She had to be brave and cunning. "I will become your Rana as Grandfather commands," she told him, then pulled his head downward and fused their lips to test him in another way.

Taken unprepared for her action, his senses whirled madly as she greedily kissed and embraced him. His arms pulled her tightly against him and he seared his lips over hers. As his body flamed and tensed with desire, his tongue danced with hers and his fingers relished the feel of her thick hair. His lips moved over her face and he enjoyed its softness and sweet smell. He inhaled the freshness of her hair, then nibbled at her ear before his lips hungrily sought her mouth again. For a time, he was lost in the wonder of this newly discovered creature and ensnared by her potent magic.

"A storm is coming, my husband. We must return to camp and wait for it to pass," she suggested as loud thunder filled her ears and passion's flames licked at her body. It was no secret that she wanted this man as much as he wanted her. It was past time for them to taste the sweet pleasures of bodies joining in blissful rapture. Surely the fierce storm that was building within their bodies was as powerful as the one nature was threatening to unleash on the land. What better way to spend such an afternoon than in her husband's arms?

Her words enabled Travis to partially clear his wits. When he leaned back, both were flushed and breathless. His gaze locked with hers. "I see a wahoo can have precious treasures as well as prickly thorns," he murmured huskily as his thumb caressed her lips and his fingers gently held her chin. "Perhaps a few pricks and pains are worth enduring to pluck such lovely flowers and delicious fruits."

She hinted boldly, "Let us return to my brother's tepee before he has need of it after his joining. The storm will surround us soon."

Travis glanced above them, then twisted to check the sky in each direction. He frowned, for many reasons. He was sitting here dallying with a ravishing woman who believed she was his wife and was eagerly offering herself to him, while dangers from foes and nature were closing in on them. This wit-stealing vixen was far too tempting to be ignored and nearly impossible to resist, Travis mused silently. He wanted her with every burning inch and tingling nerve of his susceptible body, yet he was going to have to refuse her, though it was as clear to him as a June day that if she were not Nathan Crandall's granddaughter, he would have unrolled his sleeping bag and taken her then and there. Travis was vexed for allowing himself to be talked into this false marriage with a wife who desired him and expected him to make love to her, a wife who would not understand his constant rejection of her many charms. He almost wished she had retained her fury and resistance, for her willingness to surrender to him was making it painfully hard to reject her. Of course, he admitted, her show of fiery passion could have been a cunning trick to captivate him in order to get her way. Whichever, there was only one way to cool her spirit and take the heat off him.

"Sorry, woman, but we have to ride, storm or no storm. You wasted too much time this morning with your silly games. Have you forgotten that you hate me and will never yield to me? Do not use your body and a false surrender to keep us from leaving today. A husband, not his wife, chooses when and where to unroll the sleeping mat, and I do not choose this time or place." Travis knew his words came out too harshly, punishingly, and he was instantly sorry, but he dared not apologize or explain. He had tried to come up with a clever reply that would keep her from tempting him again, for he doubted he could resist her time after time. It would not be wise for them to get too close this soon. When they reached Texas, she would have to be protected from the Caldwells and he would have to continue his fake attraction to Clarissa. Travis realized he should stop calling Rana his wife, for where they were heading, she would not be considered so. He would have to keep her away from him, even if he had to be cruel and deceitful to accomplish it.

Rana's cheeks glowed, this time with anger and humiliation. "You offer truce and friendship, then cruelly insult me," she scolded him defensively. "It is not wrong to wish to see my brother joined to my best friend. I know what I must do. I agreed to our joining to help my people and I will honor the terms of your bargain with my brother. I was not teasing you with a false surrender. My kiss was to thank you for your kindness and your vow of protection, and to seal our truce. You pretended to desire me, to choose this time and place. I did not resist your hunger, for you are my husband and I promised not to fight you again. Blame White Eagle for misleading Wild Wind with his false kisses and touches. Wild Wind will be happy if he never mates with her. But do not call her to you, then scold her for coming when it is her duty!"

Travis cursed softly through clenched teeth. He seemed to be doing everything wrong where she was concerned, and he was taking too much time trying to climb out of this bottomless pit he had dug for himself. He mumbled in English, "Hellfire, Rana, I can't tell you why I can't make love to you. It isn't right for me to touch you, and I was a damn fool to do so. Lordy, I hope you don't tempt me like that again. You don't know the truth about us."

He looked at her downcast head and sighed heavily. "Hear me, Rana," he said in Oglala. "I expect only friendship and obedience and respect from you. I will not . . . call you to me again."

She lifted her head and stared into his troubled gaze. "I do not understand,

Travis Kincade. You do not want Wild . . . Rana to be your wife? You wish Rana to live as . . . as a sister to Travis?"

"Yes, I need you to behave like my sister," he agreed defensively, although his entreating gaze belied his stinging words. A sisterly relationship was the last thing he wanted, but it offered some measure of safety until such time as he could reveal the truth. "Truce?" he coaxed hoarsely.

"If you will trust me to ride on Cloud," she responded softly.

After giving her a long, searching look, he spurred his horse forward and they joined the curious and worried Nathan. Travis told the man he would explain matters later. Right now, he needed to put distance between his and Rana's responsive bodies. "Swear you will not try anything foolish," he demanded of her. "Promise you will obey me."

"White Eagle traded for Wild Wind. She belongs to him. She will become Rana. Rana will obey the orders of Travis Kincade." She watched the effect of her words on him, carefully concealing her emotions. As Travis spoke with Nathan, Rana mentally questioned his strange English words and his curious sadness, and his denial of their blazing passion. From what she could see and hear, a sister was not what he wanted her to be. She would not tell him she could speak and understand English, for she could learn more about him this way . . .

—— *Chapter 6* ——

〜

"I HEAR CONGRATULATIONS ARE in order, Papa," Clarissa Caldwell stated sweetly as she entered her father's office. "It seems you finally squeezed out Mister McFarland. Now you own every spread that surrounds the Rocking C Ranch. Once you take it from Nathan, we'll have the largest cattle empire that ever existed. Isn't it exciting? How do you plan to root out old Crandall? He seems dug in for life."

Harrison Caldwell looked at his nefarious daughter. He admitted that Clarissa was a beautiful and seductive woman, but he knew she was also selfish and vain, and often too wild and reckless. The greedy Clarissa did not care about their ranch or property, except for the prestige, power, and wealth they represented. She did not concern herself with how her father made money, as long as she had plenty to spend. She rarely inquired about the methods her father used to deal with people, but she made certain that no one doubted or challenged the power and influence that spilled over from him to her. He wondered if Clarissa ever worried about her advancing age, for she was still unwed at twenty-eight. His gaze traveled over her ebony hair, dusky complexion, and deep brown eyes. Several times he had instructed her to use her seductive talents or devious skills to aid his plots against his enemies, or to entangle those who stood in the way of his having what he wanted. Clarissa had always enjoyed those little "assignments." She had done everything he had asked of her, except win Travis Kincade over to their side, or make Caldwell a proud father. No, he could never love or be proud of this conniving and lecherous little bitch. No doubt she would slit his throat if it suited her purposes! he mused in disgust. It was a shame a man could not trust his own child, and she could not trust him . . .

"Papa, are you listening?" she inquired, peeved at his lack of attention and affection. No matter what she did to please him or to win his approval, or what she did to annoy or punish him, she could not elicit the desired response from this man who had sired her.

"I was thinking about roots, Clarissa. We both know Nate's going to hand his ranch over to Travis. If you would put down a few roots with Kincade, I could kill Nathan and be done with all these tricky games and dangerous gunslingers. I want you to keep an eye on those last two Silas hired; they could be trouble if not handled properly."

"How close do you want me to watch them, Papa?" she asked with deceptive calm. Carrying out his little deceits meant nothing to her, but she hated him for uncaringly asking her to whore for him. If he were truly so strong and smart, he wouldn't need her! The only reasons she had done such things for him had been to exercise her power over men and to prove she could outwit them. Each assignment had taught her more about men and her father, lessons she needed in order to learn to compete in this "man's world." One day, she vowed coldly, he would pay for his vile treatment and lack of love.

"Close enough to make sure they don't interfere with our plans, girl. As soon as we're done with Crandall, we'll have everything we want. I'm going to strangle him out before winter."

Yes, Clarissa thought dreamily, she would have everything she wanted by winter. As soon as her despicable father created one of the most powerful and lucrative spreads in the West, she would get rid of the old bastard, take over the Caldwell empire, and marry Travis Kincade. This was everything she had dreamed of, and she would do anything necessary to make it a reality. She knew her father's evil secrets, past and present, for she had spied on him since the age of eight. If she had desired, she could have destroyed him with the truth, but that would have cost her her dream. She also knew Marissa's dark secrets, all of them, even one that neither of their fathers knew: the secret that Raymond had used against her dead friend . . .

A knock sounded on the door. Wes Monroe and Jackson Hayes were invited inside and Clarissa was dismissed. Harrison shook each man's hand, slapped each on the back, and complimented them on their defeat of James McFarland. "You boys did a fine job of running him out. Now, the Flying *M* Ranch is mine. The timing was perfect; nobody around to outbid me for it. I've got you boys a little bonus for working so fast and without any trouble. I like a good, clean job." He handed each man a packet of money. He had been careful to be very generous, to retain their loyalty and interest. "I want you boys to hang low for awhile. Make sure you stay out of trouble. I got one more matter for you to take care of for me;

I want you to run out Nathan Crandall as soon as he gits back from some secret trip he's making." While he was speaking, Harrison tried to remind himself not to use language that might be over the heads of these crude men, for he had found that educated speech often caused envy and dislike. He knew it was better to stay close to their level of understanding or education to avoid resentment; "working in the gully," as he called it.

"I'll pay you ten times what's in them packets," he offered, planning to get rid of these dangerous men as soon as Nathan and Travis were dead. "Just make sure you don't catch the sheriff's or U.S. Marshal's eye. I don't want anybody connecting you boys to these crimes, since you work for me. I want this matter to look real legal."

"Whatever you say, Mr. Caldwell," Wes Monroe remarked genially. "Me and Jack could use us a little rest and fun. McFarland was harder to discourage than we thought. We was trying not to damage property which would soon belong to our boss. Hell, we didn't have to kill more'n three men and forty steers. All you have to do is scare women and kids, and their men are forced to move on. When a rancher ain't got no hands, he can't run his ranch."

After the meeting, as Wes and Jackson were leaning against the hitching post outside Harrison Caldwell's office, Wes Monroe scoffed, "That old coot didn't even ask how we scared them women and kids and got their men to running off like crazy. I ain't had me that much fun since we rode with Cap'n Quantrill."

Jackson Hayes teased, "Stop bulling, Wes, you just like to rape and kill. If'n I knows you, you got plans for robbin' Caldwell and poking that bitch of a daughter. What'chu waitin' on?"

"This plan he's got going for Nathan Crandall. He'll have lots of money in his safe to buy off that ranch after he does in Crandall. We'll let him get his money together, then we'll relieve him of it. He thinks he's so damn smart and walking high over us. He's mine, Jack. I'm gonna peel him like a juicy apple, and take ever'thing he's got."

"What about that gal of his'n? Can I have her afore we move on?" his partner wheedled, for Wes was the brains of their outfit.

"Just make sure you leave me a little piece this time."

"I'll try, Wes. I just get so excited, I lose control."

"I know, Jack. I've had to clean up some of your bloody messes. Just give me a spit of time with her before you have your fun. I been watching them skirttails swish for weeks while she's walking away from me. That little bitch is coming down a few notches afore we leave."

Wes looked down the dirt street and grinned wickedly as he watched Clarissa enter a mercantile store. He was tired of moving from place to place, one hitching post away from the hangman's noose, with never enough whiskey and money and women to last long. And he was tired of taking orders from arrogant bastards like Harrison Caldwell. And he was tired of being strapped to a stupid partner like Jackson Hayes. He liked this town, and the Circle C Ranch. Maybe he would hang around a long time. Maybe he would kill Caldwell and Jackson, and marry Caldwell's daughter. Being a rich, powerful rancher with a beautiful, helpless wife sounded mighty fine to him. He had too much on Caldwell and his little brat for her to go screaming to the sheriff. Yep, he decided with a satanic grin, he just might take Caldwell's place in this area . . .

Travis, Rana, and Nathan had ridden for hours and had managed to avoid the violent storm that was currently attacking the Oglala camp. Travis kept glancing to their rear, praying that the storm would not shift and head in their direction and force them to halt their journey. He wanted as much distance as possible between them and the approaching Hunkpapa band. With luck, the storm would have delayed the hunting party's arrival. He could not imagine what would happen if the Oglalas learned the truth about his past, but he knew what the Hunkpapas would do. The sooner they were out of Lakota territory and their reach, the better.

Travis and Nathan were glad that Rana had not given them any trouble so far. Without a cross word or hesitation, she had ridden between them and had kept up with ease, making Travis proud of her. Earlier Travis had cautioned Nathan not to divulge any secrets around Rana, for a person often understood another language even if he could not speak it. He also warned himself to hold silent around her.

Rana had not spoken to either man since beginning the journey. She knew Travis was watching her with eagle eyes, ready to snatch her to his lap the moment she made a false move. She would prove how obedient and intelligent she could be, until it suited her to behave otherwise. She was aware of how often the older man's gaze slipped to her and of the warmth that filled his eyes. He seemed such a strong, gentle man. Whenever she looked his way, he would smile encouragingly. Perhaps his presence was the reason why her husband refused to touch her. No, she quickly answered herself, her husband was in a hurry. The question was why. She had noticed Travis watching their backs and saw that his body was still tense. There was an air of apprehension and mystery about him; she could sense his deep concern.

Rana did not understand this handsome male, but she knew she was strongly attracted to him, and he to her. Her emotions were in turmoil. One minute she told herself she despised him and would battle him all the way to her new home. The next, she wanted to make love to him, and was determined to do so or be told the reason why she could not. She did not like the way he could so easily control his emotions and hers. Other men had always found her beautiful and desirable, and had had to struggle inwardly to keep their hands off her; some had found they could not until she prevented them. How strange and infuriating that this half-blooded man had to be the one to stir her passions to life. How strange to want to possess and reject the same man at nearly the same time. Maybe he felt the same way, she ventured. Even if he was her husband, she could not allow him to play games with her feelings. Yet, as they rode swiftly, Rana plotted how to entice Travis while pretending to spurn him.

It was mid-afternoon when they stopped to rest and water the horses. Rana patted Cloud's forehead, then hugged him. She looked at Travis and said casually, "I will return soon." She headed into the trees, delighted that he did not stop her or question her.

"You don't think she'll try to escape, do you?" Nathan probed anxiously when she was out of hearing range and sight.

Travis removed his hat, wiped the moisture from his forehead, and replaced it. As he began unpacking something for them to eat, he replied in a playful tone, "For some curious reason, Nate, I don't think she'll try anything foolish, at least not yet. Right now, she's more concerned about disappointing her people and shaming herself than she's scared of us. If we can stay calm and friendly, maybe she will too. At least we've gotten her to accept the name Rana."

Nathan helped Travis with their light meal. "That was a sly trick, son. How long should we wait before telling her the truth? She seems like a smart girl and not one to take kindly to deceit."

"I'd say give her a week or so to get used to us before dropping it on her. That'll give her plenty of time to adjust to the news before we reach home. We're too close to the camp and she's still a little peeved with me right now. If we get her dander up, she could go hightailing it back to her brother to find out why he tricked her."

Travis explained how she had reacted to her mother's necklace and the name Rana Michaels, and he told Nathan about the nightmare she had experienced that first night. "The truth might confuse her and frighten her. We're still strangers. We've got to give her time and patience."

"You think she remembers part of the past?"

"My guess is yes. But something back there has her scared, Nate, so she doesn't want to remember it. Lone Wolf told me she used to have those bad dreams lots of times. Maybe it's nothing more than that she can't allow herself to recall the good without recalling the bad. That's how it was with me. I found it was better not to think about the past at all. Hell, you can't change it, so why keep it on your mind and let it rub you raw inside?" he declared bitterly.

"She's beautiful, isn't she?" Nathan murmured, locking his softened gaze on the girl who was approaching them slowly. Nathan did not notice when Travis absently agreed and forced his longing gaze away from the fetching sight. "She's got her mother's spirit. She's impulsive and daring, and she's tough. I won't let happen to her what happened to my Marissa. I'll kill any man who goes near her."

"Love isn't something you can control, Nate. All you can do is pray she doesn't meet another Raymond Michaels. But if you start pushing her and bossing her, I can promise you she's going to rebel. That little vixen is the most willful and infuriating creature I've ever met."

Nathan chuckled. "That sounds just like somebody I used to know," he teased, his blue eyes sparkling with mischief.

"With luck, you'll be just as successful at taming her as you were with me." Travis grinned and winked at Nathan.

"Who said I was finished with you, son?" Nathan retorted. "For a man who's down on women, love, and marriage, you sure do seem to know a lot about 'em. Shame you've never met a good woman."

Rana watched the two men teasing and laughing, and it made her feel good to see how close they were. She walked past them to the stream to wash her face and hands. She turned when Travis called her name but did not respond when he asked in English if she were hungry.

"*Loyacin hwo*, Rana?" he repeated.

"*Han*," she replied, then joined the two men. She thanked Travis for the food he handed her, then wondered why he did not scold her for not handling this female chore. She ate slowly and daintily as she watched Cloud nibble on grass nearby.

Travis asked suspiciously, "Have you finished yet?"

When Rana did not react to his words, he inquired in Oglala, "*Wanna lustan hwo?*"

She glanced at him, praising herself for her quick and clever mind. "*Han,* Travis Kincade."

The three packed their supplies and mounted, ready to continue their long journey. They rode silently and swiftly until dusk. When Travis located a spot in which he felt it was safe to camp, he told them, "We'll stay here tonight, then leave early in the morning."

Travis was pleased when Rana willingly helped gather wood and prepared their evening meal. When everything had been cleared away, the two men placed their sleeping rolls near the fire, then Travis unrolled Rana's buffalo mat between them. He even smiled when he told her to go to sleep and explained that they would have a hard day's ride ahead. He stretched out on his bedroll, knowing from past observation that Rana slept on her right side which would compel her to face him. He watched her surreptitiously.

Rana took her appointed place between the two men, lying on her back and staring at the star-sprinkled sky overhead. For a long time, she and Travis did not sleep. She was very much aware of the ever-increasing distance between her and the Oglala camp, and how each day brought her nearer to her new destiny, one that she could not envision. She recalled Lone Wolf's words: "You have trained and waited for the Great Spirit to return you to your destined path. Do not cower in fear or doubt and refuse to walk it." She shuddered with apprehension.

"Are you cold, Rana?" he inquired softly in Oglala, noting that the weary Nathan was slumbering peacefully.

"No," she responded in Oglala. "How far is it to your home?"

"*Wikcemna nunpa nais wikcemna yamni anpetu,*" he replied, giving her a time of twenty to thirty days.

As she turned her head and looked at him, their eyes fused. "There is much to learn. What if your people do not accept me?"

Travis's gaze roamed her exquisite features and flaming hair. She looked so vulnerable and insecure. He realized how intimidating this sudden change must be to her. Lone Wolf had told him she had sworn never to allow anyone to hurt her again. Like him, she had become defensive and wary. She wanted to appear tough and hard, but she was a compelling contrast of strength and softness. He smiled and reached out to caress her cheek. He said tenderly, "You are very smart, Rana. You will learn everything quickly and easily. Do not worry; everyone will like you and accept you. Go to sleep. It is late."

She smiled, her expression softening with the gentle gesture. "Is that why you chose Wild Wind?" she inquired seriously.

He chuckled. "I chose Rana because she was the woman of most beauty and value in the Oglala camp. Was it not a great honor to help your people? Do not fear me and your new life."

"Was White Eagle afraid of this new life when he left the Hunkpapa camp long ago?" she questioned curiously.

Travis rolled to his back and inhaled deeply. He wanted to continue talking pleasantly with her, but he did not like the direction the conversation was taking. "I will explain those past moons another time. I was young and bitter, and my leaving was not as yours. My mother and father were killed in battle, and speaking of such times brings pain and sadness. Is it not the same with you?" he asked pointedly.

Rana eyed him intently. She was filled with an urge to embrace him and comfort him. His tone and look had exposed such anguish, such resentment. Clearly those "past moons" had been tormenting and difficult times for this man. Perhaps that was why he had trouble revealing deep emotions and why he continually tried to avoid or to master them. He liked to be in control of himself and the situation, and emotional turmoil prevented it, or so he believed. This was a man who had been hurt deeply and who now lived too much within himself. She liked this sensitive, vulnerable, gentle side of her new husband. Suddenly she wondered if he had had a lover or a wife who had been slain in that same battle and if that were the reason he had left the Lakota lands and was reluctant to reach out to her. That speculation caused jealousy to flood her body. She had so many doubts and questions about this man.

"Yes," she admitted softly, "the past can be painful."

"One day, will you tell me what you remember of your past?" he asked gingerly, and watched her stiffen in panic.

"I wish to forget it. Do not ask," she beseeched him. "When the sun has gone to sleep on a day, it cannot be recalled or changed."

"Things that happen because of events of a past sun can be changed," he gently corrected. "Mistakes or evil deeds can be made right and old enemies can become new friends," he clarified.

"It is a mistake to leave when my people are at war."

"I cannot save the Oglalas, Rana, but I can save you. You are not deserting your people by returning to where you belong. If you stay, you can do nothing to halt their destiny, but only bring about your own suffering and death. To yield or change is not a defeat or self-betrayal."

Rana did not want to question his disquieting words. "Tell me about your home and lands," she entreated to distract him.

Travis glanced at her and grinned. "Another day, Rana. We must sleep. We have a long ride ahead. Are you restless tonight?" She sighed and nodded. He asked, "Does your heart quiver with fear?"

Rana's expression became one of annoyance. "I do not quiver in fear. I am tired. I will sleep now." She turned her back to him, rankled by his insinuation of cowardice, and she vowed to prove him wrong.

Travis knew he had said the wrong thing; he had meant "anticipation," not "fear." The problem was that often a meaning was lost through a difficulty in translation. He was sharp enough not to chuckle at her amusing reaction. "Good night, Rana. Sleep well." Travis closed his eyes, but his keen instincts remained alert through the night.

Rana did not sleep well and was irritable when Travis aroused her the following morning when dawn was barely a reality. Travis had already gathered wood, built a fire, and prepared coffee. She seized a blanket and headed downstream to bathe. When the dark-haired man questioned her obvious intentions, she sullenly replied, "*Yuzaza wacin.*"

"Hurry, and do not go far. Enemies could be nearby."

"I can defend myself," she tartly informed him. "I am not a child or a frightened girl. Will you return my knife and sheath?"

Travis studied her for a moment, then retrieved the items from his saddlebag. He handed them to her and warned, "Use it only for defense, or I will take it away. Do not anger me with silly games."

"I will use my knife to defend Wi . . . Rana against all dangers. I am smart. A weapon is not for play. Your warning insults me."

"Your behavior this morning insults me and you," he retorted. "A person should not be angry without reason. And when a person does not feel well, he should not blame or annoy others for his bad feelings. Go, bathe, and return quickly. We must eat and ride."

She started to quarrel with him, then changed her mind. It was a waste of time and energy to exchange bitter words with him. She glanced at the older man, who was watching them intently. When Nathan smiled at her, she did not respond. "I will hurry, my husband," she stated sarcastically, then glowered at him.

Travis scowled, then shook his head as he watched her departure. His troubled gaze wandered over her gently swaying hips and hair. One look into that stunning face had been enough to set his body aflame for her. He swore under his breath in Lakota as he tossed the saddlebag to the ground and reached for the coffeepot and a tin cup.

"Trouble between you two again?" Nathan inquired as he held out his cup for a refill, his gaze going from one to the other.

"Nothing I can't handle, Nate. She's in a bad mood this morning. I think she was too nervous to sleep. She realizes this trade is for real and that she's getting farther away from the Oglala camp. She's having trouble understanding a new husband who doesn't touch his wife."

"Maybe you should tell her the marriage isn't real, so she can stop worrying about becoming a wife," Nathan suggested.

"Isn't real, Nate?" he repeated skeptically. "To her, it's very real. She's been raised under Indian laws and customs. She believes in them and follows them, just like you with your white religion. Telling her our marriage isn't binding or real is like telling you there isn't a God. Or telling you your American laws aren't legal or binding, that it's all right to murder and steal. This was a crazy idea and I shouldn't have gone along with it. She's going to be furious when she discovers how we've lied to her. And she's going to be hurt."

Nathan did not know what to say or do. He could tell Travis was upset. He knew that Travis, like his granddaughter, had been raised as an Indian, raised to honor and accept Indian laws and customs. Nathan wondered if that was the problem that seemed to be harassing and confusing the young man who was like a son to him. Maybe it had been a big oversight on Travis's part; maybe he had not realized he would feel as if they were legally married inside his head and his heart. Perhaps Travis was still bound emotionally to his Indian heritage. To Nathan, the Oglala joining ceremony had merely been meaningless words. Yet he realized he would have to face the reality that it had not been viewed in that same light by Rana and Travis. And though he could not be sure, Nathan had a strong suspicion that he was right in these assumptions and speculations.

Travis's return to this area and the Lakota people had sparked old feelings and thoughts. For awhile he had become Indian again, and he had enjoyed it. Long ago he had been forced to give up this kind of life, and it had been unwise of him to confront it again. Perhaps he was still more Lakota than he had realized. His heart had surged with joy and excitement, almost as if he had been coming home and the white world was far away. No matter how much Travis told himself the marriage was not legal or binding under the white laws of his chosen people, he could not forget or ignore his Indian upbringing. Part of him said they were truly joined, and part of him said they were not. Part of him said he wanted this marriage, and part of him said he did not. He cursed his recklessness, for now he was trapped between his friend Nathan and his wife, Wild Wind. There was nothing he could do until he either convinced Nathan that the marriage was binding or convinced Rana that it was not.

While growing up in the Hunkpapa camp, Travis had witnessed many joining ceremonies. He recalled his own, envisioning Rana's touch and willingness to marry him and remembering the words and seriousness of the occasion. He recalled how he and Rana had pledged themselves to each other beneath the eyes of *Wakan Tanka,* who was the same as God to him. He remembered opening the marriage cape, her stepping inside, and his closing it around them to bind them for life. He still believed in the Great Spirit and the Indian way of life, through which he had been wed to this unique woman who trusted him. Were the Indian law and religion any less binding or sacred than the white man's? If he stood in a white man's church and repeated those same words in English, would it be any different to him, for him? He did not like being troubled by his conscience, a conscience that had been born during his years with Nathan. Now he had to think about more than himself, yet he knew that if it had not been Nathan and his granddaughter involved—

Nathan interrupted his train of thought. "You did the right thing, son. It was the only way we could rescue her. Those Indians didn't give us any choice. She'll understand once we explain everything to her."

"Do you forgive and forget when someone makes a fool of you? I know I've never forgotten or forgiven what Jeremy Kincade or Beth Lowry or Pretty Rabbit did to me and others. Just like I can't overlook what Harrison and Clarissa Caldwell are trying to do to us. Maybe you were right; we should have told Rana the truth from the beginning. She'll despise me. Who knows? Maybe she'll be delighted she isn't really tied to me. Let's drop it, Nate. Here she comes."

"You look as pretty as a field of flowers, Rana," Nathan stated, appreciatively eyeing her as Travis translated his compliment. She was wearing a clean buckskin dress with beaded designs, and her thick red hair was neatly braided and secured with decorative rosettes. Her eyes were large and bright, and her skin appeared smooth and flawless. Nathan smiled as he noticed her bare feet. He saw why Travis was attracted to this woman he had vowed to ignore. Maybe—

"*Pilamaya,* Nate," she responded, deceptively appearing calm.

After they had eaten, Travis announced that it was time to mount and ride. Rana sat down to pull on her moccasins. She was mildly surprised when Travis extended his hand to help her rise, then lifted her to Cloud's back with an ease that revealed his strength and agility. She stated mischievously, "*Pilamaya, mihigna.*"

Travis sent her a look that told her he wished he could yank her off Cloud's back and kiss her soundly. She had not missed the way his hands had lingered on her waist, or the way one had leisurely slid down her left leg, or the way his gaze had feasted on her features. Maybe it would be wise to keep touching him, she mused, and reminding him he was *mihigna,* her husband . . .

They rode for hours with Rana between them, their fast pace and the noise of the horses' hooves preventing any conversation. When they halted for the midday meal, Travis told Rana to stay with Nathan while he did some scouting.

"Do you expect trouble, my husband?" she asked worriedly, her entreating gaze meeting his intense stare.

A warm flush passed over his body. "Just being careful. I need to conceal our trail. We have been leaving one a child could follow."

"I do not understand. Do you think my people will come after you? You do not trust them?" Her large, blue-gray eyes searched his.

"You left many hungry, angry men behind," he teased roguishly. "When Rides-Like-Thunder discovers you are gone, he might come after you. If I am slain, you are free to join to another."

"Do not make jokes with me, Travis Kincade," she scolded.

"That is true, Rana, but I seek to hide our trail from enemies—soldiers and renegades," he replied honestly. "If the soldiers learn that I purchased the guns for warriors and killed the white man who tricked me, they will come after us. As soon as we can, we need to find you some clothes. Those Indian garments stand out like a dark sky. We do not need to arouse any suspicion this close to your camp. I doubt your identity is unknown to the whites and soldiers or to enemy tribes, a beautiful white girl with big blue eyes and flaming hair . . ."

"You think they would try to capture me and harm me?"

"For one reason or another," he answered vaguely. "Promise me you will stay here with Nathan and behave yourself."

"You do not trust your wife?" she probed.

Travis knew he would be gone for awhile, and he did not want to bind her and cause more trouble between them. He was afraid Nathan would not be able to handle this willful, clever female, for his friend underestimated her cunning, her daring, and her apprehension. If he used clever words and expressed faith in her, he might win her trust and obedience. "Lone Wolf told me you are as well trained as his warriors. I need you to protect Nathan. He is not as young or as quick as you are. You could flee and hide, or defend yourself. Stay alert so you can warn him of danger. But do not take any foolish chances. I love him more than my own life. Will you do this for me, Rana?"

Rana could not suppress her smile at his beseeching words and his look of concern for her safety. "I will do as you say. Be careful," she added, then hurriedly glanced away to prevent him from reading her expression. She wanted and needed to understand this man who had become such a big part of her life. She wanted to learn what he expected, and desired, from her. And she wanted to test her feelings as well as his.

"Your courage and honor are matchless. I am pleased with you."

Travis approached Nathan and related his plans. He whispered, "Keep an eye on her, Nate, and don't say anything around her."

"You watch yourself, son."

"If there's any trouble, ride fast and I'll catch up with you." He called Rana over to them and said, "Stay close and ready to leave."

Rana and Nathan watched Travis ride off into the trees. As instructed, they tended the horses and ate a light meal. When all was prepared, they sat down to await Travis's return.

"I wish you remembered English, Rana, so we could talk. Me and Travis will have to start teaching it to you before we get home. I don't want anybody giving you trouble, and I'll kill anyone who does. Lordy, we were lucky to find you. You don't know how much I love you, girl. You're going to be happy once I get you home. I won't ever let anybody harm you again. Damn them Kiowas for stealing you!"

Rana stared at him quizzically. Nathan assumed her curious look was because he was speaking English and she could not understand him. He touched her arm and smiled. "Don't worry, child. Everything will be fine just as soon as Travis explains everything to you."

A lengthy time passed and both Nathan and Rana became worried about Travis. Rana stood and walked around to master her tension. She noticed that Nathan was eyeing her as if he expected her to run off at any second. Realizing she was making the older man nervous, she took a seat near him. Her ears were straining for any noise, any indication that Travis was returning. She suddenly wondered what she would do and how she would feel if Travis were slain. They had been joined for eight suns and had not shared a sleeping mat. Maybe he was not pleased with her. Maybe he thought she was still a foolish girl. Surely he had a good reason for refusing to share a sleeping mat.

Nathan captured her hand in his and patted it with the other one. "He'll be all right, Rana. He's too smart to get into danger. I just wish he wasn't so troubled about you. It ain't good to be so distracted in enemy territory. I tried to warn him."

Rana had to grit her teeth to keep from asking, Warn him about what? And to ask why and how he was troubled over her. Maybe pretending not to understand them had been a mistake, because she could not ask questions. With Travis gone, she was missing the perfect time to obtain information from this older man who seemed to like her very much, who had eyes almost the same color as hers. She was glad Nathan was so gentle and nice, and she liked him. He vaguely reminded her of someone she could not remember, someone special who had warmed her heart. There was something about his face and voice that reached out to her. Perhaps Grandfather had put him in her dreams or visions long ago. If only she could recall them clearly, but she did not want to push herself, for too many of those dreams had been bad ones.

Travis appeared as if from nowhere, astonishing both Nathan and Rana with his skillful stealth. He frowned at them and scolded lightly, "If I had been an enemy, you two would be in deep trouble."

Rana's half-smile faded instantly, but she knew he was right. She suspected that Travis had intentionally sneaked up on them. She told him she would be ready to ride soon, then vanished into the trees.

"She been behaving?" Travis questioned anxiously.

"Not a peep out of her. We need to teach her some English, son, so I can talk to her. Any signs of danger out there?"

"Nope. I covered our trail and made a false one in another direction. I don't like it, Nate; things are too quiet. We've got us a storm brewing, and I don't mean the weather." Travis decided it was best not to tell Nathan that three of Lone Wolf's braves had been trailing them until this morning, probably for Rana's protection.

"You said Crazy Horse and his Big Bellies have been lying low for awhile. It's been months since he massacred Captain Fetterman over at Lodge Trail Ridge. And Red Cloud hasn't moved his Bad Faces Band out of the Powder River area, has he?"

"We don't have to worry about Red Cloud; he's set on keeping that Bozemen Trail closed. They're riding between the Black Hills and Little Bighorn. But you can bet Sitting Bull and his Strong Heart Society aren't sitting around doing nothing. What we have to worry about is Crazy Horse banding together those Lakotas and Cheyenne. Lone Wolf told me he's been plotting against Fort Kearny and C. F. Smith all winter. He's planning on striking at them soon. After what he did to Fetterman, the Army is ready and waiting to retaliate. It'll be a bloodbath."

"Is Crazy Horse crazy like his name?" Nathan inquired.

"That's a mistake in translation, Nate. Our word is "crazy"; theirs is "enchanted"; and believe me, he's got more magic and appeal than those soldiers can imagine. He doesn't take scalps or count *coup*, and he rides in front of his band. He's totally fearless, Nate. I doubt the Union Army has any leader as cunning and daring, and we're heading near his target area. Let's get moving," he announced, not wanting to take time to eat or rest. "Rana! *Inankni yo!*" he called loudly, telling her to hurry.

Rana appeared soon and mounted her beloved white stallion. As they rode off, she took a place at Nathan's right side, putting the older man between her and Travis. Travis did not bother to shift her, for he knew he had singed her ego and pride again.

It was past dusk when Travis called a halt to their day's ride, which had left all three of them tired and tense. While Travis thoroughly scouted the area and tended the horses, Rana helped Nathan gather firewood and prepare their meal. When the food was ready, Nathan called Travis to join them. Discarding the Indian custom for the white one, Travis instructed Rana to eat with them, not after them, and she enjoyed being treated and viewed as an equal. Travis ate silently and quickly, then unrolled the sleeping mats. Nathan wished them good night, then took his place and was soon dozing.

Rana sat staring into the fire as she brushed her hair. She was neither sad nor happy. When she took a blanket and headed for the river, Travis went after her and asked where she was going. "*Wanuwan wacin,*" she replied without losing a step.

"It is too late to go swimming and the water is too cool. Lie down on your mat and go to sleep," he ordered moodily. Travis knew he possessed the brute strength to control the stirring minx, but he had little desire to tangle with her. She provoked and enchanted him at every turn. In spite of his past female trouble and his current obligations to Nathan, he was being drawn closer to her with every passing hour.

She halted and looked at him, protesting, "I am dusty and tired. I wish to bathe before sleeping. You hurry me in the morning."

"I just want to get us safely out of this area. Several tribes are painting up for war with the soldiers, and other tribes are going to join them. I do not want us caught in the middle."

"Why do you give Indians guns, then refuse to fight with them?"

"This is not my war, Rana. I cannot take sides. I only helped your people even the odds by giving them a fighting chance for survival. I am half Indian and you have been raised by them. Soldiers would not be too friendly toward us, and neither would the Indians because we are white. You have been in that Oglala camp too long. You do not know what it is like to be trapped between warring sides, belonging to neither. I must get you out of those Indian garments and out of this Indian territory before someone guesses who you are. You do not want the soldiers using you to obtain Lone Wolf's surrender, do you?"

"No," she hastily responded. "But why did you not warn my people?"

"I did. That is why Lone Wolf traded you so readily." Knowing he had spoken rashly, he tried to cover himself. "He knew this war was heating up fast and he did not want you getting hurt by it. He loves you, Rana, but you are white. You could be a threat to them. He wants you to be safe and happy. He did what was best for everyone. Can you understand and accept that?"

"If I did not accept it, I would not be here with you. Why must you be so cold and angry with me, Travis Kincade? It is hard to leave my people and make the changes you demand. It makes me sad and angry that you do not trust me or like me." With this, she raced off toward the river, wondering how her words would affect him.

She hurriedly yanked off her moccasins and dress and tossed them aside. As she loosened the ties on her breechclout, Travis walked over to her. He seized her chin and lifted her head, intending to debate her mistaken impressions. Tears sparkled on her thick lashes and her wide eyes were somber. Her long, wavy hair settled wildly about her shoulders and reflected the moonlight, giving her a sensual aura. As she clenched her teeth, her lips formed a natural and seductive pout. She allowed the breechclout to slip from her fingers and fall to the ground, making no attempt to shield her nude body from Travis's gaze. This attractive, stimulating man was her husband, and she wanted him.

The flesh beneath Travis's light grasp was as soft and slick as an expensive satin ribbon. Her body was lithe and shapely. Where she was tanned, her skin was as golden as honey and as creamy as its texture. Where her tan stopped, her skin was as white as a fluffy cloud and as soft as freshly picked cotton. He knew he should not allow his gaze to roam her ravishing face and stunning figure, but he could not stop himself. Every inch of her seemed to call out for tender, loving caresses. She was so sleek and exquisite. Never had he viewed a more perfect woman. He yearned to let his hands explore her body, to allow his lips to follow that same trail. His respiration became ragged and his grip on her tightened slightly. His green gaze glowed with unrestrained desire. "Lordy, you're beautiful," he murmured. He was losing himself in those magnetic blue-gray eyes, and for a time he did not care. As with aged whiskey, she was utterly intoxicating. All of the times he had taken women in the past, it had been for physical release, to appease his sexual urges. It was not like that with Rana; his entire being craved her. The other women he had wanted only for a night of pleasure. But Rana he wanted completely, permanently!

Rana boldly stepped closer to him and drew his head down to hers, fusing their lips as she mesmerized Travis with her gaze. A groan escaped his lips and his arms encircled her body to mold it tightly against his. He kissed her fiercely, ravenously. His fingers tangled in her silky hair as he pressed her head to his, allowing his eager mouth to explore hers leisurely. He could feel the stimulating warmth of her body through his shirt. His hands slid down her back and, grasping her buttocks, he drew her to him. The intimate contact staggered his senses and inflamed him dangerously. He groaned again, unable to hide his rapidly fleeing restraint and mounting desire. He had craved this provocative vixen since first sighting her, and he wanted her beyond control or reason.

"Come, lie with me, my husband," she whispered seductively, pulling the captivated Travis down to the discarded blanket with her. She fastened her lips to his and feasted greedily. Her arms went under his and around his firm, supple body to stroke his muscular back. As his lips seared over her face, down her neck, and to her breasts, she writhed and caressed his lower body with her own. His actions brought her sheer bliss. While he savored one brown peak and then the other, her fingers played in his sable hair. She loved these wild, wonderful feelings he evoked and yielded eagerly to them.

All Travis could think about was possessing this enticing creature who was driving him wild with hunger for her. Never before had a woman stolen his wits and control, until Rana. He wanted to take her swiftly, and yet with maddening leisure, for she belonged to him by Indian law and by right of rescue and conquest. Desire for her had been driving him crazy for days, and he wanted to enjoy every second of this first joining of their bodies. His deft hand wandered down her supple frame, caressing and tantalizing each area as it traveled toward her unprotected womanhood, which radiated a heat in which he desperately wanted to warm himself. Lordy, he had never desired a woman so strongly or felt so possessive of one. His restraint was rapidly disappearing and he knew he could wait no longer to take her. He had to—

"Travis! Travis, where are you, son?" Nathan called loudly, his voice coming from a distance.

Travis went rigid as reality slammed hard into his gut. He leaned away from Rana, breathing heavily. "What the hell am I doing?" he murmured in disbelief. "I can't make love to you. Why did I let you tempt me like this again? You've got powerful magic."

Knowing that Nathan would continue to call and seek them, Travis stood up and straightened his shirt. He tried to master his respiration and douse his fiery passion before calling out, "Be there in a minute, Nate. Everything's fine. Rana wanted a bath, so I'm standing guard." He pulled the naked girl to her feet and whispered in her ear, "Get bathed and get back to camp as quickly as you can."

The astonished Rana gaped at her husband when he left her to join his friend as if nothing had been going on between them. Anger, embarrassment, and frustration consumed her. She could not imagine why a husband would behave as hers did. He had acted as if there were something wrong with his desiring her and with their making love. There was nothing shameful about love or sex. He had responded to her, had been hungry to possess her, even willing to do so until his friend had awakened him from his dreamy world. Travis was not a coward, she knew, so what had frightened him and quelled his passion a second time?

She eased into the chilly water to cool her own passions, but her temper remained heated. She raged aloud as she bathed roughly, "Why do you kill such good feelings and douse such wild flames of desire? Do you belong to another woman, or to her dead spirit? You are 'angry without good reason,' " she charged, using his own words. "You blazed with anger when Black Hawk tried to take what was yours, yet you refuse it. You have hurt me and shamed me deeply."

When Rana finally returned to the campfire, Nathan was dozing again and Travis was lying on his back, his hat resting over his eyes. She snatched up her sleeping mat and spread it out on the other side of the fire, away from the two men. Sullenly, she lay down and tossed a thin blanket over her trembling frame. As she was settling herself, her gaze drifted across the fire to observe Travis propped on one elbow, watching her intently. She glared coldly at him, then turned away, vowing never to allow him to treat her that way again. It was surprising how swiftly sleep came to her, despite her fury and tension.

As Travis watched her sleeping form, he realized that Rana was slowly chiseling away at his stony heart. Each day he was finding it harder to be tough and resistant. Taming her was like trying to master a wild mustang without breaking its spirit. It was like tampering with another's destiny or trying to leash pure spirit and energy, like trying to control the very essence of life itself. He asked himself, how did one capture sunshine in his hand?

He remembered how Elizabeth Lowry and Clarissa Caldwell had tried to ensnare him with their feminine wiles, and how Rana's own mother had toyed with susceptible men, if he could believe the stories he had heard about Marissa Crandall Michaels. Women's desires could prove treacherous to an unsuspecting man, as Pretty Rabbit's had been.

To make White Eagle jealous and to snare his attention, Pretty Rabbit had used Charge-A-Buffalo; she had driven him wild with desire and frustration. The warrior had loved her and had wanted her as his mate, but she had toyed with him to get at White Eagle. After she had cruelly rejected the warrior and had told him he was nothing compared to White Eagle, the warrior had been consumed by hatred and anguish. To revenge himself on White Eagle and to punish Pretty Rabbit, the warrior had lied about White Eagle's involvement with his father's evil deeds. Charge-A-Buffalo had wanted to make certain that if he could not have Pretty Rabbit, White Eagle would never have her and she would never have White

Eagle. When he had been captured, falsely accused, tortured, and scheduled for death, Pretty Rabbit had viewed his perilous predicament as the means to finally win him. But though she had died trying to help him escape, her evil scheming had kept Travis from feeling any remorse over her death.

Yet, over the years since that tragic incident, he had thought a great deal about the Hunkpapas' actions and in a way had come to understand and forgive them. His father had been a malicious enemy, and he had been a half-breed. He had left the Hunkpapas to travel with his father for two years in the white world, and perhaps they had thought he had been tainted by it. He had been at his father's side when Jeremy had been captured following his vile treachery. A courageous, renowned warrior had made charges against him, one whose hatred and feelings of rivalry were unknown to their people. He had begun to realize that with such "evidence" against him, perhaps their behavior had been logical and natural. Maybe he would have done and felt the same if the charges had been against another half-breed or white man.

Before going to sleep, Travis admitted to himself that he had learned one thing: hatred and bitterness could be a ravenously devouring disease. With Nathan's help and love, he had conquered the worst of it; and no matter what the Indians had said or might believe about him, he could face the Great Spirit with a clear conscience and an innocent heart.

Chapter 7

FOR TWO DAYS, the small group continued their journey at the grueling pace that Travis had set for them after his frustrating encounter with Rana. When they stopped to camp that second night, Travis moodily went about his tasks while Rana disappeared to bathe. He made no attempt to question her or to stop her, and Rana did not ask permission to leave camp. During the past two days Rana had been riding next to Nathan and sleeping away from the two men. It had become clear to Nathan that the two were ignoring and avoiding each other, and this behavior intrigued and worried the observant rancher. Too, he was becoming flustered by his obligatory silence, for he knew the best way to solve a problem was to meet it head-on.

Nathan now inquired seriously of Travis, "Don't you think it's about time you tell me what's bothering you, son? You've been pushing us close to exhaustion for days. There ain't no way we can stay alert and strong at this killing pace, and you haven't even tried to cover our trail. What's wrong, son? You're running like a dog with his tail afire. The same goes for Rana. You two have hardly spoken or looked at each other in two days. You've been letting her come and go as she pleases, like you don't even care if she tries to escape. I feel like I've been riding between two fierce enemies traveling under a bitter truce. Is there something you haven't told me about Rana or our situation?"

Travis tensed in dread. He should have known his actions would call Nathan's attention to him. How could he explain the truth to his best friend without increasing his worries? "I told you, Nate, I want to get us out of this territory pronto, at least past Forts Kearny and Smith. We're only two days' ride from Fort Laramie, and we'll be crossing over the Mormon and Oregon Trails on Sunday. The Indians could be watching them for wagon trains or troop movements, and the soldiers at those forts are getting plenty nervous. They're in a mood to shoot first and check around later. Our best strategy is to head overland and stay clear of forts and villages until we're out of Nebraska. I'm trying to protect you and Rana. I'll ease up in three or four days, as soon as we make Kansas. I know what I'm doing, Nate."

Nathan eyed the younger man. "Do you, Travis? Talk to me, son," he urged gravely, indicating that he did not accept his foreman's explanation.

Travis did not like deceiving the older man. Except for keeping the reasons for his originally leaving this territory a secret, he had always been open and honest with Nathan Crandall. Anguish and shame had caused him to keep silent about his father's treachery, but far different emotions were keeping him silent about this present complicated matter. By now Nathan thought he knew all about the younger man, yet Travis realized he did not even know himself where Rana was concerned.

"What's gotten into you, son?" Nathan persisted gently.

Travis inhaled deeply, feeling like his neck was in a tight noose. "All right, Nate, if you want the truth. I'll give it to you. Your granddaughter is a beautiful, desirable woman. She's trying her damnedest to become my wife in every way possible, and sometimes I have a hell of a time remembering who she is and what the real situation is between us. The faster we ride and the farther away we get from here, the sooner I can explain things to her and stop all this temptation. By the time we reach Kansas, it'll be too late for her to try anything rash or foolish. We can tell her who she is and why we came after her; then maybe we can all have some peace. But frankly I don't think she's going to understand why I married her or why the council demanded that we join."

Travis leaned against a tree as if needing its support. "It sounded like a clever idea back in the Oglala camp, like the easiest and quickest way to handle her, but I don't think so anymore. There are too many complications and feelings involved. Rana had a rough, frightening childhood, traveling from one saloon to another, watching her parents being slaughtered, enduring captivity by the Kiowas. Once she got settled in with the Oglalas and was treated like a princess for years, she became spoiled. We might as well face it, Nate; she's impetuous and stubborn, and she's too damn proud for her own good. She's been living wild and free in the forest and plains. She's been taught Lakota laws and customs. She's been taught to depend on her wits and courage—to depend on herself, Nate. Her skin is white and she's your flesh and blood, but her heart and life are Indian. She's used to sidestepping her brother to get her way, and she's had countless warriors begging for her. When she finally obeys her brother and marries a man, he doesn't come near her. It doesn't sit well with her that I'm not behaving like a husband. This situation has got to be as confusing and embarrassing for her as it is for me. It's got her ego in an uproar. Since she was seven, this is all she's known and loved. Then we walk in and make demands on her, force her to leave and change, to become civilized. It doesn't seem fair. But you're right, Nate; things can't go on this way. I've got to settle down or I could endanger all of us."

Travis straightened and rested his hands on his gun butts. Clenching his teeth, he declared sullenly, "Hell, Nate, I've never been in this kind of predicament before and I don't know how to handle it. It's got me plenty worried, and even a little scared," he admitted. "You're depending on me, Nate, and I don't want to fail you."

Nathan touched his shoulder affectionately. "You won't fail me, son, and you never have. My life was nothing but hard work and bare existence until you came along, Travis. You don't know how much you mean to me, son. I know this must be hard on you and Rana, but everything will iron out as soon as we can explain matters to her."

Travis shook his head and frowned. "I'm not so sure that won't make matters worse, Nate. She loves her brother and trusts him, and he's let her down. And we let her down. We made it look as if she didn't have enough sense or honor to understand the truth or have any say about her life. We treated her like a child or someone who couldn't think for herself, as if she didn't have any feelings or didn't deserve to know the truth. We bought her like a piece of property. We didn't ask for her understanding or cooperation. We all tricked her. And she's going to be mad at us, Nate. I know how I felt when I discovered my father's treachery. All I knew was that he had lied to me and used me. Once she hears the truth, how can she trust us and accept us? We simply expect her to take our word that we did it all for her own good? Hell, we're strangers to her!"

"I'm her grandfather, Travis," he argued sadly. "I had to get her back. I couldn't just leave her there to get tangled up in that war."

"I know, Nate, but we're asking a lot from her. She's hardly more than a child. I think the best thing for me to do is to apologize to Rana and start being nicer and easier on her. I can't blame her for acting on a lie I created. Until I can tell her the truth, I need to go along with it, at least halfway. As soon as we finish eating, I'll ask her to take a walk—see if I can't straighten things out a little bit."

"What are you going to tell her?"

"I don't know, but I have to tell her something. The longer I let her stay mad, the more she's going to be tempted to run off just to get back at me. If there's one thing I've learned, Nate, it's that women can be spiteful and selfish. They'll go to any lengths to get their wishes, or make you sorry they didn't . . . Tell me about that necklace you gave her. It seemed to make her nervous," he remarked carefully.

"I gave it to Marissa on her last visit. She wore it every day. Sometimes, when she was rocking Rana to sleep after a bad dream, Rana would hold it and rub it. It always seemed to calm her down, so I was planning to buy her one. I never got the chance. After Marissa was killed, the housekeeper found it and a doll I had given to Rana in the bottom drawer in Marissa's bedroom. I guess she left them behind so Raymond wouldn't take 'em and sell 'em for a poker stake." He paused for a moment, then continued. "Marissa and Rana both became edgy after he showed up at the ranch. What was I supposed to do, Travis? The law is on the husband's side, and she was willing to leave with him. If she had said one word against him, I wouldn't have let him take them away. I had this gut feeling she was planning to come back home. She never had a chance, but now we're giving Rana one. I kept that necklace all these years and gave it to Rana while you were gone. You think she remembers it?"

Travis replied candidly, "I think she doesn't want to remember it, or anything else about her past."

"Does that include me, son? I know she only saw me a few times, but I was hoping . . ." Nathan did not finish his wistful thought.

"You said she was happy at the ranch. Maybe it will spur her memory. One thing for certain, you need to get as close to her as possible before we reveal the truth to her. I think I'll speak to her before supper, then maybe we can all eat better. I'll return soon."

At a secluded area near the stream, Rana was also thinking and planning. She finally understood that there would be no going back to her old life and that she would have to make the best of this baffling situation. For two days she had been thinking about her new life and Travis. Somewhere out there a new destiny awaited her, and it included her mysterious husband. To keep from making herself and the others unhappy, she would have to accept the way Travis wanted things, or seemed to want them. She would have to show complete control and patience, and behave like a woman, not a child or a wild vixen. She was tired of her cold, self-imposed silence. It was making her miserable and tense, when all she wanted was to smile and be happy again. She yearned for him to like her and accept her, to be proud of her and his choice. She hated the way Travis was treating her and the way he was pushing them. His troubled spirit seemed to be driving him and she had no doubt that she was somehow to blame. Maybe she had said or done something to offend him or displease him. Maybe he believed those ugly stories about her. Maybe he doubted her reactions to him. If only he could explain his feelings and his reasons for rejecting her, perhaps they could come to some understanding.

Rana was terribly bewildered. She recalled the few stirring moments of closeness they had shared: the incident in her tepee, the kiss at the beginning of their journey, and their passionate embrace near the river. Each time, things had gone well between them until she had yielded to passion or had tried to inflame him. For some inexplicable reason, feeling desire for her angered him and caused him to lash out cruelly at her. If there were to be peace between them, she would have to keep her distance from him; she would have to live as his sister, as he had so contradictorily requested. Perhaps if she showed him her best face and ceased "tempting" him, he would settle down so they could get closer. One day she might even convince him to take her as his wife in the true sense.

With this enticing thought in mind, Rana completed her bath. Wrapping herself in a drying blanket, she washed her soiled dress so that it could dry during the warm night. Afterward, she slipped into her white garment, which she knew was her most flattering dress. She brushed her hair and allowed it to hang free down her back. Above her left ear, she secured the tiny medicine wheel made from quills in the sacred colors of blue, yellow, white, red, and black with a breath feather attached to its center. Seeing that it was nearly dark, she collected her possessions and headed toward the camp to join the men.

As she made her way back, she was surprised to find Travis waiting for her in the shadows of a tall tree. She halted before him to view his expression and to learn what he wanted. He did not look angry, only tired and troubled. She observed the way his gaze slipped over her from her head to her bare feet and she watched his troubled look increase; suddenly she regretted dressing so prettily to catch his eye and to soften his anger.

When he did not speak, she eyed him quizzically. He seemed to be having difficulty finding words, or perhaps, she mused, only the right ones. Apprehension filled her. He was so handsome and virile, and she longed to enjoy his lips and arms. At times such as this, he made her feel so unsure of herself, so vulnerable and helpless. His mere presence caused her body to warm strangely and to quiver. His look caused all thoughts to rush from her head except those of him, and it inspired her heart to beat as swiftly and forcefully as the drums during the Victory Dance. He even affected her breathing and the moisture in her mouth. As if that were not enough, he also made her legs go weak and refuse to move. No man had made her feel this way before, so weak and compliant. It was alarming, and yet very pleasant. Taking a deep breath, she looked into his eyes and waited.

"Lordy, woman, you're not going to make this easy for me, are you?" he mumbled. "How do I explain myself without making you furious with me?" He half turned and pounded his fist on the tree, for he had never before explained himself to a woman.

Rana softly replied in fluent English, "Say what is in your heart, my . . . Travis. I do not wish to cause you such pain and trouble. It is not good for us to behave as fierce enemies. What does Rana do wrong? Are you sorry you chose me? Do you wish to send me away?"

Travis faced her and stared into that upturned face with its innocent, appealing expression. Damn women for having and using such potent wiles! he cursed silently, then said aloud, "So, you do remember English. I thought as much. You're one clever and stubborn girl, Rana Michaels."

"My people did not like to hear the white man's tongue, so I did not speak it unless my brother asked it of me to question captives. Does it not please you that I can speak with you? Where we go, will you not wish me to keep the Oglala tongue a secret?"

"From now on, speak English. Why did you trick me?"

"Trick you? You did not ask if I could speak your tongue, and you did not order me to speak it. Is it strange for a white girl to speak the white tongue? Did my brother not tell you?"

"No, he didn't, and I was under the impression that you had forgotten it. You were captured as a small child and you've only heard Oglala for years. But I suspected you understood more than you let on. But that isn't what I wanted to discuss," he declared, changing the subject before he could become angered by her deceit. He had no right, he knew, for his duplicity was worse.

"Discuss?" she repeated the unfamiliar word, knowing he had a right to be angry with her for withholding her knowledge of English from him.

"Talk about," he clarified. "These last few days we've . . . I've been acting badly. I wanted to tell you I'm sorry for being so mean and hard on you. I know this change in your life must be confusing and frightening, and I haven't been making it any easier for you. I want you to understand some things about me and our marriage," Travis ventured, wanting to stay as close to the truth as possible. He had to get this particular matter straight between them, for both their sakes.

"I didn't come here looking for a wife, and I'm a little confused about finding one. You know it's the custom to choose something of great value in exchange for the guns and supplies I gave to your people. Since you were white and the war was heating up, I thought it would be a good idea to get you out of Indian territory. If what I heard was true, you were having problems in the camp. I had already asked for you in trade when they said I would have to marry you before you could leave with me. It would have been an insult to refuse to marry the sister of Chief Lone Wolf when I had been willing to trade for her. I'm not used to having a woman around, Rana, so you'll have to give me time to get adjusted to the idea. If you weren't so innocent and special, I could toss you on my sleeping mat and think nothing about it. But you are special, Rana, and I don't want to take advantage of a situation you were forced to accept. I promise you that Nate and I will do all we can to make you happy and safe. He likes you and feels drawn to you, Rana, so please be kind to him. His only daughter was killed years ago, and she looked a lot like you. That was her necklace he gave to you. For now, let's just become friends and get to know each other. Will you try to be patient and understanding? Can we have a real truce?" he inquired earnestly.

"Do you have a wife waiting for you?" she queried anxiously, aware that warriors often took more than one mate and knowing she could never share a husband, especially this rare man standing before her.

"No. You see, Rana, we're both white. We'll be living on white lands, under white laws and customs. The Oglala laws and customs are not accepted, or even recognized, by the white man. Our marriage is binding only in Indian territory and under Indian law, but we're not Indian and we won't be living here. You'll be like my sister. You'll be free. Do you understand what I'm saying?" he asked nervously.

Consternation flooded her features. She moved a few steps away from him and drifted into deep thought. Finally she turned and looked at him. "We are not joined in your eyes? You do not want me?"

Travis responded carefully, "We're not joined in the eyes and laws of the whites, and we'll be living as whites. We must obey their laws and customs. That's why it's wrong for me to make love to you. I want you to be free and happy and safe, Rana."

She realized that he had cleverly avoided her question. "You are half Indian, White Eagle. Is that half not joined to Wild Wind? Do the laws of Grandfather and your mother's people mean nothing to you? Have you forgotten all you were and knew?"

"No, Rana, I haven't forgotten. I love my people and believe in Grandfather. But I've chosen the white world and must live by its laws and ways. It troubled my spirit to join to you falsely, but I believed I was doing what was good for you. When war comes to your camp, no white girl will be safe there, from whites or Indians. I couldn't let you be killed or placed on a reservation, or worse. In war, men are evil and fierce. And I couldn't rescue you without following the wishes of your adopted people. You're very beautiful and tempting, and it's hard to remember you're not my wife. Unless we're married by white law, Rana, we can't share a sleeping mat. You're returning to the white world, so you must accept this. I can't dishonor you or use you selfishly. You have the right to choose who and what you want."

"Is there a woman you love in this land you call Texas? Is she why you hurry home and do not take Wild Wind as promised?"

He grinned at her jealous look and tone. "I have no wife, or a woman close to my heart. Come home peacefully with me, Rana. Let me . . . teach you to find your new destiny. I promise you this is how it should be. You will be able to come and go as you please. You'll be free and happy with us. Don't fight Grandfather's will," he urged.

Rana smiled, for now she understood his dilemma: he was being torn between two bloods and peoples. One law said they were not joined, and the other said they were. Was this the "truth" that had tortured him? she wondered, knowing there was a simple way to end his suffering, though it was too soon to mention it. *Oh, my love,* she thought dreamily, *you are far more Indian than you realize, and you do not wish me to be your sister!* She had wanted happiness and freedom once, but now she wanted Travis more. She had not wanted to marry and he had told her that according to white law they had not, yet she had been extremely pleased by their joining. She had wanted desperately to be allowed to be herself, yet now all she wanted was to be his!

"I do not like battling you with words each day, Travis Kincade. I promised my people I would go with you, and I will keep my word of honor." Words she had spoken to Black Hawk returned to haunt her and she repeated them hoarsely: "We are joined only in words, and false words can be broken. I will be your sister and friend. I will try to accept your ways and be happy in your lands. If it is not so by winter, you must promise to return me to my people. Do you agree?"

Travis sighed loudly in relief and smiled broadly, for he knew she would adjust. "That seems fair enough. It's a deal, Miss Rana Michaels. Let's go eat and get some sleep. I'm starving and exhausted," he announced cheerfully, holding out his hand in invitation.

Rana glanced at it, laughed softly, and teased, "Do sisters and brothers touch in this tempting manner?"

"Maybe you're right. No need to add fuel to a fire that should be left to smolder for now. Come along, sister. It's late."

As Rana followed Travis to camp, she boldly reflected, *The sun will set on your resistance sooner than you think, my love, because we are joined in the eyes of* Wakan Tanka *and in our own eyes* . . .

As the two entered the small area where they were camping for the night, Nathan instantly detected the change between them. Both were smiling and appeared lighthearted. They looked comfortable side by side and a pleasant warmth seemed to surround them. Nathan relaxed, deciding all would be fine now. He listened intently as Travis hurriedly related the essentials of his talk with Rana. He was astonished to learn that his granddaughter could speak English, but unlike Travis, he did not try to recall what he had said around her. He was too excited by the news.

Nathan smiled and laughed at the same time. Clasping Rana's hand between his, he stated exuberantly, "I'm so glad we can talk, Rana. This is going to make things so much easier for all of us. I've got so much to tell you. You're going home and—"

"Nate," Travis called to him to halt his rapid and thoughtless flow of words, "we've got plenty of time to tell Rana about her new home. It's late and we're all tired. Now I understand why Rana kept quiet about speaking English; she didn't want us to talk her ears off."

Nathan caught the hint and tried to master his rampant emotions. He was pleased with the way Travis was handling the matter, letting the facts trickle out a few at a time to keep from drowning Rana in a river of truth. "Old men do have this tendency to babble, don't they, son? Travis here doesn't do much talking, but I do. I'm real proud of him, Rana. He takes good care of me and our lands. A man couldn't ask for a better son or grandson," he stated affectionately, unwittingly misleading Rana about their relationship.

"His eyes say he has much pride and love for you, Nate. It is good for families to be close to each other. I will be happy and honored to live in your home."

"We're the ones who are happy and honored to have you join our family, Rana," Travis told her. "Now that we have a peaceful camp, why don't we all get busy with supper? Rana, I was telling Nate that it looks like there's going to be trouble in this area soon between Crazy Horse's band and the soldiers at Fort Kearny. I would like to be long gone before they start battling each other again. Do you mind riding fast and hard for a few days?"

"I understand, Travis. I will ride fast and hard at your side."

"Good," he murmured, smiling at her.

The following morning, Travis, Rana, and Nathan were in high spirits and smiled frequently at each other as they hurriedly ate and packed to leave. As Travis had requested, the small group traveled quickly, taking only short rest breaks for the horses and themselves. At one point they all burst into laughter as a herd of deer bolted across their path and startled their horses as well as the deer.

His shiny eyes revealing his genuine happiness, Nathan shouted to Rana, "Wait until you see how many we have on our ranch."

Rana had shouted back, "How big is your ranch?"

Nathan beamed with joy and pride as he replied, "A hundred and fifty thousand acres of prime grazing land. You'll love it there."

Rana instantly concluded that he was right. Excitement surged through her as the lovely scenery moved swiftly past, taking her further from the Dakota Territory and closer to Texas. Each time she glanced at the man riding to her right and slightly ahead of her, tremors of anticipation and desire assailed her. Today she felt at ease with these men; she began to believe that her new destiny held great things for her. Gone were her bitterness and anger; they had been replaced by joy and hope.

As the fast-paced journey continued, there was little conversation, for neither Rana nor Nathan wanted to distract Travis from his intense alertness. Nearing dusk, Travis rode ahead to scout the area he had selected for their camp. It was obvious to his companions that he remembered this area well, for he always seemed to know where to find water and lush grass for the animals.

As they gathered firewood and prepared their evening meal, Nathan described his ranch and home for Rana. When he told her she would have her own room and could come and go as she pleased, Rana was amazed, for she had never known such privacy and freedom before. She was also astonished by the large amount of cattle and horses Nathan owned, for it was more than those owned by several tribes combined. She decided these men must be strong and clever to control so much land and to own so many animals. She could tell that both men had deep love and respect for their land, which caused her to feel a similar respect for their great skill and success.

Nathan told Rana about the neighboring ranchers and towns, explaining as he did so about raising cattle and horses and selling them. He related colorful tales about the history of Texas and his homesteading days, and finally he told her about his wife, Ruth, and a little about his daughter, Marissa.

"Marissa . . . ," she echoed the vaguely familiar name. "It is beautiful, soft like music or the spring rain. You miss her now that she lives with the Great Spirit. It is sad to lose those we love and need. My father, Soaring Hawk, lives with *Tunkansila*. He was a great warrior and chief. My brother, Lone Wolf, walks closely in his tracks." She wanted to ask more questions about his daughter, but she sensed that the topic was painful to the old man, and to her, too, for some unknown reason.

"I know you'll miss them, Rana, but don't be angry because we're taking you home where you belong."

She looked over at Nathan and smiled. She was glad he felt she belonged with them. "I willingly go where the Great Spirit leads."

When Travis joined them to eat, he teased, "I see Nate's been talking your ears off again. He's just excited about having a woman in the house again. I think he's forgotten how much trouble they can be."

"Women give trouble only when they must," she retorted.

"To get their own ways," Travis slyly came back at her, then grinned devilishly. He sipped his coffee, eyeing her over the cup's rim.

"Do you not use clever words and deeds to get your way?"

Nathan chuckled. "She's got you there, son. This girl is smart and quick. She's going to keep us on our toes."

Travis sighed dramatically. "I'm sure of that, Nate."

When Rana excused herself to prepare for bed, Travis cautioned, "Watch what you say about Marissa, and don't mention the Kiowa attack. She could panic and bolt. Just a few more days, and I'll tell her everything."

"I'll be careful, son, but I sure am eager for her to learn she's my granddaughter. She's really settled down, hasn't she?"

"Yep, and I hate to have to upset her again." Travis did not tell Nathan that he hoped it was not an act on her part to disarm them. He knew what wily deceivers and artful pretenders women could be.

The following morning, Travis ordered Nathan and Rana to hang back while he checked the area where they would cross the Mormon Trail. As far as he could see in any direction, there was no one in sight. Satisfied, he rode back for Rana and Nathan. They were forced to go several miles out of the way to skirt a large lake and to find a place to ford the North Platte River. After riding on for miles and fording the South Platte River, they eventually came to the Oregon Trail. Again Travis told them to wait for his signal as he rode away to scout the area.

This time, Travis was gone for over an hour, causing Nathan and Rana concern over his safety. When he did return, they openly showed their relief, then noted that he was carrying several items of interest. Travis dismounted and dropped his findings on the ground. Rana and Nathan came forward to question him, curiously looking at the strange pile of possessions.

"There was trouble over there and not too long ago from the look of things. Four wagons were attacked by Cheyenne warriors. They were chased off by soldiers, probably from Fort Smith. They all left in a big hurry 'cause there wasn't any burial detail around and the Indians didn't recover their dead. They don't need these things anymore, so I took them. Rana, see if any of the clothes will fit you. If we meet up with other soldiers, it'll be best if you aren't dressed like that. Might inspire too many questions and too much time to answer them."

Rana sank to her knees while she and Travis looked through the dresses, shirts, pants, and shoes he had taken from three of the wagons. When they found several garments that seemed to be close to her size, Travis told her to change into them while he packed the others.

"She might have need of these pants and shirt later, so we'll keep them. You take these, Nate. Extra weapons might come in handy if one of ours breaks or we need some trade goods."

Nathan placed a pistol and ammunition in his saddlebag, Travis concealed another knife in his right boot, and each secured a rifle to his saddle.

When Rana returned, her nose was crinkled in dismay and she was walking clumsily.

"What's wrong?" Travis inquired.

"The dress is fine, but the moccasins do not feel good."

"Shoes, Rana," he gently corrected her. "Let me check them." He looked and felt around each one, determining that they were slightly large. "Sit down," he instructed, then wrapped torn strips of material around her feet before putting on the shoes again. "That'll have to do until I can buy you a better pair. You said you could use a bow and arrows, didn't you?" When she nodded, he handed them to her and said, "Keep these in case you need them later. Take this too," he added, handing her a larger knife in a fancily carved sheath. "When we get time, I'll teach you how to handle a gun and you can have the one I just gave Nate." He ripped off a ribbon from a dress that was too large for her and cut it in half. "Here. Tie your braids with these. Soldiers might wonder about those Lakota rosettes. Better hide that *wanapin* too. Let's get moving before those Cheyenne or the soldiers return." He packed the few supplies he had taken, then they mounted and rode away, leaving the discarded items behind.

Each day the weather became warmer and the days longer. When they camped on June ninth, Travis scouted the area thoroughly, then remained on full alert. Twice he left camp just to "take one more look around."

During the next two days, Travis ordered a more cautious pace, knowing they were only a few days' ride from Fort Kearny, the object of Crazy Horse's destructive design. They were too far out for hay gatherers or woodcutters from the fort, but not for patrols, especially during such intimidating times. Having learned that the Sioux and Cheyenne were determined to recover this area from the soldiers and homesteaders had made Travis wary and tense. He knew he could defend himself and escape danger, but he had Nathan and Rana to protect. He felt as if he were escorting them through a prairie fire with so much smoke that he could not accurately and swiftly determine which trail would lead to safety.

Sensing his concern as they sat around the fire that night, Rana coaxed, "Do not worry. We will reach home safely." Then, before she could stop herself, she asked, "Why did you leave your mother's camp and people? Did your heart feel strange stirrings returning to these lands?"

Travis focused his keen gaze across the river and nodded. Tomorrow they would be in Kansas, a day closer to the truth. "I know how much the Lakotas want to drive the white man from their lands. It cannot be, Rana, for they are strong and many and they have weapons that can slay a whole tribe or destroy an entire camp in a few hours." He did not tell her how the soldiers were using the six-year-old Gatling Gun, powerful cannons from the recent war, and dynamite, a new weapon that had been discovered last year, in order to drive the Indians off their ancestral lands and kill any resistors.

"I've lived with the white man and I know his power and greed. These lands must be shared, or the Lakotas will be pushed aside or killed. My mother's people have hunted on these lands for more winters than I can count. Her father, and her father's father, and his father have fought and died here; they are buried on the sacred mountain. Children have played and learned here. Victories have been celebrated. Enemies have been conquered and driven away. Laughter and songs have filled the air. This land is the Lakotas', and that too must pass. Once Grandfather smiled on his children; He gave us plenty to eat and protected us. Many times I rode into battle and returned with great honor. Then the white man came and wanted what was ours. Now the Lakotas must relent and change, or die. My words and fighting would change nothing, so it would be foolish to sacrifice my life for a battle already lost when the white man first set his eyes and heart on this land. My sons must be born free, where they can claim land to hunt and raise children and die in peace, a land where they will not be shamed for their mixed blood."

When he glanced at her, she was watching him with a tender expression that charged through him like a bolt of lightning. There was a deep, dreamy stare in her eyes that said she would withhold nothing from him. "I'll go check on the horses," he stated quickly, wondering why he was pouring out such private feelings and thoughts to her.

Rana grasped his arm to halt him. "Do not pull within yourself, Travis. How can I know you if you shield such feelings from me? You keep much a prisoner inside when there is comforting freedom outside. Is it wrong to share such feelings with your . . . sister?"

"Not wrong, Rana, just hard. I've never talked with anyone like this except Nate. Get some rest; it's late."

Rana watched Travis's defensive retreat, then turned to Nathan. "He carries much pain and many secrets inside his heart. Why did he leave his mother's people? Why did she marry a white-eyes?"

"I think it would be best if Travis answered those questions, Rana. The Indians gave him a hard time because he was a half-breed. That boy was hurt deeply and it isn't easy for him to talk about the past. If those Hunkpapas hadn't rejected him, he would still be a warrior. I'm glad they did, 'cause he would be fighting a losing battle. That's why we couldn't leave you there. If them Indians don't make truce with the white man, it's over for them, and Travis said they won't."

Lines of sadness marked her face. "He spoke the truth, Nate. My people will die before they yield their lands to the white-eyes."

"Your people are white, Rana," he gently reminded her.

"Only by birth. The Oglalas raised me and loved me, and my heart belongs with them. I was taught to hate and mistrust white-eyes, but I do not feel this way about you and Travis. I do not understand this, but I accept it. Where we go, are the white-eyes as you are?"

"It's like with Lone Wolf and Black Hawk, Rana; there're good and bad whites, like good and bad Indians. But don't you worry none. You got me and Travis to take care of you. We'll be a family again."

Rana looked off toward the woods into which Travis had vanished. She went over his words and Nathan's as she drifted off to sleep. Sometimes she had trouble understanding their meanings, as when Nathan had spoken of "a family again." She knew she would have to listen carefully and work hard on her English before she reached their home.

Rana realized now how fortunate she had been that Soaring Hawk had captured and for several years had enslaved a white school teacher. She had been a spirited, resilient woman who had taught Rana many things, including the importance of having an independent, bold nature, which had proven so vexing to the men in her life. For now, she would not reveal the extent of her knowledge, for she felt she could learn a great deal about Travis and Nathan as they attempted to teach her what they thought she should know.

The next morning, they resumed a similar travel pattern. Just before their noon break to rest and eat, Travis detected signs that seized his attention. He moved off to have a closer look, leaving Rana and Nathan camped near Beaver Creek. He had chosen a spot where the creek grew wide and deep and was banked heavily on one side by trees, which would provide cover during his absence. He knew the Indian tracks he had spotted were fresh, and he wanted to trail the party for awhile to make certain they had not stopped nearby or were doubling back. Less than thirty minutes after Travis's departure, trouble struck.

Rana had been about to excuse herself when, through the underbrush, she saw the band of crudely dressed soldiers dismounting and making signals about surrounding their camp. Her heart pounded in fear, for she realized that soldiers would not attack other whites unless they were evil men bent on evil deeds. Evidently they had either sighted them farther back and had trailed them here or they had discovered their fresh trail and had tracked them to this point.

She hurried back to where Nathan was sipping his coffee and shook his arm frantically.

"Bad men come, Nate. We must prepare to fight. They sneak around us in the trees. This many," she told him, holding up seven fingers. "They carry short and long guns. I believe they plan to attack us."

Nathan tossed the cup aside and grabbed his rifle and ammunition from his horse. "Get behind those rocks and stay down," he ordered as he led his horse around the rocks to drop his reins near the creek bank.

Rana did the same with her beloved Cloud, then seized her bow and arrows before concealing herself. The large creek was at their backs, but trees that could offer the villains cover grew before and on either side of them. Anxiously she waited with Nathan.

A voice called out, "Just give us what money and valuables you have, then we'll be on our way. Ain't no need to fight and die here."

Nathan caught glimpses of dirty uniforms as the men fanned out before them, and he realized they were probably deserters. He knew the Army ranks were filled with men who were dodging justice, men who sought vengeance for the outcome of Mister Lincoln's war, and men who had been toughened by frontier perils and hardships and were conscience dead from years of fighting and killing. Still, he had to try to bluff them. He shouted in return, "You best git, boys. Soldiers will be here any minute now, and you don't want them to find you attacking and robbing innocent folks. Besides, we ain't got no money to give you."

"Then we'll take your horses and guns," the voice responded.

"And leave us afoot and weaponless in Injun territory? No way."

"Then we'll have to come and take 'em," the voice replied smugly.

"Then, by God, you try it!" Nathan called out bravely, knowing it was fight or die, or worse for his granddaughter once these men got a look at her. He prayed Travis would return soon but knew he couldn't count on it. He glanced at Rana, who had dumped the arrows from the quiver and now had one poised for release. She smiled at him, warming his heart with her show of confidence and courage. "You know how to use it?" he asked.

"I can outshoot most warriors. I will help you battle them. We must fight or die. The Great Spirit will protect us and guide our aim."

Nathan grinned, for her words did not sound boastful, just honest. "Then let's give 'em a fight they'll remember."

When Nathan spotted movement to his side, he aimed and fired, winging and angering one of the men. Gunshots came from several directions at once. Nathan and Rana ducked their heads and waited for it to cease or slacken. The bullets glanced off the rocks with "pings" and "zings," sending broken chips flying here and there.

Rana peered around one rock, took aim, and caught her target in the center of his chest. She quickly seized another arrow and placed its nock on the bowstring. Since she had only six arrows, she would have to make each one count. She cautioned herself to be patient and alert. When she saw a man racing from one tree to another, she dropped to one knee beside the rock and fired at him, then swiftly flung herself behind the rock before the rapid firing of more bullets could strike her. From the man's scream of pain, she knew she had at least wounded him. She laughed happily, then reminded herself that this was not a game she played.

Nathan warned, "Don't take chances like that, girl."

"We must get many of them before they rush us, Nate. When their courage or anger mounts, they will charge like furious buffalo. We cannot shoot that fast; they would capture us. We must show them we lack all fear and are skilled fighters."

"Darnit, Rana, you're just a young girl," he reasoned.

"Today, I am a warrior," she refuted, then grinned. She readied another arrow and peered around the rock. A burst of gunfire greeted her curiosity. This time when it lessened, she bounded to her feet and fired at the man wiggling toward them on his belly. He howled and rolled over as the arrow embedded itself in his neck.

At that same moment, Nathan fired several times but missed the swiftly moving target that changed positions as the man worked his way closer to them.

For a time, both sides held their fire and the silence grew loud around them. Rana strained her ears to hear every noise, knowing the silence meant danger. Suddenly gunfire came from both sides, causing Rana and Nathan to turn back to back to answer it. Nathan's horse panicked and raced off, but Rana's loyal steed held his ground, moving about nervously as he sensed the danger. Nathan experienced a surge of fear for the safety of his granddaughter and fired wildly into the trees. Rana released two arrows and one lethally found its target in the man whom she had wounded earlier. She withdrew her knife from its sheath then and placed it nearby, for she had only one arrow left.

Another burst of gunfire captured their attention, preventing them from seeing the man who had slipped into the creek and was working his way below bank level to flank them. Slowly and silently he crawled on his stomach up the bank and inched his way toward Rana, knowing the old man, whom he assumed was her father or grandfather, would surrender once he grabbed the girl and put a knife to her throat. As the man neared Rana, something happened that he had not anticipated; Cloud reared, whinnied, and attacked him, for Rana's horse had been trained to defend her from peril.

Confusion broke out. The other men rushed them as Rana had predicted. Nathan fired, killing another one of their attackers just as he made a grab for Rana's arm. Rana accidentally discharged her last arrow when the man had grabbed her arm. Quickly she flung the useless bow aside, scrambled for her knife, and immediately engaged herself in a scuffle with the man who was being nipped by Cloud. During their fierce struggle, the knife was kicked out of her reach.

Several shots rang out and suddenly her beloved Cloud fell dead, his red blood standing out boldly against his white hide. For a time, Rana was frozen with shock and anguish, but she was spurred into action again when the dripping man lunged at her, sneering, "I'll get you, you little bitch."

Nathan's gun was empty and there was no time to reload. He grabbed the man as he shouted, "Run, Rana! Hide till Travis returns."

Rana knew the only way she could help Nathan and save herself was by securing another weapon. With men closing in on them from three sides, all she could do was fling herself over the rocks and make a dash for the weapon on the man who had fallen in the clearing. Nathan delivered a stunning blow into a wounded man's abdomen and quickly raced around the rocks to defend Rana's back and aid her escape. The three remaining men instantly pursued them.

"Back to back!" she called out to Nathan, tightly grasping the knife she had yanked from the dead man's sheath.

Nathan drew his own blade as he followed her clever suggestion, for flight had become impossible. The slender girl pressed her shoulders against Nathan's, standing poised for an attack that she thought would come quickly, though it did not. Her dress had been ripped and dirtied, and wisps of fiery hair had escaped her braids. To the men, she was a wild, stunning creature who provoked heady lust as they appreciatively and lewdly eyed her up and down, then grinned at each other.

"Well, well," the leader of the outlaw band murmured as he licked his lips in anticipation of having this entrancing vixen. "Looks like you got something more valuable than money or horses, old man. You two might as well give up, 'cause we ain't."

"*Sunka ska!*" Rana shouted, called him a white dog, then spat on the ground to show her contempt for them. She narrowed her wintry blue eyes to expose her determination to stand her ground and battle them. Surprise registered on the leader's face and he studied her once more.

"A white girl who speaks Sioux and uses a bow like that?" the second man called Curly queried suspiciously. "You men know what that means. Girl, if you weren't such a looker, we wouldn't touch none of them Sioux's leavings. How long was you their captive? You two escape them Injuns, or did the old man here trade for you?"

"You lay one finger on my granddaughter and I'll cut off your hand," Nathan threatened rashly, but Rana was too alarmed by their peril to take his slip seriously. "You boys best git while you can. When my grandson gets back with those soldiers, you'll be in deep trouble."

"You sure do talk big when the odds ain't in your favor, old man."

"What we jawin' and waitin' for? Let's take 'em. I got me a bad itch what needs scratchin'," announced the third man, named Buck.

"Me too," Curly agreed readily.

"Curly, you and Buck slow down. We ain't had this much fun in a long time. They can't stand there all day like that." The three men began to slowly, playfully circle Nathan and Rana, laughing and grinning and eyeing them like helpless prey in a steel trap.

Buck did not follow Fess's advice. "Come on, girly, let's me and you get to know each other better," he said and reached for her.

In the blink of an eye, Rana had reacted skillfully by cutting a long gash on Buck's arm. He howled in pain and retreated a few steps, glaring at Rana in disbelief. "You little savage," he sneered as he yanked his bandanna from his neck to wrap it around the gaping wound.

When Curly lunged forward Rana brought up her foot and kicked her new attacker in the groin. Almost with the same movement, she scooped up a handful of dirt and flung it into Buck's eyes. For a time, both men were disabled.

Nathan reacted spontaneously by throwing his knife into Fess's chest. Then he sprang forward to yank the blade from the man's body and stab him again. Enraged by Nathan's assault and his agony, Fess battled him with all his strength. Bloody blows were exchanged, and the men fell to the earth to continue their desperate struggle.

Before Curly could recover from the nauseating kick to his privates, Rana seized the dead man's rifle and delivered a staggering blow to Curly's jaw with the wooden butt. She heard bone and teeth shatter as the man fell backwards, trying to decide which injury to hold.

Buck had cleared his eyes enough to focus on the girl who was fighting them like a skilled soldier or a highly trained warrior. He grabbed her from behind and shook her back and forth as she kicked at his shins and clawed at his hands. "You dadburn wildcat. You're gonna be plenty sorry afore I finish with you." He whirled her around and landed a forceful slap across her flushed face, sending her staggering backward and to the ground. Buck made a diving leap on her before she could roll free, straddled her, and pinned her shoulders to the ground. He cursed as he tried to control the thrashing female.

Fess vowed coldly, "I'm gonna kill you, old man, after you watch what we're gonna do to that little bitch of yours."

Curly's head cleared and he ignored his pain in his attempt to get at Rana. He knocked Buck aside, shouting, "This gal is mine! She'll wish she'd stayed with them savages afore I let her loose," he threatened ominously as he flung himself on her. He imprisoned her hands beneath his legs and started slapping her and pulling her hair as he cursed her vulgarly.

Buck grabbed Curly's right arm and yelled, "Don't kill 'er afore we get to use her! You can punish her later. Let's git that dress off and git at 'er. She owes us plenty."

As Curly eased the pressure on her arms, Rana jerked them free and slammed her head into his broken jaw. In torment, Curly fell to his back and rolled wildly as his hands gripped his battered face.

Before Buck could seize Rana, Travis suddenly appeared behind him. He yanked him around and pounded him violently with both fists. Rana tried to stand to locate a weapon, but Curly's hands went around one ankle and impeded her search. Though she stomped on his arm and kicked his ribs, Curly held on tightly.

Travis hastily drew a knife from his boot and ended Buck's threat to anyone. As he moved to assist Rana, his keen eye caught Nathan's greater peril. Fess was hovering over the older man with a knife poised and ready to take Nathan's life. In what appeared to be one fluid movement, Travis dropped to one knee, drew his pistol, shot Fess, whirled on the ground, changed knees, yanked the second knife from his other boot, and threw it forcefully, striking Curly in the middle of his back before he could hit Rana again.

Except for the erratic respiration of the three weary survivors, deathly silence filled the clearing. Travis hurried over to Rana and asked, "Are you hurt?" His green gaze roamed her dirtied, bruised face, and he berated himself harshly for allowing such danger to befall her and Nathan.

Now that the threat had passed, reality set in on Rana. Her wide eyes scanned the area, taking in the death that surrounded them, death for which she was partly responsible. She had never killed anyone until today, and that realization staggered her senses. She looked at her bloody hands and ruined dress. Her face was sore and her body ached. She knew she looked terrible. The after-effects of facing such grim hostility and near-death struck her deeply. She was so far from home, in a land where evil whites lived and preyed on innocent people, and she was heading for a land where her new destiny loomed as a dark shadow over her head. Her control was sorely strained and she trembled and wanted to weep, but she hated to expose such fear and weakness. Without answering Travis, she walked around the rocks and stared at Cloud's body before sinking to the ground beside it. She stroked his head and neck as tears ran down her cheeks. "*Mahpiya, Mahpiya,*" she murmured in anguish, dropping her forehead to his neck to sob.

Travis and Nathan followed her and observed the tormenting scene. Travis fell to one knee beside her and gently stroked her hair as he said tenderly, "Come away from him, Rana. Don't punish yourself this way." He tried to pull her into his arms to comfort her. "I'm sorry, *micante.* I should have . . ."

Enveloped in anguish and consumed by belated shock, Rana lifted a tear-streaked face and glared at him. Why was he always so loving and enticing at the wrong times? she wondered irrationally. She was not "his heart," for he had rejected her! She interrupted him coldly, "You should have protected us. Or returned to help us. *Mahpiya* is dead. I hate all white-eyes! Do not touch me again, half-breed!"

Chapter 8

TRAVIS WINCED from what seemed to him a just attack. He too felt he was to blame for permitting her injuries, for endangering her life and Nathan's, and for getting Cloud killed. Sadness and remorse etched lines into his darkly tanned face and dulled his emerald eyes. When Nathan gently grasped his shoulder and wisely suggested, "Leave her be awhile, son," Travis looked up at him and nodded.

The two men walked away to talk privately. Nathan recounted their fierce struggle, telling Travis how bravely and cunningly Rana had fought. "I have to confess, son, I was plenty scared for us."

Together they checked the area and found seven men dead, three by Rana's hand, which did not include the injuries she had inflicted on two of the last attackers. Travis knew she was experiencing shock from the encounter and grief over her loss, but still her sharp words had cut him deeply. He understood how she must be feeling and he longed to comfort her. If she had not been trained to defend herself by Lone Wolf . . . He shuddered, refusing to complete that horrifying thought.

"We'd better get this mess cleared away, Nate, and move on. We can't let nervous soldiers find Indian arrows in these stinking deserters and blame the wrong side. I don't want innocent Cheyenne attacked because of these scum. You get cleaned up and pack your gear. You aren't hurt, are you?"

Nathan smiled warmly. "I'm fine, son. A little bruise here and there, but nothing to keep me down or still. You should have seen her in action, Travis. She put me to shame," he declared proudly.

"I saw part of it and my heart nearly stopped. When I heard gunshots, I couldn't get here fast enough. Then I didn't know who to help first. I didn't have much choice when I saw that knife gleaming over your head. I shouldn't have been gone so long."

"You can't be everywhere and do everything, son. If it weren't for Rana and you, I would be dead, so don't be so hard on yourself."

"If it weren't for you, Nate, I would have been dead seven years ago," Travis responded. "Nothing excuses my carelessness today. I knew how dangerous this area was, and I shouldn't have left you two alone. Evidently my instincts aren't as sharp as they used to be. There was a time when no man could sneak up on me," he stated in disgust.

Nathan examined Travis closely, for something was eating at the younger man. "You're bleeding, son. Let me bind that cut before we get busy."

Travis glanced absently at the wound, having forgotten about it. He knew it needed tending, so he did not reject Nathan's assistance. He removed his shirt and sat on a rock, his mind on the suffering girl.

"This isn't a knife cut, Travis. How did you get this wound? Nobody fired a gun except you," Nathan probed, suspicious.

"Like I said, Nate, my instincts are off these days. I caught up with those renegades, but they had doubled back on me. I was hit and lying on the ground before I knew they were behind me. That's what took me so long to return."

Nathan realized that Travis's survival and return meant that he had fought and overcome his red-skinned assailants. "You're lucky you weren't killed. That proves you haven't lost anything. Except maybe a little pride," the older man added, chuckling.

"You always did think I was better than I am," Travis teased.

"Nope," Nathan argued earnestly. "You always think you're less than you are. You've got to remember, son, no man is perfect, but you're as close as they come to it. Not counting a few minor injuries, we're all safe and alive, and we have Rana with us."

"I suppose you aren't counting your . . . Rana's horse. She loved that animal, Nate. We'll have to take one of those men's."

"What about the rest of their horses?"

"We'll release them. We don't want to take anything branded or marked as property of the U.S. Army. When we reach the next fort, we'll tell them what happened and make an offer to buy the horse. At least we won't have to worry about Rana anymore. She's tougher and braver than I realized." While Nathan bandaged his arm, Travis closed his eyes and envisioned her valiant struggle against the two deserters.

When Nathan finished, Travis stood and tossed his shirt on the rock to allow the blood to dry. Then he began removing the telltale arrows from the men's bodies. He searched until he was holding the six he originally had given her. After replacing them in the quiver, he looked over at Rana, who had not moved from her prior position though she had ceased her crying. She was so still and quiet that she appeared to be sleeping; yet Travis knew she was not. "Rana, you need to choose another mount from those men's horses so I can saddle him and load your gear. I'm sorry, but we have to leave quickly."

Rana pushed herself from Cloud's body and took one last look at him before standing to face Travis. "I wish to take back my cruel words to you. I spoke them when I was not myself. They were mean, and untrue. You are a skilled warrior of much honor and prowess. You have done all to protect us, and you saved our lives. I am ashamed for behaving as a hurt child. I ask forgiveness and understanding."

Relief filled Travis. "Thank you, Rana. That makes me feel better, but your words were true. I promised to keep you safe and happy. I failed. I was gone when you needed me and now your heart bleeds over *Mahpiya*'s loss. When we get home, I'll find you another special horse to take his place. Are you hurt anywhere?"

Her eyes grew misty at his soft words and sensitivity. She shook her head. "As with my brother, you carry a heavy burden to protect your family. It was wrong for me to add foolish weight to it. Do not be angry with me," she coaxed as her gaze went to his bandage and bloody arm. Concern darkened her eyes. "You are injured."

"It's fine. Nate took care of it. Do you want to wash and change clothes first or pick a horse to use?"

Rana checked her appearance. "I will choose the horse first," she replied reluctantly, wanting that necessary chore done quickly.

Rana and Travis walked to where the deserters had left their horses tethered. She looked at each of the seven mounts, then selected the best one. Travis grinned. "You'll make a good rancher 'cause you sure know good horseflesh. You constantly amaze me, woman."

Travis unsaddled the horse and led him to where Nathan was waiting. "I'll round up your horse while you and Rana get ready to ride. I doubt he ran far with his reins down."

After Travis left, Nathan turned his back while his granddaughter bathed and pulled on another dress. Rana decided that it was not the time to question Nathan about the scars on Travis's chest and back or the Lakota *wanapin* around his neck. As she was brushing and braiding her hair, Nathan explained why Travis had been delayed and how he had been wounded. Rana was glad she had apologized before learning such facts, for her apology would mean more to Travis. She was beginning to understand why the man had such a disquieting effect on her and caused her to behave so impulsively . . .

Back in the Oglala camp, Chief Lone Wolf was meeting with several Hunkpapa leaders and warriors. His dark eyes slipped around the circle to halt briefly on Sitting Bull, Gall, and Dream Hunter. When news had reached their camp about the joining of Wild Wind to a half-blooded man named White Eagle/Travis Kincade, the Hunkpapas had ridden swiftly to confer with their Oglala brothers about this man. Lone Wolf had described Travis's visit in detail and had sat stoically as the war chief, Gall, had revealed White Eagle's past to him.

"You say White Eagle claimed innocence in his father's treachery. I say his actions in my camp prove he has no hatred for the Lakotas. Many winters passed that he did not return for the yellow rocks. I say Grandfather spared his life to help us this full moon. I saw only a man of great courage and prowess, a man of complete honor and truth. Grandfather sent him to the wooden tepee of my sister's people and brought him back to our lands to claim her as his wife. It is as it should be."

"His father's blood runs in his body, Lone Wolf. He has tricked you and betrayed you as his father did your Lakota brothers. Many died long ago. We must ride after him and punish him."

"His mother's blood also runs in his body, Gall. My warriors rode with White Eagle to buy the guns, and they spoke of his courage and cunning. Others trailed him in secret when he rode from our camp. My warriors returned to say that he spoke to no enemy. He honored his words and bargain. He travels fast to return to his lands. I see why he was eager to ride like the wind; his Hunkpapa brothers wish to slay him for a black deed he did not do. Look into your hearts, my brothers. He lived and fought at your sides for eighteen winters. All tribes knew of his prowess and victories. Why did you turn your hearts against him? He has suffered much because you rejected him. I saw sadness in his eyes, then his joy to be in these lands once more, and finally there was new sadness that he could not remain. He was and is a good man. Grandfather protects him. Let this past evil die."

Dream Hunter nodded and concurred. "I say Lone Wolf speaks wisely and true. No warrior was braver than White Eagle. His *coups* were many and his heart strong and true. I say he was tricked by his father as the Hunkpapas were tricked. Many spoke against White Eagle while the pain of lost loved ones and the anger of his father's treachery burned fresh in their hearts and minds. I say that the heart of Charge-A-Buffalo and his words to White Eagle were evil. We must bury this deed."

Sitting Bull listened intently to each man before speaking. "A strange darkness seeks to cover the sky to keep sunshine from Grandfather's children and creatures. Evil rides behind this darkness, but its source is not White Eagle. White Eagle was touched by Grandfather. He has been sent to help his people and to show forgiveness for their blindness long ago. White Eagle was not our enemy then; he is not our enemy this moon. I gave White Eagle his name and *wanapin* when he returned to our camp when he was ten and six winters old. Even as a boy, he caused strange stirrings in my heart and visions in my head."

Sitting Bull drew on his redstone pipe before continuing. "When I had walked the face of Mother Earth twenty-five winters, I saw him in my visions as a mighty eagle who was forced to fly each sun and moon without rest. I saw a broken arrow, for he was of two warring bloods and could never know peace in our lands. When his father and people dishonored and betrayed him, he broke the war arrow and sought peace far away. In a later vision I saw the white eagle capture a thunderbolt with his talon, for his skill and courage were great. Around the eagle's neck I saw the *wanapin* of the War Bonnet Society. My visions have come to pass. White Eagle has found peace in another land. He returned when our Lakota brothers were painted with the War Bonnet markings. He gave them guns and supplies for defense and survival. As the thunderbolt, he has shown much power and magic. For his deeds, he earned a special *coup:* the sister of Lone Wolf, granddaughter to the man he now calls father and friend. Life is a mysterious circle like the sacred medicine wheel, my brothers. It was broken many winters past. It is whole again. We must leave White Eagle to his own destiny," Sitting Bull concluded with a wisdom that exceeded his thirty-six years.

Lone Wolf closed his eyes in relief, for Travis Kincade's destiny was now shared by his sister. He recalled the night he had revealed the joining demand to Travis and how the man had accepted the term with very little protest. He remembered the way Travis and Wild Wind had reacted to each other. Yes, he decided happily, all was as it should be. Suddenly sadness washed over him, for he knew then that he would never see Wild Wind again. He thanked the Great Spirit for the love and days they had shared. *Be free and happy, my little wildfire,* he prayed.

Travis, Rana, and Nathan rode over undulating prairie land that had been shaped by nature and held fast by endless miles of grass upon which buffalo and wild game grazed. They traveled over plains broken by occasional valleys or rolling hills. Sometimes they would not see enough trees to conceal one horse and rider, much less three of each. Other times they would ride past or through a heavy covering of them. The sky above remained a tranquil blue and the weather was glorious.

Nathan and Rana were cheerful and relaxed, having been drawn closer by their shared brush with danger and death. Rana tried not to think about the fate of her cherished white stallion, for his death meant one less bond with the Oglala people and her past life. She wondered if the Great Spirit was cutting all ties one by one as she rode toward her new life. She was dressed in white garments, riding a white man's horse, speaking the white man's tongue, living with two white men, and wearing her hair in one heavy braid down her back instead of two in the Indian style. Except for the possessions hidden in her saddlebag and the feelings in her heart, there was nothing left of her life in the Kiowa and Oglala camps. Already that world seemed so far away and long ago.

Each time their pace slowed, Nathan and Rana exchanged words quickly. Nathan had already begun to help her with English words and numbers, which he mistakenly believed she had forgotten over the years in the Indian camps. Each time they halted for a rest break or for Travis to dismount and look around, Nathan would drill Rana on what he had told her during their previous stops. Rana allowed the mostly unnecessary lessons to continue because Nathan was experiencing such pride in teaching her. She savored his patience and affection, and she enjoyed the way he bragged about her intelligence and determination to Travis, for impressing her husband thrilled her.

Nathan and Rana knew that Travis was still upset about what had happened to them the morning before. Both knew he expected a lot, perhaps too much, from himself, and they felt it would be best to leave him alone to work through his feelings.

Travis was tense and quiet, but not for the reasons they believed. His keen eyes cautiously scanned their surroundings, and he allowed nothing to distract his intense concentration today. His astute senses were constantly gathering information, studying it, sorting it, and remembering it. His entire body felt on edge, every nerve on full alert. Even his skin seemed to prickle in warning, as if everything he was or had learned was warning him of the presence of evil. His perceptions were so forceful that his body remained constantly taut, his eyes narrowed, and his teeth clenched. Anyone who knew anything about this area and its people would recognize signs of impending peril along the way, signs—both Indian and white—he had been sighting and reading all day.

Travis hoped that Nathan and Rana did not realize how worried he was, even though he had cautioned them to stay close to him and ready to respond to his orders rapidly. He had been taught trail signs and the language of blankets and feathers, and he had not forgotten them. No one could make nature speak as clearly or as loudly as the Indians. He could tell the tribe an Indian was from simply by looking at his moccasin print. He knew how to read markings, attachments, and positions of feathers to learn how a warrior had earned his *coups* and how he was ranked. He could send or interpret smoke signals. But today, it was the trail signs that disquieted him.

From the signs left behind with artfully arranged stones, deftly bound bunches of grass and carefully positioned sticks and cuttings on tree bark, Travis knew where the Indians were going, when they had passed this area, how many were in the hunting or raiding parties, and what their intentions were. It looked as if Kansas would be more dangerous traveling than either Dakota or Nebraska.

When they camped for the night, Travis waited for Rana to excuse herself before telling Nathan, "We'll make Fort Wallace a little past noon tomorrow. I want you and Rana to camp near the fort while I do some checking around. Try to discourage anybody from approaching and talking to you two. But if you get visitors, make sure she understands that everyone will be told you're my father and she's my wife. I don't want any contradictions or slipups." To make sure they each told the same story, Travis went over the details once more.

"There's been a lot of fighting going on in this area for the past year, Nate, and it's going to get worse during the summer. While you and Rana get some rest, I'll nose around the fort and see what I can learn. With any luck, I can trade that Army horse for another one and pick up a few supplies. Try to keep Rana hidden as much as possible. She's a beautiful and tempting female, and some of these men haven't seen or had a woman in ages. We don't want anybody dogging us when we leave Fort Wallace.''

Rana awoke several times during the night to find Travis's bedroll empty more often than not. When she stirred at dawn, it was empty once more. She quietly slipped from her sleeping mat and went to seek him. By then, it was obvious to her that Travis had been constantly scouting the area. She remembered his fierce concentration during the last day and a half, recalling how many times he had dismounted to study the trail. She had been distracted by her grief over Cloud's loss and her learning games with Nathan, which had revealed the older man's kindness, admiration, and patience. From now on, she would pay closer attention to the trail and to Travis's grave concern, for she already knew most of the things Nathan was trying to teach her. She reasoned that when a man of great courage and prowess became quiet and alert, it could only mean trouble or danger.

Rana was slipping through the trees, looking right and left for a sign of Travis. When she halted to listen for a clue to his location, she heard nothing. As she turned to head back for camp, she was confronted by a broad chest. Inhaling sharply, she stepped backward in astonishment as she found Travis standing within inches of her. "You drift as silently as a shadow and as secretly as a calm wind. I did not hear you move or breathe. I am happy you are not an enemy, for my hunting skills have dulled.''

Travis grinned as he told her, "If you could hear me and see me, then you would be the better hunter and warrior. Is it not best for me to have keener instincts and skills? You have proven yourself in battle, but I have no *coup* feathers to give you." He eased out of the Indian speaking style when he murmured, "I'm proud of you, Rana. Every place has its bad men and perils, including Texas; so I'm relieved you know how to defend yourself and can fight with us. It's good to find a woman who has a generous heart and a smart mind. Most of the ones I've met are deceitful, selfish bi . . . women who only think about themselves and couldn't fight their way out of an empty barn. You're very special, and I hope you stay that way.''

Rana wondered if there were clues in his insults about women that might explain his continued distance from her. If so, she decided, this was not the time to explore them. She tucked away that piece of information, declaring, "I am glad I do not displease you, Travis Kincade. In time we will come to know each other, for you are unlike other men I have known. It is good to find a man with a strong heart who thinks of others before himself and is unafraid to show gentleness when others need it. I was seeking you to ask questions. Why do you fear for our safety? Do the marks on the trail worry you? What do they say?''

"I'll explain tonight. When we reach Fort Wallace after the sun is high, I'm going to speak with the soldiers. I don't want you to be afraid, but you must be careful. When I return, I'll explain our situation. Promise me you'll stay with Nate and obey him.''

"But the bluecoats are enemies,'' she protested fearfully.

"Not anymore, Rana. You're part of the white world again. Unless we're careless, nobody will discover our secrets. Most people think I'm half-Spanish, not Indian.''

"What is Spanish?'' she inquired.

"You know how the Lakotas look and speak and act different from the Mandans or Arikaras or other Indian nations. The Spanish are one of the white nations. Texas has plenty of Spanish or half-Spanish people. I blend in without any trouble. You will too if you don't do or say anything to expose your past."

"Will the whites despise me for living with the Indians?"

"Most whites would rather see a woman die than become an Indian captive. They wouldn't understand or believe your situation, so keep quiet about it," he advised seriously.

"I will do as you say, but it will be hard. For many winters I was taught to hate and mistrust whites. I have forgotten what it is to live or be white. You and Nate must teach me such things again."

"We will, Rana," he promised, then smiled at her. "Let's get back or Nate will start to worry about us," he suggested, wary of the enticing solitude and her compelling nearness.

Later, as they neared the fort, they met several scouting and working details, which they passed without any problems. Travis was glad he had told Rana to dress in the pants and an over-sized shirt and to trap her flaming hair beneath a floppy hat. But these devices only concealed part of her beauty and shapely figure. He could not help but notice how the men who came close to them eyed her with looks of intrigue and admiration. Twinges of jealousy and possessiveness assailed him once more.

Travis halted and suggested they make camp within sight of Fort Wallace, assuming it would be safe to leave them alone this close to the voice of white authority and power. Before riding off, he reminded Nathan and Rana of their instructions, then led Rana's borrowed horse after him to explain why they had it. He hoped the commanding officer would feel obligated to let them keep it or to replace it.

Upon reaching the fort he dismounted and tied both sets of reins to a hitching post, then walked to the officer's quarters. Once inside, Travis learned that the commanding officer was at Fort Harker at a meeting with other post commanders. To the officer left in charge, he explained the trouble on the trail and turned over the personal possessions of their attackers to provide clues to the deserters' identities. The man was annoyed by the purpose of Travis's visit, for it meant reports to officials and letters to the deserters' homes. He called in one of his men, a corporal, and told him to locate a horse that Travis could buy at a reasonable price. Then he thanked Travis insincerely and dismissed him. As Travis left with the dusty corporal, he heard the officer in charge grumbling to himself about too much work, not enough pay, and several other disadvantages to Army life in the West.

The man led Travis to a small corral and told him to take his pick of the aging beasts for ten dollars. Travis glanced at the animals and scowled.

"The stallion one of your men shot was worth more than every horse you have on this fort. There isn't a mount in this corral that would last three days. You find me a decent horse and I'll pay you twenty dollars and throw in a rifle for your trouble. It's a long way to Texas, and I don't want my wife walking or riding double. I hold the Army to blame for our problem and I expect you to handle it fairly."

The offer of ten extra dollars and a rifle caught the man's interest. He thought about some horses that had been delivered two days ago but had not been branded "U.S. Army" yet. Smiling greedily, he told Travis to follow him to another corral. As they were walking, the brawny corporal began to talk freely and genially to this man who was going to help him exist more comfortably until the next payday.

"I hear you boys been having lots of Indian trouble over this way," Travis remarked evocatively.

"Yep," the man replied as he rolled a wad of chewing tobacco around before settling it on the left side of his mouth. "Them Dog Soldiers and Sioux been giving us fits since last summer. If you ask me, they're trying to take back Kansas and Colorado. Shame we can't set 'em to fighting themselves like we did those Cheyenne and Pawnee. Long as they're fighting each other, they can't fight us."

"How did you pull a trick like that?" Travis inquired with a grin.

"The Army's been giving the Cheyenne guns to make raids on the Pawnee camps. Soon as they kill 'em off, we'll light into the Cheyenne. Hell, if we could get rid of Tall Bull and Roman Nose, them Cheyenne wouldn't know how to plan an attack. General Sheridan's planning a big campaign to settle ever'body's troubles out here. He's got us guarding the settlements and roads till he gets his strategy together. After what he did to the South a few years back, ain't no doubt he'll have these savages under control by spring."

"If you have enough men left to fight by the time he gets here," Travis added, then chuckled deceptively. "From the way it sounds, you've been losing a lot of men, to Indians and deserting."

"I guess you heard about Fetterman and his defeat. Lost over eighty men in that battle. That don't include two whole detachments wiped out this past winter. When Colonel Custer passed through here not two weeks past, he found eleven cavalrymen slaughtered less than twenty miles from the fort. Circling buzzards lead 'im to the bodies. Weren't no pretty sight neither." The corporal went on to describe in detail the incident that inspired the warning, "Save the last bullet for yourself."

"Custer? Is he fighting in these parts?" Travis questioned, having heard colorful war tales about that particular man. Travis himself had not fought in a war that had had nothing to do with him.

"Yep. Seems like the Army is sending every ex-Union officer it can find out here. I suppose they think they can tame the West like they did the South. 'Course Custer's in a might of trouble these days. These last months he's been ripping up and down the Republican River trying to whip them savages or send 'em running. Guess he found out them Injuns fight harder and dirtier than them Rebs. Once he got into Colorado near them gold mines, he had men deserting in packs like hungry wolves. He was so mad he sent troops after 'em, and he caught some of 'em. We wuz told he made his regiment march a hundred and fifty miles in less than three days, hardly givin' 'em time to take a piss. Word is he's been placed under arrest for a list of charges long as my johns. I don't know if he's the biggest fool or the bravest man I ever met."

They reached the corral and Travis smiled as he eyed these new mounts. "Take your pick," the corporal offered. "Where you heading in Texas?"

"Pa and me got a ranch near Fort Worth. My brother was serving in the Army up in the Dakota Territory and got himself killed by a Sioux named Crazy Horse. Me and pa went up to fetch his widow. She was so pretty that I married her before we left the fort."

"That's what I call taking care of your family real proper. Good thing she was willing, weren't it?" the man teased, then winked.

"With no money or family, she didn't have much choice. Besides, I can be mighty persuasive when need be," he replied mirthfully.

The corporal laughed heartily. They talked on for a time as Travis craftily enticed more news from the corporal. After the deal was struck, Travis walked to the sutler's post for a drink and to see if he could pick up more information. He also wanted to buy Rana a pair of shoes.

As he was leaving, the corporal told him, "You head straight for Fort Dodge, then Fort Cobb, and you should miss them Cheyenne and Pawnee bickerings around Fort Larned. Them commissioners are trying to work out a treaty at Medicine Lodge and Fort Laramie. They're just wasting their time; ain't no treaty with savages gonna last."

Travis thought to himself that it wasn't any wonder, considering the massacres taking place at innocent, helpless villages like the one at Sand Creek, which was less than seventy miles from Fort Wallace. The Indians had been given no reason to trust the white man or to believe his paper treaties. At least the Indian "Dog Soldiers" were raiding and fighting northeast of them, for they were the ones Travis wanted to avoid the most.

Quickly returning to camp, Travis related the news to Rana and Nathan, withholding only tragic or alarming facts. "Nate, I think it would be best if we kept a guard posted tonight. I wouldn't put it past those Indians to send a few scouts to this area. This fort is almost sitting in the middle of nowhere, in the middle of their territory. Rana, why don't you keep a sharp eye while Nate and me take a nap. Nate can take the first night watch and I'll take over at midnight. Then we'll all have enough rest to be able to head out at first light."

Rana was delighted to be a part of Travis's plans, and she was pleased that he thought so highly of her skills. Before he could lie down, she insisted on checking and rebandaging his injury. She was pleased to find that the flesh wound was healing quickly, just as she was pleased by the brown ankle boots in soft leather that he had purchased for her.

Fortunately the night passed without any problems and at dawn they were already heading south. Travis kept on constant alert and set their pace accordingly. They covered a lengthy distance that day, halting to camp near Ladder Creek just as dusk dropped its shadows over the land. As he and Nathan had previously agreed, this would be the night of truth for Rana.

While Nathan and Rana set up the camp and prepared their meal, Travis scouted the area in all directions. Satisfied that it was safe, he returned to camp to sit quietly and apprehensively.

When everything had been cleared away and the three were sitting on mats near the campfire, Travis ventured hoarsely, "Rana, Nate and I have a few things to tell you. I'm not sure where to begin, so I'll let Nate start by telling you about his daughter, Marissa. Please, just hear us out and stay calm," he advised mysteriously.

Rana looked from one man to the other, then settled her quizzical gaze on Travis. "I do not understand. What troubles you?"

"Please, this is important to all of us. Listen to Nate's words and trust us," Travis coaxed worriedly, dreading her reaction.

Rana focused her attention on Nathan. Slowly and painfully he described his daughter's past: Marissa's years on the ranch, her wild and impetuous ways, her willful marriage to Raymond Michaels, what Nathan knew of their life together, and her last visit home. As he told her of Marissa's child, Rana began to fidget and breathe erratically, but still she held silent. He told Rana how Marissa and Raymond Michaels had been murdered and how his granddaughter had been kidnapped by the Kiowas. He told how he had looked for her for years, and finally had been forced to give up his futile search. He related the details of Thomas Mallory's visit and its enlightening results. He described Rana's birthmark and the scar she had received while visiting his ranch. "I'm your grandfather, Rana. My daughter, Marissa Crandall, was your mother. You used to play with that necklace when you were a little girl," he remarked when he noticed her rubbing it nervously between her fingers as she had done so long ago. He was glad Travis had repaired it and that she had agreed to wear it again. "Your mother left it at the ranch before she died. All these years I've hoped and prayed you were alive somewhere and that I would find you again. When I saw the painting of you, I cried with joy. Travis and I couldn't leave Texas fast enough. We came to the Oglala camp to find you and to bring you home where you belong. You're safe now, Rana. No one will ever hurt you again. Isn't that right, son?"

Rana whirled to look at Travis as he urged her to accept Nathan's shocking words. Many thoughts and images filled her head and conflicting emotions assailed her. They had lied to her and tricked her! This older man was her grandfather by blood and birth . . . Travis was his "son"? No, that was only an affectionate name, she decided. Travis was a Kincade, part Indian from the Lakota lands. She eyed him intently, for his part in her life intrigued her most. She was his "mission?" All along he had come after her . . . She remembered his starting to call her Rana several times and the way he had attempted to question her about her past and memory. He had told her that "mistakes and evil deeds" could be changed or corrected. Were they telling her the truth? How could this be happening after all these years?

Nathan described Marissa and stressed how much Rana favored her deceased mother. "You're my flesh and blood, Rana. How could I not come after you and do anything necessary to get you back? It was too dangerous for you to live there. You don't belong with Indians."

These revelations stunned her, and her heart drummed rapidly. She tried to resist the unexpected news. She was being taken away from all she had known and loved; and now he was telling her incredible things that denied even that reality. According to his words, she was not heading for a new destiny; she was returning to an old one that strangely frightened her, though she could not remember why. "Did you tell Lone Wolf these lies? Is that why he gave me to you? You tricked me," she accused.

Travis tried to explain his talk with Lone Wolf and their decisions, but as he had suspected, they did not sound logical or reasonable now. "We did what we had to do to get you free, Rana. Your grandfather loves you. He wants you to be safe and happy. Please understand."

Just like that, they had ridden into her life and were trying to change all she knew and was! Why would they speak such false tales? she wondered. "I do not understand. How can he love me? We are strangers. I am not his Rana Michaels. I am Wild Wind. I will return to my people."

"I can't let you do that, Rana. As with the other tribes, the Oglalas will soon be herded like cattle onto reservations where freedom and privacy don't exist but poverty and disease do. Oglala spirit will die in captivity. That's no life for you. How long do you think it would take before soldiers or Indian agents found a way to get at you? They would force you to do whatever they wanted, and you'd have to do it to protect your people. If the Oglalas did resist reservation life or rebel against it later, all they would be able to do would be run and hide or fight and be killed. I've been on the run before; it's nothing but hardship, pain, and death. We didn't want that kind of misery and peril for you. Search your heart and head, and you'll know Nate speaks the truth. Don't be afraid to trust us and accept us. You belong on the ranch with us."

She glared at Travis. "You did not come to help my people. You came to steal me. You lied. You tricked me and betrayed me."

"Only because the Oglalas made it necessary. They said we could not trade for you and take you away unless I joined to you. It was to keep the other warriors who wanted you from challenging our rightful claim on you. You are Rana Michaels! You're white, and Nate is your grandfather!" he stormed forcefully at her.

"What coward lurks inside your body, White Eagle? Why do you wait until this moon to tell me such things, if they are true?"

"Because we knew how you would react, just like you're doing. We wanted to be far away from the camp so you wouldn't try anything crazy like escaping. And we wanted to give you time to get close to us so you wouldn't be afraid. How can you be angry because your family has finally found you and you're going home? You should be happy about this news. I know it was wrong to trick you, and I'm sorry. It just sounded right and easy at the time," he admitted.

"That's why you gave my people those guns and supplies? That's why you asked for me in trade and joined to me falsely? Your words and deeds do not match, coward with a dark heart!"

Her words rankled and he scoffed, "Wild Wind was known for her disobedience and stubbornness. I did it so we could get you free and take you home with the least amount of trouble and time. There's a bloody war going on in that area, and we have a ranch to take care of. I wanted to get you and Nate out quickly and safely. And I didn't marry you falsely, because our joining isn't legal to whites, and we're white. When you want to marry, you can choose your own husband, not be traded to a man like a possession. You're free, Rana. Just like your mother, you can come and go as you please, and probably will."

"You did not like my mother?" she probed defensively.

"I never knew your mother. I've only seen her portrait."

"I do not understand. Nate calls you son," she pressed hesitantly.

Her words and expression surprised Travis, who stared at her oddly. Suddenly he grinned roguishly as he shook his head and responded, "No, Rana, I'm not your uncle by blood, but I am by law. Nate adopted me as his son years ago, like Soaring Hawk adopted you as his daughter. My legal name is Travis Kincade Crandall, but most people know me as Travis Kincade. Your mother, Marissa, was Nate's only child. During the first year after we met, Nate and I became best friends; we're like a real family now. I've been living with him for seven years and working on his ranch as his foreman. I helped him get you back because I love him and I thought I was doing the right thing for him and for you. You're smart enough to understand what we're telling you; open your heart and accept the truth. All we're asking for is a chance to correct the past. You have a home and a family. We risked our lives to claim you. Is this news so offensive?"

"Travis is like a real son to me, Rana. I begged him to help me get you back. I'm sorry we all tricked you. Travis didn't want to lie to you or marry you falsely; he did it for me and for you. The Indians made those demands and we didn't have time to argue. We were forced to go along or they wouldn't have let us have you. I was planning to give Travis my ranch until I discovered you were still alive. With Marissa dead, you two are all the family I have. When I die, I want the two of you to share the ranch. Will you come home with us? Will you give us a chance to make you happy? Will you try to understand and forgive us? All we wanted was you, my little Rana."

Rana watched the older man as he spoke. Had she discovered who she was at last, and where she had come from? she asked herself, wondering what these changes would mean to her. Nathan had touched and warmed her heart with his tale of suffering and dreams, but anger and fear had lodged there too. She thought about Travis, in light of this revelation. If she was Nathan's granddaughter, and she suspected she was, it would explain why Travis had refused to touch her, despite the fact that he desired her and felt married to her in his Indian heart. No doubt, after hearing those awful tales about her, he had expected to dislike her and to find her easy to resist. He had planned to ride in, make a trade for her, then hand her over to her grandfather. The situation had turned on him because of Lone Wolf's terms, and this intrigued her. Now Travis was caught in a painful trap —which served him right for deceiving her, she decided. He had teased her and tempted her with his kisses and gazes; now she could do the same to punish him, for he had no hold or power over her. Perhaps he too should be forced to learn a few things and to make a few changes . . .

"I will think on your words and deeds before I speak what is in my heart. This should not have been kept secret from me," she declared aloud.

Travis quickly concurred. "You're right, Rana, but that can't be helped now. We made a mistake. We've apologized and explained, so there's little more we can do. I know you've endured many dangers and changes lately, and you've been facing them bravely and with skill. We're very proud of you. But I wonder how much you learned from the Oglalas. Did you learn about patience and self-control? Are you smart enough to understand more than you can see? Or brave enough to face a new life? You've proven you have the courage and cunning to fight like a warrior, but can you behave like a woman? Can you feel and show love and kindness? Are you wise enough to accept what you know is true? And generous enough to offer us a truce and understanding? I said you were very special. I hope I wasn't wrong."

Chapter 9

FOR THE NEXT FEW DAYS, Travis watched the trail signs closely to keep them away from peril and people. From the evidence he found along the way, it seemed the Cheyenne and Pawnee were fighting bitterly over the land that had not as yet fallen under the control of the settlers or soldiers. He wished the Indians knew how the whites were duping them into killing off each other, for this was not the time for intertribal wars; this was a time to declare a truce in order to battle the more lethal enemy of both tribes. While the Indians were becoming fewer and weaker, the whites were increasing their numbers and strengths. Each year, more forts were being constructed on the Great Plains, more soldiers were being sent, and more settlers were arriving.

After crossing the Sante Fe Trail and the Arkansas River, they skirted Dodge City and Fort Dodge because Travis had no idea how Rana would act among people, and he did not trust her to be left alone with Nathan. As he had been with Marissa, Nathan was becoming too lenient with Rana, for he was blinded by his feelings for her. Nathan did not believe she could do anything wrong, and he would never have corrected her if she had because he was too happy to have recovered her and feared losing her again. He had become totally enchanted by his granddaughter, and Travis prayed this girl would not hurt Nathan as her mother had.

They passed near the Crooked Creek battle site and, on June twentieth, camped just inside what was now called Indian Territory, which would one day become the state of Oklahoma. It had been forty-seven days since they had left Texas, twenty-three days since the joining ceremony, seventeen days since they had left the Oglala camp, and five days since Rana had been told the truth about herself.

Travis did not know what to think about the exquisite redhead with steely blue eyes, for she had been behaving in a most unexpected manner, like a perfect lady or a misplaced angel. Having been told of Wild Wind's turbulent past by Lone Wolf and having witnessed her temper and willfulness in action, Travis was now suspicious of her sunny attitude and obedient demeanor, though he was pleased by her friendliness and compliance where Nathan was concerned. He found himself watching her furtively, day and night, as if she were a hot kettle that was simmering cleverly without giving off alerting steam, a kettle that he knew could burn one badly if it were touched in the wrong place. Travis felt that it would be very much in character for Rana to seek punishment or revenge—however small—for the trick they had played on her, a trick for which he seemed to be taking the brunt of the blame rather than being able to share it with Nathan and Lone Wolf. If this little wildcat were as conniving as most women he had met, he mused, she would bide her time until the right moment presented itself. He had advised, almost demanded, that she trust them; yet he did not fully trust her, for it did not seem to be Wild Wind's nature to allow herself to be tamed so quickly or easily.

Each day Travis had waited for the ground to slip from beneath him but he could do nothing more than speculate on the type of retaliation she might take. He wished he could detect some hint of a scheme so he would be better prepared to thwart her. In about eight or ten days, they would reach the Rocking C Ranch. Between here and there, they would cross more plains and prairies, an occasional rocky slope, rolling hills, several rivers, and vast Indian lands. It was these Indian lands to which Travis's attention and thoughts were drawn now as they made camp for the night.

Indian Territory had been chosen long ago as the relocation sight for the "Five Civilized Nations" from the South: the Cherokee, Creek, Choctaw, Seminole, and Chickasaw. In 1834, this entire region had been divided among these tribes, and each tribe had been assured of its ownership and authority over a certain portion of the area. During the recent North/South war, most of these tribes had sided with the Confederacy because so many of them owned slaves. Afterward, in 1866, the Government began forcing new treaties on the five nations, compelling them to cede parts of their assigned territories to the United States to be used as homes for other Indians they planned to relocate, as if their objective were to bunch all Indians into one area where they could be watched and controlled carefully and easily. The Government was, perhaps intentionally, overlooking one major problem: the Plains Indians did not like other Indians claiming their ancestral territories, especially with the help of the whites.

Travis had decided that maybe it was all a clever plot to reduce the numbers of Indians and their tribes by placing them in bloody conflict with one another, for the woodland Indians from the South had no training against the awesome skills and prowess of the Plains warriors, who were determined to hold on to their sacred lands and hunting grounds. He wondered how long it would take before everyone, Indian and white, realized that relocated Southern tribes could not coexist peacefully with the fierce Plains tribes of the Kiowa, Cheyenne, Arapaho, Comanche, and Apache Nations. He felt certain the U.S. Government would never honor the treaty they were offering the Sioux, which promised to transform most of Dakota into the Great Sioux Reservation, for that area was too rich in grazing lands and gold. The Medicine Lodge Treaty Council was scheduled to be held in Kansas within a few weeks and the Fort Laramie Peace Talks were to take place in Wyoming in the spring; Travis wondered how much, if any, difference those papers and promises would make, for he was very much aware that flowery words seldom changed ingrained feelings.

Because the Cheyenne were longtime friends and allies of the Lakotas, Travis often thought about the Cheyenne leaders he had met and had ridden with, some before he had left the Hunkpapas and some afterward. During this present journey, he had learned many new things about these men. He knew that Tall Bull and Black Kettle wanted peace with the whites and survival for their people, as did so many Indians these days. Unlike many of the "Dog Soldiers," as the whites called members of the Cheyenne Dog Men Society who were some of the most highly trained and skilled warriors who had ever existed, Chief Black Kettle was willing to accept the white man's peace treaty and go to a reservation. The leaders of the Dog Soldiers—Tall Bull, White Horse, and Bull Bear—only wanted peace; they were proud men who would never sacrifice their freedom and honor; they were not men who could laze around a reservation. No, Travis reflected, like the Lakota branch of the Sioux Nation, the Cheyenne Dog Soldiers would battle Indian and white to retain their lands and dignity. Travis felt that these Cheyenne leaders were too smart and honorable to kill off the Pawnee for the devious white man and, he decided, if he were given the opportunity to see them, he would tell them so!

During the next few days they would be traveling through the area that had been given to the Creeks, with whom the whites had made a strong treaty. Therefore Travis assumed they would not be facing any problems. If everything went as he planned, they should reach the Fort Cobb Agency within the next few days.

Travis sat near the campfire and sipped his coffee while pretending to ignore Rana, who was talking and laughing with Nathan. Every time they had stopped to rest or camp for the night, Rana and Nathan had worked together on chores or her education. The older man was teaching her about English words and numbers and had promised to teach her to read, spell, and write when they reached home. He also told her he would explain about money and shopping and would take her into town to let her practice her new skills. They used sticks, rocks, or knives and the ground to write their "lessons." When they were not studying, Nathan would relate facts about the ranch and hired hands, Fort Worth, their neighbors, her parents, Rana's childhood, and her visits to the Rocking C Ranch. Gradually Rana was able to associate her captive teacher's lessons with those Nathan provided and she began to be amazed at how much she was remembering and learning. And as Rana's knowledge and determination increased, both she and Nathan seemed to enjoy themselves more and draw ever closer.

Travis secretly observed the vivacious creature whose laughter and voice sent tremors over his weary body and called every nerve to attention. He noticed the way her grayish blue eyes sparkled with life and excitement, and the way the corners of her mouth curled playfully when she smiled. In the firelight, her skin reflected a vibrant, healthy glow, as did her long curls. He wanted to bury his hands in that thick mane of golden-red hair and tease strands of it beneath his nose. He wanted to feel her cotton-soft lips against his. His eager gaze savored them for a moment before traveling lower. Evidence of her battle with the deserters had vanished. Her lithe arms and legs, which appeared sleek and golden in the flickering light, were revealed to his scrutiny from her careless position on her furry mat. He yearned to let his hands wander over them with his eyes closed and his senses unrestricted. But his hands and lips craved more; they itched to explore every inch of her enticing body. Damn, what potent magic and temptation was sitting only a few feet from him! he cursed in frustration as he shifted from a position that was becoming uncomfortable. It was reckless to sit there watching her and hungering for her until his body ached for hers!

Travis attempted a casualness he did not feel as he left his sleeping roll and headed toward the surrounding trees. He walked to the nearby Cimarron River, yanked off his clothes, and slipped into the water. The weather was warm, but the water was still cool, especially at this late hour. He thought to himself that, with luck, maybe it would chill his passions and cool his temper. He needed to relax, and to get Rana Michaels off his mind. He had done his part to help her and Nathan; the rest was up to them. Maybe he was feeling a little jealous and left out; those two were so wrapped up in each other that they hardly noticed he was around. It sounded crazy, but he felt lonesome even in their presence! He dared not join them for fear of offending Rana and causing her to pull back from her grandfather while trying to avoid him. She had barely looked at him or spoken to him since they had had that enlightening talk with her. Funny, but he missed the way things had been going between them. The more he was around her, the more he wanted to get to know her, the more he wanted her.

Travis eyed the faint glow of their campfire, confident that he had made certain no one was around to spot it. He swam downriver then, into the shadows near the other bank, and nonchalantly draped his arms over a fallen tree. He envisioned Rana lying in the glow of dying flames, the colorful light dancing mischievously on her flesh and hair. He closed his eyes and fantasized about her beckoning him with a sensual glance and parted lips. He would leisurely remove her garments and lower his naked body to hers. His lips would drift playfully over her eyes and ears before slipping down her throat and . . . His body began to respond to his provocative thoughts. But it did not matter how much he desired her, he told himself, because she was Nathan's granddaughter. Perhaps it was her resemblance to Nathan that had touched him and softened him. With Nathan's looks and blood, surely she could not be wicked. Yet Marissa had been, his keen mind debated.

Hellfire, what did he know about women, he fumed, except bad things? After his problems with Elizabeth Lowry and Pretty Rabbit and Clarissa Caldwell's grasping pursuit, the last thing he needed was more female trouble. As with the selfish and conniving Indian maiden, the perfidious and vindictive Elizabeth Lowry had nearly gotten him killed, and the avaricious Clarissa Caldwell wanted the Rocking C Ranch as much as—if not more than—she wanted him. Then there was all that nasty gossip about Marissa . . . Were all women vain, selfish, deceitful, insensitive bitches? he wondered sullenly.

Considering the bad blood she might have inherited from her parents, Rana could be similar to the others. But if that assumption were accurate, he too could have been poisoned by his father's evil blood. If only he could understand Rana or see what was lurking inside that clever head. If only he knew how much like Elizabeth, Clarissa, Pretty Rabbit, and Marissa she was . . .

Rana looked at the deeply slumbering Nathan and smiled. He appeared so kind and loving, asleep or awake, and she was learning so much about him, from him.

He was a giving, generous person. Over the years since her mother's murder and her abduction, this man must have suffered terribly, she thought compassionately. Not knowing a loved one's fate would surely be sheer agony. Her grandfather had had no way of knowing how lucky she had been after her second capture. While she had been living happily and freely with the Oglalas, her dear grandfather had been existing on torment and loneliness and fear, at least until Travis Kincade had entered his life. She could not truly imagine the anguish her grandfather had endured long ago, and she could not bring herself to cause him more pain and sadness now. In fact, she wanted to do everything she could to make up for those lost years.

Rana knew Nathan had spoken the truth about her identity and the past. She believed he sincerely loved her and wanted her to return home with him. She could see it in his eyes, hear it in his voice, and perceive it from his spirit. Though she was still annoyed and hurt over their deceit, she was trying to accept their motives. As Travis had claimed, they had risked their lives to "rescue" her, and they had found a peaceful way to reclaim her. She would never have accepted or forgiven them if they had used soldiers to take her from the Oglalas.

It also vexed her that Travis thought he had done the right thing, especially since his tactics had included beguiling her. She became angry each time she wondered if he had actually believed those awful stories about her. She could not deny that Nathan had justified Travis's role in this scheme to reclaim her. Still, she did not like the way he had played his part, marrying her falsely and allowing her to be tempted by him. He had led her to believe she was bravely and honorably sacrificing herself to him to help her people. He had pretended she was worth a great price to him and had expected that she would be thrilled to be chosen by him. He had played with her vulnerable and naive emotions to keep his game a secret. He had made a fool of her, and she of herself, before her people. She asked herself if it mattered that he had been forced by Lone Wolf and persuaded by her grandfather to deceive her. Yes! she decided in annoyance. Yes, that irresistible rogue needed to be taught a lesson too, so he would never try to fool her again!

Rana's thoughts drifted to her Indian brother, Lone Wolf. She prayed that he and Myeerah would share a long and happy life, and she hoped to be able to visit them again one day. She thought of everything Soaring Hawk, Lone Wolf, and the Oglalas had done for her over the years. She prayed that they knew how much she loved them and appreciated their acceptance. She prayed urgently for their survival and peace.

She wondered why Lone Wolf had insisted that Travis marry her, for he had known that the union would not be consummated or considered real where they were going. Had he done it to make Travis feel responsible for her safety and happiness, particularly if something were to happen to Nathan? Or had he sensed the strong attraction between them and feared they would yield to it without being joined? Lone Wolf was perceptive and cunning, so there would have had to have been a good reason for his curious term.

Rana dreamily recalled the days since she had ridden away from the Oglala camp. She had always wanted to do exciting things, share dangerous adventures, help her people, and remain free. And yes, to live "wild" when the mood struck her! She had to admit that Travis and Nathan were providing her with the opportunities for which she had longed and had battled Lone Wolf to obtain. They were allowing her to help them in every way, to be like their partner on the trail. She had been given weapons and was expected to fight if necessary. They had permitted her to stand guard on several occasions. She knew she already possessed the "patience and self-control" Travis had questioned, for she had been forced to use them and hone them of late, though sometimes it had chafed her to practice them. Yet during the past few days she had come to realize that it was foolish to continue fighting what had been, what was, and what would be.

Rana stood up and stretched her fatigued body. She had hoped Travis would have returned to camp by now so she could go refresh herself in the nearby river. Maybe she was being too hard on him, she mused. Maybe it was time to relent slightly, for if she did not, he might lose all interest in her, and she did not want that. She knew from the sly way he had been watching her that she had him worried. She frowned, realizing that it was not good for their scout to be distracted, especially by unfavorable thoughts of her. If she were careful and wily, by the time they reached the ranch she might have him wishing they were married under the white law . . .

Rana smiled devilishly as she gathered her things. She concentrated on bringing Travis's face to mind, a face that she could have stared at all day and all night, a face on which every feature was shaped and colored perfectly. There was so much beauty and strength of character revealed in his stunning features. His expressions always imprisoned so much emotion, emotion that was tightly controlled but straining for release. How she loved to see those leaf green eyes sparkle with mischief or glow with desire or darken with vexation, for they exposed how deeply and passionately he could feel. When they were riding swiftly, the wind would blow through his dark hair and arrange it in roguish waves, as if the wind were some playful female spirit who was enchanted by him and could not resist touching him. As a doeskin drawn snugly over a tanning frame, his golden brown flesh was stretched tightly over his muscular body. She longed to run her fingers over him from head to foot and enjoy that stirring blend of softness and firmness. He was every inch the stimulating and superior warrior.

She remembered how his mouth had melted against hers and their tongues had danced together joyfully. She recalled how her body had reacted to the way his hands had moved over it. She wanted to experience those thrilling sensations again, for they had made her feel wild and free yet all the while a willing captive in his arms and under his control. If any man could tame Wild Wind, it would be Travis Kincade, for she was eager to surrender to his masterful touch.

Rana had noted that Travis had disappeared amongst the trees to the left of their camp, so she now headed toward the right. She walked to what she considered a safe distance, knowing she should not stray far even for privacy. Laying her possessions aside, she leisurely undressed, for she doubted anyone would be sneaking about at such a late hour.

Recalling the night she and Travis had touched passionately near a river, she stood on the bank for a few moments, stretching and flexing her body as sweet memories filled her mind. She inhaled the mingled fragrances nature provided and smiled dreamily, as if totally pleased with her life and her feelings. Rana braided her hair and, using a rawhide thong, secured the heavy plait to her head to avoid getting her hair soaked. Taking a cloth and soap Travis had bought for her at Fort Wallace, she gingerly made her way down the bank and into the water. She muffled a squeal as she discovered that the water was much cooler than she had imagined. She bravely splashed it on her quivering flesh, then hurriedly lathered from neck to knees. Lifting them one at a time, she soaped each leg and foot. Then she lathered her hands before tossing the cloth and soap on the bank. After washing and rinsing her face, she made her way into the deeper water to rinse off. In no hurry now, she swam around for awhile to exercise her stiff body and to warm herself.

When Rana finally returned to the bank, she could not locate her drying blanket and garments. She glanced to her right and left to see where she had placed them, but she sighted nothing. Her wet body glistened in the moonlight, and she shuddered as a breeze swept over it. Surely she had not swum that far from where she had left her possessions and entered the water! She searched the area again, mumbling curses to herself.

"*Osniyelo, Watogla Tate? Tokel oniglakin kta hwo?*" a mellow voice asked from nearby. Travis chuckled as she whirled and, blushing, tried futilely to escape the perusal of the man leaning against a tree.

His amusement did not anger her, and he sensed this. She replied in English. "Yes, I am cold, White Eagle. I have nothing to say for myself. I have done no wrong. I stayed near camp, and you always camp where it is safe. My blanket, please." She smiled as she held out her hand, trying to look calm despite the awkward circumstances. She alertly noticed that he had spoken in Lakota and had used her Oglala name. She wondered if he were feeling and thinking Indian tonight . . .

"It's 'I have done nothing wrong' or "I have not done anything wrong,' " he mildly corrected, then grinned. "What if I had been an enemy? You would have a serious problem about now," he teased as he dangled the blanket from one finger and her garments from the others. "And I don't always choose safe places to camp. Remember those deserters."

She retorted confidently, "You would not make the same mistake two times. I have no problem; you are my . . . grandfather's friend. I am safe." She made no attempt to reach for the blanket as she watched his eyes sparkle with mischief, and rapidly mounting desire. She casually removed her headband, unbraided her hair, and shook it loose to fall around her shoulders. Her eyes never left him. His sable hair was damp and wisps clung to his face and neck. His shirt was missing and his hard torso was moist; she noticed that there were wet spots on his pants and that his feet were bare, as if he had left the water quickly and recently. He seemed such a splendid, enticing male animal as he stood before her. Her heart was thudding so fiercely that simple breathing was becoming difficult.

Travis knew she was accustomed to bathing outside and around others, but, he wondered, did she feel no modesty around him? No, he told himself; it was stiff resolve and courage that kept her from fleeing or protesting over his bold intrusion. He was impressed by the way she was handling the situation. "I am your grandfather's friend, but not yours?" he questioned in amusement, potently stimulated by her naked beauty, her close proximity, and her evocative stare.

"That is your choice, Travis Kincade. You have apologized and explained your deceit. I must try to accept your words, or I must return to my . . . the Oglalas. I believe that I am Rana Michaels and that Nathan Crandall is my grandfather, as Lone Wolf believed; otherwise he would not have sent me away with you. Nate must not be hurt or made sad again. If it will make him happy, I will return to his home and learn to be white once more, as I was long ago where my memory does not reach . . . The river is cold this moo . . . tonight. It was not wise to bathe so late." She shuddered as another breeze passed over her wet flesh.

Dropping her garments, Travis stepped forward and wrapped the blanket around her, clasping the edges tightly in his balled hands just beneath her chin. As she looked into his eyes, he remarked, "No, it wasn't wise to bathe tonight. I was swimming over there," he informed her, pointing to a fallen tree that was half submerged in water.

"Why did you say nothing to stop me?" she asked softly.

"Because I didn't want to startle you and have you wake Nate with screams. Both of us swimming without clothes might have looked suspicious to him. Besides, I was enjoying myself too much," he added, grinning. "If you hadn't been so distracted by such deep thoughts, your sharp instincts would have felt my presence. With your training and skill, I'm surprised I got past you, even underwater. You are one beautiful, tempting creature, Rana Michaels. If you weren't Nate's granddaughter, I would take you here and now."

Rana laughed seductively as she placed her hands on his chest and leaned closer to him to share his body heat. "If I were not Rana, Travis Kincade would not have ridden into the Oglala camp and made trade for me and joined to me with false promises. If I were not Nate's granddaughter, I would not be here with you tonight."

In a voice that had grown husky Travis refuted smoothly, "Even if you weren't Rana Michaels, I still would have traded for you, but you would be sharing my sleeping mat now instead of having your own. Frankly, I'm almost sorry I have a new sister instead of a lovely wife." His gaze probed hers to judge how his provocative words had struck her. Her eyes were like liquid pools of blue magic that summoned him to drown in them.

"We are joined in the eyes of the Great Spirit. If you desire me so fiercely, why do you want me to be your sister and not your wife?" she reasoned bravely as her tantalizing gaze remained fused to his.

"Because I love and respect Nathan Crandall too much to seduce his granddaughter. He would despise me for taking advantage of you. I've told you, Rana, our marriage isn't legal for whites."

Rana had questioned the meaning of "legal" before; now she asked the meaning of "seduce." When Travis explained in a mixture of Oglala and English, she tried to suppress her mirthful laughter.

"What's so funny?" he asked, his brows knit in confusion.

"Did you tell my grandfather I tried to seduce you the night he called to us by the river? Is that why you were frightened and left me?"

"I was upset because I let things go too far between us that night and I left because I couldn't have resisted you if I had stayed. That wasn't the time or place for us to . . . get together, if we do. Now I understand why so many warriors were battling over you. You have powerful magic, woman, and you should learn when and where to use it. You're a cunning thief who steals a man's wisdom and control."

"How can I steal what should be mine by law and by your word of honor? Our hearts are Indian. We are joined by Indian law. If White Eagle takes Wild Wind to his sleeping mat, Rana will not tell her grandfather," she cunningly promised. She lifted one hand to move her forefinger over his lips. "If he discovers the truth, tell my grandfather I have powerful magic and I seduced you," she teased playfully.

Travis frowned in dismay. He captured her enticing hand to halt its action and argued, "*I* would know the truth. I cannot lie to him and deceive him, Rana. To him, we are not married. He trusts me, and loves me, and needs me. He has been closer to me than my own father was. You are like his own child. Taking you could destroy the bond between us and hurt him deeply. Nothing is worth that."

Rana smiled happily, for she saw he was a man of immeasurable honor. "I understand. I am pleased you love my grandfather so much. You are his true and loyal friend. I will do nothing to break the bond between you and Nate; it is special and rare. You must teach me all you have learned since leaving your mother's people. I want my grandfather to be proud of me, as he is of you. Will you be my friend and help me?"

"I've never had a female friend before. That might prove interesting. The fact is, my luck with females has been mostly bad."

"You tease me," she accused merrily as she quivered with excitement. "How can a man of White Eagle's looks and prowess not have many women chasing him? Are there some you wish me to fight off?" she jested. Snuggling closer, she murmured, "It is cold tonight. Share your warmth with me while we talk. There is much for me to learn."

Travis shook his head to prevent himself from being mesmerized by her incredible eyes. He was all too aware of the danger in standing here with her like this. "You should dry off and get dressed. You're cold, and it's too late to teach you anything tonight. We don't want Nate wondering where we are and looking for us again. He might not understand this."

"You are afraid to be alone with your sister friend?"

"Yep," he confessed between hearty chuckles.

"You are right. There is a pull between us that should not be between brother and sister. Return to camp. I will follow soon."

"Is that what you told Lone Wolf?" he questioned suddenly.

Baffled, she looked up at him. "I do not understand."

"Did you tell Lone Wolf we were drawn to each other? Is that why he demanded we marry before you could leave with me?"

"I did not speak of such things with my brother. I do not know why he forced you to join to me. You should not have agreed. He is wise and kind; he would have released me without the joining. I could not believe my ears when you asked to make trade for me and be joined to me. You forget, I did not know it was a trick until five moo . . . days ago."

He tapped her on the nose as he replied, "I think he wanted to make sure I would feel responsible for you. Then again, he could have seen or heard us and thought it would be wise to bind us together just in case we lost our heads one night by a river." His eyes twinkled roguishly.

"My brother knew you were a man of honor and control. He knew the truth about me. He knew you would not touch me. There was a reason for his demand, but I do not know it."

"One day you'll be glad you aren't bound to a rogue like me. You're free to choose your own husband, not forced to accept a stranger. I want you to be careful when we get home, Rana. You're a beautiful woman, and you'll be a rich one. Men will be chasing you."

After Travis explained the meaning of "rich," Rana told him, "I cannot choose to marry another man until I no longer feel joined to White Eagle. I was raised Indian. I do not think and feel white."

Travis stared at her regretfully. "I'm sorry I've made you so confused. In time you'll accept the way things are in the white world."

Rana had been trying to point out the fact that if he desired her so much he could marry her under white law and thereby have her without hurting Nathan. She suddenly realized that he might not want to marry her, might be glad, in fact, that the Indian ceremony was not binding. She knew it was possible for a man to desire and take a woman without loving her or wanting her as his mate. Perhaps she was reading his feelings wrong. He was always talking about her choosing and marrying another man. Maybe he did not think she was good enough for him or was the right woman for him. Nathan had said that Travis had not wanted to marry her, that he had only done so because Lone Wolf had demanded it. A painful suspicion began to gnaw at her, a suspicion that it was Nathan who wanted her, not Travis. She realized she should not be chasing him so boldly, and that realization saddened her. Quietly she informed him, "You are right, Travis Kincade. I must change or others will suffer." She stepped away from him, gathered her things, and moved into the concealing shadows.

Travis caught the change in her mood. He wished he could admit that he felt joined to her too, but he knew it would be wrong to confuse her even more. She needed time and clarity of mind to discover who she was and to adjust to her new existence. After all, he would be close at hand at all times. Besides, the ravishing vixen just might be toying with him, trying to lead him on for tricking her! He knew about the little games women played with men, games several had tried to play on him. They used their bodies like weapons, with skills to match those of the most cunning warrior. They teased, enticed, rewarded, or punished a man if he didn't follow their rules. They wanted to own a man and control him. They wanted him running after them as if he couldn't survive without them. They wanted him to pet them and spoil them. They wanted him to sacrifice everything to prove his feelings and receive their attentions only. They used him to make other men jealous, or used other men to make him jealous and nervous. They wanted him to think with his loins instead of his heart or head. They could be so selfish, so predatory, so eager to possess and consume, and so damned insidious!

He knew that women like Clarissa, Pretty Rabbit, Elizabeth, and Marissa would do anything to get their way. They did not care whom they hurt or used. Maybe Marissa's daughter was just like her mother and the others. Plenty of worthy warriors had tried to win Wild Wind as a mate, but she had rejected each of them. So why would she cast her sights on the stranger who had deceived her and had refused to acknowledge her surrender? Unless she wanted to teach him a lesson! No, he could not permit this untamed creature to come between him and Nathan. He could not allow himself to be hurt again, for he knew from experience that physical pain was nothing compared to emotional agony. No matter what Rana's motives might be, he would have to resist her.

He would never forget his near-fatal experience with Elizabeth Lowry because he had scars to remind him. That treacherous viper had pretended to be so sweet and innocent while all the while she had been trying to snare him. He had been working for her father in St. Louis and had learned by then to be nice and polite to ladies and especially to bosses' daughters. Beth had enticed and encouraged him for weeks before he finally agreed to partake of her charms, and she had had plenty of them. Thinking back, he realized his emotional wounds from the past had been too fresh during her siege. It had been twenty-two months since his torture and rejection by the Hunkpapas, which had come hard upon his father's betrayal and death and his mother's death. Maybe that nineteen-year-old, bitter, lonely, arrogant youth had needed someone to love him, to need him, to make him feel he was the most special male alive; and Beth had been an expert at such pretenses. He had been searching for something and—even knowing Beth was not it—had allowed her to distract him. Hellfire, what had really happened was he had gotten tired of making excuses not to take what she had been forcing on him!

After escaping the Hunkpapa camp, he had gone from place to place, working all kinds of jobs as he learned his way around in the white world, but never staying anywhere more than three months. He had always been careful to keep his identity and past a secret from everyone, for he knew how people felt about half-breeds. After the Hunkpapas had stopped sending warriors after him, he had slowed his pace, but he had then discovered he was merely existing from day to day. Without a home, family, identity, and purpose in life, he felt lost. Riding with a band of outlaws, he committed crimes but never got caught. As a U.S. Marshal, he fought and killed men legally. He scouted for the Army for awhile. He escorted a wagon train through Indian lands and briefly rode with fierce and cunning Apaches. He worked on a ranch, then was a bank guard for two weeks. Still he missed that sense of belonging, that feeling of pride, the stimulating adventure and thrill of being a warrior. Despite his efforts, he had been unable to find anything or anyone to fill that nagging void; and he had been unable to forget the stain on his face and honor. His father's crimes and his own rejection had eaten away at him.

Beth had entered his life at a time when he was willing to allow himself to be used, maybe as punishment. At that time, life and people meant little to him; he was just passing the days until his head cleared and his heart stopped hurting and yearning. He had taken Indian and white women in the Hunkpapa camp, but it had always been for the purpose of assuaging his lust, or as a learning experience. He had not loved Beth or desired anything permanent with her, but she had been insistent about sharing herself completely with him. And men did have their needs, he had told himself then. Even when their brief affair first began, it had not been because he had wanted her or had pursued her.

After a barn dance and a few drinks one night, Beth had sneaked into his room and had practiced her numerous skills on him; and she hadn't been a virgin. For a week, he had allowed her to share his bed, but he soon realized he was making a foolish mistake. He quickly became tired of her grasping ways and sorry attitudes, and finally he refused to see her again. He was willing to risk getting fired if keeping the job meant keeping the boss's daughter happy as well.

For weeks, Beth was furious, then suddenly she mellowed. He discovered that she was using other men to make him jealous. Beth should have known it wouldn't work, he reflected now, because he had had no feelings for her, not good ones anyway. As he continued to watch her use her wiles, sensual skills, wealth, beauty, and position, he discovered the real Beth, and he lost all respect for her. When she allowed him to find her with a man, his indifference turned to disgust. Despite what Pretty Rabbit had done to him nearly two years earlier, he had not expected Elizabeth Lowry to have such a vengeful and utterly evil streak.

One night an Indian girl who worked in the Lowry home came to him and revealed the details of Beth's scheme to entrap him. It seemed that Beth had told her father he had seduced her and she had become pregnant, though she had neglected to mention that she had also slept with many other men before and since her week with him. She was demanding that her father force Travis to marry her immediately. The Indian girl told him that Beth's accusation was a lie; she knew that Beth had twice experienced her monthly flow since he had stopped seeing her. The girl then warned him to flee St. Louis. But, like a fool, he did the same thing he had done once before, after his father's exposure; he remained to prove his innocence and courage, vowing he would not run like a guilty coward.

Beth's father would not listen to him and threatened to hang him if he did not marry his daughter. Enraged, he shouted out the names of countless men who had enjoyed Beth's charms, especially those who had taken her since him. He then challenged Beth's father to question those men or to prove his guilt, and he vowed to seek the help of the authorities in his defense. That had been another mistake. Lowry immediately ordered his daughter to pack her belongings and announced he was sending her back East to a school for girls that sounded like a prison.

As for him, Lowry hired two gunslingers to torture him and kill him, not only to prevent the Lowry name from being smeared but because Lowry wanted revenge for having his child's evil exposed to him so blatantly.

Travis vividly recalled how the ruffians had lured him into a trap with a faked note from the Indian girl who worked for Lowry, a note pleading for Travis's help. He had gone to her aid and instead had been thoroughly beaten by the two ruffians, who had then left him to die in the wilderness after stealing nearly all of his possessions. As for the Indian girl, her help in warning him about Beth's scheme had gotten her raped and murdered right before his eyes as he was losing consciousness.

But Nathan Crandall had come along, found him, and adopted him, so to speak. It had taken him months to heal, and when he had gone looking for the Lowrys, he had learned they had been robbed and slain by bandits. He had never found the two bastards who had nearly beaten him to death, but he believed that one day they would cross his path again.

Nathan had been having trouble with rustlers and renegades and had begged him to return to the ranch after his search, so he had returned and stayed to help the man who had saved his life. Time had passed, his ability to feel had slowly increased, and he had never left Nathan Crandall's side again. From the day Nathan had found him to this one, whenever he had needed a woman, he had paid for one in town.

Travis's thoughts turned to Clarissa Caldwell. Just like Beth, that little vixen had pursued him for years. But he had learned his lesson, and he had never done more than tease her with lips and hands when it had suited his purpose to taunt her or to pull information from her. Besides, he did not want to give Harrison Caldwell anything he could use to harm Nathan, or do anything that might be used to force him to leave the ranch and the man who was his best friend. He knew how much like Beth Clarissa was, and he was not about to be ensnared by the same trick twice. Just like Rana had said, he never made the same mistake two times . . .

Rana . . . Rana was nothing like those vindictive bitches who had schemed against him and had made him so cynical. He remembered how she had felt in his arms and how she had wanted him as fiercely as he had wanted her. He recalled how Black Hawk had tried to attack her, and he suddenly realized that she might turn to another man eventually if he kept pushing her away. Her expression of moments ago flashed before his mind's eye and his heart lurched wildly with desire and panic. *By damn, you're mine, Rana Michaels,* he vowed and rushed off to see what was keeping her so long.

Travis found her resting her forehead against a tree while she cried softly, her body still clad in the drying blanket and her other possessions carelessly lying on the ground. He realized how deeply he was confusing and hurting her with his contradictory words and actions. "Please don't cry, Rana," he entreated. "I really got us into a terrible mess, didn't I? Don't hate me. I didn't mean to hurt you."

"Hate you?" she echoed, lifting her head and gazing into his troubled eyes. She leaned against the tree. "That is not true. So much is happening around me and inside me. Why do you fear me and reject me and race from my side each time we touch with deep feelings?"

Travis looked at her and replied honestly, "It isn't you I fear, Rana; it's my loss of control that scares me. When there's nobody around like Nate or Lone Wolf, I can't stay clearheaded or restrained. We're too attracted to each other to be alone. Lordy, woman, you make me think and feel crazy things. No one has ever tempted me or affected me like you do. Staying around you is like tossing a match on a dry haystack and hoping it won't catch fire. You make me feel weak and reckless. I tried to return to camp to avoid more temptation, but I was worried about you." His respiration had altered noticeably and he was staring at her with intense longing, though he was afraid to touch her. He desperately wanted to yank her into his arms and kiss her again and again, yet he was frightened by what such contact would lead to. His hands were shaking and he was beginning to feel tense and damp all over from the strain on his self-control and from his burning desire for her. He warned himself to return to camp immediately, but he could not force his legs to obey his conscience's precautionary message.

Rana understood his dilemma, for she shared his feelings. They both wanted each other, needed each other, and she felt they should surrender to the battle that was raging within them. She knew how close they were to the yielding point and had already decided which path she wanted to take. Their bodies, and even the air surrounding them, were charged with emotion. Surely this was meant to be, she told herself, refusing to stop her hand from reaching up to caress his taut jawline yet knowing what such physical contact would do to both of them. It seemed as if the Great Spirit had entrapped them together, as if He had created this unique moment just for them to discover each other, as if He had lowered some magical flap for privacy to this lover's tepee of nature's construction. Travis's pull on her was too great and she could not resist it, did not want to resist it. Her instincts told her that as surely as Mother Earth was fated to change her face with each season, they were fated to change their lives and hearts this season. In a tone just above a silky whisper, she told him, "There is no reason for your fear and control. I yield to you by my choice, for I desire you. It is sad and painful to deny such needs. Is it not better to walk a path of truth and happiness? How can I remain near you if I cannot have you? Your rejections cut my heart too deeply. If your feelings match mine, why must we remain apart and in torment? How can this beautiful and powerful thing between us be evil or wrong?"

Her words, expression, tone, and nearness prevented him from retreating or protesting. He was intoxicated and utterly entranced by her. Travis grasped the hands caressing his cheeks and pressed them to his lips. As his gaze remained fused to hers and he absorbed her presence, his lips and tongue played sensuously in her palms. When she moved closer to him, his arms slipped around her body and his lips seared over her right ear. As they drifted down her throat, she trembled and swayed against him, enslaving his senses. His mouth brushed over her bare shoulder and traveled back to the hollow of her neck and up to her ear to nibble there. When Rana's arm encircled his waist and she arched her body against his, Travis's hands slipped into her cascading tresses; they cupped her head and lifted it. His eyes held hers for a heart-stopping instant before his lips captured hers in a fiery kiss that ignited their smoldering passions into a roaring blaze of urgency and reality-consuming force.

One kiss blended into another, leaving them breathless and increasing their cravings. As Travis's hands wandered over her shoulders and back, the drying blanket glided to the ground. The feel of her succulent flesh against his greedy hands drove him wild with desire. As his fingers moved over her soft curves to caress her buttocks and upward to rove over her tempting breasts, he shuddered with rising need.

Rana shifted sideways to give him more freedom to explore her aching body. He cradled her in the curve of his right arm as his mouth feasted at hers and his left hand closed over a firm breast. When its peak instantly responded and became taut with desire, his mouth was enticed to drift over her chin and down her throat to capture it, leaving behind a tingling trail of kisses. The bud danced joyfully with his lips and tongue until she urged him to share this new bliss with the other brown peak.

She was astonished by how his actions affected her from head to foot; even her tummy quivered in anticipation and delight and her legs grew weak. Her entire body was alive and aflame, as was his. Passion's fires burned brighter each moment. His mouth returned to hers and they kissed feverishly. They wanted each other instantly, fiercely, but each instinctively knew their joining should not be rushed, even if control was becoming impossible.

Travis's left hand moved past her abdomen, enticingly stroking her flesh along the way, and boldly entered the auburn forest between her sleek thighs. As it labored skillfully, eagerly, gently, his mouth worked on hers until she was limp and breathless. "Take me, Travis," she urged hoarsely, "for I burn for you."

His mouth seared over hers in a blaze of passion and he held her tightly, possessively, against his body. Suddenly an owl screeched loudly overhead, startling him and alerting him to their dangerous surroundings. "We can't, *micante*, not here, not now," he told her painfully. "Nate would be furious and hurt if he discovered my betrayal. I promised him and Lone Wolf I wouldn't do this, because of our false marriage. Besides, this place isn't safe with my senses so dulled and my mind so distracted. I want you like I've never wanted any woman, but we shouldn't have to rush our first union, or fear discovery by Nate or some enemy, or feel as if we're doing something wrong. There's a lot to be settled between us before we go any further, and we need a special time and place to come together. Lordy, you do steal my wits and control!"

Rana grasped his head between her hands and forced him to meet her compelling gaze. "We can and we must, Travis. You are mine, and I need you, as you need me. I do not care if we are not joined under the white law. You are not seducing me, or taking advantage of me, or betraying Nathan Crandall. You must not think and feel this way. This matter is between White Eagle and Wild Wind—no one else. Do not leave us burning for each other again."

Travis listened to her arguments and observed her expressions. She was being truthful with him, and with herself. He knew there would be no turning back this time, for it really didn't matter that this wasn't the best place to make love for the first time, or even that they would have to rush and remain alert.

He released her to remove his pants and drop them beside her belongings. Then he bent over and spread the drying blanket at the foot of the tree. "I can't resist you any longer, Rana. Hunger for you is eating me alive inside. Right or wrong, I must have you tonight."

They sank to the blanket together and, as they lay down, he warned, "I have never desired anything or anyone as I crave you. Once you are mine, no man will take you from me and I will never release you. The burning of flesh is nothing compared to the burning of a heart. If both do not blaze fiercely for me alone, Wild Wind, do not yield."

She clasped his face and drew it close to hers. "If yours do not burn for me alone, White Eagle, do not take me, for, in doing so, you pledge your heart, life, and honor to me." She paused for a moment to look deeply into his eyes. "But if they do burn as fiercely as mine do, you must claim me tonight, for it is torment to be near you and be denied you. Did we both not know this time would come when our eyes and bodies touched in Lone Wolf's tepee? We can no longer resist what must be between us."

Their eyes locked as each sought the other's pledge in the glowing moonlight, then both smiled. Travis lay half atop her and, for awhile, they were content to look into each other's eyes and caress lightly, lovingly. Both knew time could be short, but they savored each moment. They nibbled on each other's chins, savored each other's lips, shared warm respiration, and drowned in pools that reflected love and desire. It was a time to move with tenderness, to explore emotions as well as passions, to allow spirits to mingle as well as fiery bodies. It was a time to tame the fears and doubts that had enveloped and restrained them; it was a time to surrender to the wild winds of sweet ecstasy. It was a time for sweet, savage hearts to fuse and become one for all days.

Travis stroked her mischievous curls and teased fingers over her features as if he had been a blind man studying them. "My heart is beating loud and heavily, *micante.* I've never felt this way before, wanting a woman with more than my manhood, and it's frightening. I knew this union would come to pass the moment my eyes touched on your painted image, for I desired you even then. Yet I can hardly believe you're real, or you're here in my life, and in my arms tonight. I was afraid to reach out to you, afraid you could never feel this way about me. And I'm not a man used to experiencing or admitting fear. I've always had bad luck with women, so I've never liked or trusted many. You're so different, and that worries me. I need to know you better so I can understand what I'm thinking and feeling. Giving and sharing come hard for me."

Rana's finger teased along his neck and shoulder as she replied, "I too feared the strange feelings that attacked me. Each time you left camp, I prayed for your return. Your face gave joy to my heart and your voice stirred my soul. Lone Wolf was forcing me to join, and I was afraid to refuse. How could I explain that I desired a stranger? I have wanted you and this moment since the first night you came to my brother's tepee. When I awoke to find you gone, I feared I would not be allowed time to know you. Each time you turned away from me, it confused and pained me deeply, for I did not understand many things. Each time we touched, I knew why I had refused to join to another. In my heart, I was waiting for you, Travis Kincade, and I must have you for my life-circle to be complete and happy. This is as it should be for us."

Travis leaned forward and sealed her lips with his. They kissed and caressed until the flames of heady desire raged within their minds as well as their bodies. Very gently Travis entered her receptive womanhood, holding her possessively and fusing their lips in that special moment. He hesitated briefly to master his throbbing manhood and to allow her time to adjust to their physical bond. She had not cried out, and he assumed that her active life had allowed her to embrace this moment with little discomfort. He had known that a virgin would experience less pain if the man were gentle and patient, and he had tried to be both.

Softly he whispered, "You are mine now, *micante,* and I am yours. We have become a circle that must remain joined forever." His body shuddered then with enormous need and from the wonder of her total surrender. His sexual pleasure had never reached such heights before. He labored lovingly, carefully, until she was matching his rhythm and their bodies were working feverishly as one. Both could feel the heady tension building within and between them, building to a pitch that beat as forcefully as war drums.

Eagerly, rapidly, they climbed passion's spiral until they swayed sensuously on the precipice of victory, overcoming all doubts and hesitations, then flinging themselves over the edge of control. When her rapturous release came, her mouth and body clung to his, extracting every instant of the glorious experience and telling him to cast his own caution aside. As he seized blissful ecstasy, he murmured against her lips, "You are mine, Wild Wind, forever mine. Let no man or thing come between us. We are one now."

They lay nestled together on the thin blanket, aglow in the warmth of sated passion. Contentedly they listened to their joyous heartbeats and to the harmonious blending of music sounds created by nocturnal creatures, birds, and insects. Moonlight made its way through the trees into the small clearing and splashed across their entwined bodies. A hint of a breeze tried to rustle the leaves and branches, but they were too supple with new life to comply. The fragrance of wildflowers and the heady smell of pine teased at their noses. Serenity surrounded and pervaded them.

As the night air became cooler, they snuggled closer together, not wanting the moment or their contact to end. But they were in enemy territory and Nathan was sleeping not far away. Though neither felt tired or drowsy, both knew they needed rest and sleep for their journey.

Travis propped himself up on his elbow and gazed down at Rana. He watched how the moonlight gleamed on her shiny hair and was reflected in her entrancing eyes. His heart fluttered. He wished they could make love all night, but the hour was late and the idea dangerous, especially when he considered his reckless seduction and his rash confessions.

She smiled and asked, "Do you know how rare you are? I am glad you belong to me." She pulled his head to hers and kissed him.

"I've made plenty of mistakes, Rana, but I don't guess I turned out too badly, did I?" he jested, teasing his fingertips along her spine. He knew it was time they returned to reality, but he dreaded it. There were things he did not want to do or say, things he did not want to face.

"I would trade nothing and no one for you, Travis Kincade."

He kissed the tip of her nose. "I sure am glad I traded something for you, woman. Do you know how hard it's been to resist you? Or how hard it will be for us to avoid each other until our lives are settled?"

Rana's heart was too full of love and happiness to comprehend his last words. A dreamy haze still enveloped her. "I am glad White Eagle defeated Travis Kincade in this battle. We cannot change what is meant to be, and it hurts us and others to try."

"But sometimes we hurt others if we don't try, *micante*. Like Nate, when he discovers what happened between us tonight. I'll have to find the right words to explain our feelings and behavior to him. He trusted me to keep my word to stay clear of you. I have proven myself a man of little honor, a man of weakness."

She scolded him angrily, "Do not speak such false words! You are not to blame because we could not resist the fires that burned between us. Our Indian souls are bound as one; it was our Indian bodies that yielded. We are not children, and we cannot be forced to reveal our actions and feelings to anyone, including our family. Speak no evil of yourself. You have more strength and honor than any man I have known. Some things must be held secret; a moment such as we shared is one of those things. If you tell my grandfather, it will spoil it for us. Please, let White Eagle belong to Wild Wind in silence until the moo . . . day when Rana and Travis can share their secret. Wild Wind and White Eagle are joined and have done nothing wrong. Rana and Travis must find themselves and each other if they wish to share our life-circle."

Rana loved him, but she did not want Nathan to force Travis to marry her under the white law. She felt it was important that they share this special secret and intimacy, for she hoped it would bind them together in both worlds. She wanted him to learn to love her and trust her above anyone else, including her grandfather. She wanted him to ask her to marry him again, but this time of his own free will, not because of force or guilt. He needed the freedom to decide that he did not want freedom from her.

"Your words are true and wise, *micante* . . ." Travis began, about to ask her to marry him under the white law. But unwillingly he recalled the many problems and perils he faced, perils that could endanger Rana if he staked his claim on her too soon. He knew he would have to overcome them first; only then could he take her as his wife for a second time. For now, they needed to explore feelings: their own and each other's. They needed to learn to trust and to share completely. This thing between them was more than physical; it had to be given time and effort so that it could be allowed to flourish. He just wished he felt less guilt over duping Nathan. "I don't want anything to stain this special moment. For now, it will remain between us. We will allow Travis and Rana to seek themselves and each other, but Wild Wind will always belong to White Eagle alone."

Rana caught his hesitation and realized that something had stopped him from speaking everything that was in his heart. That aura of mystery surrounded him again, this time arriving unbidden. Though she knew that these new feelings and the situation were difficult for him, she sensed she had won him, and the thought made her smile happily. When the time came—and it would—he would explain everything to her. Until then, she would give him her love and her trust, and she would teach him to do the same with her. There was still so much they had to learn about each other and about the life they would share, she mused as she kissed him hungrily and embraced him. In Oglala, she murmured seductively, "Tonight, I am Wild Wind and you are White Eagle. When *Wi* returns with a new day, we will become Rana and Travis again."

Chapter 10

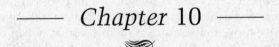

THE FOLLOWING MORNING, while Nathan was away from camp, Rana stopped her chores to ask Travis in a rush of words, "Were you angry with me because you thought I asked Lone Wolf to force you to marry me? Do you think I used the

Elk Dreamer's love medicine to snare you? Did the wicked tales about Wild Wind cause you to mistrust me?" She had decided it was time for openness and honesty between them, for she knew it was the only way they could grow closer. She had come to understand that it was not enough to love and desire a person; friendship, loyalty, trust, and respect were also vital. She knew this attraction between them was far more than physical. But did he? He seemed slightly withdrawn this morning, a little nervous, even a little guilty and embarrassed. Perhaps it was the reality of a total commitment that frightened him, for he had always appeared so independent. Or perhaps he was overly concerned about Nathan's reaction to their intimacy. Men viewed such things so differently from women. In the wilderness, life was precious and often too short, and she believed it should be lived to the fullest. She didn't want him to worry or pull back into himself, for she truly believed they had been made for each other.

Travis looked into the arresting face of the woman who had blinded him to everything except her the night before. It was intimidating to be so enthralled by another person, another power. There were so few people he admired, respected, trusted. If Rana's feelings and dreams did not match his . . . He wanted to trust her totally, but he was afraid, for he remembered the defiant, arrogant, disobedient vixen she had been, the kind of woman her mother had been, the kind most women were. And how could she love him and desire him after his deceit, with his half-blooded heritage? How could she, a beautiful, ravishing woman, want nothing from him except his love? He had always lived by his instincts, and they told him now to be wary of this bewitching woman, wary of his hunger and weakness for her. Like her, he needed time to adjust to this complicated situation and to these often alarming and novel emotions he felt. Yet, having realized all this, he still could not force himself to hold back from her completely. He stopped in the midst of saddling the horses to respond. "I wasn't mad at you, Rana. I know you didn't have anything to do with Lone Wolf's joining demand; he made it before you saw him or spoke to him after my arrival. I'm partly worried about the ranch. We've been gone a long time. Besides, you have more magic than any Elk Dreamer, *micante,* and it's driving me crazy trying to keep a cool head."

Rana smiled. "I know this magic between us is hard for you and we must travel this new path slowly and carefully. We stood beneath the eyes of the Great Spirit and spoke joining words, but the whites say they mean nothing. It is painful and confusing when the head and heart think and feel differently, or when others control your words and feelings. I was raised to accept and to honor Oglala laws and customs, to believe in *Wakan Tanka.* My head hears your white words, but my Oglala heart battles them. It is like saying to the whites the sky is green and the grass is blue when I have been taught otherwise by the Indians, as have you, White Eagle. For years I was Indian, but now I am white and must yield to the laws and customs that control my new life. You and my grandfather have asked me to make many changes quickly. Have you forgotten how it was when you left the Hunkpapas? Did your heart and life change as soon as you left your mother's lands? Was it easy and painless for you?"

He responded instantly, "No, it wasn't easy or painless, Rana. In fact, it hurt like hell and I battled those changes for two years. I didn't know where I was heading or what I was going to do. If it hadn't been for your grandfather, I would still be a hostile, bitter loner, drifting from place to place, fighting and rebelling and searching for myself—if I were still alive, that is. I was forced to leave my home; my family was dead. You're lucky; you're returning to your home and a family. Just the same, it won't be easy in the beginning. But you have people who love you and want you, people who'll help you adjust. At least you won't be alone in a world you don't understand, as I was. My past damaged me, Rana. I need time and understanding."

Travis ran his fingers through his thick sable hair and adjusted his red headband. As he attempted to decide what to tell her about his experiences, his green eyes narrowed and his brows knit, causing tiny lines to form above his nose and creating a misleading frown. He gazed at her, his look direct but uncertain. "There's so much you don't know about me, or your new life." He glanced at the ground, allowed his eyes to dart from side to side, then looked back at her.

As she awaited his reply, her puzzled expression matched his perplexed one. She recalled what Nathan had said about the Hunkpapas "rejecting" him. "You said you were 'forced' to travel a path away from your mother's lands. Will you explain your strange words? Where did you get the scars on your body? How, Travis?" She could tell he did not want to talk about his past, and probably had not revealed it to anyone but her grandfather. She was pleased he had told her this much and she hoped he would relate even more about himself, though she prayed he was not mourning a lost love. If he could be open and honest, it would mean he wanted her to understand and accept him. Yet his hesitation and tension indicated there were things he was not ready to face.

He sighed heavily. After last night, he owed her an explanation, though it would be hard to lower his guard and be candid. If he allowed her to get too close too quickly, it might impair his judgment. To relax himself, he joked, "I don't suppose you can think any worse of me than you already do. All right, Rana Michaels, I'll tell you what happened years ago in the Hunkpapa camp and why I was in such a hurry to get out of the Oglala camp and far away from Lakota lands."

Rana listened intently as Travis described his troubled past from his birth to his departure from the Hunkpapa village. He did not leave out his father's treachery or his mother's death or Pretty Rabbit's role, or how, after the Hunkpapas' torture, he had been forced to escape to avoid being executed for crimes he had not committed. His anguish and bitterness were evident to her. He had been betrayed and rejected by everyone and everything he had loved and respected. When he confessed he had been afraid the Hunkpapas would arrive and repeat the false tale to the Oglalas before he could recover her for Nathan—especially during the mix-up with the guns and the morning he had bound her and ridden off rapidly with her—she understood why he had been so aggressive and anxious to get her and Nathan out of that area with all speed. She surmised he had been right, for Indians rarely forgot or forgave a matter of broken honor. Yet she still sensed he was not telling her everything about his past.

"When I left the Lakota lands long ago, if you hadn't been a little girl I would have stolen you and taken you along with me," he teased to lighten the gloom around them. "You see, Miss Michaels, I've been nothing but trouble to myself and others since I was born. Now do you understand why I said you'd be glad you weren't joined to a jinxed renegade like me? If not for your grandfather, I'd be worse than I am. By now, the Hunkpapas have reached your camp and Lone Wolf has probably learned what he will believe to be the black truth about me. I wouldn't be surprised if he sends a band of warriors to hunt me down and rescue you. I was determined you were going home with Nate, even if I had to carry you hog-tied and screaming every mile of the way. That's where you belong for lots of reasons, including your survival. I swear I tried to honor my promise to Lone Wolf and Nate about you, but you found my weak spot and captivated me."

Travis waited for her to say something, but she just kept staring at him with those liquid blue eyes that he could not read. He prayed she wasn't sorry about last night. "I'll make a deal with you, Rana. If you decide to reject me for any reason, I'll leave the ranch and never come back, if that's what it'll take for you to remain with Nate. He turned my life around and gave me everything I needed. Seeing him happy means a lot to me. Adopted son or not, I swear I won't make any claim on the ranch. It's rightfully yours. I wouldn't want you to think I was trying to hold on to it by ensnaring you. I know I deceived you in the Oglala camp and I've broken my word about staying clear of you, so I guess you have little reason to trust me. But, please, make sure you know what you want and what you're doing."

Beyond Travis, Rana could see Nathan approaching and knew there would be no time or privacy to express her feelings. She realized how much Travis loved and respected Nathan. She was certain he had never begged anyone for anything before today, and his willingness to risk and sacrifice so much for Nathan touched her deeply. Travis had just shown her the path by which she could force him to marry her. It would be easy for her to demand that he marry her in order to be allowed to remain with Nathan and the ranch, but in her heart she knew she could not walk such a path. He had been tormented and betrayed too many times, and it would be a grave mistake for her to use any kind of coercion to win him. As he had said, he needed time and understanding. For Nathan's benefit, she declared aloud to Travis, "You said you would replace Cloud. Do you have a white stallion on the ranch?"

For a moment Travis was baffled by her question and behavior; then Nathan called out, "You two ready to ride?"

Rana smiled at her grandfather and nodded. "I'm eager to get home, Grandfather. I'm tired of riding and camping. Travis has promised to give me a horse as special as Cloud." Her gaze met Travis's as she spoke words that carried a dual meaning. "I will hold him to his words."

"If Travis said it, Rana, you can believe him. Sometimes he's a little hard to live with, but he's the best man I've ever met. I don't know what I would have done all those years if he hadn't been with me."

"You're biased, Nate," Travis teased in return, wondering which words she was going to hold him to. To Rana he said, "Let's go before he gets mushy on us." He grinned at her then, letting his eyes say far more to her than "thank-you" for the way she was treating Nathan.

* * *

When they reached the Fort Cobb Agency, again Travis left them camped nearby while he scouted the conditions in the area. He had not been gone ten minutes before Rana began questioning Nathan about this mysterious, enchanting man with whom she believed her destiny was entwined.

When Nathan discovered that Travis had divulged part of his past to Rana, he assumed it would be all right for him to reveal more facts to her. After all, he decided, they would be living together in the same house. Too, he had dreams of bringing these two young people together, for he could not imagine a better match for either one. He sensed they were being drawn to each other, and that pleased him, though he had no doubt their attraction intimidated the carefree Travis, who had a history of bad luck with women.

Nathan related what he knew about Travis's experiences with the Hunkpapas and described the incident that had brought him and Travis Kincade together, including details of Elizabeth Lowry's treacherous role in their meeting. He was not surprised when Rana asked for more information about the two women who had caused Travis to display such a grim attitude toward the female sex. As Travis had instructed, he avoided an explanation of Travis's relationship with Clarissa Caldwell, for Travis had felt she might drop innocent, though dangerous, clues to Harrison and his daughter when they eventually met.

Nathan and Rana discussed Travis's life in the Hunkpapa camp and on the ranch. Clearly she was fascinated by his adopted son. When finally they had exhausted the subject of Travis Kincade temporarily, Nathan saw the perfect opportunity to relate more information about Rana's father.

"Why did my mother marry such a wicked man?" she probed after listening intently to Nathan's words.

"I wish I knew, child. I guess love is one of those mysteries of life. Sometimes we don't use wisdom to pick the person we love. I remember when I first saw my darling Ruth," he murmured dreamily. "She was the prettiest girl I had ever laid eyes on. I couldn't think about anything until she was mine. Whenever I left on a roundup or cattle drive, I couldn't wait to get back home to my Ruthie. I hated for us to be separated, especially for months at a time. I wish you could have known your grandmother, Rana. If she hadn't died so young, your mother would have had someone to keep her straight. I should have remarried, 'cause I didn't know much about raising little girls. Sometimes it's hard to believe they're both gone forever," he mused dejectedly.

As Rana touched his arm and smiled comfortingly at him, Nathan ventured, "Maybe how I felt about Ruthie was how my Marissa felt about your father. It's a shame he was so bad. All he wanted was my ranch and money; that's why he married her. Some men are just plain greedy and evil, and they'll do anything to innocent young girls to get what they want. I tried to keep her from marrying him. I begged her to marry Todd Raines; she had been seeing him for a few months and had seemed to like him. I guess I was wrong about their feelings. She told me she didn't want to marry a poor wrangler. She knew I would have made Todd my partner if they'd married, so that wasn't the real reason she refused his proposal. She just up and ran off with that fancy gambler and crushed poor Todd's heart. If she hadn't, she would be alive today. And if Travis hadn't come along, Todd would have his place in my life now. He's still real special to me." He paused for a moment, lost in thought. "If Travis had been around, Marissa wouldn't have looked at another man. 'Course the marriage wasn't all bad." Nathan beamed as his eyes washed over Rana. "They had you, my precious little Rana. Lord knows I wouldn't take anything for you. I'm so glad I got you back."

"So am I, Grandfather," she agreed, then kissed his cheek.

Nathan declared that it was time he took a nap in order to be ready for his guard duty later that night, and as he settled into sleep, Rana watched him with deep affection. She noticed the way the dappled sunlight filtered through the trees and illuminated his blond and silver hair. His skin was leathered and lined from age and exposure to the elements, but he was still a striking man. She recalled how his gray-blue eyes filled with warmth and love and glowed with happiness each time his gaze settled on her, and she was glad fate had returned her to her family. This older man needed her sunshine in his life, sunshine that she was determined to provide for the rest of his days.

Rana had come to realize that he and Travis were right about her having no future in the Oglala lands, but she ached over the hardships she knew her adopted people would endure. Yet, as Travis had told her, there was nothing she could do to keep the Lakotas from their destiny except suffer and die along with them, which would have been her fate if she had insisted on remaining in the Dakota Territory. She hoped she could return one day to visit them, especially Lone Wolf and Myeerah. She would pray for their survival and hope they could change with the times as she had, as she was determined she would.

She was looking forward to her new life on the ranch and to winning the heart of Travis Kincade, for he warmed her soul with a strange radiance that could only be love. As she considered Travis in this light, speculations about her parents invaded her thoughts. How she wished she had known them, or could remember them. Her lack or loss of memory made her feel that something special was missing from her life. But she knew that if she worked hard, Nathan Crandall and Travis Kincade could fill the void.

Rana was giving Travis more thought than she had ever given anything in her life. She knew they could offer each other more than a physical attraction, and she prayed he would recognize that truth and surrender to it, as she was doing. They could make a good pair—fighting, working, living, and loving, side by side. She understood that his luck with women had been bad, but that could change if he would only allow it. He was skittish and wary. She needed to be patient with him, to show him she was not like those other women, who had used and hurt him. She didn't want him to feel trapped, or to claim her out of guilt.

She envisioned his handsome body, which had been scarred by so many troubles. Worse, his heart had been scarred deeply as well. His enticing body, though healed, would always carry reminders of those tragic events, but his heart could recover if he permitted her to tend it with the medicine of love. He had not expected to become entangled with her. She dreamily recalled their passionate night together, which had made her long to share many more. Perhaps he had confessed more than he had intended that night and now regretted his candor. At least she was confident that she was not in competition with another woman, dead or alive. But, she asked herself, which would be easier to battle, a real woman or painful ghosts from his past? Still, with these facts in her possession, she could understand him and better plan her winning strategy . . .

Later that night, while Travis was taking his watch, he attempted to force his thoughts from the girl who was sleeping by the campfire, for she was a powerful distraction. He could not forget how she had smiled at him upon his return that evening. She had laughed and chatted with Nathan, and with him. All afternoon he had been eager to get back to camp just to be near her, and his body had ached for hers then, as it did now. He truly enjoyed talking with her, looking at her. Her smile warmed him all over, and her voice made him quiver. He could think of nothing more pleasant than holding her in his arms while they shared their inner-most secrets and desires, unless, of course, it was making love to her. Yet, he couldn't move too swiftly with her, or she might think he wanted more from her than her love. He had to be careful around her, for they couldn't carry on a secret affair under Nathan's nose; that would have been wrong.

He had never seriously considered marriage before meeting her; now he thought about it constantly. She was causing him to experience a wide range of emotions, filling his head with hopes and dreams. And it seemed he was having the same effect on her. Was she as scared as he was about making a permanent commitment to another person? Was she just as afraid to trust him completely and risk total surrender? Would it make a difference to her, now or later, that he was a "despicable half-breed"? What if she met and wanted another man after they reached home? What if she craved a wild life, as her mother had? That would break Nathan's heart, and his too, if he allowed it. He had been independent for so long before taking on the responsibility of Nathan Crandall; now he was seriously considering adding Rana Michaels to his list of priorities, if she permitted him to do so. First, he had to make certain that this was what he wanted and needed, and she would have to do the same. She could win any man she set her sights on, and he wanted her sights on him! Where was that willful, defiant, arrogant girl others had described? How had she changed so quickly, so completely? It had taken him years! Whatever decision he made about Nathan's granddaughter, it would be a permanent one, and he vowed it would be made wisely and cautiously, and with her agreement.

In less than a week they would reach home. He would have to give her time to adjust to her new life and to the people in it. He would have to let her find herself, and he prayed she would also come to understand him. He could not get it out of his mind that they were joined, yet he was very much aware that if he staked a claim on her, he would have to be ready to back it up with a white man's marriage. In her camp, she had not wanted to marry because the cost would have been her freedom, which she prized so highly. In her new life, she could have both, whether or not her choice of a mate included him. Lord help them all if she was only seeking amusement or revenge on him. No, he refuted mentally, his Rana would never do that.

Feeling somewhat more confident, he stood and stretched, then left the campfire to scout the surrounding area.

Rana rolled to her back and sighed restively as her talks with Nathan swirled inside her head to inspire bad dreams. The black-haired man was chasing her again and spewing forth threats and crude language. For a time, all she could do was watch the terrifying action, but suddenly his words became clear. He was shouting, "You're the lowest kind of woman alive! You didn't care whose bed you crawled into, just so you got yourself diddled good. I know all about that bastard and the woods colt he sired. You mess with me, woman, and I'll tell everyone your foul secret. That little piece of information is worth a fortune, and you're gonna get it for me. You don't want your pa or that kid learning what a wicked slut you are. If I told what I know, your old man wouldn't give you a nickel and he would take that kid away from you. You ain't fit for nothing but giving men pleasure and earning money to keep my mouth shut. You try anything foolish and it's all over."

Rana shifted to her side as she subconsciously tried to block out the painful scene, but another one quickly filled her mind: "This is your last chance. I ain't gonna have nobody ruining my plans. You fool, you know who Fargo works for and I know who you been dawdling with behind my back! He can't help you, girl. He only wants what you owe him . . . You're coming with me today, and if you open your mouth, I'll fill his ears and watch all of you suffer. He'll despise you, and you'll never get a cent from him. If I toss you out, how will you and that brat live? You'd best be glad you two got me to see after you. I could stomp the Crandall name into the mud if you give me a mind to. Get your things. If this visit didn't soften him up, nothing will. Just give him a month or two, then we'll . . ."

Rana squirmed to her other side and snuggled into the furry mat. She watched the flaming-haired girl with tear-filled eyes leave the room; yet she could still see and hear the frightening man with his narrowed brown eyes. She watched him stalk toward her and could feel herself backing away from him in panic. She hated him and feared him, for he was evil and cruel. He glared at her and ordered, "Get your things packed for the last time, girl. I've found me a way out of this mess. I'm gonna have it all, and then some. Yep, me and that little dark-haired vixen are gonna take it all. Yep, we're gonna have us a real spread with no problems to bother us. She's a greedy, wicked little bitch, but I can use her help." He laughed, then pointed to a small picture of someone who appeared very much like her. "One day you're gonna be prettier than she is, but you won't be no stupid whore. Yep, little brat, you're gonna get me everything I want from your pa. Maybe when you get a little older, I might want more, since you ain't . . ."

Rana almost whimpered in her sleep as she resisted the dreams that seemed determined to haunt her. She could see this woman who looked so much like herself packing clothes in a box. For some reason she put a *wanapin* and a baby inside a tall wooden hole and closed it. Then she looked across the room and said, "No more fear or running. No more lies about me. No more degradation and threats. No matter what happens, it must end. I'm going to kill him; then we can be free and happy. I'll never let anyone or anything harm you again, my love. Once he's dead, the truth will be buried forever. I've been a coward too long and he's nearly destroyed me. Nothing can be worse than living this hell, not even the truth. God forgive me for what I've done, but it was a mistake, my love, a terrible mistake. Surely I've paid enough for it. Once it's done, I'll come home. Home . . ."

"Rana," Travis whispered as he shook her gently. "Rana, wake up." He watched her fight the nightmare, though she resisted awakening. He was baffled by the words he had overheard, yet he had a gut feeling that Rana was repeating words she had heard her mother say long ago. He wondered how she had remembered them so clearly and if she would recall them when she was awake. Evidently, if this was more than just a bad dream, he had been mistaken about Marissa Crandall Michaels. He wished he knew what the "lies, threats, and secrets" were. It seemed Raymond Michaels had had an awesome hold over Marissa if she had hated and feared him enough to plan his murder, one that fate had not allowed. Oddly, he felt sorry for Nathan's daughter, for something terrible had ruined her life. He wondered if anyone alive knew her secret.

Rana stirred and opened her eyes to look upon the smiling face of Travis. She was trembling and her eyes were moist. His gaze and touch were so tender, and she needed tenderness desperately. She refused to think about the dark dreams, which were becoming hazy now. Instead her hands rose, encircled his neck, and pulled his head down to seal their lips. She allowed him to fill her senses, to chase away her fears. When their lips parted, she murmured, "I need you, Travis. Will you hold me?"

Something in her gaze and voice exposed the depth of her need at that moment. He lay down beside her, pulled her into his arms, and rested her head against his shoulder. Cradling her like a small child, he stroked her hair. She nestled closer to him and sighed peacefully. Travis held her until she was sleeping again, this time without dark dreams. Even then he did not want to release her. It all felt so right as he lay there beneath the stars with her in his arms and his friend Nathan slumbering nearby, as if he had everything of importance within his reach. He somehow knew no peril would befall them tonight, for *Wakan Tanka* had brought them together and was watching over them. He embraced her tenderly, closed his eyes, and drifted off to sleep.

Three days later, they approached the Red River, which separated Texas from Indian Territory. It was Thursday, the twenty-seventh of June, and they expected to arrive home by Saturday. Fortunately they had not encountered any problems in Indian Territory, and they shared the excitement and joy of reaching home within two days.

Travis instructed, "I want you two to stay here while I check the current and woods on the other side. When it's all clear, I'll signal you to follow. Take it slow and easy, 'cause the river's high and fast."

Travis urged his horse into the water until it was deep enough for the animal to swim. His gaze scanned the distant bank for any sign of danger. While Rana and Nathan watched and waited, Travis and his mount gradually made their way toward the other bank, angling downriver slightly because of the strong current. Just as they reached the other side, a man jumped from behind thick bushes and fired his rifle at Travis. The bullet struck him across the left temple. Rana screamed as Travis fell backward into the swirling water and briefly disappeared beneath its fast-moving surface. As his ambusher tried to seize the stallion's reins to steal him, the horse reared and pawed, knocking the villain to the ground. The highly trained beast trampled the man's legs and arms as he yelled and vainly attempted to scramble free.

Rana's gaze strained to locate Travis in the water. Finally she sighted him bobbing along with the swift current, dazed and helpless. She shouted to Nathan, "I'm going after him! Wait here and watch for more attackers." Before Nathan could react or speak, she kneed her horse into a rapid gallop along the riverbank to get ahead of Travis. When she had covered enough distance, she urged the animal into the water and guided him to the center, where Travis was being swept toward her. With skill and in desperation, she placed the horse in Travis's watery path. When he reached her, she grabbed his shirt and pulled on it with all of her strength. It was a fierce battle, for the current was powerful and greedy, wanting to keep the handsome treasure for itself. Her hand cramped, but she refused to release her grip. Pain shot through her fingers and up her arm at the strain. The water yanked at Travis's body and she feared she would not be able to hold on to him.

Rana prayed for the strength and skill to save this man she had come to need so desperately. Her horse was also panicking and she tried to comfort and steady him with soothing words. She could tell the animal was having a difficult time struggling against the river's pull and their combined weight. She had to maintain control of the animal and her seating because she knew she could not swim to the side with Travis and, if she released him, he would surely drown. "Come on, little horse, you can make it," she encouraged the frightened animal. "That's it. Don't be afraid. Not much farther. You must help Rana, little horse. Rana will take care of you. That's a good horse," she declared, urging him onward.

Clinging to the pommel with one hand and holding Travis's head above water with the other, she prodded the horse toward the bank. Tears of pain and panic flowed down her cheeks, for she gravely doubted she could succeed. "Please help us, Great Spirit," she prayed urgently, for she knew all would be lost if she let go of Travis. She was overjoyed when her frantic prayer was answered, for the horse suddenly seemed to feel a burst of energy and strength and fought the current valiantly.

Yet it seemed as if they would never reach the other side, though this had been her only alternative when she had been unable to turn the animal around in the midst of the swirling river. She glanced down at the man whose unconscious body was pulling mercilessly on her aching arm. The attacker's bullet had torn through his headband, and she saw blood soaking it and his hair as it streamed down the side of his handsome face and neck to be absorbed by his shirt. She saw his nostrils moving steadily, indicating that he was breathing, and she wanted to pull him into her arms and cover his face with thankful kisses. Her desire went unfulfilled for the moment, for the danger had not yet passed.

Hurriedly Rana focused her gaze on the bank to make sure they were drawing nearer without drifting too far downriver. She clenched her teeth in grim determination as Travis seemed to get heavier and heavier by the second and her arm weaker and weaker. She was nearly in a state of panic by the time the horse struggled to climb out of the water. Exhausted, the animal staggered and slipped in the mud. Once his head cleared the edge of the water, she carefully released her grip on Travis and hopped off the horse, quickly tying his reins to keep him from running off. She returned to Travis and yanked on his arms until she had his upper body out of the river. Breathing erratically, she dropped to her knees beside him and called his name several times. She stroked his face, then leaned forward to kiss him. He did not awaken. She tore a strip from her sopping dress and, after removing the torn headband and stuffing it into her pocket, she bound his wound.

Having disregarded her frantic words and having crossed the river upstream in the same area that Travis had traversed, Nathan rode up, with Travis's horse in tow. He quickly dismounted and joined Rana, who was fretting over the fallen man. He gingerly removed the bandage, checked Travis's injury, then replaced it. He sighed loudly in relief. "It's just a graze, Rana. He'll be fine. Let's get him on the bank. Far as I can tell, there was only one bushwhacker, and Travis's horse took care of him."

As they worked, Nathan remarked proudly, "That was a brave and reckless thing you did, girl, but you moved and thought quickly. You worried me silly taking off like that. I knew I couldn't catch up with you two in the river; she's moving too fast. After seeing you in action before, I figured you could save him, so I hightailed it over here to help you get him out of the water. That was some rescue."

They laid Travis in a grassy area and collapsed on the ground to rest. Nathan commented to break their tension, "Lordy, he's heavy. How in heaven's name did you hold on with the river yanking on him?"

Rana smiled and replied mischievously, "I knew you would beat me if I lost your ranch foreman, and we would have been forced to do his work, Grandfather. He is our scout, so we need him." She reached behind herself to rub her complaining back near her waist, flexed her aching shoulders, then lay flat to appease her fussing body and to slow her respiration to a more normal level. She held up her left hand and gazed at her bleeding, throbbing fingertips where three of her nails had been torn loose at the quick. Tears filled her eyes, but she tried to contain them.

Travis started coughing and stirring. Rana and Nathan moved to either side of him immediately. His eyes opened to find them leaning over him with worried looks. He remembered being shot and falling into the water. He found he was soaked from head to foot, and his head was pounding. He touched the bandage and gingerly examined his left temple, though the pain caused him to wince as he assessed the extent of his injury. He knew he was lucky, for he realized it was merely a flesh wound that had struck him at just the right angle and speed to render him unconscious. He was fortunate that he hadn't drowned and that his two companions were safe. He eyed Nathan, who was wet from the hips down, then Rana, who was nearly as soaked as he was except for her hair. She seemed on the verge of tears and he tried to sit up, but Nathan's hand on his shoulder prevented it.

"You lie still, son. We're trying to stop the bleeding. You scared ten years off my life, and I ain't got none to spare," Nathan teased to ease his tension.

"What about that snake in the bushes? Was he alone?" Travis inquired sullenly, rankled with himself for getting ambushed.

"Apache did him in good, and I didn't see anybody else. Just a no-good horse thief. You rest awhile," Nathan advised.

As Nathan described the incredible rescue, Travis's gaze went to the drenched Rana, whose expression revealed pain. He noticed how tense and pale she was and how she was bravely trying to conceal something. One hand was clasped tightly in the other one, and blood was seeping through her fingers. Not only had he been rescued, but this slip of a girl had done it and at great risk to herself.

Travis insisted on sitting up. He reached for Rana's left hand and pried it free of the other one as she lowered her gaze to avoid meeting his. He had ripped off a single nail before, so he knew how badly she was hurting with three gone. Glancing at the front of his shirt, he realized it was her blood staining it, not his, just as he realized how difficult his rescue had been for her. Considering the rapid action she had taken and the anguish she had endured, she had to be the bravest and most generous woman alive. She had given no thought to her own peril and had not quit when the task had become arduous. She had literally saved his life! She was amazing, unique.

Her hand quivered in his and felt cold. Blood oozed around the ragged edges of her missing nails and raw flesh was visible. He recalled his Indian training for such injuries and that Lone Wolf had given him a *pezuta wopahte* in case it was needed on the trail. "Nate, get that medicine bundle for me. I need to take care of Rana's hand."

Travis's grip was warm and gentle, and it caused her to tremble. She was all too aware of her grandfather's presence as Travis eyed her hand and grimaced, sharing her pain. He asked why she had not told him she was hurt. She tried to pull her hand free as she softly remarked, "I will wash it and tend it. You must rest. The trail is dangerous and we have need of our scout. Do not worry over me," she urged, though what she really wanted was to fling herself into his arms and cover his face with kisses.

A half smile teased at one corner of his mouth and brightened his eyes. "Like you didn't worry over me when I was being swept away by that greedy river?" he hinted roguishly as he caressed her cheek. "From the way it's been looking, you make a better scout than I do."

She debated instantly, "We do not blame you for a tiny mistake. No man is perfect, Travis Kincade, and you must learn to accept this fact. Grandfather wants only your best, and you give it to him. Do not punish yourself for deeds that do not belong to you."

Travis eyed her strangely, for he found many interpretations in her words. Nathan handed him the medicine bundle suddenly and Travis's attention was momentarily diverted from Rana, who was able to recover her poise. "Pass me that canteen, Nate. Rana's hand needs a good washing so I can see what I'm doing." He looked overhead and added, "It's getting late; we might as well camp here for the night. Why don't you start us some supper while I tend to Rana; then we can turn in early. I think we're all tired and jumpy. When I finish, I'll scout around. Maybe I should take your granddaughter with me; she's a fearless warrior and a skilled hunter. If I come across another bushwhacker or get dizzy from this injury, I might need her protection or help."

Rana watched Travis closely and it did not appear to her that he was making a jest. His smoldering gaze inflamed her all over and his voice was as effective as a passionate caress. She was surprised he did not seem irritated at having been rescued by a woman, as she had feared. She watched him tend her fingers so lovingly, so gently. Every so often as he doctored and wrapped each finger separately, he would look up at her to ask if he was hurting her or if a bandage was too tight. His eyes twinkled with merriment as he began to massage her sore arm, then shifted behind her to move onward to her shoulders, neck, and back. She tried to tell him she was fine, but he insisted on continuing his stimulating actions, and she had to admit they felt wonderful and relaxing.

When Nathan walked off to search for wood, Travis leaned forward to murmur, "You should get out of those wet clothes and shoes, Rana. If the night air becomes chilly, you might catch cold. Besides, I'm sure they're uncomfortable. I'll stand guard while you change," he offered politely.

When she turned to respond, her shoulder brushed against his. Their bodies seemed so close and their gazes locked. Travis's right hand slipped behind her head and drew it close to his so he could fuse their lips in a much-needed kiss. When they parted, his eyes helplessly roamed her lovely features. He kissed hers shut to halt their magical, hypnotic pull. "Thanks for saving my miserable life, Rana. Go change clothes before I forget we aren't alone and I have your grandfather wanting to kill me."

Rana opened her eyes to gaze at him. She smiled and replied, "I wish we were alone, *mihigna;* then you could thank me better." She stood up, ignoring how the wet garment clung to her blazing body. She went to her pack of possessions, removed dry clothing, and headed into the trees to find a place to change. She could feel his hungry gaze feasting ravenously on her body, and she thrilled to the sensations he inspired.

Travis glanced in the direction Nathan had taken to search for firewood. He scolded himself for thinking even briefly about following Rana and making her words—"my husband"—a blissful reality. With Nathan around, they lacked the necessary time and privacy for another joining of bodies, a joining that was certain to happen again soon, for the bond between them was getting stronger each day. He went to his horse to retrieve his own dry clothing, then sought one other source of comfort. Withdrawing a bottle of whiskey from his saddlebag, he took a long swig from it. After replacing it, he gazed longingly at the area into which Rana had vanished, then cursed his bad timing as he changed clothes.

After they had eaten, an exhausted Nathan drank freely from the whiskey bottle to release his own tensions and worries, finally draining it under Travis's watchful eye. The older man then reclined on his bedroll and was soon sleeping deeply. When Travis glanced at Rana, her keen gaze was leaving Nathan's slumbering body to look at him. Their eyes met and spoke messages of intense longing.

Travis's gaze roved her enticing features and he warned himself to curb his perilous thoughts, for her expression told him she was thinking along the very same lines. He glanced at Nathan again and was assured the man would not awaken until morning. Even with him lying there, they seemed enveloped in a smoldering solitude. He went to kneel beside Rana to whisper, "I need to scout the area before we turn in. Besides, I need some fresh air and exercise or we're in trouble," he teased in a mellow voice, his green eyes twinkling.

Rana smiled and caressed his cheek. She was delighted when he bent forward and kissed her hastily before leaving the clearing. She looked at the slumbering

Nathan again, then toward the forest. Could she brazenly seduce him? She grinned. After a short time, she lifted her blanket and walked to the edge of their camp. She boldly removed her shirt and dangled it invitingly over a bush. A few feet away, she removed one boot and discarded it, then another as she moved along the path. Next, she left her pants and, lastly, her bloomers hanging on bushes to create a provocative trail to her. She spread the blanket and lay down on it, awaiting his arrival and his reaction. The night air wafted over her naked body, but it failed to cool its heat. She closed her eyes in anticipation.

"Do you know how dangerous this is?" Travis murmured as he joined her, having collected her belongings and deposited them nearby with his own. He knew this was the meaning of the message that had passed between them, and he could not resist challenging any evil or peril to have her.

"There is danger in all things, but reward in few," she replied, pulling his head down to fuse their lips.

Travis's mouth explored hers in a long, stimulating kiss. Her arms encircled his neck as his kisses seemingly branded her mouth, face, and throat as skillfully as he might brand a newborn calf or colt. Gradually all restraint left them and they clung together, quivering in each other's embrace. Each could feel the other's naked body pressing closer and closer until no space was left between them. His arms tightened around her possessively as their mouths meshed.

Travis leaned away from her to stare into her compelling eyes. Leisurely his gaze roamed her face and he marveled at her beauty, becoming inflamed at the glaze of passion in her eyes. His hand drifted into her hair, enjoying how it felt surrounding his fingers. He knew their time was limited, but, for now, all he wanted and needed was to look at her, to touch her, to feel her next to him, to absorb her surrender. He knew she was here in his arms willingly and trustingly, and that knowledge caused his spirit to soar and his heart to beat swiftly. His mouth came down on hers again, tasting her sweet desire and eagerly seeking her unbridled response. He claimed her with skill and resolve.

Rana was dazed with love and hunger for Travis. He caused her to flame and quiver all over, and she reveled in these feelings. He took control over her life, her will, her emotions. His hands moved over her flesh, tantalizing her to heightened desire. Her body seemed to urge her talented lover to invade and conquer it. So many wonderful sensations attacked her simultaneously. Her hands began to travel up and down his back and she writhed on the blanket, revealing her rising need for him.

Slowly, dreamily, Rana's fingers drifted over his sleek flesh and increased his yearning for her. Muscles bulged here and there to tempt her hands to explore them, for they revealed such strength and beauty. She felt his respiration quicken and his body shudder. She loved the feel of his flesh against hers. Hunger stormed her body and demanded feeding. Pressing closer to him, she moaned softly.

Her responses caused him to become bolder with his actions. He was sensitive and vulnerable to her every movement. His whole body burned and pleaded to fuse with hers, but he would not rush their joining. He wanted to invade her very soul and claim it as his own. The first night they had relented to passion's calling and it had been wondrous; tonight their lovemaking was sheer bliss. His hand traveled down her flat stomach and teased along her silky thighs, using long, gentle strokes, each one coming closer to her womanhood. Finally he touched that secret place, sending her world spinning with pleasure. It was ecstasy; it was rapturous torment. He wanted her to enjoy this experience to the fullest. His hands and tongue prepared her and tempted her to take him greedily and without reserve.

When he had stimulated her to the point where her body was pleading feverishly for appeasement, he slipped between her thighs and eased within her, where she greeted him with urgency and delight. He moved slowly and seductively within her receptive body, rhythmically creating a wildfire that threatened to consume them. Her breathing became erratic and her head thrashed from side to side as he brought her to the edge of conquest, then lovingly held her there to savor the wild and wonderful pleasure before carrying her over the peak.

Rana took him within her with an intensity and hunger that was exciting and stirring, and soon she had created a turbulent, wild fervor that could not be contained. As his thrusts increased in speed and purpose, she titillated him with caresses and responses that heightened his fiery desires. Their bodies were working as one, taking and giving and sharing sweet bliss.

Travis placed lingering kisses on her face and throat and shoulders, each one more possessive and tender than the last. His shaft was like a flaming torch that cried out for a merciful dousing, mercy he did not truly wish or allow. He drove into her time and time again, each stroke a blend of ecstasy and torment. She was responding to him instinctively, fiercely. When her legs draped over his and she matched his pace and urgency, he feared his control was in danger.

Rana could no longer deny her body what it craved, no matter how much she wanted to continue savoring these sensations, and she lacked the knowledge to control and pace her passions. She clung to him and kissed him savagely as her body seemed to explode into many flames and overwhelming feelings. She stiffened slightly and hugged him tightly to her.

Travis knew her release was devouring her and he unleashed his restraint to join her, allowing them to experience the sheer delight of each other and indescribable pleasure together. They rode the stallion of rapture locked in each other's arms until the wild beast was tamed and exhausted. Moisture covered their bodies and their breathing was labored. Hearts beating as one, they remained entwined until all sensation had been drained.

A tranquil afterglow surrounded and relaxed them. They snuggled together, silent for a time as the reality and meaning of this union washed over them, cooling their sated passions and sealing their bond.

Rana shifted her head to gaze into his placid expression. "I hope you are not angry with me for tempting you again. My hunger for you was so great I could not master it."

Travis responded huskily in the Lakota tongue, "I have chosen you to share my life-circle. I am your protection. I am your provider. You are mine, and I will be all things to you, as you must be all things to me. My word of honor is yours until death."

Rana's eyes misted as he tenderly repeated the stirring words from their joining ceremony, repeated them as if he truly meant them this time. Her heart overflowed with joy and love. "You are all things to me, and I am yours until death. You are the one true man who can tame the wild wind, for I do not wish to battle you or resist you."

"When we reach home, there are many things to be settled between us, Rana. I need you and I want you, but I have important matters to handle first. Trust me and wait for me," he entreated.

"Do what you must until you can come to me with an open heart."

It was very late, but they made love a second time with a tenderness and passion that entwined their hearts and sealed their destinies as one. Afterward, Travis suggested they freshen up and return to camp. They shared a quick bath and slipped back to the dying campfire, sleeping on separate sides of it to resist further temptation. From all appearances, Nathan had not stirred during their absence.

On the Circle C Ranch outside of Fort Worth, Clarissa Caldwell stared across the table at Mary Beth Sims, whose father, Clifford, owned a large hotel and fancy restaurant in town. Clifford Sims was one of the many men who owed her father heavily for several favors. Clarissa accurately suspected that her father had been discussing more than legal problems with their male guest, for this was the third time recently that Mary Beth and Clifford had been entertained in their home. It was not like her father to invite wives or children to his special dinners unless he had a lucrative purpose in mind. Clarissa knew that her father had been visiting and eating at Clifford's hotel regularly during the past few weeks, and by now she could tell that Harrison Caldwell was making crafty plans to obtain something he wanted. She recognized that covetous gleam in his eye and his anticipatory tone of voice.

Clarissa smiled deceptively as she scrutinized this woman who had obviously caught her father's attention, for he had been suspiciously secretive about his stealthy pursuit. He had not mentioned his plans for Mary Beth to her and had pretended that these dinners were part business and part social. She was certain they were not, at least not in the sense he had insinuated. She tingled with alarm and raged at his guile. Mary Beth Sims was not the kind of woman to become a man's mistress, not even a rich, powerful man like her father. Something was going on inside her father's head, something she did not like.

The green-eyed brunette was a pretty girl of eighteen who had a very shapely figure, one which her father had been eyeing furtively all evening. Harrison had been laughing and joking while the best foods and drinks were being served. He had slyly mentioned the many times he had saved Clifford's business and how he had been instrumental in getting Clifford elected to the town council. Clearly her father was preparing to call in those debts, and Mary Beth was intimately concerned.

From what she could see and hear as she observed the two men, Clarissa realized that Clifford was eager to please her father. Sims was smiling and joking easily, and cooperating fully with her father's desires. Evidently the manner of repayment was most agreeable to him. Perhaps the man had created a larger debt to Harrison than that of which she was aware, or he soon planned to increase that debt. Considering their positions and how much time and attention her father had given this girl lately, she concluded that his actions could be leading in only one direction: marriage.

Clarissa fumed as she recalled how her father had warned her to be on her best behavior each time the Simses had visited them. He was always complimenting the girl's looks and praising her wit, pretending she was the most fascinating creature alive. She wanted to laugh in her father's face for his ridiculous behavior and plans: a fifty-six-year-old man of his importance marrying a timid eighteen-year-old child! Whatever was the man thinking? she wondered angrily. After all these years of being a widower who came and went as he desired, why marry now and why this little thing? But of course, she decided peevishly, no wife would halt him from doing as he pleased.

Clarissa was aware of other facts that she doubted her father knew: Mary Beth was in love with Cody Slade, who worked for Nathan Crandall on the Rocking C Ranch, and the girl did not like Harrison in the slightest and felt ill at ease around him. Naturally Mary Beth was too much a lady and dutiful daughter to expose such feelings to either man, but Clarissa had seen how Mary Beth had glanced at Harrison when she had thought no one was watching. The girl's expression had been one of repulsion and fear. Clarissa wondered if Mary Beth was aware of what was going on before her eyes and behind her back. She also wondered if Clifford Sims would force his daughter to marry Harrison Caldwell even if she could not stand him, for evidently she could not. Yet she realized only too well that women naturally had little to say about their fates.

Clarissa lowered her head to smile spitefully as she envisioned this genteel girl refusing Harrison Caldwell's affection and proposal, as Marissa Crandall had done long ago. She could not help but imagine her father's rage and embarrassment if he were to learn how she had spied on him and Marissa years ago. The old buzzard had always underestimated her cunning and daring, and her hatred! she reflected angrily.

When she had been a child and he locked her in her room during Marissa's secret visits to his ranch, she would climb out her window, edge along the narrow balcony to his, and peek inside. Sometimes she had watched and listened for hours as the two had played in her father's bed. She had been mesmerized by their actions and the intense emotions that had flowed between them. By observing them, she had received vicarious pleasure and happiness and had savored her father's love. Little did her father suspect that he and Marissa had been the ones who had taught her all about sex and had inspired her greedy appetite. She could still remember how eager she had been to come of age and to find the courage to begin her own life of splendid enjoyment. Since her father had refused to give her love and attention, she had found plenty of men willing and eager to do so. Unfortunately, however, only Travis Kincade and Nathan Crandall had been man enough to stand against her father, and neither had become enchanted with her. But other men had loved her and desired her and had filled the void in her life, however briefly. As a child she had learned that her father did not love her or want her. She had done everything, anything, to capture his attention. His only reaction had been anger whenever she embarrassed him publicly. Yet he had not minded asking, or ordering, her to whore for him as Raymond had forced Marissa to do. What kind of father was that? she asked herself with a sneer. Her father was to blame for her behavior, for her misery, for her hatred! One day, she vowed, he would be sorry.

As the two men smoked their cigars and sipped their port and Mary Beth excused herself, Clarissa reflected on her father's past love life. She had to admit he was a handsome man and a superb catch, but she doubted he would be able to ensnare Clifford's daughter. No doubt Mary Beth would do what Marissa had done: reject her father and run off with another man; in Mary Beth's case it would probably be Cody Slade. Of course, Marissa's predicament had been vastly different from this girl's.

Clarissa knew why the blue-eyed enchantress had married Raymond Michaels: to get far away from this area so that her vile secret could be safeguarded. Poor Marissa had never imagined that a cheap saloon harlot would devastate her life with a favor and a betrayal of that favor. Nor had Marissa imagined she could not bewitch the handsome and charming gambler who had pretended to be madly in love with her in order to wed her for her money and status. Harrison had been away for months when Marissa had discovered she was pregnant; otherwise Marissa doubtlessly would have married him. If she had, the flaming-haired bitch would have fared far better than she had under Raymond's insidious hands.

She had despised Marissa for intruding on her life and for gaining a hold on her father's life and affection, a hold she had never possessed. When she had been a teenager and Marissa had returned home for visits, she had faked a friendship with the ill-fated vixen in order to find a way to destroy her. She had thought she had discovered how when she had learned of the hostility between Raymond and Nathan, for Raymond had always stayed in town while Marissa and her child had visited Nathan. She had found a clever way to meet Raymond and had sought her revenge by plotting to steal Marissa's husband, though she had remained ignorant of the couple's shocking relationship until she and the devilish gambler had begun a torrid affair. One night she overheard the sordid truth during a violent argument between Marissa and Raymond, and later confronted her lover; afterward they had shared secrets about Marissa. She had plotted with the handsome rake to get rid of Marissa and Harrison so they could marry and take possession of both ranches, using Marissa's past, present, and bastard child as their weapons. Clarissa tingled as she recalled the secret times she had made passionate love to Marissa's husband. She had hated Marissa even more for obtaining—no matter the reasons—one of the few men who had truly made her body and blood boil, for Raymond's matchless sexual prowess, abundant charms, and superb looks had been his greatest assets. If the Indians had not killed her dreams . . .

It was too late to fret over that annoying defeat. Thinking back on the whole situation, she was glad she had not become partners with Raymond Michaels, for at times he had been cruel and untrustworthy, very much like her father. Raymond had married Marissa before learning the truth about her, then had blackmailed her and made her whore to support him, just as her own father demanded she whore for him so that he might attain his diabolic ends. Marissa had married Raymond to escape her wanton trap, and Raymond had claimed to have married her for her wealth and position. Clarissa admitted she had been enamored for a time by the virile, handsome charmer, for he had had a winning way with women and had been intoxicating in bed, and perhaps his devious character had unconsciously reminded her of her father, whose love and attention she had craved yet had been denied. With her years of experience with men and life, she had learned how to handle and judge men and situations, at least most of them.

With Raymond, Marissa, and a saloon whore dead, she was the only one who knew the truth about her father's ex-mistress, though there appeared no way she could use or profit from that shocking information. She had never told her father, for she believed she might one day be able to twist that staggering truth and use it to her advantage. In time she would find a way to destroy her despicable, selfish father, as Marissa had been destroyed. Poor Marissa, she mused cruelly. She never knew the truth about her child's father, a truth that could have freed her from her nightmarish life with Raymond . . .

Clarissa thought about Marissa's last visit to the ranch shortly before her death. She had known Harrison had been up to something that day, so she had sneaked back to the ranch at night. She had witnessed the depth of his cruelty and the height of his infatuation for Marissa. What she had not known then about them or Marissa, she had learned that night as they had quarreled and battled. After Marissa's departure, she had watched her father gloat over his behavior and power and had overheard him talking to himself about his plan to murder Raymond so he could take possession of the flaming-haired witch, now that she had been properly punished for her past rejection. Determined to keep them apart, she had warned Raymond, a warning that had impelled him to flee to his death. At first she had been sad and sorry and had blamed her father; later she had calmly accepted the situation and had begun searching for another path to her victory. Looking back, she realized it would have been a careless mistake to have become partners with an untrustworthy beast like Raymond, especially since her father was steadily increasing holdings that would soon be hers alone.

After the Simses had departed, Clarissa looked at her grinning father and boldly questioned, "Papa, what do you want with a silly child like Mary Beth? I've seen the way you've been eyeing her. What are you planning?"

"Why, Clarissa Caldwell, you sound jealous," Harrison teased playfully. He realized he would have to tell her something or she might be prompted to interfere. "I've got plans for Miss Mary Beth Sims. When I take over the rest of this area, I'm going to need a proper wife to entertain my friends and clients and take care of me. Surely my daughter isn't going to be around much longer, not if she doesn't want to be called a spinster. You've got to start thinking about marriage and children. Since I'll be in need of a wife, she suits my purposes perfectly."

Clarissa argued, "Even when I marry, Papa, I can stay here to take care of you and the ranch. Who deserves to become the mistress of your new spread more than I do? I've worked just as hard as you to obtain it. Why not find a nice widow closer to your own age? I tell you, Papa, you're wasting your time and energy on her."

Harrison frowned. "Don't go telling me how to handle matters, girl. If you had done your part, Kincade would be on my side, you two would be married, and the Crandall ranch would be ours. They've been gone nearly two months. You didn't even know he was leaving, and you can't find out where they are. I'll make sure you get what's coming to you, so don't you worry none. As for my taking a wife, it isn't any of your concern or business. Surely you don't begrudge your dear father a little happiness and excitement with another woman. Pretty widow or not, I don't want any man's leavings. In case you don't have eyes, girl, I'm still a virile man, and sometimes I get itches stronger than yours. I want Mary Beth Sims to scratch them because she's pretty and young and innocent, and I can train her as I please. Your mother has been dead since '44, and I raised you all alone. Don't you think I get lonesome, and tired of using those cheap women in town?"

Clarissa wanted to shriek at him: *Like you trained that young and innocent Marissa?* but she restrained herself. "You misunderstand me, Papa," she guilefully protested. "Mary Beth has a sweetheart: Cody Slade, who works for Nathan Crandall. Even if you and her father try to convince her to marry you, I doubt she will. She loves Cody and plans to marry him. You don't want to be embarrassed by having her reject your proposal. Besides, she's such a fragile, timid creature. You need a woman with backbone, one who can stand at your side and help you run your holdings, a woman who knows how to take care of a home and a husband. Don't reach for the impossible," she entreated softly and slyly.

Harrison was vexed by his daughter's words and her attitude. "I don't care about Mary Beth's girlish feelings for Slade. She'll do as her father commands. You think Clifford would allow her to marry Slade when I've asked for her? Never. Once she gets settled in here, she'll do exactly as I say. It won't take long for her to realize how lucky she is to have married a wealthy and powerful rancher instead of a cowpuncher who can't earn in his lifetime what I spend in a year. She's got manners and breeding, and she's educated and charming. She's perfect for my needs, Clarissa, all of them. Besides, no wife of mine is going to refuse me anything or disobey me."

"Does she know that you and her father are discussing marriage?"

"Not yet. I'm giving her a taste of what I have to offer. Once I get my hands on Nate's ranch, then I'll reveal my plans for her."

"Are you sure her father will go along with you after she cries and begs to marry Cody? He loves his daughter. Surely he wouldn't force her to marry you."

"That's what you think, girl. Sims owes me plenty, and soon I'll have his neck in a financial noose. She'll do as I say, one way or another. You see, girl, her father's done a few things that the law will frown on if I choose to expose them. As his lawyer, I know all about him and his dealings. She'll agree, to keep her father from being hanged. That's something you should learn, Clarissa. Always have an alternate plan, and always know the strengths and weaknesses of your enemies and rivals. That's the only way you can succeed with your plans or defeat a foe. Just make sure you've got the guts and wits to stand firm once you make a decision to go after something or someone."

Clarissa decided she needed to learn what that "financial noose" was so that she could secretly tie it. Too, she would find some clever way to warn Mary Beth or Cody about her father's devious plan. If those two could elope before her father staked his claim on Mary Beth, it would halt his scheme. She did not want another woman in her house, especially one who could give her father a child and give her an unwanted rival for his inheritance. No matter what she had to do, she would prevent him from marrying before she could take all he owned, including his miserable life. If only Travis would return soon, she reflected, and she could find some way to win his heart and help. Women had ways of entrapping resisting men, and she vowed to use any or all of them if necessary.

Help, she mentally echoed, then smiled wickedly. If she were cunning and daring, she could beat her father at his own game with his own hirelings! If she played her cards right, as Raymond had once done, she would undermine the entire situation with the very men her father had hired to help him attain his goals . . .

—— *Chapter 11* ——

AFTER THEY HAD EATEN the next morning and were preparing to break camp, Rana handed Travis the red headband that she had removed the day before when tending his wound. "I will sew it for you later," she offered, pointing to the bullet hole. She tingled at his nearness and longed to embrace him on this new day.

Travis grinned and said, "Thanks for saving it; it's my lucky charm, or used to be. An Apache shaman gave it to me after I saved his hide. He told me to wear it every time I rode into Indian territory and the Great Spirit would protect me from all harm. It worked until yesterday when you had to save my hide," he remarked, then chuckled. His smile and laughter seemed to flow over her and coat her like warm honey, and she gave him her full attention. He observed how she was looking at him and how her cheeks flushed with desire, and his smile broadened. He wondered if she was aware of how potently she affected him. All it required to send his senses soaring was a smile, or a laugh, or a glance, or a casual touch. His blood raced inside his body as his igneous eyes roamed her features and his senses drank in her aura. Visions of her naked body lying beneath his in the moonlight filled his mind. He knew he would have to halt his fantasy, for his body was responding.

She noticed how tiny, golden brown flecks seemed to appear and dance in his green eyes when he was in a tranquil mood, a mood that caused her body to tingle and her heartbeat to increase. Little creases that suggested his sincerity and happiness teased at the corners of those entrancing eyes and deepened the lines near his mouth. He had shaved at first light and his strong jawline was now visible to her wandering gaze. She watched him remove his bandage to secure the red strip around his head, then fluff his sable hair over it, thick hair that seemed to fall into a natural part just off center and cause his wispy locks to settle in careful waves. Evidently he had used his sharp knife to keep his hair from growing too long on the top and sides or past the nape of his neck. She noted how his brows grew at an angle that gave him a devilish or arrogant look when he arched one or narrowed his leafy green eyes. His face was lean and his features well defined, as if carved by a loving and talented creator. She recalled that very little dark hair grew on his chest, not enough to conceal his scars or his muscled torso. With a smile, she debated, "It did not fail to protect you; you are alive. How did you meet this enemy shaman and save his life?" she inquired, snared by curiosity.

He did not hesitate before answering. "Years ago, I scouted for the Army for awhile, until I got tired of their lies and tricks. I was at loose ends; I didn't have any place to go or anything special to do. At the time, it seemed like a good way to learn about the white man and his world; you might say it was one of the safest ways for a half-breed to move around in dangerous territory without being trapped between two sides that hated each other. You see, Rana, whites despise half-breeds more than Indians, but they don't mind using them as trackers and scouts. At first, I didn't try to hide my mixed blood. I was too cocky and bitter to care what anybody said or thought about me. It didn't take long for me to realize how foolish that was. It caused me too much trouble; I was always having to fight or kill some man who couldn't let the matter pass. Not that I was really looking for friends or a home, though the truth would have made that impossible. That's the trouble with people; they judge you by the wrong measure and they're always looking for a way to use you to get what they want. Thing was, the Army needed my skills and Indian contacts, so they kindly overlooked my heritage," he said with a sneer, exposing his lingering resentment and the anguish he had endured since birth.

"On my last assignment, I was guiding four soldiers to a secret meeting with some Cheyenne chiefs. We came upon an Apache shaman who was on a vision quest. He was sitting on this big rock, praying and chanting for a message from the Great Spirit. The soldiers decided to have some fun, as they called it, with the old man. You see, soldiers love taking on defenseless Indians and collecting souvenirs."

She was delighted he was revealing part of his past and his emotions, though she realized how difficult it was for him to speak of these painful memories. She wondered if he was afraid she might think badly of his mixed blood and troubled past. When Travis grew silent for a time, Rana softly probed, "What happened?"

Travis looked her in the eye and calmly divulged, "I killed the bastards." When she did not appear shocked or distressed by his revelation, he continued, "I tried to talk them out of tormenting the old man and killing him, but they laughed and ordered me to stay out of it. I told them that it was bad luck to intrude on a vision quest and that the old man was harmless. The shaman just stood there with his eyes closed, chanting and waiting to die with courage and honor. I had no choice in the matter. When the battle was over, the old man smiled at me and nodded his understanding," he remarked casually, amazing her with how modestly he had revealed what must have been a fierce and dangerous battle against four soldiers and increasing her respect and admiration for him.

"The old shaman removed his headband, said a prayer over it, tied it around my head, and told me it would protect me from evil spirits. He said I could never die as long as I was wearing it. I sure am glad he didn't say I couldn't be defeated or injured, 'cause I would have known it was worthless and thrown it away a year later. He asked my Indian name, then carved those initials on a hunting knife and handed it to me. It had a thunderbird painted on the handle and he said I would receive power from it every time I used the blade. Somewhere a rattlesnake is carrying that knife and, when I find him, he's dead," he murmured coldly, his eyes glittering with hatred and desire for revenge as that infuriating betrayal and defeat flooded his mind.

"When he tried to give me his horse, I told him he was being too generous. He smiled again and said a man's life and honor were worth far more than a headband, knife, and horse. That's how I got Apache here," he told her, stroking the animal's forehead. "I don't know what the shaman whispered in his ear, but he won't allow anyone on his back but me, and I know he would give up his life for mine. He's gotten me out of many a scrape, like yesterday. He's mine until one of us dies." As if knowing his master was speaking highly of him, Apache nuzzled the side of Travis's head and brought a smile to his lips.

"How did you lose the knife?" she inquired, aware of how important those belongings and that episode were to him.

For an instant, he tensed, then forcibly relaxed his hard body. "I didn't. I was ambushed by two cutthroats when I was twenty. After they tortured me, they stole everything I had but Apache. He wouldn't let them near him. For months he had rope burns on his neck from trying to get free to save my life." Travis remembered the pistol he had been wearing that fateful day, one he had taken off a gunslinger who had challenged him to the death, a pistol that had revealed the man's prior victories in gun battles in the tiny stars notched on its butt.

Rana glanced at the animal to discover that the scars Travis had described were still visible if she looked closely. "Why did they not steal your *wanapin?*" she asked, wishing he would explain its significance, for a warrior's markings on his possessions and body told much about him. Delving into his dark past made him tense, she realized, so she probed lightly and gingerly and was ready to end the conversation the moment he desired it.

Travis absently touched the sacred token that had been carved and given to him by the legendary Sitting Bull. Only twice had it been removed from his neck —the day he had handed it to Buffalo Slayer to give to her if he did not survive his pursuit of Claude Chambers, and the day Lowry's hirelings had tried to steal it. Both times he had recovered it. "One of them cut it off, but he dropped it. Nate found it when he found me, half-dead. He took me to his ranch and brought me back to life, in several ways. That's how we met seven years ago."

"You searched for these men to slay them?" she pressed, acting as if she knew nothing of the circumstances.

"Yep, but their trail was too cold by the time I healed. The man who hired them had been murdered, so I couldn't beat any clues out of him or his . . . Nate was the first person who had accepted me and needed me since I had left the Hunkpapa camp, so I returned to the ranch to help him and stayed there. It took him years, but he settled me down. I owe him my life and loyalty, Rana," he explained pointedly. "I wouldn't want to do anything to disappoint or hurt him."

Rana watched him intently as he spoke so openly and sincerely. Every day, nearly every hour, he touched her heart more deeply. It was clear to her that he had endured a hard, painful life. She was glad he had been thrown together with her grandfather and cast into her life. "I am happy Grandfather found you and saved your life."

"Are you, Rana?" he asked, gazing into her liquid blue eyes.

She looked deeply into his before replying, "If not, he would not have found me and I would not be going home. The Great Spirit works in mysterious ways. He sent Grandfather to your side and sent you to find me to bring me home. All is as it should be."

"I'm glad you see things that way. I must admit you had me worried for awhile," he confessed, grinning at her.

"As you had me worried," she playfully retorted. "Have I not proven the bad tales about Wild Wind are false, or too great? The Oglalas did not understand how important it was for me to be as I am, to be all I am. You and Grandfather understand and accept me as Wild Wind or Rana. This makes me happy and thankful. You are good for me."

"Does this mean we can become friends now?" he hinted, allowing his appreciative gaze to wander over her from head to foot.

"We are friends, Travis Kincade, and more," she added. "I am sorry you suffered so much before meeting Grandfather, but it has made you as you are, a very special man who warms my heart. You carry the best of two bloods; be proud of both, for they are you. Promise you will never leave Grandfather and the ranch. They need you, as I need you. I will never reject you or scorn you. I am yours by choice. Lone Wolf was wise to make us join before releasing me to you."

Their gazes met and they exchanged smiles. Nathan joined them then and asked, "We ready to ride? I'm anxious to get home."

"So am I," Travis cheerfully concurred.

Rana smiled at her grandfather and nodded her agreement.

When they approached the ranch two days later, it was dusk, but they were filled with energy and anticipation. Travis and Nathan had been away for fifty-seven days; Travis and Rana had been joined for thirty-three, a fact that neither could ignore or wanted to forget.

Rana's eyes darted back and forth as the two men filled her ears with information about the ranch. As they rode under the arch, from which a large C resting on a rocker was suspended from a crossbar, her eyes grew wide with disbelief. Nathan claimed ownership for land as far as she could see and more. Fences snaked along the dirt road for miles, restraining many animals. She wondered how anyone could go hungry or be cold with so many animals, or fear any foe with so much power. It was difficult for her to comprehend the extent of Nathan's wealth and ranch. As they neared a large wooden dwelling, Nathan told her it was her new home and that he was eager to show it to her.

Not far away, she could see more wooden dwellings, which Travis told her were barns, work sheds, and bunkhouses, and he explained how each structure was used. The closer they rode to the neat settlement, the more noises she heard: men's laughter and singing, strange music, the lowing of cattle, and the neighing of horses. Travis related how Saturday and Sunday were the days the hands could relax from the week's work, with half of the men taking off Saturday and half taking off Sunday; this schedule was switched the next week, for there were chores to be done every day and the ranch could not be left unprotected. If a man had special plans, he could usually find another hand with whom he could swap days off or he could pay someone to work in his place. Usually the men would use the time to play cards or games or make music, and some would sing or dance. On Saturday, many would ride into town to visit and drink with friends who worked on this or another ranch. He did not tell her that many of them would go there to spend time with the women who worked at the Silver Shadow Saloon, as he had done on occasion. On Sunday, some would go to church or simply rest. Because it was now supper time, most of the hands had returned and were enjoying their last few free hours before preparing for the new week.

They dismounted near the house and Travis collected the reins to take the horses to the stable. Nathan instructed genially, "See if you can locate Cody while I show Rana inside. I need to know what's been going on during our absence, but I don't want the men crowding my granddaughter tonight. I'll introduce her around later."

Travis nodded, then smiled encouragingly at Rana before he walked toward the two men who were heading their way at a rapid pace. Out of her hearing range, they met and halted briefly as Travis spoke with them. The two men gazed past the handsome foreman to stare openly at the flaming-haired beauty who seemed a ghost to them. Travis chuckled as he led the men away and answered some of their questions. All he could think about was being alone with Rana, but he knew privacy would be difficult, for they would have to keep their love affair a secret for awhile. He knew he would have to settle this matter with the Caldwells before he could claim her. Travis asked the whereabouts of Cody Slade, the man they had left in charge of the ranch during their long journey; he and Nathan needed his report as soon as possible.

Rana observed their expressions before taking Nathan's arm to be escorted into her new home, a dwelling that now seemed vaguely familiar, though whether that familiarity came from her memory or from Nathan's talks she could not determine. Turning her full attention to the house, she noted that it was white with a long porch spanning the front on which had been placed six rocking chairs. Inside, Nathan intentionally began his tour to their left. She was shown an eating area that Nathan called a dining room, and a kitchen with a large pantry and side entrance. As they walked down connecting hallways that formed a *T*, Nathan pointed out three bedrooms—his, Travis's, and Marissa's old room, which would be given to her. At the door to this room Nathan remarked about the need to get her proper clothing as soon as possible. Next to her room at one end of the second hall was a bathing closet, which had been built for his beloved Ruth; at the other end of the hallway and next to Nathan's room was an office, where he did his bookkeeping. Lastly, they returned to the long front hall and entered a large but cozy sitting room with an enormous fireplace and decidedly masculine decor.

Intrigued, Rana glanced around and her gaze halted on the stunning portrait over the mantel. Nathan needlessly told her that the woman was Marissa Crandall Michaels, her mother. As Nathan placed the two paintings of Rana on either side of her mother's portrait, he murmured, "See how much you look like your mother? That's how I knew Wild Wind was my little Rana from the moment I laid eyes on these pictures."

Rana went to stand before the fireplace to study the image that had filled her dreams many times. There was no denying the obvious resemblance. She could hardly believe that the large portrait was not a likeness of her. As portions of her nightmares flashed before her mind's eye, she realized she had been dreaming about her mother; that the dark-haired villain had been attacking Marissa, not her. And if the woman in her nightmares truly was her mother, then the man must be . . . She forced such intimidating memories aside, for this was not the time or place to deal with them, and she hated to think that the cruel man in her nightmares had actually been her father.

Nathan was saying, "Rachel Raines does the cleaning, washing, and cooking for me and Travis. She's married to one of my best hands, Todd Raines. She comes in a few hours every day but Sunday to take care of us. It's a shame those two don't have any children; they're good folk." He shook his head and shrugged as he realized that Todd Raines could have been Rana's father if Raymond Michaels hadn't come along, or that he could have been his adopted son if Travis had not come upon the scene.

"You don't need a housekeeper asking you hundreds of questions and making you nervous, so I'll give Rachel a week or so off while you get settled here in privacy. I'm sure she's got plenty of canning and quilting to do; that's how she's helping Todd earn enough money to buy a little place of their own."

Nathan could tell Rana was nervous and that his chatter was distracting her, so he talked on. "Todd's away on the spring cattle drive with Mace Hunter. I think I told you Cody Slade has been looking after things while Travis and me went after you. Travis is my foreman and boss, but Mace and Cody usually take care of things for him. I've got me some good hands, Rana; you'll like my men. Only two of them are married; Todd and one of the Davis brothers. 'Course I suspect Cody will be getting hitched before winter. He's been seeing Clifford Sims's girl since summer last. Not many cowpunchers marry young. I guess because it's a hard, busy life. About five miles away I have four small houses that I rent to married hands for a small amount. That's where Todd and Rachel live, and the Davises, Darby and Lettie, with their passel of little ones. Darby's brother, Bart, works for me too, but he lives in the bunkhouse with the boys."

Rana smiled and commented, "You love your land and people very much, Grandfather. It will be good living here."

"Why don't you go to your room and get washed up and rested while Travis and me speak with Cody? We've been gone a long time and there's no telling what's been going on here. When we finish, we'll join forces in the kitchen and rustle up some chow."

Nathan filled a pitcher of water from the pump in the kitchen and carried it to her room, then showed her where the washclothes were kept. "If you need anything, Travis and me will be outside. Rest, or look around all you want. I love you, girl, and I sure am glad to have you home," he stated hoarsely, then embraced her tightly before rushing out the door.

Soon after, Travis entered Rana's room to find her standing before a closed window. When he called her name, she immediately whirled and looked at him as if she had been doing something wrong. "I brought your saddlebags and *par-fleches* so you could unpack and get settled while we talk with Cody. He escorted Rachel Raines to church and stayed over for Sunday dinner. I sent Bart Davis to fetch him." He glanced at her pitcher and noticed it was full of fresh water. "We'll have supper as soon as we finish our meeting with Cody. You need anything else before I leave?" he inquired, wanting nothing more than to remain at her side during this trying period. He wondered if memories, good or bad, were surfacing to haunt her. He knew about her past visits to the ranch, though she had been only a small child then.

While he was speaking, Rana picked up her *parfleches* and placed them in the corner of the room, as she had done in the tepee. To him, she appeared timid and apprehensive, and perhaps a little lost in the big room that he suspected she could not quite remember or did not wish to recall. As a baby or a small child, she had visited here only a few times, and many things had changed over the years. Progress had transformed much on the ranch and in the white man's world.

Travis wanted to pull her into his arms and cover her face with kisses. This privacy was too stimulating and tempting, and he was too cognizant of her allure and the big bed nearby. He dared not touch her in fear of losing his control, when someone could arrive at any moment and catch them. Here, no one knew of their Indian marriage, a union not recognized under white law. He could not tell anyone she was his wife, or be discovered treating her as such. Yet he no longer felt guilty about their involvement, even if he knew it was best to keep their relationship secret for awhile. He could not bear the thought of anyone thinking badly of her, or of Nathan believing he had taken advantage of his young grand-daughter. Twice he had made love to Rana behind Nathan's back, and he was not sure his friend and adopted father would understand his weakness. If it were another woman, perhaps; but Nathan's grandchild . . . Nathan would have expected him to have had the respect, loyalty, and strength to have waited. "Why don't you put your things in the chest?" he inquired, trying to stall his departure and help her relax.

"Chest?" She repeated the confusing word, then looked down at her own body, for she had forgotten the use of such furniture over the years. "I do not understand. Is it wrong to place them there?"

Since she seemed so nervous and sincere, Travis suppressed his amusement and retrieved her leather pouches. The room was almost as large as the entire tepee in which she had lived for ten years, and without furniture. No wonder she was baffled, he decided, certain that she would learn or recall such things. He placed the *parfleches* and saddlebags on the bed and opened them. Removing several items, he walked to the chest, opened the drawer, put the items aside, and closed it. Rana watched him quizzically, then her eyes grew wide as if she believed the wooden chest had devoured her belongings.

He patiently showed her how to use the chest and closet, promising to get her enough clothes to fill them, then explained about the bed and its covers. He refreshed her memory on the use of chairs, how to open and close windows for fresh air, the use of doors and curtains for privacy, the use of safety matches and lanterns for light, and the purpose of the chamber pot beneath her bed. Since these last instructions appeared to embarrass her, he quickly returned to the lantern to caution her about its safe use and to warn her about hot chimneys and broken glass, which reminded him to explain about the fireplace in her room, although it would not be needed until winter.

Rana followed Travis around the large room, watching and listening as he instructed her about her new surroundings. "It is easier to live in a tepee or outside," she remarked mirthfully.

Travis chuckled. "I'll show you how to use the bathing closet and kitchen later. We don't cook over open fires or fetch water from a stream, or wash our clothes and bathe in rivers. You've got lots of things to learn or remember, Rana, but Nathan and I will help you, so don't be intimidated by all these differences. Be patient with yourself; it'll take time and work, but you can do it," he encouraged confidently.

Her gaze softened. "You judge me very highly, and I am pleased. Your friends will wonder why Rana does not know such things. Will they laugh at me and tease you?" she asked worriedly.

"If anyone makes fun of you, I'll beat him senseless, or her. Just relax, 'cause Nate and I won't let anyone come near you until you've had time to learn your way around. We'll decide at supper what we're going to tell anyone who asks questions about you."

Rana's thoughts now matched Travis's earlier ones. She wanted to feel his arms around her and his lips on hers. She wanted to make passionate love and fuse their bodies into one. But this world seemed so strange and intimidating, and she needed to learn her way around it. She did not want to shame them with her ignorance or errors. She knew what whites thought about Indians, or people reared by them, or women enslaved by them. She was also aware that at any moment her grandfather or another could enter this wooden tepee and find them together, so she dared not reach out to him. She did not feel their relationship was wrong, but her grandfather might. She did not want him to become angry with Travis, or blame him. "Your sky is different," she said aloud. "I cannot read the time and season in it."

Travis smiled and stroked her hair, aware of her trembling and loosely leashed emotions. "I will teach you to read the sky over Texas, and I will teach you to read the white man's clock."

"Clock," she echoed, recalling pictures of them in the books that the teacher had guarded with her life. There was too much to learn and her family had been too kind to be fooled any longer, so Rana told Travis about the captive school-teacher and her past lessons. "If you help me, all the words and numbers will return. I will try to remember and speak as she taught me. It will be easier here where I do not have to go back and forth between English and Lakota. I wish you and Grandfather to be proud of me. I must stay in this . . . room until it is so."

Travis could not keep himself from embracing her. "You are a wonder, Rana Michaels. It's nice just being around you. Be yourself and everyone will love you, no matter how much or how little you know about the white ways. But don't rush things or they'll overwhelm you. This is all new to you; take it slow and easy. I won't let you suffer as I did."

Rana hugged him tightly. "Please help me not to shame my grandfather and my . . . you. Is it so that no one is to learn of our joining?" she queried, keeping her face nestled against his firm chest. His arms and words were so comforting, and his nearness tempting.

He tensed slightly and took a deep breath. "It must be our secret, Rana," he finally responded in a strained voice. "The whites do not accept Indian laws and customs; neither does Nathan. To him, we aren't married." He leaned back and looked into her upturned face. "Perhaps I have too much Indian blood and spirit, for it is not true with me."

When Travis heard Nathan calling him from the front porch, he gently set her aside and told her he would return later.

Rana cast a longing glance at his retreating back. She felt she could trust this man, and she hoped she could win his heart. She continued with her unpacking as he had instructed. In the bottom drawer of the tall chest she found her old doll, the one Marissa had hidden there before their fateful journey. She stared at it for a long time before lifting it and clutching it against her heart, as she had done that day long ago when Nathan had given it to her. Closing her eyes, she hugged the cherished treasure and rocked back and forth as several memories swirled around inside her head, and this time she did not try to halt them. Flashes of her last visit to the ranch, her terrifying travels with her parents, happy times with Nathan, and the receiving of this doll passed through her mind.

As if it had been a real baby, Rana lovingly snuggled the doll in her protective arms as tears rolled down her cheeks, for she remembered her mother now, just as she remembered how intimidating her father had been. She grasped Marissa's heart-shaped necklace and rubbed it between her shaky fingers. Because of Raymond Michaels's wickedness, the two precious possessions had been left behind. She recalled crying for the doll and her mother saying, "Do not fret, little one. We will return for your baby very soon. Then we will be free and happy." In light of the Kiowa attack, she was glad these treasures had survived.

As with Travis's parents, her father had been evil and her mother had married the wrong man. How she wished someone had rescued Marissa from her evil husband and had given her mother the happiness that she was experiencing with Travis. Marissa's life had been so brief and painful, and she had caused her father so much grief. For some unknown reason, Rana was convinced that Marissa had not meant to do so. If only she could discover the truth . . .

Perhaps her mother's tragedy had proven that defiance and obstinacy were bad traits, dangerous ones, and that she must cease them or she and others might suffer as Marissa had. At last the Great Spirit had sent her home to help and comfort Nathan. "I am home, Mother, and I will take care of Grandfather for you," she promised.

On his return, Cody Slade gave Nathan and Travis a shocking report on what had happened during their two-month absence. The hazel-eyed, sandy-haired man of twenty-six related infuriating news of cattle and horse rustling, the tearing down of fences, the burning of two hay fields, the surprising departure of James McFarland and subsequent purchase of his ranch by Harrison Caldwell, and the Caldwells' intense curiosity regarding their whereabouts. Anger laced his voice when he revealed how Harrison had been seeing too much of his sweetheart,

Mary Beth Sims, and told how the Caldwells had sat with the Simses in church earlier that day. He explained that the reason he had been escorting Rachel around had to do with the strange accidents that had befallen some of the women on McFarland's ranch, which had driven off many of the Flying *M* hands.

"What did the sheriff do to help Jim?" Nathan questioned.

"Wasn't much he could do, sir. Nobody would speak out; they were too scared. After McFarland lost so many hands and things got so dangerous over there, he sold out. Caldwell bought his place fair and square, or made it look that way. 'Course nobody bid against him."

"Everybody knows Harry is behind all this trouble," Nathan accused. "He's sitting around us like a tight horseshoe! I never thought Jim would weaken, but I don't blame him under those circumstances. But Harry's crazy if he thinks he's going to run us out and get my ranch. As soon as the rest of the boys get back from the cattle drive, we'll take care of those rustlers and fence cutters. We'll set out guards and handle this trouble ourselves. We'll teach that Yankee lawyer what it is to tangle with real Texans. When the election comes around, that sheriff's gonna be real sorry he's in Harry's hire. Cody, you make sure Harry doesn't get his bloody hands on Mary Beth."

"I'm doing my best, sir, but she's mighty scared. Ain't no secret Sims is beholden to Caldwell. She'll have it rough if her pa insists she marry him. I'll kill him first!" Cody vowed, imagining his love caught helplessly in that vulture's clutches.

"Maybe we should send for a U.S. Marshal to do some nosing around," Nathan suggested with mild sarcasm. "The government owes us something for holding us captive in the Union."

"Won't do any good, sir. Caldwell's covering his tracks better'n an Apache. He's been reporting the same kind of trouble we're having. It ain't nothing but a trick to look innocent. While you were gone, he hired two gunslingers; claimed they were for protection of his property and people. If you ask me, I'd bet they're the ones doing the killing and raiding. Mean-looking cusses, sir. From what I hear, they rode with that cold-blooded Quantrill, so folks around here won't rile 'em."

Hearing of Caldwell's latest deceptions caused Travis to recall how the unscrupulous lawyer had achieved his power. The Civil War had ended two years earlier and very little fighting had taken place in the Lone Star State, but many Texans were bitter over the Rebels' defeat and the terms of peace. Although most of the ex-slave owners lived in the eastern and southern parts of Texas, the aftereffects of the war were still being felt in more widespread areas. Texas had once been a republic with its own president, and she continued to feel and flaunt her streak of independence with such acts as flying the Texas flag on the same level with the American flag. Texans were proud and resilient folk, and now that the ex-soldiers had returned home and Reconstruction was underway, huge, prosperous cattle spreads were being created across this vast and rugged state.

Travis and Nathan were very much aware that during the war and shortly afterward, lawyer and rancher Harrison Caldwell had begun taking control of local politics and absorbing neighboring ranches. Well acquainted with the law, on the books and in the political offices, Caldwell had carried out his grasping process legally in the public eye and deceitfully in private. It seemed no one could stop him from achieving his dream of creating one of the largest and most lucrative cattle empires in the west.

America needed what Texas and Nathan had to offer, and Nathan had been doing extremely well until nature had begun dealing him some harsh blows. By borrowing money for survival, he had opened a door that a clever and daring thief like Caldwell could enter if Nathan could not find a way to close it soon. Years ago the Rocking C had been bordered by four separate ranches and a river; today it was bordered by the river and a horseshoe-shaped Circle C Ranch.

Travis had been silently taking in Cody's new information, reflecting that it would affect him personally by making Rana a target. "You said Clarissa has been checking around on us. What did you tell her?"

"Like you ordered, boss, I told her you two had private business and didn't tell us where you were heading or why. She's been real busy trying to uncover something. She even had that painter do her picture, but he didn't tell her nothing either. Before he left town, he came out to tell me she had been pumping him for information and that he wanted you to know he had kept his mouth shut about your granddaughter. I'm glad you two got her home safely. Bart said she looks just like . . ." Cody halted, wondering if he should mention Nathan's deceased child.

Nathan smiled knowingly and nodded. "Yep, she's almost the spittin' image of her mother. Got Marissa's spunk, too. Tell the boys to keep quiet about her; Rana needs time to get settled before people start trying to get a peek at her, especially those Caldwells. They might consider her a tangle in their plans."

Cody knew Bart had announced Rana's arrival and supplied details of her appearance to his brother, Darby, and to Rachel Raines. No matter their orders and good intentions, the hands would not be able to keep news like this quiet very long. He also knew this would be a frightening, difficult change for a young girl, particularly one to whom men would be attracted. Cody could understand Nathan's concern, and he promised to help protect Rana.

Travis ventured, "Maybe we should send a few of the boys to join up with Mace and warn him about this new trouble. We'll be in deep mud if anything happens to the cattle money. We've got that loan due at Mason's bank on August first. If we can't repay it, Caldwell will have an open door to buying us out real legal. We need to be careful and alert. I think it would be a good idea to hire a few extra men, Nate; we could round up the herds and set guards on them for awhile, at least until we can find a way to unmask Caldwell."

"Won't be easy, Travis; he's real clever. You'd best watch out for those two varmints he hired. If anything happened to you, Caldwell would find it easier to push Mister Crandall around," Cody warned, aware of the potency and importance of Travis's reputation.

"Do you know who they are?" Travis asked.

"Wes Monroe and Jackson Hayes, real bad types," Cody Slade replied. "You want me to join up with Mace and Todd?"

Travis did not respond. He was stunned by the possible identities of the two gunmen, for their first names were familiar. If he had not been badly injured and in Texas when the Lowrys had been killed, he might have been charged with their murders, for he had had a strong motive. The Lowrys had hired men called "Wes" and "Jack" to ambush him! His gut instinct told him these were the same two men who had beaten him senseless near St. Louis. If so, they were cruel and unfeeling bastards who would stop at nothing. At last he might be given a shot at revenge, or rather justice. Yet he had to be careful, for more was at stake than his own personal war with them. No doubt they had robbed and slain their boss long ago, implying that even the code of honesty and loyalty among criminals meant nothing to them. If the Caldwells felt threatened by Rana's arrival, they might sic . . .

He saw that Nathan and Cody were staring at him inquisitively. He promised himself he would handle the problem of Wes and Jack later. "I think you should stay here, Cody, and take care of some other matters for me. Pick out our three best shooters and send them. We'll talk again tomorrow."

After Cody left them, Nathan turned to Travis and asked, "Something caught your head, son; what was it?"

When Travis exposed his suspicions, Nathan looked worried. "If they remember you, son, you'll be in grave danger. You know they don't want anybody exposing them to the authorities."

"They've killed so many people I doubt they'd remember me. After supper, I'll sneak over to the Circle C. Just in case it is them and their memories are good, I'd like to sight them first."

"You're going to kill 'em, aren't you?" Nathan probed.

"Yep," he stated casually. He couldn't forget the almost lethal beating they had given him, or witnessing the Indian girl's rape and murder. Except for the Hunkpapa betrayal, once he resolved the Caldwell and Lowry matters, his past and present would be settled; and afterward he could work on his future, which looked brighter and happier since he had met Rana "Wild Wind" Michaels. He couldn't allow anyone or anything to harm her or endanger their future.

"I won't ask you to turn this matter over to the sheriff, because there isn't any proof against them, here or back in Missouri. I know you've got to take care of this, son, but do me one favor; don't get caught. I don't want you hanged for getting rid of dung like that, and you can bet Caldwell will sic the sheriff on you if you're seen."

"Don't worry, Nate. For now, I'm only going to make sure it's them. Hopefully they won't recognize me. But like the Apaches say, it's easier to kill a man than capture him. This time, they won't get away." Travis looked at Nathan and reasoned, "It isn't just for me, Nate. Those bastards have tortured and killed lots of innocent people. I have to stop them. I'm willing to swear they killed Lowry and his daughter and took more than their payment for taking care of me, and I watched them torment that Indian girl before slicing her throat. A man doesn't forget a sight like that. As I recall, the one called Jack didn't have much sense. Wes was the one who gave the orders. If he's still got my knife, I'm going to kill him with it. Trust me, Nate; I'm going to defeat them and Caldwell."

Nathan changed the grim subject. "I plan to go into town in the morning. I need to speak with Wilber Mason about my loan and see if I can learn anything about McFarland's sale. While I'm there, I'll hire a seamstress to come out and get started on some clothes for Rana, and I'll see if I can hire that schoolteacher to help her with her lessons. I think you should hang around the house until I get home. I would feel better knowing you're here to protect my granddaughter."

"You're right, Nate. We shouldn't leave Rana alone with all this trouble scattered about. When you get back, I'll check on things." Travis recalled what the two bushwhackers had done to the Indian girl who had warned him about Elizabeth's treachery and what Cody had told them about incidents involving women on the McFarland ranch. He would make certain Rana was not left unprotected for a single minute! He would also teach her how to fire a pistol and rifle tomorrow. He was glad Rana was smart and brave and knew how to fight. But even so, men like Wes, Jack, and Harrison were deadly.

Because of her injured hand, Rana was not allowed to assist Nathan and Travis in the preparation of their evening meal. As they worked, the two men taught her how to use the water pump and wood-burning stove. They showed her the pantry and explained about their foods and the use of their dishes. While the meal was cooking, Travis guided her to the bath closet in the hall and related its function. He told her that Rachel would teach her about doing the laundry when the housekeeper returned in a week. "You'll like her, Rana, and she'll be glad to help you with anything. Don't be embarrassed to ask questions."

"There is so much to learn," she murmured, feeling ignorant and insecure in this strange place.

He tenderly cuffed her chin. "I know, but you can do it. Nate's going to town in the morning, so I'll work with you most of tomorrow. I plan to teach you how to shoot a pistol and rifle, so I won't worry about you when I'm gone."

"Gone? Where are you going?" she asked as if panic-stricken.

"Just around the ranch, *micante*." He saw her smile as he called her "my heart." "I have to check a few things. We had a little trouble while we were away fetching you. Somebody's been stealing cattle and horses and cutting holes in our fences. The man who owned a neighboring ranch got scared, sold out, and left. It's best not to let this kind of trouble get out of hand."

"Another tribe raids on our lands?" she inquired in surprise. "Who would dare challenge you and Grandfather?"

Travis chuckled. "Renegade whites are trying to raid our lands, but we'll stop them now that we're home again. Don't worry."

"Rana will help you defeat them," she bravely announced.

"No, Rana will not. Rana will stay at home and study her lessons. When you've learned them, I'll teach you all about ranching, and rustling, and shooting. Then, if there's any more trouble, you can ride against the varmints with me. We both know how well you can fight; right now, your lessons are more important than helping me defeat a few raiders. Agreed?" he softly demanded, not wanting her to confront the Caldwells or Wes and Jack.

She smiled at him and nodded her head. She sensed his worry over her and it warmed her heart. He did not doubt her capabilities, she realized; he only wanted to protect her. "I will obey."

"Good." He caught her hand and, after stealing a blissful and heady kiss, led her back to the kitchen.

As they ate and Rana practiced with the utensils, Nathan told her what he and Travis had decided to reveal about her past and the reasons for her return. "We'll tell anyone who's bold enough to ask—and you can bet there'll be a few people who'll do so—the simple truth. We haven't done anything wrong and we've got nothing to be ashamed of, so why get tangled up in fancy lies? It won't take our friends long to love you and accept you. If we stick to the truth, we won't have to worry about getting our stories crossed and having people think we've got something terrible to hide. The only thing we'll keep quiet about is that false marriage between you two. Is that all right with you, Rana?"

Travis added before she could respond, "I doubt anyone will be fool enough to say anything ugly to you, or about you, Rana. If someone does, he'll answer to me. Anyone with eyes and ears can see you haven't lived as a wild savage or an abused white captive. Just remember, you don't have to explain anything to anybody. Some people will be genuinely interested and some will be downright nosy or rude. You decide how you want to handle each one, and we'll back you."

Rana smiled at both men. "Do not worry about me. Remember, for many years as Wild Wind I accepted good and bad teasing. I will not allow their words to harm me or to make me forget my honor. I will let my actions and face speak for me and prove my worth. It is good to speak the truth, for lies and tricks can do much harm."

Later that night, as Rana snuggled into her bed, she savored its comfort and softness. In spite of the awesome learning task before her, she felt happy and relaxed. The word "home" kept drifting across her sleepy mind like a peaceful cloud in a tranquil blue sky. She cuddled the doll in her arms as if it were a tangible link to her deceased mother, for it brought back good memories of nights when she and Marissa had shared this bed, had laughed and whispered and made up beautiful fantasies that had not been allowed to become realities. Yes, she decided, her destiny was here with her grandfather and her husband. *Husband,* her mind echoed, then she smiled.

With Nathan and Rana in bed, Travis stood before the fireplace in the sitting room and admired the three portraits above the mantel. His gaze finally settled on his favorite of Rana. She was so beautiful and radiant and she was so close, but so was Nathan. Lordy, how he wanted her, he reflected. It had been days since that night in the forest when she had declared that she had chosen him to share her life. She was like sunshine, and flowers, and a fresh breeze; she was a rainbow, a child, a rare treasure; she was all things good and pure and priceless. Her eyes, so large and mellow, held such magic and allure. It was as if every inch of her called out irresistibly to be touched ever so gently. Her tumbling tresses presented an enticing aura of sensuality. This angel displayed overwhelming charms and she was . . . almost his.

Travis stared at her painted image and yearned for her. He imagined her lying in bed a short distance away, waiting for him. These next weeks pretending she was his "sister" would be unmerciful, yet he needed to protect her life and reputation as much as he needed to be with her. Could he betray Nathan's trust in his own home? What if Nathan caught them together? It could damage their relationship. Even if they declared their love, would it excuse or justify their intimacy? There was no safe way they could marry until this danger with the Caldwells was past and, until they were legally wed, would Nathan understand and accept their wanton affair? It was indeed a predicament.

Travis paced the sitting room, wondering if he should go to Rana. He needed her and wanted her, but could he risk discovery? Twice he had challenged it on the trail; how long could his luck hold out? He doused the lanterns and headed toward his room.

In the hallway, Travis glanced to his left to find Rana poised in her open doorway, smiling at him and mutely beckoning him to her side. He looked toward Nathan's closed door and sighed heavily. If he learned the truth, Nathan would have to understand that he could not resist Rana or deny these passions burning within them. He quietly headed toward her. She opened the door and allowed his entrance.

Travis closed and locked the door behind him. His hands captured her body and pulled it into his embrace, creating a blissful contact. The dam that had checked their passions for many days suddenly shattered and a surge of powerful passion spilled forth. Her nearness caused his heart to race with desire. With the slowness of a snail, his hands moved over her face, down her throat, over her shoulders. His fingers deftly drifted over her bare flesh, causing her to tremble. Bending forward, he fastened his eager lips to hers. His tongue tentatively mated with hers, then darted between her lips to play joyously within her mouth. He kissed her nose, then her eyes, then sensuously attacked her ears, where his respiration caused her trembling to increase. Slowly, seductively, his mouth traveled down her neck and wandered over her shoulders. At the same time, his hands slipped up her body to capture two passion-swollen breasts and tantalize her taut peaks.

Rana shivered with longing. Her body quivered in delight. She had been waiting for him to come to her, fearing he would not. It had been too long and she craved him. Her breath came in shallow, sharp gasps as his tongue and hands brought titillating sensations to her. Suddenly her breath was stolen by feverish kisses and a fierce embrace. Her entire body experienced a rush of heat and tingling. His hands tenderly squeezed her thrusting peaks as his tongue probed her mouth. Then they slipped around her body to grasp her buttocks and fondle them, pressing her snugly against his rapidly enlarging manhood. Slowly his hands began to move up and down her body, stroking here and there.

Her fingers pushed aside his shirt and allowed it to float to the floor so she could press kisses to his throat and chest. Her arms encircled his taut body as her mouth worked its wonders. Her actions revealed her inexperience, yet she stimulated him to the edge of mindless surrender. She had craved him for days and she could not wait any longer. Her body was like an ember lying near a fire, waiting to be ignited and consumed by its heat and sparked to blazing life.

Travis's hands captured firm mounds and gently kneaded them. His mouth wandered over her face and his nose inhaled her heady fragrance. His manhood throbbed with painful cravings, flaming with a need only she could extinguish.

Their tongues touched and explored the taste of the other. Her breasts burned like two coals against his chest. He groaned in achingly sweet need of her as his lips worked between her mouth, ears, and neck, and his talented hands stimulated her body to quivering desire. Down his hand drifted, over supple breasts, past a slim waist, over rounded hips, and into a beckoning fuzzy mound that radiated a heat to rival the July sun. Slowly and provocatively his hand stroked the hardened peak it located there until their starving senses were ravenous and pleading.

"Love me," she entreated, enslaved by rapidly rising desire.

Travis could wait no longer to feel her body clinging to his. He lifted her and carried her to the bed. After placing her there, he quickly removed his clothes and joined her. He wanted to feel each sensation and to savor each emotion. She was so close, so intoxicating, so eager. He could think of nothing except her desire for him and his for her. Her flesh was as soft as Texas cotton and he longed to caress it. Her body was lithe and enticing, calling out to him to give it pleasure. Needing to feel her flesh against his, he assailed that body eagerly.

Rana's hands moved over his compelling frame. He was so strong, so firm, so sleek. It felt wonderful for her hands to glide over his body, and she relished its feel and the power she possessed to stir him to life. Her fingers roved broad shoulders and a nearly hairless chest on which muscles stood out prominently before flattening to a taut stomach and lean hips. Her respiration quickened and her insides quivered with anticipation of what lay ahead tonight. His embrace was enticing, stimulating, irresistible. It was too dark to see his handsome face, but she could envision it. Her senses were alive and alert, yet mindless and dazed. He demanded and controlled all she was, and she did not care. Her body was susceptible to his every move and touch. She wanted him to take her fully, for every area of her body and mind ached for his conquest.

Travis suppressed his groans of desire and pleasure as his hands and mouth wandered over her receptive body. Staggering sensations flooded his mind and inflamed his flesh. His lips found hers and urgently possessed them. He claimed her senses with skill and determination, wanting to be her only reality. His hunger could not be denied.

A flood of sensation washed over Rana. Her body relaxed and tensed simultaneously as he created ecstasy and torment at the same time. Some kisses and caresses sated her, while others tantalized her. Her hands grasped his shoulders and pulled him tightly against her smoldering body. She wanted . . . She needed . . .

Their contact and her eagerness were playing havoc with Travis's control. Their naked bodies clung together and their mouths fused feverishly. His shaft demanded entrance to that moist haven, which could both cool and inflame it. His hand provocatively traveled down her stomach and teased along her silky thighs, encouraging her desires to burn brighter and more fiercely. He called on all he knew about women to give her the ultimate pleasure while trying to contain his rampant need.

Rana writhed on the bed as Travis toyed with the sensitive peak, which delighted and encouraged him to continue his actions. His lips found hers and sent reality spinning. His talented lips shifted from her mouth to her breast, then back and forth, causing her to squirm beneath his artful seduction. Soon her body was pleading for appeasement. Her appetite was whetted beyond resistance or denial.

By then, nothing mattered to either except the dousing of the fires of passion that enflamed and consumed them. Yet Travis continued to use his deft hands and lips upon her pliant body. Her hands roamed his body, their pressure on it revealing the intensity of her desire. Aquiver with fierce longing, his mouth encased a taut peak and drove her wild with blissful torment. His mouth moved upward then to willfully invade hers, his hunger intense and his skill enormous. Her body was responding wildly and eagerly to his and his heart surged with joy. He soon became lost in the wonder of her love and response.

Her fingers lovingly traced the lines on his face and body. They drifted into his hair and played amongst its waves. They moved seductively over his lips, then drew his mouth to hers. Greedily she feasted at his love's well, partaking of its heady nectar. She moaned against his mouth and covered his face with kisses. As his fingers worked on her body, sliding over her throbbing peak and thrusting into her aching womanhood, she yielded her all to him, entreating more stimulation, which he eagerly and happily granted her.

At last, she murmured hoarsely and weakly, "I must have you now, my husband. Enter me and feed this hunger."

He responded huskily, "If I took you twice a day for the rest of our lives, my hunger for you could never be sated. Each time I take you causes me to want you even more." He shifted between her inviting thighs and drove gently within her encompassing womanhood. She arched upward, craving and accepting his entire length. She sighed with temporary relief, then felt the burning flames attack her once more as he moved with caution and experience. She needed him so desperately that she feverishly matched his rhythm, even as he warned her to move slowly and carefully. Wildly, skillfully, he guided and instructed her along this fiery path.

His mouth claimed hers and worked ardently before shifting its attention to her pleading breasts. As his warm, moist lips closed over one nipple, she writhed beneath him. He lifted her hips to drive more deeply into her body. He worked deftly, thrusting and thrusting until he feared she would cry out in sweet yearning. Lordy, how he wished they didn't have to be careful with their voices and actions. It was sheer agony to have to control anything tonight.

Travis could barely restrain his desire to plunge into her body over and over again until his release came. Each time he advanced and retreated, he feared it would be his final movement. She was enjoying this night too much to end it swiftly and he wanted her to claim all the pleasure she could extract or he could give. He labored to master his heated flesh, as he wanted to prod her more slowly up that mountain she was climbing so rapidly. Each time he ceased his probing to cool his blazing desire, she would wiggle and entreat him to continue. He knew she was too dazed by passion to hear or comply with his warnings, so he ceased murmuring them in her ear and labored silently to send her over love's precipice.

Rana thrilled to the way his manhood teased along the sensitive sides of the dark, damp canyon between her parted thighs. Her heart was pounding rapidly and her body was ablaze. Each time his tongue flicked over her nipples, she had to force herself not to cry out in pleasure. Her legs overlapped his and she matched his thrusting pattern. As her mouth clung to his and her hands pressed him tightly against her, she strove for the rapturous climax that had begun to melt her very core.

Their hearts and bodies were fused and their desires matched perfectly as they cast off all restraint and caution. Their bodies blended time and time again, and they unselfishly urged each other up the spiral road of passion. Higher and higher they soared, until a staggering release struck them forcefully and sent them spinning wildly back toward earth. Blissful spasms racked their bodies and tossed them on a sea of sated contentment. They lay in an embrace of love and tranquility, exhausted and enchanted.

Travis rolled to his back, refusing to release her. His heart was pounding and his body was soaked. Never had he experienced anything like this union of bodies, hearts, and spirits. It was wonderful, exciting, all-consuming, and powerful. They shared passion, tenderness, urgency, and ecstasy; they shared a beautiful love. This thing between them was good, and pure, and right; and no one would destroy it.

Rana curled against him, feeling and thinking as he did. She listened as his heartbeat and breathing returned to normal. She did not mind the wetness of his body, nor that on hers. The musky fragrance that filled the room brought a smile of happiness to her lips. His fingers were slowly, absently trailing up and down her back and she sighed happily and nestled closer to him, delighting when his embrace tightened and he rested his jawline against her forehead. A special peace filled and enveloped them. Their legs were entwined and their flesh joined as one. She closed her eyes and gradually drifted off to sleep.

Travis reluctantly drew away from her, arose, and, after kissing her damp forehead and covering her slender body, returned to his room, yearning for the time when he could remain with her night and day.

Nathan left for town the next morning after breakfast. Travis was cheerfully clearing the table and washing the dishes as Rana argued about helping with the chores, but Travis won their genial debate by kissing each bandaged fingertip and telling her, "Just keep me company while I work. Since you hurt these lovely fingers saving my hide, the least I can do is wait on you while they heal properly."

"They were injured many days ago, Travis. A little water and work will not harm them. It is wrong to be lazy and selfish."

"You can't fool me, woman. I know they're still sore and sensitive. The only water I want them in is your bath, understand?"

"You treat me like a child or a captive," she teased.

"Sometimes I think it would be easier on me if you were a child. You know good and well that if my hand were hurt, you'd be treating me this same way. Am I right?" he challenged, and her expression answered him.

When Travis went to give orders to Cody and the hands, Rana entered the water closet to take a bath. She plugged the hole with the wooden stopper and pulled on the cord to allow the wooden tub to fill itself. She grinned as she stepped into it, for she liked the ease and privacy the closet afforded. For a brief moment she could almost hear and see herself splashing in this tub long ago. When she finished, she wrapped a drying sheet around her silky frame and prepared to return to her room to dress.

* * *

Since Rana's door was ajar, Travis thought nothing about pushing it aside and walking into her room. There was a noise behind him as she reopened the closet door, which his entrance had shut on her. As he turned to locate her, he was saying, "Why don't we go for a walk and I can show—" He ceased talking and his mouth remained open, for she was nude, a vision of magic and temptation that set his passions boiling. He could not stop his gaze from instantly roaming every inch of her arresting face and figure. He had seen her naked several times in moonlit shadows, but this magnificent view in brilliant light staggered his senses and increased her enormous allure. Her shapely figure was perfect and intoxicatingly appealing. His hands itched to wander over her silky flesh, to leisurely explore curves and peaks and valleys and entreating crevices. He moistened his lips as his mouth craved to do the same. His eyes seemed to scorch her skin, to singe the flaming forest between her sleek thighs, to cause her nipples to grow hard and prominent. He smiled as he observed his effect on her, for she was glowing with desire.

Coming alert, Travis shifted nervously. "I . . . I'm sorry, Rana. I didn't know you were . . . dressing. Call me when you finish," he said, feeling he was infringing on her privacy. At other times, he had been too consumed by mindless hunger to think about his behavior and its consequences; today he was fully aware of his responsibilities and obligations to Nathan and to Rana. Could he brazenly take her every time and any place the mood struck him? Just hop into bed and make wanton love to her every time Nathan's back was turned? Damn, he cursed silently. Sometimes he hated this conscience that Nathan had inspired and despised the white man's idea of morals! As much as he wanted to be honest with Nathan about this situation, he knew he could not, for Nathan was her grandfather and he was very old-fashioned. Without a doubt, Nathan would feel betrayed and duped; he would feel Travis had dishonored his innocent grandchild and used her selfishly. Like him, Nathan would be unable to think clearly and without bias about Rana.

Retrieving the drying sheet that had slipped accidentally from her body, Rana covered herself. Had his cheeks actually flushed and his tongue twisted? she mused, warmed and amused by his behavior. Since he looked unnerved by their privacy, she asked, "This is not the first time we have been alone or touched. Why do you behave this way?"

Travis inhaled raggedly as his yearning gaze wandered over her bare shoulders and exquisite face. He revealed what he had been thinking. "No woman has ever tempted me or affected me like you do, Rana Michaels. I can't seem to keep my hands and mind off you. I'd best git out of here while I can. Somebody could come searching for me, and it would appear mighty strange for me to be locked in your bedroom with Nate gone. Much as I crave you, it's too risky for us to be together this morning," he explained, though his eyes told another story.

A fetching smile teased over her lips. "We must not feel guilt or shame over this special bond between us. It is sad we cannot tell Grandfather about it, but must we reject each other to obey laws and ways that we know are not right for us? Must we stay apart because the white-eyes say it is evil for us to be together on a sleeping mat? Must we suffer loneliness and separation because Grandfather was taught these foolish and tormenting customs? You have never dishonored me or used me selfishly; I have come to you willingly and eagerly each time. I choose to belong to you, and I care not who says my feelings are wrong or my actions are wicked. Have you forgotten how short life can be? Must we suffer painful denials by living as others demand? We hurt no one by holding our feelings and actions a secret; they are for us alone to share and know. Grandfather is gone and no one should enter your tepee uninvited. We have little time alone. Is it not best to seize each moment and joy?" She hesitated. "Do I speak and act too boldly?"

Travis realized they would be alone for hours and they had total privacy. He could read the matching hunger in her eyes, as she had in his. "Again, your words are true and wise, and spoken with great courage and daring. I must have lost my mind over you, Rana Michaels. Every time I'm near you, I want you like crazy. This pull between us is too powerful to resist, so thank heavens I don't want to fight it or have to fight it. I don't know what I would do if you didn't feel this way about me. I never thought I would hear myself saying this to any woman, but I love you, Rana Michaels, and this isn't White Eagle speaking. With everything I am and with both my bloods, I need you and I want you—today, tomorrow, and forever. I don't like sneaking around behind Nate's back and I don't like feeling guilty over taking you, but you're right about this matter remaining between us. As soon as I settle our problems on the ranch, I'm claiming you totally."

Travis stepped closer to her and gazed into her compelling face. "White Eagle desired and claimed Wild Wind's heart, body, and life; now Travis Kincade hungers to do the same with Rana Michaels."

Rana's hands slipped up his chest to capture his face between them. She went up on tiptoe to seal their lips after telling him, "Your thoughts and feelings match mine. I love you, Travis Kincade."

Travis released the drying sheet and allowed it to settle around their feet. He reached past her to lock the door, then scooped her up and carried her to the bed. After removing his boots and clothes, he lay down beside her. Had it only been a few hours since they had made passionate love in this bed? he mused. They had spoken little the night before, for it had not been a time for talking, and silence had seemed to enhance the romantic solitude of her dark room.

Her breath was stolen by the pervasive kisses he could not hold back and by his powerful embrace. He could see and feel her eager responses, her heightened desires, her love and commitment to him. His green eyes darkened with desire as his lips and hands went to work lovingly on her body.

When their bodies could tolerate no more teasing and tempting, he tenderly eased his flaming shaft inside a haven that received him ardently and gratefully. Mastering the urge to ride her swiftly and hard in order to end his bittersweet hunger, he remained motionless for a brief time, his throbbing manhood behaving as if this were the first time they had joined. He shuddered as it quivered threateningly and he concentrated fiercely on maintaining control. As he set his pattern, her legs closed over his and locked around his lower body. She worked in unison with his movements, arching to meet his rapturous entries and relaxing to endure his mandatory withdrawals. She was driving him wild with her uninhibited behavior. When her mouth nibbled on his ear and she pounded her body forcefully against his, she tempted him to race blindly and rashly for victory. He was ecstatic when she claimed her blissful prize, for he would have been unable to restrain himself any longer.

Together they rode passion's waves and were rewarded with soul-stirring pleasure. They drank from love's cup until every drop of its intoxicating liquid was drained and savored. They lay exhausted, but enlivened, in a serene setting of total contentment.

As they snuggled together in the afterglow of love, she entreated dreamily, "Tell me more about White Eagle becoming Travis Kincade."

Travis patiently repeated the story of his past to her and gave her some new information. Still he left out details of his necessary relationship with Clarissa Caldwell, the threat of destruction from Harrison, and the reappearance of Wes and Jackson in his life. He did not want this beautiful moment spoiled by such ugly and intrusive realities. This thing between them was too special to damage even with defensive lies, so he vowed to be careful about what he said and did. Besides, Rana had just arrived home; she had enough to learn and to handle without him burdening her with those distasteful and dangerous problems. Too, he was afraid she would insist on becoming a "warrior" to help him battle his foes, and he could not bear the thought of seeing her injured or slain. In a few days, he would explain about the Caldwells and their gunslingers, and why she had to stay out of that situation, and why she must allow him to dally with Clarissa. He would protect her, even from her own skill and confidence, which would cause her to insist on riding at his side.

At present, he knew she was simply very curious about him. He believed that if he was open and honest with her about himself, then eventually she would be able to look upon her own past in the same way. Therefore he was able to explain, "Right after I escaped the Hunkpapa camp, I worked several jobs to spite them, until I realized I couldn't hurt any or all Indians because of what the Hunkpapas had done to me. Besides, the only one getting hurt was me. When you aim for revenge, you always fire two arrows, and one is pointing at your own heart. That was one of my first and most painful lessons. When I became a U.S. Marshal, I think it was to give me an excuse to hunt down and kill evil men like my father and his partners so they couldn't hurt innocent people like my mother and me. I finally stopped fooling myself and endangering my life when I discovered why I had been hired. If I recall the words correctly, they went something like, 'That half-breed can get rid of lots of bastards for us and if he gets killed doing it, what does it matter?' You see, *micante,* selfish people use gullible people all the time; and people are more gullible when they're hurt or seeking revenge."

Rana nestled against his firm body and sighed peacefully. Her gaze roved each marking on his *wanapin* and each scar on his chest and arms. As if trying to determine the agony he had endured with each wound and to comfort them belatedly, her fingers lovingly traced each one. He still retained the honed body, keen instincts, and noble spirit of a highly trained warrior. She had seen him get angry but not lose his temper and control or become violent. She had seen him accept pain without even a soft whimper, and she had seen him use his courage and wits in the Oglala camp. She doubted he had ever cried out during the Sun

Dance or his torture. He was so strong and proud, yet so sensitive and vulnerable beneath that seemingly impenetrable surface.

She listened to him talk about his days with the Apaches and how much he had learned from them, even things the Lakota warriors did not know. He talked about riding with outlaws for a time, claiming it was to show the white law that he was invincible and could do whatever he wanted and no one could touch him. She heard him admit he had been trapped between two sides and could not choose which one to help or hurt, until he finally learned he was the one being harmed the most. Under Nathan's hands, he had come to accept the fact that he could not change the world, only himself. Again, her fingers traced his scarred flesh—which in no way detracted from its beauty and appeal—and caressed his virile body as she absorbed his soulful confessions. She toyed with the Lakota *wanapin* as he told her about it. He had faced so many perils and hardships and had known such anguish. Yet she realized how each incident or job had molded him and honed him into the man he was today, a man who stood above others in so many ways.

Travis kissed her, then left the room to wash up and redress. He returned shortly to find her still reclining on the bed and smiling provocatively at him. He chuckled and teased. "Don't you go looking at me like that, woman. I have no willpower where you're concerned, and Nate could return home in an hour or two. Get up and get dressed so I can show you around your new home."

Rana did as Travis suggested, rising and leaving the room to refresh herself before dressing. Travis straightened the bed and placed the doll where it had been before their heady bout of lovemaking. He gazed at it and smiled, for he knew that someday they would have a baby, and he vowed their child would never experience the pain its parents had. Strange, he hadn't given love, marriage, or children any serious thought until he had met that entrancing vixen who had practically turned his gut inside out until he had finally won her heart and acceptance. A child . . . Nothing would make him happier than making and sharing a child with Rana Michaels. After all, they were married and . . . Damn, he cursed silently. There were some problems he would have to correct as soon as possible. There was a legal entanglement that now prevented a marriage between them; there was his concern over not getting Rana with child before they were joined under the white man's law; and there was the matter of getting rid of several dangerous enemies who could be lethal threats to her and Nathan . . .

—— *Chapter 12* ——

🙡

TRAVIS SADDLED TWO HORSES and took Rana riding. Without going too far and getting out of sight in case of danger, he spent three hours telling her about ranch life and escorting her around the areas of their spread that were visible to those laboring near the wooden structures or the hands working on horseback. She was fascinated by the branding process, which he allowed her to view through his field glasses. She was concerned that the animals were being hurt, so Travis explained the procedure in detail without allowing her to approach the hectic scene. She observed the hands who were herding wild mustangs into a large corral so they could be broken and sold in two months. In the Oglala camp she had witnessed the mastering of wild horses and knew it was a dangerous task. Yet she eagerly asked Travis if she could watch what he had called "bronco-busting."

He chuckled and nodded, wondering how she would feel when she watched him nearly busting his butt and ribs on one of those wild beasts that could suddenly seem like a bundle of energy, sharp bones, and flaying hooves. Bronco-busting always gave him a sense of power and victory, and a thrill that was hard to describe to anyone who had not experienced it. There was something about challenging danger, even death, that made him come alive and sharpened his wits. He began thinking that since he was planning on a family soon—a wife and children—perhaps he should cut out some of the dangerous things he had been doing. Certainly Nathan would agree as soon as he was told of the love he and Rana shared. Soon he would become more than Nathan's adopted son and legal heir, and hopefully that would please the older man. Yet he understood that he could not legally wed Rana as long as he remained her uncle by law, a fact that would have to be altered after any threat to her was removed.

To avoid the tension of her having to meet so many strangers while she was getting settled, he stayed clear of the wranglers and the families in the married settlement. In about a week, he and Nathan would introduce her to a few people at a time, beginning with those important to the ranch, such as Cody Slade, Mace Hunter, Todd Raines and his wife, Rachel, Darby Davis and his wife, Lettie, and Bart Davis.

This first day of July was lovely and mild, and the landscape seemed to be showing its gratitude to nature by having donned its prettiest face. Travis could tell that Rana was amazed by the size of their spread and impressed by its beauty. The smiling foreman observed Rana as she twisted this way and that in her saddle to take in everything around them. Each time she looked at him to ask a question or to make a comment, their gazes met and they smiled before speaking.

He told Rana he would show her the rest of their land another day, as there was too much territory to cover so quickly and it was past lunch time. After they had returned to the stable and were heading for the house, he asked her if she would be ready and willing to learn how to handle a pistol and rifle that afternoon.

Excitedly she replied, "Yes, teach me now."

"After we eat," he informed her, then grinned. She was so full of energy, vitality, and curiosity. He enjoyed watching her and sharing time with her. She was such a rare and special woman, and he was delighted she belonged to him. He admitted to himself he was not sorry for staking his claim on her and was eager to increase it. Remembering what they had shared warmed his heart and his body. His gaze engulfed her possessively, proudly. His woman, his wife . . .

Rana smiled and her cheeks glowed as she read heartstirring emotions in his eyes. "You do not think of eating food, *mihigna*," she teased cheerfully as her eyes lovingly adored him.

Travis arched one brow devilishly and replied, "You're right, *micante*. Today it is not the rumbling in my belly that calls to me."

Rana laughed merrily, for she recalled that first night in Lone Wolf's tepee when he had scolded her with similar words. "It is good, *mihigna*, for Myeerah's tepee is too far away for me to fetch food to quiet it. We have both changed much since that first night."

Rich masculine laughter filled the air as Travis realized to what she was alluding with her jest. "Yes, we have both changed, Rana," he concurred, reaching over to caress her flushed cheek. At that moment, he did not care who was watching or what anyone thought.

"My grandfather has tamed you, and you have tamed me. I will no longer behave like a rebellious child or a wild spirit."

Travis's brows lifted and his eyes widened in surprise. Slowly the reaction faded and his gaze revealed sparkling eyes that narrowed slightly to form tiny lines at their corners. White teeth gleamed as his smile broadened and those creases deepened. Astonishingly he vowed, "I don't want to tame you, Rana; I like you and want you just as you are. You possess just the right blend of strength and softness. You're kind and generous, and you're the smartest and bravest woman I've ever met. Stay as you are, my fiery-haired temptress. You have so much spirit and life, Rana, and you make me feel good just being around you. I wish you to grow by learning, *micante*, but do not change."

She was deeply touched by his words and her eyes grew misty. "But I am stubborn and defiant," she softly refuted.

"Only because you wanted to do all the things you loved and needed to do, and the Oglalas wouldn't allow it. Here, Rana, you can do *almost* anything," he informed her, stressing the one vital word. "You have plenty of skills and talents, but you have to learn where and when to use them, especially on me," he teased.

To control his desire for her at this inconvenient time, he changed the subject. "The white man's laws and ways are different. I'll teach them to you, and you must obey them. Here, only bad men raid, and when they're captured they're punished. If we want something, we work for money, then we buy it; we never take it. If a man does wrong, we don't kill him; he's captured and punished, by jailing him or hanging him. Don't worry, I'll teach you all you need to know," he encouraged when she frowned in dismay and confusion. He tried to explain the American government, Texas laws, trials, justice, and more, but he could tell this information was overwhelming, befuddling.

She thought a minute, then asked, "What if the bad man flees before this . . . sheriff comes to . . . arrest him? This man called a lawyer—what if he tricks others with clever lies? What if the jury does not believe your charges? Will he go free?" she inquired, disliking this seemingly irrational form of justice. She insisted, "It is a man's responsibility to defend his own life and lands, and those of his family. If another does evil deeds, his guilt is known and he should die. It is right for the one who suffers from his evil to punish him."

"A white man cannot take the law into his own hands, Rana. If he does, he's guilty of breaking the law and can be punished. In America, the white lands, justice must be carried out legally. It protects an innocent person who's been falsely or mistakenly accused of a black deed, which we call a crime. Years ago I could have used a lawyer and a jury trial in the Hunkpapa camp and maybe I would have gotten a fair shake," he remarked to make his point.

She considered those words, then shook her head. "This makes no sense, Travis Kincade," she argued softly. "If a man does evil to you and the white law does not punish him, will you let him go free to harm another? Does this white justice always work?"

Travis grimaced at her painful point, for that was exactly what he would not do. Embittered or mistreated men often took the law into their own hands, just as, if necessary, he was planning to do very soon. How could he honestly tell her, "Do as I say, not as I do?" Trapped, he wondered how to answer her sincere question without lying or causing confusion in her new education.

Suddenly Rana smiled mischievously. "I understand. You must obey white laws when possible; but if justice fails you, you must appear to accept such laws while you carry out your own justice in secret, and you must not be captured while breaking these laws. Is this not so?"

"Lordy, women, you're too clever to fool or argue with. The trouble with taking the law into your own hands is you risk hurting those you love. Your family and friends can be accused of helping you and they can be punished. Besides, the white law is powerful and persistent. If you challenge it, you had better be ready to die, 'cause some of those lawmen will chase you to hell and back. I know; I did it several times when I was an Army scout and U.S. Marshal."

"What of these men who raid our lands? Why does the white law not capture and punish them?"

"The sheriff says he doesn't know who's responsible. The rustlers strike at night and nobody sees them. If people do witness their crimes, they're too afraid to give out their identities. They're like shadows, Rana, and you can't capture a shadow. Once they become real men, the law will punish them. I'm going to try to unmask them. All I need is evidence on who's behind all this trouble."

"To capture a dark shadow, you must become a darker shadow. Remember how we set traps for the sly fox and crafty raccoon? One who does mischief or evil must be snared. When you capture them, must you give them to the sheriff? Or will you punish them?"

"I'm supposed to hand them over to the law," he replied vaguely.

Rana eyed him for a few moments, then stated confidently, "You know who leads this band of night raiders. You are planning how to defeat them. Let Rana help you," she entreated earnestly.

Travis stared her in the eye as he warned, "Listen to me, Rana Michaels. These men are dangerous, and I don't want you getting hurt. Don't talk about this to anyone except me and Nate. We want you to stay close to home until this matter is settled. Understand?"

"But I can help you defeat them. Did I not prove my fighting skills on the trail? You will be in danger, and I wish to protect you."

Travis sighed heavily. "Darn you, woman, I can't be careful if I have to worry about you. In case you haven't noticed before, you are most distracting. If those men got one look at you . . ." He halted and shook his head vigorously. "No, *micante*. Please don't fight me on this. If anything happened to you, I couldn't stand it."

Rana could not suppress a happy smile. "I wish to help you and Grandfather, but I will obey."

Travis sighed in relief and cuffed her chin playfully. "Good. You don't know these people and, if you said or did the wrong thing, you could endanger all of us and the ranch. We have to be very careful and alert. You see, *micante,* until we know who's involved, we can't trust anyone. Right now, all I can do is watch and listen for clues. When I get evidence against the guilty ones, I'll let the sheriff handle them, or I will," he added with a sly grin.

As he prepared their meal, Rana observed the man who ruled her emotions. Earlier this morning he had tended her injured fingers and rebandaged them, and now he had refused to allow her to help him prepare their food or wash up afterward. Nathan arrived just as they were leaving the house to begin her pistol and rifle lessons. The session was delayed when Nathan asked Travis to join him in his office for a talk.

Nathan smiled at Rana and said, "You sit here on the porch and I'll be finished with Travis soon; then he can teach you to shoot. I talked with a woman in town this morning. She'll be coming out tomorrow to take your measurements so she can make you some clothes. And I spoke with the schoolteacher; he's agreed to come out here a few days a week to help with your lessons."

Rana hugged Nathan and said, "You are very kind and generous, Grandfather. I will wait here for Travis." She realized Nathan was worried about something and wanted to discuss it privately with Travis, and she quickly surmised it was the trouble with the evil men. She watched them go inside, then she sat down on the top step to relax and think.

Time passed as Rana awaited their return, and she was so caught up in her thoughts that she did not notice the young man who approached the house. As he sighted the beautiful, flaming-haired girl, he stared, then smiled genially. Halting at the bottom porch step, he declared, "You must be Mister Crandall's granddaughter. I'm Cody Slade. Are Mister Crandall and the boss inside?" he asked pleasantly.

Rana recognized the man's name and noted that he seemed very friendly and polite. "I am Rana Michaels. Grandfather and Travis entered the house to speak privately. We must wait here for their return," she informed him, trying to speak properly and cordially.

Cody propped his boot on the lower step to follow her advice. "I know Mister Crandall sure is happy to have you home again, Miss Rana. You're going to love it here. This is one of the finest ranches anywhere, and there's nobody better to work for than Travis and your grandfather. I've been with them since I was knee-high to a weaning calf."

Rana tried to keep the confusion that filled her at his unknown phrases from showing on her face, but she could only guess the gist of his words. She did not know how to converse with this sandy-haired, hazel-eyed male whose looks and manner were pleasing to the senses, so she remained silent and alert after she had smiled and thanked him.

Cody could not get over how exquisite she was, even though he had seen the portrait of Marissa and had been told she looked like her mother. To confront such radiance and beauty in person was stunning and gratifying. Unconsciously he indulged his stimulated senses. He had seen a few women who had been called ravishing, but all of them put together could not compete with this glorious angel before him. She looked so sweet and innocent to possess so much earthy sensuality. Everything about her seemed perfect, but it was her expressive gray-blue eyes and the fiery curls reaching to her waist that snared his attention time and time again. He wondered how Travis Kincade, who had traveled with her for weeks and was now living in the same house with her, could think about anything besides this bewitching creature. If he was not in love with Mary Beth Sims, he would feel compelled to pursue Nathan Crandall's granddaughter.

Wanting to hear that voice again, which seemed simultaneously to be able to soothe and stimulate a helpless man, Cody inquired, "Has Travis shown you around the ranch yet?"

"We rode nearby this morning," she answered slowly as she selected her words and tried to speak in the white man's style. "Travis told . . . me the ranch is too large to cover in one day. I have been away for many years and there is much to learn before I meet others."

"I guess it is a scary thing for a woman to come to a new place with so many strangers. Don't worry, Miss Rana; everyone here will help you in any way they can. You'll make friends easily and quickly."

Because of his tone and sincere smile, she did not take offense at the suggestion in his first sentence that women were prone to fear, nor did she correct him. "You are very kind, Cody Slade. Ra . . . I will need friends and help here. You are the first to speak with me; it is good to call you friend."

Cody wanted to ask all about her and her absence of eleven years, but he knew that would be too intrusive and bold. "There aren't too many girls your age around these parts. As soon as you get settled in, I'll introduce you to a close friend of mine, Mary Beth Sims. She's eighteen, and real nice. You two will like each other. She's about this tall," he related, indicating a height of about five feet, five inches. "She has green eyes and brown hair, and she's real pretty. Her father owns a fancy hotel in town. She doesn't have many friends her age, so I know she'll enjoy meeting you."

Rana observed the telltale glow that filled Cody's eyes and comprehended how much this girl meant to him. She warmed to a man who could show such deep emotion without being embarrassed. "Soon, I will ask you to bring her to visit me. It is good to have a special friend." Rana thought about Myeerah for a time and thrilled at the idea of making a good friend in her new home. If Mary Beth Sims was close to this pleasing man, she would be a very special person.

"Do you wish to sit with me until Grandfather returns?" she invited amiably, knowing he must feel awkward towering over her. Cody grinned and sat down on the middle step, within a few feet of her. "Tell me about . . . bronco-busting," she coaxed to relax him. "I saw the wild horses this morning. Travis said I could watch."

Cody eagerly slipped into an explanation of the taming procedure. As he spoke with knowledge and enthusiasm, he leaned against the next step and rested his elbow on it. Intrigued and attentive, Rana placed her chin on her hands, which were lying flat on her raised knees. Her head and Cody's were very close as he shared tales of past events.

From the hallway, Travis eyed the rankling scene on the front steps. Consumed by a novel burst of jealousy and possessiveness, he joined them, halting to hunker down behind Rana so he could boldly display his claim on her by the way he stroked her hair, then rested his hand on her shoulder. "Just what is this cowpoke filling your ears with?" he inquired jovially, concealing his irrational feelings from them.

Rana half-turned to meet his gaze and to respond, "Cody is telling me about taming wild horses. Can I choose one to replace *Mahpiya* as you promised?"

Cody observed the way Travis looked at Rana and trailed his finger across her flushed cheek as he nodded. His foreman and friend appeared to be mesmerized by those remarkably alluring eyes. Smiling, he decided that the two were deeply attracted to each other. He was pleased for Travis, for he felt this man deserved the best in a woman.

"As soon as we get them broken in, you can take your pick. Were you looking for me, Cody?" Travis queried, glancing his way.

Cody stood up and nodded. "I hired those men we talked about last night. You want to meet them and give 'em orders while they're getting settled in at the bunkhouse?"

"I'll be right along," Travis replied in a dismissing tone.

Cody smiled at Rana and told her, "It was a real pleasure meeting you, Miss Rana. If you need anything, just give me a holler." Cody noticed the way Travis tensed and frowned. Chuckling, he said to the half-blooded foreman, "See you at the bunkhouse, boss." Grinning broadly, he turned and strolled off at a jaunty pace, whistling.

Rana pondered why Travis was looking and acting so strangely. Wondering if he thought she might have said something wrong to Cody Slade, she related the entirety of their conversation. "Are you angry with me? Was it wrong to speak with your friend?"

Travis calmed himself, for he knew he had overreacted. "No, I'm not mad at you. It was all right to talk with Cody, but you have to be careful when you meet strangers. Cody might not have been a friend."

"But you and Grandfather spoke of him many times."

"I know, *micante*, but what if that man hadn't been Cody Slade?"

"Eyes do not lie, Travis Kincade. I read friendship and kindness in his. I like your friend. He is a good man, one who loves a woman named Mary Beth Sims," she reminded meaningfully.

Travis shrugged and mischievously asserted, "Must be that Indian blood acting crazy inside me. Can White Eagle help it if he's jealous and possessive of his wife, Wild Wind, when he can't claim her publicly?"

Rana laughed. "You do not trust your friend or your wife?"

"Trust any man around you? No, ma'am. You stay right here until I see my new hands." Travis chuckled heartily when her eyes filled with that now recognizable bewilderment. "Not these hands, *micante*; the men who work for us. They're called hands, cowpokes, wranglers, cowpunchers, cowboys, and a few other names."

"This white man's tongue will be hard to master. So many names, for one thing. Explain Cody's words, 'knee-high to a weaning calf'?"

Travis explained what calves and weaning were, then tried to explain slang. "He was saying he's been working here since he was a young boy, fourteen to be exact. Nate used to take in lots of young boys after their parents were killed, usually by Indians. You were right about Cody being a good man. I'm surprised he wasn't occupying the place Nate gave me. The same can be said of Mace Hunter. Those two are my best friends. I don't know how to explain the bond between me and Nate. As soon as we met, it was like father and son, and Nate insisted on making it legal so I wouldn't have any trouble getting the ranch after he died. 'Course the ranch is yours by right of blood. I was damn lucky Nate hadn't taken Cody or Mace as his son, or they might have doctored me and left me in Missouri and we wouldn't have met. Lordy, woman, listen to me rambling on and on. I never used to talk this much. Something about you just opens me up, makes me feel real comfortable, like a good pair of leather boots."

"It is the same with me, Travis. I feel I can say anything to you, and you would understand. It is good to be so close with you."

Travis gazed into her entreating eyes and stated mysteriously, "Soon, there'll be something I have to get straightened out before we can have a serious talk about our life together." He knew Rana did not realize the importance of the fact that he was legally Nathan Crandall's son and she was Nathan's granddaughter, making her his niece by law and making marriage between them impossible. Somehow he would have to find a way to void those adoption papers so he could marry Rana. Trouble was, he dared not start any obvious legal proceedings until lawyer Harrison Caldwell was out of their way. So many things appeared to be complicating his life these days, especially the matters concerning her.

Rana stood on the porch until Travis had vanished into the bunkhouse. She wanted to be near him all the time. She received so much pleasure just by looking at him or being near him. The sound of his voice seemed to tease over her entire body when he spoke. His caress and his scent enticed her, and his consuming gaze inflamed her from head to foot. She wanted to touch him, to taste him, to see him, to hear him, to enjoy him, and to share all things with him. She could not seem to get enough of him. He made her feel so calm, yet so stimulated. He made her feel as if he were everything, yet with so much more to explore or obtain. He was open, yet a mystery. He could satisfy her completely, yet leave her hungering for more. So many complex emotions filled her body, and they all centered around Travis Kincade.

Travis returned sometime later to tell Rana not to wait for him, for he was needed to instruct the new men and to make plans to overcome these new problems that had arisen. He suggested that she join her grandfather. Disappointed, Rana entered the house and headed for Nathan's office.

Nathan Crandall was leaning back in his chair and staring at the map over his desk, the one that had been altered today to indicate the unexpected enclosure of his lands by Harrison Caldwell. Over the years, Caldwell had added Sam Kelly's Box K Ranch and Harvey Jenkins's Lazy J Ranch to his Circle C holdings. Nathan had not truly been worried about Caldwell succeeding with his dream to forge a new cattle empire until James McFarland had sold out while he and Travis had been gone. If he had been here, he could have helped and advised his old friend. After his talk with Wilber Mason at the Mid-Texas Bank in Fort Worth, it had become clear from the terms of the sale and the price that Harrison Caldwell had practically stolen the Flying M Ranch, though legally, as he had supposedly acquired the other two spreads. Except for the river boundary, which was one reason why the Rocking C Ranch was so prosperous and coveted, Nathan's land was now encircled by that devious, determined rival who wanted his land and whose daughter wanted his son. They would never get either, Nathan resolved confidently.

It was hard for Nathan to imagine that he and Harrison had been genial acquaintances many, many years before. Not that they had ever been good friends, but they had been neighbors and their wives had been close. In fact, Harrison's wife, Sarah Jane, had been with his beloved Ruth when she had suffered her worst bouts of fever shortly before her death in '39. The poor creature had never recovered from that trying period, and she had been unable to face him again before her own demise in '44. One would have thought two neighboring widowers with small girls would have become good friends, but it was never to be, for Harrison Caldwell was nothing like Nathan Crandall.

Nathan admitted that perhaps he had kept to himself too much after his cherished wife's death, for he had not realized what Harrison Caldwell was plotting until the man's plans were well underway. Before he knew or suspected a thing, Caldwell was the owner of three of the four ranches that bordered Crandall holdings. While he and Travis had gone to recover his granddaughter, the last spread had been gobbled up. Ever since Caldwell's return from back east around the time Marissa had married and left home, the man had seemed bent on obtaining his ranch. It was almost as if something terrible had happened to Harry around that time to rile and embitter him, for he had become worse than ever after his return home. In the past few years, the guileful lawyer had made three offers for the Rocking C Ranch.

Nathan's mind drifted back to the day of his last overture. Caldwell had offered him any price for his ranch, saying Nathan could buy another ranch any-where and still have plenty of money to spend. Harrison had told him how impor-tant it was for a big rancher to own lots of connecting property with plenty of water and grazing land. They had talked, then argued, with Nathan vowing never to sell and Harrison claiming he would own this entire area one day.

Nathan slammed his fist down on his desk. If only he and Travis could find evidence to prove that Harrison Caldwell had driven the other ranchers away illegally. Somewhere papers and altered branding irons had to exist, as Travis had suggested on several occasions, and somewhere there was a witness who could be compelled to tell the truth. The trouble was, Harrison Caldwell was getting des-perate and was playing dirty by hiring gunslingers. Nathan hated to imagine the things happening on his ranch that had taken place on McFarland's. He could easily understand why the older man had given in to such malevolent forces.

What made things worse, if anything could be worse, was the fact that the two hirelings were the same two men from Travis's past. This posed the danger that Travis's personal feelings would get in the way of his thinking clearly. They could not expect any help from the sheriff—that had become obvious at their meeting this morning—unless the incompetent lawman was forced to take sides because of undeniable proof against Caldwell and his cohorts. If anything, the sheriff would turn on him and Travis for taking over his job and doing it efficiently and cor-rectly. It had become a touchy situation that had to be handled gingerly as well as secretly.

Nor could he expect any help or leniency from Wilber Mason. The man had come right out and admitted that his bank would foreclose on Nathan's loan after six o'clock on August first, if the debt was not paid in full. Of course, the lawyer for the bank was none other than Harrison Caldwell. Wilber Mason had even refused to discuss extending or renegotiating the loan. Clearly Caldwell was pres-suring the banker. The only way he could repay the loan and pay his hands was with the money from the cattle sale in Sedalia. He shuddered in horror when he thought of the possibility of that money being stolen. His men, under Mace Hunter and Todd Raines, had always been careful and loyal, but he was glad Travis had ordered Cody Slade to send more men and a warning to guard the cashbox.

He could still envision Caldwell's gloating face as it had been when they had met in town earlier today. He had vexed the Circle C owner by refusing to comment on his lengthy absence or to show concern over McFarland's bad luck during that absence. Neither had he told Harrison about the return or existence of his granddaughter. The insidious man would make that discovery soon enough, as would his daughter, Clarissa. Maybe news of Rana would shock the malicious vixen into . . .

"Grandfather?" Rana called to him. "Do you wish me to do some work for you? I do not understand the chores of your lands and home, so I laze here with nothing to do."

Nathan cast aside his troubling thoughts to spend time with her. "There's nothing that needs doing today, Rana. We'll let everything go until Rachel returns next week; then she can teach you about the house." In an attempt to keep her from being disquieted or embarrassed during the seamstress's and teacher's visits on Tuesday, Nathan went over what would be expected of her and the important purpose each would serve. He then gave Rana another tour of their home and explained its features in greater detail.

By the time Travis returned, she and Nathan had supper ready and waiting. It was after the evening meal was eaten and the dishes had been washed and they were drinking coffee in the sitting room that an unexpected, though anticipated, incident took place. Clarissa Caldwell arrived to see Travis, having learned of his return from her father. Even though it was nearing bedtime, the audacious woman had ridden over, after realizing with some annoyance that the handsome foreman was not coming to visit her on his second day home. To ensure their privacy, Clarissa had sent one of the hands to the house to fetch Travis to the yard.

After answering the summons at the door, Travis returned to the sitting room. He sent Rana a wry grin before he explained the rankling situation to Nathan. "Harrison Caldwell's daughter is outside and she wants to see me privately. What do you think, Nate?" he inquired casually, wondering how they should deal with Clarissa's immodest visit. Knowing that James McFarland had been squeezed out during their absence, both hoped that, in her eagerness to snare Travis, Clarissa might carelessly drop a clue about her father's activities. Yet, Travis dreaded conversing with the conniving vixen and being forced to enlighten Rana about her. He wished he had already told Rana about Clarissa and had explained their predicament with the Caldwells, especially the reasons for his past and present pretenses. He hated to imagine what Rana would think and feel about this oversight and his behavior toward Clarissa. In a way, he had promised not to deceive her or withhold vital information again, and nothing could be more vital to their relationship than a woman who was trying to captivate him while he pretended she might succeed. There was no way they could keep her from learning of the problems they were facing, and it would be in her best interest that she be well informed about them and about the people involved. He would have to see Clarissa, he decided, and get this distasteful matter over with tonight.

Neither of them wanted to subject Rana to Clarissa Caldwell this soon. That was an introduction both men wanted to put off as long as possible. Nathan saw Travis's reluctance and vexation, and he was slightly curious, for his adopted son usually enjoyed matching wits with both Caldwells, even if he could not stand either one. Maybe Travis wasn't in the mood for clever games tonight, Nathan mused. These past two months had been hard on his adopted son, and now he was facing more ghosts from his past and more danger from Harrison. Still, this task had to be done, and the sooner the better. "Considering what's been happening while we were gone, I think you should see her. Maybe you can learn something. Tell her whatever you think is best; just don't bring her inside."

Rana sensed a disturbing undercurrent in the room. From what the men had told her, Harrison Caldwell was their neighbor; yet they did not seem pleased with his daughter's visit. An aura of mystery and hesitation filled the room, making her suspicious and apprehensive. She could not understand why a woman would come to visit Travis so near to their sleeping time and why the men would need to discuss whether or not to see her. "Do you not wish me to meet this neighbor's daughter, grandfather? It is late and dangerous for a woman to be riding alone. Does she bring bad news?"

Neither man spoke for a time, which increased Rana's anxiety. Finally Travis replied, "I should have told you about Clarissa and her father before this. You'll have to meet her one day, Rana, but not tonight. She isn't the kind of woman you'll like or want to be around. I'd rather not see her tonight, but we need to know a few things—if she'll reveal them, which I doubt. Don't worry; I'll explain it all in the morning. You two go on to bed; it's late, and both of you have a busy day tomorrow. Hopefully I won't be long."

"If you and grandfather do not like her, why does she come to visit and why must you see her? Why do you refuse to allow her to enter our home?" she inquired, observing both men with rising suspicion. She knew that Travis and Nathan were not men to allow anyone to force them to do anything, so something was terribly amiss. Worst of all, her beloved looked nervous, and guilty of some wrong.

"I'll explain in the morning; just trust me," he coaxed.

Aware of how she would soon handle this distressing matter, Rana did not want to lie, so she chose her words carefully when she answered, "I will try to do as you say, but this matter is confusing."

Rana and Nathan said their good nights and went to their rooms. Travis dismissed the man who had been waiting on the front porch for further orders after delivering Clarissa's message.

The formidable man left the house to meet with Clarissa, who was pacing near the corral. The dark-haired, dusky-skinned woman halted to watch Travis Kincade's approach. Her deep brown eyes sparkled with desire and eagerness. She licked her lips in anticipation of fusing them to his. Her entire body began to warm and itch with barely suppressible lust. She could hardly wait to get this virile male in her arms, in bed or anywhere he chose. Someday and somehow she would break down his resistance; then he would be hers.

With a leisurely stride that exposed his confidence, agility, and a hint of arrogance, Travis reached her. He flashed her a devilish grin as he lazed negligently against a large post, then asked, "Isn't it a bit late for such a lovely lady to be out calling on neighbors? Cody tells me there's been some trouble in these parts while we were gone. I know you're a fearless and stubborn girl, but I'm surprised your papa let you leave home with so much danger lurking."

As her appreciative gaze roamed his face and body, Clarissa offered him a seductive pout and throaty laugh. "No man, good or bad, would dare attack Harrison Caldwell's daughter. Since you haven't come over to see me since your return, I've cast all shame aside to visit you."

Travis chuckled heartily. "I've only been back since last night."

She added petulantly, "And you were busy all day. You've been gone for months, love, and I've missed you terribly. Is this any way to greet me?" she asked provocatively, stepping forward to press her body against his intimately. "You're a cruel and selfish beast, Travis Kincade. Why do I allow you to treat me so badly?" she teased, running her fingers through his sable hair before using them to pull his head down to hers to seal their lips.

Travis was tempted to spurn her and her kiss, but he knew the only way to extract information about her father's insidious dealings was by faking a response. His arms went around her and tightened to expose his strength and control, and his mouth seared over hers, causing her to tremble with hunger. Lordy, he hated touching this woman and being nice to her! If there hadn't been so much at stake, he would have sent her on her way, after telling her how he really felt about her. Yet there were limits to his game with her; he would never bed her for any reason. It was not that Clarissa wasn't a very attractive and sensual woman, and no doubt skilled in lovemaking, but her character made her ugly and repulsive to him. During the time he had known her, he had never been tempted to accept sex from her, and she had offered it countless times. Over the years since his coming of age as a man, he had been able to separate his emotions from his sexual urges. After that perilous incident with Elizabeth Lowry, he had become very selective about whom he bedded, even on the occasions he had visited the Silver Shadow Saloon. But having taken Rana and having blended emotion with lovemaking, his feelings would never be the same. Now the only woman with whom he wanted to unite his body and share his passion was Rana Michaels. She had taught him that the act of mating was something special and that it should not be performed with just anyone, even if one's body was screaming for release.

When Clarissa's hands began to wander boldly over his body, Travis grasped them to halt the wanton display. He leaned back and taunted, "Behave yourself, woman. My cowpunchers are still up and around. We don't want them teasing their boss or thinking naughty thoughts about you. Seems a lot happened while I was gone. From what the boys have told me, it's dangerous around here for women. You'd best get home, and I'll see you in a few days."

"It's been months, Travis. I want to spend time with you. Besides, if it's so dangerous out there, you should escort me home safely," she cajoled, yearning to get him alone.

"What about those two gunslingers your papa hired? Aren't they supposed to guard you as well as Harry's property?" he jested, lifting a curl with which he began teasing her nose. "Tell me, you clever vixen, how did you sneak off with your place being watched? If you can slip past them, they must not be very good at their new job."

Clarissa chuckled at the tickling sensation. She captured Travis's hand and placed kisses over it, then erotically trailed her tongue over each finger and across his palm before suggestively and lasciviously sucking on several of his fingertips as her gaze seduced him. "When I want something badly enough, I find a way to get it," she replied breathlessly, for her actions were stimulating her to feverish desire. "If I tell you or show you how to sneak through Papa's guard line, will you use the information to visit my room tonight?" she inquired sultrily.

Travis playfully traced his forefinger from her nose, across her lips and chin, over her throat, and down her chest, to halt at the swell of her breasts where the first button on her shirt was fastened. His roguish gaze never left hers as the finger began to slip very slowly up and down her deep cleft, visibly increasing her respiration and pulse rate. He mischievously chided, "I've told you before, hot-blooded lady, I don't get involved with daughters of important or dangerous men. If Harry caught us together like that, he would skin my hide, or force me to take a wife if you were to get with child. Sorry, Clarissa, but I'm not ready to settle down or to risk getting run out of this area. I've put in my best years on this ranch and Nate has claimed me as his son and heir; I don't aim to waste or spoil that by upsetting him, 'cause you know how he feels about your papa. One of these days I'm gonna find out why those two hate each other so much. I'd bet my year's wages you know the truth, but you ain't talking."

Travis watched a telltale grin form on Clarissa's mouth, but she held her silence. "When I do get ready to settle down with a wife and home, there's one thing for sure, Clarissa. There's only one tempting female around here. I still got me a few wild years and urges left. You just be patient and obliging while I tame 'em. Now, get along. I have to get up early. Work piled up while Nate and me were on the trail. Then there's this trouble that started brewing during our absence. Harry got any idea who's behind all the rustling and fence cutting?"

Deceitfully she vowed, "If I knew anything, love, I would have told you by now. Poor Mister McFarland, he got so scared he sold out and left. I suppose he was too old and weak to put up a fight. Did you know one of his sons asked me to marry him?"

Travis frowned as he arched one brow and narrowed his green eyes, acting as if he were jealous. He winced inwardly as he lied to Clarissa to entrap her. "You'd best be glad you said no, woman. McFarland ain't got no son with guts, or they would still be over at the Flying *M* Ranch. Even if a gang of devils and demons rode in here, I would never be pushed off my land. All of my blood would soak into this dirt before I deserted it. Besides, like me, you aren't ready to settle down to marriage and children yet." They both laughed. "Nate talked with the sheriff, but that fool doesn't know anything. If you ask me, we ranchers will have to handle this matter ourselves. Maybe we should hire us some fancy gunslingers like your papa did. Except every hired gun I've ever met eventually turned on his boss and killed him. One person you can't trust is a man who hires on for money, 'cause somebody always has more money and can lure him away, or he kills you and takes more than his share of blood money. You be careful around them."

"I warned Papa those crude men might be trouble. If anything happens, Papa has only himself to blame for hiring such lowbred ruffians. I wouldn't be surprised if they've ridden as outlaws or if they try to rob Papa. You don't have to worry about me; I try to stay as far away from them as possible. But you know Papa, Travis; he thinks he can handle anyone and anything. Sometimes he's so mean to me. He became furious when I begged him to fire those beasts. Sometimes I can't wait until Papa is gone and our ranch is mine, and Nathan is gone and this ranch is yours. What an empire we could build together!" she exclaimed, wondering how he would react to her statements.

"Those dreams are a long way off, Miss Caldwell. Right now, I need sleep so I can catch up with my chores."

"You wouldn't need to catch up if you hadn't been gone so long," she scolded peevishly, finally reaching the topic that intrigued her the most. She felt she had avoided it long enough to begin questioning him without overly arousing his suspicion or annoyance. "Wherever did you go, love, and why were you away so long? Cody wouldn't tell me anything, and I was so worried about you. I think he's mad because Papa's been seeing his little sweetheart. Isn't that a laugh, Travis? A man of Papa's age pursuing a child bride? He's making a fool of himself."

"Is he really interested in Mary Beth?" Travis probed.

Clarissa wanted Travis to warn Cody to snap up the little creature before her father did, and so she confided, "It's a big secret between Papa and Mister Sims, but they've discussed marriage. That's all I need—a stepmother younger than I am! I told Papa that Mary Beth and Cody were sweethearts, but he doesn't care. Papa says he needs a wife, and she's the best choice."

"And Sims is going along with this ridiculous demand?"

"He's most agreeable. Don't you tell a soul about this, or Papa will skin me alive. He says I've been bossing him too much lately. I don't know what's gotten into him, Travis; he's behaving like a crazy man."

"I take it you won't be upset if me and Cody save Mary Beth from your father?" he teased, tugging gently on a lock of ebony hair.

"Please do, and spare me the humiliation of this absurd marriage. Let's talk about you. Where did you go, and why?"

"You'll never believe what happened in early May. Nate got news about his missing granddaughter, Rana Michaels, the one who was taken captive by Indians eleven years ago. We rode to the Dakota Territory to find this girl who favored Marissa."

The dusky-complexioned woman stared at Travis. "Well?" she probed anxiously when he did not continue. "Was it Marissa's child?"

"I'm afraid it was. She's in the house asleep right now. It cost us five thousand dollars to buy her from the Indians, and nearly cost us our lives. Seems a chief took a liking to her and adopted her as his daughter. She's been living as an Indian princess for ten years. Lordy, she's a willful, spoiled little creature. The chief named her Wild Wind, if that tells you anything about her. I practically had to hog-tie her and drag her all the way home. I've never been more tempted to turn a girl over my knee and whack her good than I was with that little brat. She fought me tooth and nail, and I probably still have scars to prove it. But it didn't take the little minx long to see that this ranch was a good thing. Knowing her, she'll probably try to weasel the entire spread out of Nate. She's a crafty little savage."

"I take it you aren't too pleased with her or her return?"

"Are you *loco*, woman? I've heard plenty of stories about her mother, and believe me, she's just like Marissa Crandall, or worse."

Clarissa scoffed rashly, "You don't know the half of it, love; Marissa was far worse than most people realized. If Nathan knew the truth, he would deny Marissa and this Rana Michaels."

Travis stared at her, sensing something mysterious in her tone and look. Clearly this woman knew some secret that few, if any, others knew. "What about Marissa?" he probed nonchalantly. "I thought you two became close friends before she was killed."

She laughed coldly, then murmured, "One day I might tell you all about Nathan's wicked daughter. What does this Rana look like?"

"You've seen the picture of Marissa over the fireplace. Let's just say that at first glance you'll think you're seeing a ghost."

Clarissa swallowed and digested this bitter information. Hatred and alarm coursed through her body. She wondered what her father would think and do when he discovered this shocking news. And, she fretted angrily, what about Rana's effect on Travis? Another Marissa to battle for the men she craved . . .

"Marissa Crandall Michaels was a very beautiful woman. If Rana favors her, then why aren't you inside with her instead of out here with me? You could have her and the ranch with one bite. No doubt her mother's whoring blood runs through her," she commented scornfully, watching how he took this insult.

"No doubt it does, but not where I'm concerned," Travis replied, having successfully concealed his fury. "She's a little brat, Clarissa, and she nearly drove me crazy. She still expects to be treated like a princess, and I won't bend to her wishes. I can't count the number of fights and quarrels we had on the trail. Damn, it's good to be home again. Facing rustlers will be a pleasant change from battling her."

"Why didn't Nathan tell Papa about her this morning?"

He scowled. "Like I said, she's little more than a savage. Nate plans to keep her hidden in the house until that schoolteacher and the seamstress can have her looking and acting half civilized."

"Is she very crude? Can she speak English?"

"Yep, the chief took a schoolmarm captive and forced her to teach the little brat English so she could question prisoners. Oh, she can look and talk white, but underneath she's wild and vicious. She's always trying to bite me or scratch me when she gets mad, and those little teeth and claws are mighty sharp. One hand's bandaged now where she broke several nails attacking me a few days ago. Her Indian father died a few months back, and she was giving her Indian brother fits. He was glad to get rid of her. Now I see why. I can tell you one thing, Miss Caldwell. I'm gonna tame that wild wind for Nate."

"What if she tames you first, my proud and carefree wrangler?"

"What if the sun doesn't rise tomorrow?" he said with a sneer.

"Tell me, love, are you really angry because she's so beautiful and she spurns you?" Clarissa held his gaze as she sought signs of deception.

Travis chuckled. "Would you like to know how many times I've kicked her off my sleeping roll? If I wanted Rana Michaels, my jealous vixen, I could have taken her plenty of times by now. Her hot blood even outblazes yours, and she has no morals or manners. She's been raised wild and free, to take whatever she wants. She rides bareback and goes barefoot, and thinks nothing of shucking her clothes and going for a swim when the mood strikes her. Her temper is as fiery as her hair. Maybe my stinging rejections riled her, 'cause I ain't sharing no bedroll with a wildcat." A playful grin crossed his face as he added, "Maybe I should relent just to have peace in the house. 'Course, like your papa, Nate would tie me to that little vixen if I shared her bed like she keeps inviting. Lordy, Clarissa, I can't think of anything worse than marrying a real bitch, can you?"

"Are you afraid Nathan might turn the ranch over to her? He did make you his son and heir. He would have to disown you."

"I won't let him, and I won't let her take it," he replied smugly.

"If you lose this ranch, love, you can marry me and take over the Caldwell holdings, which are increasing every year," she offered.

"The Caldwell empire doesn't have my blood and sweat all over it. This ranch is mine, one way or another, after Nate's gone."

"If you come home with me tonight, I'll tell you how and why you're

Nathan's only legal heir. If you get the right information and help, Rana Michaels can't claim an inch of this ranch."

"Just what are you trying to tell me without coming right out and saying it?" Travis pulled her close against him and kissed her soundly. "If you know something that can help me, spit it out," he entreated huskily, then nibbled at her ear.

"You're teasing me and tempting me unmercifully, Travis. I'm sure my lips and wits will loosen while you're making love to me."

"So, that's it, a trick to seduce me," Travis accused wickedly.

She nibbled on his lower lip and rubbed her body against his as she stated, "I swear to you I know something about Marissa that can end your worries, but you'll have to prove I can trust you."

Travis eyed her speculatively. "By sleeping with you tonight?" When she nodded, he argued, "Come now, Clarissa; I could sleep with you a hundred times and that wouldn't prove you could trust me. Don't you realize by now, if I considered you just another woman, I would bed you without a care. You mean something very special to me, so I can't use you or treat you lightly. If you can't understand or accept that, we don't need to see each other again. I have enough problems right now with the ranch and that little brat without your adding to them. Lordy, woman, you know I don't see anybody but you."

"But you don't see me enough, Travis," she wailed greedily.

"I'll tell you what. Let me get things straightened out over here and then we'll start seeing each other more, and talking seriously. I told you I ain't ready to get married yet, but we might get promised soon if things work out. Like I said, be patient and trust me."

"You aren't teasing me, are you?" she challenged.

"I don't see anybody but you, and getting promised would stop you from seeing anybody but me. I'm the one who has to worry, not you. Who could Travis Kincade Crandall choose besides the most beautiful and passionate woman around?"

Clarissa was mostly taken in by Travis's silky words, though he had actually been referring to Rana each time. Blinded by vanity and overconfidence, she naturally assumed Travis was smitten with her and would eventually marry her. If he wanted her to behave like a lady, then she would do so, at least around him. She felt he must be anxious to get his hands all over her, and would soon tire of denying himself that pleasure. Now that he was worried over his inheritance, perhaps he would come around to her way of thinking, and perhaps together they could get rid of Nathan and her father and take over both ranches. But she would have to be careful.

Rana Michaels, Marissa's little bastard, would never interfere with her plans! If necessary, she would expose the truth about Marissa's vile birth. Perhaps one day soon she would tell Travis that Marissa was not Nathan Crandall's daughter and legal heir, and that Rana Michaels was not Nathan's granddaughter. Perhaps she would tell Travis what Ruth Crandall, Nathan's beloved wife, had revealed to Sarah Jane Caldwell while in a delirium before she died. Once she had heard Ruth's secret, Clarissa's mother had never been able to look Nathan in the eye again. Travis might be relieved, and deliciously grateful, to discover that Ruth had been raped by three outlaws during Nathan's three-month absence thirty-eight years ago. Ruth had never told Nathan, even though she had borne a child of that brutal assault. Ruth's fever-dulled mind and loosened lips had even caused her to divulge which of the three villains had been responsible: a flaming-haired, blue-eyed Scotsman who had been called "Red." The old fool, Nathan, had actually believed that the baby girl named Marissa had arrived over two months early. For a fact, neither Nathan nor Marissa had ever learned about Ruth's ravishment. If Marissa had known the truth about her birth . . . But no matter now.

Perhaps she would tell Travis how Marissa had whored with her father for two years and for her husband for many years. Perhaps she would tell him that Rana was not Raymond Michaels's daughter, just as Marissa was not Nathan's child. Perhaps she would tell him who Rana's real father was. No, that would spoil her plans . . .

Travis was gazing inquisitively at the brown-eyed beauty. She had been silent for a long time. Something was running wildly through her head, and he wanted to know all about it. What, he wondered, did she know about Marissa that could affect his life, and Rana's too? "Like the Indians say, you've got a fox running around inside that pretty head. Marissa told you a big secret. What was it?"

"I'll tell you another day, my love. I should get home before Papa misses me and your hands think I'm unworthy to become your wife. As you told me, be patient and trusting a while longer."

Travis knew it would be a mistake to press her tonight, so he allowed the intriguing matter to drop. "Wait until I saddle Apache; it's too dangerous for you to be out alone, even if you were anxious to see me. Next time, woman, you control such reckless urges. In spite of what you think, some men aren't afraid of your papa. Promise me you won't go riding after dark again."

"I'm sorry for behaving so foolishly. I promise," she whispered, then kissed him ardently. She couldn't tell him she was safe because the villains worked for her father and would soon be working for her . . .

Travis left her then, but he was soon back at her side with Apache and her sorrel. He helped her mount and they rode off together.

Rana leaned against the house and closed her eyes, which forced her pent-up tears to overflow and stream down her cheeks. How she wished she could have gotten close enough to hear their words, for their behavior had seared her heart. She slipped around the house and climbed inside her room, wishing she had not crawled out her window to spy on Travis and that infuriating female called Clarissa Caldwell. She flung herself across the bed and wept as she recalled how Wild Wind and White Eagle had spent this morning in each other's arms. Was this woman the "something I have to get straightened out before we can have a serious talk about our life together"?

Suddenly Rana sat up and scolded herself. No matter how that scene had looked to her, there was probably a logical explanation for it. It was wrong to start doubting her husband, or to renounce him. She must trust him, as he had en-treated earlier, and fight for him! If she let this matter pass, it would eat her alive inside. The best thing to do was confront Travis and give him the chance to tell her the truth. Their relationship was too new and special to allow misunderstandings to damage it. She loved Travis, and she believed he loved her; so why should she suffer unnecessarily? Yes, she must give him a chance to defend himself, she decided, just as soon as he returned home.

Travis and Clarissa headed for the edge of the Circle *C* Ranch that was nearest the Caldwell house. At a safe distance, the clever Travis told her, "Now you get in that house and stay there. I don't want anything happening to you. I'll come by Wednesday or I'll see you in town Thursday." He leaned over and kissed her as if feasting on the sweetest mouth of any woman alive. He smiled and waved, then rode away.

It was late, but Travis was restless tonight, and he decided to ride along the northeast fence line, which had once bordered Sam Kelly's Box *K* Ranch. Their largest herd was grazing in that area, and he wanted to nose around before returning to the ranch. Besides, he had some serious thinking and planning to do. He would need to explain to Rana about the Caldwells and obtain her help with duping Clarissa. That wasn't going to be easy, for what woman in her right mind would want to aid her lover's pursuit of another woman, even if it was only a false chase? He had to convince Rana that Harrison and Clarissa were dangerous, that they wouldn't hesitate to destroy anything or anyone who got in their way. Rana was smart and brave; she would understand this predicament and help him, he decided. Squaring his shoulders, he rode off in search of answers, for himself and for the ranch.

Clarissa made certain that Travis had not hung back after delivering her to her ranch, then she rode off toward the cabin where Wes Monroe and Jackson Hayes were staying. There was only one horse standing near the cabin. She sneaked to a window and peeked inside to find Wes lying naked on a bunk in one corner and, surprisingly, reading a book. She smiled wickedly as she noticed he was alone, which suited her perfectly. When she knocked on the door, Wes answered, wearing nothing but a cotton sheet he had grabbed and wrapped around his hips. She watched him lower his pistol, eye her up and down, then grin pruriently.

Lacking all modesty, he leaned against the door jamb and asked, "What can I do for you, Miss Caldwell? You can see I wasn't expecting company, especially the boss's daughter. Did you need something?"

Clarissa glanced over his bare shoulder, as if checking to see if he was alone. "I need to talk about something personal," she replied, allowing her gaze to roam his face and torso. "Is your partner around?"

"Nope, and he won't be back until morning. Why don't you come inside and take a chair, if you ain't afraid of me."

"I'm not afraid of anyone, Mister Monroe," she vowed smugly. "But I want this matter to remain between you and me."

He motioned her inside and closed the door behind her. "The name's Wes to such a beautiful woman. Care for a drink?"

She nodded, then slithered seductively around the room while he fetched a bottle of whiskey and two cups. Clarissa downed the golden liquid easily and quickly, then held out her cup for another drink. She noticed how Wes was watching her as she leisurely sipped the second one. Her gaze drifted over his bare chest and legs and returned to his eyes, eyes that did not conceal his lust for her. Yes, she concluded, this man was deceitful and dangerous, and those evil qualities excited and aroused her. She would ensnare Wes with money and her charms, use him, and be done with him before he realized what was happening. When she was finished with him, she would kill him herself while he was dozing in the afterglow of sated passion, or perhaps kill him at the instant of his final release. That would be one of the most stimulating and erotic moments of her life, to watch a man's expression shift from the ecstasy of passion as he comprehends the horror of his own death. She licked her lips and smiled. "You mustn't tell my father or your partner or anyone I came here tonight. This is strictly between us. I want to hire you to do a job for me. How much will your complete loyalty cost me?"

"What kind of job would a pretty lady like you need doing?" Wes asked, pouring more whiskey into Clarissa's cup.

"I need an important man killed," she stated simply.

Wes's face revealed surprise. He eyed her keenly, then grinned. After downing the contents of his cup, he asked, "Who, and why?"

Clarissa laughed sultrily. She set down her cup, strolled to the door, and opened it. She pressed the center of her back against the frame and, on either side of her hips, clasped the edges of it with her fingers, striking a pose that caused her bosom to jut out noticeably. She rubbed her fingers over the hewn logs behind her, relishing the feel of the biting splinters and rough surface. She looked outside and inhaled the breeze that carried with it the blended odors of wildflowers and grasses. It was dark, for only a quarter moon was shining and clouds concealed most of the stars. Hints of a possible thunderstorm filled the air and she hoped it would strike, for she loved the awesome power of raw nature. The cabin smelled of cheroot smoke, whiskey, gun oil, leather, and masculine sweat: sensual and stimulating fragrances to her. When Wes joined her at the door and leaned against the other side, she murmured, "Do you ever do jobs only for the money and without questions? You didn't ask how much I'm willing to pay."

Wes straightened and stepped toward her. He trailed his fingers up her left arm and down the opening of her shirt until a button halted him. His right hand slipped over one breast and cupped it, then his forefinger and thumb kneaded the taut point between them. He was stirred by her lack of a chemise and the way her peak responded to his touch. He kept staring into Clarissa's eyes as he made move after move on her body. She returned his gaze, and not once did she attempt to stay his hands or scold him. As Wes's left hand drifted down the outside of her leg, then made its way up the inside of her thigh, he asked in a hoarse voice, "I always have to know who I'm killing and why, 'cause some jobs ain't worth the risks. Money is useless if you're put in jail or six feet under." Wes's hand made contact with a fuzzy patch between Clarissa's thighs. He realized she wasn't wearing anything but a shirt and skirt and a pair of boots. Pressing his hardened manhood against her thigh, he began to massage the greedy bud beneath her skirt. "Tell me, Miss Caldwell, what is a beautiful and desirable woman willing to pay for this important man's life?"

Clarissa undulated her hips against his hand and responded breathlessly,

"Tonight, I only want to know if you're for hire. In a few weeks, I'll tell you who and why, and how to do it. First of all, I have to make sure I can trust you to do the job perfectly and secretly."

"Unbutton your shirt," he commanded in a ragged voice. After she obeyed, he replied, "You've got a deal, Miss Caldwell, if I like your first payment tonight." His mouth closed over one breast and his finger slipped inside her moist body.

Clarissa loosened the sheet and let it fall to the floor. She grasped his manhood and murmured, "I'll make certain you don't change your mind, Wes. You do this job for me, and you can name your price."

He looked her in the eye and said, "The price is you, woman."

Clarissa smiled and drew his mouth to hers . . .

—— *Chapter 13* ——

❧

IT WAS NEARING TWO O'CLOCK when Travis reached the house. He removed his boots at the front door and entered stealthily. Taking the low-burning lantern from the front hallway, he slipped quietly to Rana's door. Deciding it was too late to disturb her, he went to his room and undressed. Before he could toss the cover aside and lie down, his door opened and Rana came inside, closing it after her entrance, and seeming not to notice that he was standing nude near his bed. Even if she had noticed his condition, it did not seem to trouble or embarrass her or deter her from her purpose.

The lantern on the bedside table gave off a soft glow, which lovingly bathed her in its adoring light and enhanced the colors of her flaming hair and gray-blue eyes. Without a word or hesitation, she came forward and halted before him, leaving only a few inches separating their bodies as she looked up into his striking face. Her yearning gaze locked with his and each absorbed the bond that stretched between them and encircled them. Only their soft breathing could be heard in the quietness. As if magically transfixed, neither spoke or moved; they just looked at each other, each sensing the other's matching need.

A light breeze played with the thin covering over the open window and sent stirring fragrances into the shadowy room. Beyond it, if they had not been so enraptured by each other, they would have heard cattle lowing, night birds and insects singing soulfully, and the distant rumble of thunder. The lantern light danced across their entranced features and susceptible bodies, highlighting certain areas as each admired the appeal of the other. It was as if all else was moving very slowly in an attempt to postpone the intrusions of a new day.

Travis lifted one hand and tenderly caressed her face, touching and enjoying each arresting feature. Rana did the same to him. They looked, and touched, and savored each other as if mesmerized. Travis's hands cupped her face and he brushed his lips so lightly over hers that it seemed their mouths were barely touching. His lips drifted lazily over her face, making contact with each rise and fall of its beloved features. His warm respiration was tantalizing at her ear as he buried his nose and hands in her thick hair. His mouth moved across her forehead and kissed each closed eye and then her nose before gently claiming her mouth. The kiss was leisurely and romantic, and ever so gradually he deepened its pressure and intensity, revealing his immense pleasure and yearning. His hands slipped down her neck and across her shoulders and he released the quilt that was wrapped around her, bringing their naked bodies together. His kisses softened once more, for he wanted this stimulating period to stir her thoroughly.

Rana's fingers trailed over Travis's firm yet pliant frame, stopping here and there to caress a bulging muscle or to admire the supple sleekness of his physique. His golden flesh felt so warm and vital, as if she were caressing the soft underbelly of a mighty buck. Her fingers traced over tiny scars that told of his battle-riddled life and enormous prowess, and she lovingly touched those that had gone much deeper than his skin. As he nibbled on her neck and shoulder, she nuzzled his ear and the side of his head. It was sheer bliss just to touch him and to be touched by him. Her hands grew bolder in their wanderings, as did his.

Travis lifted her and placed her on his bed. After dousing the lantern, he joined her. Time passed as they kissed and caressed and explored sensations that heightened their passions. There were no inhibitions or hesitations, no shame or guilt, but only the richness and beauty of their unique love. Both seemed to want to know every inch on the other's body, and how it affected the other when that area was touched and kissed in different ways. It was as if they had forever to enjoy this rapturous enlightenment, and as if they had been a part of each other longer than time itself. But fiery desires, which had been kindled so skillfully and rigidly held at a smoldering peak while they savored these stimulating pleasures, gradually seared through their control and ignited their flaming passions into one roaring blaze.

Their kisses and caresses expressed the depth and urgency of their mutual desire. As their bodies fused into one, Travis murmured against her ear, "I love you, Rana, more than anyone in my life. I waited a long time for someone special to enter my heart. Be mine forever, *micante*." He kissed her possessively, hungrily.

She felt weak and breathless from the intensity of her emotions. "I am yours forever, *mihigna*. My heart is filled with love for you. Let no one and nothing come between us, or part us."

Together they scaled and conquered the heights of blissful ecstasy and, afterward, settled peacefully in each other's arms. Travis lay on his back and cuddled her snugly against him. He continued to caress her tenderly until his breathing rate was restored to normal. "We have to talk, *micante*," he finally murmured, hating to allow anything to intrude on their meager time together, particularly the Caldwells, but knowing he should speak promptly to avoid misunderstanding.

"About Clarissa Caldwell and her father?" she asked knowingly.

Travis tensed uncontrollably, and wished he had not. "Lordy, Rana, how do I explain a dirty mess like this? I should have told you about them earlier, but it's such a bitter matter. It makes me mad every time I see them or think about them, and it riled me good when Clarissa raced her fanny over here tonight. I hope you didn't get too upset with me for meeting with her outside. By the time I escorted her home, I was so agitated I had to go riding to settle down." His tone changed noticeably as he continued. "They scare me, Rana, and I don't scare easily. They're evil, and cunning, and greedy. I don't want you getting involved with either one of them, but I doubt that's possible. Promise me you'll hear me out before you get mad, 'cause I've done some things and plan to do others that you won't like."

When he seemed to have difficulty finding the right words to begin, she coaxed, "Do not be afraid to speak what is in your heart. I love you. I will understand . . . and obey, for you would not ask me to do anything that does not matter greatly to us. We are as one now, and what harms you harms me. Reveal your fears and pain."

He hugged her fiercely. "Lordy, woman, do I even deserve you? I love you and trust you, Rana, but what I have to tell you and ask you will prove hard and painful, for both of us. And it's very dangerous."

"My father . . . I mean Soaring Hawk, told me that waiting makes it no easier, and sharing pain makes it less. Love and trust are powerful weapons, my beloved husband, and they can defeat evil if you believe in them strongly and use them against your enemies."

"I don't want to do or say anything that might cause trouble between us. I love you and need you, Rana. If you don't agree with what I suggest, I swear I won't do it, no matter what the consequences might be."

"Consequences?" she echoed in confusion.

"Things that happen because of something we say or do. Usually consequences are bad things that happen after we make a mistake," he explained. "Let me tell you about Clarissa and her evil father; then you'll see what we're up against." Travis revealed what he knew Harrison had done and what he believed the man was going to attempt. He discussed his past deceit with Clarissa and his current scheme to extract information from her by pretending she was special to him. He told her what had taken place at the corral and what had happened afterward. "I promise you it won't ever go any further than that. It makes me sick just to fake responses and touch her. It's even harder now that I have you. You'll have to play along with this game, Rana, or I'll have to stop it right now. Do you understand how dangerous it can be for all of us, especially you, if Clarissa and her father see you as a problem?"

Rana sat up and lapsed into deep thought. Several things became very clear to her: if Clarissa doubted she could win Travis, the selfish creature would consider him of little use, and his life would be in danger; also, her grandfather would be safe only as long as the Caldwells retained hope of getting the ranch peacefully through Travis and Clarissa. Until her unexpected return, Travis had been Nathan's only heir, but now that she stood to inherit the property, the Caldwells might view her as an obstacle to their evil plans. She was worried about the proximity of the two gunslingers who had once tried to murder her beloved, and deeply concerned over the evil those men could do in league with the Caldwells. Travis was right; they must join forces to unmask and overcome them.

"Rana?" Travis whispered apprehensively. He had not told Rana about Clarissa's insults and insinuations about her mother, and he feared that perhaps she sensed he was withholding something. But he refused to tell her things that could be lies and would pain her deeply. "Tell me what you think," he encouraged, sitting up beside her. He wished the room hadn't been so dark, for he yearned to see her expression; yet he could not blame her if she chose to be angry about what he had said and done with Clarissa.

She snuggled against him. "You love me, and you need my help and understanding. You will have all of them, and all of me. We must make plans and decide how much we will tell Grandfather. He will be sad if he does not know why we behave so coldly to each other."

Travis seized her and hugged her with overpowering love and gratitude. "We'll tell him how much I love you and want to marry you just as soon as this mess is over, if you'll say yes a second time."

"Are you sure you wish to make this choice so soon?"

He kissed her forehead. "As far as I'm concerned, we're already married, by our choice. All we need to do is make it legal under the white man's law. Well, what do you think about marrying me again?"

"I love you and would marry you again and again," she responded happily. "We must tell Grandfather about our love and plans for a new marriage; he will help us keep our secrets and fool our enemies. It will be good to work as a family to defeat such evil foes. But we should not tell Grandfather about this," she murmured playfully, pressing him to the bed and running her hands over his body. She kissed and caressed him feverishly, stirring new passions to life. When he was completely ensnared by heady desire, she confessed her earlier spying. They both laughed.

There were only a few hours remaining before dawn. Travis kissed Rana gently and told her she must return to her room and bed. She did as he requested, anticipating the day when such secrecy would no longer be necessary. Never had she been so happy, or so nervous about their impending actions. She snuggled into her comfortable bed and closed her eyes, pleased that she had gone to him, thereby preventing any problems.

Hours later, Rana smelled breakfast cooking. She slipped into the bathing closet to refresh herself and to dress for this busy day. As she entered the kitchen, she found Nathan sitting at the table and drinking coffee. They exchanged smiles. Nathan told her that Travis had left earlier to handle the morning chores. She ate while Nathan sat smiling at her.

"Grandfather, did Travis tell you a secret this morning?" she asked, unable to contain her joy any longer.

Nathan beamed. "Seems my family will be getting closer but not bigger real soon. I'm happy and pleased, Rana. You and Travis are perfect for each other. And I'm glad you understand about this mess with Harry's daughter. Think you two can fool her? Hiding love isn't easy," he teased, adding milk to another cup of coffee.

"We must do this until our enemies are defeated. Again we will fight side by side, Grandfather. We will be brave and cunning, and we will defeat them as we did the bluecoat foes on the trail."

"I'm proud of you, Rana, and of Travis. But I want you two to be real careful. Those Caldwells are dangerous and wicked."

"I understand, Grandfather. I will follow orders."

When the pudgy seamstress arrived mid-morning, the cheery woman was delighted with the lucrative task and the lovely girl she would outfit. She quickly took measurements and discussed clothing with Rana and Nathan, who ordered everything Rana might need or want. Mrs. Clara Dobbs told them she would begin the new wardrobe that very day and would send out a few ready-to-wear garments for Rana's immediate use. When Nathan asked the woman if she would help Rana learn how to dress properly, Clara Dobbs replied that she would be delighted to instruct Rana in any way she could. Moreover, the harrowing tale of the girl's past misfortune did not trouble Clara in the least. Mrs. Dobbs was charmed by the gentle, beautiful girl, and she was certain others would be also. With a genuine smile, the pugnosed woman bid them good day and departed with one of the hands, who would accompany her to her shop and retrieve the promised ready-made items.

After the noon meal, the local schoolteacher arrived. Nathan introduced Rana to Aaron Moore, then left the two alone in the sitting room. Aaron used his first session with Rana to question and test the extent of her knowledge. He was pleased by how much she knew and by her quick and keen intelligence. He could tell he was going to enjoy tutoring this radiant, eager pupil. Finally, he told her he would return the following day to begin their lessons. Rana was delighted when he promised he would also teach her customs, etiquette, and dancing.

After bidding the teacher farewell, Rana relaxed in the sitting room and glanced through the books Aaron Moore had left with her. She realized her journey back to the white world would be hard, but she was proud of the fact that she was learning things every hour. So far, everyone seemed so friendly and helpful. Yet she knew there were some nearby who would despise her and try to hurt her. But she had Travis and her grandfather, and together they made a happy family. Her life had changed so much since the winter snows had left the Oglala lands, and those changes had been good ones.

Rana rested an open book against her chest as her gaze traveled to her mother's portrait. Laying aside the volume, she walked to the fireplace. She looked closely at Marissa's image, then at the two portraits of herself. Comparing them, she noticed how closely she favored her mother and that pleased her, for the resemblance seemed to provide a bond between them, one that overcame even the dark barricade of death. Yet there was also an eeriness in being the reflection of another person, one who had suffered greatly in life and who had died so young and tragically. Rana wanted to know everything about her mother, but she suspected that few, if any, knew the truth or had known the woman. Intelligence and courage were reflected in Marissa's eyes, traits that should have prevented such a woman from marrying a brutal, evil man like Raymond Michaels. Even now, Rana could not imagine that man being her father, though she knew she could not alter the circumstances of her birth.

Rana wondered what her life would have been like if Marissa had married another man or had remained on the ranch after her last visit, or if Travis had arrived to find both of them living here, one older and one younger than himself. Would the sensuous Marissa have won his heart? she asked herself. A strange, unwanted jealousy consumed her as she pondered which of them might have caught Travis's eye first. Quickly Rana forced such foolish thoughts from her mind.

She was eager to meet Todd Raines, who had loved Marissa, and whom she hoped could tell her more about her mother. Her mother's past now seemed very much like the Oglala game in which a group of colored sticks were tossed into a pile to form a pattern about which one player asked a question and another player guessed the answer from the sticks' arrangement; but too many pieces were missing in Marissa's game of life to make guessing any answers possible. But perhaps Todd Raines could add a few sticks to the pile. Raines . . . Rana . . . she mused silently. How strange it was that their names were similar. Then again, she realized, Rana and Raymond were similar. If Raymond Michaels was the villain in her nightmares, the man with night hair and deer eyes, it meant she did not favor him. Perhaps it was not proper to be so happy about such a little thing, but she was.

"What drove you from your family, Mother?" she unconsciously asked aloud, empathizing with the woman who had borne her, a woman who was alive only in her dreams and almost a stranger. "Why did you stay joined to such a cruel man? I remember how he beat you and cursed you many times. All those nights I dreamed some evil man was chasing me and hurting me, it was you I saw in my sleep. Why did you not leave him or slay him? Why did you not ask Grandfather for help? I hated him, and I'm glad he's dead. How could you have endured such evil? Even love would not explain such a bond of loyalty."

Rana closed her eyes and leaned her forehead against the mantel as flashes of her past flooded her mind, remembrances that had plagued her so many times over the years that she could never forget them. Maybe there was a purpose behind her memories, and she fervently wished the Great Spirit would reveal it or push them aside forever. One dream in particular returned to haunt her, the one that had attacked her the first night she had met Travis. She knew what the white words "bitch" and "whore" meant, and she could not understand why Raymond —she could not call him father or think of him in that light—had called her mother such vile names. Had her mother actually been afraid Raymond would kill Nathan, or all of them, if she ran away? Now that she had fused her body with a man's, she recalled and comprehended other things she had witnessed; the name "Fargo" and Raymond's wicked commands caused her mind to burn with anger, contempt, and hatred for Raymond and the men who had taken advantage of her vulnerable mother. How she wished she had been old enough to protect Marissa from such torment and suffering. If only she had understood the situation and had told Nathan.

Raymond's voice shouting ". . . the truth about you and that brat . . ." thundered across her mind. "What truth, Mother? What did he mean by 'silence for money'? Why were you so afraid of him? What secret kept you bound in such evil as his slave?'' she murmured sadly.

Rana began to cry softly, for she knew some terrible evil had befallen her mother, an evil that perhaps still existed in this land and lurked nearby in secret, waiting to destroy her too. "Help me, Great Spirit; do not let this evil destroy me as it did my mother. Reveal it to me, and show me how to defeat it."

Suddenly Travis was there, pulling her around and embracing her in his strong arms. "What's wrong, *micante?* Were Mister Moore and Mrs. Dobbs so rough on you today? Don't worry, you'll learn everything soon. You're quick and smart," he murmured comfortingly as he held her snugly against him. He had watched her walk to the portrait and stare at it, and had heard her speak those baffling words. He tucked them away in his mind together with those he had overheard in Lone Wolf's tepee and those she had spoken in her sleep that night on the trail.

She admitted anxiously, "My heart races in fear, *mihigna*. Terrible dreams keep filling my head. Memories flood it like muddy waters and I cannot see through them to the bottom of my past. There is evil here and I cannot remember where or in what form."

Travis knew who held a secret about Marissa in her insidious grasp. Somehow he had to force the truth from Clarissa, for he saw that the past was tormenting his beloved and he feared that the malicious creature might find some way to use her knowledge against Rana. Somehow he had to solve the ever-increasing mystery that surrounded Marissa Crandall Michaels. Aloud, he ordered, "Forget it, love. You're safe here with me." He guided her to the settee and pulled her down beside him. "Just relax, my love, and calm down." For a long time, they sat quietly as he held her close. Finally, he teased lightly, "Do you want your grandfather to find you in tears and fire those two for upsetting you like this?"

"But it was not Mister Moore or Mrs. Dobbs."

"I know, love, but you don't want Nate to see how frightened you are. If he does, he won't let you fight these enemies with us."

Rana looked up into his eyes and inquired, "What does 'brat' mean?" She noticed that a curious expression filled his eyes.

"Where did you hear that word?" he asked in a strange tone. "It's what the whites call a really bad child, a child who's spoiled and mean as a snake, one who gives its parents great difficulty when they attempt to control it. It's a hateful and rude child you have trouble liking, one you don't want to be around if you can prevent it. Why?"

Without hesitation, she told him, "I keep hearing Raymond Michaels calling me that in my dreams. I do not understand why. I know it sounds bad, Travis, but I hate to think of him as my father."

He pulled her close to him. "No, love, it doesn't sound bad. I know how you feel. I feel the same way about Jeremy Kincade. Some men are just plain evil, Rana, and they don't deserve our love and respect, even if they're family. From what I've heard about Raymond Michaels, he didn't sound like a fatherly kind of man. Maybe he just didn't like being tied down with a small child. He liked to travel and gamble, and the kinds of places he went were not places for a little one. You probably got in his way, but not because you were a brat. When I was talking with Clarissa, I called you a brat several times to make her think you and I didn't like each other or get along," he confessed ruefully. "I'm sorry, but you know I didn't mean it."

Rana laughed. "Were you afraid I had heard it from you when I spied on you, like a brat?" she teased. "I told you, I could not hear your words from the house. But I wanted to claw out that woman's eyes for touching you as only I should touch you."

"A possessive and jealous wife—good," he remarked roguishly.

Rana kissed him, then hugged him. "I fear I am both, *mihigna*."

"When somebody asks you what that word means, what are you going to tell them?"

"The same thing you will tell anyone who asks what *micante* means," she laughingly retorted.

"Listen to me, you little brat, we have to be careful what we say and how we act around other people, even our friends, because they let secrets slip without meaning to do so," he warned.

"My son is right, Granddaughter," Nathan stated genially from the doorway. "We all have to be careful. It won't be easy to fool Harry and Miss Clarissa. I think you two should keep your kisses and hugs inside this house," he advised pointedly.

"We will, Grandfather," Rana promised happily. "When we are around your enemies, I will behave as a . . . little brat." She glanced at Travis and they both laughed.

Nathan watched Travis tickle Rana, then observed how they looked at each other. There was no doubt in his mind; they loved each other deeply and they deserved each other. His heart overflowed with joy. "I can't wait until you two are married and fill this house with my great-grandchildren. I thank the Lord every night for sending you home, Rana, and for sending Travis to me."

"So do I, Grandfather," she agreed, her loving gaze on Travis.

"Would you like to hear a secret, Papa dear?" Clarissa inquired provocatively after Harrison Caldwell had returned from town the following day. She had risen late after her wanton encounter with Wes Monroe and had discovered that her father had already left for business in Fort Worth. All day she had hoped no one would reveal to her father the news about Marissa's daughter's return.

Harrison glanced at his wayward child and asked, "If you've got something to say, Clarissa, don't be silly about it."

"Then I suppose no one's told you where Nathan Crandall went during his long absence or why?" She toyed with him, even though she knew it irritated him when she did so. Tonight she held the winning hand and she was going to savor laying it out before him, one card at a time.

"I don't give a hoot," Harrison stated, scowling at her.

"You don't give a hoot if Nathan found Marissa's missing daughter alive and well?" she inquired evocatively, grinning at him.

Harrison set aside his paper and stared at his obnoxious child. "What in blazes are you blabbering about?" he demanded.

"I thought you might be interested in knowing that Nathan located the girl and brought her home . . . a girl, I was told, who looks like her mother, or better," she casually revealed. "Evidently your hired men aren't as well informed or as talented as I am, Papa. They arrived Sunday evening, so I went to work obtaining information for my dear father. Rana Michaels could ruin your plans, so you might have to take care of her quite soon. From what Travis told me, she's quite a handful."

"Get on with it, girl," he commanded sternly when Clarissa returned her attention to the book in her hands.

The clever Clarissa had added up the clues and had realized how Nathan had learned about Rana: Thomas Mallory. "As I said, Papa, Nathan found Marissa's daughter, Rana Michaels, living with Indians as a chief's daughter. You remember how the Kiowas butchered Marissa and Raymond and abducted her little girl," she reminded him spitefully. "Nathan never gave up hoping and searching for his little Rana. When he heard about this girl who looked like Marissa, he and Travis took off to find her and look her over themselves. It was Rana, so he paid five thousand dollars for her release. Such an expenditure should have left him penniless and right where you want him with his loan at the bank coming due soon. From what I was told, Rana's beauty puts her mother's to shame. Fiery red hair and big blue eyes . . . I believe Travis said it was like looking at Marissa's old portrait, or seeing her ghost."

Harrison's mind began to race. His respiration increased and he paced unnaturally. "You don't seem distressed by having her in the house with your Travis," he taunted as he tried in vain to conceal his turbulent feelings.

"Why should I? She's a little savage and she doesn't have a claim on the ranch. Thanks to Ruth Crandall's friendship with Mother, we both know Marissa isn't Nathan's daughter, so how could Rana be Nathan's heir? After all, Travis is Nathan's legal son and heir. If Nathan tries to hand the ranch over to Rana instead of Travis, we'll just have to tell the old buzzard the truth about Marissa—all of it."

Harrison continued to pace the room, and his excitement was as obvious to Clarissa as the flush on his cheeks. She suppressed an evil grin to speculate, "I wonder if we should get rid of her, just to make certain she doesn't cause us any problems. I'm sure Mister Monroe and Mister Hayes would love to handle her for us. They seemed to enjoy their work on the McFarland ranch. Are you sure those men can be trusted, Papa? They seem awfully evil and dangerous to me."

Harrison grinned smugly and chuckled. "Don't worry, Clarissa dear, I'm holding Monroe and Hayes tightly in hand. Besides, I plan to get rid of them after they handle a few more problems for me. We'll lure them out to that old mining site on the Lazy J and drop 'em into that abandoned shaft. Hell, girl, I know their kind can't be trusted, but I'll get them before they catch on and strike at me."

"Let me lure them out there, Papa. You can depend on me to fool them, and to handle this secretly." She watched her father pour himself a sherry without offering her one. Yes, she would lure them out there, and push all three down that shaft after she had what she wanted! But she would need someone to blame for Harrison Caldwell's death, a dangerous, despicable villain whose wicked reputation was well known and feared. Everyone knew Wes Monroe was working for her father, and it would not seem suspicious if that evil beast robbed and murdered him. Afterwards, she could shoot Wes in self-defense for trying to rape her. Yes, that plan was perfect! She knew what her father was feeling now—hunger for another Marissa. She would let him discard Mary Beth and make his move on Rana Michaels. It would keep him single and occupied until their final success. But if he were to get too cocky or too close, she would reveal an astounding weapon and use it to stop him from marrying Rana Michaels . . .

"You're a wicked little bitch, Clarissa. Are you sure I can trust you? I've seen your malicious side."

Clarissa laughed as if her father had told a joke. "If you can't trust your own family, Papa, who can you trust?" she teased. "We'll be neighbors too one day. I'll be married to Travis and we'll run the Rocking *C* Ranch, and you'll have Mary Beth and run this beautiful horseshoe empire around us," she remarked, pointing to Harrison's holdings, which were shaded brightly on the map on one wall.

"Are you sure you can snare Kincade?"

"As certain as you are you can snare Mary Beth. As you tell me all the time, Papa, success is the result of clever planning. You taught me to look for a person's strengths and weaknesses, then use them against him. That's exactly what I'm doing, and I'll succeed."

"Then let's both get busy on our conquests tomorrow. This final battle is lasting too long. I'll give Nathan until August first to get out peacefully; then I'll let Monroe and Hayes handle him."

"Why a reprieve, Papa? He might get suspicious."

"Oh, I don't plan to ease up on him, girl, but I don't want to damage property too severely that will soon be mine."

"Mine, Papa," she corrected him boldly, "for all of my help. Maybe if Travis gets nervous about this Rana taking everything away from him, he might be convinced to side with us."

"Don't count on it, not if she looks like her mother. If I were you, girl, I would be plenty worried about losing him completely."

"Come now, Papa. Marissa was a cheap whore. Like mother, like daughter. Travis Kincade doesn't want a woman like that." Harrison eyed Clarissa up and down and laughed wickedly, to which Clarissa angrily replied, "I keep my affairs secret, Papa, so he doesn't know what I've done for you. You should be grateful that I obey your orders—all of them—and not be mean and insulting."

"I was only teasing you, girl. If your mother's blood had been as hot as yours, I would still be missing her today. A real man likes his woman to be a whore in bed and a lady in public. Just make sure you don't ever confuse those two roles and use them unwisely."

"I take after you, Papa. I'm insatiable, and selective."

"Well, how about using some of those insatiable and selective skills on Kincade? Don't tell me they don't have any effect on him."

"You're being mean tonight, Papa. I'm going to bed before I start doing the same," she playfully warned, leaving the room before she was tempted to do just that. How she longed for the day when she could fling his evil crimes in his face before having him killed. She decided angrily that if he did not curtail his hateful treatment of her, she would watch Wes beat him brutally before allowing the crude bastard to slay her father. Or, she mused with a grin, she might demand that privilege herself! The thought of such evil aroused her.

In her room, Clarissa pulled out a small painting of Raymond Michaels that she had kept hidden all these years. She eyed the image of the man who had once enchanted her briefly, then smiled sardonically. Perhaps she would give it to Rana, and tell that little bitch all about what her mother had done for Raymond. Perhaps she could drive Rana away, and prevent her from enticing Travis, for such a day might come if she lollygagged too long. She was all too aware of Travis's potent appeal and Marissa's magical allure, which Rana easily could have inherited. Oh, the destructive tales she could relate to Rana about her mother and Raymond! She remembered Raymond telling her how he had discovered the truth about Rana's conception, and how he had strangled the only person who had known about it besides Marissa. Now, only she possessed that valuable weapon . . .

Clarissa stood by her window, trying to catch the mild breeze. The storm had not struck last night or today and it was still humid, making her restless, but tonight she would be satisfied with the stimulation provided by her evil thoughts.

The next day, Travis spent the morning teaching Rana how to load, fire, and clean a rifle and a pistol. She learned quickly, for she possessed good instincts and had no fear of the weapons. They practiced for hours, with the sounds and smells of gunfire filling their senses. They halted finally in order to partake of the noon meal before Aaron Moore's scheduled arrival to begin Rana's afternoon lessons.

Rana spent four hours with the patient and somewhat timid teacher, who seemed smitten with her. When Aaron Moore left for the day, Travis teased, "Don't tempt him too much, *micante*, or he'll be staring at you rather than keeping his mind on your lessons."

"He is very nice, Travis, and very smart. Do not be jealous. My eyes and heart belong to you. He will not come tomorrow. He explained about the white holiday on July the fourth. It is sad that my people, the Oglalas, cannot win independence from the whites."

"I know, love, but there's nothing we can do to help them. One day, this period will be a bitter memory in history."

"Mister Moore told me about history, so I understand that word."

"Pretty soon, you'll know more words than I do, and you'll be teaching me. What do you say about us starting supper?"

Without knocking, Cody Slade rushed into the house and shouted, "Boss, you'd best get out here *pronto!* Mace and the boys are back, and it ain't good news. We sent those extra guards too late."

Travis grimaced knowingly at his words. "Please stay here, Rana, and I'll be back soon." He left instantly with Cody.

Rana hurried to the front window and observed the action taking place near the stable. She wished she could hear what was happening, or understood what had happened. She knew it was something terrible, but she also knew she should stay in the house as Travis had requested.

It seemed a very long time before Travis and Nathan returned to the house, both looking worried and angered. She went to them and asked, "What is wrong, Grandfather?"

"Bad news, Rana. The worst," he admitted sadly. "Mace was robbed on the way home. Without that money, I can't pay the bank what I owe it, and they'll take my ranch as payment."

"I do not understand, Grandfather. Who will steal your ranch? Can you not fight them? You have many war . . . men to help you."

As Nathan dropped wearily into a chair, Travis patiently explained about money, banks, loans, foreclosures, and the laws governing such things. Their predicament became clearer to her when Travis described how Harrison Caldwell could buy their ranch at a debtor's auction. "By losing that money, we've fallen right into his greedy hands, and there isn't a damn thing we can do to stop him; the law's on his side this time, and he'll use it to get this ranch."

"What about the enemies who stole Grandfather's money? Can we not go after them and recover it?" she inquired gravely.

"We could, if we knew who stole it and where they were hiding it." Travis laughed coldly. "Oh, we know Caldwell is behind the robbery, but we can't prove it. I wouldn't be surprised if those saddlebags are locked in his safe right this minute." When Rana questioned the meaning of "safe," Travis guided her into Nathan's office, showed her theirs, and explained how it worked.

"Why do we not ride to his lands and force him to open his safe and return Grandfather's money? Will the white law not help us?"

He caressed her cheek and smiled. "It isn't that simple, love. Caldwell would only deny our charges, and then he'd know we were on to him. He would hide those saddlebags where we'd never locate them. If I could sneak into his office in town and the one in his house, I could search them, for more than our stolen money. If I found something to incriminate him and his men, the sheriff would have to force him to open his safe to prove he doesn't have our money. Those saddlebags have rattlesnakes carved on them, so they're easy to recognize."

"Why do your men not tell this sheriff who did this black deed? How could they not see their faces and know them?" she reasoned.

"Harrison Caldwell is very cunning and dangerous. He's hired some deadly and clever gunslingers to do his dirty work. They sneaked up on Mace and the boys where they were camped for the night. The two cowhands Mace set out as guards were killed without a sound, their throats sliced Indian style; then one of Caldwell's men slipped into camp and took the money from Mace's side while he was sleeping. None of our cowpunchers heard or saw a thing. I should have joined them on the trail as soon as I got you and Nate home, but I had other things on my mind," he informed her with a wry grin.

"Mace said they searched the entire area the next morning and tried to track them. They finally had to give up their search because those varmints had covered their trail completely. Mace and the boys feel as bad as we do. They know we trusted them and depended on them. They don't want us to lose this ranch either. Dad-blame-it! We're out the cattle and the money, and pretty soon we'll be out of time. We know Caldwell's guilty, and we can't do a thing about it."

"These white laws and customs are bad, Travis. They do not allow the capturing of enemies and their punishment. It is wrong for the innocent to suffer."

Travis sighed heavily. "I know, *micante*, but we're trapped. We don't have any witnesses against Caldwell; we can't make accusations against him without proof and he knows it, so he'll be real careful to hide his guilt and evidence of the dirty deeds. Remember how you had no choice but to obey and yield when Lone Wolf and the Oglala Council spoke their commands, even when you disagreed with them?" She nodded her comprehension. "Until we can get evidence against Caldwell, our hands are tied. Right now, we need money, plenty of it. We have to figure out a way to get enough to exist and to repay that loan in four weeks."

"Why do you not sneak over to the Caldwell ranch and steal your money from his safe? If he does not hide it there, take his money to replace what he has stolen from us."

"That's too dangerous, love. He knows we're desperate, and he'll have plenty of guards around his place. Even if we could get into his house and safe, if we were caught we'd be in worse trouble than we are now. Much as I hate him and want to defeat him, this isn't the time to do anything reckless. It doesn't show courage, intelligence, or honor to ride into battle blind or without weapons. We have to be patient and cunning until we can trap him. I wouldn't be any use to you or Nate if I were dead or in jail. Caldwell would pounce on you two like a starving wolf on a slow rabbit. I know from experience that being innocent doesn't help much in some situations."

"This safe only opens with certain secret numbers?"

"That's right, and we don't know them. It's too heavy to steal and we can't blast it open. Too much noise. And if I know Caldwell, he'd let me beat him and shoot him before giving me those numbers."

"It's useless, son," Nathan stated dejectedly, entering the room. "We'll never see that money again, 'till Harry uses it to buy this ranch. The bastard!" Nathan exploded angrily. "I can't let him get away with this, Travis."

"Don't worry, Nate. Somehow I'll stop him. Somehow I'll find enough money to . . ." Travis grew silent and his gaze narrowed as he fell into deep thought. "That's it," he suddenly announced. "Why not? It's already been paid for with plenty of lives and suffering!" he murmured aloud, confusing Rana and Nathan.

"What are you talking about, son?"

The Rocking C foreman replied shockingly, "The gold, Nate—the gold my father took from the sacred burial grounds. I know where it's hidden, and I doubt anyone's found it yet. If I ride like the wind, I can get it and return here before Mason's bank can take our ranch and sell it to Caldwell with our cattle money. I'll be careful. It's our only hope, Nate," he reasoned when he saw Nathan begin to shake his head as worry filled his faded blue eyes.

"That gold nearly got you killed once, Travis, so don't go tempting those Hunkpapas by trying it again. Let it go, son," he pleaded. "I'd rather lose this ranch than lose you, boy, and that's God's truth."

"I can't, Nate. That part of my life is still an open wound. It's time I healed it once and for all, and this is the perfect time and way. I deserve that gold, Nate, and I've already paid for it. I'll leave in the morning, and I'll be back before this month's gone."

"I will go with you," Rana told him.

He declared gently, "No, Rana, you won't. I can travel faster and more safely alone. There isn't much time, and I need you to stay here to help Nate take care of things. Just tell everyone I went looking for the bandit's trail. Once this loan's repaid and the ranch is safe, we'll find a way to defeat Caldwell. You keep studying your books and white ways and practicing your shooting while I'm gone; then we'll take on this enemy together when I return. I need your understanding, trust, and help until this matter is settled. Nothing will happen to me, love; I promise. I'll go see Lone Wolf and get him to help me."

"Maybe Harry will settle down now that he's got our money. Ain't no need for him to do more than wait us out," Nathan speculated.

"I hope you're right, Nate, but I doubt it. It might be wise to keep guards posted. You know what kind of men he's hired, so both of you be careful. Before I leave, I'll write Clarissa a sweet little note to keep her panting after me; maybe she can keep her father in line while I'm gone. It's worth a try. Cody can deliver it for me after I'm gone. Speaking of Cody, why don't you help him and Mary Beth get married soon to get her out of Caldwell's reach? There isn't anything her father or Caldwell could do after the fact. You might want to tell Rachel to come back to work Friday, so Rana will have some company and help. Rachel can keep her too busy to worry about me."

"No, she cannot, Travis Kincade. And if you do not return in one full moon, I will come searching for you," she threatened mildly. She was so afraid for him to return to the Dakota lands, but she knew he had to go, and alone. By being stubborn or defiant, she could endanger both of their lives and his victory, so she would stay behind and do her part here at the ranch. "Perhaps you only seek to run away and not marry me again," she teased to lighten his burden.

A playful smile teased over his lips and his green eyes sparkled with mischief. In a warm tone, he warned roguishly, "No chance, my love, so make sure you don't use that false excuse to flirt with my hired hands while I'm gone. You had better be waiting for me when I return, because I've staked my claim on you. Nate, you keep a sharp eye on this restless filly for me. I wouldn't want to turn her over my knee for a good spanking the minute I get home. And another thing, Rana Michaels. Don't you dare do anything foolish or reckless. These men are dangerous and evil. Now that I've snared you and tamed you, I don't want to lose you or have you running wild again. I promise that you can be a female warrior at my side when I come home. Agreed?"

"Have I not proven I am smart and obedient?" she responded, slyly avoiding a direct answer and smiling at him innocently. She did not want to lie to him, and if anything happened while he was away . . .

Travis went into Nathan's office to write the note to Clarissa. When it was finished, he read it aloud to Rana and Nathan:

There's been some trouble over here, so I'll be gone three or four weeks. Mace was robbed of our cattle money on the way back from Sedalia. I'm heading up the trail to see if I can pick up any clues as to who took it and which way they rode off. I been doing some serious thinking about you and I don't want you fretting over me leaving again this soon. Don't tell your father how badly we need that money, 'cause I don't want him hanging over Nate's head like a vulture while I'm gone. If I can't pick up those bandits' trail, I'll be heading on up to St. Louis to see if I can locate some banker willing to settle our loan with Mason's bank. Since Nate and me stand to lose everything if I don't recover that money or I don't get a new loan, I can't ask you to wait around for me. A man's got his pride or he ain't got nothing, and no real man would take a woman for what she has. If I lose this ranch, I'll be moving on alone. So if you hear anything that can help me and Nate find these varmints who are trying to ruin us, I'm begging you, love, tell Nate while I'm gone and he can put the sheriff on them. Fact is, it's gonna be nice to get away from that little brat living with us! She's about to run me ragged around a tree. You ain't nothing like Rana Michaels.

He halted to laugh and remark, "Lordy, how true that is. If you were like Clarissa, love, Nate and I would have left you with Lone Wolf." He grinned, then continued with his note:

Don't go taking any foolish risks by trying to learn who's behind this trouble just to help me. You stay home where it's safe. I'll send you word as soon as I can. One last thing. Don't tell anybody where I'm going or what I'm doing. See you around the end of the month. Travis.

He looked at Nathan and Rana and asked, "Well, how about it?"

Nathan shrugged, but Rana responded, "If you wish to snare her heart, Travis, you must write words to give her real hope of winning you. Where you say you have been thinking seriously about her, say you will miss her or you will think of her each day you are gone. Where you say you cannot ask her to wait for you if you have no land and home to share with her, you must say you cannot ask but you hope she will wait for you and accept you even if you lose all you own. Where you say you will be moving on alone, you must add, 'Until I can find another home and work and then I will come for you.' When you speak of when you will see her again, say, 'You'd better be waiting for me when I return, because I've staked my claim on you.' I love those words, and she will love them. If she is helping her father with his evil deeds as you believe, she might try to stop him or control him if she knows she might win or lose you over what happens while you are gone."

Travis frowned in aversion. "If I say those things, *micante,* she'll be all over me when I return home. You sure you want me to say them to another woman, even if we both know they're lies?"

She smiled lovingly. "It does not matter, for I know you do this only to save us and our home from wicked foes. She is like an evil spirit that must be fooled, then defeated. When you return and pay the bank this money, you can free yourself of all evils. When she learns you have fooled her, she will become angry and perhaps reveal her evil. Say what is needed to defend our lives and home."

Travis sighed loudly. "I've been rejecting her so long, I'm not sure she'll believe this romantic letter."

Rana recalled what she had witnessed near the corral that night. "She is greedy for you; she will believe what she wishes to believe. She will think you have weakened, as she has expected."

Nathan chuckled and concurred.

"I surely hope you two are right, and that you'll beat her off me when I return home. I can always claim I didn't write this mushy message." Travis returned to Nathan's desk and wrote another letter, including Rana's bold suggestions. When he finished it, he read it to them:

I ain't one for writing letters or putting my feelings on paper where the wrong person can see them and read them. But I got some things need saying to you before I leave. There's been some trouble over here, so I'll be gone three or four weeks. Mace was robbed of our cattle money on the way back from Sedalia. I'm heading up the trail to see if I can pick up any clues as to who took it and which way they rode off. I been doing some serious thinking about you and I don't want you fretting over me leaving again this soon 'cause I'll think about you every day and I hope you do the same with me. Don't tell your father how badly we need that money I'm going after, 'cause I don't want him hanging over Nate's head like a vulture while I'm gone. If I can't pick up those bandits' trail, I'll be heading on up to St. Louis to see if I can locate some banker willing to settle our loan with Mason's bank. Since Nate and me stand to lose everything if I don't recover that money or I don't get a new loan, I can't ask you to wait around for me, but I sure do hope you will and I hope you'll still want me even if I lose this ranch. A man's got his pride or he ain't got nothing, and no real man would take a woman for what she has. If I lose this ranch, I'll be moving on alone, until I can find another job and place to live. If you're willing to marry a man with nothing and you'll wait for me while I get settled elsewhere, I'll come back for you. But I'd rather stay on the ranch if I can find a way to keep her. So if you hear anything that can help me and Nate find these varmints who are trying to ruin us, I'm begging you, love, tell Nate while I'm gone and he can put the sheriff on them. Fact is, it's gonna be nice to get away from that little brat living with us! She's about to run me ragged around a tree. You ain't nothing like Rana Michaels and you won't ever be. Don't go taking any foolish risks by trying to learn who's behind this trouble just to help me. You stay home where it's safe until I can get back. I'll send you word as soon as I can to let you know where I am and how things are going. One last thing. Don't tell anybody where I'm going or what I'm doing. See you around the end of the month, and you had better be waiting for me when I return, woman, 'cause I've staked my claim on you and told you things from my heart. Travis."

It was close to midnight when Travis sneaked into Rana's room, where she was waiting eagerly to spend this last night with him. Each longed to embrace and kiss the other urgently, for they knew that death might confront either of them shortly. They would love as if that black spirit was truly about to claim them and there would be no more happy days or blissful nights for them to share.

"I love you, Rana Michaels, and I want to marry you and let everyone know you're the woman of my heart and life."

She responded ardently, "I love you, Travis Kincade, and the Great Spirit will hear our prayers and answer them. You will return to me soon, and we will claim each other under white law. You must think of nothing and no one while you ride this dangerous trail to the Hunkpapa lands. You must think only of your safety and victory."

"Come, my beautiful wife, and soar on the wild wind with me; then later we will talk." Travis's lips and hands claimed her full attention then as they began their rapturous journey on the wings of love.

Travis lay beside her, holding her, caressing her. The door was locked and one candle glowed softly in the quiet room. For a time, he made love to her with his eyes, storing up exquisite images to carry him through the rough days ahead. Slowly he came forward until his chest grazed hers and his lips brushed over her mouth. His fingers seemingly danced over her face and through her silky hair. He rained kisses over her throat and gently devoured her breasts, bringing the brown peaks to instant life.

She groaned softly as he ignited and fanned her smoldering desires into a raging fire of blazing passion. She savored the way his experienced, talented hands roamed her body, his one hand drifting over her stomach and causing it to tighten with anticipation of the path it would forge toward her womanhood. She was stirred and tempted and could not keep from drawing his mouth back to hers and ravenously meshing her lips to his. Her hands roved his body then, stroking its tanned flesh, admiring its beauty. She closed her eyes and absorbed the stimulation of her unbridled senses. She relished the tautness of his chest as her fingers lovingly mapped his torso. One hand rose to travel through his sable hair. The other played over his body and boldly captured his rigid manhood. Lovingly she caressed its warm, smooth surface. His loins instantly responded to her touch and he writhed in pleasure. She felt him tense and relax at her tantalizing touch and she smiled happily.

Travis's lips returned to the brown nubs on her breasts and blissfully tormented them, increasing her hunger for him and what lay ahead for them this night. He saw the dreamy smile on her lips and silently vowed that this night would be unforgettable. His hands tenderly kneaded her breasts and he deftly squeezed their hard tips as his mouth drifted between them and her lips, bathing her in intense sensation. He grasped her buttocks and fondled them before pressing her core snugly against his enlarged staff, which pleaded for encompassing contact. Again his hands returned to her eager mounds to sweetly torment the thrusting peaks. Slowly and deliberately his fingers began to trail up and down her sides until one continued down her flesh into her fiery triangle and carefully, sensuously stroked the straining peak there. He could feel the tension and anticipation throbbing within her body, especially at that sensitive spot. As his mouth lavished attention on her taut nipples, a deft finger entered her entreating womanhood and moved expertly until her head was thrashing upon the bed, signaling her uncontrollable desire.

Rana's hands roamed Travis's hard, smooth frame. They teased over sinewy muscles that rippled with his movements. They wandered down his back to examine his firm buttocks that could forcefully drive his manhood into her body with such skill and delight. He was making her wild and stealing her wits. Again her fingers moved provocatively over his groin, playing in the crisp hair that surrounded his rearing stallion, so full of heat and need. She felt him trailing kisses down her stomach, and he shifted his body to continue along her thighs, taking him out of her reach. His fingers teased over her hips, ending their stimulating journey in her auburn forest, and he smiled triumphantly when she shifted her legs apart to welcome his invasion.

Travis's hand stimulated the tiny mound before he pressed kisses to it, causing her to stiffen in surprise and intense delight. He grinned as she glanced down at him, her expression questioning his action. He smiled, encouraging and relaxing her completely. His strong hands drifted up and down the insides of her silky thighs, each time barely making titillating contact with the sensitive area. He pushed aside her soft hair and his finger lovingly massaged the delicate peak. Another finger slipped within her secret haven to create a pattern that matched that of his manhood when he was thrusting deeply within her. Her moist, snug paradise told him she was eager to accept and enjoy any pleasure he wished to give her. Gently he tantalized the tiny bud, which had grown hard and hot beneath his touch. Slowly and purposefully his head bent forward and his tongue replaced the finger on the peak. He teased it with his teeth, providing a thrill she had never experienced before. His tongue flicked and circled, sometimes swiftly and sometimes leisurely. At times he would grasp it hungrily and suck upon it as he had her nipples, the action causing her to thrash wildly. Together his mouth and fingers worked to bring her to the point of torturously sweet abandon and unspeakable rapture.

Rana squirmed as the tension built within her. She wanted to relax, but found it impossible. Her body seemed taut with anticipation of something she knew would be wild and wonderful. Passion's flames licked over her body and seared it. The peak and canyon located in the core of her womanhood throbbed and pulsed as he delivered an erotic attack on them. She cautioned herself to remain alert and silent, but she feared she was losing her wits and would cry out in sheer bliss. Her hips began to arch madly as overpowering spasms assailed her, inspiring him to increase his endeavors to give her supreme satisfaction. While her womanhood was still quivering from the thrill of his success, he moved atop her and thrust his aching manhood deep within that tingling crevice. To his surprise, her passion and hunger returned instantly, indicating to both of them that her womanhood was extremely sensitive to whatever he chose to do there. As if insatiable, she responded feverishly to his thrusting.

His lips greedily drank from her hardened nipples as his hips repeatedly and seductively pounded his manhood into her receptive body. Her total surrender, her fiery responses, and her coaxing actions sorely strained his control. She was moaning against his lips and clinging to him, revealing the height of her arousal. His mouth was insistent upon hers, his tongue teasing over her lips before his own hungrily fastened on hers. She matched his pace and they worked in unison toward the mutual goal looming before them. Ecstasy exploded within her again and her teeth sank almost savagely into his shoulder as she attempted to halt her outcry of rapture and victory. He felt her clinging to him as if in fear for her life. He was charged with energy and fierce cravings, and he rode her as skillfully and wildly as a wild mustang. Together they scaled the summit and experienced the power of passion's fusion. Then slowly and dreamily they drifted back to reality.

Rana felt exhausted but totally content. This bout of lovemaking had been a journey into ecstasy beyond description or comparison. Her body felt limp and aglow; her heart was surging with love and peace. He was a skilled lover, and his sexual prowess had rewarded her greatly. He was so gentle, yet so demanding and giving. She wiped away the glistening beads of moisture from his face and smiled into his twinkling eyes. "You know many mating secrets that you must teach me," she whispered into his ear.

The candlelight flickered over her serene face as he suppressed happy chuckles, for he knew what she was feeling at that very moment and what rapture he had given her. He tingled at the memory. Drawing her ear close to his, he murmured, "I will teach you all I know, *micante,* and we will enjoy and improve our skills together when I return. There is no spot on you that I do not love and desire. There are many exciting nights ahead for us."

She shifted her head to stare into his eyes, beaming with love and anticipation. "Many nights, and many days, my love. Promise you will return safely to my lifecircle. It cannot be complete without you."

He hugged her fiercely and vowed, "With the guidance and love of *Wakan Tanka,* I will return to you, my love. But if I died this very night, I would meet the Great Spirit knowing you have given my life its true meaning and have brought me happiness beyond measure."

Their lips fused and they nestled into each other's arms, knowing and dreading what the new day would bring.

Chapter 14

SHORTLY AFTER DAWN, Travis quietly dressed and headed for the cookhouse to meet with Mace Hunter and Cody Slade, who were awaiting his arrival and final orders. Darby and Bart Davis were standing with Mace and Cody outside the wooden structure, and all four men were drinking coffee and discussing the current situation. Before Travis reached them, Todd Raines rode up and, after securing his mount's reins to a corral post, joined the small group. Travis eyed the five men as he walked toward them and realized how lucky the Rocking *C* Ranch was to have these loyal and skilled hands working on it.

After they exchanged congenial greetings, Travis told them the same false tale he had written in Clarissa's letter. He hated to deceive these good men who were his friends, but he could not allow even the slightest chance of anyone carelessly dropping a hint about him in the wrong ear or being coerced by brutal force into revealing his daring plan. Few men could hold silent while being tortured or while watching a loved one undergo such pain, and Travis knew that Caldwell was not above obtaining information by any means necessary. If he was lucky enough to retrieve the gold—their last chance to retain the ranch—he certainly couldn't risk having any of Caldwell's men ambush him and steal it.

After the Davis brothers and Todd Raines had headed off to begin their chores, Travis advised Cody Slade, "If I were you, Cody, I would settle my claim on Mary Beth Sims *pronto*. Caldwell has serious sights set on her, and I know you and Mary Beth don't want her father handing her over to that snake. If you want that girl, you'd best figure out something quick. Ask for Nate's help; he'll give it."

The sandy-haired man scowled at hearing Travis's confirmation of his suspicions. "You're right, Trav; I'll take care of it soon. I sure don't want to lose her. A woman like her comes along only once."

Cody's hazel eyes widened in surprise when Travis handed him a sealed letter and told him to deliver it to Clarissa Caldwell that afternoon. "I'm sure you'll find her in town for the big celebration. We don't want her worrying over my second absence and nagging you again," he teased devilishly and winked at his two best friends. "Mace, you decide if you want any of the boys to have time off today to go into town. I know your bunch deserves it after that long cattle drive and ride home, but this is a bad time for too many of them to be off the ranch. A holiday would be the perfect time for a surprise attack."

"You're right, and I'm sure the boys will understand and agree."

"Nathan also thinks it would be best for him to stay around here. No need to let Caldwell rile him. And he doesn't want Rana bothered."

"How is Miss Rana? I haven't seen her around. You must be keeping her locked up. Mace and the boys are real anxious to meet her," Cody remarked playfully as he stuffed the letter into his pocket.

"Cody tells me Nate's granddaughter is a real beauty, Trav. I bet you enjoy having her all to yourself. 'Course I would imagine Miss Clarissa Caldwell is not too happy about Miss Rana's return. She has heard the bad news, hasn't she?" Mace inquired with a grin. His sunny blond hair gleamed in the morning sunshine and his azure eyes glowed with undisguised curiosity. Being six feet three, Mace was at an eye level with Travis, and he studied his friend's reaction intently.

Not wanting to inspire romantic gossip about him and Rana during his absence, Travis shrugged and sighed. "Cody took a shine to her right off; too bad he already has a sweetheart. He's right, though; Rana Michaels is a real charmer, Mace, so you'd best be alert around Nate's granddaughter or you'll be following Cody's flowery path."

Cody laughed and wailed, "What's so bad about love and marriage? Especially with a radiant creature who'll inherit all this?"

"Aren't you forgetting I'm Nate's adopted son?" Travis teased casually, inspiring their laughter. "Besides, I've been working on Caldwell's only heir for years, and a man don't switch horses in midstream during a storm. I'll admit Rana is the prettiest vixen I've seen; she looks like that picture of her mother over Nate's mantel, and I've admired that beauty for years. But we all know that the most beautiful women are usually selfish and vain, and nothing but big trouble for a man."

Cody shook his head and protested amiably, "Not Miss Rana. I've never met a gentler or nicer lady. She's real smart and kind. I liked her right off, and I want her and Mary Beth to become friends."

Travis did not want to seem mean or suspicious, so he grinned and added, "You're right, Cody, but she's a mite young and willful for me. She's making Nate happy, so that's all that matters right now. You haven't been playing big brother to her, so you don't know how ornery she can be. She's bullheaded and cocky, and she doesn't like to be bossed. You two keep an eye on her, 'cause she's a wild and restless filly. I guess you can't blame her too much, considering how she was raised. She thinks she can do anything a man can do, or better, so make sure she doesn't interfere with our problems or get into trouble. She's a real handful, and you two are probably the only ones who can handle her for Nate. She should be staying close to the house, 'cause Nate's got the schoolteacher coming over nearly every day to help her adjust to our white ways. She'll straighten out soon, but be alert for any mischief or danger. After what happened to Marissa, Nate would be crushed if anything happened to his granddaughter."

"Don't worry, Trav, we'll look after Nate and Miss Rana for you," Mace replied seriously. "We'll also keep a sharp eye on the herds and fences. We've taken too many losses. You sure you don't want me to ride with you to look for those varmints? I feel responsible for losing that cattle money. I know what it means to you and Nate."

Travis empathized with his friend. "It couldn't be helped, Mace, and we don't hold you responsible. I will need your help with the payroll. We only have enough money to hand out about a third of their June pay, and I don't know what will happen this month. If you can get them to hold out for the rest of their money until the first of the month, I'll give each one ten dollars extra. Any man who has a problem with waiting, like Darby with all those kids, pay him what you can and leave off his and Todd's rent. We're all in for some rough times, Mace, so if any of the boys need to move on, tell 'em we understand and we'll get their money to them as soon as we can. If we don't recover that cattle money or get another loan, this place will be finished; then you boys will find yourselves working for Caldwell or moving on."

"No, sir! We know Caldwell is behind this trouble, so how can you stand courting his daughter?" Mace inquired boldly. "From what I see and hear, she's too much like her pa. She doesn't deserve you, Trav. You need a good woman, like Cody's sweetheart."

Cody realized their talk was moving in a private direction, so he bid Travis farewell and dismissed himself. Travis and Mace walked a short distance for privacy. The foreman inhaled deeply, then slowly released the spent air. "Listen to me, Mace. I'm not going to search for those bandits; I'm sure you and the boys didn't overlook any clues, and I'm not riding to St. Louis to seek a new loan. I have another plan in mind, but it's dangerous and it might not work. Even if it does, it'll take me a month to check it over. I told the boys that false story because

I can't risk anyone dropping clues about my whereabouts and business. Time's short, so I'll fill you in after I get back." When Travis revealed who and what Wes Monroe and Jackson Hayes were, Mace realized why Travis had to keep his impending journey a secret.

"You mean they're the ones who tried to kill you years ago?"

"That's right, but it doesn't seem as if they remember me or, if they do, they can't place me. When I return, I'm going to settle up with them. I'm telling you these things because I know you're one of the few men who would die before loosening his tongue and betraying a friend. Cody told you what happened over at the McFarland place, so you know Wes and Jackson have ways of making men talk. Watch out for those two gunslingers, Mace. I've got scars to prove bastards don't come any worse than them. As for Clarissa, that letter is only a trick to entice her to keep Caldwell off Nate's back while I'm gone. I'd bet she's as deep in this mud as her father is." He unflinchingly revealed the letter's contents to his best friend. "And as for Rana Michaels, between you and me, I plan to marry that little minx when I return."

Mace laughed heartily. "So I wasn't wrong about that sparkle in your eye. Is she willing to go along with your plans for her?"

Travis smiled and nodded. "It's strange, Mace, but the minute we met, it was like we had been waiting for each other all our lives and nothing could have stopped us from meeting. I can't explain how deeply that woman touches me. If any two people belong together and are perfect for each other, it's Rana Michaels and Travis Kincade. Lordy, I never thought I would be saying or thinking such things and surely not feeling them, but it's mighty nice," he admitted cheerfully. A worried look crossed Travis's face then, and he speculated, "You know the Caldwells think they might get this ranch through Clarissa and me marrying, so I don't want them viewing Rana as a snag in their plans. I detest that Caldwell bitch, but I'll do whatever's necessary to guard Rana and Nate from her and her father. Rana has enough problems as it is. Leaving the Indian camp to return home was hard on her, so do what you can to protect her and to help her adjust."

"I sure am glad you see through that wicked harlot. What happens if the Caldwells don't fall for your letter and deception? Miss Rana could be in real danger."

Travis mulled over that possibility. "If they get one look at her, they'll know I would never pick Clarissa over Rana. Unless Rana's really mean to me or she prefers another . . ." Travis's eyes brightened. "That's it: if she prefers another man, like the handsome and charming Mace Hunter," he suggested with a sly grin.

"You're joshing, aren't you?" Mace inquired.

"No, I'm not, old friend. If she can go along with my pretense with Clarissa, I can go along with her pretense with you." Travis related how they were planning to deal with Clarissa. "Until Rana and I can openly express our feelings, you pretend to be her sweetheart to keep her safe. Will you do this for us, Mace?"

"You know I'll do whatever you ask, Trav, but isn't this a mite dangerous? If she's as perfect and beautiful as you and Cody let on, I might become captivated by her. If you're gone too long, we might forget we're playing a game. What if we fall in love?" he teased.

Travis retorted, "Keep reminding yourself she's mine and don't play the game unless it's absolutely necessary. Time's awasting. I have to tell her and Nate good-bye and get on the trail. Take care of them and the ranch for me. If something happens and I don't . . ."

Mace interrupted, "Don't even think it, friend. I'll be here, so don't worry about anything, or anyone. Take care of yourself, Trav. I don't want to lose the best friend I've ever had."

The twenty-seven-year-old foreman said, "Give me about fifteen minutes, then come to the house. I want to introduce you to Rana myself. Will you saddle Apache for me and load my gear? And I need another strong mount. I plan to switch horses while riding to prevent too many rest stops along the way. I need to get going and get back as quickly as I can."

Travis strode quickly into the house and proceeded to explain his discussion with Mace to an uncharacteristically quiet Rana and Nathan. When he had finished, Rana nodded her head and told him, "It is a clever plan. I am grateful that your friend wishes to protect me."

The three went over their plans and stories one last time, then Nathan left the room to await Travis's departure on the front porch, knowing his adopted son and his granddaughter would appreciate some time alone.

Rana slipped into Travis's arms and snuggled against his hard body. "Be careful and return to me," she entreated in a strained voice. She had this terrible feeling that awful things were about to happen, but she did not want to worry or distract him with her fears and doubts.

Travis tightened his embrace and kissed her forehead, for he had those same feelings. Yet he knew his trip was vital. "I will, my love, and you be careful here. I promise, we'll be married real soon."

They kissed and hugged, then gazed longingly into each other's eyes, exchanging messages that held too much emotion for words to express. Finally, Travis murmured, "I have to go, love. We're running out of time. If I'm not back in twenty-nine days . . ." He sighed heavily and hugged her tightly. "Stay here and I'll bring Mace to meet you," he said.

Rana eyed the tall, handsome man who entered the room with Travis. He stood just an inch shorter than Travis and was two years older. His hair was the color of sunshine dancing on sand and his eyes were the shade of a blue pasque-flower. The creases around his mouth and eyes expressed his easygoing, happy nature and Rana found herself liking his compelling smile and genial manner. She sensed that before her stood a man of honor and prowess, much like Travis. The close friendship the two men shared was obvious in their demeanors, and she warmed to Mace Hunter immediately. He seemed a good man, and a dependable friend. They exchanged smiles and greetings.

After going over Travis's suggestion that they play sweethearts during his absence, all three left the room to join Nathan. Travis and the older man embraced affectionately, then Travis clutched forearms with Mace. Lastly and most tormentingly, Travis looked deep into Rana's eyes, then whispered, "I love you, *micante*," as he hugged her quickly.

Rana stood on the porch and watched Travis ride away, bravely holding back the tears that threatened to spill forth. She smiled and waved to Nathan and Mace as they headed off toward the stable. She knew Mace Hunter would return after her lessons to take her riding and begin their sham. She also knew that Rachel Raines would be returning to work the next day, and she looked forward to meeting Rachel and her husband. Study and keep busy, that was what she needed to do!

Harrison and Clarissa Caldwell were enjoying themselves immensely at the lengthy July Fourth celebration in town, but each kept a sharp eye for a certain, though different, person. The games, races, betting, eating, dancing, and drinking continued during the hot day without either person making an appearance.

Around two o'clock, Cody approached Clarissa with the letter from Travis, and she eagerly stole away to the livery stable to read it. She was astonished by the message and peeved over his sudden departure. She stuffed the letter into her draw-string purse to read again later, but before she could leave the secluded stable, Wes Monroe swaggered inside and attempted to have some fun then and there.

"Don't be a fool, Wes," she angrily scolded him. "We can't be seen together. This could look suspicious after you handle that job for me. Get rid of Jackson tonight, and I'll come to the cabin around ten," she offered, trying to prevent his anger or his refusal to help her.

"You're smart, woman. It would look strange for a gunslinger and a lady to be playing in the straw together. Don't be late tonight, and be ready to give me this man's name and why you want him killed."

When the celebration ended with enough time for the ranchers to get home before dark, Harrison was still tense and decided to stay in town and spend a few hours at the Silver Shadow Saloon. He had anticipated meeting Marissa's double all day and had worked himself into a mental state of constant arousal, one that needed appeasing before he went home tonight. He shouldn't have been surprised by Crandall's failure to show up today, he told himself; after all, the man would soon lose everything. No doubt Nathan was plenty worried about now. Even if Nathan and Travis suspected he was responsible for the robbery, they couldn't prove a thing, and the ranch would be his within a month. Perhaps they could work out something reasonable, if Rana were another Marissa . . .

The day had passed busily for Rana. Despite its being a holiday, Mrs. Clara Dobbs had arrived that morning to deliver several items and to fit others. After the midday meal, Aaron Moore had arrived for her lessons, for the shy teacher cared little for rowdy celebrations and was eager to work with his delightful pupil.

At five, when she was waving farewell to Moore, Cody and some of the hands returned from their chores. At twenty-six, Cody was fortunate to hold such a position of authority. The smiling man cordially and politely introduced Rana to Darby and Bart Davis. Both men had dark brown hair and brown eyes, Rana observed, and neither had looks that would tend to catch the average woman's eye. Cody explained that Darby was forty-six, with a wife named Lettie and many children, and they lived in one of the rented houses a few miles away. Bart was forty, single, and lived in the bunkhouse. Clearly the two brothers were very close, Rana mused, in looks, feelings, and personalities. Though neither had had much to say, both had been friendly and polite.

Cody asked Rana if she wanted to go riding or spend time practicing her shooting. Just as she told him she was waiting for Mace, the affable blond arrived with Todd Raines, who gaped at her as if seeing a ghost. For a time he stared at her transfixed, but Cody and Mace were too busy bantering to notice Todd's reaction.

Rana smiled at him and watched how his eyes glowed as they roamed her form from head to toe. She broke her spell over him by saying, "I am Rana Michaels, Marissa's daughter, Nathan's granddaughter. It is good to meet you, Mister Raines. Travis and Grandfather speak good words about you."

Todd murmured, "I can't believe it; you look just like your mother did years ago. They told me about you, but I wasn't prepared for this shock. I hope you'll forgive me for staring at you, Miss Rana."

Rana was delighted to meet this particular man and hoped they could become friends quickly so she could ask him about her mother. Todd was thirty-eight, the same age Marissa would have been had she lived. He had light brown hair, which some might have considered dark blond, and it shone in the approaching sunset with reddish gold highlights. His striking eyes were an unusual shade, appearing to be a mixture of silver and dark blue. His features were pleasing, and Rana speculated that his good looks had increased with age. How different Marissa's life and her own would have been if this man had won her mother's heart. She had been told his wife, Rachel, was barren and that the couple wanted a child badly. As it had been with Mace and Cody, there was something about Todd Raines that caused her to like him instantly.

Mace and Cody noticed the quick rapport and the ease with which Rana and Todd conversed. Todd explained that he had to pick up some barbed wire and head back to the men waiting for him, so he did not have long to talk. He smiled then and told Rana he would look forward to seeing her again, and she did the same. As he moved off, Todd glanced back at her several times and she watched him until he was out of sight. Their strange behavior caused Cody and Mace to exchange quizzical looks, for they had been too young to know about the fiery romance between Marissa Crandall and Todd Raines twenty years before. They only knew that after her hasty marriage and departure, Marissa had come to visit her father every two years, beginning in 1850, when Rana had been one. When she made her last, tragic visit in 1856, Cody had been fifteen, Mace, at eighteen, had only been with the ranch one year, and Todd had been married to Rachel for four years.

Still puzzled, Mace invited Rana to ride with him and, a short time later, when they had halted near a large pond to rest for a moment, Rana began asking countless questions about Todd Raines. Such excessive interest alarmed Mace. He casually stated, "I did tell you that Todd's happily married to a very sweet woman."

Rana glanced at him curiously, thinking to herself, Why would he . . . ? Suddenly Rana grinned, then laughed aloud. "I do not ask about him for myself, Mace Hunter. I asked because he was very close to my mother. I wish to become friends with him so he will tell me much about her. I was a small child when she was slain and I know little about her. Grandfather told me they almost married long ago. I think how different all would be if they had been joined. To learn about one she loved tells me much about her, and I wish to know all things. I must not ask such questions before his wife, for it would make her sad to hear him speak of another love. Do you understand?"

Mace smiled and nodded. "I understand, Rana. I never knew about Todd and Marissa, so I guess you were a shock to him since you look like your mother. I came to work for Nate when I was seventeen, so I only saw your mother once. But I can tell you, she wasn't one to forget," he murmured almost dreamily. Catching himself, he flushed lightly and said, "It's getting late. We should ride back." The sun was falling across her head, enhancing the color of her face, hair, and eyes. He smiled and remarked, "You know something? Travis is a lucky man. He said you were perfect and beautiful, and he was right."

"It is good he has a friend who knows and shares all with him, as Myeerah did with me in the Oglala camp. I miss her. Cody Slade says he will bring his love to see me and become my new friend. It is good."

Yes, Mace decided, Travis Kincade was a damn lucky man to have discovered this treasure first. He would take real good care of it for his best friend, and if Travis didn't return alive . . . No, Mace raged inwardly, nothing could and would happen to his best friend. "After you finish your lessons tomorrow, we'll do some target practice," he said aloud. "Just make sure you don't go riding without me or Cody, or Todd."

She smiled at Mace and mounted the pretty sorrel. "Did Travis forget to tell you I am very obedient and understanding?"

Mace's gaze met Rana's and they both laughed merrily.

Clarissa paced her room and read the letter again and again. The news was what she had desired, but could she believe it? Travis had been holding her off for years, so why this sudden change? Was the tough rancher going soft for her? Or was he getting worried about losing his ranch and all he owned? Did it matter to her that it was the only way she could have him? She read the letter one final time, then burned it.

It was probably a good thing he was gone right now, she told herself, for he might have been injured during her father's take-over, or he might have discovered the truth about her and her plans. And because he was gone, Travis couldn't fall for that little chit of Marissa's! Once Travis lost everything, she would look like the best catch to him, especially if her father were dead and Travis could marry her and become the owner of a vast empire. No matter his motives, she would win him and tame him. But right now, she had another man to handle. Picking up a drying cloth, she made her way to the bathing closet.

When she returned to her room after her bath, she found Wes Monroe propped lazily on her bed. She hurriedly locked her bedroom door and went to him. Keeping her voice as low as possible though she was in a burning rage, she demanded, "What the hell are you doing in here? My father could return at any time. He would fire you and disown me!"

As he placed several pillows behind him and leaned against them, Wes playfully argued, "Nobody saw me sneak in and your door's locked. We're on the second floor, so nobody can peek in your windows. If you keep your voice down, nobody will know I'm here. Sit down and talk." He grasped her hand and pulled her down beside him.

"*Nobody* doesn't matter, only my father," she sneered. "If he finds out about us, he'll get suspicious and all my plans will be ruined."

"That's who you want me to kill for you, isn't it?" he asked calmly as he untied the sash to her robe, exposing her naked body, which was still damp from her bath. He noticed her uncontrollable reaction to his words, a response that left no doubt about her prey's identity or her character. He had watched and listened, and had added up the facts and clues. This woman wanted it all, and she would kill her own father or do anything to get it. That meant she was as cold-blooded and greedy as he was, and she couldn't be trusted.

"I told you I would come to the cabin later. I was getting ready to leave. This is too risky, Wes. We can't talk or meet here."

As he fondled her breasts, he suggested erotically, "Taking you here makes it more exciting, Clarissa. Riding you like crazy within a few feet of the man you want me to kill for you and knowing he doesn't suspect a thing . . . Knowing we can't make a sound even if our bodies heat up and burn to a crisp . . . Nope, woman, this ain't risky; this is feasting on danger and making all of your senses come alive. Don't you know how much pleasure and power you can get from other people's pain? Why don't you tell me what you've got in mind for your unlucky Papa while I take another payment?" His hands went behind her back and he pulled her forward so his mouth could devour her breasts.

Clarissa thought about his stimulating words as she watched him with fascination. Her father had taken Marissa many times in the room next to hers; now she would dare to have a lover in this very house! And the man who was going to murder him! Wes was right; danger was a heady aphrodisiac and so was victory. It was all falling into place for her, and that was intoxicating. As his hand slipped between her legs, she closed her eyes and was consumed by the blissful sensations that Wes was creating up and down her quivering frame.

Suddenly he halted and pushed her aside to rise and undress. She was eager to have him feasting and laboring on her body again, and she helped him remove his garments quickly. Tossing aside her light covering, she lay down, reached for him, and drew him down to her searing body. Few men she had known had been as skilled and generous as this crude beast. Until she was finished with Wes, she would make good use of him. Soon her head began to thrash on the pillow, for Wes was driving her wild with his bold actions.

He finally rolled to his back and whispered hoarsely, "Climb on top of me and ride me good, woman. We'll talk later."

Clarissa instantly obeyed. As she rocked back and forth on him, a knock sounded on the door and her father called out, "You still awake, girl? I want to talk to you about something."

Clarissa froze and her heart pounded in fear of discovery. She gazed at Wes's wicked expression, unable to believe that he had devilishly begun to pinch her taut nipples and grin at her, knowing she could not cry out or scold him. Clarissa recalled the many times her father had hurt her and controlled her and, for a brief, maddening instant, she was tempted to cry rape and have Wes slain. But she needed him now, though she vowed she would repay him later. Harrison knocked and called out again, and Clarissa found her voice. "I'm tired, Papa; it was a long, hot day. Let's talk in the morning. I'm already in bed," she explained as she began undulating her body over Wes's again.

As Harrison argued, "It's only nine o'clock, and we have some plans to make," Wes seized Clarissa's hips and forcefully began to grind his manhood into her body. Then he pulled her forward to nibble roughly on her breasts, for the danger of Harrison's proximity and his power over her seemed to arouse him enormously. "Are you sure you don't want to get up and come downstairs for a sherry and a talk?" Harrison encouraged. He had heard about Travis's second strange departure and he wanted to learn if Clarissa knew anything about it.

Wes replaced his manhood with his mouth and hands. Tingles raced through her body. Her worst enemy was standing on the other side of that door, and, on this side, a dangerous villain was sensuously devouring her and promising to do her bidding. She felt as if she were vicariously punishing her father and she reveled in the feeling. Clarissa grinned salaciously. "I'm too tired and sleepy, Papa. I need to stay in bed tonight. I was just getting comfortable. I'll see you in the morning."

"All right, girl. We'll talk at breakfast. Have a good night," he told her, bringing a wicked smile to her lips.

"I will, Papa," she murmured softly. "Sleep well." She focused her full attention on Wes, for soon she would have to get rid of him. Hopefully, Travis Kincade was this good, or only half as good, in bed . . .

The next morning, Rachel Raines appeared for work. She was a willowy woman with dark chestnut hair and vivid green eyes. She and Rana seemed pleased with each other and soon established an easy rapport. Relieved at how well the two women were getting along, Nathan announced that he would be riding to the east pasture to see how the fence repairs were going in that troublesome area.

Rachel spent the morning teaching Rana about cooking and cleaning, and telling her about others on the ranch. Rana decided not to question the woman about her husband or their life together, at least not until they got to know each other better.

Aaron Moore arrived after the noon meal. While he and Rana worked at the dining room table, Rachel did the washing and checked on Nathan's garden, for she and one of the hands were responsible for tending it and gathering the vegetables and fruits. When Rana and Aaron took a short break from the lesson, Rachel told them she was leaving for the day and would see Rana the next morning. Rana was delighted to hear the woman had cooked a stew for supper and had left it simmering on the stove. Rachel also had biscuits ready to be baked later and had prepared tea and a cobbler with canned peaches.

Aaron Moore departed shortly after Rachel, and Mace appeared around five to take Rana to a nearby meadow for target practice. He was amazed by her natural skill with guns. As he instructed her and she obeyed, he told her many tales about the ranch and his friendship with Travis. Rana felt at ease with Mace and told him many things about her life in the Oglala camp. Since the ranch was so sorely in need of money, she did not reveal how much Nathan and Travis had paid for her return, nor did she tell Mace that she and Travis were married under Indian law. He returned her just before supper time, then conversed with Nathan for a few minutes, and the older man invited him to stay for the evening meal.

Nathan cleverly suggested, "If anybody's watching us for Harry, it might be a good idea if you're seen around the house with Rana. Out riding, you might only look like her escort. And it wouldn't hurt none if you two were seen holding hands and eyeing each other."

That day set a pattern for many to follow, with Rana steadily increasing her knowledge and skills with her books, in the house, and on the ranch. Gradually she met the other hands and they were all taken with her, each offering to do whatever he could to help her. But as she and Mace played their deceitful parts, the other men were fooled completely and made sure they did not infringe on Mace's territory.

Mrs. Dobbs finished the new wardrobe and her congenial visits stopped, but Rana felt she had learned a great deal from the affable woman. Rana knew the clothes she had made were beautiful and costly, but some were very uncomfortable for a girl accustomed to wearing supple buckskins and going barefoot. Rachel, Nathan, and Mace often teased her about those bare feet and her amusing complaints. She had gotten used to the hard western saddle, but she still preferred riding bareback, which Mace and Nathan would not allow. She missed her daily swims and frequently begged Nathan and Mace to allow her that pleasure, but all she could manage to elicit was permission to go wading in a stream.

Whenever she and Mace went riding, he would point out and explain the various ranch tasks. This was a busy season for cowhands and ranchers, and only one man appeared to have decided not to wait out the current trouble. The others agreed to continue working with partial pay until Nathan solved his problems. Some hands were engaged in structural repairs or fence mending or rounding up strays or moving cattle between pastures. Others were occupied with branding calves and colts or guarding against rustlers or breaking wild horses.

Nathan did not extend or accept any neighborly invitations; he used lost work time and catching up from his long absence as excuses to continue guarding Rana's privacy for awhile. Anyone who dropped by was greeted outside and entertained there, and at such times Rana stayed out of sight. He realized people were curious about her, but he believed they should understand she needed time to get accustomed to a whole new life. Yet, with the hands' trips into town and to other ranches, news of her beauty and appeal spread quickly. To keep their friends and neighbors from getting too curious to contain themselves, Nathan sent messages to them saying he would hold a large barbecue on the tenth of August, at which time everyone would meet his granddaughter.

Each Sunday Nathan went to church with the Raineses and answered countless questions about Rana Michaels. Most seemed to understand why Nathan did not want her overwhelmed with so many new things and people, and told him they would wait patiently for the second Saturday in August.

It had been thirteen days since Travis's departure and Rana missed him terribly. So far, the incidents of wicked mischief had been limited to several fence cuttings, the rustling of fifteen to twenty head of cattle at a time, the strewing about of hay stacks—it would have been too dangerous to set them afire, for flames could spread wildly and rapidly in all directions during this sultry July weather—the plundering of small sheds, and the opening of gates to allow horses to escape: problems that could be repaired or corrected, with the exception of the stolen cattle.

Rana had not yet been given the opportunity to speak privately with Todd Raines, but she often found him watching her intently. On this particular day, Rana turned suddenly to find Rachel observing the way she and Todd had been looking at each other. Tears glistened in the woman's green eyes and Rana followed her into the house and asked kindly, "Why do you weep, Rachel?"

Rachel dried her eyes and let them roam the features of the girl before her. "You look just like your mother, and she broke Todd's heart years ago. Every time he looks at you, he sees and remembers that pain. Your mother was . . ." Rachel held her revealing tongue.

"I am sorry my face brings such sadness and pain. Please speak, Rachel. Why did my mother hurt your husband? How did she do so? To understand my mother and myself, I must hear about the past."

Rachel answered reluctantly, "Todd was in love with Marissa Crandall and he believed she was in love with him. They were together nearly every day and they talked about marriage—until she suddenly ran off with that Raymond Michaels. It shocked everybody, 'cause he was . . ." Again Rachel fell silent and her face turned very red.

"Do not worry, Rachel, I know my father was a bad man. There is a reason why she married Raymond and died for her mistake. Why did my mother choose him over Todd Raines? It makes no sense."

Rachel's gaze wandered over Rana's entreating expression, and she knew the girl was serious. Rana's face was so much like the one that had haunted both Todd and herself for years, but there was nothing to dislike about this charming girl. The same had been true of Marissa, despite the fact that Rachel had wanted to despise the woman who had hurt her love so badly. Each time she had returned for a short visit, Marissa had seemed so sad, so lonely, so vulnerable, and so afraid. The girl whom Rachel had known during those visits long ago was nothing like the one described in the gossip she had heard then and later. And, Rachel reasoned, if Marissa had been as wicked and willful as the rumors claimed, Todd Raines would never have fallen in love with her. She wanted to help Rana, but she felt it would be wrong to reveal a mystery that would confuse and pain this sweet girl even more than she already was. Poor Marissa; something had terrified that beautiful creature and had driven her from home. But no one knew why she decided to run off with Raymond, including Todd and Nathan.

"That's something I can't explain, Rana; I doubt anyone can. I was working here during your last two visits, but I doubt you recall me. Todd married me after Marissa's second visit home in '52. I think he needed someone to help him forget your mother, but we've been very happy, except for having no children. Lord, how I wish I could give Todd a child. It would make us so happy. I used to watch Todd watching you and Marissa. I knew he still loved her and wished you two were his. I tried to hate your mother, but she made it impossible. She might have been wild and willful in her younger days, but she wasn't like that when I knew her. She was a kind, good woman, Rana, and she loved you dearly. I think she wanted to stay here on the ranch, but your papa wouldn't allow it."

Rachel peeked out the kitchen window to make certain no one was coming, then continued. "I couldn't blame Todd for his feelings, 'cause feelings are things we can't control. It took him years to get over losing her, then years to get over her death. He was one of the men who helped Mister Crandall search for you until they knew it was useless. The minute I laid eyes on you the other week, I knew how you was affecting my Todd. My poor love! All those memories must have come pouring back when he looked at you, the good ones and the bad ones. Please don't talk to him about your mama. I promise you he don't know nothing that I ain't told you. Todd's talked about her plenty, asleep and awake. He don't know why she left; that's why he suffered so. Not knowing something important is like a festering wound that won't heal. Let him get used to having you around before you say anything to him. Maybe you'll help him accept the past and get over her."

"I will not speak of my mother to him until I know the truth; then I will tell it to him, for he has earned the right to know it. You are a good wife to him, Rachel. Do not let the spirit of a dead loved one come between you. He belongs to you; fight for him. My mother is not your enemy, and I am your friend. Do not be sad or afraid."

Rachel smiled through more tears. "That's what your mother said to me the last time she was home. I was so scared Todd would fall in love with her again, and I knew she was miserable with Raymond. I was afraid they would be drawn to each other like before. Marissa saw how I was feeling. One day she put her arm around my shoulder and told me not to be sad or afraid, to trust my husband, and to fight for him if necessary. She told me she had loved Todd long ago, but as a young girl. She said she knew she had hurt him deeply, but she couldn't change the past. She refused to talk to him because she said it was best if he kept terrible thoughts about her and hated her. She believed it would make it easier for him to forget her. She was a special woman, Rana. I wish she was still alive so you could know her like I did. If anyone tells you mean things about her, don't listen to them. Hardly anybody understood or knew Marissa, and that's plenty sad."

Just then Rana moved to answer a knock at the front door and accepted a fake telegram that was signed with Travis's name. She did not bother to open it and read it, for she knew that the hired hand who had supposedly quit the ranch on July fifth was actually going from place to place to send such false telegrams to Clarissa Caldwell and Nathan as well, just in case Harrison had the telegrapher in his employ. The plan was that first a message would be sent from Springfield, then Sedalia, then St. Louis, then Springfield again, with the hopes of keeping Travis's whereabouts a secret.

Clarissa masked her outrage as she read the telegram that her father had opened and read first: "In Springfield. No good news. Sedalia next. Sending love and hope. Travis." She looked up at her father and asked, "Why did you read my mail, Papa?"

"It sounds to me as if you knew where he was going and why. Is that true, daughter?" Harrison asked coldly, angrily.

Her temper was rising and she fought to control it. "Nearly two weeks ago I told you he had left on another mysterious trip. He sent me a message by Cody Slade. I told you he said he was going to look for those bandits or try to get another loan. You read the telegram, so you know as much as I do. He hasn't found anything, and we both know he can't, so why are you angry and worried, Papa? You act like you think Travis and I are plotting against you instead of the other way around. I don't like being forced to defend myself to you."

"The whole damn thing seems curious to me!" he snapped.

"I know, Papa. That's why I told you about it. They're scared and worried over there, but we know they're trapped. Travis can't find that money because it's locked in your safe, and he can't get a loan with the debts they owe. You'll have their ranch by August first, so calm down and enjoy your imminent victory."

"It isn't like Kincade and Nate to give up so easily."

"They're not, Papa. They think they're doing all they can. What has you so upset? Is it Mary Beth Sims? You haven't seen her lately," she suggested evocatively. "Is there a problem with her?"

"The devil take that mealymouthed child!" he exploded meanly. "She isn't fit to become a Caldwell or to bear one. I told Sims today that I didn't want his daughter. I told him to marry her off to that Cody Slade; a cowpoke's wife is all she's fit to be. I didn't like her anyway, and I got tired of her refusing me. I'll find me another woman, a better and a prettier one." Visions of Marissa filled his head and he wished he could catch one glimpse of her daughter. All he had thought about since learning about Rana's existence and arrival was Marissa and their past. Somehow he had to get his hands on that girl . . .

Clarissa glared at her father's profile. She detested the dreamy look on his face and the reasons for it: Marissa and Rana. At least Mary Beth was out of her way, and she would see to it that Rana didn't mar her beautiful plans. She advised maliciously, "I think it's time to get tough with that old buzzard on the Rocking C, Papa. That cocky Nathan is climbing high and he needs to be slapped down a few rungs. Don't take any chances. He could find someone to lend him the money, so you'd better make sure he doesn't want to pay off that debt in two weeks and stay around." She smiled wickedly. "I think it's time you turned your hired hands loose over there; that's why you're paying them, to run Crandall out. If you don't let them have some fun like they did with old man McFarland, they might get bored and leave, just when you need them. The timing is perfect with Travis gone. Nobody over there will stand up to Monroe and Hayes."

"You're right, girl. I think it's about time to show Nate who's going to become the big boss soon. I'll send Fargo to fetch them. Yep, I'll make some plans with Monroe and Hayes this very afternoon."

Lone Wolf met Travis as he rode into the Oglala camp and reined in before his tepee. The two men looked at each other and smiled. "Come, sit, brother. Speak of my sister, Wild Wind, and speak of why you return to my lands when fires burn in your eyes."

Travis and Lone Wolf entered his tepee and sat on buffalo mats to talk. "There are many things I must tell you, Lone Wolf, my brother, but the words do not wish to leave my body. I must speak of much trouble in my past in these lands, and I must speak of great danger to us in the white lands. I come to seek the understanding and help of my brother, Lone Wolf, and I must return home quickly."

Lone Wolf read severe anxiety and doubt in the other man, and he knew something of great importance had brought Travis to him. "Speak, White Eagle; my heart is open to you and your words."

Travis slowly and painfully revealed his turbulent past in the Hunkpapa camp, and described all the tormenting days that had followed. "You have only my word, Lone Wolf, but I did not betray them and side with my father, whose heart was dark and evil. They left me without a people and a land and a heart for many years. They tried to take away my honor, my spirit, and my life. They left me no way to defend myself. If I had not run away, the truth would have died with me. Grandfather did not want it to end that way. He protected my life and sent me far away to find another land, people, and life. He returned my honor and renewed my spirit."

Travis explained the trouble and peril on the ranch. As had been the case with Rana, Lone Wolf had difficulty understanding white laws that prohibited Travis from punishing and slaying his enemy and recovering his belongings. Travis told the handsome and intrepid chief about the tainted gold, the "yellow rocks," which could save their lands. "Grandfather sent me into the lives and hearts of Nathan Crandall and his granddaughter, your sister, Wild Wind. I fill their hearts and lives, as they fill mine. When this danger is past and our enemy is defeated, Rana Michaels and Travis Kincade will join in the white land as Wild Wind and White Eagle joined in the Indian land. They are my heart, my life and honor, Lone Wolf, and I must defend them and protect their lands. To do this in the white world, I must have the gold, the yellow rocks, which have great value to the white man." He entreated Lone Wolf to go with him to the Hunkpapa camp and to help him convince them of his past innocence and persuade them to let him take the gold to save his lands from an evil white. This was something he hoped the Indians would understand.

Lone Wolf told Travis about the Hunkpapas' visit after Travis's departure with Wild Wind, and his words shocked and relieved the half-blooded man. "The Hunkpapas camp at a great distance from the Oglalas. We must travel far before the moon passes above us. When the new sun appears, we will finish our journey. Lone Wolf and White Eagle will speak with our Lakota brothers about the yellow rocks. It is good you come to ask for them and do not steal them. I say your words are true. But what will White Eagle do if the Hunkpapas refuse to let him take the yellow rocks?" he questioned gravely as they prepared to leave.

"I will trade all for them, Lone Wolf, for without them we will lose our honor, and perhaps our lives."

—— *Chapter 15* ——

❧

TRAVIS RECOVERED THE LAST POUCH of gold from its hiding place and packed it in his saddlebag; then met Lone Wolf's gaze and smiled. He glanced at the clear sky above them and inhaled deeply. "My heart is filled with joy and relief, my brother. My spirit chants this special *coup* of my Hunkpapa brothers. My mother's people have given back something very precious to me; they have returned my Indian heart and spirit. All has been made good again, Lone Wolf."

The young chief nodded. "It is as it must be, White Eagle. Grandfather has defeated the evil of the past. You are free of it."

"Free," Travis echoed dreamily. Yes, he was free of this tormenting part of his past. The Hunkpapas knew the truth and accepted it; he was one with them again, as it should be. Now it was time to cut the bond with this part of his life. Taking his knife, he severed the thong around his neck and removed his *wanapin*. He stared at it, then handed it to Lone Wolf. "Give this to your first son, my brother; it is a sacred bond between our two worlds. As he grows to a man, it will protect him in both worlds, as it protected me. One day the war lance will be broken between our two peoples, as the arrow is broken in the eagle's talons. He will be a leader of great power, like the thunderbolt in the eagle's grasp. He will end the bitter days of the War Bonnet Society; he will find the path to peace and survival. One day the children of Lone Wolf and Myeerah and the children of Rana Michaels and Travis Kincade will play and ride together in peace and love. They will share true friendship as we have, my brother."

Lone Wolf looked at the medallion that had been made by Medicine Chief Sitting Bull of the Hunkpapas. He understood what Travis was doing and saying. "It will be as you say, my brother. You live a new life, and the old one is gone forever. Soon such words may be true of all Hunkpapas and Oglalas. I will place this on my son's neck when he is born." Lone Wolf removed his *wanapin* and handed it to Travis. "Give this to your son, my brother. It will guard his life when he enters the Lakota lands many winters from this sun. Our hearts and lives will be joined forever, my friend."

"I must ride quickly, Lone Wolf. The days before my challenge pass as swiftly as the snows fall in winter. It is good I returned to these lands one last time. You are my friend and brother for all days."

The two men clutched forearms and locked their gazes briefly, each knowing this would be the last time they would see each other. By way of settling their old debt, the Hunkpapas had given him permission to take the "yellow rocks," and now Travis would have to get home in time to use them to thwart Caldwell. He could only pray he would make it home safely and rapidly, for it was now the eighteenth of July—two weeks before the bank loan was due—and many miles separated him from the ranch.

Lone Wolf watched Travis mount and ride away. He returned to his tepee and studied the gifts his friend had given him and his family: the *wanapin* for his firstborn son, the hair ornament for Myeerah, which Wild Wind had worn in the painting that had led Travis and her grandfather to her, the buckskin garments that Travis had worn when he had come to stake a claim on his adopted sister, several guns and knives, boxes of ammunition, warm garments for Myeerah for the winter from her friend Rana, a mirror for his beloved wife, and a special blanket in which to wrap their first child.

Lone Wolf explained the significance of the gifts to Myeerah and smiled tenderly. "Wild Wind has returned to her destiny, my wife. She and White Eagle will join in the white way and be happy. It is good. We must pray for the Great Spirit to guide her husband to her safely." Lone Wolf closed his eyes and called to mind a vision he had had recently. He smiled. Yes, he reflected, there would be a strong bond between their children one day . . .

Rana was restless, for so much was happening all around her and she felt useless, restricted. She had been studying and working hard since her arrival, but she was unaccustomed to lengthy confinement. The only privacy she had came at night in her room, and the nights seemed unbearably long as she lay in her bed alone. With Travis gone, she felt there was no one with whom she could really talk, as she once had with Myeerah. She was always watching everything she said or did, and trying to be her very best so as not to disappoint her grandfather. She was used to being in and around nature, not trapped in a wooden structure, and she felt like a captive who could not come and go as she desired. Even more difficult to combat was the helplessness she felt at not being allowed to aid those she loved.

Aaron Moore had sent word that he was ill and could not come to the ranch for her lessons today. Rachel had taken care of her chores and had left early to assist Lettie Davis with the early birth of another child. Todd Raines and several of the hands were busy mending a lengthy span of fence that had been cut the night before, while Cody Slade and others were trying to round up scattered cattle and horses. This time, in their haste, the malicious rustlers had left a carelessly concealed trail, which Mace Hunter and several men were following. If only they could catch one or two, Rana reflected, they might learn the identity of their leader, or prove it was Caldwell.

She was glad Nathan had left for a town called Dallas before this new offense had been uncovered, for he had been suffering too much during these trying days. She prayed it would not be difficult for Nathan to set aside his adoption of Travis Kincade, which would then allow them to marry. Nathan had told her he was going to Dallas to handle the matter so that Harrison Caldwell would not learn about it and become suspicious of their plans. Nathan intended to hire a lawyer there to dispatch the delicate legal problem, and he planned to return home late the following day.

Rana walked around the house several times, but there was nothing to do but wait and worry. Nathan had not realized she would be left alone today and tonight, nor had Mace Hunter when he had ridden off in pursuit of the rustlers and cattle. When word had come shortly before the noon meal that Lettie was in early labor, Rana had insisted that Rachel go to the woman and help her with the delivery. Lettie had two sons, eleven and thirteen, who would care for the smaller children, but they knew nothing of bringing a child into the world.

Rana halted near the front door and looked outside. Only two men were visible, and they were busy with chores. She was not afraid to be left alone in the house, for she knew how to defend herself. Yet worry and uneasiness plagued her and, as time passed slowly, she grew tense and irritable. Perhaps part of her distress and tension was due to the heat, for it was an oppressively hot, muggy day. What she needed was a refreshing, cooling swim.

Rana knew that the river was only a few miles from the house, and she believed she would be safe because the evil men had not attacked the ranch during the day. Why couldn't she ride there and enjoy herself for a short while? The hands would be gone for the afternoon, so who would know? Besides, she could take a gun and be very careful. Hesitating no longer, she decided to go.

Rana managed to get her sorrel and leave without being seen. She rode to a spot near the river where Mace had taken her several days before. After dismounting, she tied the reins to a bush and walked toward the inviting water. As she gazed at it longingly, she wondered if she were being rash, but before she could ponder her actions further, a man appeared from the trees. Rana drew her pistol and pointed it at him to let him know it would be unwise to attack her, if that were the motive for his approach.

The stranger did not seem alarmed or deterred by her action. He reined up near her and stared at her boldly, his mouth open and his eyes wide. As Rana studied him, she noted that he looked younger than her grandfather and was still an attractive man. His hair was dark, almost black, and his eyes were a mixture of green and brown. His body had a certain strength, but Rana could tell that he did very little physical work. She waited for him to speak.

"My God, you look just like her," he murmured in undisguised astonishment. He dismounted, dropped his reins to the ground, and came forward. He looked at the gun and her stance. "You don't need to be afraid, Rana. I'm your neighbor, Harrison Caldwell."

"I am not afraid of anything, Mr. Caldwell. The gun is for protection. Many bad things and people walk my grandfather's land. Why have you come to speak with me?" she asked bluntly, for she had guessed his identity and was therefore able to mask any outward show of emotion.

"I was out riding and I saw you standing here. I haven't had the pleasure of meeting you. Your grandfather is being very protective of you. I knew your mother, and I was shocked that you look so much like her," he replied smoothly, having mastered his surprise. "I imagine you're glad to be home again."

"Yes, it is good to return to my family and home. How did you know my mother?" she inquired politely.

Harrison laughed genially. "We were neighbors for years, Rana. Marissa used to come to my ranch to help my daughter, Clarissa, with her lessons, and sometimes she would watch Clarissa for me. It's hard for a man alone to raise a small child, especially a little girl. Clarissa and your mother were friends. She's looking forward to meeting you. Why don't you ride over one day and visit with us?" he invited.

Rana instantly thought of the safe that might be holding her grandfather's stolen money. If she could visit his ranch, she could see where it was located and how the house was arranged. If Travis could not get the gold, they could sneak into this man's house and take what belonged to them after his return. She smiled and nodded. "It is good to find new friends here. When my grandfather returns from this place called Abilene, I will ask him to bring me to meet your daughter. Grandfather went to speak with a man about horses," she lied convincingly, as she had been instructed by Nathan before his departure. "Is your ranch far away? Is it big like Grandfather's?" she asked with feigned feminine interest.

Harrison was fooled by her delicate, friendly facade and assumed that Nathan and Travis had not told her about their problems. His eyes swept over the flaming head of hair that tumbled to her tiny waist. Her complexion was as smooth as silk and playful freckles danced across her pert nose. He gazed into those large, innocent-looking, gray-blue eyes. She was even more beautiful and desirable than her mother had been, and she possessed a sweetness and artlessness that Marissa had lacked. "You should not be out riding alone, Rana. We've been having trouble with rustlers lately."

Rana laughed at his mild scolding, and the sound of it washed provocatively over the man before her. In a skillfully controlled tone, she replied, "The rustlers do not strike when the sun is high and can reveal their faces. I have a gun, and I know how to use it. I am in no danger. Do not worry over me."

Harrison laughed too. "I see you're more like your mother than looks alone," he teased jovially. "Marissa was just as headstrong and brave as you are. Still, you should be careful."

Rana smiled deceitfully once more. "You are kind to worry, Mister Caldwell, but I can take care of myself." He was looking at her as if she were her mother, and the strange look mystified and intrigued her.

Harrison concluded that since Nathan was gone, it was unlikely that anyone knew this ravishing creature was out here alone. She was a vivacious, daring young thing, and he wanted to know all about her. His mouth was dry, his palms were sweaty, his body was quivering, his heart was pounding, and his manhood was pleading. He wanted this girl with every inch of himself. "If you like, you could ride over with me now and meet Clarissa. She was home when I left, and she didn't say anything about going out today," he lied eagerly, for he knew Clarissa would be at the dressmaker's all day and he would have this girl all to himself.

Rana sensed that the man was deceiving her, for he was too caught up in his thoughts to realize that his gaze, voice, and behavior were giving him away. She noticed how he kept licking his lips and swallowing, and how his breathing indicated a racing heart. She had watched him dry his palms on his pants' legs several times. She saw the glow in his eyes and on his cheeks, and she observed how he kept shifting nervously from foot to foot. She noticed all of these things without Harrison's awareness. Rana knew she had this man duped and fascinated, and she found it impossible to avoid wondering if he had also been this taken with her mother.

She realized she was in no danger from him, at least for today. There was much she wanted to learn from him and about him, and the only way to do so was to accept his questionable invitation. "I will go with you, but I must return home soon. I must not worry those Grandfather left to protect me. Tell me about your daughter," she coaxed as they mounted.

Clarissa paced the cabin as she talked with Wes Monroe. "You're certain you left enough of a trail for them to follow without it looking odd?"

"Just like we planned, woman, so stop acting *loco*. By now, half the hands on the Rocking *C* should be chasing down that trail. When I see your papa later, I'll tell him we need to strike closer to the house tonight while those men are gone. Don't fret; I'll make sure that girl gets in the way of a stray bullet. I know my work; it'll look like an accident. Once it's done, ain't nothing he can do about it. You know this is going to cost you extra," he announced suddenly.

Clarissa halted to look at him and scoffed crudely, "Don't try that on me, you bastard. We both know how much you and Jack love killing people, including pretty women. All you have to do now is convince Papa to let you raid Crandall's stable."

"You worry too much, woman. He won't suspect a thing, not tonight or when I get ready to plug him for you. You want me to take him out quick and easy, or real slow and painful?"

"I haven't decided yet," she replied petulantly. "Right now, I just want to get rid of that little Michaels bitch before Papa gets any more silly ideas like he did with Mary Beth Sims," she explained, knowing it was Travis she wanted to protect from Rana's allure and not her father, for she had another way to halt anything that might start between Harrison and Rana.

Moving his tongue slowly over his dry lips, Wes commanded, "Forget all that for now and come here, woman."

Rana entered the house and looked around wide-eyed, as if she were astonished by its size and was appreciatively admiring it. She smiled and remarked, "Your home is very big and pretty. It is strange to live in a place with many rooms and belongings. It is much different in a tepee," she told him casually, knowing he was aware of the story of her past and concluding that her easy manner would disarm him completely. As if enthralled by the spaciousness and beauty of his home, she began to wander around, carefully studying the layout of the rooms and the objects in them.

Ushering her into the parlor, Harrison said, "I'm sorry about what happened to you, Rana. It must have been terrible for you, all those years with the Indians."

She halted her roaming to glance at him and answer, "It was not bad with the Oglalas. They stole me from the Kiowas when I was but eight winters. The Kiowas were very bad, but I was small and remember little about them. When I was taken captive by the Oglalas, Chief Soaring Hawk made me his daughter. I was very happy and free with them. But I am glad to be home again. Still, there is much to learn. The white teacher comes each day to help me, and I work hard to learn quickly. I do not wish to shame my grandfather, for many think and say I am . . . uncivilized, you whites call it. Yes?"

Harrison grinned. "Anybody who would call you a savage is blind and mean, Rana. But it isn't 'you whites,' because you're one of us."

She laughed merrily. "I forget. I was raised Indian, and change is hard and long. You are kind not to laugh at me. Grandfather knows that many people will; that is why he keeps me home until I learn much. I am brave and strong. It will hurt if they do not like me or they treat me badly, but words cannot slay a person. I wish to make Grandfather proud of me. He has been sad many years since Mother was killed. I wish to make him happy again. Where is your daughter? I wish her to tell me about my mother. I remember little about her."

Harrison replied, "She'll return soon. Why don't you look around?" he entreated. He watched Rana as she moved gracefully from one place to another as if she were on a magical journey. She was like a child filled with the wonder of Christmas. Several times her hand reached toward an object, then she would slowly withdraw it, as if afraid to touch the piece. She would ball her hands briefly as if warning herself she could break something precious or valuable. Recalling how long she had been with the Indians, he realized how new and different all of this would be for her. She was so alive and inquisitive, and he was feeling younger by the minute just observing her.

"You told me you weren't afraid of anything, Rana," he teased. "Pick it up and look at it," he encouraged when she wavered over a floral glass box and her exquisite gaze remained locked on it.

"I must not, Mister Caldwell. I would be sad if I broke something that belongs to another. I have never seen flowers that are not real, except painted ones. How strange and beautiful," she murmured, playing her naïve Indian maiden role with superb talent.

Harrison stepped forward, lifted the box, and handed it to her. "It's yours, Rana. Now you shouldn't be afraid to hold it."

Rana looked at the treasure in her hands. She widened her eyes guilefully and protested, "But I cannot take it without a reason."

"There are two reasons you should take it, Rana. First, because it's your first visit to my home and I wish you to have it; and second, because it was bought as a gift for your mother years ago, but she left before Clarissa and I could give it to her."

Rana looked at the fragile box and pondered Harrison's words. She believed it had been purchased for Marissa, but not as a gift from his daughter, and this strange perception alarmed her.

"Please take it, Rana. I will be sad if you refuse."

"I will take it because the Indians taught me it was wrong to refuse the generosity of a friend. I only wished to know why you wanted me to have it. Thank you. I will guard it carefully."

"I'll go see if any of my men know where Clarissa went and how long she'll be. You relax and I'll return shortly," he told her, pretending to know nothing of his daughter's absence.

Rana peeked out the window and watched him walk toward his stable to speak with the man working there. She hurriedly looked around his home once more, astutely memorizing where the doors and windows were located. She found his office and noticed the large safe behind an equally large desk. Excitement surged through her. She quickly studied the room, inside and outside, then returned to the parlor and was feigning fascination with the pianoforte when he returned.

She glanced up quizzically when she saw that he was alone. She listened and nodded her head as he told her the stableman had said Clarissa had gone riding. Smiling, Rana rose from her seat on the oblong bench. "I must ride for home, Mister Caldwell. The others will worry if they find me gone. I will visit another day. You are most kind and generous."

"I wish you could stay longer, but I understand. I'll ride part of the way with you, to make sure you get home safely."

Rana smiled. "If it pleases you," she agreed.

Harrison bid her good-bye at the boundary to his ranch. He didn't want any of the men seeing them together and telling Nathan about their meeting, for Nathan would surely want to keep them apart. Since it was more than likely that Rana was not supposed to be out alone, chances were she wouldn't mention their meeting either, he reasoned. "Please ride over to visit us any time, Rana. I know Clarissa is anxious to meet you."

Rana reached the stable, then made her way to the house unseen, laughing inwardly at her cleverness. When she was finally safe in her room, she placed the floral box on her dresser and stared at it intently. She wondered why her mother had been a friend to those who were now enemies of her family. Clearly this Harrison Caldwell had been in love with her mother, and now he desired her to take Marissa's place. Perhaps it had not been Clarissa whom her mother had been visiting on the Circle C Ranch long ago . . . Was it possible that her mother and Caldwell had been in love and had wished to marry, but that something or someone had prevented it? Had her mother left home and married Raymond out of spite? There were so many unanswered questions.

Rana picked up the doll from her bed and placed it beside the glass box, then laid the heart-shaped turquoise and silver pendant next to it. Her probing gaze moved from one item to the next. "What is your secret, Mother? Why did you choose a cruel beast like Raymond Michaels over Todd Raines or Harrison Caldwell? Are you the reason Caldwell hates Grandfather so intensely? What happened to you before I was born? I am sorry if you loved him, but I must make him pay for hurting Grandfather," she vowed sincerely.

It was nearing eight o'clock when Mace knocked on the front door. Rana smiled at him and invited him inside.

"I don't think that's a good idea with your grandfather gone. We don't want people talking about us. I was just making sure you're all right," he explained.

Rana looked confused. "Is it not the plan to have them do so?"

Mace looked at her oddly, then grinned. "Yes, but not that way. It's fine for us to be seen outside together, but it isn't considered nice for a lady to entertain a man when she's alone."

She reflected upon his words, then reasoned, "Why not? If we do nothing wrong, why would they think badly of us?"

"Not badly, Rana, just . . ." He hesitated as he sought the right words. "It just isn't done like that down here. A man and woman just don't spend time alone in this situation."

"Travis and Rana spent time alone in this house," she argued.

"But you're family. That's different."

"No, Mace, we are not family," she corrected him.

Mace looked disconcerted. "I don't know how to explain this to you, Rana. I just know it ain't right for me to come inside tonight."

"You whites have many strange ways, Mace Hunter," she teased.

"You whites?" he echoed mischievously.

She laughed, then asked, "Did you capture any of the rustlers?"

"Not a da . . . one, Rana. I sent a few men on ahead, but I think that trail was marked to mislead us. That makes me wonder what those bas . . . outlaws are planning tonight." Mace warned himself to calm down. He was so tired and annoyed that his tongue was hanging loose.

"You think the trail was a trick?" she inquired.

He nodded his blond head. "Yep, and I plan to put out lots of guards tonight. So if you hear anything, stay in the house and keep the doors and windows locked. And keep a gun nearby."

"It is too hot to close doors and windows, Mace."

"Then keep lights on in all the rooms so my men can see anybody sneaking around the house."

"I will. I am a light sleeper, and I can defend myself. Do not worry," she entreated confidently.

"I know you can take care of yourself. Travis told me how you and Nate fought off those deserters on the trail and how you saved his life. That's the only reason I'm not overly worried about you. He's a damn lucky man to have you, and I'm lucky he's my friend." Mace kissed her on the cheek then and left.

Nathan arrived home late the next afternoon and told Rana that the legal work had been set in motion and that the lawyer would notify him when it was time to pick up the papers in Dallas. He explained that it was a complicated matter, but he was confident it could be handled by the lawyer he had chosen.

Mace joined them for supper soon afterward and gave Nathan a detailed report of the recent events. "I can't explain it, Nate, but I was sure something was up last night. Who knows? Maybe they're watching our every move and knew we'd returned to the ranch and posted guards. Dang it! That Caldwell is a sly varmint. Doesn't look as if there's any outguessing him."

"He'll make an error one day, Mace, and when he does, we'll catch him, legally or otherwise. Presently I'm worried about Travis; if he made it, we should have gotten word from him by now.'' He glanced at Rana and frowned, annoyed with himself for his slip.

Rana smiled and squeezed his arm. "He'll be fine, Grandfather," she encouraged him tenderly, though she too felt something was terribly wrong. They had decided on a prearranged message to let Nathan and Rana know he had succeeded and was on his way home. There were less than two weeks remaining until their deadline, and the message had not arrived. Rana did not want to think about what that could mean.

After supper, Rana and Mace stood on the front porch in view of the hands near the bunkhouse and cook house, as if they were sweethearts sharing each other's company. As they talked, Mace slipped his arm around her shoulder and she rested her head against his chest. "Do you think he's safe, Mace?" she asked worriedly.

Mace comfortingly tightened his embrace for a moment, then answered, "I'm sure he is, Rana. We'll hear from him tomorrow; you'll see. Travis is cunning and smart; nothing can happen to him."

She looked up at him, her eyes pleading for reassurance. "But he's had time to send us word by now. Why has it not come?"

"I don't know, Rana, but it will." He kissed her forehead and snuggled her against him. He would not tell her that he was plenty worried too. If Travis hadn't reached the Indian camp, retrieved the gold, and left by now . . . Mace sighed heavily. He almost wished Nathan hadn't told him Travis's secret plans. Damn, he cursed to himself, it was a crazy, dangerous scheme, and it had little chance of success. Even if Travis got the gold from the Indians, how could he get it back here safely by himself, and in time to save the ranch? Mace knew Travis could do most anything he set his mind to, but this task might be too much, even for Travis.

Clarissa sat staring at her father's back. Damn you, you bastard, she silently cursed him. He had refused to let Wes and his men go near Nathan's ranch last night. In fact, he had told them to lie low until he gave further orders. She wasn't fooled. She knew he hadn't wanted Rana Michaels frightened or injured. She had seen the way her father had behaved after Rana's visit yesterday—like a dog in heat! The more she thought about his weakness for Marissa and Rana, the angrier she became, and the more her hatred and bitterness increased. "Papa, I don't understand this hesitation. You should make every move possible while Travis is gone."

Harrison turned and looked at her. He scowled. "Stop trying to run my affairs, daughter. I know what I'm doing."

"What are you doing, Papa?" she asked sarcastically.

"I'm keeping them off balance, girl. When they think I will strike, I don't. When they think I won't, I do. Mace Hunter wasn't fooled by that false trail; he was back at the ranch before dusk. I sent Fargo over there to nose around. He said they had guards posted all over the place. If I had let Wes and the boys go there, there would have been bodies to throw suspicion on me. I sent Wes and Jack down to Abilene to make sure Nate wasn't down there trying to borrow money. If he visited any of those banks, I'll know by tomorrow, and that'll keep those two busy a couple of days. You just do as I tell you, and keep your little nose out of my business."

"How can I help you, Papa, if I don't know everything?"

"You know all you need to know, girl."

"What are you planning to do next?" she persisted.

"I don't know yet, but nothing for the next few days. Let 'em relax a little and drop their guards; then I'll strike again." Harrison looked at the hostile expression on Clarissa's face. He did not want her around when he brought Marissa—no, Rana—into this house to live. He detested his daughter and wanted to punish her, and he knew that the best way to hurt a woman was to degrade her. "I need you to do something for me, girl."

"Anything, Papa," she replied sullenly, rashly.

"Fargo is getting restless. Why don't you give him a reason to hang around and stay loyal to us? We need him, Clarissa."

"*We*," "*us*," her furious mind echoed antagonistically. "What kind of reason would hold him here, Papa?" she asked with what innocence she could muster.

"You know he has a hankering for you, girl. Why don't I go into town tonight while you invite him here? I won't come back until midnight," he informed her meaningfully.

"If I invite him, Papa, he'll get the wrong idea; then I'll have him hanging around me and the house all the time."

"Then why don't I send him to the house with a message. You can offer him a drink while you read it, then let things proceed from there. You know he isn't gonna tell me he was sneaking into my daughter's bed while I was gone. You'll spark his interest, and he'll hang around waiting for another chance to get into your bloomers. Come on, girl, you're no silly virgin. You might as well enjoy your work. Before long, you'll be chained to a husband, so you'd best have fun now."

"Are you sure about this, Papa?"

"Just do whatever needs doing to keep Fargo around."

Late that afternoon, Fargo rode into town with Harrison. They stopped at the mercantile store so that Harrison could purchase some items for Fargo to deliver to Clarissa, and, shortly thereafter, Fargo was knocking at Clarissa's door, his arms full of bundles.

Clarissa answered the door in her night wrap, her hair pinned up and damp from a bath. "Fargo," she squealed as if surprised. "I thought Papa had forgotten something and had returned. I knew he said he wouldn't be home until midnight."

"He asked me to give you these things from the store," the man told her, making no attempt to keep his eyes off the way the thin garment clung to her wet body.

Aptly prepared for Fargo's arrival, Clarissa had made certain her hands would be full when she opened the door. She smiled beguilingly, her mirror and hairbrush held up before her, and asked, "Would you mind bringing them inside?" As he kicked the door closed and followed her, she pointed to the settee and said,

"You can place them there. You're very kind to do this for me and Papa. Would you like a drink? I'm sure your throat is dry. This weather is so hot."

"Don't mind if I do, Miss Clarissa. Whiskey, if it's no trouble."

"Oh, it's no trouble at all." She walked to the liquor cabinet and pretended to search for the whiskey, which she had hidden earlier near the back. She knew Fargo was staring at her and becoming aroused. "Here it is," she announced and turned to him with a smile.

Fargo joined her and took the glass. When he downed it in two gulps, she refilled it, then glanced toward the door and whispered, "You won't tell Papa if I sneak a drink, will you?"

"Course not," Fargo replied, filling his glass again.

After several drinks, Clarissa pretended to be drunk. When Fargo was filling his glass again, she casually loosened her sash, causing her wrap to gape slightly. "I think I'll find something cooler to put on," she announced. "This old rag is roasting me." She moved toward her room, knowing he would follow, and he did.

Clarissa struggled with the garment as if she were having trouble getting it off. "Let me help you," Fargo offered, removing it. He bent to kiss her neck and began running his hands over her body.

Soon he had her on the bed and was enjoying her to the fullest, and, to her surprise, she felt her body responding. They slaked their lascivious appetites until it was nearing midnight, then Fargo covered Clarissa's naked form and closed her door as he left the room.

Clarissa grinned as she heard him clearing away the "evidence" of his "seduction." She stretched and yawned. Fargo wasn't bad in bed, she mused, especially in the dark where she didn't have to look at his pockmarked face and squinty eyes. She thought about the times Raymond had forced Marissa to bed that ugly vulture, and she laughed. Perhaps the next time she did this favor for her father, she would ask Fargo a few questions about those degrading times. With a few accurate facts, she might be able to stir little Rana's memory . . .

By dusk the next day, Nathan, Rana, and Mace realized they would not be hearing any word from Travis for at least one more day. It was a very bad sign, for time was running out for them. Two hands had been ambushed and killed that afternoon, and a few of the others were getting worried. Alarmed by this added peril and dismayed by the extra work, Cody Slade suggested that the Sunday wedding he and Mary Beth had planned for tomorrow be postponed, but no one would allow it.

"If you don't do it now," Mace warned, "you might lose her. From now on, we'll post guards day and night around the ranch. I promise you she'll be fine over there with the Raineses and Davises. You've got everything set up in your new house. Do it, Cody."

"Mace is right, son," Nathan added. "Her pa is willing right now. But if Harry casts his eye on her again, it'll be too late for you."

Rana spoke up too. "Everything is ready, Cody Slade. How can you make her sad by refusing to show your courage and love?"

Todd told him, "Don't worry, Cody. Rachel and Lettie will look out for her. They keep loaded rifles ready all the time."

"That's what I'm talking about, Todd. That ain't no way to live."

"It won't be this way much longer," Todd replied.

"Then I should wait until it's better, and safe here for her."

"What you should do," Nathan advised sternly, "is snap her up while she's there for the taking. Listen, son, you know how Harry takes whatever he wants. You'd best claim her as your wife before he decides he wants her again."

"I guess all of you are right. We'll do it as soon as the preacher gets here after church tomorrow. Where do you want guards posted?"

Mace went over the evening's assignments, then everyone left except Nathan and Rana, who talked a few minutes before turning in.

Try as she might, Rana could not settle down. She lay across her bed, thinking distressing thoughts. In only twelve days her grandfather might lose his land and his heart. If Travis was not on his way back by now, he could not possibly make that deadline. And if he was on his way home, he would have sent word to them from one of the forts along the trail.

She went to her window, pushed against the thin covering, and gazed at the heavens to pray for her love's survival. He had taken such a great risk in going after that treacherous gold, she reflected.

Only a sliver of moon was showing and it was very dark outside. On such concealing nights, Oglala warriors had made secret raids on enemy camps, using skills and stealth she had persuaded her Indian brother to teach her. Long ago, on a dare, she had sneaked into an enemy camp, stolen a war shield, and sneaked home without getting caught; Lone Wolf had been furious with her and had tried to pretend he was not impressed, but she knew he had been secretly pleased that she had learned her lessons so well. He had taught her defense and escape and disguise using methods that had begun as amusing games, but there had come a time when her skills exceeded his, and his male pride had been injured. Often he had told her that these skills and practices would prepare her to meet and conquer her true destiny one day, and now she knew that the day had arrived.

Rana's keen mind began to whirl with daring plans. Saving this ranch was vital to her, because it was so important to the men she loved. She could live anywhere with them, but they loved this land and were a part of it. She truly believed it would be wrong and cowardly of her to do nothing while their enemy cleverly defeated them. If there were only a slim chance of recovering that money . . . She would not allow such speculations to continue. Her mind was set.

The daring redhead slipped into the dark pants she wore for riding and working around the house, then pulled on her darkest shirt. Taking another one of similar color, she secured it around her head to hide her flaming tresses. Strapping on her knife sheath, she concealed another, smaller blade in the long pocket that had been sewn into her knee-high moccasin, for she knew a gun might make noise and total silence was imperative. Remembering the bow and arrows in Travis's closet and confident of her skill with them, she went to fetch the quiet, lethal weapons. Cleverly and cautiously she obliterated any markings that would expose them as being Sioux, in case she was compelled to use one or more that night.

Perhaps she would not be able to reach the enticing safe or open it, but she could "nose around," as Travis called it. The more they learned, the more they would be prepared to deal with Harrison Caldwell when the moment of challenge came. She would not take any foolish chances or risk being captured, for she could imagine what that evil man would do or demand if she were to fall into his power.

The Caldwell ranch was fifteen miles away, but she could not risk taking a horse to ride there. Though she realized her stamina was not at its peak after having lazed around this house for three weeks, she knew how to travel across country and how to pace herself, thanks to Lone Wolf's training. Over this kind of terrain, she estimated she could travel a mile in ten minutes, which, allowing time for caution, would bring her there in less than three hours. Even if she could not steal a horse to ride most of the way home before releasing him, she would have time to get back before dawn.

Determined not to waste another moment, Rana climbed out her window and slipped around the house. Because she knew where Mace had posted the Rocking C guards, she could easily avoid them, and, once she had done so, she took the shortest route to Caldwell's home. Gingerly adhering to her plan, she arrived at the Circle C Ranch within the time frame she had set for herself. Within the concealment of several trees, she rested as she studied the area around the house and the other structures.

It was Saturday night and Rana assumed that most of Caldwell's hands would be in town, for if her suspicions were correct, this ranch had nothing to fear or protect from the villains who had raided other ranches and were currently attacking her grandfather's. The men who were around all seemed to be gathered in the bunkhouse, which Caldwell had placed a good distance from his home. Rana began to slip from tree to tree as she circled the house. There were no lanterns burning upstairs, which indicated that either no one was up there or those who were were in bed. There were several lanterns burning downstairs and cautiously she peered into those windows. The kitchen and parlor were empty, but she found Caldwell sitting behind his desk in his office, counting money and making notes in a large book. As she surveyed the room, she noted with mounting excitement that he was alone and the safe was open.

She sat down behind thick bushes, knowing she could do nothing but wait, watch, and listen. Because of the location of his desk and the office door, it would be impossible for her to steal into the house and into his office unobserved. She needed a miracle. *Help me, Wakan Tanka*, she prayed fervently.

Time passed and Rana was about to give up hope of any success that night. Suddenly she heard the sounds of several horses galloping into the yard followed by the low muttering of men talking. She strained to catch the words but could not. Cautiously she peered around the edge of the window and watched Harrison rise to answer the summons at his front door. Slipping to the corner of the house, she saw him join the men and begin a conversation. She assumed he did not want them to enter his office and see the tempting money on his desk. From his casual stance, she could tell he was relaxed, as if he were in no hurry to get the talk over with quickly.

Furtively she returned to his office window and climbed inside. She hurried to the safe and pushed wide the door to examine its contents. To the rear on the bottom shelf was a pair of saddlebags with rattlesnakes carved on the flaps. Seizing them, she fumbled nervously with the stubborn straps. She knew her time was short, yet her quivering fingers almost refused to work. Swiftly she removed the numerous, tightly bound packets she found within, cramming them into her roomy shirt and positioning them around her waist as she did so. Noting the many, small, decorative pillows on the settee in his office, she quietly retrieved two and stuffed one inside each saddlebag so that the missing contents might go unnoticed for a time. Then she refastened the straps and replaced the saddlebags. After carefully returning the safe door to its former position, she climbed out the window and concealed herself once more.

Her chest rose and fell rapidly with the forceful pounding of her heart, and she found it difficult to control her erratic respiration or ignore the dryness in her mouth. Her hands were trembling wildly and she felt as limp as a freshly skinned ermine pelt. No sense of power or smugness filled her; instead, she was almost overwhelmed by fear and tension. It was too soon for her to experience pride or relief or the sheer joy of success, for she was not out of danger yet. She had the stolen money, but she had to get away without being caught, stuffed as she was with the evidence of her "robbery." She prayed Caldwell would not look inside the saddlebags that night.

Feeling weak and shaky, she decided to risk riding home on a horse she would take from the corral farthest from the house and stable. She realized she would have to make her way slowly, for the paper money made a crinkling noise as she moved. Rana knew she would also have to wait until Caldwell's men had left the yard before attempting her trek to the corral, and, as she waited there in the darkness with the money packets tickling her waist, she gradually began to compose herself.

Eventually she heard Harrison returning to his office with one of the men. There the lawyer counted out some money and handed it to the other man, saying, "Pay the men for that excellent job, and make sure they hide those branding irons. We don't want Kincade or any of his boys finding them."

The other man replied scornfully, "Kincade ain't been around for weeks. What'cha think he's up to, boss?"

"I don't know, but very soon it won't matter. In two weeks the Rocking C Ranch will be mine," he boasted cockily. "When Monroe and Hayes return, make sure they come to see me immediately. I want to make certain they understand my orders and follow them to the letter." Harrison glanced up at his hireling and scoffed, "That Monroe bears close watching; he's an arrogant, dangerous son of a bitch. The damned idiot actually thought he had Mace Hunter fooled by that schoolboy trail he laid so he could raid Nate's stable. Hell, I really can't depend on anybody except you and Silas!" he lied to flatter the man. "Keep your eyes and ears open wide. I can't have any of my men's bodies showing up in the wrong places. I've worked too long and hard building this empire, and my final victory is at hand. I'll be damned if I allow some two-bit gunslinger to ruin things for me. I don't want any more burnings or shootings. It'll be my property soon and my cowpunchers. For now, I only need to scare them and harass them from time to time. There's no reason to get real nasty unless Crandall finds another loan and gets stubborn about selling out, which he won't.''

"Where's Miss Clarissa tonight?" the man asked in an eager tone.

"She went to that barn dance in town. She should be heading home soon. It wouldn't hurt if you rode that way to escort her home, if you don't mind," Harrison suggested nonchalantly.

"Don't mind at all, boss. I'll hide those branding irons in the barn, then be on my way," Fargo answered cheerfully.

"I'll walk you to the door," Harrison insisted.

The two men left the room. Fargo went outside and paid the waiting men, who then rode toward town to make the most of what was left of Saturday night by buying women and whiskey at the Fort Worth saloons. Whistling, Fargo headed for the barn with his horse's reins in one hand and the illegal branding irons in the other while, inside the main house, Harrison poured himself a drink and sat down to daydream about the vast empire he would soon control.

Without stopping to weigh the consequences, Rana set off at a cautious pace to follow the ugly man to the barn and see where he would hide the offending irons. She peered inside and watched him lift several boards to conceal the curved irons, which reminded her of the sliver of moon overhead and which easily altered the Rocking C brand into a Circle C. It was too simple for Caldwell to change their brand to his, she realized with sickening clarity. She would have to convince her grandfather to change his brand completely and into a pattern that Harrison Caldwell could not so readily alter. She moved out of sight as Fargo left the building and rode off on his horse, eager to encounter Clarissa Caldwell on her way home from town. Rana made no attempt to steal the irons, for she knew they would have to be found on Caldwell's property if they were going to serve as undeniable evidence against the villain. At least she knew where they were hidden and could tell Travis and Nathan, who would then tell the sheriff.

Rana made her way to the last corral and chose a horse. To conceal the fact of his theft, she left the gate open for others to slip out as well. She patted him for several moments and allowed him to get accustomed to her scent and touch; then she gently seized his mane and led him away from the inhabited area. He was sluggish and old, and because she was not intimidating, he went with her docilely. She mounted him bareback and guided him into a slow walk until they were out of hearing range; then she galloped toward the boundary line between the ranches. There she dismounted and left him nibbling grass, with no saddle marking to suggest he had been ridden.

Rana walked the rest of the way home, which took her over an hour in the mid-July heat. Her entire body was moist by the time she sighted the ranch, and she could feel the money sticking to her sweaty flesh. Not a breeze stirred to ease her discomfort. She was so weary, so thirsty, and she would have liked nothing more than to have been able to head for the river, strip off her clothes, and go for a soothing swim. But she did not dare. Skillfully avoiding the ranch guards, she slipped into the house and quietly made her way to Travis's room. Entering his closet, she closed the door and lit a candle. Carefully she climbed the wooden rungs that led to the attic. There she looked around for a place to hide the money until she could expose her daring deed to her grandfather.

A black trunk was positioned in one corner. She went to it and, withdrawing the packets from her shirt, stuffed the money behind it, assuming anyone who might come to search their house would look inside the trunk, not behind it. She removed the dark shirt from her head and crammed it on top of the packets to conceal them. Then she immediately proceeded to the water closet and took a long bath, hoping she would not make enough noise to awaken her grandfather. Either she succeeded or he awoke and assumed she was only trying to cool off from the stifling heat. Whichever the case, he never came to check on her.

Refreshed from the bath, she stretched out on her bed, naked and damp. It was done, she was home safely, and the money was recovered. It was nearing four o'clock in the morning and she was exhausted. Snuggling her old doll into her arms, she closed her eyes and was asleep in moments.

Travis continued his long journey between the Dakota Territory and Texas, traveling mainly at night. He found it was more comfortable to ride at night than during the heat of the day and he could more easily avoid the trouble that had begun to brew fiercely in this area if he rode under the protection of darkness. There were only twelve days remaining in which he had to cover a seemingly impossible distance. He had slept little and rested even less, but he forced himself to keep pressing onward. The telegraph lines had been cut by hostile Indians near two forts at which he had halted, and he could not afford to lose any more valuable time by seeking a place to send a telegram home. He could only hope that Nathan and Rana would realize there was a good reason why they hadn't heard from him.

Chapter 16

THE MORNING OF CODY AND MARY BETH'S WEDDING dawned bright and clear, and the beauty of the day caused Rana to look forward to her second joining with Travis, which she prayed would take place very soon. Activity in the house had been hectic all morning, with Rachel coming over to help with the preparations and Mary Beth nervously dressing and waiting for the ceremony, and Rana had not been given a chance to reveal her actions of the night before. She knew her grandfather would be furious with her at first, then proud and pleased over her clever victory.

The day was cooler than the past few scorching ones had been, and the sky was a tranquil blue, as if nature were blessing the special ceremony that was now taking place. Rana was wearing her loveliest gown in a flattering shade of sapphire, and she received many admiring stares and compliments. The defiant, daring Wild Wind seemed lost forever in the poised, demure Rana Michaels who charmed and deluded all present. With the radiant, exquisite Rana nearby, very few kept their attention on the pretty bride, but Cody and Mary Beth were too entranced with each other to notice that they were not the center of attention on their special day.

All morning and during the wedding ceremony, Rana had tried to conceal her apprehensions about Travis and about the grim situation with Harrison Caldwell, for she did not want anything to spoil Cody and Mary Beth's joining day. Yet, she was so worried about her love, and this silence increased her anxiety. For over two weeks she had told herself Travis could do anything and succeed, but panic was slowly eroding her confidence. Some perils were beyond even the bravest and cleverest man's prowess and power.

As soon as the talking and joking and celebrating began, Rana slipped away to her room to release some of the strain of her pretense. She could not imagine her existence without Travis Kincade, and she prayed for his return with all her might. How she wished he would ride up this very moment! The gold and the ranch were nothing compared to his life, she reflected despondently. She tried to tell herself she should be angry with him for leaving on such a dangerous journey, and alone. She should have gone with him! There might have been some way she could have helped him, or saved him. She remembered how she had aided him on the trail home, and she worried that another such difficulty might befall him and there would be no one around to rescue or assist him. She desperately wanted to believe he was safe and well, but if he was, why hadn't he contacted them? There was no way of knowing where he was on the trail, so she could not go searching for him as she had threatened and promised.

Mace knocked on her door and she let him come inside. "What's wrong, Rana?" he asked solicitously. "You've been in here a long time. Why don't you come back to the party? It'll be over soon. Has anyone said or done anything to upset you?"

"No, everyone has been kind to me," she replied sadly. "Why haven't we heard from Travis? How can I laugh and smile when he could be injured or in danger somewhere?"

Mace grasped her hand and squeezed it gently. Smiling, he encouraged, "You haven't known him as long as I have, Rana. I've seen him get out of pits and traps no other man could have escaped. He rescued you from the Indians, didn't he?" he reminded her.

"This time he is dealing with the Hunkpapas," she argued.

"But last time he defeated them," Mace returned.

Rana walked to her window and looked outside. "That was long ago and another helped him escape. What about those two men who attacked him before my grandfather found him nearly dead?"

"But your grandfather did find him, Rana, and saved his life, just like you saved his life when he was shot."

"That is what I mean, Mace. Each time someone helped him. This time he rides and faces evil alone. Something is wrong."

"Sometimes a man needs help, Rana, and other times he must face his challenges alone. I know he's all right and he'll return soon. You must have courage and faith. I promise you, there's a good reason he hasn't contacted us. You and Travis believe in the Great Spirit. Do you honestly think He would let you two be defeated?"

"The Great Spirit is a mystery. Sometimes His will does not match ours. Sometimes He does not answer prayers, or does not answer them as we wish. If He answered all prayers, my Indian people would not be suffering and dying at the hands of the whites. There are many things I do not understand."

"Locking yourself in this room and worrying yourself sick isn't going to change things, Rana. Come back outside and try to enjoy yourself."

As this conversation was taking place in Rana's room, Harrison Caldwell and two of his men were approaching Nathan's stable on horseback. When they reached their destination, they reined in their horses and arrogantly waited for Nathan to come and speak with them. A hush fell over the wedding party and all eyes focused on the malevolent rancher. Nathan glared at the offensive man, angry at his bold intrusion. He told the others to ignore them and to continue with the happy celebration while he went to see what Caldwell wanted.

"What can I do for you, Harry? You can see we're busy," Nathan remarked coldly as his contemptuous gaze swept over the man who was trying to destroy his existence. "Surely you didn't expect an invitation to Cody and Mary Beth's wedding?" he scoffed pointedly.

Harrison laughed. "Somebody left one of my corral gates open last night and some of my horses got loose. If you find any strays, I'd appreciate your sending them over with one of your hands."

Nathan frowned. "If I have any extra time after fighting off these filthy rustlers and fence cutters, I won't use it to round up your horses. Why don't you send your new gunslingers out to gather 'em up?"

Harrison chuckled again. "If you'd hire yourself a few good men, you wouldn't be having so much trouble, Nate. I heard your men were robbed on the way home from Sedalia. Is that why you're being so nasty and inhospitable? Are you broke? If you wish, I could make you a personal loan, with . . . say . . . this ranch as collateral? Or anything else of value you might own," he suggested, looking over the group of revelers for Rana.

"You dirty bastard! Get your ass off my ranch and take your men with you! I'll die before letting you and your kind run me off my land. Our fight isn't over yet; I've still got eleven days to pay off my loan, you vulture."

"There's no way you can come up with that much money by a week from Thursday, so give it up, Nate. I'm a rich and powerful man; I'll make you a good offer. If you wait 'til the auction, I'll be the highest bidder and you won't have anything left. You're a fool not to bargain with me now, old friend. You don't want that beautiful granddaughter of yours thrown out in the cold, so to speak."

Nathan warned, "Leave my little Rana out of this! Lord's always provided for us in the past, and He'll do so this time."

"I wouldn't count on Him answering your prayers any time soon, Nate. I'm your only hope, and you aren't being very polite or grateful."

"And I won't be, no matter what happens around here. You've been gobbling up ranches for years, but you won't get mine. Mighty strange that the ranches that have trouble are the ones you want. Somebody's got to stop your greed, and I pray it'll be me."

Harrison eyed Nathan intently, then decided Nathan couldn't have had anything to do with the daring robbery at his home. *Robbery?* Harrison's warped mind echoed the ironic term. A man couldn't actually steal his own money. If Travis Kincade had been around, he would have known who to blame. But he had seen and handled the money since Travis's departure. Or had that cunning devil really gone? Harrison scolded himself for being so foolish. Travis would have to be gone; after all, he had sent Clarissa a telegram a few days before from Springfield, Missouri.

No, Harrison concluded, Nathan wasn't in on the theft of his own cattle money. He had no one with the skill or daring to pull off such a job, and he appeared too genuinely scared about losing his ranch to have that money back in his possession. This mysterious matter would need more study and investigation. The only person with access to his safe . . . No, surely his little bitch of a daughter wouldn't dare trick him!

"If you're finished staring at me, Harry, git off my land. It ain't yours yet, and it won't be if I can help it."

Harrison's eyes drifted to the party in Nathan's front yard. He saw Rana leave the house with Mace Hunter. Gracefully she descended the steps on his arm, looking exquisite and delicate in a stunning gown. She appeared a little nervous, as if she did not wish to join the party and was being coerced into it. Perhaps crowds and strange occasions alarmed the Indian princess. She glanced toward the stable where he was still sitting astride his horse. She smiled and waved a greeting, then her cheerfulness faded suddenly as Mace spoke to her. She glanced his way again, a curious look on her face. Evidently Mace had disparaged him. After he took over this ranch, he would see to it that Mace Hunter couldn't find another job for a hundred miles!

Mace guided her over to the bride and groom, but she kept peering at him past the cowboy's sturdy body. She looked as if Mace had told her something that she could not quite believe and accept, and as if she were trying to determine the truth simply by looking at him. He wanted to believe that it troubled her to think those unknown charges could be accurate. Then Todd Raines captured her attention with his smiles and chatter. Harrison grinned sardonically, deciding that Todd was as smitten with Rana now as the younger Todd had been with her mother. Too bad, because Marissa had actually started falling for the handsome cowpoke years ago . . .

"No need to go studying Mary Beth now, Harry. It's too late. She's married to Cody Slade, and out of your filthy reach."

"Oh, I wasn't eyeing that little country lass. Who could notice her with Rana Michaels standing there? She's a beauty, Nate, a real beauty, more so even than her mother. Be seeing you around soon," he remarked, tipping his hat and riding away.

The celebration had ended and everyone had gone but Mace whom Nathan had asked to stay. Nathan told Rana he wanted to have a word with her, and now he paced the sitting room briefly before halting to look at her. He shook his head and exhaled loudly between parted lips. "Rana, I thought we'd explained to you about Harry. I don't want you smiling at him or going near him or being nice to him. Otherwise you might have him craving you as much as this ranch. He's bad, girl, real bad. He'd just as soon hurt or kill a woman as a man. Please, girl, steer clear of him."

"Your grandfather's right," Mace added. "Everyone noticed how friendly you were to him. In these parts, Rana, a man—or woman—is known by the company he keeps. You're new here, so people will wonder why Nathan Crandall's granddaughter is friendly with his enemy."

Rana looked from man to man, then smiled mischievously. "You must not worry. I will not be kind to him again; it was only to trick him. He will think you and grandfather told me bad things about him today. I did not wish him to see that I know the truth about him. He rode here to see how grandfather would look and behave today. You fooled him. I fooled him. He will think another stole the money."

Before Rana could take a breath and continue, Nathan asked in confusion, "Stole what money? What are you talking about, girl?"

"The money he stole from you, Grandfather. It was taken from his safe last night, from the saddlebags with rattlesnakes on them."

Mace stared at her oddly and inquired, "How could you possibly know about a robbery at Caldwell's place?"

"I took the money. It belongs to Grandfather. It is hidden in a room above us. He wished to see if you would act the same today. He does not suspect that you have the money or that I took it. Who would think a young girl could sneak into his home and take the money?"

Nathan and Mace were gaping at her. Mace argued, "That isn't possible, Rana. You couldn't have gotten off this ranch last night, or gotten into Caldwell's safe."

Rana laughed. "You forget, Mace Hunter, I was trained as a hunter and warrior." Without boasting, she related how she had stolen off the ranch, onto Caldwell's, into his office, and into his safe to carry out her daring scheme, then explained how she had secretly returned home. "Come, I will show you the money," she offered.

In the attic, Nathan gaped at the money in the same way he had gaped at her earlier. "This isn't possible, girl."

She hugged him and vowed, "It is, Grandfather. I did not take the saddlebags with rattlesnakes because he would have noticed they were gone. I can show you where he hides the branding irons to steal your cattle. You must not let your voice and face tell him you have the money, or he will try to take it again. You can save the ranch, Grandfather."

Mace quickly counted the money, and the amount matched that which had been stolen. "It's all here, Nate. By Heaven, she actually did it!" he remarked in astonishment as the reality settled in on him.

She nodded and confessed, "Yes, it is so. I was very frightened, but I took no chances. It is done and the danger is past."

"Took no chances?" Nathan scoffed. "Girl, you could have been arrested or killed. Why did you pull something crazy like this?"

She looked into his troubled gaze and replied softly, "Because I love you, Grandfather, and I do not wish you to lose this land that you love. He is our enemy and must be defeated. We have not heard from Travis. I feared he would not return with the gold before your time was lost. I did not wish to anger you, only help you."

Nathan embraced her tightly. "I know, and I love you too, girl," he murmured in a choked voice. "But I could have gotten both you and Travis killed trying to help me get money to save this ranch. I love this place, Rana, but not as much as you two. Harry must have checked those saddlebags this morning and found my money missing." Suddenly Nathan laughed. "I bet he's as mad as a cat with his tail stuck in the door. And with Travis gone, he won't suspect a thing."

"He will if you start acting cocky," Mace warned. "You and Rana will both be in danger if he discovers you have that money back."

Nathan nodded in agreement. "I'll hold it 'til the last minute before I settle that loan. Now I can pay the boys, Mace."

"Not yet, Nate. If you go spreading money around, you might as well admit to Caldwell you have the money. The boys will wait."

Nathan handed Mace some cash. "I'll give you a little money just in case somebody needs a few bits. We'll leave it hidden up here in case Caldwell decides to have some of his boys check my safe. I think I'll leave it unlocked so they won't blast it open."

Mace suggested, "Now that you've got the money and know where those branding irons are, we could start looking for the McFarlands and Kellys. We'll need some witnesses to support our evidence."

Nathan nodded in rising excitement. "You handle everything for me, Mace. We don't want Harry getting too nervous now that he's lost this money, so we'd best lie low and keep on like we've been doing. As for you, girl, don't go near Caldwell or his place again."

"I will stay away from him, Grandfather, and I will not be nice again. But there is more you must know," she began, then told them about her visit to the Caldwell ranch several days earlier.

Mace looked over the exquisite girl who deceptively appeared so fragile. "You utterly amaze me, woman. Travis isn't going to believe this when he gets home." Mace chuckled. "No, I suppose he will; he's seen you in action before. At least we don't have to worry about you taking care of yourself or helping out."

"I must look like nothing more than a weak woman to all others. No one must see or guess my skills, for they may be needed again."

"You're right. Besides, who would believe the truth? Any chance there's another woman like you around?" Mace asked and they all laughed.

Clarissa returned from visiting and eating with friends after church. She was all smiles, thinking that after only one more Sunday, she would sweep into that church as the owner of a vast Texas cattle empire. She halted abruptly at the parlor door to question her father's expression.

"You know anything about the money missing from my safe?" he asked bluntly to shock her into exposing herself if she were guilty.

She was taken by surprise and bewildered. "What are you talking about, Papa? You know I never take money from the cash box without your permission."

"I'm not talking about the cash box, Clarissa. Nathan's money is missing from those saddlebags in the safe."

"Missing? But how, Papa? The safe is always locked." Her gaze widened, then narrowed. "You aren't suggesting that I took it?"

"I don't know what happened to it, but it's gone. I was going to use a little of it to pay Monroe and Hayes this afternoon. I opened the flaps to find pillows from my settee stuffed inside them. All I know is, the money was there last Saturday."

"But who could have taken it, and how? Surely Nathan doesn't have it back?" she demanded angrily.

"I'm sure he doesn't. I rode over there today and he's scared stiff about losing his ranch."

Before he finished talking, Clarissa interjected, "You went to Nathan's ranch during that wedding! What will people think, Papa?"

"Exactly what I told them; we had some horses get loose last night and we were tracking them down. Nate couldn't fool me, daughter; he's plenty worried. They were having a real nice party for Cody and Mary Beth. She looked right pretty, if anybody noticed her with Rana Michaels standing there. Strike me down, if she isn't the most beautiful woman alive. She would make me a fine wife," he suggested shockingly.

"You can't mean that, Papa!" Clarissa shrieked. "Don't start dreaming about Marissa's daughter. You can't have her."

"And why is that, my jealous daughter?" he asked sarcastically.

Clarissa knew this was not the time to use her ace in the hole, so she replied, "Because Nathan would never allow it. She's a little savage, Papa. She'll humiliate you before your friends and clients."

He laughed. "She isn't as uneducated as you seem to think, Clarissa. She was ravishing today. I think you've got something to worry about over there. You sure Travis isn't hiding around here somewhere? He's the only one with the guts and wits to steal the money."

"Don't be foolish, Papa. I received his telegram the other day. He couldn't possibly have gotten home by now. You said you had the money last week, so the timing is all wrong for Travis to be involved."

"What about Monroe and Hayes? You think they have enough brains and courage to pull something like this?" he speculated.

"I thought you sent them to Abilene. Have they returned?" she asked uncomfortably, not wanting Wes around without her knowledge.

"They should return today. It's hard to believe somebody could get into my home and safe without anyone seeing a thing!"

"What about Silas, Papa? Or that Fargo? They're around all the time, and you could have left your safe open by mistake."

"They wouldn't dare rob me or try to trick me," he scoffed.

"You set Fargo up to deceive you with me, Papa. How can you be sure that's the only time he's tried it?" she reasoned, having no further use for the repulsive man after her bout with him the night before.

"Taking my daughter behind my back isn't the same as robbing my safe, girl. But feel free to work the truth out of him if you want. I don't like having somebody around I can't trust, especially when I don't know who the traitor is. You keep your eyes and ears open good."

Clarissa was not deluded; she realized that Harrison was wondering if she were to blame for the theft. From now on, she had to be very careful, for he would be watching her, or having her watched. She believed the most likely person was Silas Stern, their foreman. She looked at her father and suggested, "Why don't I see if Silas knows anything? He's the one who could pull this off with the least trouble, and he has an eye for me."

"You do that, girl, but make sure Fargo doesn't see you and get jealous. And, while you're investigating this matter for me, make sure Fargo and Monroe are whistle clean."

"Papa!" she wailed in frustration. "I can't go bedding all those men at the same time just to ask questions."

"You want us to succeed with our plans, don't you?"

"Of course, I do, but—"

"No buts, girl. You have your talents, so put them to use to make sure this situation doesn't get out of control. We're too close to having it all, Clarissa. We can't allow anyone to ruin it for us."

As always, she raged inwardly, he was using his "we" and "us" strategy again! Oh, she would obey his orders, but for her own reasons. If the money was actually gone, she wanted to know who had taken it and how. *If* the money was gone . . .

Monday morning, Nathan refused to let Harrison enter his home to discuss the purchase of his ranch. The two stood on the front porch and argued. "This afternoon, I'm sending a telegram to the Cattlemen's Association in Dallas," Nathan told his unwanted visitor. "If I can't come up with the money to pay off that loan, I'll get them to find me a suitable buyer for the ranch. I won't sell her to the likes of you, Harry."

"You won't have any choice in the matter, Nate. I'll outbid anybody who comes to her auction."

"You mean you'll get those varmints you hired to scare off any other bidders," Nathan accused. "You think I haven't realized that nobody ever bids against you. You got Sam's and Harvey's and Jim's places, but you aren't getting mine. I'll see her burned to the ground first."

"We could come to a satisfactory understanding, Nate. You have needs and I have needs. Why don't we become partners? You sign half of this ranch over to me and let me take your granddaughter as my wife, and I'll pay off your debt. When you get enough money to pay me back, I'll turn my half of the ranch over to you."

"Lord help us, you're completely *loco*, Harry! I wouldn't let you near my granddaughter, much less marry her. Get off my land!"

"What if Rana doesn't feel the same way, Nate? She might want to become the wife of the richest and most powerful man in this area. What will you have to offer her after next Thursday? Nothing!"

Having overheard their entire conversation, Rana crept out the kitchen door and signaled to Mace, who was heading in from the west pasture and was not yet in view of the porch. She ran toward him and related her cunning idea.

Mace grinned, reached down, lifted her, and set her before him on his horse. They rode leisurely toward the stable with their arms around each other. When Harrison glanced their way, they pretended not to notice him or any others as they kissed. At the stable, Mace eased her feet to the ground and then dismounted. Leading his mount toward the corral and keeping Rana snuggled close to his side, he whispered in amusement, "That should give Caldwell an eyeful and discourage his interest in you."

Rana looked up into his sparkling eyes and grinned. "It is good Travis has a handsome, unmarried friend to play this game with me."

"If Travis weren't my best friend and you were willing, we'd get hitched today," he murmured affectionately and chuckled. "I think we should ride somewhere until Caldwell leaves. We don't want him any madder at you than necessary." When she agreed, they mounted his horse again, this time with her sitting behind him and clinging to his waist, and headed off toward the nearest pond.

When they returned a short while later, Nathan laughed and remarked, "That was a clever trick, girl. You should have seen Harry's face when he saw you two all snuggly and kissy." Nathan then related the details of Harrison's visit to Mace and the two men once again praised Rana's courage.

Clarissa returned from her shopping in town to make several infuriating discoveries. Harrison had read her second telegram from Travis from Sedalia, Missouri. Her father's jealousy and wrath had been inflamed by the apparent romance between Rana Michaels and Mace Hunter, and he was furious that his attempt to bargain for Rana's hand in marriage had been rejected so peremptorily. In his rage he had ordered Wes and Jackson to poison two water holes on the Crandall ranch.

"Papa, are you insane?" she asked, panting in alarm. "What happens when we take over that ranch? How could you do something so rash? That little slut isn't worth ruining everything!"

"You let me handle my business, girl," he replied sharply. "At least we know Kincade isn't in this area. That's a real sweet message. So he misses you, does he, and can't wait to get home? I'm going to fix Nate good, and that granddaughter of his won't get Mace Hunter. What have you learned about that missing money?"

"I saw Fargo last night and Silas this morning. I don't think either of them were involved. Do you think it's safe for me to fool around with that Wes Monroe or Hayes?" she inquired innocently.

"Do what you have to do, girl. Just find out where that money is," he demanded irascibly. "They should be back at their cabin by now." He watched with a total lack of emotion as his daughter turned on her heel and left the room.

Clarissa went directly to the cabin and asked to see Wes alone. Jackson eyed her curiously, then walked a short distance away. She explained to Wes why she had come to see him, and her reason surprised him.

"You mean that old fool's lost the Crandall money? And he sent you here to seduce information out of me? What kind of bastard is he? I told him it was crazy to poison those water holes. The lying bastard said he wanted to make certain nobody else wanted that ranch. And tell me, woman, why is this Kincade sending you telegrams?"

"He's afraid he's going to lose everything, so he's trying to court me to get Papa's holdings through me. I've been faking interest to get information about Nathan's situation."

"Like you're faking with me, maybe?"

"Don't be silly, Wes. If I didn't trust you, would I tell you such things? Papa's real upset over that money—Or, I should say, over who this traitor is. I think he suspects me the most, so we'll have to be really careful from now on. It'll all be over in two weeks. Once I fire Silas and Fargo, I'll be needing a new foreman and guard," she suggested provocatively, reaching over to fondle his chest.

"Who do you think took that money?" Wes probed.

"I don't know. Maybe no one," she declared, thinking aloud. "Maybe Papa's up to something. Silas and Fargo don't have enough courage or cunning to do a job like this. I was hoping it was you, Wes."

"Well, it ain't." Wes thought about the lost money, money he had intended would come to him, one way or another. Something strange was going on . . . His thoughts suddenly veered off in a new, more enticing direction as Clarissa began to disrobe.

Tuesday morning, Mace reported the grim news to Nathan about the poisoned water holes and dead cattle. "I've got Todd and some of the boys fencing them off and Cody's moving the cattle to another pasture. Seems like we made Caldwell real mad yesterday."

"Should I pretend to be nice to him again?" Rana suggested.

"That won't work, girl, 'cause he's seen you with Mace. Anyway, it wouldn't stop him from trying to pull us down. He wants to scare me into accepting his offer for the ranch and for you. We'll stand firm."

Around midnight, the hands were called out to battle fires in two wagons of hay that had arrived too late that afternoon to be unloaded and their contents placed in the barn loft. By the time the flames were discovered, it was too late to save the hay or the wagons. Luckily they had been left in a dirt clearing, which prevented the fire from spreading to nearby structures or the dry grass.

Nathan watched the flames slowly lessen and he cursed Harrison Caldwell. He had not alerted the sheriff to the poisonings and he would not inform him about this fire. It would not do any good, for there was nothing to connect Caldwell to either crime. At least no one had been injured and no structure had been destroyed. Nathan raged against Caldwell's game of harassment and intimidation, and prayed he could withstand it.

So far, two men had been slain, and the Rocking C owner hoped he could prevent any more deaths or destruction. Nathan called together his head men and ordered, "Mace, I want you to post more guards at every vulnerable area on this ranch. Cody, do whatever you can to keep any of the men from getting nervous and quitting like they did at McFarland's place. Todd, you set a man to watch the married houses. Post him near the fire bell so he can sound it if trouble strikes over there. Make sure you tell Rachel and Lettie and Mary Beth to be real careful."

On Wednesday, there were two more fake telegrams from Travis: one sent to Clarissa and one to Nathan, both from St. Louis. The one addressed to Nathan was a trick to persuade Harrison that it was not a ruse at all, for Nathan suspected that Harrison knew about his telegrams and their contents. He hoped so, for both messages made Travis sound depressed and lonely. In them he confessed that he was failing in his tasks and would head home in a few days if nothing looked promising.

By eleven o'clock that night, Rana was so tense she could not rest or sleep. For some reason, she kept thinking about what had happened to the women on the McFarland ranch. She felt she had to make certain that Lettie, Rachel, and Mary Beth were safe, for she had this terrible feeling something was wrong over there. Dressing in her dark clothes once more, she collected her weapons and stealthily began her journey on horseback. She dismounted some distance away from the houses and walked to where the bell was located. To her horror, she found Darby Davis lying on the ground, his throat slit. Knowing there was nothing she could do for the unfortunate man, she cautiously crept to Darby and Lettie's home to discover that everything seemed peaceful within. She crept to the neighboring Raines house, but saw no one inside. Then she moved on to Cody's home to find that his new bride was not within. Alarm filled her.

Suddenly her alert ears caught a muffled noise from the trees not far away. She furtively headed that way and was stunned to see the two women, their hands bound and their mouths gagged, being taken away by four masked men. Their nightclothes were ripped and the men were running their hands over the helpless women as they urged them toward their waiting horses. Their intentions were obvious and Rana was consumed by rage. She gingerly moved closer, then fired several arrows at the villains.

There were too many trees and victims in the path of her arrows for her to be able to do more than wound two of the men. She rapidly drew her pistol then and fired over their heads. In fear of being seen or caught, the cutthroats mounted their horses and fled swiftly. Rachel and Mary Beth ran toward the bell to ring out its warning, though the gunfire had been a sufficient call for help. Rana watched them rush into their homes to conceal their torn garments. Knowing they were safe and that others would arrive soon, she made her way to her horse and home in order to protect her identity.

In less than an hour, Nathan and Mace were back at the main house. They had guessed who the rescuer had been and wanted to find out what she had seen, for they knew what she had done. Still, they hadn't revealed her secret to anyone.

Now the people of the Rocking *C* were as curious about this intrepid ghost's identity as were those on the Circle *C*.

Thursday morning Darby Davis was buried, and three hands were assigned to guard the women at night. That afternoon, a telegram arrived from Fort Wallace in Kansas saying that a rancher named Josiah Barns was not interested in buying a partnership in the Rocking *C* Ranch. Nathan, Rana, and Mace were overjoyed by the message, for it told them that Travis was safe and on his way home, though still far away.

"Even if he rode day and night, I don't see how he could possibly make it here by next week. Thank the Lord we got our cattle money back," Nathan remarked, then smiled at Rana. "Looks like that's what's going to save us. We need to defeat Harry soon, Mace, 'cause the chores can't get done with so many hands acting as guards all over the ranch."

"When Travis gets home, we'll handle Caldwell for good."

Rana was too excited to sleep much that night. The message had told them he was on his way home, but not how his mission went. She wondered what had taken place in the land of the Lakotas. She knew the men would be on full alert tonight, so she would not have to go riding. She could lie in bed and dream of Travis.

Thursday night saw no further trouble, to everyone's relief. Bart Davis moved in with his deceased brother's family to protect and support them. That afternoon, Nathan received another telegram, this one from Dallas. It informed Nathan that his papers were ready, and the rancher decided to go after them promptly in order to avoid any problems later. After all, he reflected, there wasn't anything he could do on the ranch between today and tomorrow. He told Mace to keep his eye on Rana and made her promise to stay home unless something terrible happened.

When disaster did strike late Friday night, there was nothing Rana or anyone else could do about it. The river was suddenly blocked by a dynamite blast, and all water flowing to Nathan's ranch was cut off. The poisoned water holes had been drained, and only heavy rain could fill them. The situation would become critical in a few days, after the streams dried up and the cattle became thirsty. But worse was yet to come, and on Saturday morning it did, in the form of Clarissa Caldwell.

—— *Chapter 17* ——

❦

RANA WENT TO ANSWER THE DOOR and found one of the ranch hands standing there nervously with a woman who, judging from her appearance and brazen manner, could only have been Clarissa Caldwell. The wrangler apologized for disturbing her and explained that the lady had been most insistent. Rana smiled her understanding and politely dismissed him. But before Rana could discourage Clarissa from visiting, the dark-haired woman stated belligerently, "I came to talk to you about your mother, and I'm not leaving until I do, so you might as well let me come in."

Rana realized that Clarissa was in a mood to be stubborn and hateful, and she knew this meeting could not be avoided forever. Deciding it would be best to hear the woman today and in private, Rana invited her into the sitting room. She knew her grandfather would be annoyed with her, but that could not be helped. "Speak," Rana said, as if giving Clarissa permission to begin. The woman was silent for a time as she eyed the portraits hanging over the mantel. Then Clarissa looked at her as she had the portraits, coldly and with bitterness, like a winter blizzard.

"I thought it was time we met and talked. Considering how well I knew your mother, I can understand why everyone's been trying to keep us apart. I thought you might want to hear the truth about Marissa and Raymond, and I'm sure you'd like to have this," Clarissa speculated, handing Raymond's picture to Rana, who noticeably trembled and paled. "I see you remember the brutal bastard."

Rana stared at the picture of the gambler with black hair and brown eyes who had haunted her dreams for years. "Why do you come here?" she asked, looking at the antagonistic woman before her.

"I wanted you to know what a bitch and a whore your mother was. Do you know what those words mean?" she asked hatefully, then explained their meanings and how they applied to Marissa. She told Rana how Marissa had been forced to whore to earn money to support her daughter and husband. "Marissa slept with countless men, including plenty of those who work for my father. She's even slept with some of the men on this ranch, like Todd Raines. She had poor Todd believing she loved him and was going to marry him, but she got herself pregnant and had to run off and get married to hide her sin. When Raymond found out she had tricked him, he hated her and punished her by making her whore for their living."

582 ☙ J A N E L L E T A Y L O R

"Tricked him? I do not understand. Why do you speak such evil lies about my mother? You were not her friend?" she probed.

Having decided to be crueler and more informative than she had previously intended, Clarissa echoed with an ugly sneer, "Friend? I hated her. Marissa was selfish and mean and bad. She stole the only man in my life; now her wicked daughter is trying to steal Travis or my father. Travis told me how you'd been trying to sneak into his bed. He knows you're nothing but a whore like your mother was. When he kept refusing you, did you give up and turn to Mace? You are a *bastard*, Rana Michaels. I won't let you get my father or Travis."

Rana felt she could not trust this hostile, bitter creature to be truthful. "You must go. You speak with a false, cruel tongue," she declared, regaining her composure.

"Ask Todd Raines if I'm lying," Clarissa challenged. "He knows how bad she was. Or ask Fargo, who works for my father; he's spent plenty of money sleeping with her, and he told me and Papa all about her. Ask any of the men who paid Raymond to have her for a few minutes. And you'll never guess who your father is."

"I do not care, but I am glad it is not Raymond Michaels."

"If you don't convince Nathan to sell this place to my father, everybody else will care when I spread the word about you and your mother. People will be laughing at you and avoiding you. They'll think you're just like your mother. Or worse, you little savage."

"Even if you speak the truth, I will not ask my grandfather to leave his lands. Go away; do not return. Your heart is black and evil." To frighten and punish Clarissa, Rana threatened, "If you anger me, I will take your father and force you to leave home. He has asked Grandfather to allow us to marry. I see great desire for me in his eyes."

"It isn't you he sees and desires, you little fool! If you dare try to marry my father, I'll make you wish you had never been born. I know something very bad about Marissa that I haven't told you. Raymond and I were close friends, and he told me secrets about her, and about you. I could use them to destroy your family. I'm warning you, Rana, stay away from my father and Travis." With that Clarissa stormed out of the room and out of the house.

Rana went immediately to her room and flung herself across her bed. Memories mingled with the woman's words to torment her. Clutching her doll against her heart, she cried. She had slept little the night before and was exhausted. Slowly she drifted off to sleep.

Clarissa scolded angrily, "I don't know what's gotten into you, Papa! Why would you shut off the river to land you'll own next week? Poisoning water holes, burning crops, cutting fences, stampeding cattle, ordering excessive violence—such measures aren't necessary, Papa; you'll be able to buy that ranch peacefully next week. Why cause so much damage and ill will when the land and workers will soon be yours?"

Harrison glared at her. "I've told you, girl, stay out of my business. I'm tired of your meddling. Do things my way, or get out!"

His outburst shocked her, then enraged her. "How can I remain silent when you do such foolish things? Now I learn you're proposing to Rana Michaels!" she snapped, her temper flaring, for they had been quarreling for over an hour.

"How do you know that?" he demanded furiously. "If you're spying on me, girl, I'll whip you senseless, then kick you out."

"I saw her this morning at Nathan's ranch," she admitted freely.

"You little bitch! How dare you talk with Rana! You might as well know, I am planning to marry her. Tell me what you two said. And from now on, stay away from her; you could ruin my plans."

Clarissa glared at him. "Stay away? Why, Papa? Rana is my half sister. Or didn't you know Marissa was carrying your baby when she ran away with Raymond? You can't marry your own daughter. Either you're crazy with lust for Marissa's ghost or you're ignorant of the truth. Which is it, Papa?"

"What the hell are you talking about?" Harrison shrieked.

"Haven't you figured it out by now, Papa? You were gone for months when Marissa discovered she was pregnant. She had to get away before anyone guessed her secret. That dashing gambler came along and she duped him into marrying her and getting her away before she started showing her sinful secret. But Raymond found out she had played him for the fool, and he got even with her. Didn't you ever wonder why he hated her and abused her so cruelly? And didn't you wonder why Marissa was too afraid to disobey him or leave him? For goodness sake, Papa, he was blackmailing her, threatening to expose her sins to her father and everyone. And proud Marissa didn't want that. Raymond had slowly gotten her by the throat and knew too much about her. By the time she was desperate to be free of him, it was too late."

"How do you know such things?" Harrison demanded.

"You do recall we used to be friends and do things together? One day I heard Raymond and Marissa arguing when they didn't realize I was around, and the whole filthy story came pouring out. That's what he was using to blackmail her; you know, Papa, whore for his stakes or he would expose the dirty truth about her? Marissa did it a few times to appease him, but then Raymond started demanding more and more customers. By then, she was already soiled and she was in over her head, drowning in Raymond's revenge and her dark secrets."

"Why didn't you tell me about this?" he raged at her, seeing how fiercely she hated Marissa and Rana.

Her face was lined with hostility. "Tell you I knew Marissa had been secretly whoring with my father? Tell you I knew Rana was your bastard? No, Papa, I wanted Marissa and Rana out of our lives. If she had loved you and wanted you, she wouldn't have married Raymond. She chose her prickly path and didn't try to change it. By the time I learned the truth, there was no way you could have married that cheap whore and claimed Rana as your child, and you can't claim her now. She would hate you and blame you for what happened to them. And such a revelation might cause a scandal, Papa, that is if Nathan didn't manage to kill you for what you did to his little Marissa. She wasn't much more than a child at that time, Papa. Some might suggest you raped her or misled an innocent young girl. They'll wonder why she ran off with that Michaels beast rather than marry you. Besides, if you lay claim to Rana, Nathan will disown her and she'll lose any claim to his ranch. If something did happen to block your purchase, Rana might be your only way of obtaining it."

"Is that all you care about, that stupid ranch? Did you tell Rana any of this?" he asked pointedly.

"Don't be foolish, Papa. Certainly not. I don't ever want her to know about us. Don't you realize that would give her a right to our holdings, if anything should happen to us. By revealing the truth, you'll offer them the perfect path to revenge and victory. We both know Travis doesn't love me or want me. What would happen to us if he thought he could have it all by taking the beautiful Rana as his wife? I thought maybe Marissa had confessed the truth to you and asked for your help in getting free of Raymond, but when you started talking seriously about marriage, I realized you didn't know about Rana."

Harrison had found the unexpected news staggering. "Leave me alone for a while, girl; I need to think about this," he told her, then went into his office and closed the door.

Clarissa stared at it, then grinned satanically. The old fool actually believed her! That lie would keep him distracted and mastered for awhile. If anyone were to discover who Rana's father really was, it would be a shock, especially to Rana, Travis, Nathan, Harrison, and Todd. Poor Todd; she had already been pregnant for a time when they had started falling for each other. And poor Marissa, who was too terrified and confused to realize that Todd would have married her and claimed the child. She thought about two lines from Scott's 1808 *Marmion:*

> "Oh, what a tangled web we weave,
> When first we practice to deceive!"

Terrible dreams began to fill Rana's mind. Her head thrashed wildly upon the pillow and she whimpered softly as she tried to halt them. Suddenly she cried out and aroused herself. She sat up panting and shaking. Clutching the doll tightly in her arms, she cried. Several of Raymond's statements returned to convince her that Clarissa had spoken at least part of the truth: ". . . me and that dark-haired vixen . . . greedy and wicked bitch . . . since you ain't . . ."; then Marissa's voice tormented her, "No more lies about me . . . once he's dead, the truth will be buried forever . . . terrible mistake, and I've paid for it . . . return soon . . . be free and happy . . ."

Raymond Michaels was dead, but Marissa's agonizing secrets had not died with him. Clarissa Caldwell knew them and would use them maliciously to hurt all of them if she did not get her way. Her grandfather would suffer again over Marissa's mistakes, and Travis and others would learn of her mother's past.

"What is the truth, Mother?" Rana sobbed sadly. As if Marissa were replying, Rana heard the words, *Inside the doll, little one.*

Rana shuddered and looked around the room, then glanced at the doll. She concentrated very hard to remember something her mother had told her several times: "Don't forget, little one, the truth is inside the doll. Never lose her and never tell anyone."

Rana bounded off the bed, seized her knife from its sheath, and cut off the doll's head. She stared at the rolled page that was wedged tightly within the rag stuffing, and she feared to remove it and read it. How she wished Travis were here to comfort her and help her. But she was alone, and she could not wait for his return. She closed her eyes and prayed. "Great Spirit, make me brave and strong. Help me understand. Do not allow bitterness and anger to blind me."

She pried the letter free and dropped the mangled guardian to the floor. Then she went to the bed and sat down weakly. Before unrolling the paper, she inhaled and exhaled several times to calm her racing heart and to steady her quavering hands. She had to prepare herself to confront this painful, enlightening message from the grave.

When she found the courage to read the letter, it was puzzling: "If you find this note, something is terribly wrong. Look for a final message from me in our hiding place. Remember, the little hole in the dark room, the place where we hid our treasures from the bad man."

Rana closed her eyes and tried to recall her mother's meaning. She envisioned them sitting on the floor in a small, dark area; then she saw a candle that cast glowing shadows over her mother's face. Marissa was smiling at her and her blue eyes were sparkling as she touched her finger to her lips to indicate secrecy. Marissa took a knife and pried loose a short board near the corner of a wall. She could see her mother placing things inside the black hole, then sealing it. Grasping her small hand, Marissa led her out of the darkness . . .

Rana's eyes widened, then she whirled to look at the closet in the corner of Marissa's old room. She leapt to her feet, seized her knife once more, and ducked inside the closet with a candle. Crawling to the far end, she placed the candle on the floor and searched for the special board. As she worked to pry it free, she wondered if her mother's letter and "treasures" would still be hiding there after all these years. It was possible she had removed them during that last trip. It was possible someone else had found the hiding place and taken them.

The board squeaked and yielded, then fell noisily to the floor. Apprehensively she reached inside the black hole, grasped several objects and withdrew them: a bunch of dead flowers secured with a yellow ribbon, a lock of light brown hair with reddish gold highlights bound with another yellow ribbon, an oval locket that had a broken catch and held a picture of Marissa and Todd as teenagers, a leather pouch with money inside, and a time-yellowed envelope.

Rana replaced the lock of hair, the flowers, the pouch, and the locket. Taking the candle, she left the closet, deposited the candle on the hearth for safety, then went to sit on the bed. Carefully she ripped open the envelope and slowly unfolded the fragile paper, which crackled with age. Her heart began to pound heavily and her mouth went dry. Despite the heat of the day, her hands felt cold and shaky. She dreaded to begin this new torment.

My dearest daughter Rana,

Since you are reading this letter, my little one, then I have been taken from your side, for only you know how and where to find it. If things had worked out for us as I had planned, I would have recovered and destroyed this letter before you could find it and read it.

Even as I begin, I am not sure I am doing the right thing or if I know how to tell you what I must. I wish I were there to explain these matters, little one, but it cannot be. I beg you to read this letter with love and I pray you are old enough to understand what I must tell you and why, or how, it happened.

I must reveal the truth to you as I do not want you to go on believing Raymond Michaels is your father. He is a vicious and evil man, and I curse the day he entered our lives. I was so foolish and impulsive when I was young. I wanted to taste every treat life had to offer. I was spoiled and greedy. I was stubborn and willful. Many mistakes were of my own doing, Rana, and others happened because I was so naive and trusting, though I thought I knew everything. What cruel lessons life must teach us when we care more for ourselves than others. I only wish I had been allowed to bury the dark past forever. I can be thankful that only Raymond knows my secrets and I pray he has not and will never reveal them.

Before I was seventeen, I was called the most beautiful girl in Texas, and sadly I believed it and used my beauty and charms as weapons or for foolish tricks. Many boys desired me, but I was vain and blind in heart. I trampled upon their feelings and I was forced to pay for my meanness.

We had—and may still have—a neighbor named Harrison Caldwell, a rich, handsome man whose wife died many years ago. As a young girl, I tingled and blushed each time I saw him. None of the boys my age caused me to have such feelings, so I believed I was in love with him. One day I went to deliver a message to him from Papa, and my world became confused and upturned. He had flirted with me many times, and in my vanity I thought he was in love with me. At his house that day, he offered me a strong drink and I boldly and recklessly took it. It sent my head spinning as fast as my heart was pounding. He began to kiss me and touch me and strange feelings attacked me, and I wanted to kiss and touch him back. I let him take me to his room and make love to me. For many weeks I sneaked to his home to lie with him in his bed. I told myself it was because he ordered it and I feared he would tell Papa or others what I had done. He was a skilled lover and I was charmed by him and our actions. Soon, I had to admit I liked what we were doing and I enjoyed the power I held over him, for he loved me and craved me wildly. Perhaps I was in love with love or with the feelings of mystery and wickedness. It was so exciting to explore being a woman and to have such a powerful secret and to have a real man in my control. I felt as if I were living in an adventurous dreamworld.

Over a year passed. I had learned so much about men and life and my feelings, but I had learned it in a bad way. My lovely dream had slowly faded and I realized I did not love or want this man. He had ways that were vicious and wrong. He refused to release me from our secret affair. He wanted to marry me, to keep me as his property. We argued for weeks and I refused him in every way. And I did a terrible thing during this time to test my feelings for him, which I shall explain later. I told him I did not love him or want him anymore and I said many cruel and false things to him to force him to leave me alone. Then I began to see another man. He became very angry and jealous and vowed to have me or else no other man would. I threatened to tell Papa he had raped me and forced me to do his bidding to keep him from killing Papa. He left for many months, but said he would force me to marry him on his return.

Now, I must tell you about the other man. One day my horse bolted and I was rescued by a boy my age named Todd Raines—he still works for Papa as I write this letter. When I gazed into his eyes as he held my trembling body, a feeling that I now know was true love washed over me. I wanted nothing more than to gaze into his eyes and stay in his arms forever. There was a quietness and gentleness about my feelings for him, yet he made my body flame with desire. We shared so many things, like a simple walk to gather wildflowers. We laughed as I cut his hair for a dance in town and he teased me about keeping a lock. He gave me a locket and placed our pictures inside. He was so kind and loving for one so young. How I wished I had been more like him. I kept those treasures hidden with this letter, for I could not bear to part with them. I loved him in that very first moment our eyes met and our bodies touched, and I knew he was the man I wanted as my own forever. Papa adored him and was happy for us. I hurt them both so deeply when I was forced to reject Todd. If you have found true love, little one, then you will understand what I am trying to explain.

Life had a cruel urge to punish me for my past wrongs. I discovered I was carrying a child, and I was terrified that someone, especially my beloved father or my cherished Todd, would discover the truth about me and my baby. I could not bear to tell them of my sins and past deeds, for they would hate me and think me evil. I had to break Todd's heart and reject him, and I shall never forget the pain I caused him or the love we shared. He has married another, but I know he suffers each time I return home and he sees me. But I suffer too, for I see what my sin has taken from me. How I wish I could tell him the truth, but it is too vile and destructive. How I wish you were his child —how lucky we would be today!

At times, I even wished Harrison Caldwell had been your father, so this burden would not have destroyed all I was and loved. How do I explain the truth, my little one, and not cause you to hate and scorn me as I despised myself until I almost let Raymond destroy me? How foolish I was to believe I deserved to be punished! How can I explain why I ruined our lives? I was a fool, a selfish, blind fool who made terrible mistakes. How do I explain them to myself or to you or to Todd? Your name is as close as I can ever be to him. Even now, I love him and I would give my soul for a second chance with him, but I cannot ruin his life again. I must let him go on hating me.

This is the hardest part of my confession. First, I must say I am sorry for letting you suffer at Raymond's hand. We tricked each other with our marriage. He wanted to get his hands on Papa's money through me, and I needed him to take me far away. When he learned I was carrying a child and I refused to beg Papa for money, he was very angry and mean. After you were born and he learned my secret, he became cruel and vindictive. To protect our lives and my secret, I am forced to lie with other men for money. I hate it and I hate him. When I tell you all, my little one, you will understand why I fear him and obey him. Today, we leave Papa's for the last time, for I shall kill him and return home to be free and happy, or he will slay me for trying. If he is still alive and near you, I beg you, Rana, run from him. Never let him near you. Never do anything for him. Never let him trick you or use you. He is bad and mean. Flee him, even if you must slay him. Otherwise he will destroy you as he destroyed me.

The secret he knew that held me under his control was about your real father. This was my biggest mistake and sin, my little one, not my reckless affair with Harrison or even surrendering to Raymond's brutality and blackmail. The only person who knew the truth besides me told Raymond, told him because she loved him and wanted him. How I hated her, for she was responsible for my wicked deed and for revealing it.

You see, my little one, when I was growing up I had a close friend whose father was a ranch hand for our neighbor, Harvey Jenkins, on the Lazy *J* Ranch. We did everything together until her parents were killed during the period of my secret affair with Harrison. She had no home or money, and she began to work at a private house outside town where men were entertained for a price. I sneaked over to see her one day and she was sobbing and shaking with fear. She owed the madam money for clothes and board and doctor bills, and the woman was demanding payment or she was going to throw my best friend in jail. Jail is a terrible place for a woman. We were young and gullible and did not know the woman was lying to frighten and gain control over my friend. I asked her what I could do to help, for I did not have enough money to pay her large debt.

We put all our money together, but it was not enough. I knew Papa would not give me money to pay a whore's debt. My friend told me she had a man coming over that night who would pay her enough to finish off her debt; then she would be safe and she would leave to begin a new life elsewhere. But she was in her woman's way and could not lie with him. She begged me to take her place, for the owner was mean and had beaten her many times and the law does nothing to help or protect whores. She knew about Harrison and me and knew I was no longer a virgin. She pleaded and reasoned, telling me it was the only way I could learn if I truly loved and wanted Harrison, for I had lain only with him. I was enticed and convinced because she explained that the man always insisted on lying with her in the dark and without talking. He did not want to know her name or see her face, for he always pretended she was his lost love. She vowed that the man would never know I had lain with him in her place. It sounded so mysterious and romantic and exciting. We never saw each other or spoke that night. He was a gentle man with a very nice body, but he seemed so nervous and unsure of himself, and I could do nothing but lie there and wish the deed over. I regretted my actions that very same night and refused to see my friend again for lying to me about leaving that wicked life.

I had stopped going to Harrison's bed two months before that fateful night, and I met Todd a few weeks afterward, but we did not sleep together for a long time, for he loved me and held me precious. Two months passed, and I knew I was with child, from the night with a stranger in my friend's place. There was no way I could claim the baby was Todd's or Harrison's. Todd had taken me for the first time two weeks earlier and the experience had been glorious for we had been in love. He had been afraid to rush me, and I had been equally shy with him. He asked me to marry him the night of the day I learned my tormenting secret. I had to discover the identity of my baby's father and then decide what to do. I went to her and she tried to keep the truth from me, but I forced her to speak it, to my horror. How can I tell you without tormenting you as I was tormented when I learned the truth? Sobbing, she confessed that the stranger had been Nathan Crandall, who had made his last visit to her that night. She had been so frightened and selfish that she had tricked me into sleeping with my own father! How I wish she had lied to me about him. He is not your grandfather. He is your father.

When I learned this evil truth, my heart truly broke. I knew I had to leave quickly and go far away, where no one could discover my foul deed. I had met Raymond Michaels at several barn dances and he had been trying to win me and run away with me. I saw him as the answer to my prayers. I eloped with him before anyone guessed why I was leaving home. He told me one night—before he learned of my pregnancy and my deceit—that he had married me for my money and if I ever wanted to visit home again I would have to pay him a lot of money so that he could gamble with it. He was furious when he learned I had also tricked him.

By now, you realize why I could not ask Papa for money. I refused to return home to visit for a long time. I was ashamed to face Papa and Todd. But I was so lonely and afraid and I wanted to come home. Raymond met my friend and she told him my wicked secret, for she loved him and wanted to take him from me. He killed her, Rana, for he did not want anyone else to learn the truth. He used that truth to force me to lie with other men to earn his living. I was so scared and confused and believed I deserved this punishing fate. I did what he said for a long time. When I began refusing, he threatened to kill you and Papa after telling Papa the truth about you. I couldn't let him hurt Papa or you or Todd. I was the one to blame, the evil one, the one who should suffer. But I can no longer go on this way. Surely I have paid and suffered enough. My sins were committed far away, so no one here knows about them. I must never let Papa or Todd learn how I've been living for years.

I will try to kill Raymond as soon as we get away from the ranch. Harrison hates me and is being very cruel and vengeful. Todd is married and I cannot ruin his life again. And I cannot ask for Papa's help without telling him the truth. I have no one to turn to, my little one, no one to help us and free us. Each day I grow more afraid of Raymond. He has begun to tease me about no longer needing me. He says you are the rightful heir to Papa's ranch and that he can take it through you. I do not like the way he is beginning to watch you. I see such fear and suffering in your eyes. You're happy here with your father, my father. I must try to set us free of Raymond, or die trying. I tell you these things, because, if I am gone, you will have no one to protect you from him. You must not remain with him, and you must not be drawn to Harrison. Both are evil men and they will use you for their selfish needs.

Forgive me, Rana, and please try not to hate me or judge me too harshly. I know how wrong I was about so many things, but I love you dearly and I cannot allow you and Papa to suffer anymore. Only you can decide what to do with these tormenting truths, and I pray you have found a strong, special love who will help you do what is right and best and who will give you comfort against this pain I have brought into your life and heart. If you have met Todd, then you know why I love him and wanted him. Forgive me for pressing this burden on you. I love you, little one. Do not ever doubt it or forget it.

The letter was signed, "Marissa Crandall, September, 1856," and had obviously been written during her final visit home before her tragic death. Rana read the letter again, trying to recall or understand the words that were strange to her. A variety of emotions coursed through her, but hatred and scorn were not among them.

Long ago, she had been as willful and selfish as her mother had been. She, too, had trampled on the feelings of men who had chased her. She had played with their feelings and rejected them unkindly. She knew what it was to love someone at first glance and touch, for it had been that way with Travis Kincade. How sad that she had truly loved and wanted Todd Raines, and he did not know it. She recalled how she had desired Travis that first night and wondered if that was how Marissa had felt, or thought she had felt, about Harrison Caldwell. How tragic that that mistake had led to another, more tragic one, for Marissa would not have taken her friend's place if it had not been for Harrison. Rana could not judge Marissa, for who could say what she might have done had Myeerah's life and safety been endangered? People were not invincible or perfect; only the Great Spirit was so.

She thought about Raymond Michaels and hated him even more. He deserved to die for using a helpless woman! If he had still been alive, she would have hunted him down and slain him herself.

She thought about Harrison Caldwell, who had begun the cycle of anguish that had caused her mother's torment and death. Now he was trying to destroy her grandfather—no, her father. He would pay for his evil, she vowed with fierce determination.

Her thoughts drifted to Clarissa, and she raged at the woman's maliciousness and spite. She mentally went over their conversation and wondered how much the woman knew about Marissa and her. Clarissa had said she knew "secrets about her, and you" and that Rana would never guess who her real father was. Rana prayed Clarissa did not know this destructive truth, but she feared she did. That wicked woman had pretended to be Marissa's friend, and possibly her mother had told Clarissa things without meaning to do so or because she had trusted her. If Clarissa held this awesome secret in her possession, what would she do with it? And had she revealed it to Harrison? Now she understood why Clarissa feared her father's attraction to her and what she meant when she said, "It isn't you he sees and desires!" Raymond had told Clarissa many secrets about them, but did she know about Nathan?

Nathan . . . She called his image to mind. Her father . . . Yes, she had his eyes and favored him. She could never tell him the truth, for it would destroy him to learn he had mated with his own child. How that secret must have tormented her mother. Yes, Marissa would have done anything to protect those she loved from its damage.

Travis . . . She desperately wished he were here to comfort her. What would he think about her mother's evil deeds? What if Clarissa spitefully told him everything? She was Nathan's daughter . . . How would he feel about that relationship? He loved her and she loved him, and she would tell him when the time was right, for such a secret could be harmful if it were kept from him, or if it were told to him by Clarissa.

Rana went to sit by the hearth. Lifting the candle, she burned the letter and note, then burned Raymond's picture. She took needle and thread from her sewing box and carefully repaired the doll, then laid it gently on her bed, understanding now why Marissa had left it behind. Finally she returned to the closet and concealed Marissa's hiding place. For now, she would do nothing with Marissa's "treasures."

Lost in thought she walked aimlessly around her room. Soon she realized that tears were rolling down her cheeks. Perhaps the Great Spirit had ended Marissa's suffering and removed Raymond's threat and evil, yet Clarissa's evil and threat remained. If she made an obvious move toward either Travis or Harrison, the woman might be tempted to wreak her evil vengeance. Rana doubted that Marissa had slept with any man around here other than Fargo, for she recalled that name from her bad dreams. At least Nathan and Todd had been protected from Marissa's secrets, and she would see to it that they remained so. Rana had been raised and trained to slay enemies and to seek justice or revenge. She vowed she would find a way to punish Harrison, Clarissa, and Fargo.

It was late when Nathan returned from Dallas with the papers that made Travis free to marry her. They agreed to keep them a secret until this difficult matter with Harrison was settled. Fortunately, Nathan was too busy and distracted by the damming of the river to notice how oddly Rana was looking at him and behaving. She had accepted him as her father in her heart and mind, and that reality did not trouble her. She smiled at him and hugged him tightly before he left to meet with Cody and Mace, knowing she could never call him "father."

On Sunday morning, Nathan and many of the others went to church to pray for strength and deliverance from the evil that had befallen them. Chores were being left undone as most of the men were assigned to guard duty around the ranch. Nathan had told them at a large meeting early that morning that Travis was on his way home, and he assured them that things would return to normal in another week.

Later that afternoon, Bart Davis married his brother's widow. Some might have disagreed with their decision as it came so soon after Darby's death and burial, but Rana did not. In the Indian camp, when a warrior was slain, a woman quickly took another husband to protect and to support her and her family. Bart and Lettie had been close friends for years and it seemed the best thing for all concerned.

On the Circle C Ranch, Harrison was still reeling from what Clarissa had told him the day before. He did not know what to do with or about the astounding information. But to make certain Rana would not be injured accidentally, he ordered all attacks to cease for the present. Matters would be settled Thursday, the first of August, the day Nathan's loan was due. If Nathan could not come up with the money, Wilber Mason's Mid-Texas Bank would foreclose on him Friday.

Clarissa sat at the dinner table, furtively observing her father. She had all of them right where she wanted them. Soon it would be over and everything would be hers. She smiled malevolently as she recalled her talk with Rana. Maybe she would visit her again, tell her that Nathan was her father, and threaten to expose them. If they gave her any trouble, she would. After all, there was no way Rana and Nathan could learn that Marissa was not really Nathan's daughter. She was the only one who knew that Marissa had not slept with her own father, as the troublesome slut had died believing!

— *Chapter 18* —

❧

O N WEDNESDAY, ANOTHER FALSE TELEGRAM CAME for Nathan and Clarissa from Travis, saying he was supposedly in Springfield and on his way home. The distance from Springfield was such that it appeared Travis would not return to the ranch in less than a week. This telegram delighted Clarissa because she felt everything would be settled in her favor by the time Travis arrived; then she could use her holdings and information to obtain her ultimate desire: him.

Because of the July heat, the poisoned water holes, the lack of rain, and the dammed river, the situation was becoming critical on Nathan's ranch and there was little fresh water for his cattle and horses. If not for the wells and the windmills, the people would soon have been suffering also. Mace ordered the men to dig trenches and to carry water to them to keep the animals alive until something could be done about the water supply. He also ordered guards posted on the windmills and wells, for he was very much aware of the consequences if Harrison ordered them poisoned or burned.

On Thursday, Mace helped Nathan sneak into town inside a large box in a wagon. At the livery stable, they left the wagon and horse and stole out the back way to get to the bank without being seen by anyone Harrison might have posted as a lookout. Fifteen minutes before closing time, Nathan entered the bank to see Wilber Mason and was shown into the bank president's office.

He sat before Wilber's desk and stared at the man, who squirmed nervously in his chair, not wanting to do what he knew he must. "I'm sorry, Nate, but you know I can't extend that loan," Wilber began anxiously. He hated to see this good man broken, but he was helpless.

Nathan smiled oddly, then asked, "Tell me, Wilber, have you already made arrangements for the auction and drawn up the papers to hand my ranch over to Harry?"

Wilber Mason flushed a deep scarlet and looked down at his hands, which were writhing from his tension and guilt. "You know I would help you out if I could," he stated apologetically.

"You can help me, Wilber. You can cancel that auction and tear up Harry's offer," Nathan replied calmly. He began withdrawing packets of money from his jacket, shirt, and hat. He counted them and placed them before the astonished banker. "That should settle my debt, and you can deposit the rest of this money into my account. You do still want my business, don't you?"

Wilber's mouth dropped open and his eyes widened. "Where did you . . . get so much . . . money?" he stammered in surprise.

"From an old friend," Nathan responded, then grinned. "I do have some good friends, Wilber. Relax. There's nothing you can do but take the payment and inform Harry of his misfortune. He'll be furious, but he can't blame you."

Wilber's gaze met Nathan's. Suddenly a broad grin lit his face and he laughed heartily. It was obvious the banker felt great relief and joy. Without counting the money, he took his pen and Nathan's loan papers and marked them with large, dark words: "PAID IN FULL, August 1, 1867. Wilber Mason, President, Mid-Texas Bank."

As Wilber handed Nathan his copy, he looked at the rancher and warned, "Be careful, Nate. Harrison is determined to get your ranch. There's no telling what he'll do when he hears about this," he remarked worriedly, tapping the money and papers with a warning finger.

"I know, Wilber, but I wish men like you wouldn't help make it so easy for him. It's hard to stand against evil when you're standing alone. Harry's judgment day is coming; mark my words." He picked up his papers and walked out as Wilber hung his head in shame.

Nathan returned to his ranch and made his way around it, paying his hands their salaries and adding small bonuses for their loyalty. He warned each one to be especially careful tonight, for Harrison would soon be aware of his defeat.

But Nathan could not know that Harrison had other things on his mind. The man hardly reacted when the bank teller arrived with the shocking news. Somehow he had expected it to happen and he suspected it had to do with the cattle money vanishing from his safe, a mystery that still annoyed and baffled him. Apparently Nathan had hired a clever man who was working secretly to foil his plans, the unknown hireling who had stolen the money from under his nose and had thwarted the boys' attack on the Rocking C women. He knew Nathan was still in trouble, and he was confident he would eventually destroy him and take everything he held precious. After all, Marissa was not Nathan's daughter; therefore, Nathan had no claim on Rana. How he wished Marissa had waited for his return years ago and had married him. Perhaps something had frightened her into fleeing swiftly. If he hadn't been so cruel to her on her final visit home, perhaps she would have confided in him that last night and he could have saved his love and his child. The problem was how to get his daughter without hurting her emotionally. Harrison desperately wanted the child whom Marissa had borne him, the girl who was her mother's image and his only rightful heir . . .

At two o'clock Friday afternoon, Travis galloped into town like a man pursued by demons. He hurriedly dismounted and rushed into the bank, demanding to see Wilber Mason. Inside Mason's closed office, Travis dropped his saddlebags on the desk and emptied them of numerous pouches that were bulging, as Mason promptly learned, with gold nuggets. Travis loosened the drawstrings on several to expose their contents and declared, "There's your money, Mason. And don't you dare tell me it's too late to pay off Nate's loan. You handle it personally and deposit the rest in Nate's account. Be quick and give me those papers. I'm exhausted and I want to get home."

Wilber looked from the shiny, valuable gold to the rugged man whose clothes were rumpled and dusty and who hadn't shaved for at least a month and probably hadn't bathed in that length of time. He did look exhausted and agitated. Apparently he had slept and eaten little in the past weeks, facts that the gauntness of his face and body confirmed. "Where have you been, Kincade, and where did you get all this gold?"

"From an old friend," he replied sullenly, using words that echoed Nathan's of the day before. "Hear me well, Mason; if you've set any foreclosure and auction plans in motion, you'd best end them here and now or you'll answer to me, and I'm not talking very nice these days. Now settle up Nate's account so I can be on my way."

"Evidently you haven't spoken to Nathan," he stated and smiled.

"I've been out of town since the fourth. I came straight here before you and Crandall got too busy stealing Nate's ranch."

"Like you've been stealing gold to save it?" Wilber probed.

"Not a nugget of this is stolen; it's all mine. I'll tell you what, Mason; if you hear of any gold robberies, you can notify the sheriff to investigate me. I'm sure he'll do a better job on me than he's done on all the crimes going on around here. All he'll find out is the gold is mine. Get busy 'cause I'm tired and hungry and mean."

"You can keep the gold or deposit it here, but you—"

Travis nimbly dodged around the desk, seized Mason's coat, and yanked the startled banker from his chair. Almost nose to nose, he warned, "Don't rile me, Mason. I said mark his debt paid."

"Nate's already paid off his loan!" Wilber shrieked. As Travis's hand loosened its grasp and Wilber sank weakly into his chair, he stammered, "I . . . I swear, Kin . . . Kincade. I'll show you the papers. He paid it all and deposited more money. Said he got it from an old friend, just like you did. Came in yesterday, a few minutes before closing time. I handled the transaction myself, but his ranch still isn't safe. He's had some big trouble while you were gone."

"What kind of trouble?" Travis asked as he wondered where Nathan had gotten so much money.

"The river's been dammed and there's been some burnings and shootings and water holes have been poisoned. You should have been here; he needed you," Wilber scolded, trying to regain his composure.

"Take care of this gold and make sure you weigh it accurately," Travis cautioned pointedly, then rushed to his waiting horses. Mounting Apache and seizing the packhorse's reins, he galloped for home.

Not too far behind him, a bank teller rode swiftly toward Harrison's ranch to inform him of this curious incident.

* * *

Rana heard Travis's name shouted in the yard and ran out to greet him. She did not care how he looked or who was watching as she flung herself into his beckoning arms and hugged him tightly. At that moment, thoughts of their sham were forgotten by both. He embraced her fiercely and planted kisses all over her face.

"The message did not come for so many days and we were afraid for you," she told him as tears brightened her blue-gray eyes. She searched his face and body for injuries and was relieved to find none, but she saw that the swift, arduous journey had given him a terrible beating.

"I'm safe, *micante*. The telegraph lines were down most of the way, until I reached Fort Wallace. I couldn't spare the time to keep checking locations. What's been happening here?" he inquired anxiously.

At this point, Nathan and Mace rode up. They quickly dismounted and each gave Travis a bear hug. "You had me plenty worried, son," Nate declared, "when that telegram was so late."

"We need to talk, Nate," he stated seriously.

Nathan smiled and slapped him affectionately on the back. "No need to worry, son. I paid off our loan yesterday."

"I know. I just came from the bank. I left the gold there. We shouldn't have any money problems for a long time, if ever. But how did you come up with that cash?"

Nathan grinned and suggested, "Let's get inside. We've got plenty to tell you. Mace, you come along too."

Travis listened with astonishment as Nathan, Mace, and Rana explained what had occurred during his absence. His emotions were mixed, and he kept glancing at Rana in surprise. Even though he had previously observed her mental and physical prowess, he could not help but be amazed at her feats. "We'll have to be real careful, son, 'cause I'm sure he's got his dander up by now. What we need to do is get those witnesses and branding irons and saddlebags. But tell us about your journey. You had us scared when we didn't hear from you, boy."

Travis went over the details of his trip and his accomplishments. He and Rana exchanged smiles as he talked about Lone Wolf and Myeerah. "That part of my life is finally settled," he remarked happily. His smile faded as he added, "Let's get busy settling our problems here."

Nathan told him, "As soon as we do, I have those papers that say you aren't my son anymore. Seems you two are free to marry."

Travis pulled Rana into his arms and whispered, "I love you, *micante,* and I sorely missed you." To the others he said, "We'll keep this quiet for now. We don't want Rana put in any danger. If I know Clarissa, she'll be furious, and she'll try to get her Papa that way."

After finishing their talk, Mace and Nathan left the room so that Rana and Travis could share a few moments alone. "I saw the look on your face when I mentioned her name. What is it, Rana?"

Rana told him about Clarissa's visit and his fury mounted. She smiled and nestled against his chest. "Do not worry, *mihigna;* I ordered her away. I told Grandfather nothing of her mean visit. She fears losing you and her father to me, and that fear makes her vicious, like an injured wolf. But soon the Caldwells will be defeated and we will marry."

"I need to get cleaned up and do some checking around. We'll talk about this later," he murmured, then smiled seductively.

"Yes, we will talk later," she concurred, thinking of what else she had to tell him and knowing that it was not yet the time or place.

Just as Travis was about to leave the house, a violent rainstorm broke overhead. Nathan rushed inside soaking wet and beaming with joy. Rana was here, and Travis was home safely, the loan had been paid, and the heavy rain would help replenish their vanishing water supply. He told Travis there was nothing he could do on the ranch this late in the day in stormy weather, and what he needed was a bath, shave, hot food, and a good night's sleep. Travis did not need much convincing and immediately set out to do what Nathan had suggested.

He had only intended to rest until Nathan had gone to bed, but he was so fatigued that he fell into a deep sleep and nothing aroused him—not the loud thunder or Rana as she sat on the edge of his bed and watched him for a long time. She made no attempt to awaken him; she only wanted and needed to be near him.

"See there, Papa, I told you it wasn't Travis hanging around here secretly and doing those things," Clarissa stated petulantly.

"Nor was he the one sending those telegrams, you fool. There's no way he could have gotten here today from Springfield. I don't know where he went or how he got that gold, but I intend to find out."

"Surely you can understand why he tricked me. He didn't want you to learn about the gold and rob him on the trail as you did the cattle money. What are you going to do now to force Crandall out?"

"I haven't decided, but I will. Don't you worry none, girl."

"You're hesitating because of that little slut, aren't you? You can't claim her, Papa; it would ruin everything we've worked for!"

Harrison slapped her and sneered, "That little slut, as you call her, is my daughter and your half sister. I've told you before, girl, let me handle my affairs." He stalked from the room then, shaking with anger.

I'll get you for this, you bastard, she vowed silently.

Harrison returned to the room suddenly and taunted, "Oh, yes, there's something I forgot to tell you about Nathan's recent trips to Dallas." He laughed wickedly as he related the pertinent information to a stunned Clarissa.

The next morning, Travis rode to the river to assess the damage. Seeing how it had been done, he also understood the only possible way to clear the blockage. All he lacked was dynamite, and he knew where to find some. He turned as he heard a horse approaching, and saw Clarissa riding toward him as if she had known where he would be.

She dismounted, ran to him, and tried to embrace him. He pushed her away and glared at her. "What's wrong, love?" she asked. "I've watched for you all morning. I thought you would be glad to see me."

"And I thought you'd keep your papa under control while I was gone," he retorted, slipping into the provoking role he was forced to play with her.

Assuming that Rana had not told him of her visit, Clarissa asked, "What are you talking about?" She unsuccessfully attempted to look and sound hurt and innocent.

He laughed harshly and demanded, "Get off that silly horse, Clarissa. It doesn't ride with me. We both know Harrison Caldwell is behind all this trouble and destruction. I was hoping you cared enough about me to stall him until my return so I could fight him."

"Don't be mean. I love you, Travis. I would do anything to help you and make you happy," she told him, trying to snuggle closer.

"If that were true, you would be on my side," he argued.

"Then tell me how to prove my love and loyalty!" she cried.

He answered smoothly, "Give me evidence against your father so I can have him put in jail for his crimes. Once he's out of the way and you own his ranch, then we can talk seriously—not before."

Clarissa stared at Travis. If she agreed to help him defeat her father, Harrison would retaliate by leaving everything to his "daughter" Rana. Yet if she confessed her deceit about Rana's parentage in order to stop Harrison from changing his heir, she would be exposed as a liar—if her father could be convinced she had lied to him. Now that Travis had been disowned and disinherited, perhaps he would be more vulnerable to her offerings. She had to bluff him. "I don't know anything about Papa's affairs, Travis. He's always so secretive. I don't think he trusts me, because we're so close. Why don't you beat the truth out of him or one of his hirelings?"

"You really expect me to believe you don't know anything?" he scoffed in disgust. "If we can't get your father's place, then we'd have nothing," he told her, trying to sound vexed and flustered.

"What about Nathan's ranch? You'll get it one day," she responded innocently, though her expression told him she knew otherwise, as he had suspected.

"Not unless I marry that little savage of a granddaughter! He's cut me off, hoping to force us together. If I let your papa take over, I won't get any part of this ranch, and it's mine, damnit! I'll fight him 'til one of us lands in hell, and I'll marry her if necessary."

"Never! That little bitch can't inherit Nathan's ranch because she isn't his granddaughter!" she shouted at him, then softened her voice to add, "Because Marissa isn't Nathan's daughter."

"What are you saying, woman?" he demanded eagerly, seeing she had made a rash slip in her anger.

Clarissa related the story of Ruth Crandall's death-bed confession to her mother, Sarah Jane Caldwell. "Marissa's father was a red-haired, blue-eyed outlaw! Mama told Papa, and he told me years ago, before he decided to seek another wife who could give him a son to take everything that rightfully belongs to me. I hate him and, if I knew anything that would help get rid of him, I would tell you. He can't live forever, Travis. You get Nathan's ranch by proving Rana isn't the rightful heir; then one day I'll get Papa's holdings. We'll marry and have the largest spread in this area."

Travis persisted in questioning her slip. "How do you know that it wasn't fever talking when Mrs. Crandall said such things to your mother?"

"Marissa was born six months after Nathan returned home from a four-month cattle drive, and she was fully grown as babies go. Hasn't anyone ever told you Ruth Crandall had black hair? How does black hair mix with blond to make a flaming-haired child? It doesn't."

"Obviously Nate didn't care that she wasn't his by blood."

"Nate didn't, and still doesn't, know the truth."

"And you expect me to tell him?" he inquired, fury lacing his words.

She stated coldly, "If you want the ranch badly enough, you will. Otherwise, Rana will steal it from you."

"Did Harrison threaten to expose Marissa as a bastard and she couldn't bear the shame? Is that what he told her to make her run away? Has he been trying to steal this ranch that long? Were you involved?" he demanded, attempting to evoke more answers.

"Don't be ridiculous! She ran away because she was pregnant. And she kept running because of all she had done to hide her sins."

"You certainly know a lot about her," he stated skeptically.

Clarissa's dark eyes narrowed. "I knew her and Raymond for years, but I never told her she was the bastard of an unknown Scotsman who had raped her mother. She died believing Nathan was her father."

"Did Raymond know she was pregnant? Was that his hold over her?" he probed, aware Clarissa was rashly exposing more than she had intended.

Clarissa's tone and gaze altered noticeably as she began to lie. "He made a deal with her. He was to get her away from her sinful past if she paid him money. When she tried to cheat on her part of their deal, he used it to blackmail her and to force her to whore for his gambling stakes. She should have killed the son of a bitch for beating her and degrading her. She was a fool and a weakling. She was willing to do anything to keep the truth from her father and Todd Raines!"

Although he was aware of what she had told Rana, he queried convincingly, "Todd? What does he have to do with this?"

"It seems he and Marissa discovered each other and fell in love, but, sadly, she was carrying another man's child by then. Since she hadn't been bedding Todd long enough, she couldn't tell him the child was his. She was afraid Todd and Nathan would hate her, so she bolted. She hoped to divorce Raymond and return one day, but Raymond realized what a good thing he had and used it. By the time she came to her senses, she had committed more sins and had gotten in too deep to dig her way out. Then, those nasty Indians got in her way."

"You mean she was really in love with Todd Raines?"

"Isn't that amusing? After all her running around, she found true love when it was too late. How pathetic."

He suggested doubtfully, "Something's strange here, Clarissa. I thought you said you two were friends. You sound as if you hated her."

"Why shouldn't I have? One of the men she was whoring with was my father —while she was pretending to be my friend and tutor. Why do you think he's so hot for Rana? Because she's her mother's image!"

Travis hated to think of Harrison's putting his hands on that lovely creature who had looked like his beloved. "Is Harrison Rana's father?"

"Thank heavens he isn't, or he'd leave her everything! Papa was back East during that time." She recalled what Marissa had told her friend, and what the traitorous friend had told Raymond, and what Raymond had told her about the timing of her breakup with Harrison, her affair with Todd, and her pregnancy. She had no doubt about when Rana had been conceived, but she couldn't imagine anyone else believing such a shocking accusation. "When Papa returned, Marissa was long gone and he was hopping mad. Papa had actually wanted to marry her, and he would have if she'd agreed, before or after Michaels. Haven't you figured it out by now, Travis? Revenge, that's what Papa wants with the Crandall ranch, revenge for Marissa's loss. Until he saw Rana," she added bitterly.

"Lordy, woman, what a tangled mess . . ."

"He wants Rana badly, Travis, and he would sacrifice all of his schemes to marry her, but then they would have it all if Nathan conveniently died, if you understand my meaning."

So much for her alleged ignorance of her father's life and intentions, he mused. "Not if I get her first," Travis argued, knowing she would be vexed by his words.

Clarissa knew she could not tell him the lie she had told her father, for then Travis would also believe Rana had a claim on the Caldwell holdings. Travis was right; it was a complicated and tangled mess. Maybe she should get rid of her father now and take what she could. Whatever happened, she was more than ready to get rid of Fargo, Wes, Silas, and Jackson, before one of them started trouble.

"Let me mull this over and I'll see you in a few days. Since you don't know anything about your papa's business, keep a sharp eye and ear on him, and report anything suspicious to me." With this, Travis mounted his horse and waved his farewell.

As Clarissa watched Travis ride off, she felt her anger mounting. She had said too much, and she knew he had lied to her in those faked telegrams and about his trip. Like her father, he wanted Rana, and he was only using her to get his way! She was growing weary of all these deceits and setbacks, and her passion for him was waning . . .

It was after everyone else had gone to bed for the night that Travis and Rana set into motion their plan to unblock the river. "First we steal the dynamite, then we blow it to hell," Travis explained. "Let's get our weapons ready, *micante;* this is going to be a long and busy night." He smiled into her glowing eyes and caressed her cheek.

"I am happy you are taking me with you," she murmured.

"I think you've proven you're as good, if not better, than me," he teased, then kissed her. "Sorry about last night. I was exhausted."

Rana cuddled up to his firm body and ran her fingers up his back. "We will have many nights together when this foe is defeated."

Travis's passions were stirred by her touch and fragrance. He warned huskily, "If you don't stop that, they'll begin now."

Rana laughed softly and reminded him, "We must take the weapon tonight, before he thinks to hide it. You told me it is the only way to clear the river. We must wait, but we wait together."

"You're so smart and clearheaded. I should put you in charge of this assignment." He stroked her silky tresses and gazed at her.

"It is not so, *mihigna*. My heart beats as swiftly as the war drum, and my head spins at your nearness as if I had taken the peyote button. If you kiss me again, I fear all is lost for our raid," she cautioned playfully, even though she knew her words were accurate.

"Let's get moving, wife." He gathered his bow and quiver and slung them over one shoulder. Then he checked his two knives and stuffed a rawhide strip into his pocket, for this was a night for silent weapons.

Dressed in concealing dark colors and with Rana's flaming hair covered, they rode stealthily to within a mile of Harrison's home. They dismounted and left their horses tethered, and continued gingerly on foot. Having heard from Rana about the place where Harrison was hiding the branding irons, Travis decided to look there first.

As silently and secretly as Apache warriors, they made their way to the barn. It was Saturday night and most of the hands were in town. After pointing out the area to Travis, Rana stood guard while he pried loose the boards. He grinned as his gaze touched on the branding irons and five sticks of dynamite. He removed only the explosives, stuffed them into a cotton sack, then replaced the boards.

"Let's go," he murmured against her ear, indicating his success.

They cautiously retraced their steps and headed for the dam. Rana stayed with the horses while Travis checked the blockage and carefully placed the sticks of dynamite. Time seemed to pass so slowly in the darkness and she wondered what was taking him so long. Her nerves were on edge and she continually licked her dry lips and scanned the shadows for him.

Suddenly a hand clamped over her mouth and a strong arm banded her body, locking her arms to her sides; it was not Travis's manly odor she detected and she froze.

A rough voice whispered in her ear, "Stay real quiet and still or I'll slice your throat. We finally caught you, you little sneak. Where's your partner? If you shout when I move my hand, you're both dead. Understand?" he warned, shaking her roughly.

Rana knew she had to stall for time. She nodded, then remained motionless. The hand slowly moved from her mouth. She knew the danger of shouting a warning to Travis, so she held her silence until he asked again, "Where's your partner? What's he doing?"

"Looking at the dam," she murmured softly, trying to disguise her feminine voice, forgetting her figure would give her away. She knew they could not sneak up on Travis with his keen instincts. What she had to do was entice one to go seek him; then she could battle the other one.

"Go find him and bring him over here," the voice commanded.

"It's probably Kincade. You go, Fargo, and let me guard this one," the other man argued nervously, unintentionally revealing her captor's identity.

Rana shuddered, for she knew that name. Hatred began to burn within her, and she silently vowed she would free herself and slay this man. Suddenly she was turned and shoved into the moonlight and her dark covering was yanked away. With surprise, she noted the effect of her appearance on the ugly brute.

"It can't be you. You're dead," he scoffed as he trembled.

Rana realized he thought she was Marissa, and she used that fear and hesitation to her advantage. "I have returned to punish all who harm those I love. Go from this place or I will strike you dead."

Fargo was pale and shaky. He stammered, "Don't go . . . go blaming me f-for what I did. It was . . . Mi-Mister Caldwell's orders."

"I will slay him, and I will slay you if you do not leave swiftly," she threatened, raising her voice slightly in the hope that he wouldn't notice but that Travis would be warned of their peril.

"Be quiet, girl," the other man hissed. "I'll go find her partner. Let's git this done, and git off Crandall's property. You know he's been posting guards ever'where, and that Kincade's back."

Fargo did not respond as he stared at Marissa's image in the flickering moonlight. Unaware of Fargo's involvement with Marissa, the other man frowned and slipped into the shadows to head for the dam, having been told by Harrison to check it every hour to make sure no one tried to tamper with it.

"Release me, dead man," she ordered harshly, glaring at him.

Unwittingly, Fargo obeyed. Without warning or delay, Rana yanked her knife from her sheath and buried it deep within his chest. Stunned, Fargo gaped at the knife butt protruding from his chest, then stared at the woman before him. Rana stared back, her eyes cold as ice.

"It weren't my fault," he wailed, then collapsed at her feet.

"He is dead, Mother," she whispered into the sultry night.

The other man leapt from the trees and grabbed her, striking her in the abdomen to disable her. Because of her years of Indian training, she took the blow without crying out in pain or surprise. Had she done otherwise, she might have drawn more attackers to the location, and a true warrior would never endanger his companions; he would suffer, or die, in protective silence.

The man was torn roughly from her by a leather thong around his throat. "You filthy bastard! Don't you ever touch her!" Travis warned, snarling like a wild dog. As the terrified man struggled, Travis tightened the rawhide rope until the man was dead.

He dropped the man's body to the ground, then reached for his beloved. "Are you hurt, Rana?" he asked worriedly.

She smiled and shook her head. "I knew we could conquer them," she stated confidently.

Travis glanced at Fargo's body and said quietly, "I see you got him." He was very much aware that even if one killed a man out of necessity, it was never easy, and he wondered what Rana was feeling.

She looked into his eyes and said mysteriously, "He is an old enemy. It was my right and duty to slay him. I will speak of it later."

Travis dragged the bodies into the dry river bed. "That storm has the river begging this dam for release. When she goes, she should take those bodies a long way off. You go back to the house like we planned. I'll send their horses running and cover our tracks. I'll give you twenty minutes, then I'll light the charges and get there as quickly as I can. We need to be seen there after the explosion."

"Be careful, my love," she told him as they embraced.

"You be careful, too. There might be other varmints around."

Rana quickly made her way home and slipped into the stable to return the horses to their stalls. They had ridden bareback to save time and to avoid the noise of squeaking leather saddles. Nathan had made it easy for them to move about the ranch by posting guards in places that allowed them to go and return unseen.

When she entered the house, Nathan seized her and hugged her to him. "How did it go? Are you all right?" he asked breathlessly.

"All is good . . . Grandfather. We must be ready to act." She hurriedly changed her clothes and awaited the blast, which would be heard and felt this distance away as well as on the adjoining ranch.

When it occurred, Harrison Caldwell was on his way home from town, from working off his frustrations in the Silver Shadow Saloon. He knew that if he raced to Nathan's house, he could see the guilty party returning to report. He clicked his reins roughly across his animal's shoulders and prodded him forcefully with the stirrups.

He sped to Nathan's stable, where hands were saddling horses and preparing to investigate the new blast. Nathan and Rana ran from the house toward the corral, and Travis was right behind them, buckling on his gun belt, his hair mussed from what seemed a recent arousal from sleep. They were all scurrying around like they were as surprised and puzzled as he was! If it hadn't been Travis, then who . . . ?

"What in tarnation are you doing here?" Nathan demanded.

"I was coming back from town and heard the explosion. I rode over to see what was happening." Harrison's eyes quickly went to Rana, and he smiled tenderly. "You all right, Rana?" he asked in a strange tone.

She looked at him with an inquisitive expression, then nodded. Turning away, she mounted and rode off between Nathan and Travis. As they galloped to the river, she suddenly realized why he had looked at her that way: obviously Clarissa had told him she was his child to keep him from marrying her! Would that woman do and say anything to get her way? she wondered. Stranger still, she mused, he had looked pleased!

At the river, everyone saw what had happened; the dam had been blasted away and the water was flowing rapidly and freely. Nathan twisted in his saddle to sneer at Harrison. "Looks like I have me a secret helper. Unless this is some new trick of yours, Harry. What's the matter, afraid you'll ruin the property you're trying to steal? You might as well give up, because I'm not leaving my land."

"Relax, Nate. I had nothing to do with this. But if I were you, I would find out who's responsible and learn why he's helping you. He might want your ranch more than I do." Harrison tipped his hat, then rode off. Something odd was going on, and he aimed to discover what it was and who was behind it. First, he would talk with Clarissa!

Nathan looked at Mace and suggested, "See if you can round up enough boys to move the herds near the streams. They should fill up fast. Tell 'em I'll pay 'em extra for working tonight. Things are looking sunny again," he stated, then laughed cheerfully.

Rana nestled against Travis's body and sighed peacefully, but as she recalled what she had to tell him, she stiffened slightly. Aware of her change in mood, Travis inquired softly, "What's wrong, *micante?*"

Rana told him about her mother's letter and what she had remembered that enabled her to find it. She also told him what she suspected Clarissa had told Harrison about her. "The truth must be kept secret forever or it will hurt Grandfather deeply. I can never call him father. Do you understand and agree?"

Travis tightened his embrace and murmured, "Yes, my love, I understand and agree. But there's something I need to tell you, something your mother didn't learn before she died and Nathan still doesn't know: Marissa did not sleep and mate with her father; Nathan was not her father." He explained what he knew and how he knew it, allowing the entire mystery to unravel. "Marissa did what she did because she believed she had committed a terrible sin with her father. If she had learned that Nathan wasn't her father, things might have been different."

Rana cried softly as she told him why she had slain Fargo. "He believed I was Mother and that it was she who slayed him. It was my revenge. Now, I must slay Harrison for what he did to her."

"Let me handle him, love. Once he learns he's been duped, he'll be more dangerous than ever. We'll get the evidence on him and he'll be punished. If we kill him, we'll lose with him. We have to do this legally, love—under the white man's law," he clarified.

Rana's lips touched his, for she wanted him, not more talk. It was nearing dawn and they had so little time left together, and both were very much aware that it had been weeks since they had joined their bodies and spirits. Their hungers raged, yet neither wanted to rush these precious moments.

Travis eased off her gown and gently kissed each breast tip before drifting up to ravenously devour her parted lips. Between kisses, she murmured, "It is good to have you with me again. I am lost without you." Feverishly she sealed her mouth to his.

The palm of his hand moved over her breast in a circular motion, stimulating it delightfully. Then he shifted to sear her quivering flesh with fiery kisses and burning caresses. His mouth explored and tasted her sweet desire and heady surrender. Aware of her unbridled passion, he labored lovingly and eagerly with lips and hands to arouse her to the highest peak before joining their bodies.

Her arms went around him and her hands drifted up and down his back, feeling the hardness and suppleness of his muscles and skin. He had set her entire body tingling and smoldering from his stirring actions. He tantalized and pleasured her from head to foot. Her body was aflame with need and scorching desire. Travis was controlling her, stimulating her to the center of her being. He whispered words into her ear that, coupled with his warm breath, caused her heart to race and her senses to soar like an eagle in flight. Each place he touched with lips or hands was highly susceptible to his skills, and he brought every inch of her to awareness and fiery life.

Travis's pleasure mounted as he was given free rein over her body and will. He loved her and wanted her to be a part of him forever. Her nearness, fragrance, and essence were driving him wild, but he wanted to enjoy and titillate her as long as possible. Rapturous sensations attacked him as her hands wandered over his body and her lips responded to his. Her fingers slipped into his hair and drew his mouth more tightly against hers, revealing her rising ardor.

Travis's hand enticingly roamed across her flat stomach to seek a flaming forest and a vital peak that summoned his exploration and craved his splendid skills, a place where he could heighten their desire and cause them to writhe together with barely leashed passion.

Rana's hands likewise wandered over his body, stirring his flaming need to a brighter, higher level. Her fingers teased down his sleek sides and brazenly captured the prize of love's war that could send her senses spinning beyond reality, beyond resistance or inhibition. Gently and lovingly she stroked it and absorbed its warmth to create more heat. She delighted in its strength and prowess and smoothness. With great satisfaction she felt his body shudder and she heard a deep groan escape his lips as they worked upon hers. This act of total giving and taking and sharing was so much more than she had ever imagined in her girlish dreams.

Unable to restrain himself further, he moved between her parted thighs, where she eagerly welcomed his arrival and entrance. His body was tense and his control strained as he made that first staggering contact. He tried to move calmly, leisurely, but he found it difficult to master his urgency to ride ecstasy's undulating prairie with her.

As her hand trailed up and down his back, she could feel the rippling muscles that moved as his body did. She felt him enter and withdraw, slowly, then rapidly, then slowly again. She sensed the strain he was experiencing and she arched her body to meet his and set the pace for their entrancing climb. Her responses told him when she was approaching the blissful precipice and he worked skillfully and patiently to drive them over its edge at the same time.

When the triumphant moment arrived, he muffled her cry of victory with his demanding lips. Their mouths and bodies labored and came together as one as they conquered passion's peak; then like feathers on a gentle breeze, they rapturously floated downward into a peaceful valley of contentment. Still they kissed and held fast to each other, extracting every sensation and emotion their union could provide.

They snuggled together in her bed and held each other, awed by the greater closeness and deeper bond their lovemaking had inspired. The more they were together for any reason, the more tightly their hearts and souls were bound. Both realized how much they loved and needed each other, in every facet of their lives. Incredibly, each day they were together was better than the day before. They were friends; they were partners; they were passionate lovers. They could talk and share anything, everything. They trusted each other, depended upon each other, and gave to each other. They had grown and changed together, for the better. It was a special union, unique and strong.

Because each sensed how the other was feeling and what the other was thinking, their heads turned at the same moment and their eyes fused. This time they spoke without words, and they made love slowly, tenderly.

* * *

By the next day, Harrison knew his plans were coming apart, and he did not know who to blame. He suspected that Fargo and his other hand were dead. Their horses had returned to the corral, empty, and they had been assigned to guard the dam. Yet all he could think about was Rana, or Marissa. He had to get his child back!

Clarissa entered the room and observed her father. "They were all at church this morning, gloating over their triumphs. And here you sit like you're in mourning. We're losing, Papa, and you're to blame. I'd always thought you were so strong and clever, that nothing and no one could defeat you or crush you. Have you forgotten what Marissa did to you? She scornfully rejected you. She started sleeping with Todd Raines, then ran off with that gambler. She was selfish and no good, Papa. When are you going to accept that and forget her?"

"How can I forget her, girl, when our daughter looks just like her? You're a cold-hearted bitch, Clarissa. She's my flesh and blood, and I want her. I'm going to kill Nathan and Travis; then she'll have no choice but to come home to me. Once she sees how much I love her and want her, she'll be fine. You're just worried about your inheritance, you greedy bitch. You'll have to share everything with your sister. And if you give us any trouble, I'll kick you out and she'll get it all. Do you hear me, girl?" he demanded scathingly.

Clarissa was pushed beyond control. She screamed at him, "I was crazy to lie to you to keep you from making a fool of yourself over Rana Michaels like you did with her whorish mother! That little savage isn't your child; she's Nathan's! That's right, dear Papa," she shouted contemptuously when he gaped at her as if she had gone mad before his eyes. She calmly clarified, "Rana is Nathan Crandall's daughter, not your bastard. Have you conveniently forgotten you were back East for months during that time? And you hadn't slept with her long before you left. That's right, dear Papa," she scoffed again, "I found out about you and Marissa Crandall when I was eight years old. Did you think I was blind and stupid? I knew about her countless visits to your room and I knew what you two were doing. How do you think I learned so much about sex and how pleasurable it is? From spying on you and her. All you cared about was her! You didn't love me or want me! I was glad when she left, but still you didn't shower any leftover love and attention on me, love and attention you gave her for nearly two years! I've done everything you've asked to prove my love and loyalty, but nothing matters to you. I hate you, and I hope they kill you!"

"My God, girl, you've lost your mind," he decided aloud.

"Would you like to hear the entire history of your beloved Marissa?" she asked, then shouted the shocking facts at him before he could respond. "You see, dear Papa," she finished, "Rana is Nathan's evil seed; and that flaming-haired bitch you loved so deeply was so wicked that she slept with her own father."

Harrison glared at her furiously for her deceit, for he knew she was telling the truth this time. "You forget, you malicious bitch, that Nathan isn't Marissa's father."

"What does that matter? She thought he was!"

"It was a girlish prank, a terrible mistake, and she paid for it. Are you forgetting how many times you've slept with men for a variety of reasons?" he taunted just to punish his malicious child. "Marissa was trying to help a friend, and that friend betrayed her. Nothing is worse than betrayal, Clarissa," he remarked meaningfully. "Frankly, I'm glad she isn't my daughter. I much prefer her as a wife."

"You wouldn't dare!" Clarissa screamed in outrage.

Harrison laughed coldly. "Wouldn't I? Just as soon as I can lure Nathan into a trap, I'm going to kill him myself. Then I'll sic Monroe and Hayes on Travis. Yes, I should be a happy bridegroom before winter. You'd best look hard for a husband, girl, because I don't want you around after I marry. Maybe I'll have a son this time." He strolled from the room, his laughter echoing satanically.

"Over my dead body, you bastard," she vowed. It was time to locate Wes and end this madness . . .

Chapter 19

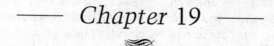

E ARLY MONDAY MORNING, the fifth of August, Harrison handed Wes Monroe a sealed letter and told him to give it personally to Nathan Crandall without letting anyone see him or the letter. "I'm going to lure my annoying neighbor into a trap and kill him myself. I've ordered my hands out of the area of your cabin so Nate and I can meet and talk privately before I put a bullet in his head. I'll tell everyone he hunted me down and tried to kill me, and I was merely defending myself. Since he hasn't made any secret of his hatred and accusations, it won't seem suspicious. After I'm done with Nate, I'll let you and Hayes take care of Travis Kincade for me; then your jobs will be over."

"What about getting control of Crandall's ranch?" Wes asked, wondering about the abrupt change in plans and Caldwell's strange behavior.

"I have another way of carrying out my wishes. I don't want any more trouble over there until I tell you to get rid of Kincade. When that's done, I'll give you two a fat bonus and then you can be on your way to your next job. See me about ten tomorrow morning." Harrison watched with satisfaction as the cocky gunslinger mounted and rode off. Once Nathan and Travis were out of his way, he would settle matters with Clarissa before claiming Rana as his bride. Evidently she had beguiled Silas Stern into helping her with some plot against him. He was convinced they were working against him, for no one else could have gotten into his safe or known about his plans in time to thwart them. It had been a mistake to let Fargo and Silas fall under his daughter's spell, but he hadn't believed she possessed so much sexual prowess and allure, or intelligence and daring. She was a cunning, conniving bitch, and she had been plotting against him for years. Soon she would pay for her treachery and betrayal, he promised himself. He walked to his corral to fetch his horse. He had one task to handle before riding to the cabin, and he had plenty of time.

Wes rode off to find Nathan and carry out his curious assignment. As soon as it was done and Caldwell left his house, he would sneak in to see Clarissa and find out what was going on. He wasn't ready to leave the area, the job, or settle for only a "fat bonus."

Wes slid off his horse near Nathan's house. He hadn't noticed anyone nearby during his cautious approach, nobody except the graying blond man sitting on his front porch reading. Wes said, "Here's a message from Mister Caldwell. He wants a private meeting with you. He gives his word on your safety, so don't be afraid to go, old man."

Nathan stared at the villainous hireling who had delivered Harrison's surprising and mystifying message. Then he read: "Meet me in one hour at the shack near my eastern boundary and we'll settle our problems once and for all. I'll make you one final offer and if you reject it, I'll make certain you aren't troubled again. There are some secrets between us, Nate, and it's time we aired them. If you want to know the truth about why Marissa left home with Michaels, come alone and come quickly. Once you hear the truth, you'll know why I've hated you for years and sought revenge. I'm tired of all our fighting, and this is a better way to settle matters. I'll be waiting, if you're brave enough to face me."

Nathan watched Caldwell's man depart and read the message again. He wondered what Marissa had to do with their conflict. She had often visited Clarissa to help her with her studies or to watch her . . . Had something happened to his daughter over there? Was Harrison responsible for his child's running away? What "secrets"? he asked himself.

Rana and Travis were out riding. Neither Mace, nor Todd, nor Cody was nearby this morning. Harrison had told him to come alone, but he had not said to keep the meeting a secret. If Caldwell were planning to harm him, he wouldn't have sent a written message for others to see. Evidently Harrison wanted to play some clever word games. Why not? he speculated. Maybe he could withdraw some important information. After all, he had been letting others take all the risks and do all the work of saving his ranch. And that crude animal of a messenger had taunted him about being afraid, singeing his manly ego. His side had been winning all the victories lately; maybe Harry wanted to capitulate in private.

He stuffed the letter into his pocket and retrieved his gun belt. Strapping it on, he walked to the corral, saddled his horse, and left, carelessly forgetting to tell anyone where he was going or why. He wanted to be early so he could hide and study the meeting area. If Harrison were setting a trap, he would be very careful and not fall into it. Besides, he needed time to locate the cabin.

Silas entered the house and took the stairs by twos to see what Clarissa wanted. She was still standing at the window after inviting him to enter the room. Turning, she smiled seductively. "Silas, we have some business to discuss. I need your help with a little problem. How would you like to help me get rid of Papa so we can marry and take over this ranch?" she asked calmly as she removed her dressing gown and let it float provocatively to her feet. "Close the door and lock it. I'm sure you don't want to be disturbed while you're . . . talking to me."

Silas Stern gaped at the naked beauty who had made such astounding suggestions, unable to move or speak. He watched her come forward gracefully, then step behind him to close and lock the door herself. She moved before him and smiled enticingly as she began unbuttoning his shirt. "Relax, Silas. Papa will be gone for at least an hour. Surely you're tired of him bossing you around and treating you as if you had no brains or feelings. He's threatening to kick me out if I refuse to marry this old friend of his. I can't, Silas, because I want you. But if I tell Papa, he'll laugh at me and punish both of us."

When she started pressing kisses on his throat and chest, he shuddered and groaned. Once she had his shirt off, his hands went to her breasts and began to fondle them. Clarissa knelt to pull off his boots, then unfastened his pants and sensuously removed them with a wanton smile. As she slowly rose, her hands played ticklishly over his eager body. She drew him to the bed and pushed him down upon it. "You will help me so we can marry, won't you, my love?" she wheedled.

Silas smiled happily. "I'll do anything for you, Clarissa."

Grasping his head, she pulled it to her breast. "We'll make plans later, my future husband. Right now, I want you too much to think clearly," she lied provocatively, having decided that Wes was too dangerous and she was not sure she could depend on him or trust him. But Silas was weak and bewitched. He would aid her and then she would find a way to kill him.

Wes tied his reins to a corral post and walked to the Caldwell house. No one was around, so no one saw him or questioned him. He slipped inside the house and went looking for Clarissa. He stood outside her door and listened to the revealing sounds coming from within. Having heard enough, he returned to the front porch to await Jackson, who arrived shortly to meet him.

"It's time we had some fun around here, Jack, then moved on. That money's gone, so we can't get much from Caldwell. When he gits back home, we'll take what he has, kill the son of a bitch, then ride out. While we're waiting, I thought we could have us some fun with his whore of a daughter. She's in there now humping Silas."

"You ain't joshing, Wes?" the man asked excitedly.

"Nope. Fact is, old friend, you can have her first and last. Unless this stick gets hard and hot, I'll pleasure myself watching you hurt her real good," Wes Monroe told him, rubbing his taut groin.

"Let's go git her," Jackson Hayes urged in rising anticipation.

"Be real quiet. We don't want to give them no warning. Yessiree, Jack, you're gonna enjoy yourself today," Wes told him, grinning malevolently.

* * *

"Say that again, Rachel," Travis coaxed in disbelief.

"Some awful man came to the door and gave Mister Crandall a letter from Harrison Caldwell. He read it, got his gun, and left. I heard some of what the man said," she began, then repeated Wes's words. "I went to check on my stew, and he was gone before I could speak to him."

Travis and Rana hurried to the corral to claim their horses, which had just been unsaddled and rubbed down. They mounted bareback and raced toward Harrison's house. Anticipating trouble and danger, they dismounted a distance from the house and moved toward it stealthily. Peering through the parlor window, they saw the obviously dead body of Silas Stern on the floor and Clarissa being tortured and raped brutally by Jackson Hayes while Wes Monroe watched and laughed. Before Travis and Rana could come to her aid, Jackson Hayes began stabbing her repeatedly as he climaxed.

Rana screamed uncontrollably as she witnessed the horrifying murder. Travis grabbed her arm and yanked her away from the window, knowing it was too late to save Clarissa's life and fearing that the noise had alerted the outlaws to their presence. Travis used Indian sign language to communicate silently with her. She nodded her understanding and hurried to obey, ashamed that she had committed such a terrible error in crying aloud.

When Wes and Jackson bounded from the house, Travis pounced on them. They struggled fiercely. To the cutthroats, Travis seemed to be nowhere and everywhere at the same time. "Where's Nathan Crandall?" he demanded as he struck one and whirled to deflect a blow from the other. "I'll kill you dirty bastards if you've harmed him!" He tripped Jackson and kicked Wes in the abdomen.

As the two men circled Travis, Wes taunted, "You'll never reach him in time. He's dead by now. Harrison lured him to our cabin to kill him. Come on, tough man, show me how you can whip me and Jack." Wes was too cocky and arrogant to draw his pistol. He assumed he could beat this man, especially when it was two-on-one.

"Then why don't you tell me where your cabin is?" Travis mocked. "I'll lick you both and be gone in a flash."

Wes tauntingly revealed its location as he drew his knife and began to wave it threateningly in Travis's face. Travis grinned sardonically. He ventured, "I bet you don't remember where you got that knife and pistol." When Wes glanced at both, then back at the man between him and Jackson, Travis replied, "You took them off me seven years ago near St. Louis, when you were working for Elizabeth Lowry's father. Right before you raped and murdered an Indian girl, then tried to beat me to death. Then you went back and murdered Lowry and his daughter. You must make it a practice to kill your bosses and their families. The initials on the handle stand for White Eagle; that's me."

Wes hesitated as he listened to this incredible tale. That instant gave Travis the edge, and he delivered a stunning blow to Wes's gut and jaw. As Wes staggered backward, Jackson attacked Travis. Rana appeared with the horses, knowing they would have to hurry to save her father. As Travis spun to miss Wes's next blow, Rana lifted her gun and fired at Jackson, striking him in the chest and killing him.

Within moments, Wes was dead and Travis had recovered his pistol and knife. He flung himself on Apache's back and they rode toward the cabin.

For awhile, Nathan remained hidden and observed Harrison as the man paced and fretted. Nathan wanted to make certain his foe was alone. He had never seen Harrison look so edgy or insecure. When he was certain no one else was around, he left his hiding place and joined him.

"You wanted to see me, Harry?" he asked as he walked to him.

Harrison turned and slowly eyed Nathan. "It's over, Nate. I finally win everything, your ranch and Rana."

"How do you see that, Harry?" Nathan argued insolently.

Harrison freely revealed his scheme to rid himself of Nathan. "I'll bet my ranch nobody knows you're here. So when I claim you came looking for me and tried to kill me, who's to prove me wrong?"

"Why didn't you hire one of your gunslingers to handle this?"

"Because I wanted the pleasure of killing you myself."

"Mind telling me why?" Nathan asked, stalling for an opening.

"Because you let Marissa marry that mean bastard and leave home. You're to blame for her suffering and death. You were too weak to control her and too damn stubborn to protect her. I was in love with her and I wanted to marry her, but that fancy gambler stole her while I was gone. You should have stopped them, Nate. She would be alive now if you had had the gumption to stand up to her or kill Michaels. You knew she was terrified of that bastard. Every time she came home, you saw she was in trouble, but you did nothing."

"You and Marissa?" Nathan murmured in disbelief.

"That's right, you fool. She should have been mine. Since she's lost forever, I plan to take Rana in her place."

"Like hell you will!" Nathan shouted in alarm, drawing his pistol and firing as Harrison simultaneously did the same.

Travis and Rana slipped from their horses and ran toward the fallen body of Nathan Crandall. He opened his eyes and smiled weakly at them. "I let him trap me," he confessed with remorse.

"Do not speak, Grandfather," Rana entreated with misty eyes and in a choked voice. "You must rest so your wound may heal."

"It's too late, girl," he murmured, then coughed as blood filled his lungs. As his strength and life began to ebb, he coaxed faintly, "Marry and be happy, like me and my Ruthie. I'll see her soon."

"Do not speak so, Grandfather," she scolded him in panic.

"Travis knows I can't make it, girl. He'll take care of you. Harry said he wanted you like he wanted Marissa," Nathan told them. With lagging strength, he repeated what Harrison had said.

"He lied, Grandfather. He wished to hurt you before he killed you. Mother did not know . . . my father was bad when she married him. Afterward, she was too proud to confess her mistake. She caused her own suffering, Grandfather, but she was going to change things. That last trip home, she had decided to leave . . . my father and return to you. She knew you would love us and protect us. It was not to be. Do not blame yourself. You are innocent. This I swear."

Nathan smiled at her. "You're a good girl, Rana. I love you."

"As I love you, Grandfather. Do not worry. We will save you."

Nathan grasped Travis's hand. "You've been a real son to me, Travis. These past years would have been empty without you. Take care of Rana. I know you love her and want her. The ranch belongs to you two." He coughed again and grew paler.

Travis looked beyond Nathan and saw that Harrison Caldwell was dead, and in that moment he understood that there was no hope for Nathan Crandall to survive. He held the dying man's hand tightly and vowed, "Don't worry about her, my father. You saved us all from Caldwell's evil. We'll be married under the white man's law very soon. We'll name our first son after you, Nate. You changed my life, and I won't ever forget that. I love you."

Nathan smiled again. "I love you, son. It's all over now, and you two can be free and happy. Don't mourn for me. I had a good life, a full one. You two made my last days happy. I can die in peace."

Nathan began to fade rapidly. His eyes fluttered and he called out, "Marissa, where are you, girl? Forgive me," he pleaded.

Rana glanced at Travis through tear-filled eyes and their gazes spoke. He nodded understanding, and she replied, "I am here, Father. I love you. I have come home to you."

"To stay?" he entreated, his mind dulled by imminent death.

"Yes, Father, to stay forever." Her heart thudded painfully.

"Will you forgive me for not helping you?" he pleaded.

"I forgive you, Father, if you will forgive me for hurting you."

"I love you, Missy," he murmured, using his pet name for Marissa.

"I love you too, Papa," she whispered in his ear and kissed his cheek. "Rest easy, Papa; I am home to stay."

Nathan smiled one last time, then relaxed in her arms, dying without ever learning of the tragic misconception that had tormented Marissa Crandall Michaels and had driven her from her home and love. "I love you, Father," she whispered one final time, knowing that the tragic secret would be buried with him and the Caldwells. The dark past was ending, and a bright future for Rana Michaels and Travis Kincade was beginning.

"I'm sorry, *micante*," Travis told her as he knelt beside the man who had saved his life long ago and had changed it so drastically. "He was like a real father to me. I know how you must be hurting."

"It is best he did not learn the truth. I will think of him as my grandfather, as it should have been. He is at peace now, as is my mother. The dangers have passed, and we must begin a new life."

By Friday, Nathan Crandall and the others had been buried. The sheriff had collected the evidence against Harrison Caldwell and notified the past owners or heirs of the Lazy *J*, Flying *M,* and Box *K* ranches to return and lay claim to them.

Since Harrison Caldwell had left a will naming Rana Michaels as his only heir, Travis and Rana discovered they owned a large, connecting spread that would one day belong to the child Rana was now certain she was carrying. With the other ranches being returned to their rightful owners, the area could be at peace once more.

Travis held Rana securely and tenderly within the circle of his arms as they stood before the mantel, staring up at Marissa's portrait. "She almost appears to be smiling at us," Travis remarked softly, nuzzling the side of her head.

Rana gazed into her mother's blue eyes, which did appear to be smiling down on them. "She has found peace, *mihigna*. The past is over. We are home, and we must begin our life together."

"I asked the preacher to come out Sunday after church to marry us. Cody and Mace are trying to keep it a secret, but they're planning a big party for us. We all know this is what Nate would have wanted us to do. Do you think we should tell everyone we're already married under Indian law?" he inquired, patting her stomach.

"You have found peace here. I do not wish others to learn of your Indian blood and torment you. They can say no words to harm me while I stand in your shadow," she declared decisively.

"It doesn't matter anymore, my love. I'm not ashamed to be half-blooded. My friends won't turn against me and others don't matter to me. I think we've all found peace, *micante*. You're not going to tell Todd anything, are you?" he ventured with mild curiosity.

"No, it is too late for such words to be a kindness."

"You sure you want to be doubly bound to me?" he teased, returning to a happier topic as he bent forward to nibble on her ear.

She quivered and warmed and leaned against him. "We are two people in each body; we must join two times."

"Good," he murmured as he turned her to face him. "That should make us twice as happy. White Eagle gets Wild Wind, and Travis Kincade gets Rana Michaels."

She looked into his eyes and smiled. "No, my love. I have you, and you have me. See, I have learned much English," she teased, then hugged him tightly. "Come, let us speak in a different way," she entreated, grasping his hand and leading him toward her room.

Saturday morning, Travis approached the family graveyard, which had been placed a mile from the house and beneath a lovely tree, whose sprawling limbs seemed to spread out protectively over those it guarded in their eternal sleep. The fence-enclosed space was a tranquil spot, and Travis had felt the need to visit it today to say a private farewell to Nathan Crandall.

Travis found Todd Raines standing over Marissa's grave, and he speculated that her funeral must have been a heartrending experience for Todd. Now there were three graves: Nathan's, Ruth's, and Marissa's. It had taken deaths to reunite them.

"I suppose I shouldn't be here," Todd murmured sadly. "It's the first time in years that I've allowed myself to visit her. It's hard to accept that they're both gone forever, Travis; they were such a big part of my life. I think the reason I could never get over her was because she left so suddenly; she left everything open and unsettled. I know a part of me will always love her and miss her, but I have a good wife who loves and needs me more than Marissa ever did or could. If I just knew why she deserted me, then I would be free of the past."

"I know what it's like to be chained to a dark past, Todd, and I wish I could help you. It's something only you can resolve."

Todd laughed. "When you rode up, I was thinking about Nate and all he did for me. He was practically a father to me too. He taught me most of what I know, or made sure I learned it. Not long before Marissa realized I was alive and set her sights on me, I had never been with a woman. You might say I was the shy, serious type. Nate said I needed to become a whole man, so he sent me to this house outside town in his place. He told me the girl wouldn't know any difference because he always insisted on darkness and no talking so he could pretend she was Ruthie for awhile. He told me he wasn't ever going to visit that whore again, so he sent me in his place to be educated. I never knew who she was, but I could tell she wanted to be any place but in bed with me. I couldn't blame her. Lordy, I was so clumsy and scared, and she didn't help relax me or teach me anything. I never went back there either, but I've never forgotten that night. In less than a month, I was seeing Marissa, and she was the only woman I wanted. She nearly destroyed me, but I think the pain would cease if I only knew why she rejected me for that no-good gambler."

Travis looked into Todd Raines's gray-blue eyes and watched the sun bring out the reddish gold highlights in his hair. He stared at Todd's eyes, his nose, his mouth, his expression. The truth was as clear to Travis as the blue sky overhead: Todd Raines had been the stranger Marissa had slept with that night; Todd Raines was Rana's father, not Nathan Crandall; and no one involved in that tragic incident had known the whole truth. Travis gingerly questioned Todd about that fateful night to make certain he was not mistaken. He was not.

Shortly thereafter, Travis returned to the house and told Rana what he had learned. She gave the matter careful thought and made her decision. "Perhaps I will be sorry one day, but I feel this must not remain our secret. To tell him I am his child gives him a new bond to the past, and that might be cruel, but he needs to hear the truth to be free. He is my father, and he has the right to know this. So many secrets in the past, and look what damage they have done. My mother's spirit cannot rest until it has made peace with the past, peace with her true love."

"You want me to bring him over here so you two can talk privately?" Travis inquired, knowing this would be hard on both of them.

Rana inhaled and nodded. "Yes, my love. Bring my father to me, and we will settle the past for all time."

"It's gonna hurt, Rana, but I think you're right."

She smiled at him. "As when you had to seek your past in the Hunkpapa camp, I must ride this lost trail alone and with courage. I will tell him all; then he can decide what to tell Rachel."

After Travis left to fetch Todd Raines, Rana retrieved Marissa's "treasures" from her closet. The wild winds that had blown destructively over Travis's life and over hers had been tamed and calmed. Their turbulent pasts were settled, and they had found love and peace together. It was time to allow Todd Raines, her father, the same opportunity for peace and contentment. She looked at Marissa's portrait and smiled. "Soon, Mother, you can rest peacefully. I have avenged the evil that befell you and I have returned your honor."

When Todd entered the room, his gaze first went to Marissa's image, then to Rana's face. Love and anguish filled his gaze, though he quickly tried to conceal his emotion. Yes, she decided, this was the right thing to do. She went to him and smiled. Taking his hand, she led him to the settee. She told him softly, "Sit. There is much I must tell you about me and my mother, secrets that have harmed many of us. It is time you knew all, so the pain and sadness can vanish from your eyes and life, as they have from mine."

Todd looked at the portrait of Marissa Crandall above him and protested, "Miss Rana, I don't think we should talk about your mother. That was long ago, and it was a bad time for me."

"Yes, *Father,* we must talk about it. We must end the secrets that drove her from your arms, for I am proof of her true love for you. As are these," she added, placing Marissa's keepsakes in his shaky hands. She smiled and nodded when he gaped at them, then at her. She murmured, "It is true; you are my father, and she loved only you. Now I must tell you all of it . . . ."

—— *Epilogue* ——

July 3, 1868

DEEP IN DAKOTA TERRITORY, in the Oglala camp, Lone Wolf was playing with his son while Myeerah nursed their daughter. The twins had been born on the eighth of March and they had been named Moon Flower and War Hawk. For the present, peace and happiness abounded in his lands and in his tepee. He looked at the *wanapin* around his son's neck and imagined how the child would grow to wear it proudly. He thought about his friend, Travis "White Eagle" Kincade, and his adopted sister, Rana "Wild Wind" Michaels, and he smiled, for he believed they too had found peace and happiness.

Myeerah looked at her husband and asked, "Why do you smile so?"

"My thoughts are of Wild Wind and White Eagle. I long to see them and speak with them. Peace fills our lands and hearts this moon, but soon a time will come when it is no longer this way. When that moon comes, I will take you and our children to live with White Eagle and Wild Wind. The season of the buffalo and the Lakota is fading swiftly, my love. We must change, or we must die. I wish our children to grow and be happy, as we are this moon. I wish them to know of their lands and people. White Eagle and Wild Wind will carry out my wishes. Many times I have dreamed of our children playing as one family. It will be so, Myeerah, for Grandfather has told me."

"Such evil days are far from this one, my husband. Forget them and share this flower of happiness."

Lone Wolf gazed into her eyes and smiled. "You are as cunning and quick as my sister, Wild Wind," he teased.

"Is that not good?" she playfully retorted, placing their daughter beside their sleeping son. They were children of one image, the image of Lone Wolf.

"Yes, it is good," he concurred, then drew her into his arms.

In Texas, on the Rocking C Ranch, Rana smiled at her husband as he entered the room. He strolled forward and looked down at her. "How're my two favorite girls today?" he asked. He watched Rana as she fed the tiny female child with fuzzy red hair and slate-colored eyes, and his heart overflowed with tenderness.

"We are fine, and happy, my love," she replied with a radiant smile. "Serrin Rose Kincade has been a very good girl today."

Travis looked at the tiny face and felt his heart lurch with joy. This bundle of bliss that had entered his life on the third of April had brought him great pride and contentment. He glanced at the shiny ring on Rana's finger, a wedding band made from the gold nuggets Sitting Bull and the Hunkpapas had allowed him to take. He had never told anyone where he had gotten them, and he never would reveal that secret.

One year ago this day, Travis had left her side to seek the gold. So much had changed during that year. Cody and Mary Beth Slade were expecting their first child. Todd and Rachel Raines had adopted a jolly baby boy and were waiting to adopt another. Bart and Lettie were happy together. Mace had fallen in love with a girl from a new family that had taken up residence nearby. The owners or heirs of the adjoining ranches had returned and their spreads were flourishing. The Rocking C Ranch was prospering far beyond anyone's imagining.

"You know who's been on my mind nearly all day?" he asked. Without waiting for her reply, he told her, "Lone Wolf. I've been doing some checking, and things are calm in that area at the moment. They've got new treaties and they should keep peace for a time. Maybe we can visit them as soon as they complete those railroads. If things get bad, we can encourage them to come live on our ranch."

"You are the kindest and most generous man I know. Lone Wolf will never leave his lands. They are a part of him, as the air he breathes or the blood of his body. Once I felt that way, but you entered my life and changed me. You, Travis Kincade, did what no other could do; you tamed the Wild Wind."

Travis laughed skeptically. "You're bound to me in two worlds, but you're still as free as a wild wind, and that's as it should be." Travis glanced at his twin son, who favored him, and he jested, "You never do anything halfway. You've made me doubly happy, Rana Michaels Kincade."

Rana joined him beside the cradles and looked down at their twins. Her arm slipped around his waist as she whispered, "Tanner Crandall Kincade is as impatient and demanding as his father. He is always first in everything: eating, wetting, crying, and loving. He is spoiled like his father."

Travis pulled her into his arms. "They're beautiful like you, Rana. I never imagined I could be this happy. The past seems so far away," he stated dreamily as he began to kiss a trail down her neck. "You aren't sorry you and Todd decided to keep the truth a secret?" he asked suddenly. "He's lost two ways; he can't claim his daughter or his grandchildren."

"He has another family and the truth would cause them suffering. The past is over." Rana turned to face him and mussed his sable hair. Her eyes met his and she coaxed, "The children are asleep, my love. Why do you not come and ride a wild wind?" She kissed him hungrily.

"Why not?" he teased. "If I can't tame it, I might as well enjoy it. I love you, Rana Kincade. Lordy, how I do love you!"

Midnight Secrets

In memory of

Roberta Bender Grossman

my publisher and friend who passed away on March 13, 1992.
I shall always remember this wonderful lady with
admiration and affection and with gratitude
for "discovering" me in April of 1981.
Everyone who knew Roberta and was
touched by her magic will miss her.

Dedicated to:

Rhonda Snider,
who has been like an adopted daughter to me for years, and still is

And,
Angelia "Angie" Holloway Hogan,
who also has been like an adopted daughter to me for years, and
still is

And,
Taylor Hogan,
Angie's first child and the Taylor family namesake

Acknowledgment and deep appreciation to the following individuals and staffs for their kind and generous help with research on this novel:

Ms. Darlene Martin, Chamber of Commerce, Jacksboro, TX
Ms. Judy Rayborn, Ft. Richardson State Park, Jacksboro, TX
Staff of Fort Leavenworth Museum in Ft. Leavenworth, KS
Pine Bluff Chamber of Commerce and Tour Center at Lake Village, AK
Chamber of Commerce, Museum, and Library at McAlester, OK
Welcome Centers at Kansas City, MO and Kansas City, KS
Welcome Center and Battlefield Museum at Vicksburg, MS
Museum at Fort Smith, AK
Garden of the Gods Campground at Colorado Springs, CO
People of Cripple Creek, CO (though I decided not to use their site)
Missouri Department of Natural Resources/Division of Parks & Historic Preservation at Jefferson City, MO
Welcome Center of AL
Welcome Centers and Tourist Bureaus of Savannah and Columbus, GA
The marvelous staff of the Augusta/Richmond County Library in Augusta, GA
And,
most of all, thanks to my husband, Michael, who made several long and rushed trips to videotape locations and to collect research materials.

Prologue

March 13, 1867
Savannah, Georgia

"**Y**OU AREN'T GOING TO DIE, Johanna Chapman; I won't let you."

"You heard what the doctor said, Ginny; it's too late."

"I won't let it be too late; I'll find a way to save you. I'll get another doctor to treat you. He'll make you well; you'll see."

"We must face the truth, Ginny; I'm going to die, very soon. There isn't much time. You must listen to me and do what I say."

"You aren't going to die. You mustn't talk. You need to rest to recover. Yesterday was strenuous for you, the move from the ship and the doctor's examination. It can't be your heart; you're only eighteen. He's mistaken."

"He said I have infection all through my body. That's why I have this fever, why I have trouble breathing, and every part of me is failing."

Ginny recalled the physician's grim words about Johanna's condition. "He's wrong about there being nothing we can do to get you well; there must be a medicine for what's wrong with you."

Johanna took a ragged breath and shook her head of matted curls. "He said there isn't. So did the doctor on the ship. There's nothing anyone can do to make me well. I've been ill for weeks and I'm sinking fast. I've accepted my fate, Ginny, and you must do the same."

"In the six years we've known each other, Johanna Chapman, have I ever lied to you?" After the girl shook her head, Ginny said, "You aren't going to die. I'll send for your father; he'll know what to do."

"You can't. I don't want him to see me end up this awful way."

A tearful and frightened Ginny said, "We've come this far, Johanna, all the way from England to America. We can't stop now; we won't. We'll make it to Texas as soon as you've recovered."

"You're ignoring reality, Ginny, and that isn't like you: I'm not going to get well, ever. I may only have a little while left."

Virginia Anne Marston looked at the feeble young woman who had been her best friend, like a sister to her, for years. She couldn't believe this tragedy was happening; she couldn't allow it to happen. Yet, there was nothing she or medicine could do to save Johanna. They needed a miracle and had prayed for one, but her dear friend worsened every hour. With tears in her hazel eyes, she vowed, "No, I won't believe that. I can't."

"You have to go on to Texas and take my place. You must do what I was going to do. If Father's guilty, you have to punish him for me and Mother."

"Don't think or talk about that trouble today. You need rest. You must take the medicine the doctor left for you; it will ease your pain."

"I need a clear head to think; I don't have much time left."

"Don't give up, Johanna, please. Fight this illness."

"I don't have any fight left in me, Ginny. I'm as weak as a baby. I can't even tend or feed myself."

"Let's talk tomorrow when you're stronger."

"I won't be here tomorrow. We have to settle this today."

"At least nap for a while. I'll get you some hot soup. You hardly ate this morning or at the noon meal. You can't get well if you don't try."

"I'm not hungry, and I'm losing this battle fast. I want to spend my last hours talking with you. Don't deny me that much."

Ginny felt as if each word was a knife in her heart. She wanted to be strong and brave for her best friend, but it was hard. "In a year, we'll be discussing the doctor's mistake over hot tea and scones."

"Don't dream, Ginny; it isn't fair to either of us. You must go to Father and pretend to be me. You must punish him."

"What if your father isn't guilty?" She thought of their recent discovery of a hidden compartment in Johanna's mother's trunk filled with letters from Johanna's father. It had also concealed money that had provided payment for their trip from England to America to reunite Johanna with her father and to aid Ginny's search for hers. "Remember the letters we found in your mother's trunk after she . . . passed away?" She watched in anguish as the girl struggled to speak between gasps for air and increasing exhaustion. She mopped beads of feverish perspiration from her friend's face with a cool cloth. She witnessed torment in Johanna's eyes and heard it in her voice.

"If Mother lied about him betraying and discarding us, why didn't Father contact me during all those years? Why didn't he come after me or send for me? Why didn't he fight for me? He abandoned her for another woman; he adopted an orphan boy and let him take my place. He loved and wanted them, Ginny, not us. He must pay for what he did. Mother died in England. I'll die returning to confront him. His selfishness destroyed us, Ginny. He must suffer as we have. I can't exact revenge; you must do it for me. Please, I'm begging you. This is my last request, my dying wish. You're my dearest and best friend, my sister in heart and soul. I can't rest until the past is settled. Only you can do that for me."

Ginny fought back tears as she watched the near-breathless girl work hard to get out those bitter words. "I love you, Johanna, but I can't pull off such a ruse. I'd never fool your father and adopted brother."

"You know everything about me, Mother, and my past. You know everything revealed in those letters we found. They can't catch you in a lie, you have all the facts. You can become me and you can obtain justice or revenge for us. We even look so much alike that people have always believed we were sisters. You can use our resemblance and all that information to fool them."

"If I failed, they could have me imprisoned for fraud, or even killed if they're as bad as you and your mother believe." Ginny kept talking to let Johanna rest for a while. "Besides, I have to search for my own father in Colorado. I haven't seen him since I was sent away to boarding school in London, six long years ago. I haven't heard from him in over eight months. I miss him and I'm so worried about him. He said someone had murdered his mining partner and was trying to kill him. He told me to keep his whereabouts secret and to remain in England until he settled his troubles and either came for me or sent for me to join him. I'm the only one from home who knows he didn't die in the war as reported."

"Your father must be dead, Ginny. If he were alive, he would have written again. If you go to Colorado unprepared and penniless, you'll be vulnerable, in terrible danger. We're almost out of money, so you don't have any safe way to get there. If you go to Father's ranch and pretend to be me, you can find a way to get money for your search. It will solve your dilemma, too."

"I couldn't steal from Bennett Chapman and escape scot-free."

"If it's necessary, you could; you must. You know you can't return home. Your stepmother and her new Yankee husband have taken control of Green Oaks. Your father has been declared dead. She ordered you never to return to the plantation; she cut off your funds."

"I know, and I hate it that I'll never see my half sister. She was born after I was sent away. My stepmother and her son were always malicious and devious. I can't go there or let them know I'm back. If it hadn't been for your mother's kindness, I couldn't have finished my last year at school. I would have been put out to fend for myself without funds, home or family and in a strange country." A bitter taste rose in Ginny's throat when she had to speak favorably of Johanna's mother whom she hadn't liked or trusted. Ginny knew Johanna had persuaded her mother to pay her expenses and the woman had done so to keep Johanna distracted and removed from her ill-gotten lifestyle. "When I locate Father, I'll repay the money she loaned to me."

"What's mine is yours, Ginny; it's always been that way between us. I don't need or want your money; I want and need your help, your promise."

Ginny wished her own mother were alive to give advice, but she had died when Ginny was eleven. That death had compelled her lonesome and tormented father into a terrible second marriage.

As if reading her line of thought, Johanna said, "Cleniece took your mother's place and Nandile took mine. Our fathers were foolish men."

"I can't blame Father for marrying again; he was so lost without Mother. But our lives would have been different if he hadn't met and married that greedy, selfish, and conniving woman. He thought I needed a mother and Green Oaks needed a mistress. He believed she would take away his pain. All Cleniece did was make us both miserable. She never liked me or wanted me around and convinced Father to send me away to school. I know he agreed because he wanted me safe and happy while he was off fighting in the war. He didn't trust her; that's why he deposited enough money in a London bank to pay my expenses for five years. He never thought the war would last so long; no one did. I would have been fine if Cleniece had sent my money. You remember Father sent me money directly from Colorado until he vanished. He was angry when he learned she had refused to support me, but he couldn't challenge her without revealing he was still alive. That witch believed I would be stranded across the ocean and be out of her hair for keeps."

Ginny helped Johanna with a drink of water and fluffed her pillows. She kept talking to make the girl stay silent and rest. "I know she and her new husband stole my home and inheritance, but I won't fight them over it. Green Oaks couldn't be the same after they've tainted it. But if they learned Father wasn't killed in the war, that he was captured and sent west as a Galvanized Yankee, and that he'd found a silver mine—they would try to lay claim to part of it. That's partly why Father refuses to contact her. After he sneaked home when the war ended and found her married to that Yankee usurper, a man my half sister believed was her father, he decided it was best to stay dead to them. His new trouble started after he returned to Colorado. How could anyone believe my father could murder a friend and partner for his share of their mine? It's absurd, and I'll help him prove it. I memorized the map he sent to me, then I destroyed it. I know how to find his cabin and I know where the claim map is hidden."

"Knowing the culprit's identity won't protect you from harm, Ginny. It's in the wilderness. Haven't you heard of wild animals and Indians?"

"I realize my plan is dangerous, but if Father is in trouble, I must help him. If he's dead, I have to make certain his killer is punished."

"Just as I have to make certain our family's betrayer and killer is punished."

"I know this man is guilty; we don't know if your father is guilty."

"He's guilty of forcing Mother to escape him all the way to England. She wouldn't run away without a good reason. When he cut off our funds to force her to come back, she still refused. For a wife to go penniless rather than return home to a rich husband does not speak well for my father. He forced Mother to become that earl's mistress to survive."

"She loved the earl, Johanna; she said so."

"The earl didn't love her. If he had, he would have divorced his wife and he wouldn't have cut off my support the moment her body was cold after promising to take care of me. At least he had the decency to return her belongings."

"Those letters we found from your father disturb me, Johanna. They contradict so many of the horrible things your mother told you about him."

"He never said he loved her or wanted her, only me, his possession. He offered to *bribe* her to return, no doubt to avoid a scandal or because he couldn't stand to lose something that belonged to him. I wonder how he explained our departure to everyone?"

"We're judging him on what your mother told you, Johanna. What if she was speaking from hurt and bitterness? What if she was being vindictive? He said she could have freedom and great wealth if she'd come home or if she would send you home: we don't know what that means. He begged for forgiveness and understanding for his past misdeeds, whatever they were, or she believed they were. He can't be all bad, Johanna. He even admitted he was selfish, a coward. He said he'd made mistakes and that he was sorry for them. We know what two of them were—his mistress and adopted son—but we don't know the story behind them." Ginny spoke with conviction, yet, she couldn't help but wonder if that assumption was correct. Bennett Chapman could be a terrible person. His "son" could be the same, as bad and mean as her own stepbrother.

Ginny looked sadly at her dear, sweet, funny, beautiful Johanna. They had been inseparable for years. They gave each other courage, strength, and solace; they were always there for each other during the good and bad times. *Don't take her from me, God.* "You're asking me to deceive your father by impersonating you when you'll be . . ."

"Gone, dead and buried here, under your name, Ginny."

Tears escaped Ginny's eyes and she quickly brushed them away to prevent upsetting Johanna. "Don't say such things; I can't bear them."

"Don't you see? If you're allegedly gone, your stepfamily will leave you alone while you search for your father. If they learn you're here, they might guess why. That could be dangerous and costly for you and your father. Before you go to him, you can settle matters for me."

"What if I can't unravel this mystery? Surely Bennett Chapman isn't going to confess any serious misdeeds. Maybe he didn't do anything wrong, Johanna. There's far more to the story than your mother or those letters revealed."

"If that were true, he would have tried to get me back. He didn't."

"According to your mother," Ginny reminded gently.

"A man with his power and wealth could have defeated my mother with ease. He had ways and means of reclaiming me. He didn't. He was too busy with his *son* to miss me or care what happened to me. He's twenty-five now, seven years older than I am. Father may have *grandchildren* by now. Even if he refused to support or contact Mother, he owed me those things. He won't even know Mother and I are dead until you tell him. That's wrong and cruel. A few short letters in sixteen years don't make up for his offenses. I deserve retribution or a logical explanation. I can't die in peace until you swear you'll get it for me because I know you won't break your word."

Ginny tried to soothe her friend's agony. "You were taken away when you were two years old, so you don't even know him. If he wasn't being honest in those letters, he'll probably pretend he was the victim of your mother's tricks. How will I know if he's lying?"

"You're intelligent; you'll know. You can watch him for clues. After he exposes himself, find a way to hurt him as he hurt us."

"*If* he's guilty. If not, what do I do? He'll be furious when he learns I'm not his daughter. He'll be devastated to discover the bitter truth."

"Not if you remain there as me."

"What do you mean? Live the rest of my life as Johanna Chapman?"

"Why not? My father is rich and powerful. He deserted me as a child; he owes me plenty. You can collect that debt for me. I'm his rightful heir, not his mistress and adopted son. There's no way anyone could ever learn the truth. It's the perfect solution for both of us. If he's guilty, drain him and punish him. If he's not, make peace and make him happy. You'll have a home, safety, all you need, for as long as you need them."

"What about *my* father?"

"You left word at school where you could be reached. If your father is alive and contacts you, then you can tell mine the truth. I'll write a letter explaining how I forced you to do this for me as my last dying wish. Find the truth for me, Ginny, so I can rest in peace."

"Let's not talk about this anymore. Please rest now and take your medicine. I know you're weak, and in pain. I can see it."

"This is the last time we'll have to talk, Ginny; I feel it all over. I can endure a little pain to spend these final hours with you. I don't want to die drugged or in my sleep or with things left unsaid."

Ginny had to relent once more. "How will I get to Texas?"

"You know where the ranch is located."

"You heard what Mr. Avery said: Train rails were cut during the war and haven't been repaired. He said stagecoach travel is worse. We were going to telegraph your father after we docked and ask for money or transportation. If I contact him and he comes here, he might discover the truth. He could send your adopted brother after me. I doubt he will be happy to have a blood heir suddenly appear."

"You were planning to travel all the way to Colorado by yourself anyhow. You'll find a way. Mr. Avery will help. Remember how he took us under his wing on the ship, how he protected us. He's a good and kind man. He helped tend me after I became ill during the voyage; he brought me here, summoned a doctor to treat me, and he and his sister are taking care of us. You know he's heading for Texas. He'll take you along with him."

"But he knows I'm not you, Johanna. He'll wonder why I'm lying."

"We can trust him, Ginny. He'll take you with him; you'll see."

"Take Virginia along with me to where?" Charles Avery asked as he entered the gloomy sickroom.

"Mr. Avery, we desperately need your help."

"No, Johanna, we can't do this. I can't do this," Ginny protested.

Though he was two inches under six feet tall, Charles sat on the edge of the bed to keep from towering over them. "Do what, young ladies?"

"Ginny must pretend to be me and get to my father's ranch in Texas. She's in danger here from her stepfamily. After I'm dead and buried as Ginny Marston she can travel there with you as Johanna Chapman."

Charles patted the sick girl's arm. "That isn't possible, Johanna dear. Only families are allowed on the wagontrain. These people are moral Christians. They wouldn't allow an unmarried young woman to travel west with a single older man, friend or not. And Virginia can't take her own wagon; they're scarce and expensive, so are supplies and mules."

Johanna gazed into his clear blue eyes that mutely apologized for having to disappoint her. At least he hadn't pretended she would recover. "She has to reach Texas, sir. Her father has enemies in Georgia and out West who might want her slain or captured. She must pretend to be me and go to Texas until she can contact him to come for her there. Father and I were going to help her. Now that I'm dying, things have changed."

Charles Avery ran his hand through his graying brown hair. He stood and said, "Let me think for a minute."

As he did so, Ginny helped Johanna with more water to wet her dry throat. They had met the lean, fifty-four-year-old Georgian on the ship from England.

They had talked every day, shared activities and amusements, eaten together, and become good and trusted friends. He had protected them from unwanted attention by sailors and other male voyagers. He had helped Ginny with Johanna after she took ill.

"I must get to Texas to my new business before the seller moves and leaves it abandoned. I can use assistance with the wagon and chores. By helping you, I'll be helping myself. She can travel as my daughter. She's the same age and physical type as Anna. The poor girl was in school up North during the war and she died recently on her way home so no one will be the wiser." Both girls looked away to give him privacy as he wiped sudden tears from his eyes. "It will be hard work, Virginia; you'll have to learn to drive a wagon and work along the trail like everyone else. The men are meeting with Steve Carr, our scout and guide, next week for training. I'm to get my wagon ready and join them Wednesday. The group is gathering at the Ogeechee River east of town. Most are heading west for new lives. The war and that so-called Reconstruction Act have ruined things for Southerners. The women begin training as soon as we finish our own, in a week or so."

Johanna grasped Ginny's hand and squeezed it with her remaining strength. "I'm begging you to do this favor for me. We've been like sisters. You know I would do it for you. Please."

"It's a wild scheme, Johanna. I could fail or get into terrible trouble."

"They'll never guess the truth. Only you and Mr. Avery will know it."

"I will not betray your confidences," Charles Avery assured. "I'll do whatever I can to help."

"Thank you, Mr. Avery. Do it, Ginny; for me, for us."

"You win, Johanna: I swear I'll carry out your last request, but only if you take at least a little of your medicine, eat something, and rest."

"That sounds like a fair bargain to me," Charles said. "I'll fetch a tray."

"Thank you, Mr. Avery. Thank you, Ginny."

Near midnight, Johanna Chapman died with Virginia Marston sitting beside her and holding her hands. She wept while Charles Avery and his elder sister, Martha, tried to comfort her. He said he would handle the burial arrangements and pay for them; he would have the young woman interred under Ginny's name. He told Ginny it would be best if she stayed in Savannah with his sister until he came for her, which would allow her time and privacy to deal with her grief and to prepare for her journey.

Ginny thanked them for their kindness and assistance. A clock chimed midnight. So many dark secrets engulfed her. She had made Johanna a deathbed promise that she must honor. With her final breath, Johanna Chapman had thanked her, then smiled and gone to sleep forever.

—— *Chapter 1* ——

❧

TWELVE DAYS LATER, Virginia Anne Marston's hazel eyes scanned the crowded and noisy area where a temporary camp was set up on the western bank of the Ogeechee River. Ginny watched the women gathered in a clearing for their instructions. Many of the fourteen laughed and chatted as if they were close friends. She reminded herself they had been given ample time to get acquainted while living there for a week or more while their husbands received their training.

"Miss Avery!" Steve Carr's sharp tone pierced her distraction. He shook her arm until she looked at him. "I need your attention, as well as your body, here this morning. We have no time to waste."

Ginny's face grew warm and flushed with embarrassment. She hadn't realized their guide had arrived and begun their lesson. "I apologize, sir, and it will not happen again," she told him. His eyes were so dark brown that they appeared as ebony as his shoulder-grazing hair. She pushed other thoughts out of her mind and came to alert, thoroughly unsettled.

"Good. As I was saying, ladies, let's introduce ourselves. You'll be living and working as one big family for a long time, so it's best to get off to a friendly start. Some of you are already acquainted, but some have been shy and kept to yourselves; and we have one new arrival this morning."

Ginny felt all gazes look in her direction for a moment.

"Sometimes you'll work alone or with your family, and other times you'll work as a group. Obedience and cooperation are a must on the trail; you are never to let personal dislikes or disagreements interfere with our purpose for being here. My name is Steve Carr; I'm your guide, scout, leader, and boss—whatever you want to call me. I'm in total control of this trip. If you can't obey me without hesitation, don't come along. If you do come with us and cause trouble along the way, you'll be left on that spot. That might sound cruel, but it's for everyone's protection. Is that clear?"

Ginny watched those dark eyes journey from woman to woman and observe each nod her head in understanding and acceptance.

She wished he hadn't embarrassed her over an innocent mistake, and when his gaze reached hers, she said, "I'll obey your orders, Mr. Carr. My name is Anna Avery. I'm Charles Avery's daughter. My father and I are moving from Savannah to Texas." Ginny noticed how Steve's powerful gaze lingered on her as if trying to penetrate her deceptive veil, or maybe that was just guilt gnawing at her for deluding these people, most of whom seemed nice.

"To get under way as soon as possible, ladies, be on time for training and practice every morning and afternoon. We'll start promptly at nine, give you a two-hour break at noon to tend your children, work until five, and quit for you to get your meals cooked, chores done, and children down for the night. The education you're about to receive will move at a swift pace. It will be hard. You'll be sore and exhausted, especially in the beginning. And some of you will be as fussy as a hungry baby past feeding time. But don't let the hardships and pains get to you. When the training is over, you'll be able to take charge of your team and wagon if anything ever happens to your husband . . . or father," he added with a quick glance at the only unmarried female present. "You'll practice along the way to keep your new skills honed. There'll be times when the men need to rest or to ride ahead to hunt fresh meat or cut firewood, so you'll be in charge of driving the wagon to camp."

Steve looked at each woman to make certain all were paying attention. "Today, we'll learn how to harness and tend your team, how your wagon works, and how to take care of it so it won't break down along the way. You won't always be able to ride, so we'll exercise daily to improve your pace, strength, and stamina. This afternoon, we'll begin with a mile walk."

"Walk a mile? After work?" Mattie Epps complained.

"Yes, and tomorrow we'll do the same. We'll increase the distance every two days by a mile. By the time we're finished, you should be able to walk five miles before riding to rest. With possessions and children and sometimes soft ground, too heavy a load will overburden the mules. If you don't take care of your animals, they won't get you far. Treat them as you would family, or better, in some cases. Your lives may depend on them."

"Why couldn't we use oxen, Mr. Carr?" Ellie queried. "They eat free grass, not high grain; and we could eat them later. Why mules?"

"Mules get five miles a day more than oxen, Mrs. Davis," Steve explained to the stout woman. "Every three days by mule team shortens your journey by a day over oxen. What you spend on grain will be less than what you would have spent on added supplies for yourselves on a longer ride. You can't eat mules, unless you get mighty desperate, but they're easier to manage and harness and they make good plow animals. Besides, outlaws don't steal a tough, stringy mule as quickly and easily as a plump, tasty ox."

As Steve grinned, other women smiled and laughed. *A sense of humor to break the tension,* Ginny decided. He sounded educated and he knew good manners, even if he had been curt to her earlier.

"What all do we have to learn?" Mattie Epps whined.

"Driving the wagon, controlling and maneuvering it, circling up for camp and safety, keeping the right pace and distance, crossing rivers, getting out of mud, repairing and replacing broken wheels, calming teams during storms, and defending yourself—things like that!"

"*Defending ourselves?* From whom?" Mattie asked.

"From bandits and raiders who still roam the land and prey on people," he explained. "If any of you have special feeding times for babies, let me know so I can set our schedule for walks around them."

Considerate, too, Ginny's impressed mind added. She noticed how he had hurried past his first sentence, perhaps to avoid scaring them.

"Any of you ladies know how to harness and handle a team already?"

Ginny watched three of the fourteen women raise their hands. She was relieved she wasn't the only novice in camp.

"How many can ride a horse?" he asked.

All but four hands lifted, and Virginia Anne Marston was delighted she was a skilled rider. She wondered if she should tell him she couldn't ride western-style but she decided not to do so, as it couldn't be much different from English sidesaddle.

"How many of you can load and fire a weapon?"

Ginny noticed how the leader grinned when everyone raised a hand, but something wasn't right about those smiles and grins. *Forced?* she mused.

"Is anyone carrying a child?" He waited a moment then pressed, "Speak up if it's true. I don't want your life or that of the baby endangered. As I told you, this is going to be a tough pace and hard work." No woman responded so Steve continued. "Do any of you have a physical problem that might affect your training or interfere with chores along the way?"

Lucy Eaves raised her hand. "I have a gimp ankle," she said, "but it rarely gives me any trouble."

Steve glanced at the slightly twisted ankle she revealed by lifting her hem. "Be sure to let me know if it does."

"Yes, sir," Lucy replied with a cheerful smile.

"Any questions or comments before we get started?" Steve's alert gaze drifted from one woman to the next around the circle enclosing him. He didn't care for this pretense of liking and helping these people, but he would do his job and do it to the best of his ability. As soon as he unmasked the culprit he was searching for, he could turn this group over to the genuine wagontrain leader who was awaiting them near the west Georgia line. "Let's get to how a wagon works and how to take care of it," he began his instructions. "Jeff Eaves, Lucy's husband, has loaned us the use of his wagon for today's lesson. Let's gather there," he told them, pointing to it.

Steve looked at the beauty who kept—annoyingly—snagging his eye and interest. "I don't think you want to train in that fancy dress, Miss Avery," he remarked. To everyone, he said, "It's best to wear your oldest clothes, ladies, not things you don't want ruined. If you own pants, those will be easier for you to move around and work in. Don't worry about looking stylish during lessons or on the trail; we'll all be too tired to notice. Let's move out now," he ordered as if leading a cattle drive to market.

The others headed toward Lucy Eaves's wagon, but Steve blocked the disquieting lady's way and asked, "Why don't you make a quick change? I'd hate to see that pretty dress spoiled; and so will you. If you hurry, you won't hold us up too long." He turned and strolled toward the other women, all of whom observed the scene with interest.

Ginny stared into his retreating back before she rushed to the Avery wagon where her trunks were stored. His two remarks had stung. She searched for something more appropriate than the promenade dress she was wearing. When she had dressed this morning in town, she hadn't considered proper attire for her lessons today. She took out a green skirt and blouse and, after drawing the privacy cord, changed clothes. As she fumbled with buttons in her rush not to "hold them up too long," she fumed, *If that was a compliment about my wardrobe, it came through the back door!* Her mother used to tell her, "Pretty is as pretty does." The same was true of handsome, and the leader certainly wasn't behaving that way. March 24, 1867, was not going to be an easy day, she fretted, if he continued to behave in this critical manner.

When Ginny rejoined the others, Steve looked her over with an expression that seemed to ask, *Are those the oldest and worst clothes you own?* She exchanged smiles with Lucy Eaves and Ellie Davis, ignoring him.

"Now, ladies, we can get started." As he pointed out parts of the wagon and harnesses, he explained their functions and care.

Ginny observed the guide with annoyance, baffled by his mercurial ways. He was on one knee as he motioned to the underpinnings of the wagon and detailed its construction. His voice was like gently rippling water as his inflections altered during his explanation. His expression was unreadable. He performed his task with skill and ease, but she sensed he was thinking about something else. Her gaze drifted over his face where not a scar or flaw was visible. Along his chiseled jawline and above his perfect mouth was the dark stubble of one day's beard growth, instead of ill-kempt, it made him appear mysterious and virile. His soft hair was as black and shiny as a raven's wing beneath the sun. She remembered he was tall, about six feet and three inches. Her eyes swept past his face of strong, rugged, and appealing features to shoulders that evinced their broadness and strength through the dark-blue cotton shirt that pulled snugly over his torso as he moved his arms to point out different areas of the wagon.

Ginny found it odd that two pistols were strapped around his waist in a camp so close to civilization. Stranger to her was the fact that they were secured with thongs to his muscled thighs in the manner she had viewed in photographs of western cowboys and gunslingers. The weapons, the initials S. C. intricately carved into the butts and resting in artistically hand-tooled holsters, looked as much a part of him as his darkly tanned flesh. No doubt they provided an important clue to his character; just as the sheathed knife that was strapped to his left leg with its handle peeking over the edge of well-worn boots should tell her he was a man who would defend himself with prowess. She wondered what this man did when he was not guiding wagontrains west, and if he were married or had a sweetheart. Surely there was far more to him, she concluded, than met the naked eye. It was unnervingly evident to her that concentration would be the toughest part of her training with a man like this as her teacher.

Steve was accustomed to doing and thinking more than one thing at a time, so he knew the beautiful female was studying him and not listening again. He almost corrected her but found it amusing that such a refined lady would find a rough man like him worth her scrutiny. He would be astonished if she could endure the training period; probably within two days she would be begging her father to remain in civilized Savannah, whining peevishly. Surely Anna had been a spoiled, pampered, and wealthy southern belle before the North had challenged the South; and it didn't appear as if the war had changed those things for her.

From his observation during the men's training, Charles Avery had not struck him as a scalawag—those greedy and traitorous Southerners who sided with Northern conquerors. He, for one, would never forget or forgive what certain Yankees had done to him in that Union prison after his capture at Shiloh. *Shu,* he had been a fool to get involved in a war that had nothing to do with him.

This particular mission wasn't to his liking, either. Unmasking the cunning man and the illegal group of his that was reported to be using this wagontrain as a cover for transporting stolen gems to a contact out West wasn't the bad part; duping these fine people was. But he always did as ordered. Somehow and someway, he must locate the sinister shipment and stop it from reaching its destination. He must prevent it from being exchanged for arms and ammunition for the Red Magnolias—a band in the Invisible Empire, the dreaded Ku Klux Klan—to use in their evil schemes. The leader of that group was clever; he knew valuable gems would not leave deep telltale wagon ruts as hauling heavy gold would and that the stones could be secreted many places in a loaded wagon or hidden compartment. It was up to him to find the treasure and to expose the culprits responsible.

To keep his mind off Miss Anna Avery, Steve looked at the gentle redhead, Ruby Amerson, who was trying to take in every word he spoke. A young mother of two babies, one a few months old and the other a little over a year, this training period was not going to be easy for her, he was sure, but she had a determined look in her eyes. He liked and respected that, and there weren't many people who extracted those feelings in him. He would do whatever necessary to get to know these people quickly so he could complete his mission and move on to his next challenge.

A child's piercing squeal had captured Ginny's attention; the guide suddenly appeared before her and said her borrowed name with cutting sharpness. Startled, she jumped and jerked her gaze to his scowling face.

"Miss Avery, you can't learn if you don't listen," he admonished with a tone seemingly meant to make her tremble in dread of punishment.

Unaccustomed to the assumed name, she hadn't responded to it immediately. She didn't like being scolded like an errant child. They exchanged challenging looks for a moment before his chilling gaze cleared her head. "I'm sorry, Mr. Carr, but I heard a child scream. I looked to see if anything was wrong."

"Children yell all the time when they're playing, Miss Avery, and I presume their fathers are tending them as ordered."

"Yes, sir," she responded to end the matter. She was miffed by his tone before the other women, who were watching in silence. Her new assessment of him was of an arrogant, rude, and demanding man.

As if reading her dark thoughts, he asked, "Why don't you help me show how to grease axles? That should keep your mind where it should be."

"I'd be delighted," she conceded as she struggled to conceal her vexation and embarrassment. Ginny noticed that only one female, a dark-haired beauty named Cathy King, seemed to find the situation entertaining.

"You'll need the grease bucket from the back," he told her, as if to let her know he didn't intend to wait on her or the others as a servant.

Ginny made her way through the group of women to the location he had pointed out earlier. Lucy, Ellie, and Ruby sent her encouraging smiles. She lifted the container from a hook and returned to her now-grinning teacher with his irritating smirk of victory. She herself did not smile as she asked, "What now?"

Steve took the bucket with a mixture of tar and animal fat, pulled out the swab, and demonstrated on one axle how to apply it in the right places and amounts. "Now, you try it on the other three."

Ginny did her best to repeat his actions. The other women followed her from wheel to wheel to observe. At the last one, she asked Steve, who had been silent along the way, if she had done the task correctly.

"All right for a beginner; you'll do better with practice. Just make sure you don't get distracted and miss a wheel or a spot. If you do, it's certain trouble." He half turned to tell the others to take a break. "But be back here at two sharp, ladies," he added.

In her annoyed state, Ginny let the swab fall lower and stain her skirt. She didn't understand why he was picking on her, unless something he'd been thinking had put him in a bad mood. When she saw what she'd done, she exhaled in irritation. She commanded herself not to let the contradictory man get to her like this.

"It's probably ruined," Steve observed, "but I warned you to wear old clothes."

"These are my oldest clothes," she retorted in a frosty tone and with a matching glare meant to silence him.

"Then you're damned lucky, Miss Avery. The others aren't as fortunate as you are. I hope you'll do your best not to create envy in them with your good looks and fine clothes."

That's a curious way to compliment a lady after you've humiliated her. "I'll do my best to behave in all respects, sir," she said, her voice dripping sarcasm. "You don't have to be so rude and mean. 'Never let personal dislikes or disagreements interfere with our purpose for being here,' you said earlier. As our leader, mine included, you could follow your own advice and be nice."

His teeth almost gritted out his reply. "I'm not here to be nice, only to get you and the others out West. If I relax as much as you've done this morning, someone could get hurt or killed. Distractions and weaknesses are dangerous. I'm paid to see that everyone—and that means you, too—arrives safe and alive; and I will, in any way necessary, even if it means being 'rude and mean.' I can't afford to be too friendly with people in my charge. If I am, some get lax, take advantage, or get rebellious. I'm sure a charming lady like you will make plenty of friends without needing me as one. See you later."

As he walked away, Ginny wondered what in the world that chiding was about, or if it even referred to her minor misconduct. She hoped he hadn't chosen her to be his example of what happened when he was disobeyed or angered. She didn't need his verbal abuse, not after what she'd suffered recently.

So what if he does have the responsibility of eighty-four people and the displeasing task of training fifteen women! she fumed. *He chose it, so he could be at least pleasant and polite.*

As her thoughts sank in, Ginny realized the seriousness of his job. Maybe he had to be bossy and demanding to maintain authority, discipline, and cooperation.

In the past, she'd had teachers like that, and their tough tactics had, in fact, worked to keep their classes in control.

In all honesty, she had provoked him, however unintentionally. She hadn't paid attention or taken the lessons with the gravity they deserved. Perhaps her conduct had come across as an air of superiority. She didn't think she was any better than anyone here. In fact, that moody guide would be surprised by what she had endured and by what loomed before her.

Ginny absently brushed at the axle-grease stain. It not only smeared but had stuck to her hand. She replaced the bucket and headed to the wagon she would share with Charles Avery, her alleged father. He had returned to town to see someone and wouldn't be back for a few days. That was good, for it gave her privacy, fewer chores, and it meant he wouldn't witness her problems before she could correct them.

She wrapped a handkerchief around her sticky hand and sat inside the wagon to stay out of view while she ate the chicken and biscuits she had brought with her. Other women were busy cooking their food or feeding their families or cleaning up after a cozy meal. She shouldn't feel guilty about not having as many chores as they did, or for having more time to rest between training periods. They were the lucky ones; they knew how to cook outside—how to cook period! She had helped Charles's sister Martha for over a week with household chores, but she had only cooked on a stove and never unattended. She stared at the pots in the wagon as if they were enemies out to get her. As much as possible, she must observe the other women and learn from them, preferably while still camped for the week. She could imagine how her ignorance in those areas would amuse Steve Carr, and no matter what she had to do to conceal her inexperience from him, she would do just that.

Ginny changed her skirt and headed to the river with soap to remove the grease from the stained one and from her hand. She knelt on a large, flat rock to work on her smelly fingers. The combination of animal fat and tar was stubborn and resisted her strongest efforts to remove it; and instead of coming off, it spread to clean areas to make a worse mess. What should—

"Use this," Steve offered over her shoulder.

Ginny jumped in surprise. "You move as quietly as a feather falling. What is it?" she asked, looking at the metal cup he was holding.

"Kerosene; it'll cut the grease. Just don't get near a flame until it's scrubbed off or you'll light up the area like a roaring wildfire. Better put cream on afterward; both of those mixtures are harsh on soft hands."

She accepted the cup of strong-smelling flammable liquid and thanked him, wondering how he knew where she was and what she was doing, and why he was being nice suddenly. She rubbed it over her hands, grateful it removed the tar. As instructed, she thoroughly scrubbed them with soap afterward.

Steve had concluded he was being too tough on Anna Avery if he was to get close enough to learn anything from her—if she and her father *were* his target, that was. Clearly she wasn't acquainted with household chores or she'd know lamp oil took off tar, so he hadn't been wrong about her pampered rearing. As she lifted her skirt to pour kerosene on its blackened area, he warned, "It'll take the color out and weaken the cloth in that area." Her response made him chuckle.

"Better faded and thin than to have a sticky mess. I can't use it again like this." She didn't look at him as she added, "It'll give me something imperfect to wear during lessons, which should please you."

She was surprised that Steve didn't comment on her last remark, but he didn't leave, either. She felt his potent gaze on her as she labored on the stain. She warmed and trembled, despite the friction between them. When her task was finished and she saw the truth of his warning, she washed and returned his cup. Holding up the garment, she murmured, "Ruined, but better. Thanks for the help."

"You're welcome, Miss Avery."

As she prepared her items to leave, she looked at him and asked, "I'm not late for class, am I? You didn't come to scold me?"

"No, you have half an hour left. Have you eaten?"

She returned to gathering her things. "Dirty hand and all." When he chuckled, she glanced at him and clarified his apparent amusement, "I wrapped it in a handkerchief so I wouldn't get tar on my food."

"I didn't see you build a fire or cook."

"I ate leftovers."

"From town, because your father ate with James and Mary Wiggins yesterday before he went to fetch you."

"I stayed in town with . . . my aunt, Father's sister, until you were ready for the women."

"A last farewell, eh? More comfortable there?"

"I wouldn't know; I've never lived or traveled on the road before for a comparison. Father insisted I stay there while you men were busy."

"It must have given him a good opportunity to make friends. The way these families are spread out across Georgia and the Carolinas, no one seemed to know any of the others until they came here. Your father must have gotten to know them by eating with a different one each night."

Ginny wondered what was behind his inquisitiveness. Wasn't, she mused, this curious behavior for a man who gave her the impression he was normally a loner and not much of a talker?

Steve watched a curious array of emotions drift across her flawless face. She had expressive green-brown eyes with tawny flecks. Her hair was light brown with golden streaks. She looked around five-and-a-half-feet tall, and was perfectly weighted to that height to be sleek and shapely. He had to admit that she possessed one of the warmest and nicest smiles he had ever seen on anyone. Her voice was pleasing and cultured; she was an educated woman, a refined lady. Steve frowned as his heart pained him with bitter resentment. "Did you hear me, Miss Avery?"

She caught the sudden edge to his voice. "Yes, every word. I didn't know you wanted a response. My father is a very genial and social man. Since he was here alone, it was natural for him to make friends with the others. I hope there isn't anything wrong with them inviting him to dinner."

He had to put distance between them. "Of course not."

"Then to which remark did you want me to reply?"

"I was just making conversation and thought you'd shut me out again."

"I'm not much of a talker, Mr. Carr. If you'll excuse me, I have important things on my mind."

Me and what I'm saying aren't important to a lady like you? "When we take our stroll this afternoon, best cover that head with a big hat. On the trail, you should keep your arms and face protected. You don't want the sun to change that soft, tawny skin to a bright and painful red or to a wrinkled brown, do you?"

She dared not look at him. "I'll follow your advice, thank you."

"We'd better get back to camp."

"I'm going now, sir. I'll put away my things and join you promptly."

"Miss Avery . . .?"

She halted her departure and turned. He hadn't moved. "Yes?"

"Stay attentive this afternoon, and from now on. I don't enjoy scolding you like a child or shaming you before the others. It breeds hard feelings."

Ginny's smile vanished. From the mellow way he'd spoken her name and his friendly words, she'd expected an apology. "Yes, Mr. Carr, it does breed ill will and could create tension in camp. I promise, from now on, I won't concentrate on anything except my lessons. I don't enjoy being humiliated for minor and unintentional mistakes."

"Even *minor* mistakes can get you killed."

"I'm positive you'll teach me and the others how to prevent any."

"I'm glad you have confidence in me, Miss Avery."

"If you weren't qualified, Mr. Carr, you wouldn't have been hired. If you'll excuse me, I have to rush or I'll be in trouble again with the boss."

"Do your best today and I'll say a good word about you to him," he jested as she prepared to leave. She halted a moment but didn't turn or reply. He watched her skirttail sway as she hurried along the path to escape him.

Ginny spread the wet skirt out to dry. *Tact is what you're missing, Steve Carr. Obviously you don't have many occasions to use it.*

She speculated on the leader. He was different from all the men she had ever met, the gentlemen and the rogues. Steve Carr was a blend of both, and he seemed to let whichever facet he wished to reveal surface at his choosing. Maybe he used that trait to keep people off balance or at a distance. Or perhaps he was playing with her from a perverse sense of pleasure at making a lady squirm.

Ginny reasoned she might be overreacting to him because of the secret she was keeping. Yet, that air of danger-if-crossed made her nervous and wary. She had seen it in his challenging gaze, a reflexive warning not to get too close or too nosey. She presumed he could slay in the flicker of an eye if need be and never worry over his lethal action. She wondered if his manner was a result of the war? Years of protecting his very life? A loss of everything and everyone he loved, so little mattered except himself and his pride?

Think only of work, Ginny. You have no time for romance or games, especially with him. Move quickly or you'll be late and provoke him to another verbal attack. She left the wagon to join the others.

—— *Chapter 2* ——

❧

STEVE INSTRUCTED THE FIFTEEN WOMEN on the feeding and watering of the mules. He showed them how to check hooves for painful and possibly crippling splits and stones. He taught them how to examine ears and teeth for problems and how to handle any they found. As he stroked the animal's forehead, he said, "A mule will bite only if he's provoked or mistreated, so don't do either one. Give them good care and affection and they'll get you where you want to go."

Ginny observed the man's gentle treatment of the creature.

"Mules don't spook easily and can be urged into place without much trouble or strength," Steve told them. He demonstrated how to put on a bridle with bit and blinkers, which the animal didn't seem to mind. He slipped on a collar, then showed them how to join the reins, straps, and bands. He added traces and backed the mule into place. With deft hands, he secured the creature to a rear whiffletree, a crossbar that held the leather contrivance fastened in place to pull the wagon. He hitched five others and put them in position, then coupled the six mules into three pairs by chain connecting two collars which kept them under better control.

A long "tongue" separated the two rows of beasts that were standing obediently awaiting their own instructions. When none came, they stood still, not even braying in impatience. They just flicked their ears to pick up sounds and swished their tails occasionally to discourage pests.

Steve told the women, "Go to your own wagon and work with your team. Get to know them and let them get to know your touch, scent, and voice. Like your youngsters, mules have different traits and personalities; it's easier to manage them if you keep that in mind. I've sent the men and children to another clearing so you won't have distractions."

Ginny was relieved the guide didn't glance at her after his last word. She gave a soft laugh when the jolly Ellie Davis asked, "Or sneak help?"

"Or sneak help," Steve echoed with a genuine chuckle. "I'll come around to help as needed. If you get into a bind, call me. This is a lot of hook-ups and leather to learn and master in one showing. I want you to hitch 'em, then let me check it, unharness 'em, then do it again. You'll practice each day until it becomes a simple chore."

"What if we can't do it alone?" Mattie Epps whined with a pout.

"We stay camped here until each one of you can do your part. The same goes for every step of the training: you learn to do it all before we leave."

"Some of us already know how," Louise Jackson snapped. "What if others can't ever manage it? We shouldn't be held up because of them. Our supplies will dwindle while we sit and wait. I think you should place a time limit on how long they can detain the rest of us."

Steve was grated by her bossy manner but suggested in a polite tone that those of the women who knew how, work with any who have trouble. "By helping them," he explained, "you help yourself because it'll speed up our departure."

"What if that doesn't work?" Louise persisted.

Steve was compelled to back down on his prior threat, which had been used to intimidate the women into doing their best or risk the outrage of fellow travelers whom they were delaying. "If you can't do any of the lessons because you aren't trying hard enough or just don't want to work, you'll be left behind after a reasonable length of time, say . . . eight days."

"That sounds fair," Louise conceded with a toss of her blond hair.

As the women went in different directions to begin their matching tasks, Ginny perceived that Louise had riled Steve Carr, even though no one else seemed to notice. From her position near him, she saw a sudden tautness enter his body and his jaw tighten. She witnessed the icy stare he bored into the blonde's back as Louise departed with a smug smirk. Ginny was surprised he had changed his decision; that showed he wasn't inflexible.

She was glad she possessed a good visual memory. She separated the contrivances into six piles. On the first mule, she repeated the harnessing process she had observed. She talked softly to him and stroked him as she worked. She prayed he wouldn't bite her or get impatient with her nervous fumblings. She'd read and seen that some animals sensed fear or incompetence and became ornery, threatening, or uncooperative.

So far, so good, she encouraged herself. When he was in gear, she tried to guide him into place at the rear of the tongue. He refused to budge! She pulled on the reins, pleaded with him, and finally berated him in whispers in one ear, "Don't be an obstinate jackass's son." The mule gave her a nonchalant glance. "Why are you giving me a hard time? Don't you want us to finish first? Do you want to get your mistress fussed at again?" The contrary beast looked the other way as if bored with her. "If you don't obey, you lazy moke," she threatened, "no sweet and delicious grain for you tonight. Please," she begged him as a last resort.

"It helps to push on his chest here and nudge his shank with your foot there," Steve advised as he demonstrated. "That tells him to back up."

Ginny saw the animal respond to the correct procedure, then stop when Steve pulled on the reins to cease movement. "How was I to know that?" she pointed out. "It wasn't in the lesson."

"An oversight, Miss Avery, since none of mine were obstinate," he observed as she and the animal obeyed and succeeded. "Next, you—"

Lifting the second set of harnesses, she interrupted, "Don't tell me, Steve. Let me see how much I remember. Correct me if I'm wrong."

He caught the use of his first name. "Continue, Anna."

She ignored his grin of amusement as she completed the task, aware of her slip and his response in kind. He had sneaked up unseen and unheard again while she was prattling like a fool to a mule. She was glad her face had not reddened like a vivid sunset to amuse him again. "Right?"

"Right, but you still have tricky connections to master. I'll check on you again later. If you run into trouble, give me a holler."

When Ginny finished and looked around to signal the scout she was ready to have her work checked, she noticed with relief that several other women were still struggling with their own chores. She motioned him over and eyed his effortless approach on long and lean legs. "Ready, Mr. Carr."

He walked around and examined each arrangement. Over the last mule's back, his gaze met hers as he said, "No mistakes. Unhitch 'em and do it again. Call me when you're finished."

Ginny was miffed that he hadn't added something like, *A good job*. Perhaps he had assumed "No mistakes" was sufficient praise.

Ginny and the others rested and chatted while waiting for the last two women, Mattie Epps and Cathy King, to finish. She knew she looked and smelled a mess: sweaty and dirty, wearing mule-and-leather cologne, and hair tousled. Since the others didn't go to freshen up, she didn't want to appear finicky by doing so. Yet, she hated feeling and being seen in this disheveled way, especially by the approaching scout who visually inspected her this time like a harnessed creature who couldn't escape.

Steve's gaze took in the sultry Cathy, a black-haired beauty with a spoiled and flirty streak he didn't like. She didn't want to go on this arduous journey, but her husband Ed had given her no choice, and she did nothing to conceal that fact or her displeasure. Steve hoped she'd cool her hot blood before her wanton behavior caused problems for him, as he had more than enough to deal with. It was obvious to him she was late on purpose to snare his attention. Mattie had pulled the same sluggard ruse but for a different reason, with hopes he would cancel the rest of her lesson today—which he hadn't. He wouldn't slack off on any of the women's training for any reason, as he'd agreed to take on this role. "Take a quick break, ladies, for water and . . . whatever needs tending before we take our walk. One mile today. Be ready to move out in ten minutes." He left to take a breather of his own.

"Walk? Exercise?" Mattie complained to Ellie. "I'm ready to drop on the ground and sleep for a year! Haven't we done enough today? We still have chores before bedtime."

"We can't balk, Mattie, or we're in trouble. We agreed to obey him."

"But I just finished, Ellie. I'm tired. You all got to rest a while."

"Because we learned and worked faster," Louise boasted.

"That was hard, and you already knew how to do it. I'll *never* have to do it. Joel will tend that chore on the trail while I tend my own. It isn't ladylike to get filthy and smelly like this; I despise doing men's labors."

"If Joel gets hurt or killed, Mattie, what then?"

In a peevish tone, she spat, "Don't be foolish, Lucy; he won't. But if he does, I'll worry about learning it then."

Louise glared at the group's whiner. "We'll all have our hands full, so learn to carry your own load now or don't go."

"That's hateful, Louise Jackson!"

"It's the truth, Mattie Epps, so stop complaining and do it. If you use only half as much energy doing your lesson as you do whining about *not* doing it, you could be finished real quick and simple."

As the two peevish women glared at each other, Lucy Eaves said, "I'm taking my break before we leave. Anyone else?" she invited.

"Me," Ginny answered, worried over Mattie and Louise's sharp words and sorry attitudes. If she were lucky, she could avoid both women on the trail, as she didn't care for dissension. Elude Cathy, too, she added, as she'd seen the married woman steal improper looks at Steve. She followed Lucy into the trees as she wondered how this lovely woman could walk miles each day on a "gimp" foot.

They trekked half a mile from camp and turned to head back the same way, their pistol-wearing leader out front and prodding them onward. He didn't slow his steady pace to aid the fatigued ones or halt to wait for intentional stragglers. Trying to get finished and rest before taking charge of active children and cooking the evening meal, hardly anyone noticed the greenery and colorful wildflowers of early spring.

Ginny did, but dared not slack off to admire them. She tried to keep as close as possible to the pace Steve set, but a stitch in her side slowed her at the end. The speed and distance he demanded on a first outing was surely unlike a leisurely Sunday stroll! No one wasted energy talking or by trying to match the steps of others for companionship or conversation.

As she entered the edge of camp alone, Steve said, "You look to be in good shape, Miss Avery, but that doesn't mean you can walk all day for a month or more unless you pick up your pace and increase your stamina. I hope you can improve tomorrow. It's hard for me to amble."

"I hope I do everything right from here on, Mr. Carr, so you'll get off my back, especially when I'm doing my best." She left him staring after her, feeling better after her curt retort. She hadn't seen him halt any of the other women to scold their speed. She didn't like being complimented then rebuked. His inconsistent behavior rubbed her nerves raw.

She hated to imagine what demands the future held for her. She glanced back to see him retracing the path to escort the tardy women home, one of whom was the flirtatious Cathy King . . . She gathered her clothes and needed items and headed to the private area the guide had designated for bathing. She passed and spoke to others who were preparing fires or meals, visiting with husbands and children, and doing various other evening chores.

She took a bath and dried herself, then tended a feminine chore that came every month with the cloth pads Martha Avery had helped her make. She buried the used one, covered the disturbed area with a rock, and donned clean clothes. She felt better after removing the grime of today's activities. She dreaded to attack the task ahead—campfire cooking—but she had to eat. As she returned to camp, Ellie Davis solved that problem for her.

The stout and jolly female halted Ginny and asked, "Anna, dear, why don't you join us for supper tonight? No need in you cooking and eating alone. We have plenty and we can get to know each other better that way."

"That's kind of you, Ellie; I'll be delighted, but only if I can help."

"Everything will be ready by the time you put away your things."

"Then you must let me do the dishes afterward."

"That's fine. Hurry before the young'uns start yelling for their food."

Ginny stored her things and returned to the Davis campsite. She smiled as Ellie's husband and their four children were introduced to her and she to them. She took the place on a bench by a table that Ellie motioned to. She bowed her head and closed her eyes as Stuart blessed the food and asked for safety on the trail ahead. Afterward, everyone was quiet, except to ask for the items they wished to be passed along. She realized the children had been taught to be still and silent while eating, so she did the same.

The dishes were done. The well-mannered children, ranging in age from eight to fourteen, were on pallets beneath the wagon. Women gathered in small groups to chat or to listen to music played on a fiddle by Ruby Amerson's husband. The perky redhead was not with him, as she was tending her two babies. She saw Steve summon the men for a short meeting on the far side of the encampment and wondered why.

To prevent disturbing the Davis children, who were trying to go to sleep beneath the wagon, Ellie suggested the two women go and sit on a quilt near a tree to rest and chat. After they were settled, she coaxed, "Tell me about yourself, Anna."

Ginny hated to deceive the sweet woman but she had to keep up her deception. It was the only way for her to reach her first destination, so she must lie with reluctance and a foul taste in her mouth.

Before Ginny began, Lucy and Ruby joined them. They chatted a while about the day's events before Ellie entreated "Anna" to relate her story.

The woman stout of heart and body said, "We shared stories last week, but—since you weren't here—we'll repeat the best parts for you later."

"Wait for me," Mary urged as she advanced in a hurry to join the group. Her damp sandy hair ringed her face with short, bouncy curls. "The boys were so full of energy I couldn't get them to settle down."

"We should have waited for you, Mary dear," Ellie said, "or come to help you finish up. Four kids are a handful; I know mine are."

"After being with their fathers all day, they get rowdy and restless. I was almost too tired to tuck them in and kiss them good night."

Lucy smiled as she brushed her long dark-blond hair before replaiting it into its thick braid. "That walk wore us all out. I think we have a slave driver for a guide," she jested.

Ruby giggled and whispered, "But he's a fine one to look at all day."

Ellie teased in a matching low tone, "You best not look too long and hard or George will hop on both of you with a brush broom."

In an exaggerated drawl, Ruby said, "It's this fiery red hair I was named for, girls; it flames me up from head to toe when I least expect it. Of course, with two babies to tend and sleeping in the open, it doesn't do me much good to tempt any man to mischief, even my beloved George."

The five women laughed at Ruby's jests and comical expression. Ginny enjoyed the warmth and rapport in the small group, and relaxed.

Ellie warned with a playful grin, "Don't let that King woman see you cast an eye on our Mr. Carr. You don't want to cat fight with her over him."

"You noticed her boldness, too?"

"We all did, Ruby dear. She's shameless and spoiled. Going to be trouble, mark my words," Ellie predicted with a woeful look.

Lucy lowered her brush. "I hope not. Mr. Carr is a nice man, just a little cocky. I like him and appreciate his help."

Ruby and Mary agreed. Ellie winked at Ginny, who didn't voice her opinion of their handsome guide. None of the others had mentioned how he picked on her, but Ginny assumed they couldn't help but notice.

"I'm afraid Louise and Mattie are also going to give him trouble. Us, too. The others seem fine. The Daniels woman is a little hateful at times, but she has a right to be bitter over her losses; those Yanks cost her husband not only the use of his leg but their home. We all have our reasons for anger, but all that can't be changed, so we'd better make the best of our new starts out West."

"You're right, Lucy dear." She glanced at the newcomer. "I suppose we shouldn't gossip about the others like this. Anna must think we're awful."

"No, I don't, Ellie. You four have become close friends. I'm glad you're letting me join your group. Thanks for including me in your circle."

The women felt she was being sincere. Ginny glanced from one to the next and smiled at each woman.

"Please go on with your story, Anna," Mary urged.

With a blend of fact and fiction, Ginny told the four genial women, "I was nineteen less than three weeks ago. My mother died when I was a child, so it makes me sad to talk about her. Father bought a ranch in Texas; that's where we'll be living. He owned several stores before the war, but Yankee taxes were eating them alive. Before they could bankrupt and be taken away, he sold them to purchase the ranch and finance this journey. My aunt owns a small boardinghouse in town; she's planning to sell it and join us later. Railroads should be repaired by then which will make an easier trip for her and it will give Father and I time to get settled."

"Was the war hard on you with him off fighting?" Ellie asked.

Ginny used an apologetic tone and expression as she admitted, "No, because I wasn't home. When things looked bad, Father sent me off to boarding school up north, in Pennsylvania. I was only thirteen, so I was scared at first. When war came, Father wouldn't allow me to return home; he thought I'd be safer there. Sherman's destructive march through Georgia proved he was right. He made me stay until school was over or things improved. When he realized that could be a long time or never and this opportunity arose, he came to fetch me by train. We only returned twelve days ago. I stayed in town while the men trained so I could visit with my aunt before departure."

"I bet you're glad to be out of Yankee land."

"I am, Mary. I hated the cold and icy winters and being with people so different from us and so far away from home. Union girls gave Dixie girls a hard time; we had to pretend to be abolitionists to keep peace. It was a coward's way out and we all hated it, but we had no choice. Some of us were tempted to escape school and come home, but we were afraid of being arrested as southern sympathizers. It was a horrible way to live. We knew we couldn't get home through enemy lines and across raging battlefields. We could have been captured and imprisoned or shot as spies. We had to hide our love and support of the South."

"How awful to live like that," Ruby murmured in empathy.

"I would have been terrified."

"Me, too, Mary," Lucy concurred. "I know you're glad to be back."

"I am," Ginny went on, "but I was shocked by the devastation I saw on the way home. I can't believe how bad things still are. I'll be glad to reach Texas. It will be wonderful to be free and proud again."

From behind the women, Steve reminded, "Texas was a Confederate state and it's under military rule like all the others in the South."

Ginny hadn't noticed his approach again, and was unsettled by his curious presence. Why wasn't he with the men? Why lurk around near the women, eavesdropping? "But it's such a big state and it's not as bad there as it is here. The man who sold Father the ranch said so. Did he lie?"

Instead of answering her, he asked, "Where is your father's ranch?"

If he knew the area, she realized, she could be exposed. Instead of saying Waco, she decided to reply that she didn't know. "You'll have to ask Father," she informed him.

As husbands joined wives in the small group, Steve responded, "I will when he returns. I have friends in Texas, so I might drop by to visit one day to see how he's doing. I like your father and enjoy his company."

Ginny didn't believe him. No matter his motive, she wouldn't be with Charles Avery, who would guard her true location. During her fabricated revelations, she'd noticed something to use as an evasion. "Why are the men armed in camp, Mr. Carr?" she asked. "Every one has a rifle within reach."

Mary's husband, James Wiggins, responded before the scout could. "Didn't Charles tell you about the gangs of ex-Yanks and freed slaves who are roaming the South like legalized criminals and attacking innocent folk?" After Ginny shook her head, James continued. "I bet most of them are riding under the cover of that Yankee Loyal League. They claim they want to train black people to become citizens but that's a pile of— Pardon me, ladies, but it riles me. They're nothing but a bunch of outlaws with government protection. Their members spy on honest folk, then attack them without just cause. They find ways to levy fines on us, our women are harassed in the streets just to provoke us, churches are entered and services interrupted, and businesses and homes are confiscated."

Lucy's husband added, "They steal, kill, rape, burn, and imprison decent folk. Some get arrested on fake charges and vanish forever."

"You're right, Jeff," James concurred. "Those Loyal League juries and judges and governors will give even a guilty Northern man a pardon or acquittal if he pays them a bribe."

"The black leagues are the worst," George Amerson stated matter-of-factly.

"I admit some of them former slaves were mistreated, but they ain't got reason to take out their hatred and revenge on every white person in the South."

Ellie looked at her mate as Stuart gave his opinion. "That new Reconstruction Act isn't going to work. Greedy carpetbaggers and scalawags and those hot-headed Radicals won't let it. That's why President Johnson vetoed it. As long as they won't readmit us to the Union, allow us to be terrorized and cheated, and keep us under their crushing boots, things will never improve down here. That's why we're getting out while we can. I don't want my children to endure the shame and anguish we've had to."

"What if some of those gangs attack here?" a worried Mary asked.

"Guards will be posted every night," the observant leader answered, "here and on the trail. That's why we circle up to camp, to be close enough to hear anyone who gets into danger. The men have their assignments. Don't worry; I check the area every evening before I turn in."

"But those raiders usually attack folk in the middle of the night."

"Stay calm, Mary love," James told his wife. "We'll be safe."

"I think it's time for everyone to settle down and turn in," Steve advised. "We all have a busy day tomorrow, especially the ladies."

The people said their good nights and went to their wagons.

Steve turned to speak to Avery's daughter to see if he could learn more from her, but she was gone, probably to avoid him. He shrugged and went to where he was camped near a tree with his horse and sat on his bedroll to think. Her tale had been enlightening, he concluded, but totally truthful . . . ? He didn't think so. Yet, there could be reasons besides involvement in the gem-smuggling scheme for her to mislead the others. He wished he could have overheard everything the women said beneath the tree, as females were more open than men and made more frequent slips. He had been giving the men their guard assignments and advising them to give their wives all the encouragement and help they could during the females' difficult training period. He had sneaked up just as Anna Avery began her personal story. When he sighted the husbands approaching, he had revealed himself to keep from getting caught and arousing suspicions in the wrong person.

He had five suspects so far: the embittered Harry Brown; Cathy's husband, Ed King, bankrupted by the Yanks; the half-crippled John Daniels; Louise's husband, Samuel Jackson who seemed deceitfully quiet and nice; and Charles Avery, about whom he was unsure and uneasy. Maybe Anna's father had fetched her from school up North to use her as a diversional cover for his dirty work, if Avery was the culprit he was seeking. The other men appeared to be open, honest, and sincere about their motives for going west and being on this particular wagon-train.

Steve knew he needed more time to study and ultimately expose his target. From years of experience, he knew how to fake a credible act. But with Anna he was at a total loss. She was unlike any woman he had met. She caused strange and annoying stirrings in him, feelings and reactions that had nothing to do with the case at hand. He found himself thinking about her too much. That had to stop or be controlled.

So did unusual and unwanted twinges of compassion and conscience these pioneers evoked in him. He assumed it was because of the sufferings they had endured during and after the war, the bitterness and resentment they felt, the loss of their roots and pride, and a tragic score that hadn't been settled. He understood such troubles only too well . . . . He didn't like getting close to people or feeling sorry for them; that created problems, distractions, and weaknesses that could interfere with his work. He must never be blinded, vulnerable, or betrayed again.

Ginny lay on a pallet inside Charles's wagon. She couldn't imagine what the next few months would bring—but she'd find out soon. It had been a difficult, tiring day. She was too edgy to sleep. In a camp filled with people, she felt alone and frightened, in spite of the four friends she'd made and many nice acquaintances. She was plagued by her deception but couldn't confess the truth. It would make her sound terrible and get her kicked off the wagontrain, not to mention getting the gentle Charles Avery into trouble for lying about their kinship.

Ginny's turbulent heart filled with grief and loneliness over the death of her best friend. At times, she believed Johanna's ploy would work like a charm; at others, she feared it wouldn't, and wished she hadn't agreed to the scheme. One thing she knew for certain: she would not emotionally and financially hurt Bennett Chapman if he were innocent. But if he were guilty . . . She'd promised! *Please, Johanna, please, God, help me know the right thing to do when the time comes.*

With Johanna gone, Ginny didn't think she could bear it if her father was dead, too. Anxiety over his safety troubled her. Until the time came to head for Colorado, she must keep worries and fears concerning him off her mind and keep her concentration on current factors.

But Johanna's loss was fresh and painful. The finality of it brought renewed anguish and tears. Ginny allowed the flow; it was needed to cleanse and calm her, especially with Steve Carr harassing her.

She couldn't understand why he picked on her. At times, he seemed to look at her with desire and interest; at others, with almost contempt and anger and a curious suspicion. If only he'd be nice for a while . . .

The scout in mind paused beside the Avery wagon during his last rounds of the evening. His keen ears heard the muffled crying inside. He wondered why Anna was weeping . . . . Because she was miserable out of her normal surroundings? Afraid of the journey and new start looming before her? Of what she was leaving behind—or who? Fears of failure? Or because he had hurt her feelings several times today?

The twenty-seven-year-old half-Indian guide didn't know why that last doubt entered his mind, unless it was the way she had looked at him at the river and after their walk. For certain he'd put obstacles in his needed path to her; he'd seen her alter her favorable opinion of him since this morning at their first meeting. He could kick himself for getting so defensive about his strong attraction to her that he overreacted and repelled her with foolish behavior. He was untouchable and unchangeable, so he shouldn't worry about her getting to him enough to cause him the problems and pains like those he'd suffered in the past. She seemed, or *had* seemed, interested in him as a man. Shouldn't he try to take advantage of that opening to obtain needed information?

He was surprised by how quickly she had learned her lessons. He could have given her well-deserved praise as he had with others to warm and to open them up to his probings. Why hadn't he? She could be his target as easily as any of the others present, who all seemed genuine so far—all except for the five men who had caused his honed instincts to go on full alert.

Ginny fed and watered the Avery mules as instructed to give them energy for their joint tasks today. The women's lesson began with how to pack a wagon and secure the load for correct balance and for protection of their possessions.

They gathered around Lucy Eaves's wagon for Steve Carr to explain the correct procedure. He told them to pack from front to back, going bottom to top along the way in three layers. Heavy and bulky items—such as stove, plow, trunks of linens, and out-of-season garments, big tools, small furniture, barrels of household goods such as curtains, and bolts of cloth—went on the bottom and were positioned to spread out their weight for stability. Lighter and sturdier possessions —kitchen items, keepsakes, cook and wash pots, churn, homemade toys, and such —came next and were safeguarded by blankets. Fragile belongings and things needed for use during travel—food supplies, dishes, weapons, clothing, and bedding—were loaded atop the high stacks.

Steve showed them how to use leather straps, cloth strips, and lengths of rope to secure the items in place for maximum protection against breakage. Lamps were suspended from hickory bows that formed the top construction of the wagon beneath its billowy covering of hemp canvas that was waterproofed with linseed oil. Other possessions were secured to the outside of the wagon box, often in wooden containers or suspended from hooks or resting on shelves, such as the fresh water barrel, an easy-to-reach weapon by the driver's seat, crates with chickens, sacks with feed, axes for chopping wood, the axle grease bucket, and saw.

"I want each of you to unload your wagon and begin from scratch," Steve told the women. "Let me check it when it's totally empty, then watch you pack and secure everything as I showed you. While I'm assisting you one at a time, the others can be doing chores or resting or visiting with friends."

"Why is this necessary, Mr. Carr?" Mattie questioned irritably. "If we pack everything we need along the way on top, we won't have to bother the other stuff until we reach our destination."

"There will be times, Mrs. Epps, when wagons have to be unloaded and reloaded. If you learn how, it will speed up those delays on the trail."

"I don't understand. For what reasons?" she pressed.

"Some rivers, the Mississippi for one, are too deep and swift to cross in wagons," he clarified. "You'll have to unload and the wheels have to be removed so we can float or ferry the wagon across, then reload after goods are taken over separately. Other times, loads and wheels have to be removed to repair broken parts. If you have belongings you know will overburden your mules and wagons, get rid of them before we depart or you might have to discard them along the trail. It's best to take them into town and sell them rather than lose their value. The ground gets real soft in parts of Mississippi and Louisiana, so heavy loads become a problem."

"I'm not leaving anything else behind!" Harry Brown's wife said.

Steve tried to appease the embittered woman. "That's fine, ma'am, and I hope it doesn't become necessary to discard anything you love along the way."

"It isn't fair," Mattie said, and Mrs. Brown nodded agreement.

"Sorry, ladies, but it's more important that you, your family, and your supplies get there than keepsakes. The mules can carry only so much."

Louise Jackson scowled at the women and almost commanded, "Stop wasting time, ladies, so we can get finished before the day's gone. The orders are clear, so accept them, bad as they might be."

"Don't be hard on them, Louise; this move is difficult."

"It's hard on everyone, Ellie, but it has to be done. Let's get busy."

Steve forced himself not to frown at the bickering females. "Women with babies and small children will begin first so they'll be ready to tend them later. Get your things unloaded and spread out for my inspection. It's best to pair off to help each other with heavy items."

Before each woman could choose her partner, Steve made his own assignments from his own study of them. Ruby and Mary became a team, as both had babies and were friends. Mattie was put with Louise so the blonde could keep the whiner moving and silent. Dependable, kind, and patient Ellie was paired with Lucy to help the woman with the bad foot. Cathy was told to work with Mrs. Brown, as the resentful older woman might keep the spoiled beauty out of his hair. The other six were put together in three teams of twos. That left Anna Avery to herself, and to him . . .

"You don't seem to have as many possessions as the others, Miss Avery, so my help should be all you need."

"The ranch Father purchased is furnished, so we don't need to carry much with us. Whatever else we need, Father said he'd buy there. He felt it would be an easier and more comfortable journey with a light load."

"You don't need to explain, but thank you for doing so," he replied. "You four teams with babies and small children begin your work now. The rest of you, do as you please for about two hours until we finish."

The women parted to go to their areas. Steve realized that none had balked enough to appear worried about what he might find in her wagon, if the wife knew what her husband might be doing on the sly. He realized what he was seeking could be hidden in the area until departure time, could be with the woman's husband today during this task, or could be in town with Charles Avery.

Steve worked with Mary and Ruby, then with the Brown woman and Cathy, then Louise and Mattie to get the mothers with babies and smallest children finished first. He soon grasped the seeming impossibility of locating a clue with this lesson, which flustered and annoyed him. He kept his feelings disguised by a feigned genial manner. He realized he couldn't search every item and container, and the stolen gems—mostly diamonds—he was seeking could be hidden anywhere and by anyone.

Steve knew his mission was dangerous, as several skilled agents had been beaten and slain while trying to solve this case. The Justice Department knew which group was involved, what their future plans included, and that the gems were being smuggled out on this trip. The many robberies to obtain payment for weapons had alerted the government to trouble and given them a trail to follow for a time. Now, it was up to him—a stranger and an experienced wagontrain scout but first-time master—to complete a mission others had died trying to solve. If this lesson didn't expose the culprit delivering the gems, perhaps large river crossings would. Surely an anxious carrier for the Red Magnolias would safeguard the pouch by removing it from its hiding spot during moments of possible endangerment, so he must keep a sharp eye out to catch the villain.

Ruby and Mary learned fast and were dismissed. Mattie and Louise took longer what with one's whining and the other's bossy delays. As hoped, Mrs. Brown prevented Cathy from trying to stay with him too long. When it came their turns, Ellie and Lucy were swift and smart. One of the other three teams cost him extra time and energy with too many goods.

So far, Steve had seen and sensed nothing to arouse suspicions. No woman had objected to him opening any container, barrel, or trunk to ostensibly see if it was packed correctly to prevent damage. He hadn't detected any location where a secret compartment could be obscured when he'd checked every wagon's underpinnings and wooden bed. He had forced himself to make small talk to evoke the women's feelings about the war, their move, and the problems being left behind. Nothing unusual had been learned. The scout dismissed the seven groups to do chores, rest, and serve their families lunch while he finished his final loading and investigative lesson for the morning: Miss Anna Avery.

—— *Chapter 3* ——

GINNY WAS SITTING on the tailgate and reading a book of epic poems by John Milton when she heard the guide give orders to the others before heading her way. She watched his approach in dread of how he would behave toward her today. Sleeves rolled to his elbows exposed hard-muscled forearms and darkly bronzed flesh. A section of ebony hair fell over his left temple and almost concealed that brow from view; its back grazed broad shoulders and made an attempt to turn under. He was clean-shaven, which stressed the squareness of a chiseled jawline. A red shirt enhanced his neat appearance and accentuated his tan. His ever-present weapons—two pistols and knife—warned of a physical prowess not to be rashly challenged. He was a fine specimen of manhood, and her heart fluttered in unbidden desire.

"Ready to begin, Miss Avery?" he asked in a mellow tone.

Ginny put the book aside and hopped down to stand before him. Attired in a split-tailed riding skirt, short boots, and shirt, she hoped she was "properly" dressed today to prevent any curt comments from him. She wanted to start off right, so she smiled cheerfully and said in a polite tone, "Yes, sir. Everything's unloaded for your inspection except for the heavy things."

Steve peered into the white-covered interior. "After I examine this stuff, I'll climb inside to check everything else. No need to pull them out. You two are traveling light, so not much to teach you."

Ginny caught an intriguing change in his tone, as if he were implying that was a curious fact. She didn't think the crowded wagon held a "light" load, but apparently for people pulling up roots and moving far away, it was. "I explained that earlier," she reminded with another friendly smile. "I've been at boarding school for six years, so most of my possessions are clothes and keepsakes; they're in those trunks there."

Steve didn't respond to her words but he did notice the practical manner in which she was dressed today. She didn't act the least bit nervous about his scrutiny, and he was glad. He opened and checked the barrels and crates filled with staples: flour, sugar, salt, pepper, rice, tea, cornmeal, coffee, baking soda, dried beans and fruits, tenderizing vinegar, cured ham, dried beef, salted bacon. "What about eggs and milk?" he asked, not noticing those items.

"Father is bringing chickens when he returns, and he made a deal with George Amerson to purchase milk from him along the way."

It looked as if the Averys were going to eat well during their trip, he concluded. He saw dishes and utensils and cooking ware that included a kettle, two skillets—small and large—coffee grinder, coffeepot, two sharp knives, a Dutch oven, and a ladle for the kettle. Avery carried several weapons—pistols and rifles and plenty of ammunition for both. There was bedding: pillows, blankets, quilts, linens, and waterproof cloths for the wet ground, as most people slept outside beneath or beside their wagons unless the weather was bad. Three crates of canned foods, including homemade soup, caught his attention. A few smaller boxes held medicines, liniments, bandages, candles, matches, writing supplies, and a sewing kit. He found no musical instruments or photograph albums. Odd, he mused, for such a civilized family . . . "You seem to have those jars of vegetables wrapped well against breakage. Some places on the trail can give a jolt to body and possession. Make sure you keep them separated with cloth or paper or you'll have a mess on your hands."

She flushed as she admitted part of the truth. "I'm not much of a cook in the open, so my aunt gave those to us to help out along the way."

Steve chuckled at her expression. In a carefully worded and toned reply to avoid offending her, he said, "I doubt fancy boarding schools would consider that chore an important lesson for a fine lady to need."

Ginny noticed the care he took with his answer and was pleased. Perhaps he had decided a truce was best for all of them. He was being courteous and pleasant, and she warmed to him. "I suppose you're right, but it puts me at a disadvantage for this trip. Ellie, Mary, Ruby, and Lucy have offered to teach me what I don't know."

Steve glanced at her to confirm his conduct was relaxing her. "You seem smart and quick, Anna, so it shouldn't be a problem for you."

She was surprised he used her first name and wondered if it was a slip. "Thank you for the compliment, Mr. Carr."

"Think nothing of it. Be back in a minute," he murmured with a smile as he rounded the wagon to check out the jockey box at the front to find tools and extra wagon parts there.

Steve returned to the spot where the woman waited for him and climbed onto the tailgate. He extended his hand and assisted her into the wagon. He hated to release his grasp but had no reason to continue it. Her hands were as soft as a cloud must be; obviously they didn't do much labor.

"Was I supposed to unload that stuff? I didn't know it was there. I was busy when Father packed the wagon, so I didn't think to check it today."

"No problem, just tools and extra parts." He glanced at the extra front and back wheels, axle, and hand-cranked jack that were stored beneath the driver's seat next to the jockey box. "Your father is certainly prepared for any accident along the trail. A smart man, Anna. You two won't have to worry about being stranded with broken parts. Let's see what else we have in here . . . Four trunks. What's inside?"

Ginny motioned to three and said, "Those are mine," then explained of the fourth, "that's Father's."

"Do you care if I peek inside?" he tested for a clue of reluctance.

Ginny knew the guide couldn't discover anything revealing about her, as she'd left her personal possessions stored at Martha Avery's boardinghouse until she sent for them. She didn't think his "peek" was necessary but gave her permission anyhow. She was confident Johanna's hidden letter wouldn't be found. "Certainly not, but I only have clothes and books, nothing fragile. I don't know about Father's trunk." Maybe Steve wanted to learn more about her . . .

Steve opened her trunks and fumbled through stacks of lovely and costly garments, lacy ladies' "unmentionables," books, inexpensive jewelry, hats, shoes, an old doll, and other items. He lifted the doll and looked at it as if admiring its workmanship. His questing fingers detected nothing suspicious concealed inside, and, oddly, he was relieved.

As if in response to an unasked question, Ginny told him, "My mother made it for me when I was a child. I never could part with it. I'll pass it on to my daughter one day."

Steve remembered that her mother was long dead and heard the love in her tone. He felt the same way about his own mother, who was still alive. "It's pretty and well made. I know it must be special to you. My best friend gave me this knife," he disclosed as he raised his left leg and touched it, "and I'd never part with it." Nor with the matching, engraved pistols from his father, worn to remind him daily of the man's treachery.

Ginny accepted the doll and gazed at it for a moment with misty eyes before she replaced it in the trunk with gentleness and care. The keepsake was the remaining link to her lost mother and she loved it dearly. If her belongings were ever threatened, it would be the first thing she would try to save. She straightened the clothes Steve had mussed.

As she worked, the scout observed her. He liked the way her light-brown hair tumbled from its highest peak to her waist in a display of curls that had gilded edges that shone under the sun like golden tips. He could tell it was soft and wished he could bury his fingers in its abundance. Her expressive eyes were a brown-green blend of allure. She had full lips that enticed a man to want to kiss it, and her nose was a perfect size and shape, as were her cheekbones and chin. She was beautiful and desir—

Ginny's gaze fused with Steve's as she turned to ask what was next. She was astonished to see a seductive and softened glow in those dark-brown depths. She stood near him in the enclosed wagon, its position on the edge of camp not allowing others to view them through the front or back openings. She felt her heartbeat quicken and her breathing alter to a swifter and shallower pace. Curious little tremors with bursts of heat attacked her body. She couldn't move or think of what to say; all she could do was return his admiring stare. She didn't even hear the voices of others or noises of animals not far away. She felt aswirl with new and powerful emotions, and captivated by the irresistible guide.

Steve lifted a long strand of hair that had several waves and curls from root to tip. "You're lucky we won't be going through any Indian territory; hot-blooded bucks would risk their lives to take a scalp like yours. Hair this beautiful would be a prized trophy."

Enthralled by the handsome and virile scout, Ginny's voice was strained as she asked, "Why would they want to kill me and scalp me?"

He looked into her wide gaze. "I doubt any warrior would; he'd keep you for himself, as his slave." At that moment, nothing would be more enjoyable than kissing her, unless it was to lay her on the bedding and make wild love to her. *Shu,* she was a powerful temptation, one he had to struggle to overcome. The way she was looking at him, she would at least accept a kiss, he was sure, but that would be reckless. Steve shook his head to clear it of the unacceptable thoughts racing inside it. "During the journey, Miss Avery, it'll be cooler if you braid it like Mrs. Eaves does. That'll keep it out of your way, too; you don't want it getting tangled on something and causing an accident." He turned from her. "Let me check your father's trunk, then we'll get that other stuff reloaded. You'll need time to eat before we begin our driving lessons this afternoon."

The short and magical spell was broken for her, too. She observed him with intrigue as he examined the contents of Charles Avery's trunk. He didn't strike her as a snoop or a thief, but he *was* oddly inquisitive. Perhaps possessions revealed a lot about people to him and he wanted to know his charges well.

Steve used his knees and hands to shove the trunks into the correct positions. "Keep them like that to stabilize your load. Hand me that rope, will you, Anna?"

Ginny obeyed and saw him cut lengths with the large, sharp knife from his left boot. He removed, used, then replaced the blade with fluid motions that said he had done that action many times; she had no doubt he could draw it from its sheath swifter than she could blink. The way he handled the huge weapon told her he was an expert with it. He secured strips around the trunks and tied their ends to the wagon sides to keep the trunks from shifting during movement. She enjoyed watching him work, but wondered why he did the task for her.

After Steve bumped his head on a lantern suspended from a frame bow, he cautioned, "Make sure you keep those empty during travel. You don't want one to fall and spill oil. Besides being a fire hazard, it stinks and can ruin things. Keep your oil container tightly closed, too."

"I will, and thanks for reminding me to check them."

"Let's get the rest of your gear stored." Steve hopped down and handed the items to her as he told her where to place them. He'd learned the Averys had the basic needs and a few extras but, he reasoned, a curiously small load compared to most who were moving west. When everything was inside, he leapt into the wagon again. He eyed her work, smiled, and said, "Good job, Anna. Just remember where and how it all goes when you have to unload along the trail. Any questions?"

"Not that I can think of, Mr. Carr. Thank you for the help."

"You're welcome, Miss Avery. Best eat before our next lesson," he suggested as he hopped to the ground. He assisted her down by a firm and strong grasp around her waist.

"Thank you again, kind sir," she said with a smile.

Steve nodded and left, unsettled by the contact with her. At least, he bragged to himself, she was as disturbed by him as he was by her.

Lucy joined her. "Here's two biscuits with ham, Anna," she offered. "And a glass of milk. It'll save you time. We've all eaten."

"Thank you, Lucy. I'm glad to be finished with one more lesson."

As they sat down for her to eat and drink, Lucy remarked, "Mr. Carr seems nicer to you today. I'm glad. He was a little harsh yesterday."

Ginny lowered the meat-filled biscuit to reply, "I'm sure everyone noticed, and I was embarrassed. I don't know why he picked on me, but he didn't do so today, thank goodness."

Lucy glanced around to make certain no one was within earshot before she whispered, "I think he's taken with you and it makes him uneasy."

"Taken with me? Why would you think that? We're strangers."

Lucy grinned and explained, "All sweethearts start off as strangers, my innocent girl. It's that instant attraction between two people that makes them pursue each other."

"Pursue each other?" Ginny repeated, then felt foolish for echoing the older woman again. "We aren't pursuing each other."

"Not yet," Lucy teased with a sly smile.

"He doesn't even *like* me; that's why he picks on me. He was just being polite today to gain a truce because I scolded him after our walk."

"He's like most men, only being defensive. Love and marriage scare men; they believe they have to resist it with all their mights. Act as if you aren't interested and he'll chase you even more."

"But I'm not interested in him or marriage," Ginny denied the truth.

"Really?" Lucy challenged with a mischievous grin.

"He *is* handsome and appealing, but . . ."

"But *what*? Will your father object to a romance on the trail?"

"No, but I will. I don't think Steve Carr is the kind of man who's interested in settling down, and certainly not with me. Besides, I think he could be dangerous."

"Being a man who can take care of himself doesn't mean he's dangerous. And don't worry about those guns; he is our guard."

"It wouldn't be wise to entice him, Lucy. He's a roaming type. He strikes me clearly as a loner and happy to be one."

"All men are loners until they meet the right woman."

"I don't think I'm the right woman to tame or change Mr. Carr."

"You might be surprised, Anna."

"If we ever got together, I would be shocked."

They shared laughter and the subject was dismissed.

Within a short time, Ruby, Mary, and Ellie joined them. The five women chatted until Steve yelled out, "Ten minutes to go!"

"Teacher's calling and class is waiting, ladies," Ellie jested.

"This is going to be a hard one," Ruby said with a sigh of dread.

"We'll do fine, partner," Mary told her with a wink of confidence.

"We'd better get ready," Lucy suggested.

Steve met with the fifteen women on either side of him at the wagon he had mounted for his demonstration. "As soon as I finish talking, each of you harness your team," he began his instructions. "We'll head westward into the open. These wheels are built to cross rough trails without breaking easily or miring down in soft ground. The front one is smaller to allow sharp turns without gouging into the wagon. The driver sits or walks on the left; don't work the team from the right or you'll confuse them. When we're on roads other wagons and riders are using, keep to the right side to avoid accidents. Most of the time, you and older children will walk to keep the team rested. I have your husbands exercising the children daily to get them into shape for the foot journey. You'll have to take turns resting on the wagon seat or lazy board," he said, pointing to a small seat jutting out from one side.

"I set the pace and you have to keep up. In the event of trouble, signal me with one gunshot if the train gets too far ahead of you. Not more than one, ladies, or you'll spook the animals into bolting. If that happens during a thunderstorm or raid, I'll teach you later this week how to react. Those are your brakes against the back wheels; the lever for them is here," he said as he motioned to it. "Use steady pressure; don't jam it tight. And don't use them unless necessary or you'll ruin them before they're really needed. If you see humps and holes ahead, avoid them. A bad one can break a wheel or an axle; that can get you stranded along the way. Make sure you keep your axles greased and rolling smoothly. That's as much your responsibility as your man's. We'll practice later on hills; they can be tricky if brakes give way. We'll go through everything today then practice daily until you can do this blindfolded. You have to know how to drive, brake, and maneuver your wagon and how to control your team on any terrain and in any weather."

Steve let his gaze drift from woman to woman as he talked to make certain all of them were listening to him and understanding and to make sure he didn't stare at Anna Avery too long. "I'll show you how to keep the right pace and distance between wagons. We'll do circle-ups tomorrow; they're tricky to learn, too. So is the use of the whip. You want to scare the animals into obedience, but you don't want to harm them. You may get hoarse because you'll do a lot of shouting at them to be heard over the noise of wheels and hooves. Your back and arms will ache at first, but they'll loosen up. It'll help if your husbands give you a good rub at night with some liniment."

Some of the women exchanged smiles of amusement.

"Have your family fed, your chores done, and your wagon loaded and ready to pull out every morning at seven. We rest for an hour in the middle of the day when it's hottest. We camp at six. Bedtime is at nine."

"We'll have that strict a schedule to follow?" Mattie asked with a pout.

"Yes, ma'am, Mrs. Epps; it keeps order. Each day, the lead wagons will be swapped with the last ones; that way, nobody has to eat dust all the time. But if you're late getting started, you fall in at the rear, no matter your assigned position. Understood, ladies?"

Some of the women nodded, some replied verbally, and a couple frowned.

"As I said, signal if you fall too far behind; it isn't safe to become a target for raiders. Don't worry about your milk cows; they'll keep pace with the mules, and so will your horse if you have one."

Ginny felt warmed by the sound of Steve's mellow voice and his nearness. She couldn't forget the sparks between them earlier, and thinking of them made her tingle. He was strong enough to take care of anything and anyone. Too bad she couldn't pursue him as Lucy had teased, as her "strict schedule" wouldn't allow it, and probably his loner attitude wouldn't permit it, either. Still . . .

"When we're in the open, you might have trouble with strong winds swaying your wagons. If it gets too bad, we'll stop to shift loads to that side to help you keep balance. A strong gust can tip a wagon on unlevel ground, especially if the load isn't packed and secured as you were taught. If you're fussy when you're tired and sore, keep to yourself in that condition so you won't pass along that irritation to others. The last two things we'll learn during this week are how to cross rivers and handle stampedes; I'll explain those when the time comes. Any questions?"

Ginny and her friends were relieved when everyone remained silent.

"Good. This is how you handle a whip and reins . . ." Steve began.

After he finished his explanation and answered questions, he sent the women to harness their teams. Only two required assistance. Milk cows and horses were tied to trees to graze, and chickens in small pens were left nearby. Steve showed the women how to make turns to leave their camping spots and how to get in line. When the formation of fifteen wagons was ready, he mounted his horse and rode to the left side of the group so he could be seen by the drivers who sat on that side of their seats. He took a place by the leader, Louise Jackson, as she knew how to handle a team and wagon, and that role swelled her bossy head even more.

"Let's move out!" Steve shouted, and waved his tan hat to those at the rear in case some couldn't hear him. He sat astride a large sorrel and signaled each one at the correct time to pull out to create a safe distance between wagons, which they were to keep unchanged as ordered.

Though little dust was stirred up during their departure in the grassy campground, he could imagine the griping from some when they hit dry-dirt locations on the trail where dust clouds would be as thick as a heavy fog or when mud was ankle-deep and mushy and wheels and hooves would fling it in all directions.

Steve watched Anna Avery click her reins and tongue to get her team moving. He was glad the six mules obeyed so he wouldn't have to ride to her and help. He didn't want the others to think he was giving her special treatment, as jealousy always sparked trouble and ill will.

The Avery mules trudged along as they reached him but kept moving. He noticed how pale and tense Anna looked. He knew that genteel lady must be shaking with panic. As if she wanted to hide those feelings from him, she didn't look his way when she passed him. Too bad he couldn't be driving that wagon and heading out on a long trip with her to spend many a secluded night under a starry—

Steve jerked himself to attention as he almost missed signaling the next woman during his distraction. *Keep your head clear!*

After the last wagon passed him, Steve patted the neck of his reddish-brown horse and murmured, "Let's go, Chuune." He galloped past each wagon to check how each female was doing. He spoke to every one, if only a few words. Again, he traveled from one end to the other as he let them practice their new skills.

The guide rode next to Louise as he told her to make a wide turn and head back toward camp. He stayed in that spot to watch each do the tricky maneuver and gave instructions when needed. He couldn't help but feel pride in himself for the good job he was doing.

He watched the woman in mind make her first turn. She had a little trouble but succeeded. She seemed proud and happy, too; she sent him a quick smile as she passed him this time. He only nodded a response to keep his surge of desire concealed from her and others.

The routine of driving and turning continued for two hours under a late March southern sun that was hot today. Steve removed his hat and used his sleeved forearm to mop the sweat away from his face. He kept his keen eyes sharp for trouble, as the armed camp would need time to respond to any threat he signaled with gunfire. A Henry rifle, a fifteen-shot repeater, rested in a long sheath on his saddle. He was an expert with it and that was no brag, just a many-times-proven fact. Fingertips on his left hand grazed the butt of a Colt-Walker .44 and absently traced the initials carved there. He halted their movement and curled them into a tight ball for a moment as he frowned in the bitterness that never released him from torment.

Ginny was exhausted. There wasn't an inch on her body that didn't protest this abuse. In spite of the wide-brimmed bonnet to shade her face, the bright sun made her squint, made her eyes and head hurt. Her flesh and clothes were damp and her face glistened with perspiration. The thick hair flowing down her back felt like a winter cloak. Tomorrow she would braid it as Steve had advised and hopefully be cooler. She wished she could wear short sleeves, but she knew the sun would bake her arms to a beet red. As for her riding gloves, they were too thin to provide enough protection from the chafing reins that had to be held tighter than a horse's. Steve had warned of the danger of dropping them and losing control of the team. With dragging reins, if the mules bolted, a rider could be bounced off the high seat that lacked a safety grip.

High? her mind scoffed. It was precariously high and rock-hard and scary. Her booted feet used the jockey box below and forward of the seat to brace herself as best she could. She still didn't feel secure, as the jostling of the wagon caused her to lose contact with her prop occasionally. Now that she knew what she was doing, she didn't have to strain to concentrate on the arduous task. She could tell the long ride ahead was going to be monotonous and demanding. Thank goodness she had her four new friends, Mr. Avery, and— *No, you don't have Steve Carr.* At that thought, her concentration vanished.

Steve joined her and shouted, "Pick up your pace, Miss Avery! You're lagging way behind!" As he moved his mount closer, he lowered his voice to a near normal tone. "I know you're tired and bored. Practice staying alert; an accident can happen or you'll get left behind if you're in the rear. The others are in the same condition, but it'll be worse on the trail when this goes on all day, day after day." He galloped off before she could respond.

Ginny scolded herself for breaking her promise not to get distracted. Steve had been justly annoyed with her. She flicked the reins, popped her whip, and shouted to her mules to increase their speed. In her rush, she was bounced about and feared losing her balance and being thrown to the ground; yet she didn't let up until the wagon was in proper position. Then she ordered herself to "alert."

She listened to the jingling of the harnesses, the snapping of traces against mule flesh, the squeaking of the wagon bed and underpinnings as she passed over bumps and dips, the rumbling of broad-rimmed wheels, the steady footfalls of twenty-four hooves, the breathing of her animals, the clinking of chains on the whiffletrees or those that linked two collars together, the shifting of extra wheels and tools beneath her location, and the yells of women giving orders to their teams.

She watched Steve sit tall in his saddle as if he were born and reared in one. She saw him go from wagon to wagon as he gave instructions and encouragement or simply observed. If she didn't get her eyes off him, she would be distracted and in trouble again, so she fastened her gaze to Ruby's wagon.

The one-mile walk later was agony to most of the women, Ginny included. This time, more of them than Mattie Epps groaned in protest, but Ginny kept her feelings to herself. She knew Steve was doing this for their own good, so she accepted the punishing task in silence and obedience.

The exhausted women stayed closely bunched on this trek and all but two returned to camp together. As it was getting late, Ginny watched the scout head out by horse to ride in the two laggers one at a time: Mattie and Cathy. He delivered the whiner to her campsite first, then fetched the dark-haired beauty, who wrapped her arms tightly around his waist.

So much for you get left behind if you can't keep up! Ginny fumed.

"Don't worry," Lucy advised. "She won't steal him from you."

Ginny met her friend's gaze and sighed. "I got into trouble again today; I suppose everyone noticed. My mind just drifted away for a while."

Neither woman saw Steve as he was about to round the Avery wagon, but halted when he overheard Lucy's next words.

"You want him, Anna. Can you leave him behind? Forget him?"

"I have to, Lucy; I don't have any choice in the matter."

"Yes, you do," the woman refuted.

"No, Lucy, I promise I don't. Are you taking a bath before dinner?"

"A cunning change of subject," Lucy teased. "Yes, right now. Jeff is starting supper for me. With my youngest being nine already, my kids don't take as much tending as those of the other women. Let's go remove this sweat and dirt."

Steve scowled. The little southern belle was playing with him, but all women were natural and uncontrollable flirts. He had been right when he guessed she couldn't be interested in a man like him. But she didn't have to mislead him when she had herself a man being left behind!

Ginny ate with Ellie and her family again, and helped do the dishes afterward. The circle of friends was too tired to visit with each other after their arduous day, so they said good night and went to their wagons.

Ginny sat on two piles of bedding with her back supported with pillows so she could read for a while by lanternlight. To allow an air flow for coolness and for the dissipation of lamp smoke, she kept on her clothes and left the ends open and the sides pushed up a few inches.

Her legs ached from the strain of bracing them on the jockey box. The bottoms of her feet hurt from the pressure against the rigid wood. Her body suffered as if every bone in it had been jarred and cracked and every muscle had been bruised and sprained. Her spine panged with torment every time she took a step. The backs of her upperarms, forearms, and wrists throbbed from the pull on them by the reins. Her fingers grumbled and stiffened from keeping her hands clutched tightly around the leather controls for hours and almost refused to hold the book she wanted to read. Her tailbone protested sitting on it, so she shifted her weight to lighten the load on the tender spot. That caused her buttocks to be vexed that another area was appeased at their expense. She wondered if sitting on a pillow would help prevent the painful bumping of vulnerable body against unyielding stone-hard seat. No, she decided, that would take away part of her already insecure balance.

She had shielded her face and arms from the hot ball overhead so fortunately she didn't have a sunburn to add to her misery. Despite the riding gloves she had worn, her hands felt bruised and sensitive; she guessed she would have blisters and blue marks on them by morning. She wished she had thicker gloves like some of the other women and Steve Carr wore as hers were too thin for adequate protection. She hadn't known special ones were needed for handling the team. When Charles Avery visited during the week as promised, Ginny planned, she would ask him to bring her a pair. She also would request several pairs of pants for easier climbing aboard and working on the wagon's high seat.

After today, she understood what Steve had meant about eating dust. Upon return to camp, she had dust in her hair, dust on her clothes, dust on her skin, dust on her eyelashes and in her eyes, and in every hollow it could find to sneak inside! She felt as if her nose was cluttered by it, even though she had used her washcloth to try to clear it of the tiny and sharp debris. She found grains inside her mouth, though she had rinsed it out many times and had eaten the evening meal. It was as if minute particles played hide-and-seek around her teeth and in the crevices of her mouth. The irritant had mingled with her perspiration to form grimy smudges when she mopped at the mess or tried to clear her stinging eyes. Though her bath had been refreshing, a longer one in a sudsy tub of warm water would have been paradise.

They had worked in an area that was an equal mixture of grass and barren ground. It was surrounded mostly by pines and live oaks, both with lacy greenish-gray moss swaying from their branches. She had noticed patches of spring flowers and wished she could have halted to pick a bunch. But that foolish action would have fallen like a stone on the serious guide.

Steve wouldn't have caught her napping at the reins if she hadn't been so lost in thought, so troubled by all her problems. But if she didn't straighten out, she worried, he might tell her "father" she couldn't travel west because she wasn't well trained enough. That would be one way of getting her out of his sight if he felt as threatened by her as she did by him.

Of course Charles Avery would not allow the scout to leave her behind. He had promised to get her to Texas, and he would. Mr. Avery, she believed, was an honest, kind, generous, and dependable gentleman. He was like a sweet and gentle uncle. On the ship and since docking, he had had plenty of opportunities to attempt to take advantage of her if her judgment wasn't accurate. He hadn't and she was certain he wouldn't. The only threats she faced were possible discovery by her stepfamily or her father's enemy, and a possible seductive siege by the irresistible scout. If he—

"Miss Avery . . ." Steve called to her from the end of the wagon.

Ginny lowered the book she wasn't reading and met his gaze.

"We need to have an understanding before this thing between us goes any further. You're trouble, woman, for me, yourself, and for everyone."

Ginny tensed in dread, wincing as she pushed her tortured body to a sitting position. His grave tone and gaze told her she had misunderstood his opening statement; he was there to scold her, not romance her. "What do you mean? I do my share and try hard. I don't complain."

"You're too easily diverted, a daydreamer. You broke your word not to become distracted again. When you do, you distract *me* by having to correct you. When I'm distracted, everyone's life is in peril."

Ginny's eyes misted from her troubles and pains. She knew he was right, and he probably found this disciplinary chore as unpleasant to dole out as it was for her to receive. "I'm sorry, Steve," she murmured. "If you'll be patient and forgiving one more time, I promise to try harder. I swear it."

Steve experienced unfamiliar twinges. He wanted to comfort the girl in her physical and emotional anguish. But how could he when part of her torment was caused by losing the man she loved? Yet, and he couldn't explain or grasp why, he didn't want to be harsh to her tonight. She looked so vulnerable and she hadn't turned a page since she'd opened the book in her hands. She was deeply troubled, an emotion he understood too well. "I'll give you another chance," he declared.

Ginny's eyes brightened with joy. "Thank you, Steve. You won't be sorry. I'll make you proud of me."

"My feelings about you aren't important, Anna; doing a good job is the only thing that counts."

"You're wrong," she refuted too quickly and strongly, then flushed.

"You care what I think?" he queried, eyeing her for signs of deceit and crafty feminine wiles to dupe him.

Her blush deepened as she admitted, "Yes, very much."

"Then prove it by being a perfect student from here on. Agreed?"

"Agreed," she said, and returned his smile.

"If you'll take that liniment from your father's medicine crate and rub it all over, you'll feel much better by morning. Don't press too hard, though, or it'll blister your delicate skin. I'd do it for you, but that isn't part of my job and wouldn't be proper."

Ginny was aroused by the thought of him smearing oily liquid over her body and massaging it in with gentle caresses. She cleared her throat to speak. "You're very kind and thoughtful, and I appreciate it."

Steve leaned against the tailgate and murmured, "I don't hear that said about me very often. Thanks."

"I would think you hear it all the time. You're so smart and . . . " she hesitated.

"Why did you stop? I'm starving for compliments from a lady."

"I don't think it's proper to tell you what I think about you."

"That bad, eh?" he questioned with a husky chuckle.

With boldness, she said, "Not bad at all, only private, too personal."

Steve felt his loins respond to her subtle message and nearness. "A hint like that certainly gives a lonely man something to ponder on his bedroll at night . . . I'm surprised you aren't married by now."

That unexpected remark took her off guard. "How do you know I'm not heading west to join my fiancé?" she queried.

Steve sealed his gaze to hers. "You would have said something to the others. Don't you women usually brag about snaring a man?"

"No more than you men boast about your conquests of women."

He laughed and teased, "Ah, a quick and sharp wit."

Ginny felt he was impressed, and that pleased her. "I speak only the truth, Mr. Carr, as I see it from observation and experience."

"You're right, Anna."

She couldn't help but challenge, "For a change?"

He grinned instead of replying. "Good night, Miss Avery."

"Steve?" she halted him, feeling overly brave at that moment. She had to know if he was only being nice or if he was interested in her.

He glued his gaze to hers and saw her fidget. "Yes?"

"I don't have a sweetheart waiting in Texas or anyone left behind."

The scout was intrigued. "Why tell me?"

"So you'll know love-pining isn't the root of my problems. Good night." She pulled on the drawstrings of the wagon and closed the back opening, then wiggled forward and did the same with the front one. She watched him stride away as she slid down the canvas on both sides.

Ginny straightened her bed and pillows. She located the liniment and lowered the lantern flame to a soft glow that would cast no provocative shadows on the thick covering. She sat down in the wagon bed and, her privacy guarded by the deep wooden sides, stripped off her garments. She followed Steve's advice; the hopefully soothing preparation pained and stung for a while as she applied it. After replacing the medicine and putting on a nightgown, she doused the light and settled herself into the most comfortable position she could find. She forced her mind to clear so she could get to sleep, knowing tomorrow would be another difficult day.

Steve saw the light go out in the Avery wagon. For the last few minutes, he had been envisioning the scene inside. His hands itched to do the chore for her. He was baffled by her enticing overtures after what he'd heard earlier. Maybe, he reasoned, he had misunderstood the talk with Lucy Eaves. Or maybe Anna had lied to him tonight or to Lucy and the other women earlier. Yet he couldn't surmise a motive for either theory. Perhaps she required a strong hand to seize her interest and to tame her. Maybe if he backed off or acted bossy she would be intrigued and taken off balance. She seemed to weaken more toward him after he was tough with her. He'd have to test that idea tomorrow to see how she responded.

Chapter 4

Ginny awoke to the sounds of animals—mules braying, horses neighing, chickens clucking, cows mooing, and birds singing—and to the voices and laughter of people. She smelled breakfasts either being cooked or just finished, especially the wafting scents of coffee and bacon and ham. Her nose wrinkled as she detected a lingering odor of liniment on her body and inside the wagon. Her complaining body protested movement. Before she could rise from bed, Ellie knocked on the tailgate to make sure her friend was awake. Ginny loosened the cord enough to peek outside and say, she was up trying to get going. "Do you ache this morning as much as I do?" she asked Ellie.

The hearty woman didn't want to say she was used to hard work and strenuous exercise, more so than her sophisticated friend. "I'm sore and stiff but faring pretty good. Do you have any liniment you could use?"

"Yes, and I did so before going to bed. Mr. Carr told me it would help lessen the pain, and I'm sure it helped. So will moving around."

Ellie smiled and nodded. "I'll save you some food. Come over when you're dressed. We're about to eat now."

"Thanks, Ellie; you don't know how much your kindness helps me."

The brunette smiled again. "Yes, I do. See you shortly." Ellie wondered if she should tell Anna that her father had paid them to help her while he was in town, then decided she would be doing it anyway, as she liked the fresh and delightful young woman. Besides, it might embarrass Anna to learn her father wasn't certain she could take care of herself alone.

Ginny tightened the drawstring and put aside the rumpled bedding. She washed her face and hands in the basin and changed clothes. Taking another of Steve's suggestions, she brushed and braided her thick hair into one long plait. It still wasn't pulled tight and severely from her face, as the abundance of tresses and the curls from root to tip didn't allow her to do so.

Ginny opened the drawstrings on both ends of the wagon. After rinsing her mouth with the mint-in-water liquid, she tossed out the contents of the basin and water bucket. She emptied the lantern and stored the flammable oil as she had been cautioned to do. She made certain everything was secured for practice today. After lowering the tailgate, she left the wagon and went to the designated area to relieve herself, then joined Ellie Davis and her family.

"Good morning, Stuart," she said, then spoke with the children. "Another lovely day for you all to play while we work our hands raw."

Everyone laughed at the comical expression Ginny made on purpose to go along with her last sentence. "I wish I could sneak off and play dolls or games with you two," she whispered to the girls.

"We'd have fun, Miss Anna; Momma made us some good ones."

"We're going fishing," the two boys told her.

"We'll have 'em scaled and gutted by the time you and Momma get done so you can cook 'em for supper," the oldest boy planned.

"If we have time while we're camped here, you'll have to teach me how to catch and clean fish," Ginny said. "I've been in a ladies' boarding school for years, so I don't know much about living outdoors and off the land."

The elder boy looked smitten with Ginny. Not one to be timid, he offered, "I can teach you, Miss Anna. It'll be fun. I'll even put the worms or crickets on the line for you."

"That's kind of you, a real southern gentleman. But if I don't learn every-thing, what would I do later when you aren't around to help?"

"Most girls don't like to hold worms and mess with them, but I'll bet you're brave enough to do it."

"I hope so. Maybe we'll have the chance to find out soon."

"You kids get your chores done and let Miss Anna eat," Ellie told the active children. "We have to be ready to do our lessons soon."

The four laughed and teased their mother about doing lessons.

Ellie ruffled her son's hair. "No matter how old you get, children, there's always something new or important to learn."

Ginny concurred, as children often listened to others more than their parents. "Your mother's right; never stop learning or trying new things." She watched the children and Stuart climb inside to collect what they needed for the day in the other clearing while Ellie was gone with their wagon.

"That's good advice, Miss Avery," Steve remarked.

Ginny turned to give him a look that asked, *Do you always sneak up on people?* "Thank you, sir. We'll be ready for work soon."

"Good, 'cause I hate getting started late. You might want to use these today," he said, handing her an extra pair of thick riding gloves. "They're a mite large for you, but they'll do the job until your hands toughen up enough to use those fancy ones you have."

Ginny accepted the scouts' offering. She glanced at the gloves, then looked at him. "Thank you, Mr. Carr; that's very thoughtful. I discovered my own pair was too thin yesterday. I was expecting to find my hands covered with blisters this morning, but all I see are red spots and bruises so far."

"Soon you'll be seeing calluses on those delicate hands, but I don't want pain anywhere on your body to distract you again. The other women are using their husband's extra gloves. A shame your father didn't get you any."

Ginny felt her high spirits lower at his unexpected mood. She wondered if she had scared him or annoyed him with her enticing behavior last night. "When he comes to visit, I'll order the proper kind from town, then return yours. I'll take good care of them."

Steve saw how his alleged motive wiped the cheerful and appreciative smile from her face. He wished he hadn't hurt her feelings, but it seemed necessary if he was going to learn how to deal with her in the most advantageous manner. He nodded, then left the two women.

Ginny frowned and murmured to Ellie, "Why does that man always have to have a hateful excuse for doing something nice for another person?"

"Loners are like that, Anna dear."

"What do you mean?"

"They use a rough air to discourage people from getting too close to them. Most have been deeply hurt in the past, so they keep people at a distance with cold actions in order that they not be vulnerable again."

"You're saying that being mean is a defensive pretense?"

"Yes. If he doesn't let anybody get close, he can't be hurt again."

"But that's foolish and wrong. Being alone and cold hurts him, too."

"Yes, but someone in torment doesn't see it that way."

"Why would a man like Steve Carr be in torment?"

"I don't know. Could be anything. Maybe something from the war. I think he's taken with you and it makes him nervous."

Ginny recalled Lucy saying the same thing and wondered if it could be true. She eyed the scout who was saddling his horse. What if that was—

"You'd better eat before he calls us," Ellie advised. She was acutely aware of the girl's strong interest in their handsome guide.

"You're right; I best hurry. I have mules to tend and harness before he thinks I'm negligent and has something new to chide me about today."

As Steve was walking past her to summon the women, Ginny halted him. "I didn't get to thank you for suggesting the liniment," she said. "It worked, and I feel better this morning."

"Think nothing of it, Miss Avery. I have to keep my ladies in good working condition. Get your team hitched and ready to leave while I tell the others to do the same." He left her staring at his retreating back, as bewildered and ensnared by him as he was by her.

You're a hard man to open up, Steve Carr. I wonder why . . .

Ginny harnessed the team and connected it to the wagon. She climbed aboard the seat and got herself settled and ready to begin practice. She could almost hear her body grumbling already. Her sun bonnet was secured by ties under her chin, and her feet were braced firmly on the jockey box.

She stared at the large gloves he had loaned her, worn over her smaller ones to make them stay in place better. They were new, so no hints of his masculine scent and odor of daily chores clung to them. His hands were large and strong, and she wouldn't mind being caressed by them. She wouldn't mind kissing him and getting to know him. If only he weren't so contradictory, so befuddling, so frustrating! She never knew what mood he was going to be in when he approached her; but maybe he didn't, either. If Ellie and Lucy were right about his fears, that would explain why he was sweet one minute and sour the next.

But her friends could be mistaken. He could be telling her he wanted to teach her but not be chased by her. That shouldn't be a problem, as she didn't have the time to do so. Their paths would separate when this journey ended in a month or so. She couldn't understand why that panged her so deeply; they were strangers, and he was as hateful to her as he was nice to her. So, she pondered, why did she like him?

That was the crux of her dilemma; she liked him, too much, too soon. She hated to think of him being plagued by anguish; she knew how that felt. Perhaps that similarity was what she sensed, what drew her to him, simply the results of a too-tender heart. But if she could soften his hardness and warm his coldness by being a friend, shouldn't she give it her best effort, no matter how he resisted? If—

"Let's pull out, ladies!" Steve yelled, then he signaled them forward one by one at the precise moment to establish correct distance and pace.

Ginny pushed aside her reverie and concentrated only on her task. It did not take her long to realize and delight in discovering that she felt more confident today. Even her balance was better, and her body didn't protest the strain on it as much as it had yesterday. She was more relaxed and in control of herself and the team.

She congratulated herself on her new skills and independence. She had mastered her grief and worries so they wouldn't be evident to others. Most of the travelers were enjoyable, particularly her four new friends. A stimulating and challenging adventure lay before her and she should make the most of it. As for what to do about the mysterious and enchanting scout, she'd decide that later.

Steve galloped his sorrel back and forth along the line of wagons stretched out in the open on flat land. All but a few of the women were doing fine with their training and attitudes. He hoped they would continue to do so when other hard lessons arrived. He was restless with this part of the mission, uneasy in a camp filled with people, and wary of the way Anna Avery got to him. He was accustomed to staying on the move with only himself to worry about and away from crowds. He was torn between wanting to rush their training and depart, and wanting to go slowly and solve the case. If he finished fast, he could get back on his own, out of reach from the beauty's temptation. He could get on to his next task, a personal one he'd delayed to accept this crucial assignment. Pretenses, lies, and cold-blooded murder—he despised them and anyone who committed them, especially against *him*.

It was difficult to act the pleasant and genial scout, and often he failed to carry off that needed ruse, in particular with Anna. But if he didn't win these people's respect, trust, and friendship, he couldn't learn anything useful from them pertaining to the sinister Red Magnolia he had to entrap.

There was no thorough way he could search the wagons for gems, and he'd used his only logical excuse to do a light inspection earlier. He would have to depend on his probing skills and instincts to glean clues. He needed to increase his rapport with the men; he'd do so this afternoon.

Steve slowed at every wagon to speak with the driver: to praise, encourage, or give helpful advice to get in the good graces of each. Most of the women smiled, chatted, and thanked him; only Mattie and Mrs. Brown frowned and merely nodded, but at least they didn't grate on his nerves with whining. Louise told him she thought everyone was trained enough to head out the next day until Steve related the other things they needed to learn. Cathy sent him a seductive look and purred like a kitten as she talked with him; Steve pretended not to notice or be affected.

"Any problems?" he asked Ginny as he rode beside her on the left.

"None that I know of, Mr. Carr. How am I doing?" she asked, keeping her gaze ahead on Mary's wagon.

"Fine. If trouble strikes, signal me." He galloped away, hoping she would wonder why he had spent so little time with her. With luck, she'd seen how much longer he had visited with the others. That should spark her curiosity and worry her, maybe provoke her to work harder to catch his eye and to please him. Most women, he assumed, wanted what they couldn't have, so Anna should be challenged to chase him.

As Steve passed her again, she ignored him. *Shu,* Anna looked appealing today. She had braided her hair as he suggested, then secured the end with a red ribbon. The thick tuft at the bottom swayed against her waist when she moved. She hadn't dared look at him and lose her pace and distance requirement. That caution meant she didn't want to annoy him with another mistake, so his scoldings, no matter their motives, were working. He had to admit she was doing an astonishingly good job. The dark-blue shirt and skirt she was wearing flattered her skin coloring, and her hairstyle highlighted her exquisite face.

Steve signaled the wagons to halt. He rode to each one to tell the women he was ready to begin corral practice. If Anna dreaded it or was vexed with him, it didn't show. He had told them before leaving that it was necessary to circle the wagons at night and sometimes on the trail itself for safety from enemy or raider attacks.

The scout walked his sorrel in a wide circle and the women followed as instructed, or tried to obey. He knew it was a tricky maneuver to guide the team ever rightward by control of the reins while not allowing a front wheel to jam into the wagon. When a team balked or got out of alignment, Steve halted the others to correct it. Sometimes he had to seize the cheekstrap or sidecheck and forcefully guide the team into place. As he did so, he told the woman involved how to better handle the reins to accomplish it from her seat. "Loosen up on your left rein and pull back on the right one to get him heading in that direction. Not too hard or he'll turn his head too sharp and resist your command. He's the leader, so the others will follow him. They have no choice; they're linked together."

Ginny was relieved the "leader" was earmarked, so she knew which one to always put on the front right side. Every time she fed, watered, or worked with her mules, she tried to earn their affection and respect so they would obey her orders without balking. So far so good . . .

It took a while for most of the women to get the procedure down, and some never stopped having trouble. When Steve halted his ride, the loop he had made was the perfect size for creating a tight ring with the right side of one wagon front almost making contact with the back left side of the wagon before it. Teams were on the exterior of the ring, adjacent to the front neighbor's wagon where they would be unhitched and led inside. That left no opening for attackers to get through their barricade. If defense was needed, he'd told them, men would stand between the jockey box and seat or behind the seat to fire their weapons, using the thick wooden bed as cover.

He shouted for the women to get down and group in the center. "On the trail, we'll leave two wagons' widths open for movement of animals and comings and goings of people for chores," he explained. "The two grain wagons joining us before we leave will drive straight into the remaining space and fill it before we turn in for the night or if trouble strikes. The animals will be corraled inside the circle to protect them from outlaws. You and your families will sleep in or under your wagons, according to weather and preference. You'll do your cooking near your wagon on the outside; keep a low campfire going at night to discourage wild animals and to prevent anyone from sneaking up on us in the dark. Any questions before we practice pulling out and doing this again?"

"If we park like this, how will we get to our things to do our chores?" Louise Jackson asked arrogantly. "What we'll use on the road is packed at the rear, out of reach from the outside. We'd have to carry things out of the circle to work, then haul them back inside. Why can't we park with our backs pointed outward? It seems just as easy and far more practical for chores. That way, the teams would already be inside when we unhitch them."

"That would make things easier for you women," he began, and saw the bossy creature gloat with smugness. "But it isn't safe, and safety is more important than ease with chores. If an attack comes, the men can defend themselves and their families better from the front of the wagon. If you'll notice, the wagon beds are high enough to pass things underneath to keep from having to walk around countless times."

Ginny was glad when Steve's authoritative tone and gaze hushed Louise, who looked miffed at being overruled. She wondered where he would camp, as he didn't have a wagon to put into the tight ring. Inside, she mused, with the animals, as there was enough room for a small campsite? Or outside, where the loner had space and privacy, as he could defend himself against any threat that might come along? Changing her line of thought abruptly, she was amazed by how he could control the color and expression in his eyes: he could make them blank and unreadable, cold and harsh and intimidating, or soft and entreating. He seemed to have masterful prowess in every area of his life and body.

"Any more questions or remarks?" he asked. The women remained silent and alert. "All right, ladies, let's pull out and do this again."

By one o'clock, they had finished the lesson and eaten lunch. Steve announced with a grin, "I'm going to let you rest and do chores for a few hours, ladies, while the men go hunting for fresh meat. I'm sure your children need some attention from you, more than just a quick visit at night before turning in. We'll start shooting lessons when I return later."

Ginny sat on a quilt beneath a shade tree away from the noise of camp. She read while Ruby Amerson's two babies napped nearby on a pallet. She had insisted on tending the children while their mother washed clothes at the river. She liked the perky redhead and knew Ruby could use the help. She didn't know much about babies, but, as long as they slept, she was sure she wouldn't have a problem. Ruby had showed her how to diaper them if it became necessary, but there was no feeding scheduled.

Ginny stopped reading a while to ponder the mysterious and appealing Steve Carr. He had avoided her today, perhaps to prevent temptation or to conceal his interest from the others and from her. He could be afraid he'd make an embarrassing error if he became ensnared by thoughts of her, and unaccustomed fear must be something he despised. Maybe the self-protective scout didn't know how to deal with or woo a woman who caught his eye. Or know how to apologize for harshness, warranted or not. Maybe he tried to do it by being nice and helpful afterward. Or perhaps he thought she was only being friendly and he could never win a woman so different from his own self. Should she show him otherwise? But why, when their paths would separate soon? She must not risk hurting herself when Steve Carr was unattainable and unchangeable.

Ginny gazed at the sleeping siblings, infant and toddler. They were precious bundles of joy with fine strawberry-blond hair and pudgy cheeks. One day, she would have a family as happy as Ruby's was. She—

Her musings halted as she saw Charles Avery walking toward her. She smiled before touching a finger to her lips and pointing to the babies to indicate quiet. She motioned for him to sit beside her. In a low tone, she said, "It's good to see you. How are things going?"

"That's what I came to ask you," he whispered with a smile.

"Fine, so far, except that contradictory Steve Carr gives me a hard time once in a while. I have to confess it's partly my fault; sometimes I have trouble paying attention during class."

The tall, lean man just responded, "It's no wonder, my dear, after what you've been through lately and what you have staring you in the face soon. I'm sorry you're having a difficult time with him; he struck me as a nice fellow."

"He is, but I rub him wrong at times, too many times."

Charles studied the curious blush on her cheeks and grinned. "Ah, so that's how it is," he teased. "You like him a great deal. What about him?"

Ginny didn't feel uncomfortable talking about her romantic feelings, as Charles Avery had a way of relaxing her. "I can't tell how he feels or what he thinks, *Father*." They shared soft laughter. "Sometimes he's nice and seems to want to become friends; other times, he's cold and rude and distant. I don't understand him at all." She related the incidents that weren't too personal. "Do you see what I mean? I'm utterly baffled." She listened to the forthcoming advice from her trusted and respected friend.

"Be nice and cooperative, Anna; he has a heavy burden on his shoulders." The name of his deceased daughter rolled easily off his tongue. Lord, how he missed his child and wife. He liked this girl and would do almost anything to help and protect her. "He may only be intimidated around a real lady; I doubt he meets and deals with many genteel women. He could be afraid that a refined lady can't learn her lessons or might not hold up during the hardships on the trail or that she will delay everyone with spoiled ways."

Ginny knew where her assumed name had come from and guessed what Charles had been thinking and feeling when he paused for a moment. Her heart went out to him for his tragic loss. The eyes that filled with torment for a while were the bluest, clearest, and gentlest ones she had ever seen. She had no doubts he liked her and that she was safe with him. "You could be right. He's nice when I'm obedient and catch on quickly. He gets mad when I don't focus my full attention on him and class."

"If he wants total concentration on him, give it to him. It is to your best interests. Besides, you might have use of him later." At her quizzical look, he explained, "A skilled guide like him would make a good scout and protector for what you have to do soon. If you agree, I can loan you the money to hire him for that service."

"Let Steve Carr take me to Colorado?" she murmured as her head filled with thoughts of what could happen between them on a secluded trail.

"Are you afraid of him? Has he done or said anything to make you think he's dangerous or untrustworthy? If he hasn't been a complete gentleman, I'll thrash him with a whip."

Ginny knew why the man got upset and why his face flushed with angry seriousness. She understood his concern. She appeased him with a touch on his rigid forearm and by assuring him Steve hadn't done anything improper or scary. *Not,* she added mutely, *like you mean.*

"He'd better not!" Charles declared angrily, balling his fists.

"I'm certain he won't, sir. I just don't want to distract him from his duties with disobedience, mistakes, or romantic overtures." Ginny turned to check on the Amerson children, who had stirred to the disturbance, but she settled them down with light pats on their backs and a soothing tone.

Her last few words told Charles Avery that she was powerfully interested in their guide. Since Carr struck him as a decent fellow, he wasn't worried about Ginny leaning in the man's direction. After all, Carr could be of great help to her soon, especially if her deception in Texas failed and if her father was truly dead. From overhearing talks between the two girls before Johanna Chapman died, he knew more about Virginia Marston and her dead friend than she realized or had confided to him.

If he didn't have his own busy schedule and problems to resolve, he concluded, he would escort her to Colorado himself. Perhaps he could after they were handled. He would make sure she knew where to locate him in case trouble arose in Texas. But if he couldn't help her if she got into peril, the skilled scout was a path she needed to open and to keep cleared for use. He would continue to encourage and advise her to do so. With the interest Ginny seemed to show in him, that shouldn't be difficult. All he had to do, Charles planned, was to make certain the scout was just as enchanted by her as she obviously was of him. If so, Steve would do anything to help and protect her. They had a long trail to cover and plenty of time for him to push the two young people together, but only if he didn't change his mind and opinion about the expert trail guide.

When Ginny faced him again, Charles said, "I'm sure you'll be fine, Anna; you're brave and smart. You know what you have to do to succeed. You have a lot at stake, so you'll make the right decisions to accomplish your goals. If the war taught me one thing, it's to do what one must for survival, victory, and happiness."

"Those are my dreams and goals, Mr.— *Father*," she corrected herself for practice. She returned his affectionate smile before continuing. "But sometimes I'm afraid I'll fail."

"That's only natural, Anna, but you won't," he assured her.

"You have more confidence in me than I do," she confessed.

"Because I know you're a strong and courageous person. Before this journey and challenge end, you'll be convinced, too."

"I hope so."

"I know so." He changed the subject. "Martha sent you a fine meal and a whole dried apple pie. I put it in the wagon before I joined you here. Is there anything else you need? I'll be returning to town soon to reach there before dark. No need to tempt evil forces to attack me."

"You will be careful and alert, won't you?" she asked with concern.

"Of course, my child, and I'm well armed for trouble."

Ginny eyed the weapon he exposed and smiled in reassurance. "I can use driving gloves. Mine are too thin for protection."

"I should have thought of that. Give me a pair of yours for size and I'll bring them tomorrow."

"I have to watch Ruby's children, but they're laying on the wagon seat." She told him about Steve loaning her an extra pair of his.

Charles grinned in pleasure. "Yes, sir, a real gentleman, just like I thought. Anything else? Don't worry about money; I have plenty."

"Only if you let me repay you later."

He smiled. "It's a deal. I'll keep an account, if you insist."

"I do. I can use pants for climbing around on the wagon; a full skirt gets tangled up and immodest at times. You can use the green riding skirt on top of my trunk for size. And boots, if you can find sturdier ones to fit. Open the trunk on the left side facing front and pull out the slippers on top. Will that be too much trouble?" she fretted aloud. "If so, I'll understand. I never considered proper attire for the trail or the training before I left town."

"Martha will assist me if I need help filling your requests. Don't worry, Anna, it's no trouble at all; honestly."

"Thank you, sir. I don't know what I would do if not for you."

Charles was touched by the unshed tears that shone in her hazel eyes. "You've been a joy to meet, to get to know, and to help, Anna. I haven't felt warm sunshine in my life since my daughter . . . died, not until I met you and . . . You know what I mean. Thank you," he said with an emotional lump in his throat.

"We're both fortunate to have met each other in a time of mutual need."

"You're right, my girl. Well," he said as he stood, "I should get moving. Take care, Anna Avery, and I'll see you tomorrow."

"Good-bye and thank you." She watched him vanish into the trees between her and camp. With Charles Avery's help and generosity, her first deception would succeed, no matter how distasteful she found it to lie to friends. As he had warned her, it was possible one of these people knew or knew *of* her stepfamily or her father, so she couldn't risk confiding her identity and ultimate goal to anyone. As for her second deception, she wouldn't think about it until the time came to begin it.

The little girl stirred and awakened. Ginny lifted and cuddled the child to keep her from disturbing the baby boy. She didn't know how much a child of fourteen months could understand, but she said, "Momma's washing clothes; she'll be back soon. Do you want . . . Anna to play with you?" She lifted a handmade toy to use to entertain the toddler along with words in a soothing tone. The child relaxed and responded, and they played.

Steve approached, observing the tender scene that tugged unbidden at his stony heart. How, he asked himself, could he behave in a cold and disinterested fashion to a woman with such warmth and appeal? Yet, he must for the sake of his mission and to protect himself. He quelled his rebellious emotions to speak with her, to continue his cunning strategy of repel, attract, repel, attract. "Babysitting, Miss Avery?"

Ginny looked over her shoulder and answered, "Yes, sir, while Ruby does the wash. She has more chores than I do, and her husband was with you."

He propped against the tree. "Why do you call me 'sir,' " he queried, forcing a mirthful chuckle and grin to surface. "I'm twenty-seven and you're nineteen; that's only eight years separating us. 'Sir' makes me feel old."

Was he, she wondered, being subtly enticing again? "Sorry, Mr. Carr. Age has nothing to do with it; a show of respect to authority does."

"Ah, yes, your fancy schooling and fine breeding are responsible."

"True," she replied, but decided not to say more until she discovered what mood he was in this time. From his casual tone and expression, she couldn't guess how he meant his last words. She remembered one teacher saying: "A smart woman knows when and how long to be silent with a trying man." The problem was, Virginia Marston fretted, was she a smart woman when it came to a difficult man—to utterly bewildering Steve Carr?

"I heard your father came to visit. Sorry I missed him." He wished he had seen Charles, as he needed time with every one of his suspects. During the successful hunt, he hadn't gleaned a single helpful clue.

Ginny sensed that his full attention wasn't on her. He was like a train with engines at both ends, each trying to pull in an opposite direction. "I ordered gloves and pants as you suggested. Father will bring them to me tomorrow. When I get them, I'll return yours. And I told Father of your kindness. He speaks highly of you."

"Does that surprise you?"

She watched a squirrel play as she answered, "No, why should it?"

"We have had our . . . differences in the last few days."

"Only because I was distracted by other matters at the wrong time."

Steve watched her closely. She seemed to avoid meeting his gaze with hers on purpose. "You're taking full blame for them?"

"No, but most of the problems were my fault."

"Then you understand why I have to be tough on you?"

"For the most part." The toddler cried in boredom and from a lack of attention, or maybe the child sensed tension in the air and it unsettled her. As Ginny focused on quieting and comforting her, the unpredictable scout left after reminding her of target practice in thirty minutes.

Steve had tested and instructed all but one woman with rifle and pistol when it came Anna's turn. He said he had made her last again because the other women with children and husbands had more chores to do. He had set up a target area a half-mile from camp to prevent frightening and disturbing the youngsters. Since Ellie's oldest children were twelve and fourteen and could watch the two younger ones for a while, Stuart Davis took the other women on their two-mile trek to let them get finished with their training today. Steve said that he or one of the other men could walk with Anna Avery when she had completed her shooting lesson.

"You said you could load and fire a rifle, right . . . ?" Steve began.

"Yes," she replied, aware they were alone and out of sight.

"Show me."

Ginny accepted the Henry rifle and studied it.

"Anything wrong?"

"Nothing, just seeing how and where it loads; weapons do vary."

"It fires .44 caliber rimfire cartridges. It's a fifteen-shot repeater with lever action and magazine loading. Any questions?"

"None." Ginny loaded the rifle without trouble. "Ready?"

"Do it."

Ginny eyed the targets he pointed out, shouldered the Henry, and fired fifteen times. "It kicks like a . . . mule," she murmured, knowing she gained another bruise.

Steve walked to the targets and checked them, then returned to her. "You're right, a skilled shot, only two misses, and I doubt by much. How did you become such an expert marksman?"

Ginny had to deceive him. "The teachers at school thought ladies should know how to protect themselves; we were at war, remember?" Actually, she had been taught because hunting was a favorite sporting diversion of the English, one every well-trained lady was expected to master.

"What about a pistol? Do you know how to handle and use one?"

"I've only fired small ones a few times."

Steve withdrew one of his Colts, unloaded it, and handed it to her. "Forty-four caliber. Six shots. Hand-cock the hammer after each firing."

Ginny took the pistol. At over four pounds and with a nine-inch barrel, it was heavy and awkward to handle. She loaded the weapon, then looked at him in uncertainty. "How do I aim?"

"Extend your arm and lock your elbow. Line up the end of the barrel with your target and pull the trigger."

Ginny obeyed with difficulty because of the pistol's weight. She exerted pressure on the trigger and a loud bang filled the air. The force of the blast jerked her hand and arm upward, sending the shot wild and high. "Not even close," she muttered as she cocked the hammer again.

Steve grasped her right wrist and put downward pressure on it as she fired another shot. "Closer, but still off. Try again."

After ten minutes and two rounds of cartridges, Ginny hit the largest target twice. "Two out of twelve is a bad score," she murmured.

"You have to learn to control a pistol's power and offset its weight. A weapon isn't much good to you if you don't know how to use it. Make it your friend, as comfortable in your hand as your palm is. You can't protect yourself if you can't hit your target, and a live one moves."

She glanced at him. "I could never kill anyone."

"When and if the time comes, you will," Steve reasoned, "and you'll be glad you're alive instead of your enemy. Think of it as gaining revenge or justice. Some people believe you can do anything for those reasons."

Ginny assumed he was referring to the recent war and lingering troubles resulting from it. "They're wrong. The war is over; we've made peace, and we're heading for new starts. The past can't be changed. Revenge only breeds more problems for innocents to get entangled with and be hurt worse."

Steve saw an opening to draw out possible clues. "The KKK doesn't think the same way you do. Of course, it's turning sour fast, forgetting why it was formed. It soon might be as bad as those Yank bands who attack Southerners."

"I don't know much about the Ku Klux Klan, only what I've been told or read. But I think it's wrong to go after black men. Most are good, kind, and honest men who only want freedom and peace. You can't blame them for the actions of those who've been deceived and provoked by the Yankees into terrorizing and punishing their ex-masters. I realize some of those gangs have gone wild and they're killing or robbing any white person, but that doesn't justify what the Klan does to innocent ex-slaves."

"You're right, and smart, too, Miss Avery. Let's get back to our task. Maybe your trouble is bad aiming. With powerful eyes like yours, you should be able to see how to do anything. Give it another try."

Ginny warmed at the almost-concealed compliment. She loaded and fired another round, and did better—three out of six. She grinned in pleasure as she looked at the scout and he commented that she was improving each time.

Steve leaned against a tree while she continued to practice. She seemed determined to become accurate and was thrilled with her success. After telling him she wasn't learning so she could kill anyone, he concluded she was trying hard only to please him. That was just what he needed . . .

When she emptied the box of shells and was hitting the target four times out of six, he said, "That's enough for today. Let's go on our stroll. I'm sure you're ready to get finished and on to relaxing or doing chores."

"Does that mean I pass the test, teacher?" she asked with a grin.

"Yep. Let's move out; we have two miles to cover."

They headed for the path he had marked earlier. Steve set the pace to match that of a moving wagon and stayed a few steps ahead of her. He didn't make small talk, as he'd been familiar enough with her for today. He was too cognizant of their solitude, the peaceful surroundings, and her appeal. If he wasn't careful, he might seize her and kiss her then and there. He would try that soon, but it was too early to get that friendly to win her favor. He had to keep telling himself that during the entire two miles.

Ginny stayed within a few steps of the tall man strolling before her. Since he didn't speak, she didn't, either. Obviously he wanted the silence and distance, so she let him have both. Besides, it wasn't wise to make an overture in this dangerously romantic setting, and she wasn't sure how he would take one from her. It was best to spend quiet and pleasant time with him rather than creating more friction between them. He was being nice and leaning her way, she realized, so she would leave it be for a while.

They returned to camp, dismissed each other, then parted.

Ginny gathered her things and went to the river for a bath. She discovered her monthly flow had ended, and she was glad. Soon, scrubbed and refreshed, she joined Ellie Davis to help finish cooking the fish the boys had caught and cleaned. She noticed that Steve had been invited to eat with the Jacksons tonight and wondered how he would tolerate the overbearing Louise and her quiet husband during the meal.

She had intended to give Steve the food Charles Avery had brought, but he didn't need it now. Two of Ellie's children didn't like fish, so Ginny gave the fried chicken to them. She saw the youngsters' eyes glow when she produced the dried apple pie from Miss Avery in town. "Eat all your dinner and you can have a slice," she advised the enthusiastic children.

Virginia Marston was relaxed and content following her successes today and Steve's easygoing manner with her. She didn't realize she was in for an enlightening and stunning lesson later that night.

Chapter 5

∽

ALMOST EVERY ONE of the men and a few women gathered around a colorful fire to talk about the evils plaguing the South. To keep from disturbing the children, the gathering was held away from the other wagons but was still close enough to hers for Ginny to overhear the chilling conversation. The barely waxing moon with its sliver of pale yellow did nothing to help lighten the setting. Only those near the blaze had their faces illuminated for recognition when they spoke.

When the talk became serious, Ginny put aside her book and doused her lantern to listen without being noticed at the side of the wagon where the canvas was slid up a few inches for fresh air.

"Some folks think strong actions should be taken to halt it, but I can't imagine what most people can do to change things. Not if they want to stay out of jail. Those Radicals are in power and they want everything done their way; they even have Secretary of War Stanton as their leader. You can't provoke a man in his position to come after you. I guess our hands are tied."

Ginny recognized Steve Carr's voice; she hadn't taken him for a man interested in or concerned with politics and reforms. Hadn't he implied he only needed and took care of himself? Odd. . . .

"Ain't much an honest man can do until the South is free of Yankee control and we get our own governments back in power," Stuart Davis said.

Daniels disagreed. "What we need is stronger 'Black Codes' like ever'body voted in 'cept Tennessee. Like them Mississippi boys said, we live under the threat of Yankee bayonets and crazy words from misguided foreigners. We done did away with slavery, so why can't ever'body be happy and leave us be? Ex-slaves can't be citizens of this great country; they can't socialize with us or rule us from political offices handed to them by crazy Yanks. We'll do as we're ordered, let 'em be safe, but we don't have to like it or be friends with them or have 'em crammed down our throats."

"Us Georgia boys don't cower to Negroes. If they're caught lazing around, we arrest 'em and jail 'em or fine 'em. It's all legal, too."

Ginny couldn't see who had made those remarks. She wished she could, as a Georgian might know— Harry Brown's explosion halted her thoughts.

"Hellfire, our own President can't help us! The Army Act won't allow him to give it orders; they have to come through General Grant. I say, a President, no matter how I hate him, should be in control of the country, not them contrary and greedy Radicals. Hellfire, the South's been chopped up into five military districts with a general over each, all because we wouldn't accept that Fourteenth Amendment. They expect us to agree that Africans are citizens and can vote? They can hold office and we can't 'cause we fought against the Union? We can't file claims for slaves they took away or for property they burned and looted just for the meanness of it. We can't even get loans to see us through bad times; they let carpetbaggers steal our land and homes on unpaid taxes they levy on us to pay for a war we lost. We're all dead broke. Why should we vote in and then obey laws that go against us? Hellfire, we ain't even part of the Union again! Africans have more rights than we do! If we even pass air the wrong way, they punish us."

"They do the same to businesses," Ed King added, "They keep us disfranchised and rule every manner of transportation and sales. With those carpetbaggers running over us with the help of scalawags, we don't have a chance of recovering. They stole my dairy business, but I'll build a new one in Texas. They won't get that one without a bloody fight."

"You think those Yanks will ever pull out of the South?" Ellie asked.

"No conqueror ever retreats or gives back what he's won. They think they did us a favor with that Amnesty Act, but it only helped the rurals."

"I know what you mean, Ed," James Wiggins said. "Any man who was a high officer or had money before the war has to personally beg the President for one. I refused to bend my knee to him or any Yank."

"We could have won the war if Ole Jeff Davis and most of us hadn't been so genteel," Jeff said. "If we'd done forays into the North before Abe hired such good generals to fight us, they would have been too weak and scared to strike."

"The Yanks ain't got no room or right to be high and mighty!" Daniels fumed. "They're forgetting they had slavery, too, nigh unto 1805. When they leaned toward industry, they didn't need slaves no more; but we did for our plantations. They asked us to abolish it, that whole institution of slavery, but we couldn't. They ruffled lots of feathers when they demanded it in '30. I never knowed any southern gentleman who abused his property; they was too valuable to beat and cripple, like they near crippled my leg from no treatment in that prison. The Yanks had no right to take our property away and attack us. They just used slavery as an excuse to destroy us, to come down here and take over. They ain't nothing like us, so they don't understand us. They think we're stupid and backward 'cause we talk slow and easy and different."

"Hellfire," Brown spat. "They don't care about Africans! They're already abandoning and ignoring their *rights*. We'll make it back in spite of them."

"It all started with that Missouri Compromise in '50," Ed King said. "We should never have agreed. Then, the way they acted over that Dred Scott case was stupid; it didn't matter if his master moved to a free state; that didn't give him a right to sue for his freedom or become a citizen. But when they blockaded our ports and captured southern territory, they challenged us beyond restraint, even those of us who didn't have slaves and never would. We had to join our friends and families to battle them."

"Weren't much of a country anyway," Daniels said. "We had one constitution and a President and congress, but not much unity beyond them. States and towns handled their own affairs. What did the government do for us? Very little, so why should we be more loyal to the Union than the South?"

"It was the railroads' and telegraphs' fault. Progress be damned! Made everybody get too close and cozy, too easy to reach and control."

"You're right, Ed," James said. "Every section was being threatened or exploited by another. We were being pulled apart at the seams, which weren't strong to begin with. The Englanders hated the westerners because too many folks were moving that way and could raise and sell crops cheaper than them. The westerners knew the easterners were using them and considered them trash. The South was rich and genteel and powerful so those Yanks couldn't stand it. Yes, sir, they used slavery as an excuse to attack. They even praised that vicious John Brown when he made that bloody attack at Harper's Ferry on whites to free his own kind."

The quiet Samuel Jackson spoke up. "I've seen the papers, so I know the real figures: less than three hundred fifty thousand out of six million Southerners owned slaves; fewer than two thousand had one hundred or more; most only owned four or less."

Again, Ginny couldn't recognize the voice of the speaker in the shadows who said, "It didn't help Georgia none that she was the power of the Confederacy. Her rails, port, and three arsenals kept our side alive until Sherman destroyed them. He even captured Jeff Davis at Irwinville."

"The Yankee bastard should have been shot!" Daniels shot out. "He ordered and allowed his men to do things beyond cruelty, even for wartime."

"I bet the KKK would love to get their hands on him for a few hours," George said. "They're big in Alabama where we'll be passing soon. Right in the heart of the Confederacy's birth, our first capital at Montgomery."

"If you men got rid of Radicals, carpetbaggers, scalawags, and that Loyal League," Cathy scoffed, "we wouldn't have to pull up roots and move; we wouldn't have to tuck our tails between our legs like beaten dogs and flee. This is our land, so why hand it over to greedy Yanks? We can all join the Klan and fight back. The Invisible Empire is strong and fearless. The soldiers have to catch you before you can be jailed or punished. If we're clever, we won't get caught. It's worth a try. Surely somebody here knows how to reach members."

Ed King changed the subject after scowling at his beautiful wife and scolding, "Don't be foolish, Cathy. Those are dangerous words to speak aloud. You never know when spies are around. Besides, you don't know what you're talking about; the Klan is as dangerous as it is helpful. I heard that Sherman and other Union officers have been assigned out west to whip the Indians like they whipped the Rebs. Word is, everybody's demanding Indian control by placing them on reservations or by destroying them. With so many citizens moving west, the government will have to respond."

"Yeah," Daniels scoffed, "Sherman is commander of the Military Division of the Missouri. I hope them redskins lick him and his troops worse than they did us. Serve 'em all right to get killed and scalped after what they done to us. Maybe those redskins will do a job on them we couldn't."

"Mrs. King is right to a point; if we could fight back, we wouldn't have to leave. But we can't; it's too dangerous. That Klan is going crazy."

"How is that?" Steve questioned Mattie Epps's husband.

"Yeah, Joel. I hear they're doing a good job of protecting Southerners and running out bad Yanks and Africans. Hellfire, they done got the vote and got themselves schools. Next, they'll be taking over," Brown sneered in disgust.

"Schooling might help them," Ellie reasoned. "Learning helps anybody. Even if you don't believe that, it's wrong to burn their schools and churches and homes. It'll only provoke more of them to attack whites."

"I hear only educated and rich men are Klan members," Louise remarked. "That's why they wear hoods, so they can't be recognized and caught. They only raid troublemakers and Yankees, and those traitorous scalawags. Half the things they're accused of doing are actually done by those Loyal Leaguers in disguise. I think they deserve praise for their courage and cunning. I wouldn't mind being a Klanswoman. If I were, I'd lead my group to great victories. Our name would be known the country over."

"So would news of your captures and hangings."

"We wouldn't get caught, Ellie, we'd be too clever. We'd scare the pants off those Yankee thieves and killers."

Again, Ginny struggled to pierce the darkness to see who spoke next. "Those Yankee courts don't help us; they only help their kind and Negroes. If it wasn't for the Klan, we'd be in sorry shape. Most say General Dudley DuBose is the leader in Georgia, but the law can't prove it. I say they're patriots, good men being forced to fight evil any way they have to."

Steve marked Carl Murphy off his mental list of suspects, even though he hadn't been included on it earlier. No culprit, he surmised, was fool enough to say an important leader's name aloud. He listened as Louise Jackson began spouting her knowledge of matters.

"I saw their creed published in a newspaper. Some journalist got his hands on a copy and exposed it. It didn't help the Yankees' claims against them because it said it was to 'protect the weak, the innocent, and the defenseless, from indignities, wrongs and outrages of the lawless, the violent, and the brutal,' and so forth, 'especially the widows and orphans of Confederate soldiers.' It even said it was to 'protect and defend the Constitution of the United States, and all laws.' It sounds good to me."

"Me, too," Daniels said. "You don't see the 'so-called' *law* capturing and punishing those Loyal Leaguers or gangs of 'so-called' soldiers. But catch a Klansman and he's strung up high on the spot or tossed into the worst hellhole of a prison they can find. You're in deeper trouble if you're a high officer, say a Grand Dragon. Or a Den member of the Red Magnolias."

Steve wondered why John Daniels would mention the very unit the law was trying to expose. Most feared to even whisper the name of that secret society. *A trick,* he pondered, *to throw off suspicion?*

"Who are the Magnolias?" Cathy inquired.

"A small but powerful Den. Their symbol is a white magnolia blossom dipped in blood or one painted with red dripping from it. Their costumes are scarlet, a fearsome sight to behold. If you ever find one of their signs on your porch, you best run for your life."

"It's the war." Ellie ventured, "That's what did it to them. Made them cold and hard. Made them willing to do anything for revenge."

Jeff Eaves asked Steve if he was in the war.

"Yes, like most men."

"For which side?" Harry Brown asked.

Steve had to reply, "Wasn't but one right side, the Confederacy."

James Wiggins asked him where he had fought.

"Here and there, mostly in Mississippi, Tennessee, and Kentucky."

"Let's not talk about the war anymore tonight," Ellie suggested. "It's late and everybody's unnerved. George, why not play us a relaxing song?"

"Sure, ma'am, be happy to." Ruby's husband lifted his fiddle from his lap and began a merry tune to calm everyone before bedtime.

As he listened, Steve knew why he hadn't told them he had been captured at Shiloh in April of '63 while trying to save a man's life. Nor would he mention how he had been imprisoned and harrowed, and most of all how he had been released to become a Galvanized Yankee. He knew how most Southerners hated and viewed such soldiers as traitors and cowards.

He told himself he shouldn't have been in the war in the first place, so why stay in a "hell hole," as John Daniels had called Union prisons? Why be tormented emotionally and physically or watch others be treated that way? Why watch men die in fear, pain, and denial when you could be out West in fresh air, free, far from the horrors of war, and doing good and brave deeds instead of rotting away for years? Who wouldn't accept the Yanks' offer? Other Rebs had done the same thing for a variety of reasons. Some were fed up with war and killing, some realized how futile and wrong the fighting was, some were plagued by utter despair, some were suffering from lost courage, some wanted hope for new roots elsewhere, and some didn't want to be forced to change sides to battle family and friends as the other price for release.

Despite the good Galvanized Yankees had done during the war—helping with road and fort building, stringing or restringing or guarding telegraph lines and relay shacks, carrying mail, protecting and guiding survey crews, rescuing Indian captives, and other jobs—they were labeled yellowbellies and betrayers by the South and they were pushed aside by the Union they had helped. Dishonored and discouraged, many had become outlaws, rustlers, gunfighters, and worse after their releases in '65; some had become his missions to track down and halt.

Steve felt he was one of the lucky ones, and good fortune hadn't been too kind to him in the past. The compromise had given him a place to work, a way to earn respect, to get survival training, to hone his skills and instincts, and to make a few good friends. He could have escaped at any time, as he had often worked alone, but he hadn't. It wasn't because of loyalty to his releasers or fear of recapture, but out of what he was gaining from the situation. It had suited his needs, so he had done his assignments; he had continued to do most of those same tasks afterward.

Steve sensed eyes on him from the Avery wagon. He wondered what Anna thought about all she'd heard. If her father was the villain he was seeking, did she know about his evil involvement with the Red Magnolias? Did she approve? Had she been duped into believing the Invisible Empire was doing good and necessary work? He wished Charles Avery had been present tonight to air his opinions. He hoped Anna's father could be eliminated as a suspect. If he was the guilty one, what would happen to the refined beauty?

Steve told himself he couldn't worry about that possible future predicament, couldn't worry about the repercussions to families and friends of *any* criminals who were slain or imprisoned. He had been easy on her today. Tomorrow he must be repelling, but not rough, just ignore and avoid her enough to concern her and challenge her.

Practice began at nine. When all women showed they were proficient in harnessing, driving, and circling up, Steve said it was time for their next lesson: handling runaways, stampedes, and calming terrified teams.

The women emptied one wagon of its load so three at a time could practice: a driver with two assistants standing behind her. The others waited their turns in a group but were ordered to pay attention, not chat.

"Mrs. Jackson, you be our first driver. Mrs. Amerson and Martin, you two be the riders. I'll spook the team with gunfire. Usually it's gunshots from raiders or thunder that sets them off. When one team takes off, the others generally follow. The lead wagons must get their teams slowed and controlled as quickly as possible. Just do as I say." He spoke to everyone at once, but only Louise nodded with smugness.

"If you lose the reins, hang on to the seat until I halt the team. You observers make sure your drivers don't fall off. Grab an arm or handful of clothes to keep her aboard. Pull her back into the wagon with you if need be. Any questions?" None came, so the scout asked if they were ready to leave.

Louise sent him a confident nod. Ruby and Mrs. Martin braced themselves for the wild ride ahead.

Steve drew his pistol and fired shots within inches of the mules' hooves and whizzed bullets past their twitching ears. The startled animals bolted instantly, jerking the wagon into motion. The pounding of hooves, squeaking of wagon, and women's yells filled the air. Dust and severed grass were flung up by hoof and wheel alike.

As instructed, Louise Jackson "let them have their head" to see if the frantic beasts would overcome their fear and settle down or get winded soon and slow by themselves. Steve galloped alongside the runaway team to be nearby if help was needed and to protect the women from injury.

When the winded team began to slow, Louise pulled back on the reins and shouted commands for them to halt. At the right moment, she worked the brake lever and the wagon stopped.

Steve looked at the grinning female who grated on his nerves most of the time. "Good, Mrs. Jackson. Now, drive it back for the next team to do it."

Lucy Eaves drove for Mrs. Hammond and Mrs. Brown without trouble.

Ellie drove for "Anna Avery" and Mary Wiggins, again without trouble.

When it came time for Cathy King to be the leader for Mrs. Murphy and Mrs. Franks, she fretted, "I'm so scared, Steve. Must I?"

"Don't worry, Mrs. King; you're in no danger; I'm here."

"That's the only reason I have the guts to try this," she told him.

"You'll do fine, just like the others did," the scout encouraged.

But the dark-haired beauty didn't "do fine." She lost the reins almost immediately and screamed for Steve to rescue her.

Ginny watched the racing team speed up as the reins dragged the ground. She was glad she hadn't been assigned as a driver, but only because she hadn't wanted to make a mistake. Ellie had managed the team with skill and courage, and she had bragged about her friend. She had the wicked suspicion that Cathy King had let go of the reins on purpose. She watched the sultry beauty lean over and grab Steve by the neck, forcing him to take her onto the saddle with him to keep her from falling to the ground from the lofty seat. The other women must have suspected the same ruse because they glanced at one another and frowned.

Steve turned the control over to Mrs. Carl Murphy and put Cathy inside the wagon from the rear. He told her to go forward while the other woman did the demonstration. "Pay close attention, Mrs. King. You might need this knowledge later. This lesson could save your life."

"I won't have to do it again, will I?" she pleaded.

"Not today. Maybe later. Let's get moving." He took his position by the team. "They're winded already, Mrs. Murphy, so they shouldn't bolt long. I hate to scare and run them again, but you all didn't get a good enough lesson. Ready?" he asked, and the woman nodded.

When the wagon returned, Mattie Epps was told to drive for Mrs. Daniels and Hackett. The constant whiner glared at the boss and declared, "It's too dangerous. I won't get injured before we even begin this stupid journey. You didn't make Cathy do it, and I won't, either."

Steve gritted his teeth and clenched his jaw. "Mrs. Daniels, why don't you show your team how it's done?" he said. "Stampedes don't happen often, so everyone doesn't have to do it. You just need to know how to respond if it does. Watching is enough for now."

"I'll do it. I ain't scared. No worse than battling a Yankee attack."

"Hang on, ladies," he told the other two, and Mattie scowled at him.

Ginny was amazed and pleased Steve didn't make each one of them drive. She was impressed by his expert horsemanship and physical prowess. She wondered if there was anything the skilled man couldn't do. She had no doubts they were safe in his care, no matter the perils ahead.

"I was terrified," Cathy said. "I could have been thrown off and broken every limb in my body." When no one replied or gave her sympathy, she was miffed. "You pulled my hair, Sue Murphy," she chided her teammate.

"That was the only thing I could grab to keep you from falling."

"It still hurts," Cathy complained, rubbing her scalp.

"Stop groaning and pay attention," Louise scolded her.

"You have room to talk; you know about teams and wagons. We don't."

"If you kept your mind where it should be, you would, too, by now."

"What does that mean?" Cathy demanded, eyes blazing in anger.

"You know very well what I mean. Now, be silent."

Cathy glared at Louise Jackson, then at "Anna Avery" for a moment.

Ginny wondered if the dark-haired vixen was jealous of her, as that was the look she had been given.

* * *

While the others were eating lunch and after he'd finished his, Steve went to scout
for appropriate river locations for the women's lesson in water crossings this afternoon. During his absence, Charles Avery came to deliver his "daughter's" order
and to see how she was doing with her lessons.

Ginny took a stroll with him so they could speak in private. She told him
about the training and her successes. She thanked him for the items and supplies
he had brought, but assumed the food he'd given Ellie was a thank-you for all the
meals she—"his daughter"—had shared with the Davises. Afterward, she related
the alarming talk she had overheard last night.

"That would be Carl Murphy," he enlightened her to the Georgian's identity.
"He's a hothead, so avoid him. I hope the others hush up about this Klan business; we don't need a spy in camp pulling down the Yanks on us."

"Is what they said true, sir?" she asked in concern.

"In a way. Some men have gotten into the Klan to wreak revenge on Yankees
and their cohorts for the horrible things done to them during the war and after it
ended. Some are reckless and downright mean and trying to settle personal
grudges. But most are honest and decent men who just want to protect Southerners from more cruelties."

"But killings and burnings aren't the right way to obtain justice."

"What would you suggest they do?"

Ginny gave that question deep and serious thought. "I don't know."

Charles smiled and advised, "Well, don't worry your pretty head about it.
Soon, we'll be far away from such perils."

"I'm glad, sir, because I don't want trouble to interfere with our journey. We
both have grave matters to handle."

"And we will, my girl, you wait and see. But I'd best get back to town. I have
a last business meeting this evening. I'll return for good in a few days. Yessiree,
this will all be behind us next week."

"We'll be on our way soon," she murmured, dread and excitement filling her
from head to foot.

"Any more problems with our handsome guide?" he queried as they headed
back to camp.

"Not really," Ginny replied. "Right now, he's ignoring and avoiding me as
much as possible."

"That tempted by you, is he?" Charles jested.

"If you say so, sir."

"He is, mark my words. Give him the space he thinks he wants and needs
while coaxing him toward you, girl. Don't forget what I told you; you might need
him and his skills one day soon."

That idea both thrilled and alarmed her. "He'll probably be hundreds of miles
away from me when and if that time arrives."

"Somehow I don't think so," Charles murmured, his grin broadening.

She told her racing heart to slow. "We'll see."

"Yes, sir, we surely shall. Good-bye, Anna."

"Good-bye, sir. *Father*," she corrected with a warm smile.

* * *

When Steve returned to camp, Ginny handed him his borrowed gloves and thanked him for them. "Father brought me these," she said, holding out the new pair. "Are they all right?"

Steve grasped one hand as if he was examining them for quality and sturdiness. "Yep, I see I missed his visit again." He released her hand.

Ginny was moved by their brief contact. "Yes," she murmured, "he didn't stay long. He'll be joining us soon."

Steve eyed her closely. "I'm sure that makes you happy."

With a blend of truth and deception, she responded, "It does. We've been separated for six years. It's time to get reacquainted. We had so little time together after my return home from boarding school."

"What kind of man is your father, Anna?"

"Just how he seems: kind, generous, charming—a gentleman."

"You aren't biased in his favor, are you?" he teased.

She returned his smile. "Isn't it natural to be so?"

His tone and expression altered uncontrollably. "I reckon."

Ginny surmised that he didn't sound convinced and decided he might be an orphan, which would explain why he was such a loner. She was intrigued and touched by the bitterness that glittered like black ice in his dark eyes. A clue to him? she wondered.

"Have you eaten?" He suddenly veered away from the topic of parents, and after she had nodded in the affirmative, he said, "We go to work soon. I'll see you later."

"Steve?"

He stopped and turned. "Yes, Miss Avery?"

"You're doing a fine job with our training. Thank you."

He tipped his hat, didn't smile or thank her, turned, and departed.

What an enigma you are, Steve Carr! Should I try to solve it?

At two o'clock, the women met at the river in their wagons.

Steve halted them at the first location he had chosen. They gathered around him as he gave his final instructions. "We'll start shallow and work our way to deeper areas. This first site will give you a feel for moving through water and soft bottoms. Once you approach the bank, keep going; don't allow your team to stop to drink or rest. If you do, your wheels will mire down. Goad them extra hard on entering and leaving; that lets the mules get a quick grip when they're changing surfaces. Some rivers will be the most treacherous ground to cover. If your wagon starts leaning to one side, don't panic; you're probably just hitting a low place. Keep your pace steady and don't let your mules slack off or sense you're not in control of them. When we hit deep water later, if we have problems, I'll explain then how to deal with them. Along our route, we'll probably have to hitch up extra teams to get enough power and strength to cross some rivers. That causes delays, but it can't be helped. If there are no questions, let's get busy, ladies."

* * *

By the time that lesson was over and their two-mile walk was behind them, the women were exhausted from the arduous exertions. Most of them flopped down on grassy areas to rest before beginning evening chores.

Ginny prepared a plate from the food Charles Avery had brought to her and left it on the rock ring that enclosed Steve's campfire. She knew he would return soon from selecting a deeper site for their river crossing practice tomorrow. When he did, he would find a nice meal, including apple pie, awaiting him. She hoped that would please him.

She joined the Davises for dinner, and delighted the children with another tasty dessert. After the dishes were done, she helped Mary Wiggins repair torn clothing for her four children. She had noticed and questioned Ellie about the fact there were no children in the camp between the ages two and six. Ellie had explained that those ages would correspond with the war years, when so many men were absent! Those few born at the war's end or shortly afterward were the results of men returning home earlier than other soldiers because of injuries.

She hoped things would settle down for the devastated South. It would be wonderful for life to get back to normal. She prayed nothing would happen to create new hostilites and troubles. If wicked and well-intended groups on both sides ceased their vengeful and greedy attacks on each other, peace and healing could come. *Please, Lord, let it be so.*

When she and Mary had completed the task, Ginny smiled at the perky woman with bouncy curls and said, "I want to thank you and the others for helping me learn my chores. It'll make it easier for me on the trail. I'm afraid household tasks weren't part of our studies at school. They depended on mothers to teach them to their daughters."

"You said your own mother has been dead for a long time?" Mary queried.

"Yes, since I was eleven. I still miss her." Longing filled Ginny's heart, so she changed the subject. "Sometimes I feel so ignorant not knowing the things most females do."

"You can't be blamed for that, Anna, so don't feel bad. You were away a long time. I'm sure you're happy to be home."

From the corner of her eye, Ginny noticed Steve leaning against a tree nearby and wondered how long he had been standing there and listening, and why? She pretended not to see him and said what she must, what would mask any possibly unusual behavior between her and Charles. "Yes, I am. I missed my father very much. It's been too long. We've both grown and changed during our separation; it's almost . . . like meeting for the first time and having to learn about each other all over again."

"That could be fun, like a game," Mary ventured.

"You're right; I hadn't thought of it that way."

"The others are gathering soon for conversation and maybe some music," Mary reminded her friend. "Why don't you join them? I'll be along as soon as I get the children tucked in. And thank you for the help with sewing."

"That's one of the few feminine things I can do," Ginny quipped.

"And do very well," Mary complimented her skill.

They exchanged a few words before Ginny left. As she did so, she noticed Steve was no longer around the Wiggins area. *Quiet as a mouse, you stealthy creature. What reason do you have to be furtive with me?*

As she headed for the meeting spot, Ginny pondered if she could be mistaken about thinking he watched everyone in a curious manner, and her more than the others. After what she'd heard last night from her wagon, she fretted about him being a Loyal Leaguer who was trying to ferret out Klan members. Ed King had warned his talkative wife to silence for that very reason. Others had mentioned how spies were used to gather "evidence" against Rebel whites to justify an attack on them. It didn't matter, she reasoned, that the scout had a southern accent, as plenty of them had sided with the Union.

You're being silly, Ginny. Steve is too expert to be a fake wagontrain leader. Maybe he just likes to know his charges well, pick out the possible troublemakers, and deal with them to prevent problems along the way. Or maybe he has a personal interest in you. For certain, there's more to that cunning guide than meets the eye. Whatever the answer, you need to solve the mystery soon, before you become more ensnared by him.

"That's mighty heavy thought, Miss Avery. You really pull deep into yourself when you're distracted. I've been walking beside you for fifty feet and you didn't know I was here. Be glad I'm not an enemy or you'd be in danger. I'm worried about this saddle-napping you do."

Ginny halted and looked at him. With scant moonlight and illumination from the fire, she could barely make out his expression; after she squinted and strained to do so, it was unreadable. The combination of his darkly tanned flesh, ebony hair, and black garments made him almost as invisible as a new moon. He smelled fresh, as if he recently had a bath. She was impressed that a trail man took such care with his body and clothes. The only things ever a little slack in his grooming were a habit of not shaving until evening and of mussing his hair with his fingers, yet those things oddly enhanced his appeal. Her study only required seconds, but it seemed longer. "Don't be worried, Mr. Carr. I simply have a special matter on my mind tonight. I didn't realize I needed to stay alert in camp, not with an expert gunsman and plenty of guards around to protect me. Besides, with your enormous skills, I bet you could sneak up on a bird and capture it."

Steve was aware he had been scrutinized, and it aroused him. He murmured in a husky tone, "Is that a fancy way of complimenting me?"

Ginny felt warm, shaky, and tingly being so close to him in the dark. How she wished things could settle down between them, but perhaps it was best if they didn't. The stars fall down if he wasn't already too tempting! If he ever pursued her seriously, she'd never be able to resist him. "No, you're the one with that skill, too. I wouldn't be surprised if you sneaked up on me so you could scold me for another lapse of attention."

He chuckled and grinned, revealing snowy teeth. In a mirthful tone with left hand over his heart, he said, "Why, Anna, you wound me deeply with that accusation."

Ginny frowned at him for his jest. "Do I indeed? I would imagine few things get to you, Mr. Tough Scout."

Steve fingercombed his hair as he prepared his answer. "You're right, but those few things are real special or they wouldn't work on me."

She struggled to appear poised and unaffected by him and his words. "I would certainly hope so."

Steve gave her a swift and close eyeing. She was as enticing as a wagon of gold. Her hazel gaze sparkled with interest and conflict. Her light-brown hair, or maybe dark tawny, snaked its way from her crown to her waist in wriggling curls and waves. Her lips called to him to kiss them. Her flawless skin urged him to stroke it. Could he? Should he? Not yet. "You're a strange filly, Anna Avery, different from all the others."

"I hope so: I'd hate to be exactly like everyone else. I'd prefer to be a pink cloud in a sky filled with white ones."

"Ah, pink, a soft and warm and lovely color, not stand-out bold and fiery like red. Good choice. What color would I be if I were a cloud?"

Ginny was surprised by his question and response to her whimsical remark. To let him know how he often treated her, she said with bravery, "Black. You're stormy, unpredictable, threatening, and powerful."

Steve took her comparisons to have dual meanings, as her mood implied. "That sounds about right. You're a good judge of character."

She had half expected—more accurately, *hoped for*—him to refute, explain, or apologize. "I hope so," she murmured again to pique him. To escape the disturbing banter, she left him to join the others, and he tagged along without another word.

Following light conversation, one of the men asked Steve to tell them about Texas.

Steve knew it was the duty and custom for leaders to entertain and enlighten travelers with stories and information. He used an easygoing manner as he complied. "She's big, with mountains and valleys westward, forests in the eastern part, and desert in the western section. Lots of flat, open prairies and grasslands. Most areas have rivers or streams. You have to be careful of flash floods in low-lying sections; they can sweep away horse and rider or even a wagon in the blink of an eye. Her weather isn't ordinarily bad, but she can boil your brains in summer and freeze your bones in winter if she takes a mind to. She's like a divided horse, half tamed and half wild."

Steve had everyone's attention and interest, so he assumed he was doing a convincing job. "Cotton, cattle, and farming are her big interests. The Revolution with Mexico for independence ended in '45. *Bandidos* still raid across the Rio Grande sometimes, but they stay near the border for a quick escape, far from where any of you will settle. Right now, she's still excluded from the Union; she tried to get back but they wouldn't allow it. They elected a Unionist governor last year and voted on a new constitution that renounced slavery. Hasn't helped yet. Military law rules her under Radical control and that new Reconstruction Act but there's little trouble from either one. General Sheridan is in command of the Texas-Louisiana district; I'm sure all of you recall his name from the war."

"Damn right we do!" Brown sneered, and others nodded agreement.

Steve didn't give the men time to start rehashing their grievances. "Texans are proud, stubborn men who know how to fight," he said, and related their deeds during the war. "She had legendary lawmen who could face down an entire mob or gang alone; the Union put Rangers out of power fast to prevent any threat from them."

"You said there wasn't much trouble there?" a man asked Steve.

"Very little trouble with gangs of soldiers or raiders like you have here. Texans have occasional problems with rustlers on ranches and outlaws along stageline routes. She's too big and spread out to entice many villains to work there; they'd have to do too much riding."

"Do you do this kind of thing—escort wagontrains—all the time?"

"Not all the time," Steve answered Mrs. King's question, "but I've made my share of trips across country. Mostly I've taken trains from St. Louis to the Far West, to Arizona and California or to Colorado and the Oregon Territory. It's mostly gold and silver that draws folks there. Outlaws, too."

"What do you do when you aren't escorting wagontrains?" Cathy asked.

"A little bit of everything and anything, ma'am."

The dark-haired beauty persisted. "Such as?"

"Guard for gold and silver shipments or freight lines, shotgun for stage-coaches, scout and guide for the Army or private companies, Indian fighting: you name it and I've probably done it or will do it." He chuckled.

"Indian fighting?" Cathy's husband echoed. "In Texas?"

"West Texas has problems with Apaches and Comanches, but none of you are heading there. Most of the trouble is northward in the Dakota lands. The Sand Creek massacre in Colorado started the worst of it. The Indians made treaty in '51, but it's been broken too many times and ways to count. They're working on a second one now and hope to have it signed by fall. It'll be a wise move; those Indians are powerful and cunning and fearless; they won't surrender their lives and lands without heavy bloodshed on both sides. You'd think everybody had had enough of killing."

Ginny fretted over the knowledge of fierce Indian trouble in the area where her father supposedly lived. Without help and protection, how could she get there safely? She halted her frantic musings to listen to the rest of Steve's revelations.

He talked about Chivington's massacre, the Indians' retaliation, and the Bozeman Trail conflict. He finished with the tale of a cocky officer's fatal battle with the legendary Crazy Horse. "Fetterman was led into a cunning trap with his men and slaughtered with the ease of throwing a stone. Some of his troops were part of Sherman's bloody campaign through this state."

"Served 'em right after what they did here!" the Georgian declared.

"Yesiree, maybe them redskins will take revenge for us," Brown murmured with a happy smile and a glitter of hatred in his eyes.

"You said we won't have trouble with outlaws in Texas?" one man asked.

"Not much, maybe a little along stage and mail routes."

"You ever killed an outlaw, had a shootout with one?" another asked.

"I try to mind my own business and keep out of trouble. You should never challenge a man or provoke one to challenge you unless you're certain you can outdraw and outshoot him. Never covet a gunslinger's reputation. There's a say-ing: 'Live by your guns and you die by them,' and it's true."

"You surely know how to handle your weapons," someone else observed.

"It's my job. Besides guiding you folks, I have to protect you." Steve took the interest off him by saying, "The bad ones work the Missouri, Kansas, and Arkansas areas. Most of them are leftover Jayhawkers or men from Quantrill's raiders."

"We've heard of him, read unbelievable stories in newspapers," Jeff Eaves said. "He was killed in '65, wasn't he?"

"Yep, in Kentucky. He led federal troops on a wild chase for years. People's opinions of him differ from good to bad, from misguided patriot, to heartless thief, using the war for his own profit and glory. His band killed innocents and burned and looted both sides: that's been proven," he added when two men looked about to argue in favor of the notorious man.

When neither spoke, Steve continued. "War taught men to kill and some to enjoy it. Some outlaws seem born mean and greedy; others are driven to it out of revenge. Folks say the worst ones from Quantrill's band haven't stopped killing and robbing innocent folks since the war ended."

Steve noticed that no one asked about the Jayhawkers: plundering marauders who had been antislavery raiders in Kansas, Missouri, and their bordering states. He began tales about notorious outlaws and their criminal deeds.

"They must have people giving them shelter or they'd be caught by now."

"I'm sure they do, Mrs. Wiggins," Steve told Mary. "Some folks see them as famous, and others are afraid to turn down their . . . *requests.*"

"They should be Jim Crowed like Negroes are. Segregated, like we do those Galvanized Yankees! You ever met those traitors during your travels, Steve?"

"Plenty of them in the West."

"You mean they admit what they done?" Brown scoffed.

"They don't think they have anything to be ashamed of, Harry. Nor do most folks out West; those men did too much good to be rejected and insulted. Much as you and others despise them, it might be wise to keep those feelings to yourselves or you'll offend new neighbors and friends who might have personal reasons to like them. You have them everywhere out there: many stayed after the war and made fresh starts alone or sent for their families. Most won't return to the South because they are viewed as traitors."

"We sure didn't *want* them back here, the stinking polecats! Nothing but a bunch of betrayers and gutless weaklings. I won't befriend one."

"What are Galvanized Yankees, Mr. Brown?" Lucy asked.

"Let Steve tell you; I can't stand the taste of the words on my tongue."

Steve explained what they had done out West.

Ginny, who had listened quietly and intently, spoke up. "I don't understand, Mr. Carr. If they did so much good and all they wanted was to get out of horrible Yankee prisons, why was that so bad?"

"Hellfire, girl, are you crazy?" Harry Brown shouted. "They betrayed our side, went against their own families and friends."

"How so, Mr. Brown?" she pressed to learn more about her Galvanized Yankee father and his possible motive for remaining out West.

"They went over to the side of the damned Yankees who was killing their people and robbing them or burning them out! A decent and brave man don't do nothing to help his enemies. Nothing!"

"You're saying you think it would have been better if they had stayed in those awful prisons instead of doing good work that didn't harm the South?"

"I spent plenty of time in a prison, but I wouldna ever gone over to the Yankees' side. About cost me my leg, too!"

"But what they did out West will help all of us who are going there. Isn't that worth something, worth forgiveness and compassion?"

"Hell, no, girl, it ain't!"

Steve was about to jump into the hot talk, as he didn't like how Brown was looking at or speaking to Anna Avery, who was only asking questions to grasp the tragic situation. She had a tender and compassionate heart that moved him. He was relieved when both people went silent so he didn't have to cause any conflict.

As people chatted about less serious topics, Ginny drifted into deep thought. She knew the embittered and vengeful man couldn't be reasoned with or appeased. It was evident a few others present didn't like what those ex-Rebel soldiers had done but those didn't feel or react as strongly, thank goodness. She realized that if she was faced with a similar choice, she would have done the same as her father had, following his capture at Stones River at Murfreesboro in early '63. That was how Mathew Marston had gotten to Colorado, and tonight's revelation could prove a partial answer as to why he had remained. He had done some of the jobs Steve Carr had mentioned, and she was proud of him for doing so. She was glad he hadn't stayed in prison and suffered needlessly. Why couldn't these men see that it was better to live and build rather than kill and destroy? She could hardly wait to reach her father's side and be reunited. No joy could be greater than to see his smiling face again.

Ginny sneaked a look at the virile scout, who was silent and alert. After what she'd learned, could she take Charles Avery's suggestion about hiring Steve as her guide and protector? Perhaps she shouldn't keep her deathbed promise to Johanna Chapman. Perhaps she should head straight to Colorado to begin her search. Maybe she should make her final decision after she got to know the mysterious scout better, and after she learned if he was indeed available to be hired.

For all she knew, Steve could be heading back immediately to escort another wagontrain to Texas or farther west. That would place enormous distance between them. What if she never saw him again after this journey ended? Despite their many conflicts, that wasn't what she wanted. She wanted— *Stop thinking such foolish things, Ginny Marston! It's impossible for more reasons than you can count on both hands. Forget about winning Steve Carr. Forget your silly romantic notions. Your goal is to reach Colorado and find your father, not find a husband along the way . . . Certainly not a quicksilver and enigmatic male,* her mind added.

Ginny told herself she was inexperienced and, maybe even ignorant when it came to men and romance. She had been instructed to think of serving and pleasing her mate first and her family second, never herself, to defer to her husband's whims and desires at all times. One was to look and behave her best at all times: be charming, demure, ladylike, and servile. One's only goal should be to find the "proper" man, wed him, bear his children, and cater to his needs. It was believed that a woman was nothing without a husband, no matter if she had talents and skills elsewhere. She must have a mate to be respectable and accepted. She must be taken care of, not fend for herself. Only females in the lowest class supported themselves and remained unwed, even if not by their choice, but the result of cruel fate.

Surely, Ginny thought, there was more in life for a woman. There must be other challenges and rewards. Why was wanting and needing more than a husband so wrong, so unacceptable by society? What made a man stronger and smarter and braver? Didn't their lessons this week prove a woman could do the same tasks and take the same risks men did? Why must a woman only cower, bend a knee, and serve?

Until she met Steve Carr, she hadn't been tempted to pursue a man. She hadn't met one who caused such flames to burn in her body or such hungers to torment her soul. But dare she follow through with her temptation? Dare she risk a broken heart if she lost the chase, as Steve was probably unattainable? Dare she risk tossing obstacles into the difficult and dangerous path she must travel?

Chapter 6

STEVE GUIDED THE WOMEN to an Ogeechee River location where the water was deeper and swifter and where the banks had more of an incline. After repeating their instructions of the previous day, he added a caution he had forgotten: "Watch out for large rocks in stream beds; they'll bust a rim or a spoke. If a river is too bad on the trail, we'll have to use an extra team to help pull wagons across. That causes delays but can't be helped. We'll have to ferry or float wagons across the worst sites; it slows us more when wheels have to be removed along with loads then replaced on the other side. Now, if nobody has a question, let's get moving."

Ginny was apprehensive but not terrified. Her biggest worry was making a mistake that would cause Steve to scold her. She kept her concentration at peak level and used everything he had taught her. Paying attention was simpler when the handsome man wasn't close.

At one point, Steve had to climb aboard Cathy King's wagon to get it unstuck after the dark-haired woman let it halt in midriver and mire down, on purpose Ginny surmised with annoyance. She watched how the two of them had to sit close and snug on the short seat with bodies touching. She witnessed how Cathy brazenly and wantonly gazed into the scout's eyes and thanked him for rescuing her. She fumed, knowing she would have been scolded whereas Cathy didn't receive the slightest reprimand. For all she knew, the guide didn't care about the woman's marital status; Cathy certainly didn't. If the sultry flirt had her way, she would entice Steve into the woods to roll on the ground, and he might go! In England, she had heard gossip about men having mistresses or fiery moments in the arms and beds of wedded women. Her anger mounted with her jealousy. She warned herself to cease her distraction.

After the women made two successful crossings in a row, the smiling teacher told them to take a break then meet for self-defense lessons.

The women gathered near camp, some reluctant about this class. But even with scowls or pouts, everyone listened to Steve's instructions about how to fight and defend oneself. When he asked for a volunteer to help him demonstrate several ways to respond to an attack and to gain escape, Cathy King almost leapt forward with eagerness for contact with him.

Ginny observed as Cathy giggled and practically fondled Steve as he showed them what to do if someone grabbed them. She fumed more and more as time passed.

When Steve had finished his demonstration, he turned to the women. "The secret is to be quick, to take your attacker off guard and by surprise. If you can't find something nearby to use as a weapon to club him with, react fast and flee . . . Who's next?"

As if by prearranged signal, Ellie, Lucy, Ruby, and Mary pushed Ginny into the human circle and shouted, "You, Anna."

Ginny balked and protested, "I paid attention; I don't need to do it."

"If she doesn't want to, Steve, I'll continue to be your target," Cathy said coyly.

"That's all right, Mrs. King, but thank you anyhow. Come and give me a try, Miss Avery. Prove you wouldn't be helpless and vulnerable if you were to be attacked."

Ginny was challenged to make an attempt to best the grinning man. She prayed she could do it, but the supplication wasn't heard above. As she tried to do as Steve had instructed and shown, she was tossed to the ground and pinned there with a knee to the small of her back while he roped her like a calf for branding. With her hands and feet bound behind her and lying on her stomach, she was relieved she was wearing pants today, thanks to Charles Avery's generosity. She wanted to scream curses at the chuckling man but refused to be goaded into bad behavior before others.

Steve withdrew the knife from his boot and sliced through the short rope he had snatched from around one gunbutt and used to capture the now-infuriated woman with blazing eyes. "See, without training and practice, you can be taken quick and easy by a determined man. Try me again."

Ginny tried to entangle his ankle and flip him over her shoulder. She found herself lying on the ground with Steve straddling her and his hands imprisoning her wrists to the hard earth. She felt his knees touching her sides and was staring up into a cocky—seductive?—expression. She wanted to shriek for him to get off her! She knew no one could see his face, the look he was giving her. For a crazy instant, she wished they were alone and wished he would lower his body to hers and . . . Turbulence raced through her as she feared he was playing with her, trying to humiliate her in front of the others. She narrowed and chilled her gaze.

Steve was inflamed by the contact, by the way she first looked at him. Her breathing was rapid and shallow, and her chest rose and fell from exertion, straining against the taut material of her shirt. Perspiration gleamed on her exquisite face, and she was dusty. Her hair was flared around her head like a light-brown pillow. *Shu,* what he would give to bend forward and kiss that parted mouth. He would give even more to rest his body atop and within hers. He had stalled her release too long, so he stood and pulled her up with him. "Try me again."

"This isn't a fair test, Mr. Carr. You're on alert, whereas you said our real opponents wouldn't be. How can I take you by surprise when you're awaiting my attack and prepared to parry it?" Before he could answer, Ginny lowered her chin as if to catch her breath and calm her anger. The moment Steve relaxed, she lunged forward and slammed him in the gut with her head, knocking him to the ground. She fled to the safety of the ring of women and turned to gloat at him for her clever escape.

Steve looked at her from his seat on the grass and said without smiling, "See, even a man on guard can be fooled and beaten. Who's next?"

When it was time to break for lunch, everyone had practiced with Steve. As Ginny headed for her wagon to wash up for the meal, the roguish scout caught up with her and murmured in a tone only she could hear, "You need a bath, Miss Avery; you're a mite dirty and sweaty after scuffling with me."

Don't let him provoke you to say or do something foolish, Ginny. "You're right, as always, but it will have to wait until this evening. If I'm late for afternoon class, I'll be curtly scolded," she retorted and kept walking.

Steve dropped by the Davis campsite before her arrival to thank Ellie for the food she had left for him last night, which had included apple pie.

"It wasn't me, Mr. Carr; it was Anna. Her father brought it to her. Since she eats with us, she gave it to you. She's a kind and thoughtful young woman. She's really trying hard to do good with her lessons. It must be terribly hard for a girl who hasn't had a mother to teach her much, and she's been away from home and her father for so long. She's lived such a sheltered existence, so this challenge must be difficult for her."

"You're probably right, ma'am. Thank her for me, will you?"

"It would mean more to her if it came from you," Ellie suggested, as she sensed the attraction between them and thought them a good match.

He nodded and left. He wondered why Anna would do such a kindness and keep it a secret. Wouldn't she want the credit? Of course, he mused, she figured he'd seek out the thoughtful person and discover it was her! She was a sly and wily female after all.

That afternoon they walked for three hot and tiring miles. Ginny passed Steve as she entered camp and refused to glance his way or speak. She told herself that maybe he couldn't decide how he felt or how to behave. If she ignored him for a while, maybe that would coerce a decision from him.

Dark, threatening clouds moved overhead before meals were cooked and served and evening chores were done. The wind increased in force and intent; it yanked at limbs, clothes, hair, and canvases. A heaviness in the air warned of an imminent storm. Menacing rumbles said it would lash out at them any moment.

Everyone hurried to prepare for its assault. Baths were skipped or taken swiftly. Possessions were either stored inside or placed underneath the wagon on water-proof cloths.

Ginny took all the precautions with the animals and wagon she had learned. While she was checking and securing the mules' ropes and stakes, the storm struck with a fury. A torrential rain poured down in a rush before she could finish and dash inside. The beasts were startled by the loud thunder and flashes of lightning. She patted and spoke soothingly to them until they calmed. When she turned to head for the wagon, she saw Steve running toward her, as drenched as she was.

"Anything wrong?" he questioned, gazing at the water dripping from her face and at the soaked curls plastered to her face. Her shirt did the same clingy task on her chest but he pretended not to notice.

She explained what she was doing over the loud and combined noises of rain, wind, and thunder. "I'm finished now and going inside."

"You don't have your tarp on the front. A rain this heavy will seep inside and ruin things. I'll help you." He grasped her hand and pulled her to the wagon. He climbed onto the tongue, lifted the jockey box lid, and withdrew a large water-proof cloth. He showed her how to toss it over the box and seat, then secure it in place. The way he positioned one edge created a valley that allowed rain to run off left and right of the wooden bed. "Let's get inside and see if anything needs moving out of the water."

Steve leapt aboard the tailgate, hauled her up as easily as lifting a feather, then closed the opening behind them. He saw that the center of the wagon was clear of obstacles, as she hadn't put down her bedding yet. He moved forward and checked for puddles at the front. "Nothing to worry about, just a little damp." He handed her several items that needed moving out of possible harm's way if wind ripped the cover loose. "That should do it. You best get dried off and changed before a chill sets in."

"Thank you for the help. I'm sorry I didn't know about the tarp."

"Think nothing of it, Miss Avery; it hasn't been the subject of a lesson yet."

As they stepped over a crate, Ginny's foot was snagged by the fastener and she lost her balance. Steve grabbed for her, and both began falling toward the back. The motion of their actions caused the bedding to topple to the floor before they reached it, softening their landing. Steve was half atop Ginny, so she was captive between him and the soft bedding.

Steve chuckled and remarked as he patted the feather mattress, "That was good timing; or both of us might have been injured."

Ginny noticed that he didn't move off her; nor did she push him aside. "Thank you for the rescue," she murmured, unsettled and wary.

"You're welcome, Anna." He pushed wet curls from her face as he smiled. "You're soaked."

Ginny couldn't help but smile in return. "So are you, Steve."

Without lifting his elbow from near her shoulder, he leaned his head forward and fingercombed his sable hair. "A mess, eh?"

"No," she heard herself murmur. His virile body felt like a copper bedwarmer on a wintry night. She couldn't break his powerful hold on her gaze. His dark-brown eyes were glowing and his mood was entreating. It was almost as if she could hear them beckoning: *Kiss me; love me, Ginny.* Her eyes drifted over his rain-slick face and settled on his mouth.

Steve observed her actions and felt her tremble. "Cold?" he asked, though he knew she wasn't. He wondered if she realized he was also aquiver with desire. His body felt aflame. A curious tension held him rigid and refused to allow him to leave her. He knew that was what he should do, and pronto.

Ginny's hands rested against his broad chest. She felt his heart pounding against her fingertips and palms; it surprised and pleased her to have such a powerful effect on him. Her gaze was drawn back to his as she finally shook her head to his query. His mood was mellow and enthralling, as was his dark gaze. Almost against her will, her fingers seized his shirt and pulled him toward her.

Steve responded to the unspoken invitation. His mouth covered hers and parted her lips. His fingers wiggled into her drenched hair, clasped her head, and held it still as his mouth worked hungrily at hers. A groan escaped his throat as he pressed closer and tighter against her. The lightning outside couldn't be charged with more energy than he was.

Ginny's arms banded the dazing scout's waist. She clung to him, stroked his back, and urgently returned his kiss. A surge of unfamiliar heat licked over her flesh. Love claimed and ruled her heart.

A thunderbolt crashed loudly outside and vibrated the wagon. The mules nearby brayed in panic. Steve came to his senses and leaned away from Ginny. Her cheeks were flushed with passion and her eyes were glazed by it. She wanted him as much as he wanted her. If they weren't in a camp filled with people—any one of whom could approach any second and discover this reckless scene—he would make her his. He would brand her with a love she would never forget, remove, or match.

Ginny blushed as reality and his withdrawal destroyed the dreamy illusion. She didn't know what to say or do; they had gotten carried away by desire. She recalled she had been the one to initiate it, to encourage it. What must he think about her, a so-called lady entreating . . . seduction?

"I've been wondering for days what that would taste and feel like. You've learned your wiles well, Miss Avery; you're one powerful temptation. I'd best get out of this hot box before we both say and do something foolish."

"You're right, Mr. Carr. I apologize for . . . behaving so badly and rashly. You're also a powerful temptation, and I'm unaccustomed to . . . " Surely he recognized an innocent without her admitting to being one. "I don't know what possessed me to act that way," she lied. "I'm ashamed and embarrassed. Please don't tell Father I lost my wits."

"Don't worry, Miss Avery, I won't. He might horsewhip me for letting the situation get out of control. I promise it won't happen again." He told himself he was only inching closer to her because of his mission, and he dared his troubled mind or racing heart to argue with him.

"Thank you, and I'll also make certain it doesn't." She watched Steve loosen the cord and hop over the tailgate. She heard the thud and squish of his boots against the softening ground. She commanded herself to get up and resecure the opening against the bad weather.

Ginny flopped down on the bedding and rested a forearm over her eyes. She had the urge to cry in frustration but fought it down. *How could you have been so stupid, so wanton? You rebuke Cathy King, then behave as badly or worse. Whatever got into you, Virginia Marston? You've never acted like this before. Damn you, Steve Carr, you have too strong of a pull on me. I have to be extra careful around you in the future.*

When the storm lessened near dusk but still didn't cease, tents of tarp were put up for cooking underneath. Grassy spots were chosen to cut down on mud. The men built fires, and smoke soon curled around the shelter's edges. When the flames were right, meals were begun by the women.

Ginny put on a rain slicker and helped Ellie Davis as usual. She doubted anyone had seen Steve enter, remain too long, and depart her wagon; the storm had been in full force and all wagons had been closed tightly against its intrusion.

As she worked, she wondered whether Steve was attracted to her and just being defensive, or if he had, as men were said to do, merely taken advantage of something offered, or if he truly wanted her to leave him alone. She was to blame for the heady incident, so she shouldn't fault him for responding. Still, it would be unfair—was *cruel*—for him to play with her emotions, to abuse her weakness for him. She ordered herself to forget about Steve and the intoxicating moment for now.

The scout was joining the Kings for supper. From the corner of her eye, she saw Steve and Cathy laughing and chatting. She couldn't forget how the woman clearly craved him. Nor could she halt the flood of envy and jealousy that surged through her. It was almost as if Steve knew of her gaze upon him and was behaving that way on purpose. She should be angry but it tormented her.

It rained most of the night, and Ginny slept little. Part of her restlessness had to do with the two Davis girls sleeping with her. They were active even in slumber and she was unaccustomed to bedmates. She had offered to let them stay so Ellie and the others would have more room inside their cluttered wagon where the weather had driven them. It had been a kindness that was taking its toll on her. As dawn approached, the weary Ginny was exhausted and tense.

Ginny watched Steve chat with Cathy after breakfast. What difference did it make, she fumed, that the bold woman had approached him? That Steve didn't say a few polite words and walk away as he should have to prevent suspicions in others, particularly in Ed King, who had to be blind or stupid not to be aware of his wife's flirtation? Maybe the Kings wanted something special from the scout and Cathy was softening him up to get it.

How far, she worried, had the relationship between Cathy and Steve been taken? Had they stolen kisses and caresses during walks when they were last to return or those times he had gone back to fetch her? Had Cathy sneaked into the woods to meet with him? Would Steve Carr do such a wicked and dangerous thing? Surely not, as he took his job too seriously and was too proud to risk humiliation.

Besides, the virile male had spurned her in the wagon yesterday when she had practically begged him to seduce her. She had lost her wits and self-control, and he had been the one to use his to halt their behavior. *Just because he didn't want you that way doesn't mean he doesn't want Cathy. After all, she's experienced and hot-blooded, you're only— Stop it, Ginny; you're letting this get to you too much.*

The next morning, Steve said, "Thanks to a timely rain, this is the perfect day to practice driving through and getting out of mud." He gave them instructions before they hitched their teams and began the lesson.

Since keeping the correct pace and avoiding perilous spots were the main two safety measures, Ginny paid the most attention to them.

It was almost time for lunch. Once or twice they had halted to rehearse getting started again after a stop with wheels sunk into mire. Only a couple of women had gotten stuck or couldn't get moving again and had required Steve's help. Neither of them was Cathy King who, Ginny assumed, was smart enough to realize she couldn't be all over the scout all the time.

They headed for rest and food. Two wagons became stuck in the overworked ground, as Steve had chosen a saturated dirt area that had been trampled by them into mush. One was Ginny's, who tried her best to free the captive wagon so he wouldn't have to help her in her foul mood.

Steve sent the others onward to camp with Louise Jackson in charge. He helped the other woman first, as she wasn't mired down as deeply.

Before the scout reached Ginny, she took an ax and trudged through graspy earth to chop off pine limbs from nearby trees. She hauled them to the wagon, got down on her knees, and worked them around and under the captive rim; that would give it something to grip for pulling out of the mud hole. She had seen carriage drivers in England use this method. She was about to climb aboard to test her solution when Steve arrived.

He looked at the draggled female, eyed her work, and said, "That's clever, Miss Avery, but what if no tree limbs are around on a prairie?"

Ginny mused a moment, then walked to the side. She ignored the mud she was getting on her hands and clothes to kneel and remove the limbs. She went to the front, opened the jockey box, and took out a hammer. She walked to the back and climbed inside, then unloaded a sturdy crate and shoved it to the ground. She didn't say a word as she took the box apart and laid the hammer and nails on the tailgate. She used the wood slabs as she had the limbs. Within minutes, she was free, and no wooden piece had been broken, only one cracked a little. She hopped down—glad she was in pants and boots again today—and put the crate together again. She left it in the back to wash off the mud before replacing the items she had removed. When the hammer was returned to its location, she climbed aboard and said, "All done. See you in camp."

Steve had observed in silence. He was impressed by her quick wits. She was definitely learning how to take care of herself. As he watched her, he couldn't get the passionate scene in her wagon off his mind. He had to make sure it happened again soon. He rode up beside her and unwisely teased, "You and your clothes will need a good scrubbing, Miss Avery. I'm surprised a lady would roll in the mud like that."

Her overcrowded mind retorted, *Better than rolling in the grass with another man's wife! Don't let him provoke you, Ginny. You're just tired and edgy and miserable, and angry. Show him you can control your temper.* "I know it's unlike a lady not to look her best, but there are times when she can't; this is one of them. It's more important to do my lessons and appease my teacher than to look ready for a Sunday stroll."

"Then you've learned one of the most important lessons of all: never let anything or anyone stand in the way of doing what you must."

"That advice couldn't come from a more appropriate source."

"Appropriate . . . suitable," Steve murmured. "Yep, you're right."

For a moment, Ginny had thought he didn't know that word, and she was amazed he did. But actually, she admitted, he seemed quite educated.

After they reached camp, Ginny unhitched the team and led them to the river to drink. She carried a bucket along to rinse off most of the mud, as it would surely be uncomfortable after it dried. She staked them near her campsite as usual and stored the harnesses underneath the wagon. Just to pique Steve, she didn't take a bath, only washed her face and hands. Nor did she change clothes or brush and rebraid her mussed hair. She was relieved the other women didn't groom themselves, either.

The women took their three-mile walk following lunch, because Steve said it was going to storm again later and they needed to get their chores and meal preparations completed earlier than usual.

Ginny hung back with Lucy Eaves. Her bad ankle was swollen and slowing her friend's pace. Ginny knew it must be aching and suggested she fetch Steve to give Lucy a ride to camp.

Lucy thanked her, but refused. "I have to do this for myself. It'll be fine by morning; it always is. It's just the wet weather bothering it. Why don't you go on ahead? I'll be fine. I'm ruining your pace."

"I don't care about that. Our demanding teacher will understand," Ginny told her, but wasn't convinced he would. She never knew what to expect from the unpredictable creature.

Steve didn't say a word to either woman as they entered camp. He knew why they were slow. He saw how brave and determined Lucy was and how thoughtful Anna was. An idea came to mind and he went to work on it.

"You don't have to do this, Anna," Lucy protested, but she was inwardly delighted.

"Yes I do. We're friends. You keep that foot in saltwater soak while I do the chores. Just correct me when I go astray. You know I'm not well trained in the kitchen," she reminded with a laugh.

After the Eaves family and Ginny ate the meal she had cooked, Ginny made Lucy sit down while she did the dishes and put things away. She helped Jeff prepare everything for the approaching storm.

Afterward, she sat on the ground and rubbed liniment into Lucy's ankle, foot, and calf. "Am I hurting you?" Ginny asked as she gently but firmly massaged the aggravated area.

Lucy smiled and sighed almost dreamily. "No, and you're so kind to tend me this way. I feel like a pampered child; it's heaven."

"You deserve good treatment. I'll do this again tomorrow."

Ginny hurried to get her own chores and preparations finished, then gathered her things and headed for the designated bathing area to scrub off the mud and to wash her filthy garments. She wasn't about to share her bed with mud or to dirty the wagon with it. When she heard voices around the bend in the path, she ducked behind some bushes after she recognized one as Cathy's and the other as Steve's. She told herself the action was silly, but she didn't want to meet and speak with either one. They passed her concealed location and stopped ahead, out of hearing range. Ginny refused to risk exposing herself. She must wait in concealment until they left and hoped that would be soon.

Steve was annoyed with the dark-haired beauty for seeking him out in the woods. He knew, if discovered, it would appear improper and could be hazardous to his mission. He was tired of the woman grasping at him and offering herself. He suspected he was going to have to be harsh with her to make her behave. When she pleaded for a stop to the exhausting walks, he told her, "You need the stamina, ma'am. You'll soon be doing it daily on the trail, so you'd better get used to it now."

"You could tell the others I have a good reason I can't do it, perhaps a bad ankle or leg like Lucy Eaves has."

"I don't lean toward lies and tricks, Mrs. King; they cause trouble."

"I could reward you," she purred, pressing her body close to his and lacing her fingers behind his neck. She tried to kiss him.

Steve grasped her hands and worked them free, careful not to get any telltale scratches from her nails. He captured her chin to keep her from rising to attempt another kiss. "Don't do this, Mrs. King."

"Why not? I want you, and you want me."

"That isn't true. Don't force me to embarrass you with the truth."

Ginny couldn't watch any more. She hated the way Steve cupped the woman's face. She couldn't bear to see them kiss, so she gingerly slipped from her hiding place and escaped the tormenting scene.

The rain began before Ginny finished washing her shirt and pants and cleaning her boots. Her clean skirt and blouse would get soaked before she reached cover but she didn't care; they would dry. The drops felt cool, refreshing, soothing, even stimulating to her weary body and troubled spirit. She stuffed her things into a cloth sack and flung the laundry over one arm to head back.

The downpour increased and played mischief with her vision. Peals of thunder boomed overhead and lightning flashed in zigzag patterns. She assumed everyone was inside their wagons by now so there was no one who knew she was gone and would worry—or so she thought. She almost collided with Steve Carr as she hurried along the path. Blinking away raindrops as she looked up into his sullen expression, she said, "I'm coming; I'm coming."

"Get to your wagon, woman! Don't you realize it's dangerous to be away from camp alone? With the storm's noise and everybody inside, a scream for help wouldn't be heard. If anything happened to you, Anna, I'd be held to blame. Why take this foolish risk?"

"I was helping Lucy. Her ankle looked awful. She can't walk like the rest of us. You're mean to force her to aggravate it with exercise."

Steve knew what she had been doing. "There are times she'll have to walk, Miss Avery. She knows and accepts that; she doesn't complain."

"She wouldn't, and you know it," Ginny told him. "She won't have to walk. When she can't drive her wagon, she can drive mine, and I'll walk."

"What about your father?" Steve reminded and tested her.

"He has a horse; he can ride him. There are times when a person can't do his share of the work and others have to help them."

Steve sensed anger and tension. "You're in a foul mood today."

"Why shouldn't I be? You pick at me half the time. I don't appreciate being hog-tied for your amusement or constantly corrected like a bad child. You're mean to me and Lucy. Since you obviously don't like me, Mr. Carr, why not leave me alone? Stop playing spiteful games with me."

"What do you mean?" he asked, looking confused and intrigued.

"Do you want the truth?" she challenged, egged on by her strain. *Be honest, Ginny, so you can clear the air.*

"Of course," Steve murmured without thinking of the consequences.

"A few times you've reacted too strongly, even if you had just cause for your annoyance. You have a heavy responsibility for a lot of people; I realize that. But you and I rub each other wrong. I'm a friendly and open person; you're the opposite; our differences somehow offend and irritate you. You mistake those traits as false pretenses and womanly wiles. In clear terms, you think I'm a fake, spoiled, can't or won't learn the lessons, will delay the journey, make you look bad, and will be too friendly to you. You don't believe a lady can carry her weight on the trail. Whether or not it's intentional, you're tougher on me than on the others."

"How do you know what I think or feel?"

"Actually, I don't," she admitted, "because you keep me in a constant state of confusion and tension with your contradictory behavior, but that's the impression you've given me. Correct me if I'm wrong."

"I thought you had confidence in me."

"I do. I believe you're a very capable teacher and skilled guide."

"But you have a low opinion of me as a person?"

"No. I just don't think you like me or trust me or that you're fair to me."

"Do you think I should give you special treatment?"

"That isn't what I mean. Louise and Mattie and . . . others give you a hard time, unjustly I'll add, but you aren't mean to them. Why single me out to be scolded and embarrassed so many times?"

Steve came up with a logical explanation. "You need toughening up the most. Your distractions endanger me, yourself, and the others; I've explained that to you. What Mrs. Jackson, Epps, and . . . others do is annoying but not dangerous. I see no need to make them behave worse by reprimanding them. But with you, corrections improve your progress and you don't get spiteful and rebellious, or I didn't think you would."

"I'm to take that as a compliment?" she scoffed, ignoring the storm.

Steve did, too. "Why, Miss Avery, I do believe you've been hiding a naughty and defiant streak. You have more sides and surprises to your personality than a box," he teased to relax them both. As he did so, he cupped her face as he'd done with Cathy while setting the vixen straight.

The same scene came to Ginny's tormented mind and she was provoked to warn, "Don't make fun of me, you bastard."

Steve went rigid and glared at her. He was piqued into a rash reply. "Yep, so I guess it comes natural for me to act like what I am."

Ginny was stunned and she gaped at him. He was serious! Telling the truth! On purpose? Was that the root of his—

"Sorry if I shocked you, Miss Avery; it slipped out."

Even though he was the one to apologize for a change, he did it with a sarcastic tone and expression. Her pleading heart went out to him. "I'm sorry, Steve; I didn't mean to say that. You made me angry with your amusement at my expense. I like you and want to be friends, to have peace, a truce."

She looked genuinely contrite but he discarded her plea. "Don't be sorry or feel pity for me. I'm not the only bastard alive. The way some men and women carry on, who can be sure of their parentage? Take that King woman; her children could be fathered by three different men. If she doesn't stop working on me to become number four, she'll be sorry."

Was that what influenced his feelings and behavior toward women? Toward her? At least, she had misunderstood the scene she had witnessed earlier. "I'm sorry you hate your mother so much."

Steve stared at her strangely. "I don't; I love her."

She realized he didn't mention his father, if he knew who he was. She didn't query him about the touchy subject. But why blame and hate the man involved and not the woman? Odd . . .

He was so drawn to her that he rebelled. "Just a friendly warning, Anna, if you have your sights set on me, don't. I'm not available."

"You're married or you have a sweetheart?"

"Neither; past, present, or future. No place in my life for either one. A man like me only needs himself to tend."

"That sounds awfully cold and hard and lonely, Steve."

"Maybe so, but it suits me fine. I never allow myself to become vulnerable to other people's demands or put myself in a position to suffer defeat. You shouldn't, either. Be strong and smart, and you won't."

"You don't trust anyone or let anyone get close?" she asked.

"Nope, I just trust myself."

"That's a hard way to exist, Steve."

"Hasn't been so far."

"You don't ever want to change your life?"

"Nope."

"I don't believe you."

"Why not?"

"Who would want to live that way on purpose?" she reasoned. "Besides, you're too special to be alone forever."

"Am I? A man like me will take whatever a woman offers him, even if he doesn't feel the same way she does. Beware of devils like me, Anna Avery. We're dangerous and untrustworthy and selfish." *And I'm worse things you don't even know about.*

Afraid of me, are you? "Is that a challenge to find out? To prove to you that you're wrong about yourself?"

"Maybe so, because you're one tempting woman, but don't accept it. When you've had time to think about me carefully, you'll realize I'm right, that I'm worse than any violent storm could be. Get back to camp now; the storm's getting worse and it isn't safe out here alone. Don't do this again."

Ginny grasped double meanings in his words. "Ste—"

"Don't push, woman, or you'll be sorry. Better listen to me and heed my words while I'm in a rare generous mood. Git!" he ordered.

Ginny obeyed him, but didn't want to leave him or stop talking.

Steve watched her hurry out of sight when what he really wanted was to yank her into his arms and cover her mouth with kisses. He leaned against a tree and took several deep breaths to calm himself. He was angry for making his reckless admission and for behaving like a fool. *Niiguyaa,* he must have a head full of stones! But his heart no longer felt like one, and that worried him. Whyever had he told her such a humiliating and bitter secret? Because she had unsettled him—taken him off guard—with her words, expressions, and allure. But she was *ntu'i izee,* bad medicine.

After she tossed her sack inside the wagon, Ginny hung her soaked garments over a rope she had suspended between two trees to allow them to dry. Drenched, she checked on the nervous mules and went to the Davis wagon.

After leaving Steve and while she was doing her tasks, she pondered this man she desired. She could imagine the anguish and hardships he must have endured without a loving father's name, guidance, affection, and influence. It must have been a terrible cross to bear. Perhaps his mother had been ravished, or been a "soiled dove" who had gotten pregnant on the job, or had chosen to love and surrender to an unattainable man, one like her son had become.

Steve Carr was clearly a man in torment, with deep resentments, a scarred heart and troubled soul, and a tragic past. By his own admission, he didn't want to trust or get close to anyone, especially a woman. She was beginning to grasp why he was so moody, defensive, and wary. He had become self-contained, stubborn, and tough to protect himself against being hurt again; but he was unaware that he was his biggest enemy and torturer. Without realizing it, he had become more like his father than he knew, or wanted to be, or would admit. She was positive he didn't comprehend how much he needed love, comfort, and peace. Maybe his slip hadn't been an accident; maybe his lost soul was reaching out to her for those things.

When Ellie responded to her call, Ginny said, "Give me a minute to get into dry clothes, then let Stuart bring the girls over for the night."

"We don't want to be trouble, Anna; we'll have to sleep this way on the trail during bad weather."

"No need to be cramped before it's necessary," she teased. "Truly, it's no bother and everyone will be more comfortable."

Ginny sat in a nightgown on the mattress with the two girls. She was tired and needed a good night's sleep, but she needed a diversion more. The youngest provided it because she was afraid of the loud rain and thunder. "Let's play a game," she suggested. "Let's close our eyes and make guesses what the storm sounds like to us. Ready?" Ginny asked when they agreed. When both answered at the same time, she said, "I'll be first. Listen to the rain; it sounds like your mother . . . frying chicken or bacon. The thunder sounds like . . . your father hunting and firing his rifle."

"It sounds like furniture moving upstairs," the oldest ventured.

"You're right," Ginny said, and the game continued.

Afterward, she entertained and distracted them with stories her mother and father had told her as a child. At one thunderous boom, the youngest girl leaned closer to her. Ginny embraced her and soothed, "Snuggle close and I'll protect you. When I was a little girl and scared of storms, my mother left a candle burning and sang to me."

Ginny had the light low and the lantern secured to prevent an accident. She sang softly to the girls until both were asleep, one on each side of her. She smiled in satisfaction and closed her eyes, relaxed and weary enough to slumber herself tonight.

Steve moved away from the Avery wagon, wishing he could be cuddled in Ginny's arms. She was right; he was too tough and inconsistent with her, but he had good reason and he wasn't certain he could stop his ruse. She was the most invigorating breath of air he had ever taken. She had good and enticing traits. He liked being with her and talking with her. He warmed under the shine of her smile. He quivered under the sound of her voice. He flamed with desire for her.

A wife, home, and children were things he hadn't ever considered or wanted for himself. Then, Anna Avery had appeared on the scene and made them come to mind too often, made them look and feel compelling at times. That was crazy, he told himself. He had no room for them in his life, no place for them in his embittered heart. He resented the fact she even teased such dreams over his mind. Perhaps being around so many families was also to blame for him thinking so wildly and foolishly. What did he know about romancing and loving a woman, a lady like Miss Anna Avery?

Love . . . Jump off that stallion before you break your neck trying to tame it. Don't go near her with thoughts of capturing and mastering her.

Steve quelled his rebellious emotions and went for a ride on Chuune. He would finish the women's training tomorrow, give them Sunday for final preparations, then pull out on Monday, April first. He hadn't unmasked the culprit he was seeking, but he would during the journey. If it turned out to be Charles Avery, he might kill the man for endangering and involving his daughter! What would he do about her, with her, if Charles was guilty? The spirits help both of them if she was part of the crime in progress!

As he galloped along on Chuune's back to release his tension, he knew that several people were in for big surprises in the morning.

Chapter 7

SATURDAY MORNING, Ginny went to help Lucy Eaves with chores before their final training began. The woman showed her the sturdy crutch Steve Carr had made for her to help her walk better during the daily exercise and on the trail. She heard of how the scout had offered to let her friend skip that difficult task, and that Lucy had refused. Ginny was pleased but dismayed with herself for her verbal attack on him about the matter. Why hadn't he told her about this? It wasn't something he'd done since her criticism of him, which revealed he possessed compassion. Again, it was made clear he wanted to conceal or deny good traits. Remorse and guilt flooded her. As soon as she completed Lucy's chores, she sought him out.

"Steve, I want to apologize for what I said on the path yesterday. Lucy told me what you've done for her. I was wrong to misjudge you and to be so hateful. I was in a wicked mood from lack of sleep. I shouldn't have taken out my tension on you. Please forgive me."

"There's nothing to forgive, Miss Avery. It's my job to see that everyone does their jobs. She needed help, so I provided it."

"You can pass it off lightly if you wish, but I won't. In spite of what you think your motive was, it was nice and thoughtful. You aren't as cold and heartless as you believe and try to pretend to be. I'm sure you must have suffered in your life, but you can let the past go if you want to badly enough."

"With your help and sacrifice, Miss Avery?"

Tears glittered in her hazel eyes as she looked at him. She tried to convince herself it was a defensive action, but it hurt; it hurt for him. Her voice was strained as she replied, "I know it's hard for you to accept words of gratitude, but these come from the depths of my heart."

"Don't do this to yourself; don't make me out to be something I'm not. Being responsible for people you're in charge of doesn't mean I have a tender heart like you do. That's fine for you, just not for me. I've told you and shown you what kind of man I am, a bastard in more than birth."

Ginny shook her head in disagreement. "If you think kindness and compassion are weaknesses, you're wrong, Steve. Sometimes people do get hurt when they take risks, but life isn't much without the times you succeed. If you aren't the man I believe you to be, you would have taken what I offered and cared nothing for its effect on me."

Gazing into her entreating eyes and lovely face, it required a moment for him to think clearly enough to find a deceitful reply. "I care about my survival and my job; playing with you could destroy them."

"You can tell yourself that was your motive, but I don't believe it."

He locked gazes with her. "What do you think my motive was, *is?*"

Ginny decided to gamble for the whole pot. "I think you feel the same way I do and that scares the dickens out of you."

Steve narrowed his eyes and he dared not ask her what those feelings were. "You think I'm a coward, a weakling?"

"Only with your feelings," she explained. "You're willing to risk everything or anything—even your life—on physical challenges, but refuse to risk anything on emotional ones. Taking physical chances can kill you; emotional ones might only wound and can heal with time and another try."

"Some wounds never heal, Anna. Never."

"Because you pick at them, keep them open and raw, untended. You refuse to allow anyone to help treat them."

He realized he had to extricate himself from this unsettling talk. "Unless you've lived my life, you'd never understand it or me. Advice is easy to give, but taking it isn't. Even if I did feel as you do, whatever that is, it wouldn't change things. I'm a loner and I'll remain a loner till I die."

Ginny feared she couldn't reach him, and perhaps that was for the best. It was selfish and reckless to try to convince him to take a risk that could hurt both of them if it failed. "You aren't the only one who's scared of risks and who's suffered and been cheated in life."

Something in her voice and expression reached deep into his gut and twisted it. "How would a lady like you know anything about suffering?"

Tears pooled along the rims of Ginny's eyes, but she kept them from overflowing and spilling down her cheeks. "It would shock you."

"Teasing from Yankee girls and being away from family for years in an expensive boarding school isn't the end of the world, Anna."

"It has nothing to do with that. Yes, I've had what most people would believe is a pampered existence, but you don't really know me or what . . ." Ginny lowered her lashes to compose herself before she revealed too much to a beguiling stranger. She had the overwhelming urge to sob. When she lifted her eyes again, she was poised, but curious anguish was still visible to the man before her. "Forget it," she said. "I just came to thank you, not unload my burdens. Your shoulders are too full as is. Besides, we don't know each other well enough to share such a serious talk. I'll see you later, Mr. Carr."

He grasped how he had hurt her and spurned her. He couldn't help but reach out to her, even though he told himself it was only to save his mission, to repair the bridge needed to get to her. "Anna, tell me—"

She didn't face him while replying. "No, Mr. Carr; you solve your problems and I'll solve mine." She walked away with head held high.

Steve ran certain words through his keen mind: "Problems . . . Unload my burdens . . . Other worries . . . Feel the same way I do . . . Suffered and been cheated . . ." What had she been about to tell him, to let slip? Why hadn't he allowed her to confess whatever troubled her? What would "shock" him? Her "burdens" had to do with more than him, and he should have let her expose them. She could hold valuable clues to his case and he had forced her to keep her hands balled. He wondered if it had been intentional on his part; once he solved this case, he would be gone.

The group met around a wagon in the next clearing: they used the Avery one because it had fewer things to unload, and Charles had the necessary tools for today's training task. Before they started the lesson, Steve told the others how "Miss Avery" had gotten free of the mud hole and praised her wits; that surprised and pleased Ginny.

"You should remember those tricks in case you need them later. Now, let's learn how to remove and replace a wheel. We won't break anything here to learn how to do repairs, but I'll tell you how they're done."

"Why learn this? Our husbands and the other men will do it."

Steve explained to Mattie Epps and others, "If your husband is alive and uninjured, you're right. And, if you don't get stranded or leave the wagontrain for some reason, you're right. But what if you're wrong?"

"Why would anyone do that?" the complainer asked.

"Husbands can get hurt and killed and too sick to work. If one of those hardships strikes, sometimes people don't go on, or they decide to head to the nearest town to settle or recover there, or they decide to give up and turn back. Once you leave the wagontrain, you're on your own. If you break a wheel or part, who's going to do the change or repair? Are you going to sit there waiting and hoping for help to come along? Supplies could run out or robbers could come by before that happens. I won't force any of you to learn this lesson, but don't say I didn't give you fair warning it could be needed."

After those words, no one left the area or refused to participate in the lesson. They used Charles Avery's jack to lift the wagon by the axle assembly. They took turns turning the crank, removing the wheel, replacing the wheel, and lowering the contrivance.

When every woman knew the procedure and could respond accurately to questions about other repairs, they broke for lunch, then took their four-mile walk. Afterward, Steve met with them for final instructions.

* * *

At four o'clock, the scout announced, "You're trained and ready, ladies. Be sure to practice and hone your new skills on the trail; don't let them get rusty. This evening and tomorrow, get your final chores and preparations done. We leave Monday morning at seven sharp. You're dismissed until that time, except for your exercise tomorrow; you don't want to get stiff and soft by skipping a day. I'll be heading to town soon to tell the grain wagon drivers we're finished and to join us tomorrow. If any of your husbands want to come along to get supplies, he's welcome to ride along with me. All of you did a good job, so I doubt anyone will have trouble along the way."

Loud cheers rose among the women.

Ginny climbed aboard the wagon, drove it back to her campsite, and un-hitched the team. She went inside to make certain everything was in its correct place and was secured, as others had helped her reload.

"Miss Avery?"

She turned, walked to the back, and knelt to speak with the scout.

"Do you have a message for your father I can deliver? Anything you need him to bring when he comes tomorrow to join us?"

"Nothing I can think of, Steve, but thank you for the offer."

"See you later."

"Good-bye, Steve, and thanks."

He tipped his hat, nodded, and left.

So much for not having human kindness, Ginny thought with a smile. It slowly faded as she mused, *Or did you only want an excuse to see where and how you think I lived? Checking me out, my inquisitive guide? Why?*

Ginny shook her head in displeasure. *Don't be so suspicious of him. Just because he's being nice doesn't mean he has an ulterior motive.* Yet, she had a strong feeling he did; perhaps it had been something in his tone of voice or in his expression that gave her that feeling. After all, Steve Carr wasn't a man to do anything without a good reason, his own reason.

Ginny let the matter drop and went to see Ruby Amerson. "Why don't I watch the children while you get your wash done?" she offered. "I don't have as much, so I can do mine afterward."

"That's so kind of you, Anna. It'll be a big help. George went into town with Mr. Carr to replenish some of our supplies."

"It will be fun and educational; just tell me what to do."

Ginny scrubbed her clothes at the river. After she finished each item, she laid it on a blanket to keep from soiling it while she worked on the others. She realized ironing was impossible in camp and on the trail, so she could imagine how some of the cotton garments would look a rumpled mess soon.

She heard a distant gunshot and remembered some of the men had gone hunting. She was relieved they hadn't had any trouble while camped there, and prayed they wouldn't on the trail.

* * *

Steve leaned against a tree at his campsite. His supplies and gear were ready to move out; they always stayed ready for a quick departure. None of the men who had gone into town with him had done anything suspicious. Either the gems were hidden in a wagon, concealed near camp, or would arrive with Charles Avery tomorrow. He had stopped by the boardinghouse for a minute on the pretext of telling Charles their schedule. The man hadn't been home, so his older sister had taken the message. The friendly woman had sent Anna some treats and a shawl that he would pass along to her when she returned from chores.

Steve concluded the boardinghouse was clean, large, and had been successful, but not enough so to earn wealth or provide a high social status. From Anna's possessions, schooling, and genteel breeding, he had expected something very different. He told himself it was because Charles, preparing for this move west, had sold his home and business and moved in with his sister. Steve wished he could have gotten a look at something indicative of Charles's old lifestyle which could tell him more about the man. He also wished he had arrived in time and had the chance to do more study on Avery and the other men. At present, he didn't know who to watch most carefully.

Steve joined Ginny as she hung her wash to dry. She glanced at him and smiled. "It's hard to believe we'll be heading west on Monday."

"You're looking forward to it?"

Ginny gazed into space over the rope clothesline as she thought of seeing her father. "Yes, very much. I can hardly wait to arrive."

"Better enjoy the journey. After you get there, you'll have lots of work to do . . . Your aunt sent you some surprises; I put them in your wagon."

Ginny halted work to look at him, "You went to see her?"

"I dropped by to tell your father we'd be leaving Monday. He wasn't home, so I left word with your aunt."

What if someone had told him Mr. Avery's daughter was dead when he asked for directions? she fretted. What if someone mentioned a recent death and burial of another girl, a stranger who had just docked from England? Surely not, as the scout didn't appear or sound suspicious of her. "That was nice of you," she said and concentrated on her task.

Steve wondered why she looked unsettled by his mention of the visit to her home. Maybe she had lost more because of the war than she had hinted at and hoped no one in camp discovered they were near what she might think were dire straits. He'd keep alert to—

"What's this, Mr. Carr?" one of the Davis boys asked as he drew Steve's knife from his boot sheath while the scout was distracted.

Steve reacted instantly by grasping the blade and yanking it from the startled child's hand. "That's sharp and dangerous, Son; don't ever play with knives or guns."

"I'm sorry, sir; I won't do it again. I better go."

Ginny and Steve watched the embarrassed boy run off to play with the others. She looked at the scout's hand as he replaced the weapon and saw red staining his palm. "You're bleeding. Let me see your hand."

Steve looked at the injury. "Just a nick. Doesn't hurt much."

Ginny captured and eyed his hand. "It needs tending. I'll—"

"Don't trouble yourself."

"It won't be any trouble."

"I can take care of it; I always take care of myself."

"That blood should prove you're human just like everyone else. You don't have to be so strong all the time. It won't hurt to open up a little and let people in. You might be surprised to learn you like it. That wound could become infected. It will be easier for me to bind it. Besides, I need the practice; you can tell me what to do. I insist, Steve, no arguing." She captured his wrist and pulled him toward her wagon. "Sit up here while I take care of it. Let me fetch the medicine box."

Steve did as she said, sat cross-legged on the tailgate. He watched her get the medicine box and a basin of fresh water.

Ginny washed the oozing scarlet area with gentleness, but blood continued to flow from the cut. "It doesn't look deep enough for stitches, so that's good." She dapped stinging medicine on the slice, but the man didn't wince or move. She wrapped a clean bandage around his hand, then used his thumb and wrist to secure it in place. "That's better. I'll check it and change the bandage tomorrow."

"Thanks, Dr. Avery, you did a good job."

Ginny returned his smile and quipped, "See, it wasn't so bad to let someone help you for a change. You do it plenty for others."

"I suppose not," he relented a little. He realized she hadn't released his injured hand yet; it was cupped tenderly in hers, and the contact felt wonderful. Too stimulating, he warned himself and moved it.

Steve eased off the tailgate and turned to her. "The things from your aunt are over there." He pointed to a small pile. "See you later."

Ginny observed his retreat before she tossed out the bloody water and put away the medicine kit. She returned to hanging up her laundry. She was amazed he had given in to her request, spoken as an order. It had been enjoyable, despite the circumstances, to tend and to touch him. The more time she spent with him, the more she wanted him to remain in her life.

The sliver of a moon attempted to give adequate light to the shadowy landscape; its task was aided by fires here and there whose colorful flames leapt upward and sent curls of smoke in the same direction. The ebony sky was filled with bright stars. A refreshing breeze stirred mosses, branches, and grass blades. The ground was still soft from two days of rain. Nocturnal birds, insects, and creatures sent forth their sounds into the night. Frogs and crickets were particularly abundant. Some wagons were aglow from lanternlight inside. Laughter and voices could be heard wafting on the wind. Most seemed content to rest and relax tonight at their own campsites before doing their final chores tomorrow.

Ginny strolled into the shadows opposite her wagon. Steve joined her immediately without startling her. She grinned and explained, "I wasn't going far, boss; I remember your caution about the danger of being away alone. I love nighttime:

the stars, the moon, the shadows, the nocturnal sounds, the calm of it all. You have to be in the darkness to experience them better.''

''If we were out West, you wouldn't be safe even this close to camp and guards. A trained warrior could sneak up to kill you, rob you, or capture you without making a sound to alert others.''

''Then I'm glad we're here tonight. Have you . . . tangled with many Indians in your travels?''

''Yes and no,'' he replied as he envisioned her as his captive.

''Explain that,'' she encouraged to keep him talking.

''I've done Indian fighting, and I've also made friends with some.''

''Friends?'' she echoed in surprise.

''I do have some, Anna. I just don't make them easy and often.''

''You constantly amaze and confuse me, Steve Carr. Who are you?''

''Nobody, so what do you mean?'' He tensed as he wondered if he had done or said something to cast suspicion on himself, on his mission.

''Where are you from? How do you live?''

''Out West and by whatever catches my interest. I stay on the move so I'm not in one place very long.''

''No home? You travel all the time?''

''Yep, I prefer it that way.''

''Where did you attend school?''

''What?''

''You sound educated to me.''

''That surprises you for a cowpoke, a trail duster?''

''Nothing I learn about you should surprise me. You're quite a puzzle.''

''My mother.''

It was her turn to be baffled. ''What?''

''My mother taught me and had me tutored. Thought it would help get me accepted in the 'right' places and with the 'right' people.''

''From your bitter tone, it didn't. So you instantly dislike people like me? I'm sure life was tough and painful for you on your own.''

''Despite what you think, Anna, I haven't had a bad life. I'm good at what I do, and I like it.''

''Do you ever hire out as a private guide?''

He was intrigued. *A clue?* ''Why?''

''Just wondered. Do you?''

''I have, and I'd do it again if the money and challenge were there.''

Ginny dropped that idea for the moment. ''You said you don't let people get close so you won't be vulnerable and get hurt. How could I hurt you?''

''Don't you know, Anna?''

''I hope so, but I'm not sure. Do I make you as nervous as you make me? Do you push me away because you don't like me or because of Cathy?'' The last question slipped out before she could prevent it.

''Mrs. King? Ah, yes, so it is noticeable to others. I was afraid of that. I set her straight when she waylaid me in the woods yesterday. I'm lucky I didn't get clawed up by that coy little cat when she was grabbing at me. I had to struggle to control my temper. I don't like women who paw me.''

"I imagine many women chase you during your travels."

"Some."

"Do you . . . spurn all of them?"

"Mighty nosy, aren't you?" he jested and gently tugged on a curl. "Should I start questioning you about your lovelife?"

"I don't have one and have never had one."

"That's hard to believe, a beautiful and desirable woman like you."

"It's true, by choice. I've never met a man I wanted to get to know better, until now."

"Until now?" he repeated, asking himself if he should press onward to ensnare her or retreat to avoid this sensitive topic.

Ginny's gaze fused with Steve's. "Until you."

"You want to get to know me? Why?"

"Because you're interesting, different, appealing. Because I like you. Because I think we could become good friends. Is that being too bold?"

"It's mighty direct for a lady."

"Is that why you're afraid of me, because I'm a lady?"

"Ladies give men like me trouble and aggravation."

"How so, Steve?"

"For all reasons you mentioned last night when you scolded me, and because they want and need what I can't and won't give them."

"Why is friendship so terrible to give?"

Steve clasped her face between his hands, gazed deeply into her eyes, and asked, "Is that all you want from me, Anna Avery? I don't think so."

"I honestly don't know *what* I want from you, Steve. It's confusing."

"I know, Anna, and it's trouble for both of us; it's impossible."

"Why?"

"I'm not the settling-down kind. Look for a husband in Texas."

"What was it you said to me; 'Advice is easy to give, but hard to take?' I'm not searching for a husband, Steve, in Texas or here with you."

"You're not the kind to have . . . unmeaningful . . . amusement."

She was relieved when he chose his words with care. "I . . ."

When her words trailed off before refuting his statement, Steve bent forward and kissed her. His tongue danced with hers. He pulled her tightly against him. Scorching heat licked over his body. He yearned to possess her then and there. He felt her tremble in his embrace. She was so warm and willing and eager with her responses, with the way she kissed him, with the way she clung to him, with the way she stroked his back. He knew it would be wonderful to teach her lovemaking, to experience it with her. But what would happen after she surrendered to him? Would she endanger his mission? Would he become too distracted by her to solve it? Would it blind him to the Averys' possible involvement in his case? Would she become clingy and demanding, or would she get painfully hurt by him?

The intensity of Steve's kisses and hunger, and those of her own, alarmed Ginny. Strange and powerful longings filled her, and she knew their names were Desire and Passion. She wanted to be introduced to them; she wanted to get to know them. But they could be enemies, could be dangerous, could be captors. She relished his fiery kisses and tender caresses as long as she dared without losing her wits. When she realized the hunger was increasing, as was the pleasure, she pushed away from him. "I can't . . . do this, Steve."

"I know, Anna; that's what I was trying to prove to you."

Ginny looked into his eyes and doubted his claim. He couldn't convince her he wasn't as aroused as she was. "Just because I can't do something reckless here and now doesn't mean I don't want to, Steve."

"Wanting something badly and taking rash action to get it aren't the same, woman. Keep a strong will and a clear head, Anna Avery, and don't allow a man like me to take advantage of you."

Ginny knew he had the power to capture her heart and claim her innocence if he really tried; the fact he wouldn't do either told her he cared about her more than he realized or would admit. "That's easier for you than for me, Steve, because you're experienced with these things."

"Not with a woman like you, Anna. You should steer clear of me; I'm untrustworthy and dangerous." He was trapped between two forces. One urged him to take what she offered and what he wanted for his own pleasure and to aid his mission; the other warned and pleaded for him to let her escape his clutches to be kind.

Ginny didn't know if his advice was an evocative challenge or an honest warning. "Couldn't we become friends and take this slow and easy?"

"I'm tempted, but it wouldn't work. I won't mislead you, Anna."

"Are you telling me to come after you at my own risk?"

"No, I'm telling you I'd probably let you catch me for a while, but only for a while, Anna. That I know for certain. You strike me as a woman who'd want more from a man, who'd suffer later."

"So you're spurning me to protect my feelings?"

"Maybe. I just know it's crazy to leap on a stallion that can't be tamed."

"I believe you have the skills to master anything you want to. Doesn't a man keep a valuable stallion after he's tamed it and branded it?"

"Some only love the challenge of breaking them in. Then they sell them or release them back into the wild."

"And it never bothers you that it carries your brand?"

"Hasn't yet."

"But it might with me so you don't want to take the chance?"

"Maybe."

"You never want to commit yourself, do you?"

Steve studied her for a moment. Maybe she was smarter and braver than he knew; she had learned her lessons well in the past week. Maybe she was using cunning wiles he couldn't perceive to lure him into her clutches to get him, as she'd subtly hinted, to guide them to the Averys' contact out West. She could be working with Charles on an evil scheme, out of loyalty to her father or out of a misguided belief the Klan was doing good things. As with most Southerners, she did have cause to hate Yankees and to seek revenge. There was only one way to find out: challenge her to pursue him, let her think she'd caught him, and see what happened. If he was wrong about her and she got hurt from his ruse . . . He'd deal with that possibility later. If she didn't need him for something important, his imminent words should frighten her and send her running for cover!

"How's this for being clear as a mountain stream? Damn right, I like you and you get under my tough hide. Damn right, I want you, and want you badly. Damn right, I'd take you if given the chance, and take you every time I could. Damn right, I'd leave when the time came for us to part ways; and it would come, Anna, never doubt that for a moment."

Ginny watched his retreat with an open mouth and stunned wits. He had admitted his affection and desire for her! He would love her and he would leave her. Or would he? Could she change him? Or not so much change him as help him get over the past. What would it be like to love him, to win him, to marry him, to have his children, to share his life, to take him to Colorado with her?

Ginny milked the cow as Ellie Davis had taught her, then helped with breakfast and the clean-up chores.

A religious service was held under the trees with Bible reading, singing, and praying. In spite of many complaints, they had begun their training last Sunday on the "Lord's Day." By this one, the men and women were ready to begin their trek the next day.

The women took their four-mile walk while husbands watched children. Afterward, the men took theirs. It was everyone's last task before making all final preparations to depart. They had the remainder of the day off, to work, to rest, and to have fun.

The two grain wagons and drivers arrived in camp: Hollister and Brent. The leader met with them and gave them their instructions.

After lunch, Ginny and other women went to the river for a last bath and shampoo before hitting the dusty and demanding trail. She lathered her long hair as she thought about Steve and last night. He had been distant again today and that troubled her. She couldn't decide whom he was trying to protect the most: him, her, or both of them? Would she ever understand and reach him? He wouldn't be afraid of her and avoid her unless . . .

Don't push it, Ginny. It might complicate matters and you don't need more problems. You don't know him well enough to reveal your secrets. Doing so can paint you black to him. He already doesn't trust people; then you confess you're a deceiver! He'll think you're like the others—or worse.

While Ginny was gone, Charles Avery arrived and joined the group.

Steve walked over to speak with the man who was attaching his chicken pens to his wagon and stowing supplies. "Good to see you."

Charles glanced up and smiled. "My sister gave me your message; thanks for coming by yesterday. I was already planning to head out today. I thought it was best to let Anna have privacy during her training. How did she do, Steve? Any problems?"

Steve was intrigued by what he thought was a slip: how could she "do badly" in front of him if she'd been away at boarding school for six years and had just returned? "No problems to amount to anything. Training was tough on all the women, but Miss Avery did fine. You should be proud of her."

Confusing the two girls as he sometimes did—his lost child and Virginia Marston, his alleged daughter—Charles answered with remarks about both. "I am; she's a smart girl; she can do anything she sets her mind to. She made the best grades of her class. They wanted her to become a teacher, but Anna wants more of a challenge in life."

"Such as?" Steve asked casually as he helped with the task.

Charles centered on their ruse, as he honestly liked Ginny. "She doesn't know yet, but I won't be surprised by anything she attempts."

"She'll do fine at whatever she tries if she keeps her mind on it. The only trouble she has is with bouts of distraction."

"She told me she had trouble concentrating and you scolded her."

Steve gave the same explanation he had given her, and no apology.

"I fully understand and agree, and I told Anna so. She promised to do better and obviously she kept her word." Charles glanced around to make sure no one was close enough to overhear what he was about to say. He had decided to get the scout and Ginny matched up for she would need the man's help and protection soon. He was sure Carr would keep his confidence, as he seemed that kind of man. "This is between us, Steve, but it might explain why she behaved like that in the beginning. When she came to camp, she'd just lost her best friend since childhood, she died in Anna's arms right before I started my training. That's really why I left her in town with my sister; I thought she needed privacy to grieve and begin to recover. Don't tell her I told you; it would upset her to know you'd be nice because of her suffering. She's a proud girl. She also has me to deal with; we've been separated for six years, so she's having to get used to me again. While she was up North, she lost her home, and the war ravaged everything she knew and loved. I collected her and I'm rushing her off to the Wild West. She just needed time to adjust to all those changes. Do you understand?"

Steve nodded and continued helping Charles to secure the fowl pens. He knew what it was to lose a best friend, a home, and more. He now knew the reason why she'd been weeping that night; and she'd had no one to comfort her. Twinges of guilt for his behavior and suspicions chewed at him. He had been too tough and cold; she was so very vulnerable. It was surprising she'd come to like him. She should have confided in him about her troubles. She probably assumed he wouldn't understand or, if he did, it wouldn't make a difference in his treatment of her. Yet she had tried, he remembered, and he'd prevented it. Lost a best friend to death . . .

At least her best friend had died, he mused with bitterness, not been murdered and . . . But the cold-blooded killer would be tracked down and punished as soon as he completed this mission. He had promised himself: no more defeats, distractions, and unfinished business to prey on his mind. He would—

"That has it done, Steve; thanks for the help. You promise you won't tell Anna what I told you?" the graying man reminded.

"You have my word of honor, sir."

"That's the most important thing a man can have and give to another."

"Yep, but the war almost took it away from us Rebs. We promised to do a lot of things—protect our homes, families, friends, and land, but we couldn't keep those vows. I guess we'll all accept that defeat one day."

"One of the hardest losses a man can suffer is that of his pride. Things wouldn't be so bad in the South if the Yankees would let us have a little bit of it back. They're determined to keep us cowered and conquered."

Steve listened and watched for clues. "I don't see that there's much we can do about that, sir, until they change their minds and actions."

"I'm afraid you're right, Steve, and it really sticks in my craw."

"Mine, too, sir. But as you said, there's nothing we can do about it. Of course, some of the men here think differently."

Charles came to alert. "What do you mean?"

Steve tried to sound and look nonchalant. "Oh, there's been a lot of wild talk at night about the Klan and what they're doing. Some of the men think they're in the right."

"And you don't?"

Steve pretended to think a moment, shrugged, and replied, "I'm not sure what I believe, sir. A man can't always trust everything he hears and reads, so I don't know if they really do all they get blamed for."

"Would you ever join up with a group like that to punish the ones who've made us suffer and continue to make us suffer so much?"

Steve faked deep thought again. "I can't honestly say one way or the other, sir. I've never run into any Klan members. I don't know the truth about them."

"I have. They struck me as decent, honest men who are protecting their friends and families and what little they have left from the war."

"But what about all the lynchings, burnings, and lootings they're blamed for?" Steve reasoned.

"I don't suppose they're doing anything worse than those Yankee marauders and foragers, like Sherman and his troops did here in Georgia."

"But isn't the Klan attacking innocent men?"

"From what I hear and read, it's carpetbaggers, scalawags, Loyal Leaguers, cruel ex-officers, and troublemaking Negroes they focus on."

"Does that give them the right to retaliate in such a deadly way? They could make mistakes and kill innocent people, and some don't obey rules."

"Who can say what's right or wrong when it comes to war, hatred, revenge, and justice? If things were set right in this country and courts didn't go against us, there wouldn't be a place or need for societies like—"

Ginny returned and halted their conversation. She glanced at Steve, then looked at Charles Avery. She behaved as she thought she should. She smiled and embraced the older man. "It's good to see you, Father."

"It's good to be here, Daughter. Steve was telling me how well you've done with your training. I'll get a look at it for myself on the trail."

She stood there with Charles's arm around her shoulder. "It was hard, Father, but we all survived his lessons."

"If you two will excuse me, I have chores of my own to tend. Good day, Miss Avery, sir." Steve nodded at the woman and left them alone.

"That young man likes you, girl," Charles told her.

"He what?" she asked. "Did he tell you that?"

"Not exactly, but he was softening up your father to get to you."

"What did he say about me?"

"Nothing much; just bragged on how well you'd done this week."

"It's about time; he's usually stingy with compliments or he walks them through the back door."

Charles laughed. "That's because men get skittish around girls they like and want; they're scared of making mistakes and scaring them off while they get up the courage to court them."

"Court me?" she repeated and laughed. "I can imagine a moody loner like Steve Carr coming to our wagon at night to ask your permission to take a stroll in the moonlight with me," she teased.

"He might surprise you and do just that."

"Surprise me? It would shock me to wits' end."

Ginny helped Lucy Eaves cook, serve the meal, and do the dishes. She and Charles ate with the couple and their three children. They enjoyed talking with Jeff and Lucy, and they seemed to enjoy the Averys.

Afterward, almost everyone met in the camp center around a glowing camp-fire to sing, chat, listen to music, dance, and laugh—except those few who be-lieved it was wrong to dance on Sunday. It was a celebration of the end of their work and the beginning of an adventure, and all were in a cheerful and relaxed mood. Music came from a harmonica, a "squeeze-box," and George Amerson's fiddle. Toes were tapping on the ground. The older children observed or joined in on the merriment.

Charles talked with Ed King, and Ginny did so with her women friends.

"Go ask him to dance," Ruby suggested with a grin.

"I couldn't. He might not know how and might be embarrassed. Besides, it would be forward of me," Ginny replied, knowing George's wife meant Steve. She was greatly tempted to be bold.

Steve wished he could check out the chicken coops Charles had brought with him. He knew the birds would make too much noise. He had attempted to inspect them while helping Charles but failed. When he saw Cathy King eyeing him, he knew she was about to ask him to dance. He prevented that by approach-ing and asking Anna Avery, who looked astonished. Steve grasped her hand and pulled her forward to join other couples.

As they moved around the campfire, he chuckled and whispered, "See, woman, no broken or stomped toes. I can do a few refined things. If you're still interested, we can be friends, Anna, but take it slow and easy."

Ginny dared not look up into that handsome face. She was amazed by the revelation of this new skill: he was an excellent dancer. She was also amazed he had chosen her as his first partner, shown interest in her before the others. She decided not to play coy. Instead, she murmured, "Slow and easy it is, sir."

Steve loved the feel of her in his embrace, savored her hand in his, feasted on her beauty, enjoyed her hair grazing his arm, and inhaled her clean and perfumed fragrance. "We leave tomorrow at seven. Make sure you're ready so I won't have to ruin our truce with another scolding."

Ginny had difficulty thinking about anything but the irresistible man she was touching and smelling. He was reaching out to her, however cautiously. "I'll make certain I'm ready for any challenge by morning."

"*Any* challenge, Anna?"

She met his roguish gaze. "Yes, Steve, *any* challenge."

——— *Chapter 8* ———

❧

"WAGONS, HO!" STEVE SHOUTED, and signaled them with a wave of his tan hat to follow his lead as they left the campsite near the Ogeechee River on April 1, 1867. His deception was in progress but hadn't provided much information to date. Soon, he promised himself, the case would be solved.

Seventeen wagons—fifteen families and two hauling grain—moved out to head west. Of the eighty-four people present, those old enough to be aware of things were happy to be seeking fresh starts away from the war-ravaged area. Steve Carr on his sorrel led and scouted the trail. Men and women either drove their wagons, walked beside them, rode for a while on them, or sat astride nearby horses. Some older children walked, too, for as long as they could, while toddlers and babies rode inside. Few talked, in an effort to conserve energy. Cows and horses roped to tailgates ambled along at the pace set by leader and mules—a few times sending forth whinnies, moos, or brays. Occasionally a chicken clucked or a rooster crowed, startled by unfamiliar movement and noises.

Water sloshed back and forth in covered barrels secured to the outsides of wagon beds. The wide rims of wheels rumbled along easily on the mixture of grass and hard dirt beneath them. Sounds of trampling hooves, shaking canvases, creaking leather, jangling harnesses, and squeaking wood were heard.

The Old South of Georgia was being left behind, as were previous lives. New starts were before the travelers, who assumed they would never return to their lost homes. All of that was gone, just as the Indians who had once lived in the area, who, too, had been pushed westward, but to reservations in the Oklahoma Territory. The days of gentility, chivalry, hospitality, culture, charm, wealth, and leisure were things of the past; or so everyone present believed. The "Planter's Society" that had made the South great had also destroyed it.

Miles south of middle Georgia, the flat terrain was covered in a sandy topsoil over hard clay and with verdant grass and scattered wildflowers. Virgin forests of pine, oak, and other hardwoods greeted travelers with a vision of green. Here and there, graceful magnolias and dainty hollys joined the scenery to beautify it. They journeyed through woods, meadows, and fields, where cotton, cattle, corn, and other crops once flourished; many were now overgrown with weeds.

As Ginny walked beside the Avery wagon, she reflected on her last talk this morning with the man driving it. He had asked if she was ready for the "challenges and adventures" that lay ahead. She had said, "Yes," but a mixture of emotions filled her: panic, doubt, excitement, and sadness. *I wish I could forget my problems and promises, get on a horse, and ride to Colorado.* Yet, more trouble and peril could await her there, especially if her father was dead. It was frightening to think of being stranded alone in that wilderness with its many hazards and threats. It was scary to think of becoming a target for her father's enemy. Yet, each mile trekked took her closer to her father and hopefully to success. She wanted to tell her friends the truth, but it would get her and Mr. Avery kicked off the wagon-train and stranded without its protection and guidance. She couldn't do that; the kind man had done too much for her and Johanna.

She wanted Steve, but if she confessed the truth to him, he'd never believe her or trust her again. She didn't want to increase his bitterness and mistrust or risk him thinking horrible things about her or risk breaking her heart. It was better to let him see and remember her as Anna Avery, a lady, a tempting romance, a friend.

Ginny wondered if Johanna's adopted brother was anything like Steve Carr. Perhaps all western men were similar in character and behavior. He was two years younger than Steve, but he could have fought in the war and been changed by it as so many men had. Were he and Mr. Chapman as close as they had been years ago? Had losing Johanna altered the rancher's feelings and actions? Mr. Chapman had given up his only child for another man's son; he had given up his wife for a mistress. Had he ever regretted those decisions? What kind of man would want two women at the same time? Ginny didn't think she was going to like or respect Johanna's father.

She looked at the man silhouetted against the blue sky. Last night had been such fun, but he was ignoring her today. Steve sat astride his sorrel and kept a steady pace. A rope hung from the butt of his sheathed rifle. His saddlebags bulged with clothes and other small possessions. A blanket, slicker, and bedroll were secured behind his cantle. A cloth sack with supplies and cookware swung from the horn. Two Colts with his initials were strapped to his waist and thighs, and the knife was resting in its boot sheath. His red shirt could be sighted easily by anyone needing him.

Ginny walked as much as she rode or drove, and she was glad now that Steve had insisted on daily exercise to increase her stamina and strength. But she worried each time he galloped past to check on everyone, always on the other side of the wagon and never glancing her way. At lunch, Steve didn't approach her; and he left early to scout the trail ahead for problems. They crossed the Canoochee River and other streams and creeks without trouble or delay. Along the waterline she saw cypress trees with lacy moss draped over their branches and with their gnarled roots exposed.

On the land outside of Savannah, they passed lingering reminders of Sherman's "March to the Sea." She viewed signs of the horrible and tragic destruction: burned and looted plantations and homes, collapsing barns, weather-beaten sheds and outhouses, lonely churches, and broken-spirited Southerners who were trying to eke out a living in the midst of ruins. Some farms and once-grand houses were deserted and rundown or occupied by squatters. Many fields hadn't been replanted, but some—belonging to carpetbaggers, she presumed—showed tiny green sprouts. A few had workers in them, white and black, but paid for their labors now, not slaves. She wondered how Green Oaks had fared the war and Cleniece's ownership.

I wish I could go to Texas, tell Johanna's father the truth, then head for Colorado, with Steve. Would you hold me to my promise, Johanna, if you knew I had fallen in love, and honoring it might destroy that love and me? I wish you were here so we could talk and you could tell me what to do. Everything has gotten so complicated. I made a promise to you and I have to keep it or I'll feel guilty for the rest of my life for letting you down; I owe you that much. I have to stay silent on the journey because I owe Mr. Avery that much. To confess the truth to my friends and Steve wouldn't change things; it would only make them worse.

Penniless, homeless, alone, Ginny had no current alternative except to continue on to the ranch. She couldn't keep taking advantage of Mr. Avery's generosity. She couldn't force Steve to love her. She had no choice except to carry out the secret she had promised Johanna that sad night.

At dusk, Steve halted them to camp in the edge of a cool and shady forest. Charles built the fire and she "cooked" their meal, opening and warming two jars of canned soup with ham from his sister. She mixed and fried cornbread in a skillet and prepared coffee as Ellie had taught her. They also drank milk Charles had purchased from Stuart Davis.

After the meal, Ginny used water from the barrel to wash the dishes. At that point, she didn't have to worry about conserving it, as they would pass enough rivers and streams for refills. She helped Charles grease the axles and tend the team after she fetched grain in a bucket from Hollister. The mules also grazed on grass, but had to be supplemented daily with feed to keep them in good condition. She thought Steve was smart for providing the feed service so wagons wouldn't have to bear the extra weight of heavy grain sacks. When both finished, they went their separate ways.

As Ginny chatted with her four women friends, she noticed that Charles Avery had spoken with Ed King and was with Harry Brown and John Daniels at present. Later, he visited with Carl Murphy, the Georgian.

When he returned to their site, she expressed her concern about Murphy. "Do you know him? Can he expose our ruse?"

Charles patted her arm and coaxed, "Don't worry, girl; nobody can expose us. Nobody here knows my Anna's fate. No one knows you recently docked. Even if any checking was done on us, no one could discover anything."

That relieved Ginny, who didn't want to be caught in lies.

Within twenty minutes, the camp was quiet and slumbering.

Tuesday, the pattern and pace established on the first day became routine. The Georgia plains stretched out before them, an area that would have been a sea of white from cotton if the war hadn't occurred and if it were late summer. The terrain stayed flat and easy to travel. Trees of pine and hardwood remained the same. Sometimes they passed ponds with lilypads floating atop, creating a serene sight.

The next day, a landscape of various shades of green continued. A low hill—more of a gentle incline and decline—appeared once in a while. Only twice did the line of wagons journey on dirt roads. Usually it went through forests, over untilled farmland, and across unused pastures with torn-down fences. They crossed the Ohoopee River with its slow-moving black water and fifty-feet width and a swift stream here and there.

On Thursday, they traversed areas abundant in oak, flowering plum, cedar, and chinaberry. The only difference in the terrain were spots of uneven flatland. Everything was verdant and growing, as many trees and bushes were evergreens and Georgia's winters were mild. Sometimes they saw old churches with cemeteries. They were fortunate to have a wooden bridge for crossing the wide, deep, and swift Oconee River; they did it one at a time, given their heavy loads and its advanced age. More streams and creeks greeted them before they halted for their fourth day on the trail.

Ginny noticed that during the last few days Steve and the two grain wagon drivers camped together and ate together unless some of the families invited the men to join them for the evening meals. She had seen the scout visit around the camps each night, but he always seemed to reach theirs while she was away on chores or for chats. She surmised it was intentional and was twice tempted to approach him to ask why. She decided to let him unravel his defensiveness alone. She had seen him riding and talking with other men on horseback during the day, including with her companion while she drove the wagon. She was grateful to the guide for his tough lessons, as they were paying off.

Charles kept telling her how taken with her the scout was, but Steve's contradictory behavior didn't reveal or even suggest that. Four days, she fretted, without a touch, a word, a smile, or a kiss! She yearned for all, or for only one, of them. She couldn't grasp why he was treating her this way after what he'd said that last night in camp.

Ginny was tired each night and was sleeping well in the wagon, with Charles slumbering beside or underneath it on a bedroll. Few people talked after turning in because the closeness of the circle prevented privacy. Baths had merely been fast wash-offs, as they hadn't camped at a river site since leaving. Thanks to the jars of canned soups and vegetables from Charles's sister, and to the simplicity of trail food, preparing tasty meals hadn't been difficult so far. The routine was set and would continue for weeks.

Friday, between long spans of flatland, more very low-rolling hills appeared than in past days; they were so gentle with their rises and falls that they presented no hardships for the strong teams and only required a slightly slower pace. They reached an offshoot of the Ocmulgee River, some dense patches of scrubs to their right and left, and soft spots Charles called "attempts at creeks."

In some locations, countless pines had concealed the ground with their dead straw and were currently sending out pollen to attack everything in sight. Ginny kept the wagon openings closed to prevent the yellow dust from covering their possessions. It coated canvases, sweaty animals, and perspiring people with sunny-colored grime. It caused some travelers to respond with sneezes, watery eyes, runny noses, and headaches.

In camp that night, Charles borrowed a horse and gear from Ed King to teach Ginny how to ride western saddle. Finally she had told him she walked when not resting or driving because she only knew sidesaddle and feared making a fool of herself or causing an accident with an error. She was delighted to discover how easy it was to master. They were gone twenty minutes when Steve joined them. Ginny was surprised and pleased, although he rode next to Charles, not her.

"Enjoying yourselves?" the scout asked from his sorrel.

"Most assuredly," the grinning Charles replied.

"Yes" came her succinct response. *Let him stew as I have!*

Steve leaned forward, looking past Charles to speak to her. "I see your training is paying off, Miss Avery; you're doing fine."

Ginny kept her gaze ahead, on the scenery and off him. "Yes, it is, and thank you for the many lessons."

The men chatted for a while before the sly and determined older man said, "I think I'll head back now. This body isn't used to so much exercise. Steve, would you escort Anna back when she finishes her ride?"

Before the scout could answer, an embarrassed Ginny said, "That won't be necessary, Father, I'm ready to return to camp, too."

"I don't mind at all, Anna," Steve told her. "It's still early."

She didn't want him to think this ride was a ruse to capture his attention or be forced to spend time with her. "No thank you, Mr. Carr. I'm tired and have things to do before bedtime. Let's go, Father." Ginny pulled on the reins, turned her horse, and started riding.

Steve and Charles exchanged apologetic looks and shrugged.

"You have been ignoring her, son," Charles hinted, "and women are sensitive creatures who need attention."

Steve was surprised by the remarks. "Miffed with me, is she?"

"Yes, I'd say she's that all right. Too bad, because she likes you and misses you. I'd hate to see anything spoil your friendship."

"What are you suggesting, sir?"

"Anna can use good friends right now; she has a lot of adjusting to do, and they can help ease her burdens. During her training, she came to respect, admire, and depend on you. I guess she feels cut off from that strength and that shoulder to lean on she'd gotten accustomed to. I don't know what would become of her if anything happened to me. Anna's strong and smart and brave, but she's lived in a sheltered environment for six years under the guidance and protection of the teachers. I'm not sure she knows how to deal with people and situations. She left the South when it was beautiful and safe; she returned when it was scarred and dangerous. We love each other, but we're like strangers because we were separated for so long. She left as a girl and returned as a woman; I've changed, too. The war was on, so any letters we might have written to keep us acquainted couldn't even get through. Her best friend was with Anna at school; they were like sisters; her death hit her hard. She has a lot to learn about people and life, so I'd be grateful if you help her. See you in camp, son. And will you join us for supper tomorrow night?"

"What will Anna have to say about that?"

"She'd be delighted, I'm sure. So will I. See you in camp."

Steve watched Charles catch up with his daughter and join her. He had a strong feeling the man was trying to push him and Anna together. He wondered why a gentleman would want a "saddle tramp," as he'd been called more than once, to court his most precious possession. Suspicion and curiosity flooded his body. A gut instinct told him Charles Avery wanted something particular from him. It could be help on his new ranch, as he'd be a greenhorn in his new existence. Or it could be as a guide to an evil rendezvous, as Anna had hinted earlier, if her query was more than casual conversation. Or it could be as a gift to his cherished daughter, if she craved him enough to seek and receive her father's assistance. Or it could be as a protector if an accident or death befell the man on the trail or until she was settled on the new ranch or needed returning to her aunt. Whatever the older man's motive was, Steve needed to learn it quick.

As they rode along, Ginny asked Charles what the two of them had said to each other.

"We were talking about guard assignments and what's ahead. I hated to come after you too fast after you took off like that, so I chatted with him a while. Why didn't you stay with him, girl? The perfect opportunity was there."

Ginny explained her reason, and Charles concurred and apologized. But the man knew he had sparked interest in the scout toward her, and he was glad of it. Most of what he had said about Ginny and her father was true, so he had sounded convincing, and he knew Steve wouldn't repeat it to her. Getting the skilled westerner bewitched by Ginny, Charles believed, would fill everyone's needs.

The wagontrain halted the next day at five, as some men needed to hunt for fresh meat while it was still light enough to do so. Charles Avery left with them after saying he was off to get rabbits for roasting over a spit.

A clear sky and early-rising full moon promised a lovely evening. While Ginny was cooking over the fire Charles had built before leaving, Steve approached the Avery campsite. She was frying cured ham, cooking biscuits in a Dutch oven, and getting coffee ready to perk. She glanced up at the smiling scout, then returned her gaze to her tasks.

"Did you need something, Mr. Carr? Father isn't back yet."

She was polite but cool. The things Avery had disclosed to Steve in confidence raced through his mind at lightning speed. "He invited me for supper. Is that all right with you, Anna?"

Her head jerked up, her eyes wide in surprise. "He did?"

"I guess he forgot to mention it to you."

She quickly recovered her poise and was courteous. "He did, but it's all right, if you don't mind what we're having tonight. Father wanted ham, red-eye gravy, scrambled eggs, biscuits, and coffee." Now she understood why Charles had asked for the simple fare; she could manage it without mistakes or much work. He should have told her about inviting Steve, should have asked her permission.

The man comprehended she was genuinely unaware of the invitation and assumed the sly Charles had kept it from her on purpose. "Sounds and smells delicious, if you have enough and don't mind my joining you two."

"Oh!" she shrieked as she realized the ham would burn soon if she didn't tend it quickly. "Don't say it," she warned the scout.

He was baffled. "Say what, Anna?"

"That I'm distracted again and ruining dinner," she replied.

"I wouldn't, not when I'm the cause—or hope I am." She didn't glance up or respond, so he ventured, "You're annoyed with me, so I should explain my . . . 'contradictory,' you once called it, behavior."

"You don't have to tell me anything. You don't owe me excuses."

He noticed she said 'excuses,' not 'reasons.' "Yes, I do, Anna."

"Why?" she asked, stealing a quick glance at him. "You said 'take it slow and easy.' We've both kept our word, so there is no problem."

"I didn't mean we should have no contact."

"That hasn't been my intention or doing, Steve. Surely I'm not expected to chase you down to be friends. That isn't proper."

"I know it's my fault, but you've kept your word too well."

Ginny set the cooked meat aside and covered it. She shifted the pot to the edge so the coffee wouldn't perk over the spout. She had been taught by Ellie not to peek at the biscuits and let out the heat, so let them be. Pleased things were under control, she looked at Steve, who was hunkered down across the fire. "That's all until Father returns and I can cook the gravy and eggs. I believe you were talking about our avoiding each other. I'm confused, Steve. You get unsettled if I'm too bold, but you also get unsettled if I'm too reserved. Frankly I'm not sure what the middle ground is with you so bear with me until I find that tricky location. It's been six days since we pulled out and we've barely spoken or been near each other. Since you didn't come around, I assumed you wanted to be left alone for a time. You said making friends was hard for you, so I don't want to push. How exactly do you prefer me to behave? What exactly is it you expect and want from me? I can't obey rules when I don't know what they are."

He sat down and crossed his legs. "I'm sorry, Anna, but a man like me makes few, if any, female friends; I reacted too strongly. After we danced and talked so much that night, I was worried others might think we'd gotten too close and they'd be watching us for mischief. The best two reasons for firing a leader are incompetence and . . . You know what I mean."

She hadn't been prepared for an apology and explanation from him. "You're avoiding me to protect your job?"

"It isn't amusing or unimportant."

"I didn't laugh or dispute you."

"Your eyes did, woman, and I'm serious. I can't lose this job."

"Don't you think it looks more suspicious to others for you to avoid me like cholera rather than to visit me as you do them?" Ginny reasoned.

He shrugged and admitted, "I hadn't thought of it that way, but you're right. With your father's permission and help, I can probably visit you without any suspicion." He leaned forward to whisper, "Some people would enjoy making problems for anyone. I've given some of them a hard time, and you're a woman to be jealous of. I can't anger them by showing special treatment to you." *For crucial reasons you don't know,* his mind added. He was having a difficult time deciding the best way to handle each person.

Ginny deliberated his words and concluded they had merit. Cathy could be spiteful after a spurning, or Louise or Mattie could be vindictive after stern and embarrassing words of correction, or one of the men could think they were trained well enough to go on alone if Steve vexed him too much. She certainly didn't want to do anything to get him fired. "You asked his permission to see me?"

Steve shifted in uneasiness. "No. But he guessed I wanted to, and gave me the opportunity."

"He likes and respects you. He sees no harm in our being friends."

"Maybe he's wrong to trust me around you," he muttered.

Ginny hoped she understood the meaning of those words. "Why, because you have wicked intentions of leading me astray?" When he frowned at her jest, she said, "I was only teasing. You can't do that without my agreement and cooperation. He trusts me and doesn't tell me what to do or think, so stop worrying. Now I have to fetch the eggs."

Steve leapt to his feet, took the basket from her grasp, and said, "I'll do it for you. I need a breather. Serious talk tenses me." He ducked under the wagon to the inner circle where the pens with cushioning nests of hay were attached to the bedside. He checked each one to see if a bag of gems could be hidden there: none. He removed the eggs and returned to her.

To calm the nervous man, she made light talk. "Thank you, Steve. You saved me from getting pecked again. One of those hens hates me."

He chuckled. "Not really. She's only a mother hen protecting her unborn babies."

Steve wanted to bite his tongue for replying, "That's what mothers are for, to defend their own." *Shu,* she was relaxing him too much!

With caution, Ginny inquired, "What's your mother's name, Steve? What is she like? You said she was still alive. Where does she live?"

He didn't look at her to answer, "Rose. She's beautiful, gentle, kind, and unselfish to a fault. She lives in Arizona. Your Mother is dead, right?"

"Yes, she died when I was eleven. She had the same traits as yours. I still miss her. I doubt anyone ever gets completely over the loss of a parent."

"It can be done if necessary." More rash words had shot from his lips unbidden, and he warned himself to clear his wits.

"Did you . . . Do you . . ." She halted on second thought.

"Know who my father was?" he finished for her, guessing her question accurately. Since he had made the slip, he'd test her feelings about his illegitimacy.

Ginny heard the bitterness and resentment plaguing the man she loved. She wished she hadn't begun the topic. "I'm sorry, Steve, that's being too nosy about a painful subject."

"Yes, Miss Avery, it is. For now," he added for some crazy reason.

"The last thing I'll say about it is that it doesn't bother me; it doesn't influence my opinion of you. I'm only sorry it torments you so deeply. I won't ever mention it again. How about a cup of coffee? I can't promise it's good, but I hope it won't be the worst you've ever had." She laughed.

"You're quite a woman, Anna Avery," he murmured.

Charles returned, grinning as if he was the happiest man alive. "Hello, you two. Did I hold up supper?"

"Not really, Father. It gave Steve and me time to talk for a change. Any luck?" she asked, noting his hands were empty.

"None, I'm afraid. But some of the others made kills; one even got a deer. That'll be sweet eating for days. I'll get washed up for supper."

As Ginny prepared the red-eye gravy and readied the eggs to scramble, Steve asked, "Does your father always stay dressed up?"

She laughed, then speculated, "A habit, I suppose, from years of being a businessman. I imagine a formal attire is like a second skin to him by now. Sort of like those pistols and knife are to you, my well-armed protector. I bet you're so accustomed to wearing them, you don't realize they're there, until you need them."

"Point made," he murmured with a grin.

"Does that make you a gunslinger? I've read books about them."

"Nope. A gunslinger earns his living by them; I don't, or try not to."

The food was eaten with enjoyment and little talk. Afterward, the men drank coffee and chatted while Ginny washed the dishes in a basin nearby. She listened closely to what they said.

"Where is your ranch, sir?" Steve inquired over sips of not-bad-tasting coffee.

Charles was impressed with the manners and intelligence of the man before him. He realized Steve Carr wasn't an ordinary man or drifter. Somewhere in his past, the scout had been schooled and taught. Yes, he assured himself, Steve was a good match for Ginny. Charles finished his coffee and set the cup aside. "Outside of Waco. I got a good deal on it. One hundred acres with seventy-five steers, a few cows and horses, and two pigs. It has a nice house and barns, but I'll have a few repairs and changes to make. The hands and foreman have agreed to stay on; they'll teach me what I need to know about raising and selling cattle. It's called the Box F now, but I'm told it will be simple to alter that mark to the Box A with a special branding iron."

"Yep, that'll be easy to do. It sounds good to me, sir."

"It will be, Steve. You're welcome to come by anytime to visit."

"Maybe I will, sir. I'd like to make sure you get settled in all right. You'll like Texas and that area. War hardly touched it. You won't see the ugly scars there that you see in these parts."

"How glorious, praise the Lord. It certainly will be nice not to have these same horrible reminders in the place where we're trying to make a new start. Ever thought about ranching, Steve? Or ever been a foreman or cowhand?"

"I've been just about everything, sir. I like ranching, but haven't decided if that's where I want to be when I shake the last trail dust from these boots. I have a roaming spirit, too restless to stay put long. Guess that's why I enjoy leading or scouting for wagontrains; always on the move."

"What about your homestead and parents, Son?"

As Charles leaned forward to refill his coffee cup, he didn't see the look Steve sent Ginny, but she did and understood its meaning, its plea to conceal the humiliating secret he had told her.

"They're dead, sir. Been on my own since sixteen." That was why he still scolded himself for joining the Confederate Army; he had no home and land to defend. He had done it to protect those of friends and his mother.

Charles looked surprised and intrigued. "You're mighty well bred and cultured for a man who was an orphan on the road."

Steve smiled and feigned a look of modesty. "Thank you, sir; that's mighty kind of you. I put eight years of schooling under my belt and hat before . . . and I do read most of the time, try to learn all I can. I've been lucky to have smart friends along the way who've taught me plenty."

"Like dancing?" Charles asked with a sly wink.

"Yep. A major's wife at one of the forts where I was scouting forced me to learn. She said that was one skill every young man should have. When she first took hold of me, I thought I had four feet and they kept getting tangled. She used music boxes for practice, and I finally got the know of it. I knew I had to or she wouldn't let up on me. Strange as it sounds, the crabby driver of freight wagons was the one who taught me how to mend my clothes and take care of them."

Ginny had the feeling that most of what he was saying was the truth. That bewildered her. How could he have done so well for himself and been touched by so many others, yet still be so tormented and such a loner? He was a complex and mysterious man. She wished she knew more about him, *everything* about him. She dared not press for more information and cause him to close up to her. She must allow him to reveal things at his own pace. After all, she had plenty of secrets of her own! She dared not expose them, not when he was learning to trust her. Besides, there was a strong probability that he would leave her behind when the journey ended, no matter what happened between them.

After Steve left the wagon, Ginny and Charles took a stroll to speak in privacy.

"Why did we tell everyone such things?" she asked him. "You purchased a mercantile store in town. What will Steve and the others think when they learn we deceived them about a ranch as well as being kin?"

"It won't matter; by then, you'll be safe at the Chapman ranch. I want Steve to believe we're rich in case you decide to hire him. Besides, westerners think more highly of ranchers than of storeowners."

"Won't he think it's odd I'm going to Colorado without my father?"

"Not if you tell him you have a brother there who you're going to visit while I get the ranch fixed up. When you reach your destination, you can confess the truth, if you wish. Don't tell him anything before then, Anna. He'll think that if you can lie about one thing, you'll lie about another, about *all* things. Never forget that he's a wary and proud man. You don't want him to get his feelings and pride hurt and take off leaving you stranded."

"You're right, and I'll be careful. But—"

"Listen well to me, Anna: some people put on good fronts when inside they're bad, or just confused and misguided. They'll use you and trick you, then get rid of you by discarding you or killing you. Steve Carr seems like a good man, but we could be wrong about him. Don't risk getting hurt or betrayed," he urged. "Wait until you're convinced beyond even a tiny doubt that he's totally dependable and trustworthy."

"I agree, sir, and I'll follow your good advice. What I was about to question was the lie about a brother. I don't want to make up one now in case I don't need to use that ruse; it could complicate matters for us if we mention details about him that don't match. When and if the time comes to hire Steve, I'll think of something credible to tell him. I'll say we didn't mention such a close family member because you two had a serious disagreement years ago and don't have anything to do with each other anymore."

Charles was intrigued. "About what?"

Ginny mused a moment. "Your son, my brother, sided and fought with the Yankees, so you disowned him in a moment of anguish, anger, and disappointment, and he's angry with you for being a Rebel, a traitor to the Union and his country. That actually happened with some families, so it should work. I'll say that now that the war is over and things have calmed, I'm going to see him to try to make peace between you two."

Charles beamed with excitement and pleasure. He grasped her hand and squeezed it gently. "You're quick and smart, Anna. It's perfect. That way, our stories won't conflict and expose us."

"I'm getting good at deceptions. Too good," she murmured in dismay. "I don't like having to lie and trick people, especially friends."

Charles put empathetic pressure on her hand. "Sometimes it can't be helped, girl. With so much at stake, this is one of them. You can't allow anything or anybody to stop you from accomplishing what you must do. I'm proud of you, girl; Anna and you would have been good friends; you're so alike."

Ginny watched him drift off into melancholy thought. She knew that her similarity to his daughter was part of the reason Charles Avery liked and helped her, and it was why he could be trusted implicitly. He was a good and kind man. Charles didn't realize that Steve would refuse to be hired by her when he discovered she wasn't Anna and there was no ranch, nothing but lies. Nor would either know how or where to locate the other when her departure time arrived or if he decided to visit the nonexistent ranch. She didn't know why the mercantile store was a secret, but she assumed Charles had a private reason for keeping it one, and so would she.

They journeyed over matching terrain on Sunday, except for crossing the Ocmulgee River five miles from camp. Although very wide, it wasn't deep, so caused no delay. They had a short religious service during the noon break then continued traveling until dusk to camp forty miles south of Macon. Meals and chores were completed and visits began.

Ginny took a stroll, and Steve joined her when she was out of sight of the others.

"Sorry I had to lie to your father last night," he said. "If he knew the truth about me, he would make sure I didn't get within fifty feet of you."

"I understand. We've been apart for so long and we've both changed so much that I can't honestly say if you're wrong or right. But it's best to take no chances. Besides, it's none of his or anyone's business."

"But it doesn't bother you I'm a . . ."

She watched him lower his head and take a deep breath. "No, Steve, I swear. It wasn't your fault, or even perhaps your mother's."

"She chose him of her free will. Knowing the awful truth about him, she . . . yielded to him and bore his bastard son anyway."

Ginny detected anguish but no bitterness toward his mother. Would he feel the same about her if she "yielded" to him and got into trouble? Would he do as his father had long ago and refuse to wed her? Would he let anyone or anything saddle him with responsibilities and restraints he didn't want? "She must have loved him deeply."

"She did, and I can't blame her for that."

"But you blame him for . . ." She stopped and said, "I'm sorry, Steve; I promised not to do this again, nose into your life."

Vexed with himself, he admitted, "I started it, like a fool trying to switch himself with a limb."

Ginny ventured in a tender tone, "Maybe because you need to talk about it to someone who cares and understands so you can get rid of your torment and deal with the truth. You've kept it pent up for years. It's ready to burst from confinement."

"You're right, but I'm not ready to talk about it, not yet."

"When the right time comes along, you will," she contended. "I know you will." He didn't look convinced. "Maybe it's had a good side, Steve; it could be what's driven you to become so strong and independent. Troubles have a way of doing that for us. If everything in life was easy, where would we get our strengths and courage? What would hone our skills and wits? What would make those good things and times so wonderful and rewarding?"

Steve's gaze locked with her hazel one. "For such a young and sheltered woman, you know a lot, Anna Avery."

Ginny sent him a bright smile. "That's one of the best compliments you could pay me. Thank you."

"No flattery, woman, just the plain truth."

The moon was full. A breeze wafting over them was cool. The green and quiet setting was romantic and private. They were alone.

Steve's alert ears checked for sounds of anyone nearby. He heard nothing to stop him from pulling her into his arms, and she came willingly and freely. They shared several kisses, their eager lips meshing with gentleness and leisure, then swiftness and urgency. Their fingers caressed, giving and receiving pleasure. He trailed kisses over her face, then claimed her pleading mouth once more.

When he realized they were becoming too aroused, he ordered himself to recover self-control and to clear his wits. He rested his cheek against the top of her head while hers nestled against his broad chest. He felt her tremors of desire. He wanted and needed her so badly. He wished they were alone somewhere else so he could make love to her. Yet, that might be a painful experience, to know her and lose her. If he got that involved with Anna, it could mean trouble and pain for both of them. He didn't have anything to offer her, not yet, not any time soon, if ever. Without his changing, a bond between them was impossible; and he wasn't sure he could change or *wanted* to change. If he couldn't make a promise to this special woman, how could he take her?

Ginny felt and heard Steve's heart thudding rapidly and heavily in a fierce need that matched the one storming her body. It felt good, right, perfect in his arms. She knew she wanted more than hugs and kisses from him and, if they were elsewhere, she would challenge the unknown. He had lied to her "father" for a good reason, so perhaps he would be forgiving and understanding of her deceits. She had to learn if he was softening toward her.

"When this is over, Steve, why not come with me to . . . work?"

He noticed she hadn't said with *us*. "Where?"

"To . . . the ranch or wherever."

He caught her hesitation and prayed it didn't mean anything sinister. Surely the Klan wouldn't send a woman to do their task! But who would suspect an innocent-looking beauty? His heart pounded in dread and his guts twisted into painful knots. To evoke information and clarification, he said, "I have another task waiting for me when I finish this one."

"Is there anything I can say or do to change your mind?"

Don't make me wrong about you, woman. "I can't, Anna; I made a promise, and it's important. I will come to visit you afterward."

She understood important promises and having to honor them, but a "visit" wasn't all she wanted from him. Yet, it was a good start. "How long will the next job require?" she asked.

"Maybe weeks, maybe months. I don't know yet."

"What if, . . ." *I need you, pay you, persuade you?* her mind enticed.

"What if what?" he asked when she halted and tensed.

"The ranch doesn't work out and Father moves again or returns to Georgia? How could we locate each other?"

"Leave a message for me with the Waco sheriff."

She looked at him wide-eyed. He was acquainted with the lawman where Charles alleged to own a ranch? "The sheriff? You know him?"

Steve worried over the sound of her voice, the expression in her eyes, and the way she went almost stiff in his embrace. He knew there was something he must check out when he reached Columbus and could send a telegram. "No, but most towns have one," he lied, "and that's how messages get passed. Give him a dollar and he'll do the favor for you."

"We'll need a guide if we return to Georgia or move elsewhere."

"Then I'll make sure I stay in touch; I'd like to have this same job again."

"How did you get it in the first place?"

As he toyed with long curls, he murmured, "Newspaper."

"What do you mean?"

"The company that arranges and outfits wagontrains advertises in newspapers in the South and East. They knew of me, so they hired me as leader and scout. A lot of folks are moving west these days, but most to the Far West. I usually head out of Missouri on the Oregon, Sante Fe, or Mormon trails. This trip sounded good for a rest and change. No prairies, mountains, or Indians to worry about. The company tells the leader where the best stops are and has preparations made for him along the route."

"You know the Midwest well, don't you?"

When she focused on that particular area, Steve's anxiety increased. He had been told that Missouri was the rendezvous point for the villain to meet his contact. "Yep, traveled most of it many times. Tell me where you need to go and I can get you there safely. Maybe even for no charge."

Ginny hated to leave him, but it was perilous to remain longer in the tempting location. "If I ever need to make a trip there, I'll hire you. It's getting late. We should return to camp before we're missed." She kissed him again before they parted.

Steve lay on his bedroll staring at stars and clenching his teeth over and over until they ached. *Getting later than you think, Anna, because you're becoming too inquisitive about certain things.*

Chapter 9

O**N MONDAY, THE SOIL BECAME REDDER AND HARDER** on the western side of Georgia but the shape of the terrain altered little. They saw few snakes and animals; no doubt the approach of the noisy wagontrain frightened them away. They skirted two areas where fenced cattle grazed and finally reached the wide and deep Flint River and camped, as it was too late in the day to begin the lengthy crossing. That allowed people to have extra time for chores and relaxing and for thorough baths. Many had worn the same garments several days so this was a welcome stop.

Women gathered in different areas at the water to wash clothes. Lucy, Mary, Ellie, Ruby, and Ginny chatted while they worked together. Ginny helped Ruby tend her babies while her husband hunted with some of the men. In camp, other husbands or older children tended small ones so the women could work. Steve rode to the farm nearby to let the owner and his helpers know they had arrived and would be ready for ferry assistance in the morning as prearranged.

Ginny asked Lucy about her ankle and learned it was doing fine, giving credit to the support crutch Steve had made for her. She heard from her friends that the irritable women in the group had behaved themselves.

Ruby looked at Ginny. "Our handsome scout has been paying you much attention, Anna." The redhead grinned, as did the other three.

"Is that bad?" Ginny asked, testing his worry about dissension.

"Only if you don't want him to," Mary answered. "You do, don't you?"

"I like him," Ginny admitted with a light flush to her cheeks.

"That's good," Ellie told her. "He would make a fine husband."

"Husband? We haven't gotten that close and I doubt we ever will."

"Keep trying," Ellie encouraged, and the others nodded agreement.

"I'm not certain Steve Carr is the marrying kind."

"You can convince him otherwise," Ruby said with confidence.

"I'm sure you can, Anna," Lucy added in a coaxing tone.

"If a man is shy or reluctant, a woman has to lead him with cunning bridle to the trough to drink from her charms, just like a stubborn mule."

"But how does a woman capture a man's total interest?" Ginny asked.

Ruby smiled at Ginny and replied, "Just be yourself, Anna. How could he help but like you and want you? He isn't blind, old, or taken. And you have an advantage, girl; you're the only single lady available."

"That doesn't matter to Cathy," Ellie whispered, "but she must have gotten a stinging rebuff because she's left him alone for a while."

"She has to know our scout is enchanted by Anna," Mary said.

"If she's the jealous and spiteful type, she could cause trouble for us."

"Don't worry, Anna, we won't let her."

"Thank you, Ellie. I wouldn't want anyone to get the wrong idea and try to have Steve fired out of vindictiveness."

"You work on him with all your might, and we'll make sure no one interferes. Right, ladies?" Ruby, Mary, and Lucy nodded their agreement.

After their baths, the two Davis boys entreated Ginny to fish with them. "If we catch enough, Momma says we can cook 'em for supper. Please help."

Ginny looked at the elder boy and realized he had a case of boyish infatuation on her. She smiled at him and said, "Why not? Let's go, but you'll have to teach me how."

Hooks had been baited and lines tossed into the river many times with good results when Steve returned and joined them. The scout grinned at Ginny and noticed how the boy was disappointed by his arrival.

"We can use another fisherman, Mr. Carr. If we catch enough, we're frying them for dinner. If you help, you can join us," she tempted.

"How could any man resist an offer like that?" he replied. He located and cut a sturdy limb, then attached line and hook. As he secured a small hunk of old meat as bait, he said to the subdued boy, "You're skilled at this, son; I'm sure your parents are proud of you. I bet you wouldn't have any trouble fending for yourself and them if need be." The boy beamed with pride and pleasure, and was won over to Steve's side.

Ginny hauled in a catfish with laughter and squeals that amused and delighted Steve. The fish thrashed in the air, then on the bank. "I'm not taking him off," she murmured with more laughter. "The last one pricked my fingers with those sharp fins."

The fourteen-year-old removed the fish and rebaited her line. He added it to the growing string that dangled in the water to keep them fresh.

When the task was finished, the group had plenty of catfish and two other kinds to feed nine people. Steve and Stuart skinned or scaled, gutted, and cleaned the mess. Ellie and Ginny rolled them in a mixture of cornmeal, salt, and pepper, with a smidgen of flour. As the fish began cooking, a delightful aroma wafted over the area. Ellie prepared hushpuppies, and Ginny provided several jars of canned vegetables.

While they all worked or observed, Ginny asked Steve, "Does the Klan really do all those awful things some of the men have mentioned?"

Getting worried about helping them? "I don't know. Why?"

"Mr. Brown and Daniels and a few others speak so strongly in their favor that I'm confused. The North did do horrible things to the South, so I'm not sure I can blame them feeling as they do. If the Loyal Leaguers and other gangs—white and black—continue to terrorize Southerners, who will stop them if not the Klan? The Yankee-controlled courts and laws don't protect them. I wonder which is worse: do nothing or risk overdoing? People have suffered so much already; I hate to see more."

Steve was in a quandary: If he spoke against the Klan, she would hush if guilty; if he didn't and she wasn't involved, she'd get a bad opinion of him. Luckily he didn't have to answer, as the meal was ready.

Mattie scowled and complained as she unpacked her wagon at the riverbank, "Why couldn't we cross on a bridge? This is lots of work."

"Bridges north and south of here were destroyed by the Yankees and haven't been rebuilt, ma'am," Steve explained once more. "We'd have to travel too far out of our way to take the next one."

"More time than it takes to unpack, ferry across, and repack?"

"That's right, Mrs. Epps," Steve responded. He was hard pressed to control his annoyance with the whiny woman who'd carried on childishly since they began this task after eating breakfast and cleaning up the campsite. Travelers worked together on both banks to unhitch and reharness teams and to unload and reload wagons. Hired men from nearby towns helped ferry the people, teams, wagons, and loads across the eight-foot depth on separate trips because of their heavy weights and large sizes. Steve was in an unsettled mood because no one had acted strangely, as if they were protecting valuable gems. He'd hoped this chore would provide him with a clue.

Later, they crossed railroad tracks that stretched between Macon and far below Andersonville. They camped not many miles above the site.

After the evening meal and chores, men chatted about its significance. It was a well-known Confederate prison camp for captured Yankees. Nearly fifty thousand of the Northerners had been incarcerated there, and thirteen thousand of them had died during captivity and were buried on the vast acreage.

"No more died there than Rebs died in their harsh prisons. Woulda been more if not for those traitors who joined 'em. If them Galvanized Yanks hadn't done all their work out West, we'd have had less of 'em to fight."

Harry Brown snarled like a wild dog. "Hellfire, the Klan ortta go after them traitors, too! If I was a member, we would."

Others gave their opinions until rain sent the men and women rushing to their wagons for cover. Later, some sat beneath them to play cards.

One man watched and listened. He absently touched his waist where a pouch was secured under a blousy shirt. Soon, he vowed, the Red Magnolias would have the arms and ammunition needed to seek and punish the Yanks for what they did to the South. His Den would make those vicious attackers only too happy to pull back of the Mason-Dixon Line! When he reached Dallas, the plan would go into motion. He would meet his contacts and journey with them to Missouri to exchange the gems.

Two days later at four o'clock, the wagontrain halted to camp near the Chattahoochee River, a few miles south of Columbus on the border. They had journeyed two hundred twenty miles in eleven days to cross Georgia, the largest state east of the Mississippi and the lengthiest one to traverse.

Some of the men headed for town to restock supplies. The grain wagon drivers did the same. Women tended chores and children.

Charles talked Ginny into going to Columbus to eat, bathe, shop, and stay at a hotel overnight. She did her chores and secured the wagon openings against rain. She took a small cloth satchel with her possessions, mounted a borrowed horse, and they left.

The scout met with a stranger—Luther Beams, called Big L because of his size. The real leader would pose as Steve's helper and be ready to take over if the special agent solved his case and had to leave. Luther had agreed without hesitation to assist the crucial mission that riled him.

"I'll tell the others you're to be obeyed as quickly as I am. You'll be in charge tonight. I have to ride into Columbus to send two telegrams. I won't return until morning. One of my suspects is staying there overnight, so I'll need to watch him." He was glad he hadn't said *them* or *her*. "You keep your eyes and ears open here for anything suspicious."

Steve approached Ginny's door to invite her to take a stroll. He was relieved her father was at the other end of the hall and had turned in for the night, early. One telegram was on its way to the Georgia agent to have him investigate if Charles Avery really had a daughter, one this woman's age. It was possible her name wasn't Anna Avery and she wasn't kin to the older man. If she wasn't Anna, he'd have a strong clue to work on. If she was, he could breathe easier. The second telegram was on its way to a Texas agent, asking him to investigate if Charles Avery had purchased the Box F Ranch near Waco. He had requested answers as quickly as possible, and said he would check for them in Montgomery and Jackson and Vicksburg. He anticipated those responses with a blend of dread and hope.

Steve tapped on the door marked with the number the desk clerk had given to him, and Ginny responded. She appeared surprised to see him. She peeked into the hall, saw no one, and pulled him inside in a rush. She closed the door, locked it, and looked at him.

Ginny was so glad to see Steve that she acted without thinking about what she was doing—bringing a man into her room, and in her state of dress! "We can't be seen talking this time of night in a hotel. What are you doing here? Why aren't you back in camp?"

Steve noted how she was attired, in a white cotton nightgown patterned with dainty and colorful flowers. It had long sleeves, buttoned to the throat, and reached her ankles, so she was well covered. Yet, the reality of what the garment was and the heady setting enflamed him, almost caused him to lose sight of his mission, his real reason for coming—to get closer to her. The uncertainty about her was driving him wild; he had to be convinced she was what he hoped she was: an innocent beauty attracted to him.

"No one saw me; I was careful. Your father went to his room and doused his light fifteen minutes ago. My partner joined me here, so he's in charge of camp tonight. I came to invite you to take a stroll. I didn't think you'd be turning in so early."

"I wasn't. I couldn't go out alone, so I planned to lie in bed and read. We had fun. We shopped and ate grandly downstairs and took long baths. I wish I had known sooner and I wouldn't have gotten un— Oh, my goodness!" she said with a blush as she remembered what she was wearing. "I don't have a robe with me. I only answered the door because I thought it was Father. Dear me, this is most improper and embarrassing."

Steve smiled and murmured, "You look beautiful, Anna. I'm sorry I intruded on your privacy. I'll leave so you can read and relax. I'll see you in camp tomorrow. We have a lot of busy days ahead."

Without privacy, her mind hinted. "You didn't intrude, Steve, and I'm happy to see you. I'd rather talk with you than read."

Steve looked her in the eye. "I'm not sure it's wise for me to visit with you here. You're much too tempting, woman. All I can think about is yanking you into my arms and kissing you."

"Why don't you?" she enticed with bravery as her wits dazed.

"If I did, I would be too ensnared by you to quit there. I want you, Anna, more than I've ever wanted a woman before, for any reason. Every time I see you or hear your voice, I catch on fire."

Ginny lifted her hands to caress his face. He turned his head to kiss the palm of one, then did the same with the other. She trembled and he did, too. His fingers closed over hers and he gazed deeply and intently into her hazel eyes. She didn't attempt to pull away.

"You have too much power, Anna. How could I not want you?"

"How could I not want *you,* Steve? You make me feel so strange, so weak and shaky. When you touch me, and sometimes when you only look at me or speak to me, I feel as if I'm standing naked beneath a blazing sun and it's scorching my flesh. My heart races like a runaway carriage. I can't think clearly. It feels good and it feels scary. Why do you do this to me?"

The more she said, the more Steve's eyes glowed and the more his smile broadened.

Somehow, both knew what was going to happen between them tonight, what they had craved for what seemed more like an eternity. They no longer had the strength—or desire—to resist. Each knew they could part forever soon. Each also knew loving would bring them closer, a bond each needed.

Steve cupped her face and kissed her with tenderness and longing. Ginny responded joyously. It only took moments for their kisses to become urgent with rising need.

Ginny wanted this night with all her soul and she loved this man with all her heart. Johanna's death had taught her that life could be short, cruel, and demanding. She had to seize this precious moment while it was available. She murmured against his lips, "I don't know what to do. You'll have to show me."

Her shyness and admission touched his heart. Near a whisper at her ear, Steve said, "Don't be afraid of me, Anna, or of making love. We can't deny what we want and need. Resisting each other is too hard." He drifted his lips down her throat and back to her mouth.

Ginny's hands encircled his waist and she pressed closer against him. Her mood encouraged him to continue arousing her. Her fingers stroked his back and relished the feel of his hard frame. She felt aswirl in an unfamiliar and yet instinctively familiar pool, with powerful currents of desire and mystery lapping at her body.

Steve's hands slipped into her long and thick tresses. Each kiss fused into another and another; each caress led to an even bolder one. He guided her toward the lamp and doused it, all without interrupting their kisses and caresses. He thought it would be better for her this first time if there was darkness to protect her modesty and to ease her introduction to a man's naked body. As his mouth lavished adoration on her neck, his deft fingers unfastened the buttons of her gown. He worked the garment off one shoulder, his hand tugging on the sleeve. She assisted him by withdrawing one arm then the other. The gown slipped to the floor around her bare feet. He worked the bloomer laces free and allowed them to join the other garment. He felt her movements as she stepped out of them and nudged them aside with her toes. Contact with her bare flesh heightened his desire and increased his pleasure. His hands were like greedy and starving creatures who feasted on her breasts and soft curves.

Ginny was amazed by how brave and bold she was being. She was glad he had put out the light so she could use her other senses to get to know him this first time. But next time, she planned ahead to her surprise, she wanted the light on so she could see him. Her breasts were taut and tingling and their buds stood out in rigid yearning. She learned why when Steve kneaded and kissed them. Her body reacted to the blissful new sensations from head to foot.

Steve lifted her and laid her on the bed. Rapidly, he was out of his clothes. He lay on his stomach with his hips beside her and with his chest over hers. Some instinct or past advice told him to kindle her smoldering coals into a roaring blaze before he took her. He trailed his lips and fingertips over every area of her face, neck, shoulders, and breasts. One hand stroked her abdomen, along her thighs, and inched its way up their inner surface. He used evocative stroking to arouse her to a writhing and breathless state, one which wouldn't allow her to halt him when he touched her most private places.

Ginny couldn't have halted him; her will was stolen, along with her breath. She wanted him so much that a curious bittersweet torment flooded her mind and body. She realized this tantalizing period was leading to something wonderful. She felt her body straining and pleading for something more, much more. Steve was being so gentle, so skillful, so tender, and so filled with the same desire for her.

Steve knew there was no turning back for either of them. He wished he could view the expression on her face, within her greenish-brown eyes. He wished he could send his gaze on a leisurely journey over her body. His hands were mapping and exploring her well, but seeing it all would enhance his delight. He savored every touch with hand, body, or mouth.

Ginny's lips teased over his shoulder and nibbled at his neck. Her fingers roamed the same welcoming territory and trekked onward into his silky hair of midnight black. She didn't need the lamp's glow to tell her how he looked; she had memorized every inch of his face. It was time to seek and yield to her destiny. "Whatever comes next, Steve, I'm ready to challenge it," she murmured in an emotion-strained voice.

Steve thought she was moist and eager enough to be prepared for his entry. He believed he would be able to please her, even though tiny doubts chewed at his mind, as he'd never been with a virgin before. Anna was different, innocent. He gently moved atop her, kissing her deeply as he eased inside her. He halted when she moaned in discomfort.

Ginny realized why he stopped. "I've heard it only hurts a moment," she whispered, "so do what you must, quickly, then wait a minute."

Steve followed her advice. She gasped, winced, arched her body toward his, and clenched her teeth. He didn't move, fearing he had injured her. He didn't know what he should say or do at that point. He waited while she brought her erratic breathing under control and relaxed. He seared her mouth with kisses, branding them as his own.

"It's all right now," she murmured, hoping that was true.

With gentleness and caution, Steve moved within her, and was relieved when she didn't flinch or cry out or tell him to withdraw. He worked with slow delibera-tion to rekindle her doused flames. Soon, she was responding feverishly again, and he increased the pace of his thrusts.

Ginny's discomfort vanished and pleasure returned—no, *heightened*. Her fin-gers trailed over his face and torso. His broad chest was hairless and firm; it teased against her swollen and sensitive breasts. She had assumed this physical act would be wonderful with Steve, but it was beyond measure or description.

Steve labored lovingly until she writhed and moaned with need. Pride and joy surged through him when he fulfilled it. Toward the end, she had caught his pace and matched his rhythm until rapturous release came. Her mouth and body clung to his to extract every moment of the glorious experience. He did the same, reveling in the throes of ecstasy, in the wonder of her total surrender to him.

As they lay nestled together, neither knew what to say—if words were even necessary in the golden aftermath of something so beautiful and special!

After a while, Steve kissed her and finally spoke. "I have to leave, Anna. We don't want anyone to find me here like this. I'll see you in camp tomorrow."

Ginny surmised he was tense and uncertain about the intimate situation, probably feared what demands she would make on him. It should surprise and please him when she made none, not yet anyway, not aloud. She smiled into the darkness and murmured, "Good night, Steve."

The sated and anxious man calmed a little when she responded in that careful manner. He couldn't say what the future held for them, but he knew he wanted her again and again. He rose, dressed, strapped on his pistols, and told her good-bye. "Lock the door after me, and don't open it again without asking who's there. I don't want anything to happen to you."

Ginny saw him in the hall light when he opened the door and slipped out quietly. She went to obey his protective order. She leaned against the door for a minute, took a deep breath, then returned to bed. She cuddled against the pillow where his head had rested; his scent clung there. "I love you, Steve Carr," she whispered, "and I want you so much. Please let this bond you to me. Please love me and want me, too."

Steve listened outside Charles Avery's door to make sure the man hadn't sneaked out to meet anyone. He heard snores from inside and relaxed. He had allowed himself to get distracted again by Anna Avery, and he wasn't sure that tying her so tightly to him was a smart idea at this point. But he couldn't help himself, and that worried him even more. It was bad for him if she was guilty; it was wrong of him if she weren't.

After crossing the powerful and sometimes treacherous Chattahoochee River by ferry, the wagontrain was in Alabama, birthplace of the defeated Confederacy. They had skilled help from local hired men. Yet, the strong currents, depth, and width of the river made it an almost all-day task. Again, Steve observed the travelers with a keen eye, but no one behaved as if he or she feared the loss of valuable gems. He wondered if the reports had been wrong or if the Red Magnolias' plans had changed.

As soon as the ferrying was completed, everyone rested before chores and meals and visits. Steve spent that time with Luther Beams, something Ginny noticed and assumed was another defensive action.

For the next four days, they journeyed through an area that appeared evergreen with a thick plant cover, countless pines and some hardwoods, and widespread mistletoe on branches. At rivers and ponds, they saw black cypress and waterlilies and willows; in many locations, they encountered bamboo and cane thin enough not to block their way. They passed north/southwest railroad tracks and traveled through sleepy rural communities where homes were scattered, people were poor, and farmers and sharecroppers worked fertile fields. As with other southern states, Alabama had a long and mild growing season, a hundred days more than in the North.

At first, the eastside landscape was a mixture of low, gentle hills, stretches of flat lowlands, an occasional steep incline or decline, dense forests, rivers, and streams of various widths. The Indian Trail, oldest one to the Atlantic, was pointed out to them, along with churches and cemeteries.

Then, a section of consistent hills appeared and caused them to move slower for a while. The dirt became redder, a sturdy clay. They crossed spots that though marshy, gave no one trouble, nor did the endless creeks. More oaks and magnolias began to blend in with pines and cedars. Farms were being worked. Abundant morning glories on fences and bushes greeted them each day in pink, white, blue, and lavender.

Everyone noticed the lack of war devastation in the rural location. It gave them a time to relax and forget it for a while. The talk in camp at night was genial and hopeful. Music and stories were heard more than complaints or grim memories.

On Tuesday evening, they camped fifteen miles below Montgomery, birthplace of the Confederacy and its first capital. It was a land of white-supremacy beliefs, but under military rule now because Alabamians had refused to ratify the Fourteenth Amendment, as had most other southern states. It looked as if war hadn't touched this area or, if it had, damages had been repaired and concealed.

Ginny helped her companion with their daily chores; greasing axles, fetching grain and tending the mules, checking the water barrel supply, cooking, and washing dishes, and making any repairs needed to the gear. In the past four nights since entering Alabama, she also had assisted her friends with chores or by babysitting, as that helped to distract her from Steve's behavior.

Those who hadn't gone into town in Georgia to restock supplies did so. Steve also went to Montgomery, and in a strange mood, she noticed. Since Charles, her "father," didn't suggest going, she had no way to meet with the man she loved again. She missed him and longed for him. She feared that their intimacy and brief closeness had Steve panicked. She didn't know how to convince him otherwise. It had taken a lot of patience and self-control to let him have the space he needed, but she didn't know how long she could exist in . . . limbo. He was so capable of dealing with the problems and needs of others but not with his own. As for exposing feelings, she fretted, he made sure he didn't commit that mistake, that weakness. But why, she reasoned, was it so terrible for their unwed scout to court a single lady?

Steve was keeping his distance again. He always seemed on alert and inquisitive. Sometimes he appeared to look for a reason to visit with certain men. She felt as if there was a particular motive for him being so watchful and curious, one she couldn't surmise. She hoped and prayed his mystery didn't include ensnaring her to aid it.

After eating, she chatted with Luther "Big L" Beams. "How long have you and Mr. Carr been partners?" she asked.

The real wagontrain leader smiled and replied, "This is our first job together, but surely not our last. I'm enjoying working with Steve. He went on ahead to train all of you while I brought up the rear with preparations. From what I've seen, he did a fine job of teaching everyone."

"He did, Mr. Beams, and we're all grateful . . . How did you two meet?"

"The company hired both of us."

Ginny talked with him a while longer and realized she wasn't going to learn anything new about Steve, as she had hoped. She saw how skilled and experienced and easygoing Luther Beams was by observing him with others around camp, on the trail, and while relating stories at night. It seemed to her as if the company should have hired Beams as the leader and Steve as scout and assistant. She wondered why they hadn't.

In Montgomery, Steve observed the three men who were his suspects as they shopped and talked with locals, but nothing out of the ordinary took place, to his disappointment. He wanted to be in camp with Anna; no, in the nearest hotel room with her. He couldn't get their passionate night off his mind. She was closer to him than anyone ever had been except his mother, and, as a child, his deceitful father. He wanted to get even closer to her, but determined not to do so until he had the truth about her, and until his next task was finished. The telegram in his pocket from Georgia informed him that Charles Avery had a nineteen-year-old daughter named Anna, but that didn't mean "his" Anna was that woman. If only the telegram from Texas had been awaiting him, he would know if Charles had purchased the Box F Ranch in Waco, would know if they were honest, would know if she was worth risking his heart and soul to pursue. It would be a long and tormenting stretch to Jackson and a reply, if one was awaiting him there.

Steve knew he was avoiding her too much again, but he couldn't be near her without wanting her, without fear of betrayal chewing at him, without risking exposure of his feelings by the look on his face.

For the next three days, Ginny stayed busy during the daytime rotating drive shifts with Charles Avery and James Wiggins because Mary came down with an illness that plagued her with vomiting, diarrhea, dizziness, and weakness. The three Wiggins children spent time during the day in the Avery wagon to prevent an excess burden on James's team with Mary and the toddler riding inside. At night, she tended to her ailing friend's chores and children. Only the youngest one—eighteen months old—gave any problem, as she couldn't seem to understand why her mother couldn't take care of her.

The driving hadn't been too difficult for Ginny, even the numerous back-to-back streams at one point or the creek with its boulders to be avoided to prevent broken wheels. In the lush location, they had sighted armadillo, fox, rabbit, squirrel, a few deer, one bear, and several poisonous snakes.

That night, they camped at the Alabama riverbank where they could bathe and do washing. Ginny and her friends insisted a slowly recovering Mary rest while they did her laundry along with their own.

Steve watched the generous woman as she worked so hard and long to help her friend. He had done James's hunting several times, and the man was grateful for the fresh meat for his family. In spite of his apprehension about discovering that Anna was involved in criminal mischief, Steve joined her as she finished her washing. His heart pleaded: *Please don't confess anything terrible to me when I probe for clues.* "You've been mighty busy these past few days, Anna. I bet you're exhausted and sore. James tells me his wife is better, so you shouldn't have double duty much longer. I'm sure you can use the rest."

"You've been a big help to them, too, Steve. And please don't say, 'It's part of my job.' Accept gratitude and compliments when they're deserved."

"Yes, ma'am," he drawled, and chuckled. "You all right, Anna?"

"Of course. Why shouldn't I be?" She glanced at him and smiled, as his tone and gaze waxed serious and concerned.

"Have you ever done anything you know was wrong or realized later it was; something you're sorry for and wish you could change?"

Ginny stared at him as she tried to read his expression. Was he referring to their lovemaking? Was he seeking a kind way to reject her? "Not that I can think of on the spur of the moment. Have you?"

Steve noticed how she tensed and her smile faded. "I suppose an answer depends on who's judging the situations. People have different opinions about what's right and what's wrong. Even Christians don't honor their Ten Commandments all the time. They say not to kill and steal, but the North and South do it to each other, the whites and Negroes do it to each other, and the whites and Indians do it to each other out West. Some folks think it isn't stealing if you take something from an enemy. The Brownses and Danielses say it's a sin to work or have fun on Sunday, but they talk about hatred, revenge, and killing half the time. Where is the line drawn between right and wrong? Life can be a bad place to live with people stirring up more trouble."

To understand, she asked, "Like the Klan and other secret groups?"

"Can't really say. What do you think?"

Ginny assumed he was searching for anything to talk about except their feelings for each other. *For now, let him.* At least they were together. "I suppose the Klan has good and bad points."

Why mention only that one? "Would you side with them?"

"Me? Not unless I had a strong motive for doing so."

"Lots of folks think they do. It's expanding and spreading."

Ginny locked her gaze with his. "That worries you, Steve? Do you think they'll give us trouble along the way?"

"I hope not."

"Why should they? We're Southerners escaping Yankee perils."

"Innocents get injured and killed during a war, Anna, and the Klan has declared war on their conquerors."

"Somehow I can't believe Southerners would attack loyal Southerners."

"Like you believe Galvanized Yankees aren't traitors and cowards to be hunted down and punished by Klan members?"

Did he know who she was? Who her real father was? Was he tracking down Virginia and Mathew Marston for . . . Surely not. Her father's enemy couldn't know she'd be on this wagontrain or even back in America! And surely he wasn't a secret Klansman seeking "traitors and cowards" to slay in revenge! "Of course they aren't. Why would you think of them?"

Steve noticed her change of tone and expression, as if fear and doubt of him had entered her mind. Odd . . . "It jumped into my head while I was making crazy talk to keep me distracted from you." He grinned wryly.

Ginny relaxed but wasn't sure he told the truth. "Ah, yes, I do recall you don't like distractions. That means I certainly don't want to be one."

"But you are, woman. A big one."

"I'm sorry. What can I do to correct my innocent mistake?"

Steve drifted his gaze over her silky hair and skin. He yearned to stroke them. "Be patient and understanding while I work out a few things."

Ginny read desire in that almost-black gaze, and she warmed with it herself. "Don't pull you closer but don't repel you, either?"

Steve's hands itched to touch her. "You're smart, Anna; thanks."

"I'm trying to be, Steve. It's hard at times because I miss you."

"Miss me? But I'm around every day. My mind couldn't be any closer to you."

She wanted to ask, *What about your heart?* "The same is true for me."

"Then we're both in good shape or in deep trouble."

Ginny laughed and replied, "That's an unusual way to put it, but I get your meaning, and you're right . . . Now I have to go see if Mary needs anything before bedtime. It's getting dark."

Steve hadn't noticed; he'd been too absorbed with her. "I'll walk you back to your wagon."

"Is that a wise idea?"

"Probably not, but I'll do it anyway."

She gathered her things and returned to camp at her lover's side. "Good-bye, Steve."

That word twisted his gut. "You mean, good night, don't you?"

"Every time we part, it's like a short and painful good-bye."

"One day . . . Good night, Anna."

Ginny watched his retreat. *One day we won't have to say good-bye?*

Crossing the wide, deep, and swift Alabama River the next morning was slow and treacherous work. So was crossing the Tombigbee River two days later. Without bridges or hired helpers at either site, the wheels and possessions had to be removed, the wagons floated across, the goods and mules and people rafted over, and everything replaced. Under the supervision of Steve and Luther, the travelers worked in groups to speed up the task. Nothing went wrong, and the scout gathered no clues for his mission.

For a time, the terrain was swampy as they journeyed over hills and "lumpy" land, as Charles called it. They traveled to the state line, having traversed two hundred miles across Alabama in ten days. They camped there for an extra day for rest, chores, and repairs.

Ginny was delighted by the lengthy stop, which gave Steve the opportunity to eat dinner with them one night. Afterward, he remained to play cards and chat with Charles. She even fried fruit fritters from canned Georgia peaches for the men to enjoy as dessert with steaming, rich coffee.

Both men smiled and complimented her, and she beamed with joy and pride. She observed Steve as he visited with Charles. Every day she came to love, want, and need him more and more. She savored his friendship and glowed under his glances. *Two states down,* she told herself, *and two and a third to go before parting or committing.*

A new state came. Mississippi was much like Georgia and Alabama: pines and oaks, red clay, rich vegetation, mostly flatland with an occasional rolling hill, and many streams.

On the third day in the lush area, trouble struck.

Charles felt the jolt as a rear wheel dropped hard into a deep pothole and he heard weakened wood snap. He pulled out of line and halted his team, then he leapt down and looked at the damage: two busted spokes. He knew a change was needed or the unsupported area of rim would bend. He yelled to the last wagon driver, "Keep going, Carl; Anna and I will change the wheel and catch up by camptime. You won't be far ahead."

Carl Murphy nodded and continued on without stopping to help.

Ginny eyed the damage. "We can do it; Steve taught us how."

They worked swiftly to unload everything heavy. They moved light things aside to reach the extra wheel and jack. Charles positioned the jack beneath the axle and began turning the crank to lift the wagonbed.

Steve glanced back and saw the Avery wagon off to the side of the rutted trail. He told Luther Beams to continue onward while he went back to help them, as camp was less than an hour away. He galloped to the location and dismounted. "You should have signaled me."

"I was afraid gunfire might spook the teams. We have rifles nearby," he said, pointing to two on the ground. "Anna said you'd trained her to help out, so I figured we could change it and join you in camp."

"She's right, but it's dangerous to be too busy to stand guard."

They changed the wheel and reloaded the wagon. Ginny had to relieve herself before heading out and entered the woods to do so.

Within minutes, Charles and the scout heard a scream, then her voice shouting, "Steve, help me!"

"Get your rifle! Guard the wagon while I see what's wrong. Stay here!" Steve ordered, drawing his pistols and racing into the forest.

Charles wondered if it was a cunning trick by Ginny to get Steve alone. He'd do as told until someone shouted for assistance.

Steve was frantic as he headed toward her, yelling he was on the way to rescue her. He saw her backing away from a log positioned between them, her face pale and her wide gaze on the ground. He heard the reason why: a timber rattler. "Don't move, Anna," he commanded and was relieved to see her obey. He turned and shouted to Charles, "A snake, but don't worry. I'll get him."

Charles grinned and mentally thanked the crawly creature. He leaned against the wagon to savor what he hoped was a lengthy wait.

Steve reholstered one of his pistols. He killed the snake with the other, then bent to remove its rattlers with his knife. He stuffed them into a shirt pocket before joining the trembling woman. "Are you all right?" he asked gently.

She watched him wipe the snake's blood on his fingers onto his pants leg. "I am now. I was going to skirt him, but he moved right or left every time I did. I was afraid he was going to take off after me."

"They do that sometimes when you spook them." He pulled her into his arms to comfort her, overwhelmed by desire for her.

His mouth closed over hers, and she responded eagerly. One kiss fused into another until both were breathless and quivering with a need for more. They dared not lose their wits, as time was short. They kissed and embraced a final time, then parted with reluctance.

"*Shu,* woman, what you do to me," he said in a ragged voice.

"And what you do to me, Steve Carr," she responded with a smile.

In camp, Mary Wiggins met them. "You two are joining us for supper. It's the least I can do to repay all the wonderful care you gave me."

Ginny and Charles ate with the Wigginses while Steve ate with the Davises. The yearning couple didn't speak again that night, and very little during the next two days before they camped south of Jackson.

Charles suggested they visit a hotel in town for relaxation, and Ginny readily agreed, as Steve was going into town himself.

It was ten o'clock when Steve approached her room. He was dismayed that a telegram from the Texas agent said he'd been delayed in his task and to expect an answer when he reached Vicksburg in three days. The troubled man knew it was reckless, but he had to see and hold her tonight.

Ginny responded to the soft knock at her door, assuming and hoping it was Steve. She smiled when she saw him. "I'm glad you came," she whispered, and pulled him inside the room.

"I brought you a present, something for protection." He held out a small derringer in a miniature holster. At her confusion, he explained, "It straps to your thigh or calf for concealment. It's always better if an enemy doesn't know you're armed. Wear it every day, Anna. Please."

His concern touched her deeply. "Why don't you show me how to strap it on?" she suggested, lifting her nightgown to above her knees.

Their gazes meshed and both knew what they wanted to show each other.

Chapter 10

❧

"**Y**OU CAN STRAP THE DERRINGER on here," he began, securing the short belt to her shapely calf, "so you can reach under your skirt or pants to grab it quickly when needed. Or," he continued as he unfastened the buckle, "you can put it here." With quivering fingers, the scout placed the small holster a few inches above her knee. "A dress will hide it, and you can get to the pistol easily." His hand remained on her silky thigh.

Ginny withdrew the derringer, studied the weapon, and reholstered it. She kept her foot propped on the bed so he wouldn't move his hand away. "That's very clever. Thank you, Steve."

He pulled a box of low-caliber cartridges from his vest and held them out to her. "Here are the bullets for it. If you have a pocket in whatever you're wearing at the time, keep a few extras handy. I have another box to use for target practice. I wanna make sure you can put a few holes in whatever you aim at." When he saw the same expression he had during her weapons lesson, he added, "At least wound and stop an enemy if you can't force yourself to kill one."

Ginny undid the buckle and laid the holstered weapon on the table, along with its ammunition. "This is very kind of you, Steve, but I should pay you for it. You work hard for your money. I'll ask Fa—"

"It's a gift; and I can afford it. Didn't cost much. Besides, Miss Avery, I did it for a selfish reason: I wanna be sure you stay safe and alive."

"That kind of selfish is wonderful, my protective scout. The only present I have in return is this," she murmured, and kissed him.

When it ended, she gazed into his eyes, as dark as night and as fiery as black coals. His nearness and touch were breathstealing. Her fingers traced his rugged features. "You're the most handsome and irresistible man I've met, Steve Carr. You make me think and do crazy things. You have a powerful hold over me, and I don't know whether to be happy about it or afraid."

Steve stroked her flushed cheek and drifted his forefinger over her parted lips. "You do the same to me, woman." His arms tightened around her body and his mouth covered hers. Exhilaration filled him.

Ginny knew she loved him and wanted to marry him, but was sure he wouldn't consider such a dream until he worked through his troubles and resolved the reasons for his bitterness. This was perhaps the last time they could share intimacy before the journey ended; she needed to bond him to her as strongly as possible, to soften his heart and to open his mind's eye to the reality of his feelings for her. A loner like Steve wouldn't do and say such things as he had if they didn't have deep meaning behind them. She had to get him past his fears so he'd recognize and accept the truth. She pressed tightly against him, kissing him with feverish desire and hugging him with soul-deep feelings.

Steve's mouth feasted at hers with ravenous hunger. He also realized how short their remaining time together was, perhaps shorter than either of them knew. It was difficult not to yank off their garments, fall to the bed, and ride away to splendor within her. She was eager and responsive. He had dreamed day and night of having her again; now that precious moment had come.

Thoughts of Ginny's troubles vanished in the golden glow of their loving. It was as if thousands of butterflies were trapped inside her body and fluttering against her skin as they sought to break through to freedom. Simultaneously she felt relaxed and tense as her anticipation mounted. No man had ever made her feel this way, and probably no other man could. She craved his kisses, his embraces, his touch. No flames could sear her body and heart as his possession did. She yearned to become one with him again tonight, and for countless times in the future. Even if her behavior, her uncontrollable surrender, was dangerous and reckless, she could not stop herself from claiming what she needed.

Steve relished her sweet mouth, and clean skin. His lips varied between long and firm kisses where their tongues touched, to light and brief ones where his lips scouted hers from end to end. He wanted to take her fast; he wanted to take her slow; he wanted her completely. His hands roamed her clothed body with stirring caresses as he increased their suspense, until he could endure the barriers between them no longer. He removed her gown, with her eager assistance. He stripped off his weapons, boots, and garments—again with her bold help. He lifted her and carried her to the inviting bed and placed her there. For a moment he felt vulnerable without his ever-present Colts and knife, and knowing his wits were dulled by passion.

Ginny had already tossed aside the covers. She kept her gaze locked to his as he smiled down at her. She had to read what was exposed in his eyes, to see it was tenderness and desire. She didn't ask him to put out the lamp, and he didn't do so. With courage and elation, her gaze slipped over his masculine body. His bronze physique appeared flawless; the few scars here and there did not detract from his near perfection. His muscles were well honed, creating a potent landscape of ridges, valleys, and plains. His weight was ideal for his height. She noticed that he had little body hair growing on his arms and legs, and none on his tawny chest. Yet, his ebony hair was thick and lush, his stubble when he needed a shave was heavy and black, and the crispy fuzz around his . . .

Ginny blushed as she realized she was examining him like she had seen gamblers do with prize horses before placing their bets at the races. Her feminine curiosity had gotten the better of her. When her gaze rejoined his, he seemed to be savoring every inch of her the way she had visually adored him.

Steve had expected her body to be as compelling as her face, but it was even more exquisite than he had imagined. Her complexion reminded him of a ripe peach from her home state. Some would call her hair lightest brown and others, darkest blond. Her eyes were like pools of green with brown magic submerged in them. No artist could have created a more lovely beauty; one probably could mix colors forever and not find the correct shades to capture her. The seven-inch difference in their heights made her the perfect size to fit in his embrace. From the glow on her cheeks and in her eyes, she was as pleased and enticed by what she saw as he was. Obviously she recalled how much pleasure he had given her and was too highly inflamed to be either modest or afraid at the sight of his arousal.

Steve lay down half atop her. His mouth roved her face, neck, and shoulders. His lips returned to hers and sealed them in a kiss that could enlighten her to his deepest and most protected feelings. The contact with her bare skin caused him to tremble with swiftly mounting desire. He trailed his fingers over her as they mapped and explored her terrain. His mouth trekked with leisure down her throat and to her breasts.

Ginny moaned in bliss at the wild and wonderful sensations. Her fingers wandered into his ebony hair and thrilled themselves with its softness. They left the midnight location to roam his sleek torso. He was strong and firm, but supple. She was consumed by an overpowering need to be locked against him, but couldn't seem to get close enough after his mouth returned to hers. He was like a sorcerer working his spells and enchantments on her, and she didn't want to break them, ever.

Steve cupped and stroked her firm breasts. He quivered with joy every time his hands or mouth touched them, as did she. His body was awash in a flood of tormentingly sweet sensations. He hadn't experienced such feelings with saloon girls, as only his body had sought and found physical release with them. With Anna, his heart and mind were involved in taking her. She seemed more relaxed and eager tonight, as she knew what lay ahead—that thrilled him, as it said how much he had pleasured her last time. He kissed her closed eyes, the tip of her nose, the crest of her chin, the ridges and hollows of her cheeks, her ears, and her mouth. He let his tongue dance with hers, as he had danced with her in camp.

Ginny thrashed her spinning head and aching body. He was assailing her wits and heightening her desire. Her strained voice urged, "Please, Steve, take me before I die of longing."

His lips captured hers as he slid his manhood within her. Obviously there was no discomfort this time because she arched to meet every thrust and clung to him. She was yielding herself freely, totally, and ardently. He took her in those same ways.

Passion's flames leapt and scorched their bodies as they caressed, kissed, and moved as one. Love's fire burned out of control. The tension within them built to an almost staggering point as they reached the pinnacle together. Their pulses quickened, as did their pace. Bursts of ecstasy shot through them. Their kiss went on and on, making them breathless and lightheaded until, at last, they rested in each other's embrace.

Steve's voice was husky and tender as he murmured in her ear, "That was the best experience I've had in my entire life, Anna. Thanks."

Ginny was overwhelmed by her love for him. "You're a good teacher in many areas, Steve Carr," she replied, aware it was still too soon to press him for a permanent relationship or an admission of love. "Of course I have a lot more to learn, if you don't get weary and bored with my lack of experience and vexed with my distractions. Blame yourself. You are quite wit-stealing, my talented scout."

Steve propped his elbows on either side of her head, careful not to entrap and pull her touseled hair as it spread out on the pillow. "You're the big distraction, woman. Half the time, all I think about is you."

"Only half the time?" she drawled, putting on a look of disappointment. "You control my thoughts and feelings most of the time."

"If I thought about you any more than I do, we wouldn't travel ten feet safely. As for getting 'weary and bored' with you, it will never happen, woman. If you gave me any more pleasure than you do, I'd go wild. You best have mercy on me and take it easy or I'll be stalking you day and night."

"I wouldn't mind. That might be fun."

"But bad timing, Anna," he responded in a serious tone. He needed to prevent either of them from saying revealing words too soon.

"I know, for both of us. After we get things settled in our lives, we can see if we want more from each other than this. Is that fair?"

Apparently, he decided, his necessary caution had worked, and he was relieved. "Sounds like a good offer to me. What do you have to settle?" he asked as his mind shifted with reluctance from romance to his mission.

"Starting a new life. How about you, my secretive scout?"

"Secretive? Me? What do you mean?"

Ginny wanted to do probing of her own but quickly learned it would be futile. "I've seen how you watch people. You're mighty inquisitive for a scout. You look as if you're trying to discover everyone's secrets."

Steve chuckled. "Only those that could cause me trouble on my job."

"Like *I* cause you trouble?" she teased, his answer unconvincing.

"This kind of trouble, I like," he replied and nibbled at her neck.

Ginny used her hand to smother her laughter. "Me, too."

Steve leaned back and gazed into her merry eyes. He pondered how he had gotten to this refined lady so quickly—unless she wanted him to do so. Was he *all* she really wanted from him? How could he know for sure? They were so different: she, a genteel, pampered southern belle; he, a half-breed bastard and all saddle tramp. *Are you real, Anna Avery? Can I trust you? Can I accept the consequences if you're—*

"Why are you staring at me like that?" she inquired, feeling unsettled by the intensity of his gaze.

"Like what?" he murmured, kissing the tip of her nose.

"Like you're a voracious predator who's searching for my weaknesses before attacking me."

"I am. Haven't you realized that by now?" he jested.

As Steve's mouth and hands returned to her pliant body, Ginny had an alarming feeling he had lied or masked his real meaning. What, she mused in panic, did she really know about this man she loved? He could be anybody, anything. Should she trust him? Would he use, betray, and discard her when they reached Dallas? But how could he make love to her so tenderly if he didn't care about her? She reasoned it was probably only her guilt about deceiving him that played tricks on her mind, or maybe he had been probing his intimidating feelings for her before he had spoken. Soon, she was lost in the wonder of what he was doing to her.

* * *

The group stayed camped below Jackson the following day for several men to make repairs on their wagons. The grain supply was replenished, chores were done, and visits exchanged.

Ginny wished she could have remained in the hotel room with Steve all day and another night, but that was impossible. Several men from town had arrived to chat with the travelers, to gather news from Georgia and other locations, and to relate all the horrific details of the Yankee conquest of that area and the fearsome destruction it had caused.

Ginny wished the depressing talk would stop. She didn't want to imagine what had been done at beautiful Green Oaks in Georgia, her lost home. She wasn't surprised when a query was voiced concerning the existence of the Ku Klux Klan in Mississippi.

The local man answered that "no group had been organized yet, but that if things got worse or didn't improve, they would indeed form one."

As Ginny listened, she was glad she'd hadn't witnessed and endured those tragedies and terrors. Since entering Mississippi, she had viewed lingering and chilling reminders of vast destruction, still visible two years after it had ended. She heard and saw bitterness and hatred in the Mississippians, as she had in Georgians. It had been war, she admitted, but some things couldn't be justified even under that word. She was sitting in the dark in the Avery wagon and knew she couldn't be seen, but she saw Steve standing near the conversing group of people. She observed him closely as he took in every word spoken, every expression used, and every person present. What, she mused, had the scout so intrigued?

They broke camp on time Tuesday morning and crossed the wide Pearl River without problems, as it wasn't deep or swift.

Steve was edgy and alert. He surmised that he might not unmask the culprit until Dallas, their termination point, unless the telegram he was expecting in Vicksburg gave him a clue. The closer he came to a response, the more he dreaded what he might learn.

Ginny continued to study the moody and mysterious scout who had won her heart. This morning, he had ridden close enough to touch her calf and find his present to her missing. He had scolded her, telling her in an almost curt tone, "Put that pistol on during the next stop and never be without it, not even in camp. Wear it dawn to dusk, woman; I mean it."

She told herself she should be happy he was so protective of her, but his concern seemed to have an underlying motive she couldn't grasp.

On Wednesday, May first, they crossed the Natchez Trace and Big Black River. Widely spaced rolling hills of mostly pine and cedar with a few magnolias allowed for a comfortable ride and steady pace. As the sun was setting, they halted near Vicksburg: "Gibraltar of the Confederacy" whose conquest had begun the gradual fall of the South. Because they were close to civilization, they didn't have to circle-up as on the trail, which allowed for welcome privacy between wagons.

The Mississippi River wasn't far from camp. Its width and depth and its swift and unpredictable currents would make it the most treacherous and time-consuming crossing. This was where accidents and losses might occur. The famous river was down a steep slope with countless evergreen trees between it and camp, so the water wasn't visible. The hilly terrain was dotted with numerous mounds, some manmade earthworks from the war; the men called them redoubts, redans, and lunnettes. Damage by gunboat blasts to land, trees, and property was still noticeable and heartrending, although Mother Nature and local inhabitants were doing their best to heal the numerous scars. Twice they heard horn blasts from steamboats that plied their trade on the river. They had journeyed for seven days to traverse one hundred forty miles of Mississippi, and the sight of the famed river and nearby town filled everyone with excitement.

"We'll rest tomorrow and get ready to challenge our most dangerous river on Friday," Steve announced. "I suggest a night of fun and rest."

Everyone happily concurred. Meals were eaten and chores were done with haste. Music, merriment, and dancing began as soon as children were put to bed.

Steve stayed in camp, hating to imagine what he would discover in the morning. He realized that if the villain he must defeat was Charles Avery, that could call a halt to his relationship with Anna. This might be the last enjoyable evening with her. Besides, he excused his reluctance, the telegraph office was surely closed by now.

Residents who had seen or heard the wagontrain approach came to visit and bring treats for fellow Southerners. They joined in the fun.

One related that Vicksburg had been a gambler's paradise at one time because of the riverboats. When crime became a problem, the locals had put an end to it in '35 by ordering them out of town within a day or face brutal consequences of "thirty-nine lashes at the public whipping post." He reported with a comical grin how the threat had worked on almost all of the professional gamblers and their "fancy women." He went on to entertain the travelers with colorful tales of famous thieves who had worked the Mississippi and the Natchez Trail.

Conversation naturally veered to the past war with the North. Another local told them about the steamboat *Sultana* that picked up released Yankee captives in April of '65. "She took on too many fur her size and power: twenty-five hunnerd prisoners and others piled aboard. More 'an eager to git outta the dangerous South. Squeezed into her tighter 'an blood in a tick after a good feeding. She blew up near Memphis, burned, and sank. Word was fifteen hunnerd went down with her. Some couldn't swim and some was too weak to do it, and that river has powerful currents in some places no man could survive."

Ginny listened until she couldn't endure any more grim talk. She was relieved when several men took up their instruments and played cheerful tunes. She saw couples dance and others snack on the sweet treats of southern hospitality. Many chatted, laughed, sang along, clapped hands, or tapped toes.

"Why don't we join them?" Steve suggested to Ginny, nodding to the dancers.

"Dare we risk being so close?" she jested. "I might lose my wits."

Steve grinned. "Who can blame me for yielding to temptation?"

"Or me," she replied, and slipped into his beckoning arms.

Their first dance was fast and lively; the second one was slow enough and with sufficient distance from others to permit whispered talk.

"We're lucky we haven't had any problems with storms and mud," she remarked. "Bad weather always seems behind us. I hope it stays that way."

Steve didn't know if he agreed or not, as storms would slow their progress. If he received good news tomorrow, it would give him more time with Anna, but would lengthen his mission and delay his other task. He wanted both jobs finished so he could . . . He frowned as he realized his future action was controlled by the information in that telegram. "Less than three weeks and four hundred miles to go, Anna," he murmured.

She wondered what Steve had been thinking to bring such a scowl to his handsome face. He was so tense tonight, and that worried her, yet he had asked her to dance twice and appeared reluctant to leave her side. Something heavy was weighing on those powerful shoulders, and she feared the burden somehow had to do with her. She tried to relax him with light talk. "I know; Father told me today. It sounds like a long time, but it will pass so swiftly. These last four and a half weeks have raced by."

Steve pushed aside his worries to concentrate on her. "That's because you stay so busy and are having so much fun," he jested.

"In spite of the work and hardships, Steve, it *has* been enjoyable. I'll never forget this journey. Of course, since we've encountered no perils, I'll have to embellish it to make it colorful for my children and grandchildren. I'm sure you'll have countless adventures to relate to yours one day."

Words the haunted man had thought and believed for years leapt from his lips before he could halt them. "I don't plan to have either one. I wouldn't make a good father, or a good husband."

Ginny assumed he had taken her innocent statements as pressure for a commitment. She faked merry laughter and teased, "You could be right; a trail man wouldn't be around enough to fill their many needs."

Steve forced chuckles, too. She was generous to release him from his trap. "That's a fancy and kind word for saddle tramp."

Ginny broadened her smile and slipped a seductive tone into her voice. "A saddle tramp doesn't work to earn his living or have routes and schedules to follow. You do lead a free life without attachments, but you aren't an idle wanderer. You aren't ill-kempt, worthless, or irresponsible."

Steve leaned back and stared at her. He grinned and asked, "What brought on those compliments?"

Ginny sent him a beguiling look that said she wasn't going to answer. "Father says we're going into Vicksburg tomorrow to spend the day and night. If you're going, too, perhaps we could share the day."

Steve squeezed her hand and lowered his voice even more to whisper in a husky tone, "What if I want more than the day with you?"

Ginny trembled with desire and her cheeks glowed. "I hope you do. We only have Shreveport left between here and Dallas."

Steve caught her meaning: one more town and one last chance to have privacy. "Let's have lunch, a long stroll, sup— dinner, and . . ."

Ginny's body felt as if he was setting it afire with his provocative words. She couldn't wait to be alone with him again. She had only a few chances left to win his heart before they arrived in Dallas. She wished they could sneak from camp to kiss and embrace. They didn't have to make love every time they were alone, only be together.

"Well?" Steve prompted. "You want to spend time with me?"

She gazed into his dark eyes. "Sounds perfect to me, Mr. Carr."

Steve reacted to the intoxicating plans in the same manner. He was aching with need for her, and more than physical need. She made him feel good in many ways. "Sounds perfect to me, Miss Avery. Now, let's change the subject before our expressions expose us as naughty children."

"Sounds very wise to me, Mr. Carr," she replied, and grinned.

Steve left the following morning before the Averys did. He picked up the telegram and read it. His emotions were a mixture of anger and sadness, of disbelief and confirmation of doubts. As he had suspected, Charles Avery had not purchased the Box F Ranch, hadn't purchased any ranch or property; there wasn't a Box F near Waco! He had been deceived! Ginny's father was the sly culprit.

Dread washed over the scout's body and anguish flooded his mind. What remained to be learned was if Anna knew the dirty truth about her father and— Spirits help him—if she was involved in the vicious scheme.

All he could do was wait for them to reach town. In bitter resentment, Steve resolved to take advantage of Charles's encouragement to pursue his daughter. He must confront her in private. *Shu,* he hated to search for the truth! Either she was innocent and would despise him for duping her and arresting her father, or she was guilty of complicity and of tricking and betraying him and would go to prison with Charles. Even if guilty, could he condemn her to such a terrible fate? Didn't love and loyalty to her father and misguided beliefs count for anything with the law? How should he know, as he didn't have love or loyalty to his father?

Be innocent, Anna, or I can't help you, not without destroying all I've worked for and without sacrificing vengeance for my best friend. If you've lied to me and used me, how can I ever trust you again?

"We're here to see Mr. Avery," a stranger said to the oldest Davis boy.

"That's his wagon over there, sir." The youngster pointed to it.

"Much obliged," the gang leader said, and guided his friends that way.

As five roughly clad males approached the wagon, Ginny eyed the well-armed and crude-looking men who made her nervous even at a distance.

"We're looking for Charles Avery. Is he here?"

Ginny's wary gaze drifted from man to man. "My father went to view the river with some of the men. He'll return soon."

"Your father? We didn't know he was bringing his daughter along."

"You know him? You're friends of his?"

"Yep, we've come to get him and take him to a meeting."

She was confused and apprehensive. "What do you mean? We're heading for Dallas on the wagontrain. Was he expecting you to meet him?"

"Yep, but we're a mite early. We have a business deal."

Ginny was uneasy. She didn't like the unkempt . . . *ruffians,* she decided with aversion. "What kind of business do you have with my father?"

"Private, Miss Avery, 'less he's already told you about it."

"He hasn't mentioned anything like this to me." She glanced around to see if anyone was close enough to rescue her if these men presented a threat. She saw the group returning from the river. With relief, she said, "Here he comes now . . . Father, you have visitors."

Charles looked the five men over as he asked how he could help them.

Ginny grasped that the leader had lied, that they were strangers. Her anxiety increased.

"We're here to take you safely to where you need to go."

Charles was as angry as his look and tone sounded. "This wasn't part of the plan. You're supposed to meet me in Dallas."

"Plans changed, Avery, and we had no way of getting in touch with you. This one's better. It'll save everybody a lot of time and saddlesores. Graham will meet you in Little Rock 'stead of St. Louis."

Ginny was more worried about Charles leaving with such crude-looking men than she was concerned about this unexpected event playing havoc with her own plans. "What's going on, Father?"

Charles patted her arm and smiled. "Nothing for you to worry about, Anna. You boys will have to meet me in Dallas as prearranged; I can't change my schedule. I have to get my daughter there and see her settled in before we take our little business trip."

"Afraid that ain't possible, Avery."

"And why not?" Charles demanded.

"I have orders to bring you with me. And we've already been seen here. Too many dangerous questions will be asked. Too many suspicions aroused. You catch my drift?"

"Then you shouldn't have come here. Everything was going fine, just like we planned. No one suspected me. This will bring trouble to me and to my daughter after we leave."

"Can't worry about that. The good of the cause is the only important thing. Ain't that right?"

Good of the cause echoed across Ginny's mind and alarmed her. She surmised Charles Avery had a deception of his own in progress, one he hadn't told her about. He was vexed by this kink in his scheme, whatever it was.

"Get the goods and your gear and let's move out fast. Bring her along."

"She stays here. She isn't part of this." Charles grasped her hands in his. "Anna, you take the wagon on to Dallas," he ordered. "You'll do fine alone; you're well trained. I have to go with these men. Don't fret, girl, Steve will take good care of you if you need help. You do what you have to do."

Ginny gleaned the clues in his words for her to carry on with her deceptions.

"What's going on?" she pressed in fear. "What's wrong? You didn't tell me about this trip."

"Nothing to worry about, Anna, just do what you came to do."

"Ain't smart or safe to leave her behind," the leader said. "Not after people get curious about you."

"They wouldn't have if you'd done as planned," Charles scoffed.

"Time's important, Avery; you'll find out why very soon."

"Nothing is as important as keeping my identity and mission a secret."

"Too late to worry about that. Let's get moving. Get your stuff ready to pull out, too, Miss Avery."

"I told you she isn't coming with us. Anna stays here and goes on to Dallas on the wagontrain."

"She's coming with us, Avery. The law could be on to us anytime. We might need her for cover. You got the goods with you?"

"In a safe place. I'll turn them over to Graham when I see him."

Luther Beams had been observing the incident and catching a strange word here and there. He walked over and asked, "Got a problem, folks?"

"I'll be leaving the wagontrain with my friends," Charles said. "Anna is continuing on to Dallas with you and will wait for me there to join her. I trust you and Steve will look out for her?"

The gang leader fingered his gun butts. "No, sir, that ain't a smart idea. Your daughter is coming along with us." When Big L started to bring his rifle upward to ready it for trouble, the leader warned, "You don't want to do that, mister, too many nice folks around here might get hurt. Why don't you lay aside that rifle until after we're gone?"

"What's this about, Avery?" Luther Beams asked as he obeyed.

"Private business," Charles replied.

From what he'd been told by the authorities who asked for his help, Big L realized what was taking place, but he dared not risk challenging five armed men who looked as if killing could be second nature to them.

"You two get your stuff and let's get out of here. We need her along for protection. Nobody will follow and shoot if a woman prisoner is with us."

"Prisoner?" A wide-eyed Ginny repeated the chilling word.

Charles comprehended he couldn't change the men's minds. He looked at Ginny. "I'm sorry, Anna, but you'll have to come with us for a while. Don't worry; you'll be safe. I promise."

"What about my things, Father? Are we taking the wagon with us?"

"Nope," the leader answered for Charles. "We're riding horses."

"I don't have a horse," Ginny told the man who had been doing all the talking.

With a wicked grin, the boss said, "I'm sure one of these nice folks will lend you one. They don't want any trouble with us."

Ginny grasped his meaning, as did Big L and Charles. "*Steal* one?"

"*Borrow* is a nicer word, Miss Avery."

That would entice the authorities to pursue them, Ginny knew. Once questions started being asked, the entire truth about her identity might be exposed. "Stealing is against the law," she protested. "We'll get into trouble."

"You don't have to steal; I will. Rollie, you and Slim find her a good mount. Avery, you and your daughter stuff some things in a bag. Now."

"What about all my possessions?" Ginny persisted.

"The wagon will have to be left here," Charles answered.

"What if they're stolen before we return?"

Big L surmised that Anna didn't know what was going on and was being taken as a hostage by the ruffians. "Don't worry, Miss Avery; your friends will take turns driving your wagon to Dallas. Your belongings will be waiting for you at the company office in a few weeks."

"Thank you, Mr. Beams, but I can't put you all to such trouble."

"Won't be no trouble at all, miss. You've done plenty for others, so they won't mind helping you out. You best go with your father and his friends; we don't want trouble and injuries in a camp of women and children. Steve will take care of everything when he returns from town."

Ginny caught his hints. Fear gripped her heart as she thought about Steve getting weary of awaiting her, returning soon, and having a gun battle with these . . . outlaws. Nor did she want to endanger any of the people in camp. She had placed herself in Charles Avery's care; now she was in the midst of his troubles. "You're right. Thank you, sir."

Ginny climbed into the wagon, lifted a cloth satchel, and packed clothes for the trail in it. From the corner of her eye, she checked to see if she was being watched. Not close enough, she concluded, for the men to see her drop extra cartridges into her skirt pocket for the holstered derringer strapped to her thigh. She was told to rush by the man at the tailgate.

Ginny realized she was helpless to disobey, but, thanks to Steve's tough training and precautions, she wasn't vulnerable in other ways. She would do as she was told and await the opportunity to escape. She must watch the route taken carefully so she could retrace it afterward. She admitted with sadness that she had misjudged Charles Avery in some areas; he obviously was up to no good and had used her as a protective cover for his "mission." Yet he had tried to help her, to have her left there. His failure meant he had no control over these rough villains, a realization that frightened her.

Within five minutes, she and Charles were mounted and being led from the campsite. She was on a horse taken from a wickedly smiling Cathy King, as Ed was in town. Ginny waved to her four watchful friends and sent them a look that said she wasn't leaving willingly.

The seven galloped south for miles to a stream and rode in it for a time. They veered northeast, with one man hanging behind to cover their tracks, skirted Vicksburg, and headed northwest toward Arkansas.

Ginny feared no trail or clues were being left for anyone to follow and come to her rescue. She glanced back at the large city perched on steep hills, and its cobblestone streets. Her last sight of town was of the Greek Revival courthouse on its highest point. Before concentrating on memorizing their route, she thought of Steve Carr futilely awaiting her arrival in town to share the day and a glorious night together. What would he do when he discovered she had been taken against her will? He couldn't quit his job and cast aside his responsibilities to chase after Charles Avery's daughter. No matter what Steve felt about her, his duty and job would come first. She was sure he would allow the local law to take a course of action.

Steve paced at the corner of Clay and Washington streets as he watched for the Averys' arrival. Time passed, too much. It was after the lunch hour, so Charles must have changed his mind about the diversion. He mounted up and rode for camp, to be told a shocking story there.

"What do you mean, Anna was abducted by her father's friends?"

"Miss Anna was taken captive, Steve. I could tell she wasn't involved in these evil doings. Mr. Avery tried to leave her behind, but that leader—a bad sort— wouldn't let him. They stole Mr. King's horse and forced her to go with them. She looked real scared and worried, but she didn't have a choice. They hinted they would shoot up the camp if she refused or I challenged them, so both of us obeyed. They rode south hours ago. When you took so long, I sent one of the men to search for you in town. You must have missed him on the way back." Luther related all he'd heard and seen.

"I have to go after them, Big L; you have to take over here."

"Don't worry about us; we'll do fine. Just catch those devils and help Miss Anna. One more thing, Steve. As they were mounting up, the leader whispered a warning to me. He said if anybody followed them, Miss Anna would be killed. I think he meant it. Out loud he told me they'd release her soon. He lied and she's in big danger. I don't believe Mr. Avery has any control over them, but he don't know it yet."

They talked a few minutes before the troubled man gathered his possessions and supplies and took off after them.

Steve rode south, hours behind them. He speculated they were heading for New Orleans to exchange the stolen gems for arms and ammunition. That would give Avery access to a ship to transport his cargo to Savannah and into the clutches of the Red Magnolias. He couldn't allow that to happen. He must not fail in this mission.

Steve rebuked himself for not keeping his mind on the assignment. If he'd returned to camp after getting the revealing telegram, he could have captured the gang and recovered the gems this morning. This case could be settled by now. Instead, both the villains and gems were gone. So was Anna. He wondered if she had promised to meet him in town to get him out of the way so they could join their contacts. Maybe what Luther Beams witnessed was nothing more than a pretense to conceal her involvement. Maybe she cared for him, suspected trouble, and had kept him out of danger with a pretty lie. Or was that too much to hope for, her love and innocence? He'd know the truth when he caught up with them soon.

—— *Chapter* 11 ——

❧

VIRGINIA MARSTON AND CHARLES AVERY were ferried across the wide Yazoo River on a large raft that didn't seem sturdy enough to the trembling female to bear their weights or to be safe in the tricky currents. Rolling hills of lush grass, wooded knolls, and sand-colored soil gave way to fertile black flatland of the delta region where cotton grew in abundance and the moist ebony dirt clung to hooves and was kicked up behind them. They journeyed westward of a dense forest of mostly pine, oak, and willow, with occasional magnolia and dogwood. They crossed numerous creeks where cypress with huge bases grew at their sides. They passed plantations at a distance, some repaired and some fallen into ruin during and since the bitter and bloody conflict with the Union. They saw fields of rice and corn. To Ginny, it looked as if the residents of this area were recovering slowly from the horrors of the war.

The group of seven traveled as fast as the terrain would permit and took few rest stops. The gang continued to watch for pursuers over their shoulders, and finally stopped concealing their getaway trail. They rode in close proximity that warned Ginny, along with Bart's words, not to "make a break for it." She was glad her body was in better condition now than it had been before her intense training period with Steve and from weeks of exertion on the wagontrain.

So far, the ruffians hadn't given her trouble. The leader promised her safety on the trail and release in Little Rock, but she distrusted him and his men. Although the muckers talked and joked with Charles and he with them, an intimidating tension filled the air. Charles tried to mask his apprehension, but Ginny's worried senses penetrated it.

She was afraid, but assumed it was best to put up a brave front. She discouraged any conversation and disdained all attempts at friendliness. She knew that haughtiness often kept even roughened types at a distance. She hoped that pretense would work for her. But every mile of the way she was conscious of the holstered derringer strapped to her right thigh and the extra bullets in her skirt pocket, cushioned by a handkerchief. She wisely did not expose it and wouldn't until the right moment presented itself. She knew she could not take on five armed and dangerous men. She must wait to get one alone, disable him as Steve had taught her, and flee. She hoped she would remember the route they were taking and paid close attention to it.

By flatboat, they crossed the mighty Mississippi, a river to evoke wonder and terror. The ferrymen kept on alert for treacherous "boilings" and eddies in the swift blue currents and for ever-shifting sandbars. It was noisy at both banks where sucking and gurgling sounds chewed ravenously at land and debris and where vegetation was thick and verdant.

In Arkansas, they encountered a heavy tracery of rivers and streams in the lowland that would, Ginny prayed, slow their progress for a while. Yet the flat and open landscape allowed for a lengthy visibility, and she saw no one in pursuit. At dusk, the leader halted them not far inside the watery stateline: fifty miles from Vicksburg, the man she loved, and her possessions.

Ginny was exhausted and sore from a nerve-wracking and long ride. The food being cooked—fried salt pork and grits, served with strong coffee and warmed biscuits—did not appeal to her even though she was hungry. She knew she must keep up her strength, though, so she forced herself to eat. She heard frogs and crickets and saw fireflies flickering here and there. She studied her surroundings carefully in case she was compelled to flee trouble. This area did have sluggish creeks and stagnant ponds and names with "bayou" attached, but it was nothing like those in southern Louisiana, Georgia, and Mississippi. The terrain was called swampland, but it wasn't what she'd imagined a real swamp to be. In spots the ground was wet, spongy, and densely vegetated, but she'd seen no uncrossable marshes, quagmires, alligators, poisonous water snakes, or other bog creatures she associated with one. Yet this area was spooky at night and fraught with hidden perils, so she must escape during the day when she had light to guide her steps.

An inquisitive fox darted back into the trees and vanished before one of the men could shoot it with his drawn rifle and a mean grin on his face. She hated to imagine how these men would act in a few days after they wearied of her arrogance. If they tried to ravish her, she would fight them to the death.

Death . . . Ginny trembled, thinking the word. They might silence her with death to protect their evil scheme. She might never see her father again, or Mathew Marston could be dead already. Steve could be murdered if he came after her. To stay alive and safe to return to her loved ones, she must remain alert and cautious and brave. She must depend on the skills her lover had taught her for protection and freedom. At the time, she hadn't realized how important his tough training would become to her.

Ginny massaged her grumbling shoulders and neck and the muscles at the back of her waist. Riding horseback all day, she decided, was more demanding than walking and driving a wagon, or perhaps it was only a reaction to the activity. During the day, they had encountered boatmen, several riders, hunters, and fishermen, and had seen workers in fields, but she hadn't shouted for help from sources she considered futile. She was in a perilous predicament, but she must survive and find her father and Steve Carr again.

Charles joined her away from the men. They lay on bedrolls beside each other. "I'm sorry I got you into this, Ginny," he whispered. "Don't be scared. Those men are hired to do a job and wouldn't dare betray their boss. Don't worry, they won't harm either of us."

He didn't sound convinced to her. Ample space between them and the bandits and the excessively loud croakings of many frogs allowed them to speak softly without being overheard. The separation was permitted because the horses were close to the gang and Bart had pointed out that, "nobody's fool 'nough to escape into a swamp at night."

"What is this all about, Mr. Avery?" she asked. "I have a right to know why I was abducted."

He reasoned she would discover the truth soon, so it wouldn't matter if he revealed it now. "I'm a carrier for the Red Magnolias. I have a crucial mission to accomplish for them."

Ginny stared at him, his features visible beneath a three-quarter waxing moon. She recognized the name of a powerful unit of Klansmen. During the journey, she had learned that most Invisible Empire members honestly believed they had formed the secret organization to combat Yankee and ex-slave terrorism in the vulnerable South. But as in all large groups of rebels, the Ku Klux Klan had members who went beyond protection and justice to obtain personal revenge and greedy desires. "Carrier? For what?"

Charles patted his waist, "Gems, mostly diamonds, worth a fortune. We're exchanging them for arms and ammunition from Timothy Graham in St. Louis, and we're hiring scouts to track down our enemies."

"What enemies, sir?"

"Men like Sherman, who ravaged the South, and Loyal Leaguers, who are still ravishing our land. We're going to punish them, kill them, so they can't do this to anybody again."

"Track down and . . . assassinate them?"

"Punish them for what they did, for what they're still doing to us. To stop Negro gangs they're inciting, arming, and training to loot and kill us. They're sicking embittered ex-slaves on us like starving dogs on juicy meat. Most of us didn't even own slaves; those who did, never abused them. They didn't believe in cruelty, and such property was too valuable to maim. We can't take attacks lying down like cowards. But we can't risk fighting back in the open or exposing our- selves as Klansmen. If we succeed, the South will rise to her past glory. We'll be free, safe, and powerful once more."

"But what you're planning to do with this . . . 'mission' is murder, Mr. Avery. You can't be a part of it. You're too good and kind; too gentle. The war is over; let it die."

"Like my Anna died? Raped, beaten, and murdered by Yankee soldiers. She's not the only woman that happened to because of the war. Other members have wives, daughters, mothers, and sisters those beasts have ravished or terrorized or slain. With these," he said, patting his waist again, "they can be located and punished. My sweet and innocent Anna and others can be avenged."

"With *what*, Mr. Avery? You have the gems hidden on your body?"

"In a pouch around my waist. I don't want those men to know what I'm carrying or to where. They probably think it's money or a voucher or a promissory note. Once our scouts find the bastards we want, they're dead."

Scouts? her mind echoed. Steve was a skilled one for hire, and Charles had constantly and eagerly pushed them together. She fretted over the possibility of their being secret cohorts. Steve had been inquisitive and observant; he could have been interrogating her and spying on everyone else for this very reason. He could have gotten wind of this "mission" and been seeking the carrier, a boss to approach for his next job. Steve had insisted she be armed at all times. Had he suspected this trouble and prepared her to defend herself? No, she argued with herself, he wouldn't take a wicked job like this.

"Were you wooing Steve Carr to become one of those scouts?" she probed. "Is that why you wanted him ensnared by me, your daughter?"

"No, Ginny girl. I meant, hire detectives. I only wanted Steve to be willing to guide you to your father. You see now why I couldn't, and can't, go with you. Steve Carr is a good and honest man, a skilled guide and expert shooter. I thought you might need his help and protection after we parted and if things didn't work out in Texas." Charles sighed heavily and frowned. "After this, he probably wouldn't let you hire him for any amount. He's also proud and stubborn. If you meet again, you'll defeat any hope with him if you continue being Anna Avery or if you confess you lied. Either way, he'll never trust you again. Men can deceive, then expect and get forgiveness, but if a woman deceives them, they take it as an attack or unforgettable treachery. Besides, it's dangerous and foolish to travel with a man who feels that way about you. You'll have to find another way to get you to Colorado. I'm sorry I messed that up for you."

Ginny feared those grim words were true, but only time and Steve's reaction could convince her. She worried over what her friends at the camp were thinking about her. Possibly they had added up the clues and realized her "father" was committing a more terrible deed than horse-stealing. They might even think she was a clever and disguised party to it. Her four friends . . . She missed them already and hoped they wouldn't believe such awful lies about her.

No doubt Cathy King was delighted to have her gone. And no doubt the theft of their horse would give her an excuse to cry on Steve's shoulder!

Steve . . . Would he try to trail and rescue her? But how, when fourteen families were in his care? Would the law come to help her soon? Would they be fooled by the false trail the men had marked southward?

The following day they were riding again by eight o'clock. The Arkansas lowland was green and beautiful. Past or present crops of cotton, rice, and maize stretched before their gazes for what looked like miles in several directions. They skirted inhabited areas to avoid contact with farmers and sharecroppers, just as they did where cattle grazed on lush grass. The few hills they crossed were so low and gentle that they could more accurately be called uneven terrain. Sprinklings of hardwoods broke what sometimes seemed like prairie land. They spooked deer, quail, squirrel, and rabbit, a few times, turkey and opossum.

During one rest stop, Bart told her that people in the northern and western sections of the state were fiercely independent and suspicious of strangers. He said many, especially in isolated mountain regions, were backward, poor, and rough. He disclosed that Union loyalty had been "strong and thick" in the northern region, and fights still broke out between ex-Confederates and ex-Union sympathizers. "You don't wanna git caught by none of them mountain boys, Miss Anna," the leader ended his chat. "You'd never see a town or friendly face again. You'd be kept like a slave to 'em till you die, or git too old or belly-fat to serve 'em."

Ginny didn't have to be told what "belly-fat" meant. She shuddered as she realized she could escape one peril and fall into another one.

Friday night they camped west of Barthalomeu Bayou at dusk, having used all hours of daylight available.

The following night they camped fifteen miles southwest of Pine Bluff. Charles tried to persuade Bart to allow his "daughter" to ride into town where she could take a comfortable steamboat or keelboat down the Arkansas River to the Mississippi to Vicksburg or upriver to Little Rock and meet them there. Bart used the possibility of danger to her as an excuse to continue holding her captive. He claimed that too many Union troops had stayed in Pine Bluff or returned there since its capture in '63 for her to go unnoticed. Bart alleged the big town, where some of the first shots of the war had been fired, was perilous because of rough landing workers and tricky gamblers who plied their trades on the riverboats that docked there.

Sunday night they halted on the Ouachita River. Hills were steeper in this area, some with rocky sides exposed. Woods surrounded the site. Many trees had branches low to the ground, and underbrush was thick, telling her there were excellent hiding places nearby if she could escape.

By that time, Ginny understood what Charles was doing and why, but she did not agree and told him so. She was worried about his sinister plans with the Red Magnolias, worried about him, and worried about the bold, lustful looks the men had been giving her since Friday.

It had poured yesterday, and her soaked shirt had clung to her breasts. The offensive men had sent her lewd smiles, nudged each other and winked, and licked their lips as if in anticipation of tasting a treat. She had chided herself for not packing a slicker but hadn't thought about it at the wagon during her panic. She had used a dripping blanket to cover her shoulders and halt their leering. She knew time for action was slipping away and that she must escape the next day. She couldn't wait for aid to come. Even if someone was pursuing them, she reasoned, they had traveled too fast to be overtaken.

Ginny knew she looked a mess. She intentionally didn't groom herself and risk creating more appeal to the ruffians. She was miserable in the dirty, sweaty, and mussed state. She yearned for the day it would no longer be a necessary precaution.

"Ginny, I don't trust these men," Charles whispered. "We're heading west now, but Little Rock is northeast of us, so they aren't taking us there for a meeting. Tomorrow, I'll demand they release you. If they refuse, I'll hold a gun on them until you make your escape. When I give you the word, you ride out of here and keep riding as fast as you can, northwest to Hot Springs." At her baffled look, he explained, "I've been to Little Rock and Hot Springs before and, best I remember, the mineral springs should sit at eleven on a clock from our present position. If you're afraid you'll get lost, just follow the river. It's a longer route but will get you there. Once we begin our ruse, no matter what you hear, don't look back or return."

"I have a derringer strapped to my leg, Mr. Avery," Ginny revealed in a whisper. "Steve gave it to me and taught me how to use it. If I help, we can escape together. They'll kill you after I get away from them."

Charles exposed what was necessary to persuade her to cooperate, as he felt it was the horrible truth. "I think that's what they already have in mind for me very soon. I don't believe they're guiding us to Timothy Graham; I think they've turned greedy and traitorous and plan to take the payment for themselves. I'm not afraid to die, girl. I faced death many times during and since the war. I love you, girl, and I don't want to see you hurt. I'm more concerned about your safety and survival than I am about failing this mission. Another member can replace me, but nobody else can save you. You know what these men will do to you the moment I'm dead. I can't let happen to you what happened to my sweet Anna."

Tears clouded her hazel eyes. "I can't let you risk your life for me."

"I got you into this and I'll get you out. Please don't argue. Even if we both drew on them, these men won't care if we shoot two of them while the other three gun me down to rob me and . . . hurt you."

She admitted he was right. It pained her to know he would probably die helping her, as the cutthroats would have no reason to hold him prisoner. She was angered by their helplessness, terrified of the grim fates looming before them in the morning. "All right, sir."

"Good girl. Get some sleep. You'll need it."

Ginny lifted her satchel. "I'm going upriver to take a bath and change clothes. I'll return in about twenty minutes."

"Halt, Miss Anna!" the leader shouted at the departing woman. "You don't wanna go trying nothing crazy and riling me."

Ginny looked at him and scoffed, "Attempt escape without a horse, weapon, or supplies and in an unfamiliar wilderness? I'm not a fool, Bart, and my father is in your care. I can't stand being so filthy and disheveled a minute longer. I'm going, so don't try to stop me or I'll pitch a fit."

Bart scowled but said, "Slim, you go guard Miss Anna. And behave yourself or you'll answer to my fists and irons."

Ginny found a site close to the woods for hiding after she made her break. She trembled in suspense and prayed for Charles's endangered life. She waited a few minutes, then called out, "Slim, a snake!"

The outlaw joined her in a hurry, "Where?"

"There, at the edge of the bank near those weeds and my things."

Slim stepped closer to the water and looked in that direction. "I—"

Ginny clobbered his head with a large rock. She tossed one pistol into the river so he couldn't use it on Charles and kept the other. She was tempted to return to camp and help him escape with her, but that would be futile against four men. She assumed he didn't stand a chance of saving himself and that troubled her, so much that she changed her mind.

Ginny bound the unconscious man's ankles and wrists with his shirt and belt then gagged him with his bandana. She drew her derringer, as she felt she could control her accuracy better with its lighter weight. She checked the bullet chambers and sneaked to camp, a weapon in each hand. To avoid startling and distracting her companion and giving the bandits time to react, she must wait until the right moment to expose herself. Charles had said he would delay the men when they became suspicious of her lengthy absence and decided to investigate. While she was reasoning what to do next, Bart took matters out of her hands.

"That gal of yourn is taking too long. Rollie, go check on 'em."

Charles drew his pistol. "Don't any of you move," he ordered.

"What the— Don't be a fool, Avery; it's four to one. You can't shoot all of us before the rest clear leather and fire."

"Ah, yes, but which one will it be who dies?" Charles bluffed.

"You probably can't hit the side of a stage anyway."

"But I can, and I will," Ginny vowed coldly as she stepped into the clearing with two weapons pointed in the men's direction. "Let's tie them up and get out of here, Father," she said, accustomed to calling him that.

"Mount up and ride, Anna. I'll keep them covered then follow you."

"We leave together. Unbuckle your gunbelts, you scoundrels."

"You're making a big mistake, girlie. You—"

"The mistake was yours when you kidnapped me. See that canteen beside you?" Ginny fired at it and water gushed from a bullethole. "Does that convince you I know how to use these? And I will if you don't obey me fast and easy with one finger only." Ginny cautioned herself not to get carried away with her daring ruse. She wasn't "Little Pearl" from the ten-cent pocket novels she had read, about a fictional western heroine who could do anything a man could and most of the time better. She was lucky her reckless demonstration had worked; it wouldn't have if Steve hadn't insisted on weapons lessons and target practice.

"Do as the lady says, boys."

"What?" the other three shouted at the same time.

"Do it," Bart snarled like a provoked animal. "We don't want to be sleeping on our bedrolls like Slim probably is. She's serious."

All four unfastened and dropped their holsters to the ground.

"Step away," Ginny ordered, and Bart made his men obey again.

Charles collected the holsters and backed to the horses. He kept glancing at the outlaws as he saddled two of them in a rush. He mounted while Ginny kept her weapons aimed on the scowling men, then did the same for her. He glanced at the alert woman, smiled, and thanked her for coming back for him. They kneed their mounts to gallop to safety.

Having grasped Bart's hint, the men dashed for their bedrolls and fetched rifles from beneath covers as the leader gave his orders. All aimed and fired. Charles was wounded in the shoulder and fell off his horse, which kept galloping. Ginny's mount was shot in the neck and leg and both tumbled to the ground.

"Run!" Charles told her as he tried to get to his dropped weapon.

Ginny glanced back and saw the four men racing toward them. She couldn't help Charles further. Nor could she take time to aim and fire, as four armed villains were approaching them with haste. She ignored Bart's shouts for her to halt as she raced toward the woods. She heard the leader order a man to go after her.

While Rollie searched for her and Ted fetched the runaway horse, Bart scoffed at the wounded Charles, "You're a fool, Avery, if you think we'll let you git away with the money."

"I don't have any money. I only wanted to get us away safely."

"You musta figured we was going to take it from you today."

Charles winced in pain. "I had the feeling you'd try. You're the fool, Bart. The Klan will hunt you down and kill you for this outrage."

"We ain't afraid of no men in silly costumes."

"You should be; they're powerful and dangerous. They'll find you. They'll make you wish you'd never had a greedy bone in your body."

"We'll tell 'em we was attacked and you was killed. If you had any money with you, we don't know nothing about it."

"Money" would be the exposing word, and Charles smiled at knowing he'd be avenged. "They'll know you're lying. You're dead men."

"Nope, you are," Bart said, and shot him twice in the heart. "Search his stuff, Kip. Let's git that money and the gal and ride outta here. We'll enjoy her in camp tonight, make her sorry she ever gave us trouble."

Kip grinned and stroked his crotch.

Bart chuckled. "Calm yourself; you'll get your turn after me."

Kip tossed Charles's things in all directions but found no money.

"He must have it on him," Bart suggested.

Kip yanked off the dead man's coat and checked it. "Nothing, boss." He searched Charles's pants pockets. "Not here."

As Bart flipped Charles over, he felt something besides flesh beneath his dark shirt. He ripped it open and grinned when he saw the leather pouch. He removed it and looked inside. "What the devil!"

"Cut a lizard in half, boss, them's diamonds and more."

Bart chuckled. "Yep, and I bet they're worth plenty. Lookie how they sparkle. Ain't they real pretty. We're rich, in high cotton."

Rollie joined the two men, looking mad and breathing hard. Slim trailed him with a bloody injury and embarrassed expression. Ted rode up with Charles's horse and dismounted. All five eyed the glittering treasure.

"Where's the gal?" the leader asked. "You got her tied to a tree?"

Rollie exhaled in annoyance. "I cain't find her, boss, but Slim's all right. She wacked him bad with a rock. Needs binding."

"Did you search real good? I got me a score to settle with her. After I finish, you boys can have yore fills, too. After we git tired of 'er, we can give 'er to some of them mountain boys if they give us any trouble."

"She's hiding better 'an a coon with hunting dogs sniffing after her. She's real smart, but she'll have to show herself soon. We'll wait."

"Yeah," Kip agreed, "we'll outwit her. I'm second with her, boys."

"Why you?" Ted asked, licking his lips in eagerness.

Kip reminded, "I was last with the other girl. She was 'bout used up when it came my turn to shoot in her. So was the two before her."

Bart looked at the gems and thought about a posse coming to recover them and the chestnut, as horse-stealing was a serious crime in the West. "With these, we can git us all the women we want, women we won't have to force to do what we want and like, women for each of us. Anna cain't git far without a horse or supplies. We'll leave her to the buzzards. Probably wouldn't be no good hump no way. Let's git moving."

Rollie didn't know how right he was, as Ginny had climbed a tree and concealed herself among branches with thick foliage. She'd shinnied up many a tree as a child and was relieved she remembered how and could still accomplish the feat with speed. She'd heard two shots and guessed what they meant: Charles Avery was dead. She had eluded Rollie but hadn't relaxed her guard. She assumed the gang would come looking for her again, and she feared their retribution. She heard horses gallop away but dared not show herself in case it was a trick to lure her out of hiding. Even if the evil men were gone, she was still in a dangerous predicament. Life had never looked blacker for her than it did at that moment.

Ginny remained in the concealing tree until late afternoon. She finally climbed down, drew her pistol, and sneaked to camp, praying the ruffians were gone. She watched and listened for another hour before assuming they had left her to her fate. All horses and gear had been taken, except for the mount shot from beneath her. She knew the bullets hadn't gone astray; the men had wanted her alive to . . . She shuddered at the thought.

The distraught female walked to Charles Avery's body, knelt, and wept for his loss. He had been a good and kind man, only a misguided and tormented one. After what he'd suffered during the war and the tragic murder of his daughter, she understood what had driven him to this desperate act. She had no way to bury him, was not even able to cover him with rocks or a blanket to protect his body from scavengers.

The Kings' horse had died during the day and she raged at the men for not putting him out of his misery. She knew that was true because Charles had three wounds to his body, the one that had felled him and two in his chest, those she had heard from her hiding place. It was obvious the men had found his concealed cache and stolen it, which was no doubt their intention all along. They had taken his money and watch, too. They had left nothing behind for her to use: no canteen, blanket, or food.

Don't panic, Ginny. You'll get out of this mess. Think.

She remembered the satchel she'd left at the river. She hurried there and recovered it. At least she had a change of clothes, soap, a washcloth, and a brush. In her pocket, she had extra cartridges. And safety matches, she realized with a smile of relief. She had the river for water to drink. She had two weapons with which to hunt for food. She had strong legs, thanks to plenty of exercise on the trail and Steve's lessons, to walk to civilization and help. It was early May, so the nights wouldn't get too chilly. The thing to remember was to stay alert and to keep moving.

You can't head northwest to Hot Springs, Ginny reasoned, *that's the way their tracks lead. You don't know where or how far away Little Rock or another town is. There's nothing back trail for miles, and if you don't stick close to the river, you won't have a water supply and you don't know how far the next one is. You could use— No, the Kings' horse didn't have any saddlebags to use as makeshift canteens.*

She couldn't think of any use for the left-behind saddle to aid her survival. She'd heard and read that Indians used animal stomachs and bladders for water containers, but she couldn't cut open the horse to do the same. Besides, she didn't have a knife.

Think, Ginny. She should get as far from there as daylight permitted. She prayed for Charles Avery's soul and began walking in a knee-high section of the Ouachita River to hide her tracks. She didn't remove her shoes and was glad she was wearing ones that laced snugly above the ankle and prevented excessive water from filling them. Her skirt tail was pulled from the back, between her legs, and looped over the waistband in the front to keep a soaked hem from slowing or tripping her.

It wasn't long before that precaution didn't matter; the water level reached her waist and then her breasts. Fortunately it was a clear blue hue that didn't cause her to worry about invisible creatures and perils. Balance was difficult and arm strain was the result during those minutes when she tried to hold her satchel over her head to keep it dry. Soon that was also futile. A few times she swam side-armed through deep areas to keep from leaving the water and giving a persistent villain a trail to find, which proved to be tricky with the satchel she refused to discard. Once she even hitched a short ride on a floating log that allowed her to rest except for kicking her legs to keep her moving. She realized her action would also deny the law a trail to follow; that couldn't be helped. She wasn't going to take any risk of being captured again.

It was dusk when she halted and climbed onto the bank where the Caddo River joined with the Ouachita. She ached all over from trudging and swimming in the river. She lay on her back for a while and rested. Her stomach growled in hungry protest.

"You'll have to wait until morning when I can hunt something to cook," she murmured as she stroked it.

Ginny used eye and ear to check the location and detected nothing to alarm her. Miserable, she stripped off her garments and bathed in the river, aware her modesty had lessened since meeting Steve Carr. She used wrung-out clothes for wiping off and donned clean but slightly damp ones. Pants would have been better for riding, but her concealed weapon was easier to get at with a skirt. She was relieved to find the satchel was waterproof, as promised by the seller, though some moisture had sneaked inside around the opening. Having brought along two skirts and shirts, she draped the water-dabbled extra set over tree limbs to dry.

Ginny felt better after taking a bath and brushing the tangles from her long hair. She braided it to prevent more during the night, then scrubbed the soiled clothes and hung them over branches to dry. She put aside her belongings, gripped the derringer in her hand, and lay down on the grass to sleep. She used the satchel as a pillow and one of her garments to cover her shoulders and arms. The heavy bag had been a nuisance to carry all day, but she might need the changes of clothes or Slim's confiscated pistol with its six bullets. Many times she had quelled the urge to toss the weapon aside and was lucky it hadn't gotten waterlogged.

At last her empty stomach and fatigued body allowed her to fall asleep. Her hand relaxed and the derringer slipped from her grasp.

Ginny heard birds singing. Her stomach growled. She yawned and stretched. Reality flooded her and she opened her eyes with reluctance to test it. She was lying on the ground beneath a tree, so it hadn't been a bad dream. She caught sight of a dark figure from the corner of her eye, shrieked in surprise, and jerked to an upright position against the tree. She gaped at the man sitting cross-legged nearby. "How did you find me? I traveled in water all afternoon."

"A Comanche warrior taught me how to move across the land without being seen and how to know somebody had passed before me even if he covered his tracks with skill," Steve explained. "Be it on dirt or in water or by foot or on horse, it matters not to me. But you did a good job, Anna. The average man or tracker couldn't have located you, or surely not this fast."

Ginny realized it was only confidence in himself that caused him to speak the truth without conceit or thought that it might sound like bragging. One thing she was certain of was that Steve possessed enormous prowess. But one thing he didn't possess was a proper greeting. There wasn't a glad-to-see-you or comforting smile in return, and she wondered why he seemed . . . almost cool and wary. His ebony gaze, as usual, was as impenetrable as a moonless night. He appeared on rigid alert that was understandable under the circumstances. Except for a tan low-crowned hat lying beside him, he was attired all in black, even down to his gunbelt and holsters. His sable hair was finger-tousled, and dark stubble grew along his jawline and above his mouth. If not for his aura of mystery and reserve, she would fling herself into his arms and cover him with kisses. "I had a good teacher, a very demanding scout. I'm happy to see you. I was afraid no one would come after us or would be misled by that false trail Rollie made."

He caught her use of the man's first name and wondered why she seemed so calm after what she'd endured. He had expected her to leap into his arms with joy and shower him with praise and thanks, and was miffed when she didn't. He was mystified by why she looked and behaved as if nothing out of the ordinary had happened. "That false trail didn't trick me for a minute. I realized in a hurry you weren't heading for New Orleans or someplace southward. Took me a while to get the news and to catch up because I waited in town for you until one. They pushed you hard and fast, but you didn't hold 'em back any. It would have helped me if you had found cunning ways to slow 'em down a mite."

Ginny asked herself if his tone and expression had bewildering edges of accusation to them. "I dared not provoke them, Steve; they were evil men. I tried not to call attention to myself. I even skipped all my customary grooming until last night. The way they were eyeing me was scary."

Steve noticed how beautiful and fresh and desirable she looked, too much so for his troubled and doubting state of mind to handle. "You've had a rough time of it. I could tell what happened back there in the last camp."

Ginny's thoughts had been diverted by her rescue and handsome lover. His remark brought back the horror of yesterday. "They killed . . . him. We tried to escape, but . . . It was awful. I didn't even have a way to bury him."

As she cried in grief, Steve pulled her into his arms. He was glad he had finally gotten a normal reaction from her. Perhaps she was in shock; he'd seen Indian and war captives act strangely upon their rescue. To get at the truth, he must be patient and sly. The telegram from Texas sparked suspicions about her, as did possible slips by her during the wagontrain journey. It was hard to believe she didn't know in advance there was no ranch in Waco, no fresh start ahead. Yet he didn't find it impossible that her own father would misuse her this way; his had deceived and betrayed him long ago. He also knew from experience that women could be cunning and dangerous criminals. He had chased, exposed, and captured a female rustler, a murderess, and a bank robber. Those vixens had done their deeds willingly and eagerly, but Anna might have been ignorant of the real situation or acting out of loyalty to her father.

Ginny snuggled into Steve's strong and protective embrace. She allowed the cleansing tears to flow for a while. She had endured a terrible ordeal, but she was safe now. Her love was holding her and was stroking her back with tenderness. After she composed herself, she asked, "What about the wagontrain? How could you leave it?"

Steve was affected by her contact, her smell, her voice, and the pain of possibly having lost her. "I put Big L in charge; he's better trained than I am."

Ginny's heart fluttered. "You left to come after me?"

He used a misleading answer. "Did you think I wouldn't?"

She looked up into his dark eyes and murmured, "Thank you, Steve. I was so scared. I tried to remember everything you taught me. Your training was the only reason I survived and was able to escape. I'll never again complain or refuse any lesson you want to teach me."

Pride flooded him from her sincere words, at least he presumed they were honest. If she was only a good deceiver, he worried, he could be wrong. "I'm glad you finally understand and accept why I was so tough on you. This untamed land can be a dangerous place, Anna."

She stared into his softened gaze and her heart warmed. "You're the best thing that's ever happened to me. Thank you for being here when I need you." She craved him so much that she couldn't stop herself from pulling down his head to seal their lips.

Steve's body flamed with a need that dulled his warring senses. In spite of his anger and doubts about this woman, he had been desperate to locate and rescue her. He had been filled with anxiety during every mile he traveled, praying he wouldn't come upon her discarded body along with Avery's, praying the gang wouldn't be so intoxicated by her beauty that they brutally ravished her. If the villains had harmed her, he would have tracked them to the end of the world and slain them, slowly and painfully as the Indians had taught him long ago. Guilt over deluding her had been his riding companion, and would be until he was certain she was totally innocent. If she was cleared, she might never forgive him for tricking her. He might never possess her again. That thought drove him to surrender to her.

Ginny's heart pounded with excitement and her flesh burned with desire. She was glad she had bathed and changed clothes last night. Steve's unspoken summons for her to yield her all to him was clear, loud, powerful, and irresistible.

He was as consumed by her as she was by him. They experienced an urgent, almost desperate, yearning to fuse their bodies into one. Their mouths meshed many times with hungry, deep, and feverish kisses. They sank to the grass, locked in each other's arms.

Steve's eager hands stroked her breasts through the material of her shirt. His lips worked over her face, her ear, and down the silky column of her throat. His tongue teased into the hollows there as his quivering fingers unbuttoned the fabric obstacle and found no chemise to create another one. His cheek nuzzled her bare chest until his mouth reached a rosy-brown peak and fastened onto it. He lingered and stroked it for a minute, then drifted his tongue toward the matching bud nearby. He lavished delight between the two mounds and caused her to moan and thrash with white-hot passion. His hand traveled downward and worked its way underneath her skirt, which had been hiked up by her movements. His fingers inched to her warm moistness, entered it, and stimulated another peak to pleasure.

Ginny was adrift on a spellbinding cloud of enchantment. She ached to merge her body with his, as the core of her womanhood demanded almost immediate appeasement. Everything he did to her heightened her hunger for him. She stroked his hair, neck, and shoulders. Her fingers wanted to clutch him tightly to her. She had feared never seeing him again. What had seemed the darkest moment of her life was becoming the brightest one. Ever so often his stubble scratched her skin, but she didn't care, if she noticed. She was too lost in the wonder of Steve Carr and the power of what he was doing to her.

Steve's mouth returned to hers. His teeth nibbled at her lips. He kissed her several times, short and light, then long and deep. Tension mounted within him. Self-control was difficult to maintain any time he touched her. Her responses and satisfaction made it even harder to master himself. His heart thudded forcefully. No challenge had ever been as potent as she was. No nourishment as filling. No experience as rewarding. No fear as great as losing her to death. She was his! For now.

Ginny clung to him, wanting and needing him fast. She savored his taste and feel. Her actions coaxed him to take her swiftly. She didn't know how long she could accept this bittersweet torment.

Troubled hearts, dazed minds, yearning souls, and ravenous bodies craved and sought comfort. Ginny relaxed her thighs as Steve's hand nudged them apart. Both trembled in suspense and eagerness. They kissed as he unfastened his pants and, with her help, slid them past his hips. Without removing her garments, she assisted him with getting through the privacy opening in her bloomers. They tingled with rapture as they were united. In minutes, they were moving almost fiercely, with Steve embraced securely by her encircled legs. Their pace was swift and rhythmic, building to a climactic and stunning release. They relaxed in each other's arms, not moving or speaking until their erratic breathing and racing hearts returned to normal.

Then Steve withdrew and rolled to his back. He didn't know what to say or do following the heated episode that had taken place so unexpectedly. "We'd best wash up," he said, trying to sound composed. "You must be starving."

Ginny also felt slightly awkward after the uncontrollable coupling. She was glad he didn't apologize for his feverish behavior, as she'd evoked it. "Your perception and skills are enormous. You see and know everything."

"I wish I did, woman," he murmured, then stood, stripped, and entered the water. After he had washed and had left it, he dried off with the skirt she tossed him. He sent her a half-smile and nod of thanks, then put on his clothes.

Steve built a fire and warmed beans while she freshened up in the river and redressed. When she finished, he said, "Let's eat and get moving. We have a long way to travel before dark."

Ginny assumed he didn't want to chat because this total privacy and recent intimacy had made him skittish again. Yet, she allowed it to tell her he must care deeply for her or he would pass it off casually. The fact he couldn't discuss it and it made him nervous misled her, warmed her heart.

After they finished the scant meal and loaded his gear, Steve coaxed them to get moving. "Mount up with me until we find you a horse," he said.

She smiled. "I'll be so glad to get back to the wagontrain."

Steve noticed she had forgotten about her father, a proper burial for him, and the brutes who had abducted her and stolen the gems. "We aren't heading to rejoin the others. I'm going after that gang."

Ginny hadn't forgotten about Charles Avery but had pushed the man and his murder to the back of her mind to avoid suffering over them. She couldn't ignore the fact there might have been something she'd done wrong that had gotten him killed. Nor did she want to think about where she would be at this moment if she hadn't escaped and Steve hadn't rescued her. "Please don't, Steve. Let the authorities catch them and punish them. You don't have to take revenge because of me. I wasn't harmed."

Steve pulled her up behind him, ignoring her words. "Hold on around my waist. We have lots of territory to cover; they have a good lead on me."

"Please don't," Ginny persisted as they headed off at a gallop to return to the last campsite to begin his frightening task. "There are five of them. They're well armed and dangerous. I have faith in your skills, Steve, but you're only one man. Don't go after them, at least not alone."

Steve's body stiffened. His voice was monotone as he revealed, "It's my real job, Anna. I have orders to go after them and bring them to justice."

Somehow Ginny knew his two words had nothing to do with being a wagontrain leader and scout. "What do you mean, it's your 'real job.' "

Chapter 12

❧

Ginny's nerves were taut, her heart pounded, and she held her breath in dreaded anticipation of his response. Somehow she sensed there was a secret and powerful reason for him coming after them that had nothing to do with his love for her or wanting to rescue her. Somehow she felt his answer was going to be detrimental to their relationship. She wanted to cry and scream before he admitted some awful and damaging truth. She waited and agonized over the destruction of her beautiful dream.

Steve could sense the fear and doubt and the tension exuding from her. With his own large measure of those same emotions chewing at him, he responded, "I have to catch them and recover those stolen gems."

Ginny told herself she shouldn't have been shocked by his reply but she was. "You know about the gems he was carrying?"

Steve surmised she would see and hear enough along the way to grasp what he was doing, so he might as well get his task into the open, here and now. He couldn't risk her distracting reaction at a perilous moment. "Yep, but I couldn't figure out where they were hidden or who the culprit was. Charles Avery had me duped good and that doesn't happen often. I figured the carrier would expose himself at river crossings while trying to protect his delivery. Your father never did. From the marks on his belly, I know where and how he hid them, but that didn't occur to me earlier."

"I don't understand, Steve. You sound as if . . ."

"I was assigned to expose the man carrying the gems, get them back, and capture him and his contacts. I was, Anna, and I'll finish my assignment now that I have a clear trail to follow."

He sounded so nonchalant about such a serious matter! "Assignment?"

"Yep. I accepted a job to solve a tricky case for the law and a friend of mine. It sounded different and challenging. It's turned out to be more trouble and aggravation than I ever imagined. For a while there, I was afraid I would fail ·this time. The closer we got to Dallas without clues, the more concerned I became. Your father was very cunning."

"But you're a scout and guide, a wagontrain leader."

"Not this time; that was Big L's wagontrain I was using for cover. He's taken over and he'll lead them the rest of the way. He kindly allowed me time alone with everyone to get acquainted before he joined us in Columbus. It was important for everyone to accept me and like me as their leader."

"Using?" Ginny murmured, and realized how many times she was echoing his staggering words, words she didn't want clarified this way.

"Yep, to catch a Red Magnolia member and stop their evil plans. Big L agreed to let me pretend to be boss of his wagontrain until I exposed the culprit. It took longer than I figured. Big L was ready to take over the moment I had to leave. I shouldn't have wasted time in town waiting for you, but I wanted to speak with you in private after getting that telegram that pointed to Charles. If I'd headed back pronto, I could have captured all of them in camp and been on my way to my next job. I'm already late leaving, and there's another cunning man to . . ." He finished *unmask*, rather than *kill*.

He sounded eager to be done and gone, even from her. This "job" explained why he had seemed so inquisitive. She had agonized over deceiving him and others and how to confess the truth when he had been doing that same thing all along. She didn't know the real Steve Carr any more than he knew the real her. "You're a spy?"

Steve had half expected her to guess accurately: Special Agent for the Justice Department. For as long as possible, he needed to keep that identity a secret. "Sort of, with this particular job. I accept all kinds."

Including gunman for hire? "Can we stop to discuss this?"

"Nothing to discuss and no time if there was. Lost too much already hanging around town to talk to you and leaving their trail to rescue you. Every minute I waste they put more distance between them and me." Steve skirted the outlaws' last camp where her father lay dead and unburied to keep her from having to endure that bloody sight again. When he reached the authorities with his prisoners, he'd report the location of the body for proper interment for Anna's sake. He already knew which direction the cutthroats had taken, so he followed it.

Alarming suspicions and realities filled Ginny. Though Steve believed she was "the culprit's" daughter and surely suspected she might be involved, he had made passionate love to her this morning. He hadn't come to rescue her. He even sounded annoyed at losing time doing so. He had come after the Red Magnolia member, the gems, that gang, and the contact in . . . "His name is Timothy Graham."

"Whose name?" Steve asked, distracted while pondering if he should apologize for the fact his last statements sounded cold and cruel.

"The contact for the arms and ammunition. The meeting place was changed from St. Louis to Little Rock, or so those men told us. I doubt they spoke the truth; they only wanted to steal the gems for themselves."

Damn you, woman! "So you knew all along. I feared as much but hated to believe such a fine lady could be involved in something so wicked."

After all they had shared, Ginny was pained by his doubts of her. How could she have misjudged him so badly, and he, her? He had beguiled her to aid his task, not pursued her from his own desire. That meant he was cold-blooded, ruthless, and would take any step necessary to help him achieve his goal. Her heart chilled for a time. "No, Mr. Carr, I knew nothing about it. I learned those things on the trail here."

The truth or a trick, Anna? "Why tell me?"

"To help you catch them and stop them from carrying out their plans."

"Why?" he asked, his neck bent to study the gang's trail.

"Because they're wrong and what they're doing is wrong."

"Including your father's part in it?"

Ginny refused to tell her traitorous lover the truth about her identity. He had lied to her, used her, and betrayed her love and trust. She had been shocked and hurt, and now she was angry. Yet she couldn't refuse to help prevent a horrible crime. "He was misguided, Mr. Carr, with what he believed was good cause. I'm sure he isn't the only one who ever made a terrible mistake." She could not stop herself from trying to evoke guilt and remorse in him for how he'd hurt her. "One of those causes was the rape, beating, and murder of my sister by a Yankee gang of so-called soldiers," she alleged. "The Loyal League-controlled courts and officials said there wasn't any evidence against them, so they went free. That was on top of losing our home, land, and business to Yankee deceits. Hate, he had reasons for it. Revenge, he craved it. Justice, he deserved it. Such things have happened to other members. But what he told me the Red Magnolias have in mind I know is wrong and can provoke worse cruelties against Southerners. One cannot fight evil with evil or hatred with hatred and win anything worthwhile. Most of the Klansmen believe what they're doing is right and necessary, but I admit there are wicked members who do things just as horrible as what Northerners and ex-slaves are doing to Southerners. I didn't know he was a Klansman or about his 'mission,' as he called it. If you don't mind, I'd rather not talk anymore. Besides, that's all I know."

Steve hoped she was telling the truth. The anguish in her voice and tragic tale she'd told moved him to say, "I'm sorry, Anna, for everything. This matter is like a powder barrel and the Klan is holding a torch ready to explode it. I have to do my job any way I can."

Ginny fought back tears. Just as she thought there was a silver lining to the dark cloud she was under, Steve had vanquished it and blackened it even more. Some of her torment was replaced by ire. "That's supposed to excuse your traitorous actions, you bastard? 'Sorry' is only a word, and I doubt you have enough good inside of you to mean it. But what can one expect from a creature born and reared as you were?"

Steve tensed. He hated the sound of those cruel words from her lips, lips that had kissed him and had hinted at loving him. He had endured too many bitter disappointments and harsh experiences in his life to suffer another one with her. He had lost her, so he must protect himself against hurt. "I warned you long ago I was a sorry bastard in more than birth."

Ginny's warring heart accused, *No denial? No explanation?* "I should have believed you; it was probably the only time you spoke the truth to me. Are you arresting me?" Was that why he had wasted time to rescue her?

"Are you involved? I thought you were trying to tell me you aren't."

His asking the question told her he wasn't convinced she was innocent. If that was how he felt after being so close to her, there was nothing she could say or do to persuade him otherwise. "No, but I doubt you'll believe me. Don't worry, I'll have no trouble clearing myself."

"That's good, Anna, because you wouldn't like prison."

"You sound as if you're acquainted with such a place."

"I am. During the war those Yanks had fun with us Rebs at their mercy."

Ginny was shocked again. He had been a prisoner-of-war. There was no guessing what horrors and abuses he had endured. That atop his troubled past had hardened him. No wonder he was so self-contained and distant. No wonder he did as he pleased with little concern for others. How could she ever understand him, trust him, and forgive him? Or forget him? "But you're working for the Union now, your past enemies and tormentors."

"Yep."

"Trapping Southerners who are mostly trying to defend themselves?"

"There's only one side now, Anna, the right one. The United States."

"And you're a patriot doing a glorious mission to save it?"

"I'm a workingman who loves challenges, not much more."

"The infernal job! No one and nothing else matters but doing it with perfection. You didn't answer: Am I your prisoner?"

"Nope, it's just not safe to send you off alone and I can't spare the time to take you to a town. You're better off with me for a while. But do exactly as I say. Both our lives could depend on your behavior and obedience. After I capture those men, I'll take them and you to the nearest town. You can decide there what you want to do next. It would probably be best to return to your aunt in Georgia. There's no ranch in Texas."

"How do you know there isn't? When did you check on it?"

"I telegraphed the man who hired me when I was in town."

"When? Which stop?"

"Does it matter?"

To her, it did, considering their intimate relationship. "Yes."

"I don't think so. Why do you want to know when and where I learned you and your father were lying to me?" He felt her stiffen and her grip around his waist tighten. He didn't want to quarrel. He wanted her to have time to comprehend what he was doing and why it was so important; he wanted her to have time to settle down; he wanted her to have time to realize she must confess anything she knew that might be helpful to him, the mission, and to herself. "Would you stop the distracting chatter so I can concentrate on tracking that gang of outlaws?"

Ginny was provoked. "Why? You're so skilled you can probably do it blindfolded! You had no trouble finding and capturing me."

He noticed she didn't say, *rescuing* me. "None at all. If they hadn't been so stupid, they could have found you first. Hush up, woman, before they hear us coming and set an ambush. I doubt you want to be taken captive by traitors to the cause again. Despite what you think, Anna, I am trying to protect both our lives. Control your anger or you'll get us both killed. Don't blame me because your father got you into this crime and I'm the one solving it. Be glad I am or you could be in worse trouble."

Ginny stayed silent after that warning, but not totally because of it. She was confused by his words and mood. She didn't know what he was thinking and feeling. In fact, she didn't know him at all. Her heart kept telling her to confess everything and see how the truth affected him. But her mind warned that would complicate matters, and would cause him to doubt and disrespect her even more.

Besides, he had proven himself untrustworthy and traitorous. She must wait and see.

Steve guided Chuune onward at a walking trot that allowed him to track the men. Anna's weight wasn't enough to be an added burden for the big and strong sorrel. He tried to keep his attention on his task, but the woman clinging to him made it difficult. He felt her, smelled her, touched her, heard her breathing, and desired her like crazy. He prayed she was innocent and honest.

Ginny was lost in confusion and anguish. *You're a hard and cold man, Steve Carr. I'm not sure I want to win you even if you beg my forgiveness. The bad instincts and feelings you've born, bred, and nourished for so long will always be stored somewhere inside you, ready to sprout and grow if the right provocation came along. I doubt anyone or anything can change you enough to . . . Let it go, Ginny. It's too late; he's seen to that. You can't trust him. I loved you so much, Steve. I wish you hadn't done this to me, to us.*

Ginny craved solitude so she could cry out her heart to alleviate the torment inside of it. She knew it would take a long time to get over this cruel experience and this elusive man. She had to be strong, brave, and work hard to succeed. Soon, they would part forever. Then she could start healing and forgetting, things she couldn't do in his presence. She had important challenges of her own ahead to distract her from him and to occupy her thoughts. She was bitter over his deluding her and she was tempted to seek vengeance. But spite and hatred were two-edged swords that could slice her more deeply than she was already cut. Besides, those wicked emotions were responsible for this bitter situation, for Charles's criminal actions, for her being here, and for Steve's troubled character. She hated the things that had made him this way, that had ruined their lives.

Don't let them destroy you, too, Ginny Marston.

The full moon that night illuminated their campsite. They hadn't halted until dark so Steve could use every ray of light for tracking. Ginny hadn't spoken to him after he silenced her, only nodded or shook her head to respond to his questions or comments. She hadn't trusted herself to speak without either crying or ranting at him.

They had stopped for a while to chew on dried beef and corn dodgers, downed with water from his canteen. They had ridden most of the time but walked on occasion for the sorrel to rest, with her on one side of the animal and him on the other. He had spoken a few times to tell her the men seemed to be riding slowly deeper into the Ouachita Mountains, and looked as if they were headed for Indian Territory. They were a day ahead of them, he had elaborated, and they might catch up in two days or less if the gang kept up its present pace and they could maintain theirs.

Steve roasted a rabbit over a spit that he'd shot, cooked johnnycakes, and perked coffee—all without asking her to assist him or looking as if he expected her to do so. Nor did she offer to help, as he was accustomed to doing his own chores and seemed to prefer it that way. It was apparent he knew what he was doing and had plenty of experience on the trail.

You're too self-contained, Steve; you don't need anybody.

After he handed her a plate of food and cup of steaming coffee, she took them and thanked him without meeting his piercing gaze.

Steve was unsettled by her silence and anguish. "So, you can still talk," he provoked. "I figured you'd lost your tongue back there."

Ginny glared at him and reminded in a toneless voice, "You ordered me to silence, remember? Since then, you haven't given me permission to talk and said our survival depended upon my strict obedience. Even if you had, I have nothing to say to you, Mr. Carr. You're a liar and deceiver."

He had expected her to feel this way, but it still got to him that she had reacted so strongly. Obviously she hated him now. "Don't worry, Anna, you'll have to endure me for only a few more days. That should please you."

"I'm sure both of us will be delighted to end this offensive matter."

His gaze narrowed as he retorted, "Is that a fact?"

Ginny determined not to let him provoke her into a silly or cutting quarrel. If he was trying to hurt her to push her away from him, she wouldn't cooperate at her expense. If he was being himself for a change, she didn't want to view that side of him. She ate her food and drank her coffee, and found everything delicious. She noticed Steve ate from the skillet and with his fingers because he had only one set of utensils and dishes. That told her the loner was not prepared for company. "You cooked, so I'll clean up the mess. It was good. Thank you."

"No need. Besides, I don't let anybody scratch my skillet. Doesn't cook good that way." He went to the stream, used sand to scrub it, then returned to grease and dry the surface. "A good skillet has to be kept conditioned. I've had this one a long time, seen a lot of things with me."

Ginny wanted to scoff, *How nice,* but she didn't. In fact, she was impressed by his many skills and the way he could take care of himself and others. Maybe she shouldn't blame him totally for the kind of man he had become. Perhaps she should blame his background and the cruel war and the many other unknown and embittering incidents. But people had endured times just as hard and hadn't become liars and deceivers and haters. *That isn't completely true, Ginny. Think about some of the people you met on the wagontrain, yourself, Charles Avery, and your own father. Everybody has a thirst for survival and battles obstacles in the only way open to them.* She certainly shouldn't have called him a bastard, as that fact was so painful; he had . . . trusted her with that secret in a moment of weakness and she had fired it at him like a lethal bullet. Why? Bad language and cruelty weren't normal responses for her.

Perhaps, she reasoned, it was because she was hurting so much and had struck out in pain. Perhaps all the untimely deaths in her life had changed her: her mother, Johanna's mother, her best friend, Mr. Avery, possibly her father, and almost herself. She had confronted so much evil and devastation since her return to America. Perhaps all of that put together was making her resentful and rebellious toward the cruelties in life and the harsh demands from fate. Soon, she would have to seek revenge on Bennett Chapman for her best friend; she had lost the man she loved; and she might not find her father alive. It wasn't fair to witness and endure so much pain. Why must it be—

Steve shook her arm to get her attention as she hadn't heard his voice. "You use the bedroll, Anna. I'll use the blanket. Take any spot you want, but not too far from me and my guns. Get settled now so I can douse the fire. We don't want it being seen by unwelcome visitors."

Ginny noticed how gentle his tone was and pretended to ignore it. "Don't trouble yourself over my comfort, Mr. Carr. I'll use the blanket or sleep on the ground. I don't want to take your bedroll." *Your smell on it will keep me awake all night and create fires I don't need!*

"I'm used to hugging the ground, Anna, you aren't. If you don't get proper rest, you'll fall out of the saddle and delay me. It's a precaution not a kindness, so you don't need to refuse out of hurt pride or spite."

Ginny wasn't convinced his tender gaze agreed with his words. Was he being nice for selfish reasons or hiding his unwanted concern for her behind feigned ones? No matter the truth, she didn't argue and refuse. It didn't take her long to confirm the reason for her reluctance: the bedroll exuded his fragrance. Its manly smell made her flushed and restless. She damned him for affecting her this way.

"Here, it'll help you sleep," Steve offered fifteen minutes later.

"What is it?" Ginny didn't reach for the cup he held out to her.

"Whiskey, enough to put you out for the night. Neither of us can rest with you tossing around like that bedroll's full of biting ants."

"Is this supposed to loosen my tongue for a confession?" she quipped.

Unnerved, Steve snapped, "You said you didn't have one to make, so I'll take your word until you or something proves otherwise. You've been through a lot recently, so I thought it would help you relax. You don't have to worry about me taking advantage of you in a weakened condition."

"You've changed since this morning? How nice for the both of us," she scoffed, grabbed the cup from his grasp, and downed the strong liquid. She choked and coughed. Her eyes widened and watered, sending tears down her glowing cheeks. Steve tried to pat her on the back, but she yanked away and glared at him. Between coughs, swallows, and ragged gasps of air, she scolded, "Damn you! I . . . can't . . . breathe. My . . . throat and . . . stomach's on fire." She drank water from the canteen he held out and recovered. "You should have warned me to sip it slowly."

"You didn't give me a chance to warn you, woman. You'll be all right in a minute. Actually it's best to get it inside fast so it can get to work. Lie down, close your eyes, and you'll be asleep in no time."

Ginny did as he suggested. A mellow feeling spread through her body. A swirling sensation filled her head that made her feel as if she were drifting on clouds. Her lids were too heavy to open and she yielded to the effects of the potent magic. She was warm and cozy and serene. The gentle hand stroking her cheek and hair felt wonderful. But the heady kiss with sweet and soft lips was even better, though she could barely respond. She let the overwhelming sensations sweep her away.

Tenderness tugged at Steve's heart, knowing all she had suffered. He was well acquainted with torment and hated that she must endure it. He owed it to her and to himself to help her avoid more. Perhaps she had made mistakes, but who hadn't? He must free her from this grim situation so she wouldn't wind up as he had. Inside, Anna Avery was a good person; she didn't deserve what could happen to her because of what her father had done. Maybe he wasn't guilty either, but it was too late to change that fact. If they had met under different circumstances and were different people . . . But they hadn't and they weren't. What he was, if or when she learned the whole truth, would kill any good feelings she had for him. He was dreaming, fooling himself, if he believed for one minute she could love and accept him. How could she, a stranger, when his own father couldn't? "Good night, Anna, you'll be safe with me."

Unable to open her eyes or think clearly, Ginny murmured, "Good night, love." She sighed dreamily and went limp.

Steve sat beside her for a while, caressing her face and touching her hair. His fingers toyed with the wisps that had escaped her braid. He hadn't been able to stop himself from kissing her. He had seen her inhaling his scent on the bedroll and suspected—hoped—that was what had unsettled her. They had made such urgent and passionate love this morning; the heady episode was fresh in his mind, yet also seemed so far in the past. He could have been kinder and easier on her today; after all, she had just lost her father.

Fathers! he scoffed. *They can be more treacherous than your worst enemy. I want to trust, you, Anna, but I couldn't stand for you to betray me and reject me like he did. I don't know what I would do to you if you did. It's best if we don't find out who's the more skilled deceiver between us.*

Ginny chided herself for being too cognizant of Steve's closeness. The constant rubbing against him, hearing his voice, inhaling his scent, gazing at his handsome face, and speculating on excuses for his actions gnawed at her nerves and defenses against him. Doubts kept working on her. Maybe he was angry, disappointed, and hurt because he believed she had duped him. Maybe his behavior and words were his own kind of defense against being used and injured. Maybe he was afraid he would lose her if she had to go to prison, which was possible if a Loyal Leaguer court tried to punish her "father" and his group through her. Would the law believe her when she said she wasn't Anna Avery? Would it matter if she weren't? She had been with Charles and they had carried off a dangerous and cunning deception. The Yankee officials might not believe she wasn't informed and involved in it. After all, she had lost much to the war. If she had to summon her stepfamily as witnesses to her identity to save her life and avoid prison, that would expose her father's lies to them. With Mathew Marston missing in Colorado and possibly dead, she couldn't call on him for help. Her life had too many entanglements that could be exposed. Charles had warned her that to tell the truth or to continue her ruse was hazardous, so there was only one thing left to do. As soon as Steve released her, she needed to get far away from this threat, to go to the Chapman ranch.

Ginny covertly watched Steve. He seemed bothered, too. While riding and obviously in deep thought, his hand had covered hers around his waist and he had stroked them unaware of his action. Another time, he had thrown his arm behind her waist to steady her balance on a downhill section, then left it there longer than necessary. She sensed his thoughts were on her. He desired her, of that she was certain. But was it only a physical craving? Was it against his will? Had he been entrapped in his ruse to ensnare her for clues? Did he care for her more than he wanted to? More than he would admit to her or to himself? How could what they shared— *Don't do this to yourself, Ginny. It didn't mean the same thing to him it did to you.* She wished her heart hadn't added, *Not yet, not that he realizes. He can't believe someone could love him and want him as much as you do.*

Steve moved quietly to keep from awakening the weary woman until breakfast was cooked. He'd been compelled to give her some whiskey again last night as a sleeping potion. Something was wrong. She was too subdued for the woman he had gotten to know along the wagontrain journey. Where were her spunk and spirit? Why wasn't she yelling at him and cursing him? Why no demand for an explanation or more information? Was she silent and tense because she was grieved over her father's loss and hurt over his and Charles's deceits, or was she only afraid he'd discover her guilt as he continued to investigate this case?

Ginny stirred and inhaled deeply. She smiled and sighed in pleasure. Odors of coffee, biscuits, and bacon teased at her nose and stomach.

Steve nudged her shoulder. "Wake up, sleepyhead, or I'll eat all of this myself. I'm starting the eggs now, so get moving, woman."

Ginny sat up and rubbed her eyes. She looked in the skillet, then at him and asked, "How? Where?"

Steve grinned and said, "I have my ways."

"There's a town nearby?" she asked.

Steve misunderstood her surprise for eagerness to be gone from him. "Nope, only a farm. You don't want to go there. There's just a man and two sons."

"Did you steal those?" she asked, nodding at the eggs.

Steve glanced at her and scowled. "Nope. Why do you always think the worst of me, Anna?" He stirred the eggs swiftly in agitation.

She knew she'd piqued him. "Isn't that what you do with me?"

He looked at her again. "I have good cause, don't you think?"

"And I don't? I would never use innocent people the way you have, pretending to like them while spying on them." Guilt flooded her as she realized that was exactly what she planned to do to Bennett Chapman in Texas.

Steve noticed her curious reaction and strange expression. She wasn't being honest with him, but at least a guilty conscience made her cheeks color and her lovely hazel eyes blink too fast. "Like you did with me for your father? Distracting me so he could carry out his wicked task? Did you two suspect an agent might be after you?"

At that unsettling moment, she didn't notice the word he used to describe himself. "That isn't true! I didn't know about this crime!"

"So you do agree and believe it is a crime?"

"Of course it is!" Ginny ordered herself to calm down. "What did you mean when you said the gems were stolen? How did the authorities know a carrier was on the wagontrain?"

Steve saw no harm in answering her. "Stolen by bandits here and in England. Special Agents added up clues, investigated, and learned of the Red Magnolias' plot. Several of them were murdered for getting too nosy. The man who hired me knew your wagontrain was the cover, what the deal was, and where it was supposed to take place. What he didn't know were the names of the men involved; the agent died before revealing them. I was told to recover the gems and unmask the villains. It sounded simple and quick, but it hasn't been either one.''

Stolen gems . . . That was why Charles Avery was in England and aboard the same ship to America! Agents murdered . . . That meant the assignment was dangerous for Steve. He could be eliminated, too.

"Why did your father fetch you from that fancy boarding school up North? Was it to use you as his cover? You two weren't moving to Texas!"

"I didn't know he hadn't bought property there." Charles had told her he had purchased a mercantile store in the town of Waco, but he had lied. On the trail, he had confessed the whole truth to her, too late.

"I know you're his daughter, not just a cunning hired accomplice."

"You do? How?"

"I checked that out, too."

Ginny knew Anna's death was a secret to Georgians, as it had taken place in another state. "Before or during the journey?"

Steve wished he hadn't exposed that precaution. "During."

"Did you check out anyone else?"

"Nope."

"Why not?" Surely others had made him suspicious, too.

Steve dished up the food and poured the coffee. "After what happened between us, the reason for my action should be obvious."

Attracted to a suspect, she mused, or something else? "Perhaps to a man like you. When did you get your answer?"

He had to learn how much she knew and how deeply she'd been involved. That was the only way to find a means to extricate her from guilt. "In Montgomery I learned you were his daughter. In Vicksburg while waiting for you, I learned there was no ranch."

Ginny took the plate and cup as she reflected on those dates. He'd checked on her after their first night together in Columbus and on both of them after their second night together in Jackson. He had suspected her and Charles but had still made love to her at the first available opportunity. His suspicions had increased, yet he did so again. After being convinced Charles was his target, he had planned — "Were you going to confront me before or after we . . . were together in Vicksburg?"

His look said *After,* but his mouth didn't reply. He had taken her again after her rescue and before exposing his task. Why? A last time before his damaging revelations terminated their relationship? Again, why?

He realized she didn't say, *made love,* and that troubled him, along with her expression. No matter what he said to justify, excuse, or explain his behavior, it wouldn't change things and perhaps would make them worse. "Things and people aren't always what they seem, Anna."

She fused her gaze to his. "I agree, Mr. Carr. I think we've both proven that to each other, more than either of us realizes."

"Enough cutting talk, woman. Let's eat and then ride out."

*　*　*

Ginny decided she would be polite and friendly today to relax Steve with hopes he would open up to her so she could learn the whole truth. She asked at one break, "How can you tell how far ahead of us they are?"

He was surprised at her question and new, pleasant mood. "Condition of their tracks shows how long ago they were made." He explained his meaning.

"But how do you know if what's a day old here will be a day old a mile ahead? What's to prevent them from backtracking and ambushing us?"

He tensed. "Backtracking? How do you know about that trick?"

Ginny told him about the novels she had read to acquaint her with the West before moving there.

Steve smiled and relaxed but didn't laugh at her. "It isn't like that out here. Now would you mind telling me what happened in that last campsite? I haven't wanted to ask while your pain was too fresh."

Ginny related not only the episode there but all that occurred along the way since her kidnapping. She saw him paying close attention to her.

"I'm impressed, Anna. How did you learn to climb trees?"

"When I was a child. And I have you to thank for the other skills that saved my life. Despite the trouble between us, I am grateful to you for that."

He mellowed and warmed. "You used them well."

"Including the derringer you gave me."

"Are you wearing it now?" She trembled when he touched her leg.

"All the time, as you ordered, Steve. Afraid I'll pull it on you?"

He caught the switch to his first name. "That wouldn't be smart and you're no fool. I'm your only hope of getting out of here alive."

"I know, so I'll behave myself."

Steve grinned and chuckled. "I'm glad to hear that, woman."

"Were you around camp long after I left?"

"Worried about what your new friends might think about you?"

"Yes."

"Don't be; they like you and believe you were abducted."

"But you don't?"

Steve decided he should lighten up on her. "Actually, Anna, I do. I believe your father was, too." At her look of astonishment, he added, "Villains often betray each other. If they were good men, they wouldn't be doing what they do. That gang came after you two early just to rob you. They would have shot up the camp and taken you by force if you had both refused to leave with them. You saved innocent lives by complying and placing your own in danger. But that still doesn't excuse what your father was planning to do, what he would have done if he hadn't been killed. Even if you were involved or involved only as his cover, I'll release you soon as a reward for your unselfish actions in camp."

Ginny was dismayed that he continued to harbor doubts about her. She couldn't persuade him he was wrong without revealing secrets about herself, secrets she didn't trust him with yet. Surely it would be worse if he suspected she was a habitual deceiver. Later, she would send him a letter explaining the truth and telling him her whereabouts in case he wanted to find her; she would send it in care of the wagontrain company. If he had gotten in contact with Luther Beams and they were close enough to do this task together, surely Luther would know where and how to find Steve. By that time, they would know how they felt about each other. Her intrusive challenges would be finished one way or another. If for no other reason, she would contact him to tell him how mistaken he had been.

They halted at dusk, close enough to overtake the gang the next day. In the last fading light of day, Steve scouted the area to make certain his assumptions were correct. He learned that no one was within striking distance of their campsite, north of Mena, a town of sparse population. They had encountered many streams, a few springs, and steeper hills today. The gang was headed into the rugged terrain of the Ouachitas, unique for stretching east to west rather than from north to south as most mountain ranges did. Not far ahead was Rich Mountain, the highest peak in the oldest and largest national forest in the South. He had no doubts they would overtake the outlaws before noon tomorrow, and he was grateful she hadn't slowed him down. He had been able to conserve Chuune's strength by skirting the bases or crossing the lower sections of the highest hills. He had trained her well, and she didn't complain when the going was hard. She was a remarkable, strong, and brave woman, the kind he would want. If only . . . *Don't dream!*

Steve returned to find the evening meal ready for him.

Ginny served the fried salt pork, biscuits, beans, and coffee. "It won't be as delicious as your food, but it'll save you time and work tonight."

"Much obliged, Miss Avery," he remarked, and sat down.

"Have you ever thought of carrying two sets of dishes with you?"

"Too much trouble and not enough space. Everybody I meet has their own provisions with them. Drifters like me have to travel light and fast."

"Don't you ever get tired of staying on the move and being alone?"

"Pour me some more coffee, will you?"

Ginny knew he normally would get it himself. It was a ruse to make her forget her question while he ignored it. She "obliged" him again.

They finished eating in silence, then did the chores together.

As she took her place on the sleeping roll, she asked, "What will happen tomorrow when we catch up with those ruffians?"

Steve was lying within a few feet of her as he insisted on doing each night for protection, a pistol on either side of him. He looked at her as he answered. "You hang back and hide while I capture them."

Her gaze fused with his. "As simple as that, Steve?"

"Nothing is ever simple, Anna. Haven't you learned that by now?"

"Yes, but I wish . . ."

"You wish what?" he coaxed, quivering with desire for her. *Shu,* if things went wrong tomorrow, they could be dead before nightfall.

"I wish life weren't so hard and dangerous and cruel. There are five of them, Steve. You could be . . ."

"Killed?" Her worried gaze and use of "you" instead of "we" moved him.

"Don't say that!" she cried, then lowered her gaze from his.

Steve propped his right elbow on the ground and rested his chin on his fist. "If you stay hidden, Anna, they won't get you again."

"I wasn't worried about me. I meant, not only about me."

"Who else is there to worry about? Surely you don't care about those bastards who captured you and tried to rape you."

"Of course not."

"Then who?" he persisted, needing to hear her name him.

Ginny wondered why he was pressing her for an answer he didn't want to deal with tonight or any time soon—or perhaps never. Should she give him one more chance to recognize and accept his feelings for her, one last chance? She needed to know for certain there was no hope for a future with him. Perhaps more importantly, she needed to know if what they'd shared meant anything to him. She could always blame the potent whiskey for causing her to lose control. They could be dead tomorrow, so what happened between them tonight wouldn't matter. "I'm too tense to sleep. Can I have another drink from your bottle?"

"You're developing a bad habit, woman, depending on this."

"You're right, and I really don't want it. What I do want, is to know if what happened between us was all lies and deceptions?"

Steve's gaze locked with hers. "No, Anna, it wasn't. I care about you and want you. To ensnare you that way wasn't part of my assignment. You took me by surprise and I'm still not sure how to deal with you. As soon as this job is over, I have another important one I can't refuse. I don't know how long it'll take to solve. And I don't know where our trail could take us afterward, if anywhere. I've never ridden this road before and I'm not certain I know how. To tell the truth, I can't swear I want to ride it or *can* ride it. I'm a loner and that works best for me. And there are other things about me that can block the path between us."

Ginny watched and listened with a conflicting mixture of joy and sadness, with despair and hope, with courage and cowardice. He had sketched her a clear and honest picture. "Do they have to block the path between us tonight or until you must leave?"

Did he understand her right? "You can do better than me, Anna; you're a fine lady. I'm nothing" . . . *But a half-breed bastard who's broken plenty of laws to uphold others. I have nothing to offer you but trouble and hardship. No home, little money, and little respect from others.*

"You're wrong, Steve; you're the best man I've ever met. You have so much to give if you'll only let yourself. Until you can open up, I'm not asking for any promises. I only want you for as long as I can have you. If you must ride away, I won't try to stop you. I'll wait for you to return."

Her words touched him deeply, but he was afraid to believe and accept them; his bitter past had taught him that much. "Don't, Anna. If I leave, I won't come back. Don't ruin your life waiting for something to happen that never will; I know from experience. I'm not worthy of a woman like you, so I can't keep pulling you to me. I realize now that's wrong and cruel."

He had said, "*If* I leave." "Will that stop how we feel about each other? How much we want each other? How much I . . . care about you?"

"Don't care about me, Anna, I can hurt you more than you realize."

"Your warning is too late, Steve: I care and I hurt now." She closed her eyes, causing the pool of tears in them to overflow and run into her hair.

Steve moved to her side. He stroked her hair and kissed at the tears as he entreated, "Don't cry, Anna; I'm sorry it has to be this way." His fingers cupped her chin between them and his thumbs dried the wetness on the flesh beneath her eyes. He kissed her forehead and the tip of her nose. The backs of his fingers lightly rubbed her flushed cheeks then drifted back and forth under her chin. They wandered down her neck and caressed its silky lines. "You're so beautiful and tempting." He trembled at contact with her. He felt weak and nervous, unsure if he should proceed.

Steve's fingers halted to rest along one cheek while his thumb moved over her parted lips. When she kissed, nibbled, and teased it with her tongue, his breathing grew fast and shallow. His body burned for hers as fiercely as the hot desert sun on the sand. His pulse raced like a wild mustang that was fleeing capture across hilly terrain. His heart pounded in his ears. He rolled to his back. "*Shu*, Anna, what you do to me."

Ginny couldn't let him withdraw and stop when she was trembling with anticipation and desire. Her skin tingled and blazed where he had touched it. She wanted all of him pressed to her. With boldness, she moved atop him, looked into his smoldering eyes, and kissed him with feverish need. Her eager hands roamed over his hair, face, throat, his whole body, then her lips followed the same trail.

Steve didn't know if he should lie still and enjoy her stimulating and unexpected siege or take control of it. Mercy, he couldn't lie still, not with her warm breath filling his ear and her hot tongue tantalizing it. Her brown mane surrounded his head and tickled him. Her body fondled his with seductively squirming motions. Her mouth and hands pleasured his flesh *in all directions.* He took a deep breath of what should have been steadying air, but it wasn't, not when she unbuttoned his shirt and let her tongue circle the nipples on his hairless chest. He hadn't realized that could be arousing to a man, but it was. He writhed as her fingers explored every inch of his torso. He couldn't suppress a moan when her flattened palm drifted back and forth across the evidence of his desire. He was astonished when she unfastened his pants and dipped her hand inside them to grasp his throbbing manhood. He shuddered. His head was dazed by hunger and his body ached with it.

Ginny was too aroused to travel this new adventure slowly. She felt brave and daring. She was just as aroused as he was. All her senses were aware of how much he wanted her.

Steve could hold himself pinned to the ground no longer. He grasped her by the forearms and guided her to her back. When his quivering fingers couldn't unfasten one of her shirt buttons, to his surprise, she seized both sides and yanked, popping off the last obstacle against his approach. She hastily undid the ribbons of her chemise and shoved it from his path. His mouth wasted no time in trekking down her neck, across her chest, and to the exposed mounds that beckoned his conquest. One of his hands hurried down her thigh, grasped a handful of skirt, and lifted it so his fingers could pass beneath. He called on all of his experiences, knowledge, and skills to pleasure her and himself.

Swept to a high level of urgent desire, they united their bodies. They kissed and caressed as they searched for the ultimate pleasure, and soon found it.

In the afterglow of their shared rapture, they cuddled together and slept on the bedroll in each other's arms.

* * *

Ginny recovered the button she had jerked off in her eagerness. She had bathed, dressed, and eaten. Steve had done so, too. They had exchanged smiles and casual talk this morning, but nothing was mentioned about their passionate lovemaking. As the sun came into view, they were loaded and ready to mount, to seek the perilous challenge ahead.

Steve climbed upon Chuune's saddle then assisted her up behind him. "No talking today, Anna. I can't be distracted for an instant. We'll catch up with them around noon, whether they slow or stop."

Five-to-one odds thundered inside her head. Ginny trembled.

"Don't be afraid; I'll protect you. Just do everything I say."

"Protect both of us, Steve." She snuggled her cheek against his back and embraced him tightly. As she loosened her grip, she laughed and quipped, "I'm finished now, and I'll behave for the rest of the day."

He was appreciative of the hug. "After I let you off to hide, don't show yourself no matter what you see or hear. Understand?"

"Yes, sir," she replied, knowing she'd obey him just as she had obeyed Charles Av—She winced as she recalled that her help hadn't saved his life and might even have cost it. She knew it was futile to beg Steve to turn aside from his job. *Help us to survive today,* she prayed. *I love him and need him so much. He feels the same way about me and will admit it one day soon. Please, God, protect us.*

Steve nudged the sorrel's sides and they headed toward an unavoidable confrontation with the cold-blooded gang.

Chapter 13

THEY PASSED RICH MOUNTAIN, where the view of the forested landscape beyond looked like a rolling sea of green waves with a hazy blue veil hovering close to their verdant crests. Wildflowers in many colors and sizes grew in abundance on hillsides where tall grass was moved by breezes. Broken white clouds with dark-blue bases and paintbrush splashes dotted the sky. Though emerald and azure bodies of water in streams and ponds were visible from that height, the Ouachitas weren't that high and rugged when compared to the north Georgia mountains Ginny had seen.

* * *

Steve halted his sorrel on a densely treed hill that allowed him to see without being seen. He dismounted, then helped Ginny down. "Wait for me here. I'll return for you as soon as I can. Keep alert for trouble." When she started to protest, his fingers tapped her lips. "No arguing. I can move faster and quieter alone. If I'm not back by three o'clock, start walking northeast to Waldron; it's about twenty miles from here." He pointed to the spot where the sun would be at that intimidating hour. He placed a compass in her hand and told her how to use it to find the town.

Ginny watched him unload his gear and remove his saddle. "Why are you leaving those here? And why are you telling me how to reach civilization?"

"In case something goes wrong. I don't think it will, but it's best to be prepared for problems so you won't panic and fall into the clutches of that gang. I'll cover my trail so they can't find you. If it takes longer than I figure, I'll catch up with you on the way to Waldron. Make sure you take supplies, a blanket, and canteen with you." He nodded toward his pile of belongings and explained, "An Indian once told me to remove anything that makes noise when you're trying to sneak up on enemies. That's why I'm leaving them here, not because you'll need them if anything happens to me."

Ginny half believed him. She squeezed the compass and thought of his orders. He was showing care and concern again without being obvious. "I suppose he taught you how to ride bareback, too?"

He checked his pistols and knife. "Yep, that and plenty of other stuff I use in my work. Those tricks and skills are what's kept me alive so long."

"Let me help, Steve. I can shoot."

"You'd be too distracting. I trust your skills, Anna, but not mine with you in danger. Stay here. I mean it, woman, or you'll get both of us killed. Don't worry about me, I've done this plenty of times; have even gone after more men. They're not far ahead, so I'll return before you have time to miss me."

She stalled his departure by asking how he could tell.

He pointed to an area in the valley below their lofty perch. "Smoke about a mile away. Either they've decided to stay camped there for a while or they're getting a mighty late start today. Or maybe they're just nervous about heading into Indian Territory; they're almost sitting on its border."

"You sure that's the gang you're after?"

"Yep." Steve swung himself onto the sorrel's back. He hated to leave her behind, but he couldn't risk her life. Nor could he bring himself to admit anything rash.

Don't distract him with reckless confessions, Ginny! "Be careful."

Steve read more than a polite caution in her voice and expression. "Always, Anna," he replied huskily. "You do the same. I'll be back soon." He smiled at her and headed down the hill.

Ginny leaned against an oak and kept her frantic gaze glued to the smoke rising above the pines below. She didn't want to think about Steve getting killed. It was too far, even if she ran, to catch up with him and to assist him. He had left her this far away on purpose, as she'd told him how she'd disobeyed "her father's" orders to keep out of peril. All she could do was wait and worry, and pray she saw Steve Carr before three o'clock.

* * *

Steve sneaked toward the outlaws' camp. One man, supposedly out of sight to any visitor, was standing guard. He knew the others couldn't see either of them as he used stealth to approach and strike the cutthroat on the head with his gun butt. He bound and gagged his first prisoner: Rollie.

He slipped closer, relieved that dense underbrush concealed him. He observed the crude men, registering their names and speech patterns. It was apparent they intended to linger there at least for today, for horses were unsaddled, bedrolls were still on the ground, and a stew pot was simmering on the fire. The gang was lazing against trees while they drank coffee and whiskey. He couldn't rush four armed bandits, so he waited for an opening.

One came when Kip said, "Fry a lizard in oil, I gotta go take a grunt."

Steve made his way without noise to the spot the man had chosen. As soon as the outlaw finished, he clobbered, bound, and gagged his second prisoner. He was happy the task was being made easy for him, yet he knew it was reckless to get cocky or to lower his guard for an instant.

Mimicking Kip's voice and style of speaking, Steve called out, "Stomp a lizard's tale, my boot's hung in a foxhole! Help me, Ted!"

"Git yourself loose, you clumsy fool," came the unwanted reply.

Steve gave it another try before attacking the camp. "Lizard's toes afire, if I move, I'll fall into my grunt! Come on, Ted."

The outlaw grumbled but came to help. Steve captured his third man. He knew the others would get suspicious soon, so he prepared to take the last two with daring and hopefully by surprise. With a Colt in each hand, Steve leapt into the open and shouted, "Drop your weapons; you're under arrest." Bart and Slim grabbed for their guns, Slim's borrowed from Kip because their female prisoner had taken his. Steve wounded one in the hand, causing his pistol to drop to the ground. He winged the leader in an arm, but not before Bart got off a shot that went wild. Having disabled all five, Steve finally relaxed.

The Special Agent tended their injuries and tied them to trees. He fetched the others and did the same with them. He doused the fire and saddled a horse. "I'll be back for you boys soon." He mounted Chuune and rode to get his companion, taking along the roan stolen from Charles Avery for Anna to use.

Three shots echoed across the valley and caused Ginny to tense in fear. She strained to hear others but none came. There were five men, she fretted, so how could Steve defeat them with three bullets? Surely those vicious beasts wouldn't surrender to a verbal threat. Did that mean . . .

Ginny heard horses approaching. She concealed herself, the derringer in one hand and Slim's pistol in the other. Steve had told her long ago she could kill a man if her life was threatened . . . but could she? If it was those villains, recapture meant they'd—

"It's me, Anna. You can come out; everything's fine."

Ginny jumped from her hiding place and raced toward him. "Steve! You're all right. I was so worried. I heard three shots. What happened?"

The victorious man warmed to the hug she gave him; it kindled the desire to make love to her. This wasn't the time or place for being intimate, though, so he used nonchalance to quell the urge. He looked down into her anxious gaze as he related his tale.

"See, I told you not to worry," he said in conclusion.

Ginny wanted embraces, kisses, caresses, and tender words. She, too, realized she couldn't give or receive them at that time. She saw how reserved he was acting, how eager he was to get back on the trail as he saddled his sorrel and loaded his gear in a rush. Yet she hated to lose this opportunity, which could be their last time together. From here on in, they would have five ruffians with them. Once they arrived at their destination, Steve would take off to the other job he had mentioned. "You captured five dangerous men that easily and quickly?"

"Yep, but they weren't on guard and never got a chance to fight back."

"You amaze me," she murmured as she returned his compass and handed him a canteen to hang over the horn. "I certainly wouldn't want to be your enemy."

Steve glanced at her and grinned. "Thank you for the compliment. Now let's get moving. I don't want to lose my prisoners and have to track them down again."

As she mounted, Ginny inquired where they were heading.

"To Fort Smith, around fifty miles north of us. We should make about fifteen of those before nightfall and cover the rest tomorrow. With the terrain ahead and five men in ropes, it'll take longer than it ordinarily would. I'll turn them over to the commander there, then telegraph my boss they're in custody. He can figure out how to get them to the right prison."

Ginny had seen the long leather pouch dangling over his left arm upon arrival; he had rolled it later and packed it inside his saddlebag. "Your boss will be pleased with the good job you've done; you've recovered the stolen gems, captured the gang, and . . . unmasked the Red Magnolia member."

Steve glanced at her when she hesitated. "I'll notify the Army to recover your father's body and bury it." He said, assuming that was the reason for her unease. "You won't have to worry about being arrested, Anna, I won't mention you in my report."

Ginny leaned back in the saddle and pressed her feet against the stirrups to balance herself on the downhill slope. "That wouldn't be wise, Steve; others knew about my presence on the wagontrain. You don't want your boss to think you're covering for me for a personal reason."

"You're right. I'll tell him I investigated you and found you innocent, so I released you. He'll accept my word."

She wished he had admitted what she hoped was the truth and was slightly depressed when he didn't. "Thank you, Steve. Be assured you aren't mistaken; I wasn't involved."

"Even if you were, Anna, I'd still let you go."

That admission touched her. *Tell me more, my love.* "Why?"

"Because I like you and it would have been a mistake on your part. Either way, you've suffered enough and lost plenty because of your father's evil deed, and I'm sure you wouldn't do anything like this again."

That wasn't the answer she wanted, but she didn't press for the desired one. "You're very kind and generous."

On level ground, he suggested, "Let's pick up our pace before you swell my head with more compliments."

They reached the campsite, where five sullen men were bound. Ginny saw Bart's gaze widen in shock, then narrow and chill. She noticed the wound on his arm and the one on Slim's hand. In a way, she was surprised Steve hadn't killed any of them, and she remarked on that.

The Special Agent used the Federal Marshal rule to explain. "Men like me get paid for the number of miles we cover to capture criminals and for live ones we turn in. If we kill a target or prisoner, we don't get paid for him and *we* have to pay to bury him." The truth was, he always tried to bring in suspects alive for questioning and punishment.

"I see you got help, eh?" Bart scoffed at her.

Ginny glared at the offensive man. "The best, can't you tell? He captured all of you as easily as picking cotton from a ripe boll."

"Did he give you them gems he took from us?"

"No, they weren't mine; they were stolen. He's turning them over to the authorities to be sent back to their proper owners."

The leader sneered. "What you gonna do when we reach town and you join us in a cell, Miss Anna? Think you'll be safe from the Klan's reach? Or from the law's? One or the other will git you for what you done."

"I won't be in any danger from either side because I wasn't involved in Father's scheme or in yours. You'll hang for murdering him."

Bart feigned shock. "That's a damn lie, girl. Your pa wouldna been kilt if you two hadna gotten greedy and tried to git away with the Klan's payment. Your pa weren't the contact, *you* was. You can fool that hired man with you but you won't fool the law, and the Klan knows what you are. They'll make you pay good for trying to cheat them."

Ginny gaped at the man. "You're crazy, Bart."

"Crazy for not catching on to you afore it was too late. I don't see why you turned on us; we done just like your telegram said; We pretended to kidnap you to hide your part in this. We woulda split the gems with you two if you'da told us what you had planned. You're crazy if you think we'll keep our mouths shut and take your punishment atop ours."

Ginny realized Steve was keeping quiet and listening carefully to the brute's wild rantings. "Whatever you're trying to pull, Bart, it won't work."

" 'Cause you think the law will take a *lady's* word over ours? Once they capture Graham and he talks, your trick is up. You shouldna tried to run and we wouldna shot your horse and pa. And if he hadna tried to shoot me whilst he was down, I wouldna kilt him in self-defense."

"Self-defense? You murdered him in cold blood. You would have killed me, too, if I hadn't escaped."

"We was with you for days. We had plenty of time to kill you and rob you if that was our plan. Why would we haul you all this way to do it? When did we ever pull a gun on you or tie you up? Never! We didn't shoot till you two was galloping off with them gems the Klan needs. That's probably why Graham sent us after you two early, 'cause he knew you couldn't be trusted. You two was planning to disappear with them gems, wasn't you?"

Ginny looked at her love. "He's lying, Steve. He's only trying to save his neck by incriminating me. Besides, Bart, you made a slip; you said we telegraphed you to meet us early, then you said Graham changed the plans and sent you after us early."

"Graham sent us after we got that crazy telegram. You two musta needed us as guides and guards 'cause you had the law closing in on you. I bet you was planning to escape us soon as we got you clear of trouble."

Steve finally intruded. "You might as well hush up, Bart. I've been investigating Miss Avery for a long time; I know she's not involved. You're wasting your breath trying to trick me."

"She's the one tricking you, lawman," the leader argued. "What did she give you to git you on her side, a good roll or two in the grass?"

Steve's gaze darkened and narrowed and his body stiffened in warning. "Don't push it, Bart, or you won't make it to the Fort Smith stockade."

"Akst the boys; they'll tell you like I did."

"It would be lies like yours are," Steve retorted. "Let's go."

Ginny was relieved by those confident words and Steve's anger. Surely that meant he believed *her,* not *them.* She was glad Bart fell silent and the others didn't speak up to concur with his ruse.

They journeyed through woodland to open spaces. Steve kept control of the gang by roping their horses together by their bridles. The captives sulked and sent the quiet and alert couple lethal looks.

Ginny was tense the entire ride, fearing the law wouldn't be as trusting and generous with her as their hired man was. She prayed that Bart wouldn't continue to claim she was a Klan member and carrier and, if he did, they wouldn't believe him.

At dusk, they halted to camp on the Poteau River. Steve and Ginny prepared a meal large enough to serve all of them. They ate first, then he stood guard over the gang without cutting their hands free while they devoured their food. Steve bound them to trees to spend the night in a secure state. The couple took their places near a cozy fire to pass the dark hours in light slumber until morning came.

Ginny had noticed Steve's ability to fall asleep and awaken instantly. She also noticed that his features seemed to become hardset the closer they came to town, and she wondered why. Something she couldn't read was reflected in his gaze and revealed in the stiff way he sat in his saddle or moved about when dismounted. This shadow closing over him worried her. She wished he would explain his curious mood.

They ate a quick and light breakfast, saddled up, and got underway by seven to cover the last leg of their journey to Fort Smith, Arkansas.

They traversed more forest land and rode into open, wooded terrain, with trees scattered about. They took the Waldron Road and passed near Massard

Prairie, where Rebels had routed Union troops in July of '64 in a glorious victory. They skirted the western edge of town and headed for the fort. They arrived at six o'clock on Saturday, May eleventh.

Ginny couldn't understand why Steve was taking the prisoners to the army post at Fort Smith instead of to the town marshal or sheriff. She didn't want to query him before the captives, though, so she stayed mounted as ordered while Steve spoke briefly with an officer at such a distance they couldn't be overheard.

Ginny gazed at her surroundings. The post consisted of both two- and one-story buildings: officers' quarters, soldiers' barracks, storehouses, commissary, guard house, hospital, kitchens, bakery, telegraph office, stables, and other structures she didn't recognize. A pole about a hundred feet high with a large flag that displayed only thirty-six stars until Nebraska's would be added soon stood prominently dominant. In the open terrain, she realized it could be seen for miles, as was intended. A rock wall about four feet high encircled the fort that was nestled in a bend of the wide, blue Arkansas River. Situated on a high sandstone bluff, it was safe from flooding and could repel attacks by water. Ruins of an earlier one were visible on a nearby knoll. From the sizes and amount of structures and the number of men she saw moving about, she guessed about two thousand soldiers were assigned there. This time of day, it was quiet.

She recalled what Steve had told her about Fort Smith during their midday break, and his alleged motive for doing so. The original fort had been constructed as an outpost in enemy territory to handle problems between the neighboring Osage and "intruding" Cherokee Indians, following the "Trail of Tears" from the South. A military presence became more important in '39 when immigrants feared Indian uprisings and demanded more show of force in the area. The increase in Indians in nearby Oklahoma Territory was due to the influx of tribes from the southern states. Steve told her about a Grand Indian Council in '65 where new treaties were written to take effect last year, an action that cost the Indians half of their promised lands and was based on their siding with Confederates during the war. He related tales of glorious battles fought by the Cherokees, mostly under General Stand Waite, an Indian who was now a tobacco grower and curer.

When she had questioned him about why he was revealing so much about Fort Smith, he had shrugged and claimed she might want to settle there and, even if not, she would be there for some time while earning money to get back to her aunt in Georgia. That wasn't the answer she had expected or wanted and didn't query him further about the town or her future.

She was convinced he was well acquainted with Fort Smith; for all she knew, he could have been born and raised here. Perhaps he wanted her to stay around while he decided what to do about her. If only he'd tell her how he felt and what he wanted from her, she could make a decision about him.

Her rambling thoughts halted as the captain took charge of the gang. She was relieved Bart and the others didn't try to implicate her again before they were led toward the guard house by a detail of three soldiers.

Steve mounted and said, "Follow me, Anna. Jake told me where to find a good hotel that's reasonable and safe."

Ginny's heart fluttered with excitement, but she didn't ask him why he didn't know of one since he was familiar with this town. *Alone at last,* she thought happily. But Steve registered her at the desk and paid the clerk, then said he had to return to the post to finish his report to the captain, Jake Cooper, and to turn the stolen gems over to the commander.

"Will you be back in time to join me for dinner?" she asked, a curious sensation of dread washing over her at his reserved mood.

He didn't glance at her as he replied, "Nope, so don't wait for me. I have a lot to do tonight. Good-bye, Anna."

Ginny's heart hammered in her chest. Her pulse raced. Her throat was constricted by warring emotions. He said nothing about seeing her tomorrow or later. In fact, his last two words sounded like a final farewell. With others nearby, she couldn't question him at the desk, and he left too fast for her to follow him outside to do so.

From the hotel porch, she watched him ride down the dirt street toward the fort, and felt as if he were riding out of her life. She wanted to chase after him, declare her love, and entice an admission from him. But she couldn't and she mustn't. When he was out of sight, she went inside and to her lonely room. She didn't fail to realize this hotel was on the far end of town from the post, too far to walk if she were tempted to follow him. One of the owner's sons had taken charge of her horse and, by now, it was unsaddled and stabled. It was foolish to saddle him again and go find Steve Carr.

Don't worry, Ginny, he wouldn't desert you like this. Would he?

Ginny ate a quick meal, then took a bath and washed her hair in the water closet on the second floor. She paced her room while worrying about Steve. She pondered where he was and what he was doing and why he refused to visit her tonight. She wondered if it was because his "assignment" was over and he no longer needed her for clues, or if he truly had business keeping him away, or if he was running scared again.

Ginny prayed he wasn't seeing a woman in one of the brothels she had noticed on their way to the hotel. There was no way she could search for him, for the town was too large and unfamiliar, her hair was wet, and it was too late and dark for a stroll.

Steve Carr, she decided irritably, was exasperating! It was past midnight, so it was clear he wasn't coming to see her. She was tired and edgy and should go to bed. If there was something to learn—good or bad—she would discover it tomorrow.

Sunday at dawn, Steve mounted his sorrel and rode out of town. Once more he was heading to roam the countryside to test his prowess against criminals. He had done it for years, but the glow of excitement didn't warm him today. Long ago he had chosen to pit himself against lawbreakers and perils to prove he was a man to himself and to his father and to the others who had scorned him because he was a half-breed bastard. He hadn't chosen to be a gunslinger because he didn't want the hassle of a reputation to maintain or to be always looking over his shoulder for someone who wanted to take his place. His badge and license proved he was a man of authority, one not to insult or challenge. He had solved many cases and been praised by many government officials, so wasn't it time he accepted and believed he was worthwhile, not a nobody or a nothing? If that were true, he wouldn't have this important job, wouldn't have friends, wouldn't have tempted Anna to surrender to him.

Steve told himself he couldn't risk seeing Anna Avery before he left, as the meeting could evoke too many questions he wasn't yet willing to answer. Being apart for a while would give them time to clear their heads and to probe their feelings. He had work to do before he let her fill his thoughts and rule his actions. He had telegraphed his superior from the fort last night and had sneaked to the hotel and left money with the owner for Anna to use for her room and board and other needs. He had left a note with Captain Jake Cooper to give to her and hoped she accepted his explanation. The words he had penned to her from his warring heart drifted through his troubled mind:

> Anna,
>
> I have to leave to turn in the gems I recovered and finish my assignment in Missouri. As soon as I capture those to blame and file my report, I'll return for you. Wait for me here and don't worry about me; I've done this kind of thing plenty of times. I left you enough money with the desk clerk to pay for food and board during my absence. If it takes longer to solve this case than I guessed, Captain Cooper's wife will hire you at her dress shop in town. Stay close to the hotel and be careful. I don't want anything to happen to you. Stay armed, woman. If all goes fast and well, I'll rejoin you within a couple of weeks. When I return, we need to have a serious talk about us.
>
> Steve

They had been together almost all the time ever since they first met. He needed to put distance between them to test her pull on him. She had become his one weakness. He had to make certain his attraction to her wasn't just physical. He could accomplish that only away from the temptation of her. He couldn't stand it if she rejected him as his father had, and she might just do that after she learned the rest of the truth about him: his half-Indian blood. Too many whites hated and avoided Indians, and half-breeds were looked down on more than full-blooded Indians. Most wanted Indians killed or confined to reservations. If she had known he was worse than a bastard, she might never have made love to him. Before he revealed his intimidating secret, he had to make certain he would fight to win her, would do anything to persuade her it didn't matter. And if he was willing to go after her, he had to be convinced he wouldn't be facing a losing battle, because not once had she said she loved him and wanted to marry him.

Marry . . . That was a scary thought. If they did wed, what kind of life could they have? Where? He had so little to offer a woman who had had everything from birth. Why would she want him as a husband and the father of her children? Could he endure her scorning him? Could he find the courage before his return to Fort Smith and her to ask her to commit herself to him? Maybe the future depended upon what he learned from Timothy Graham. He was certain Bart's claims had been wild and vengeful rantings, and he prayed he wouldn't find out otherwise. *Be trustworthy, Anna Avery, or* . . .

* * *

As Ginny dressed, she reflected on the decision she had made during a restless night that included awakening many times and pacing the floor a few of them. She was going to tell Steve everything about her today, everything. Perhaps he sensed she was withholding something from him and that made him even more wary of her. If she opened up to him, maybe he would open up to her. Before things went any further between them or they went their separate ways, she had to know where—if any place—she stood with Steve Carr, the man she loved. She would confess everything. She would discover today how that information affected him and how he felt about her. She couldn't put this off any longer.

Ginny went downstairs to eat and to see if there was a message from Steve. Perhaps he was waiting for her. Anticipation and dread flooded her. *Don't let him be angry,* she prayed. *Don't let him reject me. Help him to understand and accept what I've done. Please let him feel the way I do.*

"Miss Avery, your brother left a message for you," the clerk told her.

Brother? That told her Steve Carr couldn't be from Fort Smith or his lie about their relationship wouldn't work on the man. "What is it?"

The clerk handed her an envelope. "He gave me this for you before he left town."

Ginny stared at him. "Left town? When?"

"Last night, Miss Avery," he replied, looking surprised.

"I thought he was leaving this morning. I suppose he was too rushed to wait or I misunderstood him," she said to conceal her pain.

"He said you'd be staying with us for a while. Is everything satisfactory?"

Those words calmed her a little, as she prayed the letter said to wait for him. "Yes, wonderful. Thank you." Ginny returned to her room to read the message in private. She ripped open the envelope and gaped at its contents: only money, enough to support her for a few weeks. She looked between each bill and inside the envelope once more as she felt there must be an enclosed scrap of paper with a few words. But there was nothing.

Ginny was stunned, her heart was tormented, and her mind was dazed. How could he ride away like this? No good-bye. No warning. No mention of a return. She stared at the money with parted lips and wide-eyed disbelief. She fretted that he was paying her off as some . . . *fille de joie.* Why hadn't he at least included a short note of explanation? Just a few words would have been sufficient. Gone . . . He didn't want her. He was deserting her, betraying her. He had told her he had another job waiting that could take weeks or months. He could be going anywhere, be miles away by now. He hadn't asked her to wait for him. She remembered his words on the trail; "If I leave, I won't come back. Don't ruin your life waiting for something to happen that never will." Had that been all the message he felt was necessary? He had said, "I'm sorry it has to be this way." So was she, undeniably more than he was!

After all that had happened between them, how could he do this cruel thing? He had turned in his prisoners, but what about the gems? They were worth a fortune, perhaps one large enough to tempt even an honest man, and surely a penniless drifter. Yet he had tracked and captured the gang easily and quickly like a trained expert. Was there still more to Steve Carr than what he alleged? Was there a crucial reason he couldn't expose the truth to her? How could she check out her suspicions?

No matter his motive, he had done her wrong. Anger seeped into her body and dulled some of the shock and agony. How dare he use her and discard her this way! What reason could justify his behavior? None, she concluded.

As the hours passed, she began to doubt herself and him. Maybe she wasn't what he needed and wanted. Maybe he never had real feelings for her, only lust. How could she have misjudged him so badly? Or had she? There was one place she could check for him or news of him. Until she gathered the truth, it was unfair to suspect him of wrongdoing.

Ginny went downstairs and had her horse saddled and brought to the front. She rode to the fort and asked to see Captain Jake Cooper.

The private in charge of the officer's affairs told her, "Sorry, ma'am, but he left about dawn to handle a sudden problem in Indian Territory."

"Did Steve Carr go with him?"

"Don't know any Steve Carr, ma'am."

"The man who brought in the five prisoners yesterday."

"Him? No, ma'am. He talked with the captain last night and left town. Is there a problem I can help you with?"

"Thank you, but no. When do you expect Captain Cooper to return?"

"About a week, ma'am. I can tell him you want to see him."

"That won't be necessary; I'll be gone by then. Thank you."

Ginny returned to her room. She paced and worried. *Mother, Father, Johanna, if only one of you were here to advise and comfort me.* She didn't know what to do or think. She realized she could stay there forever and he might never come back. If he needed time away from her, should she give it to him? Would that do more harm than good to their uncertain relationship? She wondered if she should go on to Texas. *Let him worry for a change. If he wants me, he has the skills to search for me and find me.* She asked herself if she should give him today, perhaps a few days, to change his mind and return. *Yes, that's only fair.* Perhaps he hadn't thought a message was necessary or had forgotten to include one in his rush to depart. Perhaps he thought she trusted him enough to realize he would come back soon. Maybe it was an innocent mistake. Surely he would grasp his oversight then send her a message by letter, telegram, or friend.

But the next day passed without word from Steve. Ginny's hope dwindled and her apprehensions increased. Her troubled thoughts and misty gaze kept shifting to the packet of money, causing her to dread its meaning. Though he had deserted her, he hadn't left her without funds for her support, at least for a while. Yet the money could have been left only to ease his conscience for what he'd done to her. But a man, a drifter, couldn't have much money to spare. Where had he gotten it? A bounty payment on the outlaws? An advance on his salary for his assignment? No matter, she could either use it to wait here for a miracle or use it to get to Texas. There wasn't enough to do both, so a difficult decision was at hand.

*　*　*

By Monday morning, Ginny had convinced herself she must accept reality: Steve had betrayed her and abandoned her, just as Bennett Chapman had done to Johanna. Now, she fully understood how her friend had felt. As Johanna had, what she truly wanted was a logical explanation and happy reunion, not revenge. Yet, it was different with Mr. Chapman. He was a father; it was his duty, responsibility, and moral obligation to love, protect, and support his own child. He owed his daughter something and she must collect that long-overdue debt as she'd sworn to do on Johanna's deathbed.

She couldn't force Steve to love her or to return to her. She couldn't do anything about his cruel desertion, as she could about Bennett's. If Steve was that kind of man, he was wrong for her. He would bring her more anguish than joy. She must put him out of her mind and heart. She must focus on her original goals of locating Bennett Chapman and Mathew Marston. It would not be simple or painless to get over Steve, but she must get him off her mind and set her important tasks in motion.

Besides, she had realized that Steve's boss, the government, might not be as trusting and lenient with her as the scout had been. Either someone might believe Bart's accusations or Timothy Graham could lie about her. She couldn't ignore the possibility that something might incriminate her. The law could come after her at any moment. There were no witnesses she could call upon who wouldn't create problems for her and her father. She needed to get to the Chapman ranch and stay there until the investigation was completed. She needed Johanna's identity to hide behind for protection of her life and freedom.

She considered telegraphing Bennett for travel money and refusing to accept Steve's, but she decided that required too long of a wait. She could repay Steve later, if she ever located him in the future. If they were fated to be together, destiny would cross their paths again. Until then, she had work to do. She mustn't spend valuable time, emotions, and energy on self-pity. She got busy on her new goal.

Ginny sent her two extra sets of clothes to a laundress. She put the money in her skirt pocket and pretended to take a stroll to view the town, as she dared not ask for directions. In spite of dirt streets and few sidewalks, she realized how large and lovely the town was. It was busy and noisy this morning, so she mostly went unnoticed. She passed many businesses and the people who worked in them, passed schools, churches, and houses she was certain were fancy bordellos.

She saw the Missouri & Western Telegraph office, but had decided against sending Bennett Chapman advance warning of her impending arrival, as a telegram could be recalled and traced. Steve had told her most of these businesses and merchants had been here before 1860 when the last census of the area was taken and listed the population at over seven thousand. She saw Federal Marshal Luther White's office, and cringed in anxiety. Steve had related information about that lawman: he had strong Union feelings and ties, had been appointed by Lincoln, and was also a doctor. Surely a fiercely loyal Union man wouldn't lean kindly toward a suspected Klanswoman. She hurried past that office.

The town seemed to be expanding to the south and east with rapid growth. She noticed construction in many locations where laborers worked with skill and efficiency. Steve had told her that outside of town were farms of all sizes. Soldiers, from the post and ex-military men from both sides in the war, were everywhere. She suspected a few of the rough-looking men were gunslingers and outlaws. She saw some Indians and remembered Steve had said the neighboring land was Indian Territory. She hoped there wasn't terrible trouble there that might delay her plans.

She halted and pretended to window shop so she could listen in on two soldiers standing nearby whose words had caught her interest.

One said, "I don't wanta be sent to Texas where them Injuns are kicking up a fuss again. Myers and his unit should be at Belknap by now."

"I thought Fort Belknap was abandoned before '60."

"It was, but Texas troops used her during the war, and the Army's using her again until Richardson is built near Jacksboro. Hell, that's only seventy miles from Injun Territory. The boys at old Fort Richardson were split up last month and sent to Belknap and Buffalo Springs. They'll all go back to Richardson when she's underway in a few months. Some of the rest of us might be sent down afterward. I sure hope it ain't me."

"Did Myers take that pretty wife of his with him?"

"Cora's to join him in the next month or so was what he said. Too bad she won't have time to get lonely and lean toward you, right, Harry?"

"Maybe she will. Being so far out of town, she hardly sees anybody. Most folks around here don't even know she's alive and out there. She'll probably need help with the farm and chores, don't you think?"

As the two men drifted into lewd whispers, Ginny left the scene. She relaxed when she saw the sight she wanted. She went into the stagecoach office and purchased a ticket to Fort Belknap for Tuesday morning under the name of Mrs. Cora Myers. She told the agent she was going to meet her husband who had been transferred from Fort Smith to Fort Belknap. She assumed the man couldn't know every soldier at the nearby post, and he appeared to believe her. While he prepared her ticket, she chatted cunningly about what she had overheard the two soldiers say. She had studied the map and schedule on the office wall while he was busy with someone else, so she knew the Oxbow Route would put her about one hundred and twenty miles from Dallas. She could either go to the Texas fort and catch a stage to Dallas from there or she could catch one to her real destination, the Chapman ranch, on a spur route after they entered the Lone Star State. The trip would require four and a half days. By Saturday night, she figured, she would be near or at the Chapman ranch, out of danger from any repercussions from her ruse as Anna Avery.

During her return stroll, she entered a nearby store and bought one simple dress for the journey ahead, all she could afford. After she reached the hotel and put away her purchase, she took Charles Avery's horse and saddle to a farm near the edge of town and sold them for less than their value. She told the happy buyer she wanted to make certain her beloved animal had a good home and she couldn't be sure of that if she sold him to one of the stables in town. Her action would make tracking her harder for Steve or for anyone else, as he could be assigned to come after her if things went wrong. There was one last precaution to take: She told the desk clerk, who was also owner of the hotel, that she was departing on a steamboat for home the next day and paid him to give a letter to her "brother" when he returned.

Ginny readied herself to leave in the morning. She took a bath and ate a good meal downstairs, her last for many days. Her laundry had been returned, so she packed her scant belongings. She hoped the wagontrain would arrive in Dallas soon so she could recover the rest of her possessions. Of course, everything could be replaced except for the doll her mother had made for her as a child. She hadn't wanted to risk losing it on the trail with that awful gang, and she would be glad to be out of the same town with them. If possible, she could see her four friends again in Texas.

Ginny looked around the room. Every precaution had been taken. The skilled Steve might be able to track her movements and locate her. If he did come after her, she hoped it was for the right reason. She thought about the message waiting for him with the hotel owner:

Dear Steve,

If I've misunderstood your motive for leaving me here without a word or note, I'm sorry, but what am I to think? I don't want to believe you would use me, betray me, and desert me in this cruel way. But it appears as if I've been paid off like a strumpet you hired to share your bed on a few occasions or have been paid off to soothe your conscience for deceiving me. Perhaps I was wrong to think there was something special between us. Your disappearing without a word tells me I was mistaken about you and about us. Perhaps you'll have a reasonable explanation when we see each other again, if we do.

I was going to confess everything to you Sunday morning, but you deserted me and took away that opportunity. I'm not convinced you'll return and get this letter, but I felt I owed you this much, although you didn't do the same for me. You'll be told soon where to locate me, if you have a desire to do so.

I can't wait around to see if you'll come back because I have an important and secret task to do. After your desertion and tricks, surely you grasp why I'm not disclosing it. In about a month or two, I'll send you a letter in care of Captain Cooper to tell you where I am. Perhaps by then, we'll both be ready to be honest about our lives and feelings. We've duped each other more than once, but perhaps there's still a chance for us to forgive each other and have a happy future together. If you care about me like I care about you, check for my message later. I'll pray I didn't misjudge you. I'll miss you.

Love, Anna

On Tuesday morning, Ginny was assisted into the brown stagecoach with its sunny yellow trim by a polite and friendly gentleman. If any passenger knew or suspected she wasn't Mrs. Cora Myers, none called her bluff. Yet her heart raced, her body quivered, and her tension increased. She heard the driver give commands to the team by words and whip. The coach jerked and creaked. She was on the way to become Johanna Chapman and would soon decide if she must be cruel or kind to her best friend's traitorous father. She was leaving Fort Smith and her misadventures behind. If only she knew if she were also leaving her love behind forever.

—— Chapter 14 ——

ARKANSAS WAS QUICKLY LEFT BEHIND. The stage crossed into Oklahoma Territory, more frequently called Indian Territory because the Osage, the Five Civilized Tribes of southeastern America, and other Indian tribes lived there. At first they journeyed near the Poteau River which caused bittersweet memories to fill Ginny's head; Their last night on the trail had been spent on the banks of that river. She didn't want thoughts of Steve to trouble her, so she distracted herself with recalling as many as possible of the often amusing rules posted at the station for Stagecoach Etiquette.

As other passengers talked with each other and a few times with her, Ginny stuck to her fabricated story. It was obvious, to her relief, that no one knew Cora Myers or her husband because nobody cast her a doubtful or suspicious glance. Nor had the three men who were riding outside: a driver and two well-armed guards.

She gazed out the window as she realized a stage journey was more bouncing, bruising, and jarring than one on a wagon. The pace was faster and more dust was kicked up because of the rapid speed and any motion was more noticeable as passengers were jostled against each other. The confines were close and tight in the small coach with its three benches. Nine people were crowded together three to each hard wooden seat. Fortunately she had one of the best seats, located behind the driver. The middle one had no back rest and those on it constantly bumped knees with those on the rear seat. With little breeze coming through the tall and narrow windows, she could imagine how the cramped interior would smell in a few days as people went without baths. She hoped it didn't rain, which would compel them to lower the leather shades and block off all fresh air.

A mixture of sounds filled Ginny's ears: luggage thudding against the wood of the coach, the jangling of harnesses and snap of a whip in the jehu's hand, the flick of reins on horse flesh. She listened to the driver's shouts as he urged the animals to a faster pace, the rumbling of wheels and pounding of twenty-four hooves against hard ground, and the voices of passengers as they chatted to while away the boring hours.

A routine was established immediately upon their departure. The half-wild horses were run at a swift pace for sixteen miles. At the end of that leg in two hours, they halted at a relay station where the exhausted team was unhitched and a new one was harnessed in less than ten minutes while the passengers stayed aboard. The process was repeated twice more until a twenty-minute lunch break and driver change during their third stop. Two more rapid runs lasted about two hours, when they halted at almost primitive home stations for the night. The schedule allowed for eighty miles travel each day with five stops. In a little over four days, they would reach Fort Belknap.

It didn't take the Kiamichi region long to become a familiar sight of mostly flat terrain with verdant bushes, trees, and grass. A little variety came by lunchtime; with scattered rocks and a scrubland look where even cottonwoods, oaks, and redbuds grew along waterlines. Hills and ridges greeted them before their third short stop where biscuits with fried meat were downed with coffee and milk. The customary meal was a rushed and almost tasteless one; taken at the station near the end of the Poteau River and south of the San Bois Mountains.

Their next stop was at Wilburton, which according to one man was notorious for sheltering outlaw hideouts in the nearby sandstone cliffs and caves. Four passengers got off and two more got on the stage.

During the last leg of the first day's travel, buffalo, deer, antelope, and coyote were seen foraging. Ginny realized what lush and beautiful grazeland they were crossing, the property of the Indians by treaty. One of the men mentioned how cattle drives passed through this area on their way to market, which reminded her of Bennett Chapman and the reluctant deception looming before her.

Ginny was relieved that no Indians, outlaws, or rustlers attacked them while traversing this perilous region. She didn't know what kind of trouble had drawn Captain Jake Cooper into this neighboring territory in such a hurry, but they hadn't seen any trouble, nor had the station keepers known of any. She prayed it continued to be safe for all of them.

Each time they halted, dust surrounded the stage and team and wafted inside the coach, causing most passengers to cough. At morning boarding, at lunch and at dusk tonight, polite men assisted her from the stage. The home station was comprised of corrals, stables and smithy for the horses, privy, and two crude shacks where the keeper, sometimes with a family and his workers, lived in meager conditions.

Following a scant meal, men slept on the floor, driver and guards on bunks, and women with the keeper's wife or in a separate room. Ginny longed for a bath and privacy. At least she had been allowed those treats on one wagontrain. That last word stirred up memories she didn't want to think about tonight, so she pushed them aside to get much needed rest and sleep.

They passed west of the Jack Fork Mountains, crossed several large creeks, and saw woods without the pines she had become accustomed to before entering Indian Territory. By the end of the second day, she learned there was little money available for feeding passengers a good supper. Mostly it was beans, corn-dodgers or biscuits, and meat the keeper had shot or trapped: antelope, deer, and rabbit which was usually cooked too long.

* * *

The third day, rolling hills didn't slow their progress as the stage skirted the highest ones. She saw where farmers were raising corn, maize, cattle, and horses. As they crossed the Red River, the Texas border, her anxiety mounted. She was exhausted and dust-covered by the time they halted for the night beyond the Gainsville stop where three passengers had gotten off and four had joined them. She longed to take a spur route to Dallas, but thought it best to continue on to her alleged stop to conceal her ruse in case the law investigated the missing "Mrs. Cora Myers."

On the fourth day, majestic mesas appeared between the east and west forks of the Trinity River. Abundant mesquite, cactus, rocks, flash flood areas, and lush grass greeted her. The lunch break was better, as it was on Main Street in Jacksboro where supplies were easier and cheaper to obtain, and three passengers deboarded. Including her, there were five left, giving them unaccustomed and welcome room in the coach.

But Ginny learned while eating that there was no town at Fort Belknap, so she'd be stranded there and noticeable to curious eyes of soldiers. Too, another stage was due at four o'clock, heading for Dallas, which was about eighty miles away. She made the decision to alter her plans. She went outside and told the Fort Smith driver, "I received a message from my husband. He wants me to await him here where accommodations are better. I'll need my satchel."

Ginny watched the noisy stage depart in a cloud of dust. She waited a few minutes, then walked to the adjoining office and purchased a ticket for her real destination as Miss Johanna Chapman. One more night on the trail, she mused, before she began her next deception.

As she sat on the porch to await her ride in an hour, doubts plagued her about her impending ruse. Perhaps it was wrong to take justice into her hands, and especially *revenge* if she discovered it was well deserved. There were terrible accusations against Bennett Chapman from the lips of Johanna's mother. Ginny reflected on them to motivate her. Stella had said it took her years to get pregnant with Johanna, then she'd dared to birth a girl as the firstborn. When Ben learned she could have no more children, especially a son, he ignored and mistreated her. She claimed he had married her only to be his "brood mare" and arm decoration. Ben had wanted a son so badly that he had adopted a ten-year-old boy who lived and did chores on the ranch. He and Ben had become inseparable. Ben had lavished all of his love and attention on the boy and he had taken a mistress. The time came when Stella could no longer accept such cruelties, so she took Johanna and left for England to be far from Ben.

Stella had told Johanna that Ben had even asked her if Johanna was his daughter and seemed to doubt she was. Ben had not forced them back home because, according to Stella, she threatened to expose all of his dirty secrets to his friends, neighbors, and even the law. Stella alleged that Ben loved his image and position and wanted to avoid a scandal so much that he left them in peace, and never contacted them again.

Ginny remembered her crying friend's painful words as they sat on the floor next to the trunk: "I was always told that Father didn't love me or want me, that he never wrote me or tried to get me back. But here are his letters to me and Mother that prove it wasn't true. If she lied about that part, perhaps she lied about other parts. I must learn why Mother left him. And why Father allowed her to take me away and keep me from him. I must seek the truth, Ginny, in America, in Texas, as soon as possible. If Father acted out of cruelty, I must find a way to punish him. If he is innocent of Mother's claims, I must tell him the truth about me and her."

Johanna's death had placed that task on her shoulders. Ginny worried over how Ben would react to "Johanna's" sudden arrival. She fretted over what Ben's adopted son would think. She had made her rash promise to Johanna in a moment of weakness and anguish. She had left Fort Smith in a moment of panic and torment. What she should have done, she now realized, was head for Colorado to search for her own father, not come here to investigate and possibly punish or hurt the father of her best friend. But she had no choice but to go on with her daring scheme, as almost all of the money from Steve was spent. Nor could she remain in Jacksboro and work to earn enough to head further west.

She eyed her surroundings. She saw the building called Old Fort Richardson, which the soldiers had evacuated. The town was rowdy and noisy but had lovely sandstone structures from local sources. Many of the businesses must have been aimed at the soldiers who had pulled out recently, but now catered to rough-looking men of questionable character. She overheard tales of Indian raids that chilled her blood and made her glad she would be gone soon. She realized the close proximity to Indian Territory and the recent uprisings were the motives for reopening Fort Belknap and for impending construction of a larger Fort Richardson, a mile outside of town. She would be happy to leave this town.

Late the following day, the coach halted at the Dallas depot. Ginny collected her satchel and walked to a small hotel she hoped was inexpensive and clean. She found it to be both and sighed in relief. Despite her dusty and wrinkled appearance, she decided to have dinner downstairs before she bathed and washed her hair, as she couldn't go into the eating area later with her long tresses wet and they required hours to air dry.

After a delicious meal, she approached the desk clerk and asked if he knew of a man named Bennett Chapman. "He owns a ranch nearby," she explained.

"Yes, Miss Chapman, a fine gentleman. Are you kinfolk?"

"Yes, I am. I'll need directions to the Circle C Ranch tomorrow." Even if the clerk recalled the name she was using, it wouldn't seem odd for her to need directions, since Johanna had left Dallas at the age of two.

The man smiled. "Mr. Chapman will be in town in the morning for Sunday services at the church down the street. You could meet him there or have a message sent to the pastor to have him visit you here."

"Thank you, sir, that's very helpful. Good night."

Ginny took a long bath and scrubbed her light-brown hair. She wanted to look her best for the meeting, and she would find that difficult enough with the simple cotton dress she had saved for the occasion.

As she paced her room, Steve Carr took lodging in her mind. There was so much distance separating them, more than in miles. It was possible that nothing and no one could change him. Perhaps they would never meet again to find out if she was wrong. Perhaps he could never be the marrying and settling down type. Maybe all he could do was take whatever was offered to him then ride away, back to his self-imposed lonely existence. He was so complex, so contradictory: good and bad, strong and weak, giving and unrelenting, and tender and tough. If only he would soften up long enough for her to—

Stop fooling yourself, Ginny; he's probably unattainable.

Sunday morning she dressed with care. She was scared, nervous, and reluctant to initiate her ruse as Johanna. She scolded herself once more for not using Steve's money to get her to Colorado, then dismissed her error, which was too late to correct. At least she looked enough like Johanna and knew enough about her best friend's life to stand a good chance of duping Bennett Chapman and the people in Dallas. She had to find a way to get money to search for Mathew Marston. From the warnings in his past letters, she dared not telegraph him in Colorado City. She was trapped; it was carry out her scheme or . . . *What?*

Ginny walked to the church down the street and took a seat near the back. Several people looked at her and smiled or nodded. She almost felt as if she were holding her breath as she quivered inside. A man across the aisle greeted a friend who had just entered. "Howdy, Ben," she heard him say.

Ginny tensed and observed, in case it was her . . . target. The man was well-dressed, nice-looking, and alone. His hair—a blend of black and gray—was combed neatly. He stood just under six feet and had a sturdy build. If he was Bennett Chapman, that wouldn't surprise her since he had carved a huge cattle ranch from a wilderness while battling Indians, inclement weather, and other perils. As the newcomer's gaze drifted over the people nearby, she noticed he had brown eyes and a gentle smile. Many furrows etched his forehead and numerous creases fanned from his expressive eyes; If this was the man she sought, Ginny couldn't guess if they'd come from an age of forty-nine, his work beneath the sun, or from painful emotions. Surely even a cold and cruel man, she reasoned, would suffer from the losses and hardships Bennett Chapman had endured.

Two older women sitting beside her shared their hymnal during the singing. After the preacher began, Ginny wanted to flee the building. The last thing she needed today was a sermon on the Ten Commandments about stealing, lying, "shewing mercy unto . . . them that love me," and honoring "thy Father": all the things of which she might soon be guilty. Yet the service finally ended the torment.

Ginny hurried outside and watched the people leave. A few stopped and greeted her, and she thanked them but didn't encourage conversation. She listened for names and heard the man she'd watched in church called "Ben" by some and "Mr. Chapman" by others. Her heart drummed in suspense and panic. She wondered if her mouth would speak and her feet would move when ordered to do so. Would a guilty conscience entice her gaze and expression to expose her bold lies? She must keep reminding herself how important this ruse and her success were to Johanna and to herself. When he finally approached a buggy to depart, Ginny walked to him and asked, "Sir, are you Bennett Chapman?"

The man lowered his leg from an attempted mount and turned to face her. His inquisitive gaze locked to her guarded one. "Yes. May I help you?"

Be direct, simple, and quick, Ginny. "I'm Johanna. I've just arrived from England. Mother is dead. I wanted to meet my father." The man was stunned speechless. He stared at her as if fearing to believe his eyes and ears. Then, his brown gaze glowed and teared.

"You're Johanna? My precious, lost Johanna?"

She commanded herself to reply, "Yes, sir, I am." She watched him look her over from head to foot. "Please excuse my appearance, as I lost my things during the trip here. This simple dress was all I could afford." He continued to stare in silence that made her nervous. "Do you doubt I'm your daughter?"

"Of course you're my Johanna. You favor your mother greatly."

She didn't read the anticipated hatred in his softened gaze or hear resentment in his emotion-choked voice. Yet she probed, "Is that bad?" She calmed a little when Ben smiled at her and shook his head. She didn't know how to respond when he hugged her and laughed merrily. She felt uneasy when he held her at arm's length and studied her with a loving gaze.

"My child, you're home at last. I feared I'd never lay eyes on you again. I don't know what to say. This is such a shock. A wonderful surprise."

He looked genuinely delighted and moved. "I hope so, Father. I didn't know where else to go. I have no money left. You're my only family. Am I welcome here?"

Ben laughed and hugged her again. "Yes, yes, my girl. I've wanted you back since your mother stole you from me so long ago."

"Stole me?"

Ben glanced around, then suggested, "Let's go home to talk. There's so much we have to tell each other."

"I'm staying at the Klems Hotel. It's all I could afford."

"But you'll come home with me, won't you? Please."

This was her last chance to back out of the scheme. "I . . . ."

"Of course you will, my only daughter. Let's fetch your things and be on our way." He looked her up and down. "You've grown into a beautiful young woman, Johanna. I'm so proud of you and so happy you've returned. Wait until Nan and Stone see you. They won't believe this wonderful news."

She feigned ignorance of those names. "You've married again?"

"No, no," he replied quickly. "Nan is my housekeeper and Stone is my adopted son, adopted before you were taken from me. Of course you wouldn't remember Nan and your brother; you were only two when Stella cheated me out of my daughter . . . What did she tell you about me?" he asked abruptly.

Ginny concluded he looked worried and scared. "Very little, Father. She didn't like to speak of you or the past, even to me."

"She's dead, you say?"

"Yes, in February, from a winter chill in the chest. I used what little money she left to sail to America. I came here by wagontrain and stage. It was horrible, but I'll tell you about my misadventures later."

"You won't ever have to worry about money or be afraid again, Johanna. I promise everything will be safe and wonderful for you from now on."

"Thank you, Father."

"Let's go home; you've been gone too long."

Ginny smiled and said, "Yes, Father, we've been apart too long."

Ginny stared at the stone arch as they drove beneath its large, encircled C. They had been riding on Chapman land for over an hour. The spread was beautiful and enormous, with fences, cattle, horses, and cowboys scattered here and there. Numerous structures came into view over a grassy hill: barns, outbuildings, corrals, and a large house.

Ben halted the horse on a verdant knoll and motioned over the terrain. "Home, Johanna. All of this will belong to you and Stone one day."

"Is my . . . brother here so I can meet him?"

"Not at present, but he'll be home soon. He's away taking care of some business. Stone's lived here since he was a child. He did a lot to make the ranch as grand as you see it. The boy needed a father, needed a family. He was so special that I adopted him when he was ten. He's like my real son, Johanna, but that takes nothing of me away from you. I hope you agree it's only fair to split the ranch with him."

Ginny wondered if Ben had indeed showered all his affection and attention on his "son" as Stella had told Johanna? Love for Stone was obvious in Ben's eyes and voice. "Of course I agree, Father. I'm eager to meet him."

"He'll be thrilled to see you. He adored you. I wish you two could have been raised together. He was sad after Stella . . . But let's forget that for a while." He clicked his tongue and the reins to continue their ride.

When she reached the house, Ben leapt down and shouted, "Nan! Nan! Come see who I've brought home! She's back! My beloved Johanna has returned to me!"

Ginny looked at the lovely fortyish woman who hurried onto the porch. Her silky black hair was in a neat bun at the nape of her neck. With her dark eyes, complexion, and hair, she looked Spanish to Ginny.

"Johanna . . ."

Ginny heard the name leave Nan's lips in a whisper of amazement. She watched the neatly dressed woman come to greet her with enthusiasm. They exchanged smiles and studied each other quickly. Suddenly Nan embraced her with what seemed to be honest joy and affection.

"It's so good to have you home again, little one. Your father has ached and prayed for your return. This is a blessed day."

"Stella died a few months past, so Johanna decided to return home."

Ginny noticed a strained look on Nan's face at that unexpected news. The woman glanced at Ben as if to see how he was taking it. The two exchanged smiles that told Ginny they were close friends.

"I'm sorry about your mother. Come inside. Tell us everything."

The woman entered the house with her satchel. When Ginny glanced at Ben in bewilderment, the man smiled and explained to her that Nan had been with the family since before she was born. She's one of us. I couldn't do without her. You'll love her."

Once inside, Ben said, "Nan, show Johanna to her room. She can freshen up there before we sit down to eat."

Ginny followed the slim woman to a room that astonished her.

Nan smiled and said, "He has kept it ready in anticipation of your return since the day you left. It's cleaned every week and redecorated every five years as things get old and faded. He wanted it to be perfect when you came home, which he always prayed and believed you would. He selected everything in here himself. Sometimes I'd find him sitting on the bed thinking about you, sometimes crying over the loss of you. He loves you so much, little one. Every Christmas and birthday he bought you a present; they're all in your drawers. He never shipped them because Stella refused to . . . I'm sorry; that isn't something I should talk about. You must still be grieving."

"I'm recovered now, but thank you for your kindness. This room is beautiful." Ginny looked at the sensitive woman and murmured, "I don't know you, Father, or this house. It feels strange to be here."

Nan placed her arm around the girl's back and patted it. "You were only two years old, so of course you don't remember us or the house. Don't worry; everything will be familiar soon. I'm so happy you've come home, Johanna. Your father has missed you so much."

"What's he like, Nan? And is that what I should call you?"

"You called me Nanna, but Nan is fine now that you're grown. You've become such a lovely young woman, Johanna. He'll be so proud of you."

Ginny wondered if Nan didn't answer her question on purpose. "Why did Mother leave him and take me away?" she asked and saw Nan grimace.

"I shouldn't be the one to discuss such matters with you. Ask him. But wait a while, Johanna, please. The past is a terrible burden he's carried for years. Let him be happy for a while. He deserves some peace, and your return can give it to him. Allow time for you two to get acquainted. Let's go join him. We have a great deal of catching up to do."

Over a lengthy and delicious meal with Ben and Nan, Ginny related all that had happened to her: her voyage to America, her ruse with Charles Avery, her abduction by outlaws, her rescue by the scout Steve Carr, and her trip to Dallas.

"The man deserves a reward if he can be located," Ben said. "With all that trouble and danger, it's a miracle you survived. You've shown real courage and cunning, Johanna, a true daughter of mine."

"Thank you, sir. It was scary at times and hard at others. That scout was tough on us during training, but his lessons saved my life and got me here. If I had known what kind of evil plans Mr. Avery had, I wouldn't have gotten involved in them by pretending to be his daughter." She related more information about Charles, his motives and his scheme to help her get through this difficult meeting.

Ben sighed. "I can understand how the war could drive a man—may Avery's soul rest in peace now—to take reckless action. We all have moments of weakness.

We were lucky the war didn't touch here much and that Reconstruction government, as they call it, doesn't give me or my neighbors any trouble."

"I'm glad, sir, because it's terrible other places. You can't imagine the awful sights and bitterness I've witnessed on the way here." She disclosed some of those things to him and saw him frown in dismay.

"I'm thankful I didn't join the fighting or see such horrors. The Lord's been good and merciful to me. He brought you back to me, with Mr. Carr's help. If we can reach him, I'll repay the money he gave you—probably a lot for a workingman like him. Tell me what happened to your mother?" he asked abruptly.

Ginny was surprised by the sudden change of subject. She glanced at the quiet woman nearby, her expression asking Ben if she should speak freely in front of Nan.

"It's fine, girl. Nan's been with me since before I met and married your mother. She's . . . like a sister to me, an aunt to you. We don't have any secrets between us; we live and work too closely for them to intrude."

From what she'd perceived so far, Ginny decided that Ben loved his daughter. He couldn't seem to take his glowing and often misty eyes off her. He smiled and laughed every few minutes as if he were releasing an overabundance of joy in his heart to keep it from bursting. That pleased, confused, and dismayed Ginny. Perhaps, she mused, his past mistakes had been the results of flaws that might have been corrected over the years. Either Ben or Stella—or both—had lied about the past. But which one, why, and about what?

"If you prefer, Johanna, I can leave the room."

Ginny realized her thoughtful silence had been misunderstood. She smiled and said, "No, Nan, that isn't necessary. Father says you're part of the family, so you should stay and listen. It's such a painful story that I didn't know if he wanted to hear it alone. I'm sure her death came as a shock to him, as did my unexpected arrival." Ginny summoned more courage to gather clues. "Please don't think badly of me, but I'm going to speak the truth, mean and ugly as it may sound. At times Mother was a confused, selfish, and impulsive woman. But you know that from experience, Father, and you must remember it, too, Nan. I loved her dearly, but she made many mistakes. It was wrong of her to leave home, to keep me so far away and out of touch, and to live as she did."

"Don't worry about speaking the truth, Johanna," Ben entreated. "We both know you're right about her. She married me because I was wealthy and successful. I married her because she was beautiful, genteel, charming, and should have made a perfect wife and mother. But what I saw on the outside wasn't like her inner self. I won't blame everything on her; we were both wrong in many ways. We were ill-suited, and it caused us both a lot of suffering. She had to be free and I couldn't hold her, short of ripping all of us apart. I kept thinking she'd come to her senses and return. I should have come and fetched you home. At first, I didn't want you trapped between warring parents, and I honestly believed a baby girl needed her mother more than her father. Despite her many faults, she was a good mother and loved you dearly. Time just got away from me. I was working hard to keep this ranch and to make it prosper. The country was getting in bitter turmoil over the slavery question; trouble was springing up everywhere all during the fifties. Then secession and war came along. I couldn't find it in me to take sides, as both were wrong."

He took a deep breath and released it before continuing. "I wasn't a coward, but I had to stay here and protect my ranch from Yankees and rustlers and land grabbers—your land one day, Johanna, yours and Stone's. I thought that if I didn't support Stella in the fancy lifestyle she loved, she'd tire of living hand-to-mouth and return home. I certainly couldn't see her working to support the two of you; she'd been too pampered. I told her I would send ship tickets anytime she wanted them. I let too many years pass without taking a stand for you. I'm sorry, Johanna, and I hope you'll forgive me. I never meant for you to go wanting, but I couldn't trust Stella to use any money I sent to travel home. How did you live over there?"

Ginny was disappointed to learn some of those facts. Ben hadn't known how they were surviving and he had the money for their support, but he had tried to use it for leverage against Stella. Yet he freely and apologetically admitted he was wrong to do so. Perhaps his intention to drive a penniless Stella home justified it in his mind. But why couldn't he have taken a month off from his precious ranch to check on his child to make sure she had food and shelter? As she had told Steve, sorry was only a word if the feelings inside didn't match it. "Mother spent all the money she took from you when she ran away. When it ran out, she became . . . the mistress of an English lord."

Ben straightened in his chair. "She *what!* Stella let my daughter see her living in sin? My God, Johanna, I'm so sorry you had to exist that way. I can't believe she would become a kept woman. She was too proud and vain. I assumed she'd married again under English law, without divorcing me."

"Mother believed he loved her and would eventually marry her, but it wasn't true. Perhaps that's why she never divorced you, in case she ever needed to return home. The older I became, the more the earl considered me an intrusion. He paid to have me placed in a boarding school in London when I was thirteen. I rarely saw either of them afterward. It wasn't bad there. I learned to become a lady and received a good education. I had a best friend who came from Georgia, she was like a sister to me; we returned home to America together on the same ship. After Mother died in February, the earl cut off my support. While I was going through her things, I found enough money to pay for my trip to Dallas. There was a letter inside one trunk from you, begging her to send me or bring me home."

Ginny saw the man tense and pale, as if in dread of what had been written in that letter. She doubted he could recall every one he had penned to her, so she told him what it said, and saw him relax. She wished it had revealed the secret he seemed to fear her learning, as his reaction told her there was a terrible mystery to be solved. "I wanted to meet you, so I came here. I suppose I can be as impulsive and reckless at times as Mother."

"You did the right thing, Johanna. The smart thing. I'm glad."

"It was scary after docking in Savannah and seeing what the war had done in America during my long absence. Mr. Avery seemed so nice and trustworthy. It was the only way I could get to Texas. The stage ride from Fort Smith was just as scary. I was afraid to telegraph you from either town, afraid you'd tell me not to come."

"How could you ever think I didn't love you and want you?"

Ginny used her feelings and worries about her own father to facilitate her answers. "It's been so long since we were separated. I don't even know you, and I didn't know you'd written me."

"We'll have the rest of our lives to get acquainted. We're together, Johanna, and I'll never let anything tear us apart again; I promise. I hope you don't blame me for your mother's wickedness and weaknesses. I know she had come to hate me and she wanted to leave me. I couldn't divorce her or deny you like she wanted me to. I kept hoping and praying she'd come to her senses, realize what she had here, and return."

For Johanna and herself, Ginny responded, "I wish she had. It's terrible for a daughter to grow up not knowing her father."

Ben finished his chilled coffee and smiled. "This has been a long and straining talk for both of us. You should rest after your long journey. We'll talk again tonight and tomorrow and for many days to come."

"You're right, Father; I *am* exhausted and this *has* been difficult." Ginny rose and left the table after smiling at Ben and Nan, who hadn't spoken during the strenuous conversation.

She entered what should have been Johanna's room and looked at her surroundings. The cherrywood furniture was of skilled craftsmanship. The floors were highly polished, with a floral rug concealing the center of the room. The coverlet, chair, and curtains were also in a matching floral design in muted shades of green, blue, and pink on ivory. A silver comb and brush lay on the dresser, along with a vase of flowers and bottles of cologne. The oil lamp was hand-blown glass, and brass candleholders were on the wall on either side of a mirror over a low chest. It was an expensively appointed and lovely room, and Ginny wished Johanna were there to see and enjoy it.

She stretched out on the comfortable bed and prayed the worst of her deception was over. Not once had either Ben or Nan looked at her as if they suspected she was an imposter. She was surprised that neither one seemed to wonder if Stella had sent her here for revenge or monetary gain. They appeared to accept her with open arms, which sent twinges of guilt through Ginny. From here on, she needed to glean clues to make her final decision; but she must work slowly and carefully to prevent arousing any suspicions. And there was one more hurdle to overcome: Stone. She hoped he would be as easy to dupe as Ben and Nan had been. Considering what "his sister's" return could cost him, he might resent her presence. *If you can see me and hear me, dear Johanna, I hope I am doing the right thing. This is so much harder than either of us realized it would be.*

Ginny turned onto her side and looked across the room. Didn't what she see and all she'd learned convince her that Ben loved his daughter and was contrite over the past? She got off the bed and went to the dresser. She rummaged through each drawer, eyeing the presents Johanna had never received, had never known about. That tragedy pained Ginny's heart. There were dolls and other toys for a child. There were necklaces, scarves, fancy ribbons, books, a writing set, expensive stationery, shawls, beaded purses, brooches, and more items appropriate for the daughter of a wealthy parent. It would have made Johanna ecstatic to have received only one of these gifts. It was cruel and spiteful of Stella to have denied them to her daughter. It was selfish and cowardly of Ben not to have made certain she did get them. How terrible to be caught between two warring parents. Yet Johanna had done well on her own, partly because of Virginia Marston. They couldn't have loved each other more or been any closer if they had been sisters. Once more, Ginny grieved over Johanna's loss.

She had to quell the brief desire to hurt Ben as he'd hurt her best friend. What was the truth about Ben, Stella, and the shrouded past? Did he truly love and want Johanna? Was she more than property to him? If not for that coin stuck in the corner of Stella's trunk, she and Johanna wouldn't have even known her father had tried to reach her and recover her many times. Had Stella lied when she accused Ben of being abusive? How could a woman who had lived in open sin for years and who had threatened to blackmail her husband with a scandal be trusted? On the same hand, how could a man who had allowed himself to lose his daughter to avoid that scandal be trusted and respected? Who would have believed the Ben she saw could be cruel to his wife and baby? Yet Ben had feared that threat enough to give up his only child. If, Ginny mused, that was the only threat Stella had held over his head. Besides, Ben had Stone, who was loved and accepted as his blood son.

"Why shouldn't my traitorous father support and protect his daughter?" Johanna had asked her. "He refused to do so years ago. He forced Mother and me into a terrible situation. He sinned, and he must pay. My Mother is dead because of him. I've lived in loneliness and fear because of him. Promise me you'll learn the truth about my father and the past. Promise me you'll make him suffer as he made us suffer. But if he isn't guilty of the things Mother said, give him a little happiness before you tell him I'm gone. Let him see and enjoy me through you; we're so much alike."

Oh, Johanna, do you realize what you asked of me? What if I make the wrong choice? What if he kills me after he learns the truth? What if Ben's adopted son doesn't want me back to share the ranch with him? This midnight secret can prove to be more dangerous than either of us imagined.

The next four days passed swiftly and more easily than Ginny had imagined they would. Ranch life was fun and interesting. She came to like Ben, Nan, the foreman, Buck Peters, and all the hands. It was clear everyone admired and respected Bennett Chapman. She enjoyed riding the range, learning new skills, and getting to know Johanna's father. But the longer she continued her ruse, the more she came to trust and admire him, to be convinced he had changed over the years, to believe Johanna would have loved and accepted him, would have forgiven him. The longer her deceit continued, the harder it became to expose the truth and the deeper she became ensnared.

Ginny was certain it would break Ben's heart to discover the cruel deception and to learn his daughter was dead. She didn't know how much longer she could go on tricking him. This ruse of daughter and father caused her to yearn for her own father. She was so worried about him. The length of time between his last letter and her departure created doubts about his survival and fears about confronting his enemies. What if she couldn't prove he had been murdered and unmask the culprit? What if the silver mine had been claimed by someone else? What if she made it to Colorado and found nothing and was stranded there? Would it be so horrible of her to live out her days as Johanna Chapman? Yes, because she *wasn't* Johanna.

If only Stone would get back so she could study the two men together; she could discover then if the adopted man meant more to Ben than Johanna did, as Stella had alleged. She had sneaked into his room once to see what she could learn about him. There were plenty of clothes in the drawers and closet of the neat masculine room—casual and dress garments. Yet she found it strange and intriguing that most of them appeared new or hardly worn. She surmised Stone had those he favored and wore most frequently with him on his trip. She held up several items and decided he was over six feet tall and had a lean build. There were no photographs in his room or in the house to tell her how he looked. But there was a portrait of Stella and Johanna hanging over the fireplace in the parlor, painted before they left home. There were many books in Stone's room, so obviously he liked to read. But she found no letters or keepsakes to reveal more about him.

She had noticed that Ben and Nan didn't talk about Stone. When she'd asked questions about him, they had told her they wanted her to meet him and form her own opinion. She thought that odd since he was "her brother" and Ben's acclaimed "joy and delight," according to Stella.

Ginny had ceased asking any questions and just observed. She knew Ben's room was on one end of the bottom floor of the two-story house and Nan's was on the other. No woman had ever been mentioned by anyone. Ginny wondered if he had a lady friend nearby as he didn't leave home except to ride with his hands. If Stella had told the truth about his lusty diversions, perhaps he no longer enjoyed them at his age.

Too, Ben could have become romantically interested in Nan over the years, living in such close proximity with her for so long. Ginny suspected Nan had a deeper and stronger affection for Ben than a cook and housekeeper who was like a "sister" to him would normally possess. Sometimes she caught Nan gazing at Ben with what appeared to be love and desire in her eyes. Now that Ben was free, perhaps they could explore their feelings. That would be romantic, Ginny decided with a smile.

Love and romance . . . Where had they gotten her? Into pain and loneliness, she replied to herself. *Where are you, Steve? Do you miss me as much as I miss you, or at all? Have you even returned to Fort Smith to check on me? Should I write or telegraph you, tell you where I am? No, not yet . . . as soon as I finish my task here. I love you and want you so much. Please feel the same way about me.*

Friday, news came that the wagontrain from Georgia had arrived in town. Ben persuaded her to let the boys recover her possessions to prevent friends of the outlaws from discovering her whereabouts and coming to seek revenge on her for helping to capture them. She sent letters to Lucy, Mary, Ruby, and Ellie. She explained the "truth" to them and asked for their addresses to write them in the future. She hated not seeing them a last time, but Ben's advice seemed wise.

When Justin "Buck" Peters returned with her possessions, Ginny thanked the foreman. She hurried to her room to read notes from her four friends with whom she had shared so much. Steve hadn't returned to the wagontrain, and the journey from Vicksburg had passed without trouble.

Ginny unpacked her clothes, and Nan helped her put them away. She lay her prized doll on the bed, her heart overjoyed by its safe return. She told Nan it was a gift from a friend at school, and the woman believed her.

As Ginny dressed for dinner, she thought of the money in the drawer nearby. Ben had given it to her so his "Johanna" wouldn't feel vulnerable again as she had since "her mother's death." Ginny knew it was a sufficient sum to buy a stage ticket to Colorado City, as she'd asked the agent the amount in Dallas before leaving the station. She had given Ben six days of happiness and release from his tormenting guilt. She couldn't punish him for his past deeds because she didn't believe he deserved it, as he had whipped himself enough over the years for his mistakes. Ben would have Nan and his "son" to comfort him after he learned the awful truth of his daughter's death. What reason did she have to stay on the ranch a day longer? She had fulfilled her midnight secret to Johanna as best she could. She had her friend's letter to back up her claims. Why stay?

The following morning told her: her monthly flow began. It would require three days to complete, three days better spent here than cooped up like chickens in a coach where baths weren't possible. Tuesday, she decided, she would make a decision about when to tell Ben the truth and when to depart, if the deception didn't cause him to throw her out instantly.

At least she wasn't pregnant, something she hadn't considered in the heat of passion with Steve Carr. How tragic and ironic it would be for his first child to be born in his father's footsteps, an embittered bastard. Love could compel people to do foolish and reckless things. But was love worth any price one had to pay, any sacrifice one had to make? She couldn't answer, considering what she had done and would do for the love of Johanna, her father, and Steve Carr.

She hadn't asked Ben why Stella had left; she would allow him to carry that damaging secret to his grave. She decided she would confess and leave the ranch next week.

At Fort Smith, the man in Ginny's thoughts and dreams was receiving grim news on his twenty-eighth birthday. Steve couldn't believe she was gone from his life. Her letter to him was bittersweet. He was angry she hadn't gotten his explanation; Captain Cooper hadn't returned until after her departure. No one had seen her leave. She wasn't listed as a boat passenger or a stage passenger. Her horse was gone. He had asked Jake if there was a soldier named Myers who had been sent to Texas, the only female traveling alone that day. He had despised hearing there was, and her name was Cora, a brown-haired woman of around twenty years.

Why, Steve worried, had she vanished? How had she done it with such cunning and thoroughness? Even with his skills, it was hopeless to track her now after so much time had lapsed. This loss, atop that of his best friend, gave him feelings of loneliness and anguish, more intense than any he'd endured before meeting Anna. She had told him he picked at his wounds, kept them raw and open, and refused to let anyone, including her, help tend and heal them. He had realized that was true. She had told him that when the right time and circumstances came along, he would be ready and willing and eager to let go of the painful past. He knew now that Anna was that circumstance and this was the time for a fresh beginning.

He admitted that his troubles had molded him into a strong man, as she'd said, even stronger than he had comprehended until she entered his life. The bitterness eating at him was destroying him, might have destroyed his only hope for a bright future if Anna decided not to contact him. Steve couldn't blame her for disappearing, as his behavior did appear uncaring and traitorous. That wasn't true. He had come to realize he loved and wanted Anna Avery. Now, she possibly was lost to him, lost because she didn't know of those feelings he'd been afraid to expose to her. He was worried about the mystery hinted at in her letter. She could be in danger this very minute and he was helpless to rescue her. Spirits, he hated that feeling.

He wondered what task she had to do, where, what lies she had told him, and what she had wanted to confess. If only he'd seen her that night before he left. If only he hadn't left her escape money or given it to Jake. If only he'd put his note in with the money. He had trusted the clerk with the cash but not with a private message he had feared a nosy person might read.

It was too late for hindsight. On the wagontrain she had reached out to him, but he had pushed her away. "You solve your problems and I'll solve mine," he had told her. He could have learned her secrets long ago if he hadn't been stubborn and defensive. She admitted lying to him in the letter so, when he found her again, she should be as understanding and forgiving as he would be with her. She loved him and wanted him; wasn't that what her message implied? The next month or two would be terrible for him, waiting and hoping she didn't change her mind. He had told Jake Cooper he would keep in touch by telegram. He could hardly wait to hear from her so he could go to her and tell her the overdue truth.

He prayed she hadn't deceived him about being involved with the Klan. Timothy Graham hadn't known anything about her when he was arrested in St. Louis, or claimed he hadn't. Surely she had been only escaping the traitorous gang when he rescued her on the trail. Surely she wasn't heading back South to aid the KKK again, to help them replace their losses, and to succeed where her father had failed. From what she'd told him, she had just motives for being vengeful. Wherever she had gone, he hoped she was safe and that he would hear from her sooner than she'd said. While he was waiting, he would take care of another tormenting matter, then complete one final job: finding and killing his best friend's murderer.

Ginny fretted over allowing twelve days to pass since her arrival without finding the courage to expose her identity and ruse to Ben and Nan. She accused herself of being a coward, afraid of causing Ben pain, afraid of leaving these happy surroundings to place herself in peril in Colorado on the slim hope her father was still alive. What if she wrote to Steve in care of Captain Cooper, told him where to locate her, and asked him to come guide her to Colorado? What if he hadn't returned to Fort Smith? What if he *never* returned to Fort Smith? What if he was dead, too, which was a possibility as he lived such a dangerous existence? Could she throw away all she had here on the ranch to chase uncertain dreams? She must, as she had no right to Johanna's life. She had given Charles joy by playing his Anna. She had given Ben joy by playing his Johanna. It was her father's turn to receive joy. Both deceptions had been trouble and anguish. It was time to be herself.

Tomorrow, she would go into town and send Steve a telegram. She would pray she meant enough to him for him to come help her out of this predicament. As soon as she heard from him or he arrived, she would tell Ben everything and hope he forgave her.

She continued to dress for dinner, one of the most enjoyable times of the day. Yet she was apprehensive and didn't know why.

Ben smiled and said, "Stone, you're finally back, Son. I have a surprise for you; your sister's returned from England. And Stella is dead."

The younger man looked stunned. "Johanna's here?"

"Yep, and she's beautiful. You don't have to worry; I told you half of this ranch is yours when I die. Nothing can change that; it's in my will."

Stone saw the glow in his father's eyes. He had to struggle not to let bitterness storm through him. "Did you tell her about me?" He watched Ben lower his head in shame. Well-deserved, he decided.

"No, Son, and you know why I can't. Please understand."

"Protection of the Chapman name is the most important thing to you," Stone accused. "Not me or Mother or your precious Johanna."

"It's your name, too, Son. You don't want it stained, either."

"Mine by adoption only. I'd rather have it the right way. Being your half heir isn't as important as people knowing what blood runs in my veins. All my life I've had to lie about who and what I am. How can you say you love me and want me when you've denied me since birth, when you made me a bastard in everyone's eyes? My mother has loved you and served you for almost thirty years. Even after Stella found out about us and left, you still refused to marry her. Now that she's dead, you'll probably still find excuses not to do it. Yet you claim you love her and want her, too."

Stone closed the distance between them to tower over his slump-shouldered father. He knew he was hurting the man, but he couldn't stop himself, as he wanted to open Ben's eyes. Now that he knew what love was, he had ammunition to fire at the man who had denied and hurt him and his mother, had hurt Johanna and *her* mother. First he had to wound his father, then help heal that injury for all their sakes. "How could a decent man take two women to his bed at the same time? You selfishly and cruelly used both of them, Father. You've cheated all of us. You still don't think Mother is good enough to be Mrs. Bennett Chapman because she's Apache, enemy and scourge of the whites. Because I carry your blood, I'm good enough to be adopted and to inherit half of your ranch, but because my mother is Indian and I'm a half-breed I don't deserve for people to know I'm your son, that I have the Chapman name by right of birth and blood. I loved you. I worked for you and with you for years. I would have done anything for you. I wouldn't have known the truth about myself if I hadn't overheard you and Stella quarrel that day because you'd have never told me. For the rest of my miserable life, you'd have let me think I was the bastard of an Indian . . ." He could never call his beloved mother a whore as most had whispered but never dared to say aloud because she was under the protection of Bennett Chapman. "I even had to pretend she wasn't my mother so no one would guess the truth about you two. That isn't fair, Father. Can't you understand that?"

"I've hurt you worse than I realized, Stone, and I'm deeply sorry. But this isn't the time to beat the past like a disobedient dog. Johanna will be down shortly, Son. She doesn't know about us and this isn't the time or way for her to learn that awful secret. Let's talk about this later, please."

"It is always 'later' with you, Father. Have you ever feared it might be too late for us when you decide to acknowledge me? When I have children, I want them to know who their grandparents are, what their bloodline is."

"Times and people change, Son."

"Not that I've seen, and I've been everywhere. People will always hate and reject Indians because people like you refuse to show your acceptance of them. I need peace, Father. That's why I came home, to seek it. If we can't settle this soon, it will be too late for us. Is that what you want?"

Ben looked at his troubled son. "Be patient with me, Stone. I know you're right. I've been a coward for too long about a lot of things. I love you. Let me find the best time and way to explain this to your sister before we reveal the truth to everyone. I will, Son, I promise. Soon there will be no more lies and denials. But let's drop it for now; I hear Johanna coming."

"All right, Father, one last chance." He needed a strong drink to calm his tension after the difficult talk and before a reunion with his "sister."

As Ginny entered the room she noticed the man with his back to her and his head lowered as he poured a glass of whiskey from a liquor cabinet. She tensed when she surmised it must be Stone and deceitful work loomed before her.

"Your brother's home, Johanna. Stone, you remember your sister . . ."

The man turned and his jaw went slack. His dark eyes widened in disbelief, then narrowed in suspicion. What pretense was she pulling now? How had she discovered his carefully guarded identity? What did she want from his family with this daring ruse? Force them to force him to marry her for dishonoring her? Women did that. Before he could think whether or not to expose her, he murmured, "Anna Avery, what are you doing here?"

Ginny went pale and trembled. Her heart pounded. Her lips parted. Her eyes gaped at him in shock. Her gaze slipped to the two Colts with S.C. on their butts: not for Steve Carr but for . . . Stella had lied or been wrong about Stone's age; he wasn't twenty-five! He had deceived her all along! He had made her feel sorry for him by claiming to be an embittered loner, a penniless drifter, a worthless bastard! She had loved him, believed him, surrendered to him! He was just like his father, a selfish user of women! He had told those lies to justify deserting her after they . . . Heavens above, if she truly had been Johanna . . . "You're Stone

Chapman, Ben's adopted son? You lied to me, you sorry . . ." Anger and resentment choked off her remaining word. How could he have been so cruel and cold?

"You two look and sound as if you've met before," Ben remarked.

Stone and Ginny looked at a curious Ben, having forgotten his presence during their shock. Both wondered what to say and do now.

Chapter 15

⚘

"WE HAVE, FATHER. He's the man I told you about, the one on the wagon-train," Ginny finally replied, "the one who rescued me from those outlaws during the time I was pretending to be Charles Avery's daughter. He told me his name was Steve Carr, and I believed him, believed everything he told me."

Stone realized she looked genuinely stunned to see him and to learn this news, but he hesitated to trust her and resisted believing her. He recalled how she'd invited him to come home with her, but never suspected she meant to *his* home. But she wasn't Johanna Chapman; she couldn't be Johanna; it must, his troubled mind reasoned, be another trick. "Pretended to be Avery's daughter?" he scoffed. "You're saying you aren't?"

Ben chuckled and said, "Of course she isn't, Son; she's Johanna. She told me all about her adventures with you while she was trying to get home to us."

Stone's narrowed and chilled gaze glared into the woman's eyes, which were filled with . . . panic and anguish. If she wanted him as a man, why claim to be kin? Of course, he was allegedly adopted! Was her scheme to insinuate herself into his family, win and wed him, then confess her deceit? What if the real Johanna came home and exposed her? Yet she looked so alarmed and so vulnerable, so betrayed by him. Maybe the little trickster hadn't known Steve Carr was really Stone Chapman. Could he allow her to carry out her pretense so he could have her? No, because there was a vital secret she didn't know that would prevent that. Only by exposing her could he have her, if he could trust and forgive her. "All about them, Father?"

"Yes," Ben answered, ignorant of the situation between them. He hurriedly glossed over what he had been told about the reasons she'd left England and how she'd made it home. "Saints be praised, I have you to thank for saving her life. She said you were tough on her, but we're both glad you were. Her daring ruse as Anna Avery held surprises she hadn't expected. I'm happy you were there to help her. One of those undercover jobs of yours, I suppose. It's dangerous to be a Special Agent for the Justice Department, Stone. I wish you'd give it up and come back to the ranch for keeps. We need you here, Son . . . Well, aren't you going to hug your sister?"

The last word sliced through Stone like a white-hot knife carving out his resentful heart. After hearing Ben's revelations—things only the real Johanna could know—he couldn't delude himself. When he'd told the Fort Smith hotel clerk he was her brother, he couldn't have imagined that would prove to be the case. Spirits help them, he had made love to his own half sister! Thank the Spirits she didn't know the wicked truth. Johanna believed he was adopted, no blood kin to her, so she didn't realize what they had done . . . Unless Stella had told her daughter the truth about him. If so, she knew and must be tormented to discover who Steve Carr really was.

As Ben went into deeper detail about their adventures, Stone didn't listen to the tale he already knew. He was angry and bitter that he'd finally found a woman to love, only to learn she was his sister and a future together was impossible. He had to find a way to forget his forbidden feelings for her. Worse, if she didn't know the truth, and he prayed she didn't, he couldn't tell her why he would reject her. If she had returned home for revenge or for profit, her greed and hatred had ruined both of their lives. If only they had trusted each other enough on the trail to confess their secret identities before things had gone too far between them. He had himself to blame; she had tried to confess to him several times, and he had halted her. He cursed Fate for allowing this cruel trick to be played on them. How could he accept what he had done? How could he stop desiring her? How could he forget she desired him, might love him, and might be devastated by the awful truth? He hadn't deserted her at Fort Smith as she believed, yet she planned to contact him soon. What was she thinking at this difficult moment?

Ginny wasn't listening to Ben, either; she was ensnared by doubts and questions. How could she expose her lies to her traitorous love and his deluded father? Yet anger at her ruse might soften the news of Johanna's death. She feared both men might aim their vengeance at her, perhaps have her arrested for her dishonest action, as it could be labeled fraud. If only she'd told "Steve" she was Virginia Marston. Of course that would have evoked a much different confrontation at this time. She would already be exposed by Stone. She didn't know or trust the man she loved, so she mustn't confess the truth yet, even to soothe Stone. She would leave an explanatory and apologetic letter behind when she left for Colorado. From what she'd observed on the trail, he wasn't one to dupe. After pretending to be Anna and Johanna, he'd think her a liar and greedy schemer; he'd never believe she loved him and had made reckless mistakes.

If Stone had feelings for her, he would behave differently at this moment. Being adopted, he had no reason not to reach out to her. Unless he couldn't get past the word "sister" and was worried about seducing his adopted father's daughter. They weren't blood kin, nor were Johanna and Stone, so they hadn't committed incest. Perhaps he resented her for being Johanna and for returning to share Ben's love and possessions. Maybe he didn't love her and feared she'd make demands on him. Perhaps it was only hurt pride over being fooled by her, and the belief the love she proclaimed was also a lie. She longed to reveal the truth about everything, but something about Stone compelled her to stay silent for now. Despite all he had done to her, she loved him and wanted him. There was so much she wanted to say and to ask, but not in front of Ben. She must speak with Ste—no, Stone—in private first. How could he scorn her when he was a liar and deceiver, too?

With recovered wits and poise, Ginny said, "Mr. Avery did have a daughter named Anna, Stone. What I said about her was true." She gave a partial explanation for her pretense as Anna Avery. "You know why I left Fort Smith if you returned there and was given my letter."

"I did, but you never got mine." He pulled it from his pocket and handed it to her. He quickly realized he shouldn't have, but he couldn't yank it from her grasp and evoke curiosity in Ben. "Jake Cooper had it but never got a chance to pass it along because he was called away on a mission. Doesn't matter. You're home now and safe."

Ginny was thrilled and astonished to discover he had left her a message; she could hardly wait to read it. She stuffed the paper into her dress pocket. "We'll talk later. We have a lot of catching up to do."

Stone caught a hint in her tone about what she wanted to discuss with him. He couldn't allow it, not yet. She had been duped by Avery and had been drawn to Steve while vulnerable and grieving over her mother's loss, not over that of a best friend as Charles had told him. "We'll have plenty of time to talk later."

"Maybe we should talk tonight, Son," Ben said.

Stone also caught the hint in his father's tone and gaze, and froze in despair. He couldn't let Johanna learn they'd sinned against the Bible and the law by surrendering to their feelings for each other. He'd have to convince his father to conceal their secret forever. It was ironic and agonizing that the reason he'd wanted it exposed had turned out to be the reason it couldn't: his love for this woman. He should never have lowered his guard and taken her. Spirits help him, he still loved and desired her! "No, Father, this isn't the right time to finish discussing that private matter. We'll do it at a much later date. Dead business is better left buried."

"If you say so, Son," Ben replied, confused but relieved. "You two chat a minute while I tell Nan to set another plate on the table. I'm glad you're home, Son; we can be a real family now."

After Ben left the room, Ginny and Stone stared at each other.

"Why did you lie to me?" she asked. "Was it only so you could seduce me then ride away with me thinking you were too embittered to commit yourself to me or to any woman? You have love, a family, and a good life here. All those things you told me were only to make me susceptible to your siege. You aren't a scout or hired manhunter; you're a lawman, a secret agent. You used me and betrayed me, Stone. Why?"

When tears filled her hazel eyes, he couldn't resist pulling her into his arms and telling her how sorry he was. She nestled her face against his chest, and he felt her tremble. He had to be gentle, compassionate, and comforting without confessing his love and while letting her down as easily as possible. He realized for the first time that he had honor, deep feelings, and a conscience. He was surprised to discover those traits and emotions within him. "I've never done this with a woman before and I didn't mean to do it with you. I was attracted to Anna Avery, but I didn't want to be caught by her; I tried to tell you that many times." *Shu*, it was hard to lie to her, to bring her more anguish, to touch her without kissing her, to master his craving for her. "I am a bastard by birth; I didn't lie about that part. My father has never claimed me, and Ben's adopting me doesn't make up for that denial. I don't live here and I only came for a short visit. Ben and I didn't get along. I came to settle our differences, then ride on to . . . do another job."

Ginny wasn't sure what he was telling her. She had to make him be clearer before she decided how to make her confession. "You don't understand, Stone; this is all my fault. I should have told you who I am. Things can still work out for us; we aren't kin. I want you."

Stone forced them apart. His turmoil was enormous and knifing. He was consumed by love and desire for her. He had to end it here and now. "Forgive me, Johanna, but there can't be *anything* between us. I like you and I enjoyed being with you, but that's all. I can't love you. Our little deceits with each other were painful and costly. We have to forget what happened between us; and it won't happen again, I promise. If it were anybody except you who had duped me, I would kill her. Nothing riles my temper more than lies and ruses. You're a beautiful woman and a mighty tempting one, so I couldn't resist making love to you. I shouldn't have."

Was he saying his feelings had been nothing more than physical desire? How could he speak so coldly about "lies and ruses" when he himself practiced them? She fused her somber gaze to his impenetrable one. "Then you don't feel the same way about me that I feel about you?"

Stone forced himself to reply, "No, and I'm sorry. I couldn't tell you who and what I was on the trail, but I would have returned to Fort Smith and confessed the truth. Despite how I tricked you, I didn't want you pining over me. I had to complete my assignment and make certain you weren't involved. If you had been, you could have betrayed me to other Klansmen. I sensed you were withholding things, but I never suspected what they were. If I could change what happened between us, I would. Anybody who does what I did to you for selfish reasons isn't worth dried mud on your boot. You were suffering from your mother's loss and caught up in a scary pretense, so you turned to me because you thought I was a strong shoulder to lean on. I'm not the man for you."

She had to make a last, desperate attempt to reach him. "Yes, you are. We must believe we were thrown together for a special reason. We can resolve this matter. I love you, Stone. I've loved you and wanted you since that first day in Georgia. No matter what happens between us, I'll always feel that way. You aren't and you'll never be a brother to me. I want us to have a life together, here or anywhere."

Stone feigned a scowl. "Spirit help us if that's the truth."

"It is. I know I've deceived you in the past and you have cause not to trust me, but I swear I'm telling the truth about my feelings for you."

"Forget me," he ordered. "Forget what happened between us."

Ginny caressed his cheek. "Never, and I don't want to. I love you."

Stone stepped away from her disturbing reach and touch. "Then we're in trouble. I never meant to hurt you, Johanna, and I hate hurting you tonight. You'll come to realize I'm not right for you. I don't feel the same way about you. It was physical, nothing more. Don't ever tell Father you love me and we . . . If you do, I'll leave and never return." He knew he had to leave tonight anyway to put distance between them.

Ginny winced at the cruel disclosure and his threat. Yet something urged her not to believe him. She thought, *You're home now, so I'll prove to you you're wrong about us. I'll tempt you and chase you every minute I can. You won't be able to resist me.* But if what he said was true, she best not expose herself to this dangerous man.

Ben returned and smiled at both moody people. "Nan said supper will be ready in about twenty minutes." She'd also told him she'd heard her son arrive and had been listening to their talks.

"I need to see . . . Aunt Nan a minute," Stone said, "I'll speak with you later, Father. You, too, Johanna. It's good to see both of you again." Stone left the room to visit a moment with his mother before he left for a while.

Ben smiled at the nervous woman. "Did you and Stone have a nice chat? You both look a little edgy. Is there a problem between you?"

"No, Father. We just had a tiny quarrel before he left Fort Smith. I can't blame him; he did believe I was Anna Avery and that I might be involved in that assignment he was working on with the Klan. He is miffed with me for not telling him who I am, but he'll get over that soon. We thought we'd become friends, even though we continued to deceive each other. I think that was because we both had some secrets we were afraid to expose."

Ben looked as worried as he felt. "You two aren't . . . I mean, you didn't come to like each other too much, did you?"

Ginny forced out merry laughter. "Of course not. Stone acted as hard and cold to me as his name. He was tough on me, but he's nice. I like him. I hope he'll be around a long time so we can get better acquainted."

"I hope so, too. We've had problems in the past, but we're ready and willing to make peace now."

"That's good, Father, because you both deserve it."

After a short while, Ben suggested that they go to the table.

Nan entered the dining room. "Stone had to leave, Ben," she informed him. "He's gone. He said not to worry, that he'll return in a week or two."

"Gone without a word," Ben murmured. "Is he all right?"

Nan smiled at the worried man to calm him. "He's fine, Ben. He just didn't want to say good-bye to you two. He only had a short time to visit. He's working on a very important job. He was in a rush, but promised to return very soon," she stressed. "Now, dinner is ready."

Somehow Ginny managed to eat the delicious meal and to make light conversation. She couldn't surmise why Stone had departed in such a hurry. Perhaps he needed to get away from her. Temptation or remorse? To give both of them time to adjust to and accept their real identities? At least he had said he would return soon, she could work on him then or confess and leave.

When the meal finally ended, Ginny needed to be alone. She might have found her love again, only to lose him to his unrequited emotions. She sensed a curious strain in the air, though Ben and Nan tried to conceal it. Something was afoot, she decided. The two looked worried and sad, and hadn't mentioned Stone again. Was it true he didn't live here? Was it true there were problems between the two men? Had finding her here—the blood child and other heir to the ranch—created more trouble? Perhaps Stone had given Nan a message to pass to Ben. "I'll help you clear the table, Nan. I'm exhausted tonight. So much has happened today."

"You go on to bed, Johanna. I'll help Nan."

Ginny pretended to do as he suggested, but his eagerness to get her out of the room intrigued her. She saw Ben rise to assist the unusually quiet woman. She pressed herself against the wall to listen to their talk.

"Why did he leave in such a rush, Nan? Was he upset?"

"I heard what you two said to each other before Johanna joined you. That was hard for him, *Tsine,*" she pointed out, calling him "my love" in Apache as she always did in private. "You two must make peace. You must learn to forgive, to understand, to accept each other. He's your son, Ben. It's only natural for him to want everybody to know that truth. He's had to live a lie all of his life. People wouldn't dare insult Stone Chapman to his face, but they do so behind his back. If you hadn't adopted him, they wouldn't let him sit in the same room with them. People hate Apaches; that's why you couldn't marry me, why you couldn't lay claim to our son. He needs you, Ben, your love and acceptance. This bitter life he's lived has almost destroyed him. He's reaching out to you; reach back before it's too late."

Ginny couldn't believe what she was hearing: Stone was Ben and Nan's child. Ben had adopted his own bastard son. Nan was Apache, not Spanish. Stone was half Indian, what some people called a half-breed. He knew the truth and wanted his father to acknowledge him. Ginny's eyes widened and her heart thudded. That meant Stone was Johanna's half brother and knew it. That meant he thought he had made love to his . . .

"Do you think Johanna knows about Stone?" Ben fretted aloud.

"How could she, *Tsine,* unless Stella was that cruel?"

"Stella was cruel, cold, and vengeful. She stole my daughter from me when she learned about you and Stone. She threatened a terrible scandal if I went after Johanna. Lordy, how I wanted that girl back. I loved her and needed her, just like I do Stone. I should have called Stella's bluff. I shouldn't have let Johanna suffer all those years. I shouldn't have let Stone suffer all those years. I've been a selfish coward, Nan. I should have married you and dared anybody to scorn me for doing so. How could I have been such a blind fool? How could I have believed I needed a white wife, a genteel lady? I'm partly to blame for Stella's wicked flaws."

"No, *Tsine,* she had them before she married you."

"When Johanna learns Stone is our son, she'll hate me and I might lose her again. She'll think Stella had good reason to leave a man who loved another woman and had a son with her."

"But you weren't married to Stella when we had Stone."

"But we loved each other when I married her and we've never stopped loving each other. Johanna doesn't know how evil her mother was. After she learned she couldn't give me any more children, she didn't want me to touch her again. But she let other men do it. She laughed in my face plenty of times when I accused her of what I knew was true. Every trip she made she carried on like a harlot. But she was smart enough not to be seen by the wrong people. I tried every way I could to get my daughter back: I threatened to expose her wickedness and I even tried to bribe her. I'm not even convinced she wanted Johanna, she just didn't want me to have her. Lordy, that woman was so cruel, I'm almost happy she's dead. How can I break my child's heart by telling her such things? But if I don't, she'll never understand about you and Stone, about why I didn't come after her."

"You fear Stone will tell her when he returns soon? He won't, *Tsine*, he understands why we can't reveal the truth."

"Does he, Nan? It isn't fair to him."

"You're leaving him half of this ranch. You gave him your name."

"That isn't enough for a father to share with his only son."

"Stone Thrower is a man, *Tsine*, a strong and brave man, a smart man. He accepts what cannot be changed. He told me this before leaving."

"You heard what he said to me earlier, so what changed his mind?"

"If you claim him, *Tsine*, he'll be branded a bastard publicly. Our sin and love for each other will be exposed. He only wanted to see if you loved him enough to take such risks. You were willing, so that filled his hunger. He said it would be wrong and painful to all of us for the truth to come out now. He urged me to beg you not to tell Johanna. He said he will be content to live his life as your adopted son."

"But will *I*, Nan? Stella hated him because she knew how much I loved him. She despised him because he was half Indian. Many times she tried to get me to send that 'little Injun orphan' away. That's what she called him! She didn't mind your being here because you served her hand and foot. She was jealous of every minute Stone and I spent together."

"Which were many, *Tsine*; Stone Thrower was like your shadow."

"He loved me so much before he learned of my deceit."

"He still loves you. If not, he wouldn't keep returning."

"Every time he leaves home, I miss him. I hope he returns for good, and he and Johanna get along."

"They did as children. No matter what Stella thought or said, you didn't give one child more love and attention than the other."

"I kept thinking if I let Stella have her way, she'd relent. But she never did. She died with her sins on her head."

"Stella could not accept you loved me, not her. She could not accept I gave you a son when she couldn't. She was proud and vain."

"I should have beaten some sense into her. I should have locked her in her room and never let her take Johanna away."

"You could never harm anyone, *Tsine*, not even her."

"Much as I came to hate and resent her, I'm sorry she ended up in such a bad way. I'm sure she's scarred our daughter with her wickedness."

"Johanna seems fine to me. Don't worry about her. She's proven she has her father's blood, his courage and strength. So does our son. When he returns, we will be a real family at last. I couldn't love Johanna more if she were my daughter. I'm so happy she's come home."

"What would I do without you, Nan?"

"Or I without you, *Tsine*, my love?"

"We'll have to be careful with Johanna in the house. But one day it—"

"Do not speak such beautiful words until they can come true. When the hatred of my people lessens, then we can speak of a future as one. But things are growing worse these days instead of better. You must not risk your name and place in this land. People would not sell and buy cattle from a man with an Indian wife and half-breed son. The truth could destroy you."

"I'm not sure I believe that anymore. Stella is gone; I'm free. Why would it be so despicable to marry the woman I love, the woman I've loved for thirty years?"

"We both know why, *Tsine*, we both know why."

Ginny crept to Johanna's room, having risked eavesdropping long enough to glean a few clues to help her make her final decision. She asked herself how Ben could not grasp how hurt and humiliated Stella had been when she discovered his longtime romance with another woman, a trusted woman who shared their home, a woman who had borne her husband a son. Surely Stella's vengeance, even if wrong, was understandable, perhaps even normal under those circumstances. She pondered how Nan could be the lover of a man who had married another woman, could share a relationship with him beneath the same roof that his wife did. How could their son, because Stone knew who his father was, accept such conditions as laid down by his deceitful parents? Was he just as selfish and greedy? Did he only want his share of this wealth? He had his father's name and was accepted as Stone Chapman, but everyone believed he was a bastard.

Bastard . . . Her lover hadn't lied about experiencing the sting of that word. Yet he was fortunate he was loved and wanted enough by his father to be at least half claimed by Ben.

Had he rejected her downstairs because he believed they were half brother and sister? Or did he truly not want her? It seemed as if Stone was always fleeing difficult situations rather than confronting them. He had been hurt so many times in the past that she couldn't blame him.

What will you do to me when you discover my deception? You'll be happy I'm not Johanna and you haven't sinned with your sister. You won't have to risk Ben thinking you seduced his daughter for spite. Will you be understanding and forgiving? Will you be angry and vengeful for how I've hurt and duped you and your father? Will you be glad you're sole heir to this ranch? Will you want me as Virginia Marston?

Ginny waited two days for Stone to get over his shock and return so she could speak with him before talking to his father. She couldn't stop thinking about the letter Captain Cooper hadn't given to her. Did it mean Stone loved her and wanted her, or was that interpretation wishful dreaming on her part? Was he only going to "return for you" to guide her back to Georgia to Miss Avery? Was his "serious talk" only going to tell her what he had said the other night: not to pine over him, that his seduction of her was only the result of a physical need and weakness?

By Saturday night, June first, he hadn't returned, and she realized he might not come back any time soon. He had told her his next job could take weeks or months; she couldn't wait that long to get on with her personal task in Colorado.

With the truth in his possession and her gone, Ben could tell Stone, if he contacted his father, that he had no reason to stay away from the ranch.

Stalling the inevitable only made it worse for everyone, especially for her. She needed her father, and Stone might be lost to her. If that was not the case, he'd know this time where to locate her at least, as she'd written him an enlightening letter. Perhaps it would be best if Ben told him the truth and if she wasn't present for his reaction.

Ginny walked downstairs and into the parlor where Ben was reading. "Mr. Chapman, I have to speak with you about a grave matter."

Ben lowered his newspaper and stared at her in confusion. "Why did you call me Mr. Chapman, Johanna? Is something wrong?"

"Yes, sir. Plenty. I don't know how or where to begin." She saw the man tense and grimace in dread of what might come from her lips. From the corner of her eye, she noticed Nan halt in the doorway.

"Is it about you and Stone? Did something happen between you two on the trail? You both acted so strangely. Is that why he left so suddenly?"

Ginny's heart pounded in matching dread. She didn't ask Nan to leave, as Stone's mother had a right to hear the truth. "Yes . . . and no, sir. I honestly don't know why Stone left as he did. I don't know what he thinks and feels about me, but I love him and I'd hoped he loved me," she revealed.

Ben paled. The paper shook then fell to the floor. "*What?*"

"As Anna Avery, I fell in love with Steve Carr."

"But you can't love him; he's your brother."

"No, sir, he isn't. I love him and want to marry him. I'm not—"

"That's impossible!" Ben shouted in dismay. He glanced at Nan, who stood motionless at the doorway, her face pale and body shaky.

"Only if Stone doesn't love me and want me," Ginny replied. "The other night he coldly spurned me. But I don't believe he doesn't love me, even if he honestly thinks he doesn't. I think, I *hope*, he left for a while to prevent me from causing a scene by pressing the matter. Only if I reveal the truth to everyone can we resolve this."

"He could never marry you. He's your brother, Johanna, by blood. He's my real son, not adopted, mine and Nandile's. Oh, my God, that's why he tore out of here like a blue norther! He loves you, too."

Ginny kept herself from blurting out the shocking truth too soon. "I hoped he was falling in love with me. He denied it and rejected me before leaving. I'm praying he deceived me about his feelings."

"Did you hear me, Johanna? You're his half sister. This can't be. The Lord is punishing me for my past sins. He's let my children fall in love. God forgive me for keeping such painful secrets. What shall we do?" he murmured, looking at his secret love who stared at them both in disbelief and anguish.

"I'm leaving, sir, tomorrow or Monday, whichever you say."

"You can't. We'll work this out. I love you and need you."

Ginny made her tone and gaze as gentle as she could. "No, sir, you love and need Johanna. I'm not Johanna. I'm not your daughter, Mr. Chapman. I'm Virginia Anne Marston. Johanna and I were best friends at school. She asked me to come here and pretend to be her."

"Is this an act of revenge?" He questioned in angry despair.

"Not at all, she didn't hate you. She wanted to come home. She couldn't, so she sent me. Everything I've told you about her and Stella is true."

"This was a test, eh? I'll write her to come home immediately."

"You can't, sir. Johanna is . . . She's . . . She died on March thirteenth in Savannah, shortly after we arrived from England."

Ben leapt from his chair, the newspaper crackling beneath his boots as he crossed to her. He grasped her forearms and fused his gaze to hers, "Why are you doing this, Johanna?" he fumed. "So you can have Stone? You can't pretend you are another girl so you can live in sin."

Ginny wanted to escape his firm grasp and pleading gaze but she couldn't even try to do so. "I *am* Ginny Marston, sir, I swear it. Let me tell you all I know, then we can discuss it." She guided him to the couch, helped them both to sit down before her wobbly legs gave way, and faced the astonished man. She related her story as slowly, carefully, and compassionately as she could. "That's the truth, Mr. Chapman," she said in conclusion. "I loved her as a sister and did as she asked. I couldn't let you go on believing I was Johanna." She stood and looked down at him. "I'll leave immediately. I didn't want to hurt you, but I can't remain here any longer as your daughter. I must go search for my father, and I pray he's still alive."

"You lying, scheming witch," Ben cried out in pain. "How could you be so cruel? My Johanna would never do this to her father. You thought you'd come here and trick money out of me after her death. You're only confessing now because you know Stone will unmask you and kill you."

"No, Ben," Nan said from the doorway. She walked hurriedly to them. "Ginny has given you a part of your Johanna you could never have had if she hadn't come here. Can't you see how alike they are? I believe her. You owe her kindness and understanding for honoring Johanna's last wish; it must have been hard for her. You owe them to her for being honest. If she wanted anything from you, she would continue her ruse."

In torment, Ben accused, "She thinks she can get her hands on my ranch through my son, have him and everything else she wants."

"That isn't true, sir. I don't want your ranch or your money; I didn't want to do this for Johanna. I do want Stone, because I love him and I've been good for him. Hate me if you must; maybe that will help you accept Johanna's loss easier. Stella lied to her all those years, but she still loved you and wanted to come home. You would have been so proud of her. She was the most wonderful person I've ever known." Tears welled in Ginny's hazel eyes and rolled down her flushed cheeks. "I miss her so much. We couldn't have survived those years alone at school if we hadn't had each other. She . . ." Ginny couldn't control the tears and anguish that flooded her heart.

Nan embraced her and cried with her because she believed her. Now she grasped Stone's suddenly black mood and his rush from the house: her son loved and wanted this woman. Ginny had changed and softened his heart. Their Life Circles had crossed many times because they were destined to overlap and become one. To deny and resist the truth would bring great suffering and defeat to all involved. The Great Spirit was at work in Stone Thrower's life; His hand was guiding her son toward his rightful path and fate: to Ginny and to peace with Ben. She must convince all of them this was meant to be.

When a small measure of control returned, Ginny said, "She would have loved it here and been so happy. When I saw her room and all those gifts you'd bought for her that she never received, it almost broke my heart. You don't know how happy it would have made Johanna to have gotten only one of them, only one letter, one word, one visit. It was wrong and cruel of Stella to hurt her just to spite you. I met Stella many times, so I believe all you said about her. I never told Johanna I didn't like or trust her mother because I didn't want to hurt her. I wish she could have lived to be here with you. It would have meant so much to her.

"I don't agree with what you did in the past, sir, but I understand it. Marry Nan and be happy," Ginny felt she had to give her opinion. "Don't care about what others might say; life is too short to deny yourselves one minute of joy together. Acknowledge Stone; he needs that so much, sir." Her eyes teared again as she said, "Somehow I think Johanna can see us and knows you didn't abandon her . . . I'll leave now. I'm sorry, sir, truly I am. It seems I've made too many mistakes lately trying to help myself and others. I'll leave a letter for Stone on the bed; please give it to him. He deserves to learn the truth from me."

Nan told the man she loved what she had been thinking earlier. "It is fate, Ben. Do not make it harder on our son to accept the truth."

Ben surmised that this young woman was what had changed his son and was the reason Stone had returned to make peace and why he had mentioned children and grandchildren. His beloved daughter was lost forever, but he still had his son. He had come to like Ginny, and her motive for fooling him had come from the heart. Nan was right; Ginny had given him his daughter for a while. And, if Stone loved her and married her, he could lose him by rejecting her. He mustn't allow anguish and resentment to color his judgment. He halted her exit. "Stop! Don't go, Ginny. Please tell me more about her," he added in a strained voice.

Ginny turned and looked at the anguished man. "I'll tell you all I learned." She took a seat again and related the story of how they'd met, become best friends, how they'd lived in England, and returned to America. She revealed how Johanna was buried under Ginny's name and where. She asked Ben to bring his daughter's body home for reinterment. "Ask me anything you wish, sir, and I'll try to answer."

"Why didn't you confess this when Stone arrived?"

That wasn't the question she had expected. She blushed. "It's very complicated, sir. I've told you about our adventures together as Anna and Steve. I fell in love with him, but he had such bitterness and pain locked up inside and refused to allow anyone to get close to him." Ginny related some personal details about her feelings, but left out their physical relationship, which they probably suspected by now anyhow. Surely they of all people realized love and passion were irresistible and powerful.

"When he came home, I assumed he had lied to me about his troubled past. I believed he had deserted me in Fort Smith. You see, he left a letter for me with a friend, but I never received it. After he impulsively gave it to me the other night, I read his words to mean he did have deep feelings for me. But he treated me so distantly, spurning me completely. And then he left. I'm ashamed to say I eavesdropped on you and Nan after dinner that night. I realized Stone thought he . . . was falling in love with his sister, at least I hope that's why he rejected me and was troubled enough to leave. You see, Stella never told Johanna that secret, and it wasn't in any of the letters from you that we found. I was trying to give you as much time with 'Johanna' as possible, but I realized I had to end this ruse to keep from hurting everyone more. I came to like and respect you so much that I even wished at one time I never had to tell you. I had trapped myself and didn't know how to get free. In hindsight, the entire deception was foolish and cruel. So much happened so fast that I didn't think clearly or act wisely, but that's no excuse for what I did to you. I should have come here, told you the truth, then left. I'll admit, knowing my father might be dead and being so happy here, it was tempting to stay where I was loved and safe, but I want my father. I love him and miss him. I'm so afraid for him."

As tears brightened her hazel eyes, Ginny admitted, "Maybe I stalled so long and carried out this ruse because I'm afraid to go to Colorado and discover he's dead."

"Is there anything I can do to help, Ginny?"

"You've been too kind and generous already, Mr. Chapman. I don't deserve that after how I've duped you."

"You brought me the truth and a period of sunshine. If you hadn't been with Johanna all those years, she would have been miserable, and she would have died alone and frightened in Savannah. And I would have died never knowing she loved me and tried to get back to me. I owe you something for that."

"There is one thing you can do, sir: you can loan me stage fare to Colorado City. I'll return it by mail after I find my father. If he's . . . gone, I'll take a job there and repay you."

"Of course I'll do that. But why don't you wait until Stone returns? He can guide you there and protect you along the way."

"I think Stone will need time to adjust to the truth after you tell him. I feel it would be a mistake to wait for him. Stone's a proud and troubled man. I've fooled him many times before, so another time might be more than he can accept and forgive. In the heat of his anger, he could say and do irreparable damage to any future relationship we might have. Besides, I'm only hoping and praying he feels the same way I do. He's never told me he loves me and wants me. In fact, he's always tried to convince me of the opposite."

Ginny decided to be bold and brave to help Ben understand and reach out to his son. "He tried to tell me he was a nothing. For such a strong and confident man in most areas, Stone has a low opinion of himself. He can't stand the thought of defeat or weakness, yet he's vulnerable in ways he doesn't admit. He doesn't believe he has anything to offer another person and he doesn't want to risk being hurt by getting close to anyone. He keeps a tight rein on his emotions, but I've seen the good and gentle side of him. He tries to protect himself by being cool and reserved. But I've seen him smile, laugh, show kindness and compassion, and risk his life for others; I think he shocked himself when he recognized feelings in himself he didn't know he possessed. I think he's softened and changed since we met; I hope because of me. He's a very special man with a lot of love inside him."

Ginny knew she might be going too far but she had to help her love. "For

Stone to accept himself and to discard the burdens of the past, you have to accept him, Mr. Chapman. He has to know you love him and will do anything for him. Now that I know the truth about him, it helps me understand him better. He loves you and needs you. I believe that only you can save your son. Even though you adopted him, he still feels rejected by you. As for me and Stone, if I've seen him for the last time, I want to remember him the way I knew him as Steve Carr. I don't want him to feel he has to hurt me to prove he doesn't want me. Until he loves and accepts himself, he can't love and accept me. Does that make sense?"

Nan smiled. "Yes, Ginny, it does. You know my son well, and I think you're right about leaving. It would be best for Stone to have time to think this out before he sees you. People in pain often strike out at those they love, it is only they who have the power to truly hurt you. We'll speak to him when he returns, and I'm sure he'll come after you."

Ginny's heart fluttered. "You do?"

Nan smiled again. "I will be surprised and disappointed if he doesn't."

"So will I," Ben added, his heart too heavy to allow him to smile at that moment. "When do you plan to leave? And how much money do you need for your ticket and expenses?"

"Monday morning, sir, but the money you gave me is plenty."

"I'll give you another fifty dollars for any unexpected problems. Send for more if you need it. And if you don't locate your father, you're welcome to return here."

Ginny was surprised and touched at his kindness. "Thank you, Mr. Chapman, Nan. You've both been wonderful to me. I'll pack tomorrow and go into town by dusk. The stage leaves early in the morning."

"Buck will drive you, if you're certain you won't stay longer."

"I can't, sir. One last thing: I didn't want you to think I was using this to soften and sway your opinion of me, so I waited to give it to you." Ginny withdrew a letter from her pocket. "This is from Johanna to you, explaining what she asked me to do and why. She wrote it in case I needed help to get out of trouble with you and perhaps the authorities. Please remember she didn't know the truth when she wrote it. All she had to base her feelings on were Stella's lies and those hazy letters from you that contradicted Stella's false claims."

Ben took the letter, almost dreading to read it. "Thank you, Ginny."

"Good night, sir. Good night, Nan. Thank you both again."

Monday morning, June third, Ginny climbed aboard a coach in Dallas to head for Gainesville to connect with the Oxbow Route to retrace her recent journey from Fort Smith. From there she would travel on to Tipton, Missouri, and across Kansas to Colorado City. It would require fourteen days to complete her journey.

She was dressed in a dark-green traveling skirt and jacket with a cream-colored blouse. Her long hair was pinned atop her head and partly covered by a fashionable ivy hat. Her money was pinned inside her chemise as Nan advised to protect it from stage robbers. She was taking only part of her possessions; the rest she left at the ranch, along with her doll. When Ben sent for his daughter's body, he would recover the rest of her things, along with Johanna's, from Martha Avery.

She had spent a restless night in the hotel after bidding Ben and Nan farewell yesterday afternoon. Ginny was glad the letter from Johanna had been a kind and loving one that would help Ben accept her ruse. The couple, despite their grief, seemed happy about the future before them.

Ginny had hoped Stone would appear before her departure, but he hadn't. When he returned home, he would be given the explanatory letter she had left with his mother. She prayed he would be understanding and forgiving, and that he loved her.

She caught herself from lurching forward against another passenger as the driver popped his whip and set them into rapid and jostling motion. She was on the way to her next and final deception, again using the name Anna Avery while she searched for her father—or his killer.

Chapter 16

☙

VIRGINIA MARSTON JOURNEYED across the beautiful Ozarks, over rolling green hills, through fertile valleys, past famed battlesites, and onto grassland that would almost extend to her destination. While the fatigued and bruised Ginny prepared to spend a restless night near Fort Leavenworth, a tormented Stone Chapman dismounted at his home, and spoke a silent prayer. *Spirits have mercy on both of us because I have to get this settled for my sister's sake. I can't let her suffer like I'm doing.*

He entered the house to find his father sitting at his desk. The rancher looked at him, then blinked back tears. Tears of joy and relief? Stone mused. He watched Bennett rise as if an old and beaten man.

"I'm glad you're home, Son," Ben said as he approached him. "I was afraid you wouldn't return. I've missed you and worried about you." Since Ginny exposed the awful truth and left for Dallas a week ago, the house had been too quiet. It had affected him like losing his daughter a second time. Grief and loneliness had plagued him, as had a fear of also losing his son, both resulting from his foolish and selfish mistakes.

Stone didn't know what to do when his father embraced him. Taken by surprise and sensing something was terribly wrong, he asked in an emotion-hoarsened voice, "Where's Johanna?"

Ben's arms dropped to his sides and his graying head lowered as he barely got out the painful words, "She's dead." Ben's head lifted with teary eyes as he continued. "But I have my son back. I love you, Stone, and I need you. I know I haven't been a real father to you, but I want that to change. Please help me do it."

The younger man's heart felt as cold as ice and as rigid as his name. His father's words and mood had registered in his mind, but his pounding heart could respond to only one thing. "She's . . . dead? How? When?"

"She became gravely ill during her return voyage from England," Ben murmured in anguish. "She died shortly after she reached America. Lord have mercy on my soul, I didn't even get to see my child again."

Stone feared the man had gone mad with grief and guilt. "What are you talking about, Father? She was here when I left over a week ago."

Ben's wits cleared and he hurried to explain, "No, Son, she's buried in Savannah. The woman we met was her best friend, like a sister to my lost Johanna. Ginny is the one who tended and buried Johanna, with Mr. Avery's help. My child had been deceived by her wicked mother. Stella told her awful lies about me. Ginny made her a deathbed promise to come here to wreak revenge and justice on me for betraying her. But the girl was too tender-hearted to carry it out. After she learned the truth from me, she confessed her ruse. She told me and Nan everything after you left. When she discovered you and Johanna were related she realized why you took off so fast. She didn't want to hurt any of us, so she confessed to her ruse and left."

Stone's heart drummed. His mouth felt dry. His head was dazed for a few moments. "She isn't my half sister?"

"No, her best friend. Ginny was heart-stricken over Johanna's loss; she loved my daughter. She told me all about their years at boarding school and how she got here from Savannah with your help."

Stone was astonished to learn it was only a ruse, like the one she pulled on the wagontrain with Avery. The woman he'd made love to wasn't his sister. The cunning vixen was a skilled pretender to dupe him twice.

Ben was bewildered by his son's reaction. If Stone loved Ginny, he should be shouting with joy over this news; for some unknown reason, he wasn't. "She told me the truth after you left like a bandit in the night. She would have told you, too, if you hadn't sneaked off. She was very contrite, Son, and I understand her motive."

"She certainly took her time getting a guilty conscience and spilling the truth. I'll bet she wouldn't have done it if I hadn't shown up and scared her witless. She knew she dared not cross me again. She came here to torment and punish you, but you understand and forgive her?"

"Yes, Son. You of all people should comprehend vengeance and bitterness as powerful motives to hurt someone. We've done terrible things to each other, Stone; I want to end the past; I want peace. I love you and need you. I will never call you my adopted son again; I swear. You're a Chapman, my only flesh and blood and heir; this ranch will be all yours one day."

Those admissions touched Stone deeply, but he couldn't deal with them yet. "Where is this Ginny? She and I have a few things to settle."

"She left the ranch and Dallas after her confession and plea for forgiveness. We know why you ran from her and why she's giving you time to cool your temper." Ben related Ginny's disclosures and assumptions about him. "She loves you, but she's afraid you won't understand and forgive her. *Do* you love her?"

The younger man paced as those stunning revelations flooded his mind. She seemed to know him well, but he didn't know *her*, not the real woman. He'd met "Anna Avery" and "Johanna Chapman," but not this Ginny woman. What if she wasn't anything like the women she had pretended to be? She lied and duped with ease and skill. Or did she? Hadn't he always perceived she was being dishonest and had a dreadful secret? Did she love and want "Steve Carr" or the heir to the Chapman ranch and fortune? "Gone where?" he asked.

"To Colorado to join her father. That's where she was heading after a visit here with Johanna, but Johanna never made it home. She's afraid for his life; someone is apparently trying to murder him and steal his silver strike."

Stone's heart skipped several beats and his body chilled as additional suspicions gnawed at him. "What's her real name, Father?"

"Virginia Anne Marston. Her father is—"

"Mathew Marston," he interrupted, gritting out the name. Now he grasped why she had escaped him again, terrified of his wrath.

Ben noticed his angry reaction. "You know her father?"

"Yep, I know the bastard. He killed my best friend, Clayton Cassidy. They were partners in that silver strike she mentioned. I was chasing him before I had to leave to join Jo— Ginny's wagontrain to catch Charles Avery and his gang. I'm heading there now to . . ." Stone narrowed his gaze.

"My Lord in heaven, Son, you aren't going there to kill her father? You can't. If he's guilty of a crime, arrest him, but don't do this to Ginny."

"Her claims of love for me are only another trick to protect her father from me and justice. Matt probably told her about me and Clay, may have even sent her here to ensnare me. If Matt is dead, Ginny may believe I killed him, so she came to wreak revenge on me after Johanna died and gave her a path. How can I trust her again? She's lied too many times."

"You're wrong, Son. They were friends for years, since they were girls of thirteen. I read your sister's letter to me telling all about them."

"How do you know this Ginny woman didn't write it just to fool you?"

"She didn't, Son. Please don't be hard on her. She loves you. I'm sure she doesn't know about you and Clay and her father. She would have told me. You're afraid to believe her because you don't want to be hurt again. Ginny's known heartache, too. Let me tell you about her . . ." Ben related what she had revealed about her difficult life.

Stone wondered if what Ginny had told his father was true. If it was, did it change anything—change what she'd done, change what and who she was? "You want to protect the conniving woman who deceived us?"

"She had good call, Son, and a good heart. I told you her life's story, Stone; she's suffered plenty, as we have. Don't hurt her more. Please."

Hurt her, his mind shouted, *after what she's done to me? She let me think she was Anna Avery! She let me think she was my sister and I had made love to her! She's Matt's daughter, greedy and sly just like him! Well, I have a big surprise for you, Ginny Marston, one you'd never imagine . . .*

"She left a letter for you, Son. And something strange. A doll." Ben walked to his desk, withdrew both, and returned to hand them to Stone.

"Do you understand this?" Ben asked, nodding to the doll.

Stone fingered the keepsake in confusion and anguish. "No, I don't," he finally replied. He wondered if what he feared to believe was true: that she did love and want him. Yet every time a black cloud vanished, another one took its place over their heads: Mathew Marston and his crime would come between them and prevent any hope of a future between them. "I need to be alone for a while. I'm going to my room."

"You won't take off again without seeing me first?" Ben entreated.

Stone looked at his father; the man had been changed by this event; he read that in Ben's eyes, tone, and posture. "No, Father, I won't. It's past time for us to make peace. We'll do it before I ride out on my last mission. When I finish it and return home, it will be to stay."

Ben hugged his son once more, and this time Stone responded.

"I'll tell your mother the good news. You don't know how happy this makes me, Son. We'll be a real family at last. My beautiful Apache Sunflower has agreed to marry me. We'll wait for your return for the ceremony."

Stone was astonished again. "You're marrying Mother?"

Ben smiled. "As soon as you return. It's about time, past time. She's the only woman I've ever loved. It's time the world knew and accepted our feelings for each other."

"I'm glad, Father. Tell her I'll speak with her later."

Stone went to his old room and sat on the bed. His thoughts and emotions were in turmoil. Dare he open and read the message she had left for him? Would it be the truth, as she'd promised in her Fort Smith letter? Or would it be another cunning deception? Did she know who he really was—Clay's heir and avenger on her father—and wanted to trick him into not taking either of those roles? Would beautiful lies in her missive affect his feelings and actions in a foolish way? No, he vowed coldly as he cautioned himself to remember she wasn't Anna Avery or Johanna Chapman.

His half sister . . . She was dead, buried not far from where he had trained this beguiling vixen for her trip to torment him and his father. Stella had taken Johanna away when she was two and he was ten, but he remembered the child who had owned their father's heart and loyalty. He would never get to meet and know the woman she had become. Yet, he was grateful the woman he had made love to wasn't his sister. He would grieve for Johanna's loss in his own time and way. For now, he had to . . .

Stone's hands shook as he ripped open the envelope:

Dear Stone,
 You know the wicked truth by now and must hate me. To say I'm sorry will mean little or nothing to you at this point. I know giving you my two most prized possessions—myself and my doll—will not make up for the pain and bitterness you're feeling.
 I admit I tricked you many times, but my reasons seemed right at those moments. You also tricked *me* many times. If you had told me you were Stone Chapman, I would never have done what I did to you, with you. So often I wanted to confess the truth but things you said or did halted me. I sensed you were hiding something powerful and I feared to trust you. After you dumped me in Fort Smith as if I were

used-up supplies, I had no choice, I believed—except to come here for help. I was hurt and confused and afraid because I didn't know you hadn't deserted me. I also feared I'd become entangled again in the Klan crime and had no one to prove my true identity and innocence. I wanted to hide here until I was out of danger.

I'm sure your father told you he loaned me the money to reach *my* father in Colorado. He said he would explain my past to you so you'd understand why I left and where I'm going. I suppose I knew all along I couldn't carry out my promise to your sister, but I loved her so much that I agreed in a moment of anguish.

I was going to tell you everything in private before confessing to your father but you left too quickly. I'll be out of your life when you get this letter and I'll understand if you make that forever. Please don't allow the mistakes I've made to increase your torment. Make peace with your father; he's a good man, even though he made cruel mistakes. He loves you and needs you and he's sorry. Give him the chance to make everything up to you. This is the moment both of you have waited for, so don't throw it aside.

I hope you can understand and forgive me one day. I'll never forget what you've done for me and what you mean to me. I'll always regret what might have been between us . . .

Love, Ginny

Stone read it again then squeezed his eyes closed. *Do I believe you this time, Ginny Marston? It won't matter after I do what must be done to your father. I understand love and promises between best friends; that's why I'll have to kill Matt, if the snake's still alive.* Stone rose from the bed and headed for a long and overdue talk with his father and mother.

Monday morning, the ranch foreman galloped to the house with bad news. "Rustlers struck again last night in the south pasture. Made off with fifty prime steers, one of our best bulls, and about ten horses. Two of the boys are dead and one's wounded. I'll round up some hands and we'll track 'em down. Raid was early last night so they have a good start on us. It'll probably take a few days to catch 'em and bring back the stock."

Ben was angered and dismayed. "That'll leave us too short of men here. Pick three hands who are good with rifles, Buck, and I'll ride with you. Tell the boys to guard Nan and the house while we're gone. Son, I have to go."

Stone read Ben's reluctance to miss a minute of his visit and imminent departure, but his father's decision was the only one he could make. Stone knew chasing the bandits was perilous and he didn't want to risk losing Ben to an ambush. "I'm coming with you. When a rustler goes to killing, he's dangerous and tricky. You might need my help and guns."

Ben smiled. "Thanks, Son. You're better at dealing with criminals than we are. Let's ready supplies and move out in ten minutes."

Stone realized this episode would delay his trip, and perhaps that was intentional. Surely the trouble here could be cleared up in less than a week. It would take him about thirteen days to cross the Texas panhandle and northeast corner of New Mexico Territory to reach Colorado City. He should be finished here and on the trail shortly before Ginny reached her destination.

Be there and be ready to face me, woman, with the truth for once.

Forts Riley, Harker, and Hays and numerous other relay and home stations were left behind as Ginny's stage rumbled across the vast Kansas plains. They journeyed on the Smoky Hill Road that ran beside a river by the same name from Fort Riley into Colorado. The combination of occasional low, rolling hills, long stretches of flat terrain, scant trees except near waterlines, outcrops of rocks, and the seemingly endless span of grass became monotonous and nerve-wearing to several passengers. But not so to Ginny, who had never viewed anything like the landscape before her gaze.

She saw countless buffalo, deer, antelope, and foxes. She noticed a few Indians at a distance and was relieved they didn't attack the coach. Hills became more frequent as they neared the border. Afterward, she watched the Big Sandy River for twenty-five miles as it snaked along beside them in the arid region. She enjoyed the beauty of countless wildflowers, plants with blades that resembled mini yuccas, waving tall grass, several varieties of sagebrush, and amaranth that eventually became tumbleweeds. The openness in all directions amazed her.

Nights had been cool in this region for mid-June, making her thankful for her long sleeves and shawl. Days were often windy, with some gusts swaying the stage and stirring up choking dust on the dirt road.

They crossed the Rush, Horse, and Pond Rivers and passed a prairie dog town where she saw many furry creatures scampering about or standing tall and alert on mounds. The Rocky Mountains appeared on the horizon. Colorado City would be their last stop of the day, and Ginny could hardly eat her scant lunch as she stared at the awesome sight.

A passenger told her that the first gold strike—made by men from her home state of Georgia—was on Cherry Creek not far from Colorado City. In '58 the shout had been: "Pike's Peak or bust." The man gave a wry grin as he related that many had "gone bust."

During the last leg of the journey, Ginny watched snowcapped Pike's Peak grow in size as the stage neared its base where her destination awaited her. Her gaze picked out lofty ranges of towering slopes, sharp and rugged mountains, exposed rocks and lofty summits, and upturned foothills. Passes, valleys, canyons, and sandstone hogbacks filled her line of vision, their coverings and splotches of white telling her that winters in the high country were long, rough, and demanding. She couldn't imagine why her father had fallen in love with this wild area and remained here after the war.

The closer she rode to the city, the larger and taller those peaks and ridges became. Verdant foothills seemed covered in emerald fuzz of evergreens and hardwoods of late spring. Soil in shades of red ranging from vivid to dull, and rocks dotted the landscape. Nearing sunset, the tallest range and summit were like a pearly-pink ridge that drifted up into a startlingly blue sky. Ginny found the azure, green, white, and red colorings a striking contrast. She watched clouds and fog slowly lower themselves like cozy blankets over the jutting and chilly terrain.

Over the next rise, Colorado City sprang into view, nestled on relatively flat land at the base of the uplifted terrain. Apprehensions flooded her. She was afraid she wouldn't be able to locate her father, afraid she wouldn't be able to find a proper job before Bennett Chapman's money was spent, and afraid she'd never see Stone again. She hadn't expected Colorado City to be so large and settled. She relaxed as she realized it wouldn't be a small and rough and filthy town.

Yet as the stage entered the outskirts, Ginny realized she might have made part of that assumption too soon. She saw tents, shacks, lean-tos, and log cabins with animals and clutter around them that were interspersed with nice homes and businesses of many sizes and kinds. Freight wagons were backed up to stores either to unload or having unloaded their wares. Men were moving goods—picks, shovels, wheelbarrows—inside their stores for the night to prevent them from being stolen.

It was active and noisy this time of evening as work ended and recreation began. She heard laughter, shouts, muffled talk, and a contrasting blend of music from dance halls, brothels, and saloons. A mixture of smells filled the air, most from the preparation of food at eating establishments, some merely marked Grub or Eats. She saw ill-kempt men in shabby garments strolling the streets, others loitering at night places that appeared elegant and expensive, drunks lying against wooden structures, and scantily clad females enticing customers to spend their money at these locations. People milled everywhere she looked. This was a town of mixed inhabitants, a town of the rich and poor and the in-between, of the famous and infamous and the nobodys. She had learned those facts from several of her fellow passengers.

After the coach halted, the driver told Ginny, "You wait tilst I'm finished here, Miz Avery, and I'll see you to a nice boardin' house. You don't want any of that trash takin' charge of you and yore possessions." He made his remarks scornfully as he nodded to shabby men hawking business from newcomers. "They'll git you outta sight and rob you clean. You'll have to be careful here. Never go out after dark 'less yore with an escort who's well armed and good with his guns. No minin' town is safe fur a lady. Some of them men have lost everythin' they came with and will do anythin' to git another grubstake. A few of 'em have struck pay dirt and lost it faster 'an they dug it out. Gold fever kin be a dangerous sickness."

Ginny was fatigued, dusty, and sore. She was eager to be on her way but wisely waited for the kind driver to escort her. The man borrowed a wagon from the coach company, loaded her belongings, and took her to Hattie Sue Pearl's Boarding House. After introductions were made, the stocky female with graying hair in a loose bun led Ginny inside and to her new "home" of two small rooms—sleeping and sitting—and showed her where the bathing closet and privy were located.

Suppertime had passed, but Hattie warmed leftovers for her. The two women sat at the kitchen table, chatting. Ginny related the terrible conditions in the South since the war ended to Mrs. Pearl. "I'm an orphan," she began her fabricated reason for coming to the town. "I lost my home and family, everything, during the war. I tried to work and make a new life there, but it's impossible until things change. I read about Colorado and decided to move here. It might sound impulsive and rash but I had to get away to make a fresh start. With all the mining and progress here, surely there are good jobs available for a strong and dependable woman. Who knows, I might find a proper husband."

The older woman grinned. "Please call me Hattie." They exchanged smiles before she said, "I think you're a brave and smart girl. I came from Mississippi three years ago and I'm earning good money. My husband and son were killed in that awful war and I lost everything, too, except for gold and jewels I kept hidden from them thieving Yanks. I used them to build this place and to invest in one of the hotels down the street. We got us plenty of unmarried men who have enough looks and gold to make a woman's heart flutter. I have my eye on a couple of prospects myself. I'm sure you'll have no trouble finding you a rich young man to snare."

"First, I need to find a job. My resources won't last very long. I lost everything to a Yankee carpetbagger. A friend loaned me traveling money. I was fortunate the driver brought me here to you. I've heard the hotels and most lodgings charge a small fortune for room and board."

"They do 'cause they can get it. Men who can't afford niceties live in awful conditions, some bedding down in alleys and begging for grub. When miners or prospectors come to town to rest and sport, they pay what you ask 'cause they think they'll find more gold the next day. After spending scary months down in somebody else's mines or scratching for nuggets on creeks and rivers, they're desperate for company and good food and a good loving, if you know what I mean." Hattie's eyes twinkled with mischief. "I know of a job that'll last a week at Mr. Trevers cat and book store. His wife needs a rest something fierce, been sickly. He mentioned it to me just today."

"Why cats and books?" Ginny inquired about the odd mixture.

Hattie chuckled. "All kinds of men in these parts, Anna. They need books to en'ertain and relax them after work in town or shoveling dirt all day, and cats make great pets and mousers. Camps and shafts are overrun with rats and mice, so they ain't hard to feed and tend. I've seen wagons bring as many as a thousand on one load and sell 'em faster than fleas multeeply on a dog. I'll take you to meet John in the morning. Mary Jane will be happier to see you than a bull in a pasture of eager cows. Them miners and cats keep 'er busy and she's in sore need of rest."

"That sounds wonderful, Hattie. I love both books and cats."

"Like I said, it'll only last a week. Unless John makes a bigger profit with a beauty like you working there," she jested. "It'll be a start, give you time to learn your way around and meet folks here. A beautiful and genteel lady will be in big demand. Don't let nobody hire you cheap and work you hard; too many jobs around here for that. You could earn a fortune if you like singing and dancing and making merry with men. We got more than our share of them kinds of places. Some men squander their whole earnings in one night in some of them holes."

From Hattie's look and tone, Ginny realized she wasn't serious. "I'm not interested in working there, quick and easy fortune or not," she clarified.

"Good girl. Just testing you," Hattie teased with a grin. "A real lady."

Ginny liked the friendly woman in her mid-forties who kept a clean lodging, was an excellent cook, and seemed kind and trustworthy.

"The water's hot if you're ready to wash off that coat of dust."

"Thank you, Hattie, and I'm more than ready. I haven't had a proper bath in ages."

"You're to feed and water the cats every day, Miss Avery," John Trevers said, "and make sure their pens are clean. I don't want none getting sick and dying on me; they're too valuable. When the men come in to check the books, make sure they wash their hands first. Talk to them and you'll know what to show them." They discussed the stock for a while, then John grinned and said, "Sounds like you know your books and writers. Good. I can use you from today until Saturday night. I'll pay you sixty dollars for the week's work and one extra for every sale you make. Does that suit you?"

Ginny smiled, as the salary he offered was a generous one. She concluded the high pay and his wife's need of rest must mean business was good and that she was in for a busy and hectic week. "Perfect, Mr. Trevers. I promise to work hard, be on time, and do a good job for you, sir."

The man thanked Hattie before the genial boardinghouse keeper left. He showed Ginny where everything was located and let her begin her chores before the store opened in twenty minutes.

As she worked, Ginny thought about her father. She couldn't ask around about him and tip off his enemy. Hopefully if he was in town, he'd see her and contact her. If not, she had a cunning plan in mind.

She also thought about Stone Chapman. She wondered if he had returned home and discovered the truth about her second deceit. Would he be glad she was out of his life or would he come after her? She loved him and missed him so much. She prayed he would understand and forgive her for duping him again, and would arrive soon. She could use his help and protection. Steve was a skilled agent and might be able to trace and find her father faster than she could, alone and inexperienced. It had been eighteen days since she'd last seen him, and she had an emotional and physical ache for him. She could close her eyes and envision him in detail, imagine his gentle touch and blazing kisses. Yet it was more than his handsome looks and virile prowess that drew her to him. He was the man with whom she wanted to share her life.

Mr. Trevers unlocked the front door for customers to enter and command her full attention with purchases and questions about felines and books.

Tuesday, as she was about to leave Trevers's Cats & Books to deliver two animals to a customer to be used for mousers in his restaurant, Ginny met Frank Kinnon, the man mentioned in her father's letters as a possible enemy of his. She listened to and observed him with interest.

John introduced them and told her, "Frank owns the bank and assay office next door, among his many businesses around town, and a thriving ranch ten miles away. Frank is rich, and powerful, Miss Avery, so be wary of him," the friend teased. "Oh, yes, Frank's also a bachelor."

Ginny watched the two men shake hands and chuckle. According to her father's missives, Frank Kinnon was also evil, selfish, and greedy, and perhaps a murderer of Matt's partner, Clayton Cassidy.

"I see John is keeping his new helper busy. Don't let him overwork you as he did his poor wife."

Ginny smiled at the pleasant and polite man in his late thirties. He appeared very distinguished in his expensive suit and with the silver streaks at his temples. "So far, Mr. Trevers has been a perfect boss."

"See, Frank, I'm not a slaver like Mary Jane says," John jested.

As the two men chatted, Ginny pretended to check the latches on the two cages to stall for more time to observe Frank. He was nice-looking, almost handsome. His dark hair was cut and combed neatly. His blue eyes sparkled with vitality, amusement, and secretiveness, and with desire when they touched on her. She wasn't surprised when he invited her to join him for dinner the next night, but the offer filled her with apprehension.

"O'Rourke's is a fine restaurant, Miss Avery. I'm sure you'll enjoy the excellent food and atmosphere. Please accept. I'll be a perfect gentleman."

She couldn't comprehend why she hesitated since she needed to get close to him in order to cull clues. "I don't know, Mr. Kinnon; we're strangers."

John provided help for his eager friend. "You'll be safe with Frank, Miss Avery. You can trust him to honor his word. I'm sure you two will become good friends. He might even be able to help you find another job next week."

Ginny made certain she behaved as a proper lady and didn't appear smitten by the valuable suitor, as that was how the man was behaving. "If you say it's all right, Mr. Trevers, I'll accept." She turned to Frank. "I'm staying at Hattie Sue Pearl's Boarding House. I'll require time to freshen up and change after work. You can call for me at seven-thirty."

"Perfect, Miss Avery, see you tomorrow night."

Ginny hoped she didn't blush or fidget beneath his fiery blue eyes. "I'll return soon, Mr. Trevers," she told her boss as she lifted the two cages and headed toward the door. She left the men talking. Before she was halfway down the street, Frank Kinnon hurried to overtake her and pulled the cages from her hands.

"Let me help you with these."

Ginny forced a warm smile. "You needn't bother, sir, I can manage them. I only have another block to go. I'm sure you're busy."

"Not too busy to assist and protect a beautiful lady. We have many rough men here, and I wouldn't want you to get a bad opinion of our town if some of them approached you. In a place like this, we have few ladies, but not for long. The whole state of Colorado is growing fast. Gold, silver, furs, and ranching make it enticing. Besides, I need the exercise."

Ginny eyed his powerful physique from the corner of her eye and knew it was an excuse to spend more time with her. She should be glad she'd seized his interest, but he made her nervous nevertheless. He made her think of a starving man with a juicy treat before him. She decided not to play the coquettish southern belle to ensnare him tighter as that could be hazardous. She wasn't convinced she could carry out her ruse to let him romance her while she beguiled information from him.

They strolled past the many businesses, banks, offices of attorneys and doctors, many clothing and mercantile stores, and three saloons with gambling. Across the street she had seen a meat market, smithy, Brown's Hay & Feed, two freight companies, the Leavenworth & Pike's Peak Express Company with mail delivery, and Farrell's Drugs. Farther down, she noticed more businesses and more hotels and lodgings, restaurants, a church, and, oddly, many brothels and dancehalls. They reached her destination, delivered the cats, accepted payment, and returned to the store. Ginny smiled and thanked him, as his warning had been correct; if he hadn't been with her, gawking men might have approached her.

"My pleasure, Anna. I look forward to our dinner tomorrow night."

"Good-bye, and thank you for the escort, Mr. Kinnon."

"It's Frank, Anna. Please."

"Good-bye, Frank." Ginny watched the grinning man enter the building next door. She went to the store's back room to eat the lunch Hattie had packed for her, her mind drifting to what she knew and what she needed to learn.

Her father had written her that the only man who knew about his silver strike was the one who had assayed the rich ore: Frank Kinnon. He had related, "If his tests are accurate, the future mine will bring in great wealth and fame." Lincoln's Homestead Act of '62 had opened up this area to settlement: anyone could claim up to one hundred sixty acres of land. Mathew Marston had filed his claim in Denver at the Colorado General Land Office under the name of V. A. Marston for Virginia Anne Marston, not in this town to prevent Kinnon or others from knowing where it was located. Her father and Clay had found "a rich vein, one most prospectors would have missed even if standing atop it," its bluish-gray and bluish-black "rocks" deceptive to the ignorant and inexperienced. He had told her that gold was easier to find and collect, but not so with silver, which was embedded with other minerals and had to be separated. It required knowledge, work, equipment, and skill. It was almost mandatory to have investors because silver mining was expensive, took many workers to dig and to smelt, and others for hauling and guarding shipments.

Another assayer had been with Frank Kinnon that day and had prevented the man from lying to her father. Frank had been forced to reveal that the ore sample contained a high percentage of pure silver and little refining would be required. It was estimated that "each ton of ore will yield one thousand dollars in gold, four thousand in silver, and additional money in lead and quartz." Matt had kept his find a secret until he could work out the details for mining it because news of a strike would lure countless men into his area, men after the gold, men who would overlook or ignore the silver, men who would create problems. He had registered his land claim after he and Clay had pretended to lead spies to the right location and after Clayton Cassidy and another prospector had been killed and burned in a cabin. Matt didn't know if anyone—especially the villain and his cohorts—knew he wasn't the second man slain that day. Her father was supposed to leave the area to seek those needed investors and protectors, but she didn't know if he had made it out alive.

His letter had warned of claim-jumpers, widespread thievery, lynchings, murders, corrupt or incompetent politicians and assayers and claims officials or surveyors, and the overworked special agents who tried to uphold the laws and capture criminals. The El Paso Claims Club had run Colorado City in '58 and had meted out justice and punishment to wrongdoers; they still had powerful members, including Frank Kinnon.

But the wealth available here was too tempting for some men to worry about how they collected it. Fur trade was bountiful in the mountains, and warm clothes were expensive. Farmers nearby raised much-needed food and charged exorbitant prices, as did freighters who brought in goods. Shops charged outrageous prices for supplies and equipment. It was relatively safe from Indians who had been defeated in '65; only a few attacks troubled settlers on rare occasions. It was the greedy white man who threatened those innocent and law-abiding fellow white men in this territory.

Ginny understood why her father couldn't expose his find and why he couldn't accuse Kinnon of murder. She grasped why he needed investors and why he had to remain "dead" until he found them for protection. But what, she wondered, was taking him so long and where was he now? If Stone were here, she would have asked him to guide her to the cabin where her father might be hiding out until his plans were finalized.

But one precaution she needed to take now was to be prepared to flee in the event Kinnon discovered her identity and motive for coming to Colorado. Without arousing suspicion, she must buy a horse, supplies, and rifle, and keep them stored in her room at Hattie's.

Saturday night, Ginny was having her third dinner of the week with Frank Kinnon. They had spent most of the day sightseeing at the Manitou Cliff Dwellings and enjoyed a picnic at the springs nearby. Tomorrow he was showing her the Garden of the Gods; they would share another meal in that ancient setting. She hadn't feared being with him away from town, as several armed men tagged along as guards against daring villains. She had agreed to the outings because she needed to learn her way around in case disaster struck and she was compelled to flee.

Obviously Frank had let everyone in town know he had "staked his claim" on her because no other men had dared to approach her. The Trevers were pleased by her "conquest" and urged her to continue it, as Frank would "surely propose marriage as soon as he thinks it's proper." In one way, she was glad he had prevented any competition for her as it allowed her to concentrate on her target. In another way, it alarmed her to have him too enamored of her. She was glad he was being cautious and leisurely in his pursuit. She could imagine how cruel a wicked man like him would be if he learned the truth about her. Before that day came, she must either find her father or find a way to prove Frank was a criminal.

"You look lovely tonight, Anna. I'm so happy you came to our town."

Ginny tried to appear poised but was unsettled by his ravenous gaze feasting on her. She hadn't allowed anything personal to occur between them, but she was sure he would attempt to kiss her soon and would eventually propose marriage. She hadn't decided yet how to handle those incidents. But if her ruse became perilous or if his chase became too swift and demanding and she couldn't slow things down between them, she was prepared for her escape. If only Stone would come to help her, she mused in brief panic, but she couldn't depend on that happening. "Thank you for the compliment, Frank; you're such a kind and polite gentleman. So far, things are going fine for me. I finished my last day with Mr. Trevers, so I'll be seeking another job Monday. Do you know of anyone who needs help?"

"That's my surprise for tonight: I do, if you'd like to go to work for me. The woman who did my records and letters at the assay office eloped with a miner sweetheart who struck it rich this week. Can you begin Monday? That is, if you think I'll make a good boss."

Ginny couldn't believe her good fortune—a way to get inside his files and view his records to check out her father's accusations. With luck, there was enlightening and damaging evidence in his office that she could use against him. "That sounds wonderful, Frank. Thank you, and I accept."

He chuckled. "You didn't even ask about salary and hours," he teased.

"I'm certain you'll be fair with me. Won't you?" she asked, and smiled.

"Of course I will. I'll make it such a good offer and such excellent working conditions that you won't ever search for a replacement position."

Ginny was relieved their meal arrived; it compelled him to release her hand that he had grasped and was stroking with his thumb as he stared into her eyes. She was grateful he wasn't rushing her, and she did all she could think of to make certain he continued his sluggish pace. Yet Frank Kinnon was clearly a virile man who went after what he desired; she wasn't sure how long she could stall him if he pressed for a commitment. For the present, behaving as a lady and acting skittish seemed to work in her favor.

"This is delicious," she murmured of the tender roast beef.

"It should be; I raised it on my ranch. You'll have to come out and visit one day. It's beautiful. I promise you'll love it."

"Perhaps, one day," she replied in a cordial tone. "It's too soon to come calling on a handsome bachelor. I'm sure you understand."

"Of course, Anna, but one day soon will come quickly."

"Perhaps," she said again, then flashed him a demure smile. For once, she was glad she was prone to blushing, as it aided her pretense, though wine and her apprehensions were really the cause, not feelings for the evil man. She realized she didn't feel guilty over duping him, as he deserved it.

"I would never do or say anything to upset you or to embarrass you, but I see I have done so."

"I'm certain you wouldn't, Frank. You're a fine gentleman. I'm happy we became acquainted so quickly as Colorado is a wild and dangerous place. You make me feel safe here. I treasure our friendship."

"She's a state of boom towns and ghost towns, a place where fortunes can be made and lost in the same day. I wouldn't allow anyone or anything to harm you, Anna. Whatever you need or want, just ask me."

"You're much too generous and kind, but thank you."

"When the right time comes, I want to be very generous with you."

As if she misunderstood him, she responded, "You said you would pay me a fair salary, so I believe you."

"That isn't what I meant."

"I know." Her point made, she changed the subject. "Have many big strikes have been made near here? There's so much I don't know about mining. Which is better to find, gold or silver? You will let me watch you assay one time and teach me all I need to know to be a good employee?"

"I'm a rich and powerful man who's accustomed to getting what he wants, so forgive me for racing after the most beautiful and desirable woman in town. I don't mean to appear pushy."

Ginny lowered her lashes and smiled as he hadn't answered her questions. "Those are advantages, Frank, not flaws or weaknesses, so don't apologize for having them. I'm sure you realize you make me a little nervous. We've only known each other for less than a week. You must be patient with me."

"You don't know how refreshing it is to meet a lady like you out here. But I promise to behave myself and to control my eagerness to win you. Now, to answer your questions. We've had many big strikes in Colorado since '58 but most of them have been in other towns and up in the high country. Most of those have been in gold, but there's plenty of silver in there somewhere and lucky the man who strikes it. I've assayed ore that would make a prospector's eyes bulge. I'll teach you all you want to know. If you find assaying enjoyable, you can become my assistant. The process is simple but requires training and a good eye, especially with silver. Sometimes its tricky to detect by sight alone. I have several books on it you might find interesting. I'll loan them to you. After you read them, ask me any questions you want. Within a week, you'll probably catch gold or silver fever."

Ginny didn't want to appear suspiciously intrigued. "I can't see myself grubbing in the dirt or living as I've heard those miners and prospectors do."

Frank chuckled and nodded his head. "You're right. Dreams of riches craze them, Anna. It's much easier and cleaner to live off of their fantasies here in comfort and safety. In those camps, men *exist*, they don't live or enjoy life. They're plagued by poverty, illnesses, accidents, fights and bad tempers, loneliness, attacks by thieves or claim-jumpers, depression, disappointment. Hazardous weather condition, poor food or starvation, and freezing hands from mountain streams wear them down. Gold fever takes its toll on them."

As their desserts arrived, she knew the time remaining for questions was getting short. "How do prospecting and mining work? Can they dig anywhere?"

"Yes and no. A man can stake a claim and work it or he can skip from site to site, and if he finds gold or silver can stake a claim there on the spot. Men work alone or in groups. Often they form companies, sometimes doing their own work and sometimes hiring men to do it for them. If a strike is big, a company is best for protection and results. Sharing a lot of wealth is better than eking out a little alone. That's especially true of silver; it's hard and expensive to mine."

Ginny noticed how many times he mentioned silver and wondered if that was a clue. She smiled innocently and asked, "Why silver?" She listened as Frank told her the same things her father had in his letter. His mood and expression exposed his greed for the shiny metals. "That's fascinating, Frank. Have you ever considered investing in a claim or mine?"

"I have invested in two and both should be paying off soon. Don't tell anybody, but I have an advantage being an assayer. Sometimes men bring in samples, that they have no idea the worth of. I get paid a nice fee for steering them to investors and for advising ignorant prospectors they need them. It's true, so nobody is hurt and I make an added profit."

She saw him sipping too often from his wine glass and hoped its potent effect would loosen his evil tongue. With cunning and desperation, she evoked, "It's good to put people who need each other in touch. Have you ever found something in an assay that a prospector or miner missed? I'm sure they would pay plenty for such information."

"Rarely."

Ginny caught a hint in his voice that said he wasn't being honest. "Perhaps one day you will find something special and become famous for being behind the biggest strike in this state."

"If that happens, I hope I'm involved as an investor."

"Or an owner. If a man doesn't realize what he has and offers to sell it to you, why shouldn't you purchase it? Fortunes are made on others' ignorance and greed . . . My goodness, that must sound terrible. I didn't mean to cheat someone. I just meant, if . . . Oh, my, how to explain myself?"

Frank chuckled. "No need, Anna. I understand."

Ginny was positive he didn't and prayed he misunderstood and misjudged her. "I'm glad because sometimes simple words can sound so cold and cruel and deceitful. Someone mentioned salting to me. What does that mean?"

"It's when a claim or mine is worthless or used up and the man tosses out nuggets to fool a buyer. That can get the seller killed or lynched fast."

Wide-eyed, she murmured, "I imagine so, if he isn't long gone by the time a mistake is discovered. Wouldn't a buyer bring samples to someone like you to be tested before he makes his purchase?"

"Usually not. Greed, Anna, the dream of striking it big, makes him foolish. He thinks he's making a good deal when he's being cheated."

"Don't such men deserve each other?" she asked.

"I guess so. You haven't told me why you came here."

Ginny was prepared for that question and fabricated, "I hate to tell you, Frank, but you deserve the truth." As if reluctant, she related the tale she had told Hattie and others. "Most of that is true, but there's more. I trust you, so I'll be honest with you. Besides, someone could arrive any day to expose me and get me into trouble." She noticed how that caught his interest. "My parents are dead and I did lose everything from the war. But my father, Charles Avery, was connected with the Ku Klux Klan." In case he checked on her, as a man in his position had the money and means to do so, her false tale should be foolproof. She related what had happened on the wagontrain, except for Stone's part in it. "I had to get away from the South before I was accused and arrested for being involved with his doings. I wasn't, Frank, but I doubt I could convince the authorities. I thought this was far enough away to be safe, to make a fresh start. Am I awful for not telling you sooner? You must be terribly disappointed with me."

"Of course not. It must have been awful for you. I'm glad you came here. Don't worry about anyone or anything harming you here."

Ginny knew she had intrigued and ensnared him. "Thank you, Frank. Now it's late so I should be getting home."

"You'll be at work Monday morning at eight?"

"Yes, I promise. You won't be sorry for hiring me."

"I'm certain I won't."

At the boardinghouse, Ginny bid him good night and allowed him to kiss her cheek. She walked to her rooms dreading what tomorrow's activity and Monday's challenge would bring. She realized it might have been too early to begin her ruse, but that couldn't be helped now. *Stone, my love, where are you? I need you.*

—— *Chapter 17* ——

Frank let Ginny into the bank and locked the door behind her after speaking to several customers who were waiting outside to do business with him. He smiled and asked if she was ready to begin the new job.

"Nervous, but ready," she responded, then forced a return smile. This was her perfect opportunity to search for clues and to win his confidence, so she told herself to be alert. She mustn't become distracted or reckless for an instant, something "Steve Carr" often had scolded her for doing during her training. She quickly dismissed her love from mind and observed her surroundings.

Four clerks stood behind a long U-shaped counter getting ready to open for business in twenty minutes. Frank whispered for her to notice that the workers had either no pockets or stitched-down ones in their trousers to prevent hiding places if they became tempted to steal a nugget or coin. The counter and floors were highly polished wood, but, as Frank whispered to her again, there were no chairs or sitting areas supplied to entice customers to remain inside the large room longer than necessary. He said she would grasp why when the bank became crowded and noisy soon.

In every corner there was a guard armed with a rifle at the ready to discourage or to defeat robberies. Most propped their buttocks on stools to keep from becoming overly fatigued or cramped during a long day of standing. She saw all the guards and clerks eye her for a moment. No doubt, she concluded, they also knew their boss had a "claim" on her.

Ginny looked at a large sign on one wall: The Frank Kinnon Bank. A clock was mounted on the opposite one. In the elbow of the waist-high counter was a shed-type case with scales for weighing gold dust, flakes, and nuggets, Frank said.

"It's glassed on the customer's side to keep wind from scattering gold dust on the scales when the door is opened and closed. It also lets customers witness the handling of their property to prevent any problems. Want a peek inside the safe before it's locked?"

"Yes. I've never been inside one before."

Frank guided her around the counter and to the large metal "closet." While blocking everyone's view, his deft fingers twirled the combination dial on the heavy door. With brute strength, he pushed the door aside and motioned her into the small, dark area that held numerous shelves from floor to ceiling. Using a lamp, Frank adjusted it to give her a good view of the contents: bills, coins, pouches of gold in three forms, ingots of silver and gold, and samples of ore on trays.

"What do those mean?" she asked, pointing to names on some bags.

"Men either sell me their gold and silver or they store it here for a fee. Whenever they need some, they have the clerks weigh out the amount they want. They sign a paper inside the pouch telling when and how much they withdrew and how much is left. Storing it here keeps them from carrying around large amounts and risking being robbed. It also keeps some men from being tempted or tricked into spending it all in one night after they get drunk and lose their wits at the gambling tables."

Ginny tried to read the names in a hurry to see if her father's or Clay's was among them and stalled for more time by saying, "That sounds very intelligent to me. What happens to a man's gold if he dies?"

"If I hear about a misfortune, I date his pouch and hold it for one year for family or partners to claim. If no one does, it becomes mine. Those eight on that shelf are patiently waiting to jump into my pocket."

Ginny's heart fluttered as her gaze touched on her father's name on a fat pouch. She wished she could peek inside to see what the date was but dared not show her interest to the man nearby. She was worried about finding it on that gloomy shelf, but Mathew Marston had been reported dead. She didn't want to imagine that might be true or to think about Frank taking something that belonged to her if Matt was gone. "There's a fortune here. Have you ever been robbed?"

"No. I keep four guards on duty day and night. It's expensive, but it increases business because men know their earnings are safe with me."

"What if something happened to you? How would they open the safe?" How, she mused, could she get her hands on her father's property?

"I'm the only one here who knows the combination. If I died, the governor has the combination in his safe. It's about time to open, so let's get in the back where we work." As he locked the enormous safe, Frank told her, "The clerks keep the banking records, but I check them every night for errors. You won't have any tasks out here."

On the back wall was a door into another section, over which a sign read: Frank Kinnon, Assay Office. He led her into a hallway and closed the door. "Nobody comes back here unless invited or by appointment." He motioned to three doors as he explained, "That's my assay room, my office, and where you'll work. I make notes which you'll write up in a report form twice: one copy for me and one for the customer. They're kept in a file in my office and it's always locked when I'm out. You'll also copy letters for me because my script, as you'll soon discover, is terrible. You'll keep the office books: charges, payments, supplies, and so forth."

Ginny followed him into the "laboratory," a clean but cluttered room. She laughed, "I almost feel as if I'm in jail; every window and door has bars."

Frank chuckled. "A man can't be too careful when he's responsible for so much wealth. It would shock you to know how much money and precious metals are in that safe. If anything happened to them, the men around here would lynch me in a second. I have to protect my business and reputation."

"It appears you're doing a good job with both."

"Thank you, Anna. Please look around and ask all the questions you wish."

Ginny glanced at cabinets that held supplies used in his trade. There were several long work tables. One had lines of metal weights and a scale. Another held a small crusher, a vise and hammer for sizing samples, many wooden trays to hold them, flux and burners and crucibles for tests, tongs for lifting hot objects, thick jars of nitric acid, and paper with ink and pen for recording results. "How does this process work?" she asked after he explained the use of each item, though many were obvious or were marked.

As he removed his coat, rolled up his sleeves, and put on an apron to protect his clothes, he said, "Pull up that stool and I'll give you a lesson while I do this sample. Kelly's coming by later today for his answer."

Ginny realized he was absorbed by his task or he would have fetched the stool for her. She sat close to the table as Frank Kinnon worked and talked to observe this man her father mistrusted and feared.

"I use chemicals and heating techniques to determine how much precious metal or mineral is in a sample. Most are scattered throughout. Flux helps melt it into what's called a button. It separates into slag, which is tossed out, and a button of mostly lead and hopefully something valuable. The button is melted to get out the impurities and to leave a dore bead, usually gold or silver, or a combination of both. I weigh the bead and record the figure. Next comes nitric acid bath to remove any silver. This is one of the trickiest and most dangerous steps; acid can burn worse than any flame. I weigh the gold I recover and subtract that amount from the first figure to determine how much, if any, silver is there. Take a look: gold with no silver tracings. Nuggets men find in streams don't need assaying; their value is obvious and their payment is easy to determine by weight. Mining gold is different; if it's embedded in rock, it has to be freed by pick and smelting."

"Fascinating," she murmured.

"No tests are necessary if a prospector brings in fool's gold. A trained eye can spot pyrite instantly, but it's tricked many an innocent man. It's sometimes used to dupe ignorant buyers into thinking they're getting a valuable claim."

Ginny looked at the samples of pyrite and gold Frank showed her. "You said silver was harder and more expensive to mine. How is it done?"

"Ore has to be crushed, calcined, washed, smelted, and cast into bullion. Stop me if I confuse you. Calcine is to convert ore into calx by roasting it in a way that it's exposed to air and oxidizing. Silver is a pure metal, but it's embedded in or with other materials, such as gold, quartz, lead, or copper. Most prospectors overlook it because of its color; they discard gray or blackish or bluish rocks without realizing what they've found. It requires lots of men, work, equipment, and money to extract it. A company needs furnaces and vats for removing roasted ore, then laborers to cut and haul wood and feed fires. They need smelters and crushers, and diggers and haulers. They require a water supply and trained men to cast silver into bricks. It takes guards for the diggings, company, and transport, plus drivers and wagons and teams. Silver mining is big business, Anna."

That explanation helped her to grasp her father's problems better. "My goodness, it sounds like it. Is that why you didn't get involved in it?"

"I haven't found a promising silver mine to invest in, only gold."

"You said you have books I can study?"

"Yes, over there on that shelf. Take what you want."

"I think it would be best if I familiarize myself with all of this since I'll be working here and living in this area. You're smart and skilled and I'm very impressed. It's going to be interesting and fun working here with you."

"It's good to know your surroundings. If you have any questions or problems, come to me. I won't mind being interrupted by you."

"Thank you, Frank. Oh, my," she said, and feigned a look of dismay. "Shouldn't I call you Mr. Kinnon at work?"

"No need. We'll see few people back here."

"What do you want me to do first today? Do I have a routine to follow?"

Frank related her tasks and schedule, then showed her to her office. "If you need anything, call me. I'll be back here or out front."

Ginny sat down, smiled, and watched him leave. She read over the notes she was supposed to copy neatly into a ledger and glanced at the reports she was to write out afterward. It was going to be a busy day. Before she began her first task, she wondered if Frank had requested information about her from any sources back South. He hadn't mentioned the half-true, half-false story she had told him about herself last week. If he suspected her of wrongdoing with the Klan or of coming here to seek a rich husband, it didn't show or didn't matter to him.

At least, she realized, there wouldn't be a pregnancy complicating her life, as her monthly flow began this morning. Yet she wanted to have Stone's children and, every time he touched her, the last thing that came to mind was worry over getting pregnant. Probably she was lucky his seed wasn't growing inside her as he might be lost to her forever. Three weeks ago today she had left Dallas. If he had returned home as promised and been told the truth, there had been enough time for him to reach Colorado City, if he wanted to come after her. Perhaps he didn't and never would. She ordered herself not to think about Stone Chapman right now as it evoked too many doubts, fears, and pains.

Ginny closed her eyes and envisioned the bulging leather pouch in the safe with her father's name attached. She could use that money to search for Matt; rather, to pay a detective to ferret out the truth. She was trapped in a bind: she couldn't get answers without asking questions, but she couldn't ask questions without exposing herself.

Soon, she promised, she would find a way to get at the truth.

All of Thursday, Ginny knew something was afoot. Frank Kinnon smiled, whistled, grinned, and hummed continuously. He dropped in for little chats. He adored her from head to foot with his eyes. He invited her to join him tomorrow for "a special dinner."

Anxiety nibbled at her as she feared he was going to propose. Whatever would she do and say if he offered marriage? She couldn't marry him just to extract clues. If he was that serious, dealing with him might become difficult. She hadn't expected her target to fall in love with her. Desire her; perhaps and hopefully. Love her; that was trouble. Propose; that was incredible. He could be her father's mur— *No, Ginny, don't think such horrible thoughts. You need more time to glean clues but Frank might not allow either one. Better come up with an alternate plan.*

Shortly before quitting time, Ginny was putting away the letters and reports in Frank's office that she'd done while he finished work in the assay room. She noticed a file marked *MM.* She glanced into the hallway and heard the man humming, obviously still busy working. Quickly she snatched out the file and read two papers inside. The same notes and figures in her father's last letter were recorded there, with the conclusion: *high grade silver ore, 80 to 90 percent pure.* Mathew Marston's name wasn't listed nor was a location of the strike, but she was certain this file was about her father. It was dated last June, a year ago. Yet her father's pouch of gold or silver was still in the safe so a year, according to Frank's rule, hadn't passed since its deposit. Her father's last letter to her had been dated July of '66 after Clay's death and his departure to seek investors: almost a year had passed. Would such a task require that long? And why no word from him since then? Unless he feared the wrong person might be watching her and might get their hands on any enlightening missives . . .

Ginny heard Frank coming down the hall, and panicked a moment. Thinking fast, she tossed the two files and other papers to the floor. She muttered to herself, "Look what you've done, Anna." She knelt to retrieve them.

"What's wrong?" Frank asked from the doorway.

Ginny looked up and sent him a wry smile. "I was pulling out the Maples file and another one came along with it. I dropped everything trying to replace it without putting down the stack. I'm sorry, but nothing looks damaged. I'll have this mess straightened up shortly. Two pages don't have names, so I don't know where they go."

Frank came over and knelt to assist her. He took the two papers and slipped them into the file marked *MM.* He chuckled and said, "That's one claim I'd like to invest in, but nobody knows where it's located. It could be anywhere in the Rocky Mountains or even in another state."

"What do you mean, Frank? Why does it only have initials?"

Frank squatted and looked at her. "Sometimes prospectors and miners don't trust local assayers or want news of their findings to leak out prematurely, so they carry their samples a long distance to have them tested. In this case, I understand why. I don't know where that sample was taken from, but it's one of the richest grades of silver I've seen."

Ginny watched him stare at his hands, then ball his fists until his knuckles whitened, that bittersweet vision seemed to bring a greedy and frustrated look to his face. Frank stood and helped her to her feet. He stuffed the file back into place, right where the name Marston would go.

"If there's as much silver and gold embedded in the area as the ore they brought me implies, it'll be one of the biggest and best strikes ever made. That's how I know nobody's found it; there has been no big headline in newspapers across the country and it's been a year. They would have been wealthy and famous men. It's worth millions, almost pure. Lot of gold, too. It came out easy, so little refining will be required. I'd surely like to invest in whoever's company finds this strike. It even tempts me to go searching for it myself."

"I don't understand, Frank. It's already been found. You've tested the sample. Do you know the men? Have you seen them in town?"

"I knew both of them, but they were murdered last summer, probably by common thieves. No claim was ever filed at the local land office by Mathew Marston and Clayton Cassidy. The location of the silver remains unknown to this day."

Ginny was relieved she was able to control any outward reaction to his disclosures. He was relaxed and he trusted her, yet she must make sure to sound only curious. "Surely someone else will find it one day. There are so many men working the mountains that it can't remain a secret forever."

"But remember what I told you—silver is often overlooked by ignorant and inexperienced men. Matt and Clay recognized it from working a mine."

"It's a shame they were killed; it could have meant plenty of jobs and more progress in Colorado. What happened?"

"Their bodies were found in a burned cabin. Undertaker said both were shot first. Their mules and gear outside were used to identify them."

"Perhaps whoever attacked them forced them to reveal where the strike was located before they were murdered."

"That couldn't have happened, Anna, or it'd be big news by now."

"What if this villain staked a land claim and he's biding his time before mining it until the time he won't fall under suspicion by the law?"

"I thought of that. I tried to help solve the crimes by checking to see who registered claims here. But there's been nothing suspicious to date."

Ginny didn't dare remind him he'd said the strike could be anywhere and asked him if he'd checked with other land offices, such as the one in Denver. "I suppose you're right: it may never be found or not for a long time; their killers, too. A crime like that must be too old to solve even for a detective."

"I actually hired one to see if he could backtrack on them, but it was futile. I even thought for a while that somebody else may have been in the cabin and one of them escaped. That couldn't be true because nobody's seen or heard from either man and Marston has a gold pouch in the safe that he wouldn't leave behind."

Ginny gave a sympathetic sigh. "What a shame, to die just before you become rich. Did they have families? Does anyone here try to reach kin following accidents and deaths?"

"Cassidy had no family. Marston has a daughter in England, but nobody knew how to reach her or even knew her name. And she could be married and have a different one by now. They stayed here after being Galvanized Yanks for years in the state. Seemed like good men to me."

"How awful for a person's father to be dead and not know it."

"I wish I could learn more about her. If Matt sent her any news or maps, I could handle a mining company for her. We'd both be rich."

Ginny feigned an interested look. "Did you try hard to locate her?"

"Yes, but without a name or town, it was impossible. I checked with the Army, but they didn't have any records revealing anything about her. If I could just come up with the right clues, I'd be first in line to take over the claim from a criminal I'd exposed."

"You said one of them might still be alive. Why would he disappear?"

"I can't imagine."

"Nor can I. It would be nice to own a mine of such value. This has given me an idea. You could start another business, Frank: let men register their identities and prospecting locations or claims with you; then, when or if something happened to them, their families could be notified about inheritances. They could carry papers telling whoever found them to contact you for a small reward for their help. You could charge a fee and I could handle the records."

"That might be an excellent idea. I'll think about it this weekend."

She turned and finished her filing. She didn't actually expect him to act on her idea; she had used it to help dupe him.

A clerk knocked on the door and said, "We're closed, sir. You ready to check up?"

"Coming in a moment. You go home and rest, Anna. And don't forget about our special dinner tomorrow night."

She smiled and assured him she wouldn't.

Ginny finished her bath and returned to her room. She had eaten with Hattie and two other boarders, as the others were out for the evening. She was ready to turn in for the night, because she was emotionally and physically fatigued from her labors and discoveries today. She dreaded facing Frank tomorrow as she suspected what he had in store for her later that night. She locked her sitting-area door and entered the other room. She barely suppressed a scream as her gaze noticed the man half lying on her bed with his booted feet on the floor.

Ginny gaped at him as questions filled her head and spilled forth, "Stone, how did you get in here? Did anyone see you? How did you find me? Surely you didn't ask around to locate me?"

He sat up, exhaled, and looked at her. Light-brown hair tumbled over her shoulders and drifted to her waist. Hazel eyes were wide with astonishment and suspense. Her lips had remained parted after their rush of words. One hand gripped the edges of a night robe to keep it closed; the other held bathing needs with a damp drying cloth thrown over her forearm. *Shu,* she was beautiful and tempting with little—yet in another way, a vast—distance between them. He finally managed to speak. "Hello, Ginny Marston."

She stared at him and tried to ascertain his mood. The fact he hadn't leapt upon her and attacked her with harsh words or blows told her he had himself under rigid control. Her gaze took in the image of irresistible manhood. He wasn't an illusion, this man she loved clad in all black and with a short beard as if in disguise. Yet, neither had he leapt from the bed and taken her into his arms as she'd hoped when they next met. It was hard not to rush to him. At last, he was here. "Your father told you everything?"

Stone scooted to the end of the bed and propped one elbow on the wooden footboard. He placed his unshaven chin on the backs of curled fingers and drilled his gaze into hers. Before he answered, he wondered why she remained frozen in the doorway instead of hurrying to his aching arms. "Him and your letter. So, I finally meet the real woman. You aren't Charles Avery's daughter and you aren't Bennett Chapman's daughter. You've had a lot of fathers along your route to here. Have you found yours?"

"No. I was told just today that he and his partner were murdered last year, but I know—I hope—that isn't true."

"What is true, Ginny?"

She walked to the bed and sat down near him. After he shifted to face her, she confessed everything to the man she loved and prayed he felt the same about her and believed her. "I know Father wasn't in that cabin, but I don't know where he is now or if the killer got to him later. If he's still alive, I can't understand why he hasn't contacted me. I'm sure Frank Kinnon's involved and I'm slowly gleaning clues from him."

"It sounds as if you're as good at deceptions and investigations as I am." He saw her wince as if he'd insulted her or struck her a physical blow. "Don't fret, I didn't ask about Virginia Marston, because Father told me about your dangerous predicament. I arrived this morning and I've watched the bank most of the day after I saw you enter at lunch and not come out again. I followed you here and waited until it was safe to sneak inside. I would have come sooner but we had trouble with rustlers at the ranch." He explained his meaning. "You might be pleased to learn Father and I have made peace and my parents are getting married as soon as I return home."

I *return, not* we? "That's wonderful news. I'm happy for them and for you. Please congratulate them for me. How soon are you leaving?"

He was baffled by her reaction of sadness and anguish to a mention of departure that should delight her and her father if they wanted him out of the way. If only he knew what she knew about the matter tormenting him. He dreaded to ask out of fear she might lie to him again, even if only out of mistrust or caution. He must wait and see how much she revealed.

Both felt the strain within themselves and the other. Each wanted to reach out but waited for the other one to do it first.

"I haven't decided. What you did to me and my family was wrong, Ginny, but I understand your motives. I want to thank you for giving Father a little of Johanna and for halting your ruse before it lasted too long." He witnessed a look of surprise and relief; then, sadness dulled her eyes again.

"Is that all you came to tell me, that you won't seek revenge?"

"No, I wanted to tell you, for one thing, I'm glad you aren't Johanna."

When he didn't say more, she probed, "Why?"

"Because she and I, as you discovered, were blood kin. It knifed me badly to learn I had made love with my sister and knew I had to hurt her again."

Be bold and brave, Ginny, or you'll never extract the truth, whatever it might be. "Did you say those cruel and painful things to me that night only to discourage me, or did you truly mean them? Were you only trying to halt things between us because you thought our relationship was wrong and had no future, or were you trying to convince me of your genuine disinterest? Was it just physical attraction for you, Stone, nothing more? Do you still want to discard me now that you know I'm not your sister or Anna Avery? Did my two deceptions destroy all respect and affection you had for me? Did they destroy any hope or chance of us building a future together?"

Stone gazed at the daughter of the man who had murdered his best friend, a man he'd sworn to kill. That was an impending task she might or might not know about, one that would affect the "chance" she was questioning. Clay's message had told him that Matt was acting strange. "I don't think I kan trust him ennymore," he had written Stone. "He's balking on filing our klaim. He says we have to keep it a sekret. I've had krazy akseedents with only Matt around. He's been my friend and partner but I'm skared to trust him. If ennything happens to me, my share of the klaim is yours. Here's the map and paper saying so. You know I don't have no family and yore my best friend. You saved my life more than once. If Matt balks, force it out of him. It's worth a fortune, Stone. That's what the assayer told us. If you kan kome help me with him, pleze hurry."

Stone felt there must be valid reasons for Clay distrusting Matt after the two men had been together for years as Galvanized Yankees and prospectors. With Clay dead and the land in the Marston name, Matt believed he owned it all. He had learned that Matt had registered the claim in Denver under Ginny's initials. He knew the strike's location, so he didn't need Matt or Ginny to lead him there. It wasn't the wealth that he wanted; he wanted Clay's killer exposed and punished. This thing with Kinnon, he reasoned from experience, was a smokescreen like Indians sometimes used to conceal or protect their retreats across prairieland. If Matt wasn't guilty, he would have gone to the law; he would have helped them find and punish the killer of his friend and partner. Yet, even if there was a slim possibility Matt was innocent, Matt'd let the murderer go free just to keep the strike for himself. Perhaps he was off searching for investors as Ginny had said and he'd show up one day and plead ignorance of Clay's death and his own alleged one. Those were points he'd investigate soon.

Had Matt mentioned Stone in his letters to Ginny? Was duping him her real reason for impersonating his sister? Did she know about his lethal quest and inheritance? Those questions plagued him. If he asked them, would she be honest? His father had told him how she had escaped Fort Smith and his reach; she was cunning and brave. She'd come here alone and was doing fine by herself. His mother had urged him to—

"Stone, why did you really come here? A letter could have said all you have." Ginny was worried over his lengthy silence and impenetrable stare. "Does it take this long to decide how you feel? Was what I did so terrible that you can't understand it or forgive me?"

The Special Agent was skilled at tracking, outwitting, and exposing criminals. He was experienced at confronting troubles head-on with speed and accuracy and without fear. Somehow those traits deserted him tonight in Ginny's presence. She looked innocent and vulnerable, honest and tormented. "A letter can't look you in the eye when it talks. But even face-to-face, you can't always tell if someone is being honest with you; we've both proven that."

"Except for the false claims I made about my identity, I was myself with you,"

Ginny assured him. "I don't think the same is true of Steve Carr and Stone Chapman; you two are much alike yet greatly different. You're the stranger in this room." She didn't stop to think it might be the short beard that made him look different, mysterious and almost intimidating. "Even if you can't forgive me and don't want a personal relationship with me now or ever, please let me hire you to help find my father." *I have to keep you here until you realize the truth. You love me and want me, you stubborn creature. I need time to prove it to you.*

"You want *me* to help you look for Mathew Marston? Why?"

Ginny misunderstood why he stressed the "me." "You're a skilled tracker and agent. I don't know how or where to search for him. I know to work on Frank Kinnon, but he's getting too—It's just so hard and scary working alone on a dangerous and enamored man. Do you despise me too much to help me? I'll pay whatever I can." *Stay and work with me, Stone. Give us time together to get past this strain between us.*

Ignoring the evocative deception he had in mind, he admitted the truth. "I don't hate you, Ginny. I haven't stopped wanting you for a moment since the day we met in Georgia. Things have been crazy and it takes getting used to. I have to deal with all these changes and deceits. But they weren't all your fault. I did my share of lying and tricking and provoking you to do more than you wanted to do. At the ranch when I thought you were my sister, I was tormented and stunned. I had to turn you against me, and I had to leave there fast. I made love to you on the trail because I wanted you and needed you. You, Ginny, not just your body. *Shu,* woman, don't you realize how you get to me? I've never wanted or needed anything more than you, not even for my father to acknowledge me as his son. When I learned the truth about your two ruses, yes, I was angry. And I was disappointed, hurt, and confused. I'm sure you've felt the same way many times with me. I didn't come here to punish you or toss you aside. I came because you were mine and I want you to be mine again . . . Why are you crying?" he asked as he moved closer and brushed away the tears rolling down her cheeks.

"I was so afraid I'd lost you, more afraid than I've ever been in my life. I love you, Stone. I've tried not to press you because you're so . . ."

"Skittish as a horse near a branding iron?"

His broad smile warmed her very soul. It was enticing and devilish and tugged at the corners of his wide mouth until it parted his lips and exposed even, white teeth. His dark eyes glowed with emotions that matched her own. She was no longer tired or afraid; her senses were alive and alert. He was utterly arresting, and she was susceptible to his charms. "I'm so glad you're here. I want you so much. It's been too long since you've held me and kissed me. Lordy, how I've missed you. Can you forgive me?"

For almost anything. He pressed kisses to her brow, nose, and lips. As his mouth left hers, he murmured, "Surely you know you're the only woman for me." His bearded chin gingerly moved aside the robe so his tongue could taste the clean flesh of her shoulder and neck.

"You're the only man for me, Stone." Ginny's arms tightened around him as she sought surcease for a yearning deeper and stronger at that moment than her physical desire for him. Her heart was so full of love, joy, and relief that she feared it might burst. Her body soon blazed with fiery passion. She wanted all of him.

She lacked the strength and wits to deny what they both craved, a union of bodies despite any consequences. She surrendered to his intoxicating kisses and stirring caresses.

Stone longed to reveal everything within his heart and mind, but he couldn't until he confronted Matt and held the entire truth within his grasp. His hold on her was too new and fragile to risk breaking with a stunning confession about their mutual target. Maybe she was right and there was another villain to blame for Clay's death. If so, they would unmask him together. If Matt was innocent, it would be rash to expose his speculations and create new problems between them.

As Ginny kissed and caressed him and changed his line of thought, it seemed to Stone as if she entreated his touch and response as proof of his feelings and claims, as a way of evoking reassurance from him. It was true, she was the only woman who could have reached him and saved him from the destructive ravages of the past. His hands peeled the robe off her body to reveal creamy skin that beckoned his lips and mouth. With expertise and enraptured by her, he stormed her bared flesh with deft hands and captivating lips as he explored her curvy regions and flat planes.

Ginny hugged him possessively because she believed he was yielding his all to her. She unbuttoned his shirt and removed it, then trailed fingers over his iron-muscled body. She yearned to make tender and passionate love to him. Nature and her entire being demanded she respond to the urgent messages passing between and within them. She gave free rein to those emotions and unleashed every inhibition.

Stone was enthralled by her urgency and his own. His head seemed as if it was spinning in a whirlwind. He parted them to hurriedly remove his boots and pants, as his weapons and hat were hanging over a chair nearby. He turned back to her to find her naked and her hand extended in a sweet invitation. Her hazel eyes beckoned. His fingers buried in her hair as his hand pressed her head closer to his to seal their mouths in a breath-stealing kiss. His embrace tightened and he refused to release her for a long time. His needs and kisses became urgent and demanding but he tried not to rush and to be gentle. He groaned in rapidly mounting desire. "I said you were a dangerous distraction and irresistible temptation; I was right."

"So are you, my love." Though smoldering with hot desire, she was dreamily aware of each kiss and caress, each sensation. She felt his hunger for her in his touch, heard it in his tone, and read it in those dark eyes that enslaved her.

Stone realized her desire was as tangible and evocative as a physical caress. Weeks of starvation for her ignited his body to a flaming torch, fires that licked precariously at his resolve to take her with leisure. His molten body covered hers and shared its seething heat. He was almost afraid to caress and kiss her lest his control be vanquished and he succumb to its coaxing to take her with swiftness.

He leaned over and tantalized her taut breasts with his lips while his hands drifted downward to stimulate her womanly center with love and tenderness. When his mouth returned to hers, their kiss fused into a savage and feverish bond. Their need so great, he eased between her thighs and slid himself within her, then halted to master his wavering control. Never had he taken a woman who enticed his manhood to seek bliss the moment he entered her body. She ensnared him with a speed and ease that nearly hurled him beyond reason and willpower. She smelled fresh as spring air and was as hot as the sultriest summer day.

Ginny's hands traveled from Stone's sable hair to his bronzed torso. His body was beautiful, strong, and stimulating. She arched to meet his hips each time he withdrew and entered her again. Her body responded to his instinctively, but what instinct didn't supply, he did. She writhed as his lips, hands, and movements worked magic upon her. She tried to relax, to give him full mastery over the situation, and to abandon her will to his; she couldn't stay still, not with him assailing her wits and body. The sensations he created were wonderful and intense. She tingled. She flamed. She wanted every instant of this union.

Urged onward by his insistent desire, Stone increased his pace and deepened his kisses. She was holding nothing back from him and that filled him with happiness.

Ginny felt her body quiver with suspense. Only Stone could quench this thirst for appeasement. "I want you and need you, my love."

"And you shall have me." He carried them to the peak of pleasure where she stiffened a moment and moaned in ecstasy. Her grip on him tightened and she pressed herself closer to him. He swept her over the precipice and beyond . . .

Blissfully sated, they didn't break or release their hold on each other. They snuggled together as their bodies quieted and glowed in passion's aftermath. They felt peaceful, warm, and happy.

Ginny nestled her cheek to his chest. With eyes closed, she sighed dreamily. She felt his fingers wander through her mussed hair and over her damp flesh. She smiled when he placed light kisses over her face. She felt safe, tranquil, and fulfilled in his arms.

Stone relaxed. Beyond any doubt, he loved her. He had taken other females but never *made love* to them; he knew the difference now. Ginny was totally satisfying in all ways. That was the secret to happiness and contentment: love. He rolled to his side and gazed at her. "Tell me everything about you again. I want to know every detail about my Ginny Marston."

It was nearing midnight when she finished relating her history from birth to this moment. "The last thing to tell you about Frank Kinnon is that I think he's going to propose to me tomorrow night. How can I discourage or stall him without breaking my hold over him?"

Stone knew he had to stay out of Kinnon's sight and remain unshaven to conceal his presence from a man who could recognize and expose him. If she was right, Kinnon or someone else could be guilty rather than Matt. If that proved to be true, it would be wonderful because he wouldn't have to hurt Ginny or risk losing her. "I don't want him touching you or kissing you, woman. I feel jealousy firing in me already. You saw your father's pouch in the safe and those reports in the file. What else could you learn from him? He won't confess he murdered two men. If you ask questions, he'll get suspicious. It's time to quit that job and stop taking chances."

"If I quit or suddenly change my behavior, he *will* get suspicious."

"Change your behavior? Have you been enticing him?"

Ginny toyed with his beard. "Not exactly. It wasn't necessary."

"I can believe that. You stole my heart and eye the first time we met."

She nibbled on his hairy chin. "Good, and I'll never return them."

"Back to Kinnon. You go to work as usual tomorrow but don't do anything to arouse his curiosity. I'll figure out what to do about him while you're gone. You may need to see him for dinner, let him propose, then ask for time off from work to consider his offer. That'll give us the opportunity to think this out. I don't like it, but it might be the only path open to us for now."

"Sounds clever to me. I'm sure it will work . . . Where will you stay?" she abruptly changed the subject.

"Are you asking me to leave?" he jested, nipping at her lips.

"It would expose us if you're found here with me. Besides, this is dangerous. Babies can come from wild sport like this."

He cupped her face between his hands and locked their gazes. "Doesn't matter at this point, Ginny love, if you'll marry me soon."

Her eyes widened and her lips parted. "You're asking me to . . ."

Stone chuckled, then kissed her forehead. "You look shocked that I love you and want to marry you. I thought both were obvious by now."

"I am and I'm not," she said amidst hugs and kisses.

Stone chuckled again. "I take your reaction to mean yes."

"Yes, yes, yes," she murmured in a happy rush. "Those are the most beautiful words I've ever heard. I love you, Stone Chapman."

"I love you, too, Ginny. We have to make sure nothing comes between us again to separate us." The moment that caution left his lips he wanted to cringe in dread of what he must do.

Her fingers teased his dark beard. "What could possibly go wrong, my roguish lawman? We love each other and have been honest with each other."

"Set a wedding date fast while I'm being brave," he pretended to tease.

"We should wait until after we locate Father."

I need to rope you quick, woman. "Why? We can get hitched as soon as possible. I don't want any children of mine born like I was."

He seemed afraid of losing her, which touched her deeply. "You won't lose me, Stone, so don't worry about hurrying me to the preacher. I'm wearing your brand on my heart and body already. I want my father there."

"It doesn't bother you I'm a . . ."

"You aren't a bastard. Your father has claimed you. You have his name."

"That wasn't what I was going to say. Have you forgotten I'm part Indian, part Apache? Our children will carry Indian blood."

"I love you, Stone, every part of you. Nothing changes my feelings."

"You don't know much about me, woman."

"Then tell me everything, just like I told you."

"You know how I was born and what my father's denial did to me, and maybe some of that damage was my fault because I reacted so badly to the situation." He reminded her of how he'd been adopted and had discovered Ben was his father through overhearing a quarrel with Stella. "As far back as I can remember, I was told to call my mother Aunt Nan to keep people from gossiping about her, from calling her an Indian whore. Her name, Nandile, means Sunflower; she was an Apache chief's daughter."

"You're the grandson of a chief? What a marvelous thing to tell our children and grandchildren. Be proud of that heritage, Stone."

"Father was captured by her tribe to exchange for arms and supplies to fight the white man. But Ben proved himself a great warrior and friend, so they gave him his freedom. When he left their camp, he took her with him. She's been his lover for almost thirty years. Ben always said they couldn't marry because people hated and mistrusted Indians, especially the feared Apaches, so it might ruin him. I always said I didn't understand and called him a coward and weakling, but I suppose I see his point now. Love and desire can make people do crazy things; you've taught me that much. I loved you and wanted you, but I was too scared to tell you. Maybe the same was true with Father; he feared the repercussions. Since leaving home, I've witnessed the hostilities between the two sides. When you're the one involved in a nasty situation, you can be blind to reality."

"That's true, my love, but that's how we learn and grow. We're all human, so we have flaws and weaknesses. Sometimes we think problems are bigger than they are, and sometimes we make them larger so we'll have an excuse to ignore them . . . How did you get your name? It's so unusual."

"Mother named me Stone Thrower after my grandfather when he was a child. Ben kept the first part of it when he adopted me at age ten. I loved and trusted him and I believed until recently that he had betrayed me; I believed he used my mother and misused Stella, bad as she was, and she was bad, Ginny. I stayed at the ranch for years trying to punish him, but it only hurt both of us. I ran away at sixteen to find myself. I spent time with my mother's people and was taught many warrior skills. But a half-breed didn't fit in there, and I didn't like raiding. I wandered into the white man's world and did odd jobs but didn't seem to fit anywhere. I was confronted by the problems he'd tried to explain to me and Mother." He related many of the troubles he'd had in his early years as a result of being part Indian.

"I even worked as a Texas Ranger for three years. But things got too hot with the Apaches and I couldn't bring myself to help kill my mother's people or push them onto some filthy and barren reservation. When the war started, I saw it as an escape from my problems, another chance to use and hone my skills. But I was captured by Union soldiers in April of '63. I shouldn't have joined the war; it wasn't part of my world. But I was looking for something, something I didn't understand, not until I met you, Ginny Marston." He kissed her, then smiled. "I was trying to save a man's life when I was taken prisoner. After months of torture and captivity, I was asked if I wanted to become a Galvanized Yankee and serve my sentence in the Army out West. In July, I was on my way to a new life."

Ginny brightened. "My father was, too. He was captured at Stones River at Murfreesboro in early '63. He served at forts in and near here. He stayed after the war and did prospecting. He didn't want to return to Green Oaks and intrude on his family's new life; they all believed he was long dead and that didn't seem fair. Where did you go? What did you do?"

"They guessed I was a half-breed, so they figured they could use me to help out with Indian problems. I worked as an interpreter, scout, guide, guard, and plenty of other things that I mentioned that night in camp. When the war ended, I did much the same things, but for pay then. I agreed to help the Yanks because I wanted to be free, to stay on the move, to learn all I could for survival, and to get away from such cruelties. Two years ago, I met Warren Turner from the Justice Department. He was impressed by some of my missions and asked me to become a Special Agent. The work is exciting and stimulating. I thrived on the danger, challenges, and victory. I craved and needed the importance and respect I received from my successes. I liked having white men forced to depend on a half-breed for their lives and safety, forced to follow one's orders. Warren and I became friends; he's my superior. I've sent him a letter of resignation. I plan to return to the ranch and live there, if that suits you, Ginny. You will be my wife soon. We'll inherit it one day."

"What about my father and the silver strike?"

Stone hoped wealth wasn't that important to her; he didn't think it was. "He can run it if he's still alive. If not, you can form a company to do it. You said you know where the strike is, and the land is registered in your name so nobody can steal it from you."

"There's one point that needs handling if Father's gone: his partner. If Clayton Cassidy has family somewhere, part of the strike is theirs. Father said he had no relatives, but I'd like to make sure of that."

That moved Stone deeply and convinced him she was being honest. "If they're distant, why would they deserve it? You'll need investors, but all of this can be discussed and decided another time. It's late and you need sleep, woman. I'll sneak out, bed down someplace, and see you tomorrow night after your evening with Kinnon."

"I dread that, but it might help us learn something."

"Just don't go too far to dupe him."

"I won't, so don't worry. If there's one thing I've learned since leaving England, it's how dangerous and dark midnight secrets can be."

Stone prayed his remaining secret wouldn't be long or damaging, and he would confess it soon. To do it now might evoke suspicions. She needed him and, if she learned the truth about him, she might turn against him and find herself in danger. It was possible Matt had her duped and was deserting and betraying her as he was doing to the rest of his family in Georgia. When she discovered the truth about her father, he needed to be at her side. "I love you, Ginny. Whatever happens, you have me."

She cuddled against him. "I love you, Stone Chapman. I can hardly wait for this to be over so we can begin our new life together in Texas."

"I'll work hard to make sure it's very soon."

"Nothing can ever come between us again," she murmured as she kissed him, unaware that terrible "nothing" would appear within hours.

— *Chapter 18* —

~

"WHAT?" Ginny heard the shout come from Frank Kinnon's office next to hers. Muffled voices reached her ears then another shout of "Damnation!" She wondered what had evoked her boss's anger. Surely, she fretted, she hadn't been exposed. Her apprehension mounted as she strained to eavesdrop, but she couldn't make out what was being said. She saw a shabbily dressed prospector pass her room while counting gold coins in his dirty grasp. Her tension mounted as she waited to see if he came to confront her. Two guards passed her office and entered Frank's, to stay only a few minutes.

She went to check out the matter. "What's wrong, Frank? I heard shouting. Is there a problem? Can I help?"

"That damn Special Agent is back in town again! Joe saw him and he's asking sneaky questions around the miners' tents and in the saloons. If he keeps looking for Clay's killer, he'll find that strike before I do."

Ginny tensed in dread of Stone being the agent mentioned and rashly exposing her. Yet Frank had said *again* and *keeps looking* . . . The pacing and scowling banker seemed so unsettled by the news that he spouted off a rush of disclosures that soon amazed and distressed her.

"Maybe Clay told him where the silver is located before he died. I wouldn't be surprised if Chapman knows and he's come to see if anyone's working the area. Maybe he was in on the strike and the claim is registered to him. I never thought to investigate that possibility. Hell, he could have been a third partner in the diggings; they were all friends. I'd better go to the land office and check it out. I'll soon see if Chapman's been fooling me."

Ginny was stunned by the intimidating hints in his words. "Wait. What are you talking about, Frank? You're so upset that you're not making sense. Did someone cheat you?"

"It's about that Marston-Cassidy silver strike, the one I told you was worth a fortune. A lawman named Stone Chapman was their friend; he served with them in the Army during the war and they worked odd jobs together. He and Clay were real tight for years, best friends. Chapman was away on a mission when Matt and Clay were murdered, I think scouting for a supply train for Captain McDougall of Company B in Denver. When he returned and heard the news, he was like a wild man. He's been here twice looking for the killer. He left the last time in early March, and I was hoping he'd given up and wouldn't return. Now, he's back again to thwart me."

Friends: Matt, Clay and . . . Stone? Her love wasn't a stranger here? Left in March to accept another assignment: the Ku Klux Klan mission. *This* was the "next job" he had mentioned to her several times? Her father had never written to her about Stone Chapman, but Ginny didn't doubt the truth of what Frank Kinnon was telling her because, if he even suspected who she was, he would have taken her to his ranch to question and then beat the truth from her. He wasn't even observing her for a reaction, so her identity and goal were definitely unknown to him. It sounded as if her boss had checked out the agent in the past, no doubt for clues to the silver. When the irate man started talking again, she listened carefully.

"From the questions he asked last time, he had a wild idea Matt's still alive and he's the one who killed Clay to get everything. He's back nosing around for clues. From what Joe reported, Chapman still thinks Matt's alive and is the murderer. It's crazy; Matt wouldn't desert such a rich strike or fail to stake a claim on it. He must be dead. My detective couldn't find news of him anywhere and what man would lay low for a year when he has a fortune to dig out? I have men taking samples everywhere to see if I can find a match to the one Matt and Clay brought in. So far nothing. Chapman can complicate matters for me. I know he won't rest until Clay's killer is found and punished, probably by his guns, and he's damn good with them."

Ginny didn't want to believe what she was hearing but sensed it was accurate. Stone hadn't come to fetch or help her, only to entice her to lead him to her father so he could . . . Kill or arrest him? How could he know her father and think him capable of cold-blooded murder? If her traitorous lover wasn't up to no good, he would have shared this information with her last night. The moment Ben had exposed her name, destination, and goal, he had guessed who she was, and might have known from the start. To conceal her shock and anguish, Ginny faked anger and disappointment. "That's awful, Frank. You've done more work to find it than he has. It would be terrible for him to ride in and snatch it away. Do you think this Mathew Marston is still alive? Do you think he killed his partner?"

"No, or he would have shown up or been located by now. He must have been the second man in the cabin. Chapman can't have evidence otherwise. He told the authorities here he didn't have proof it wasn't Matt."

"You think this Stone Chapman knows where the silver is hidden? You think he may have been a third partner? Maybe he wants Mr. Marston imprisoned or slain so he can get full control of the strike."

"It's possible, Anna. I'm having him watched to see what I can learn. Joe's pointing him out to my two boys and they won't let him out of sight. Maybe, with luck, he'll lead them to the strike."

"That's good, Frank, and very smart. You said he's a lawman, a Special Agent. Perhaps he's only trying to solve a criminal case; he does have a personal interest in it. Perhaps he doesn't know where the claim is located. I hope not. You've dreamed of owning it for so long."

Frank grasped her hands in his and gazed into her eyes. "I hope it'll be ours, Anna. I want you to marry me. I love you."

Ginny feigned astonishment. "You're . . . proposing to me?" He smiled and nodded. "But we've only known each other for less than two weeks. This is so sudden and unexpected. I don't know what to say, other than I'm flattered and taken by complete surprise. You're the most sought-after bachelor in town. Why me, Frank? And why so soon?"

"Love doesn't work on a schedule, Anna. This caught me by surprise, too. Sure, I've wanted and searched for a proper wife, but I couldn't find one. Then you appeared in my life, the perfect woman for me. I can give you anything you want, with or without that strike. I own many businesses, a prosperous ranch, a big house here in town, and investments in other areas. I'm a leading citizen of Colorado City and the state. I'm rich and powerful. People like and respect me. I have friends in high places, so nobody from your past could ever harm you under my protection. We'll have a beautiful family and give them the best of everything. You'll be the belle of Colorado City, Miss Anna Avery, if you'll become my wife."

She pretended to ponder his proposal for a minute and to fidget in uncertainty. "This is such an important decision, Frank. I need time to think. You don't know how tempted I am to say yes this very moment, but that wouldn't be fair to either of us. I must make sure it's *you* I love, not all you can give to me. Let's cancel our dinner tonight and allow me time to make the right decision. I'll see you Sunday and give you my answer then. All right?" *That will give me time to escape both yours and Stone's clutches.*

"Take off now. It's only a few hours to quitting time. Rest and think hard, Anna. I love you and I won't take no for an answer. If you don't love me now, you will one day. There's nothing wrong with marrying me knowing that, and you won't be duping me if you expose your feelings."

"That doesn't seem fair to you, Frank."

"Having you is the most important thing. Whether you love me or not, you'll make me a good wife, the perfect companion and partner. Now I need to get to the land office before it closes for the day. If I don't find anything registered there, I'll telegraph the one in Denver. By Monday, I'll have an answer about a claim registered under the name of Chapman or Marston or Cassidy. I'll call for you Sunday evening at six. Say yes, Anna, and you'll never be sorry."

"Whatever happens, Frank, I'll never be sorry I met you. I've learned so much from you. I promise you'll have my answer by Sunday night."

Ginny had no choice except to allow Frank to embrace and kiss her. Needing to dupe him, she responded demurely. "Please don't come around to influence me to say yes. I have to do what's right for me, for us."

"Sunday night it is, Anna. I know you'll agree."

Ginny and Frank parted outside the bank. Without being obvious, she checked her surroundings several times to make certain she wasn't being followed by her traitorous lover or by Kinnon's men. By now, Stone should be concealed or trying to shake his tails. She knew he was skilled enough to realize he had shadows, so precaution should keep him away long enough for her to elude him. If she confronted him, he would deceive her again and she couldn't bear that, not today. If he loved her and trusted her, he would have confided this secret last night. Stone must have been shocked to learn her identity from his father, but his knowledge couldn't be kept a secret for long. Surely he was intelligent enough to realize the risk of damaging their relationship was greater from her discovering he'd deceived her again than from a brief misunderstanding and suspicions that could be explained as coincidences and destiny. He could have told her at least part of the truth about their entwined pasts and given his old friend the benefit of doubt.

She must find her father first to help prove his innocence. Besides, she couldn't risk Stone exposing her to Kinnon, as his reckless and inexplicable investigation could do at any moment. How strange and cruel that mischievous fate kept throwing them together and yanking them apart. Every time things looked sunny and peaceful, new conflicts and dark clouds appeared. Perhaps they were ill starred.

Hattie's Boarding House came into sight and she hoped Stone hadn't taken refuge in her rooms. When she reached them, she was relieved to find both empty. With haste, she changed into a shirt, pants, and boots. She packed a few garments in saddlebags, and loaded the cloth sack with supplies, and filled her canteen. She strapped her derringer near her calf, then concealed a knife she'd purchased in her boot. She belted a new holster around her waist and slid the pistol taken from Slim into it. The rifle was loaded and more cartridges for all three weapons were stuffed into pockets of her flannel jacket. Months ago Stone had told her to keep extras close at hand for emergencies. He had taught her plenty she would use now to escape him and to protect herself in the wilderness. She dreaded heading into the mountains alone where countless men were seeking their fortunes, but she had no choice. Because of his rash probings, by Monday, Frank would know about a claim seventy miles away in the name of V. A. Marston. She couldn't let Kinnon beat her to the cabin and capture her father in case Mathew Marston was hiding out there from both men. If Stone knew the cabin's location and followed her there, she would force the truth from him and would convince him he was pursuing the wrong man. With Kinnon and a Special Agent after him, her father wouldn't, couldn't, return to town. Matt wasn't safe here and neither was she anymore.

Stone knew he'd been recognized, despite his short beard and all his precautions. He'd tried to ask his questions about Marston and the fire last year as cunningly as possible, but one of the prospectors had gotten suspicious. Within the last hour, he'd picked up two shadows, men he'd seen with Frank Kinnon yesterday. That annoyed but didn't surprise him as the banker had been searching for the claim since last year. Since he'd done the assaying and the strikers were dead, it wasn't odd for him to seek the rich site. He'd checked out Kinnon the last time but found nothing suspicious about the man. As far as everyone knew, Kinnon was an honest and upstanding citizen who'd never had any accusations against him to sully his good name. Yet, if Matt was being stalked or framed, it was up to him to help his old friend prove it. And if trouble had befallen Matt, Ginny needed him to help and protect her from that same threat.

Stone sipped a whiskey in a saloon that would be filled with customers soon; a big and noisy crowd would make it easier for him to lose his trailers. While he waited, his keen mind worked on his problem. Matt was the missing piece to the puzzle and he must find him before he could put it all together. If only Matt had sent him a message for help or left an explanatory note in the cabin, he could have solved Clay's killing by now and Matt would be in the clear. If Ginny's father had thought he couldn't trust the law or the officials in these parts, Matt should have known he could trust him. The fact Matt was also hiding from him created doubts of the older man's innocence. Or maybe his own troubled past was causing him to think evil of the man.

As soon as it was dark, he'd sneak to Ginny's room to wait for her to return from her dinner with the banker—and that one had better not touch her! He'd confess everything to her and trust her to believe him. Maybe she didn't realize her father might have changed during their long separation; she hadn't seen Matt since she was thirteen. The man had endured a bitter war where killings and cruelties had become second nature for many. Imprisonment, a loss of his plantation and family, and hardships in the wilderness must have worked on him. Matt was allowing his other daughter and wife to believe he was dead but he'd kept in touch with Ginny until last summer. Didn't that mean Matt loved and wanted his oldest child? Yet didn't he realize that news of his enormous strike would spread all over the country and expose him to his discarded family? Perhaps Matt was seeking investors so the mine and company wouldn't bear his name; perhaps he'd be a silent partner to protect his holdings from claims by other kin.

As he finished his drink, Stone knew he would have to persuade Ginny that her father might be a criminal. Yet, during this next talk, he needed to be totally honest with her. With Kinnon on to him and perhaps his true target, it was time to get Ginny out of town to safety. Before dawn's light came, they needed to sneak away to the cabin ten miles north of Weston Pass. If Ginny refused to listen or trust him tonight, he would rope and gag her, then haul her there where he could convince her in private! *Matt Marston, you'd better be innocent for her sake! Don't force me to lose the woman I love because I have to arrest you and send you to prison.*

As she completed preparations for departure, Ginny agonized over the dark span between them. While snuggled in her bed at midnight, Stone had led her to believe everything was golden and a bright future loomed ahead. She had not reached him and changed him. An evil monster dwelled between them, one Stone refused to slay. Love had blinded her to the real man and to the staggering facts. He knew how confused she was about her father; yet he had kept secrets that could explain certain matters about the past. His hatred, bitterness, and desire for revenge were apparently more important to him than their love, *if* he loved her. Until he confessed all to her and truly changed, there was no hope for them. If it must end between them, she wanted it to happen before more damaging evidence against him surfaced. If she was mistaken, he would find her and convince her of it.

Ginny penned a note to Hattie, who was out with a man who was attempting to woo the older woman. She revealed that Frank had proposed and she was going to Denver for a few days to consider her answer. She asked the woman to take care of her possessions until she returned. She twirled and stuffed her hair beneath a wide floppy-brimmed hat with a pinch-creased crown that concealed part of her face. She donned the oversize jacket that hid her curvy figure. She had eaten cold fried chicken and biscuits while she worked to avoid a revealing campfire in the hills later and she had wrapped extra food in a clean cloth to save her time and work for tomorrow.

Ginny checked outside in all directions before she went to the barn and corral out back to saddle her horse. She attached her supplies and saddlebags, then mounted. From sightseeing trips last week with Frank, she knew which road she needed to take. It was Friday at five o'clock; the town was busy and noisy enough that she should go unnoticed in her disguise, and she was visibly well armed to discourage trouble. There were about three to four hours of daylight left to assist her escape, time to get miles away and concealed in the forest. She scanned her surroundings and, seeing no one, she left the boardinghouse corral to head for her destination, about four days' ride from town.

Stone had finally shaken both men and sneaked to the boardinghouse barn to hide in the hayloft until later. He'd heard someone below him and stayed still and quiet. When the person had gone outside after saddling a horse, he'd peeked through a crack and seen his Ginny sneaking off alone and obviously prepared for a long trip! Astonishment, dismay, and confusion had kept him from exposing himself to her or to anyone who might join her.

Stone reasoned that she knew where the cabin was located and must be heading there. But why leave without him or not even telling him? If he hadn't been concealed here, she would be long gone before he was wise to her ruse. She had been such a genteel lady when they'd first met, but she'd learned plenty of tricks and skills since that day months ago. Stone read panic in her behavior and posture, and he wondered about the cause for them. Perhaps Matt had gotten a message to her to join him somewhere in the foothills. Or maybe she had decided to look for her father at the cabin. That was rash and dangerous, and not including him was suspicious. He would shadow her to seek the truth but not reveal himself unless she got into trouble.

Shu, *woman, you said you told me everything. Said you loved me and trusted me. Why are you sneaking off like this? Maybe you knew I was keeping something from you and that caused you to doubt me and bolt. Or maybe you're just choosing your father over me. Mercy, Ginny love, how can I help you, protect you, and win you if you keep running away from me?*

Ginny avoided the two toll roads that snaked into the foothills, ways of getting wagons and supplies inland. As she rode northwestward, she glanced at Pike's Peak and was relieved she didn't have to head in that direction or scale the towering summit that was still capped with snow despite the fact it was almost July. Yet many sharp ridges, plateaus, valleys, meadows, canyons, and rugged terrain lay between her and the secluded cabin. The lofty range before her was intimidating and beautiful. The landscape's colors were almost startling in their vividness: the sky overhead was an intense blue; trees, grasses, and bushes were various shades of green; upturned hills and boulders of red sandstone blazed like fire beneath the sun; and snow atop peaks or trapped in crevices of grayish brown or crimson rock was a pristine white.

She passed near Manitou Springs where ancient cliff dwellers had lived, hundreds of years ago. She rode through the edge of the Garden of the Gods and was fascinated by the unusual formations in red-and-white sandstone, some reaching two to three hundred feet tall. She followed the map's instructions, which she had committed to memory, staying within sight of the northernmost toll road but out of view from any travelers or workers on it. She knew the road and the stream near it would be her markers for a long time.

Gradually the elevation increased but not fast enough to create a hardship on the horse or herself. Her pace was slow, but the ride wasn't difficult, yet. Pines and scrubs clung tenaciously to rocky cliffsides, creating a lovely contrast of emerald and vermilion. She ventured between rugged hogbacks with verdant coverings of piñon, oaks, juniper, alder, and birch. She saw trees twisted and stripped by the forces of harsh nature and creeks of swift, clear water which she discovered was cold when she halted to rest near one and drank from it. It had been warm today, but she knew the air would cool fast when dusk arrived in the mountains that engulfed her. The light jacket already felt good, but Stone's embrace, she mused dreamily, would have been better.

Don't do this to yourself, Ginny. He's left behind for now. Until Father explains his part in their past, you can't trust him.

The long and lonely journey continued. She needed to put as many miles as possible between her and Colorado City before dark closed in around her. It was fortunate there were no strikes and prospectors in the area she was covering, for now anyway. She skirted a rocky cliff where a stream of icy water shot over the precipice with a loud roar and in a burst of white. During her ride, she saw and heard squirrels, rabbits, chipmunks, bison, and pronghorn. Once, she and a moose startled each other in a low marshy place near a nature-made pond.

When she reached the highest elevation since departure, Ginny paused to glance back at Colorado City in the flatland far below her. It looked as small and alone as she felt in the heights around her and the vast expanse of the land before her. *Continue or turn back?* she asked herself.

There was no choice; she was committed. Frank wouldn't know she was missing until Sunday evening and might be fooled until Monday by the message in her note to Hattie and the possessions left behind. He might believe she had panicked and traveled to Denver to put distance between them, and perhaps search for her there. She hoped so as that would give her more escape time. But even if she headed back this minute, she wouldn't reach town before Stone realized she was gone, if he found a way to get to her room tonight. She couldn't imagine what he would do when he discovered she had vanished again.

Damn you for lying to me last night. Can I ever trust you again? Ginny forced him from mind after warning herself to stay alert.

The forest-covered Rampart Range to her right was steep and rugged, and she was glad she didn't have to cross it. She heard a wagon rumbling down a slope on the road and paused behind bushes to stay out of view. She reached the point where it veered southwest beyond Cascade Creek; that knowledge supplied her present location. She was glad she'd practiced drawing the map from memory and she could close her eyes and visualize it with clarity.

Dusk approached and told Ginny she must halt soon to camp. At least a near full moon was rising to prevent the woods from being pitch dark on her first night out alone. That and having eaten before her departure would enable her to skip lighting a fire whose flames could be sighted and odor smelled by the wrong person. She was compelled to guide her mount into a rushing stream to avoid rough and uneven terrain. As they walked in the chilly water, she strained her ears to catch any sound of prospectors panning or camping ahead. She prayed she would see danger before it struck, as her view was restricted by twists of the hilly banks. By the time the terrain allowed her to leave the water, she'd only encountered animals coming to drink and she'd spooked them. She passed Sand Gulch and saw a cabin on one hillside with smoke leaving its chimney to reveal it was occupied. She rode onward, the elevation steadily increasing but the evergreen pass aiding her chore.

Not far ahead she stopped for the night at Crystola Creek. She unsaddled the horse to let him drink and graze. If peril came while she was sleeping, surely he would make enough noise to awaken and alert her. She spread a borrowed blanket on pinestraw-covered ground and placed her weapons beside it.

In the near darkness, Ginny heard all kinds of sounds. Nocturnal birds called to each other. Animals moved about in the brush, a browsing deer actually coming close before he sniffed her presence and darted away. Frogs and crickets were abundant near the water. It was chilly as she nestled into the blanket for warmth. When breezes stirred foliage and limbs, her imagination fashioned them into scary threats. Her heart pounded and pulse raced. She trembled. A few times, her teeth chattered. It didn't help to try to convince herself she was being childish and cowardly. At last, exhaustion allowed her to sleep.

Stone crept close to her position, tossed a blanket over him, and slept nearby to guard her. He wanted to ease her fears but needed, if he could, to wait until she exposed her motive for running away.

On Saturday Ginny crossed the South Platte River and trekked through Wilkerson Pass in the lower mountain range. She was surrounded by trees of various types: a world of vivid green with smells she found refreshing and heady. Purple fringe, daisy, columbine, and monument plant gave certain areas beautiful splashes of color; so did the numerous butterflies and other insects working on them. She smiled as a pair of red foxes paused to watch her pass before returning to their playful rolls in the grass, and almost laughed aloud when a fat porcupine waddled across the trail and caused her mount to prance and whinny in fear of tangling with those sharp spines. She saw many large hares leaping for cover and wondered how one would taste roasted over a fire until crispy brown. Mule deer and elk grazed in meadows and only lifted their heads a moment to make certain she wasn't a threat to them. She listened to squirrels chattering in trees and noisily feasting on the seeds inside pinecones. It was an awe-inspiring territory that was lovely and peaceful for the time being.

For the past two nights Ginny had refused to fret over the three men in her life and allow such thoughts to distract her concentration. She didn't want to worry and suffer over her father's survival. She didn't want to fear over Frank's vengeful pursuit. She didn't want to agonize over Stone's possible betrayal and treachery.

But she could no longer keep the men from her thoughts. She scolded herself for not giving Stone a chance to explain before she acted on impulse from anguish and shock. It was probably foolish and dangerous to have ridden into this vast wilderness alone. Anything could happen to her. She could have an accident and be far from help. She could be attacked by a band of men like Bart's gang. She could encounter a perilous wild animal; already she had seen two large bears this morning. She could fall prey to a renegade Indian or a desperate prospector driven mad from defeat and solitude. She could miss a marker and get lost, as mileage was difficult to judge in the rugged terrain. No matter that Stone was misguided and mistaken about her father, she was certain he loved and wanted her and wouldn't harm her. It had been stupid to take off without speaking with him and bringing him along. He must be thinking horrible things about her.

She had warned him that Kinnon was dangerous, though Stone could take care of himself; if Kinnon believed he knew where the silver was located, he could try to beat the information out of him or even ambush and kill him. Stone could be in danger this instant. Probably the only reason Kinnon hadn't attacked Stone so far was because the villain knew he was a lawman whose murder would entice other agents to investigate and possibly unmask him. Kinnon had no way, she hoped, of knowing what Stone may have written in his official reports about him.

Without a doubt, the moment that telegram arrived from Denver with a claim listed under V. A. Marston, Kinnon would head for the same location she would reach on Tuesday. If Stone didn't arrive soon after she did and her father wasn't there, she must ride to the closest town for protection while she decided what step to take next.

She retrieved her attention as she saw a distant cliffside honeycombed with tunnels. Sluices and flumes snaked their way down rocky walls to a place where workers waited to separate gold from gravel and sand. Men with rakes, picks, shovels, and wheelbarrows labored under the late-June sun or in the near darkness of shafts. She watched a while, then journeyed onward until she found a sheltered area near Wilkerson Pass and camped.

Monday, July first, Ginny left the dense forest for a time to travel across a plateau of scattered trees, scrubs, and rolling grassland. She used the fieldglasses and compass she had purchased in Colorado City to spy her markers and to provide the right direction. She continued to be successful in avoiding gold-seekers and fur trappers on creeks and streams. She skirted the area where she saw a grassy hillside dotted with shaft entrances, some disappearing inward and others downward. Many men were mining the obviously productive site. Tents, shacks, lean-tos, and dugouts were scattered nearby for shelter and sleeping. Wagons and teams waited to be filled with gathered ore to be taken to a smelter or a Sampling Works, as she saw no processing structure. At the latter, Kinnon had told her that ore was purchased, assayed on the spot, and the miner paid, with a deduction for smelting and transporting charges. She made certain to go unnoticed.

Before Ginny camped that night in a gulch, she checked the sky and air for signs of rain to prevent being trapped during a flash flood. Kinnon had told her how many men ignorant of this area were killed that way.

She had finished her chicken and biscuits Saturday night. Yesterday she had risked a fire long enough to cook johnnycakes, warm beans from a tin, and to brew coffee, but she had doused it the moment her meal was ready. She did the same tonight. Tomorrow, she would eat the leftover bread and dried beef. She had been fortunate to have a constant water supply along the way. She longed for a relaxing and muscle-soothing bath but couldn't risk being caught naked and unarmed by man or beast.

When she finished eating, she stretched out her sore body on the blanket. This time, she dreamed of Stone when she slept.

Tuesday she crossed another section of the South Platte River, a well-worn animal or Indian trail, and a creek with large boulders piled in a right-angle bend: all markers on her mental map, which told her she was still on the right path and nearing the cabin. Forest enclosed her again. Ridges of rippling hogbacks filled her line of vision and peaks towered in most directions. Weston Pass southward and Mount Lincoln northward stood out as two of the tallest, with the cabin she sought located halfway between the two majestic points that were guiding the remainder of her journey.

Shortly after midday, Ginny spied the rustic cabin perched on a large shelf of a steep hillside with a swift stream at its base. It looked unreachable on its lofty perch of sharp and slick rock. The relatively flat ledge and three cliffsides were strewn with trees to provide wood for winter fires and cooking. She wondered how her father and Clay had constructed the sturdy dwelling in such a difficult place. A ladder was raised to prevent entry to trespassers or attackers, but she knew how to lower it. The place appeared to be deserted for a long time. She watched for a while but heard and saw no one nearby.

Ginny rode to the stream and dismounted. "Father! Matt Marston! Are you here?" she yelled. "Is anybody inside? Father, it's Ginny!"

There was no response, which distressed her. She wondered if he was at the silver site but doubted it because there was no horse or mule nearby, or any tracks fresh or old. All she heard was the rushing of the stream and birds singing. She guided her horse across the cold water to a grass spot, then dropped his reins. She unloaded her supplies and possessions in case something endangered him and he abandoned her.

She stood below the ladder and gazed up at it. She didn't like how rickety the climbing device looked and wondered if it was too old for safe ascent. But if her father had left a message there for her, she must—

"Do you know how to lower the ladder and get inside?"

Startled, Ginny whirled, her eyes wide, her mouth agape, and her hand going to the butt of Slim's pistol. "Stone! How . . ." He looked so handsome and she was so happy to see him that she almost flung herself into his arms before reality returned with his too quick reply.

"I've been on your tail since you deserted me. You did a good job of leaving unseen and getting here safely. You're smarter and braver than I realized, woman. I've been guarding you day and night during the journey."

"Guarding me or letting me lead you to my father so you can kill him?"

"So, you did know the truth all along, just as I feared and suspected."

Stone's hazy answer tormented Ginny's heart and she was glad her father wasn't there to confront and challenge this beloved enemy.

—— *Chapter* 19 ——

GINNY GLARED AT HIM as she tried to conceal her anguish. "You're sadly mistaken, Mr. Special Agent. I didn't know about your lies and sinister plans until you riled Frank so badly Friday that he tattled on you."

Stone tensed in dread. "What did he tell you about me?"

"The truth, Mr. Traitorous Chapman."

Stone realized that this conversation wasn't going to be easy. "What is 'the truth' Ginny?"

"Why didn't you tell me you knew both my father and Clay? Why didn't you tell me you've been here many times, that on some of those visits you came searching for my father to kill him for something he didn't do? He would never murder anyone, especially not Clayton Cassidy." Before he could respond, she said, "We'd better prepare for an attack by Frank's men. He said he was having you followed so you probably led them straight here. They'll kill us both to get information. I was wrong about you. I thought we had been honest with each other. I told you everything about me and thought you'd done the same."

"Then why did you take off like that? You didn't even allow me to explain. You believed what Kinnon—a stranger and your target—said over what the man you claim to love and trust told you. And don't worry about Kinnon's men; I lost them Friday afternoon before I sneaked to Hattie's barn to wait for you to get back from your romantic dinner with your boss."

To clear the oppressive air between them, Ginny knew she must be cooperative and honest and pray he would be, too. "I'll admit it was foolish and dangerous to take off like I did," she began her explanation, "but I was too hurt and angry and scared to think straight, and I was too far along on the trail to turn back when my head cleared. Besides, Frank telegraphed Denver to check on three names for land registration: Marston, Cassidy, and Chapman. He'll get a response Monday and I'll be exposed, thanks to your reckless nosing around. He thinks you might have been a third partner in the strike and that you filed the claim for yourself. He suspects you know where it is. Did you already know about this location?"

"Yes, because Clay left his half of the claim to me. He sent a map and will before his death. Besides, the location is listed in the Denver General Land Office."

She gaped at him. "You . . . own half of this claim?"

Her reaction told him she hadn't known that fact. "I was Clay's best friend, like his family. He has no other kin . . . You're saying you ran only because you'd be exposed Monday and because you thought I'd lied to you?"

Ginny noticed how he quickly changed the subject. "For those reasons and to save my father's life. Frank said you three were in the Army together, were friends. How can you believe Father could do such a thing?"

"Your father isn't the same man you left at thirteen, Ginny. He's ridden through hell a few times since then and it's obviously changed him. I suspected him because of Clay's last message to me." He repeated what the letter had said. "Clay didn't trust him anymore and I can't tell you why, other than those curious accidents and Matt's strange behavior. I do know Matt didn't file the claim until after Clay was dead, and he put it in your name. It seemed to me as if he disappeared for his own gain instead of helping the law find Clay's killer. He didn't even ask for my help in solving the crime. What was I supposed to think, Ginny? And how could I confess such things to you right after we finally reconciled? I didn't want to lose you, at least no sooner than necessary. I wanted as much time with you as possible before I had to confess something that might tear us apart again. I was going to tell you everything when I saw you Friday night, but that didn't happen. You left before I had the chance." Stone grasped her by the forearms. "Don't you understand I was afraid of losing you because of who I am and what I must do? If Matt's guilty, I have to arrest him and see him punished. I owe it to Clay. But if he isn't to blame, I'll help clear him and protect him; I promise. What more can you expect of me? I've sworn to bring in the killer."

His words moved her. He had acted unwisely but from good motives, something she understood from her own foolish actions. "Believe me, Stone, it isn't my father."

"Wanting that to be true doesn't make it so. This is the third father to come between us. I hated to defeat Charles Avery because I knew it would hurt my Anna. I hated to desert Ben, but I knew staying home would hurt my Johanna more. Now I hate to chase Matt because it can hurt you, maybe destroy our future together. Please don't let that happen, Ginny. I love you and need you. Mercy, woman, why do you always put me in a bind?"

She wanted to fling herself into his arms and kiss him, but more needed to be said first. "Don't you think my father was also hurt, afraid, and confused? His partner and friend was murdered and somebody tried to kill him. He probably knows even you don't believe him and are chasing him. If a friend doubts his innocence, why should he think the law would believe him? He could be dead and buried somewhere."

Stone pulled her into his arms. "Don't cry, love. I'm sure he's alive. If we can only find him and learn the truth, things will be all right."

Ginny leaned back and looked into his eyes. "What if he can't prove he's innocent, Stone? What if Clay's killer is never found? Can he be arrested and imprisoned on suspicions alone?"

"No, Ginny, he can't. But he's made it look bad for himself, so he'll be investigated. Have you told me everything you know?"

"Yes. It's Frank Kinnon's wicked deed; I'm certain of it." She related how the man had behaved and what he'd said when he'd discovered Stone was back in town. "He wants this claim so badly, he's obsessed."

Stone stroked her flushed and dampened cheeks as he reasoned, "Why would he kill Matt and Clay before they revealed where it was? If he'd gotten the truth from them, he'd have the mine going by now. He wouldn't still be searching for clues or be riled by my return."

"I realize it doesn't make sense to kill the only sources of information for something you crave, but I'm sure there's an explanation. Maybe his men made a mistake in killing both partners. Maybe they didn't realize both men were in the shack when they fired on it and burned it. Maybe Frank thought he could get to me or to you." With reluctance she added, "Maybe it wasn't Frank. Maybe it was a common thief."

Stone felt he had to point out that couldn't have been the case. "Their animals and possessions weren't stolen," he explained. "And the two men inside were shot then burned beyond recognition for some reason I can't figure. But I suppose a spark from the fire or a lantern shattered during the shooting could have set off the blaze. Shacks of dry wood fire up fast and easy. It's possible the fire wasn't set on purpose, or maybe Matt could have done it afterward to dupe the killer into thinking him dead. They were identified by those belongings left outside. I figured somebody wanted to make certain the remains were believed to be those of Mathew Marston and Clayton Cassidy."

"You mean 'somebody,' as in my father?"

"Yes, Ginny, that's how it looked to me. I guessed Matt's things were left behind as proof he was there, but we both know he wasn't the second victim. I discovered that by the fact, he registered the claim days after the incident. The minute I heard V. A. Marston, I knew who that was. Matt took off from the shack with nothing, went to Denver and registered the claim, then vanished. You said he wrote to you that he was searching for investors. His claim was safely staked, so why did he flee, Ginny? Where is he now? What's taking so long to announce the biggest strike this territory has known? With that assay report, he should have investors begging to be part of his new company. Why doesn't he seek help and protection from the law? Why doesn't he contact me, his new partner? Why didn't he mention me to you or explain this suspicious mess to you?"

The speculations didn't sound good for Ginny's father. "I don't know," she admitted. "Maybe Clay didn't tell him he left his share to you. He must have been afraid for his life or he wouldn't have sent me the map and told me to wait for him in England. If something hasn't happened to him, he would have written again by now."

"Letters get lost or slowed down or stolen during robberies. You and Johanna left London in late February. Maybe you missed a letter from him."

"If so, Ben should have it by now. We asked for all mail to be forwarded to us at the ranch. I was to visit with her before I came here, before she died and everything went crazy. You would have loved her, Stone. She was wonderful, special. I miss her terribly. It wasn't fair for her to die so young. It wasn't fair for her to never reach home and make peace with your father." More tears spilled forth as bittersweet memories filled her head.

Stone cuddled her in his comforting arms, his hand stroking her back and hair. "That's how I felt about Clay, Ginny. A best friend is hard to lose and harder to replace. What happens to us if Matt . . . is guilty?"

She gave his question serious thought. "Don't worry, he isn't."

Stone couldn't help but envy the total faith she had in her father when she had lacked it in him. He told himself she'd had good reason to doubt him, and he didn't refute her.

Ginny saw his concerned reaction. She smiled and coaxed, "Don't worry. Whatever happens won't affect our relationship. Just don't be the one to arrest him. Do that much for me, for us. I love you, and I believe you did what you thought was right. We have a lot to learn about each other but we'll have plenty of time—our whole lives."

He almost held his breath as he entreated, "You mean that?"

She hugged and reassured him, "Yes, Stone. I love you and I'll marry you. We'll settle things here and return to Texas to live."

"When?"

His elation and excitement made her smile. "I don't know how long this will take. What do you think?"

He deliberated a few moments. "I don't know. I've investigated this several times before and found no clues to lead me to Matt or to the killer. Do you think if we form a company of our own, Matt will show himself?"

"If he hears about it, I suppose so. Wouldn't you think he'd keep his eyes and ears on this area no matter where he is?"

"I would think so. So you agree to my plan?"

"Yes, but I prefer to put the mining company in your name until my family in Georgia can be given the news if Father is alive. They think he was killed during the war. Hearing he lived and never contacted them would come as a shock. I'm also sure my stepmother and stepbrother will try to claim part of the earnings. I don't want to have anything to do with them. I told you how they cut me off when I was stranded in England."

"I'll handle any problems for you."

"Thank you." A whinny from her horse pulled her eyes in that direction but nothing appeared wrong and Stone didn't go to investigate. "Why don't we get inside? I'm starved and tired. We can talk more later."

"That's a good idea. I'll lasso the ladder and pull it down."

"No need." She walked to where bushes and vines grew along the rocks. Her fingers probed until she located a rope. "Yank on this."

Stone obeyed and the ladder released and lowered noisily to within a few feet of the ground. "Clever." He whistled for his horse and the well-trained animal came galloping forward from the woods.

"Father made one like this for me when I was a child. I had a small house in a big tree and this is how I reached it. I loved doing boy's things; that's why I needed to go off to school to learn to become a lady."

Ginny gathered her supplies and possessions while Stone unsaddled both horses and fetched his gear. He steadied the shaky ladder while she climbed to the top. She lowered the rope he had given to her to drape over her shoulder. He tied cloth sacks to it and she hauled them upward. The action was repeated until all the goods were on the wooden landing.

Stone scaled the squeaking rungs with caution and agility, his weight heavy on them. He pulled up the device and locked it in place, to tower above the cabin. "Now, we won't be disturbed or endangered. Chuune will guard your horse for us."

She glanced down at the reddish-brown sorrel with its light mane and tail. "What does his name mean? I presume it's Indian."

"It's Apache for *friend,* and he's surely been that for years."

"He's magnificent and smart and loyal."

"Like my new best friend: Miss Virginia Anne Marston."

Ginny smiled and hugged him. "You're my best *chuune,* too."

Thunder rumbled in the distance and Stone glanced that way. "Going to rain later. Let's get inside and check for any clues."

Ginny felt the threat of a powerful storm, but not from nature. It came from intense emotions building within her body at having the man she loved near.

Stone opened the door and pushed it ajar. With fingers grazing his pistol butts, his keen eyes scanned the interior. "It's safe."

The cabin was dim because the wooden shutters were closed, the walls were of thick logs, and their bodies blocked much of the sunshine. Her eyes adjusted and her gaze moved about the last home of her missing father.

"I'll open the windows for fresh air and light," he said, cognizant of what she must be experiencing.

While he did his task, Ginny carried in their belongings and closed the door. She glanced around once more, trying to envision a southern plantation gentleman in such barren and musty surroundings. It was a big change from Green Oaks and the luxury he had known there. The cabin was small, dusty, and smelly. Its only furnishings were two bunks, a table, two chairs, a stove, and one large cabinet containing dishes, cookware, and supplies. A few garments hung on pegs, looking pathetic in their rumpled and faded state. A pair of well-worn boots with crusted mud and snowy cobwebs rested on the floor near one bed. A deck of old poker cards were scattered on the eating table; more cobwebs displayed themselves there and on the two chairs to tell how long it had been since they'd been used or wiped. Rusty splotches on the stove said it too, hadn't been used in ages. Everything revealed a layer of thick dust and no fingerprints to indicate they'd been touched recently. A look of long abandonment brought sadness to Ginny's heart.

Her somber gaze locked with Stone's, who'd clearly come to the same conclusions. It seemed obvious, but she said, "He hasn't been here."

"That doesn't mean he isn't alive somewhere, love. Have faith."

Sensing nothing of her father in the meager room, she walked onto a rock porch out back that was covered by a shed-type roof and supported by two rough poles. There, she noticed rusting prospector equipment: picks and shovels and pans. Overhead were hooks for hanging garments to dry or for suspending meat to cure. She tried to imagine her genteel father living in this rustic setting and working under arduous conditions. He had not been much of an outdoorsman except for occasional hunting, but had become one to be a miner. His hands had been soft and little exposure to sun had not tanned or wrinkled his face. She wondered how he would look when she saw him again after many ravages had worked on him.

Mathew Marston had lived and worked as a prosperous and refined southern gentleman. What she saw here told of a man who knew hard work and sacrifice, a man without wealth and comforts, a man without the amenities of civilization, almost without the bare essentials and necessities for survival. Fate in the guise of bitter and greedy war had taken so much from him and changed him, as Stone suggested. He had endured prison and many losses and hardships, so many denials and torments, according to Stone. He had lacked a devoted family during his dark hours to give him support. He had been compelled to accept and adjust to his losses alone. She hadn't noticed this shocking effect on him in his letters, but this harsh setting exposed it in vivid and heartrending detail. *Oh, Father, what has life done to you?* Tears eased down her cheeks, and Stone hurried to wrap his loving arms around her for solace. When her weeping was controlled, she told him what she had been thinking and feeling.

Stone had also been in deep thought about the past. He had called to mind days and nights with Clay and Matt. "It's like this for many men now, love; war does that. Being on the wrong or losing side makes it worse. A man's pride takes a beating; when that happens, either he gets stronger and tougher or he gives up. But Matt was a good and kind man. I'm sure I misjudged him. I wasn't in any frame of mind to be clear-headed; I allowed Clay's curious accusations to cloud my wits. Something must have happened after I saw them that last time to cause trouble between them."

Ginny stiffened and paled. She sealed her gaze with Stone's and asked, "What if Clay is the one still alive? What if he filed the claim? What if my father wrote that letter before he was killed and Clay mailed it to me?" Ginny shook her head. "That isn't right; it had news of Clay's murder in it."

Stone tensed, too. "Are you sure it was in your father's handwriting?"

She mused a moment. "Almost positive. But I didn't examine it closely. I had no reason to suspect it wasn't from him. If Clay wrote it, why send me a map? Why register the land in my name?"

"If Matt was in the shack, you'd be Clay's partner. And putting your name on the deed would conceal him as the survivor. He could be waiting for you to get worried and come looking for Matt. Maybe he didn't want to put bad news in a letter."

"We'll have to wait and see who shows up, or if anybody does."

"You're right. No need to waste energy on wild thoughts. I want to check out those woods, make sure nothing looks unusual there. I'll be back soon, love."

Ginny looked at the verdant trees. She noticed a stack of chopped wood that was rotting, the sharp cliffs that would guard their flank and sides, and a rapid waterfall shooting over one precipice. She walked to that lovely scene, silently complimenting her father for selecting an easily defensible site with wood and water sources. With adequate supplies, a person under siege from villain or weather could hold out here for a long time. Between two jutting rocks was a hunk of gradually dissolving soap that would have been gone by now if not for its protective shelter. It and a raggedy drying cloth lying over a limb implied the spot was used for bathing. As Stone joined her, she moved closer and stuck her fingers under the rush of water, then shrieked and jerked them away. "It's almost freezing! I need a bath desperately, but I'm going to start a fire and warm water first."

Stone locked his arms around her waist and smiled when she leaned back against him. "Sounds good to me, but I'm used to washing off in cold streams and icy creeks. I'll be done before the first bubble rises in your pot."

She turned in his embrace to find him grinning. "You aren't serious?" He nodded and chuckled. "You're going to stand under that arctic flow?"

"Yep, soon as I shuck these clothes." He unbuckled and put aside his weapons. He doffed his boots and clothing and stepped under the cascade of invigorating liquid to wet his body. When his hair and body were wet, he stepped from beneath the flow to tend his task. With his back to her, he worked the soap free of its prison and whistled as he lathered himself.

"Ouch!" she wailed. "How can you stand that? Just the spray and wind from it are chilling me."

Stone glanced over his shoulder and grinned. "It's not bad. You get used to it fast after the first shock. Livens you, woman, and cools you off. I need that about now or we won't get supper anytime soon."

Eat? her mind challenged as she stared at him and let his voice wash over her. *Who could be hungry for food at a time like this?* She couldn't think or do anything at this moment except gaze at the irresistible man before her. His darkly tanned body appealed to all her senses. His flesh was taut and smooth. Few scars were visible and none were detracting. His broad chest was hairless. He was lithe and sleek. His firm muscles rippled with each movement. Her gaze drifted over strong shoulders, powerful arms, narrow waist, firm buttocks, and long legs. Fiery desire attacked her. On impulse she yanked off her clothes and joined him, backing into the flow. She gasped in shock as the cold water dashed over her skin and created goosebumps and shivers. "You li-lied, St-Stone; it's li-like ice."

He chuckled in amusement. "Not for long, my brave filly; a good rubbing will warm you." Using his bandanna and sliver of soap, he moved her long hair aside and briskly washed her neck, back, and arms. Then he turned her and lathered her breasts, passing the cloth over them with tantalizing leisure. He sent her a mischievous grin and asked, "How do you like this bath, Mrs. Chapman, if you don't mind me practicing that name?"

"Since I've used so many with you, my love, please do. It sounds wonderful." She gave a dreamy sigh. "*This* feels wonderful, frozen and all. My hair's soaked, so I might as well scrub it, too. I can't get any colder."

"I'll do it," he volunteered eagerly. He washed and rinsed it twice as instructed by a laughing Ginny.

She turned and murmured, "Marvelous hands, kind sir; you can use them on me any time you wish. I'm so limp I feel as if I could melt."

"How does this please you, Mrs. Chapman?" he asked as his mouth covered hers in a searing kiss and their tongues danced playfully. He enjoyed the feel of her slippery hands on his face as she caressed it. "Or this?" Stone's deft hand continued its delightful task and grew bolder as the soapy cloth was worked downward past her ribs, waist, and hips.

Ginny trailed her fingers over his slick body, his actions staggering to her spinning head. Despite the temperature of the water and breeze over her flesh, she blazed inside and his skin felt warm to her touch. His mouth left hers and trekked down her throat to tease her sensitive breasts. She closed her eyes a moment and her head seemed to roll around on her neck like a slowly spinning toy top. She looked down as his tongue drew circles around her taut nipples. With smoldering eyes, she watched the intimate action, feeling no modesty. The beauty of their love flooded her soul. When his mouth returned to hers, she feasted upon it.

Stone rubbed his body against hers to increase her warmth and pleasure. His gaze roamed her face before his fingers caressed the silky skin there. One thumb moved over her parted lips and he felt her tremble. She glowed with radiance from love and desire. "You're so beautiful, Ginny. Do you realize how you get to me?" he asked, voice thick with emotion.

Her gaze took in his dripping sable hair, damp lashes encasing dark and sparkling eyes, and the clear drops running down his stubbled face. "I hope it's the same powerful way you affect me."

He quivered with yearning as her lips and tongue made love to his thumb, sending torrid messages to every part of his being. His soul and loins throbbed to possess her fully. His breathing quickened. "You're the first woman who's stolen my heart. I haven't been able to get you off my mind since we met. It was hard understanding and accepting what you do to me. I was afraid if I ever weakened but couldn't win you I'd be tormented for life, and I'd had my share of suffering. I couldn't believe a woman like you—the most precious in the world—could want a half-breed bastard. I've almost lost you so many times, Ginny, that it scares me to think about them."

"You'll never lose me, my love, never. You're the only man I've ever wanted, or ever will. So many times I was terrified you didn't love me or would never admit it. I was afraid that I was too blinded by love to realize you didn't feel the same way. I couldn't bear to lose you, Stone Chapman."

"When I'm near you, Ginny, I want to kiss you, touch you, hold you. I want to hear you laugh and see you smile and watch everything you do. I want to talk with you and be with you. I want to protect you and make you happy. If I don't watch out, my flaming beauty, you'll totally consume me."

"How can fire consume fire, my love? You engulf me head to foot."

"*Shu*, it's strange hearing me say such words. I've never talked about my feelings before and tried to keep them bridled, but I want you to know them, all of them, all of *me*, Ginny. You're the most important thing that's ever happened to me. I never knew such feelings existed in me. But you make it easy for me to feel them and share them. You've been a terrible distraction, woman. You stole my attention and time and energy without even trying. My wits were so dulled I made mistakes in thinking. I'm sorry for tricking you in the past. I promise it won't happen again."

Those admissions sent potent charges through her. Yet he looked a little uncomfortable at being so open for the first time in his life. To help him get past the difficult moment, she smiled and quipped, "I didn't mean to be a distraction, Stone, only an irresistible attraction."

He nibbled at her lips, grasping her thoughtful ruse and appreciating it. "From here on, woman, I'm keeping a keen eye on you. If I don't, you'll be leading me around like a mustang on a rope and have me too tamed to keep my mind on other things when it's necessary."

"We certainly can't have that, now can we?" she teased. His touch and nearness assailed her head to foot. "I've missed you and wanted you so much, Stone." She placed her hands around his neck, drew down his head, and covered his mouth with hers. The moment she had craved—and feared lost—arrived in glorious splendor. She yearned to taste and share his tender and torrid passion. He was such a powerful force. When he kissed her, he stole her breath away. When he touched her, she lost her will to him. She became shameless with him, a wanton and greedy creature.

He groaned in desire and tightened his hold on her. He kissed each feature on her face as he murmured over and over that he loved her. His hand renewed its prior task and eased the soapy cloth between her thighs to bathe and stimulate the core of her womanhood.

Ginny felt as if the very essence of her being was under beautiful siege, and she willingly surrendered. Every inch of her was alive, aware, eager, aflame. Her secret place enticed, summoned, begged him to conquer it and enslave her. "You're driving me mad, Stone. I need you now."

Stone hurriedly rinsed the soap from their bodies, lifted her, and carried her into the cabin. He lay her on a bunk and took a position half atop her on the narrow space. His mouth and hands went to work to brand every part of her as his. He trembled with need as soft moans escaped her throat and she writhed from the flames he kindled. He wanted her so badly and quickly that he feared to enter her too soon and lose mastery over himself.

Ginny pulled him closer. "If you don't feed me now, I'm going to starve from hunger for you."

Stone obeyed her urgent command, each stroke and thrust evoking another and another. He tried to take deep breaths and think of other things to help retain his control, but it soon became impossible. Ginny *made* it impossible by responding to him with such ardor that his mind couldn't think straight. When he halted a moment to recover himself, she continued to drive him wild. He cautioned in a husky voice, "Be still a minute, love. I'm barely restraining myself."

Entrapped in a swirling vortex of desire, she coaxed, "No need to wait, Stone. I'm more than ready for you."

That was all the invitation and encouragement he needed.

Ginny thrashed upon the bunk and kissed him with total abandon. Love's music wafted over her mind and body, rapidly increasing in pace and volume. As if the most magical violin in the world was playing, passion's strings struck the sweetest notes she had ever heard. Its stirring and romantic chords touched her very soul with harmony and pleasure. Faster and louder the strains flowed over her until a crescendo thundered in her ears. She clung to him in rapture.

Blood pounded through Stone's being like drums during an Apache victory dance. "I love you, Ginny Marston, I love you."

They kissed deeply and then, breathless and sated, they nestled together to share their contentment and joy. At last, they were one in mind, heart, and body, and a bright future awaited them.

Stone held her and kissed her with such tenderness, gentleness, and possessiveness that she almost cried with happiness. He belonged to her now of his own free will and admission.

As if reading those thoughts and sharing those conclusions, Stone murmured, "You're all mine, Ginny. We'll never be parted again. I promise, never another secret from you."

They rested and relaxed for a while, then Ginny's stomach growled as breakfast was far behind her. Stone smiled and said, "Suppertime's calling. Let's rinse off and dress. I'll make a fire in the stove and we'll cook together while you dry your hair before you get too chilled."

"If I freeze again, I know somebody who can heat me up in a delightful manner." She kissed him seductively.

"He will be more than willing to obey after supper and a rest."

"This is wonderful," Ginny murmured as she ate a hot meal and sipped coffee, snug in a blanket and cozy cabin with the man she loved.

"Yep, it surely is, woman. I can get used to this kind of living. I know the perfect spot on the ranch to build our house."

"Don't you think we should ask your father's permission first?"

"He'll agree. He'll be happy to have his son and new daughter settle down there. And he'll be after us to give him grandchildren quick. So will Mother. I told her how I feel about you and she spoke in your favor."

That news pleased Ginny. "If we keep practicing, I'll be with child before we say 'I do.'"

"Not if we get married in Denver. Why not do that? Why wait any longer?"

Her pulse raced with anticipation. "Are you sure you're ready to give up the trail for a demanding wife, confining home, and noisy children?"

"Sounds more than appealing to me, woman."

"My goodness, you have changed, my once-skittish guide," she teased, slipping a morsel of bread into his mouth.

Stone captured her fingers and licked them clean. His dark eyes glittered with strong emotion. "*You* changed me, Ginny. Thanks. You made me show my best side around you. I didn't even realize I *had* one until you pulled it out of me. If anybody had told me in March I would be getting married in July, I'd have thought him loco."

"I can say the same thing. I never expected to meet anyone like you. Steve Carr swept me off my feet and Stone Chapman kept me there."

"We're perfect for each other, Ginny," he said in a serious tone.

"Yes, my love, we are. Fate must have believed the same thing because she kept throwing us together. Isn't it wild how coincidences work sometimes? First the wagontrain, then the ranch, and now here."

"Amazing. My guiding spirit is showing me favor this year."

"You'll have to tell me all about your mother's people one day."

"Soon they'll be gone. White men will wipe them out or imprison them on confining reservations that will slay their spirits and bodies."

"I'm sorry, Stone; that must be hard for you and your mother."

"It's the way of life, Ginny, for the stronger to survive. The whites have more people and better weapons for the battle to possess all."

"And more greed. Maybe things will change and peace will come."

He shook his head and lowered his cup. "Never."

"That's what you said not long ago about yourself changing. And look at me, a pampered southern belle making it through the wilderness alone because of all I learned from a tough scout. Change is possible. *Anything* is possible; we're proof of that."

Stone grinned and nodded. "You're right, woman."

They ate in silence for a few minutes, then Ginny asked, "What will we do next about settling matters here?"

"Let's rest tomorrow and leave for Denver on Thursday. I'll telegraph Father to see if a letter from Matt came for you. While we wait for his answer, we'll get married and set our mining plan into motion. A lot of big companies are in that area. We won't have trouble finding investors and someone to run it for us if we have to leave for home."

"Perfect. We'll be safe there, too, from Frank. Maybe Father will . . ."

"Many signs indicate Matt hasn't been here in a long time. I'll look around tomorrow to see if anyone else has been nosing around the claim. Nobody can get to you up here while I'm gone for a few hours."

"I would scrub this filthy place while you're out, but we'll be leaving the next day so no need to waste energy better spent on other things."

"You're right again, woman. Yep, I lassoed me a smart filly."

"I'll get the dishes done and the beds freshened. Too bad they're nailed to the walls and can't be pulled close together; and they're so narrow."

"That wouldn't be smart anyway. If Matt returned, it would be hard to explain that to a protective father." He chuckled, then suggested, "I'll do the dishes and you get us ready to turn in. We'll have to shut the windows soon; storm's almost atop us. Not much oil in the lantern to keep it burning much longer. I guess we'll have to sit in the dark until we go to sleep." He chuckled again and winked at her.

Ginny adored seeing him so relaxed and happy. "Sit, indeed," she quipped. "I lie down to rest—and to do other things."

"Don't put me in a fire like a branding iron, woman," he warned, "or I'll be all over you with my mark."

Ginny looked at her arms and legs, then peeked down the blanket covering her naked body. "You mean you missed some places earlier? I was certain every inch of me had a tiny *S. C.* on it. Of course, I could be wrong. You'll have plenty of time to examine me and correct any oversights."

"With a temptation like that, I'd better do my chore fast or it'll have to wait until morning. Get to work, woman."

They shared laughter and exchanged smiles, then got busy.

Twenty minutes later, a storm broke overhead. Stone closed the shutters to keep out the slanting rain and latched them against the wind yanking them open.

He bolted both doors, though he doubted anyone could get to the cabin, especially with the hidden pull rope curled on the landing and the ladder out of reach. To make certain no one could lasso it and lower it, he had tied it securely in the raised position.

"We'd better put out the lantern or we won't have any oil left for tomorrow night. You ready to turn in?"

Ginny grinned. "Yes, sir. I removed the musty bedding and put ours down. Which one do you want, right or left?"

"To start with, the one you're in."

Ginny loosened and dropped the blanket around her to her feet. She sat down. "We'll try this one tonight and the other one tomorrow night."

Stone smiled as he removed his pants. He walked to her and placed the lantern on the floor. He doused it and joined his love for the next hour . . .

Ginny stirred and stretched like a contented feline. She realized what had awakened her: the smell of food and coffee. She sat up and her loving gaze found her future husband working at the stove. "Good morning," she greeted him.

Stone turned, smiled, and responded, "And a beautiful morning it is, but not as beautiful as you are. Breakfast is almost ready."

The shutters and doors were open. The storm had ceased and bright sunshine flooded the cabin. She heard birds singing and the waterfall and stream gushing from their recent refills. A fire crackled in the stove and food cooked upon it. "How did you do all this without awakening me?"

"You were exhausted from lack of sleep on the trail. You got plenty of exercise yesterday and a relaxing bath. A hot meal filled your belly, and I was quiet as a mouse stealing corn from a crib."

"You're marvelous, Stone Chapman. Most men would have pushed the woman out of bed to do these chores. Thank you."

"That would be silly and selfish when I can do them just as well. I'm used to tending myself and you needed your rest. But if you take a nap while I'm gone, you can stay up later tonight."

"Yes, sir," she responded amidst laughter, securing the blanket around her. She washed her face and hands in a basin that was bent in several places. She pushed saddening thoughts from her mind of her father doing the same thing. She brushed and braided her hair, then asked how she could help.

"Pour the coffee and take a seat, ma'am."

Stone served her biscuits, fried ham that was cured to perfection, and red-eye gravy. He took the chair across from her.

Ginny leaned forward, closed her eyes, and inhaled the delectable odors rising from her plate and cup. "Paradise, my love."

Stone ate while he observed her savoring every bite as if it were the best food she had ever put in her mouth. *Shu,* how he loved watching her, being with her, talking with her, and doing things to make her happy. She appreciated and warmed to the smallest kindness from him. He realized it wasn't the size of a deed or gift that made it special; it was the love and thoughtfulness behind it. He was impressed that for a woman who had possessed so much in her life, it didn't require wealth or pampering to satisfy Ginny. Without a doubt, they could be content anywhere together.

As she sipped the last of her coffee, she asked, "What are you thinking about?"

"Daydreams . . ." he murmured. "I never put any stock or hope in them until you came along, Ginny. You fill my head with plans for us. Do you know how much I love you and how proud I am to have you? You make every part of me feel alive."

She rose, rounded the table, and leaned over to hug and kiss him. Stone pulled her down into his lap. His fingers roamed her face with a light touch and snailish pace. She nestled her head against his bare chest and listened to the pounding of his heart.

Her eyes widened. "You shaved."

Stone laughed with amusement. "About time if I don't want to scratch this pretty face again."

She stroked his jawline and added, "Or cover this handsome one."

They kissed and caressed until passions blazed and had to be cooled with a heady bout on the bunk.

Both were bathed and dressed and saying good-bye for a while. Ginny raised the ladder after Stone reached the ground and secured it as he'd shown her. She watched him check the cliffside to make certain there was no way anyone could get to her during his absence.

"Stay out of sight, woman, until I call your name. Don't answer anybody else. There are dangerous and desperate men in this territory. They'll pull any kind of trick to get up there. Even if they say they're wounded or starving or whatever, don't come out or help. Understand?"

"Yes, sir. Be careful and come back soon."

"I'll do both," he mounted his sorrel, then, vanished into the trees.

Ginny closed the front door and looked around the cabin. The campfire had been put out to prevent smoke from alerting anyone to her presence. Yet if someone came close, her horse would expose her. If she didn't respond, he could be stolen. At least she could fire her rifle and frighten away a thief.

You heard him: he said don't show yourself or talk. Obey, woman. Woman, that was his motive, she decided; he didn't want anybody to know a female was here by herself. Men alone for months could become just as hungry and greedy for a woman as they could for gold. She remembered how Bart and his gang had lusted for her and what they'd planned for her. Stone was right: She must stay hidden no matter what she saw or heard.

It was late afternoon when he returned. She hugged him and kissed him the moment his boots touched the landing. "I'm so glad you're safe."

"If this is the welcome I'll get after a short separation, imagine what it would be like if I were gone for a week!"

Ginny poked him in the stomach. "I'd take a brush broom to your backside, Mr. Chapman, if you deserted me for that long."

He threw back his head and laughed. "I can feel it. Ouch. I'll confess now that it'll be necessary to leave you once a year when we return to the ranch. Ever hear of cattle drives? They take several months."

She had read about them in dime novels. "Yes, but I'll go with you."

He kissed the tip of her nose. "You can't bring babies and children along like on a wagontrain. It's too dusty and dangerous."

"That's a sneaky trick to get time away from your wife."

"Maybe Father will leave me in charge of the ranch until he's too old and feeble to make such a long and hard trip."

"Is that another sneaky way of enticing me to give in to letting you go?"

"Of course not," he vowed with a broad grin.

"We'll see if you tire of me and start joining the boys for diversions."

"Where do you get ideas like that, woman? I'm your man."

"In England, many men have mistresses and lovers. In America, too."

"Not Stone Chapman. One woman is enough for him: you, Ginny."

She blushed. "I suppose I sound silly and jealous. I just love you so much and winning you was so hard. I don't want to lose you for any reason."

He cupped her face and locked their gazes. "I promise you'll have me forever, woman. I love you. Besides, no other female would want a man like me. I'm too stubborn and tough. Look what a time you've had with me."

"Any woman would give a fortune to have you. And I'm glad you were too blind to realize that truth before we met. If you asked me to walk away from this strike to have you, I would."

Stone knew she was telling the truth and it touched him deeply. "I wouldn't ask you to give up what's rightly yours."

"And half yours," she reminded.

"The claim wasn't filed while Clay was alive and it's in your name. He's not here to dispute it. By law, it belongs solely to you if Matt's . . ."

"That doesn't matter to me. Clay was a partner and he willed his share to you. Now, either you and my father are partners or *we* are."

"Do you realize what some women would do with what you own? I don't think you understand how much it's worth."

"Frank said millions over time. Money is wonderful, Stone, especially when you don't have any. But wealth doesn't make one happy. My family had plenty of money and prestige, but it didn't keep us from losing everything. Love and friends are more important. I would give up this claim if I could bring my Johanna and your Clay back to life and have my father returned."

"I believe you, Ginny, so would I. We'll have everything we need at the ranch and we can work for anything else we desire."

She brightened. "We could help your mother's tribe. A fortune could buy a large cattle spread where they could live in peace and pride. It can buy clothes and food and a school. We don't have to turn them into whites, but we *can* help them adjust to the strange world engulfing them."

Love surged through him. "You're amazing, woman, always thinking of others, like you did with your friends on the wagontrain. It could work."

"Then we'll do it."

"What if your father's still alive? The strike would be his, not yours."

"But half will be yours, remember?"

"Not if Matt refuses to acknowledge Clay's partnership and will."

"If he wants to keep his daughter, he won't contest your claim."

"You would do that for me, for my people?"

"Yes, Stone. When I marry you, we become as one. I owe you even more loyalty than I would my father. The same is true for you: a husband, the Bible says, cleaves to his wife, not his parents. It's cruel, damaging, and wrong to side with parents against your mate. I hope you agree."

"Yes, my beautiful and precious love, I do with all my heart."

"Now, tell me what you found out there."

"No signs of anyone nosing around. Even if ore was found, nobody can stake a claim or start a mine; that's what's needed to remove the silver."

"Did you find the second map Father mentioned to me?"

"Nothing to even hint one had been there. Must have changed his mind about drawing out the locations of the veins. It would have been a dead giveaway if it had been found. He must have figured if the property fell into your hands, all you had to do was hire a skilled miner to find them. Smart action."

"Yes. Now what about putting a little food in our stomachs for energy?"

He grinned. "Just what I need about now: nourishment and you."

Thursday morning, they were ready to leave for Denver. The shutters and doors were closed and the cabin was straightened. Stone lifted their supplies, lingering to say, "It's only seventy miles, but it'll be slow traveling. It's high mountains and rugged passes all the way. We'll be heading into heavy prospecting and mining country, so we'll have to stay alert."

"No fooling around on the trail?" she hinted with a grin.

"That's right, woman, but we'll be there soon. Denver has good food and hotels with soft beds. We can do those things we missed in Vicksburg. We can—" Stone pressed his fingers to her lips before she could question his action. "Somebody's out there," he whispered, on full alert.

She heard Chuune neigh in warning, then a bone-chilling shout.

"Come on down, Mr. Chapman, Miss Marston. If you don't, we'll starve you out or burn you out if you force my hand. We can camp here for as long as it takes. There's no escape. Be smart and don't rile me further."

Ginny panicked. "My heavens, Stone, it's Frank Kinnon! This soon?"

Chapter 20

∾

"W E'LL BLUFF OUR WAY past them, love. Once we're in the forest, we can lose them. Trust me and obey." Stone explained his daring plan in a rush.

"Come out, you two, or we'll start firing!" Kinnon shouted again.

Stone pulled Ginny into his arms and fused their lips as if saying a bittersweet farewell. Frightened for their lives, she clung to him and kissed him with feverish desire, stormed by a mixture of emotions. She wished there was time for more words and another union of bodies. She didn't want to break their holds on each other. She didn't want to challenge impending danger. She didn't want to lose him forever. When he murmured his love, hugged her tightly, and meshed their mouths again, she trembled and prayed it wouldn't be the last kiss they ever shared.

"You're provoking me to attack, Chapman!" Frank shouted.

She realized Stone hated to separate and endanger them as much as she hated for him to do it. The tender look in his dark eyes made her heart beat faster. "I love you so much. We have to survive this."

"We will, my love. Be strong and brave. We have to begin our ruse."

Stone opened the door and yelled, "Hold your fire, Kinnon, until you see what I've got to bargain with. Attack and your fiancée will be the first one to die." He shoved Ginny into sight with faked roughness, a pistol pointed at her head, and her hands appearing to be bound behind her back.

"Help me, Frank!" Ginny shrieked. "He kidnapped me Friday night and said he would kill me if you don't do as he says. Don't let him hurt me."

The banker ordered his men to be calm, but to stay alert.

"Better listen to her, Kinnon, or your future bride is dead."

"You can't fool me, Chapman. I know who she is."

"So do I: your woman, the one you plan to marry. If you love her, you'll save her hide by following my orders. I'll trade her to you for a confession that you killed Clay Cassidy and Matt Marston."

"Are you crazy? I know this land is in her name. She's Marston's daughter, isn't she? You two came to town to trick me. You disappeared together because you knew I was on to you. I received some interesting news from Denver on Saturday. Told us where to come to find you two."

"You're a fool, Kinnon. Virginia Marston Blake is in London. She doesn't know the strike is filed in her name, and I didn't plan to tell her either about that or her father's death until I had his killer behind bars. I trailed you to the telegraph office Friday, so I knew you wouldn't be fooled much longer. Course you got here sooner than I expected."

Stone was at the ready to return gunfire and to yank his love inside if the desperate ruse failed. His keen eyes took in the attackers' number, positions, and arms; and he mentally plotted how to respond to an assault. "I was about to leave you a note on the ladder with my offer, then hide her in the woods. I did some checking in town and learned you'd found yourself this pretty thing to wed. Everybody knows you've staked your claim on her and dared any man to come near her. You even talked with a jeweler about furnishing gold to make her a wedding band. That sounded like mighty serious intentions to me. I gambled you'd do about anything to save her skin and get her back. We both know you murdered Matt and Clay. Give me a confession and she'll live."

Ginny clutched a loaded pistol in her hidden grasp as she entreated, "Please, Frank, help me. He's crazy! He means it. He thinks you killed those two men. I told him he was wrong, but he doesn't believe me. Do something to convince him he's made a terrible mistake."

"You lied to me and duped me, woman!" Frank accused. "You're in on this scheme to entrap me! You're Matt's daughter, aren't you?"

Ginny feigned astonishment, terror, and distress. "No, I didn't, I'm not; I swear. I can prove I'm Anna Avery; telegraph my aunt in Savannah. I'm not that Miss Marston. I'd never heard of Mathew Marston or the silver until you mentioned them to me. I'm not part of your quarrel with this lawman. You can't let him harm me, and he'll do it. I'm so afraid. Please help me."

"I can't trust you, woman."

Ginny noticed doubt in the man's expression. She pressed the tiny advantage. "You said you loved me and wanted to marry me. Now you won't do anything to save my life. This silver strike you both mentioned means more to you than I do. To think I was going to say yes to your proposal. You're as wicked and mean as he is." She glared at Stone and challenged, "A lawman can't do something like this. Let me go, you beast!" She pretended to try to jerk free of the grasp of his arm across her chest.

Stone struggled with her a moment and visually tightened it. "Not so fast, woman. Be still and shut up or I'll give you a blow on that lovely face. Better make a deal fast, Kinnon, she's annoying me."

"There's nothing to work out, Chapman. You can't escape."

"If I die, so does she." As Stone stroked her flushed cheek with the weapon's cold barrel and she flinched, he said in a defiant and cocky tone, "Mighty young and pretty to have her face and body smashed on those rocks down there. If you want her back unmarred and alive, better do as I say."

Ginny screamed and thrashed as if in panic. "You can't do this! Frank, please, do something, anything. You have lots of armed men. Force him to release me." She began to cry, relieved she could summon the fake tears.

"Shut up, woman!" Stone ordered. "I can't think with you bawling like a calf who's lost its mother. You picked yourself a sorry man, so accept the truth. What's it to be, Kinnon, a shootout or a trade?"

"The only thing I'll trade is your life for hers."

Stone sent forth sarcastic chuckles. "That's not the deal I want. As long as I have her, you won't attack and risk her taking a stray bullet."

"You can't remain up there long, Chapman. Supplies run out. I bet you only have enough for a few weeks. I can send for more and outwait you."

"If I run out of food, Kinnon, I'll have to feast on something else. I'll have me a taste or two of your sweet thing." Stone nuzzled his head against hers. "Yep, if you don't cooperate, might as well enjoy myself before I die."

Ginny wriggled in his grasp and jerked her head away from his. "You animal! You wouldn't dare touch me! I'll kill you first!"

"That'll be a little hard, Miss Avery, all tied up and at my mercy. I'll probably give you more pleasure than a stuffy old banker could."

"Leave her be, Chapman, or you're a dead man! We'll compromise. I'll give you half of this strike in exchange for her. It's worth millions. Touch her and I'll have you sliced into little pieces and fed to buzzards."

Stone comprehended that he had infuriated his target and that Frank was no longer positive she was Virginia Marston. "You ain't in no position to make that compromise, Kinnon. Matt's daughter in England owes half of this land. Clay left me the other half before you did him in."

"He *what*? You knew all along where this claim was located?"

"That's how I knew where to come. I guessed you'd be along soon. You just messed up my schedule a mite. It's the confession or nothing."

"If you think I'm confessing to murders I didn't commit, you're crazy. I'm not going to prison for something I didn't do. Sure, I want this claim, but I didn't kill Matt and Clay to get it. You think I'm fool enough to shoot the only two men who knew where the silver is?"

"Then who did kill them?" Stone scoffed.

"If you've been doing any clever investigating, lawman, you'd know I've been trying to learn that same thing. At first, I guessed it was a claim-jumper. When time passed and nobody started a mine the size this one would be, I decided I was wrong. It must have been bandits, or maybe they shot each other in a dispute."

"You expect me to buy that load of empty barrels? Do better, Kinnon. Put something valuable and tempting in them. I already own half of this claim, so that isn't an acceptable trade. What I want is Clay's killer. If one of your men exceeded his orders, turn him over to me and we'll be settled."

"If you harm her, you can't get away, and the law won't look kindly on a Special Agent for kidnapping and abusing an innocent lady, and certainly not on murdering one. You wouldn't dare harm her. You're bluffing."

"Sorry, love," Stone whispered as the hand over her chest snaked to her hair, seized a handful, and yanked her head backward.

Ginny screamed in surprise and pain. "Stop it! You're hurting me! Frank, do something!" She wiggled her shoulders and head to break free as she pleaded with her captor to halt his torment and release her. She was relieved that during her shock she hadn't exposed the weapon behind her.

"You'll pay sorely for hurting her! I'll rip you apart with bare hands!"

Stone eased his grip on the light-brown mane as he chuckled and taunted, "You'll have to capture me first, and that ain't likely to happen. I think we'll go inside, Kinnon, while you give your choice some thought. You have two hours to make a decision. Take any longer than that and I'll be overly tempted to sample your sweetie's treats." Stone backed her into the cabin and closed the door as Frank shouted another warning.

"You're dead, Chapman, if you touch her!"

Stone holstered his pistol and guided Ginny to the floor. "Let's stay down in case they start shooting. These thick walls are impenetrable but these shutters and front door aren't. We'll let him stew a while and get worried about what I'm doing to you in here. At least we've got him baffled about who you are. He's mighty hungry for you, my love, so he won't act rashly." He looked into her eyes. "Sorry about pulling your hair." His fingers massaged her tender scalp. "There was no way to warn you of what was coming. You were quick-witted to keep your pistol hidden. I'm proud of you." He closed his mouth over hers and kissed her deeply.

Ginny responded as if her survival depended on his nourishing nectar. When their lips parted, she gazed at him. "Will we get out of this alive? Do you believe he'll let us leave when you demand to use me as escape cover?"

"I think so, but I'm not sure. That silver has him crazed. He wants it and you, my love. If it comes to taking one or the other, I just don't know which he'll choose. He's already rich, but he's greedy. He should think he stands a better chance of getting you away from me if we're on the ground."

"I pray your cunning ruse will work. You think he believed my act?"

"I hope so. You did a good job out there of confusing him about your identity." He trailed his fingertips over her silky skin and smiled. "If I weren't retiring soon, we'd make a good pair of agents."

Ginny knew he was attempting to calm and distract her from their peril. She ruffled his sable hair and teased her fingers over his strong features. "If this is similar to your regular missions, no thanks. One day you'll have to tell me about your past adventures. From the ones I shared with you, you've certainly led a dangerous and exciting life." She had to be persuaded of imminent success. "What now?"

Stone shifted to lie on his back and warmed when she cuddled against him. "We wait for two hours and try to force his hand."

Ginny's fingers toyed with the buttons on his shirt, then her palm flattened on his chest. She felt the steady beating of his heart beneath her hand. Despite the perils outside, she wanted him this very moment. She wondered if it was crazy to be thinking of such wanton things in the face of death. She decided, it was normal to desire the one you loved, to want to end one's existence locked together as closely as possible. "Are you sure there's no other way out of here?"

"Not unless you're a goat or a ram or a puma. If we tried to scale those cliffs behind us, they'd see us and circle around before we reached the other side, which we couldn't, since they're too steep and slick." Yet Stone knew if it came to the last minute of hope, he'd try that—*anything*—to save her. He didn't want to die but he'd faced that possibility many times; he didn't fear it, not if it meant Ginny would survive. If he did have to sacrifice his life for hers, he prayed she was carrying their child so she'd have something of him to comfort her and to compel her to stay brave and strong.

"There's no place to hide in here or on the shelf," Ginny murmured. "Why would Father build in an area where he could be trapped?"

"It's a good place for defense against enemies and wild animals. Besides, love, this cabin is sitting atop part of the very thing Kinnon craves."

She stared at him. "You mean we're sitting on a silver vein?"

"Yep, a rich one, high grade, almost pure. Plenty of it, too."

"That's very clever of them. Who would think to prospect under a cabin? What if we sign over the land in exchange for our freedom?"

"He wouldn't let us go, not once he learned we are the real owners."

"Why did you tell him Clay left you his half?"

"To get his attention off you as full owner and to let him know not to go shooting at either of us too impulsively."

"But he could decide I'm V. A. Marston and that he can get the claim in his greedy hands by slaying you, partner, and holding me prisoner. If he killed both of us, what would happen to ownership of this land? Could he stake it?"

"Nope, and I'm sure he realizes that. Our families would inherit our shares, so he has to take them from us with legal signatures. No matter how rough it gets, love, never—I mean *never*, woman—admit to him you're Ginny Marston. You'll have to keep him duped until you can escape him."

She grasped the meaning behind his alarming words: if he was murdered. "We live or we die together, Stone Chapman. I'm not going to him."

He rolled half atop her, cupped her face, and imprisoned her gaze. "Listen to me, Ginny. It's crazy and wrong for both of us to die, if it goes that far." He shifted to caress her abdomen as he said, "You could be carrying our child so you might have his life to think of, too. You also have to think of what losing both of us will do to our families. I've ridden a hard and fast trail, woman, and stared death in the face lots of times and it never troubled me. Then I found you and changed. More than anything, I want to live and be with you. If it's too late to snatch more time from the Great Spirit's hands, though, let me die like a man, die knowing you and perhaps our baby are safe. Do whatever you must to survive for all of us. Swear to me you will. You also have to do this for my mother and father."

"I can't. I love you and need you. I can't live without you."

"You can and you must, woman. If you really love me, live for me."

She wanted to protest but knew he wouldn't argue the matter. When he pressed for her promise, she gave it with reluctance and in a strained voice. "Perhaps he'll relent to your demand," she sighed. "If you were alone, could you get out of this?"

"What do you mean? Surrender to him in exchange for my release?"

"No. If I pretended to overpower you and got down the ladder, could you escape without me to worry about?"

"No way, woman, would I turn you over to that devil while I'm alive."

"But if you're free and we're both alive, you can rescue me. This standoff won't last long, Stone. We need a backup plan. I won't lose you."

"If we have to, we'll stay up here until they get tired and careless. We have enough supplies for two weeks if we're careful. I won't do anything rash. I'll try picking them off one at a time with my rifle."

"After you shoot the first one, they'll take cover. He won't give up, Stone, no matter how long it takes to starve us out and win. I wouldn't be safe with him because I couldn't dupe him for long if he tried to touch me. And I'd never be able to escape because he's sure to mistrust me for a while and have me guarded. If he lets us leave with only your promise to release me down the trail, I'll be shocked. We must stay up here until our supplies are gone. Maybe help will come before they're depleted."

"That isn't likely to happen, Ginny love; there aren't enough men to defeat Kinnon and his gang. They'd kill anybody who tried to rescue us, or anyone who witnessed what's going on here. It's us against them."

"At least we'll have two more precious weeks together. Longer if we don't eat much to extend our supplies. We have water. They can't get up here to attack or disturb us. If Frank balks, why risk death sooner than necessary?"

"The longer we're alone where anything could be happening between us, the less Kinnon's gonna want you back and the madder he'll get. A crazed man is unpredictable. But you're right about not being safe with him. I can't allow him to capture you."

"Then we are trapped, and trying to outwait him won't make a difference. If Frank rejects your bluff, we're doomed, my love."

Stone knew he had to give her comfort and hope, so he made up a deception to possibly use. "I can leap off the cliff onto Chuune's back and gallop off. At least half of them will chase me. Kinnon will figure you're tied up and I'm going for help. I'll either ambush my pursuers or elude them in the forest, then sneak back to disable the others."

"That's a wild chance, Stone. You could be killed."

"Might be our only one if he's determined to outwait us, or decides you aren't Anna Avery, or if he's willing to sacrifice whoever you are for the strike." He smiled and caressed her cheek tenderly. "Don't worry, Ginny love, I've jumped off higher roofs and boulders than that cliff out there. Landed in my saddle every time." He chuckled. "Chuune knows that whistle. It'll work fine."

"They'll see you, Stone, and shoot at you at close range."

He kissed the tip of her nose. "Not if I do it after dark."

"There's a full moon. They'll see you and come running."

"It'll happen too fast for them to react. I'll take them by surprise. Once I'm on the ground, I can pick them off like I did Bart and his men."

"Bart and his gang weren't expecting your attack. Frank knows you're skilled and determined to get him. He'll be on alert for cunning tricks. There are too many of them and only one of you."

"I've fought more men alone than he has out there. But I need an advantage. I don't have one up here, and not while you're in danger. We may have no choice. Please trust me and do what I say when the time comes."

Ginny didn't want her love to risk his life on such a hazardous ploy, but she knew Stone Chapman had the prowess to carry out his daring idea. "I do trust you and I will obey. But if they start firing at you, I'm going to give you cover with my rifle. I'm a good shot because I had a good teacher. I don't care if it tells him I'm on your side. I'll pin them down while you get yourself concealed." She was relieved when he grinned and didn't argue. To get away from the distressing subject a moment, she asked, "Do you think there's any truth to his claim he didn't do the shootings and burning?"

"Nope. I think you and Matt are right; he's the target I want."

Ginny smiled and hugged him. "Thank you for believing us."

They began sharing kisses and caresses until their deadline arrived.

A rider approached the anxious banker's location in the edge of the dense forest. He dismounted, glanced at the band of men, and asked in a polite tone, "Frank Kinnon, what are you doing on my claim?"

"So, you *are* alive, just as Chapman suspected. He wants to find you and kill you. Looks like I saved your life by getting to him first. I have the sorry bastard pinned down in your cabin. He'll surrender soon."

"Stone Chapman? He's up there?"

"That's right, Matt, with your daughter. Isn't that a surprise?"

"With my daughter? That's impossible. Ginny lives in England. Even if she came to America, she doesn't know where this claim is located."

"She didn't have to know; Chapman brought her here."

"Stone and Ginny don't know each other. I've never mentioned him to her. He's a lawman, Kinnon. This is crazy. What did he do to provoke you?"

"A few weeks ago, a beautiful woman came to town. She went to work for me and we got real close. I was going to marry her until I found out she was your daughter and the strike's filed in her name: V. A. Marston. She and Chapman took off for this cabin Friday when they realized I had caught on to their scheme. We trailed them and have them trapped up there."

"She's an imposter. They're lying. Ginny hasn't had time to get here since her last letter, which said nothing about a trip to Colorado. She's to stay there until I send her and Robert the money to join me. Something's amiss. What 'scheme' are you talking about? How does my land figure into it? And it *is* in my name: Virgil Aaron Mathew Marston. I was named after Mama's three brothers who were killed in the last war with England. That clerk must have left off the *M* in V. A. M. Marston. It's on my deed."

"Maybe Virginia talked her husband into letting her come search for you or persuaded him to bring her. Haven't seen him, though."

"Robert would never allow such foolishness and Ginny's an obedient wife. The woman up there isn't my daughter; she can't be. If she thinks she can impersonate Ginny to take over my claim, she's wrong. If Stone's in on her lies, he's wrong, too. I'll tell them so right now. But why are you—"

"What does your daughter look like?"

"Flaming red hair and blue eyes, about five feet three inches tall, slim. Why? What's going on? Nobody's stealing my claim, not even a past friend and his female cohort. Whatever scheme he has in mind, it won't work. I'm alive and this land is mine. But it isn't like Stone Chapman to work with another agent, and he's never shown any real interest in a woman. Are you sure she came here willingly? Stone's one to use any trick to accomplish his missions. He hates defeat. Maybe he planned to force her to pretend to be my Ginny to entice me out of the cabin if he found me here. I know he thinks I killed his best friend, but he's wrong and I'll tell him so. Why don't you explain what's happening here before I go talk to him?"

"Chapman said he kidnapped my fiancée to use her to force me to sign a confession that I killed you and Clay. When I found out about the claim registration on Saturday, I surmised she was your daughter and that her behavior with me was a trick to help him expose me. Obviously it isn't."

"Why would Stone think you were involved? That's crazy."

"That's what I told him, but he doesn't believe me. Where have you been? Why did you disappear after Clay's death? And why have you come back now?"

Mathew Marston related clever answers to those questions.

"Your timing is a little suspicious. First she comes, then Chapman, then you: all within a few weeks of each other. Mighty strange to me."

"Not if Stone's been tracking me and knew I was about to return. If he's got it in his head that I killed Clay, or you did, I'll have to convince him otherwise. Let me talk to him and get this matter cleared up."

"I can't let you join him, Marston. We have him outnumbered."

"Then keep my weapons down here."

"He probably has extra ones you can use to help him."

"Then I'll speak to him from the ground. I don't have to go up there. I need to set him straight on some matters. I don't want him terrifying an innocent young woman on such foolish notions about you or me."

"You think you can talk him into coming out and giving up the girl?"

"I'll try my best. I don't want her harmed and I want him to stop chasing me. I have work to do, a mine to get going."

"If he's dead, he can't trouble you again."

"I don't want him killed or injured. He was my friend for a long time. Clay lied to him about me. Things will be fine when he hears the truth. Besides, you can't gun down a lawman without terrible repercussions."

"He's stubborn and he might not believe you. We'll have to trick him to flush him from the cabin. I don't want Anna harmed."

"Who is Anna?"

"Anna Avery, my fiancée, the woman he's holding captive."

"I thought you just said she's Stone's cohort and impersonating Ginny."

"That was a trick to see if you and Stone are working together."

"We aren't. What I can't understand is why he's trying to force a confession out of you when he thinks I killed Clay. It could be he thinks we did it together and he's after both of us. We'll do it your way. But no shooting. I don't want his agent friends coming after me."

The two men walked into the clearing before the stream. "Chapman! Chapman, I have a new deal for you!" Frank shouted.

"What now? Time isn't up yet," Ginny fretted and held Stone tightly.

"Don't worry, love, I won't let him get you. Stay down while I see what he wants. He's in a quandary; he doesn't know if you're lying."

"Use me for cover again," she urged.

"No, you've taken enough risks already."

"Yes, Stone. Until he's sure I'm tricking him, he won't shoot me."

Stone cracked open the door and shouted, "What is it, Kinnon? I'm busy getting to know your woman. I can see why you wanted her so badly. I would, too, if she wasn't so enchanted by a varmint like you."

"You bastard! Accept my bargain or your friend's dead! He showed up in the nick of time to save your hide. We all thought he was dead, but here he is, my prisoner. Let Anna go and you can have your friend in exchange. We'll ride out and forget everything. All I want is her. That's my offer."

"Friend?" Ginny murmured. "What friend? Clay?" she hinted.

"I'll have to take a peek."

Ginny grabbed his arm and restrained him as she said, "No. He'll shoot you the minute you show yourself. It's a trick. He probably has rifles aimed on the door. I would look, but I don't know Clayton Cassidy."

"You're lying, Kinnon," Stone yelled, "and I won't fall for any tricks! I guess you don't want your woman back. Too bad for her."

"It's me, Stone, Matt Marston. I just returned. What's going on here? What are you doing up there? Why did you take his fiancée hostage?"

An astonished Stone looked at a pale-faced Ginny.

"Father . . . That beast has my father prisoner! What shall we do?"

Stone was worried about the suspicious timing of Matt's return.

"We can't let Frank torture and kill him. We have to do something."

"It's been years and you've probably changed. Will he recognize you?"

Ginny nodded and replied in dismay, "Yes, I look like my mother. He'll be so stunned to see me here and in danger, I'll be exposed. My heavens, Stone, he has all of us captive now. We'll never escape. He'll torture us until we sign over this claim; then he'll kill us anyway."

"I won't let that happen, Ginny. If Matt can't get a look at you, he can't expose you. We'll still call our bluff and ride out of here. I'll hide you in a safe place and return to rescue your father. You have to do as I say."

"But—"

"No buts, Ginny. Didn't I teach you the importance of obedience during your training in Georgia? Remember how I tricked and captured Bart's gang? I'm experienced and skilled at this kind of ruse. But I can't let you be around to distract me and endanger all of us. You have to trust me."

"If you cover my head, Frank will be suspicious. You need a shield."

"I have an idea . . ." Stone prepared her for initiating it, then shouted, "Coming out, Kinnon, but she's first. Better relax those trigger fingers."

Ginny was guided through the door, a wide bandanna secured over her mouth and nose. Her hair was pulled back and stuffed beneath the floppy-brimmed hat. At that distance and with her face partially concealed, the couple hoped their disguising ruse would work. She ordered herself not to do anything to arouse suspicion as her gaze sought her father below. Matt was standing with Frank Kinnon; he was smiling and appeared to be relaxed.

Stone grinned. "Hope you don't mind that I gagged her, Kinnon. Got tired of her chatter and crying. Matt, my treacherous old friend, what brings you back after so long? I was finally convinced you were dead, but my first thought was accurate after all. Your timing is mighty strange. I was about to trade Kinnon's sweetheart for a confession he murdered you and Clay." The Special Agent's tone altered to one of coldness and accusation. "Where have you been, you sorry snake? What happened at that cabin last year? Were you and Kinnon working together all this time? Have you been hiding in the woods until he needed to use his ace? It won't work, old friend. You'd shoot me in the back the moment it was turned."

"You're wrong, Stone," Matt argued. "About me and about Kinnon. He wasn't the one who attacked me and Clay; it was a gang of claim-jumpers after Pete's diggings, not after us or ours. Why would I kill him? He saved our lives that time at Perry's Ford when we were captured by those redskins. He walked into their camp and used himself as bait to get us free. He was my friend, my partner. Remember what we said that day: nobody could take us when we had friends to help. I'm here to help you get out of this mess. Trust me like we trusted Clay that night."

Stone prayed he wasn't wrong about thinking Matt was sending him masked clues and that he was reading them right. If that was true, everything would be fine. There was no way to relate his hopeful assumption to Ginny, so he had to continue his act of suspicion. "You expect me to believe that mush and give up my advantage? If you didn't kill Clay or have him killed, why hide from me for a year?"

"I wanted to send for you, Stone, but I didn't know what you were thinking. I was scared you'd shoot before asking questions. Clay said he'd written to you to come after me if anything happened to him, and it did, but not by my hand or order. I don't know why he became so mixed up in the head. He had a few curious accidents and accused me of being behind them. I wasn't, Stone; you must believe that. I would never harm Clay. I ran because I was afraid people would think I'd murdered him; you can't blame me, not after the way he was talking and acting before he died."

"Why'd you come back now? Your timing is mighty coincidental."

Matt rubbed his thighs as he explained, "I was laid up for months in Virginia City with two broken legs and a busted shoulder; almost died twice. Two varmints attacked me and robbed me clean, pushed me off a cliffside and left me for dead. Some miners found me and carried me to town. I can thank Dr. Lynch for patching me up and saving my life. He was almost sure my walking days were over, but I was determined to prove him wrong. It took months to get on my feet again. Legs still hurt if I ride or stand too much. I had to work a long time to earn enough money to pay Andrew because I always take care of my bills. Doc Lynch let me stay at his home and he took good care of me, so I owed him. I also had to earn enough money to buy a horse, saddle, and supplies to get back to my claim. I didn't want to write Virginia for any money and worry her into coming here to check on me. This territory is too wild and dangerous for a refined and gentle lady. I'd told her in my last letter it would be a long time before I wrote again, so I knew not hearing from me wouldn't overly concern her. By now, I hoped the trouble and danger were over for me here. I decided that once I got the mine going, I'd have enough money and power to clear myself and catch the guilty parties."

"You're him or the man beside you is, or both of you are to blame."

"Stone, Stone, don't be fooled by Clay's crazy accusations. Kinnon is the one who assayed the ore sample for us. He asked about investing in the mine. I liked him and was impressed with him. Before we could talk, Clay and I were attacked and I had to get out of sight. I decided to ask Kinnon to become one of my partners. I'll need a good banker, one close by, a well-known and respected man who can protect me against unjust charges for murder. Please come down and let's get this nasty misunderstanding straightened out. You don't want to keep frightening that innocent young lady. You can't blame Kinnon for being riled by your treatment of her. After we settle things here, we'll catch Clay's killers."

Stone gave a derisive laugh. "You think Kinnon's gonna let me live if I turn over his girl? No way, Matt. He won't let you live, either, past partner or promise of future partner. He wants that silver too badly."

"Matt's right," Frank argued. "I was only riled because you stole my woman and tried to accuse me of murder. I'll be satisfied to be an investor."

Stone laughed once more. "Yeah? What about your earlier threats?"

"I told you, you riled me by kidnapping and abusing my Anna."

"When you got here, you didn't even believe she *was* your Anna. You thought she was Matt's daughter, my cohort. You were going to attack both of us. Trust you to let me ride away unharmed and alive? Do you think I'm loco? You'd sacrifice your own mother to get your hands on that silver."

"I know she isn't Virginia Marston Blake. Matt's daughter has red hair and blue eyes. It was only a bluff to get you to release her. I know the woman with you is Anna Avery. I love her and plan to marry her. I'm sorry, Anna dear, for scaring you while I was trying to persuade him to let you go."

Ginny struggled in Stone's hold to let the man know she'd heard him. Yet she was confused by the lies everyone was telling.

"Listen to him, Stone," Matt urged, "he's speaking the truth. He didn't attack us. He didn't kill Clay. I didn't murder Clay. This can all be worked out if you come down and discuss it. You're a lawman, remember? We'll answer your questions. Surely you realize we wouldn't dare harm you and provoke other agents to come after us. We'll put up a reward for Clay's killers. We'll hire skilled detectives to locate and arrest them. I want myself cleared, and Kinnon wants to get out from under suspicion. Don't forget half of this strike is yours. You can't profit from Clay's love and generosity if you kill us. Let's all shake hands and work out a deal to get our mine going."

"Let me think about your offer for a minute," Stone replied.

"I'll forgive you and forget about this, Chapman, if you stop it before it goes any further. I can understand how your grief over the death of your best friend could cloud your wits. But isn't it better to become friends and partners rather than shooting each other? You know you don't want to harm Anna and get into trouble with the law you're supposed to uphold. You've investigated me long enough to know I'm a man of my word. I promise, no revenge."

"You'll be getting just what you want, Kinnon: the girl and the silver. I guess I will, too: the silver and Clay's killers when we catch them. Matt will, too: the silver and exoneration. I suppose it's a good bargain for all of us. No shots have been fired at each other, so maybe . . ."

"Do it, Stone, come down and talk," Matt coaxed. "Do it while I'm in a position to help you two. If you stay up there, everything could go wrong."

"How will we get down?" Ginny whispered through the bandanna. "They'll shoot you as soon as your shield is missing. He's making Father say those things, so don't believe them. At least force Frank to send his men out of firing range but keep them in sight to watch for tricks."

Stone realized that was an excellent idea. He gritted out without moving his lips, "Don't worry. Matt's on to him."

"*What?*" she asked, her eyes wide with confusion and fear.

"What's your answer, Chapman?" Frank shouted. "You're stalling."

"We're coming down. No tricks, Kinnon. I'm tying her wrist and mine to the same rope. If you shoot me and I fall, so will she. Keep your word and nobody will get hurt." While her body blocked the men's view, Stone pretended to cut her bonds free but was actually taking the pistol from her hands and sliding it into his belt. He pulled the knife from his boot, cut a strip of rope, and secured it around his wrist first and then hers. "Duck behind a tree when I give the word," he whispered.

"But—"

"Don't worry; it's all right."

"Come on down before I get nervous and impatient, Chapman. You've frightened and mishandled my fiancée long enough. Hurry."

"I want your men to holster their weapons and move to that clearing over yonder while we talk," Stone yelled. He motioned to one a distance away, right where he wanted the gang. He quelled his grin.

"Us lay down our arms while you keep yours?" Frank replied.

"If you're duping me, Kinnon, I'll have time to defend myself. You're armed, so hold your pistol on me if you like. Then if you're trying to pull something, we'll shoot each other. That's only fair since I'm outnumbered."

"How do I know you won't shoot me anyway?" Frank asked.

"Because your boys would get me before I could escape. I'm good, Kinnon, but not that good so I can take down ten men before they killed me. You get Anna as soon as I'm convinced we can make a deal."

Frank smiled. "Agreed, Chapman. Boys, put up those pistols and walk over there. I'll signal you if there's trouble."

After the gang obeyed and only Kinnon was close enough to be a threat to their safety, Stone headed down the ladder first and Ginny followed a few rungs above him, their wrists linked by the rope. The aging ladder groaned and protested, but Stone knew it would hold up long enough to get down.

As his boots touched the ground, he helped Ginny make the final descent. With an uncocked Colt to her back and her walking before him, they approached the men. Ginny worried over her father recognizing her and wondered why he had said she had red hair and blue eyes, and why he hadn't reacted when Frank called her Virginia Blake. It was difficult to be near him and to look at him as if he were a stranger; he made it easier for her when he didn't take notice of her. Apparently his mind was elsewhere. She didn't have time to study his physical changes while listening to the crucial talk.

"Well, speak up and convince me," Stone coaxed.

"Untie and ungag Anna first. Let her come over here with me."

"Give up my cover?" Stone teased.

"You don't need her anymore, partner. I gave my word. I'll keep it. Besides, you're armed, so she's still in danger. I won't risk her life by trying anything reckless with you."

Stone eyed the man closely and knew he was lying. He smiled and said, "All right, partner. No need to create more ill feelings."

Stone freed a nervous Ginny. *No,* she wanted to shout. *Don't let Father see me! He'll expose us from shock!* She lowered her head as the bandanna was removed so the hat would conceal most of her face.

"Come here, Anna, you're safe now, my love."

Ginny hurried to stand beside Frank with her back to her father. The villain smiled at her and put an arm around her waist. To play her part, she returned the smile and cuddled against him for a moment, hating to do so. She noticed he kept a cocked pistol in his other hand, aimed at Stone's broad chest. She was glad when Frank removed his repulsive arm, but she kept her back to her father and dared not sneak a peek at him.

"No need for this now," Stone said. "You're blocking me as a target for your men. But I warn you, Kinnon, if you use that pistol, I can clear leather and fire on you before I hit the dirt."

Ginny panicked when Stone holstered his Colt and Frank didn't. To make matters worse, her father had no gun. "I have to sit down, Frank, my legs are wobbly and I feel weak all over. This has been a terrifying and exhausting experience for me. You should be punished, you insufferable beast," she said to Stone.

"Sorry, Miss Avery, but I thought it was a necessary action. It's obvious I was mistaken. I apologize."

"That doesn't excuse your vile behavior, does it, Frank? He should be horse-whipped for abducting me."

"Relax, my dear," the banker said, "this will be over soon."

Ginny sat on the ground behind Frank. With relief, she decided her father hadn't recognized her voice. She couldn't grasp why Stone hadn't used her distracting act to get the upper hand. With caution she worked the derringer free and eased it into her jacket pocket, fingers locked around it, with one on the trigger. Before leaving the cabin, Stone had ordered her not to do anything until he gave a signal: *Duck.*

The youngest man hinted, "I'm not hearing anything from you two."

"It's like I told you, Stone," Matt said, "we didn't have anything to do with Clay's murder. We'll ride back to town together and meet with a lawyer to get our plans into motion. We'll be partners in the Ginny M. Mine."

"I don't think so," Frank announced, brandishing his pistol.

"What do you mean?" Matt asked, taking a few steps backward.

"That will give me two partners too many."

"Hold on, Kinnon; you can't be in on the mine unless me and Stone let you join us. We each own half."

"If Chapman's dead, you own it all. If you sign it over to me, I own it."

"We aren't killing Stone! And I'd never sell my half."

Ginny couldn't believe Stone made no attempt to draw his weapons, as only Frank was armed and nearby. Why didn't he get the drop on the villain and use him as a hostage? He just stood there watching and listening.

"I have heirs, Kinnon," Stone said, "so my share wouldn't go to Matt."

"It will if you sign it over to him, and you will, Chapman."

"Why would I do that?"

Frank explained with a wicked grin, "To save his life. I'll kill him, slowly and painfully, if you don't cooperate."

"This was a trick," Stone accused. "You two are working together."

"No, Stone, you're terribly mistaken," Matt argued.

The lawman eyed his old friend. "Tell me, Matt, how hard will he beat you to convince me you aren't his partner in crime?"

Frank did the answering. "He isn't my partner, Chapman. This is the first time I've seen him since he disappeared last year. If I have to, I'll kill both of you and force the claim from your daughter. Now that I know who and where she is, I'll take it from her."

"You go near my daughter and I'll kill you!" Matt warned.

"How will you do that, Matt, when you'll both be bulging out some buzzards' bellies? I'm going to enjoy finishing you off, Chapman. You made a big mistake taking my woman."

Ginny felt she had to get close enough to take action soon. She stood and asked, "What are you doing, Frank? It sounds as if . . ."

"He's trying to double cross us," Stone finished for her with a scowl. "Let the snake talk, Miss Avery; I'd like to know the truth before I die."

Ginny couldn't understand why Stone didn't give the signal, as he had seen her pocket her small weapon. "Don't you call my Frank names."

"It's all right, my sweet," the banker said. "I have tough skin."

Matt looked at his daughter, "I'm sorry you have to witness such a crime, Miss Avery. Your fiancé had us both fooled. If I were you, I wouldn't marry a low-down skunk like him."

Before she could halt herself, Ginny half turned and looked at Matt. At her slip, her pulse raced and her heart pounded. Yet, he said nothing!

"Let me handle this, Anna. These are bad men and they deserve to die. Soon we'll be rich beyond your dreams. Matt promised me a share of the mine, then backed out on me. I have a right to it. I promise to make you forget this incident. You'll be happy with me."

Ginny knew her father must have recognized her as he was staring into her face, a reflection of her mother's, the woman he had loved beyond measure. Something, she decided, was going on that she didn't grasp. Her father and lover were trying to keep from exposing her. It seemed as if they were working together to try to extract an admission of guilt from Frank Kinnon. But if that were true, Stone would have told her; he had promised no more secrets between them. "I don't agree with what you're doing, Frank, but I'll trust you to do what's best for us," Ginny said. "I don't want you going to prison for a mistake you made last summer. I love you and want to marry you. Just don't . . . deal with them with me watching."

"Why don't you join my men over there until I'm finished here?"

Stone couldn't allow that to happen. "Why not stay and watch him kill us?" he sneered. "I should have known you'd be just like him. You two deserve each other. She's as greedy as you are, Kinnon. I'd be careful she doesn't learn from your example and double cross you one day."

"She's perfect for me: beautiful, refined, a real lady. She deserves to be dressed in silks and satins, to travel the world, to have people bow down to her like a queen. I can give her all of that."

To help keep her with them, Matt scoffed, "With our silver. If you're going to kill us anyway, why should we turn over our claim?"

"To be given a quick and easy death and to keep me away from Ginny."

"You did kill Clay like Stone said, didn't you, Kinnon," Matt accused. "And you tried to murder me that same day last summer?"

"That action was a little premature. The boys thought you'd led them to the right claim. I told them to get rid of you two as soon as they had the location of it. I was furious when you two 'died' with your secret intact. Even when Chapman kept asking questions about you and searching for you, I believed you were dead. This time, you will be. The giveaway was in registering the claim after you were supposedly dead. Very clever to do it in Denver where I wouldn't think to look. The date told me you hadn't died in the attack. That's probably what tipped off Chapman you were still alive. If he hadn't come nosing around again, I wouldn't have found out the truth. It's amusing you two are old friends who didn't trust each other."

Suddenly Frank burst into raucous laughter. "What am I thinking? I don't need either of you to sign your shares over to me. The strike is registered in the name of V. A. Marston; she will be the sole owner when you two are dead. Cassidy's name isn't on file, so he can't leave Chapman half of something he never owned. I won't have any trouble getting the land from Matt's daughter. I'll bring her here from England, tell her I have her father prisoner, get her to sign everything over to me to save his life, then . . . You catch my drift. It will be as easy as taking a toy from a small child."

Ginny panicked when the ruthless villain moved his pistol closer to Stone's body. "No, Frank, it won't," she refuted, jabbing her derringer into his side. "Do anything I don't like and I'll shoot; the bullet will enter your kidney and you'll bleed to death, a slow and painful death. Ask Stone and he'll tell you what an expert I am with firearms. Let's not alert your men. Holster your pistol and keep smiling."

"What are you doing, Anna? I have it all figured out. We'll be rich."

"*I'll* be rich, Frank, but *you'll* be in prison for murder. Put up your pistol, now. Don't drop it, just holster it," she warned.

The banker gaped at her in disbelief. "You're going to kill them and pin it on me? Use my plan to get everything for yourself?"

"Of course not. You're going to prison for murdering Clayton Cassidy."

"Are you a Special Agent working with Chapman?"

"No. The gun, Frank, put it away. I don't want your boys to attack. You could get shot by accident. I want you to go on trial and be punished."

"Are you Clay's kin? Or his woman?"

"Neither. If you don't disarm yourself instantly, I'm going to shoot."

"Then why are you helping these men and doing this to me?"

When Frank shoved the weapon into its holster, Ginny relaxed. Now she could tell him the shocking news. "I'm saving them because one is my father and the other is the man I love and am going to marry." When Frank glared at her, she said, "Keep quiet or you'll be trapped in the middle of a shootout with your men."

"You're . . . you're Virginia Marston Blake, Matt's daughter? But you're already married. Matt and Stone said so, to Robert Blake."

"No, and I've never been married, but Stone and I are to wed soon."

Frank paled and gritted his teeth aloud. "You bitch, you tricked me."

"That's right, with my love's help. Stone, if you'll take over here, I can speak with my father; it's been years since we've seen each other. Then we'll have to figure out how to get away from Frank's men."

"That won't be necessary, Ginny, my friends have them in custody. Stone and I were enjoying your arrest so much that we allowed you to finish it. Take over, Stone, it seems my daughter has a few things to tell me."

In that moment of distraction for everyone, Frank growled like a wild animal, grabbed Ginny's wrist, twisted the derringer around, and fired it as he shouted, "No man will have you if I can't!"

Chapter 21

～

A BULLET WHIZZED through Ginny's jacket and past her side without wounding her. She didn't even notice the scream that escaped her lips. Stone leapt on the enraged man, wrestled him to the ground, and pinned him there. Soldiers rushed forward from concealment and took control of Frank.

The lanky officer in charge said, "You're under arrest for the murder of Clayton Cassidy and the attempted murders of these three people."

"It's a lie! A trick! I'm innocent!"

The officer told the wild-eyed and shaking banker, "We heard it all, Mr. Kinnon, so save your breath for the trial."

Soldiers bound and led a mumbling Frank away to join his captured men. The defeated villain kept glancing back at the woman who had betrayed him, the woman he loved and had tried to murder.

"Stone, you remember Captain Andrew Lynch, don't you?" Matt said.

The Special Agent and the man in blue shook hands and exchanged smiles. "I surely do remember who gave us orders every day for years after we reached Fort Wise. How have you been, Andy?"

"Fine, Stone, a little saddlesore. Didn't get to rest in Denver before Matt hauled me here to help him. Seems we arrived at the perfect time."

"You certainly did. Sneaked up and took them without firing a shot. You still have your cunning skills," Stone complimented, then glanced at his love. "Ginny, this was our commanding officer when we were released from that Union prison and sent west as Galvanized Yankees. He taught us plenty and kept most of the recruits alive with his skills and courage. Andy, Miss Virginia Anne Marston, Matt's daughter and soon to be my wife."

Andrew and Ginny shook hands and smiled. "A pleasure and an honor, sir. Thank you for the rescue."

"Congratulations," Andy responded. "Never thought to see the day when a woman, especially a fine lady, would snare this renegade. I hope you'll be very happy. Does this mean you'll be retiring?"

Stone wondered if Matt was shocked by this news and would be disappointed with his daughter's choice. "Yep. I've done my last mission. Gonna give ranching a try. My father has a large spread in Texas. He's been trying to lure me home for years to join him."

"And she changed your roaming ways?" Andy jested.

"Yep, she surely did. I'm lucky we met."

Matt wanted to know every detail about how that event had occurred, but he would probe it later in private. "You're a grown woman, Ginny, a *beautiful* woman like your mother. Lordy, how I've missed you, girl."

Ginny went to her father and hugged him. For a few minutes they remained in a loving and comforting embrace while they experienced the joy of being together again. Their hearts were full of love and their minds filled with relief. They leaned back to study each other with moist eyes.

"You look wonderful, Father," she said, though he had lost weight, half his brown hair had grayed, tiny wrinkles etched his tanned face, and he needed a shave from many days' growth of wiry whiskers. "I was so worried about you when you didn't write again."

Matt stroked her mussed hair, hugged her once more, and disclosed that he had written two more times, in October and in late February.

"I didn't receive either letter, Father, nothing since last July. The first one must have gotten lost and the second one would have arrived after I left London that month. I came by wagontrain and stagecoach. I've been in Colorado City since the middle of last month. It's so good to see you."

Matt stroked his thick mustache as he grinned and said, "You and Stone took me by surprise being at my cabin and with your little ruse up there. We rode Kinnon's tail almost the whole way here but didn't expect to find you two present. We overheard your talk and carried on with our trap."

"How did you know to come here today?" Stone asked.

"I was in Denver finalizing plans with my investors when Kinnon telegraphed the land office for information. It alerted us to his renewed interest and to possible trouble. I told the others he was the man who had assayed the ore sample and gotten all sparkly-eyed; then it was no time hardly before Clay was murdered. I suggested I hurry back to see what was going on with him because I was certain he'd had Clay killed. I'd already seen Andy when he arrived, so I explained matters to him and talked him into helping me settle this problem. When Kinnon left town with his men Sunday morning, we followed him. I decided the best place to trick him into confessing was at the very site he craved and in what he thought was privacy. Andy agreed. Kinnon fell right into the pit we dug for him."

"Thank goodness you came, Father. We were running out of ideas fast. Stone was talking about sacrificing his life to save mine."

Matt smiled at her and placed one arm around her shoulder. He looked at his old friend. "Thank you, Stone, for protecting her."

Stone's dark eyes visually caressed Ginny's face, and his gaze softened and glowed. "She would have given her life for me, too. She's the bravest and smartest woman I've ever met. You should be very proud of her; I am."

"You won't believe all the things he's taught me, Father, or the adventures we've shared. We'll tell you about them later."

Matt felt the powerful and tender bond between them and noticed the way they looked at each other: they were undeniably in love. "When Kinnon called out for Miss Marston to show herself, my heart almost stopped. Then Stone came outside with you as his captive and saying you were Kinnon's fiancée. You were begging for help from the man I was trying to snare for murder. I was totally shocked and confused. I didn't know if Stone was truly using you to outwit Kinnon or if you two had somehow connected and were attempting to entrap him yourselves."

Matt looked at the man who loved his daughter. "You were mighty rough with her, Stone, but I was certain you wouldn't really harm her. You took a big gamble using her for cover to dupe Kinnon. I'm glad you gave him that deadline so we'd have time to outmaneuver him."

"I'm still dazed by seeing you, Father, and discovering this cunning hoax. Don't blame Stone for our dangerous deception; we were hopeful our ruse would succeed. I've been letting Frank court me for weeks—as Anna Avery—so we were almost positive we could fool him. At least confuse him long enough to escape. We didn't have any choice."

Matt sent her a smile of understanding and acceptance. "I gave Kinnon a false description of you because I had to keep him believing the woman with Stone was Anna Avery. I pretended to believe he was innocent of that trouble last summer. For a scary minute, Kinnon hinted that the three of us were working as a team. He suggested killing Stone, but I told him I'd clear your head. He's the one who came up with the idea how to entice you outside so I could talk you down."

"I almost fainted, Father, when I heard your voice and name. I lost all hope of us getting away from that evil man."

"I'm sorry I frightened you, Ginny, but I had to get you two to come down. I knew you wouldn't be in much peril, not with soldiers hidden in the woods and ready to defend us. I was sure Kinnon would get cocky and chatty and unmask himself. It was a risk, I admit, but I had to take it to clear up this matter. He confessed, thank goodness. I was only worried Stone wouldn't understand and cooperate."

"You were cunning with your words, Matt. I caught your clues about Perry's Ford, Andrew Lynch, Virginia Blake, and the deceitful description of Ginny. At least, I *hoped* I was reading your hints right."

"I was praying you'd catch them and trust me, Stone. I was certain you'd remember you were the one who saved me and Clay from those Indians and how you'd done it with hidden soldiers. I hoped using the same name you had for her would tip you off that I'd been eavesdropping."

"You did a good job, Matt, Andy. So did your daughter. It was Ginny's idea to send Kinnon's men upstream out of firing range. I wanted to let her know not to worry, but I couldn't risk Kinnon seeing us whisper."

"I had no clue it was a trap, even though Stone mumbled for me not to worry," Ginny said. "I was afraid you'd be so shocked to see me, Father, that our deception would be exposed. When Stone holstered his pistol and made no attempt to attack Frank, I was petrified."

"I guessed that Matt had been lurking nearby from the start when he used the name Blake." Stone looked at the observant Captain Lynch. "I'm glad Kinnon exposed himself before witnesses, Andy; the law may have thought I had selfish reasons to let Matt go and to use Kinnon as a scapegoat. I'm sorry, Ginny, but I couldn't alert you to what was going on."

"I tried to keep my head down and my back to you, Father, to conceal my identity. I finally realized something was afoot when I turned before thinking and you didn't react to me. At first, I thought maybe it was to protect me, but then I sensed it was something more. I thought Stone wasn't attacking because he was afraid of endangering me. I shouldn't have let down my guard after Frank holstered his weapon. Stone will tell you I have a bad habit of being distracted at the worst times. He's tried to cure me of it, but I have occasional relapses." She wiggled her finger in the bullethole in her jacket. "We're lucky none of us got shot."

"We sure are, Miss Marston," Andy agreed. "It's good to see my past troops haven't lost their skills or forgotten their training. Stone, Matt, and Clay were three of my best soldiers. We shared good and bad times."

"That's the most you've said since we arrived, Andy," Matt teased. "He's still not much of a talker, is he, Stone? 'Course we haven't given him a chance to get many words in."

"Papa always said a boy couldn't hear and learn when he was running his mouth like a racing horse, so I guess it became habit to be quiet. Except when I'm giving orders, then I can out shout the loudest of men or women. Times like those, my men wished I'd stayed quiet."

Everyone laughed at Andy's amusing grin and tone.

"It's good to see you again, Andy," Stone repeated his earlier words.

"I've missed you riding with me, Stone," the officer responded. "I always knew I could depend on you more than anybody to obey without thinking about any peril involved. No matter what happened, I knew you would never take off and leave any of us in danger. Some of the boys I've had since you left would desert their own mothers to save their hides. My duty is up next month. I'll have to find me something like ranching to do. And find me a pretty lady to marry like you have. You're lucky."

"More than lucky," Stone amended. "She's perfect in every way."

Ginny felt a flush race over her body as he complimented her. Not only had he learned to express his feelings to her but he no longer concealed them from others as if they were something to be ashamed of. She read love, pride, and happiness in his expression. She had her father and future husband with her, and all were safe. She felt alive and aglow and bubbling with energy and anticipation. "You're biased, Mr. Chapman. Besides, I'm the fortunate one. If not for you, I'd be in terrible trouble by now. You're right about him, Captain Lynch, he's the bravest and most dependable man I've ever met."

"When did you two meet?" Andy asked. "How? Where?"

"On Sunday morning, March the twenty-fourth in Savannah, Georgia," Ginny answered with a radiant smile. The officer had earlier referred to Stone as being a Special Agent, so she didn't think it too revealing to explain that he was on a mission and was posing as the guide and leader for the wagontrain she was taking west. "Are you the one who taught him to be such a tough and demanding teacher?" she laughed and asked. "He worked us women every day as if he was drilling soldiers until we almost collapsed each night. But it was worth every pain and irritation. By the time he finished our lessons, we could do anything the men could do, and sometimes better. We owe our lives, safety, and success to him."

"That was a lucky coincidence, you two meeting like that so far away."

"More than luck, Captain Lynch, *destiny*. Stone's sister and I were best friends during our years at boarding school in London. We were heading for the Chapman ranch after we docked in Savannah. Since we met, our lives have been entwined. Haven't they, Stone?"

He chuckled and concurred. "The strange part is, I was working as Steve Carr and she was traveling as Anna Avery; we didn't know for a while we had two connections: her father and my sister."

Andy was intrigued. "Why under a false name, Miss Marston? Didn't Stone's sister burst his cover?"

Ginny related her connection with Johanna and her subsequent ruse. When she had finished, she was aware her father hadn't asked any questions or made comments. Stone hadn't stopped any disclosures yet, so she assumed all she'd said so far was all right with him; in fact, he was smiling and nodding agreement. But the next part of the story was too personal to tell someone who was a stranger to her, so she laughed and raced beyond it to all that had happened after and how she finally connected with Stone in Texas and wound up here in search of her father.

"That is quite an adventure, Miss Marston."

"Please call me Ginny."

"If you'll call me Andy."

No one spoke for a few minutes as Ginny pondered if she'd talked too freely before telling her father such important things.

"What happened here last summer, Matt?" Stone finally asked in reluctance. "Between you and Clay, I mean."

"I'll explain everything later, Stone. Andy wants to eat, then head for Denver. He has to be back by Monday night. He can make it by using Kenosha Pass and getting started soon. If you don't object, I'll offer Andy the job of heading up our mine and transport guards, if he's interested in being a boss, choosing his own men, and making a good salary."

"A great idea, Matt. What about it, Andy? Need time to think on it?"

"Nope, sounds good. I'll give it a try. Thanks."

The men shook hands on the deal. "I'll contact you from town later," Matt said. "We'll spend the night here and discuss a few family and business matters. It appears I have a lot to learn about my daughter and partner."

Ginny saw her father glance back and forth between her and Stone and knew one topic that intrigued him was the extent of their relationship. She wondered if it was obvious how far it had gone. Would he be angry with her and Stone? Would he, she fretted, object to their marriage?

By two o'clock and with about seven hours of daylight left, the soldiers and prisoners were on their way to Denver. The three left behind for the night were relieved to have privacy. Ginny, Stone, and Matt sat near a campfire and sipped coffee. It seemed as if each of them was waiting for another one to begin their long-anticipated conversation.

"Well, Matt," Stone prompted, "you ready to talk about Clay?"

"You realize now that I didn't kill him. I understand why you'd suspect me and I don't blame you. I know how bad it looked. After we made our strike here, we took a sample of the ore to Frank Kinnon. We'd met him a few times when we were in town and we both liked him, thought he was trustworthy. But I saw how Kinnon eyed the ore. He told us the truth about it being high grade and almost pure and what the mine would be worth. He asked to become an investor and we told him we'd think about it. I could see his palms itching and his eyes burning to have a stake in our diggings." Matt leaned forward on the rock seat as he recalled that time.

"I was worried because I knew we were being watched and followed. I tried to explain the dangers to Clay, tried to convince him we needed to file our claim in Denver and to be careful. He couldn't seem to grasp or accept what I was saying. It was as if he'd also become blinded by the idea of wealth. I'd never seen Clay act like that before. He changed after Kinnon told us the value of our strike. After being poor all his life and living hand-to-mouth as we did while prospecting, I guess I can understand how such news could affect him like that. I told him we needed investors we could trust, but he wanted to file in Colorado City, bring Kinnon in on the deal, and start mining immediately. I convinced him to pan and dig here and there for two weeks to get enough gold for supplies and to dupe anybody trailing us. But he got impatient and downright nasty with me on a few occasions."

Matt looked sad as he reflected on the deterioration of the friendship and Clay's baffling mental state. "When we'd meet up with other men, I'd almost have to gag him to keep him from boasting about being rich. He wanted to go into town, reveal the news so he could get credit or a loan, and use the money to live it up with women and gambling. He was almost uncontrollable, Stone. He had several curious accidents and started looking at me strangely. His girth strap came loose and his tent caught fire and some other things. He finally accused me of trying to get rid of him, said I had chosen this location and found the silver and wanted it all to myself. That wasn't true; I'd never felt that way. I didn't have to be greedy; there's enough silver here to make us rich a hundred times. I was worried, and I was unconvinced he wasn't behind those episodes to force my hand. He wanted to announce the strike to everyone that very week. I tried to tell him how dangerous and unwise that would be. Every time a big one is revealed, prospectors flood the area. I said we had to keep quiet until we worked out the details of our company. I suggested filing it in Ginny's name to protect us. Clay refused and got angry."

Matt sipped coffee to wet his throat. "We stopped by Pete's new shack until I could be sure we'd lost our shadows. While I was in the woods relieving myself, I heard gunshots. I stayed where I was for a while because I didn't have a weapon with me. When I sneaked back later, Clay and Pete were dead. I knew it wasn't a thief because our horses and belongings hadn't been taken. In a way, I'm to blame for Pete being killed. I shouldn't have led Kinnon's men to his location. They must have thought it was ours and that they were getting rid of us. I knew when the bodies were found, the culprit would realize he'd missed me. I burned the cabin to conceal my escape."

Matt waited for Stone to object to that action, but he didn't. Nor did Stone protest or refute what he was hearing about their deceased mutual friend. "I disguised myself, took Pete's mule and gear, left my belongings, and sneaked into town. I found out that Kinnon filed on the land Pete had been prospecting. I heard that me and Clay were declared dead, so I let everyone continue to think that. I hurried to Denver and registered this claim in the name of V. A. Marston, then sent Ginny a map and a warning. You received them?"

After she nodded, Matt explained, "I didn't file in Colorado City because some surveyors and officials were close friends of Kinnon's. I was afraid if I showed myself, Kinnon would sic his friends on me and frame me for Clay's murder because I had a damn good motive for getting rid of him. I decided, if I stayed 'dead,' the killers might be caught by a smart lawman like you, Stone. I didn't want any shadow of doubt cast on me. There was no hurry to mine the silver; it wasn't going anywhere and the claim was safe. I knew Clay had written to you. I hoped you'd come and investigate and find evidence to clear me. I also realized that if I announced the strike, the killer might never be found because there'd be no reason to expose himself. I reasoned that when I got everything set, I would use myself to entrap the murderer as I did today."

Matt looked at Ginny, then at Stone. "Do you understand that I couldn't allow myself to be charged with murder and that I needed time to find somebody I could trust to help me unmask a rich and respected man like Frank Kinnon?" They both nodded. "I decided it was best to head for other parts—Montana, Arizona, Nevada, and California—to study silver mining and to locate investors, men who would have the power and wealth to protect me and help me. I'm not a coward, Stone, but I knew how bad it looked for me. I knew how much Kinnon wanted my claim. I realized there were corrupt officials who could be bribed to frame me. I had no proof against him, and who would take my word over his?"

"You can stop worrying now, Father; it's over and we're all safe."

"I think you did the right thing, Matt, and I believe you."

"Thanks, Stone; that means a lot to me."

"Are you all right, Father? Why didn't you send for me sooner?"

"What I said about my broken legs and busted shoulder was the truth. The only place I visited was Virginia City. That trouble kept me there for almost a year. I couldn't decide when to return and see how things stood here. I didn't know how or where to reach you, Stone. And I didn't want to worry Ginny with such bad news. I wrote her in October that everything was going fine, but that letter must have been lost or stolen during a stage robbery. I sent you money in February to sail for America this month. I told you to take the train to St. Louis and telegraph me from there so I could come for you. I concluded my problems would be settled by the time you got here in August."

"You should have told me the truth, Father. You were hurt and in trouble and you needed me."

"I was afraid you'd come here and I'd be too injured to protect you. This is wild and dangerous territory, girl. Men can get crazy or desperate. Tell me, Stone, what did Clay write to you?"

The younger man related what had been in their friend's last message to him. "I'm sorry for doubting you, Matt, but it did look suspicious to me."

"I understand. In your place, I'd have thought and done the same thing. I didn't know Clay had given you his share of the claim, but that's not a problem. Now that I know I have a partner, I'll have to work out a new agreement with the investors I've chosen. They're awaiting news in Denver. I'll telegraph them from town in a few days. Dr. Wilton Clancy, the man who saved my life in Virginia City, is one of them. I hope you don't mind that I've put things into motion without conferring with you first."

"Of course not. Whatever you do is fine with me. I plan to be a rancher in Texas with my father. I've asked Ginny to marry me and she's agreed. We'll be living there, but you're welcome to visit anytime. Do you have any objections to me joining your family?"

From the time they had spent together today, Matt could read the changes in Stone Chapman, which were clearly results of meeting and loving his Ginny. He had always believed the young man had plenty of good traits and strong emotions inside him but was fearful to expose them. It was obvious Ginny had brought the best in Stone to the surface and the man had dealt with his bitter past, whatever that was, as he hadn't talked much about it to him. Matt saw her reach for her sweetheart's hand and squeeze it, then smile. "From the way my daughter looks at you and speaks about you, I doubt it would make a difference if I did. But don't worry, Stone, I think you'll make Ginny a perfect husband and me a fine son-in-law. I can see that you've resolved and discarded any troubles tormenting you. This is the most I've seen you smile since we met years ago. The hardness in your eyes is gone. The chip's off your shoulder. You were always your own worst enemy, Son, but I'm convinced you've made peace with yourself."

Stone's thick voice exposed his feelings. "Thank you, Matt. You won't be sorry you've entrusted her to me. I love her very much and she's been the best thing that's happened to me. I was riding a self-destructive trail until I met her, but she changed that for me."

Ginny smiled at Stone and her father but didn't speak because she wanted them to get closer and thought any words might disrupt the special moment.

Matt sighed and told them, "I hate to lose her so soon after our reunion. This news does come as a big surprise, but I'm happy with your decision. I think you two have a bright future ahead. Now, I want to hear more about you two meeting and getting here." His inquisitive gaze focused on his daughter. "What's this about traveling with a stranger who was dangerous and evil? You should know better, Virginia Marston! What did they teach you all those years in that fancy boarding school?"

"Charles Avery wasn't a totally evil man, Father. He was a tormented and misguided one. We liked each other, and I was never in any peril from him. Besides, he couldn't harm me with Stone and so many people around on the wagontrain. I don't know if you've heard about what's happening in the South since the war ended. I couldn't believe what I saw after docking there. The South is like a captive to the North; they rule it with an iron hand. Many people lost everything because of the war. Husbands, fathers, sons, and brothers were killed. Women, children, elderly parents, and orphans must fend for themselves. There was so much wanton destruction, more than was necessary to win a war. It left people without homes and ways to support themselves. Horrible things are taking place and Southerners are still suffering terribly."

She caught a breath before going on. "The North has many secret and dangerous organizations, like the Loyal League. They claim their purpose is to help ex-slaves learn to become citizens, but they also arm, train, and coax resentful ex-slaves to attack vulnerable whites. None of the instigators or villains are ever punished or halted. I can grasp why men like Mr. Avery would become bitter and desperate, but that does not justify what they're doing to equally innocent blacks and whites. Wicked men on both sides must be stopped, Father, by our government."

When Matt didn't interrupt, she continued. "Some men in the South have formed a secret group whose purpose, they claim, is to fight terrorism and injustices and to protect their lives, families, and homes. It's called the Invisible Empire, the Ku Klux Klan. They dress in flowing robes and hoods to conceal their identities from victims and witnesses. Mr. Avery was a member of the most notorious Den." She related the deceased man's personal motives about becoming involved with the nefarious group, the Red Magnolias.

"Mr. Avery's Den wanted money for arms and ammunition for their battles and to locate and murder officers whose orders almost destroyed the South, like Sherman who crushed Georgia. They got the payment for those plans through robberies in the North and in foreign countries, including England—mostly valuable, untraceable gems. Mr. Avery was chosen to deliver the payment to a man in Missouri who was going to fill their order. The Justice Department assigned Stone to unmask the carrier and stop them. It was a dangerous mission; several agents had been murdered while gathering information, so he pretended to be Steve Carr, our guide for the wagontrain. But things went wrong in Vicksburg." She explained all that had transpired until their arrival in Fort Smith.

"Lordy, girl, you could have been killed many times! You shouldn't have taken such risks, Ginny."

"Thanks to everything Stone taught me, Father, I did fine."

"I can see that you did. I'm proud of you, Ginny. Stone, too. But what happened to his sister? Why did you continue to pretend to be Anna?"

Ginny looked at her love as if to ask how much to reveal.

Stone smiled and replied, "Tell him the truth about me and her."

Ginny talked about the close friendship with the girl who had been like a sister to her and the relationship and repercussions of Ben's love for the Apache woman.

"They had a son together: Stone." She saw Mathew Marston glance at the other man for a moment. She continued the story of the fragmented Chapman family, Stella's death, then her misadventures as Anna Avery and why she had used that identity on the wagontrain.

She decided not to confess her Johanna deception with the Chapmans and would ask Ben not to mention it to her father when they met. Nor would she tell him about the many misunderstandings and love affair with Stone since their meeting. "I hid out from the authorities while visiting Johanna's father. I had left Steve Carr a message telling him where to find me. I knew, if he felt the same way I did, he would come after me when his mission was completed."

Ginny knew that Stone would catch the deletions and deceits in her story, would understand, and agree with her motive. She continued to relate the events leading up to the present one that had halted their departure to Denver. She told him the rest of the plan they'd had in mind and finished with a point important for her father to know. "Nandile is still Mr. Chapman's housekeeper. They love each other and plan to marry soon. She's a kind, beautiful, and wonderful lady, Father. You'll like her. You'll like Mr. Chapman, too. He's a good man. In many ways, he reminds me of you."

"I'm a Chapman by birth and adoption," Stone affirmed, telling Matt his father had only recently acknowledged him. "I didn't know I was Bennett's son until I was ten and overheard him and Stella quarreling before she took off with my half sister. We had problems over the years because I resented how I was born and because he refused to marry my mother, but we love each other and we've made peace," he explained. "Does it bother you that I was born a half-breed bastard? Do you think that makes me unworthy of Ginny?"

"No, Son, and it helps me understand what drove you. I'm sure you endured a hard life and plenty of troubles. During our Army years, I saw both sides of the Indian dispute, so I grasp your father's dilemma. I'm glad he's found the courage and strength to marry the woman he loves. Besides, I can't speak badly of him for marrying Stella. After I lost Ginny's mother, I married a woman I didn't love for all the wrong reasons. I wouldn't be surprised to learn she and Stella are a lot alike —greedy and selfish women who snare men while they're vulnerable. My second wife took up with a Yankee carpetbagger after I was reported dead. I have another daughter, six years old, who I've only seen once, near the time she was born before I was called away to war. Amanda doesn't know me; she probably thinks that Yankee who stole Green Oaks is her father. I went back after the war to let them know I was alive. Clay went with me. You were up in Dakota on a long mission. Remember? Everything was lost. She was married and expecting his child. I didn't show myself. We returned west and started prospecting."

Matt stared unseeingly into the forest. "I still haven't written to my wife and baby. I decided it was best for all of us if I remained dead to them. It didn't seem fair to Amanda to disrupt her life, and going back couldn't change anything for me with the plantation and my lost family. Soon, though, I'll have to contact Cleniece. I'll need a good lawyer to handle our divorce, or whatever one does under such mixed-up circumstances."

"You should do it quickly, Father, before you announce the strike. Once that greedy woman hears how rich you are, she'll swear she's still married to you and leave her Yankee mate. Even if she loves her new husband—though I doubt she can love anyone—her son will persuade her. You remember how he is. I told you how they abandoned me after you were reported dead. I was ordered never to come home again. Get the divorce first to prevent problems with her. If she doesn't want to tell Amanda about you, you can still send money for her support."

"From what Ginny's told me about them, Matt, she could be right," Stone added. "A strike this size will be news all over the country. She's bound to hear about it."

"I agree and I'll handle the matter immediately."

Ginny wanted to ask how Stone, Matt, and Clay had met and what things they'd done together. She decided those questions should wait until another time when all their torments and losses were less painful. She concluded they had been placed in the same Army unit after they had arrived in the West. His motives for becoming a Galvanized Yankee were probably the ones her love had mentioned that night on the wagontrain trail.

"We'll head for town in the morning and put our plans into motion," Matt said. "I'm sure you two want to leave for Texas next week. If you can hold off for a month until August third, I can finish here and make it to the ranch in time to give away my daughter to a fine man I'll be proud and pleased to call son."

"That sounds like a fine date for a wedding to me, Matt, and I'm sure my parents will agree to that date for theirs. What do you think, Ginny?"

"Waiting only one more day is too long, but I agree."

They talked, laughed, and planned until it was time to cook and eat.

"Before we begin chores, I'm taking a bath in that freezing water," Ginny said with a playful grin. "I'm not heading off on a four day ride in this sweaty condition. Why don't you two chat about old times until I return?"

Matt chuckled and said, "I see you located my chilly shower."

"I saw the soap and drying cloth and stuck my fingers under the flow. If you can suffer through something like that, I can, too. I guarantee I won't take long. Ignore any screams you might hear."

The men chuckled, then watched her scale the rickety ladder.

"She's very special and precious," Stone murmured as if to himself.

"She certainly is, Son. She favors her mother. Lordy, I miss that woman. You never get over losing a love like that; nobody can replace it."

"As Ginny hinted, I was too stubborn for a while to recognize and accept what she could give to me. I had a hard time believing she could love and want a man like me or that I could give her what she deserves. I do love her with all my heart, Matt, and I'll take good care of her. I can't imagine losing her as you lost your wife."

"You two will be fine, Son," the older man said with confidence. "I'm glad you were here today so we could make peace. It's time for new beginnings. I look forward to having a happy and close family again."

"So do I, Matt, for the first time."

The two men looked at each other, smiled, and changed the subject.

*   *   *

Supper and chores were completed. Matt and Ginny lay on the two bunks. Stone rested on the floor in his sleeping roll. The cabin was quiet except for the sounds of breathing and dark except for the slanting light from a full moon. Through the windows came a cool breeze, the rushing sound of the stream below, and combined noises of nocturnal creatures and insects.

Ginny enjoyed the tranquility of the moment. It was July Fourth, Independence Day. They were free and safe and content. A bright future awaited all of them. Problems and perils were things of the past. Surely no more dark clouds would appear to hover over and threaten them.

—— *Chapter 22* ——

GINNY, STONE, AND MATT ARRIVED in Colorado City near dusk on Monday without any problems befalling them on the trail. They reached Hattie Sue Pearl's boardinghouse and astonished the woman with their story about Kinnon being arrested for the murder of Clayton Cassidy. Nothing was mentioned about the silver strike, but they told her they had all worked together to set a trap for Frank and it had succeeded. The woman was delighted to meet Stone and Matt and fascinated by the exciting tale.

Following the delicious meal she prepared for them, Stone and Ginny took a stroll while Matt and Hattie talked and laughed over a cup of coffee.

At the corral, Stone gazed at her and noticed how moonlight flowed like silky water over her. It brought out the golden tones in her hair and skin as if to announce her value. "You're so beautiful," he murmured. "I can't even glance at you without wanting you. How do you have such power over me?" He pulled her into his arms and kissed her. He quivered with desire. His lips roamed her face, sampling every inch of its satiny texture. His hand moved her long tresses aside so he could taste her neck and nuzzle her ear. His playful nips caused her to tremble and giggle. "Ginny love, you're driving me wild and I can't have you tonight. A month seems like forever."

Her fingertips trekked over his face as she replied, "It's twenty-six days, my love, and it does sound like forever. How shall we manage until then? We haven't been alone for days. With our separate trips staring us in the face, we won't even see each other for two weeks. Why can't we travel together? I have a horse, too. Father could rent one instead of using mine and selling him before he leaves. Besides, we've been on the trail in private before. Why must I go by stage? I'm dying for you."

Stone's fingers stroked her curls and caressed her face. They moved over her lips, and both trembled with mounting desire. "I know, love, but we can't sneak off together from Matt. And there's no way me and Chuune could keep pace with a near runaway stage. We'll head south and swing over to Dallas and reach there about the same time you do. Then, woman, I won't ever let you out of my sight again. For now, we'll have to be satisfied with stolen kisses and hugs. At least we're together."

"For one more day, and for the rest of our lives after we reach Texas. Two weeks without even seeing you . . ." She rested her head against his chest and listened to the steady drumming of his heart. "It would be easier if I didn't know what it was like to have you completely. I never want to be separated from you again."

"You know I can't sell Chuune or leave him behind," he said, gazing fondly at the sorrel.

"I know. Who would have thought I'd become jealous of a horse?"

They shared laughter, then remained there for an hour, holding each other and sharing kisses and talking of their future.

Ginny's body felt light and her head dreamy. His lips were sweet and stirring each time they captured hers. His fingers drifted up and down her back, an action more stimulating than soothing. Her arms encircled his body as her mouth fastened with greed to his.

When their passions threatened to kindle too high, Stone suggested they go inside before they lost their heads. With reluctance, she agreed, and Ginny went to her rooms to cool her blazing body and to long for the day her lover would be at her side.

On Tuesday, the investors in the future Ginny M. Mine arrived to discuss business with Matt in private. Captain Andrew Lynch had met with them and reported the successful trap and Matt's impending trip to Colorado City. They were not upset about learning there was a previously unknown partner in the company and seemed pleased to meet Stone Chapman. They decided to keep the news concealed for as long as possible.

Afterward, Stone telegraphed his parents to relate their victory and their imminent departure for Texas tomorrow. With a stroke of luck, he met an ex-soldier who was heading home to Texas and hired him to deliver Chuune to the ranch. He knew the sorrel understood when he whispered in the stallion's ear to go with the other man.

It was at the evening meal that the two young lovers noticed how taken Matt and Hattie seemed to be with each other.

When they strolled again after supper, Stone and Ginny held hands as they kept looking at each other, smiling and halting every few minutes to kiss and embrace. Aware of the peril of becoming too aroused, they made certain to control their heady desire, also aware it wouldn't be for long.

Stone grinned and hinted, "I have a big surprise for you, woman."

"What? Tell me."

"I'm coming with you on the stage tomorrow." He explained the details.

* * *

Thursday morning, July eleventh, Ginny and Stone left by stage for the Chapman ranch. Matt remained behind to conclude his business in time to leave by the following Friday to join them. The journey through Kansas, Missouri, Arkansas, and Oklahoma Territory to reach Texas didn't seem as long and as monotonous to Ginny as the trip in the opposite direction had, since she and Stone were pressed together in a coach for fourteen days and too cognizant of their physical contact during every mile. Also, two of the stops were made in towns with cozy, romantic, and private hotels . . .

Ginny sighed dreamily in Stone's arms. "This is wonderful."

He lifted his head and gazed down at her with an expression of mischief and passion. His eyes slipped over her tousled hair. "That's what you said in Fort Smith," he teased as his tongue traced patterns down her throat and across her collarbone to her breasts.

Ginny's hazel eyes sparkled with the memory. "You took me for a ride down a new trail, my lusty guide, and gave me another adventure I hadn't known existed. Perhaps I should interrogate you, Mister Lawman, about where you acquired such knowledge and skills."

"Don't be jealous; I've never used them on a woman before. You're just so delicious and I was so hungry that I couldn't resist tasting you from head to foot." His tongue flicked over her breasts and made her quiver. His mouth captured one peak and tantalized it before doing the same to the other one. His hands caressed her warm and supple body, fondling each curve and mound and plane they encountered. He savored his potent effect on her. He shifted to lie half atop her so his lips could explore hers. He tried to go slowly, but it was hard to control his ache for her.

Ginny responded with unbridled need as he claimed her. No matter how many times they joined, she never had enough of him and it took only a touch or look to intoxicate her. He sent her senses spinning. Her hands roamed his muscled back and shoulders. They played in thick hair as shiny black as a raven's wing beneath the sun. Her flesh quivered and pleaded from his burning kisses and searing caresses. There wasn't an inch of her that wasn't sensitive to his ardent attack. Wild and wonderful emotions assailed her. She always wanted to travel love's journey in leisure with him but his actions evoked her to race faster and faster toward victory. As his fingers roved down her stomach to seek out the hidden place that heightened her desires, she moaned and writhed.

Ginny clung to his sinewy frame, surrendering her all to him in a near-wild frenzy. All doubts and worries left behind, she let him guide her where he willed. He was strong, yet his touch was as gentle and light as sunshine playing over flowers. She was like a slender limb being blown to and fro by a powerful wind that shook her to her core. "I love you so much, Stone Chapman."

"I love you, Ginny," he replied in an emotion-thickened voice.

Ginny rolled him to his back and almost leapt upon him. She dropped kisses as light as feathers on his face, then confined his head between her hands to ravish his mouth with hers. Her lips went from feature to feature as they traced each one. She wandered down his neck and over his hairless chest. She smiled and blazed as he moaned and squirmed as he'd made her do at their last stop. Her exploring hand trekked down his torso and claimed the prize it sought.

Stone trembled and moaned at the stimulating action as her lips and hands played over his body. He wanted to let her continue with her blissful torment, but he also wanted to seize her and make swift love to her. "Mercy, woman, you have me boiling like a pot of coffee on hot coals."

Ginny laughed and teased, "Like you perk me every time you take me? This is far more sporting when I participate." She returned to work on him.

Soon, Stone was compelled to flip her to her back so he could take them to the golden summit.

Together they gathered priceless nuggets of glittering splendor. They wanted nothing less than total love, commitment, and appeasement. Their mouths meshed to prevent joyful outcries of pleasure achieved. They kissed and caressed as their sated bodies cooled and relaxed.

Stone turned to his side and drew her into the curve of his body. She snuggled against him, using his arm as a pillow. Her fingers roamed the tawny terrain of his chest. Both were amazed and awed by how simple contact or a mere look could enflame their passions to such soaring heights. They loved and felt loved. They took and they gave and they shared. No doubts troubled their dreamy thoughts; no uncertainties teased their hearts. They were separate beings, yet one in spirit and goal.

"You're mine, Ginny Marston, forever."

"Yes, my love, forever."

Bennett and Nandile awaited the beaming couple when the coach halted in Dallas on the twenty-third. They let the cloud of dust go by and their loved ones get out before they rushed forward for hugs and kisses.

"Heavens be praised, Son, it's good to have you home again. Ginny, I'm happy you roped this boy and convinced him to settle down. You did what nobody else could, not even Stone himself: you gave me back my son."

"He was difficult to catch, sir, but I tired him out and lassoed him."

"I'm sure my son didn't put up too much of a battle," Nan jested as she stood there smiling with Stone's arm around her shoulder. Yes, she told herself, this was destiny; this was Stone Thrower's rightful Life-Circle. Just as Bennett Chapman, she added with immense joy, was hers.

Stone laughed. "How could I get away when I had all of you pushing us together? I never stood a chance of escaping three ropes."

Ginny relaxed when she saw that neither Ben nor Nandile held any resentment toward her for her deception. It warmed her heart to see him and his family so happy. It had been a long and tough battle to get close, but they had won it together. In the heavy southern drawl she had lost while living in London, she purred, "Stone Chapman, are you accusing me of using my wiles unfairly and charging them of assisting me?"

His other arm pulled Ginny close and embraced her as he chuckled. He dropped a kiss on her forehead and smiled at her. "You needed all the help you could get, woman, and thank goodness you received it. I would have stormed my way into Colorado City if my parents hadn't talked sense into me. They beat down my pride and forced me to see the truth."

"Let's get your things and go home, Son. We have a lot to share."

On the way to the ranch, they chatted about the younger couple's adventures and about the double wedding to take place soon.

"What about round-up and the cattle drive, Father?"

"Don't worry, Son, I wouldn't pull us away from our new brides that soon. Buck can handle them this year."

Nandile grinned and told Ginny, "Our men have changed, my new daughter, when their work comes second to love. I'm too dazed to think."

"Now, Mother," Stone teased, "you're the one who ordered me to go fetch this girl and bring her back. I'm only being an obedient child."

"You're no longer Stone Thrower. You have become a strong and proud man, a smart one, too. The Great Spirit has smiled on both of us."

"Yes, *Shima*, He has." It was good to finally call her his mother.

The following day was spent in making plans for the double wedding in eleven days. Friends were written and ranch hands delivered the invitations to them, including those to Ginny's four friends from the wagontrain who had settled in or near Dallas. She was eager to see them again and looked forward to swapping tales. She explained her ruse about being Johanna Chapman as necessary to protect her from vengeful attacks by friends of Charles Avery or Bart. She lightly glossed over her real identity and motives.

While she was writing, Ginny penned a letter to Charles Avery's sister Martha in Savannah to give the woman comfort and enlightenment about her brother's loss. She knew that Negroes and Indians must be accepted one day or terrible times were ahead for all three clashing cultures.

As they worked, she enjoyed Nandile's company and realized—as did Sunflower—they got along very well. She listened with enthusiasm as the woman told her many things about her beloved fiancé. Ginny wanted to hear more about the Apache people, especially her tribe. She wanted to relate the plans she and Stone had mentioned at the cabin but thought it wise to wait until she was certain they could carry them out for her band. She learned that Nandile's parents were deceased and her tribe was far away. Yet, they contacted Nan occasionally to relate their whereabouts.

Meanwhile, Stone and Ben went to study the site where the ex-lawman wanted to build his new home. It was located atop a rolling hill with verdant trees scattered about and a stream-fed pond nearby. One could see for miles from up there and the view was lovely. It seemed as if the green landscape fused with the azure heaven in all directions. Birds sang and a variety of wildflowers abounded in colorful splendor.

"I wanted to check this with you, Father, and get your permission before I show it to Ginny. It's close to you and Mother but still private for us, about a mile from the house. If there's an emergency, a bell could be heard at that distance. And there's plenty of water and grass. It's perfect, isn't it?"

Ben eyed the setting, thought of their reason for being there, and sent Stone a broad smile. "Yes, Son, it is. We'll start immediately, as soon as you and Ginny decide what kind of a house you want."

"We haven't talked about that." Stone laughed. "Big enough for us and children but plenty of space so they don't get underfoot at the wrong time."

Ben chuckled. "Grandchildren . . . A new chance to do things right this time. I didn't with you and Johanna. I'm sorry, Stone, and I'll do anything to make it up to you."

"You have, Father, by acknowledging me and accepting Ginny. If we have any control over it, there'll be lots of tiny Chapmans running around soon."

"Your mother and I will be overjoyed. I love you, Son, and I'm glad you're home for good. Thank God you've forgiven me for hurting you."

"I love you, too, Father. I never stopped, hard as I tried. After I met Ginny and learned what love was about and saw how I resisted the truth, I came to understand what you'd endured because of those same things. I behaved just like I always accused you of doing. I was selfish, denying my feelings, avoiding responsibilities, punishing and hurting myself and others, and being too blind to see my mistakes. I was more like you than I realized. It's a good thing we both changed and softened or we'd have lost the most important people in our lives. It's over now. We have peace."

Later, Ginny and Stone visited Johanna's new grave. The body had been sent by train to Vicksburg, then brought the rest of the way by wagon, as had the possessions that had been left in Savannah with Martha Avery.

Ginny knelt and lay flowers where the headstone would be placed soon. "I wish she were alive and here to share everyone's happiness."

Stone bent and clasped her hand in his. "I'm sure the Great Spirit is allowing her to do so where she is. She'll always live in our memories, my love. She's a special part of each of us."

"You're right, Stone. Good-bye, Johanna, my sister."

"Good-bye, Johanna, *shi-k'is 'ikee naaghan*," he murmured, too.

As Ginny looked at the mound, she knew the Chapmans loved, believed, and accepted her. And they would have done so even if her father's last letter hadn't been forwarded from school to the ranch to prove she had intended to come here in the beginning not to impersonate Johanna but to visit as her friend. If she and Stone ever had a daughter, her name was ready.

By the time they reached the house, the ex-soldier was reining in with Chuune in tow. The two seemed happy to be reunited. As always, it amazed Ginny that the animal was so smart, seemed almost human.

Mathew Marston arrived on August first. He was beaming, and spoke often of Hattie Pearl. Two of the investors, mining experts, had been left in charge of ordering equipment and finalizing preparations. "So far no news has leaked out. I hope we can keep it that way until that lawyer I hired straightens out the legal entanglements of my marriage. I'm sure Cleniece will be shocked to learn she has two husbands. Hopefully she'll also want things unraveled fast. I'll decide later if I should keep out of Amanda's life. That depends on what Cleniece tells me."

"What's best for Amanda is what you must do, Father, hard as it might be."

Matthew nodded, then told Ginny that he had recovered the pouch of gold he had on deposit in Kinnon's safe, and that the authorities seized control of the bank until its fate is decided.

Saturday, friends gathered in the Chapman house to observe and to help celebrate the marriages of Stone to Ginny and Bennett to Nandile. They stood before the minister as he began the joint ceremony. "Friends and loved ones, we are gathered in this loving home today to join these two couples in the holy bonds of wedlock. Our Father in Heaven and all of you are here to witness this happy occasion. Who gives these fine women into marriage?"

Stone said, "I do," as he placed his mother's hand in his father's, then kissed her cheek. The three exchanged heartfelt smiles.

"I do," said Matt, then placed his daughter's hand in that of his old friend and partner. He kissed Ginny's cheek and shook Stone's other hand. He stepped back to stand with the other guests, beaming with pride. He wished his beloved wife—her mother—could be with them today. Or Hattie. Matt's heart thudded with excitement as thoughts of the woman far away came to his mind. He felt his loins stirring with desire. It had been a long time since he had experienced such potent feelings.

The clergyman said stirring words, read appropriate scriptures from the Bible, then asked them to exchange their vows. For a while, none of the four was aware of their guests. The older couple went first. Ben faced Nandile as their words were spoken from deep within their hearts. For them, this day was a glorious victory following a thirty-year conflict.

Stone gave Ginny's hand a gentle squeeze as he watched his parents speak their vows. He realized they were as much in love as they had been when they met so long ago, a powerful love that had given him birth, one that had never dulled over the years and never would. Nandile wore a pale-blue dress that enhanced her dark-brown eyes, tawny skin, and silky black hair that flowed down her back like a tranquil river. Stone thought she was beautiful and radiant. He glanced at Ginny, who was clad in a soft yellow dress that brought out the sunny highlights of tresses that tumbled down her back in waves and curls. His breath caught in his throat and tightened his chest. She was his forever.

Ginny noticed how handsome the two grooms looked in their dark suits, white shirts, and polished boots. She trembled in elation and anticipation of this special moment they were sharing and of what would follow soon.

"Do you, Stone Chapman, take this woman, Virginia Anne Marston, to be your lawfully wedded wife, to love, honor, and cherish her in sickness and in health, in good times and in bad, for richer and for poorer, until death do you part?"

Stone gazed into her hazel eyes as he replied, "I do, with all my heart and all I possess." *Shu*, she looked so exquisite! He quivered with desire. Thank the Good Spirit he had found her and won her.

"Do you, Virginia Anne Marston, take this man, Stone Chapman, to be your lawfully wedded husband, to love, honor, and cherish him in sickness and in health, in good times and in bad, for richer and for poorer, until death do you part?"

Ginny's softened gaze remained fused with Stone's engulfing brown one. "I do," she said, then added the same stirring words he had, "with all my heart and all I possess." No words or emotions had ever been truer, more meaningful, or sweeter to her.

"The ring," the minister prompted Stone, who seemed lost for a time in the wonder of his love. He lifted it from the young man's palm. "A circle without an end, as true love and marriage should be. Slide it on her finger, and repeat after me: With this ring, I thee wed until death."

Stone slipped the gold band in place, kept his fingers on it, looked into her eyes and said, "With this ring, I thee wed until death."

Ginny clasped his hands and repeated after the minister, "This ring I accept as a bond of our wedlock until death."

Ben and Nandile looked at each other and smiled. They were ecstatic by what they witnessed and shared with their son. They had come full circle like the ring on Sunflower's finger: the three were together again as a close family. The young woman joining their lives today was responsible for their joy. They would all be grateful to her forever.

The clergyman had each of the four place their left hand on his Bible, one atop the other, then covered them with his own. "By the authority granted to me by our Heavenly Father and the great state of Texas, I pronounce you man and wife," he said to Ben and Nan. He looked at Stone and Ginny. "I pronounce you man and wife. What God hath joined together, let no man put asunder. Gentlemen, you may kiss your brides."

At last, Ben and Nan thought, they didn't have to conceal their love. At last, they could hold hands, embrace, and reveal their feelings in public without fear of exposing their forbidden love. If anyone scorned them, so be it. They deserved this moment, each other, and the sunny future beckoning them onward. They hugged and kissed.

Ginny and Stone wished they could mesh their mouths longer, but this wasn't the time and place. Later, it would be . . . They listened as the preacher spoke his final words and said a prayer to end the bonding ceremony.

He turned the newlyweds to face their guests. Standing between them and with an arm around the shoulder of each, he said, "Friends, I present to you Mr. and Mrs. Bennett Chapman." He moved to do the same with Ginny and Stone. "I also present to you Mr. and Mrs. Stone Chapman. May both of your unions be long and happy. God bless you all. Amen."

The witnesses cheered and congratulated the glowing couples. A merry party ensued. Ginny chatted with her friends, who were excited and intrigued by her many adventures, though they weren't told about Stone's secret mission to foil the Red Magnolias. The incident was disguised as a jewel theft that he was assigned to solve and that he couldn't act until the gang was exposed. Ruby, Mary, Lucy, and Ellie whispered mirthful and romantic advice to the blushing bride.

Food and drink were abundant. Stone and Ginny danced, laughed, fed each other treats, and had fun with friends. Others watched and joined in on the activities. Even Lucy with her gimp ankle moved around the dance area with her husband. Everybody's fresh beginning seemed to be working out, evidenced by the cheerful smiles, elated moods, and genial behaviors of all.

Ginny danced with her father several times, and they chatted about Hattie again. She suspected there might be another wedding soon, in Colorado. She shared Matt's happiness at finding new love and believed Hattie to be a good choice. Yet she didn't press him about a decision and acknowledgment of his feelings. She wanted him to enjoy the heady mystery and stimulating chase of a special experience, his second one.

When she took a break to refresh herself, Ginny thought about the doll lying on her bed in the house. She wished her mother could share this day with her. Perhaps, as with Johanna, both women were observing her happiness.

Stone whirled Ginny around and around as his gaze refused to leave hers. The August heat almost went unnoticed, as their minds were filled with other thoughts of what awaited them later. They were eager to be alone to consummate their vows with fiery passion.

At seven, the guests realized it was time to head to their homes before dark overtook them on the road; and it was time to leave the two pairs of newlyweds in romantic seclusion. Congratulations and best wishes were offered a final time. Farewells were exchanged and plans for future gatherings were made. At last, all friends and ranch hands were gone.

Ben glanced at his son, winked, and flexed his sturdy body. "I don't know about you two, but Nan and I are exhausted from so much activity at our ages. We're turning in. Cleanup can wait until morning."

Stone sent his father a smile of gratitude. "So are we. Young or not, we're tired, too. Ready to call it a day, Mrs. Chapman?"

Ginny glowed as she replied, "Yes, my husband."

Ben looked at Nan. "You ready to call it a day, Mrs. Chapman?"

Nan grinned at Ginny and used her same words, "Yes, my husband."

Embraces and kisses were shared before they parted for the night.

Later in their bedroom, Ginny revealed, "Something was supposed to happen the day we arrived here, my love, but it didn't, and hasn't, yet."

A beguiling grin flickered over his face and settled in his dark eyes. "What was that, woman? What did I forget?"

Ginny unbuttoned his shirt, peeled it off his shoulders, and snuggled against his chest. Her fingertips made tiny circles there. "You didn't remember not to get me pregnant before we stood before a minister."

Stone captured her face and lifted it to look into her compelling eyes. "Are you sure, Ginny love?"

She raised on her tiptoes to kiss him before admitting, "No, but my monthly visit has never been late before. If it's true, it happened at Hattie's or the cabin or on the way here, so I'm not far along, a month or less."

"That's wonderful news, my love. A baby . . . Our baby . . . If it's true, Ginny Chapman, we'll have our new home finished just in time for his birth—or hers. A father . . . Me, Stone Chapman, a father . . ."

Ginny saw how his dark eyes glowed with joy and pride. She knew he would make an excellent parent. He would shower their children with love, protection, and attention. He would make certain they were happy and would never suffer as he had. He was free of his bitter and imprisoning past, and he belonged to her. Never again would another midnight secret come between them.

Stone scooped her into his arms and carried her to the bed. He lay half across her body as a playful grin danced in his eyes. "Wait until Warren Turner hears about this news. He'll be as stunned as he was about my retirement. If Washington weren't so far, he'd have come to the wedding. This isn't another one of your daring deceptions to make me stay home to watch you grow with our child, is it, my clever filly?"

"No, Mr. Suspicious Chapman. If I ever tricked you again, you'd send that tough and demanding scout, Steve Carr, to abduct me and punish me. We have so much to be thankful for, Stone. We're going to be so happy."

"Yes, my love, we are. What shall we do now?" he teased.

"I bet with a little cunning and investigating, my ex-Special Agent, you could find a clue to lead you in the right direction to solve your current mission. With your skills and prowess, your job shouldn't be hard."

Stone nuzzled her face with his and murmured in a voice made husky with love and desire, "This is one job I'll gladly scout for."

Virginia Marston Chapman grinned and enticed, "Then let's ride, my love, toward paradise together," and they did.

Born in Athens, Georgia, Janelle Taylor is the prolific, highly successful, award-winning author of more than thirty novels. Seven of her books have appeared on *The New York Times* bestseller list, including *Moondust and Madness, Savage Conquest, Stolen Ecstasy* and featured in this Wings Books collection, *First Love, Wild Love*. More than 26 million copies of her books are in print worldwide. Ms. Taylor currently lives in Evans, Georgia.